A Glossary of Literary Terms

文学术语词典

(中英对照)

第10版

[美] M.H.艾布拉姆斯（Meyer Howard Abrams）
杰弗里·高尔特·哈珀姆（Geoffrey Galt Harpham） 著

吴松江 路雁 朱金鹏 朱荔 崔侃 林淼 余艳 张文定 编译

版权局著作权合同登记　图字：01-2013-5153
图书在版编目（CIP）数据

文学术语词典：第 10 版：中英对照 /（美）艾布拉姆斯（Abrams, M. H.），（美）哈珀姆（Harpham, G. G.）著；吴松江等编译 . —北京：北京大学出版社，2014.11
ISBN 978-7-301-24998-7

Ⅰ. ①文… Ⅱ. ①艾… ②哈… ③吴… Ⅲ. ①文学－对照词典—汉、英 Ⅳ. ①Ⅰ-61

中国版本图书馆 CIP 数据核字（2014）第 243990 号

A Glossary of Literary Terms
M. H. Abrams & Geoffrey Galt Harpham
Copyright © 2013 by Wadsworth, a part of Cengage Learning.
Original edition published by Cengage Learning. All rights reserved.
Peking University Press is authorized by Cengage Learning to publish and distribute exclusively this bilingual edition. This edition is authorized for sale in the People's Republic of China only (excluding Hong Kong, Macao SAR and Taiwan). No part of this publication may be reproduced or distributed by any means, or stored in a database or retrieval system, without the prior written permission of the publisher.

本书双语版由圣智学习出版公司授权北京大学出版社独家出版发行。此版本仅限在中华人民共和国境内（不包括香港特别行政区、澳门特别行政区及中国台湾）销售。未经授权的本书出口将被视为违反版权法的行为。未经出版者事先书面许可，不得以任何方式复制或发行本书的任何部分。

Cengage Learning Asia Pte. Ltd.
151 Lorong Chuan, #02-08 New Tech Park, Singapore 556741

本书封面贴有 Cengage Learning 防伪标签，无标签者不得销售。

书　　　名：	文学术语词典（第 10 版）（中英对照）
著作责任者：	[美] M. H. 艾布拉姆斯　杰弗里·高尔特·哈珀姆 著
	吴松江　路雁 等编译
责 任 编 辑：	徐文宁
标 准 书 号：	ISBN 978-7-301-24998-7/I·2827
出 版 发 行：	北京大学出版社
地　　　址：	北京市海淀区成府路 205 号　100871
网　　　址：	http://www.pup.cn　新浪微博：@北京大学出版社　@阅读培文
电 子 邮 箱：	编辑部 pkupw@pup.cn　总编室 zpup@pup.cn
电　　　话：	邮购部 62752015　发行部 62750672　编辑部 62750112
	出版部 62754962
印 刷 者：	天津联城印刷有限公司
经 销 者：	新华书店
	720 毫米×1020 毫米　16 开本　55.5 印张　1000 千字
	2014 年 11 月第 1 版　2024 年 2 月第 6 次印刷
定　　　价：	138.00 元

未经许可，不得以任何方式复制或抄袭本书之部分或全部内容。
版权所有，侵权必究
举报电话：010-62752024　电子信箱：fd@pup.cn

出版前言

　　M. H. 艾布拉姆斯（Meyer Howard Abrams）是当代欧美文学理论家和批评家中的大师级人物。1912年7月23日，他出生于美国新泽西州一个贫寒的犹太家庭，父亲是名建筑油漆工。1930年他考入哈佛大学攻读英语文学专业，成为家中第一个大学生。他念大学时正值美国经济大萧条时期，有人劝他早点工作，他却说："现在工作不好找，与其干着不喜欢的活还挨饿，不如做我感兴趣的文学挨饿。"1934年他取得学士学位，同年获得奖学金赴英国剑桥学习，师从英国新批评大师理查兹（又译瑞恰兹）教授（I. A. Richards, 1893—1979）。

　　理查兹是20世纪大师级的文艺理论家，也是西方大家中对中国有着特殊感情的学者。理查兹从1920年代起就在剑桥讲授文学批评理论，并最早把语义学和心理学引入文学理论和文学批评。他与奥格登合著《美学原理》(1921)、《意义的意义》(1923)，独自完成《文学批评原理》(1924)、《实用批评》(1929)等文学理论和文学批评史上划时代的著作，成为西方文艺理论界新批评派的权威。1927年，理查兹到远东旅行结婚，在日本小住后来到北京。这次中国之行给他留下美好印象，1929年他应邀在清华大学外语系任教，1931年返回剑桥。30年代初，理查兹成为奥格登发起的"基本英语"运动的领袖。1936年，理查兹来到中国，在赵元任、胡适、叶公超、陈翰笙等的支持下，在中国推动"基本英语"运动，直到1938年由于中国进入全面抗战而终止。回到英国，他一直在哈佛任教，直到退休。1978年，寄寓剑桥的理查兹接到北大校长周培源代表"前同事、前学生"赠送的礼物和访问中国的邀请，大喜过望。尽管重病在身，他还是抱着"去是死于胜利，不去是死于失败"的信念决定重返中国。1979年5月，理查兹来到中国，在桂林、杭州、上海、济南、青岛周游演说，6月在青岛病倒，被紧急送入北京协和医院。

7月，中国政府派人护送昏迷的理查兹回国，但他却一直没有醒来。9月7日，理查兹在剑桥逝世，终年86岁。作为20世纪文学理论和文学批评的一代宗师，理查兹除了留下多部具有深远影响的著作，还培养了一批杰出的文学理论家和文学批评家，其中燕卜荪和艾布拉姆斯是最出名的两位弟子。

  燕卜荪(William Empson, 1906—1984)于1925年进入剑桥学习数学。他兴趣广泛，除有数学天赋，对人文科学亦甚感兴趣。在大二读了T. S. 艾略特的文学论文后，产生了转系的念头。1928年10月他转入英文系，跟随系主任理查兹教授研究英国文学。燕卜荪才华横溢，在1929年度的考试中拿下数学和英文两个全校第一。在剑桥，他还是位颇有名气的青年诗人。在理查兹"实用批评"理论的影响下，燕卜荪在1930年出版了《晦涩的七种类型》，轰动西方文学理论界。1931—1934年，燕卜荪在东京大学教英语。1936年，理查兹在中国推广"基本英语"，燕卜荪表达了想在中国任教的愿望。在理查兹的推荐下，1937年燕卜荪来到北京大学任教。不久日本发动侵华战争，北大南迁，与清华、南开一起先后组建长沙临时大学和西南联大。燕卜荪与北大师生一起南下，风餐露宿，同甘共苦。他(当时他的中文名叫安浦生)和叶公超、莫泮芹是长沙临时大学期间外文系仅有的三名教师，也是北京大学来长沙73名教员中唯一一名外国人。在与中国师生一起忍饥挨饿中，燕卜荪还用他出众的诗歌才华写下了哲理长诗《南岳之歌》，展示了临时大学师生乐观的精神和坚强的信念，表达了他对中国人民的深沉之爱。在昆明西南联大，在十分艰苦的办学条件下，燕卜荪为中国高等教育事业奉献了他的聪明才智，为中国培养了一批研究西方语言文学的杰出人才。一代知名学者王佐良、李赋宁、杨周翰、许国璋、袁可嘉及诗人穆旦、郑敏等，都在西南联大受过他的教诲。1940年燕卜荪休假回国，因反法西斯宣传需要，留在英国BBC电台任编辑，但在西南联大的北大教师名册上依然有他的名字。1946年底，燕卜荪再次回到北大任教。他在学生中享有较高声望，1948年出版的《北大1946—1948》一书中对他有这样的描述："燕卜荪是理查兹的弟子，因而对'晦涩''基本英语'都下过工夫，他是现代英国有名的诗人之一；他讲莎士比亚，是细琢细磨……他对学生运动颇为关心，他的夫人最近亦参加反对美国扶植日本的大会。"他在中国经历了中国抗日战争和解放战争的动荡岁月，也亲历了新中国的成立。当大批西方人离开中国时，他却选择留在中国。1952年，中国大学开始进行全国性的院系调整，北大、清华、燕京等院校的外语系合并成北京大学西方语言文学系。但是教师聘用名单上却没有燕卜荪的名字，这对很想继续在北大任教的燕卜荪来说无疑是个重大打击。在从好友那里知道了校方的难处后，燕卜荪恋恋不舍地离开了北大。回到英国，燕卜荪在谢菲尔德大学英文系一直任教到1971年退休。燕卜荪的著作除了上面提到的成名作，还有《诗集》(1955)、《弥尔顿的上帝》(1961)等。鉴于燕卜荪在学术研究、诗歌创作和教育上的杰出贡献，他的母校剑桥大学于1974年正式授予他名誉博士学位，这位被除名的剑桥才子，时隔44年终于获得母校高度的肯定。1979年，英国女王授予他爵士头衔。

艾布拉姆斯小燕卜荪6岁，入理查兹门下也晚燕卜荪6年。1934年艾布拉姆斯在理查兹的指导下研究英国文学时，燕卜荪正在东京大学讲授英国语言文学。在理查兹的引导下，艾布拉姆斯重点研究英国18世纪诗人及批评家塞缪尔·约翰逊和塞缪尔·柯勒律治，并于1937年和1940年先后获得文学硕士和哲学博士。二战中，艾布拉姆斯供职于为美军服务的哈佛大学心理声像实验室。战争结束同年，他被聘为康奈尔大学英文系教授。

艾布拉姆斯在康奈尔大学任教达半个多世纪，是该校1916级荣休讲座教授。他是康奈尔大学人文研究中心的开创者，勇于创新，积极改革，营造了一个开放、宽松、互相尊重的学术环境，招聘和吸引了一批优秀学者到康奈尔任教、讲学、研究，其中包括乔纳森·卡勒、希利斯·米勒、拉尔夫·科恩、雅克·德里达等知名学者，大大促进了康奈尔大学的人文学术研究。艾布拉姆斯桃李满天下，著名批评家哈罗德·布卢姆、后现代作家托马斯·品钦等都出自他门下。艾布拉姆斯著述丰富，最有名的为三部经典：(1) 1953年出版的理论著作《镜与灯——浪漫主义文论及批评传统》，(2) 1957年出版的文学工具书《文学术语词典》，(3) 1962年主编的文学教科书《诺顿英国文学选读》。当今研习英美文学及文学理论的学者、教师和学生，几乎人人都读过这三本书。

艾布拉姆斯的《镜与灯》是在其博士论文的基础上不断修订扩充而成，当然，其源头则可追溯到他在理查兹的指导下对英国浪漫主义诗歌和诗歌理论的研究。在英国剑桥期间，艾布拉姆斯还通过理查兹见到了1923年诺贝尔文学奖得主爱尔兰诗人、剧作家叶芝和T. S.艾略特，并阅读过艾略特在出版前送给理查兹的诗歌批评。《镜与灯》从英国诗歌理论出发，主要讨论了西方浪漫主义文学理论的文学批评，同时对西方文学理论做了一个全面的梳理和总结，从历史和现实两个方面重新阐述和归纳了"模仿说""实用说""表现说""客观说"："模仿说"不仅仅是现实主义文论的美学追求，也是浪漫主义文论追求的目标；"实用说"强调艺术的直接功能，在实用主义批评派和新批评派批评中也得到发扬；"表现说"是浪漫主义文论的基本特征；"客观说"则注重批评的客观性和科学性。艾布拉姆斯还提出了文学批评的四大要素：1. 作品 (work)；2. 世界 (universe)；3. 艺术家

(artist)；4. 欣赏者(audience)。在这个由作品、世界、艺术家和欣赏者四大要素构成的框架上，艾布拉姆斯采用了一个方便实用的三角形模式，将"作品"这个阐述对象摆在中间，世界、艺术家和欣赏者处在三个边上。运用这样一个坐标和图式，可以把阐述艺术作品本质和价值的尝试划分为四类，其中有三类主要是用作品与另一要素（世界、欣赏者或艺术家）的关系来解释作品，第四类则把作品视为一个自足体单独进行研究。艾布拉姆斯对四大要素的概括和三角形坐标的阐述，至今仍有重大价值。

《镜与灯》出版后产生了巨大影响。文学批评大师勒内·韦勒克认为，这部文学批评史著作是美国学术界在这一领域作出的最卓越贡献。美国《现代语言研究》认为，这本书对思想史、英国文学、批评理论、美学等多个领域都有永久的意义。《时代》文学副刊评论认为，过去四十多年文学理论界曾有过多次规范文学观念的尝试，这本书是最成功的，它把丰富的历史研究与清晰的思想表述完美地结合起来。美国《当代文学》上的书评认为，这本书是过去30年内出版的对文学批评贡献最大的五本著作之一。21世纪初，在Modern Liberary评出的过去100年内英语写作的100部非虚构类作品中，《镜与灯》排在第25位。早在《镜与灯》出版第二年，它就获得了克里斯汀·高斯奖，为二战后欧美文学研究与批评设立了权威性的标准，同时也奠定了艾布拉姆斯在文学理论界的大师地位。

北京大学出版社早在1989年就出版了由郦稚牛、张照进、童庆生翻译的中文版《镜与灯》，时任北大英语系主任李赋宁教授在1988年12月6日为中文版所写的序言中，回忆了其1985—1986年在康奈尔大学访学时与艾布拉姆斯的结识和友好的交往。李赋宁先生与艾布拉姆斯的导师理查兹相识，并受业过理查兹的学生燕卜荪，因此对同是理查兹的学生艾布拉姆斯有着特殊的感情。在序言中，李赋宁教授高度评价了《镜与灯》的学术成就和研究方法："艾布拉姆斯是一位传统的人文主义学者，他的文学研究方法既是传统的，又是科学的。他把历史、传记、校勘、训诂、出处、类型、风格研究与心理学、美学，以及人生的阅历和智慧有机地结合在一起，因此他的研究成果具有极强的说服力和启发性，发人深省，令人信服。此外，艾布拉姆斯教授主编的英国文学选读教科书《诺顿英国文学选读》和他独立编写的《文学术语词典》已占领了全世界的大学课堂。"李赋宁先生认为，艾布拉姆斯的英国文学研究和教学的贡献具有世界意义。艾布拉姆斯向李赋宁教授表达了他热爱中国文化、渴望到中国访问和讲学的愿望。北大英语系也准备在《镜与灯》中文版出版之际邀请艾布拉姆斯访华，到北大讲学。但因1989年中国发生的事件，这一愿望未能实现。到90年代，艾布拉姆斯已是80多岁的耄耋老人,到北大访问的愿望已无法实现,只能是留在他的无限的想象中。如今李赋宁先生已经作古,艾布拉姆斯也已是 102 岁高龄,我们祝愿老人健康长寿。2002 年,北大出版社编辑《未名译库》,《镜与灯》再次列入出版规划。2003 年,北大出版社再次向牛津大学出版社购买了《镜与灯》的中文版权,并于 2004 年出版了由王宁教授校订的新版《镜与灯》,受到了学术界的欢迎。

艾布拉姆斯编写的《文学术语词典》自 1957 年出版以来,成为英语世界文学专业的必读书,被译成多国文字。北大出版社在出版了《镜与灯》后的第二年,便推出了由朱金鹏、朱荔翻译的《文学术语词典》。当时的书名定为《欧美文学术语词典》,主要是考虑到本书涉及的文学术语范围都是欧美文学。1990 年的中文翻译版是根据本书 1981 年第 4 版译出的。2003 年北大出版社向牛津大学出版社再次购买《镜与灯》的版权时,也向汤姆逊公司购买了《文学术语词典》1999 年第 7 版的中文版权,艾布拉姆斯在新版中对原条目做了调整,增加约 50 余条,并对部分条目做了改动。在 2013 年出版的第 10 版中,作者对每个条目都作了修改,并新增 30 个条目。

艾布拉姆斯对本书的多次修订,体现了他在不断变化的人类社会文化和文学创作及批评环境中与时俱进的科学态度和求真精神,值得中国的文学研究者和文学教育者认真学习。近 20 年来,西方学者编写了多种文学术语类辞书,其中较有影响的有《简明牛津文学术语词典》和《文学术语与文学理论词典》,两者所收条目远远超过艾氏的《文学术语词典》,但却难掩后者的光彩。艾氏的词典条目少而精,阐释很有特色,初版所收条目只有 100 多条,第 10 版增至 234 条,所设条目不仅包括当代西方文学的重要术语,也包括数千年来西方文学史上的重要名词术语,涵盖了文学史、文学批评和文学理论。西方文学历史悠久,名作、事件、思潮、理论繁多,想要在较短时间内对西方文学有一个基本把握,谈何容易?但如果一个人能对艾氏词典的条目有深入理解,认真阅读条目涉及的主要作品,那他一定能对西方文学有一个基本把握,这也正是为什么艾氏词典自问世以来长期被世界上许多大学采用为教材或教学参考书、受到一代又一代学子欢迎、至今畅销不衰的原因。

这篇出版前言用了较多的篇幅介绍了理查兹和燕卜荪、艾布拉姆斯的师承关系及其各自在文学研究方面取得的成就,并特别介绍了他们三位与中国文学界的特殊联系,我们相信这种联系还会继续进行下去。

《文学术语词典》第 4 版中译本在我社以《欧美文学术语词典》为名出版后已经 20 多年了,艾氏的词典又先后出了 6 种新版(第 7 版为艾氏独立完成的最后一版，2004年第8版、2008年第9版、2013年第10版均为艾布拉姆斯与杰弗里·高尔特·哈珀姆合作完成），重译和出版新版是我们多年的愿望，但因原来的译者或移居海外，或另有他事，使得这个计划一直未能如愿进行。2008年推出第7版，书名还原为《文学术语词典》，译文由吴松江先生主持和主审，参与翻译的有吴松江、崔侃、林淼、余艳等，朱金鹏、朱荔两位先生虽然未能参加第7版翻译，但他们的开创性工作为第7版翻译提供了一个很好的基础，将他们两位列为译者实乃理所应当。这次出版的第10版，又由译者路雁在第7版的基础上全部校译一遍，并补译第7版未译的参考书目和补充阅读书目。全书英文人名译名以商务印书馆《英语姓名译名手册》（第4版）为准，书名已有中文译名的以中文译名为准。为了便于读者检索查阅，页面上方页码均系原书页码，文中引用页码即指这一页码。本书采用中英文对照形式出版，一是便于读者在阅读译文时联系原文，加深对条目的理解，不至于被译文中的误解所误导；二是便于读者对译文中的问题和错误提出批评意见，汇聚众人之力，使本书的谬误之处降到最低，最大限度地裨益广大读者。

北大培文教育文化公司一直致力于引进国外优秀的学术著作和教材图书。近年来先后引进出版了《全球通史》《美国人民》《艺术与观念》《看电影的艺术》，以及一批心理学、社会学、电影等方面的图书，受到广大读者的欢迎。这次引进国外经典词典，并用中英对照形式出版，对我们来说是一次新的尝试，也是一个考验，我们真诚地欢迎专家学者、业界及读者朋友对我们的工作提出批评建议，共同为把书做好、多做好书而努力。

北大培文教育文化公司

2014年10月

目 录

出版前言 1

前　　言 9

致　　谢 13

如何使用本书 15

中文条目索引 16

文学术语 3

作者索引 847

Preface

Literary studies are always on the move. The purpose of this tenth edition of *A Glossary of Literary Terms* is to keep the entries current with innovations in critical views and methods, to take into account important new publications in literature, criticism, and scholarship, and also to take advantage of suggestions for improvements and additions, some solicited by the publisher and others volunteered by users of the *Glossary*.

All the entries have been reviewed, and most of them have been revised in order to improve the clarity, precision, and verve of the exposition, but above all, to bring the entries up to date in their substance and their lists of suggested readings. This edition adds 30 terms to the *Glossary*, including substantial new essays on *cognitive literary studies, detective story, graphic novels,* the *grotesque, Idealism,* and *romance novel.* The book now encompasses discussions of more than 1,175 literary terms. Books originally published in languages other than English are listed in their English translation. We avoid references to websites, since these are often unstable, and variable in their content.

A Glossary of Literary Terms defines and discusses the terms, as well as the critical theories and viewpoints, that are used to classify, analyze, interpret, and narrate the history of works of literature. The component entries, together with the guides to further reading included in most of them, are oriented especially toward undergraduate students of English, American, and other literatures. Over the decades, however, the book has proved sufficiently full and detailed to serve as a useful and popular work of reference for advanced students, as well as for the general reader with literary interests.

The *Glossary* is organized as a series of succinct essays, listed in the alphabetic order of the title word or phrase. Terms that are related but subsidiary, or that designate subclasses, are identified and discussed under the title heading of the primary or generic term; in addition, words that are often used in conjunction, or as mutually defining contraries, are discussed in the same essay. The essay form makes it feasible to supplement the definition of a literary term with indications

前　言

文学研究总是在不断变化。《文学术语词典》（第10版）的目的是为了使各个条目跟随批评观点和方法上的创新，关注新近的文学、批评和学术出版物，同时也采纳读者所提建议对旧版予以改进和充实，这些建议有的是出版社收集到的，但更多的还是本书使用者主动慷慨地提供的。

所有的条目都经过了重新修订，其中多数都做了改写，目的是使所有的论述尽可能做到明晰、精确、富有生气，但最重要的是，尽量扩大范例和参考文献的范围。新版增加了30个条目，对下列每个术语分别编写了实质性的新条目：*认知文学研究、侦探故事、图像小说、奇异艺术风格、唯心主义、浪漫小说*。现在书中讨论的文学术语超过1175个。一些非英文出版物也按其英译版列出。我们避免参阅网站，因为网上的术语内容不够稳定，经常变来变去。

本书解释和论述一些常用于分类、分析、诠释以及著述文学作品史的术语、批评理论和视角。所收录的条目和大部分条目中所列出的与之相关的深入阅读书目，主要面向英美文学和其他文学专业的大学本科学生。不过，几十年的实践证明，对高年级学生和喜爱文学的普通读者来说，这同样是一部实用和受欢迎的参考读物。

本书按标题词或用语的字母顺序排列，提供了一系列简明的论说文。一些相关但是附属的术语，或被认为是次类的术语，会在主要或总称术语的标题下予以解释；同样，常常一同出现或互为解释的一些条目，则会在同一条目中一同予以论述。以简明论说文的形式解释术语，有助于说明一个术语随时间变迁其意义的变化及

of its changes in meaning over time, and of its diversity of meanings in current usage, in order to help readers steer their way through the shifting references and submerged ambiguities of its varied applications. In addition, the discursive treatment provides an opportunity to write entries that are not only informative, but pleasurable to read. The alternative organization of a literary handbook as a dictionary of terms, defined singly, makes dull reading and requires excessive repetition and cross-indexing. It may also be misleading, because the application of many terms becomes clear only in the context of other terms and concepts to which they are related, subordinated, or opposed.

In each entry, **boldface** identifies terms for which the essay provides the principal discussion, and *italics* indicate terms that are discussed more fully elsewhere in the *Glossary*. It should be noted that all the literary terms discussed in the *Glossary*, whether they serve as the title of an essay or are defined within an essay, are presented in a single sequence, arranged in alphabetic order.

The aim of this tenth edition of the *Glossary* remains the one announced by the author of the first edition: to produce the kind of handbook he would have found most valuable when, as an undergraduate, he was an eager but sometimes bewildered student of literature and literary criticism.

其当前用法的多样性，为读者梳理出一些与之相应的参考文献并了解到其在文学应用中内在的一些歧义。另外，以更广阔的视野讨论文学术语，有利于作者把条目论述得既清晰可用又易懂可读。文学术语若是以术语词典的方式进行编写，对每个术语以定义的方式单独加以解释，不仅会使阅读变得枯燥乏味，而且会出现大量的重复以及大量注明互见索引的现象；同时还会产生误导，因为许多术语的使用和用法只有在与之相关或隶属或对立的其他概念的语境中才会显得清晰可辨。

在每个条目中，**黑体字**表示该条目会对其做重点阐释；以*斜体字*形式出现的术语则表示尽管其在该条目中出现，但在其他条目中会予以更详尽的阐释。应该注意的是，书中讨论的所有文学术语，不论它们是论说文的标题或是在论说文中得到解释，都已按英文字母顺序编排呈现出来。

新版的目的依然沿承第 1 版中作者的宣称：编写一本他念大学时觉得最有价值的手册，那时他还是文学和文学批评专业一名充满热情但有时却不知所措的大学生。

Acknowledgments

This edition, like preceding ones, has profited greatly from the suggestions of both teachers and students who proposed changes and additions that would enhance the usefulness of the *Glossary* to the broad range of courses in American, English, and other literatures. The following teachers, at the request of the publisher, made many useful proposals for improvements:

Michael Calabrese, *California State University, Los Angeles*
Kyle Grimes, *University of Alabama at Birmingham*
Salwa Khoddam, *Oklahoma City University*
Elona K. Lucas, *Saint Anselm College*
Sherryll S. Mleynek, *Marylhurst University*
Mary-Antoinette Smith, *Seattle University*
Stephen Souris, *Texas Woman's University*

As in many earlier editions, Dianne Ferriss has been indispensable in preparing, correcting, and recording the text of the *Glossary*. Matt Spears has also been a helpful member of the Cornell team. Michael Rosenberg, publisher at Cengage Learning, continues to be an enthusiastic supporter of each new edition. Joan Flaherty served as our development editor, and Divya Divakaran was our project manager at PreMediaGlobal.

致　谢

就像此前所有版本一样，新版从师生们的建议中获益匪浅，他们提出了可以改进和充实的地方，促进了新版的实用性，拓宽了其在英美文学和其他文学专业的适用范围。应出版人之求，下列老师提出了许多有用的改进建议，他们是：

迈克尔·卡拉布雷斯，加利福尼亚大学洛杉矶分校
凯尔·格兰姆斯，阿拉巴马大学伯明翰分校
萨尔瓦·霍达姆，俄克拉荷马城市大学
埃隆纳·K.卢卡斯，圣安塞姆学院
谢里尔·S.姆利内克，玛丽赫斯特大学
玛丽－安托瓦妮特·史密斯，西雅图大学
斯蒂芬·苏里斯，德州女子大学

与许多早期版本一样，在新版内容的准备、改正和复制上，戴安娜·费丽丝一直都是不可或缺的人选。马特·斯皮尔斯也一直都是康奈尔团队中一名给力的成员。圣智集团的出版人迈克尔·罗森伯格始终都是每次新版的热心支持者。琼·弗莱厄蒂是我们的拓展编辑，迪夫亚·迪瓦卡兰则是我们的 PreMediaGlobal 项目经理。

How to Use This Glossary

All the terms discussed in the *Glossary* appear in a single alphabetic sequence. Each term that is not itself the subject of the entry it identifies is followed, in **boldface**, by the number of the page in which it is defined and discussed. This is then followed by the page numbers, in *italics*, of the occurrences of the term in other entries, in contexts that serve to clarify its significance and illustrate how it is used in critical discourse.

Some of the listed terms are supplemented by references to a number of closely related terms. These references expedite for a student the fuller exploration of a literary topic, and make it easier for a teacher to locate entries that serve the needs of a particular subject of study. For example, such supplementary references list entries that identify the various types and movements of literary *criticism*, the terms most relevant to the analysis of *style*, the entries that define and exemplify the various literary *genres*, and the many entries that deal with the forms, component features, history, and critical discussions of the *drama*, *lyric*, and *novel*.

Those terms, mainly of foreign origin, that are most likely to be mispronounced by a student are followed (in parentheses) by a simplified guide to pronunciation. The following markings are used to signify the pronunciation of vowels as in the sample words:

ā	fate	ĭ	pin
ă	pat	ō	Pope
ä	father	ŏ	pot
ē	meet	oo	food
ĕ	get	ŭ	cut
ī	pine		

Authors and their works that are discussed in the text of the *Glossary* are listed in an *Index of Authors* at the end of the volume. To make it easy to locate, the outer edges of this *Index* are colored gray.

如何使用本书

书中论及的所有文学术语,都是按照英文字母顺序编排而成。每个不是条目主要论述的术语后面,都会接着一个黑体字印刷的页码,在这一页码该术语得到解释和讨论;紧接着是用斜体字印刷的页码,这是该术语在其他条目中出现的页码,在其他条目中阐明了该术语在文学批评用法中的意义并说明了其作用。

本书对一些比较普遍或宽泛的术语增补了许多密切相关的术语。这些参考资料可以促进学生更完整地去探讨一个主题,同时也使教师更容易找到研究某一特定课题所需要的条目。例如,增补的参考资料可分辨出论述文学*批评*的各种类型和运动的各个条目、分析*文体*最相关联的术语、界定和举例说明文学*类型*各种类别的各个条目,论述*戏剧*、*抒情诗*、*小说*的形式、构成特征、历史及评论的许多条目。

可能会被学生读错的术语,其中大多数是外来词,其后(在括号内)附有简化读音指南。下面的标记被用来说明例词中元音的发音:

ā	fate	ĭ	pin
ă	pat	ō	Pope
ä	father	ŏ	pot
ē	meet	oo	food
ĕ	get	ŭ	cut
ī	pine		

书中论及的作者和他们的作品,都列入全书最后的"作者索引"。为了便于查找,这一索引的外边缘涂成了灰色。

中文条目索引

A

哀歌 …………………………………… 101
哀史 …………………………………… 189

B

巴洛克风格作品 ……………………… 24
柏拉图式恋爱 ………………………… 292
悲剧 …………………………………… 408
悲伤感 ………………………………… 270
悲喜剧 ………………………………… 411
背景 …………………………………… 363
比喻语 ………………………………… 130
编年历史剧 …………………………… 50
编年史 ………………………………… 51
表现主义 ……………………………… 117
表演诗歌 ……………………………… 271
布鲁姆斯伯里团体 …………………… 31

C

超文本 ………………………………… 167
超现实主义 …………………………… 392
陈词滥调 ……………………………… 51
崇高 …………………………………… 389
辞藻华丽的章节 ……………………… 326

D

达尔文主义文学研究 ………………… 74
打油诗 ………………………………… 93
当代批评理论和运动 ………………… 405
地方色彩 ……………………………… 200
第一人称、基调和言念 ……………… 286
典故 …………………………………… 12
叠句 …………………………………… 337
定型反应 ……………………………… 379
定型情景 ……………………………… 379
定型人物 ……………………………… 378
读者反应批评 ………………………… 330
短篇小说 ……………………………… 365
对话批评 ……………………………… 85
对偶 …………………………………… 15

F

翻案诗 ………………………………… 266
反讽 …………………………………… 184
反英雄 ………………………………… 14
仿古 …………………………………… 16
讽刺 …………………………………… 353
风景诗 ………………………………… 406
否定能力 ……………………………… 235
浮夸之辞 ……………………………… 31
符号论 ………………………………… 357

G

感伤谬误 ……………………………… 269
感伤主义 ……………………………… 363

感受力与想象力 119
哥特小说 151
格律 217

H

哈莱姆文艺复兴 157
涵义与表义 63
合唱队 49
黑人艺术运动 29
后结构主义 308
后殖民主义研究 306
滑稽讽刺作品 37
话语分析 89
荒诞派文学 1
黄金时代 151

J

机智、幽默与滑稽 420
及时行乐 44
即兴喜剧 57
假面歌舞剧 210
降神 85
教诲文学 88
接受理论 336
结构主义批评 381
解构主义 77
警句 110
具体与抽象 60
具像诗 61

K

凯尔特文艺复兴 45
科幻小说与幻想作品 356
客观的与主观的 261
客观对应物 261
口头诗歌 264
夸张与含蓄 166
垮掉派作家 26

L

籁歌 191
浪漫小说 351
灵瞬 111

M

马克思主义批评 203
谩骂 183
美国的超验主义 412
美国文学各时期的划分 273
美术 133
梦幻体 95
民间传说 135
民谣 23
摹仿 171
牧歌 268
墓畔诗人 153
幕和场 3

N

内心独白 370
拟声词 264
逆说 267
女性主义批评 121

P

俳句 157
批判 71
批评 67

Q

七大罪 364
奇迹剧、道德剧和插剧 224
歧义 13
骑士传奇 48
骑士恋 66
启蒙运动 106

奇异艺术风格……………… 155
前拉斐尔派画家和诗人……… 315
巧思妙喻…………………… 58
轻松诗……………………… 191
情感谬误（又译感受谬误）…… 6
情感文学…………………… 360
情节………………………… 293
情节剧……………………… 211

R

人文主义…………………… 161
人物与人物塑造……………… 45
认知文学研究………………… 52

S

三一律……………………… 405
散文………………………… 318
尚古主义与进步论…………… 315
社会主义现实主义…………… 368
神话………………………… 230
审美意识形态………………… 3
生态批评…………………… 96
诗的破格…………………… 300
诗的正义…………………… 299
诗节………………………… 375
诗意辞藻…………………… 298
十四行诗…………………… 370
史诗………………………… 107
史诗明喻…………………… 109
史诗戏剧…………………… 110
试金石……………………… 407
视角………………………… 301
释义与阐释学………………… 176
书籍………………………… 32
书籍版本…………………… 33
书籍版式…………………… 34
书籍史研究…………………… 34

抒情诗……………………… 201
属性形容词………………… 113
双关………………………… 325
思想与感受的分裂…………… 91
颂…………………………… 262

T

题旨与主题………………… 229
通感………………………… 398
同性恋理论（又译酷儿理论）…… 327
头韵………………………… 10
图画叙事…………………… 152
突降与突降法………………… 25
颓废派文艺………………… 75

W

唯美主义…………………… 4
唯心主义…………………… 168
维多利亚时期与维多利亚时期
　的特点…………………… 418
伟大的生存（环）链………… 154
委婉语……………………… 115
文本批评…………………… 402
文本与书写（书面文字）…… 400
文化研究…………………… 72
文体………………………… 384
文体学……………………… 387
文学………………………… 199
文学惯例…………………… 64
文学经典…………………… 41
文学类型…………………… 148
文学社会学………………… 368
文艺复兴…………………… 338
文字误用…………………… 203
问题剧……………………… 317
乌托邦和反面乌托邦………… 416
无韵诗……………………… 30

X

喜歌 …… 112
喜剧 …… 54
喜剧性调剂 …… 57
戏剧 …… 93
戏剧独白诗 …… 94
现代主义和后现代主义 …… 225
现实主义与自然主义 …… 334
现象学与文学批评 …… 289
象牙塔 …… 188
象征 …… 393
象征释义和寓意释义 …… 180
象征主义运动 …… 397
小说 …… 252
谐音与非谐音 …… 115
心腹 …… 62
心理距离与感情介入 …… 92
心理学与精神分析批评 …… 319
新古典主义和浪漫主义 …… 236
新历史主义 …… 244
新批评 …… 241
形式与结构 …… 137
形式主义 …… 138
性别批评 …… 146
性格喜剧 …… 57
修辞格 …… 345
修辞学 …… 342
修辞学批评 …… 344
虚构小说与真实 …… 128
叙事和叙事学 …… 233
叙事语法 …… 233
玄学派诗人 …… 215

Y

押韵 …… 348
哑剧和默剧 …… 266
言语行为理论 …… 372
仪轨 …… 82
移情与同情 …… 103
异化效果 …… 7
意识流 …… 380
意图谬误 …… 175
意象 …… 169
意象主义 …… 170
隐喻理论 …… 212
应景诗 …… 262
英国文学各时期的划分 …… 278
英雄剧 …… 159
英雄双韵体 …… 158
影射小说 …… 351
影响与影响的焦虑 …… 173
尤弗伊斯体 …… 116
语言学在文学批评里的应用 …… 193
寓言 …… 7
寓言诗 …… 119
原型批评 …… 16
韵律学 …… 319

Z

杂文 …… 114
赞美诗 …… 165
张力 …… 400
传记 …… 27
侦探故事 …… 84
自白诗 …… 62
自然神论 …… 83
自由诗 …… 142
作品基调 …… 18
作品删节 …… 37
作者和作者身份 …… 19

A Glossary of Literary Terms

文学术语词典

Literary Terms

abstract (language): **60**; *169*.

absurd, literature of the: The term is applied to a number of works in drama and prose fiction which have in common the view that the human condition is essentially absurd, and that this condition can be adequately represented only in works of literature that are themselves absurd. Both the mood and dramaturgy of absurdity were anticipated as early as 1896 in Alfred Jarry's French play *Ubu roi* (*Ubu the King*). The literature has its roots also in the movements of *expressionism* and *surrealism*, as well as in the fiction, written in the 1920s, of Franz Kafka (*The Trial, Metamorphosis*). The current movement, however, emerged in France after the horrors of World War II (1939–45) as a rebellion against basic beliefs and values in traditional culture and literature. This tradition had included the assumptions that human beings are fairly rational creatures who live in an at least partially intelligible universe, that they are part of an ordered social structure, and that they may be capable of heroism and dignity even in defeat. After the 1940s, however, there was a widespread tendency, especially prominent in the *existential philosophy* of men of letters such as Jean-Paul Sartre and Albert Camus, to view a human being as an isolated existent who is cast into an alien universe; to conceive the human world as possessing no inherent truth, value, or meaning; and to represent human life—in its fruitless search for purpose and significance, as it moves from the nothingness whence it came toward the nothingness where it must end—as an existence which is both anguished and absurd. As Camus said in *The Myth of Sisyphus* (1942),

> In a universe that is suddenly deprived of illusions and of light, man feels a stranger. His is an irremediable exile.... This divorce between man and his life, the actor and his setting, truly constitutes the feeling of Absurdity.

文学术语

A

abstract (language)：抽象（语言） 60；*169*。

Absurd, Literature of the：荒诞派文学

　　荒诞派文学指那些共同认为人类的状况在本质上已荒诞不经、这种状况只有通过自身荒诞的文学作品才能得到恰当表现的戏剧和小说作品。荒诞文学的基调和剧作理论已先见于 1896 年阿尔弗雷德·雅里的法文剧作《于布王》（又译《乌布王》）中。荒诞派文学亦起源于*表现主义*和*超现实主义*运动，以及弗朗兹·卡夫卡作于 1920 年代的小说（《审判》《变形记》）。然而，在第二次世界大战（1939—1945）的恐怖经历之后出现在法国的荒诞派文学运动，则是对传统文化和文学中的基本信仰与价值标准的反叛。这一传统观念包括这样的假设：人是具有理性的动物，他赖以生存的世界至少是部分可知的；在有秩序的社会结构里，人是其中的一个组成部分；即便他置身逆境也不会丧失自己的英雄气概与尊严。然而，1940 年代后，出现了尤以让－保罗·萨特和阿尔贝·加缪等文人的*存在主义哲学*为突出代表的普遍倾向。他们认为：每个人都是沦落异乡的孤独的生灵；这一人类世界不存在固有的真理、价值标准与任何意义；人生只不过是对生存目标和存在意义的徒劳的探索过程，人生本自虚无，并终将化为虚无；人生的存在是件既痛苦又荒诞的事。就像加缪在《西西弗斯的神话》（1942）中写到的：

> 在一个突然失去了幻想与光亮的世界中，一个人就会感到自己是异乡人，是陌生客。他的流放无可补救……人与人之间，演员与背景之间的这种脱节，正是让人感到荒诞之处。　　（杜小真译）

Or as Eugène Ionesco, French author of *The Bald Soprano* (1949), *The Lesson* (1951), and other plays in the **theater of the absurd**, has put it: "Cut off from his religious, metaphysical, and transcendental roots, man is lost; all his actions become senseless, absurd, useless." Ionesco also said, in commenting on the mixture of moods in the literature of the absurd: "People drowning in meaninglessness can only be grotesque, their sufferings can only appear tragic by derision."

Samuel Beckett (1906–89), the most eminent and influential writer in this mode, both in drama and in prose fiction, was an Irishman living in Paris who often wrote in French and then translated his works into English. His plays, such as *Waiting for Godot* (1954) and *Endgame* (1958), project the irrationalism, helplessness, and absurdity of life in dramatic forms that reject realistic settings, logical reasoning, or a coherently evolving plot. *Waiting for Godot* presents two tramps in a waste place, fruitlessly and all but hopelessly waiting for an unidentified person, Godot, who may or may not exist and with whom they sometimes think they remember that they may have an appointment; as one of them remarks, "Nothing happens, nobody comes, nobody goes, it's awful." Like most works in this mode, the play is absurd in the double sense that it is grotesquely comic and also irrational and nonconsequential; it is a parody not only of the traditional assumptions of Western culture, but of the conventions and generic forms of traditional drama, and even of its own inescapable participation in the dramatic medium. The lucid but eddying and pointless dialogue is often funny, and pratfalls and other modes of slapstick are used to give a comic cast to the alienation and anguish of human existence. Beckett's prose fiction, such as *Malone Dies* (1958) and *The Unnamable* (1960), presents an *antihero* who plays out the absurd moves of the end game of civilization in a nonwork which tends to undermine the coherence of its medium, language itself. But typically Beckett's characters carry on, even if in a life without purpose, trying to make sense of the senseless and to communicate the uncommunicable.

Another French playwright of the absurd was Jean Genet (who combined absurdism and diabolism); some of the early dramatic works of the Englishman Harold Pinter and the American Edward Albee are written in a similar mode. The early plays of Tom Stoppard, such as *Rosencrantz and Guildenstern Are Dead* (1966) and *Travesties* (1974), exploit the devices of absurdist theater more for comic than philosophical ends. There are also affinities with this movement in the numerous recent works which exploit **black comedy** or **black humor**: baleful, naive, or inept characters in a fantastic or nightmarish modern world play out their roles in what Ionesco called a "tragic farce," in which the events are often simultaneously comic, horrifying, and absurd. Examples are Joseph Heller's *Catch22* (1961), Thomas Pynchon's *V* (1963), John Irving's *The World According to Garp* (1978), and some of the novels by the German Günter Grass and the Americans Kurt Vonnegut, Jr., and John Barth. Stanley Kubrick's *Dr. Strangelove* (1964) is an example of black comedy in the cinema. Some playwrights living in totalitarian regimes used absurdist techniques to register social and political protest. See, for example, *Largo Desolato*

或如创作了《秃头女高音歌手》(1949)、《惩诫》(1951)和其他一些**荒诞戏剧**作品的法国作家尤金·尤内斯库所说:"一旦切断宗教的、形而上学的、先验的根基,人就感到茫然若失;他的一切行为也都变得毫无意义、荒诞不经而又徒劳无益。"尤内斯库在评论荒诞派文学的混合基调时认为,"当人们沉溺于毫无意义的事物中时,只会显得荒唐怪诞,他们的遭遇只能用带有嘲弄色彩的悲剧形式来体现。"

侨居法国巴黎的爱尔兰作家塞缪尔·贝克特(1906—1989)是荒诞派文学运动中在戏剧和散文体小说两方面最杰出、最有影响的人物,他经常用法文写作,然后又译成英文。他的剧作,如《等待戈多》(1954)和《最后一局》(1958,又译《结局》),采用摒弃现实场景、逻辑推理和条理清晰的连贯情节的戏剧形式,来反映丧失理性、无助的、荒诞的生活。《等待戈多》描写两个流浪汉在荒野中徒然无望地等待一个不明身份的人——戈多。戈多此人若有若无,两个流浪汉时而记得与戈多或许有过约会,如其中一人说:"什么事也没有发生。谁也没来,谁也没去。这太可怕了。"就像大多数同类戏剧一样,该剧的荒诞性也具有双重意义:它是滑稽怪诞、非理性和毫无意义的;它还通过戏谑模仿,刻意讽刺西方文化的传统观念与传统戏剧的传统手法和形式,甚至对它自身不得不沿袭的戏剧形式也予以嘲弄。剧中那些清楚直白但却又自我绕弯并且毫无意义的对话往往是荒唐可笑的。像"跌跤"之类插科打诨的形体动作也被借用来表现人类存在的异化及悲痛。贝克特的散文体小说,如《马洛纳之死》(1958)和《无名的人》(1960),在试图通过破坏语言自身这一媒介的连贯性的非作品中,塑造出一位在文明的终结游戏中结束了其荒唐行为的**反英雄**。但贝克特笔下典型的主人公,即便是在毫无目标的生命历程中,也一如既往地试图从无意义中找到意义,在无法交流处进行交流。

另一位法国荒诞派剧作家是让·热内(他融荒诞主义与恶魔主义于一体);与此相似的还有英国剧作家哈罗德·品特和美国剧作家爱德华·阿尔比早期的一些戏剧作品。在汤姆·斯托帕德的早期剧作如《罗森克兰茨和吉尔登斯特恩都已死去》(1966)及《滑稽的模仿》(1974,又译《戏谑》)中,剧作家为了促成滑稽而非含有哲理的目的,也运用了荒诞戏剧的表现手法。与荒诞派文学运动密切相关的许多近期作品采用了**黑色喜剧**或**黑色幽默**的表现手法:描绘在光怪陆离或噩梦般的现代世界里,邪恶、天真幼稚或无能的人物在尤内斯库称为"悲剧性闹剧"中扮演的角色,其情节同时具有滑稽可笑、恐怖与荒诞的色彩。例如约瑟夫·海勒的《第二十二条军规》(1961),托马斯·品钦的《V》(1963),约翰·欧文的《盖普眼中的世界》(1978,又译《加普的世界观》),以及德国作家君特·格拉斯和美国作家小库特·冯尼戈特及约翰·巴思的一些小说。斯坦利·库布里克导演的《奇爱博士》是一部黑色喜剧的代表影视作品。一些身处集权统治社会的剧作家则运用荒诞手法对社会和政治予以抨击和针砭。例如

(1987) by the Czech Vaclav Havel and *The Island* (1973), a collaboration by the South African writers Athol Fugard, John Kani, and Winston Ntshona.

See also *wit, humor, and the comic,* and refer to: Martin Esslin, *The Theatre of the Absurd* (rev. 1968); David Grossvogel, *The Blasphemers: The Theatre of Brecht, Ionesco, Beckett, Genet* (1965); Arnold P. Hinchliffe, *The Absurd* (1969); Max F. Schultz, *Black Humor Fiction of the Sixties* (1980); Enoch Brater and Ruby Cohn, eds., *Around the Absurd: Essays on Modern and Postmodern Drama* (1990): and Neil Cornwell, *The Absurd in Literature* (2006).

For references to the *literature of the absurd* in other entries, see pages 47, 185, 227.

absurd, theater of the: 2.

accent (in meter): 217.

accentual meter: 217.

accentual-syllabic meter: 217.

accentual verse: 221.

accidie (ak′ sidē): 364.

act and scene: An **act** is a major division in the action of a *play*. In England this division was introduced by Elizabethan dramatists, who imitated ancient Roman plays by structuring the action into five acts. Late in the nineteenth century a number of writers followed the example of Chekhov and Ibsen by constructing plays in four acts. In the twentieth century the most common form for traditional nonmusical dramas has been three acts.

Acts are often subdivided into **scenes**, which in modern plays usually consist of units of action in which there is no change of place or break in the continuity of time. (Some recent plays dispense with the division into acts and are structured as a sequence of scenes, or episodes.) In the conventional theater with a **proscenium arch** that frames the front of the stage, the end of a scene is usually indicated by a dropped curtain or a dimming of the lights, and the end of an act by a dropped curtain and an intermission.

action: 46.

àdversarius (adversär′ ĭus): 354.

aesthetic distance: 92; 235. See also *empathy and sympathy.*

Aesthetic ideology: Aesthetic ideology was a term applied by the *deconstructive* theorist Paul de Man, in his later writings, to describe the "seductive" appeal of *aesthetic* experience, in which, he claimed, form and meaning, perception

捷克的瓦茨拉夫·哈维尔的《悲情声声慢》(1987)和南非作家阿瑟·福哥德、约翰·卡尼、温斯顿·恩特肖纳合著的《孤岛》(1973)。

也可参见：*机智、幽默与滑稽*。参阅：马丁·埃斯林所著的《荒诞派戏剧》(1968年修订版)；戴维·格罗斯弗格尔所著的《亵渎者：布莱希特、尤内斯库、贝克特和热内的戏剧》(1965)；阿诺德·P.欣奇利夫所著的《荒诞派》(1969)；马克斯·F.舒尔茨所著的《60年代的黑色幽默小说》(1980)；伊诺克·布拉特与鲁比·科恩合编的《以荒诞派为中心：现代与后现代戏剧论文选》(1990)；尼尔·康韦尔所著的《文学中的荒诞》(2006)。

其他条目中提及"荒诞文学"的地方，参见第47、185、227页。

absurd, theater of the：荒诞戏剧　2。

accent (in meter)：(格律中的)重音　217。

accentual meter：重音格律　217。

accentual-syllabic meter：音强－音节格律　217。

accentual verse：强音诗歌　221。

accidie：倦怠　364。

Act and Scene：幕和场

　　幕是*戏剧*情节发展的主要划分形式。英国伊丽莎白时代的剧作家效仿古罗马戏剧将剧情组织成为五场，从而把"幕"这一形式引进英国。19世纪后期，一些作家又仿照契诃夫和易卜生的做法把戏剧划分为四幕。20世纪传统的非音乐剧通常划分为三幕。

　　幕通常又可再分为**场**，场在现代戏剧里是情节发展的最基本环节，在一场戏里，地点不变，时间的连贯性不被打断。(一些近期的戏剧没有幕的划分，而是由一连串的场或情景组成。)在设有**拱形舞台**的传统剧场里，幕布落下或灯光变暗表示一场戏结束，帷幕落下及幕间休息则代表一幕剧结束。

action：行为　46。

adversarius：对立者　354。

aesthetic distance：审美距离　92；*235*。也可参见：*移情与同情*。

Aesthetic Ideology：审美意识形态

　　*解构*主义理论家保罗·德·曼在其晚期著作中用审美意识形态这一术语来描述那种"有诱惑力的"审美经验，他声称，在这种审美经验里，形式和意义、感知

and understanding, and cognition and desire are misleadingly, and sometimes dangerously, conflated. Such a conflation, he held, is manifested in some formulations of Nazi politics as an artful remaking of the state. In de Man's view, the concept of the aesthetic came to stand for all *organicist* approaches not only to art, but to politics and culture as well. The experience of literature, he argued, minimizes the temptation of aesthetic ideology to confuse sensory experience with understanding, since literature represents the world in such a way that neither meaning nor sense-experience is directly perceptible. See de Man, *Aesthetic Ideology* (1996); and Marc Redfield, *Phantom Formations: Aesthetic Ideology and the Bildungsroman* (1996).

In *The Ideology of the Aesthetic* (1990), the Marxist theorist Terry Eagleton presented a history and *critique* of "the aesthetic," noting the many "ideological" perversions and distortions of the concept. Originally articulated in terms of freedom and pleasure, and therefore possessing an "emancipatory" potential for humankind, the aesthetic has often been appropriated by the political right so as to represent the essence of a reactionary ideology, which works most efficiently when it seems not to be working at all. (See *ideology* under *Marxist criticism*, and for essays on this subject, refer to George Levine, ed., *Aesthetics and Ideology*, 1994.)

aesthetic movement: 4.

Aestheticism: In his Latin treatise entitled *Aesthetica* (1750), the German philosopher Alexander Baumgarten applied the term "aesthetica" to the arts, of whicn "the aesthetic end is the perfection of sensuous cognition, as such; this is beauty," In present usage, **aesthetics** (from the Greek, "pertaining to sense perception") designates the systematic study of all the *fine arts*, as well as of the nature of beauty in any object, whether natural or artificial.

Aestheticism, or alternatively the **aesthetic movement**, was a European phenomenon during the latter part of the nineteenth century that had its chief headquarters in France. In opposition to the dominance of science, and in defiance of the widespread indifference or hostility of the middle-class society of their time to any art that was not useful or did not teach moral values, French writers developed the view that a work of art is the supreme value among human products precisely because it is self-sufficient and has no use or moral aim outside its own being. The end of a work of art is simply to exist in its formal perfection; that is, to be beautiful and to be contemplated as an end in itself. A rallying cry of Aestheticism became the phrase "l'art pour l'art"—**art for art's sake**.

The historical roots of Aestheticism are in the views proposed by the German philosopher Immanuel Kant in his *Critique of Judgment* (1790), that the "pure" aesthetic experience consists of a "disinterested" contemplation of an object that "pleases for its own sake," without reference to reality or to the "external" ends of utility or morality. As a self-conscious movement, however, French Aestheticism is often said to date from Théophile Gautier's witty defense of his assertion that art is useless (preface to *Mademoiselle de Maupin*,

和理解、认知和欲望被错误地有时则是危险地混为一谈。他认为，这样的混为一谈，表现在纳粹政治的一些构想上，用来巧妙地改造国家。在德·曼看来，得到所有*有机论者*支持的审美观念，不仅为艺术所用，也为政治和文化所用。他认为，文学经验最大限度地减少了审美意识形态的诱惑，混淆了感官体验与理解，因为文学展现世界的方式，使得意义或感官体验都不会被直接感知到。参阅：德·曼所著的《审美意识形态》（1996）和马克·雷德菲尔德所著的《幽灵的形成：审美意识形态与成长小说》（1996）。

在《审美意识形态》（1990）一书中，马克思主义理论家特里·伊格尔顿，呈现了"审美"的历史和批判，指出了这一概念的许多"意识形态的"歪曲和曲解。原本与自由和快乐相连，并因此拥有一种"解放"人类的潜能，审美往往被政治右派据为己有，用来代表一种反动意识形态的本质，它在看上去一点不起效的时候其实最有效。[参见：*马克思主义批评*里的*意识形态*，关于这一问题的论述，参阅：乔治·莱文主编的《美学与意识形态》（1994）。]

aesthetic movement：唯美主义运动 **4**。

Aestheticism：唯美主义

德国哲学家亚历山大·鲍姆加登在其 1750 年出版的用拉丁文写成的《美学》中，用"美学"这一术语来指艺术，在这些艺术中"美学的目的就是感性认识的完善，这就是美"；在当前的使用中，**美学**（源自希腊语，"用感官去知觉"）指对所有*美术*，以及任一事物（无论是自然的还是人造的）中美的性质的系统研究。

唯美主义或**唯美主义运动**是 19 世纪晚期以法国为中心波及欧洲的一种文艺思潮。为了抵制当时占据主导地位的科学和挑战中产阶级社会对不宣扬功利主义或教化道德价值观的任何艺术的普遍冷漠乃至敌视，法国作家提出了这样一种艺术宗旨，即艺术品是人类成果中最有价值的东西，之所以这样，正是因为艺术品是傲然自足的，除了自我存在，别无其他任何功利或道德目的。一件艺术品的目的仅仅在于其以完美无瑕的形式存在；换句话说，唯美唯思即是其本身的目的。唯美主义的呼声最终演变成为"**为艺术而艺术**"的口号。

唯美主义的历史根基源于德国哲学家伊曼纽尔·康德在其所著的《判断力批判》（1790）一书中提出的理论，即"纯粹"的审美体验是对"自愉自乐"的审美客体的一种毫无功利色彩的沉思冥想，这种体验超越了艺术品自身的现实性或"外在"的实用价值及道德标准。然而，通常认为，法国唯美主义作为一场自我意识的运动，始于泰奥菲尔·戈蒂耶对艺术非实用论的机智辩解[见《莫班小姐》

1835). Aestheticism was developed by Baudelaire, who was greatly influenced by Edgar Allan Poe's claim (in "The Poetic Principle," 1850) that the supreme work is a "poem *per se*," a "poem written solely for the poem's sake"; it was later taken up by Flaubert, Mallarmé, and many other writers. In its extreme form, the aesthetic doctrine of art for art's sake veered into the moral and quasi-religious doctrine of life for art's sake, or of life conducted as a work of art, with the artist represented as a priest who renounces the practical concerns of worldly existence in the service of what Flaubert and others called "the religion of beauty."

The views of French Aestheticism were introduced into Victorian England by Walter Pater, with his emphasis on the value in art of high artifice and stylistic subtlety, his recommendation to crowd one's life with exquisite sensations, and his advocacy of the supreme value of beauty and of "the love of art for its own sake." (See his Conclusion to *The Renaissance*, 1873.) The artistic and moral views of Aestheticism were also expressed by Algernon Charles Swinburne and by English writers of the 1890s such as Oscar Wilde, Arthur Symons, and Lionel Johnson, as well as by the artists J. M. Whistler and Aubrey Beardsley. The influence of ideas stressed in Aestheticism—especially the view of the "autonomy" (self-sufficiency) of a work of art, the emphasis on the importance of craft and artistry, and the concept of a poem or novel as an end in itself, or as invested with "intrinsic" values—has been important in the writings of prominent twentieth-century authors such as W. B. Yeats, T. E. Hulme, and T. S. Eliot, as well as in the literary theory of the *New Critics*.

For related developments, see *aesthetic ideology, decadence, fine arts*, and *ivory tower*. Refer to: William Gaunt, *The Aesthetic Adventure* (1945, reprinted 1975); Frank Kermode, *Romantic Image* (1957); Enid Starkie, *From Gautier to Eliot* (1960); R. V. Johnson, *Aestheticism* (1969). For the intellectual and social conditions during the eighteenth century that fostered the theory, derived from theology, that a work of art is an end in itself, see M. H. Abrams, "Art-as-Such: The Sociology of Modern Aesthetics," in *Doing Things with Texts: Essays in Criticism and Critical Theory* (1989). Useful collections of writings in the Aesthetic Movement are Eric Warner and Graham Hough, eds., *Strangeness and Beauty: An Anthology of Aesthetic Criticism 1848–1910* (2 vols., 1983); Sally Ledger and Roger Luckhurst, eds., *The Fin de Siècle: A Reader in Cultural History, c. 1880–1900* (2000). A useful descriptive guide to books on the subject is Linda C. Dowling, *Aestheticism and Decadence: A Selective Annotated Bibliography* (1977). In recent years, the concepts of the aesthetic and of beauty have been revisited, often in a spirit of renewed appreciation, by philosophers and literary critics alike. See George Levine, ed., *Aesthetics and Ideology* (1994); Elaine Scarry, *On Beauty and Being Just* (1999); Arthur C. Danto, *The Abuse of Beauty: Aesthetics and the Concept of Art* (2003); Jonathan Loesberg, *A Return to Aesthetics: Autonomy, Indifference, and Postmodernism* (2005); Denis Donoghue, *Speaking of Beauty* (2003); John Armstrong, *The Secret Power of Beauty* (2004); and Susan Stewart, *The Open Studio: Essays on Art and Aesthetics* (2005). Berys Gaut and Dominic McIver Lopes, eds., *The Routledge Companion to Aesthetics* (2d ed., 2005), is a useful collection of historical and descriptive

(1835)序言]。深受埃德加·爱伦·坡美学思想"最高超的诗作是'为诗而作的诗'"["诗歌原理"(1850)]影响的波德莱尔使唯美主义得以继续发展,后来,福楼拜、马拉梅及许多其他作家继承了唯美主义的衣钵。发展到极致阶段时,"为艺术而艺术"的美学观点转变为"艺术家要为艺术而生活"或"将生活当成一件艺术品"的道德准则和类似于宗教的信念,并将那些摒弃世俗追求的艺术家视为福楼拜等人所说的"美之宗教"的传教士。

法国的唯美主义思想通过沃尔特·佩特传入维多利亚时代的英国。佩特强调创作技巧的别具匠心和艺术风格的精巧玄妙在艺术中的价值,主张以高雅的情感充塞个人生活,同时还宣扬美的无上价值和"为艺术而爱艺术"的观念。[参阅:佩特所著《文艺复兴史研究》(1873)一书的结论一章。]唯美主义的艺术主张及道德规则也在阿尔杰农·查尔斯·斯温伯尼和1890年代的英国作家奥斯卡·王尔德、阿瑟·西蒙斯、莱昂内尔·约翰逊及艺术家J. M. 惠斯勒、奥布里·比尔兹利等人的作品中得到体现。唯美主义所强调的某些主张,特别是艺术作品的"艺术自治"(艺术自足)、强调技巧与艺术性的重要性、诗歌与小说独立于生活或是具有"内在"价值等,对20世纪著名作家W. B. 叶芝、T. E. 休姆、T. S. 艾略特的创作,以及*新批评*的文学理论都产生了重要影响。

相关发展情况参见:*审美意识形态、颓废派文艺、美术、象牙塔*。参阅:威廉·冈特所著的《美的历险》(1945,1975年重印);弗兰克·克默德所著的《浪漫的想象》(1957);伊妮德·斯塔基所著的《从戈蒂耶到艾略特》(1960);R. V. 约翰逊所著的《唯美主义》(1969)。关于18世纪产生"艺术品自身即是目的"这一理论(源自神学)的知识界与社会条件,参见:M. H. 艾布拉姆斯所著的《以文行事:艾布拉姆斯精选集》(1989)一书中的"像这样的艺术:现代美学社会学"。唯美运动中实用的论著选集,参阅:埃里克·沃纳与格雷厄姆·霍夫合编的两卷本《陌生与美丽:1848—1910审美批评文集》(1983);萨利·莱杰与罗杰·卢克赫斯特合编的《世纪末:1880—1890文化史读本》(2000)。关于该主题相关书籍的实用性描述指南,参阅:琳达·C. 道林所著的《唯美主义与颓废主义:选择性注释书目》(1977)。近年来,一些哲学家和文学批评家重新评估了"审美"与"美"这两个概念。参见:乔治·莱文主编的《美学与意识形态》(1994);伊莱恩·斯卡里所著的《论美与公正》(1999);阿瑟·C. 丹托所著的《美的滥用:美学与艺术的概念》(2003);乔纳森·罗斯伯格所著的《重回美学:自治、冷漠与后现代主义》(2005);丹尼斯·多诺霍所著的《谈谈美》(2003);约翰·阿姆斯特朗所著的《美的隐秘力量》(2004);苏珊·斯图尔特所著的《开放的工作室:艺术与美学论文集》(2005)。贝伊斯·高特与多米尼克·麦基弗·洛佩斯合编的《劳特里奇美学指南》(2005年第2版)是一本非常有用的

essays on the aesthetic. A comprehensive reference work is Michael Kelly, ed., *Encyclopedia of Aesthetics*, 4 vols. (1998).

For references to *Aestheticism* in other entries, see page *168.*

aesthetics: 4; *3.*

affective fallacy: In an essay published in 1946, W. K. Wimsatt and Monroe C. Beardsley defined the affective fallacy as the error of evaluating a poem by its effects—especially its emotional effects—upon the reader. As a result of this fallacy "the poem itself, as an object of specifically critical judgment, tends to disappear," so that criticism "ends in impressionism and relativism." The two critics wrote in direct reaction to the view of I. A. Richards, in his influential *Principles of Literary Criticism* (1923), that the value of a poem can be measured by the psychological responses it incites in its readers. Beardsley later modified the earlier claim by the admission that "it does not appear that critical evaluation can be done at all except in relation to certain types of effect that aesthetic objects have upon their perceivers." So altered, the doctrine becomes a claim for *objective criticism*, in which the critic, instead of describing the effects of a work, focuses on the features, devices, and form of the work by which such effects are achieved. An extreme reaction against the doctrine of the affective fallacy was manifested during the 1970s in the development of *reader-response criticism*.

Refer to: Wimsatt and Beardsley, "The Affective Fallacy," reprinted in W. K. Wimsatt, *The Verbal Icon* (1954); and Monroe C. Beardsley, *Aesthetics: Problems in the Philosophy of Criticism* (1958), p. 491 and chapter 11. See also Wimsatt and Beardsley's related concept of the *intentional fallacy*.

affective stylistics: 332.

African-American writers: 274; *249.* See *Black Arts Movement; Harlem Renaissance; performance poetry; slave narratives; spirituals.*

Age of Johnson: 282.

Age of Sensibility: 282.

Age of Transcendentalism: 275.

Agrarians: 277.

agroikos (ăgroi′ kŏs): **378.**

alazon (ăl′ ăzŏn): **378**; *184.*

Alexandrine (alexan′ drĭn): **219**; *94.*

关于美学的历史和描述性文章合集。迈克尔·凯利主编的四卷本《美学百科全书》(1998)则是一本综合性参考书。

其他条目中提及"唯美主义"的地方，参见第168页。

aesthetics：美学　**4**；*3*。

Affective Fallacy：情感谬误（又译感受谬误）

W. K. 维姆萨特和门罗·C. 比尔兹利在他们1946年共同发表的论文中，把"情感谬误"解释为根据读者的感受，特别是感情上的效果，来评价诗歌的错误做法。这种谬误致使"作为深究细品之物的诗歌趋于埋没"，而对诗的批评则"流于印象主义和相对主义"。这两位批评家对 I. A. 理查兹在其颇有影响的《文学批评原理》(1923)一书中提出的观点作出了直接回应，理查兹认为诗歌的价值可以通过其在读者心中激发起的心理反应加以衡量。后来，比尔兹利改变了其原有主张，承认"看来并非只有凭借美的事物赋予欣赏者的种种感受才能对它进行评价"。这种修正后的文学批评学说主张*客观批评*，即批评家不应绘声绘色于作品给自己的感受，而是要着重分析作品取得艺术感染力的特征、手段和形式。1970年代发展起来的*读者反应批评*对情感谬误学说进行了激烈的抨击。

参阅：维姆萨特与比尔兹利合写的文章"情感谬误"，重印收入 W. K. 维姆萨特所著的《语像》(1954，又译《词语偶像》)；门罗·C. 比尔兹利所著的《美学：批评哲学中的问题》(1958)第491页及第11章。也请参阅维姆萨特和比尔兹利的相关概念：*意图谬误*。

affective stylistics：感受文体学　**332**。

African-American writers：非裔美国作家　**274**；*249*。参见：*黑人艺术运动、哈莱姆文艺复兴、表演诗歌、奴隶故事、灵歌*。

Age of Johnson：约翰逊时代　**282**。

Age of Sensibility：情感时期　**282**。

Age of Transcendentalism：超验主义时期　**275**。

Agrarians：平均地权论者　**277**。

agroikos：乡巴佬　**378**。

alazon：骗子　**378**；*184*。

Alexandrine：亚历山大体　**219**；*94*。

alienation effect: In his *epic theater* of the 1920s and later, the German dramatist Bertolt Brecht adapted the *Russian formalist* concept of "defamiliarization" into what he called the "alienation effect" (*Verfremdungseffekt*). The German term is also translated as **estrangement effect** or **distancing effect**; the last is closest to Brecht's notion, in that it avoids the negative connotations of jadedness, incapacity to feel, and social apathy that the word "alienation" has acquired in English. This effect, Brecht said, is used by the dramatist to make familiar aspects of the present social reality seem strange, so as to prevent the emotional identification or involvement of the audience with the characters and their actions in a play. His own aim in drama was instead to evoke a critical distance and attitude in the spectators, in order to arouse them to take action against, rather than simply to accept, the state of society and behavior represented on the stage.

On Brecht, refer to *Marxist criticism*; for a related aesthetic concept, see *distance and involvement*.

allegorical imagery: 8.

allegorical interpretation (of the Bible): **181**.

allegory: An allegory is a narrative, whether in prose or verse, in which the agents and actions, and sometimes the setting as well, are contrived by the author to make coherent sense on the "literal," or primary, level of signification, and at the same time to communicate a second, correlated order of signification.

We can distinguish two main types: (1) Historical and political allegory, in which the characters and actions that are signified literally in their turn represent, or "allegorize," historical personages and events. So in John Dryden's *Absalom and Achitophel* (1681), the biblical King David represents Charles II of England, Absalom represents his natural son the Duke of Monmouth, and the biblical story of Absalom's rebellion against his father (2 Samuel 13–18) allegorizes the rebellion of Monmouth against King Charles. (2) The allegory of ideas, in which the literal characters represent concepts and the plot allegorizes an abstract doctrine or thesis. Both types of allegory may either be sustained throughout a work, as in *Absalom and Achitophel* and John Bunyan's *The Pilgrim's Progress* (1678), or else serve merely as an episode in a nonallegorical work. A famed example of episodic allegory is the encounter of Satan with his daughter Sin, as well as with Death—who is represented allegorically as the son born of their incestuous relationship—in John Milton's *Paradise Lost*, Book II (1667).

In the second type, the sustained allegory of ideas, the central device is the *personification* of abstract entities such as virtues, vices, states of mind, modes of life, and types of character. In explicit allegories, such reference is specified by the names given to characters and places. Thus Bunyan's *The Pilgrim's Progress* allegorizes the Christian doctrine of salvation by telling how the character named Christian, warned by Evangelist, flees the City of Destruction and makes his way laboriously to the Celestial City; en route he encounters characters with names like Faithful, Hopeful, and the Giant Despair, and passes through places

Alienation Effect：异化效果

1920年代及其以后，德国剧作家贝尔托尔特·布莱希特在其所著的《史诗戏剧》中把*俄国形式主义批评家*提出的"陌生化"概念转换成"异化效果"。这一德文术语也被译为**陌生化效果**或**间离效果**；后者最接近布莱希特的本义，因为它消除了"异化"一词在英语中所具有的迟钝、麻木不仁、社会冷漠等负面内涵意义。布莱希特认为这一效果被戏剧家用来使人们所熟悉的当今社会现实变得生疏奇异，以免观众出现感情认同或介入剧中角色及其行为之中。相反，他自己的戏剧目的是使观众与角色及其行为保持距离，以批判的态度来对待舞台上发生的事件，以此引发观众行动起来进行反抗，而不是简单地接受舞台上呈现的社会现实和行为方式。

关于布莱希特，可以参阅*马克思主义批评*中的相关论述；与该术语相关的美学概念，参见：*心理距离与感情介入*。

allegorical imagery：寓言形象　8。

allegorical interpretation (of the Bible)：(圣经中的) 寓言释义　181。

Allegory：寓言

无论是以散文还是诗歌的形式出现，寓言都是一种叙事文体，作者通过构造人物、情节，有时还包括场景的描写，构成完整的"字面"意义，即第一层意义，同时传达另一层相关的意义。

我们可以把寓言划分为两种主要类型：(1) 历史与政治寓言：借助字面上描写的人物与情节指代或"讽喻"历史人物与事件。在约翰·德莱顿所著的《押沙龙与阿奇托菲尔》(1681) 中，大卫王象征着英王查理二世，押沙龙代表他的私生子蒙默思公爵，引用圣经故事中押沙龙对他父亲的反叛（《撒母耳记下》13—18）来象征蒙默思公爵对国王查理的反抗。(2) 观念寓言：故事里的人物象征概念，故事情节用于传达、阐明抽象的训诲或论点。这两类寓言体裁既可能贯穿同一作品的始终，如德莱顿的《押沙龙与阿奇托菲尔》和约翰·班扬的《天路历程》(1678)，也可能只用于一部非寓言作品的某个情节，最著名的例子是约翰·弥尔顿《失乐园》(1667) 第二卷中撒旦与他的女儿"罪恶"和"死亡"（象征他们乱伦而生的儿子）相遇的一段描写。

观念寓言作品主要以拟人手法表现美德、邪恶、心灵状态、生活方式、人物类型等抽象概念。寓意较明显的这类作品通过人物和地点的名称来道破所指。班扬所著的《天路历程》就是这样表现基督救世的教义的。书中描写：基督徒经传道者指点，逃离"灭亡城"，历尽艰辛奔赴"天城"，路逢名为"忠信""盼望""绝望"等人，途经"灰心潭""死荫谷""虚华集市"。以下原文摘录可以表现出其

like the Slough of Despond, the Valley of the Shadow of Death, and Vanity Fair. A passage from this work indicates the nature of an explicit allegorical narrative:

> Now as Christian was walking solitary by himself, he espied one afar off come crossing over the field to meet him; and their hap was to meet just as they were crossing the way of each other. The Gentleman's name was Mr. Worldly-Wiseman; he dwelt in the Town of Carnal-Policy, a very great Town, and also hard by from whence Christian came.

Works which are primarily nonallegorical may introduce **allegorical imagery** (the personification of abstract entities who perform a brief allegorical action) in short passages. Familiar instances are the opening lines of Milton's *L'Allegro* and *Il Penseroso* (1645). This device was exploited especially in the *poetic diction* of authors in the mid-eighteenth century. An example—so brief that it presents an allegoric tableau rather than an action—is the passage in Thomas Gray's "Elegy Written in a Country Churchyard" (1751):

> Can Honour's voice provoke the silent dust,
> Or Flatt'ry soothe the dull cold ear of Death?

Allegory is a narrative strategy which may be employed in any literary form or genre. The early sixteenth-century *Everyman* is an allegory in the form of a *morality play*. *The Pilgrim's Progress* is a moral and religious allegory in a prose narrative; Edmund Spenser's *The Faerie Queene* (1590–96) fuses moral, religious, historical, and political allegory in a verse *romance*; the third book of Jonathan Swift's *Gulliver's Travels*, the voyage to Laputa and Lagado (1726), is an allegorical *satire* directed mainly against philosophical and scientific pedantry; and William Collins' "Ode on the Poetical Character" (1747) is a *lyric* poem which allegorizes a topic in literary criticism—the nature, sources, and power of the poet's creative imagination. John Keats makes a subtle use of allegory throughout his ode "To Autumn" (1820), most explicitly in the second stanza, which personifies the autumnal season as a female figure amid the scenes and activities of the harvest.

Sustained allegory was a favorite form in the Middle Ages, when it produced masterpieces, especially in the verse-narrative mode of the *dream vision*, in which the narrator falls asleep and experiences an allegoric dream; this mode includes, in the fourteenth century, Dante's *Divine Comedy*, the French *Roman de la Rose*, Chaucer's *House of Fame*, and William Langland's *Piers Plowman*. But sustained allegory has been written in all literary periods, and is the form of such major nineteenth-century dramas in verse as Goethe's *Faust, Part II*; Shelley's *Prometheus Unbound*; and Thomas Hardy's *The Dynasts*. In the twentieth century, the stories and novels of Franz Kafka can be considered instances of implicit allegory.

Allegory was on the whole devalued during the twentieth century, but has been reinvested with positive values by some recent theorists. The Marxist critic Fredric Jameson uses the term to signify the relation of a literary text to

讽喻鲜明的特性：

> 此时，基督徒正一个人孤孤单单地走着。他远远瞥见一个人穿过田野迎面而来。正要擦肩而过时，两人刚好打了个照面。来人名叫世故先生，住在拜俗城，那是一座大城，离基督徒来的地方不远。
>
> （苏欲晓译）

一般而言，非寓言作品也可以在某些段落章节中使用**寓言形象**（即把抽象的概念拟人化，用来描写简短的寓言情节）这种手法。弥尔顿《快乐的人》和《沉思的人》（1645）的开头部分就有这种人们熟悉的范例。*诗意辞藻*中的 18 世纪中期作家尤其爱用寓言形象。例如，托马斯·格雷的《墓畔哀歌》（1751）短短两行就展现出一幅寓意深刻而非刻意叙事的画面：

> "荣誉"的声音能激发沉默的死灰？
> "献媚"能叫死神听软了耳根？
>
> （卞之琳译）

寓言是任何文学形式或体裁都可采用的一种叙事技巧。16 世纪早期的《每人》就是这样一则*道德剧*形式的寓言故事。《天路历程》是叙事散文体的道德、宗教寓言。埃德蒙·斯宾塞的《仙后》（1590—1596）则是集道德、宗教、历史、政治寓言于一体的*传奇诗篇*。乔纳森·斯威夫特的《格列佛游记》第三卷（《拉普他与拉嘎多游记》）（1726）为寓言性*讽刺*小说，旨在暴露当时的哲学和科学学究们的迂腐自大。此外，威廉·柯林斯的寓言*抒情诗*《诗人颂》（1747），把诗人创作想象力的性质、源泉与威力这一文学批评的议题寓言化了。约翰·济慈在他的《秋颂》（1820）里精湛地运用了寓言手法，其中最精彩的要数第二节，他把秋季寓拟为收获的场景和活动中的一位女性形象。

寓言早在中世纪就已成为人们喜闻乐见的一种文学形式，当时产生了不少名著，尤其是以*梦幻体*的诗歌-叙事模式创作的寓言，描写叙述者昏昏入睡后所经历的寓言化梦境。这种体例包括 14 世纪但丁的《神曲》、法国寓言长诗《玫瑰传奇》、乔叟的《名望之屋》（又译《声誉之宫》）、威廉·朗格兰的《农夫皮尔斯》。寓言创作遍及各个文学时期，一些世界名著就是用寓言形式写成的，如 19 世纪著名的诗体剧作：歌德的《浮士德》第二部、雪莱的《解放了的普罗米修斯》、托马斯·哈代的《列王》。20 世纪弗朗兹·卡夫卡的短篇与长篇小说，可被认为是含蓄的寓言体故事的范例。

寓言在 20 世纪总体上受到了贬低，但近来一些理论家一直在给予其正面评价。马克思主义批评家詹姆逊用这一术语来表示文学文本与其历史潜文本、其

its historical subtext, its "political unconscious." (See Jameson, under *Marxist criticism*.) And Paul de Man elevates allegory, because it candidly manifests its artifice, over what he calls the more "mystified" concept of the *symbol*, which he claims seems to promise, falsely, a unity of form and content, thought and expression. (See de Man, under *deconstruction*.)

A variety of literary *genres* may be classified as species of allegory in that they all narrate one coherent set of circumstances which are intended to signify a second order of correlated meanings:

A **fable** (also called an **apologue**) is a short narrative, in prose or verse, that exemplifies an abstract moral thesis or principle of human behavior; usually, at its conclusion, either the narrator or one of the characters states the moral in the form of an *epigram*. Most common is the **beast fable**, in which animals talk and act like the human types they represent. In the familiar fable of the fox and the grapes, the fox—after exerting all his wiles to get the grapes hanging beyond his reach, but in vain—concludes that they are probably sour anyway: the express moral is that human beings belittle what they cannot get. (The modern expression "sour grapes" derives from this fable.) The beast fable is a very ancient form that existed in Egypt, India, and Greece. The fables in Western cultures derive mainly from the stories that were, probably mistakenly, attributed to Aesop, a Greek slave of the sixth century BC. In the seventeenth century a Frenchman, Jean de la Fontaine, wrote a set of witty fables in verse which are the classics of this literary kind. Chaucer's "The Nun's Priest's Tale," the story of the cock and the fox, is a beast fable. The American Joel Chandler Harris wrote many Uncle Remus stories that are beast fables, told in southern African-American dialect, whose origins have been traced to *folktales* in the oral literature of West Africa that feature a trickster similar to Uncle Remus' Brer Rabbit. (A **trickster** is a character in a story who persistently uses his wiliness, and gift of gab, to achieve his ends by outmaneuvering or outwitting other characters.) A counterpart in many Native American cultures are the beast fables that feature Coyote as the central trickster. James Thurber's *Fables for Our Time* (1940) is a recent set of short fables; and in *Animal Farm* (1945) George Orwell expanded the beast fable into a sustained satire on Russian totalitarianism under Stalin in the mid-twentieth century.

A **parable** is a very short narrative about human beings presented so as to stress the tacit analogy, or parallel, with a general thesis or lesson that the narrator is trying to bring home to his audience. The parable was one of Jesus' favorite devices as a teacher; examples are his parables of the good Samaritan and of the prodigal son. Here is his terse parable of the fig tree, Luke 13:6–9:

> He spake also this parable: A certain man had a fig tree planted in his vineyard; and he came and sought fruit thereon, and found none. Then said he unto the dresser of his vineyard, "Behold, these three years I come seeking fruit on this fig tree, and find none: cut it down; why cumbereth it the ground?" And he answering said unto him, "Lord, let it alone this year also, till I shall dig about it, and dung it. And if it bears fruit, well: and if not, then after that thou shalt cut it down."

"政治无意识"之间的关系。（参见：*马克思主义批评*中的詹姆逊。）保罗·德·曼认为寓言坦率地展现了它的技巧，故将寓言提升到他所说的**象征**这一更多"费解"的概念之上，在他看来，象征似乎虚假地允诺了一种形式与内容、思想与表达的统一。（参见：*解构主义*中的德·曼。）

许多文学体裁都可以划归为寓言的特殊形式，它们通过描述某些情节的来龙去脉，有意来暗示相关的第二层含义：

寓言故事（又称**道德故事**）是短篇叙事散文或诗篇，反映抽象的道德主题或人类行为准则，结尾时往往由叙述者或某一角色以*警句*形式道出道德的至理名言。最常见的是**动物寓言故事**，其中各种动物按照各自代表的人物类型说话行动。在尽人皆知的狐狸与葡萄的故事里，狐狸在使尽诡计后因为得不到高高悬挂的葡萄就悻悻地说：葡萄准是酸的。这个故事揭示的寓意是，人类往往会贬低他们自己得不到的东西（现代的"酸葡萄"一词就源自这则寓言）。动物寓言是存在于埃及、印度、希腊的一种非常古老的文学形式。西方文化中的动物寓言故事主要出自公元前6世纪一个叫伊索的希腊奴隶（这一看法可能有误）。17世纪法国诗人让·德·拉封丹写了一系列风趣诙谐的寓言诗，堪称这类文学的经典。乔叟的"尼姑教士讲的故事"里公鸡和狐狸的故事也是一篇动物寓言。美国作家乔尔·钱德勒·哈里斯写了许多属于动物寓言的雷默斯大叔的故事，这些故事用美国南方黑人方言来讲述，其渊源可以追溯到西非口头文学中的*民间故事*，他们把骗子塑造成类似雷默斯故事中的兔子兄弟（**骗子**是故事中的主人公，他一贯地耐心地运用自己的阴谋诡计和如簧巧舌，以机智或诡计取胜别的主人公，从而最终达到自己的目的）。与之相对应，在北美文化的动物寓言故事中，草原狼被塑造成主要的骗子。詹姆斯·瑟伯所著的《当代寓言》（1940）是一部近期的短篇寓言故事集。乔治·奥威尔所著的《动物庄园》（1945）则是把动物寓言扩展成为一部关于20世纪中期斯大林统治下的俄国极权主义的讽刺作品。

醒世寓言是关于人类自身的短篇叙事故事，它通过含蓄的比拟和对比使人从故事情节中领悟出寓言所要阐明的普遍主题或训诫。这是基督最擅长的一种训导方法，例如在圣经中他就乐善好施者与浪子回头这一主题所作的讲述。这里例举《路加福音》（13：6—9）里基督以无花果树为题的简洁的醒世寓言故事：

> 主还讲了这样一个寓言故事：一个人有一棵无花果树，栽在葡萄园里。他来到树前找果子，却找不着，就对管园的说："看哪，我这三年，来到这无花果树前找果子，竟找不着。把它砍了吧，何必白占地土呢！"管园的说："主啊，今年且留着。等我周围掘开土，加上粪，以后若结果了便罢，不然，再把它砍了。"

Mark Turner, in a greatly extended use, employs "parable" to signify any "projection of one story onto another," or onto many others, whether the projection is intentional or not. He proposes that, in this extended sense, parable is not merely a literary or *didactic* device, but "a basic cognitive principle" that comes into play in interpreting "every level of our experience" and that "shows up everywhere, from simple actions like telling time to complex literary creations like Proust's *A la recherche du temps perdu*." (Mark Turner, *The Literary Mind*, New York, 1996.)

An **exemplum** is a story told as a particular instance of the general theme in a religious sermon. The device was popular in the Middle Ages, when extensive collections of exempla, some historical and some legendary, were prepared for use by preachers. In Chaucer's "The Pardoner's Tale," the Pardoner, preaching on the theme, "Greed is the root of all evil," incorporates as an exemplum the tale of the three drunken revelers who set out to find and defy Death and find a heap of gold instead, only to find Death after all, when they kill one another in the attempt to gain sole possession of the treasure. By extension the term "exemplum" is also applied to tales used in a formal, though nonreligious, exhortation. Thus Chaucer's Chanticleer, in "The Nun's Priest's Tale," borrows the preacher's technique in the ten exempla he tells in a vain effort to persuade his skeptical wife, Dame Pertelote the hen, that bad dreams forebode disaster. See G. R. Owst, *Literature and the Pulpit in Medieval England* (2d ed., 1961, chapter 4).

Proverbs are short, pithy statements of widely accepted truths about everyday life. Many proverbs are allegorical, in that the explicit statement is meant to have, by analogy or by extended reference, a general application: "a stitch in time saves nine"; "people in glass houses should not throw stones." Refer to *The Oxford Dictionary of English Proverbs*, ed. W. G. Smith and F. P. Wilson (1970).

See *didactic, symbol* (for the distinction between allegory and symbol), and (on the fourfold allegorical interpretation of the Bible) *interpretation: typological and allegorical*. On allegory in general, consult C. S. Lewis, *The Allegory of Love* (1936), chapter 2; Edwin Honig, *Dark Conceit: The Making of Allegory* (1959); Angus Fletcher, *Allegory: The Theory of a Symbolic Mode* (1964); Rosemund Tuve, *Allegorical Imagery* (1966); Michael Murrin, *The Veil of Allegory* (1969); Maureen Quilligan, *The Language of Allegory* (1979); Jon Whitman, *Allegory* (1987).

For references to *allegory* in other entries, see page 88.

alliteration: Alliteration is the repetition of a speech sound in a sequence of nearby words. Usually the term is applied only to consonants, and only when the recurrent sound is made emphatic because it begins a word or a stressed syllable within a word. In Old English **alliterative meter**, alliteration is the principal organizing device of the verse line: the verse is unrhymed; each line is divided into two half-lines of two strong stresses by a decisive pause, or *caesura*; and at least one, and usually both, of the two stressed syllables in the first half-line alliterate with the first stressed syllable of the second

马克·特纳从更广泛的意义上认为,"醒世寓言"是"用一个故事影射另一个故事"或其他许多故事,不论这种影射是有意的还是无意的。他提出,广义上,醒世寓言不仅仅是一种文学或*教诲*手段,还是"一种基本的认知原则",该原则用于解释"我们体验的每一个层次"并被"广泛应用于从说明时间这一简单动作到如同普鲁斯特写作《追忆似水年华》这样复杂的文学创作中"。(马克·特纳:《文学思想》,纽约,1996。)

劝谕性故事是通过一个具体实例来阐述一篇宗教布道文的主题。这种创作手法流行于中世纪,一些历史性的和传奇性的劝谕性故事为传教士广泛收集采用。乔叟的"卖赎罪券者讲的故事"中,卖赎罪券者以"贪婪是万恶之源"为题讲述了这样一个劝谕性寓言故事:三个寻欢作乐的人去寻找和反抗"死神"时发现了一堆金子,结果各自为了独吞财宝互相残杀,全都送了命。广义上讲,"劝谕性故事"也可用于指代非宗教性但又严肃认真的劝世作品。在"尼姑教士讲的故事"中,乔叟笔下的"公鸡"就是借用了这种劝谕手法对多疑的爱妻母鸡珀特洛特夫人讲了十个寓言故事,苦口婆心地说明噩梦预示灾祸的道理。参阅:G. R. 奥斯特所著的《文学与中世纪英格兰的布道》(1961年第2版)第4章。

谚语是广为流传的概述生活哲理的一些短小精练的句子。许多谚语也属于寓言范畴,它们形式简明,借以类推或外延意义,具有广泛的实用性:像"防微杜渐";"自身有短,休惹他人"等。参阅:W. G. 史密斯与 F. P. 威尔逊合编的《牛津英语谚语辞典》(1970)。

参见:*教诲文学*、*象征*(关于寓言与象征之区别)、*象征释义*与*寓意释义*(对圣经四重寓意的解释)。关于寓言的一般论述,参阅:C. S. 刘易斯所著的《爱情的寓言》(1936)第2章;埃德温·霍尼格所著的《黑色的比喻:寓言的形成》(1959);安格斯·弗莱彻所著的《寓言:一种象征模式理论》(1964);罗斯蒙德·图夫所著的《寓言/讽喻意象》(1966);迈克尔·马林所著的《寓言的帷幕》(1969);莫琳·奎里根所著的《寓言的语言》(1979);乔恩·惠特曼所著的《寓言》(1987)。

其他条目中提及"寓言"的地方,参见第88页。

Alliteration:头韵

头韵是一串相近的字词中相同音素形成的重复。通常它指的是辅音,尤其是词首辅音或词内重读音节辅音的复用。在古英语的**头韵格律**中,头韵是诗行的主要组织手法:诗节之间不押韵,每行由*行间停顿*分割为前后两个半行,各有两个重读音节。前半行的两个重音节,或者至少是一个,与后半行中第一个重读音节

11 ALLITERATION

half-line. (In this type of versification a vowel was considered to alliterate with any other vowel.) A number of Middle English poems, such as William Langland's *Piers Plowman* and the romance *Sir Gawain and the Green Knight*, both written in the fourteenth century, continued to use and play variations upon the old alliterative meter. (See *strong-stress meters*.) In the opening line of *Piers Plowman*, for example, all four of the stressed syllables alliterate:

> In a *só*mer *sé*son, when *só*ft was the *só*nne....

In later English versification, however, alliteration is used only for special stylistic effects, such as to reinforce the meaning, to link related words, or to provide tone color and enhance the palpability of enunciating the words. An example is the repetition of the *s*, *th*, and *w* consonants in Shakespeare's Sonnet 30:

> When to the *s*essions of *s*weet *s*ilent *th*ought
> I *s*ummon up remembrance of *th*ings past,
> I *s*igh the lack of many a *th*ing I *s*ought
> And *w*ith old *w*oes new *w*ail my dear time's *w*aste....

Various other repetitions of speech sounds are identified by special terms:

Consonance is the repetition of a sequence of two or more consonants, but with a change in the intervening vowel: live-love, lean-alone, pitter-patter. W. H. Auden's poem of the 1930s, "'O where are you going?' said reader to rider," makes prominent use of this device; the last stanza reads:

Assonance is the repetition of identical or similar vowels—especially in stressed syllables—in a sequence of nearby words. Note the recurrent long *i* in the opening lines of Keats' "Ode on a Grecian Urn" (1820):

> Thou still unravished br*i*de of qu*ie*tness,
> Thou foster ch*i*ld of s*i*lence and slow t*i*me....

The richly assonantal effect at the beginning of William Collins' "Ode to Evening" (1747) is achieved by a patterned sequence of changing vowels:

> If aught of oaten stop or pastoral song,
> May hope, chaste Eve, to soothe thy pensive ear....

For a special case of the repetition of vowels and consonants in combination, see *rhyme*. For references to *alliteration* in other entries, see page *140*.

形成头韵呼应。(在这种格律中,元音之间也可以构成头韵。)一些中世纪英国诗歌沿袭了这种古老的头韵法,并且在运用中变换翻新,例如:威廉·朗格兰所著的《农夫皮尔斯》和浪漫传奇《高文爵士与绿衣骑士》。这两部作品都作于14世纪,沿用了古体头韵的各种变体形式。(参见:*强音诗歌*。)例如,《农夫皮尔斯》开篇第一行的四个重音节全部押了头韵:

> 初夏风和日丽,阳光和煦……　　　　　　　　　　　　(沈弘译)

不过,在后来的英诗韵律中,头韵只是用于达到特定的文体效果,如加强语义、衔接相关字词,或是造成音色效果和加强字词发音的清晰感。如莎士比亚第30首十四行诗中就有以辅音 s、th、w 形成的头韵:

> 我有时醉心于沉思默想
> 把过往的事物细细品尝
> 我慨叹许多未曾如愿之事
> 旧恨新怨使我痛悼蹉跎的时光……　　　　　　　　　(辜正坤译)

其他类型的音素重复也各有所称:

辅音韵为两个或两个以上连续辅音的重复,但插入的重读元音有所变化。如 live-love, lean-alone, pitter-patter。W. H. 奥登在作于1930年代的《何往?》(版权未授,请参旧版。——译注)这首诗里出色地运用了辅音韵的表现手法:

> (略)

半谐音:同一行里一串相近字词相同或相似元音的重复,尤其是重读音节里这样的元音复用。请注意以下济慈《希腊古瓮颂》(1820)开头两行中长元音 i 的复用:

> 你委身寂静的完美的处子,
> 受过了沉默和悠久的抚育……　　　　　　　　　　(穆旦译)

而威廉·柯林斯《黄昏颂》(1747)的开篇则是通过连续的同元音与准元音变换来取得醇美的半谐音效果:

> 如果一切的麦笛或牧歌不曾停止,
> 愿这纯洁的夜啊,抚慰你谦恭的耳朵……

有关元音与辅音的综合使用,参见:押韵。其他条目中提及"头韵"的地方,参见第140页。

alliterative meter: 10.

allusion: Allusion is a passing reference, without explicit identification, to a literary or historical person, place, or event, or to another literary work or passage. In the Elizabethan Thomas Nashe's "Litany in Time of Plague,"

> Brightness falls from the air,
> Queens have died young and fair,
> Dust hath closed Helen's eye,

the unidentified "Helen" in the last line alludes to Helen of Troy. Most allusions serve to illustrate or expand upon or enhance a subject, but some are used in order to undercut it ironically by the discrepancy between the subject and the allusion. In the lines from T. S. Eliot's *The Waste Land* (1922) describing a woman at her modern dressing table,

the *ironic* allusion, achieved by echoing Shakespeare's phrasing, is to the description of Cleopatra's magnificent barge in *Antony and Cleopatra* (II. ii. 196ff.):

> The barge she sat in, like a burnish'd throne,
> Burn'd on the water.

For discussion of a poet who makes persistent and complex use of this device, see Reuben A. Brower, *Alexander Pope: The Poetry of Allusion* (1959); see also John Hollander, *The Figure of Echo: A Mode of Allusion in Milton and After* (1981); Edwin Stein, *Wordsworth's Art of Allusion* (1988); Christopher Ricks, *Allusion to the Poets* (2002), and *True Friendship: Geoffrey Hill, Anthony Hecht, and Robert Lowell Under the Sign of Eliot and Pound* (2010).

Since allusions are not explicitly identified, they imply a fund of knowledge that is shared by an author and the audience for whom the author writes. Most literary allusions are intended to be recognized by the generally educated readers of the author's time, but some are aimed at a special coterie. For example, in *Astrophel and Stella*, the Elizabethan *sonnet sequence*, Sir Philip Sidney's punning allusions to Lord Robert Rich, who had married the Stella of the sonnets, were identifiable only by intimates of the people concerned. (See Sonnets 24 and 37.) Some modern authors, including Joyce, Pound, and Eliot, include allusions that are very specialized, or else drawn from the author's private reading and experience, in the awareness that few if any readers will recognize them prior to the detective work of scholarly annotators. The current term *intertextuality* includes literary echoes and allusions as one of the many ways in which any text is interwoven with other texts. See Joseph Pucci, *The Full-Knowing Reader: Allusion and the Power of the Reader in*

alliterative meter：头韵格律　10。

Allusion：典故

　　典故是没有明确关联性的转变参照，类比某一文学或历史人物、地点或事件，或是另一篇文学作品及章节。例如伊丽莎白女王一世时代托马斯·纳什的《瘟疫年的祈祷》：

　　　　光亮从空中降落，
　　　　年轻美丽的女王们死去了，
　　　　尘埃蒙上了海伦的眼睛，

最后一行中未指明的"海伦"引用了特洛伊城海伦的典故。多数典故都是用于阐明或展开或渲染主题，但也有一些则是通过主题与典故不一致之处来达到反讽贬低的目的。例如诗人 T. S. 艾略特在《荒原》（1922）中对一位在时髦的梳妆台前的现代妇女所作的描写（版权未授，请参旧版。——译注）：

　　　　（略）

这个反讽的典故是对莎士比亚诗句的间接效仿，它引自莎剧《安东尼与克莉奥佩特拉》第二幕第二场第 196 行及其下各行，指的是对克莉奥佩特拉富丽堂皇的大游艇的描写：

　　　　她所坐的大船，像发亮的宝座，
　　　　在水上放光。　　　　　　　　　　　　　　（查良铮译）

　　有关惯于综合运用典故手法的诗人的论述，参阅：鲁本·A. 布劳尔所著的《亚历山大·蒲柏诗歌的典故》(1959)；亦可参阅：约翰·霍兰德所著的《回声之影：弥尔顿及其后典故的模式》(1981)；埃德温·斯坦所著的《华兹华斯的典故艺术》(1988)；克里斯托弗·里克斯所著的《诗人们的典故》(2002) 和《真正的友谊：艾略特和庞德标记下的杰弗里·希尔、安东尼·赫克特、罗伯特·洛威尔》(2010)。

　　由于典故并未被明确地标识出来，这就意味着作者和他的读者都应具备相当丰富的知识才能正确理解典故的含义。多数文学典故都能为与作者同时代受过一般教育的读者所领会，但有些典故的读者对象却是针对某个特殊的小圈子。例如，在伊丽莎白女王一世时代的*十四行组诗*《爱星者和星星》中，菲利普·锡德尼爵士所运用的关于迎娶了组诗中的星星斯特拉的罗伯特·里奇勋爵的双关典故，恐怕只有那些对此颇为熟知的人们才能理解（参见十四行组诗 24 和 37）。但是一些当代作家，包括乔伊斯、庞德、艾略特，经常运用一些极其特殊的或是基于个人阅读与个人经历的典章故事，他们知道只有少数读者借助高水平注释者挖掘性的研究工作才能看懂。目前所用的*互文性*这一术语把文学模仿和典故视为任何不同文本之间相互交织的多种方式之一。参阅：约瑟夫·普奇所著的《全知的读者：西方文学传统中的典故与读者的能力》

Western Literary Tradition (1998); and Gregory Machacek, "Allusion," *PMLA*, Vol. 122 (2007).

ambiance: (ăm′ bēäns), **19**.

ambiguity: In ordinary usage "ambiguity" is applied to a fault in style; that is, the use of a vague or equivocal term or expression when what is wanted is precision and particularity of reference. Since William Empson published *Seven Types of Ambiguity* (1930), however, the term has been widely used in criticism to identify a deliberate poetic device: the use of a single word or expression to signify two or more distinct references, or to express two or more diverse attitudes or feelings. **Multiple meaning** and **plurisignation** are alternative terms for this use of language; they have the advantage of avoiding the pejorative association with the word "ambiguity."

When Shakespeare's Cleopatra, exciting the asp to a frenzy, says (*Antony and Cleopatra*, V. ii. 306ff.),

> Come, thou mortal wretch,
> With thy sharp teeth this knot intrinsicate
> Of life at once untie. Poor venomous fool,
> Be angry, and dispatch,

her speech is richly multiple in significance. For example, "mortal" means "fatal" or "death-dealing," and at the same time may signify that the asp is itself mortal, or subject to death. "Wretch" in this context serves to express both contempt and pity (Cleopatra goes on to refer to the asp as "my baby at my breast, / That sucks the nurse asleep"). And the two meanings of "dispatch"—"make haste" and "kill"—are equally relevant.

A special type of multiple meaning is conveyed by the **portmanteau word**. "Portmanteau" designates a large suitcase that opens into two equal compartments, and was introduced into literary criticism by Humpty Dumpty, the expert on semantics in Lewis Carroll's *Through the Looking Glass* (1871). He is explicating to Alice the meaning of the opening lines of "Jabberwocky":

> 'Twas brillig, and the slithy toves
> Did gyre and gimble in the wabe.

"Slithy," Humpty Dumpty explained, "means 'lithe and slimy'.... You see it's like a portmanteau—there are two meanings packed up into one word." James Joyce exploited this device—the fusion of two or more existing words—in order to sustain the multiple levels of meaning throughout his long dream narrative *Finnegans Wake* (1939). An example is his comment on girls who are "yung and easily freudened"; "freudened" combines "frightened" and "Freud," while "yung" combines "young" and Sigmund Freud's rival in depth psychology, Carl Jung. (Compare *pun*.) "Différance," a key analytic term of the philosopher of language Jacques Derrida, is a portmanteau noun which he describes as combining two diverse meanings of the French verb "différer": "to differ" and "to defer." (See *deconstruction*.)

(1998);格雷戈里·麦查塞克所写的文章"典故",载于《美国现代语言学协会会刊》2007年第122卷。

ambiance:气氛 19。
Ambiguity:歧义

在一般意义上,"歧义"往往指文风上的缺陷,即本应明确具体的措辞或语意却表现得含混晦涩。自从1930年威廉·燕卜荪发表《晦涩的七种类型》(又译《朦胧的七种类型》)以来,该词已被广泛运用于文学批评,代表诗歌创作的一种手法——用某一词或词组指两个或更多的不同事物或者表示两种或多种相异的态度与情感。**语义重叠**和**复义**是这种语言表达方法的代名词,它们具有避免对"歧义"一词产生贬义联想的优点。

在莎剧中,克莉奥佩特拉激怒毒蛇后说道(《安东尼与克莉奥佩特拉》第五幕第二场第306行及其下各行):

> 来,你杀人的毒物,
> 用你的利齿咬断这一个
> 生命的葛藤吧。可怜的蠢东西,
> 张开你的怒口,赶快完成你的使命,　　　　　(朱生豪译)

她的这一席话含有多层语义。例如:"杀人的"一词的意思是"致命的"或"致死的",同时也表示这条毒蛇本身是垂死的或是必有一死的。又如"毒物"在文中既表示蔑视又含有怜悯之情(克莉奥佩特拉接下去又把毒蛇比作"我怀里的乳婴,吸吮着乳汁睡去")。同时"赶快完成"也包含着"快"与"杀"两层相关联的意思。

合并词是语义重叠的一种特殊形式。"合并"是指一个有着两个同样隔层的大的旅行衣箱,它是由路易斯·卡罗尔《镜中世界》(1871)里描写的那位语义专家汉普蒂·丹普蒂引入文学批评领域的,他对爱丽丝解释了《捷波瓦奇》开头几行的意思:

> 这是灿烂而滑动的土武斯,
> 在摇摆中旋转和平衡。　　　　　(赵明菲译)

汉普蒂·丹普蒂解释说:"滑动就是'光滑'与'流动'……你看,这就是一个合并词,两个意思装在一个词里了。"詹姆斯·乔伊斯为了在他的长篇梦境小说《芬尼根的觉醒》(1939)中取得语义的多重效果而充分运用了这种修辞手法,即把两个或更多的词混合在一起。例如他对"yung and easily freudened"的姑娘们所作的评论中,freudened混合了frightened(害怕)与Freud(弗洛伊德:奥地利精神分析学家)两个词,而yung则包含了young(年轻)与Jung(西格蒙德·弗洛伊德在深层心理学方面的劲敌卡尔·荣格)两个词义。(对比:*双关*。)又如,语言哲学家雅克·德里达提出的重要的语言分析术语differance(异延),他描述为混合了法文动词differer(使不同)的两个不同意思:"differ"(相异)和"defer"(拖延)。(参见:*解构主义*。)

By his analysis of ambiguity, William Empson helped make current a mode of *explication* developed especially by exponents of the *New Criticism*, which greatly expanded awareness of the complexity and richness of poetic language. The risk is that the quest for ambiguities will result in **over-reading**: excessively ingenious, overdrawn, and sometimes contradictory explications of a literary word or passage.

For related terms see *connotation and denotation* and *pun*. For a critique of Empson's theory and practice, refer to Elder Olson, "William Empson, Contemporary Criticism and Poetic Diction," in *Critics and Criticism*, ed. R. S. Crane (1952).

American literature, periods of: 273.

American Renaissance: 274.

anachronism (anăk′ rŏnism): **300.**

anagnorisis (anagnō′ rĭsĭs): **297;** *409.*

anapestic (anapĕs′ tik): **218.**

anaphora (ană′ fora): **345.**

anatomy (in satire): **354.**

anecdote: 365.

Anglo-Norman Period: 280.

anglophone authors: 285.

Anglo-Saxon Period: 279.

annals: 51.

antagonist (in a plot): **294.**

anthropocentric: 97.

anticlimax: 25.

antifoundationalism: 309.

antihero: The chief person in a modern novel or play whose character is widely discrepant from that of the traditional protagonist, or *hero*, of a serious literary work. Instead of manifesting largeness, dignity, power, or heroism, the

通过其对歧义的分析，威廉·燕卜荪帮助促成了一种文学*解说*方式的流行，这一方式尤其得到*新批评*倡导者的发展，从而大大提高了对诗歌语言复杂性和丰富性的认识。风险在于，过分探究语义的重叠歧义会引起**过度解读**：添枝加叶，夸大其词，有时甚至会出现对同一文学词语或段落自相矛盾的解释。

相关术语参见：*涵义与表义*、*双关*。对燕卜荪的理论和实践的批评，参见：埃尔德·奥尔森所写的文章"燕卜荪、当代批评与诗意辞藻"，收入 R. S. 克莱恩主编的《批评与批评家》(1952) 一书。

American literature，periods of：美国文学各时期的划分　273。

American Renaissance：美国的文艺复兴时期　274。

anachronism：时代错误　300。

anagnorisis：发现　297；*409*。

anapestic：抑抑扬格　218。

anaphora：首语重复法　345。

anatomy（in satire）：(讽刺中的) 剖析　354。

anecdote：轶事　365。

Anglo-Norman Period：盎格鲁－诺曼时期　280。

anglophone authors：英语作家　285。

Anglo-Saxon Period：盎格鲁－撒克逊时期　279。

annals：年鉴　51。

antagonist（in a plot）：(情节中的) 对立角色　294。

anthropocentric：人类中心主义　97。

anticlimax：突降法　25。

antifoundationalism：反基础论　309。

Antihero：反英雄

反英雄指的是现代小说或戏剧中其品行与读者心目中严肃文学作品里传统的主角或*英雄*形象相去甚远的主要角色。与伟大、高尚、威严或英勇的英雄形象相反，

antihero is petty, ignominious, passive, clownish, or dishonest. The use of nonheroic protagonists occurs as early as the *picaresque* novel of the sixteenth century, and the heroine of Defoe's *Moll Flanders* (1722) is a thief and a prostitute. The term "antihero," however, is usually applied to writings in the period of disillusion after the Second World War, beginning with such lowly protagonists as we find in John Wain's *Hurry on Down* (1953) and Kingsley Amis' *Lucky Jim* (1954). Notable later instances in the novel are Yossarian in Joseph Heller's *Catch-22* (1961), Humbert Humbert in Vladimir Nabokov's *Lolita* (1955), and Tyrone Slothrop in Thomas Pynchon's *Gravity's Rainbow* (1973). The use of an antihero is especially conspicuous in dramatic tragedy, in which the traditional protagonist had usually been of high estate, possessing dignity and courage (see *tragedy*). Extreme instances are the characters who people a world stripped of certainties, values, or even meaning in Samuel Beckett's dramas—the tramps Vladimir and Estragon in *Waiting for Godot* (1952) or the blind and paralyzed old man, Hamm, who is the protagonist in *Endgame* (1958).

See literature of the *absurd* and *black comedy*, and refer to Ihab Hassan, "The Antihero in Modern British and American Fiction," in *Rumors of Change* (1995). For references to *antihero* in other entries, see page 2.

antimasque: 210.

antinovel: 258.

antipathy (antĭp′ athy): **105.**

antistrophe (antĭs′ trŏfē): **262.**

antithesis (antĭ′ thesis) is a contrast or opposition in the meanings of contiguous phrases or clauses that manifest **parallelism**—that is, a similar word order and structure—in their *syntax*. An example is Alexander Pope's description of Atticus in his *Epistle to Dr. Arbuthnot* (1735), "Willing to wound, and yet afraid to strike." In the antithesis in the second line of Pope's description of the Baron's designs against Belinda, in *The Rape of the Lock* (1714), the parallelism in the syntax is made prominent by *alliteration* in the antithetic nouns:

> Resolved to win, he meditates the way,
> By *f*orce to ravish, or by *f*raud betray.

In a sentence from Samuel Johnson's prose fiction *Rasselas* (1759), chapter 26, the antithesis is similarly heightened by alliteration in the contrasted nouns: "Marriage has many *p*ains, but celibacy has no *p*leasures."

antithetical criticism: 174.

antitype: 181.

anxiety of influence: 173; *323.*

反英雄体现的是卑鄙、下流、消沉、愚蠢或奸诈的人物品行。早在 16 世纪的*流浪汉小说*中就已经出现了非英雄主人公，笛福在《摩尔·弗兰德斯》(1722) 中塑造的女主人公就是一个小偷和妓女。但"反英雄"这一术语主要出现在第二次世界大战后人们的梦幻破灭以后的作品中。我们可以从约翰·韦恩的《误投尘世》(1953) 和金斯利·埃米斯的《幸运的吉姆》中找到这样地位卑微的反英雄主角。约瑟夫·海勒《第二十二条军规》(1961) 中的约瑟连、弗拉基米尔·纳博科夫《洛莉塔》(1955) 中的亨伯特·亨伯特、托马斯·品钦《万有引力之虹》(1973) 中的蒂龙·斯洛思罗普是后来小说中这类角色的杰出代表。在戏剧性的悲剧中，反英雄的使用尤其引人注目，传统上的主人公往往貌似尊贵典雅而又英勇无比（参见：*悲剧*）。在一些极端的例子中，主人公置身于一个没有确定性，没有信仰，甚至没有任何意义的世界中，例如塞缪尔·贝克特剧作中的妓女弗拉基米尔和《等待戈多》(1952) 中的伊斯塔根，或《最后一局》(1958) 中那位又瞎又残疾的主人公老汉姆。

参见：*荒诞派文学、黑色喜剧*，参阅：伊哈布·哈桑所写的文章"现代英美小说中的反英雄"，收入其所著的《变革的谣言》(1995)。其他条目中提及"反英雄"的地方，参见第 2 页。

antimasque：滑稽穿插戏　210。

antinovel：反小说　258。

antipathy：反感　105。

antistrophe：相衬诗句　262。

Antithesis：对偶

　　对偶是相邻的短语或句子在意义上的对比或反衬，从而在句法上形成**平行结构**，即*句法*上相似的词序和结构。例如，亚历山大·蒲柏在《致阿布斯纳博士书》(1735) 中对阿蒂克斯的描写："乐于伤害，却怯于下手。"蒲柏在《卷发遇劫记》(1714) 中描写男爵对贝林达施计的第二行中，以对偶名词的*头韵*突出了句法上的平行结构：

　　　　决意去获取，他思忖着该如何去做，
　　　　是强力去夺，还是欺骗诱惑。

塞缪尔·约翰逊的小说《拉塞勒斯》(1759) 第 26 章中有这样一组对偶句，同样是通过对比名词的头韵来强化对偶效果："结婚多有苦衷，而独身毫无乐趣。"

antithetical criticism：对立批评　174。

antitype：反原型　181。

anxiety of influence：影响的焦虑　173；*323*。

aphorism (ăf′ ŏrism): **111**.

apocrypha (ăpŏk′ rĭfa): **41**.

apologue: **9**.

aporia (ăpŏ′ rēa): **80**.

apostrophe (apŏs′ trŏf ē): **345**.

apothegm (ăp′ othĕm): **111**.

applied criticism: **68**.

appropriation (in reading): **247**.

Arcadia (arkā′ dia): **268**.

archaism: The literary use of words and expressions that have become obsolete in the common speech of an era. Spenser in *The Faerie Queene* (1590–96) deliberately employed archaisms (many of them derived from Chaucer's medieval English) in order to achieve a poetic style appropriate to his revival of the medieval *chivalric romance*. The translators of the King James Version of the Bible (1611) gave weight, dignity, and sonority to their prose by a sustained use of archaic revivals. Both Spenser and the King James Bible have in their turn been major sources of archaisms for Milton and many later authors. When Keats, for example, in his ode (1820) described the Grecian urn as "with *brede* / Of marble men and maidens *overwrought*," he used archaic words for "braid" and "worked [that is, ornamented] all over." Abraham Lincoln achieved a ritual solemnity by biblical archaisms in his "Gettysburg Address," which begins, "Fourscore and seven years ago."

Archaism has been a standard resort for *poetic diction*. Through the nineteenth century, for example, many poets continued to use "I ween," "methought," "steed," "taper" (for candle), and "morn," but only in their verses, not their everyday speech.

archetypal criticism: In literary criticism the term **archetype** denotes narrative designs, patterns of action, character types, themes, and images which recur in a wide variety of works of literature, as well as in myths, dreams, and even social rituals. Such recurrent items are often claimed to be the result of elemental and universal patterns in the human psyche, whose effective embodiment in a literary work evokes a profound response from the attentive reader, because he or she shares the psychic archetypes expressed by the author. An important antecedent of the literary theory of the archetype was the treatment of myth by a group of comparative anthropologists at Cambridge University, especially James G. Frazer, whose The *Golden Bough* (1890–1915) identified

aphorism：警语　111。

apocrypha：伪经　41。

apologue：道德故事　9。

aporia：反逆性　80。

apostrophe：呼语法　345。

apothegm：格言　111。

applied criticism：实用批评　68。

appropriation (in reading)：（阅读中的）挪用　247。

Arcadia：阿卡迪亚　268。

Archaism：仿古

　　仿古指的是在文学写作中使用在某一时期的日常用语中已经废弃的词语和表达方式的做法。斯宾塞在《仙后》(1590—1596)中刻意运用仿古这种手法（其仿古语汇多出自乔叟的中世纪英语），旨在形成一种与他复兴中世纪*骑士传奇*相一致的诗歌风格。詹姆斯国王钦定本圣经(1611)的译者通过仿古使译文格调庄重、高雅，语言响亮。斯宾塞的作品与钦定本圣经又成为弥尔顿和许多后世作家仿古的主要辞源。例如，济慈在其颂歌(1820)中把希腊古瓮描写成"上面缀有石雕的男人和女人"，他使用古字"brede（刺绣）"取代"braid"，用"overwrought"取代"worked（即镶边）"。亚伯拉罕·林肯在《葛底斯堡演说》中以模仿圣经的古语开始："Fourscore and seven years ago"（八十七年前），取得了一种仪式性的庄重肃穆的文体效果。

　　仿古成了*诗意辞藻*的惯用手法。例如，整个19世纪，不少诗人仍在使用 I ween（我以为）、methought（据我看来）、steed（骏马）、taper（蜡烛）、morn（早晨）等古语，但仅限于诗句中，而非在其日常口语中。

Archetypal Criticism：原型批评

　　在文学批评中，**原型**这一术语是指在范围广泛的各种文学作品，以及神话、梦幻乃至社会礼仪中反复显现并可识别的叙事策略、行为模式、人物类型、主题和意象。这些反复出现的现象常被认为是人类精神世界中基本的和普遍的模式的体现，其在文学作品中的生动再现会激起用心读者的强烈反响，因为他或她能分享作者所表现的心理原型。原型文学理论的一个重要前身是剑桥大学一批比较人类学家对神话的分析，尤其是詹姆斯·G.弗雷泽，他所著的《金枝》(1890—1915)

elemental patterns of myth and ritual that, he claimed, recur in the legends and ceremonials of diverse and far-flung cultures and religions. An even more important antecedent was the depth psychology of Carl G. Jung (1875–1961), who applied the term "archetype" to what he called "primordial images," the "psychic residue" of repeated patterns of experience in our very ancient ancestors which, he maintained, survive in the *collective unconscious* of the human race and are expressed in myths, religion, dreams, and private fantasies, as well as in works of literature. See *Jungian criticism*, under *psychoanalytic criticism*.

Archetypal literary criticism was given impetus by Maud Bodkin's *Archetypal Patterns in Poetry* (1934) and flourished especially during the 1950s and 1960s. Some archetypal critics dropped Jung's theory of the collective unconscious as the deep source of these patterns; in the words of Northrop Frye, this theory is "an unnecessary hypothesis," and the recurrent archetypes are simply there, "however they got there."

Among the prominent practitioners of various modes of **archetypal criticism**, in addition to Maud Bodkin, were G. Wilson Knight, Robert Graves, Philip Wheelwright, Richard Chase, Leslie Fiedler, and Joseph Campbell. These critics tended to emphasize the persistence of mythical patterns in literature, on the assumption that myths are closer to the elemental archetype than the artful manipulations of sophisticated writers (see *myth critics*). The death/rebirth theme was often said to be the archetype of archetypes, and was held to be grounded in the cycle of the seasons and the organic cycle of human life; this archetype, it was claimed, occurs in primitive rituals of the king who is annually sacrificed, in widespread myths of gods who die to be reborn, and in a multitude of diverse texts, including the Bible, Dante's *Divine Comedy* in the early fourteenth century, and Samuel Taylor Coleridge's "Rime of the Ancient Mariner" in 1798. Among the other archetypal themes, images, and characters frequently traced in literature were the journey underground, the heavenly ascent, the search for the father, the Paradise/Hades dichotomy, the Promethean rebel-hero, the scapegoat, the earth goddess, and the fatal woman.

In his influential book *Anatomy of Criticism* (1957), Northrop Frye developed the archetypal approach—which he combined with the *typological interpretation* of the Bible and the conception of the imagination in the writings of the poet and painter William Blake (1757–1827)—into a radical and comprehensive revision of the foundational concepts of both the theory of literature and the practice of literary criticism. Frye proposed that the totality of literary works constitute a "self-contained literary universe" which has been created over the ages by the human imagination so as to assimilate the alien and indifferent world of nature into archetypal forms that satisfy enduring human desires and needs. In this literary universe, four radical **mythoi** (that is, plot forms, or organizing structural principles), correspondent to the four seasons in the cycle of the natural world, are incorporated in the four major *genres* of comedy (spring), romance (summer), tragedy (autumn), and satire (winter). Within the archetypal mythos of each of these genres, individual works of literature also play variations upon a number of more limited archetypes—that is, conventional patterns and types that literature shares with social rituals as well as with theology, history,

分析了他认为发生在相隔遥远、各不相同的文化与宗教中传奇和仪式里的神话及礼仪的基本模式。原型文艺批评的另一更为重要的理论渊源是卡尔·G. 荣格（1875—1961）的深层心理学。荣格用"原型"指代他所谓的"原始意象"，即我们原始祖先经验的反复模式的"心理残余"，他认为，"原始意象"在人类的*集体无意识*中传承下来，并在神话、宗教、梦幻、个人想象和文学作品中得以再现。参见：*精神分析批评*中的*荣格批评*。

莫德·博德金所著的《诗歌中的原型》（1934，又译《诗中的原型模式》），推动了原型文学批评理论的发展，1950、1960年代是这一理论的鼎盛时期。一些原型批评家丢弃了荣格的作为这些模式深层来源的集体无意识理论；用诺斯罗普·弗莱的话来说，这一理论是"多余的设想"，"不管是怎么来的"，反复再现的原型就在那里。

在从事各类**原型批评**的批评名家中，除了莫德·博德金，还有 G. 威尔逊·奈特、罗伯特·格雷夫斯、菲利普·惠尔赖特、理查德·蔡斯、莱斯利·菲德勒、约瑟夫·坎贝尔。这些批评家趋向于强调文学作品中神话模型的持续存在，他们认为，神话比高超的作家的艺术作品更接近于原型（参见：*神话批评家*）。死而复生的主题往往被认为是原型中的原型，它以季节的转换和人的生命的有机轮回为依据；这种原型被认为是发生在每年帝王献身的原始仪式中和广为流传的神仙以死求生的神话中以及众多的各类文学作品中，包括圣经、14世纪早期但丁的《神曲》、1798年塞缪尔·泰勒·柯勒律治的《古舟子咏》。文学作品常常追溯的其他原型主题、形象和人物还有地狱行、升天堂、寻找圣父、天堂–地狱二分法、普罗米修斯式的反叛英雄、替罪羊、人间女神，以及有诱惑力的女性。

诺斯罗普·弗莱在其颇有影响的著作《批评的剖析》（1957）中，发展了原型批评方法：他结合圣经中的*象征释义*和威廉·布莱克（1757—1827）这位诗人兼画家的诗作中的想象意念，从根本上全面修正了传统文学理论和文学批评实践的基础性概念。弗莱认为文学作品在整体上构成了一个"自主自足的体系"，这一体系产生于人类想象力的历史积累，从而把异化的陌生的自然界融入原型模式，以满足人类持久的欲望和需求。在该文学体系中，与自然界四季循环运动相对应的四种基本**主题**（即情节形式，或称之为结构组织原则）具体化为喜剧（春天）、传奇（夏天）、悲剧（秋天）、讽刺（冬天）四种主要的*文学类型*。在这四种文学类型的原型主题范围内，每一种类型的个别文学作品中的原型也会出现许多更为有限的变体——即文学作品与社会仪式以及神话、历史、法律和事实上所有的

law, and, in fact, all "discursive verbal structures." Viewed archetypally, Frye asserted, literature turns out to play an essential role in refashioning the impersonal material universe into an alternative verbal universe that is humanly intelligible and viable, because it is adapted to universal human needs and concerns. Frye continued, in a long series of later writings, to expand his archetypal theory, to make a place in its overall scope and on different levels for including many traditional critical concepts and procedures, and to apply the theory both to everyday social practices and to the elucidation of writings ranging from the Bible to contemporary poets and novelists. See A. C. Hamilton, *Northrop Frye: Anatomy of His Criticism* (1990).

In addition to the works mentioned above, consult: C. G. Jung, "On the Relation of Analytical Psychology to Poetic Art" (1922), in *Contributions to Analytical Psychology* (1928), and "Psychology and Literature," in *Modern Man in Search of a Soul* (1933); G. Wilson Knight, *The Starlit Dome* (1941); Robert Graves, *The White Goddess* (rev. 1961); Richard Chase, *The Quest for Myth* (1949); Francis Fergusson, *The Idea of a Theater* (1949); Philip Wheelwright, *The Burning Fountain* (rev. 1968); Northrop Frye, "The Archetypes of Literature," in *Fables of Identity* (1963); Joseph Campbell, *The Hero with a Thousand Faces* (2d ed., 1968). In the 1980s, *feminist critics* developed forms of archetypal criticism that undertook to revise the male bases and biases of Jung and other archetypists. See Annis Pratt, *Archetypal Patterns in Woman's Fiction* (1981), and Estella Lauter and Carol Schreier Rupprecht, *Feminist Archetypal Theory: Interdisciplinary Re-Visions of Jungian Thought* (1985).

For discussions and critiques of archetypal theory and practice, see Murray Krieger, ed., *Northrop Frye in Modern Criticism* (1966); Robert Denham, *Northrop Frye and Critical Method* (1978); Frank Lentricchia, *After the New Criticism* (1980), chapter 1. For references to *archetypal criticism* in other entries, see pages *149, 297, 323.*

archetype (ar′ kĕtīp): **16**.

argument (in narrative forms): **108**.

art for art's sake: **4**.

article: **114**.

aside, the: **370**; *63, 64.*

assonance (ă′ sōnăns): **11**.

atmosphere: Atmosphere is the emotional tone pervading a section or the whole of a literary work, which fosters in the reader expectations as to the course of events, whether happy or (more commonly) terrifying or disastrous. Shakespeare establishes the tense and fearful atmosphere at the beginning of *Hamlet* by the terse and nervous dialogue of the sentinels as they anticipate a

"散乱的言语结构"所共有的传统模式及类型。从原型视角出发,弗莱认为文学终将在变客观物质世界为可供选择的言语世界的过程中发挥至关重要的作用,后者是对人来说清晰易懂而又能独立存在的,因为它适合于人类基本的和普遍的需求和兴趣。弗莱后来又在其很多论著中继续阐释他的原型批评理论,目的是在包括许多传统批评概念和程式在内的总体范畴内和不同层面上为原型理论确立一席之地,并使该理论运用到自圣经直至当代诗人和小说家的社会实践和作品阐释中去。参阅:A. C. 汉密尔顿所著的《诺斯罗普·弗莱:对他的批评的剖析》(1990)。

除了上面提到的著述,还可参阅:C. G. 荣格所写的文章"分析心理学与诗歌的关系"(1922),收入《分析心理学文集》(1928),"心理学与文学",收入《追寻灵魂的现代人》(1933);G. 威尔逊·奈特所著的《星光灿耀的天空》(1941);罗伯特·格雷夫斯所著的《白色女神》(1961年修订版);理查德·蔡斯所著的《神话的探求》(1949);弗朗西斯·弗格森所著的《剧院的想法》(1949);菲利普·惠尔赖特所著的《燃烧的源泉》(1968年修订版);诺斯罗普·弗莱所写的文章"文学中的原型",收入其所著的《同一的寓言》(1963);约瑟夫·坎贝尔所著的《千面英雄》(1968年第2版)。1980年代女性主义批评者发展了各种原型批评形式,着手修订了荣格和其他原型批评理论家的男性视野和偏见。参阅:安妮斯·普拉特所著的《女性小说中的原型模式》(1981),埃斯特拉·劳特与卡罗尔·施赖尔·鲁普雷希特合编的《女性主义原型理论:跨学科的荣格思想》(1985)。

关于原型理论和实践的讨论和批评,参阅:默里·克里格主编的《现代批评中的诺斯罗普·弗莱》(1966);罗伯特·德纳姆所著的《诺斯罗普·弗莱与批评方法》(1978);弗兰克·兰特里夏(又译伦特恰瓦)所著的《新批评之后》(1980)第1章。其他条目中提及"原型批评"的地方,参见第149、297、323页。

archetype:原型 **16**。

argument (in narrative forms):(叙事体作品中的) 论点 **108**。

art for art's sake:为艺术而艺术 **4**。

article:文章 **114**。

aside, the:旁白 **370**;*63, 64*。

assonance:半谐音 **11**。

Atmosphere:作品基调

作品基调是指弥漫在文学作品的部分章节或整部作品的情感气氛,它可以唤起读者对事件发展趋势的预感,无论这种趋势是吉是(往往是)凶或是灾难性的。在《哈姆雷特》的开头部分,莎士比亚通过描写卫士等待鬼魂再现时的那段简短、紧张的对话,为全剧烘托出一种紧张恐怖的基调;柯勒律治通过

reappearance of the ghost; Coleridge engenders a compound of religious and superstitious terror by his description of the initial scene in the narrative poem *Christabel* (1816); and Hardy in his novel *The Return of the Native* (1878) makes Egdon Heath a brooding presence that reduces to pettiness and futility the human struggle for happiness for which it is the setting. Alternative terms frequently used for atmosphere are **mood** and the French word **ambiance.**

For references to *atmosphere* in other entries, see page *152.*

aubade (ō bäd′): **229.**

Augustan Age (awgŭs′ tan): **282.**

author and authorship: The conception of an author in ordinary literary discourse can be summarized as follows: **Authors** are individuals who, by their intellectual and imaginative powers, purposefully create from their experience and reading a literary work which is distinctively their own. The work itself, as distinguished from the written or printed texts that instantiate the work, remains a product accredited to the author as its originator, even if he or she turns over the rights to publish and profit from the texts to someone else. And insofar as the literary work turns out to be great and original, the author who has composed that work is deservedly accorded high cultural status and achieves lasting fame.

Since the 1960s this way of conceiving an author has been put to radical question by a number of structural and poststructural theorists, who posit the human *subject* not as an originator and shaper of a work, but as a "space" in which conventions, codes, and circulating locutions precipitate into a particular text, or else as a "site" wherein there converge, and are recorded, the cultural constructs, discursive formations, and configurations of power prevalent in a given cultural era. The author is said to be the product rather than the producer of a text, or is redescribed as an "effect" or "function" engendered by the internal play of textual language. Famously, in 1968 Roland Barthes proclaimed and celebrated "The Death of the Author," whom he described as a figure invented by critical discourse in order to set limits to the inherent free play of the meanings in reading a literary text. See under *structuralist criticism* and *poststructuralism.*

In an influential essay "What Is an Author?" written in 1969, Michel Foucault raised the question of the historical "coming into being of the notion of 'author'"—that is, of the emergence and evolution of the "author function" within the discourse of our culture. The investigation would include such inquiries as "how the author became individualized," "what status he has been given," what "system of valorization" involves the author, and how the fundamental category of "'the-man-and-his-work criticism' began." Foucault's essay and example gave impetus to a number of studies which reject the notion that the prevailing concept of **authorship** (the set of attributes possessed by an author) is either natural or necessitated by the way things are. Instead, historicists conceive authorship to be a *cultural construct* that emerged and changed drastically, in accordance with changing economic conditions, social circumstances, and institutional arrangements for the writing

叙事诗《克利斯托贝尔》(1816) 中开始场景的描绘烘托出一股凝聚着宗教与迷信的恐怖基调；哈代在他的小说《还乡》(1878) 中，把埃格登荒原描绘成一片乌云笼罩的境地，这种背景使人们为追求幸福的斗争变得渺小而徒劳。作品基调也常被称为**氛围**或法语词**气氛**。

其他条目中提及"作品基调"的地方，参见第 152 页。

aubade：晨歌　229。

Augustan Age：奥古斯都文学盛世　282。

Author and Authorship：作者和作者身份

普通文学话语中的作者概念可作如下概括：**作者**是那些凭借自己的才学和想象力，以自身阅历和他们对一部文学作品特有的阅读经验为素材从事文学创作的个人。作品本身与例示其存在的书写或印刷文本不同，它的所有权仍属作者本人作为创始人所有，即使作者把文本的出版权转让给他人并由此从中获利。因此，只要文学作品是大手笔并且是原创的，那么其作者理应荣获崇高的文化地位并享有持久的声誉。

但自 1960 年代以来，许多结构主义和后结构主义理论家对"作者"这一概念的这种界定方法提出了根本上的质疑。他们断言，人类"*主体*"是不能成为一部作品的创作者和塑造者的，而是作为规则、符号以及通用的措辞等融合而成为一篇特殊文本的一个"空间"，或是作为一个融合并记录盛行于特定文化时期文化观念、无序组合及权力结构的"场所"。作者被视为文本的产品，而非文本的制作者，或是被重新描述为由文本语言的内部游戏产生的"效果"或"功能"。最有名的是，1968 年罗兰·巴尔特振聋发聩地宣称并庆贺"作者的死亡"，他把作者描述成一个由批评话语产生的客体，以此限制在阅读文学文本时固有存在意义上的自由游戏。参见：*结构主义批评*、*后结构主义*中的相关论述。

米歇尔·福柯在其 1969 年所写的颇具影响的文章"何为作者？"中提出了"'作者'这一概念的历史性形成"——即在我们的文化话语内出现并得以发展的"作者功能"。这一研究并探讨了诸如"作者何以个性化"、"作者享有何种地位"、关于作者的"评估系统"是什么、"'作者及其作品批评'这样的基本范畴是如何'开始'的"等一些具体问题。福柯的文章及实例促进了许多研究工作，这些研究反对对**作者身份**（作者所具有的属性）这一概念所作出的业已被公众接受的界定，即作者身份既是自然所为，又是事物使然。相反，历史主义者认为作者身份是在西方世界过去若干世纪的发展过程中，随着不断变化的经济条件、社会环境、写作和销售图书的制度设置而出现并相应急剧

and distribution of books, over many centuries in the Western world. See *new historicism*.

Cultural historians have emphasized the important role, in constructing and reconstructing the concept of an author, of such historical developments as:

1. The shift from an oral to a literate culture. In the former, the identity of an author presumably was not inquired after, since the individual bard or minstrel improvised by reference to inherited subject matter, forms, and literary formulae. (See *oral poetry*.) In a culture where at least a substantial segment of the population can read, the production of enduring texts in the form of written scrolls and manuscripts generated increasing interest in the individual responsible for producing the work that was thus recorded. Many works in manuscript, however, circulated freely, and were often altered in transcriptions, with little regard to the intentions or formulations of the originator of the work.

2. The shift, in the course of the fifteenth and sixteenth centuries, from a primarily manuscript culture to a primarily print culture. (See *book*.) The invention of printing greatly expedited the manufacture and dissemination of printed texts, and so multiplied the number of producers of literary works, and made financially important the specification of the identity and ability of an individual writer, in order to invite support for that individual by the contemporary system of aristocratic and noble patronage. Foucault, in addition, proposed the importance of a punitive function in fostering the concept of an author's responsibility in originating a work, which served the interests of the state in affixing on a particular individual the blame for transgressive or subversive ideas.

3. The emphasis in recent research on the difficulties in establishing, in various periods, just who was the originator of what parts of an existing literary text, which was often, in effect, the product of multiple collaborators, censors, editors, printers, and publishers, as well as of successive revisions by the reputed author. See *multiple authorship* under *textual criticism*.

4. The proliferation of middle-class readers in the late seventeenth and eighteenth centuries, and the attendant explosion in the number of literary titles printed, and in the number of writers required to supply this market. Both Foucault and Barthes, in the essays cited above, emphasized that the modern concept of an author as an individual who is the intellectual owner of his or her literary product was the result of the *ideology* engendered by the emerging capitalist economy in this era. Other scholars have stressed the importance of the shift during the eighteenth century, first in England and then in other European countries, from a reliance by writers on literary patrons to that of support by payments from publishers and booksellers. A result of the booming literary market was the increasingly successful appeal by writers for copyright laws that would invest them, instead of the publisher, with the ownership of the works that they composed for public sale. These conditions of the literary marketplace fostered the claims by writers that they possessed originality, creativity, and genius, and so were able to produce literary works that were entirely

变化着的一种"*文化建构*"。参见：*新历史主义*。

文化历史学家从以下方面强调了历史发展在建构和重构"作者"这一概念中所起的重要作用：

(1) 从口头文化向书面文化的转变。在口头文化阶段，作者的身份也许没有人去考究，因为那是一些游吟诗人或歌手参照传统的题材、形式、文学惯例进行即兴创作。（参见：*口头诗歌*。）在大多数民众具有阅读能力的文化环境中，以书卷和手稿形式生产不朽文本会引发个人对生产书面作品产生越来越大的兴趣，作品也就因此被记录下来。不过许多以手稿形式存在的文学作品随处流传，文稿内容在抄写过程中经常被随意改动，并且很少考虑原创者的意图或文本的原本格式。

(2) 15到16世纪，以手抄本文化为主向印刷本文化为主转变。（参见：*书籍*。）印刷术的发明大大促进了印刷文本的制作与传播，进而大大增加了文学作品创作者的数量，这使得详细说明作者的个人身份和才华具有重要经济意义，可以争取当时的贵族统治社会和贵族对作者个人的资助。另外，福柯还指出惩罚功能对于作家形成一种创作的责任感的重要性，这有利于国家追究特定个体破坏性或颠覆性的言论。

(3) 近期研究的重点和难点是，确定在各个不同时期到底谁是现存文学文本某个部分的原创者，而事实上，文学文本往往是由许多合作者、编审、编辑、印刷者和出版者，以及著名作家不断修订的产物。参见：*文本批评中的多重作者身份*。

(4) 17世纪晚期和18世纪，中产阶层读者激增，伴随而来的是印刷体文学种类数量的激增和为满足这一市场需求而涌现的大批作家。福柯和巴尔特在上文援引过的文章中强调指出，作家的现代概念，一个是自己文学作品的知识产权人的个体，是这个时代出现的资本主义经济所形成的意识形态的结果。其他学者则强调指出，18世纪，从作者依赖文学创作的资助到出版商和销售商支付稿酬这一首先发生在英国、随后遍及欧洲其他国家的转变，具有重要意义。文学市场繁荣所引发的结果是，作者越来越成功地呼吁制定版权法，授予他们——而非出版商——为在公众市场上销售而创作的作品的所有权。这样的文学市场环境鼓励作者声称他们拥有原创性、创造性和才华，因而能够产生出全新的文学作品。

new. They made such claims in order to establish their legal rights, as authors, to ownership of such productions as their "intellectual property," in addition to their rights (which they could sell to others) to the printed texts of their works as "material property." Historians of authorship point out that the most emphatic claims about the genius, creativity, and originality of authors, which occurred in the *Romantic Period,* coincided with, and was interactive with, the success of authors in achieving some form of copyright protection of an author's proprietary rights to the literary work as the unique product of his or her native powers. See Mark Rose, *Authors and Owners: The Invention of Copyright,* 1993; Martha Woodmansee, *The Author, Art, and the Market: Rereading the History of Aesthetics,* 1994; and the essays by various scholars in *The Construction of Authorship: Textual Appropriation in Law and Literature,* ed. Martha Woodmansee and Peter Jaszi, 1994. Paulina Kewes' *Authorship and Appropriation: Writing for the Stage in England, 1660–1710* (1998) is a study of the cultural and economic factors that determined the status of an author in the later seventeenth and early eighteenth centuries.

Historicist scholars of authorship have succeeded in demonstrating that there has been a sustained interplay between the economic circumstances and institutional arrangements for producing and marketing literary texts and some aspects of the conception of authorship, or of ideas associated with authorship. The radical further claim, however, that the modern figure and functions assigned to an author are in their essentials a recent formation, resulting from the distinctive conditions of the literary marketplace after the seventeenth century, does not jibe with historical evidence. Some two thousand years ago, for example, the Roman poet Horace wrote his verse-epistle, the *Ars Poetica,* at a time when books consisted of texts copied by hand in rolls of papyrus. (See the entry *book.*) Horace adverts to a number of individuals from Homer to his friend Virgil who, he makes clear, are individuals who conceived and brought their works into being, and thus are responsible for having achieved their specific content, form, and quality. A competent literary author—Horace refers to him variously as *scriptor* (writer), *poeta* (maker), and *carminis auctor* (originator of a poem)—must possess a natural talent or genius (*ingenium*) as well as an acquired art; this author purposefully designs and orders his *poema* in such a way as to evoke the emotions of his audience. The bookseller, Horace indicates, advertises his commodities locally and also ships them abroad. And if a published work succeeds in instructing and giving pleasure to a great many readers, it is a book that not only "makes money for the bookseller," but also "crosses the sea and spreads to a distant age the fame of its author." Clearly, Horace distinguishes between material and authorial, or intellectual, ownership, in that the author, even if he retains no proprietary interest in a published book, retains the sole responsibility and credit for having accomplished the work that the text incorporates. (See M. H. Abrams, "What Is a Humanistic Criticism?" in *The Emperor Redressed: Critiquing Critical Theory,* ed. Dwight Eddins, 1995.)

Another revealing instance is provided by the publication of the First Folio of Shakespeare's plays in 1623. As writings intended for the commercial

他们作出这样宣称的目的是为了确定身为作者的法律权利,除了拥有其著作的印刷文本作为"物质产权"这一权利(他们可以将其转卖给他人),还拥有其著作生产的"知识产权"。一些研究作者身份的史学家指出,发生在浪漫主义时期的作者对拥有自己的才华、创造性和原创性所提出的最强烈的要求,与他们成功取得对文学作品这种凝结着自己天赋才智的独特产品的某种形式的版权保护是一致的,而且是互相影响的。参阅:马克·罗斯所著的《作者与所有权人:版权的发明》(1993);玛莎·伍德曼西所著的《作者、艺术与市场:重读美学史》(1994);各派学者的文章参阅:玛莎·伍德曼西与彼得·贾西合编的《作者身份的建构:法律与文学中的文本挪用》(1994)。保利娜·克韦斯所著的《作者身份与挪用:1660—1710年间英国的为舞台写作》(1998),研究了17世纪下半叶和18世纪早期决定作者地位的文化和经济因素。

  从事作者身份研究的历史主义学者已经成功地阐明了生产和营销文学文本的经济环境与制度设置之间存在着的持续的相互作用,和对作者身份或是与作者身份有关的观念的理解的一些方面。然而,有的学者认为,作家被赋予的现代身份和功能就其本质而言是在近世形成的、是源自17世纪后特殊的文学市场环境的,这种更为激进的观点与历史证据不相吻合。例如,大约两千年前,罗马诗人贺拉斯创作完成了他的书信体诗文《诗艺》,当时的书本是手工誊写的草纸卷。(参见:*书籍*。)贺拉斯提到了包括从荷马到他的朋友维吉尔在内的许多诗人,他明确表示,这些诗人是构思并使他们的作品问世从而决定了作品的内容、形式和质量的个体。一位合格的文学作品的作者——贺拉斯提到他自己时用了不同的称谓,如作家、作者和诗人——必须具备一种与后天习得的艺术才华一样重要的创作天赋或才华;这一作者在创作诗歌时,经过刻意构思和设计诗作的结构和情节,以激发他的听众的情思。贺拉斯指出,书商不仅在当地推销他的商品,还在国外发行。因此,如果一部作品出版后能成功地给许多读者施行教化和带去乐趣,那么这部书不仅能"让书商赚到钱",还能让"作者名扬四海,声誉永垂"。显然,贺拉斯对作为物质形式的作品和作品的作者或知识的所有权之间的关系作了区分,作者即使仍然没有从已版的书中获得版权利益,也仍然独自享有与该书相应的责任和声誉,因为是他完成了文本。[参阅:M. H. 艾布拉姆斯所写的文章"什么是人文批评?"收入德怀特·埃丁斯主编的《重新穿上衣服的皇帝:对批评理论的批判》(1995)。]

  另外一个具有代表性的事例就是1623年出版的莎士比亚的第一部对开本剧

theater, Shakespeare's plays were a collaborative enterprise in which textual changes and insertions could be made by various hands at all stages of production; the resulting products were not Shakespeare's property, but that of his theatrical company. Furthermore, as Stephen Greenblatt remarks in the Introduction to *The Norton Shakespeare* (1997), there is no evidence that Shakespeare himself wanted to have his plays printed, or that he took any "interest in asserting authorial rights over a script," or that he had any legal standing from which to claim such rights. Nonetheless, as Greenblatt points out, seven years after Shakespeare's death his friends and fellow actors Heminges and Condell were confident that they could sell their expensive *folio* collection of his plays by virtue of the fact, as they claimed in a preface, that their printed texts were exactly "as he conceived them" and represented what he himself had "thought" and "uttered." The identity of the conceiver of the plays, serving to attest to the authenticity of the printed versions, is graphically represented by an engraved portrait of Shakespeare by Martin Droeshout in the front matter. The First Folio also included a poem by Ben Jonson, Shakespeare's friend and dramatic rival, "To the Memory of My Beloved, The Author Mr. William Shakespeare." In it Jonson appraised Shakespeare as the equal of the Greek tragic dramatists Aeschylus, Euripides, and Sophocles; lauded him as not only "The applause! delight! the wonder of our stage!" but also as an individual who, by the products of his innate abilities ("nature") even more than his "art," was "not of an age, but for all time!"; and asserted that his "well-turned" lines reflect the "mind, and manners" of the poet who had fathered them. It would seem that, in broad outline, the figure and functions of Horace's "auctor" and of Jonson's "author" were essentially what they are at the present time, in ordinary critical discourse.

See the entry *sociology of literature*. In addition to the items listed above, refer to Frederick G. Kenyon, *Books and Readers in Ancient Rome* (1951); A. J. Minnis, *Medieval Theory of Authorship* (1984); Wendy Wall, *The Imprint of Gender: Authorship and Publication in the English Renaissance* (1993). Roger Chartier, in "Figures of the Author," *The Order of Books* (1994), describes the diverse functions assigned to an individual author, from the late Middle Ages through the eighteenth century.

authoritative (narration): 302.

authorship: 19.

autobiography: 27.

automatic writing: 226.

avant-garde (ă′ vŏn-gard″): 227.

本。作为为商业舞台创作的剧本，莎士比亚的剧本是众人合作的结晶，在舞台演出过程中文本经历了许多人的修改和删减；因此，最终的剧本并不属于莎士比亚本人，而是属于戏剧演出公司。此外，正如史蒂芬·格林布莱特在《诺顿莎士比亚》(1977) 的序言中所言，没有证据证明莎士比亚本人希望自己的剧作能够印刷出版，也没有证据证明他对"拥有剧本的创作权感兴趣"，或是声称拥有上述权利的法律地位。格林布莱特指出，尽管如此，在莎士比亚去世七年后，他的朋友兼演员同事海明格斯和康德尔自信地声称，他们会出售他们拥有的昂贵的莎士比亚对开本剧本合集，正如他们在前言中所称，依据事实，他们所印的文本正是"莎士比亚所创作的"，而且代表了莎士比亚本人的"所想"和"所言"。用以证实印刷本真实性的剧作者身份，通过在原稿前页上印有马丁·德罗肖特为莎士比亚所雕的肖像，明确地体现出来。首部对开本中也收录了莎士比亚的朋友、戏剧上的对手本·琼森的一首诗《为了纪念我钟爱的朋友、作者威廉·莎士比亚先生》。琼森在诗中把莎士比亚与古希腊悲剧作家埃斯库罗斯、欧里庇得斯、索福克勒斯相提并论；赞扬他不仅是"我们舞台的掌声！乐趣！奇迹！"而且是一位先天能力（"天赋"）胜于"艺术"的、"不属于一个时代，而是所有时代"的天才；琼森还声称，莎士比亚"措辞巧妙"的诗行反映了这位曾经酿就这些诗句的诗人的"思想和行为"。大体而言，在当代普通批评话语中，本质上还能看出贺拉斯的"诗人"和琼森的"作者"的身份和功能的当代含义。

参见：*文学社会学*。除了上举书目，还可参阅：弗雷德里克·G. 凯尼恩所著的《古罗马的书籍与读者》(1951)；A. J. 明尼斯所著的《中世纪作者身份理论》(1984)；温迪·沃尔所著的《性别的印记：英国文艺复兴时期的作者身份与出版》(1993)。罗杰·夏蒂埃在其所著的《书本的秩序》(1994) 中"作者的形象"一章里描述了中世纪后期至 18 世纪期间作者个体被赋予的不同功能。

authoritative (narration)：权威（叙述） 302。

authorship：作者身份 19。

autobiography：自传 27。

automatic writing：自动书写 226。

avant-garde：先锋派 227。

B

ballad: A short definition of the **popular ballad** (also called the **folk ballad** or **traditional ballad**) is that it is a song, transmitted orally, which tells a story. Ballads are thus the narrative species of *folk songs*, which originate, and are communicated orally, among illiterate or only partly literate people. In all probability the initial version of a ballad was composed by a single author, but he or she is unknown; and since each singer who learns and repeats an oral ballad is apt to introduce changes in both the text and the tune, it exists in many variant forms. Typically, the popular ballad is dramatic, condensed, and impersonal: the narrator begins with the climactic episode, tells the story tersely in action and dialogue (sometimes by means of dialogue alone), and tells it without self-reference or the expression of personal attitudes or feelings.

The most common stanza form—called the **ballad stanza**—is a *quatrain* in alternate four- and three-stress lines; usually only the second and fourth lines rhyme. This is the form of "Sir Patrick Spens"; the first stanza also exemplifies the abrupt opening of the typical ballad, and the manner of proceeding by third-person narration, curtly sketched setting and action, sharp transition, and spare dialogue:

> The king sits in Dumferling towne,
> Drinking the blude-red wine:
> "O whar will I get a guid sailor,
> To sail this schip of mine?"

Many ballads employ set formulas (which helped the singer remember the course of the song) including (1) stock descriptive phrases like "blood-red wine" and "milk-white steed," (2) a *refrain* in each stanza ("Edward," "Lord Randall"), and (3) **incremental repetition**, in which a line or stanza is repeated, but with an addition that advances the story ("Lord Randall," "Child Waters"). See *oral poetry*.

Although many traditional ballads probably originated in the later Middle Ages, they were not collected and printed until the eighteenth century, first in England, then in Germany. In 1765 Thomas Percy published his *Reliques of Ancient English Poetry* which, although most of the contents had been revised in the style of Percy's era, did much to inaugurate widespread interest in folk literature. The basic modern collection is Francis J. Child's *English and Scottish Popular Ballads* (1882–98), which includes 305 ballads, many of them in variant versions. Bertrand H. Bronson has edited *The Traditional Tunes of the Child Ballads* (4 vols., 1959–72). Popular ballads are still being sung—and collected, now with the help of an electronic recorder—in the British Isles and remote rural areas of America. To the songs that early settlers brought with them from Great Britain, America has added native forms of the ballad, such as those sung by lumberjacks, cowboys, laborers, and social protesters. A number of recent folk singers, including Woody Guthrie, Bob Dylan, and Joan Baez, themselves compose ballads; most of these, however, such as "The Ballad of

B

Ballad：民谣

　　简单来说，**流行民谣**（又称**民间歌谣**或**传统歌谣**）是一种口头流传、讲述故事的歌谣。因而它属于叙事类民歌，源自口头并流传于文盲或半文盲民众间。多数情况下，一首民谣首先由一人所作，其作者不详；但每位歌手在学唱和演唱过程中，都会对歌词和曲调有所改动，因此，同一首民谣会有许多不同版本。戏剧性、简洁和客观的叙事口吻是流行民谣的典型特征；歌者一开始就进入高潮段落，通过动作和对话（有时只有对话）简明地讲述故事，不附加个人所指、态度或情感。

　　最常见的民谣形式，被称为**民谣体诗节**，是四个和三个重音节交替的四行诗，通常只有二、四两行押韵。《帕特里克·斯彭斯爵士》采用的就是这种形式，其第一段也表现出民谣惯用的陡然开篇、第三人称叙事手法、简略的场景和行为描写、急剧的情节转换和简洁的对话等特征：

> 邓弗林镇上坐着国王，
> 喝着血一样红的酒：
> "啊，我哪里去找好水手，
> 来驾驶我这艘好船？" 　　　　　　（黄灿然译）

大多数民谣都会采用一些固定的模式（以帮助歌手记忆歌曲）：(1) 描述性的陈词套语，如"血一般红的酒""奶一样白的马"；(2) 每一段中有一个叠句（"爱德华""兰德尔老爷"）；(3) **递增的重复**，即重复某行或某段，但内容有所增加以推进故事情节（"兰德尔老爷""童泉"）。参见：*口头诗歌*。

　　尽管许多传统民谣可能源自中世纪晚期，但其收集与出版却是始于 18 世纪，先是在英国，继而在德国。1765 年，托马斯·珀西出版了《英国古诗拾遗》（又译《英诗辑古》），在很大程度上唤起了民众对民间文学的广泛兴趣，尽管其中多数内容经过重写已具有珀西时代的风格。弗朗西斯·J. 蔡尔德主编的《英格兰与苏格兰民谣集》(1882—1898) 基本上是一部现代民谣集，共收录 305 首民谣，其中许多是变体版本。伯特兰·H. 布朗森编辑了四卷本《童谣的传统曲调》(1959—1972)。如今在英伦三岛和美国的边远乡村，民谣仍为人们传唱，并借助电子记录器加以录制收集。在美国，那些由早期居民从英国带来的歌谣已被赋予当地的民谣形式，例如传唱于伐木工、牛仔、劳工和社会抗议者中间的民谣。包括伍迪·格思里、鲍勃·迪伦、琼·贝兹在内的许多当代民歌手自己也进行民谣创作；但其中大多数，

Bonnie and Clyde" (about a notorious gangster and his moll), are closer to the journalistic "broadside ballad" than to the archaic and heroic mode of the popular ballads in the Child collection.

A **broadside ballad** is a ballad that was printed on one side of a single sheet (called a "broadside"), dealt with a current event or person or issue, and was sung to a well-known tune. Beginning with the sixteenth century, these broadsides were hawked in the streets or at country fairs in Great Britain.

The traditional ballad has greatly influenced the form and style of lyric poetry in general. It has also engendered the **literary ballad**, which is a narrative poem written in deliberate imitation of the form, language, and spirit of the traditional ballad. In Germany, some major literary ballads were composed in the latter eighteenth century, including G. A. Bürger's very popular "Lenore" (1774)—which soon became widely read and influential in an English translation—and Goethe's "Erlkönig" (1782). In England, some of the best literary ballads were composed in the *Romantic Period*: Coleridge's "Rime of the Ancient Mariner" (which, however, is much longer and has a much more elaborate plot than the folk ballad), Walter Scott's "Proud Maisie," and Keats' "La Belle Dame sans Merci." In his *Lyrical Ballads* of 1798, Wordsworth begins "We Are Seven" by introducing a narrator as an agent and first-person teller of the story—"I met a little cottage girl"—which is probably one reason he called the collection "*lyrical* ballads." Coleridge's "Ancient Mariner," on the other hand, of which the first version also appeared in *Lyrical Ballads*, opens with the abrupt and impersonal third-person narration of the traditional ballad:

> It is an ancient Mariner
> And he stoppeth one of three....

See W. J. Entwistle, *European Balladry* (rev. ed., 1951); M. J. C. Hodgart, *The Ballads* (2d ed., 1962); John A. and Alan Lomax, *American Ballads and Folk Songs* (1934); D. C. Fowler, *A Literary History of the Popular Ballad* (1968). For the broadside ballad see *The Common Muse*, ed. V. de Sola Pinto and Allan E. Rodway (1957).

ballad stanza: 23; *376.*

baroque (ba rōk') is a term applied by art historians (at first derogatorily, but now merely descriptively) to a style of architecture, sculpture, and painting that emerged in Italy at the beginning of the seventeenth century and then spread to Germany and other countries in Europe. The style employs the classical forms of the *Renaissance*, but breaks them up and intermingles them to achieve elaborate, grandiose, energetic, and highly dramatic effects. Major examples of baroque art are the sculptures of Bernini and the architecture of St. Peter's cathedral in Rome.

The term has been adopted with reference to literature, with a variety of applications. It may signify any elaborately formal and magniloquent style in verse or prose—for example, some verse passages in Milton's *Paradise Lost* (1667) and Thomas De Quincey's prose descriptions of his dreams in

如《邦妮与克莱德之歌》（关于一个臭名昭彰的恶棍及其女友的故事），已远离蔡尔德民谣集里那种古朴、英雄诗般的民谣风格，而更接近新闻报道性的"宽页传单上的民谣"。

宽页传单上的民谣（又译市井歌谣）是印在大幅单张单面纸（称为宽页）上的民谣，内容涉及时事、人物、事件，配以人们熟悉的曲调。宽页传单上的民谣自16世纪开始就流行于英国的街头巷尾和乡村集市。

传统民谣在总体上对抒情诗的形式和风格产生过极大影响。传统民谣也孕育了**诗谣**：一种刻意模仿传统民谣的形式、语言和主题的叙事诗。德国的一些重要诗谣创作于18世纪后期，其中包括G.A.伯格创作的非常流行的《勒诺》（1774）——其英译版很快就成为广为传阅、颇具影响的民谣——和歌德的《魔王》（1782）。英国一些最著名的诗谣产生于*浪漫主义时期*，如：柯勒律治的《古舟子咏》（不过，其篇幅长度和情节的复杂性要远过于民谣）、沃尔特·司各特的《骄傲的梅赛》、济慈的《无情美人》。在《抒情歌谣集》（1789）中，华兹华斯以《我们是七人》为开篇诗，把叙述者当做行为者；在《我遇到的村舍少女》中，把叙述者作为第一人称的故事讲叙者，这也许是他之所以把自己的诗集冠以"抒情歌谣"的原因之一。另一方面，柯勒律治创作的《古舟子咏》，其最早版本同样出现在《抒情歌谣集》中，却是以传统民谣突如其来客观的第三人称叙述者的口吻开篇的：

> 他是一个年迈的水手
> 从三个行人中他拦住一人　　　　　　　　　　（顾子欣译）

参阅：W. J. 恩特威斯尔所著的《欧洲民谣》（1951年修订版）；M. J. C. 霍加特所著的《民谣》（1962年第2版）；约翰·A. 与艾伦·洛马克斯合著的《美国民谣与民谣歌曲》（1934）；D. C. 福勒所著的《流行民谣文学史》（1968）。关于宽页传单上的民谣，参阅：V. 德·索拉·平托与艾伦·E. 罗德威合编的《大众的缪斯》（1957）。

ballad stanza：民谣体诗节　　**23**；*376*。

Baroque：巴洛克风格作品

该术语被艺术史学家用来描述（起初具有贬义，但现今仅仅是客观性描述）始于17世纪初意大利而后又遍及德国和欧洲其他国家的建筑、雕塑和绘画的艺术风格。这种风格采用*文艺复兴*的各种古典形式，但又将其拆开，使之相互融合，以取得精巧华丽、充满生机、富于戏剧性的艺术效果。巴洛克风格艺术作品的主要代表作有贝尔尼尼的雕塑和罗马的圣彼得大教堂。

该术语一直被应用于文学艺术中，有多种用法。它可以指代诗歌或散文中任何精致庄重和富丽堂皇的风格，例如弥尔顿《失乐园》（1667）中的一些诗节和托马斯·德·昆西《一个吸鸦片英国人的自白》（1822）中对他梦境的散文体描写，

Confessions of an English Opium Eater (1822) have both been called baroque. Occasionally—though oftener on the Continent than in England—it serves as a period term for post-Renaissance literature in the seventeenth century. More frequently it is applied specifically to the elaborate verses and extravagant conceits of the late-sixteenth- and early-seventeenth-century poets Giambattista Marino in Italy and Luis de Góngora in Spain. In English literature the metaphysical poems of John Donne are sometimes described as baroque; but the term is more often, and more appropriately, applied to the elaborate style, fantastic conceits, and extreme religious emotionalism of the poet Richard Crashaw, 1612–49; see under *metaphysical conceit*. Refer to René Wellek, "The Concept of Baroque in Literary Scholarship," in *Concepts of Criticism* (1963).

The term "baroque" is derived from the Spanish and Portuguese name for a pearl that is rough and irregular in shape.

bathos and anticlimax: **Bathos** is Greek for "depth," and it has been an indispensable term to critics since Alexander Pope, *parodying* the Greek Longinus' famous essay *On the Sublime* (that is, "loftiness"), wrote in 1727 an essay *On Bathos: Of the Art of Sinking in Poetry*. With mock solemnity Pope assures his readers that he undertakes "to lead them as it were by the hand.... the gentle downhill way to Bathos; the bottom, the end, the central point, the *non plus ultra*, of true Modern Poesy!" The word ever since has been used for an unintentional descent in literature when, straining to be pathetic or passionate or elevated, the writer overshoots the mark and drops into the trivial or the ridiculous. Among his examples Pope cites "the modest request of two absent lovers" in a contemporary poem:

> Ye Gods! annihilate but Space and Time,
> And make two lovers happy.

The slogan "For God, for Country, and for Yale!" is bathetic because it moves to intended **climax** (that is, an ascending sequence of importance) in its rhetorical order, but to unintended descent in its reference—at least for someone who is not a Yale graduate. Even major poets sometimes fall unwittingly into the same rhetorical figure. In the early version of *The Prelude* (1805; Book IX), William Wordsworth, after recounting at length the tale of the star-crossed lovers Vaudracour and Julia, tells how Julia died, leaving Vaudracour to raise their infant son:

> It consoled him here
> To attend upon the Orphan and perform
> The office of a Nurse to his young Child
> Which after a short time by some mistake
> Or indiscretion of the Father, died.

The Stuffed Owl: An Anthology of Bad Verse, ed. D. B. Wyndham Lewis and Charles Lee (rev. 1948), is a rich mine of unintended bathos.

Anticlimax is sometimes employed as an equivalent of bathos; but in a more useful application, "anticlimax" is nonderogatory, and denotes a writer's deliberate drop from the serious and elevated to the trivial and lowly in order

都可称为巴洛克风格作品。有时——尽管在欧洲大陆比在英格兰更为常见——它作为一个指代时期的术语，专指17世纪后文艺复兴时期的文学作品。但多数情况下，巴洛克风格作品专指16世纪晚期和17世纪早期意大利的贾姆巴蒂斯塔·马里诺和西班牙的路易斯·德·贡戈拉两位诗人刻意雕琢的诗句和过分夸饰的构思。在英国文学中，约翰·多恩的玄学派诗歌有时也被归入巴洛克风格作品之列；但该术语更常见、更适于指代诗人理查德·克拉肖（1612—1649）精致的风格、奇异的构思、极端的宗教感情主义。参见：*玄学派巧思妙喻*中的相关论述。参阅：韦勒克所著的《批评的概念》（1963）中的"文学研究中的巴洛克概念"一章。

术语"巴洛克风格作品"源于西班牙语和葡萄牙语中对未经加工、形状不规则的珍珠的称谓。

Bathos and Anticlimax：**突降与突降法**

突降是希腊语"深处"的意思。自从1727年亚历山大·蒲柏戏谑模仿希腊作家朗吉努斯的著名散文"论崇高"撰写了"论诗歌中的突降技巧"，突降就成为文学批评家一个不可或缺的批评用语。蒲柏曾俏皮地向读者许诺，他要"手挽手地引他们缓缓下山……'突降'到山的深处、山底、尽头、中心点，以领略真正的当代诗艺之粹！"从此，"突降"一词便一直被用来表示文学作品中非意识的格调跌落——正当作品格调力图变得凄楚或激昂或升华时，作者却因行文过甚而弄巧成拙，致使作品的格调一落千丈或变得浅薄可笑。蒲柏在例证中引用了当时的一首诗《两位缺席情侣的谦恭乞求》：

众神！除了时空消灭一切吧，
以使得两位情侣幸福。

口号"为上帝，为祖国，为耶鲁！"也具有突降色彩，因为其在措辞顺序上有意达到**层进**（即在重要性上依次提升），但在所指上却形成非意识降格——至少对非耶鲁毕业生是如此。有时，就连大诗人也会在不经意间跌入这样的修辞格中。在《序曲》（1805，第9卷）的初稿中，威廉·华兹华斯在讲述过沃德拉库和朱莉娅这对时运不济的情侣的故事后，又讲述起朱莉娅如何死去，把乳婴留给沃德拉库扶养：

这是她留给他的慰藉
抚育失去母亲的孤婴并履行
一个保姆的职责关照他幼小的孩子
时日不长，因为父亲的某些过失
或轻率，孩子死去了。

温德姆·路易斯与查尔斯·李合编的《猫头鹰标本：劣诗选》（1948年修订版）是一个有关无意识突降的宝藏。

突降法有时可用作突降的代名词；但在更为实际的应用中，"突降法"并不具有贬义，它表示为了造成喜剧性或讽刺性的艺术效果，作者故意笔锋一转，从

to achieve a comic or satiric effect. Thus Thomas Gray in his *mock-heroic* "Ode on the Death of a Favorite Cat" (1748)—the cat had drowned when she tried to catch a goldfish—gravely inserts this moral observation:

> What female heart can gold despise?
> What cat's averse to fish?

And in *Don Juan* (1819–24; I. ix.) Byron uses anticlimax to deflate the would-be gallantry of Juan's father:

> A better cavalier ne'er mounted horse,
> Or, being mounted, e'er got down again.

battle rapping: 271.

beast fable: 9.

Beat writers: Beat writers identifies a loose-knit group of poets and novelists, in the second half of the 1950s and early 1960s, who shared a set of social attitudes—antiestablishment, antipolitical, anti-intellectual, opposed to the prevailing cultural, literary, and moral values, and in favor of unfettered self-realization and self-expression. The Beat writers often performed in coffeehouses and other public places, to the accompaniment of drums or jazz music. (See *performance poetry*.) "Beat" was used to signify both "beaten down" (that is, by the oppressive culture of the time) and "beatific" (many of the Beat writers cultivated ecstatic states by way of Buddhism, Jewish and Christian mysticism, and/or drugs that induced visionary experiences). The group included such diverse figures as the poets Allen Ginsberg, Gregory Corso, and Lawrence Ferlinghetti and the novelists William Burroughs and Jack Kerouac. Ginsberg's *Howl* (1956) is a central Beat achievement in its breathless, chanted celebration of the down-and-out and the subculture of drug users, social misfits, and compulsive wanderers, as well as in representing the derangement of the intellect and the senses effected by sexual abandon, drugged hallucinations, and religious ecstasies. (Compare the vogue of *decadence* in the late nineteenth century.) A representative and influential novel of the movement is Jack Kerouac's *On the Road* (1958). While the Beat movement was short-lived, it left its imprint on the subjects and forms of many writers of the 1960s and 1970s; see *counterculture*, under *Periods of American Literature*.

Refer to Lawrence Lipton, *The Holy Barbarians* (1959); Seymour Krim, ed., *The Beats* (1960); Ann Charters, ed., *The Portable Beat Reader* (1992); Brenda Knight, ed., *Women of the Beat Generation: The Writers, Artists and Muses at the Heart of a Revolution* (1996); Jonah Raskin, *American Scream: Allen Ginsberg's "Howl" and the Making of the Beat Generation* (2004). Holly George-Warren has edited a collection of essays, reviews, memoirs, and interviews: *Rolling Stone Book of the Beats: The Beat Generation and American Culture* (1999).

For references to *Beat Writers* in other entries, see pages *29, 76, 277*.

beginning (of a plot): **296.**

严肃高尚的格调跌落到轻浮卑贱。在仿英雄体诗《祭爱猫之死》(1748)中,托马斯·格雷对爱猫偷捕金鱼不成反遭落水身亡之灾,沉痛地作出了如下的道德短评:

> 什么样的女人心灵才蔑视金子?
> 什么样的小猫不喜爱鱼? （黄绍鑫译）

此外,在《唐·璜》(1819—1824)第一章第九节中,拜伦是这样用突降法降低唐·璜之父自诩的英勇气度的:

> 从来没有一个骑士,不论是骑上马的,
> 或者是骑上了又跳下来的,能比荷塞更加出色。 （朱维基译）

battle rapping：战斗说唱 271。

beast fable：动物寓言故事 9。

Beat Writers：垮掉派作家

垮掉派作家指的是 1950 年代后半期至 1960 年代初期,一些诗人和小说家由于共同的社会观念——反现有秩序、反政治、反理性——而结成的一个松散的集团,他们反对主流的文化、文学和道德价值观,主张无拘无束的自我实现与自我表现。垮掉派作家经常在咖啡馆和其他公共场所在鼓乐或爵士乐的伴奏下表演。(参见:*表演诗歌*。)"垮掉"有两层含义:"被击垮"(被当代压抑性的文化所击垮)和"自得其乐"(很多垮掉派作家通过信奉佛教、犹太教和基督教的玄想之说和/或靠吸食毒品引起的幻觉,修炼成一种狂喜的精神状态)。该集团里的人物形形色色,其中有诗人艾伦·金斯堡、格雷戈里·柯尔索、劳伦斯·弗林哥蒂和小说家威廉·巴罗斯、杰克·凯鲁亚克。金斯堡的《嚎叫》(1956)是垮掉派的核心代表作,它声嘶力竭地为潦倒者和这个吸毒成性、不满现实、被迫流离的亚文化群体引吭高歌,同时也表现他们因放纵情欲、嗜毒成幻、迷恋宗教而引起的神志和感官的错乱。(对比:19 世纪后期*颓废派文艺*的流行。)杰克·凯鲁亚克的《在路上》(1958)是垮掉派小说最具影响的代表作。垮掉派运动的寿命虽然短暂,但在创作主题和形式上,对 1960 年代和 1970 年代的许多作家留下了深刻的印记。参见:*美国文学各时期的划分中的反文化运动*。

参阅:劳伦斯·利普顿所著的《神圣的野蛮人》(1959);西摩·克里姆主编的《垮掉派》(1960);安·查特斯主编的《垮掉派便携作品集》(1992);布伦达·奈特主编的《"垮掉的一代"中的女性:位于革命核心的作家、艺术家和缪斯》(1996);乔纳·拉斯金所著的《美国尖叫:艾伦·金斯堡的"嚎叫"与"垮掉的一代"的形成》(2004)。霍利·乔治-沃伦主编了一本由随笔、评论、回忆、采访组成的合集:《滚石垮掉派作品集:"垮掉的一代"与美国文化》(1999)。

其他条目中提及"垮掉派作家"的地方,参见第 29、76、277 页。

beginning (of a plot)：(情节中的) 开始 296。

beliefs (in reading literature): **129**.

bibliography: 32; *35*.

Bildungsroman (bĭld" ungsrōmän'): **255**.

binary opposition: 79; *328*.

biography: Late in the seventeenth century, John Dryden defined biography neatly as "the history of particular men's lives." The name now connotes a relatively full account of a particular person's life, involving the attempt to set forth character, temperament, and milieu, as well as the subject's activities and experiences.

Both the ancient Greeks and Romans produced short, formal lives of individuals. The most famed surviving example is the *Parallel Lives* of Greek and Roman notables by the Greek writer Plutarch, c. AD 46–120; in the translation by Sir Thomas North in 1579, it was the source of Shakespeare's plays on Roman subjects. Medieval authors wrote generalized chronicles of the deeds of a king, as well as **hagiographies**: the stylized lives of Christian saints, often based more on pious legends than on fact. In England, the fairly detailed secular biography appeared in the seventeenth century; the most distinguished instance is Izaak Walton's *Lives* (including short biographies of the poets John Donne and George Herbert), written between 1640 and 1678.

The eighteenth century in England is the age of the emergence of the full-scale biography, and also of the theory of biography as a special literary *genre*. It was the century of Samuel Johnson's *Lives of the English Poets* (1779–81) and of the best known of all English biographies, James Boswell's *Life of Samuel Johnson* (1791). In our own time, biographies of notable women and men have become one of the most popular of literary forms, and usually there is at least one biographical title high on the best seller list.

Autobiography is a biography written by the subject about himself or herself. It is to be distinguished from the **memoir**, in which the emphasis is not on the author's developing self but on the people and events that the author has known or witnessed, and also from the private **diary** or **journal**, which is a day-to-day record of the events in one's life, written for personal use and satisfaction, with little or no thought of publication. Examples of the latter type are the seventeenth-century diaries of Samuel Pepys and John Evelyn, the eighteenth-century journals of James Boswell and Fanny Burney, and Dorothy Wordsworth's remarkable *Journals*, written 1798–1828, but not published until long after her death. The first fully developed autobiography is also the most influential: the *Confessions* of St. Augustine, written in the fourth century. The design of this profound and subtle **spiritual autobiography** centers on what became the crucial experience in Christian autobiography: the author's anguished mental crisis, and a recovery and **conversion** in which he discovers his Christian identity and religious vocation.

Michel de Montaigne's *Essays*, published in 1580 and in later expansions, constitute in their sum the first great instance of autobiographical self-revelation

beliefs（in reading literature）：（阅读文学中的）信念　**129**。

bibliography：书目学　**32**；*35*。

Bildungsroman：主人公成长小说　**255**。

binary opposition：二元对立关系　**79**；*328*。

Biography：传记

　　17世纪晚期，约翰·德莱顿把传记简明地定义为"特定人物的生平"。如今，该术语指的是相对全面地记述某个特定人物的一生，包括表现其性格、气质、社会背景，以及传主的活动和经历。

　　古希腊罗马时期的传记都是记叙人物的一些短暂而又刻板的人生片段。流传至今、最负盛名的传记作品是希腊作家普卢塔克（约46—120）创作的关于希腊罗马社会名流的《名人列传》；1579年由托马斯·诺斯爵士译成英文，成为莎士比亚罗马题材戏剧的创作素材。中世纪传记作家的作品既有关于帝王言行的普通编年史，也有**圣徒传**：那些风格雷同、往往是以虔诚的传奇故事而非事实为依据的基督圣徒的生平传记。英国正宗的、相当翔实的世俗传记产生于17世纪；当时最杰出的传记作品是艾萨克·沃尔顿于1640—1678年间创作的《名人志》（包括诗人约翰·多恩和乔治·赫伯特的短篇传记）。

　　18世纪，完整的传记作品在英国已蔚然成风；作为一种独特的文学类型，传记理论也呈繁荣之势。该世纪是属于塞缪尔·约翰逊的《诗人传》（1779—1781）和詹姆斯·鲍斯韦尔的《约翰逊传》（1791）这一传记中最为杰出的作品的时代。如今，社会名流的传记是最为人们喜闻乐见的文学形式之一，往往至少会有一部传记高居畅销书之列。

　　自传是传主本人为他/她自己而作的传记。它与**回忆录**不同，回忆录不是侧重于作者自己的成长历程，而是主要记录作者所知道或目睹过的人物和事件。自传也有别于私人**日记**或**日志**，日记或日志记录每日发生在自己日常生活中的琐事，其目的是为满足个人使用或消遣，很少或不以出版为目的。例如：17世纪塞缪尔·佩皮斯和约翰·伊夫林的日记，18世纪詹姆斯·鲍斯韦尔和范妮·伯尼的日志，以及多萝西·沃兹沃斯写于1798—1828年间而直到她去世很久才得以发表的著名的《日志》。第一部描述详尽完整，同时也是最具影响的自传是圣奥古斯丁写于公元4世纪的《忏悔录》。这部深刻细腻的**精神自传**，展示了基督徒自传的主要内容：从作者苦闷的精神危机到平复再到灵魂的**皈依**，记录了他对自己基督徒身份的认可和对宗教使命的发现。

　　米歇尔·德·蒙田发表于1580年的《随笔》及其后来的扩充本成为首部自传体作品自我展示的伟大典范，这种自我展示是为了其天性爱好，而非为了宗教或

that is presented for its inherent interest, rather than for religious or didactic purposes. Among later distinguished achievements in secular autobiography are Rousseau's *Confessions* (written 1764–70), Goethe's *Dichtung und Wahrheit* ("Poetry and Truth," written 1810–31), the autobiographies of Benjamin Franklin, Henry Adams, Sean O'Casey, Lillian Hellman, and Gertrude Stein (published in 1933 under the title *The Autobiography of Alice B. Toklas*), and *The Autobiography of Malcolm X* (1964). Many spiritual histories of the self, however, like John Bunyan's *Grace Abounding to the Chief of Sinners* (1666), followed Augustine's example of religious self-revelation centering on a crisis and conversion. An important offshoot of this type are secular autobiographies that represent a spiritual crisis which is resolved by the author's discovery of his identity and vocation, not as a Christian, but as a poet or artist; examples are Wordsworth's autobiography in verse, *The Prelude* (completed 1805, published in revised form 1850), or the partly autobiographical works of prose fiction such as Marcel Proust's *À la recherche du temps perdu* (1913–27), James Joyce's *Portrait of the Artist as a Young Man* (1915), and Ralph Ellison's *Invisible Man* (1965). In recent years, the distinction between autobiography and fiction has become more and more blurred, as authors include themselves under their own names in novels, or write autobiographies in the asserted mode of fiction, or (as in Maxine Hong Kingston's *The Woman Warrior*, 1975) mingle fiction and personal experience as a way to get at one's essential life story (see the entry *novel*).

On biography: Donald A. Stauffer, *English Biography before 1700* (1930) and *The Art of Biography in Eighteenth-Century England* (1941); Leon Edel, *Literary Biography* (1957); Richard D. Altick, *Lives and Letters: A History of Literary Biography in England and America* (1965); David Novarr, *The Lines of Life: Theories of Biography, 1880–1970* (1986); Linda Wagner-Martin, *Telling Women's Lives: The New Biography* (1994); David Ellis, *Literary Lives: Biography and the Search for Understanding* (2000). Catherine N. Parke, *Biography: Writing Lives* (1996), includes a chapter on "Minority Biography." On autobiography: Roy Pascal, *Design and Truth in Autobiography* (1960); Estelle C. Jelinek, ed., *Women's Autobiography: Essays in Criticism* (1980), and *The Tradition of Women's Autobiography from Antiquity to the Present* (1986). The importance of autobiography in the Victorian period in England is discussed in Avron Fleishman, *Figures of Autobiography* (1983), and Linda H. Peterson, *Victorian Autobiography* (1986). For an extended discussion of Augustine, Rousseau, and Beckett, see James Olney, *Memory and Narrative: The Weave of Life-Writing* (2001). John N. Morris, in *Versions of the Self: Studies in English Autobiography from John Bunyan to John Stuart Mill* (1966), deals with both religious and secular spiritual autobiographies. M. H. Abrams, in *Natural Supernaturalism* (1971), describes the wide ramifications of spiritual autobiography in historical and philosophical as well as literary forms. In a highly influential essay on "The Autobiographical Pact" (1974), Philippe Lejeune argues for an historical view of the self as expressed in autobiography; reprinted in Paul John Eakin, ed., *On Autobiography* (1989). Paul John Eakin's *How Our Lives Become Stories: Making Selves* (1999) is an account of autobiography that draws on cognitive science, memory studies, and developmental psychology; see also Eakin's *Living Autobiographically: How We Create Identity in Narrative* (2008).

说教目的。在后来的世俗自传作品中，杰出代表作有卢梭作于1764—1770年间的《忏悔录》，歌德作于1810—1831年间的《诗与真》，以及本杰明·富兰克林、亨利·亚当斯、肖恩·奥凯西、莉莲·赫尔曼、格特鲁德·斯泰因（1933年以《艾丽斯·B.托克拉斯自传》为名发表）等人的自传，以及《马尔科姆·X自传》。许多精神自传，例如约翰·班扬的《罪魁蒙恩记》(1666)，以奥古斯丁的宗教自我展示为样本，主要记述精神危机和灵魂的皈依。此类传记中的一个重要流派是作者通过发现自我和身为一个诗人或艺术家而非基督徒的使命而解决精神危机的世俗性自传；如华兹华斯的诗体自传《序曲》（完成于1805年，1850年以修订版出版），或如马塞尔·普鲁斯特的《追忆似水年华》(1913—1927)、詹姆斯·乔伊斯的《一个青年艺术家的画像》(1915)、拉尔夫·埃利森的《隐形人》(1965)等半自传体小说。近年来，随着作者本人以实名出现在小说中，而自传又以所谓的小说模式写成，或是[像在玛克辛·汉·金斯敦（即汤婷婷）的《女勇士》(1975)中那样]将小说与自我经历融为一体来记录某人主要的生平故事，自传与小说之间的区别已经变得越来越模糊（参见：*小说*）。

关于传记，参阅：唐纳德·A.斯托弗所著的《1700年前的英国传记》(1930)和《18世纪英国传记的艺术》(1941)；利昂·埃德尔所著的《文学传记》(1957)；理查德·D.奥尔蒂克所著的《生活与信件：英美文学传记史》(1965)；戴维·诺瓦尔所著的《生命之线：1880—1970年间的传记理论》(1986)；琳达·瓦格纳-马丁所著的《讲述女性生活：新传记》(1994)；戴维·埃利斯所著的《文学生活：传记与追寻理解》(2000)。凯瑟琳·N.帕克所著的《传记：书写生活》(1996)中包括一章"少数群体传记"。关于自传，参阅：罗伊·帕斯卡尔所著的《自传中的设计与真实》(1960)；埃丝特尔·C.杰利内克主编的《女性自传：批评论文集》(1980)和《从古代到现代的女性自传的传统》(1986)。阿夫伦·弗莱施曼所著的《人物自传》(1983)和琳达·H.彼得森所著的《维多利亚时期的自传》(1986)，讨论了英国维多利亚时代自传的重要性。关于对奥古斯丁、卢梭、贝克特的扩展讨论，参见詹姆斯·奥尔尼所著的《记忆与叙事：生命书写的编织》(2001)。约翰·N.莫里斯在《自我视野：从约翰·班扬到约翰·斯图尔特·穆勒的英国自传之研究》(1966)中论述了宗教和世俗精神自传。M.H.艾布拉姆斯在《自然的超自然主义》(1971)中讲述了精神自传的历史并描述了其在历史和哲学以及文学当中种类繁多的各种形式。在一篇极具影响力的文章"自传契约"(1974)中，菲力浦·勒热纳从历史主义视角论证了自传中表述的自我，这篇文章重印收入保罗·约翰·埃金主编的《论自传》(1989)。保罗·约翰·埃金所著的《我们的生活如何变成故事：塑造自我》(1999)，利用认知科学、记忆研究和发展心理学方面的知识来解释自传；也可参阅：埃金所著的《自传式地生活：我们如何在叙事中创造认同感》(2008)。

Black Aesthetic: 29.

Black Arts Movement: The Black Arts Movement designates a number of *African-American* writers whose work was shaped by the social and political turbulence of the 1960s—the decade of massive protests against the Vietnam War, demands for the rights of African-Americans that led to repeated and sometimes violent confrontations, and the riots and burnings in Los Angeles, Detroit, New York, Newark, and other major cities. The literary movement was associated with the Black Power movement in politics, whose spokesmen, including Stokely Carmichael and Malcolm X, opposed the proponents of integration, and instead advocated black separatism, black pride, and black solidarity. Representatives of the Black Arts put their literary writings at the service of these social and political aims. As Larry Neal put it in his essay "The Black Arts Movement" (1968): "Black Art is the aesthetic and spiritual sister of the Black Power Concept. As such it envisions an art that speaks directly to the needs and aspirations of Black America" and "to the Afro-American desire for self-determination and nationhood."

The **Black Aesthetic** that was voiced or supported by writers in the movement rejected, as aspects of domination by white culture, the "high art" and modernist forms advocated by Ralph Ellison and other African-American writers in the 1950s. Instead, the black aesthetic called for the exploitation of the energy and freshness of the black vernacular, in rhythms and moods emulating jazz and the blues, dealing especially with the lives and concerns of lower-class blacks, and addressed to a black mass audience. The most notable and influential practitioner of the Black Arts was Imamu Amiri Baraka (born LeRoi Jones) who, after an early period in Greenwich Village as an associate of Allen Ginsberg and other *Beat* writers, moved to Harlem, where he founded the Black Arts Repertory Theater/School in 1965. Baraka was distinguished as a poet, a dramatist (his play *Dutchman* is often considered an exemplary product of the Black Arts achievement), a political essayist, and a critic both of literature and of jazz music. Among other writers of the movement were the poets Etheredge Knight, Sonia Sanchez, Haki Madhubuti, and Nikki Giovanni; the authors of prose fiction John Alfred Williams, Eldridge Cleaver, and James Alan McPherson; and the playwrights Paul Carter Harrison and Ed Bullins.

The revolutionary impetus of the Black Arts Movement had diminished by the 1970s, and some of its pronouncements and achievements now seem undisciplined and crudely propagandistic. But its best writings survive, and their critical rationale and subject matter have served as models not only to later African-American writers, but also to Native American, Latino, Asian, and other *ethnic* writers in America. For a later emergence, on the popular level, of antiestablishment poetry by African-Americans, see *rap* under *performance poetry*.

The *Black Aesthetic*, ed. Addison Gayle (1971), includes essays that were important in establishing this mode of criticism by Ron Karenga, Don L. Lee, and Larry Neal, as well as by Gayle himself. See also Imamu Amiri Baraka, *Home: Social Essays* (1966), and editor with Larry Neal of *Black Fire: An*

Black Aesthetic：黑人美学　29。

Black Arts Movement：黑人艺术运动

　　黑人艺术运动指的是一大批非裔美国作家，他们的作品脱胎于1960年代动荡不安的社会和政治环境中，当时，大规模的反越战运动和非裔美国人争取民权的运动导致接二连三的有时甚至是暴力的社会对抗，在洛杉矶、底特律、纽约、纽瓦克和其他一些大城市爆发了骚乱和焚烧事件。文学运动在政治上与黑人权利运动相联系，其代言人，包括斯托克利·卡迈克尔和马尔科姆·X，反对种族混合和种族同化的倡议，倡导黑人分离主义、黑人尊严、黑人团结。黑人艺术运动的代表作家以他们的文学作品为这些社会和政治目标服务。正如拉里·尼尔在他的评论文章"黑人艺术运动"（1968）中所写："黑人艺术是黑人权利概念在美学和精神上的姊妹。它以此构想一种艺术形式来直接表达黑人美国的需求和渴望"以及"美国黑人对自主和国家认可的期望"。

　　黑人美学是由此次运动中的作家倡导和发起的，以抵制1950年代由拉尔夫·埃利森和其他非裔美国作家鼓吹的在白人文化各领域中占主导地位的"高雅艺术"和各种现代派艺术形式。黑人美学号召作家发掘黑人方言在模仿爵士乐和蓝调音乐的节奏和基调上的活力与清新，尤其是反映社会底层黑人的生活和忧虑，并以广大黑人为其具体的艺术服务对象。最有声望、最具影响的黑人艺术实践者要数伊马穆·阿米里·巴拉卡（原名勒罗伊·琼斯），他早期在格林威治村与艾伦·金斯堡和其他*垮掉派*作家合作共事过，后来移居纽约哈莱姆区，并于1965年在那里建立了黑人艺术剧团剧院/学校。巴拉卡是位杰出的诗人、剧作家（他的剧作《荷兰人》一向被认为是黑人艺术成就的代表作）、政论家，以及文学和爵士乐批评家。此次运动中的其他作家还有诗人埃瑟里奇·奈特、索尼亚·桑切兹、黑基·马德胡布蒂、尼基·吉欧万尼；小说家约翰·艾尔弗雷德·威廉斯、埃尔德里奇·克利夫、詹姆斯·阿伦·麦克弗森；以及剧作家保罗·卡特·哈里森和埃德·布林斯。

　　到1970年代，黑人艺术运动最具革命性的推动力逐渐式微，在今天看来，其某些主张和成就显得任性和具有宣传功利色彩。但其最优秀的作品则流传下来，他们的批评理论和创作题材不仅是后世非裔美国作家，而且成为美国本土以及生活在美国的拉美、亚洲和其他*民族*作家的典范。关于后来在大众层面出现的非裔美国人反对正统流派的诗歌，参见：*表演诗歌*中的*说唱*。

　　艾迪生·盖尔主编的《黑人美学》（1971）收录了罗恩·卡伦格、唐·L. 李、拉里·尼尔及其本人为建立这种批评模式而写的一些重要文章。另可参阅：伊马穆·阿米里·巴拉卡所著的《家：社会论文集》（1966）及其与拉里·尼尔合编的

Anthology of Afro-American Writing (1968); Stephen Henderson, *Understanding the New Black Poetry* (1973); and the text, biographies, and bibliographies for "The Black Arts Movement: 1960–1970" in *The Norton Anthology of African American Literature*, ed. H. L. Gates, Nellie Y. McKay, and others, 1997.

black comedy: 2.

black humor: 2.

Black Mountain poets: 277.

Black writers: 274. See also *African-American writers*.

blank verse: Blank verse consists of lines of *iambic pentameter* (five-stress iambic verse) which are unrhymed—hence the term "blank." Of all English metrical forms it is closest to the natural rhythms of English speech, yet flexible and adaptive to diverse levels of discourse: as a result it has been more frequently and variously used than any other form of versification. Soon after blank verse was introduced by the Earl of Surrey in his translations of Books 2 and 4 of Virgil's *The Aeneid* (about 1540), it became the standard meter for Elizabethan and later poetic drama; a free form of blank verse remained the medium in such twentieth-century verse plays as those by Maxwell Anderson and T. S. Eliot. John Milton used blank verse for his epic *Paradise Lost* (1667), James Thomson for his descriptive and philosophical *Seasons* (1726–30), William Wordsworth for his autobiographical *Prelude* (1805), Alfred, Lord Tennyson for the narrative *Idylls of the King* (1891), Robert B.owning for *The Ring and the Book* (1868–69) and many dramatic monologues, and T. S. Eliot for much of *The Waste Land* (1922). A large number of meditative lyrics, from the *Romantic Period* to the present, have also been written in blank verse, including Coleridge's "Frost at Midnight," Wordsworth's "Tintern Abbey," Tennyson's "Tears, Idle Tears" (in which the blank verse is divided into five-line stanzas), and Wallace Stevens' "Sunday Morning."

Divisions in blank verse poems, used to set off a sustained passage, are called **verse paragraphs**. See, for example, the great verse paragraph of twenty-six lines which initiates Milton's *Paradise Lost*, beginning with "Of man's first disobedience" and ending with "And justify the ways of God to men"; also, the opening verse paragraph of twenty-two lines in Wordsworth's "Tintern Abbey" (1798), which begins:

> Five years have bast; five summers, with the length
> Of five long winters! and again I hear
> These waters, rolling from their mountain-springs
> With a soft inland murmur.

See *meter*, and refer to Moody Prior's critical study of blank verse in *The Language of Tragedy* (1964). For references to *blank verse* in other en ries, see pages *64, 93, 142*.

《黑火：非裔美国作品选》(1968)；斯蒂芬·亨德森所著的《理解新的黑人诗歌》(1973)；H. I. 盖茨和内利·Y. 麦凯等人编著的《诺顿美国黑人文学选集》(1997)中为"黑人艺术运动：1960—1970"提供的文本、传记及参考文献。

black comedy：黑色喜剧　2。

black humor：黑色幽默　2。

Black Mountain poets：黑山诗人　277。

Black writers：黑人作家　274。也可参见：非裔美国作家。

Blank Verse：无韵诗

无韵诗由*五步抑扬格*（有五个重音节的抑扬格诗行）诗行组成，行与行不押韵，故称"无韵诗"。在各类英语格律诗歌中，无韵诗最接近英语口语的自然节奏；无韵诗结构灵活，适合于各个不同层次话语的格调，因此它的运用比其他诗歌形式更为常见和多样化。（大约在1540年）萨里伯爵在翻译维吉尔的《埃涅阿斯纪》第二卷和第四卷时把无韵诗引入英国，很快，这种形式就成为伊丽莎白时期及后世诗体剧本的标准格律；无韵诗的一种自由形式仍然是20世纪马克斯韦尔·安德逊和T. S. 艾略特等人从事诗体剧本创作的艺术形式。约翰·弥尔顿的史诗《失乐园》(1667)、詹姆斯·汤姆逊寓描述和哲理于一体的《四季》(1726—1730)、威廉·华兹华斯的自传体长诗《序曲》(1805)、阿尔弗雷德·丁尼生勋爵的叙事诗《国王歌集》(1891，又译《国王叙事诗》)、罗伯特·布朗宁的《指环与书》(1868—1869)和许多戏剧性独白诗，以及T. S. 艾略特的《荒原》(1922)中的大部分内容，都采用了无韵诗的形式。自浪漫*主义时期*至今，许多沉思性的抒情诗歌也是用无韵体创作的，如柯勒律治的《霜夜》、华兹华斯的《丁登寺》、丁尼生的《眼泪枉流》（为五行一节的无韵诗）、华莱士·史蒂文斯的《礼拜日的早晨》。

无韵诗往往把各展开部分分开，称为**诗段**。例如弥尔顿《失乐园》中杰出的26行开篇诗段，以"关于人类最初违反天神命令"开篇，以"向世人昭示天道的公正"结尾；同样，华兹华斯的《丁登寺》(1798)是以22行诗段开头的，其开篇如下：

> 五年过去了，五个夏天，还有
> 五个漫长的冬天！并且我重又听见
> 这些水声，从山泉中滚流出来，
> 在内陆的溪流中柔声低语。　　　　　　　　（汪剑钊译）

参见：**格律**，参阅：穆迪·普赖尔在其所著的《悲剧的语言》(1964)中对无韵诗的评论研究。其他条目中提及"无韵诗"的地方，参见第64、93、142页。

Bloomsbury Group: Bloomsbury Group is the name applied to an informal association of writers, artists, and intellectuals, many of whom lived in Bloomsbury, a residential district in central London. This group of friends began to meet around 1905 for conversations about the arts and issues in philosophy. Its members, who opposed the narrow post-Victorian restrictions in both the arts and morality, included the novelists Virginia Woolf and E. M. Forster, the painters Duncan Grant and Vanessa Bell (Virginia Woolf's sister), the influential art critics Clive Bell and Roger Frye, the iconoclastic biographer of Victorian personages Lytton Strachey, and the famed economist John Maynard Keynes. Some members were linked not only by common interests and viewpoints but also by complicated erotic liaisons, both heterosexual and homosexual. The Bloomsbury Group had an important influence on innovative literary, artistic, and intellectual developments in the two decades after the First World War, which ended in 1918. A memoir by the son of Clive Bell and Vanessa Stephen is Quentin Bell, *Bloomsbury Recalled* (1997). See Leon Edel, *Bloomsbury: A House of Lions* (1979); S. P. Rosenbaum, ed., *The Bloomsbury Group: A Collection of Memoirs and Commentary* (1995); and Rosenbaum, ed., *A Bloomsbury Group Reader* (1993).

Bombast: Bombast denotes a wordy and inflated diction that is patently disproportionate to the matter that it signifies. The magniloquence of even so fine a poet as Christopher Marlowe is at times inappropriate to its sense, as when Faustus declares (*Dr. Faustus*, 1604; III. i. 47ff.):

> Now by the kingdoms of infernal rule,
> Of Styx, Acheron, and the fiery lake
> Of ever-burning Phlegethon I swear
> That I do long to see the monuments
> And situation of bright-splendent Rome;

which is to say: "By Hades, I'd like to see Rome!" Bombast is a frequent component in the heroic *drama* of the late seventeenth and early eighteenth centuries. The pompous language of that drama is parodied in Henry Fielding's *Tom Thumb the Great* (1731), as in the noted opening of Act II. v., in which the diminutive male lover cries:

> Oh! Huncamunca, Huncamunca, oh!
> Thy pouting breasts, like kettle-drums of brass,
> Beat everlasting loud alarms of joy;
> As bright as brass they are, and oh! as hard;
> Oh! Huncamunca, Huncamunca, oh!

Fielding points out in a note that this passage was specifically a *parody* of James Thomson's bombastic lines in *The Tragedy of Sophonisba* (1730):

> Oh! Sophonisba, Sophonisba, oh!
> Oh! Narva, Narva, oh!

"Bombast" originally meant "cotton stuffing," and in Elizabethan times came to be used as a metaphor for an over-elaborate style.

Bloomsbury Group：布鲁姆斯伯里团体

布鲁姆斯伯里团体是一个由作家、艺术家和知识分子组成的非正式团体，其中许多人都住在布鲁姆斯伯里——伦敦市中心一个住宅小区。1905 年左右，团体里的朋友开始聚会，讨论艺术和哲学方面的问题。其成员，反对后维多利亚时代对艺术和道德的狭隘限制，包括小说家弗吉尼亚·吴尔夫和 E. M. 福斯特，画家邓肯·格兰特和瓦妮莎·贝尔（伍尔夫的妹妹），有影响力的艺术批评家克莱夫·贝尔和罗杰·弗莱，批判传统信仰的维多利亚时期人物传记作家利顿·斯特雷奇，著名经济学家约翰·梅纳德·凯恩斯。对部分成员来说，将其联系到一起的不仅是共同的兴趣和观点，还有复杂的情欲关系，既有异性恋又有同性恋。1918 年第一次世界大战结束后的二十年间，布鲁姆斯伯里团体对标新立异的文学、艺术和智识发展产生了重要影响。克莱夫·贝尔和瓦妮莎·斯蒂芬的儿子昆汀·贝尔写有一部回忆录《布鲁姆斯伯里回忆记》（1997）。参阅：利昂·埃德尔所著的《布鲁姆斯伯里：名人屋》（1979）；S. P. 罗森鲍姆主编的《岁月与海浪——布鲁姆斯伯里文化圈人物群像》（1995）和《布鲁姆斯伯里团体读本》（1993）。

Bombast：浮夸之辞

浮夸之辞指与所指事物明显不相吻合的冗长浮华、言过其实的措辞。即使像克里斯托弗·马洛这样优秀的诗人在其诗作中也时有华而不实的现象，例如浮士德的一番陈述（《浮士德博士》，1604；第三幕第一场第 47 行及其下）：

> 现在我凭阴间的王国，
> 凭那有阴河及永冒烈焰的
> 火湖的王国立誓愿
> 我渴望着看一看辉煌的
> 罗马城的名胜和形势；　　　　　　　　　　（戴镏龄译）

其实这里所要表达的只是"冥王，我想看看罗马！"17 世纪晚期和 18 世纪早期的*英雄剧*中常有浮夸之辞。亨利·菲尔丁在其讽刺喜剧《大姆指汤姆的生与死》（1731）中对英雄剧中的浮夸之辞作了一番戏谑模仿。例如在该剧第二幕第五场著名的开场白中，小情人大声赞叹：

> 哦！哈恩卡米尤卡，哈恩卡米尤卡，哦！
> 你凸起的胸部，像黄铜制成的鼓样，
> 撞击出永恒的响亮的欢快之音；
> 它们鲜艳如黄铜，而且，哦！坚挺如黄铜；
> 哦！哈恩卡米尤卡，哈恩卡米尤卡，哦！

菲尔丁在注释中指出，这一段落是戏谑模仿詹姆斯·汤姆逊的《索弗尼斯巴之悲剧》（1730）中的诗句：

> 哦！索弗尼斯巴，索弗尼斯巴，哦！
> 哦！纳尔瓦，纳尔瓦，哦！

"bombast"（"浮夸之辞"）的原意是"棉花填料"，在伊丽莎白时代用以比喻冗长浮华言过其实的措辞风格。

bomolochos (bōmŏl′ ŏkŏs): **378**.

book: In its inclusive sense, the term designates any written or printed document which is of considerable length, yet is light and durable enough to be easily portable. Studies devoted to the identification of the authorship, dates of issue, *editions*, and physical properties of books are called **bibliography**.

In ancient Greece and Rome the standard form of the book was the double papyrus roll. **Papyrus**, which had been developed in Egypt, was made from the papyrus reed, which grows profusely in the Nile delta; the stems of the reed were cut into strips, soaked, and impregnated with paste. The texts were **manuscripts** (that is, written by hand), and were inscribed in columns; as the reader went along, he unwound the papyrus from the right-hand roll and wound it on the left-hand roll.

In a very important change in the form of the book during the fifth century of the Middle Ages, papyrus rolls were superseded by the parchment or vellum codex. **Parchment** was made from the skins of sheep, goats, or calves which were stretched and scraped clean to serve as a material for writing. **Vellum** is sometimes used interchangeably with "parchment," but is more useful as a term for an especially fine type of parchment that was prepared from the delicate skin of a calf or a kid. To make a **codex** (the plural is "codices"), the parchment was cut into leaves; as in the modern printed book, the leaves were stitched together on one side and then bound. The great advantages of the codex over the roll were that the codex could be opened at any point; the text could be inscribed on both sides of a leaf; and the resulting book was able to contain a much longer text than a manuscript roll. In its early era, the codex was used primarily for biblical texts—a single volume could contain all four Gospels, where a roll had been able to encompass only a single Gospel.

In the course of the Middle Ages, many monasteries had **scriptoria**—rooms in which scribes copied out texts; often, a number of scribes copied texts that were dictated by a reader, in an early form of the mass production of books. To make especially fine codices—at first for religious, and later for secular texts, including works of literature—the manuscripts were **illuminated**; that is, they were adorned by artists with bright-colored miniature paintings and ornamental scrolls. Since all kinds of parchment were expensive, written surfaces were sometimes scraped off, then used for a new text. Such parchments are called **palimpsests** (Greek for "scraped clean"); often, the original text, or in some cases multiple layers of texts, remain visible under an ultraviolet light.

Paper, invented by the Chinese as early as the first century AD, was introduced to Europe by the Arabs in the eighth century, after which it increasingly replaced parchment. Early paper was made from linen and cotton rags; later, technology was invented for making paper from the pulp of wood and other vegetable fibers. The use of paper was essential for the invention of printing. The Chinese had been printing from carved wood blocks since the sixth century; but in 1440–50, Johannes Gutenberg introduced in Germany a new craft of printing from movable metal type, with ink, on paper, by means

bomolochos：丑角　378。

Book：书籍

  书籍广义上指任何有相当长度/篇幅又轻便耐久易携的手抄或印刷文献。致力于鉴别图书的作者身份、出版日期、版本及其物理属性的研究叫**书目学**。

  在古希腊罗马，标准的书籍形式是双纸莎草卷。**纸莎草**，一直发展于埃及，来自尼罗河三角洲生长繁茂的纸莎芦苇；将纸莎草的茎剖为长条，浸泡后黏贴到一起使其饱和，就可制成长卷。文本是**手抄稿**（即，手写而成），按列书写；读者在阅读时，右手滚动展开纸莎草，左手滚动合上纸莎草。

  中世纪的5世纪，书籍形式上发生了一个非常重要的改变，纸莎草卷被羊皮纸或牛皮纸抄本所取代。**羊皮纸**由绵羊、山羊或小牛的皮制作而成，这些皮被拉伸和刮干净，用作书写的材质。**牛皮纸**有时可与"羊皮纸"交替使用，但是作为一个术语更常用来指一种上佳的羊皮纸，由精密的小牛/小山羊皮质做成。为了做成一个**抄本**（复数形式是"codices"），要把羊皮纸切成页；就像在现代印刷书籍中一样，书页要顺着一边缝合起来，然后装订。抄本相比卷本最大的优点是，它可以在任何一个地方打开；文稿可以写在一页纸的两面；形成的书比起手抄卷能够容纳更多文稿。在其早期年代，抄本主要用于抄写圣经——一卷就可容纳所有的四福音书，而一个羊皮纸卷一直只能容纳一本福音书。

  在中世纪，许多寺院/修道院都有**缮写室**——抄写员在里面抄写文稿的房间；经常是这样，一个朗读者口述内容，一些抄写员进行抄写，这是图书大众生产的一种早期形式。为了制作上佳的抄本——一开始是宗教文本，后来是世俗文本，包括文学作品——手抄本被进行**彩饰**；也就是说，它们会被艺术家配上色彩明亮的微型图画和涡卷形装饰。由于所有类型的羊皮纸都很昂贵，写好的表面有时会被刮去，然后写上新的文稿。这样的羊皮纸叫做**重写羊皮纸卷**（希腊语中的意思是"刮干净"）；经常是，原初的文稿，或者在一些例子中是多重文稿，在紫外线下仍能看出。

  纸，早在公元1世纪就已由中国人发明出来，在8世纪由阿拉伯人引入欧洲，在那之后，它很快就取代了羊皮纸。早期的纸是用亚麻和破布为原料制造而成，后来，技术进步，用木浆和其他植物纤维来造纸。对印刷术的发明来说，纸的应用必不可少。自从6世纪以来，中国一直用雕刻好的木版印刷；但在1440—1450年间，德国的约翰内斯·古登堡采用了一种新的印刷技术：给金属活字涂上油墨，

of a press that was tightened by turning a levered screw. Within the next half century this cheap method of making many uniform copies of a book had spread throughout Europe, with enormous consequences for the growth of literacy and learning, and for the widespread development of the experimental sciences. See Elizabeth Eisenstein, *The Printing Press as an Agent of Change: Communications and Cultural Transformations in Early Modern Europe*, 2 vols., 1979.

The term **incunabula** (ĭn' kyoonăb" yoolă; the singular is incunabulum) designates books that were produced in the infancy of printing, during the half century before 1500. "Incunabula" is Latin for "swaddling clothes" or "cradle."

From the mid-seventeenth century on, there was a great increase in literacy and in the demand by the general public for literary and all other types of books. The accessibility and affordability of books was greatly expedited, beginning in the nineteenth century, by the invention of machines—powered first by steam, then by electricity—for producing paper and type, printing and binding books, and reproducing illustrations. In the twentieth century, and even more in the present era, the primacy of the printed book for recording and disseminating all forms of information has been challenged by the invention and rapid proliferation of electronic media for processing texts and images.

Refer to the entries on *book editions, book format, book history studies*, and *textual studies*. For the history of the book trade from classical Greece through the twentieth century, see F. A. Mumby, *Publishing and Bookselling: From the Earliest Times to 1870* (5th ed., 1974), and Ian Norrie, *Mumby's Publishing and Bookselling in the Twentieth Century* (1982). On the making, format, and history of printed books, see Ronald B. McKerrow, *An Introduction to Bibliography for Literary Students* (rev. 1994).

book editions: In present usage, **edition** designates the total copies of a book that are printed from a single setting of type or other mode of reproduction. The various "printings" or "reprints" of an edition—sometimes with some minor changes in the text—may be spaced over a period of years. We now identify as a "new edition" a printing in which substantial changes have been made in the text. A text may be revised and reprinted in this way many times, hence the terms "second edition," "third edition," etc.

A **variorum edition** designates either (1) an edition of a work that lists the textual variants in an author's manuscripts and in revisions of the printed text; an example is *The Variorum Edition of the Poems of W. B. Yeats*, ed. Peter Allt and Russell K. Alspach (1957); or else (2) an edition of a text that includes a selection of annotations and commentaries on the text by previous editors and critics. (The term "variorum" is a short form of the Latin *cum notis variorum*: "with the annotations of various persons.") *The New Variorum Edition of Shakespeare* is a variorum edition in both senses of the word.

See *book*, and refer to Ronald B. McKerrow, *An Introduction to Bibliography* (rev. 1965); Fredson Bowers, *Principles of Bibliographical Description* (1949); Philip Gaskell, *A New Introduction to Bibliography* (1972).

用一台拧紧杠杆螺钉固定好的印刷机，印到纸上。在接下来的半个世纪中，这一给一本书制造出许多一模一样副本的廉价方法传遍欧洲，由此产生的巨大后果是：识字学习得到增长，实验科学得到广泛发展。参阅：伊丽莎白·爱森斯坦所著的两卷本《作为变革代理人的印刷机：早期现代欧洲的交流与文化转型》(1979)。

古版本（单数形式为"incunabulum"）指的是1500年前50年内印刷术处于初始阶段时印制的所有书籍。incunabula一词是拉丁语，意指"襁褓期"或"婴儿期"。

从17世纪中期开始，随着读写能力提升，普通大众对文学和其他类型书籍的需求大增。从19世纪开始，通过机器的发明——先由蒸汽驱动，后由电力驱动——用来生产纸和铅字，印刷和装订书籍，复制插图，书籍的可得性和可购性迅速实现。在20世纪，在当今时代表现更甚，印刷书籍记载和传播各种信息的主导地位，一直受到存储文档和图片的电子媒介的发明及其快速扩散的挑战。

参阅条目：*书籍版本、书籍版式、书籍史研究、文本研究*。关于从古希腊到20世纪的书业史，参阅：F. A. 姆贝所著的《出版与书籍销售：从最早的时代到1870年》(1974年第5版)和伊恩·诺里所著的《12世纪Mumby的出版与书籍销售》(1982)。关于印刷书籍的制作、版式和历史，参阅：罗纳德·B. 麦克罗所著的《写给文科学生的书目学入门》(1994年修订版)。

Book Editions：书籍版本

在当前的用法中，**版本**是指由原稿一次性排版印刷而成的或以其他形式再版的书册。一个版本的不同"印刷本"或"重印本"——有时会在文本中出现细微的变化——会间隔几年。我们现在所谓的"新版本"是指出现许多更改的文本。文本可以多次修订和重印，因此就有"第二版""第三版"等这样的称谓。

集注本指的是：(1) 集中了一个作家手稿的不同版本和印刷本的修订文本而形成的版本；例如《叶芝诗歌集注本》[彼得·奥尔特与罗塞尔·K. 奥尔斯帕奇合编(1957)]；或(2) 收集了先前编辑和批评家对原文本所作的注释和评论的版本。（术语"集注本"是拉丁文cum notis variorum的简写形式，意思是"包含不同人的评注"。）《新莎士比亚集注本》是一部囊括上述两种含义的集注本。

参见：*书籍*；参阅：罗纳德·B. 麦克罗所著的《书目学入门》(1965年修订版)；弗雷德森·鲍尔斯所著的《书目描述原理》(1949)；菲利普·加斯克尔所著的《新书目学入门》(1972)。

book format: **Format** signifies the page size, shape, and other physical features of a book. The printer begins with a large "sheet"; if the sheet is folded once so as to form two "leaves" of four pages, the book is a **folio** (the Latin word for "leaf"). When we refer to "the first Shakespeare folio," for example, we mean a volume published in 1623, the first *edition* of Shakespeare's collected plays, the leaves of which were made by a single folding of the printer's sheets. A sheet folded twice into four leaves makes a **quarto**; a sheet folded a third time into eight leaves makes an **octavo**. In a **duodecimo** volume, a sheet is folded so as to make twelve leaves. The more leaves into which a single sheet is divided, the smaller the leaf, so that these terms indicate the dimensions of a book, but only approximately, because the size of the full sheet varies, especially in modern printing. It can be said, however, that a folio is a very large book; a quarto is the next in size, with a leaf that is nearly square. The third in size, the octavo, is the most frequently used in modern printing.

As this book is open in front of you, the page on the right is called a **recto** (Latin for "on the right"), and the page on the left is called a **verso** (Latin for "turned").

The **colophon** in older books was a note at the end stating such facts as the title, author, printer, and date of issue. In modern books the colophon is ordinarily in the front, on the title page. With reference to modern books, "colophon" has come to mean, usually, the publisher's emblem, such as a torch (Harper), an owl (Holt), or a ship (Viking).

book history studies: Investigations of all the factors involved in the production, distribution, and reception of recorded texts. Separate stages in this process—especially with reference to literary texts—had for many centuries been subjects of inquiry; but as a defined, systematic, and widely recognized study of the overall process, book history did not emerge until the 1980s. Within a few decades, this area became the subject of special journals, books, and learned conferences, and is increasingly being taught in university courses.

Traditionally, the production and dissemination of recorded texts had been conceived mainly as a self-contained and one-way process, in which the author conceives and inscribes a text, the publisher and printer reproduce the text in multiple copies, and the competent reader interprets the text in order to reconstitute the author's originating conception. From this age-old view, the current discipline of book history differs in three principal ways:

1. Traditional dealings with each stage in the production and dissemination of literary texts had been normative and evaluative. That is, literary authors were judged to be good or bad, major or minor; bibliographers set out to establish a single valid text, free from what were called "corruptions" by agents other than the originating author (see *textual criticism*); and interpretations of the text by readers were judged to be right or wrong, good or bad, sensitive or insensitive. In contrast, current exponents of book history tend to be objective and nonjudgmental. All contributions to a recorded text, whether by the author or other agents, and whether intentional or accidental, are taken into account; literary books,

Book Format：书籍版式

版式指的是书本页面的尺寸、形状和其他外观特征。印刷工首先面对的是一面大"**印张**"；如果印张对折一次成四个印页的两"叶"，成书为**对开本**（拉丁语，意为"叶"）。例如，我们所谓的"第一部对开本莎士比亚文集"指的是1623年印刷工采用这种方式装订出版的莎士比亚戏剧集。印张折叠两次成四张八页版，称为**四开本**；折叠三次则成为八张，称为**八开本**。印张折成十二张时则为**十二开本**。印张折叠次数越多，开本越小，因此以上各种开本的名称是用于表示书籍的尺寸的，但也不尽然，因为印张本身的尺寸或有不同，尤其是在现代印刷工艺中。总的来说，对开本书籍的尺寸很大，四开本次之，页面近似方形。八开本列居第三，是现代印刷最常采用的版本。

当打开本书置于你面前时，右侧的一页称为**正页**（拉丁语，意为"在右边"），左边的是**反页**（拉丁语，意为"翻动"）。

在老式书籍中，**出版者商标**一般置于最后，依次注明书名、作者、印刷厂家、出版日期。在现代书籍中，出版者商标一般置于前面的扉页上。现代书籍的出版者商标通常已成为代表出版商的标志，如火炬（哈珀）、猫头鹰（霍尔特）、船只（维京）。

Book History Studies：书籍史研究

书籍史研究是指对记录文本的生产、发行和接受中涉及的所有因素进行的调查研究。这一过程中的不同阶段，尤其是文学文本，许多世纪以来一直是调查研究的主体；但是作为一个明确的、系统的、得到广泛认可的对整体过程的研究，书籍史直到1980年代才出现。短短几十年里，这一领域成为专门期刊、书籍和学术会议的主题，并正越来越多地在大学课程中得到讲授。

传统上，记录文本的生产和传播一直主要被视为一个自足和单向的过程，在这一过程中，作者构思和写出文本，出版印刷商复制多个副本，有能力的读者解释文本，为的是重新建构作者原初的想法。从这一古老的观点来看，当前的书籍史研究在以下三个主要方面有所不同：

1. 关于文学作品生产和传播每个阶段的传统处理办法一直是规范和评价。也就是说，文学作者会被判定是好还是坏，是重要或是次要；目录学家着手建立一个单一的有效文本，不存在代理人经手的"讹误"（参见：*文本批评*）；读者对文本的阐释，被判定是对还是错，好或坏，敏感或不敏感。相比之下，当下的书籍史研究倾向于保持客观，不加评判。记录文本的所有促成因素，无论是作者或其他代理人，无论是有意还是无意，都要考虑在内；文学书籍，

together with all other texts, are regarded as "commodities" that are marketed to readers, their "consumers," in order to make a profit; and the diverse responses to the text by different classes and groups, whether elite readers or mass audiences, are paid equal and neutral attention.

2. The book historian does not view the making and distribution of a book as a one-way process from author through publisher and printer to reader. Instead, Robert Darnton—an important early formulator of the point of view and procedures of book history—proposed in 1982 that historians view the "life cycle" of a book as a "communications circuit" that runs from the author through the publisher, printer, and distributors to the reader, and back to the author, in a process within which the reader "influences the author both before and after the act of composition." ("What Is the History of Books?," in *The Kiss of Lamourette: Reflections on Cultural History*, 1990.) In accordance with this perspective, book historians conceive all stages of the life cycle of a book to be interactive. The author, for example, is subject to the demands of the publisher, who estimates the market demands of readers; while the readers also directly influence the author who, in composing a work, anticipates the preferences of a potential audience.

3. In defining the overall "communications circuit," Robert Darnton emphasized also that book history deals with "each phase of this process ... in all its relations with other systems, economic, social, political, and cultural, in the surrounding environment." D. F. McKenzie, who, like Darnton, was influential in describing and exemplifying the emerging practice of book history, described the new development in *bibliography* as "a sociology of texts" that considers "the human motives and interactions" at each point in "the production, transmission, and consumption of texts." ("The Book as an Expressive Form," in *Bibliography and the Sociology of Texts*, 1986; rev. 1999.) Book history, that is, deals with the formation and dissemination of a text, not as a self-contained process, but as one that at every stage is affected by, and in turn may influence, the economic, social, and cultural circumstances of its time and place.

Applied to the long-term development of ways of recording and communicating information, book history deals with the sequence of revolutionary changes that occurred when an oral culture was succeeded by a *manuscript* culture; when the era of written texts in turn gave way, in the mid-fifteenth century, to a primarily print culture; and when, as the result of new technologies that began in the twentieth century, printed books and materials were increasingly supplemented—and to some extent displaced—by film, television, the computer, and the World Wide Web. (See *oral poetry* and *book*.) An influential work that deals with the impact on Western civilization, science, and the arts by the change from script to print is Elizabeth Eisenstein, The *Printing Press as an Agent of Change* (2 vols., 1979).

The major focus by book historians has been on the era of print, and especially on the diverse circumstances that affect each stage of the

连同所有其他文本,被视为"商品"销售给读者——它们的"消费者"——为的是赚取利润;不同阶层和群体对文本有不同的反应,无论是精英阶层的读者或是大众读者,都会给予平等和中立的关注。

2. 书籍史学家不认为图书的制作和分销是一个单向的过程:从作者出发,经过出版印刷商到读者。相反,罗伯特·达恩顿——这一观点和书籍史流程一位早期重要的奠基者——在1982年提出,历史学家认为一本书的"生命历程"就像是一个"传播循环",从作者出发,通过出版商、印刷商、分销商到达读者手上,然后回到作者那里,在这一循环过程中,读者"无论在创作之前还是之后都影响着作者"["什么是书籍史?"收入其所著的《拉莫莱特之吻:有关文化史的思考》(1990)]。按照这一视角,书籍史学家认为,一本书的生命历程的所有阶段都是互动的。例如,作者受到出版商的要求的影响,出版商会预估读者市场的需求;而读者也会直接影响作者,作者在写作时会预计潜在读者群体的喜好。

3. 在确定整体的"传播循环"时,罗伯特·达恩顿还强调指出,书籍史研究"这一过程的每个阶段……在复杂的社会背景下,包括经济、社会、政治、文化等各方面要素。"D. F. 麦肯齐(他像达恩顿一样,在描述和例证新兴的书籍史方面颇具影响)描述了新的发展:将书目学视为一种"文本社会学",在"文本的生产、传播和消费"每一个点上都考虑到"人类的动机和互动"。["作为一种表现形式的书籍",收入其所著的《书目学与文本社会学》(1986,1999年修订版)。] 书籍史在研究文本的形成和传播时,不是将其作为一个自足的过程,而是作为一个在每个阶段都会受到其所处时间和空间中经济、社会、文化环境的影响,并会反过来影响它们的过程。

关于记录和传播信息的方式的长期发展,书籍史论及历史上发生的一系列革命性变化:口传文化被抄本文化替代;书面文本时代又在15世纪中叶让位于印刷文化;作为20世纪出现的新技术的结果,印刷书籍和材料正在越来越多地成为电影、电视、电脑和万维网的补充——在一定程度上则是被其取代。(参见:*口头诗歌*、*书籍*。)关于从书写到印刷的转变对西方文明、科学、艺术所产生的影响,一本有影响力的著作是伊丽莎白·爱森斯坦所著的两卷本《作为变革代理人的印刷机》(1979)。

书籍历史学家关注的焦点一直是印刷时代,尤其是影响印刷书籍的生产、分

production, distribution, and reception of the printed book. To cite a few prominent examples:

D. F. McKenzie has emphasized the contributions to the book, not only by the author, the author's literary advisers, and copyeditors but also by the book designer and the printer who—often with little or no consultation with an author—determine the typography, spatial layout, illustrations, paper, and binding of a book. All such nonverbal, material features of a book, McKenzie insists, are not neutral vehicles for the printed word, but have an "expressive function" and contribute to the meaning of the verbal text. (See D. F. McKenzie, *Bibliography and the Sociology of Texts*, 1986; also, for similar views about the signifying function of the material features of a book, Jerome McGann, *The Textual Condition*, 1991.)

A prolific and influential contributor to book history is the French scholar Roger Chartier, especially in his emphasis on recorded facts about the differing ways in which diverse readers have received and responded to printed texts. He has, for example, studied the literacy rates of various classes and groups of people at different times and places. He has chronicled the shift from the public to the private reading of texts, and in private reading, the change from reading to oneself aloud to reading in silence; this last practice, according to Chartier, "fostered a solitary and private relation between the reader and his book," "radically transformed intellectual work," and greatly expanded the reader's "inner life." Chartier also analyzed the degree to which people in particular localities, employing diverse "social and cultural practices" in their reading, created a diversity of interpretations of a single text. (Roger Chartier, *The Culture of Print: Power and the Uses of Print in Early Modern Europe*, 1989; and *Forms and Meanings: Texts, Performances, and Audiences from Codex to Computer*, 1995.) Other scholars have chronicled the emergence of mass audiences for printed books and journals, and have compared the literary preferences and responses of a mass audience with those of elite readers and critics. (Richard Altick, *The English Common Reader: A Social History of the Mass Reading Public, 1800–1900*, 1957, rev. 1998; Jonathan Rose, "Rereading the English Common Reader," *Journal of the History of Ideas*, Vol. 53, 1992.) There are also numerous studies of the variety of factors that affect the reception, interpretation, and evaluation of literary books. Jane Tompkins, for example, investigated the importance of an influential coterie of friends, reviewers, and magazine editors in establishing and sustaining the reputation of a novelist. (*Sensational Designs: The Cultural Work of American Fiction, 1790–1860*, 1985.) And in *A Feeling for Books*, 1997, Janice Radway shows that the panelists in the Book-of-the-Month Club—founded in the 1920s, and still flourishing—have made their selections not in accordance with a general criterion of literary excellence, but by matching books to the tastes and preferences of specific groups of readers in the literary marketplace.

For studies of individual stages in the production and reception of literary books that have contributed to book history, see the latter-day developments described in the entries on *author and authorship, reader-response criticism, reception-theory, sociology of literature,* and *textual criticism.* All the researchers

配和接受每个阶段的不同情况。这里举几个突出的例子：

D. F. 麦肯齐已经强调指出，对一本书作出贡献的不单是作者、作者的文学顾问、文字编辑，还有这本书的设计师和印刷者——他们经常是在很少或根本就不征求作者意见的情况下便决定了一本书的字体排印、空间布局、插图、纸张和装订。麦肯齐坚持认为，一本书所有这些非语言的材料特性，对印刷文字来说并非无足轻重的工具，而是有一种"表达功能"并对言语文本的意义有所贡献。[参阅D. F. 麦肯齐所著的《书目学与文本社会学》(1986)；也可参阅杰尔姆·麦根所著的《文本情境》(1991)，该书对一本书物质特性的表达功能持有与麦肯齐相似的看法。]

一位多产的和有影响力的书籍史贡献者是法国学者罗杰·夏蒂埃，他的研究重点在于有记载的关于形形色色读者接受和回应印刷文本的不同方式的事实。例如，他研究了不同时代和地方不同阶级和群体的识字率。他记载了从公众阅读（文本）向私人阅读文本的转变，以及在私人阅读中，从对着自己大声朗读到沉默阅读的变化；夏蒂埃认为，这最后一种做法，"在读者与他的书之间确立了一种孤独和私人的关系"，"从根本上改变了知识分子的作品"，大大扩展了读者的"内心生活"。夏蒂埃也分析了在何种程度上特定区域的人在他们的阅读中采用多样化的"社会和文化惯习"，创造了对单一文本的多样化诠释。[罗杰·夏蒂埃所著的《印刷文化：印刷机在早期现代欧洲的力量与使用》(1989) 和《形式与意义：从抄本到计算机的文本、表演和观众》(1995)。] 其他学者则记载了印刷书籍和期刊的大众读者的出现，对比了大众读者与精英读者和评论家的文学喜好和反应。[理查德·奥尔蒂克所著的《英国的普通读者：1800—1900年间大众阅读社会史》(1957, 1998年修订版)；乔纳森·罗斯所写的文章"重读英国普通读者"，载于《观念史杂志》1992年第53卷。] 也有许多关于影响接受、解释和评估文学书籍的各种因素的研究。例如，简·汤普金斯调查了有影响力的朋友、评审和杂志编辑形成的小圈子，在建立和维持一位小说家的声誉上所起的重要性。[《杰出的设计：美国小说的文化成果，1790—1860年》(1985)。] 贾尼丝·雷德威在其所著的《书的感觉》(1997) 中表明，成立于1920年代并且至今仍在蓬勃发展的"每月一书俱乐部"的成员，在作出他们的选择时，不是按照一般优秀文学的标准，而是通过匹配文学市场上特定读者群的口味和喜好。

关于促生书籍史的文学书籍的生产和接受中各个阶段的研究，参见：*作家和作者、读者反应批评、接受理论、文学社会学、文本批评*中描述的当代发展。

mentioned in this entry on book history studies are represented in the anthology, *The Book History Reader*, edited by David Finkelstein and Alistair McCleery (2002). Influential works, in addition to those already referred to, are: Marshall McLuhan, *The Gutenberg Galaxy: The Making of Typographic Man* (1962); Robert Darnton, *The Business of Enlightenment: A Publishing History of the Encyclopédie, 1775–1800* (1979); Walter J. Ong, *Orality and Literacy: The Technologizing of the Word* (1982); D. F. McKenzie, "The Sociology of a Text: Orality, Literacy and Print in Early New Zealand," *The Library*, 1984, pp. 333–65; John Sutherland, *Victorian Fiction: Writers, Publishers, Readers* (1995); Geoffrey Nunberg, ed., *The Future of the Book* (1996); Adrian Johns, *The Nature of the Book: Print and Knowledge in the Making* (1998).

bourgeois epic (boor′ zwä): **109**.

bourgeois tragedy: 410.

bowdlerize: To delete from an edition of a literary work passages considered by the editor to be indecent or indelicate. The word derives from the Reverend Thomas Bowdler, who tidied up his *Family Shakespeare* in 1818 by omitting, as he put it, "whatever is unfit to be read by a gentleman in a company of ladies." Jonathan Swift's *Gulliver's Travels* (1726) and *The Arabian Nights*, as well as Shakespeare's plays, are often bowdlerized in editions intended for the young; and until the 1920s, at which time the standards of literary propriety were drastically liberalized, some compilers of anthologies for college students availed themselves of Bowdler's prerogative in editing Chaucer.

Breton lay: 191.

broadside ballad: 24.

bucolic poetry (byookŏl′ ik): **268**.

burlesque: Burlesque has been succinctly defined as "an incongruous imitation"; that is, it imitates the manner (the form and style) or else the subject matter of a serious literary work or a literary *genre*, but makes the imitation amusing by a ridiculous disparity between the manner and the matter. The burlesque may be written for the sheer fun of it; usually, however, it is a form of *satire*. The butt of the satiric ridicule may be the particular work or the genre that is being imitated, or else the subject matter to which the imitation is incongruously applied, or (often) both of these together.

"Burlesque," "parody," and "travesty" are sometimes applied interchangeably; simply to equate these terms, however, is to surrender useful critical distinctions. It is better to follow the critics who use "burlesque" as the generic name and use the other terms to discriminate species of burlesque; we must keep in mind, however, that a single instance of burlesque may exploit a variety of techniques. The application of these terms will be clearer if we make two preliminary

本条目中提及的所有书籍史研究的研究者都在下面这本选集中有所展现：戴维·芬克尔斯坦与阿利斯泰尔·麦克利里合编的《书籍史读本》(2002)。除了已经提到的，其他有影响的作品还包括：马歇尔·麦克卢汉所著的《古登堡星系：印刷人的形成》(1962)；罗伯特·达恩顿所著的《启蒙运动的生意：百科全书出版史，1775—1800》(1979)；沃尔特·J. 翁格所著的《口述和读写：词语的技术化》(1982)；D. F. 麦肯齐所写的文章"文本社会学：早期新西兰的口述、读写和印刷"，载于《图书馆》1984 年第 333—365 页；约翰·萨瑟兰所著的《维多利亚时期的小说：作者、出版商与读者》(1995)；杰弗里·纳伯格主编的《书籍的未来》(1996)；阿德里安·约翰斯所著的《书的本性：印刷与形成中的知识》(1998)。

bourgeois epic：市民史诗　　109。

bourgeois tragedy：市民悲剧　　410。

Bowdlerize：作品删节

作品删节指删除一部文学作品中编辑认为是粗俗或下流的章节。该词源自托马斯·鲍德勒主教的名字，他在 1818 年整理《家用莎士比亚选集》时删去了他认为"绅士不宜读给女士听的内容"。乔纳森·斯威夫特的《格列佛游记》(1726)、《天方夜谭》和莎士比亚的戏剧也是经过删节而成为儿童读物的；直到 1920 年代，语言的得体性标准已大为解放，有些大学生文选的编辑在编辑乔叟作品时仍在使用删节的特权。

Breton lay：布列塔尼籁歌　　191。

broadside ballad：宽页传单上的民谣　　24。

bucolic poetry：田园诗　　268。

Burlesque：滑稽讽刺作品

滑稽讽刺作品被简明地定义为"不相称的模仿性作品"；即它模仿某一严肃文学作品或某一文学*类型*的方式（形式和风格）或题材，但由于方式和题材之间的滑稽性的不协调，致使这种模仿变得滑稽可笑。这类作品可以完全是为取乐所作，但常常是作为一种讽刺形式出现的。讽刺的对象可以是所模仿的某一特定作品或文学类型，也可以是与所模仿的不相一致的题材，或是（往往）二者兼顾。

"滑稽讽刺作品""戏谑作品""效颦作品"三者有时可以交替使用；然而如果简单地把三者视为等同，就会抹杀它们之间实用的重要差异。因此，最好依照批评家的做法，把"滑稽讽刺作品"作为一个类属概念，而用其他概念区别这一类属作品中的不同类别。但我们必须记住，仅从一部滑稽讽刺作品中就可以区分出许多不同类别来。如果我们作如下两类初步的区分，这些术语的用法将会更加清晰：

distinctions: (1) In a burlesque imitation, the form and style may be either lower or higher in level and dignity than the subject to which it is incongruously applied. (See the discussion of levels under *style*.) If the form and style are high and dignified but the subject is low or trivial, we have "high burlesque"; if the subject is high in status and dignity but the style and manner of treatment are low and undignified, we have "low burlesque." (2) A burlesque may also be distinguished according to whether it imitates a general literary type or genre, or else a particular work or author. Applying these two distinctions, we get the following species of burlesque.

I. **Varieties of high burlesque**:
   A. A **parody** imitates the serious manner and characteristic features of a particular literary work, or the distinctive style of a particular author, or the typical stylistic and other features of a serious literary genre, and deflates the original by applying the imitation to a lowly or comically inappropriate subject. John Phillips' "The Splendid Shilling" (1705) parodied the epic style of John Milton's *Paradise Lost* (1667) by exaggerating its high formality and applying it to the description of a tattered poet composing in a drafty attic. Henry Fielding in *Joseph Andrews* (1742) parodied Samuel Richardson's novel *Pamela* (1740–41) by putting a hearty male hero in place of Richardson's sexually beleaguered heroine, and later on Jane Austen poked good-natured fun at the genre of the *gothic novel* in *Northanger Abbey* (1818). Here is Hartley Coleridge's parody of the first stanza of William Wordsworth's "She Dwelt among the Untrodden Ways," which he applies to Wordsworth himself:

   > He lived amidst th' untrodden ways
   > To Rydal Lake that lead,
   > A bard whom there were none to praise,
   > And very few to read.

   From the early nineteenth century to the present, parody has been the favorite form of burlesque. Among the gifted parodists of the past century in England were Max Beerbohm (see *A Christmas Garland*, 1912) and Stella Gibbons (*Cold Comfort Farm*, 1936), and in America, James Thurber, Phyllis McGinley, and E. B. White. The novel *Possession* (1990), by the English writer A. S. Byatt, exemplifies a serious literary form which includes straight-faced parodies of Victorian poetry and prose, as well as of academic scholarly writings.
   B. A **mock epic** or **mock-heroic** poem is that type of parody which imitates, in a sustained way, both the elaborate form and the ceremonious style of the *epic* genre, but applies it to narrate a commonplace or trivial subject matter. In a masterpiece of this type, *The Rape of the Lock* (1714), Alexander Pope views through the grandiose epic perspective a quarrel between the belles and elegants of his day over the theft of a lady's curl. The story includes such elements of traditional epic protocol as supernatural

(1) 滑稽讽刺模仿作品在形式与文体的层次和格调上可以高于或低于所滑稽模仿的作品。（参见：文体中关于层次的论述。）如果形式、文体高雅而主题浅薄平庸，我们称之为"上等滑稽讽刺模仿作品"；如果主题庄重高雅而文体手法粗俗低劣，我们称之为"下等滑稽讽刺模仿作品"。(2) 滑稽讽刺模仿作品也可以根据所模仿的是一般的文学类型或类别，还是某一具体的作品或作家来加以区分。运用这两种划分方法，我们就可以区分出滑稽讽刺模仿作品的以下各种类型。

一、上等滑稽讽刺作品的种类

（一）**戏谑模仿**作品：模仿某篇文学作品严肃的手法或特征，或某一作家独特的文体，或某一严肃文学类型的典型文体和其他特色，并通过表现粗俗的或滑稽的风马牛不相及的主题来贬低被模仿者。例如：约翰·菲利普斯的《耀眼的先令》(1705)是对约翰·弥尔顿《失乐园》(1667)史诗风格的戏谑模仿。它夸张地运用《失乐园》高雅的表现形式，描写一位衣衫褴褛的诗人在四面透风的顶楼从事创作的情景。亨利·菲尔丁的《约瑟夫·安德鲁斯》(1742)把理查逊笔下受到淫威诱惑的女主人公变成一个强健热诚的男主角以戏谑模仿塞缪尔·理查逊的小说《帕美勒》(1740—1741)。后来，简·奥斯丁又在《诺桑觉寺》(1818)中善意地取笑了哥特小说类型。以下是哈特利·柯勒律治对威廉·华兹华斯《她住在人迹罕至的地方》一诗中第一节的滑稽模仿，用以描写华兹华斯本人：

> 他住在人迹罕至的地方
> 就在赖德尔湖畔，
> 那儿没人去颂扬他这位吟游诗人，
> 也几乎没人去读他的诗。

从19世纪早期一直到现在，戏谑模仿一直是滑稽讽刺模仿作品中受人青睐的一种形式。20世纪戏谑模仿的天才作家包括英国的马克斯·比尔博姆 [参见他的作品《圣诞花环》(1912)] 和斯特拉·吉本斯 [《寒冷舒适的农庄》(1936)]，美国的詹姆斯·瑟伯、菲利斯·麦金利和 E. B. 怀特。英国作家 A. S. 拜厄特在其小说《占有》(1990) 中展示了一种严肃的文学形式，其中包括对维多利亚时期诗歌和散文以及学术性文章直面的戏谑模仿。

（二）**模拟史诗**或**仿英雄体诗**：是指那类戏谑模仿的诗作，它持续模拟史诗宏大精细的形式和庄重高雅的文体，却用来陈述平庸琐碎的题材。在著名代表作《卷发遇劫记》(1714) 中，亚历山大·蒲柏从崇高的史诗角度来记述一场美女与雅士为卷发遭劫一事进行的争吵。故事

machinery, a voyage on board ship, a visit to the underworld, and a heroically scaled battle between the sexes—although with metaphors, hatpins, and snuff for weapons. The term *mock-heroic* is often applied to other dignified poetic forms which are purposely mismatched to a lowly subject; for example, to Thomas Gray's comic "Ode on the Death of a Favorite Cat" (1748); see under *bathos and anticlimax*.

II. **Varieties of low burlesque**:
   A. The **Hudibrastic poem** takes its name from Samuel Butler's *Hudibras* (1663), which satirized rigid Puritanism by describing the adventures of a Puritan knight, Sir Hudibras. Instead of the doughty deeds and dignified style of the traditional genre of the *chivalric romance*, however, we find the knightly hero experiencing mundane and humiliating misadventures which are described in *doggerel* verses and a ludicrously colloquial idiom.
   B. The **travesty** mocks a particular work by treating its lofty subject in a grotesquely undignified manner and style. As Boileau put it, describing a travesty of Virgil's *Aeneid*, "Dido and Aeneas are made to speak like fishwives and ruffians." *The New Yorker* once published a travesty of Ernest Hemingway's novel *Across the River and Into the Trees* (1950) with the title *Across the Street and Into the Bar*, and the film *Young Frankenstein* is a travesty of Mary Shelley's novel *Frankenstein*.

Another form of burlesque is the **lampoon**: a short satirical work, or a passage in a longer work, which describes the appearance and character of a particular person in a way that makes that person ridiculous. It typically employs **caricature**, which in a verbal description (as in graphic art) exaggerates or distorts, for comic effect, a person's distinctive physical features or personality traits. John Dryden's *Absalom and Achitophel* (1681) includes a famed twenty-five-line lampoon of Zimri (Dryden's contemporary, the Duke of Buckingham), which begins:

> In the first rank of these did Zimri stand;
> A man so various, that he seemed to be
> Not one, but all mankind's epitome:
> Stiff in opinions, always in the wrong;
> Was everything by starts, and nothing long....

The modern sense of "burlesque" as a theater form derives, historically, from plays which mocked serious types of drama by an incongruous imitation. John Gay's *Beggar's Opera* (1728)—which in turn became the model for the German *Threepenny Opera* by Bertolt Brecht and Kurt Weill (1928)—was a high burlesque of Italian opera, applying its dignified formulas to a company of beggars and thieves. A number of the comic musical plays by Gilbert and Sullivan in the Victorian era also include elements of high burlesque of grand opera.

融会了传统史诗惯用的手法,如超自然的情节机制、乘船出航、寻访阴曹,以及男女之间可称为英勇的争斗——尽管双方的武器只是唇枪舌剑、帽针和鼻烟。仿英雄体诗往往指其他刻意用格调庄重的诗体牵强附会地表现浅薄低劣的主题;例如托马斯·格雷的滑稽诗作《祭爱猫之死》(1748);参见:突降与突降法中的相关论述。

二、下等滑稽讽刺作品的种类

(1) **休迪布拉斯式滑稽诗**得名于塞缪尔·勃特勒的《休迪布拉斯》(1663),该诗通过描写清教徒骑士爵士休迪布拉斯的奇遇,嘲讽了僵化的清教主义。与传统的骑士传奇描写英勇事迹及其崇高的艺术风格相反,在这类作品中,我们看到的是由打油诗和荒唐可笑的俗语所描述的这位游侠庸俗蒙羞的遭遇。

(2) **效颦**作品是以滑稽平庸的方式和风格表现崇高的主题来嘲讽某一作品。正如布瓦洛在描述一篇效颦维吉尔《埃涅阿斯纪》的作品时所言,"使得狄多和埃涅阿斯说起话来像泼妇与恶棍。"《纽约人》上曾发表过一篇效颦欧内斯特·海明威的小说《跨过河流,进入森林》(1950) 的作品,其题目是《跨过街道,进入酒吧》;电影《年轻的弗兰肯斯坦》则是效颦玛丽·雪莱的小说《弗兰肯斯坦》。

滑稽讽刺作品的另外一种形式是**讽刺诗**:一篇篇幅短小的讽刺作品,或一部长篇中的一个段落,旨在通过描写某个特殊角色的相貌和性格特征从而使得该角色显得滑稽可笑。它通常采用**讽刺漫画**的手法,借用词语描述(犹如平面造型艺术)来夸张或扭曲某个人物独特的外在形象或个性特征,以取得滑稽效果。约翰·德莱顿的《押沙龙与阿奇托菲尔》(1681) 中就有这样一首著名的描写津里(与德莱顿同时代的白金汉公爵)的25行讽刺诗,它是这样开头的:

> 在津里站立着的第一排中;
> 他显得真是个多面手,似乎
> 不是一人,而是所有人类的缩影:
> 观念僵化,且总是谬误;
> 一切事情都是有始无终……

现代意义上的"滑稽讽刺作品"作为一种戏剧形式,历史上源自通过不相适宜的模仿而嘲讽严肃戏剧的剧目。约翰·盖伊的《乞丐的歌剧》(1728)——后来成为贝尔托尔特·布莱希特与库尔特·魏尔《三分钱歌剧》(1928)的范本——是对意大利歌剧的上等滑稽讽刺模仿作品,把其中高雅的客套话强加于一伙乞丐与小偷的对白之间。维多利亚时期吉尔伯特与萨利文创作的不少滑稽音乐剧,也包含有对大歌剧的上等滑稽模仿成分在内。

See George Kitchin, *A Survey of Burlesque and Parody in English* (1931); Richmond P. Bond, *English Burlesque Poetry, 1700–1750* (1932); Margaret A. Rose, *Parody: Ancient, Modern, and Post-Modern* (1993). Anthologies: Walter Jerrold and R. M. Leonard, eds., *A Century of Parody and Imitation* (1913); Robert P. Falk, ed., *The Antic Muse: American Writers in Parody* (1955); Dwight MacDonald, ed., *Parodies: An Anthology* (1960); John Gross, ed., *The Oxford Book of Parodies* (2010).

参阅：乔治·基钦所著的《英语中的滑稽讽刺和模仿讽刺概览》(1931)；里士满·P.邦德所著的《1700—1750年间英国滑稽讽刺诗》(1932)；玛格丽特·A.罗斯所著的《古代、现代和后现代的戏谑模仿》(1993)。文集可以参阅：沃尔特·杰罗尔德与R.M.伦纳德合编的《嘲讽与戏仿的世纪》(1913)；罗伯特·P.福尔克主编的《滑稽可笑的缪斯：戏谑模仿的美国作家》(1955)；德怀特·麦克唐纳主编的《戏谑模仿作品选》(1960)；约翰·格罗斯主编的《牛津戏谑模仿作品集》(2010)。

cacophony (kăkŏf′ ōnē): **115**.

caesura (sĕzyoor′ ă): **221**; *10,158*.

canon of literature: The Greek word "kanon," signifying a measuring rod or a rule, was extended to denote a list or catalogue, then came to be applied to the list of books in the Hebrew Bible and the New Testament which were designated by church authorities to be the genuine Holy Scriptures. A number of writings related to those in the Scriptures, but not admitted into the authoritative canon, are called **apocrypha**; eleven books which have been included in the Roman Catholic biblical canon are considered apocryphal by Protestants.

The term "canon" was later used to signify the list of secular works accepted by experts as genuinely written by a particular author. We speak thus of "the Chaucer canon" and "the Shakespeare canon," and refer to other works that have sometimes been attributed to an author, but on evidence that many editors judge to be inadequate or invalid, as "apocryphal." In recent decades the phrase **literary canon** has come to designate—in world literature, or in European literature, but most frequently in a national literature—those authors who, by a cumulative consensus of critics, scholars, and teachers, have come to be widely recognized as "major," and to have written works often hailed as literary *classics*. The literary works by canonical authors are the ones which, at a given time, are most kept in print, most frequently and fully discussed by literary critics and historians, and—in the present era—most likely to be included in anthologies and in the syllabi of college courses with titles such as "World Masterpieces," "Major English Authors," or "Great American Writers."

The use of the term "canon" with reference both to the books of the Bible and to secular literature obscures important differences in the two applications. The biblical canon has been established by church authorities vested with the power to make such a decision; is enforced by authorities with the power to impose religious sanctions; is explicit in the books that it lists; and is closed, permitting neither deletions nor additions. (See the entry "Canon" in *The Oxford Companion to the Bible*, 1993.) The canon of literature, on the other hand, is the product of a wavering and unofficial consensus; it is tacit rather than explicit, loose in its boundaries, and always subject to changes in the works that it includes.

The social process by which an author or a literary work comes to be widely although tacitly recognized as canonical has come to be called "canon formation." The factors in this formative process are complex and disputed. It seems clear, however, that the process involves, among other conditions, a broad concurrence of critics, scholars, and authors with diverse viewpoints

cacophony：非谐音　115。

caesura：行间停顿　221；*10, 158*。

Canon of Literature：文学经典

　　希腊单词"kanon"指的是一种度量标杆或度量尺，被引申用来指代列表或目录，后来指被宗教权力机构确立为真正神圣经文的《犹太教圣经》和《新约》中的书目目录。与神圣经文相关但却没有被确立为圣经经典的许多其他作品被称为**伪经**；但被罗马天主教奉为经典经文的十一部作品却被新教视为伪经。

　　后来，"canon"（经典）一词又被用来指真正由某位作家创作的、又经专家认可的世俗作品的书目。因此我们说"乔叟经典"和"莎士比亚经典"，而把那些有时被人们归属于某位作者但又被众多编辑认为证据不足以断定作者身份的作品视为"伪作"。近几十年来，**文学经典**这一术语开始用来指在世界文学，或在欧洲文学中，但主要是在民族文学中那些历来被批评家、学者和教师一致认可并被公认为"重要的"、写出被尊为文学经典的那些作家。出自经典作家之笔的文学作品在某一特定时期内大都不断地印刷出版，文学批评家和历史学家经常对其进行充分的探讨研究，而且——在当今时代——极有可能被文选收录并被大学课程的教学大纲所采用并冠以"世界名著""英国重要作家"或"美国伟大作家"等标题。

　　"经典"这一术语既指圣经又指世俗作品，从而模糊了这两者之间的显要区别。圣经经典是由获得授权的宗教权力机构认定并由具有制定宗教法令的权力机构实施、目录明确、不容增减的封闭性作品 [参见《牛津圣经词典》（1993）中的条目"经典"]。相对而言，文学经典则是非官方的、非确定性的公众共识的产物；是默认的而非明确的，范围模糊，入选作品往往可做更改。

　　一位作家或一部作品被公众广泛地默认为经典的社会过程被称为"经典的形成"。该形成过程中的各种因素既复杂又有争议。但可以肯定的是，除其他条件之外，持有不同观点和感受能力的批评家、学者和作家在该过程中能够达成广泛的共识；

and sensibilities; the persistent influence of, and reference to, an author in the work of other authors; the frequent reference to an author or work within the discourse of a cultural community; and the widespread assignment of an author or text in school and college curricula. Such factors are of course mutually interactive, and they need to be sustained over a period of time. In his "Preface to Shakespeare" (1765) Samuel Johnson said that a century is "the term commonly fixed as a test of literary merit." Some authors of the past century such as Marcel Proust, Franz Kafka, Thomas Mann, and James Joyce—probably even more recent writers such as Vladimir Nabokov and Milan Kundera—have achieved the prestige, influence, assignment in college courses, and persistence of reference in literary discourse to establish them in the European canon; others, including Yeats, T. S. Eliot, Virginia Woolf, and Robert Frost, are already secure in their national canons, at least.

At any time, the boundaries of a literary canon remain indefinite and disputable, while inside those boundaries some authors are central and others marginal. Occasionally an earlier author who was for long on the fringe of the canon, or even outside it, gets transferred to a position of eminence. A conspicuous example was John Donne, who from the eighteenth century on was regarded mainly as an interestingly eccentric poet. T. S. Eliot, followed by Cleanth Brooks and other *New Critics* in the 1930s and later, made Donne's writings the very paradigm of the self-ironic and paradoxical poetry they most admired, and so helped elevate him to a high place within the English canon. (See *metaphysical poets*.) Since then, Donne's reputation has diminished, but he remains prominent in the canon. (On Donne's altering reputation, see Ben Saunders, *Desiring Donne: Poetry, Sexuality, Interpretation*, 2006.) Once firmly established, an author shows considerable resistance to being disestablished by adverse criticism and changing literary preferences. For example, many New Critics, together with the influential F. R. Leavis in England, while lauding Donne, vigorously attacked the Romantic poet Shelley as embodying poetic qualities they strongly condemned; but although a considerable number of critics joined in this derogation of Shelley, the long-term effect was to aggrandize the critical attention and discussion that helps sustain an author's place in the canon.

Since the 1970s, the nature of canon formation, and opposition to established literary canons, has become a leading concern among critics of diverse theoretical viewpoints, whether deconstructive, feminist, Marxist, postcolonial, or new historicist (see *poststructuralism*). The debate often focuses on the practical issue of what books to assign in college curricula, especially in required "core courses" in the humanities and in Western civilization. A widespread charge is that the standard canon of great books, not only in literature but in all areas of *humanistic* study, has been determined less by artistic excellence than by the politics of power; that is, that the canon has been formed in accordance with the *ideology*, political interests, and values of a dominant class that was white, male, and European. As a result, it is frequently claimed that the canon consists mainly of works that convey and sustain racism, *patriarchy*, and imperialism, and understate or exclude interests and

经典作家会对其他作家的作品产生持久的影响,其名字会在其他作家的作品中经常被提及;经典作家或作品在一文化团体的话语中常会被人们提及;经典作家或作品普遍被选作学校或大学课程中的学业内容。这些因素彼此之间理所当然地相互作用,而且,它们理应持续一定的时期。塞缪尔·约翰逊在《莎士比亚绪论》(1765)中写道,一个世纪的时间"一般来说是用以检验文学价值的时间段"。一些20世纪作家,如马塞尔·普鲁斯特、弗朗兹·卡夫卡、托马斯·曼和詹姆斯·乔伊斯——也许甚至包括弗拉基米尔·纳博科夫这样新近的作家——似乎已经取得了经典作家的声誉、影响力、被选入大学课程、在文学话语中常被人们提及这样一些能在欧洲经典中确立他们地位的成就。其他像包括叶芝、T. S. 艾略特、弗吉尼亚·吴尔夫和罗伯特·弗罗斯特等在内的一些作家,似乎已经稳稳地占据了至少是民族经典作家的地位。

文学经典的界限在任何时期都是不确定的和有争议的,即使同属经典作家,有些处于核心位置,有些则处于边缘。有时,长期处于经典的边缘位置,甚或是在经典圈子之外的作家,又会成为杰出的经典作家。约翰·多恩就是一个显著的例子,自从18世纪以来,他一直被视为是一位有趣的行为怪诞的诗人。T. S. 艾略特及其后的克利安斯·布鲁克斯和1930年代及其后的*新批评家*,把多恩的作品推崇为最让他们景仰的自我嘲讽和玄学派诗歌的典范,从而使他高居英国经典作家之列。(参见:*玄学派诗人*。)此后,多恩的声望有所降低,但仍属杰出的经典作家。[关于多恩变化的声誉,可以参阅本·桑德斯所著的《欲望多恩:诗歌、性爱与阐释》(2006)。] 有的作家一旦稳固地登上经典作家的宝座,就会对敌对的批评和变化了的文学偏好表现出强大的抗拒力。例如许多新批评家与英国颇有影响的F. R. 利维斯一道,在赞美多恩的同时,对浪漫主义诗人雪莱所体现的诗作品格予以猛烈的抨击和遣责;尽管有数量可观的批评家加入到贬损雪莱的行列中,但其长期效应却是扩大了对批评的注意与争论,反而有助于延续诗人在经典作家之列的地位。

自1970年代以来,经典形成的本质,以及与已确立的文学经典的对立,成为解构主义、女性主义、马克思主义、后殖民主义或新历史主义(参见:*后结构主义*)等理论观点相异、派别不同的批评家关注的首要问题。争论的焦点往往集中在一个实际问题上,即何种作品可选入大学课程,尤其是选入像人文学科和西方文明这样必修的"核心课程"。人们纷纷指责,不仅在文学领域,而且在人文学科研究的各个领域,伟大作品的经典评价标准已不再以作品的艺术价值为主,而是以权力政治为主;即经典形成的依据是*意识形态*、政治利益,以及白人、男性和欧洲社会精英阶层的价值观。其结果是,认为经典主要是由那些表达和支撑了种族

accomplishments of blacks, Hispanics, and other ethnic minorities, and also the achievements of women, the working class, popular culture, homosexuals, and non-European civilizations. The demand is "to open the canon" so as to make it **multicultural** instead of "Eurocentric." (As applied to literary scholarship, "multicultural" designates the movement to redress what are asserted to be the errors and injustices of a history dominated by Europe-centered historians, so as to make it represent adequately the cultural contributions of races and groups that have been hitherto marginalized or ignored.) Another demand frequently voiced is that the standard canon be stripped of its elitism and its "hierarchism"—that is, its built-in discriminations between high art and lower art—in order to include such cultural products as Hollywood films, television serials, popular songs, and fiction written for a mass audience. A radical wing of revisionist theorists, to further their political aim to transform the existing power structures, demand not merely the opening, but the abolition of the standard canon and its replacement by currently marginal and excluded groups and texts. In another extreme form of multicultural thinking, adherents claim that culture constructs its own social reality, so that any assertions of knowledge, truth, or value are relative—that is, the claims are valid only within that particular culture. (Refer to *cultural constructs* in the entry on *new historicism*, and *relativism* in the entry on *poststructuralism*.) See Satya Mohanty, *Literary Theory and the Claims of History: Postmodernism, Objectivity, Multicultural Politics* (1997); and James Trotman, ed., *Multiculturalism: Roots and Realities* (2002).

The views of defenders of the standard canon, like those of its opponents, range from moderate to extreme. The position of many moderate defenders might be summarized as follows: Whatever has been the influence of class, gender, race, and other special interests and prejudices in forming the existing canon, this is far from the whole story. The canon is the result of the concurrence of a great many (often unexpressed) norms and standards, and among these, one crucial factor has been the high intellectual and artistic quality of the canonical works themselves, and their attested power to enlighten and give delight, and to appeal to widely shared human concerns and values. (See *humanism*.) Moderate defenders agree to the desirability of enlarging the canon of texts that are assigned frequently in academic courses, in order to make the canon more broadly representative of diverse cultures, ethnic groups, classes, and interests; they point out, however, that such changes would not be a drastic innovation, since the educational canon has always been subject to deletions and additions. They emphasize also that the existing Western, English, and American canons include notable examples of skepticism, of political radicalism, and of the toleration of dissent—features of the accepted canon of which the present proponents of radical change are, clearly, the inheritors and beneficiaries. And however a canon is enlarged to represent other cultures and classes, moderate defenders insist on the need to maintain a continuing study of and dialogue with the diverse and long-lasting works of intellect and imagination that have shaped Western civilization and constitute much of Western culture. They point to the enduring primacy, over many

主义、父权制和帝国主义的作品所构成，是为使黑人、拉丁美洲和其他少数民族的利益和成就，以及使妇女、工人阶级、大众文化、同性恋和非欧洲文明的成就边缘化或对其加以排斥服务的。人们要求"开放经典"以便使其表现**多元文化**而非仅仅"以欧洲为中心"。[当用于文学学（即学院式研究）中时，"多元文化"指一种运动，该运动旨在纠正被确认为是欧洲中心论历史学家所主导的历史错误和不公，以便充分呈现此前一直被边缘化或被忽视的种族和群体作出的文化贡献。]另外一种经常可以听到的呼声，要求标准的经典之作应除掉精英统治和"等级主义"——即对高雅艺术和低级艺术之间固有的歧视性区别——目的是为了将诸如好莱坞电影、电视连续剧、流行歌曲和通俗小说等文化产品包括在内。一派激进的修正主义理论家，为了改变现有的权力结构而推进其政治目的，不仅要求开放经典，而且要求废除权威经典之作，由处于边缘位置和遭受排斥的团体和作品取而代之。在多元文化思维的另一种极端方式中，拥护者宣称：文化会建构它自己的社会现实，因此，任何知识、真理或价值观的主张都是相对的——即，这些宣称仅在那一特定文化中才是有效的。（参阅：*新历史主义*条目中的*文化建构*和*后结构主义*条目中的*相对主义*。）参阅：萨蒂亚·莫汉蒂所著的《文学理论与历史宣称：后现代主义、客观性、多元文化政治》(1997)；詹姆斯·特罗特曼主编的《多元文化主义：根源与现实》(2002)。

　　权威经典的辩护者如同那些反对者一样，其观点也是由温和到极端，不一而足。大多数温和派辩护者的立场可以概括如下。在形成现有经典的过程中，不论阶级、性别、种族和其他特殊利益和偏见的影响如何，都远不是关键性因素。经典是由许多（常常是无法陈述的）标准和规范达成共识的结果，在这些标准和规范中，一个关键因素是经典作品本身具有的高度的理性和艺术价值，及其久经验证的启蒙和愉悦读者的力量和对人类普遍关心的问题和共有的价值观的关注。（参见：*人文主义*。）温和派辩护者赞同扩大在学术课程中经常选用的经典作品的选录范围，从而使得经典之作能够更广泛地代表不同的文化、种族团体、阶层和利益；但他们也指出，这种变化不会是一种急剧的革新，因为具有教化功能的经典作品往往是可做删减和添加的。他们还强调指出，现有的西方、英国和美国的经典作品中包括对已确立的思维方式所持的怀疑论、政治激进主义和对异己的宽容——显然，当今激进的理论家和主张改变的倡导者，正是公认的经典作品所具有的这些特征的继承人和受益者。尽管经典之作扩展到可以表现其他的文化和阶层，但温和派辩护者仍然坚称有必要持续细察形成西方文明和构成西方文化主体的各种不朽著作所表现的理性和思想，并与之进行对话。他们针对的是数世纪以

centuries, of such Western authors as Homer, Plato, Dante, and Shakespeare. They also remark that many theorists who challenge the traditional English canon, when they turn from theory to applied criticism, attend preponderantly to established authors—not only Shakespeare, but also Spenser, Milton, Jane Austen, Wordsworth, George Eliot, Whitman, Henry James, and many others—and so recognize and confirm in practice the literary canon that they in theory oppose.

For discussions of the nature and formation of the literary canon, see the collection of essays edited by Robert von Hallberg, *Canons* (1984); John Guillory, *Cultural Capital: The Problem of Literary Canon Formation* (1993); and Wendell V. Harris, "Canonicity," *PMLA*, Vol. 106 (1991), pp. 110–21. Questioners or opponents of the traditional canon: Leslie A. Fiedler and Houston A. Baker, Jr., eds., *English Literature: Opening Up the Canon* (1981); Jane Tompkins, *Sensational Designs: The Cultural Work of American Fiction, 1790–1860* (1985); Barbara Herrnstein Smith, *Contingencies of Value: Alternative Perspectives for Critical Theory* (1988); Jonathan Culler, *Framing the Sign: Criticism and Its Institutions* (1988), chapter 2, "The Humanities Tomorrow"; and Darryl L. Gless and Barbara H. Smith, eds., *The Politics of Liberal Education* (1990). Defenses of the traditional canon: Frank Kermode, "Prologue" to *An Appetite for Poetry* (1989); the essays in *The Changing Culture of the University*, a special issue of *Partisan Review* (Spring 1991); Harold Bloom, *The Western Canon* (1994).

For references to *canon of literature* in other entries, see page *307*.

cardinal sins: 364.

caricature: 39.

carnivalesque: 86.

Caroline Age: 281.

carpe diem (car′ pĕ dē′ ĕm), meaning "seize the day," is a Latin phrase from one of Horace's *Odes* (I. xi.) which has become the name for a very common literary *motif*, especially in lyric poetry. The speaker in a carpe diem poem emphasizes that life is short and time is fleeting in order to urge his auditor—who is often represented as a virgin reluctant to change her condition—to make the most of present pleasures. A frequent emblem of the brevity of physical beauty and the finality of death is the rose, as in Edmund Spenser's *The Faerie Queene*, 1590–96 (II. xii. 74–75; "Gather therefore the Rose, whilst yet is prime"), and, in the seventeenth century, Robert Herrick's "To the Virgins, to Make Much of Time" ("Gather ye rosebuds, while ye may"), and Edmund Waller's "Go, Lovely Rose." The more complex poems of this type communicate the poignant sadness—or else desperation—of the pursuit of pleasures under the sentence of inevitable death; for example, Andrew Marvell's "To His Coy Mistress" (1681) and the sustained set of variations on the carpe

来西方第一流的文学大家,如荷马、莎士比亚和但丁。他们也认为,许多挑战传统英语经典的理论家,当他们从理论转向应用批评时,主要关注的是一些成名的重要作家——不仅是莎士比亚,还有斯宾塞、弥尔顿、简·奥斯丁、华兹华斯、乔治·艾略特、惠特曼、亨利·詹姆斯和许多其他作家——因此在实践中也就承认并确认了他们在理论上所反对的文学经典。

有关文学经典的本质和形成的论述,参阅:罗伯特·冯·哈尔伯格所著的《经典》(1984);约翰·基洛利所著的《文化资本:文学经典形成的问题》(1993);温德尔·V.哈里斯所写的文章"正典性",载于《美国现代语言学协会会刊》1991年第106卷第110—121页。对传统经典提出质疑或反对的有:莱斯利·A.菲德勒与小休斯顿·A.贝克合编的《英语文学:敞开典律》(1981);简·汤普金斯所著的《杰出的设计:1790—1860年间美国小说的文化成果》(1985);巴巴拉·赫恩斯坦·史密斯所著的《权变性的价值:批评理论的替代视角》(1988);乔纳森·卡勒所著的《符号构形:批评及其体制》(1988)第2章"明日的人文学科";达里尔·L.格莱斯与巴巴拉·H.史密斯合编的《自由教育的政治》(1990)。为传统经典辩护的有:弗兰克·克莫德所著的《诗歌的爱好》(1989)一书的"序言";《宗派评论》(1991年春季卷)专刊"改变中的大学文化"中的文章;哈罗德·布鲁姆所著的《西方正典》(1994)。

其他条目中提及"文学经典"的地方,参见第307页。

cardinal sins:基本罪过 364。

caricature:讽刺漫画 39。

carnivalesque:狂欢化 86。

Caroline Age:查理时期 281。

Carpe Diem:及时行乐

"carpe diem"是出自贺拉斯《歌集》(第一卷第六首)中的一个拉丁文短语,意为"及时行乐",现已成为一种常见的文学*题旨*——抒情诗中尤为常见。此类诗歌中的言语者强调人生短暂、岁月如流水,从而告诫他的听众,常常是不愿改变自身情境的贞女,要尽情享受眼前的快乐。诗人多用玫瑰花象征容貌娇艳的短暂和最终死亡的必然,如埃德蒙·斯宾塞的《仙后》(1590—1596,第二卷第七章第74—75行;"故尔采摘玫瑰,要趁花俏叶茂。");17世纪罗伯特·赫里克的《致处女:及时行乐》("好花堪摘须及时")和埃德蒙·沃勒的《快,可爱的玫瑰》。这类诗歌更为错综复杂的杰作都表达了一种面对不可避免的死亡时渴望爱情的深切悲哀或绝望;如安德鲁·马韦尔的《致羞涩的情人》(1681)和维多利亚

diem motif in *The Rubáiyát of Omar Khayyám*, translated by the Victorian poet Edward FitzGerald. In 1747 Lady Mary Wortley Montagu wrote "The Lover: A Ballad," a brilliant counter to the carpe diem poems written by male poets; in it, the woman explains to her importunate suitor why she finds him utterly resistible.

catalectic (kătălek′ tĭk): **218**.

catastrophe (in a plot) (kătăs′ trŏfē): **296**; *409, 412*.

catharsis (kăthär′ sĭs): **408**.

Cavalier poets: 281.

Celtic Revival: The Celtic Revival, also known as the **Irish Literary Renaissance**, identifies the remarkably creative period in Irish literature from about 1880 to the death of William Butler Yeats in 1939. The aim of Yeats and other early leaders of the movement was to create a distinctive national literature by going back to Irish history, legend, and folklore, as well as to native literary models. The major writers, however, wrote not in the native Irish (one of the Celtic languages) but in English, and under the influence of various non-Irish literary forms. A number of them also turned increasingly for their subject matter to modern Irish life rather than to the ancient past.

Notable poets in addition to Yeats were AE (George Russell) and Oliver St. John Gogarty. The dramatists included Yeats himself, as well as Lady Gregory (who was also an important patron and publicist for the movement), John Millington Synge, and later Sean O'Casey. Among the novelists were George Moore and James Stephens, as well as James Joyce, who, although he abandoned Ireland for Europe and ridiculed the excesses of the nationalist writers, adverted to Irish subject matter and characters in all his writings. As these names indicate, the Celtic Revival produced some of the greatest poetry, drama, and prose fiction written in English during the first four decades of the twentieth century.

See Herbert Howarth, *The Irish Writers* (1958); Phillip L. Marcus, *Yeats and the Beginning of the Irish Renaissance* (1970), and "The Celtic Revival: Literature and the Theater," in *The Irish World: The History and Cultural Achievements of the Irish People* (1977). Declan Kiberd, *Inventing Ireland* (1996), deals with the Irish writers as exemplary modernists. For the influence of anthropology on Irish revivalists, see Gregory Castle, *Modernism and the Celtic Revival* (2001).

character and characterization:

1. The **character** is the name of a literary *genre*; it is a short, and usually witty, sketch in prose of a distinctive type of person. The genre was inaugurated by Theophrastus, a Greek author of the second century BC,

女王时代的诗人爱德华·菲茨杰拉德翻译的以及时行乐的各种形式为题旨的《欧玛尔·海亚姆的鲁拜集》。玛丽·沃特利·蒙塔古夫人作于1747年的《情人:情歌集》,机智地反驳了出于男性诗人之笔的以及时行乐为主题的诗歌。诗中的女主人对纠缠不休的情人解释了,为什么在她眼中,他的诱惑是完全可以抵制得住的。

catalectic:异体抑扬格 218。

catastrophe (in a plot):(情节中的) 结局 296;*409, 412*。

catharsis:情感陶冶 408。

Cavalier poets:骑士诗人 281。

Celtic Revival:凯尔特文艺复兴

凯尔特文艺复兴又称**爱尔兰文学复兴**,指大约1880年至1939年威廉·巴特勒·叶芝逝世期间爱尔兰文学卓越的创作时期。在这次文学运动中,叶芝和这次运动的其他早期领导者的目标是通过追溯爱尔兰的历史、传说、民间故事和本土文学原型,创立具有爱尔兰民族特色的文学。然而,一些主要作家并不是用爱尔兰文(一种凯尔特语言)而是用英文写作,并且受到种种非爱尔兰文学形式的影响。许多作家的创作题材也日益转向爱尔兰的现代生活风貌,而不是她古老的过去。

除叶芝外,爱尔兰文学复兴的重要诗人还有"AE"(即乔治·拉塞尔)和奥列弗·圣约翰·戈加蒂。剧作家包括叶芝本人、格雷戈里夫人(也是复兴运动的主要资助者和宣传者)、约翰·米林顿·辛格以及后来的肖恩·奥凯西。小说家有乔治·莫尔、詹姆斯·斯蒂芬斯、詹姆斯·乔伊斯,尽管乔伊斯弃离爱尔兰旅居欧洲大陆并且有过嘲讽爱尔兰民族主义作家的过激言论,但他的全部作品都注重表现有关爱尔兰的题材和人物。正如这些名字所表明的那样,凯尔特文艺复兴运动造就了20世纪头40年一些用英语创作的最杰出的诗歌、戏剧和小说作品。

参阅:赫伯特·豪沃思所著的《爱尔兰作家》(1958);菲利普·L. 马库斯所著的《叶芝与爱尔兰文艺复兴的开始》(1970)和《爱尔兰世界:爱尔兰人民的历史与文化成就》中的"凯尔特文艺复兴:文学与戏剧"。德克兰·凯伯德所著的《创造爱尔兰》(1996),将爱尔兰作家视为典范的现代主义者予以论述。关于人类学对爱尔兰复兴运动者的影响,参阅:格雷戈里·卡斯尔所著的《现代主义与凯尔特文艺复兴》(2001)。

Character and Characterization:人物与人物塑造

1. **人物素描**是一种文学类型的称谓;是作者以简洁、诙谐的白描手法勾勒出的某一类典型的人物形象。公元前2世纪(应为公元前4世纪——译注),古希腊作家泰奥弗拉斯托斯创作的生动逼真的《人物

who wrote a lively book entitled *Characters*. This literary form had a great vogue in the early seventeenth century; the books of characters then written by Joseph Hall, Sir Thomas Overbury, and John Earle influenced later writers of essays, history, and fiction. The titles of some of Overbury's sketches will indicate the nature of the form: "A Courtier," "A Wise Man," "A Fair and Happy Milkmaid." See Richard Aldington's anthology *A Book of "Characters"* (1924).

2. **Characters** are the persons represented in a dramatic or narrative work, who are interpreted by the reader as possessing particular moral, intellectual, and emotional qualities by inferences from what the persons say and their distinctive ways of saying it—the **dialogue**—and from what they do—the **action**. The grounds in the characters' temperament, desires, and moral nature for their speech and actions are called their **motivation**. A character may remain essentially "stable," or unchanged in outlook and disposition, from beginning to end of a work (Prospero in Shakespeare's *The Tempest*, Micawber in Charles Dickens' *David Copperfield*, 1849–50), or may undergo a radical change, either through a gradual process of development (the title character in Jane Austen's *Emma*, 1816) or as the result of a crisis (Shakespeare's *King Lear*, Pip in Dickens' *Great Expectations*). Whether a character remains stable or changes, the reader of a traditional and realistic work expects "consistency"—the character should not suddenly break off and act in a way not plausibly grounded in his or her temperament as we have already come to know it.

E. M. Forster, in *Aspects of the Novel* (1927), introduced new terms for an old distinction by discriminating between flat and round characters. A **flat character** (also called a **type**, or "two-dimensional"), Forster says, is built around "a single idea or quality" and is presented without much individualizing detail, and therefore can be described adequately in a single phrase or sentence. A **round character** is complex in temperament and motivation and is represented with subtle particularity; such a character therefore is as difficult to describe with any adequacy as a person in real life, and like real persons, is capable of surprising us. A *humours character*, such as Ben Jonson's "Sir Epicure Mammon," is a flat character who has a name which says it all, in contrast to the roundness of character in Shakespeare's multifaceted Falstaff. Almost all dramas and narratives, properly enough, have some characters who serve merely as functionaries and are not characterized at all, as well as other characters who are left relatively flat: there is no need, in Shakespeare's *Henry IV, Part I*, for Mistress Quickly to be as globular as Falstaff. The degree to which, to be regarded as artistically successful, characters need to be three-dimensional depends on their function in the plot; in many types of narrative, such as the *detective story* or adventure novel or *farce* comedy, even the protagonist is usually two-dimensional. Sherlock Holmes and Long John Silver do not require, for their excellent literary roles, the roundness of a Hamlet, a Becky Sharp, or a Jay Gatsby. In his *Anatomy of Criticism* (1957), Northrop Frye has proposed that even lifelike characters are identifiable variants, more or less individualized, of stock two-dimensional types in old literary genres,

谱》(多译《品格论》),开创了人物素描这一文学类型。这一文学形式在 17 世纪初期颇为流行;当时的约瑟夫·霍尔、托马斯·奥弗伯里爵士、约翰·厄尔等的人物素描作品对后世的历史撰写和散文、小说的创作产生了一定的影响。从奥弗伯里部分素描作品的篇名就可看出这种文学形式的特性,如《谄媚者》《聪明人》《漂亮快活的挤奶姑娘》。参阅:理查德·奥尔丁顿的选集《人物肖像集》(1924)。

2. **人物**是戏剧或叙事作品所描写的人,读者将其理解为拥有特定的道德、才智和情感特征,并通过人物的话语和其特有的话语方式——**对话**——与他们的所作所为——**行为**——进行推断,从而解读作品中的人物。支配人物言行的性情、愿望和道德本质的基础称为人物的**动机**。在一部作品中,人物的观念和性格可以保持基本"稳定"或始终如一 [如莎士比亚《暴风雨》中的普洛斯彼罗,查尔斯·狄更斯《大卫·科波菲尔》(1849—1850)中的米考伯],人物也可能会通过自身的逐步发展 [如简·奥斯丁《爱玛》(1816)中的标题人物爱玛] 或由于经历危机(如莎士比亚的《李尔王》、狄更斯《远大前程》中的皮普)而发生性格和观念的突变。无论作品中的人物观念或性格特征是稳定的还是变化的,传统作品和现实主义作品的读者总是期望作品中的人物具有"连贯性"——人物不应出乎情理之外地突然中断读者业已了解的其性格特征或表现出一反常态的性情特征。

E. M. 福斯特在《小说面面观》(1927)中通过辨别干瘪的人物和丰满的人物,为旧式人物形象区分提出了两个新颖的术语。福斯特指出,**干瘪的人物形象**(也称**模式化人物**或"平面人物")产生于只描写"单一思想与气质",缺乏足够细致的个性表现,因此仅需只言片语便可完全勾勒出来。**丰满的人物形象**具有复杂多面的性格与动机,是通过深入细腻的描写而刻画出来的;因而,刻画这类人物不亚于再现生活中活生生的人,是难以完美无缺地予以呈现的,也如同真实的人物一样会让我们感到意外。*诙谐人物*,如本·琼森的"老饕财神爵士",是一个平面人物,同莎士比亚笔下多面性的丰满的人物福斯塔夫相比较,这一名字就足以说明诙谐人物的一切特征。几乎在所有的戏剧和叙事作品中都有一些只作陪衬而不加刻画的角色以及其他一些相对干瘪的人物形象:如莎士比亚在《亨利四世》第一部中对奎克利夫人的描写就不如福斯塔夫那样丰满,因为没有必要这样去做。对人物进行何种程度的立体化描绘,以取得成功的艺术效果,取决于他们在情节中的作用;在许多叙事类作品如*侦探故事*、历险小说或*闹剧*中,甚至连主人公也常是平面式形象。舍洛克·福尔摩斯和朗·约翰·西尔弗,就其卓越的文学角色而言,无需塑造成像哈姆雷特、贝基·夏普或杰伊·盖茨比那样圆润丰满的形象。诺斯罗普·弗莱在《批评的剖析》(1957)中提出:即便是逼真的人物形象,也无非是原有文学类型中定型人物模式的变体,只不过是多少加以个性化而已,

such as the self-deprecating "eiron," the boastful "alazon," and the "senex iratus," or choleric old father in classical comedy. See *stock characters*.

A broad distinction is frequently made between alternative methods for **characterizing** (that is, establishing the distinctive characters of) the persons in a narrative: showing and telling. In **showing** (also called "the dramatic method"), the author simply presents the characters talking and acting, and leaves it entirely up to the reader to infer the motives and dispositions that lie behind what they say and do. The author may show not only external speech and actions, but also a character's inner thoughts, feelings, and responsiveness to events; for a highly developed mode of such inner showing, see *stream of consciousness*. In **telling**, the author intervenes authoritatively in order to describe, and often to evaluate, the motives and dispositional qualities of the characters. For example, in the terse opening chapter of *Pride and Prejudice* (1813), Jane Austen first shows us Mr. and Mrs. Bennet as they talk to one another about the young man who has just rented Netherfield Park, then (in the quotation below) tells us about them, and so confirms and expands the inferences that we have begun to make from what has been shown.

> Mr. Bennet was so odd a mixture of quick parts, sarcastic humour, reserve, and caprice, that the experience of three-and-twenty years had been insufficient to make his wife understand his character. Her mind was less difficult to develop. She was a woman of mean understanding, little information, and uncertain temper.

Especially since the novelistic theory and practice of Flaubert and Henry James, a critical tendency has been to consider "telling" a violation of artistry and to recommend only the technique of "showing" characters; authors, it is said, should totally efface themselves in order to write "objectively," "impersonally," or "dramatically." Such judgments, however, privilege a modern artistic limitation suited to particular novelistic effects, and decry an alternative method of characterization which a number of novelists have employed to produce masterpieces. See *point of view*.

Innovative writers in the twentieth century—including novelists from James Joyce to French writers of the *new novel*, and authors of the dramas and novels of the *absurd* and various experimental forms—often presented the persons in their works in ways which ran counter to the earlier mode of representing lifelike characters who manifest a consistent substructure of individuality. Structuralist critics undertook to dissolve even the lifelike characters of traditional novels into a system of literary conventions and codes which are *naturalized* by the readers; that is, readers are said to project lifelikeness upon codified literary representations by assimilating them into their own prior stereotypes of individuals in real life. See *structuralist criticism* and *text and writing (écriture)*, and refer to Jonathan Culler, *Structuralist Poetics* (1975), chapter 9, "Poetics of the Novel."

See *plot* and *narrative and narratology*. For the traditional problems and methods of characterization, including discussions of showing and telling, see in addition to E. M. Forster (above), Percy Lubbock, *The Craft of Fiction*

如古典喜剧中自我贬损的"愚人"、善于吹嘘的"骗子"、"愤怒的女祭司"或性情暴躁的老父亲。参见：*定型人物*。

叙事作品中用来进行**人物塑造**（即塑造独特的人物形象）的手法往往大致分为两类：展示与讲述。**展示手法**（又称"戏剧性手法"）是指作者只是呈示人物的言行，而完全让读者去分析推论那些隐藏在人物言行背后的动机与气质。作者不仅可以展示人物外在的言行，而且可以展示人物内在的思想、情感，以及对事件的反应；关于展示内心世界的高超手法，参见：*意识流*。用**讲述手法**塑造人物时，作者在描述的同时掺杂个人意志，经常对人物的动机与气质予以评价。例如在《傲慢与偏见》（1813）简短的开头一节，简·奥斯丁首先通过贝内特夫妇对内瑟菲尔德公园年轻新房客的谈论向我们展示了这两个人物，然后向我们讲述他们（见以下摘录），从而证实和扩展了读者从作者的展示过程中对人物作出的推测。

> 贝内特先生可真是个古怪人。他喜欢插科打诨，爱挖苦人，又不露声色，变幻莫测，他太太积攒了23年的经验，还是摸不透他的性情。相反太太的心思就很容易暴露了，她是个智力贫乏、孤陋寡闻、喜怒无常的女人，一遇到不称心的事，她就自以为神经衰弱。她一辈子最重要的事就是嫁女儿；她一辈子最大的乐趣就是访友拜客和打听新闻。
>
> （张小余译）

尤其是自福楼拜和亨利·詹姆斯的小说理论和实践问世以来，有一种批评倾向认为"讲述"手法是反艺术的，并且倡导只使用"展示"手法塑造人物；作者应当完全隐藏自己的存在，以便做到"客观""不介入"和"戏剧性"的描写。然而，这种观点赋予了一种具有局限性的现代艺术手法以特权，而这种手法只能对某些特殊类型的作品产生艺术效果，而且贬低了人物塑造的另一种手法，许多小说家正是通过这另一种手法写出了不朽的著作。参见：*视角*。

20世纪的创新作家，包括从詹姆斯·乔伊斯到法国的新小说作家，以及*荒诞戏剧、小说及实验*各种不同形式的作家，常在作品中以违反常规的手法塑造人物，即他们不是通过展示人物个性特征的一致性来塑造逼真的人物形象。结构主义批评家甚至着手把传统小说中逼真的人物形象分解为被读者*归化*的文学惯例和符号系统；即通过读者把人物形象同化成各自先前现实生活中的人物类型，从而赋予那些符号化的文学形象以真实感。参见：*结构主义批评、文本与书写（书面文字）*；参阅：乔纳森·卡勒所著的《结构主义诗学》（1975）第九章"小说的诗学"。

参见：*情节；叙事和叙事学*。关于人物塑造的传统问题与手法，包括对展示和讲述两种手法的论述，除了上文提到的 E. M. 福斯特外，另可参阅：珀西·卢伯克

(1926); Wayne C. Booth, *The Rhetoric of Fiction* (1961), especially chapters 1–4: and W. J. Harvey, *Character and the Novel* (1965). On problems in determining dramatic character, see Bert O. States, *The Pleasure of the Play* (1994); and on the disappearance of traditional characterization in *postmodern* drama, Elinor Fuchs, *The Death of Character* (1996). On the formal distinction between primary characters (*protagonists*) and minor characters, see Alex Woloch, *The One vs. the Many: Minor Characters and the Space of the Protagonist in the Novel* (2003). In *The Economy of Character* (1998), Deidre S. Lynch describes the shift, especially in the second half of the eighteenth century, from external signs and actions to subjective states, as indicators of character.

character, the (a literary form): **45**.

characterizing: 47. See also *distance and involvement; empathy and sympathy*.

chiasmus (kīăz′ mŭs): **346**.

Chicago School (of criticism): **138**; *172*.

chivalric romance: Chivalric romance (or **medieval romance**) is a type of narrative that developed in twelfth-century France, spread to the literatures of other countries, and displaced the earlier *epic* and heroic forms. ("Romance" originally signified a work written in the French language, which evolved from a dialect of the Roman language, Latin.) Romances were at first written in verse, but later in prose as well. The **romance** is distinguished from the epic in that it does not represent a heroic age of tribal wars, but a courtly and chivalric age, often one of highly developed manners and civility. Its standard plot is that of a **quest** undertaken by a single knight in order to gain a lady's favor; frequently its central interest is *courtly love*, together with tournaments fought and dragons and monsters slain for the damsel's sake; it stresses the chivalric ideals of courage, loyalty, honor, mercifulness to an opponent, and elaborate manners; and it delights in wonders and marvels. Supernatural events in the epic usually were attributed to the will and actions of the gods; romance shifts the supernatural to this world, and makes much of the mysterious effect of magic, spells, and enchantments.

The recurrent materials of medieval chivalric romances have been divided by scholars into four classes of subjects: (1) "The Matter of Britain" (Celtic subject matter, especially stories centering on the court of King Arthur). (2) "The Matter of Rome" (the history and legends of classical antiquity, including the exploits of Alexander the Great and of the heroes of the Trojan War); Geoffrey Chaucer's *Troilus and Criseyde* belongs to this class. (3) "The Matter of France" (Charlemagne and his knights). (4) "The Matter of England" (heroes such as King Horn and Guy of Warwick). The cycle of tales which developed around the pseudohistorical British King Arthur produced many of the finest romances, some of them (stories of Sir Perceval and the quest for the Holy Grail) with a religious instead of a purely secular content. Chrétien

所著的《小说的技巧》(1926);韦恩·C.布思所著的《小说修辞学》(1961),尤其是书中前四章;W. J.哈维所著的《人物与小说》(1965)。关于确定戏剧性人物的问题,参阅:伯特·O.斯泰特斯所著的《戏剧的愉悦》(1994);关于后现代戏剧中传统人物塑造手法的消失,参阅:埃莉诺·富克斯所著的《人物之死》(1996)。关于主要人物(主人公)和次要人物之间的正式区分,参阅:亚历克斯·沃洛克所著的《一个人对许多人:小说中的次要人物与主人公的空间》(2003)。戴德丽·S.林奇在其所著的《性格经济学》(1998)中,描述了尤其是在18世纪下半叶从外在的符号和行动到作为人物标示的主观状态这一转变。

character, the (a literary form):人物素描(一种文学形式)　45。

characterizing:人物塑造　47。也可参见:*心理距离与感情介入*;*移情与同情*。

chiasmus:交错配列法　346。

Chicago School (of criticism):(批评中的)芝加哥学派　138;*172*。

Chivalric Romance:骑士传奇

　　骑士传奇(或**中世纪传奇**)是12世纪发端于法国,后传入其他国家,并取代了早期的*史诗*及英雄体文学形式的一种叙事体文学类型。["罗曼司"一词原指用法语(由古罗马语的一种方言拉丁语衍生而成)写成的作品。]骑士传奇起初采用诗体形式,后来也用散文形式。**传奇**与史诗的不同之处在于,传奇表现的不是充满部落战争的英雄时世,而往往是举止文雅、彬彬有礼的宫廷、骑士时代。它通常描写单身骑士**追求**意中人以讨其欢心的故事,故事的主题通常是*骑士恋*,并伴有骑士为了意中人而进行马上比武和降龙伏妖的壮举。这类作品注重表现英勇、忠诚、荣誉、对对手的宽容、典雅考究的仪表等骑士风度,并热衷于描写壮举和奇迹。史诗中的超自然事件通常源于神的意志与行动,骑士传奇则把超自然的世界转换成自然世界,并大肆渲染魔法、符咒和妖术的神秘气氛。

　　学者把中世纪传奇的常见题材划分为四种类型:(1)"不列颠题材"(凯尔特题材,尤其是以亚瑟王的宫廷为中心的故事)。(2)"罗马题材"(古代历史和传说,包括亚历山大大帝的功绩和特洛伊战争英雄的业绩);杰弗里·乔叟的《特洛伊罗斯与克里西德》就属于这一类别。(3)"法兰西题材"(查理曼大帝和他的骑士们)。(4)"英格兰题材"(像霍恩王和沃里克的盖伊等英雄的故事)。英王亚瑟历史传说的一系列故事产生出了许多优秀的传奇作品,其中有些(如珀西瓦尔爵士和探寻"圣杯"的故事)具有宗教色彩而不是纯粹的世俗故事。

de Troyes, the great twelfth-century French poet, wrote Arthurian romances; German examples are Wolfram von Eschenbach's *Parzival* and Gottfried von Strassburg's *Tristan und Isolde*, both written early in the thirteenth century. *Sir Gawain and the Green Knight*, composed in fourteenth-century England, is a **metrical romance** (that is, a romance written in verse) about an Arthurian knight; and Thomas Malory's *Morte d'Arthur* (fifteenth century) is an English version in prose of the cycle of earlier metrical romances about Arthur and various of his Knights of the Round Table.

See *prose romance, Gothic romance, romantic comedy,* and *romance novel.* Refer to L. A. Hibbard, *Medieval Romance in England* (rev. 1961); R. S. Loomis, *The Development of Arthurian Romance* (1963) and *The Grail* (1963); the anthology *Medieval Romances,* ed. R. S. and L. H. Loomis (1957); and *The Cambridge Companion to Medieval Romance,* ed. Roberta L. Krueger (2000). For the history of the term "romance" and modern extensions of the genre of romance, see Gillian Beer, *The Romance* (1970); and for Northrop Frye's theory of the mythical basis of the romance genre, see the entry in this *Glossary* on *myth.* For references to *chivalric romance* in other entries, see pages 16, 39, 66.

choral character: 50.

chorus: Among the ancient Greeks the chorus was a group of people, wearing masks, who sang or chanted verses while performing dancelike movements at religious festivals. A similar chorus played a part in Greek tragedies, where (in the plays of Aeschylus and Sophocles) they served mainly as commentators on the dramatic actions and events who expressed traditional moral, religious, and social attitudes; beginning with Euripides, however, the chorus assumed primarily a lyrical function. The Greek ode, as developed by Pindar, was also chanted by a chorus; see *ode.* In *The Birth of Tragedy* (1872) the German classicist and philosopher Friedrich Nietzsche speculated that, at the origin of Greek tragedy, the chorus—consisting of goat-like satyrs—were the only figures on the stage. They were presented as attendants and witnesses of the suffering, death, and self-transformation of their master, the god Dionysus. Later, in Nietzsche's view, actors were introduced to enact the event that had originally been represented only symbolically, and the chorus was reduced to the role of commentator.

Roman playwrights such as Seneca took over the chorus from the Greeks, and in the mid-sixteenth century some English dramatists (for example, Norton and Sackville in *Gorboduc*) imitated the Senecan chorus. The classical type of chorus was never widely adopted by English dramatic writers. John Milton, however, included a chorus in *Samson Agonistes* (1671), as did Shelley in *Prometheus Unbound* (1820) and Thomas Hardy in *The Dynasts* (1904–8); more recently, T. S. Eliot made effective use of the classical chorus in his religious tragedy *Murder in the Cathedral* (1935). The use in drama of a chorus of singers and dancers survives also in operas and in musical comedies.

During the Elizabethan Age the term "chorus" was applied also to a single person who, in some plays, spoke the prologue and epilogue, and sometimes

12世纪伟大的法国诗人克雷蒂安·德·特鲁瓦创作了一些亚瑟王传奇；德国的骑士传奇有沃尔夫拉姆·封·埃申巴赫的《帕尔齐法尔》和哥特菲尔德·封·斯特拉斯伯格的《特里斯坦和伊索尔德》，两部作品都创作于13世纪早期。《高文爵士与绿衣骑士》是创作于14世纪英国的一部**格律传奇**（即用诗歌形式写就的浪漫传奇），描写的是亚瑟王属下一位骑士的故事；托马斯·马洛礼的《亚瑟王之死》（15世纪）是根据亚瑟王和他的圆桌骑士的一系列早期的格律传奇用英文创作的散文体传奇。

参见：*散文体传奇、哥特式传奇、爱情喜剧*。参阅：L. A. 希巴德所著的《英国中世纪传奇》（1961年修订版）；R. S. 卢米斯所著的《亚瑟王传奇的发展》（1963）和《圣杯》（1963）；选集：R. S. & L. H. 卢米斯夫妇合编的《中世纪传奇》（1957）；罗伯塔·L. 克鲁格主编的《剑桥中世纪传奇指南》（2000）。关于术语"传奇"的历史和传奇文学类型的现代运用，参阅吉利恩·比尔所著的《传奇》（1970）；诺斯罗普·弗莱关于传奇文学类型的神话基础理论，参见：*神话*。其他条目中提及"骑士传奇"的地方，参见第16、39、66页。

choral character：唱白人　50。

Chorus：合唱队

合唱队是古希腊时期的演唱班子，每逢宗教节日盛典，他们便头戴面具载歌载舞进行表演。类似的合唱队也出现在希腊悲剧（如埃斯库罗斯和索福克勒斯的悲剧）中，其作用主要是作为评论员解说戏剧行为和事件，表达传统道德、宗教观念、社会态度；但从欧里庇得斯开始，合唱队的功能主要在于抒情。品达创始的希腊颂歌也被合唱队吟唱；参见：*颂*。在《悲剧的诞生》中，德国古典学家和哲学家弗里德里希·尼采推断，在希腊悲剧的起始，合唱队——由羊人萨提尔组成——是舞台上唯一的人物。他们作为随从出现，见证他们的主人受苦受难、死亡和自我转化。后来，在尼采看来，演员被引入进来表演此前一直仅被象征性地呈现的事件，合唱队被简化为评论员的角色。

以塞内加为代表的罗马剧作家继承了希腊人的合唱队表现形式，16世纪中期，一些英国戏剧家（如诺顿与萨克维尔在《戈尔伯德克悲剧》中）效仿塞内加式的合唱形式。古典的合唱形式一直未被英国剧作家广为采用。但在约翰·弥尔顿的《力士参孙》（1671）、雪莱的《解放了的普罗米修斯》（1820）和托马斯·哈代的《列王》（1904—1908）中，采用了合唱队的表现手法；现代作家 T. S. 艾略特在其宗教悲剧《大教堂凶杀案》（1935）中，有效地运用了古典合唱队的表现形式。歌剧和音乐喜剧中仍然沿用着戏剧里歌唱家和舞蹈家合唱队的表现形式。

在伊丽莎白时代，"合唱队"这一术语也用来指代剧中宣读开场白和收场白，

introduced each act as well. This character served as the author's vehicle for commentary on the play, as well as for exposition of its subject, time, and setting, and the description of events happening offstage; examples are in Christopher Marlowe's *Dr. Faustus* and Shakespeare's *Henry V*. In Shakespeare's *Winter's Tale*, the fifth act begins with "Time, the Chorus," who requests the audience that they "impute it not a crime / To me or my swift passage that I slide / O'er sixteen years" since the preceding events, then summarizes what has happened during those years and announces that the setting for this present act is Bohemia. A modern and extended use of a single character with a choral function is the Stage Manager in Thornton Wilder's *Our Town* (1938).

Modern scholars use the term **choral character** to refer to a person within the play itself who stands apart from the action and by his or her comments provides the audience with a special perspective (often an *ironic* perspective) through which to view the other characters and events. Examples in Shakespeare are the Fool in *King Lear*, Enobarbus in *Antony and Cleopatra*, and Thersites in *Troilus and Cressida*; a modern instance is Seth Beckwith in O'Neill's *Mourning Becomes Electra* (1931). "Choral character" is sometimes applied also to one or more persons in a *novel* who represent the point of view of a community or of a cultural group, and so provide norms by which to judge the other characters and what they do; instances are Thomas Hardy's peasants and the old black women in some of William Faulkner's novels.

For the alternative use of the term "chorus" to signify a recurrent stanza in a song, see *refrain*. Refer to A. W. Pickard-Cambridge, *Dithyramb, Tragedy and Comedy* (1927) and *The Dramatic Festivals of Athens* (1953); T. B. L. Webster, *Greek Theater Production* (1956).

chorus (in a song): **337**.

Christian humanism: 162.

chronicle plays: Chronicle plays were dramatic works based on the historical materials in the English *Chronicles* by Raphael Holinshed and others; see *Chronicles*. They achieved high popularity late in the sixteenth century, when the patriotic fervor following the defeat of the Spanish Armada in 1588 fostered a demand for plays dealing with English history. The early chronicle plays presented a loosely knit series of events during the reign of an English king and depended for effect mainly on a bustle of stage battles, pageantry, and spectacle. Christopher Marlowe, however, in his *Edward II* (1592) selected and rearranged materials from Holinshed's *Chronicles* to compose a unified drama of character, and Shakespeare's series of chronicle plays, encompassing the succession of English kings from Richard II to Henry VIII, includes such major artistic achievements as *Richard II*, *1 Henry IV*, *2 Henry IV*, and *Henry V*.

The Elizabethan chronicle plays are sometimes called **history plays**. This latter term, however, is often applied more broadly to any drama based

间或也介绍每幕剧情的一位角色。剧作者借助该角色评论剧情，同时向观众阐明戏剧主题、时间、背景，以及描述发生在舞台以外的情节；例如在克里斯托弗·马洛的《浮士德博士》和莎士比亚的《亨利五世》中。在莎士比亚《冬天的故事》第五幕中，首先出场的是名为"时间"的唱白角色，他请求观众"让我如今用时间的名义驾起双翩／把一段悠长的岁月跳过请莫指斥／十六个春秋早已默无声息地度过"（朱生豪译）。接下来是他对 16 年沧桑的概述并说明本幕戏的场景是波希米亚。桑顿·怀尔德《小城风光》（1938）中的舞台监督，是近代戏剧在广义上对单个角色唱白功能的应用。

现代学者用**唱白人**这一术语指代那种作为剧中人但又不介入情节的角色，他／她通过评论剧情为观众提出认识剧中人物与事件的特殊视角（往往是具有讽刺意味的视角）。如莎剧《李尔王》中的弄臣、《安东尼与克莉奥佩特拉》中的伊诺巴勃斯、《特洛伊罗斯与克里西德》中的瑟赛蒂兹；在现代戏剧中，这样的例子有奥尼尔《哀悼》（1931）中的塞思·贝克威思。"唱白人"一词有时也用于指称*小说*中的一人或多人，代表某一团体或文化群体的观点，以提供评价作品中其他角色及其所作所为的准则；如托马斯·哈代作品中的农夫和威廉·福克纳一些小说中的黑人老太太。

"合唱"还可用来指称一首歌曲中的重复段落，关于这一用法，参见：*叠句*。参阅：A. W. 皮卡德－坎布里奇所著的《赞美诗、悲剧和喜剧》（1927）与《雅典的戏剧节》（1953）；T. B. L. 韦伯斯特所著的《古希腊戏剧作品》（1956）。

chorus (in a song)：(歌曲中的) 合唱部　　337。

Christian humanism：基督教人文主义　　162。

Chronicle Plays：编年历史剧

编年历史剧是指以拉斐尔·霍林希德等人编著的英国《编年史》中的历史素材为依据的剧作；参见：*编年史*。1588 年英国战败西班牙无敌舰队后，国内出现的狂热的爱国主义，激发了人们对有关英国历史的戏剧的需求，于是，编年历史剧在 16 世纪后期风靡一时。早期的编年历史剧只对某个英王执政时期内的事件作罗列式的松散描写，并主要依赖在舞台上呈现喧闹的战役、盛大的庆典和其他壮观场面来取得演出效果。然而，克里斯托弗·马洛在创作《爱德华二世》（1592）的过程中，对霍林希德的《编年史》作了筛选和重新组织，从而创作了一部情节统一的人物剧；莎士比亚创作了从查理二世到亨利八世的系列编年历史剧，其中具有高度艺术成就的有《查理二世》《亨利四世》第一部与第二部及《亨利五世》。

伊丽莎白时代的编年历史剧有时称为**历史剧**。这一称谓常常泛指任何以历

mainly on historical materials, such as Shakespeare's Roman plays *Julius Caesar* and *Antony and Cleopatra*, and including such recent examples as Arthur Miller's *The Crucible* (1953), which treats the Salem witch trials of 1692, and Robert Bolt's *A Man for All Seasons* (1962), about the sixteenth-century judge, author, and martyr Sir Thomas More. G. B. Shaw titled one of his plays, which dealt with historical matters, *St. Joan: A Chronicle Play in Six Scenes* (1923).

E. M. W. Tillyard, *Shakespeare's History Plays* (1946); Lily B. Campbell, *Shakespeare's "Histories"* (1947); Irving Ribner, *The English History Play in the Age of Shakespeare* (rev. 1965); Max M. Reese, *The Cease of Majesty: A Study of Shakespeare's History Plays* (1962). For a *new-historicist* treatment of Shakespeare's history plays *Henry IV, 1 and 2*, and *Henry V*, see Stephen Greenblatt, "Invisible Bullets," in *Political Shakespeare: New Essays in Cultural Materialism*, ed. Jonathan Dollimore and Alan Sinfield (1985).

chronicles: Chronicles, the predecessors of modern histories, were written accounts, in prose or verse, of national or worldwide events over a considerable period of time. If the chronicles deal with events year by year, they are often called **annals**. Unlike the modern historian, most chroniclers tended to take their information as they found it, making little attempt to separate fact from legend. The most important English examples are the *Anglo-Saxon Chronicle*, started by King Alfred in the ninth century and continued until the twelfth century, and the *Chronicles of England, Scotland, and Ireland* (1577–87) by Raphael Holinshed and other writers. The latter documents were important sources of materials for the *chronicle plays* of Shakespeare and other Elizabethan dramatists.

chronological primitivism: 316; *151.*

classic, a: 236; *41.*

classical: 236.

cliché: Cliché is French for "stereotype"—that is, a metal plate with a raised surface of type, used for printing. In its literary application, "cliché" signifies an expression that deviates enough from ordinary usage to call attention to itself and has been used so often that it is felt to be hackneyed or cloying. "I beg your pardon" or "sincerely yours" are standard usages that do not call attention to themselves; but "point with pride," "the eternal verities," "a whole new ballgame," and "lock, stock, and barrel" are accounted as clichés; so are indiscriminate uses in ordinary talk of terms taken from specialized vocabularies such as "alienation," "identity crisis," "interface," and "paradigm." Some clichés are foreign phrases that are used as an arch or elegant equivalent for a common English term ("aqua pura," "au courant," "terra firma"); others are over-used literary echoes. "The cup that cheers" is an inaccurate quotation from William Cowper's *The Task* (1785), referring to tea—"the cups / That cheer but not inebriate." In his *Essay on Criticism* (II. 11. 350ff.), Alexander

史素材为主的剧作，例如：莎士比亚的罗马剧作《尤利乌斯·恺撒》和《安东尼与克莉奥佩特拉》，近代的有阿瑟·米勒关于1692年一桩塞勒姆女巫案的《炼狱》(1953)和罗伯特·博尔特关于16世纪托马斯·莫尔爵士这位法官、作家和烈士的历史人物剧《不朽的托马斯·莫尔》(1962)。萧伯纳给他的一部涉及历史问题的剧作定名为《圣女贞德：六幕编年剧》。

参阅：E. M. W. 蒂利亚德所著的《莎士比亚的历史剧》(1946)；莉莉·B. 坎贝尔所著的《莎士比亚的"历史"》(1947)；欧文·里布纳所著的《莎士比亚时代的英国历史剧》(1965年修订版)；马克斯·M. 里斯所著的《威严不再：莎士比亚历史剧研究》(1962)。关于新历史主义者对莎剧《亨利四世》第1、2部和《亨利五世》的论述，参阅：斯蒂芬·格林布拉特所写的文章"看不见的子弹"，收入乔纳森·多利莫尔与艾伦·辛菲尔德合编的《政治的莎士比亚：文化物质主义新论文集》(1985)。

Chronicles：编年史

编年史为现代史的前身，是以散文或韵文形式记叙一段相当长时期内国内或国际事件的书面史料。连年记载历史事件的编年史常称为**年鉴**。编年史作家与现代历史学家不同，他们很少对历史事实与传说加以区分，所见所闻尽收笔下。英国最重要的编年史是《盎格鲁－撒克逊编年史》(其所记内容始于9世纪的英王阿尔弗烈德直至12世纪)和拉斐尔·霍林希德等人编著的《英格兰、苏格兰、爱尔兰编年史》(1577—1587)。后一本书中的史实成为莎士比亚编年历史剧和伊丽莎白时代剧作家创作素材的重要来源。

chronological primitivism：年代尚古主义　316；*151*。

classic，a：经典　236；*41*。

classical：古典　236。

Cliché：陈词滥调

陈词滥调是铅板的法语叫法——即，一个上面有着凸起铅字的金属板，用于印刷。在其文学用法中，"陈词滥调"指为引人注目而过于偏离普通用法并因使用频率过高而显得陈腐或厌腻的用语。像"请原谅"或"您忠诚的"是标准用语，不再引人注意；而"深感荣幸""永恒的真理""完全是一种新情况""一股脑儿地"等则被视为陈词滥调。同样，在日常交谈中，不加区分地运用"异化""性格认同危机""界面""范式"等一些专业词汇，也属滥用词汇。有些陈词滥调是外来语，用作点缀或用于普通英语词语以取得格调上的对等（如"净水""陆地"）；另外，还有因为过度模仿文学经典的诗句而造成的陈词滥调，如"杯盏宜人"就是对威廉·柯珀《任务》(1785)一诗的断章取义，意指饮茶——"杯盏宜人而不醉人"。

Pope comments satirically on some clichés that early eighteenth-century **poetasters** (untalented pretenders to the poetic art) used in order to eke out their rhymes:

> Where'er you find "the cooling western breeze,"
> In the next line, it "whispers through the trees";
> If crystal streams "with pleasing murmurs creep,"
> The reader's threatened (not in vain) with "sleep."

See Eric Partridge, *A Dictionary of Clichés* (4th ed., 1950), and Christine Ammer, *Have a Nice Day—No Problem! A Dictionary of Clichés* (1992).

climax (in a plot): **296**.

climax (rhetorical): **25**.

close reading: 242; *80*.

closed couplet: 158.

closet drama: 94.

codex: 32.

cogito: 290; *311*.

cognitive literary studies: Cognitive literary studies, also known as **cognitive poetics**, is an approach to literature from the viewpoint of cognitive science, which is associated with the fields of artificial intelligence, computer science, cognitive and evolutionary psychology, neuroscience, and linguistics. Cognitive science seeks to understand the workings of the human brain and explains language and other forms of communication in terms of mental states and the mental processes of cognition. Cognitive literary study, accordingly, approaches literature as a function of the brain rather than as a means of representation or expression. In this respect, cognitive literary study sets itself apart from both literary *formalism* and the *New Criticism*, which treat the literary work as independent of the author's thoughts or intentions, and critical approaches such as *new historicism* and *cultural studies*, which assume that literature is largely determined by factors in the external environment.

A rough distinction can be made between cognitive studies that use literature as a source of information about the brain, and those that use researches about the brain as a way to understand literature better.

1. In the first type, the object of study is literary language, especially stylistic features, such as metaphor and analogy, that involve complex mental processes. Literary language is treated as a rich body of evidence for human cognitive capacities such as the ability to register impressions, form

亚历山大·蒲柏在《批评论》（第二部第十一章第350行及其下）中辛辣地评论了18世纪早期**冒牌诗人**（没有天赋而妄装诗人）为了填词补韵而使用的陈词滥调：

无论何处你遇到"凉爽的西风"，
下一行里必有风"耳语于丛林中"
倘若再见清澈的溪水"潺潺流过"
拜读者定遭"睡神"的威胁。

参阅：埃里克·帕特里奇所著的《陈词滥调词典》（1950年第4版）；克里斯蒂娜·安默所著的《祝你今天愉快——没问题！陈词滥调词典》（1992）。

climax (in a plot)：(情节中的) 高潮　296。

climax (rhetorical)：(修辞学中的) 层进法　25。

close reading：细读　242；*80*。

closed couplet：闭合双韵体　158。

closet drama：文房剧　94。

codex：抄本　32。

cogito：自我　290；*311*。

Cognitive Literary Studies：认知文学研究

认知文学研究，又称**认知诗学**，是一种从认知科学的角度来看文学的方法，与人工智能、计算机科学、认知和进化心理学、神经科学和语言学等领域联系在一起。认知科学旨在了解人类大脑的工作机制，从精神状态和认知心理过程去解释语言和其他传播交流形式。因此，认知文学研究也就将文学视作大脑的一种功能，而不是视作一种陈述或表达的手段。在这方面，认知文学研究将其自身与*文学形式主义*、*新批评*区别开来，这两者将文学作品视作独立于作者的思考或意图，并与如*新历史主义*、*文化研究*这样的批判研究方法区别开来，这两者认为文学作品很大程度上受到外部环境因素的决定。

在将文学视作一种大脑的信息来源的认知研究，与将研究大脑作为一种更好地理解文学的方式的认知研究之间，可以做一粗略区分。

1. 在第一类中，研究的对象是文学语言，特别是文体特征，如比喻和类比，其中涉及复杂的心理过程。文学语言被视为人类认知能力的丰富证据，如能够存储印象，形成概念，处理信息，交流意识状态，使

concepts, process information, communicate intentional states, use symbols, and produce narratives. The idea of **conceptual metaphor**, initially developed by George Lakoff and Mark Johnson, has been particularly influential. The fact that a number of metaphors occur in numerous languages (e.g., "the river of time," or "life is a journey") supports, they claim, the hypothesis that the mapping, in these cases, between conceptual domains corresponds to neural mappings in the brain. (See the cognitive view in the entry *metaphor, theories of*; also refer to George Lakoff and Mark Johnson, *Metaphors We Live By*, updated ed. 2003, and Lakoff and Mark Turner, *More than Cool Reason: A Field Guide to Poetic Metaphor*, 1989.) Some work in this area uses imaging technology to observe the brain's responses to literary stimuli, including *rhythm* and *rhetorical figures*, especially metaphor.

2. In the second type, cognitive studies undertakes to illuminate literature by reference to properties of the brain. One way to do so is to refer to studies that demonstrate the human capacity to construct imagined worlds, to track multiple sources of information, or to apply a "theory of mind"—that is, the ability to understand the mental states of other people—and then to use these studies to explain the cognitive motivation of such features of literature as *free indirect discourse* (in which the thoughts of fictional characters are represented in the voice of the narrator), or the ways in which literature enlists the emotional responses of the reader, such as concern or sympathy for fictional characters.

Cognitive literary study often allies itself with *Darwinian literary studies*, by arguing that the literary processes of the brain reveal adaptive qualities of human existence that have served the evolutionary interests of the human species.

For cognitive poetics, see Elena Semino and Jonathan Culpeper, eds., *Cognitive Stylistics: Language and Cognition in Text Analysis* (2002); and Joanna Gavins and Gerard Steen, eds., *Cognitive Poetics in Practice* (2003). Peter Stockwell's *Cognitive Poetics: An Introduction* (2002) attempts to construct a bridge between linguistic analysis and accounts of the reading experience. In *Literature and the Brain* (2009), Norman Holland surveys recent empirical work that illuminates the brain's response to the various kinds of cognition. In *Reading Minds: The Study of English in the Age of Cognitive Science* (1991), Mark Turner argues that the human mind is inherently linguistic and literary, with a unique capacity for "conceptual blending." For an example of the use of imaging technology in studying the response to literary language, see Philip Davis, "Syntax and Pathways," *Interdisciplinary Science Reviews* 2008 (33.4), 265–77. For instances of the "theory of mind" approach, see Lisa Zunshine, *Why We Read Fiction: Theory of Mind and the Novel* (2006); and Blakey Vermeule, *Why Do We Care about Literary Characters?* (2010). Bruce McConachie and F. Elizabeth Hart, eds., *Performance and Cognition: Theatre Studies and the Cognitive Turn* (2006) gathers a number of essays that apply the cognitive approach to drama.

用符号，作出叙述。最初由乔治·雷柯夫和马克·约翰逊提出的**概念隐喻**这一想法一直特别有影响力。他们声称，许多语言中都有的一些隐喻（如，"时间的长河"或"生命之旅"）这一事实支持该假说：在这两个例子中，概念域之间的映射对应于大脑中的神经元映射。[参见：隐喻理论中的认知观点；也可参阅：乔治·雷柯夫和马克·约翰逊合著的《我们赖以生存的隐喻》（2003年修订版），以及雷柯夫与马克·特纳合著的《超越冷静理性：诗性隐喻分析指南》（1989）。] 这一领域的一些工作采用成像技术来观察大脑对文学刺激的反应，包括韵律和修辞格，尤其是隐喻。

2. 在第二类中，认知研究尝试通过参考大脑的属性来阐明文学。这样做的一个方式是，参照那些表明人类有能力构建想象世界，跟踪信息的多个来源，或采用"心智理论"——也就是说，能够理解别人的心理状态——的研究，然后使用这些研究来解释像*自由间接话语*（虚构人物的思想通过叙述者的声音表达出来）这些文学特征的认知动机，或者是阐释文学寻求读者情感反应的方式，如关心或同情虚构人物。

认知文学研究经常将*达尔文主义文学研究*引为盟友，认为大脑的文学过程揭示了人类存在的适应特性，服务于人类物种的进化利益。

关于认知诗学，可以参阅：埃琳娜·塞米诺与乔纳森·卡尔佩珀合编的《认知文体学：语篇分析的语言和认知》（2002）；乔安娜·加文斯与杰拉德·斯蒂恩合编的《认知诗学实践》（2003）。彼得·斯托克韦尔所著的《认知诗学导论》（2002），尝试在语言分析和阅读体验描述之间搭起一座桥梁；诺曼·霍兰在其所著的《文学和大脑》（2009）中，调查了近来阐释大脑对各种认知的反应的实证研究。在《阅读心灵：认知科学时代的英语研究》（1991）中，马克·特纳认为，人的心灵在本质上是语言和文学，具有独特的"概念整合"能力。使用成像技术研究对文学语言的反应的一个例子，可以参阅菲利普·戴维斯所写的文章"语法和路径"，载于《跨学科科学评论》2008年（33.4）第265—277页。采用"心智理论"方法的实例，参阅：丽莎·祖恩夏因所著的《我们为什么读小说：心智理论与小说》（2006）；布莱基·弗穆尔所著的《为什么我们关心文学人物？》（2010）。布鲁斯·麦康纳基与F.伊丽莎白·哈特合编的《演出与认知：戏剧研究和认知转向》（2006），收集了一些用认知方法研究戏剧的文章。

cognitive poetics: 52.

cognitive rhetoric: 343.

collective unconscious: 323.

Colonial Period: 273; *311.*

colophon (kŏl′ ŏfŏn): 34.

comedy: In the most common literary application, a comedy is a fictional work in which the materials are selected and managed primarily in order to interest and amuse us: the characters and their discomfitures engage our pleasurable attention rather than our profound concern, we are made to feel confident that no great disaster will occur, and usually the action turns out happily for the chief characters. The term "comedy" is customarily applied only to plays for the stage or to motion pictures and television dramas; it should be noted, however, that the comic form of *plot*, as just defined, also occurs in prose fiction and narrative poetry.

Within the very broad spectrum of dramatic comedy, the following types are frequently distinguished:

1. **Romantic comedy** was developed by Elizabethan dramatists on the model of contemporary *prose romances* such as Thomas Lodge's *Rosalynde* (1590), the source of Shakespeare's *As You Like It* (1599). Such comedy represents a love affair that involves a beautiful and engaging heroine (sometimes disguised as a man); the course of this love does not run smooth, yet overcomes all difficulties to end in a happy union. Many of the boy-meets-girl plots of later writers are instances of romantic comedy, as are *romance novels* and many motion pictures, from *The Philadelphia Story* to *Sleepless in Seattle*. In *Anatomy of Criticism* (1957), Northrop Frye points out that some of Shakespeare's romantic comedies manifest a movement from the normal world of conflict and trouble into "the green world"—the Forest of Arden in *As You Like It*, or the fairy-haunted wood of *A Midsummer Night's Dream*—in which the problems and injustices of the ordinary world are dissolved, enemies reconciled, and true lovers united. Frye regards that phenomenon (together with other aspects of these comedies, such as their frequent conclusion in the social ritual of a wedding, a feast, or a dance) as evidence that comic plots derive from primitive myths and rituals that celebrated the victory of spring over winter. (See *archetypal criticism*.) Linda Bamber's *Comic Women, Tragic Men: A Study of Gender and Genre in Shakespeare* (1982) undertakes to account for the fact that in Shakespeare's romantic comedies, the women are often superior to the men, while in his tragedies he "creates such nightmare female figures as Goneril, Regan, Lady Macbeth, and Volumnia." See also *gender criticism*.

cognitive poetics：认知诗学　52。

cognitive rhetoric：认知修辞学　343。

collective unconscious：集体无意识　323。

Colonial Period：殖民地时期　273；*311*。

colophon：出版者商标　34。

Comedy：喜剧

　　在最常见的文学用法中，喜剧是指一种虚构性作品，其素材经过筛选和编排，主要用来愉悦我们：剧中人物和他们的困窘引发的不是我们的忧心愁绪，而是我们愉悦的会意，我们确信不会有大难临头，剧情往往是以主人公如愿以偿为结局。"喜剧"这一术语习惯上只适用于舞台剧或电影和电视剧；然而应该指出，就像现在界定的，这种喜剧式*情节*也出现在小说和叙事诗歌中。

　　在广义的戏剧性喜剧范畴内，常可划分出如下几种类型：

1. **爱情喜剧**：是伊丽莎白时期剧作家在同时期散文体传奇的模式上发展起来的一种戏剧形式，如托马斯·洛奇的散文体传奇《罗莎琳德》(1590)是莎士比亚《皆大欢喜》(1599)的原始素材。这类喜剧表现的爱情故事中的女主人公美丽迷人（有时为女扮男装）；恋爱过程并非一帆风顺，但经排忧解难终结良缘。后世作家的许多有关青年男女幽会的情节描写也属于这类爱情喜剧，包括爱情小说和从《费城故事》到《西雅图不眠夜》的许多电影也属于此类。诺斯罗普·弗莱在《批评的剖析》(1957)中指出：莎士比亚的部分爱情喜剧体现出由充满矛盾与烦扰的现实世界转向"绿色世界"，如《皆大欢喜》中的阿登森林，或《仲夏夜之梦》中仙女出没的树林。在这样的"绿色世界"中，原有现实世界中的疑难和不公消解了，敌手言和，有情人终成眷属。弗莱把这种情形（连同这些喜剧的其他方面，如作为喜庆结局的社会礼仪：婚礼、盛宴、舞会）作为一种证据，证明喜剧情节源自庆贺春天战胜寒冬的原始神话和礼仪。（参见：*原型批评*。）琳达·班伯在《喜剧女性，悲剧男性：性别研究和莎士比亚作品中的文学类型》(1982)中，致力于论述这样一个事实，即在莎士比亚的爱情喜剧中，女性总是优越于男性，但在悲剧中，他"创造出了诸如高纳里尔、里根、麦克白夫人和瓦卢米尼亚这样一些梦魇般的女性形象"。也可参见：*性别批评*。

2. **Satiric comedy** ridicules political policies or philosophical doctrines, or else attacks deviations from the accepted social order by making ridiculous the violators of its standards of morals or manners. (See *satire*.) The early master of satiric comedy was the Greek Aristophanes, c. 450–c. 385 BC, whose plays mocked political, philosophical, and literary matters of his age. Shakespeare's contemporary, Ben Jonson, wrote satiric or (as it is sometimes called) "corrective comedy." In his *Volpone* and *The Alchemist*, for example, the greed and ingenuity of one or more intelligent but rascally swindlers, and the equal greed but stupid gullibility of their victims, are made grotesquely or repulsively ludicrous rather than lightly amusing.

3. The **comedy of manners** originated in the **New Comedy** of the Greek Menander, c. 342–292 BC (as distinguished from the **Old Comedy** represented by Aristophanes, c. 450–c. 385 BC) and was developed by the Roman dramatists Plautus and Terence in the third and second centuries BC. Their plays dealt with the vicissitudes of young lovers and included what became the *stock characters* of much later comedy, such as the clever servant, old and stodgy parents, and the wealthy rival. The English comedy of manners was early exemplified by Shakespeare's *Love's Labour's Lost* and *Much Ado about Nothing*, and was given a high polish in **Restoration comedy** (1660–1700). The Restoration form owes much to the brilliant dramas of the French writer Molière, 1622–73. It deals with the relations and intrigues of men and women living in a sophisticated upper-class society, and relies for comic effect in large part on the wit and sparkle of the dialogue—often in the form of *repartee*, a witty conversational give-and-take which constitutes a kind of verbal fencing match—as well as on the violations of social standards and decorum by would-be wits, jealous husbands, conniving rivals, and foppish dandies. Excellent examples are William Congreve's *The Way of the World* and William Wycherley's *The Country Wife*. (See *The Cambridge Companion to English Restoration Theatre*, ed. Deborah Payne Fisk, 2000.) A middle-class reaction against what had come to be considered the immorality of situation and indecency of dialogue in the courtly Restoration comedy resulted in the *sentimental comedy* of the eighteenth century. In the latter part of that century, however, Oliver Goldsmith (*She Stoops to Conquer*) and his contemporary Richard Brinsley Sheridan (*The Rivals* and *A School for Scandal*) revived the wit and gaiety, while deleting the indecency, of Restoration comedy. The comedy of manners lapsed in the early nineteenth century, but was revived by many skillful dramatists, from A. W. Pinero and Oscar Wilde (*The Importance of Being Earnest*, 1895), through George Bernard Shaw and Noel Coward, to Neil Simon, Alan Ayckbourn, Wendy Wasserstein, and other recent and contemporary writers. Many of these comedies have also been adapted for the cinema. See David L. Hirst, *Comedy of Manners* (1979).

4. **Farce** is a type of comedy designed to provoke the audience to simple, hearty laughter—"belly laughs," in the parlance of the theater. To do so

2. **讽刺喜剧**用于嘲讽政治方针与哲学信条，或通过嘲弄破坏道德或习俗准则者的荒唐来抨击社会的混乱秩序。（参见：讽刺。）早期的讽刺喜剧大师是希腊作家阿里斯托芬（前450—前385），他的戏剧嘲讽当时的政治、哲学及文学创作。莎士比亚的同期作家本·琼森创作的讽刺作品或（有时称为）"矫正喜剧"，如他创作的两部喜剧《狐狸》和《炼金术士》，把骗子的卑鄙狡诈、巧取豪夺及其牺牲品的贪婪轻信、愚昧无知表现得怪诞荒唐、令人生厌，而不是让人感到轻松愉悦。

3. **风俗喜剧**源于希腊剧作家米南德（约前342—前292）的**新喜剧**[与阿里斯托芬（前450—前385）的**旧喜剧**相对而言]，公元前3世纪至公元前2世纪，罗马剧作家普劳图斯和泰伦斯发展了这一剧种。他们的作品描述青年恋人的沉浮并且塑造了为后世喜剧沿用的各种定型人物，如智慧的仆人、年迈守旧的父母、富贵的情敌。英语风俗喜剧的早期代表作有莎士比亚的《爱的徒劳》和《无事生非》，后来通过**王政复辟时期的喜剧**（1660—1700）得到高度完善。王政复辟时期的喜剧形式汲取了法国作家莫里哀（1622—1673）不朽剧作的精华，反映的是貌似高雅实则尔虞我诈的上层社会中男女之间的风流韵事。它的喜剧效果主要体现在机智精彩的对白中——常采取机智应答的形式，即唇枪舌剑、机智的口头论战——以及那些自命不凡的智者、争风吃醋的丈夫、暗中合谋的情敌、纨绔子弟违反社会习俗与体统的可笑行为上。这类喜剧的杰出代表作有威廉·康格里夫的《如此世道》和威廉·威彻利的《乡下女人》。[参阅德博拉·佩恩·菲斯克主编的《剑桥王政复辟时期戏剧指南》（2000）。]由于中产阶级反对在文雅的王政复辟时期的喜剧中出现这种被他们认为是伤风败俗的情境和污言秽语的对白，从而使得该剧种被18世纪的感伤喜剧所取代。然而，18世纪后半期，奥利弗·哥尔德斯密斯（《委曲求全》）和他同时代的理查德·布林斯利·谢立丹（《情敌》《造谣学校》）又恢复了王政复辟时期喜剧的机智和妙趣横生的对白，而摒弃了污秽的言词。19世纪初期，风俗喜剧再度销声匿迹，但自A. W. 平内罗和奥斯卡·王尔德[《认真的重要性》（1895）]，经乔治·萧伯纳和诺埃尔·科沃德，再到尼尔·西蒙、阿伦·阿克博恩、温迪·瓦色斯坦等许多杰出剧作家和其他一些当代作家之笔又得到复兴。这些喜剧中的许多作品也已被改编成电影。参阅：戴维·L. 赫斯特所著的《风俗喜剧》（1979）。

4. **闹剧**是喜剧的一种类型，其目的是逗引观众发出天真、衷心的大笑，用剧界的行话来讲就是"捧腹大笑"。为了实现这个目的，

it commonly employs highly exaggerated or caricatured types of characters, puts them into improbable and ludicrous situations, and often makes free use of sexual mix-ups, broad verbal humor, and physical bustle and horseplay. Farce was a component in the comic episodes in medieval *miracle plays*, such as the Wakefield plays *Noah* and the *Second Shepherd's Play*, and constituted the matter of the Italian *commedia dell'arte* in the Renaissance. In the English drama that has best stood the test of time, farce is usually an episode in a more complex form of comedy—examples are the knockabout scenes in Shakespeare's *The Taming of the Shrew* and *The Merry Wives of Windsor*. The plays of the French playwright Georges Feydeau (1862–1921), relying in great part on sexual humor and innuendo, are true farce throughout, as is Brandon Thomas' *Charley's Aunt*, an American play of 1892 which has often been revived, and also some of the current plays of Tom Stoppard. Many of the movies by such comedians as Charlie Chaplin, Buster Keaton, W. C. Fields, the Marx brothers, and Woody Allen are excellent farce, as are the Monty Python films and television episodes. Farce is often employed in single scenes of musical revues, and is the standard fare of television "situation comedies." It should be noted that the term "farce," or sometimes "farce comedy," is applied also to plays—a supreme example is Oscar Wilde's *The Importance of Being Earnest* (1895)—in which exaggerated character types find themselves in ludicrous situations in the course of an improbable plot, but which achieve their comic effects not by broad humor and bustling action, but by the sustained brilliance and wit of the dialogue. Farce is also a frequent comic tactic in the theater of the *absurd*. Refer to Robert Metcalf Smith and H. G. Rhoads, eds., *Types of Farce Comedy* (1928); Leo Hughes, *A Century of English Farce* (1956); and for the history of farce and low comedy from the Greeks to the present, Anthony Caputi, *Buffo: The Genius of Vulgar Comedy* (1978), and Albert Bermel, *Farce: A History from Aristophanes to Woody Allen* (1990).

A distinction is often made between high and low comedy. **High comedy**, as described by George Meredith in a classic essay *The Idea of Comedy* (1877), evokes "intellectual laughter"—thoughtful laughter from spectators who remain emotionally detached from the action—at the spectacle of folly, pretentiousness, and incongruity in human behavior. Meredith finds its highest form within the comedy of manners, in the combats of wit (sometimes identified now as the "love duels") between such intelligent, highly verbal, and well-matched lovers as Benedick and Beatrice in Shakespeare's *Much Ado about Nothing* (1598–99) and Mirabell and Millamant in Congreve's *The Way of the World* (1700). **Low comedy**, at the other extreme, has little or no intellectual appeal, but undertakes to arouse laughter by jokes, or "gags," and by slapstick humor and boisterous or clownish physical activity; it is, therefore, one of the common components of farce.

See also *comedy of humours, tragicomedy*, and *wit, humor, and the comic*. On comedy and its varieties: G. E. Duckworth, *The Nature of Roman Comedy* (1952); Elder Olson, *The Theory of Comedy* (1968); Andrew Stott, *Comedy*

闹剧常运用高度夸张或极其滑稽的各类人物形象，把他们安排在出人意料而又荒唐的情境中，并大量采用插科打诨、粗俗的口头幽默和肢体嬉闹与喧哗等手法以求得闹剧效果。闹剧是中世纪奇迹剧（例如韦克菲尔德的戏剧《挪亚》和《牧人剧之二》）中喜剧情节的一部分，并且是文艺复兴时期意大利即兴喜剧的组成部分。在历史悠久的英国戏剧中，形式比较复杂的喜剧中往往包含闹剧的成分，如莎士比亚的《驯悍记》和《温莎的风流娘儿们》中的喧嚣场面。法国剧作家乔治·费多（1862—1921）在剧作中大量运用与性有关的幽默和暗示，完全属于闹剧；同样，布兰登·托马斯1892年创作的美国剧《查利的姑姑》也是一部彻头彻尾的闹剧，曾经多次公演。汤姆·斯托帕德的一些当代剧也属闹剧之列。喜剧演员查理·卓别林、巴斯特·基顿、W. C. 菲尔兹、马克斯兄弟和伍迪·艾伦出演的电影，以及"巨蟒小组"出演的电视剧和电影，也是极其出色的闹剧。独幕音乐表演剧与电视"情节喜剧"也常常采取闹剧形式。需要注意的是，术语"闹剧"有时称为"闹剧喜剧"，也可用来指代戏剧 [王尔德的《认真的重要性》(1895) 是一个卓著的例子] 中夸张的类型人物发现他们在一种不可置信的情节中处于滑稽荒唐的情境中，但他们获取的喜剧效果并非来自粗俗的幽默和喧嚣的场面，而是来自连续的对白所体现的机智和才华。闹剧也是荒诞戏剧里一种常见的喜剧手法。参阅：罗伯特·梅特卡夫·史密斯与 H. G. 罗兹合编的《不同类型的闹剧》(1928)；利奥·休斯所著的《百年英国闹剧》(1956)；关于自古希腊至今闹剧和世俗喜剧的发展史，参阅：安东尼·卡普蒂所著的《演滑稽角色的男低音歌手：低俗喜剧的天才》(1978)，阿尔伯特·伯梅尔所著的《闹剧史：从阿里斯托芬到伍迪·艾伦》(1990)。

喜剧常被划分为高雅喜剧和世俗喜剧两种类型。正如乔治·梅瑞狄斯在其经典文章"喜剧的观念"(1877) 中所阐述的，**高雅喜剧**通过展示人们的愚蠢、自负、失检等行为，引发观众"理性的笑声"，即在观众对剧情保持感情上的超然态度的基础上发出的深思笑声。梅瑞狄斯在风俗喜剧中发现了高雅喜剧的最高表现形式，这种形式体现在聪慧、善辩、匹配的情侣之间的智斗中（有时相当于现今的"爱情决斗"），如莎士比亚《无事生非》(1598—1599) 中的班尼迪克和比阿特丽斯，以及康格里夫《如此世道》(1700) 中的米拉贝和米拉芒。作为另一极端的**世俗喜剧**很少或不去触动观众的理性，只是利用笑话或"插科打诨"，或借用粗鲁的幽默、喧闹或丑角表演来引人发笑。因此，它通常是闹剧的组成部分。

参见：*性格喜剧*；*悲喜剧*；*机智、幽默与滑稽*。有关喜剧及其各种类型，参阅：G. E. 达克沃思所著的《爱情喜剧的本质》(1952)；埃尔德·奥尔森所著的《喜剧理论》(1968)；安德鲁·斯托特所著的《喜剧》(2005)。关于喜剧与

(2005). On the relation of comedy to myth and ritual: Northrop Frye, *Anatomy of Criticism* (1957), pp. 163–86; C. L. Barber, *Shakespeare's Festive Comedy* (1959). On comedy in cinema and television: Horace Newcomb, *Television: The Most Popular Art* (1974), chapter 2; Steve Neale and Frank Krutnik, *Popular Film and Television Comedy* (1990).

comedy of humours: A type of comedy developed by Ben Jonson, the *Elizabethan* playwright, based on the ancient physiological theory of the "four humours" that was still current in Jonson's time. The **humours** were held to be the four primary fluids—blood, phlegm, choler (or yellow bile), and melancholy (or black bile)—whose "temperament" (mixture) was held to determine a person's both physical condition and type of character. An imbalance of one or another humour in a temperament was said to produce four kinds of disposition, whose names have survived the underlying theory: sanguine (from the Latin "sanguis," blood), phlegmatic, choleric, and melancholic. In Jonson's comedy of humours each of the major characters has a preponderant humour that gives him a characteristic distortion or eccentricity of disposition. Jonson expounds his theory in the "Induction" to his play *Every Man in His Humour* (1598) and exemplifies the mode in his later comedies; often he identifies the ruling disposition of a **humours character** by his or her name: "Zeal-of-the-land Busy," "Dame Purecraft," "Wellbred." The Jonsonian type of humours character appears in plays by other Elizabethans, and remained influential in the *comedies of manners* by William Wycherley, Sir George Etheredge, William Congreve, and other dramatists of the English Restoration, 1660–1700.

comedy of manners: 55; *57*.

comedy, sentimental: 361.

comic, the: 420; *353*.

comic relief: Comic relief is the introduction of comic characters, speeches, or scenes in a serious or tragic work, especially a drama. Such elements were almost universal in *Elizabethan tragedy*. Sometimes they occur merely as episodes of dialogue or horseplay for purposes of alleviating tension and adding variety. In more carefully wrought plays, however, they are integrated with the plot, in a way that counterpoints and enhances the serious or tragic significance. Examples of such complex uses of comic elements are the gravediggers in *Hamlet* (V. i.), the scene of the drunken porter after the murder of the king in *Macbeth* (II. iii.), the Falstaff scenes in *1 Henry IV*, and the roles of Mercutio and the old nurse in *Romeo and Juliet*.

See Thomas De Quincey's famed essay "On the Knocking at the Gate in *Macbeth*" (1823).

commedia dell'arte: Commedia dell'arte was a form of comic drama developed about the mid-sixteenth century by guilds of professional Italian actors.

神话、礼仪的关系，参阅：诺斯罗普·弗莱所著的《批评的剖析》(1957) 第 163—186 页；C. L. 巴伯所著的《莎士比亚的欢庆喜剧》(1959)。关于影视喜剧，参阅：霍勒斯·纽科姆所著的《电视：最受人欢迎的艺术》(1974) 第 2 章；史蒂夫·尼尔与弗兰克·克鲁特尼克合著的《受欢迎的电影及电视喜剧》(1990)。

Comedy of Humours：性格喜剧

性格喜剧是*伊丽莎白时代*剧作家本·琼森根据当时仍然流行的古代有关"人体四液"的生理学理论发展起来的一种喜剧类型。所谓的**人体四液**，是指当时认为的四种主要体液——血液、粘液、胆液（或称黄胆汁）、郁液（或称黑汁），它们的"质"（合成）被认为决定着一个人的身体状况和性格特征。据说任何一种体液质的失调都会导致形成四种性情——乐观自信型（源自拉丁语"血红色"）、迟缓冷漠型、暴躁易怒型、消沉忧郁型。这些名称一直沿用至今。在琼森的性格喜剧中，主要角色无一不是体液失调的，各自的主导体液造就了他们畸形或怪癖的秉性。琼森在他的喜剧《人各有癖》(1598) 的"前言"中详尽地阐述了自己的理论，并在后期的喜剧创作中为这一模式作了示范；他通常把**性格人物**的名称与其主要性格倾向联系起来，如"繁忙之地的热心人""手艺完美女爵""正人君子"。琼森式的性格人物类型也出现在伊丽莎白时代的其他剧作中，并且对威廉·威彻利的*风俗喜剧*、乔治·埃思里奇爵士、威廉·康格里夫及其他一些英国王政复辟时期（1660—1700）的剧作家产生过一定影响。

comedy of manners：风俗喜剧　　55；*57*。

comedy, sentimental：感伤喜剧　　361。

comic, the：滑稽　　420；*353*。

Comic Relief：喜剧性调剂

喜剧性调剂就是把带有喜剧色彩的角色、话语或场景引入严肃剧或悲剧、尤其是戏剧作品中的一种创作手法。*伊丽莎白时期的悲剧*作品中几乎都有这些成分。这些成分有时只是作为穿插对话或喧闹的情节，起到缓解紧张气氛、丰富剧情的作用。但在优秀的戏剧中，这些起调剂作用的成分则是情节的组成部分，用于烘托强化严肃或悲剧的意义。喜剧成分用于悲剧的例子有莎士比亚《哈姆雷特》（第五幕第一场）中的掘墓人；《麦克白》第二幕第三场中，国王被害后仆役的醉酒；《亨利四世》第一场中福斯塔夫的一出戏；《罗密欧与朱丽叶》中茂丘西奥与老保姆的作用。

参见：托马斯·德·昆西所写的经典文章"论《麦克白》中的敲门声"(1823)。

Commedia dell'arte：即兴喜剧

即兴喜剧起源于 16 世纪中期的意大利，是由职业的意大利戏班演出的一种

Playing *stock characters*, the actors largely improvised the dialogue around a given **scenario**—a term that still denotes a brief outline of a drama, indicating merely the entrances of the main characters and the general course of the action. In a typical play, a pair of young lovers outwit a rich old father ("Pantaloon"), aided by a clever and intriguing servant ("Harlequin"), in a plot enlivened by the buffoonery of "Punch" and other clowns. Wandering Italian troupes played in all the large cities of Renaissance Europe and influenced writers of comedies in Elizabethan England and later in France. Shakespeare's *The Taming of the Shrew*, Rostand's *Cyrano de Bergerac*, and Molière's *The Misanthrope* drew on conventions of the commedia. The modern puppet shows of Punch and Judy are descendants of this old Italian comedy, emphasizing its components of *farce* and buffoonery.

See Kathleen M. Lea, *Italian Popular Comedy, 1560–1620* (2 vols., 1934); Martin Green and John Swan, *The Triumph of Pierrot* (rev. 1993), which traces the influence of Pierrot from 1860 to 1930 and beyond; Domenico Pietropaolo, ed., *The Science of Buffoonery: Theory and History of the Commedia dell'Arte* (1989). See also two books by Robert F. Storey: *Pierrot: A Critical History of a Mask* (1978) and *Pierrots on the Stage of Desire* (1985), which tracks the persistence of Pierrot in nineteenth-century French literature and pantomime.

common measure (in meter): **376**.

Commonwealth Period: 281.

competence (linguistic): **195**.

complication (in a plot): **296**.

conceit: Originally meaning a concept or image, "conceit" came to be the term for figures of speech which establish a striking parallel, usually ingeniously elaborate, between two very dissimilar things or situations. (See *figurative language*.) English poets of the sixteenth and seventeenth centuries adapted the term from the Italian "concetto." Two types of conceit are often distinguished by specific names:

1. The **Petrarchan conceit** is a type of figure used in love poems that had been novel and effective in the Italian poetry of Petrarch, but became hackneyed in some of his imitators among the Elizabethan sonneteers. (See the entry *sonnet*.) The figure consists of detailed, ingenious, and often exaggerated comparisons applied to the disdainful mistress, as cold and cruel as she is beautiful, and to the distresses and despair of her worshipful lover. (See *courtly love*.) Sir Thomas Wyatt (1503–42), for example, in the sonnet "My Galley Chargèd with Forgetfulness" that he translated from Petrarch, compares the lover's state in detail to a ship laboring in a storm. Another sonnet of Petrarch's translated by Wyatt begins with an *oxymoron*

喜剧形式。演员在演出*定型人物*时，根据剧情说明——该术语仍然用于指代一部戏剧的简洁概要，注明剧中主要人物的出场顺序以及剧情的大体进程——尽情地自编台词，即兴表演。典型的即兴喜剧往往描写一对青年恋人得到足智多谋的仆人（"丑角"）的帮助，智胜有钱的老父亲（"傻老头"），同时通过"潘趣"和其他丑角的插科打诨活跃剧情。文艺复兴时期，意大利戏班的足迹遍布欧洲各主要城市，他们表演的即兴喜剧对英国伊丽莎白时期的许多喜剧作家以及后来的法国戏剧家莫里哀都产生过一定影响。莎士比亚的《驯悍记》、罗斯唐的《西拉诺·德·贝尔热拉克》和莫里哀的《恨世者》都吸收了喜剧的传统手法。现代的"潘趣和朱迪"（滑稽木偶剧）就是从这种古老的意大利喜剧演变而来，主要展示其*闹剧*性和插科打诨的表演。

参阅：凯瑟琳·M.李所著的两卷本《1560—1620年间意大利流行喜剧》（1934）；马丁·格林与约翰·斯旺合著的《小丑的胜利》（1993年修订版），描述了1860—1930年间及之后丑角的影响；多米尼克·彼得罗保罗主编的《滑稽的科学：即兴喜剧的理论与历史》（1989）。也可参阅罗伯特·F.斯托里所著的两本书：《小丑：面具批评史》（1978）和《欲望舞台上的小丑》（1985），描述了丑角在19世纪法国文学和哑剧中的持续存在。

common measure (in meter)：（格律中的）普通韵律　376。
Commonwealth Period：共和国时期　281。
competence (linguistic)：（语言学中的）语言能力　194。
complication (in a plot)：（情节中的）纠葛　296。
Conceit：巧思妙喻

"巧思妙喻"原指概念或意象，后来用作修辞术语表示令人称奇的对比：即在两类截然不同的事物或情形之间炮制出的别出心裁的类比。（参见：*比喻语*。）该术语由16、17世纪的英国诗人从意大利语"矫揉造作的文体"（concetto）改写而来。巧思妙喻通常以具体名称分为两类：

1. **彼特拉克式巧思妙喻**是用于爱情诗歌中的一种修辞格，在意大利诗人彼特拉克的笔下显示出其新奇、动人的修辞效果，但经伊丽莎白时期有些十四行诗人的模仿而变得陈腐乏味。（参见：*十四行诗*。）这种修辞格以细腻、精巧、总是夸张的对比手法形容少女的高傲，其冷酷淡漠恰似其美貌，同时表现她的崇拜者的苦闷与失望。（参见：*骑士恋*。）例如，托马斯·怀亚特爵士（1503—1542）在他翻译的彼特拉克的十四行诗《被遗忘的航船》中，把求爱者的困境细腻地比喻成一艘在惊涛骇浪中挣扎行进的航船。在怀亚特翻译的另一首彼特拉克的十四行诗中，以*逆喻*（又称"矛盾修辞法"）开篇，

describing the opposing passions experienced by a courtly sufferer from the disease of love:

> I find no peace; and all my war is done;
> I fear and hope; I burn and freeze in ice.

Shakespeare (who at times employed this type of conceit himself) *parodied* some standard comparisons by Petrarchan sonneteers in his Sonnet 130, beginning

> My mistress' eyes are nothing like the sun;
> Coral is far more red than her lips' red:
> If snow be white, why then her breasts are dun;
> If hairs be wires, black wires grow on her head.

2. The **metaphysical conceit** is a characteristic figure in the work of John Donne (1572–1631) and other *metaphysical poets* of the seventeenth century. It was described by Samuel Johnson (1709–84), in a famed passage in his "Life of Cowley," as "wit" which

> is a kind of *discordia concors*; a combination of dissimilar images, or discovery of occult resemblances in things apparently unlike....
> The most heterogeneous ideas are yoked by violence together.

The metaphysical poets exploited all knowledge—commonplace or esoteric, practical, theological, or philosophical, true or fabulous—for the vehicles of these figures; and their comparisons, whether succinct or expanded, were often novel and witty, and at their best startlingly effective. In sharp contrast to both the concepts and figures of conventional Petrarchism is John Donne's "The Flea," a poem that uses a flea who has bitten both lovers as the basic reference for the lyric speaker's argument against a lady's resistance to his advances. In Donne's "The Canonization," as the poetic argument develops, the comparisons for the relationship between lovers move from the area of commerce and business, through actual and mythical birds and diverse forms of historical memorials, to a climax which equates the sexual acts and the moral status of worldly lovers with the ascetic life and heavenly destination of unworldly saints. The best known sustained conceit is Donne's parallel (in "A Valediction: Forbidding Mourning") between the continuing relationship of his and his lady's soul during their physical parting, and the coordinated movements of the two feet of a draftsman's compass. An oft-cited instance of the chilly ingenuity of the metaphysical conceit when it is overdriven is Richard Crashaw's description, in his mid-seventeenth-century poem "Saint Mary Magdalene," of the tearful eyes of the repentant Magdalene as

> two faithful fountains
> Two walking baths, two weeping motions,
> Portable and compendious oceans.

描写求爱者受相思病煎熬对爱情既幸福又痛楚的两种截然不同又交织在一起的情感体验：

> 我无法平静；我的斗争已经结束；
> 我害怕又渴望；我燃烧又冰冻。

莎士比亚（他本人有时也采用巧思妙喻手法）在他第130首十四行诗中戏谑模仿过一些彼特拉克式十四行诗人的惯用比喻：

> 我情人的眼睛可一点不像太阳；
> 珊瑚都比她的嘴唇要红润得多：
> 如果雪能算白，她的胸膛就暗黑无色；
> 如果秀发如丝，她的头上就满是黑铁。

2. **玄学派巧思妙喻**是约翰·多恩（1572—1631）和17世纪其他一些玄学派诗人特有的一种修辞手法。塞缪尔·约翰逊（1709—1784）在其"考利传"（1779—1781）里一个著名段落中，把这种巧思妙喻描绘成一种"机智"，它

> 是一种对立物之间的捏合；是把截然不同的意象结合在一起，或是从外表绝不相似的事物中发现玄妙的相似点……把最不伦不类的思想概念强行捆到一起。

玄学派诗人用作喻矢的素材包罗万象：平凡的、深奥的、现实的、神学的、哲学的、真实的或传说的，应有尽有；这些比喻，无论其简洁还是深邃，都表现出新奇诙谐、妙趣横生、令人称奇的修辞效果。约翰·多恩的《跳蚤》与传统的彼特拉克式概念和比喻都形成了鲜明的对照，诗中以跳蚤叮咬一对恋人为基本参照，比喻抒情说话者反对女子对他的追求的反抗。在多恩的《圣徒追封》中，随着诗歌主题的展开，多恩表现恋人关系的比喻由经商、买卖到现实和神话中的各种鸟类以及历史记载中的不同形式，直至进入高潮时，把世俗情侣间的性行为和道德状况同超凡圣徒的禁欲生活和升天理想等同起来。多恩最著名的巧思妙喻（在《莫为分离悲伤》中）莫过于把自己和情人各居天涯、心心相印的关系比作绘图员所用圆规两脚的协调动作。理查德·克拉肖在其17世纪中期的诗作《圣女玛丽·马格德琳》中以其超常的夸张才思创造的玄学派巧思妙喻，成为人们广为引用的范例，诗人这样描写马格德琳忏悔时的一双泪眼：

> 两汪忠实的喷泉
> 两个会走的清池，两个哭泣的动体，
> 随身携带的丰盈的海洋。

The metaphysical conceit fell out of favor in the eighteenth century, when it came to be regarded as strained and unnatural. But with the strong revival of interest in the metaphysical poets during the early decades of the twentieth century, a number of modern poets exploited this type of figure. Examples are T. S. Eliot's comparison of the evening to "a patient etherized upon a table" at the beginning of "The Love Song of J. Alfred Prufrock," and the series of startling figurative vehicles in Dylan Thomas' "In Memory of Ann Jones." The vogue for such conceits extended even to popular love songs, in the 1920s and later, by well-educated composers such as Cole Porter, for example:

> You're the top!
> You're the Coliseum
> You're the top!
> You're the Louvre Museum.
> You're a melody from a symphony by Strauss
> You're a Bendel bonnet,
> A Shakespeare sonnet,
> You're Mickey Mouse.

Refer to Rosemod Tuve, *Elizabethan and Metaphysical Imagery* (1947), and K. K. Ruthven, *The Conceit* (1969).

conceptual metaphor: 53.

concrete and abstract: In standard philosophical usage a "concrete term" is a word that denotes a particular person or physical object, and an "abstract term" denotes either a class of things or else (as in "brightness," "beauty," "evil," "despair") qualities that exist only as attributes of particular persons or things. A sentence, accordingly, is said to be concrete if it makes an assertion about a particular subject (T. S. Eliot's "Grishkin is nice ..."), and abstract if it makes an assertion about an abstract subject (Alexander Pope's "Hope springs eternal in the human breast"). Critics of literature, however, often use these terms in an extended way: a passage is called abstract if it represents its subject matter in general or nonsensuous words or with only a thin realization of its experienced qualities; it is called concrete if it represents its subject matter with striking particularity and sensuous detail. In his "Ode to Psyche" (1820) John Keats'

> 'Mid hush'd, cool-rooted flowers, fragrant-eyed,
> Blue, silver-white, and budded Tyrian

is a concrete description of a locale which interinvolves qualities that are perceived by four different senses: hearing, touch, sight, and smell. And in the opening of his "Ode to a Nightingale," Keats communicates concretely, by a combination of literal and figurative language, how it feels, physically, to experience the full-throated song of the nightingale:

至 18 世纪，玄学派巧思妙喻因被视为矫揉造作而失去人们的青睐，但在 20 世纪初期，随着人们对玄学派诗人再度表现出极大的兴趣，一些现代诗人也采用了玄学派的比喻手法。例如：T. S. 艾略特在《普鲁弗洛克的情歌》中把傍晚比喻成"昏倒在桌子上的患者"。迪兰·托马斯在《纪念安·琼斯》中也运用了一连串令人叹服的比喻。这种巧思妙喻的盛行甚至波及 1920 年代及其后一些由受过良好教育的作曲家所创作的流行情歌中，如科尔·波特创作的《你是最棒的》。

> 你是最棒的！
> 你是罗马竞技场
> 你是最棒的！
> 你是卢浮博物馆。
> 你是施特劳斯交响曲中的旋律
> 你是班德尔软帽，
> 莎士比亚的十四行诗，
> 你是米老鼠。

参阅：罗斯蒙德·图夫所著的《伊丽莎白时期意象与玄学派意象》(1947) 和 K. K. 鲁思文所著的《巧思妙喻》(1969)。

conceptual metaphor：概念隐喻　　53。

Concrete and Abstract：具体与抽象

传统哲学把用于表示特定的人或物的名词界定为"具体名词"，而把表示一类事物或特定的人或物的属性的名词（如"明亮""美丽""罪恶""绝望"）界定为"抽象名词"。相应地，阐明一个特定主体的句子被认为是具体的（如 T. S. 艾略特的句子"格里施金是个好姑娘……"），阐述一个抽象主体的句子则为抽象的（如亚历山大·蒲柏的"但愿人心春长在"）。然而，文学批评家常把"具体"和"抽象"这两个概念加以引申运用到文学批评中：如果一篇文章只是概括性地或用非感官词汇陈述其题材，或者对其被体验过的品质陈述得远不够详尽，那么这篇文章就是抽象的；如果题材陈述得鲜明详尽，并运用具体细腻的感官词汇，那么就是具体的。如济慈《心灵颂》(1820) 中的一段描写：

> 在寂静、清凉中绽放的花丛里，看着芬芳的、
> 蓝色的、银白色的和紫红色的花蕾

这是对一场景的具体描写，其中触及四种感官功能：听觉、触觉、视觉和味觉。而在《夜莺颂》的开头，济慈并用直叙与比喻两种手法表述了聆听夜莺放声歌唱时内心感受的细节：

> My heart aches, and a drowsy numbness pains
> My sense, as though of hemlock I had drunk,
> Or emptied some dull opiate to the drains....

It is frequently asserted that "poetry is concrete," or, as John Crowe Ransom put it in *The World's Body* (1938), that its proper subject is "the rich, contingent materiality of things." Most poetry is certainly more concrete than other modes of language, especially in its use of *imagery*. It should be kept in mind, however, that poets do not hesitate to use abstract language when the area of reference or artistic purpose calls for it. Keats, though he was one of the most concrete of poets, began *Endymion* with a sentence composed of abstract terms:

> A thing of beauty is a joy forever:
> Its loveliness increases; it will never
> Pass into nothingness; ...

And some of the most moving and memorable passages in poetry are not concrete; for example, the statement about God in Dante's *Paradiso*, "In His will is our peace," or the bleak comment by Edgar in the last act of *King Lear*,

> Men must endure
> Their going hence, even as their coming hither;
> Ripeness is all.

See John Crowe Ransom, *The World's Body* (1938); Richard H. Fogle, *Imagery of Keats and Shelley* (1949), chapter 5.

concrete poetry: Concrete poetry is a recent term for an ancient poetic type, called **pattern poems** or **shaped verse**, that experiments with the visual shape in which a text is presented on the page. Some Greek poets, beginning in the third century BC, shaped a text in the form of the object that the poem describes or suggests. In the Renaissance and seventeenth century, a number of poets composed such patterned forms, in which the lines vary in length in such a way that their printed shape outlines the subject of the poem; familiar examples in English are George Herbert's "Easter Wings" and "The Altar." Prominent later experiments with pictorial or suggestive typography include Stéphane Mallarmé's *Un Coup de dés* ("A Throw of Dice," 1897) and Guillaume Apollinaire's *Calligrammes* (1918); in the latter publication, for example, Apollinaire printed the poem "Il pleut" ("It rains") so that the component letters trickle down the page.

The vogue of **concrete poetry** is a worldwide movement that was largely inaugurated in 1953 by the Swiss poet Eugen Gomringer. The practice of such poetry varies widely, but the common feature is the use of a radically reduced language, typed or printed in such a way as to force the visible text on the reader's attention as a physical object and not simply as a transparent carrier of its meanings. Many concrete poems, in fact, cannot be read at all in the conventional way, since they consist of a single word or phrase which is

>我的心在痛，困顿和麻木
>
>刺进了感官，有如饮过毒鸩，
>
>又像是刚刚把鸦片吞服……
>
>（查良铮译）

一般认为"诗歌是具体的"，或如约翰·克罗·兰塞姆曾在《世界的躯体》(1938) 中所言：诗歌恰当的主题是"事物丰富多变的物质性"。当然，大多数诗歌比语言的其他形式显得更加具体，尤其体现在意象描绘方面。然而，应该记住，一旦诗歌的所指或艺术创造目的需要时，诗人也会毫不犹豫地运用抽象语言。济慈是行文最为具体的诗人之一，但在《恩底弥翁》这首诗的开头，他全部使用抽象词语：

>美丽的东西是永恒的：
>
>它的美随时间而增；也永远不会
>
>化为无物；
>
>（王佐良译）

一些最动人心弦和令人难忘的诗句也并非是具体的。例如：但丁在《天国篇》中有关上帝的陈述："我们的安宁寓于上帝的意志之中。"又如《李尔王》最后一幕中埃德加凄凉的评论：

>人们的生死都不是可以
>
>勉强求到的，你应该
>
>耐心忍受天命的安排。
>
>（朱生豪译）

参阅：约翰·克罗·兰瑟姆所著的《世界的躯体》(1938)；理查德·H.福格尔所著的《济慈和雪莱的意象》(1949) 第5章。

Concrete Poetry：具像诗

具像诗是近来人们对古代**图案诗**或**形状诗/拟形诗**的一种称谓，其诗行经过排列在页面上构成视觉形状。早在公元前3世纪，一些希腊诗人就开始把他们的诗文组成诗歌所要表现或暗示的事物的形状。在文艺复兴时期和17世纪，许多诗人都创作过这样的图案诗，诗中诗行长短不一，以致排印后能勾画出诗歌所表现的主题；英诗中常见的例子有乔治·赫伯特的《复活节的双翼》和《祭坛》。此后，以图像或排印造型为试验创作出的杰出具像诗有斯蒂芬·马拉梅的《骰子一掷绝不会破坏偶然性》(1897) 和纪尧姆·阿波利奈尔的《加利格朗姆》(1918)。阿波利奈尔后来发表的图案诗《雨》经过排印，组成字母犹如纷纷滴落的雨珠。

具像诗在世界范围内的风行，很大程度上是由瑞士诗人尤金·冈林格于1953年发起的。此类诗作千姿百态，然而它们的共同特征在于使用极度压缩的文字，经过书写排印使诗文聚合成一个实物图像映入读者的眼帘，而非仅仅是其含义的清晰的载体。事实上，很多具像诗是根本无法用传统方式去阅读的，因为它们包含的

subjected to systematic alterations in the order and position of the component letters, or else are composed of fragments of words, or of nonsense syllables, or even of single letters, numbers, and marks of punctuation. In their shaped patterns, concrete poets often use a variety of type fonts and sizes and different colors of type, and sometimes supplement the text with drawings or photographs, while some of their shapes, called "kinetic," evolve as we turn the pages.

America had its own tradition of pattern poetry in the typographical experiments of Ezra Pound, and especially e. e. cummings; see, for example, cummings' "r-p-o-p-h-e-s-s-a-g-r" in which, to represent the way we at first perceive vaguely, then identify, the leaping insect, scrambled sequences of letters gradually order themselves into the word "grasshopper." Prominent practitioners of pattern poems in the shape of the things that they describe or meditate upon are May Swenson (*Iconographs*, 1970) and John Hollander (*Types of Shape*, 1991). Other Americans who have been influenced by the international vogue for concrete poetry include Emmett Williams, Jonathan Williams, and Mary Ellen Solt.

Collections of concrete poems in a variety of languages are Emmett Williams, ed., *An Anthology of Concrete Poetry* (1967); Mary Ellen Solt, ed. (with a useful historical introduction), *Concrete Poetry: A World View* (1968); see also Dick Higgins, *Pattern Poetry: Guide to an Unknown Literature* (1987). For a noted early eighteenth-century attack on pattern poems, see Addison's comments on "false wit" in the *Spectator*, Nos. 58 and 63.

concretize (in reading): **289**.

confessional poetry: Confessional poetry designates a type of narrative and lyric verse, given impetus by the American Robert Lowell's *Life Studies* (1959), which deals with the facts and intimate mental and physical experiences of the poet's own life. Much confessional poetry was written in rebellion against the demand for impersonality by T. S. Eliot and the *New Critics*. By its secular subject matter, it differs from religious *spiritual autobiography* in the lineage of Augustine's *Confessions* (c. AD 400). It differs also from poems of the *Romantic Period* representing the poet's own circumstances, experiences, and feelings, such as William Wordsworth's "Tintern Abbey" and Samuel Taylor Coleridge's "Dejection: An Ode," in the candor and sometimes startling detail with which the confessional poet reveals private or clinical matters about himself or herself, including sexual experiences, mental anguish and illness, experiments with drugs, and suicidal impulses. Confessional poems were written by Allen Ginsberg, Sylvia Plath, Anne Sexton, John Berryman, and other American poets. See Diane Middlebrook, *Anne Sexton: A Biography* (1991); "What Was Confessional Poetry?" in *The Columbia History of American Poetry*, ed. Jay Parini (1993); Adam Kirsch, *The Wounded Surgeon* (2005).

confidant: A confidant (the feminine form is "confidante") is a character in a drama or novel who plays only a minor role in the action, but serves the

只是能适应其组成字母排列顺序和位置的体系变换的一个单词或短语，或者是由支离破碎的字词、毫无意义的音节，甚至是单一的字母、数字和标点符号组成的。在具像诗的造型上，诗人常会使用不同的印刷字体、型号和油墨颜色，有时还配以插图或照片，有些被称为"活性具像诗"的造型还会随页面的翻动而演变。

美国拥有它自己的具像诗的传统，埃兹拉·庞德，尤其是 e. e. 卡明斯曾经从事过图案诗的创作实验。例如卡明斯的作品"r-p-o-h-e-s-s-a-g-r"，它表现的是我们起初依稀地觉察到，继而认定是跳跃的蝗虫的反应过程，随着这个反应过程，拼凑起来的字母也逐渐组合成"蝗虫"（grasshopper）这个字。以其所描述或沉思冥想的某一事物形状从事图案诗创作的著名诗人是玛丽·斯温森 [《图像》(1970)] 和约翰·霍兰德 [《图像的类型》(1991)]。受到具像诗世界性风潮影响的其他美国诗人有：埃米特·威廉斯、乔纳森·威廉斯、玛丽·埃伦·索尔特。

不同语言的具像诗集可以参阅：埃米特·威廉斯主编的《具像诗选》(1967)；玛丽·埃伦·索尔特主编的《具像诗：世界视角》(1968)，其中包括一些有价值的历史性回顾；也可参阅：迪克·希金斯所著的《图案诗：一种鲜为人知的文学的指南》(1987)。18 世纪早期抨击具像诗的著名论文有艾迪生发表在《旁观者》第 58、63 期上的评论文章"虚假的机智"。

concretize (in reading)：(阅读中的) 具体化　289。

Confessional Poetry：自白诗

自白诗指的是在美国人罗伯特·洛威尔的《人生写照》(1959) 的推动下流行起来的一种叙事和抒情的诗歌形式，用以表现诗人自我生活中的真实事件、私人的内心写照和肉体体验。许多自白诗是为反对 T. S. 艾略特和*新批评家*所倡导的客观性写作要求而兴起的。有别于以奥古斯丁《忏悔录》（约公元 400 年）系谱为代表的宗教式*精神自传*，自白诗表现的是世俗主题。自白诗也有别于*浪漫主义时期*的诗歌，后者描写诗人的境遇、经历和情怀，如威廉·华兹华斯的《丁登寺》和塞缪尔·泰勒·柯勒律治的《沮丧颂》；自白诗则直言不讳地披露诗人自己的一些令人瞠目结舌或客观如实的生活细节，包括性体验、精神痛楚和疾病、吸毒、自杀冲动。创作自白诗的诗人有艾伦·金斯堡、西尔维娅·普拉斯、安·塞克斯顿、约翰·贝里曼和其他一些美国诗人。参阅：戴安娜·米德尔布鲁克所著的《安妮·塞克斯顿传》(1991)；杰伊·帕里尼主编的《哥伦比亚美国诗歌史》(1993) 中的"何谓自白诗？"；亚当·基尔希所著的《受伤的手术师》(2005)。

Confidant：心腹

心腹（其阴性形式是"confidante"）是戏剧或小说作品中的一种配角，他／她

protagonist as a trusted friend to whom he or she confesses intimate thoughts, problems, and feelings. In drama the confidant provides the playwright with a plausible device for communicating to the audience the knowledge, state of mind, and intentions of a principal character without the use of stage devices such as the *soliloquy* or the *aside*; examples are Hamlet's friend Horatio in Shakespeare's *Hamlet*, and Cleopatra's maid Charmian in his *Antony and Cleopatra*.

In prose fiction a famed confidant is Dr. Watson in Arthur Conan Doyle's stories about Sherlock Holmes (1887 and following). The device is particularly useful to those modern writers who, like Henry James, have largely renounced the novelist's earlier privileges of having access to a character's state of mind and of intruding into the narrative in order to communicate such information to the reader. (See *point of view*.) James applied to the confidant the term **ficelle**, French for the string by which the puppeteer manages his puppets. Discussing Maria Gostrey, Strether's confidante in *The Ambassadors*, James remarks that she is a "ficelle" who is not, "in essence, Strether's friend. She is the reader's friend much rather" (James, *The Art of the Novel*, ed. R. P. Blackmur, 1934, pp. 321–22).

See W. J. Harvey, *Character and the Novel* (1965).

conflict (in a plot): **294**.

connotation and denotation: In a widespread literary usage, the **denotation** of a word is its primary signification or reference; its **connotation** is the range of secondary or associated significations and feelings which it commonly suggests or implies. Thus "home" denotes the house where one lives, but connotes privacy, intimacy, and coziness; that is the reason real estate agents like to use "home" instead of "house" in their advertisements. "Horse" and "steed" denote the same quadruped, but "steed" has a different connotation that derives from the chivalric or romantic narratives in which this word was often used.

The connotation of a word is only a potential range of secondary significations; which part of these connotations are evoked depends on the way the word is used in a particular context. Poems typically establish contexts that bring into play some part of the connotative as well as the denotative meaning of words. In his poem "Virtue" George Herbert wrote,

> Sweet day, so cool, so calm, so bright,
> The bridal of the earth and sky....

The denotation of "bridal"—a union between human beings—serves as part of the *ground* for applying the word as a *metaphor* to the union of earth and sky; but the specific context in which the word occurs also evokes such connotations of "bridal" as sacred, joyous, and ceremonial. (Note that "marriage" although metrically and denotatively equivalent to "bridal," would have been less richly significant in this context, because more commonplace in its connotation.) Even the way a word is spelled may alter its connotation.

进入情节的机会不多，但却是男女主人公值得信赖，可以吐露心声、焦虑和情感的密友。因此，剧作家可以巧妙地借助这种配角向观众表明主人公的身世、情思和意向，而不必使用*内心独白*或*旁白*之类的舞台表现手法。例如：莎士比亚《哈姆雷特》中哈姆雷特的朋友霍拉旭，《安东尼与克莉奥佩特拉》中克莉奥佩特拉的女仆卡尔蒙。

阿瑟·柯南道尔的舍洛克·福尔摩斯故事（1887 年及其后）中的华生博士是小说中运用心腹的典范。对亨利·詹姆斯等现代作家而言，心腹这种表现手法显得弥足珍贵，他们已经在很大程度上放弃了以往小说家进入小说人物内心世界以及进入叙事与读者直接交流对话的特权。（参见：*视角*。）詹姆斯又称心腹为**笔偶**，该法文词原意是木偶表演者表演木偶时所用的牵线。在评价《大使》中斯特西尔的心腹玛丽亚·戈斯特雷时，詹姆斯认为，她只是个"笔偶"，"事实上，她并不是斯特西尔的朋友，而是读者的朋友。"［詹姆斯所著的《小说艺术》（1934 年 R. P. 布莱克默主编）第 321—322 页。］

参阅：W. J. 哈维所著的《人物与小说》（1965）。

conflict (in a plot)：(情节中的) 冲突　294。

Connotation and Denotation：涵义与表义

在较普遍的文学用法上，一个词的**表义**是指其基本意思或所指，其**涵义**则是指其通常所体现或隐含的第二层意义或联想和情感意义。因而，"家"就指代一个人生活的住所，但也隐含着隐私、亲密、舒适等内在涵义。正是因为这个缘故，房产商在打广告时喜欢用"家"来代替"房屋"一词。英文中"horse"和"steed"指代同一四足动物。但由于"steed"一词曾广泛用于骑士或传奇叙事作品中，因此它又有着不同的涵义。

一个词的涵义仅仅是其第二层意义中潜在的一系列意义，其中任何一种涵义的联想都取决于该词使用的特定语境。诗歌尤其是通过建立上下文来发挥字词的涵义和表义的。乔治·赫伯特《美德》一诗的开篇：

良辰凉爽，宁静，明朗，
天地婚配成双。

（赵甄陶译）

"婚礼"（bridal）一词的表义，即人和人之间的结合，用作*隐喻*天地合一的*基础*；但在特定的诗文语境中，该词的出现又使人联想到庄严、欢乐、仪式等涵义。[注："marriage"（婚礼）一词尽管在韵律和表义上与"bridal"一致，但在该语境中，其意义显得不够丰富，因为它的涵义已经趋于平淡。]词的写法甚至也有可能改变它的涵义。

John Keats, in a passage of his "Ode to a Nightingale" (1819), altered his original spelling of "fairy" to the old form "faery" in order to evoke the connotations of antiquity, as well as of the magic world of Spenser's *The Faerie Queene*.

> Charmed magic casements, opening on the foam
> Of perilous seas, in *faery* lands forlorn,

consonance: 11.

constative: 373.

constructs (social and discursive): See *social constructs*.

Contemporary Period: 277. See also *Modern Period*, in *Periods of English Literature*.

contextual criticism: 243.

conventions:
1. In one sense of the term, conventions (derived from the Latin term for "coming together") are necessary, or at least convenient, devices, accepted by tacit agreement between author and audience, for solving the problems in representing reality that are posed by a particular artistic medium. In watching a modern production of a Shakespearean play, for example, the audience accepts without question the convention by which a *proscenium* stage with three walls (or if it is a **theater in the round**, with no walls) represents a room with four walls. It also accepts the convention of characters speaking in *blank verse* instead of prose, and uttering their private thoughts in *soliloquies* and *asides*, as well as the convention by which actions presented on a single stage in less than three hours may represent events which take place in a great variety of places, and over a span of many years.
2. In a second sense of the term, conventions are conspicuous features of subject matter, form, or technique that occur repeatedly in works of literature. Conventions in this sense may be recurrent types of character, turns of plot, forms of versification, or kinds of diction and style. *Stock characters* such as the Elizabethan braggart soldier, or the languishing and fainting heroine of Victorian fiction, or the sad young men of the lost-generation novels of the 1920s, were among the conventions of their literary eras. The abrupt reform of the villain at the end of the last act was a common convention of *melodrama*. *Euphuism* in prose, and the *Petrarchan* and *metaphysical conceits* in verse, were conventional devices of style. It is now just as much a literary convention to be outspoken on sexual matters as it was to be reticent in the age of Charles Dickens and George Eliot.

约翰·济慈在其《夜莺颂》(1819) 的一节中，改用"美女 (fairy)"一词的古体形式 (faery)，为的是使人联想起其古老典雅的涵义，同时引发人们对斯宾塞《仙后》中奇境的联想。

> 蛊惑着神奇的窗扉，下面是险恶的海。
> 浪花翻滚，在那仙境，却这么荒凉。　　　　　（赵瑞蕤译）

consonance：辅音韵　11。

constative：表述句　373。

constructs (social and discursive)：(社会和话语) 建构　参见：社会建构。

Contemporary Period：当代时期　277。也可参见：英国文学各时期的划分中的现代时期。

contextual criticism：语境批评　243。

Conventions：文学惯例

1. 就该术语的第一层意义而言，文学惯例（该术语源自拉丁语，意为"聚合在一起"）是必要的或至少是一些得心应手的手法，由作家与观众达成默契共同接受，解决在再现现实时某一特定艺术形式所面临的难题。例如，在观看莎剧的现代演出时，观众会完全接受拱形舞台用三面墙（若是**圆形剧场**则没有墙壁）代表实际上有四面墙壁的屋子这一惯例。剧中人物的道白采用无韵诗而非白话，并通过内心独白和旁白道出他们的内心思绪，而且，呈现在单一舞台上不足三小时的剧情可以代表发生在很多地方且跨越数年的事件，诸如这些惯例也都被观众所接受。

2. 从该术语的第二层意义上讲，文学惯例也是反复出现在文学作品中的题材、形式和艺术手法的一些显著特征。这种意义上的文学惯例可以是常见的人物类型、惯用的情节转折手法、格律形式或各种措辞手法与风格。定型人物的例子有伊丽莎白时代作品中的吹牛士兵、维多利亚女王时代小说中忧郁憔悴时常昏厥的女主人公，以及 1920 年代"迷惘的一代"小说中的感伤青年。他们分别是各自不同文学时期的人物惯例。在全剧尾声，反面角色的幡然悔悟是情节剧常见的惯例。散文作品的尤弗伊斯体、诗歌中的彼特拉克式和玄学派巧思妙喻，则是创作风格上的惯例。当今文学作品对性问题的直率正如查尔斯·狄更斯和乔治·艾略特时代对它的回避一样都属于文学惯例。

3. In the most inclusive sense, common in structuralist criticism, all literary works, no matter how seemingly realistic, are held to be entirely constituted by literary conventions, or "codes"—of genre, plot, character, language, and so on—which a reader *naturalizes*, by assimilating these conventions into the world of discourse and experience that, in the reader's time and place, are regarded as real, or "natural." (See *structuralist criticism* and *character and characterization*.)

Invention was originally a term used in theories of *rhetoric*, and later in literary criticism, to signify the "finding" of the subject matter by an orator or a poet; it then came to signify innovative elements in a work, in contrast to the deliberate "imitation" of the forms and subjects of prior literary models. (See *imitation*.) At the present time, "invention" is often opposed to "convention" (in sense 2, above) to signify the inauguration by a writer of an unprecedented subject or theme or form or style, and the resulting work is said to possess **originality**. Repeatedly in the history of literature, innovative writers such as John Donne, Walt Whitman, James Joyce, or Virginia Woolf rebel against reigning conventions of their time to produce highly original works, only to have their inventions imitated by other writers, who thereby convert literary innovations into an additional set of literary conventions. (For a discussion of the history and uses of the concept of originality, see Thomas McFarland, *Originality and Imagination*, 1985.)

There is nothing either good or bad in the extent or obviousness of conformity to pre-existing conventions; all depends on the effectiveness of the use an individual writer makes of them. The *pastoral elegy*, for example, is one of the most conspicuously convention-bound of literary forms, yet in "Lycidas" (1638) John Milton achieved what, by wide critical agreement, ranks as one of the greatest lyrics in the language. He did this by employing the ancient pastoral rituals with freshness and power, so as to absorb an individual's death into the universal human experience of mortality, and to add to his voice the resonance of earlier pastoral laments for a poet who died young.

See M. C. Bradbrook, *Themes and Conventions of Elizabethan Tragedy* (1935); Harry Levin, "Notes on Convention," in *Perspectives of Criticism* (1950); Graham Hough, *Reflections on a Literary Revolution* (1960); and the issues *On Convention* in *New Literary History*, Vols. 13–14 (1981 and 1983). For references to *conventions* in other entries, see pages *66, 300.*

conversion: 27.

Copernican theory (kōpŭr′ nĭkan): 340.

copy-text: 402.

correspondences: 397.

cosmic irony: 186.

3. 从总体意义上说，正如结构主义批评理论通常认为的那样，一切文学作品，无论其显得多么逼真，都完全是由文学类型、情节、人物、语言等的惯例或"代码"所构成。读者通过把这些惯例同化为被他们所处的时代和地域当做真实的或"自然"的话语和经验的世界，从而归化这些惯例。（参见：*结构主义批评*、*人物与人物塑造*。）

文学创新原为修辞理论中的一个术语，后来用于文学批评，指演说家或诗人对题材的"发现"；尔后，又用以区别对以往文学模式的形式和题材的刻意"摹仿"，意指一部作品中的创新成分。（参见：*摹仿*。）目前，"文学创新"往往与"文学惯例"（与前面所述的第二层意义）恰好相反，意指作家在创作题材或主题、形式或风格上的标新立异，这样的作品被认为是**富有创造性的**。文学发展史呈现出这样一种周期反复：约翰·多恩、沃尔特·惠特曼、詹姆斯·乔伊斯、弗吉尼亚·吴尔夫等创新作家打破各自时代文坛上居于统治地位的文学惯例，创造出高度创新的作品，而他们的创新成果又经其他作家的模仿，转换成另一套新的文学惯例。[关于"创造性"这一概念的历史及应用的讨论，参见托马斯·麦克法兰所著的《创造性与想象力》(1985)。]

对原有文学惯例的摹仿在程度或明显性上并无好坏可言：一切取决于作者摹仿所产生的艺术效果。例如*牧人哀歌*是一种最显明地受文学惯例制约的文学形式，然而约翰·弥尔顿在《利西达斯》(1638)中却取得了为批评界广泛认可的成就，成为英语中最杰出的抒情诗之一。他的成功之处就在于在运用古老的田园礼仪时能赋之以新意和活力，从而把个人的死亡融入整个人类的死亡经历，同时把自己的声音汇入早期牧人哀歌悼念诗人英年早逝的共鸣声中，从而加强了自己的哀思。

参阅：M. C. 布拉德布鲁克所著的《伊丽莎白时期悲剧的主题及惯例》(1935)；哈里·莱文所著的《批评视角》(1950)中"关于文学惯例的注解"；格雷厄姆·霍夫所著的《对文学革命的反思》(1960)；相关论述参阅《新文学史》第13—14卷（1981年和1983年）中的"论文学惯例"。其他条目中提及"文学惯例"的地方，参见第66、300页。

conversion：皈依　27。

Copernican theory：哥白尼理论　340。

copy-text：复制–文本　402。

correspondences：对应　397。

cosmic irony：命运反讽　186。

counterculture: 277; 76.

country house poem: 407.

couplet: 375.

courtesy books: 339.

courtly love: A doctrine of love, together with an elaborate code governing the relations between aristocratic lovers, which was widely represented in the lyric poems and *chivalric romances* of western Europe during the Middle Ages. The development of the *conventions* of courtly love is usually attributed to the **troubadours** (poets of Provence, in southern France) in the period from the late eleventh century through the twelfth century. An influential book, written in Latin in the latter twelfth century, was Andreas Capellanus' *De arte honeste amandi*, translated into English as *The Art of Courtly Love*. In the conventional doctrine, love between the sexes, with its erotic and physical aspects spiritualized, is regarded as the noblest passion this side of heaven. The courtly lover idealizes and idolizes his beloved, and subjects himself to her every whim. (This love is often that of a bachelor knight for another man's wife, as in the stories of Tristan and Isolde or of Lancelot and Guinevere; it must be remembered that marriage among the upper classes in medieval Europe was usually not a relationship of love, but a kind of business contract, for economic and political purposes.) The lover suffers agonies of body and spirit as he is put to the test by his imperious sweetheart, but remains devoted to her, manifesting his honor by his fidelity and his adherence to a rigorous code of behavior, both in knightly battles and in the complex ceremonies of courtly speech and conduct.

The origins of courtly love have been traced to a number of sources: a serious reading of the Roman poet Ovid's mock-serious book *The Remedies of Love*; an imitation in lovers' relations of the politics of feudalism (the lover is a vassal, and both his lady and the god of love are his lords); and especially an importation into amatory situations of Christian concepts and ritual and the veneration of the Virgin Mary. Thus, the lady is exalted and worshiped; the lover sins and repents; and if his faith stays steadfast, he may be admitted at last into the lover's heaven through his lady's "gift of grace."

From southern France the doctrines of courtly love spread to Chrétien de Troyes (who flourished from 1170–90) and other poets and romance writers in northern France; to Dante (*La Vita Nuova*, 1290–94), Petrarch, and other writers in fourteenth-century Italy; and to the love poets of Germany and northern Europe. For a reader of English literature the conventions of courtly love are best known by their occurrence in the medieval romance *Sir Gawain and the Green Knight*, in Chaucer's *Troilus and Criseyde*, and later in the Petrarchan subject matter and the *Petrarchan conceits* of the Elizabethan sonneteers.

"Courtly love" is a modern term that does not occur in medieval texts, and there has long been a debate whether courtly love was limited to medieval

counterculture：反文化运动　277；76。

country house poem：乡村诗　407。

couplet：对句　375。

courtesy books：礼仪书籍　339。

Courtly Love：骑士恋

　　骑士恋与支配贵族恋人之间关系的复杂习俗，是中世纪西欧抒情诗歌和*骑士传奇*广为表现的一种爱情主义。骑士恋这一*文学惯例*通常被认为是由11世纪后期至12世纪期间的**行吟诗人**（法国南部普罗旺斯地区的诗人）发展起来的。12世纪晚期用拉丁文写成的一本有影响力的书由安德烈亚斯·卡佩拉努斯所著，英文名叫《优雅之爱的艺术》。传统的爱情主义认为，异性间的爱情，包括其性爱和肉体方面的精神化，被视为尘世间最崇高的情感。骑士恋者往往把自己的意中人理想化、偶像化，并为她倾倒得俯首帖耳、唯命是从（这种爱情常常表现为单身骑士对他人之妻的迷恋，正如特里斯坦与伊索尔达，或兰斯洛特与格温娜维尔等故事中所描写的那样；必须注意到的是，中世纪欧洲上层社会贵族之间的联姻往往不是出于爱情，而是出于功利与政治需要达成的一种契约）。由于意中人的傲慢和任性，追求者经受着肉体和精神上的磨难与痛楚，但他忠心不渝，在与骑士们的战斗中和在复杂的宫廷礼仪的言谈举止中，用忠诚和循规蹈矩的骑士风度来证实自己的爱慕之情。

　　骑士恋产生的渊源是多方面的：对罗马诗人奥维德的严肃讽刺作品《爱之矫正》严肃认真的解读；对封建主义政治影响下情人关系的模仿（追求者是仆从，意中人和爱神是他的主子）；尤其是在爱情中输入了基督徒的观念和礼仪，以及对圣母玛丽亚的崇敬之情。这样一来，意中人的身份也就变得高贵起来，成为崇拜的偶像；而追求者则触犯圣训并进行忏悔；如果他忠心不移，终会得到意中人的"恩惠"而进入情人的天堂。

　　骑士恋主义从法国南部流传开来，法国北部的诗人克雷蒂安·德·特鲁瓦（活跃于1170—1190年间）和其他诗人与传奇作家，意大利的但丁（《新生》，1290—1294）、彼特拉克和14世纪意大利的其他作家，以及德国和北欧的爱情诗人都传承了这一文学题材。对英国文学的读者而言，最著名的骑士恋这一文学惯例出现在中世纪传奇《高文爵士与绿衣骑士》、乔叟的《特洛伊罗斯与克里西德》，以及其后伊丽莎白时期十四行诗人运用的彼特拉克式题材和*彼特拉克式巧思妙喻*中。

　　骑士恋是一个现代术语，在中世纪的文本中并未出现过；长期以来，人们一

literature and to elegant conversation at courts, or whether to some degree it reflected the actual sentiments and conduct in aristocratic life of the time. What is clear is that its views about the intensity and the ennobling power of love as "the grand passion," of the special sensibility and high spiritual status of women, and of the complex decorum governing relations between the sexes have profoundly affected not only the literature of love but also the actual experience of "being in love" in the Western world, through the nineteenth century and (to a diminished extent) even into our own day of sexual candor, freedom, and the feminist movement for equivalence in the relations between the sexes. Some feminists attack the medieval doctrine of courtly love, as well as later tendencies to spiritualize and idealize women, as in fact demeaning to them, and a covert device to ensure their social, political, and economic subordination to men. See *feminist criticism*.

Refer to C. S. Lewis, *The Allegory of Love* (1936); A. J. Denomy, *The Heresy of Courtly Love* (1947); F. X. Newman, ed., *The Meaning of Courtly Love* (1968); Denis de Rougemont, *Love in the Western World* (rev. 1974); Roger Boase, *The Origin and Meaning of Courtly Love: A Critical Study of European Scholarship* (1977); David Burnley, *Courtliness and Literature in Medieval England* (1998). For skeptical views of some commonly held opinions, see D. W. Robertson, "Some Medieval Doctrines of Love," in *A Preface to Chaucer: Studies in Medieval Perspectives* (1962); Peter Dronke, *Medieval Latin and the Rise of European Love-Lyric* (1965–66); E. Talbot Donaldson, "The Myth of Courtly Love," in *Speaking of Chaucer* (1970). For reappraisals of the role of women in the tradition, see Andrée Kahn Blumstein, *Misogyny and Idealization in the Courtly Romance* (1977); R. Howard Bloch, *Medieval Misogyny and the Invention of Western Romantic Love* (1991); Slavoj Žižek, "Courtly Love, or Woman as Thing," in *Metastases of Enjoyment* (1994).

For references to *courtly love* in other entries, see page *48*.

crisis (in a plot): **296**.

criteria (in criticism): **67**.

criticism: Criticism, or more specifically **literary criticism**, is the overall term for studies concerned with defining, classifying, analyzing, interpreting, and evaluating works of literature. **Theoretical criticism** proposes an explicit **theory** of literature, in the sense of general principles, together with a set of terms, distinctions, and categories, to be applied to identifying and analyzing works of literature, as well as the **criteria** (the standards, or norms) by which these works and their writers are to be evaluated. The earliest, and enduringly important, treatise of theoretical criticism was Aristotle's *Poetics* (fourth century BC). Among the most influential theoretical critics in the following centuries were Longinus in Greece; Horace in Rome; Boileau and Sainte-Beuve in France; Baumgarten and Goethe in Germany; Samuel Johnson, Coleridge, and Matthew Arnold in England; and Poe and Emerson in America. Landmarks of theoretical criticism in the first half of the twentieth century are

直对骑士恋仅是局限于中世纪文学和宫廷中高雅的话题,还是在某种程度上反映了当时贵族生活中的真实情感和行为争论不休。然而,可以肯定的是,作为"崇高感情"的爱情的力量是强烈而高尚的,女子具有特有的敏感性与很高的精神化地位,以及支配两性间关系的复杂礼仪等骑士恋主义观念,不仅对西方的爱情文学,而且对热恋中的真实体验,以及对整个 19 世纪,甚至(在稍低的程度上)对我们这个时代两性间的性开放、性自由及为争取男女关系中平等地位的女性主义运动,都产生了深刻的影响。一些女性主义者对中世纪的骑士恋主义,以及后来把女性精神化、理想化而事实上却在贬低女性并以此作为一种隐蔽的策略确保女性在社会、政治、经济地位上从属于男性的趋势予以了抨击。参见:*女性主义批评*。

参阅 C. S. 刘易斯所著的《爱情的寓言》(1936);A. J. 德诺米所著的《骑士恋的异端》(1947);F. X. 纽曼主编的《骑士恋的意义》(1968);丹尼斯·德·鲁热蒙所著的《西方世界里的爱情》(1974 年修订版);罗杰·博厄斯所著的《骑士恋的起源和意义:欧洲学界批评研究》(1977);戴维·伯恩利所著的《中世纪英格兰的优雅与文学》(1998)。关于对人们通常所持观点的怀疑性论述,参阅:D. W. 罗伯逊所写的文章"一些中世纪爱情教义",收入其所著的《乔叟序言:中世纪研究视角》(1962);彼得·德朗克所著的《中世纪拉丁传统与欧洲爱情抒情诗的兴起》(1965—1966);E. 塔尔博特·唐纳森所著的《谈谈乔叟》(1970) 中的"骑士恋的迷思"。关于对传统中女性作用的重新评价,参阅:安德烈·康·布鲁姆斯坦所著的《宫廷爱情中的厌女症与理想化》(1977);R. 霍华德·布洛克所著的《中世纪厌女症与西方浪漫爱情的发明》(1991);斯拉沃热·齐泽克所著的《快感大转移》(1994) 中的"骑士恋,或作为物的女性"。

其他条目中提及"骑士恋"的地方,参见第 48 页。

crisis (in a plot):(情节中的)关子　**296**。

criteria (in criticism):(批评中的)标准　**67**。

Criticism:批评

批评,或更具体地称之为**文学批评**,是研究有关界定、分类、分析、解释和评价文学作品的一个总的术语。**理论批评**是在普遍原则的基础上提出的明确的文学*理论*,并确立了一套用于鉴别和分析文学作品的术语、区分和分类的依据,以及用于评价文学作品及其作者的**标准**(原则,或规范)。亚里士多德的《诗学》(公元前 4 世纪)是理论批评最早的、具有持久重要影响力的论著。在后来的数世纪中,最具影响的理论批评家有希腊的朗吉努斯;罗马的贺拉斯;法国的布瓦洛和圣伯夫;德国的鲍姆加登和歌德;英国的塞缪尔·约翰逊、柯勒律治和马修·阿诺德;美国的坡和爱默生。20 世纪前半叶具有划时代意义的理论批评论著有

I. A. Richards, *Principles of Literary Criticism* (1924); Kenneth Burke, *The Philosophy of Literary Form* (1941, rev. 1957); R. S. Crane, ed., *Critics and Criticism* (1952); Erich Auerbach, *Mimesis: The Representation of Reality in Western Literature* (trans. 1953, reissued 2003); and Northrop Frye, *Anatomy of Criticism* (1957).

Since the 1970s there have been a large number of publications—Continental, American, and English—proposing diverse radical forms of critical theory. These are listed and dated in the entry *theories and movements in criticism, recent*; each theory in that list is also given a separate entry in this *Glossary*. For a discussion of the special uses of the term "theory" in these critical movements, see *poststructuralism*.

Practical criticism, or **applied criticism**, concerns itself with particular works and writers; in an applied critique, the theoretical principles controlling the analysis, interpretation, and evaluation are often left implicit, or brought in only as the occasion demands. Among the more influential works of applied criticism in England and America are the literary essays of Dryden in the *Restoration*; Dr. Johnson's *Lives of the English Poets* (1779–81); Coleridge's chapters on the poetry of Wordsworth in *Biographia Literaria* (1817) and his lectures on Shakespeare; William Hazlitt's lectures on Shakespeare and the English poets, in the second and third decades of the nineteenth century; Matthew Arnold's *Essays in Criticism* (1865 and following); I. A. Richards' *Practical Criticism* (1930); T. S. Eliot's *Selected Essays* (1932); and the many critical essays by Virginia Woolf, F. R. Leavis, and Lionel Trilling. Cleanth Brooks' *The Well Wrought Urn* (1947) exemplifies the "close reading" of single texts which was the typical mode of practical criticism in the American *New Criticism*. For an example of practical criticism applied to a single poetic text, see Stanley Fish, *Surprised by Sin: The Reader in Paradise Lost* (2d ed., 1998).

In practical criticism, a frequent distinction is made between impressionistic and judicial criticism:

Impressionistic criticism attempts to represent in words the felt qualities of a particular passage or work, and to express the responses (the "impression") that the work directly evokes from the critic. As William Hazlitt put it in his essay "On Genius and Common Sense" (1824): "You decide from feeling, and not from reason; that is, from the impression of a number of things on the mind ... though you may not be able to analyze or account for it in the several particulars." And Walter Pater later said that in criticism "the first step toward seeing one's object as it really is, is to know one's own impression as it really is, to discriminate it, to realise it distinctly," and posed as the basic question, "What is this song or picture ... to *me*?" (preface to *Studies in the History of the Renaissance*, 1873). At its extreme this mode of criticism becomes, in Anatole France's phrase, "the adventures of a sensitive soul among masterpieces."

Judicial criticism, on the other hand, attempts not merely to communicate, but to analyze and explain the effects of a work by reference to its

I. A. 理查兹的《文学批评原理》(1924)、肯尼思·伯克的《文学形式原理》(1941, 1957年修订版)、R. S. 克莱恩主编的《批评家与批评》(1952)、埃利希·奥尔巴赫的《摹仿论：西方文学中现实的再现》(1953年英译, 2003年再版) 和诺斯罗普·弗莱的《批评的剖析》(1957)。

自1970年代以来，欧陆、美国和英国涌现出大量论著，提出了各种各样新颖的、激进的批评理论形式。这些论著在*当代批评理论和运动*条目中罗列出并注明了出版日期；在本书中，对该条目中的每一理论都单列条目进行论述。关于术语"理论"在当代批评运动中的一些特殊用法，参见：*后结构主义*。

实用批评或**应用批评**注重评析具体作家与作品；在实用文学批评中，用于指导分析、解释和评价的理论原则往往被忽略，或在偶尔需要时才加以运用。英美两国更具影响力的实用批评论著包括德莱顿《复辟》中的文学随笔；约翰逊博士的《诗人传》(1779—1781)；柯勒律治的《文学传记》(1817) 中论述华兹华斯诗歌和他关于莎士比亚的讲演的章节；1820、1830年代威廉·黑兹利特关于莎士比亚和英国诗人的演讲；马修·阿诺德的《评论文集》(1865年及其后)；I. A. 理查兹的《实用批评》(1930)；T. S. 艾略特的《论文选集》(1932)；以及出自弗吉尼亚·吴尔夫、F. R. 利维斯和莱昂内尔·特里林之手的许多批评随笔。克利安斯·布鲁克斯的《精制的瓮》(1947) 是对单纯的文本加以"细读"的一个范例，这是美国新批评实用批评的典型模式。对单一诗歌文本进行实用批评的例子，可以参阅斯坦利·费什所著的《为罪恶所震惊：〈失乐园〉中的读者》(1998年第2版)。

实用文学批评常又分为印象主义批评和分析批评：

印象主义批评试图以文字来表现一个具体章节或一部作品的直观品质，即作品对批评家造成的直接反应（"印象"）。正如威廉·黑兹利特在《论天才与常人之识》(1824) 中所说："人们是凭感觉而不是理智去判断事物的，即通过大脑对许多事物的印象……尽管可能无法对这种印象作出细致的分析或解释。"后来，沃尔特·佩特认为，在批评过程中，"客观认识事物的第一步，就是要真实、清晰地辨析和认识自己得到的印象"，并要提出这样一个基本问题："这首歌曲或这幅图画……对我来说是什么？"[《文艺复兴史研究》(1873) 前言]当印象主义批评模式走向极端时，就成了像阿纳托尔·法朗士所说的：是"敏感的心灵在名著宝库里的探奇"。

另一方面，**分析批评**不只是试图呈现作品的艺术效果，更是要通过参照文学

subject, organization, techniques, and style, and to base the critic's individual judgments on specified criteria of literary excellence.

Rarely are these two modes of criticism sharply distinct in practice, but good examples of primarily impressionistic commentary can be found in the Greek Longinus (see the characterization of the *Odyssey* in his treatise *On the Sublime*), Hazlitt, Walter Pater (the locus classicus of impressionism is his description of Leonardo's *Mona Lisa* in *The Renaissance*, 1873), and some of the twentieth-century critical essays of E. M. Forster and Virginia Woolf.

Types of traditional critical theories and of applied criticism can be usefully distinguished by their orientation—that is, according to whether, in defining, explaining, and judging a work of literature, they refer the work primarily to the outer world, or to the reader, or to the author, or else treat the work as an independent entity:

1. **Mimetic criticism** views the literary work as an imitation, or reflection, or representation of the world and human life, and the primary criterion applied to a work is the "truth" and "adequacy" of its representation to the matter that it represents, or should represent. This mode of criticism, which first appeared in Plato and (in a qualified way) in Aristotle, remains characteristic of modern theories of literary realism. See *imitation*.

2. **Pragmatic criticism** views the work as something which is constructed in order to achieve certain effects on the audience (effects such as aesthetic pleasure, instruction, or kinds of emotion), and it tends to judge the value of the work according to its success in achieving that aim. This approach, which largely dominated literary discussion from the versified *Art of Poetry* by the Roman Horace (first century BC) through the eighteenth century, has been revived in *rhetorical criticism*, which emphasizes the artistic strategies by which an author engages and influences the responses of readers to the matters represented in a literary work. The pragmatic approach has also been adopted by some *structuralists* who analyze a literary text as a systematic play of codes that produce the interpretative responses of a reader.

3. **Expressive criticism** treats a literary work primarily in relation to its author. It defines poetry as an expression, or overflow, or utterance of feelings, or as the product of the poet's imagination operating on his or her perceptions, thoughts, and feelings; it tends to judge the work by its sincerity, or its adequacy to the poet's individual vision or state of mind; and it often seeks in the work evidences of the particular temperament and experiences of the author who, deliberately or unconsciously, has revealed himself or herself in it. Such views were developed mainly by romantic critics in the early nineteenth century and remain current in our own time, especially in the writings of *psychological* and *psychoanalytic critics* and in *critics of consciousness* such as Georges Poulet and the Geneva School. For a reading of literary criticism itself as involving self-expression, see Geoffrey Galt Harpham, *The Character of Criticism*, 2006.

作品的主题、结构、表现手法与文体，以及依据批评家个人评价文学杰作的具体批评标准，来分析和解释作品的艺术效果。

印象主义批评和分析批评在实际运用中很少表现出截然不同的性质，然而在希腊的朗吉努斯（参见他在《论崇高》中有关《奥德赛》人物塑造方面的评论）、黑兹利特、沃尔特·佩特[他在《文艺复兴史研究》(1873)中对达芬奇的《蒙娜丽莎》的描绘成为印象主义批评最权威的章节]，以及20世纪 E. M. 福斯特和弗吉尼亚·吴尔夫的一些评论文章中，可以看到偏重于印象主义批评的一些很好的例子。

传统批评理论和应用批评理论类型的区别标准在于它们的取向不同，即在对一部文学作品进行解释和评价时，是以外界因素为主要依据，还是以读者或作者为主要依据，或者是否把作品视为一个自足的实体。

1. **摹仿式批评**认为文学作品是对世界和人类生活的一种模仿或反映或再现，衡量作品的依据是看它是否"真实地"和"准确地"再现了它所表现或应该表现的题材。这种文学批评方式最初出现在柏拉图和（在一定意义上说是）亚里士多德的论著里，现在仍然是现代现实主义文学理论的一个特点。参见：摹仿。

2. **实用主义批评**认为文学作品的创作目的在于对读者产生艺术感染力（如给观众以美感、教益或引起各种感情冲动），并以此作为衡量作品价值的标准。从罗马诗人贺拉斯的诗作《诗艺》（公元前1世纪）开始一直到18世纪，这种文学理论一直主导着文学论坛，如今又通过修辞学批评得到复兴。修辞学批评方法强调的是艺术策略，即作者借助艺术策略引导和影响读者对作品所表现的题材的反应。实用主义文学批评方式也被一些结构主义者所采用，他们把文学文本分析成生成读者理解反应的一套系统性的文字符号的游戏。

3. **表现主义批评**主要探讨文学作品与作者的关系。它把诗歌解释为感情的表达、洋溢和喷发，或者是诗人的想象力作用于其直觉、思维和感情的结果；它评价作品的依据是看作品是否真实或充分地反映了作者的想象与意境；同时，它经常会在作品中发掘证据，证明作者在作品中自觉或不自觉地表露出其自身的特定气质与经历。这些理论观念主要是由19世纪早期浪漫主义文学批评家发展起来的，在当今我们这个时代仍然流行，尤其表现在诸如乔治·普莱（也译布莱）和日内瓦学派这样的心理学与精神分析批评家和意识批评家的著作中。关于将文学批评自身看做与自我表达有关，参阅：杰弗里·高尔特·哈珀姆所著的《批评的特征》(2006)。

70 CRITICISM

4. **Objective criticism** deals with a work of literature as something which stands free from what is often called an "extrinsic" relationship to the poet, or to the audience, or to the environing world. Instead it describes the literary product as a self-sufficient and autonomous object, or else as a world-in-itself, which is to be contemplated as its own end, and to be analyzed and judged solely by "intrinsic" criteria such as its complexity, coherence, equilibrium, integrity, and the interrelations of its component elements. The conception of the self-sufficiency of an aesthetic object was proposed in Kant's *Critique of Aesthetic Judgment* (1790)—see *distance and involvement*—was taken up by proponents of *art for art's sake* in the latter part of the nineteenth century, and has been elaborated in detailed modes of applied criticism by a number of important critics since the 1920s, including the *New Critics*, the *Chicago School*, and proponents of European *formalism*.

An essential critical enterprise that the ordinary reader takes for granted is to establish a valid text for a literary work; see the entry *textual criticism*. Also, criticism is often classified into types which bring to bear upon literature various areas of knowledge, in an attempt to identify the conditions and influences that determine the particular characteristics and values of a literary work. Accordingly, we have "historical criticism," "biographical criticism," "sociological criticism" (see *sociology of literature* and *Marxist criticism*), *psychological criticism* (a subspecies is *psychoanalytic criticism*), and *archetypal* or *myth criticism* (which undertakes to explain the formation of types of literature by reference to the views about myth and ritual in modern cultural anthropology).

For a detailed discussion of the classification of traditional theories that is represented in this essay, see M. H. Abrams, *The Mirror and the Lamp* (1953), chapter 1, and "Types and Orientations of Critical Theories" in *Doing Things with Texts: Essays in Criticism and Critical Theory* (1989). On types of critical approaches, refer also to René Wellek and Austin Warren, *Theory of Literature* (rev. 1970). Histories of criticism: *Classical Criticism*, ed. George A. Kennedy (1989); Bernard Weinberg, *A History of Literary Criticism in the Italian Renaissance* (2 vols., 1963); René Wellek, *A History of Modern Criticism, 1750–1950* (7 vols., 1955ff.); *The Cambridge History of Literary Criticism* (multiple vols., 1989–). On criticism in the earlier nineteenth century see Abrams, *The Mirror and the Lamp*; on twentieth-century criticism, refer to: S. E. Hyman, *The Armed Vision* (1948); Murray Krieger, *The New Apologists for Poetry* (1956); Jonathan Culler, *Structuralist Poetics* (1975) and *Literary Theory: A Very Short Introduction* (1997); Grant Webster, *The Republic of Letters: A History of Postwar American Literary Opinion* (1979); Frank Lentricchia, *After the New Criticism* (1980); Chris Baldick, *Criticism and Literary Theory, 1890 to the Present* (1996).

Convenient anthologies of literary criticism are A. H. Gilbert, ed., *Literary Criticism, Plato to Croce* (1962); Lionel Trilling, ed., *Literary Criticism: An Introductory Reader* (1970); Hazard Adams, ed., *Critical Theory since Plato* (2d ed., 1993). Anthologies that focus on recent criticism include: Hazard Adams

4. **客观批评**把文学作品看成是通常被称为独立于诗人、读者和外部世界的"外在"事物来加以研究。它把文学作品描述为一个自足自主的实体或独立的内在世界，必须将其自身视为是审美的目的，因此要以其复杂性、一致性、均衡度、整体性和作品各组成部分间的相互关系等"内在"准则对其进行分析与评价。审美客体的自给自足这一观点是康德在《审美批判》（1790）中提出的（参见：*心理距离和感情介入*），19世纪后期被为艺术而艺术的倡导者所接受，1920年代以来，包括新批评家、芝加哥学派、欧洲形式主义等流派在内的一些重要批评家又以应用批评的模式对客观批评进行了详尽的阐释。

普通读者认为，一部文学作品理应有一个有效的文本；参见：*文本批评*。与文学相关的知识领域多种多样，为了认识决定一部文学作品的特色和价值的条件和影响因素，就要把文学批评划分成不同的类型。因此，就出现了"历史批评""传记批评""社会学批评"（参见：*文学社会学*、*马克思主义批评*）、*心理学批评*（可再分为精神分析批评）、*原型批评*、*神话批评*（即以现代文化人类学中关于神话和礼仪的理论为依据来解释文学类型的形成）。

关于对出现在本文中的传统理论的分类，可以参阅以下详尽论述：M. H. 艾布拉姆斯所著的《镜与灯》（1953）第1章，《以文行事：艾布拉姆斯精选集》（1989）中的"批评理论的类型与方向"。关于文学批评方法的类型，也可参阅：勒内·韦勒克与奥斯汀·沃伦合著的《文学理论》（1970年修订版）。关于文学批评史，参阅：乔治·A. 肯尼迪主编的《古典批评》（1989）；伯纳德·温伯格所著的两卷本《意大利文艺复兴时期的文学批评史》（1963）；勒内·韦勒克所著的七卷本《现代批评史：1750—1950》（1955年及其后）；多卷本《剑桥文学批评史》（1989— ）。关于19世纪早期的文学批评，参阅：M. H. 艾布拉姆斯所著的《镜与灯》；关于20世纪文学批评，参阅：S. E. 海曼所著的《武装起来的洞察力》（1948）；默里·克里格所著的《诗的新辩护士》（1956）；乔纳森·卡勒所著的《结构主义诗学》（1975）与《文学理论入门》（1997）；格兰特·韦伯斯特所著的《文学界：战后美国文学观点史》（1979）；弗兰克·兰特里夏所著的《新批评之后》（1980）；克里斯·鲍尔迪克所著的《批评与文学理论：从1890年到现在》（1996）。

实用文学批评文集有：A. H. 吉尔伯特主编的《文学批评，从柏拉图到克罗齐》（1962）；莱昂内尔·特里林主编的《文学批评导读》（1970）；哈泽德·亚当斯主编的《柏拉图以来的文学理论》（1993年第2版）。近期文学批评文集有：

and Leroy Searle, eds., *Critical Theory since 1965* (1986); Vassilis Lambropoulos and David Neal Miller, eds., *Twentieth-Century Literary Theory: An Introductory Anthology* (1987); David Lodge, ed., *Modern Criticism and Theory* (1988); Robert Con Davis and Ronald Schleifer, *Contemporary Literary Criticism* (rev. 1989); and the most inclusive, Vincent Leitch and others, eds., *The Norton Anthology of Theory and Criticism* (2001). Suggested readings in current types of critical theory are included in the entry of this *Glossary* for each type.

For collections of essays on topics in late twentieth-century theory and criticism, see Michael Groden and Martin Kreiswirth, eds., *The Johns Hopkins Guide to Literary Theory and Criticism* (1994); Frank Lentricchia and Thomas McLaughlin, eds., *Critical Terms for Literary Study* (2d ed., 1995).

For the many types of critical theory and practice, see *anxiety of influence; archetypal criticism; art for art's sake; Chicago School; contextual criticism; theories and movements in recent criticism; critics of consciousness; Darwinian literary studies; deconstruction; dialogic criticism; ecocriticism; feminist criticism; gender criticism; linguistics in modern criticism; Marxist criticism; New Criticism; new historicism; phenomenology and criticism; postcolonial studies; psychological and psychoanalytic criticism; queer theory; reader-response criticism; reception theory; rhetorical criticism; Russian formalism; semiotics; sociological criticism; speech-act theory; structuralist criticism; stylistics.*

criticism, theories and movements in recent: 405.

critics of consciousness: 290.

critique: Critique is often used to designate an especially robust and searching kind of criticism; it suggests a rational analysis of an intellectual position, or of a work incorporating that position, with a sharp eye especially for errors, confusions, or harmful implications. The term glances back to the German philosopher Immanuel Kant, who wrote three *Critiques* (of Pure Reason, Practical Reason, and Judgment), published 1781–90. The fact that Kant's use of "critique" suggests a rigorous reliance on reason, implies confidence in human autonomy, and is associated with Kant's looking forward to human emancipation (see *Enlightenment*) has made the term especially congenial to Marxist thinkers. The use of "critique" is associated particularly with the writings on "critical social theory" of the Frankfurt School, a group of neo-Marxists that included Walter Benjamin, Herbert Marcuse, Theodor Adorno, Max Horkheimer, and Jürgen Habermas (see under *Marxist criticism*). For brief and influential position statements, see Horkheimer, "Traditional and Critical Theory," in *Critical Theory* (1992); and Adorno, "Resignation," in *The Culture Industry* (2001).

cultural constructs: 245; *328.* See also *social constructs.*

cultural materialism: 250.

cultural poetics: 249.

哈泽德·亚当斯与勒罗伊·瑟尔合编的《1965年以来的批评理论》（1986）；瓦西里斯·兰布罗普洛斯与戴维·尼尔·米勒合编的《20世纪文学理论选集》（1987）；戴维·洛奇主编的《现代批评和理论》（1988）；罗伯特·康·戴维斯与罗纳德·施莱弗尔合著的《当代文学批评》（1989年修订版）；以及最全面的文森特·利奇等人合编的《诺顿理论与批评选集》（2001）。关于当代批评理论类型的一些推荐书目，本书在各理论类型的条目中都有收录。

关于20世纪晚期理论和批评主义这一主题的文章合集，参阅：迈克尔·格洛登与马丁·克雷斯沃斯合编的《约翰·霍普金斯文学理论和批评指南》（1994）；弗兰克·兰特里夏与托马斯·麦克劳克林合编的《文学研究的批评术语》（1995年第2版）。

关于批评理论和实践的诸多类型，参见：影响的焦虑、原型批评、为艺术而艺术、芝加哥学派、语境（上下文）批评、当代批评理论和运动、意识批评、达尔文主义文学研究、解构主义、对话批评、生态批评、女性主义批评、性别批评、语言学在文学批评里的应用、马克思主义批评、新批评、新历史主义、现象学与批评、后殖民主义研究、心理学与精神分析批评、同性恋理论、读者反应批评、接受理论、修辞学批评、俄国形式主义、符号论、社会学批评、言语行为理论、结构主义批评、文体学。

criticism, theories and movements in recent：当代批评理论和运动　405。

critics of consciousness：意识批评家　290。

Critique：批判

批判经常被用来指一种特别强劲和锐利的批评，它暗示对一种知识分子立场的理性分析，或是对持有那一立场的著作的理性分析，特别是对其中的错误、混乱或有害影响保持敏锐的审视。这一术语的使用可以追溯到德国哲学家康德那里，他写有三大批判（《纯粹理性批判》《实践理性批判》《判断力批判》，1781—1790年间出版）。康德对"批判"这一术语的使用，严格依赖理性，意味着对人类自主性的信心，与康德对人类解放（参见：*启蒙*）的期许联系在一起，这一事实使得这一术语尤其与马克思主义思想家意气相投。"批判"这一术语的使用，特别与法兰克福学派的"批判社会理论"著作联系在一起，法兰克福学派是一个新马克思主义者群体，其中包括沃尔特·本雅明、赫伯特·马尔库塞、西奥多·阿多诺、马克斯·霍克海默、尤根·哈贝马斯（参见：*马克思主义批评*中的相关论述）。关于这一立场简短而有影响力的声明，参阅：霍克海默所著的《批判的理论》（1992）中的"传统理论和批判理论"；阿多诺所著的《文化工业》（2001）中的"屈从"。

cultural constructs：文化建构　245；*328*。也可参见：*社会建构*。

cultural materialism：文化唯物主义　250。

cultural poetics：文化诗学　249。

cultural primitivism: 315.

cultural studies: Cultural studies designates a cross-disciplinary enterprise for analyzing the conditions that affect the production, reception, and cultural significance of all types of institutions, practices, and products; among these, literature is accounted as merely one of many forms of cultural "signifying practices." A chief concern is to specify the functioning of the social, economic, and political forces and power structures that are said to produce the diverse forms of cultural phenomena and to endow them with their social "meanings," their acceptance as "truth," the modes of discourse in which they are discussed, and their relative value and status.

One precursor of modern cultural studies was Roland Barthes, who in *Mythologies* (1957, trans. 1972) analyzed the social conventions and "codes" that confer meanings in such diverse social practices as women's fashions and professional wrestling. (See Barthes under *semiotics* and *structuralism*.) Another was the British school of neo-Marxist studies of literature and art—especially in their popular and working-class modes—as an integral part of the general culture. This movement was inaugurated by Raymond Williams' *Culture and Society* (1958) and by Richard Hoggart's *The Uses of Literacy* (1958, reprinted 1992), and it became institutionalized in the influential Birmingham Centre for Contemporary Cultural Studies, founded by Hoggart in 1964. In the United States, the vogue for cultural studies had its roots mainly in the mode of literary and cultural criticism known as "the new historicism," with its antecedents both in poststructural theorists such as Louis Althusser and Michel Foucault and in the treatment of culture as a set of signifying systems by Clifford Geertz and other cultural anthropologists. (See under *new historicism*.)

A prominent endeavor in cultural studies is to subvert the distinctions in traditional criticism between "high literature" and "high art" and what were considered the lower forms that appeal to a much larger body of consumers. Typically, cultural studies pay less attention to works in the established literary *canon* than to popular fiction, best-selling romances (that is, love stories), journalism, and advertising, together with other arts that have mass appeal such as cartoon comics, film, television "soap operas," and rock and *rap* music. And within the areas of literature and the more traditional arts, a frequent undertaking is to move to the center of cultural study those works that, it is claimed, have been marginalized or excluded by the *aesthetic ideology* of white European and American males, and particularly the works of women, minority ethnic groups, and colonial and *postcolonial* writers. Radical exponents of cultural studies subordinate literary studies and criticism to political activism; they orient their writings and teaching toward the explicit end of reforming existing power structures and relations, which they consider to be dominated by a privileged gender, race, or class. For the contributions of Stuart Hall—a leader in British cultural studies—to discussions of culture, race, and ethnicity, see David Morley and Kuan-Hsing Chen, eds., *Stuart Hall: Critical Dialogues in Cultural Studies* (1996).

Many cultural studies are devoted to the analysis and interpretation of objects and social practices outside the realm of literature and the other arts;

cultural primitivism：文化尚古主义　315。

Cultural Studies：文化研究

文化研究是一项跨学科课题，目的是为了分析那些影响各种类型的制度、实践和文学作品的生产、接受和文化意义的环境因素；在这些因素中，文学仅仅是作为文化许多"能指实践活动"的形式之一。文化研究中主要关注的是，具体说明据说是产生文化现象的所有形式并赋予它们以社会"意义"、"真理"、人们谈论它们的话语模式及其相应价值和地位的社会、经济、政治力量和权力结构的功能。

现代文化研究的先驱之一是罗兰·巴尔特，他在《神话学》（1957，1972年英译版）中分析了赋予诸如女性时尚和职业摔跤这些社会活动以意义的社会习俗和"代码"。（参见：*符号论*、*结构主义*中关于巴尔特的叙述。）现代文化研究的另一先驱是以文学艺术——尤其是大众和工人阶级模式的文学艺术——为研究对象的英国新马克思主义学派，该学派把文学艺术作为整个文化不可或缺的组成部分。这一文化研究运动是由雷蒙德·威廉斯的《文化与社会》（1958）和理查德·霍格特的《文化的用途》（1958，1992年重印；又译《识字的用途》）所引发的，并于1964年由霍格特组建成颇具影响力的专门机构"伯明翰当代文化研究中心"。在美国，文化研究的兴起主要植根于被称为"新历史主义"的文学和文化批评模式中，其先驱既包括路易·阿尔都塞和米歇尔·福柯这样的后结构主义理论家，又包括视文化为一系列能指体系的克利福德·格尔茨和其他文化人类学家。（参见：*新历史主义*中的相关论述。）

文化研究的主要目标是颠覆传统批评中关于"高雅文学"和"高雅艺术"与那些吸引大量消费者而被认为是庸俗的文学艺术形式之间的区分。相对于文学经典这样的成名著作，文化研究更加关注大众通俗小说、畅销浪漫史（即爱情故事）、报章杂志、广告，以及其他诸如卡通滑稽剧、电影、电视"肥皂剧"和摇滚*说唱*等能够吸引广大观众的艺术形式。而且，在文学和更为传统的人文学科领域内，文化研究更加致力于把研究中心推向被欧洲或美国男性白人所持的*审美意识形态*所边缘化甚至排除在外的那些作品，尤其是女性、少数民族，以及殖民地和*后殖民主义*作家的作品。激进的文化研究的倡导者把政治行动主义置于文学研究和批评主义之上，他们的著述和学说观点瞄准这样一个明确的目标：改革他们认为是由享有特权的性别、种族和阶层主宰的现有的权力结构和关系。关于英国文化研究领军人物斯图尔特·霍尔在对文化、民族和民族性的论述上作出的贡献，参阅：戴维·莫利与陈光兴（台湾）合编的《斯图尔特·霍尔：文化研究的批评对话》（1996）。

许多文化研究都致力于去分析和解释文学及其他艺术领域之外的事物和社

these phenomena are viewed as endowed with meanings that are the product of social forces and conventions, and that may either express or oppose the dominant structures of power in a culture. In theory, there is no limit to the kinds of things and patterns of behavior to which such an analysis of cultural "texts" may be applied; current studies deal with a spectrum ranging from the vogue of bodybuilding through urban street fashions, and from cross-dressing to the social gesture of smoking a cigarette.

See the journal *Cultural Studies*, 1987–; also Catherine Belsey, *Critical Practice* (1980); Andrew Ross, *No Respect: Intellectual and Popular Culture* (1989); Lawrence Grossberg, Cary Nelson, and Paula Treichler, eds., *Cultural Studies* (1992); Anthony Easthope, *Literary into Cultural Studies* (1991); Richard Klein, *Cigarettes Are Sublime* (1993); Valda Blundell, John Shepherd, and Ian Taylor, eds., *Relocating Cultural Studies: Developments in Theory and Research* (1993); Terry Lovell, ed., *Feminist Cultural Studies* (2 vols., 1995); Houston A. Baker, Jr., Manthia Diawara, and Ruth H. Lindeborg, eds., *Black British Cultural Studies: A Reader* (1996); Mark Seltzer, *Serial Killers I, II, III* (1997); Mieke Bal, *The Practice of Cultural Analysis* (1997); Simon During, ed., *The Cultural Studies Reader* (2d ed., 1999); Simon During, *Cultural Studies: A Critical Introduction* (2005); Andrew Edgar and Peter Sedgwick, eds., *Cultural Theory: The Key Thinkers* (2d ed., 2007). M. Jessica Munns and Gita Rajan, eds., *A Cultural Studies Reader: History, Theory, Practice* (1995), traces cultural studies as far back as Matthew Arnold in the Victorian era, then through the structural anthropology of Claude Lévi-Strauss to many current practitioners. For references to *cultural studies* in other entries, see page **52**.

cyberfiction: 167.

cyberpunk: 357.

会实践活动；这些事物和活动被视为蕴涵着一定的意义，是社会力量和习俗的产物，既可表现又可对抗某一文化中占主导地位的权力结构。理论上，对可用来分析的文化"文本"而言，其事物类别和行为方式是没有局限的；当前文化研究涉猎的范围包括从健美运动的风行到市井时尚，从穿戴异性服饰到吸烟的社会姿态，等等。

参阅：期刊《文化研究》(1987—   )；凯瑟琳·贝尔西所著的《批判实践》(1980)；安德鲁·罗斯所著的《不尊重：知识分子与大众文化》(1989)；劳伦斯·格罗斯伯格、卡里·纳尔逊与葆拉·特雷克勒合编的《文化研究》(1992)；安东尼·伊索普所著的《文学至文化研究》(1991)；理查德·克莱因所著的《香烟：一个人类痼习的文化研究》(1993)；瓦尔达·布伦德尔、约翰·谢泼德与伊恩·泰勒合编的《重新定位文化研究：理论和研究发展》(1993)；特里·洛弗尔主编的两卷本《女性主义文化研究》(1995)；小休斯顿·A. 贝克、曼西亚·迪亚瓦拉与鲁斯·H. 林德堡合编的《黑人英国文化研究读本》(1996)；马克·塞尔策所著的《连环杀手 I II III》(1997)；米尔克·巴尔所著的《文化分析实践》(1997)；西蒙·杜林主编的《文化研究读本》(1999 年第 2 版)；西蒙·杜林所著的《文化研究：批判入门》(2005)；安德鲁·埃德加与彼得·塞奇威克合编的《文化理论：重要思想家》(2007 年第 2 版)。杰茜卡·芒斯与吉大·拉姜恩合编的《文化研究读本：历史、理论与实践》(1995)，回顾了远至维多利亚女王时代的马修·阿诺德，包括克劳德·列维–斯特劳斯的结构人类学在内，直至当今许多文化研究者的研究。其他条目中提及"文化研究"的地方，参见第 52 页。

cyberfiction：赛博小说   167。

cyberpunk：电脑朋客   357。

dactylic (dăktĭl' ĭk): **219**.

Dadaism: 392.

Darwinian literary studies: The application to literature of Charles Darwin's theory of evolution, especially the evolutionary concepts of the struggle for existence, and the survival of those individuals and groups best adapted to their environment. The movement was begun in the mid-1990s by scholars who argued for a wholesale refashioning of literary studies to bring them into conformity with the findings of biological science, especially the theory of evolution. Darwinian literary studies were one of several new areas of investigation that were developed simultaneously with, or soon after, Edward O. Wilson's *Sociobiology: The New Synthesis* (1975), which proposed that evolutionary pressures and results play a significant role not only in animal societies, but also in human culture. These investigations applied evolutionary principles to the fields of psychology, anthropology, and epistemology (the study of how human beings acquire knowledge).

The first major publication in Darwinian literary studies was Joseph Carroll's *Evolution and Literary Theory* (1995), written in express opposition to the various modes of *poststructuralist* criticism, with their exclusive focus on textual or linguistic features and their treatment of culture in independence from biology. Carroll proposed, instead, that literary works should be studied as articulations of the vital needs and interests of human beings, viewed as adaptively evolved organisms. This approach, he claimed, would enable critics to discover in works of literature, beneath their myriad details of character and plot, a structure of motives, cognitive predispositions, and behavior that, as the result of an age-old process of evolution, is specific to the human species.

Many Darwinian studies focus on the analysis of themes in literature, especially those that deal with human reproductive behavior in sexual competition and the selection of mates, and with the formation of social alliances and of family relationships. When applied even to such unlikely seeming works as those of Jane Austen, for example, such an approach stresses the fact that they typically involve men who compete for women in their socioeconomic attributes of money and rank, and women who compete for men in their attributes of youth and beauty. When applied to the Homeric epics, the Darwinian approach views these works as a series of stories in which men— Paris, for example, who abducted Helen of Troy from Agamemnon—compete with one another, fundamentally, not for power, status, or wealth, but for the most desirable sexual mates.

Such thematic analyses have been criticized as drastically reductive, even vulgar. Another, more theoretical approach has emerged in the Darwinian movement that is concerned less with the analysis of particular works than in the ways that literature in general represents the elemental features of

dactylic:扬抑抑格 219。

Dadaism:达达主义 392。

Darwinian Literary Studies:达尔文主义文学研究

指用查尔斯·达尔文的进化论尤其是其物竞天择适者生存的进化概念来研究文学。这一运动始于1990年代中期，由那些认为应该大规模重新进行文学研究使其与生物科学尤其是进化论的研究结果相一致的学者发起。达尔文主义文学研究是一些新研究领域之一，这些新领域的发展与爱德华·O.威尔逊的《社会生物学：新的综合》(1975)的出版相同时或在其后不久，该书提出，进化压力和结果不仅在动物社会，而且在人类文化中也起到了显著作用。这些研究将进化原则应用到心理学、人类学和认识论（研究人类如何获取知识）领域。

达尔文主义文学研究的第一部重要作品是约瑟夫·卡罗尔的《进化和文学理论》(1995)，作者反对各种*后结构主义*批评模式，后者仅仅关注文本或语言特征，没有从生物学角度去考虑文化。相反，卡罗尔建议，应该将文学作品作为与人类切身需求和利益相连去进行研究，视为适应进化的生物。他声称，这样做可以使批评家在文学作品中发现，潜藏在人物和情节的无数细节下面的动机、认知倾向和行为的结构，这一结构是古老进化过程——具体说就是人类物种进化的结果。

许多达尔文主义研究都集中于分析文学的主题，尤其是涉及性竞争和配偶选择这样的人类生殖行为，以及社会联盟和家庭关系的形成。当应用到那些看上去似乎不太可能的作品，像简·奥斯汀的作品时，这种方法强调这样一个事实，即它们通常都会涉及用金钱和地位（他们的社会经济属性）去争夺女性的男性，和用其青春和美貌（她们的属性）去争夺男人的女人。当应用到荷马史诗时，达尔文主义的方法将其视作一系列故事，在故事中，一个男人，例如从阿伽门农那里诱拐走特洛伊的海伦的帕里斯，与另一个男人竞争，从根本上来说，双方争夺的不是权力、地位或财富，而是最理想的性伴侣。

这样的专题分析一直被批评为极度简单化，甚至低俗。另外，在达尔文主义的运动中也出现了更多的理论方法，较少关注分析具体作品，更多关注文学大体上展现人类生活基本特征的方式。这方面的一本重要著作是罗伯特·F.斯托里的

human life. A key work was Robert F. Storey's *Mimesis and the Human Animal* (1996), which proposed a "biogrammar" of the human species that stressed such aspects of literature as its representation of human sociality and of elemental human motives and mental functions. Storey then applied his biogrammar to an analysis of the major *genres* of narrative, tragedy, and comedy, which he treated as highly developed forms of evolved and adaptive—or, in tragedy, of maladaptive—responses to evolutionary pressures; each genre, he claimed, had its distinctive kind of "phylogenetic" history of adaptive evolution.

Another type of Darwinian approach to literature is the study of how the basic activities of writing and reading literary works contribute to the adaptive fitness for survival of the human organism, by developing useful patterns of response, mapping out social relations, depicting intimate kin relationships, clarifying our understanding of our fundamental nature, and in general, helping us to make sense of the environing world. Some studies in this area of literary investigation use methods, such as statistical analyses, which ally them with the social sciences rather than the *humanities*.

For an overview of Darwinian literary studies, and of their relation to other fields such as evolutionary philosophy and *ecocriticism*, see Joseph Carroll, *Literary Darwinism: Evolution, Human Nature, and Literature* (2004). The initial anthology of Darwinian approaches to literature was Jonathan Gottschall and David Sloan Wilson, eds., *The Literary Animal: Evolution and the Nature of Narrative* (2005). For a wide-ranging, undogmatic application of the Darwinian perspective to a diversity of literary texts, see David P. Barash and Nanelle R. Barash, *Madame Bovary's Ovaries: A Darwinian Look at Literature* (2005). Among other relevant studies are Brian Boyd, *On the Origin of Stories: Evolution, Cognition, and Fiction* (2009); Marcus Nordlund, *Shakespeare and the Nature of Love: Literature, Culture, Evolution* (2007); and Jonathan Gottschall, *The Rape of Troy: Evolution, Violence, and the World of Homer* (2008).

dead metaphor: 131.

death of the author: 311.

Decadence, the: In the latter part of the nineteenth century, some French proponents of the doctrines of *Aestheticism*, especially Charles Baudelaire, also espoused views and values that developed into a movement called "the Decadence." The term (not regarded by its exponents as derogatory) was based on qualities attributed to the literature of Hellenistic Greece in the last three centuries BC, and to Roman literature after the death of the Emperor Augustus in AD 14. These literatures were said to possess the high refinement and subtle beauties of a culture and art that had passed their vigorous prime, but manifested a special savor of incipient decay. Such was also held to be the state of European civilization, especially in France, as it approached the end of the nineteenth century.

《模仿和人类动物》(1996)，书里提出了一种人类物种的"生物语法"，强调文学作为展现人类的社会性与基本的人类动机和心理功能的这些方面。然后斯托里用他的生物语法来分析主要的叙事、悲剧和戏剧*文学类型*，他将其视为面对进化压力高度发达的进化和适应（或者，在悲剧中则是适应不良）形式；他声称，每一种文学类型在适应进化上都有其独特的"系统发生的"历史。

另一种类型的达尔文主义文学研究方法是，研究写作和阅读文学作品这些基本活动，是如何有助于人类有机体的适应性生存，通过发展出有用的反应模式，映射出社会关系，描绘出亲密的亲属关系，澄清我们对我们本性的了解，在一般情况下，帮助我们理解包围我们的世界。这方面的一些文学研究使用了像统计分析这样的方法，将它们与社会科学而不是人*文科学*结为一体。

对达尔文主义文学研究，以及它们与其他领域如进化哲学和生态批评主义之间的联系的概述，参阅：约瑟夫·卡罗尔所著的《文学达尔文主义：进化、人性与文学》(2004)。第一部文学达尔文主义研究选集是乔纳森·戈特沙尔与戴维·斯隆·威尔逊合编的《文学动物：进化论与叙述的本质》(2005)。关于广泛的、非教条地从达尔文主义视角去看文学作品的多样性，参阅：戴维·P. 巴拉许与纳尼尔·R. 巴拉许合著的《包法利夫人的卵巢：达尔文主义文学观》(2005)。其他相关研究有布赖恩·博伊德所著的《论故事的起源：进化、认知和小说》(2009)；马库斯·诺德隆德所著的《莎士比亚和爱情的本质：文学、文化、进化》(2007)；乔纳森·戈特沙尔所著的《强暴特洛伊：进化、暴力与荷马的世界》(2008)。

dead metaphor：亡隐喻　131。

death of the author：作者的死亡　311。

Decadence, the：颓废派文艺

19世纪后期，法国一些*唯美主义*学说的倡导者，尤其是查尔斯·波德莱尔，也赞同后来演变成被称为"颓废派"运动的观点和价值观。颓废派文艺（其倡导者并不认为它含有任何贬义）是以公元前最后三个世纪的古希腊文学和公元14年奥古斯都大帝死后罗马文学的特征为根基。这些文学作品被认为具有高雅精美的文化艺术特征，并已超越其全盛时期，但却弥漫着一股刚刚萌发的特殊的腐朽之味。这也被认为是一直持续到19世纪末的欧洲文明（尤其是在法国）的情形。

Many of the precepts of the Decadence were voiced by Théophile Gautier in the "Notice," describing Baudelaire's poetry, that he prefixed to an edition of Baudelaire's *Les Fleurs du mal* ("Flowers of Evil") in 1868. Central to the Decadent movement was the view that art is totally opposed to "nature," in the sense both of biological nature and of the standard, or "natural," norms of morality and sexual behavior. The thoroughgoing Decadent writer cultivates high artifice in style and, often, the bizarre in subject matter, recoils from the fecundity and exuberance of the organic and instinctual life of nature, prefers elaborate dress over the living human form and cosmetics over the natural hue, and sometimes sets out to violate what is commonly held to be "natural" in human experience by resorting to drugs, deviancy from standard norms of behavior, and sexual experimentation, in the attempt to achieve (in a phrase echoed from the French poet Arthur Rimbaud) "the systematic derangement of all the senses." The movement reached its height in the last two decades of the nineteenth century; extreme products were the novel *À rebours* ("Against the Grain"), written by J. K. Huysmans in 1884, and some of the paintings of Gustave Moreau. This period is also known as the **fin de siècle** (end of the century); the phrase connotes the lassitude, satiety, and ennui expressed by many writers of the Decadence.

In England the ideas, moods, and behavior of the Decadence were manifested, beginning in the 1860s, in the poems of Algernon Charles Swinburne, and in the 1890s by writers such as Oscar Wilde, Arthur Symons, Ernest Dowson, and Lionel Johnson; the notable artist of the English Decadence was Aubrey Beardsley. In the search for strange sensations, a number of English Decadents of the 1890s experimented with drugs and espoused what were conventionally held to be extranatural modes of sexual experience; several of them died young. Representative literary productions are Wilde's novel *The Picture of Dorian Gray* (1891), his play *Salomé* (1893), and many of the poems of Ernest Dowson.

The emphases of the Decadence on drugged perception, sexual experimentation, and the deliberate inversion of conventional moral, social, and artistic norms reappeared, with modern variations, in the *Beat* poets and novelists of the 1950s and in the *counterculture* of the decades that followed.

See Mario Praz, *The Romantic Agony* (1933); A. E. Carter, *The Idea of Decadence in French Literature, 1830–1900* (1958); Karl Beckson, ed., *Aesthetes and Decadents of the 1890s* (1966); Richard Gilman, *Decadence: The Strange Life of an Epithet* (1979); Ian Fletcher, ed., *Decadence and the 1890s* (1979); G. H. Pittock Murray, *Spectrum of Decadence: The Literature of the 1890s* (1993); and Jane Desmarais, *A Cultural History of Decadence* (2008). A useful descriptive guide to books on the subject is Linda C. Dowling, *Aestheticism and Decadence: A Selective Annotated Bibliography* (1977). For references to *decadence* in other entries, see page **156**.

decasyllabic couplet (dĕk′ asĭlă″ bĭk): **375**.

颓废派的许多基本文艺理论出自泰奥菲尔·戈蒂耶在波德莱尔《恶之花》(1868)"前言"中对波德莱尔诗歌的描述中。颓废派文艺运动的核心观点认为，在生物性和标准，或者说道德和性行为的"自然"准则的意义上，艺术与"自然"是截然对立的。彻底的颓废派作家在风格上追求高雅的技巧，而且题材往往奇异古怪，他们回避自然有机体和本能生命的繁殖力和勃勃生机，喜欢给充满生机的人类穿上华丽的盛装和给自然的色调施以浓妆，有时还打破被认为在人类经历中是"自然"的常规而诉诸吸食毒品、偏离标准的行为准则和进行性实验，试图取得"一切观念体系的错乱"（法国诗人阿尔蒂尔·兰波之语）。该运动在19世纪后20年发展到顶峰阶段；其激进的代表作有 J. K. 于斯曼的小说《逆流》(1884)和古斯塔夫·莫罗的一些绘画。这个时期也被称为**世纪末日**；这一短语蕴涵了许多颓废派作家所表达的倦怠、厌腻和无聊这样一些情绪。

在英国，颓废派的思潮、情绪和行为体现在1860年代初阿尔杰农·查尔斯·斯温伯恩的诗作中，到1890年代，又体现在奥斯卡·王尔德、阿瑟·西蒙斯、欧内斯特·道森和莱昂内尔·约翰逊等作家的作品中；英国颓废派的著名艺术家是奥布里·比尔兹利。1890年代，英国的许多颓废派人士为了追求奇异的感受而吸食毒品，追求被传统视为反常的性体验模式；他们中的有些人英年早逝。其文学代表作有王尔德的小说《道林·格雷的肖像》(1891)、戏剧《莎乐美》(1893)和欧内斯特·道森的许多诗作。

1950年代，颓废派对毒品幻觉、性试验的迷恋，对约定俗成的道德、社会和艺术准则的肆意颠覆，又以现代的变体形式重新出现在*垮掉派*诗人及小说家和其后几十年的*反文化*运动中。

参阅：马里奥·普拉茨所著的《浪漫的痛苦》(1933)；A. E. 卡特所著的《1830—1900年间法国颓废文学的观念》(1958)；卡尔·贝克森主编的《1890年代的美学家与颓废派艺术家》(1966)；理查德·吉尔曼所著的《颓废派文艺：一种奇怪的生活》(1979)；伊恩·弗莱彻主编的《颓废派文艺与1890年代》(1979)；G. H. 皮托克·默里所著的《颓废派文艺的光谱：1890年代的文学》(1993)；简·戴马雷所著的《颓废文化史》(2008)。琳达·C. 道林所著的《唯美主义与颓废派文艺：选择性注释书目》(1977)，是一部关于该主题各种论著的实用性描述导读著作。其他条目中提及"颓废派文艺"的地方，参见第156页。

decasyllabic couplet：十音节对句　　375。

deconstruction: Deconstruction, as applied in the criticism of literature, designates a theory and practice of reading that questions and claims to "subvert" or "undermine" the assumption that the system of language is based on grounds that are adequate to establish the boundaries, the coherence or unity, and the determinate meanings of a literary text. Typically, a deconstructive reading sets out to show that conflicting forces within the text itself serve to dissipate the seeming definiteness of its structure and meanings into an indefinite array of incompatible and undecidable possibilities.

The originator and namer of deconstruction is the French thinker Jacques Derrida, among whose precursors were Friedrich Nietzsche (1844–1900) and Martin Heidegger (1889–1976)—German philosophers who put to radical question fundamental philosophical concepts such as "knowledge," "truth," and "identity"—as well as Sigmund Freud (1856–1939), whose *psychoanalysis* violated traditional concepts of a coherent individual consciousness and a unitary self. Derrida presented his basic views in three books, all published in 1967, entitled *Of Grammatology, Writing and Difference*, and *Speech and Phenomena*; after that date he reiterated, expanded, and applied those views in a rapid sequence of publications.

Derrida's writings are complex and elusive, and the summary here can only indicate some of their main tendencies. His vantage point is what he calls, in *Of Grammatology*, "the axial proposition that there is no outside-the-text" ("il n'ya rien hors du texte," or alternatively "il n'y a pas de hors-texte"). Like all Derrida's key terms and statements, this has multiple significations, but a primary one is that a reader cannot get beyond verbal signs to any things-in-themselves which, because they exist independently of the system of language, might serve to anchor a determinable meaning.

Derrida's reiterated claim is that not only all Western philosophies and theories of language, but all Western uses of language, hence all Western culture, are **logocentric**; that is, they are centered or grounded on a "logos" (which in Greek signified both "word" and "rationality") or, in a phrase he adopts from Heidegger, they rely on "the metaphysics of presence." They are logocentric, according to Derrida, in part because they are **phonocentric**; that is, they grant, implicitly or explicitly, logical "priority," or "privilege," to speech over writing as the model for analyzing all discourse. By logos, or **presence**, Derrida signifies what he also calls an "ultimate referent"—a self-certifying and self-sufficient ground, or foundation, available to us totally outside the play of language itself, that is directly present to our awareness and serves to "center" (that is, to anchor, organize, and guarantee) the structure of the linguistic system, and as a result suffices to fix the bounds, coherence, and determinate meanings of any spoken or written utterance within that system. (On Derrida's "decentering" of structuralism, see *poststructuralism*.) Historical instances of such claimed foundations for language are God as the guarantor of its validity, or a Platonic form of the true reference of a general term, or a Hegelian "telos" or goal toward which all process strives, or an intention to signify something determinate that is directly present to the awareness of the person who initiates an utterance. Derrida undertakes to

Deconstruction：解构主义

解构主义是指文学批评中阅读作品的一种理论和实践方法，它质疑并主张"颠覆"或"破坏"这样一种理论，即语言系统建立在足以确立文学文本的范围、连贯性或整体性及其确定性意义的基础上。解构主义阅读方式的典型特征是，试图展示文本自身中对立的因素，把文本的结构和意义在表面上的确定性消解为不可调和的和难以确定的不确定性碎片。

解构主义的创立者和命名者是法国思想家雅克·德里达，解构主义的先驱包括德国哲学家弗里德里希·尼采（1844—1900）和马丁·海德格尔（1889—1976），他们对诸如"知识""真理""同一性"等基本的哲学概念提出了激进的质疑；此外还有西格蒙德·弗洛伊德（1856—1939），他的*精神分析*学说打破了那种认为个人的意识本身是独自连贯和一元的传统观念。德里达在1967年发表的《论文字学》《书写与差异》《语音与现象》三部著作中阐述了他的基本观点。他在随后接连发表的论著中又重申、扩展和应用了自己提出的那些理论观点。

德里达的著作复杂而又晦涩，以下摘要仅仅体现出他的作品的一些主要倾向。在《论文字学》中，他认为自己的观点的优势是他所谓的"核心主张是认为没有文本以外的世界"。与德里达所有的关键性术语和陈述一样，这一陈述同样具有多重所指，但其首要所指是认为读者不能因为事物本身是独立于语言系统之外，就能超越言语符号而触及任何可建立某一可确定意义的事物本身。

德里达反复强调，不仅所有西方哲学和语言理论，而且所有西方语言的运用，以至全部西方文化，都是以理性（词义）为中心（或译"**逻各斯中心主义**"）；即：它们是以"标识语"（希腊语中指"词"和"理性"）为中心或基础；或如他采用海德格尔的表述，认为它们是依赖于"在场的形而上学"。根据德里达的观点，它们之所以是词义中心的，是因为它们又是**语音中心的**；即：它们或明确或含蓄地认为，作为分析所有话语的模式，口头语较之书面语具有逻辑上的"优势"或"特权"。德里达用标识语或**在场**指代他所谓的"最终所指"——即自我证实和自主自足的基础或根据——这种所指完全处在语言自身的游戏之外，直接呈现在我们的意识中，并作为语言系统结构的"中心"（即建立、组织和保证语言系统结构），从而能够确定该系统内任何口头或书面语的使用范围、连贯性和确切意义。（关于德里达对结构主义的"去中心化"，参见：*后结构主义*。）被当做语言基础的历史例证有：上帝保证语言的有效性；或一个一般的词的真实参照的柏拉图式的形式；或黑格尔的所谓所有活动力争达到的"终极"或目标；或一种表示确定某一事物的意图，这种意图直接显现在发出言语的人的意识中。德里达试图证实，

show that these and all other attempts by Western philosophy to establish an absolute ground in presence, and all implicit reliance on such a ground in using language, are bound to fail. Especially, he directs his skeptical exposition against the phonocentric assumption—which he regards as central in Western theories of language—that at the instant of speaking, the "intention" of a speaker to mean something determinate by an utterance is immediately and fully present in the speaker's consciousness, and is also communicable to an auditor. (See *intention*, under *interpretation and hermeneutics*.) In Derrida's view, we cannot help but say more, and other, than we intend to say.

Derrida expresses his alternative conception, that the play of linguistic meanings is "undecidable," in terms derived from Saussure's view that in a sign system, both the *signifiers* (the material elements of a language, whether spoken or written) and the *signifieds* (their conceptual meanings) owe their seeming identities, not to their own "positive" or inherent features, but to their "differences" from other speech sounds, written marks, or conceptual significations. (See Saussure, in *linguistics in modern criticism* and in *semiotics*.) From this view Derrida evolves his radical claim that the features that, in any particular utterance, would serve to establish the signified meaning of a word, are never "present" to us in their own positive identity, since both these features and their significations are nothing other than a network of differences. On the other hand, neither can these identifying features be said to be strictly "absent"; instead, in any spoken or written utterance, the apparent meaning is the result only of a "self-effacing" **trace**—self-effacing in that one is not aware of it—which consists of all the nonpresent differences from other elements in the language system that invest the utterance with its "effect" of having a meaning in its own right. The consequence, in Derrida's view, is that we can never, in any instance of speech or writing, have a demonstrably fixed and decidable present meaning. He concedes that the differential play (*jeu*) of language may produce the "effects" of decidable meanings in an utterance or text, but asserts that these are merely effects, and lack a ground that would justify certainty in interpretation.

In a characteristic move, Derrida coins the *portmanteau* term **différance**, in which, he says, he uses the spelling "-ance" instead of "-ence" to indicate a fusion of two senses of the French verb "différer": to be different, and to defer. This double sense points to the phenomenon that, on the one hand, a text proffers the "effect" of having a significance that is the product of its difference, but that on the other hand, since this proffered significance can never come to rest in an actual "presence"—or in a language-independent reality Derrida calls a **transcendental signified**—its determinate specification is deferred from one linguistic interpretation to another in a movement or "play," as Derrida puts it, *en abîme*—that is, in an endless regress. To Derrida's view, then, it is difference that makes possible the meaning whose possibility (as a decidable meaning) it necessarily baffles. As Derrida says in another of his coinages, the meaning of any spoken or written utterance, by the action of opposing internal linguistic forces, is ineluctably **disseminated**—a term which includes, among its deliberately contradictory significations, that of

这些以及所有西方哲学企图建立一种在场的绝对基础以及在使用语言时所有对这种基础的绝对依赖都是注定要失败的。他特别把怀疑的矛头对准语音中心论——他把语音中心论视为西方语言理论的核心——即在言语的瞬间，言语者要用言语表达某个确定的事物的"意图"就能立即完整地呈现在言语者的意识中，而且也能够传达给听者。（参见：*释义和阐释学*中的*意图*。）依照德里达的观点，我们所说的必定总是比我们本来想说的要多，而且还会有其他含义。

德里达提出了他的另一概念，即认为语言意义的游戏是"不确定的"，这一概念用源自索绪尔观点的术语表达，即在符号系统中，*能指*（一种语言的物质成分，不论是口语还是书面语的）和*所指*（它们的概念意义）两者表面上的同一性并不取决于它们自身"实证的"或固有的特征，而是取决于与其他语言的发音、字符及概念含义之间的"区别"（参见：*语言学在文学批评里的应用*、*符号学*中关于索绪尔的论述）。德里达从这一观点推论出他的激进主张，认为在任一特定话语中，用以生成一个词的所指意义的特征是从来不会以其实证的同一性在我们眼前"在场"的，因为这些特征和它们的含义只不过是一个差异的网络。但另一方面，也不能断定这些同一性特征绝对"缺场"；相反，在任何口语或书面语中，其表面意义仅仅是"自我消失"的**踪迹**——这种自我消失在于人们没有意识到它——它由语言系统中的其他成分之间所有缺场的差异构成，这些差异赋予言语自身以具有某种意义的"作用"。德里达认为，其结果是，在任何口语或书面语中，从来没有明显的固有而又确定的在场意义。他承认，语言的差异游戏能产生话语或文本中确定意义的"效果"，但他又断言，这仅仅是些效果而已，它们缺乏可用以证明阐释的确定性的基础。

德里达的特别之处是他创造了*合词*——**异延**这一术语。他解释说，在该词中用"-ance"代替"-ence"，表示法语动词"differer"所含"差异"和"延缓"两种意思的混合。这一双重意义指的是这样一种现象，即一方面，一个文本提供的具有意义的"效果"，该意义是差异的产物；但另一方面，由于所提供的这一意义永远不可能停留在一个实际的"在场"——或一个独立于语言之外的现实中，德里达称之为**超验所指**——其意义的确定便在由一种语言的解释向另一种解释的运动或"游戏"中被延缓了，正如德里达所言，这是一种无穷尽的回归。因此，在德里达看来，正是差异使意义成为可能，它必然要阻碍这种（作为一种可确定意义的）可能性。正如德里达在创造另一个新词时所言，通过语言内部对立的确切意义的作用，任何口语或书面语的意义都不可避免地被**播撒**——这一术语在其刻意对立化的多种含义中包括：

having an effect of meaning (a "semantic" effect), of dispersing meanings among innumerable alternatives, and of negating any specific meaning. There is thus no ground, in the incessant play of difference that constitutes any language, for attributing a decidable meaning, or even a finite set of determinately multiple meanings (which he calls "polysemy"), to any utterance that we speak or write. (What Derrida calls "polysemy" is what William Empson called "ambiguity"; see *ambiguity*.) As Derrida puts it in *Writing and Difference:* "The absence of a transcendental signified extends the domain and the play of signification infinitely" (p. 280).

Several of Derrida's diverse skeptical procedures have been especially influential in deconstructive literary criticism. A cardinal procedure is to subvert the innumerable **binary oppositions**—such as speech/writing, nature/culture, truth/error, male/female—which are essential structural elements in logocentric language. Derrida shows that such oppositions constitute a tacit hierarchy, in which the first term functions as privileged and superior and the second term as derivative and inferior. Derrida's procedure is to invert the hierarchy, by showing that the primary term can be made out to be derivative from, or a special case of, the secondary term; but instead of stopping at this reversal, he goes on to destabilize both hierarchies, leaving them in a condition of undecidability. (Among deconstructive literary critics, one such demonstration is to take the standard hierarchical opposition of literature/criticism, to invert it so as to make criticism primary and literature secondary, and then to represent, as an undecidable set of oppositions, the assertions that criticism is a species of literature and that literature is a species of criticism.) A second operation influential in literary criticism is Derrida's deconstruction of any attempt to establish a securely determinate bound, or limit, or margin, to a textual work so as to differentiate what is "inside" from what is "outside" the work. A third operation is his analysis of the inherent nonlogicality, or "rhetoricity"—that is, the inescapable reliance on *rhetorical figures* and *figurative language*—in all uses of language, including in what philosophers have traditionally claimed to be the strictly literal and logical arguments of philosophy. Derrida, for example, emphasizes the indispensable reliance in all modes of discourse on metaphors that are assumed to be merely convenient substitutes for *literal*, or "proper" meanings; then he undertakes to show, on the one hand, that metaphors cannot be reduced to literal meanings but, on the other hand, that supposedly literal terms are themselves metaphors whose metaphoric nature has been forgotten.

Derrida's characteristic way of proceeding is not to lay out his deconstructive concepts and operations in a systematic exposition, but to allow them to emerge in a sequence of exemplary close readings of passages from writings that range from Plato through Jean-Jacques Rousseau to the present era— writings that, by standard classification, are mainly philosophical, although occasionally literary. He describes his procedure as a "double reading." Initially, that is, he interprets a text as, in the standard fashion, "lisible" (readable or intelligible), since it engenders "effects" of having determinate meanings. But this reading, Derrida says, is only "provisional," as a stage toward a second, or

具有意义效果（"语义"效果）、在无数其他可能的意义中分化输导意义、否定任何确定的意义。因此，在构成任何语言的连续不断的差异游戏中，认为任何口头或书面语具有一个可确定的意义、甚或具有有限的一系列明确的多种意义（他称之为"多义性"）的属性是毫无根据的。（德里达所谓的"多义性"就是威廉·燕卜荪所谓的"歧义"；参见：*歧义*。）正如德里达在《文字与差异》中指出的："超验所指的缺场，无限扩大了含义的领域及游戏的范围"（第280页）。

德里达的几处质疑对解构主义文学批评产生了特殊的影响力。最重要的做法就是颠覆无数的**二元对立关系**：如言语／文字，自然／文化，真理／谬误，男性／女性，这些都是词义向心语言的基本结构成分。德里达指出，这些对立构成了一种被人们默认了的等级秩序，在这个等级秩序中，前者拥有特权和优势，后者则处于派生或下等的地位。德里达的做法就是通过表明后者可被证明是前者衍生出来的，或者说是前者的一种特殊形式，从而把这一等级秩序颠倒过来；但他并没有就此罢休，他接着继续瓦解这两种等级秩序，使之处于不可确定的状态中。（在解构主义批评家中，解构的其中一种表现就是把文学／批评之间标准的等级对立关系颠倒为批评是第一位的，而文学是第二位的，然后将其描述为一组不可确定的对立关系，认为批评是文学的一种类型，文学是批评的一种类型。）德里达解构主义对文学批评方法的第二个影响是，试图为文本建立一种牢固的确定性的范围、或者说是界限或边缘，从而区分文本的"内部"与"外部"。其三是他对所有语言使用中，包括哲学家传统上认为是严格的哲学文字和逻辑观点的表述中固有的非逻辑性或"修辞"的分析——即语言使用中不可避免地依赖于*修辞格和比喻语*。例如，德里达强调，在所有的话语模式中，都必不可少地依赖隐喻这种仅仅被当做*字面*或"恰当"意义的便利的代用语；他继而试图说明，隐喻一方面不会被缩减为字面意义，但另一方面，据推测，文字本身就是隐喻，只不过它们的隐喻本质已被人们所遗忘。

德里达独特的分析方式并没有系统地阐述、设计出他的解构概念和操作方式，而是让这些概念和方式出现在从对柏拉图到让－雅克·卢梭直至当代作品的一系列示范性细读中——按标准的分类，这些作品中尽管也有文学作品，但主要是哲学作品。德里达把他的解构过程称为"双重阅读"。即他首先按通常的方式视作品具有"可读性"（易读的或可理解的），因为作品生成了具有确定意义的"效果"。但德里达认为，作为向第二阶段或解构"批评阅读"过渡的这一阅读阶段仅仅是"暂时性的"，这种阅读把暂时性的意义播撒为一系列不确定的含义，他认为，这些含义总

deconstructive "critical reading," which disseminates the provisional meaning into an indefinite range of significations that, he claims, always involve (in a term taken from logic) an **aporia**—an insuperable deadlock, or "double bind," of incompatible or contradictory meanings which are "undecidable," in that we lack any sufficient ground for choosing among them. The result, in Derrida's rendering, is that each text deconstructs itself, by undermining its own supposed grounds and dispersing itself into incoherent meanings in a way, he claims, that the deconstructive reader neither initiates nor produces; deconstruction is something that simply "happens" in a critical reading. Derrida asserts, furthermore, that he has no option except to attempt to communicate his deconstructive readings in the prevailing logocentric language, hence that his own interpretive texts deconstruct themselves in the very act of deconstructing the texts to which they are applied. He insists, however, that "deconstruction has nothing to do with destruction," and that the standard uses of language will inevitably go on; what he undertakes, he says, is merely to "situate" or "reinscribe" any text in a system of difference which shows the instability of the effects to which the text owes its seeming intelligibility.

Derrida did not propose deconstruction as a mode of literary criticism, but as a way of reading all kinds of texts so as to reveal and subvert the tacit metaphysical presuppositions of Western thought. His views and procedures, however, have been taken up by literary critics, especially in America, who have adapted Derrida's "critical reading" to the kind of *close reading* of particular literary texts which had earlier been the familiar procedure of the *New Criticism*; they do so, however, Paul de Man has said, in a way which reveals that new-critical close readings "were not nearly close enough." The end results of the two kinds of close reading are utterly diverse. New-critical explications of texts had undertaken to show that a great literary work, in the tight internal relations of its figurative and paradoxical meanings, constitutes a free-standing, bounded, and organic entity of multiplex yet determinate meanings. On the contrary, a radically deconstructive close reading undertakes to show that a literary text lacks a "totalized" boundary that makes it an entity, much less an organic unity; also that the text, by a play of internal counterforces, disseminates into an indefinite range of self-conflicting significations. Some deconstructive critics claim that a literary text is superior to nonliterary texts, but only because, by its self-reference, it shows itself to be more aware of features that all texts inescapably share; that is, its fictionality, its lack of a genuine ground, and especially its patent "rhetoricity," or use of figurative procedures—features that make any "right reading" or "correct reading" of a text impossible.

Paul de Man was the most innovative and influential of the critics who applied deconstruction to the reading of literary texts. In de Man's later writings, he represented the basic conflicting forces within a text under the headings of "grammar" (the code or rules of language) as opposed to "rhetoric" (the unruly play of figures and tropes), and aligned these with other opposed forces, such as the "constative" versus "performative" linguistic functions that

是包含着一种**反逆性**（逻辑学术语）——"不可确定的"难以调和或矛盾的意义导致的不可逾越的僵局或"双重困境"，对此，我们缺乏充分的依据作出选择。在德里达的描述中，其结果是，每一文本都是这样自我解构的：自我瓦解其假定的基础并自我消解成解构主义读者既没有提出也没有产生的非连贯性的意义；解构仅仅是"发生"在批评阅读过程中。此外，德里达宣称，他别无选择，只有以流行的逻各斯主义语言才能表述出他的解构式阅读方法，因此他自己的阐释性文本也以其用来解构他人文本的同样方式自我解构。但他强调"解构不等于破坏"，而且语言所有的标准用法还必将延续下去；他声称自己所从事的仅仅是使任一文本"处于"一个差异的体系中或者说是"再登记"，从而表明文本自身具有的那种貌似可理解的效果的不稳定性。

德里达并不是把解构主义作为一种文学批评模式提出来的，而是作为阅读各种文本的一种方式并以此揭示和颠覆西方思想中被默认的形而上学的假说。但是他的观点和方式被文学批评家，尤其是美国的文学批评家所采纳，他们借用德里达的"批评阅读"方式来*细读*一些特殊的文学作品，这就是早期*新批评*所熟悉的方式；但保罗·德·曼认为，他们通过采用德里达的阅读方式发现，新批评的细读法"尚不够细"。这两种细读的最终结果截然不同。对于文本的阐释，新批评所从事的是表明一部伟大的文学作品，以其比喻和自相矛盾的意义的紧密内部关系，构成了一个多元而又意义明确的独立完整的有机统一体。相反，典型的解构主义细读则是试图表明，文学文本缺乏能使之成为一个实体的"整体化"界限，更不用说使之成为有机统一体；同时，文本通过内部对立的确切意义的游戏，把自身消解成一系列不确定的自我冲突的含义。文学文本比非文学文本优越，但这仅仅是因为文学文本通过自我参照，表明其自身更加意识到一切文本都不可避免地共有的一些特征：如虚构性，缺少真正的依据，尤其是其显著的"修辞性"或比喻手法的运用——这些特征使得对文本的任何"正确阅读"或"合理阅读"都成为不可能。

保罗·德·曼是位最具创新精神、最有影响的批评家，他把解构主义原理应用到解读文学作品中。在德·曼后期的著作中，他在"语法"（语言符号或规则）和相对的"修辞"（不受约束的比喻语和比喻游戏）的标题下，描述了文本内部基本的冲突因素，并把这些冲突因素与其他对立因素，如由约翰·奥斯汀所区分的"施为"与

had been distinguished by John Austin (see *speech-act theory*). In its grammatical aspect, language persistently aspires to determinate, referential, and logically ordered assertions, which are persistently dispersed by its rhetorical aspect into an open set of nonreferential and illogical possibilities. A literary text, then, of inner necessity says one thing and performs another, or as de Man alternatively puts the matter, a text "simultaneously asserts and denies the authority of its own rhetorical mode" (*Allegories of Reading*, 1979, p. 17). The inevitable result, for a critical reading, is an aporia of "vertiginous possibilities."

Barbara Johnson, once a student of de Man's, has applied deconstructive readings not only to literary texts, but to the writings of other critics, including Derrida himself. Her succinct statement of the aim and methods of a deconstructive reading is often cited:

> *Deconstruction* is not synonymous with *destruction*.... The deconstruction of a text does not proceed by random doubt or arbitrary subversion, but by the careful teasing out of warring forces of signification within the text itself. If anything is destroyed in a deconstructive reading, it is not the text, but the claim to unequivocal domination of one mode of signifying over another. (*The Critical Difference*, 1980, p. 5)

J. Hillis Miller, formerly the leading American representative of the *Geneva School* of consciousness-criticism, later became one of the most prominent of deconstructors, known especially for his application of this type of critical reading to prose fiction. Miller's statement of his critical practice indicates how drastic the result may be of applying to works of literature the concepts and procedures that Derrida had developed for deconstructing the foundations of Western metaphysics:

> Deconstruction as a mode of interpretation works by a careful and circumspect entering of each textual labyrinth.... The deconstructive critic seeks to find, by this process of retracing, the element in the system studied which is alogical, the thread in the text in question which will unravel it all, or the loose stone which will pull down the whole building. The deconstruction, rather, annihilates the ground on which the building stands by showing that the text has already annihilated the ground, knowingly or unknowingly. Deconstruction is not a dismantling of the structure of a text but a demonstration that it has already dismantled itself.

Miller's conclusion is that any literary text, as a ceaseless play of "irreconcilable" and "contradictory" meanings, is "indeterminable" and "undecidable"; hence, that "all reading is necessarily misreading." ("Stevens' Rock and Criticism as Cure, II," in Miller's *Theory Then and Now*, 1991, p. 126, and "Walter Pater: A Partial Portrait," *Daedalus*, Vol. 105, 1976.)

For other aspects of Derrida's views see *poststructuralism* and refer to Geoffrey Bennington, *Jacques Derrida* (1993). Some of the central books by Jacques

"表述"两种语言功能（参见：*言语行为理论*）排列在一起。从语法角度来说，语言一贯追求确定性、能指性、富有逻辑性的有序陈述等功能，而这些功能又被其修辞功能持续不断地消解为一系列开放的非能指和非逻辑的可能性。于是，一篇文学文本从内部需要出发，所表述的与所施为的也就不相一致，或正如德·曼对这一问题的表述，文本"同时肯定而又否定它自身修辞模式的权威性"[《阅读的寓言》(1979) 第 17 页]。对批评阅读来说，不可避免的结局就是"不稳定的可能性"的反逆性。

曾师从德·曼的芭芭拉·约翰逊不仅把解构主义阅读方式应用到文学文本中，也将其应用到其他批评家的著作中，其中包括德里达本身。她对解构主义阅读的目的和方法所作的简洁明了的论述常被人们引用：

> *解构不是破坏的同义词……对一文本的解构并非无端的怀疑和任意的颠覆，而是仔细梳理文本自身在含义上的对立意义。如果一切都被解构阅读破坏了，那么文本就不成其为文本了，而是声称一种能指模式对另一种能指模式明白无误的主宰。*
>
> [《批评的差异》(1980) 第 5 页]

J. 希利斯·米勒曾是意识批评*日内瓦学派*在美国的主要代表人物，如今则成了最著名的解构主义者之一，他尤其以把解构主义批评阅读应用于小说中而著称。米勒关于自己批评实践的陈述表明，把德里达为解构西方形而上学的基础而发展起来的概念和方式，应用到文学作品的分析和批评中，其结果是多么的大相径庭：

> *解构主义作为一种解读作品的方法是通过深入细致地进入每部作品文本的迷宫来实现的……解构主义文学批评家利用这样的追溯过程来寻找研究对象系统中的非逻辑成分和所研究的文本中可以把文本全部解开的线索，或者说是在搜寻可以使整幢房屋倾倒的那块已经松动的石头。确切地说，解构主义是通过表明文本早已自觉或不自觉地破坏了自己立身的基础来实现其掘基解构的。它并非要肢解文本的结构，而是要证明文本本身已经自行解构了。*

米勒得出的结论是，任何文学文本，作为"互不相容"或"矛盾对立"的各种意义的一种无休止的游戏，是"不可确定"或"不可推断"的；因此，"一切阅读必然导致误解。"["史蒂文斯的岩石和作为疗法的批评，II"，文章收入米勒所著的《此时与彼时的批评》(1991) 第 126 页；"沃尔特·佩特：部分肖像"，载于《代达罗斯》1976 年第 105 卷。]

有关德里达观点的其他方面，参见：*后结构主义*；参见：杰弗里·本宁顿所著的《雅克·德里达》(1993)。德里达一些重要论著的英译版及其英译时间，

Derrida available in English, with the dates of translation into English, are *Of Grammatology*, translated and introduced by Gayatri C. Spivak (1976); *Writing and Difference* (1978); and *Dissemination* (1981). A useful anthology of selections from Derrida is *A Derrida Reader: Between the Blinds*, ed. Peggy Kamuf (1991). *Acts of Literature*, ed. Derek Attridge (1992), is a selection of Derrida's discussions of literary texts. An accessible introduction to Derrida's views is the edition by Gerald Graff of Derrida's noted dispute with John R. Searle about the speech-act theory of John Austin, entitled *Limited Inc.* (1988); on this dispute see also Jonathan Culler, "Meaning and Iterability," in *On Deconstruction* (1982), and Geoffrey Galt Harpham, "Derrida and the Ethics of Criticism," in *Shadows of Ethics: Criticism and the Just Society* (1999). Books exemplifying types of deconstructive literary criticism: Paul de Man, *Blindness and Insight* (1971), and *Allegories of Reading* (1979); Barbara Johnson, *The Critical Difference: Essays in the Contemporary Rhetoric of Reading* (1980), and *A World of Difference* (1987); J. Hillis Miller, *Fiction and Repetition: Seven English Novels* (1982), *The Linguistic Moment: From Wordsworth to Stevens* (1985), and *Theory Then and Now* (1991); Cynthia Chase, *Decomposing Figures: Rhetorical Readings in the Romantic Tradition* (1986). Expositions of Derrida's deconstruction and of its applications to literary criticism: Geoffrey Hartman, *Saving the Text* (1981); Jonathan Culler, *On Deconstruction* (1982); Richard Rorty, "Philosophy as a Kind of Writing," in *Consequences of Pragmatism* (1982); Michael Ryan, *Marxism and Deconstruction* (1982); Mark C. Taylor, ed., *Deconstruction in Context* (1986); Christopher Norris, *Paul de Man* (1988). For the range of deconstructive literary criticism, refer to Martin McQuillan, ed., *Deconstruction: A Reader* (2001); for a positive assessment of this criticism, see Christopher Norris, *Deconstruction: Theory and Practice* (3d ed., 2002).

Among the many critiques of Derrida and of various practitioners of deconstructive literary criticism are Terry Eagleton, *The Function of Criticism* (1984); M. H. Abrams, "The Deconstructive Angel," "How to Do Things with Texts," and "Construing and Deconstructing," in *Doing Things with Texts* (1989); John M. Ellis, *Against Deconstruction* (1989); Wendell V. Harris, ed., *Beyond Poststructuralism* (1996). Essays that oppose the theory and practice of deconstruction are collected in *The Emperor Redressed: Critiquing Critical Theory*, ed. Dwight Eddins, 1995, and *Theory's Empire: An Anthology of Dissent*, ed. Daphne Patai and Will H. Corral, 2005.

For references to *deconstruction* in other entries, see pages *3, 163, 196, 245, 331, 401.*

décor (dā kōr): **364**.

Decorum: Decorum, as a term in literary criticism, designates the view that there should be propriety, or fitness, in the way that a literary *genre*, its subject matter, its characters and actions, and the style of its narration and dialogue are matched to one another. The doctrine has its roots in classical theory, especially in the versified essay *Art of Poetry* by the Roman Horace in the first century BC. It achieved an elaborate form in the criticism and composition

参阅:《论文字学》,1976年佳娅特亚·C.斯皮瓦克译介;《书写与差异》(1978);《播撒》(1981)。有关德里达的实用的选集,参阅:佩吉·加缪夫主编的《德里达读本:盲目之间》(1991)。德里克·阿特里奇主编的《文学行为》(1992)是一部德里达论述文学文本的选集。杰拉尔德·格拉弗主编的关于德里达与约翰·R.塞尔针对约翰·奥斯汀提出的言语行为理论的著名争论的著述《有限公司》(1988),是一部介绍德里达学术观点的简明易懂的作品。关于这一争论,也可参阅:乔纳森·卡勒所著的《论解构主义》(1982)中的"意义与可重复性",杰弗里·高尔特·哈珀姆所著的《道德的阴影:批评与公正的社会》(1999)中的"德里达与批评伦理"。举例说明解构主义文学批评类型的著述有:保罗·德·曼所著的《不察与洞见》(1971)和《阅读的寓言》(1979);芭芭拉·约翰逊所著的《批评的差异:当代修辞阅读文集》(1980)和《差异的世界》(1987);J.希利斯·米勒所著的《虚构与重复:七部英国小说》(1982)、《语言的瞬间:从华兹华斯到史蒂文森》(1985)和《此时与彼时的批评》(1991);辛西娅·蔡斯所著的《解剖人物:浪漫主义传统中的修辞阅读》(1986)。有关对德里达解构主义理论及其在文学批评中的应用的论述可以参阅:杰弗里·哈特曼所著的《拯救文本》(1981);乔纳森·卡勒所著的《论解构主义》(1982);理查德·罗蒂所著的《实用主义的后果》(1982)中的"作为一种书写的哲学";迈克尔·瑞恩所著的《马克思主义与解构主义》(1982);马克·C.泰勒主编的《语境中的解构主义》(1986);克里斯托弗·诺里斯所著的《保罗·德·曼》(1988)。关于解构主义文学批评的范围,参阅:马丁·麦奎兰主编的《解构主义读本》(2001);关于对这一批评的积极评价,参阅:克里斯托弗·诺里斯所著的《解构主义:理论与实践》(2002年第3版)。

部分对德里达的评论以及解构主义文学批评的实践者及其著述,可以参阅:特里·伊格尔顿所著的《批评的作用》(1984);M.H.艾布拉姆斯所著的《以文行事》(1989)中的"解构的天使""如何以文行事""理解与解构";约翰·M.埃利斯所著的《反对解构主义》(1989);温德尔·V.哈里斯主编的《超越后结构主义》(1996)。反对解构主义理论及其实践的文章收入德怀特·埃丁斯主编的《重新穿上衣服的皇帝:对批评理论的批判》(1995)和达夫妮·帕泰与威尔·H.科拉尔合编的《理论帝国:对立观点选集》(2005)。

其他条目中提及"解构主义"的地方,参见第3、163、196、245、331、401页。

décor:布景　364。

Decorum:仪轨

仪轨作为文学批评术语,指文学*体裁*、题材、人物及其行为,以及叙事与人物对话风格等之间的匹配得体或适宜。该学术观点源于古典理论,尤其是公元前1世纪罗马诗人贺拉斯的诗体随笔《诗艺》中。在文艺复兴和新古典主义时期,

of literature in the Renaissance and the *Neoclassic* age, when (as John Milton put it in his essay *Of Education*, 1644) decorum became "the grand masterpiece to observe." In its most rigid application, literary forms, characters, and style were each ordered in hierarchies, or "levels," from high through middle to low, and all these elements had to be matched to one another. Thus comedy must not be mixed with tragedy, and the highest and most serious genres (epic and tragedy) must represent characters of the highest social classes (kings and nobility) acting in a way appropriate to their status and speaking in the *high style*. A number of critics in this period, however, especially in England, maintained the theory of decorum in only limited ways. Thomas Rymer (1641–1713) was an English proponent, and Samuel Johnson (1709–84) was a notable opponent of the strict form of literary decorum.

See *neoclassic and romantic, poetic diction*, and *style*, and refer to Vernon Hall, *Renaissance Literary Criticism: A Study of Its Social Content* (1945). Erich Auerbach's *Mimesis* (trans. 1953, reprinted 2003) describes the sustained conflict in postclassical Europe between the reigning doctrines of literary decorum and the example of the Bible, in which the highest matters, including the sublime tragedy of the life and passion of Christ, are intermingled with base characters and humble narrative detail, and are treated with what seemed to a classical taste a blatant indecorum of style. For Wordsworth's deliberate inversion of traditional decorum at the beginning of the nineteenth century, by investing the common, the lowly, and the trivial with high dignity and sublimity, see M. H. Abrams, *Natural Supernaturalism* (1971), pp. 390–408. For references to *decorum* in other entries, see pages *237, 298*.

deep structure (linguistic): **198**.

defamiliarize: 139.

deictic (dīk′ tĭk): **233**.

deism: A widespread mode of religious thought that manifested the faith in the supremacy of human reason during the European *Enlightenment* in the latter part of the seventeenth and the eighteenth centuries. Deism has been succinctly described as "religion without revelation." The thoroughgoing deist renounced, as violating reason, all "revealed religion"—that is, all religions, including Christianity, which are based on faith in the truths revealed in special scriptures at a certain time and place, and therefore available to only particular individuals or groups. The deist instead relied on those truths which, it was claimed, prove their accord with universal human reason by the fact that they are to be found in all religions, everywhere, at all times. Accordingly the basic tenets of deism—for example, that there is a deity, discoverable by reasoning from the creation to the creator, who deserves our worship and sanctions all moral values—were, in theory, the elements shared by all particular, or "positive," religions. Many thinkers assimilated aspects of deism while remaining professing Christians. Alexander Pope, without renouncing his

仪轨在文学批评与创作实践中得到了高度发展，（正如约翰·弥尔顿在其1644年发表的《论教育》中所言）仪轨已经成为人们"奉行的金科玉律"。在应用过程中，仪轨最严格的标准是要求文学形式、人物和创作风格均按照等级或"档次"从高档到中档再到低档排列，所有这些要素都必须相互匹配。因此，喜剧不能与悲剧相混合，最高尚和最严肃的文学类型（如史诗与悲剧）则必须以*高雅的风格*描写行为举止与其身份地位和谈吐相匹配的上流社会的人物（如国王和贵族）。然而，这一时期的一些批评家，尤其是英国批评家，只是有限地奉行了这种仪轨理论。托马斯·赖默（1641—1713）是位英国的仪轨理论倡导者，而塞缪尔·约翰逊（1709—1784）则以反对文学仪轨的严格形式而著称。

参见：*新古典主义和浪漫主义、诗意辞藻、文体*。参阅：弗农·霍尔所著的《文艺复兴时期的文学批评：对其社会背景的研究》（1945）。埃利希·奥尔巴赫所著的《摹仿论》（1953年英译版，2003年再版）介绍了欧洲后古典文艺时代居于支配地位的仪轨文学理论和圣经文体之间的长期争论，圣经中包括耶稣基督诞辰和蒙难这样庄严的悲剧在内的极为严肃的题材是与凡人琐事混同描写的，因此在古典主义者看来，这在文体上显然是不得体的。关于19世纪初华兹华斯通过用最高贵最崇高的文体描写平常的、低下的、琐碎的人或事而刻意颠倒传统仪轨的做法，参见：M. H. 艾布拉姆斯所著的《自然的超自然主义》（1971）第390—408页。其他条目中提及"仪轨"的地方，参见第237、298页。

deep structure（linguistic）：（语言学中的）深层结构　198。

defamiliarize：陌生化　139。

deictic：指示词　233。

Deism：自然神论

　　自然神论是一种广为流传的崇尚人类理性的宗教思维方式，17世纪晚期和18世纪欧洲的*启蒙运动*以推崇人类理性为特征。自然神论曾被简明地描述为"没有天启的宗教"。彻底的自然神论者否认所有反理性的"天启的宗教"——即包括基督教在内的在某一特定时间和地点受特定经文启示而对真理产生信仰的所有宗教，因此，这种宗教只属于某个特定的个人或团体。自然神论者则信奉那些在任何时间、任何地点的所有宗教中存在的经证明与整个人类理性相一致的真理。因此，自然神论的基本教义——例如，神是通过从宇宙万物到造物主的理性推理而被发现的，他值得我们信奉并且认同所有的道德价值观——在理论上是所有特定的或"确实存在"的宗教所共有的。许多思想家尽管仍然信奉基督教，但已接受了自然神论的一些观点。亚历山大·蒲柏尽管没有放弃对天主教的信仰，

Catholicism, expressed succinctly the basic tenets of deism in his poem "The Universal Prayer" (1738), which begins

> Father of all! in every age,
> In every clime adored,
> By saint, by savage, and by sage,
> Jehovah, Jove, or Lord!

deliberative oratory: 343.

demotic style (dĕmŏt′ ik): **385.**

denotation: 63.

dénouement (dā noo män′): **297.**

descriptive-meditative lyric: 406.

detective story: A narrative that centers on the sustained, analytic investigation by an amateur or professional detective of a serious crime, usually a murder. Typically, the crime is committed in a closed environment that limits the number of possible suspects. This type of *plot* was given its standard form by the short stories of Edgar Allan Poe ("Murders in the Rue Morgue," 1841, and "The Purloined Letter," 1845), and later by the most widely known of all detective fiction, the short stories and novels about Sherlock Holmes by Arthur Conan Doyle, published mainly in the 1890s.

The 1920s and 1930s was the period of many major detective stories by four Englishwomen: Agatha Christie (author of more than eighty novels and creator of the Belgian detective, Hercule Poirot, and of the doughty amateur investigator, Miss Jane Marple), Dorothy Sayers (creator of Lord Peter Wimsey), Ngaio Marsh, and Margery Allingham. Since that time women have continued to be the primary authors of detective novels, including the prolific American Mary Roberts Rinehart and the English authors P. D. James and Ruth Rendell.

Through the first two decades of the last century, the typical detective story involved well-mannered upper-class characters in a well-to-do milieu such as a country house. In the 1920s male writers in America inaugurated the **hard-boiled detective story**, set in mean urban environments, and featuring violent actions in the pursuit of gangsters and other vicious criminals by a "private eye," notably Raymond Chandler's Philip Marlowe and Dashiell Hammett's Sam Spade. Detective stories have been favored recreational reading, and the subject of critical writings, by a number of eminent literary figures, including T. S. Eliot, W. H. Auden, and Jacques Barzun.

Mystery novels (or more shortly **mysteries**) are a large class that includes detective stories, in addition to any other novels that focus on the solution of a problem, or of the source of a series of ominous events. Notable early examples are Ann Radcliffe's Gothic romance, *The Mysteries of Udolpho*

但他在诗歌《环球祷告》(1738)中简明地表现了自然神论的基本教义，诗的开头这样写道：

> 万众之父！千秋万代，
> 四面八方，
> 圣徒、蛮人、圣贤都对您崇拜，
> 无论是耶和华、朱庇特，还是耶稣基督

deliberative oratory：审议性的雄辩术　343。

demotic style：通俗文体　385。

denotation：表义　63。

dénouement：结局　297。

descriptive-meditative lyric：描述－沉思式抒情诗　406。

Detective Story：侦探故事

一种叙事，重点在于业余或职业侦探对严重罪行（通常是谋杀案）所进行的持续的分析调查。通常情况下，所犯罪行是在一个封闭的环境中，从而限制了可能的犯罪嫌疑人的数量。这种*情节*类型的标准形式先是埃德加·爱伦·坡的短篇小说〔《莫格街谋杀案》(1841)和《失窃的信》(1845)〕，后来则是所有侦探小说中最广为人知的柯南·道尔主要在1890年代出版的有关福尔摩斯的短篇故事和小说。

1920、1930年代是一个由四位英国女性所写的许多主要侦探故事出版的时期：阿加莎·克里斯蒂（超过八十本小说的作者，比利时侦探赫尔克里·波洛和刚强的业余侦探简·马普尔小姐这两个人物的创造者），多萝西·塞耶斯（彼得·温西爵士的创造者），奈欧·马许和玛格丽·艾林翰。自那时以来，女性一直是侦探小说的主要创作者，包括美国多产的玛丽·罗伯茨·莱因哈特，以及英国作家P. D. 詹姆斯和露丝·伦德尔。

上世纪前二十年间，典型的侦探故事都会涉及生活在富有的环境下如乡间别墅里彬彬有礼的上层阶级人物。1920年代，美国男性作家开创了**硬汉派侦探故事**，背景设置在低劣肮脏的城市里，其特色是暴力行为，透过一位"私家侦探"去追捕黑帮和其他恶性犯罪，比较知名的有雷蒙德·钱德勒塑造的菲利普·马洛和达希尔·哈米特塑造的山姆·史培德。侦探故事一直受到休闲阅读的青睐，并成为许多批判性文章的主题，这些文章出自一些著名文学人物之手，包括T. S. 艾略特、W. H. 奥登和雅克·巴赞。

神秘小说（或其简短形式**mysteries**）是一大类，包括侦探小说，以及任何专注于解决问题或解决一系列不祥事件的缘由的其他小说。值得注意的早期例子是安·拉德克利夫的哥特式传奇《奥多芙的神秘》(1794)，和威尔

(1794), and the Victorian novel by Wilkie Collins, *The Moonstone* (1868), about the mystifying disappearance of a very valuable diamond.

The **thriller** designates any novel which features a rapid sequence of sensational events; often, such novels represent hairbreadth escapes of a protagonist from relentless and terrifying pursuit by sinister enemies. This type of fiction was inaugurated by William Godwin's *Caleb Williams* (1794), in which the hero flees malignant persecution by an employer whose guilty secret he has discovered. The term "thriller" was first applied to fiction in pulp magazines, and is now most frequently used for such popular writings, with formulaic plots and thin characterization, as the spy stories by Ian Fleming about James Bond. The term "thriller," however, is sometimes extended to apply to the much more complex and sophisticated spy fiction by authors such as John le Carré and Anthony Price, as well as to Alfred Hitchcock's cinematic masterpieces of suspense and terror, including *Rear Window* and *Vertigo*. Detective stories, mysteries, and thrillers constitute a major proportion of motion pictures and of television dramas.

See the ground-breaking "Introduction" by Dorothy Sayers to her anthology, *The Omnibus of Crime* (2d ed., 1931); and Julian Symons, *Bloody Murder* (3d ed., 1993); Jacques Barzun and Wendell Hertig Taylor, *A Catalogue of Crime* (rev. and enl. ed., 1989); P. D. James, *Talking about Detective Fiction* (2009); *The Oxford Companion to Crime and Mystery Writing* (1999).

deus ex machina (dā′ ŭs ex mak′ ĭna) is Latin for "a god from a machine." It designates the practice of some Greek playwrights (especially Euripides) to end a drama with a god, lowered to the stage by a mechanical apparatus, who by his judgment and commands resolved the dilemmas of the human characters. The phrase is now used for any forced and improbable device—a telltale birthmark, an unexpected inheritance, the discovery of a lost will or letter—by which a hard-pressed author resolves a plot. Conspicuous examples occur even in major novels like Charles Dickens' *Oliver Twist* (1837–38) and Thomas Hardy's *Tess of the D'Urbervilles* (1891). The German playwright Bertolt Brecht *parodied* such devices in the madcap conclusion of his *Threepenny Opera* (1928). See *plot*.

diachronic (dīakrŏn′ ik): **193**.

dialects: 196.

dialogic criticism: Dialogic criticism is modeled on the theory and critical procedures of the Soviet critic Mikhail Bakhtin who, although he published his major works in the 1920s and 1930s, remained virtually unknown to the West until the 1980s, when translations of his writings gave him a wide and rapidly increasing influence. To Bakhtin a literary work is not (as in various *poststructural* theories) a text whose meanings are produced by the play of impersonal linguistic or economic or cultural forces, but a site for the dialogic interaction of multiple voices, or modes of discourse, each of which is not merely a verbal but a social phenomenon, and as such is the product of

基·柯林斯所写的维多利亚时期的小说《月亮宝石》(1868)，关于一个非常有价值的钻石神秘失踪之谜。

惊险小说指任何一部具有一系列快节奏的耸人听闻的事件这一特点的小说，这样的小说往往描绘主角间不容发地逃离无情的敌人险恶而可怕的追杀。这种类型的小说由威廉·戈德温的《凯莱布·威廉斯》(1794)所开创，书中的主人公逃离雇主的恶意迫害，因为他发现了雇主罪恶的秘密。术语"惊险小说"最早是指低俗杂志上刊登的小说，现在常指通俗读物上的小说，有着公式化的情节和单薄的人物塑造，就像伊恩·弗莱明塑造的关于詹姆斯·邦德的间谍故事。不过，"惊险小说"有时也会延伸指像约翰·勒卡雷和安东尼·普赖斯这些作家所写的很多更加复杂而深奥的间谍小说，以及希区柯克的悬疑和恐怖电影杰作，包括《后窗/偷窥》和《迷魂记》。侦探故事、神秘故事和惊险故事构成电影和电视剧的主要部分。

参阅：多萝西·塞耶斯为其文集《犯罪文选》(1931年第2版)所写的具有开拓性的"序言"；朱利安·西蒙斯所著的《血腥谋杀》(1993年第3版)；雅克·巴赞与温德尔·赫蒂希·泰勒合著的《犯罪目录》(1989年修订增加版)；P.D.詹姆斯所著的《谈谈侦探小说》(2009)；《牛津犯罪和神秘写作指南》(1999)。

Deus ex Machina：降神

该术语是拉丁文，意为"从机械里出来的天神"。它描述的是一些希腊戏剧作家（尤其是欧里庇得斯）在一出戏的结尾，借用舞台上的机械设施把神降到舞台上，通过他的审判和意旨解决剧中人物的两难境地的一种舞台表现手法。这一术语如今被用来指代那些牵强附会和不切实际的表现手段——如一个泄露隐情的胎记、一笔出人意料的遗产、失而复得的遗嘱或密信——束手无策的作者以此解决一个情节。查尔斯·狄更斯的《雾都孤儿》(1837—1838)和托马斯·哈代的《德伯家的苔丝》(1891)等名著中也都有这类鲜明的范例。德国戏剧作家贝尔托尔特·布莱希特在《三分钱歌剧》(1928)轻率的尾声里用戏谑模仿的手法嘲讽了对降神手法的滥用。参见：*情节*。

diachronic：历时 193。

dialects：方言 196。

Dialogic Criticism：对话批评

对话批评是在苏联批评家米哈伊尔·巴赫金的理论和批评方式的基础上建立起来的一种批评模式。尽管巴赫金在1920年代和1930年代就已发表出版了他的一些主要著作，但他对于西方学界而言仍然是陌生的，直到1980年代，他的著作的译本才为他赢得了广泛且急剧增大的影响力。在巴赫金看来，文学作品不是（如在不同的*后结构主义*理论中）由没有人情味的语言或经济或文化力量的游戏产生意义的文本，而是多种声音或话语模式交互对话的场所，其中每个声部不仅仅是种语言现象，也是一种社会现象，因此，文学作品是由特定阶级、社会群

manifold determinants that are specific to a class, social group, and speech community. A person's speech does not express a pre-existent and autonomous individuality; instead, his or her character emerges in the course of the dialogue and is composed of languages from diverse social contexts. Each utterance, furthermore, whether in actual life or as represented in literature, owes its precise inflection and meaning to a number of attendant factors—the specific social situation in which it is spoken, the relation of its speaker to an actual or anticipated listener, and the relation of the utterance to the prior utterances to which it is (explicitly or implicitly) a response.

Bakhtin's prime interest was in the novel, and especially in the ways that the multiple voices that constitute the text of any novel disrupt the authority of the author's single voice. In *Problems of Dostoevsky's Poetics* (1929, trans. by Caryl Emerson, 1984), he contrasts the **monologic** novels of writers such as Leo Tolstoy—which undertake to subordinate the voices of all the characters to the authoritative discourse and controlling purposes of the author—to the **dialogic form** (or "polyphonic form") of Fyodor Dostoevsky's novels, in which the characters are liberated to speak "a plurality of independent and unmerged voices and consciousnesses, a genuine polyphony of fully valid voices." In Bakhtin's view, however, a novel can never be totally monologic, since the narrator's reports of the utterances of another character are inescapably "double-voiced" (in that we can distinguish therein the author's own accent and inflection), and also dialogic (in that the author's discourse continually reinforces, alters, or contests with the types of speech that it reports).

In *Rabelais and His World* (trans. 1984), Bakhtin proposed his widely cited concept of the **carnivalesque** in certain works of literature. This literary mode parallels the flouting of authority and temporary inversion of social hierarchies that, in many cultures, are permitted during a season of carnival. The literary work does so by introducing a mingling of voices from diverse social levels that are free to mock and subvert authority, to flout social norms by ribaldry, and to exhibit various ways of profaning what is ordinarily regarded as sacrosanct. Bakhtin traces the occurrence of the carnivalesque in ancient, medieval, and Renaissance writers (especially in Rabelais); he also asserts that the mode recurs later, especially in the play of irreverent, parodic, and subversive voices in the novels of Dostoevsky—novels that are both dialogic and carnivalesque.

In an essay on "Discourse in the Novel" (1934–35), Bakhtin develops his view that the novel is constituted by a multiplicity of divergent and contending social voices that achieve their full significance only in the process of their dialogic interaction both with each other and with the voice of the narrator. Bakhtin explicitly sets his theory against Aristotle's *Poetics*, which proposed that the primary component in narrative forms is a plot that evolves coherently from its beginning to an end in which all complications are resolved (see *plot*). Instead, Bakhtin elevates *discourse* (equivalent to Aristotle's subordinate element of *diction*) into the primary component of a narrative work; and he describes discourse as a medley of voices, social attitudes, and values that are not only opposed, but irreconcilable, with the result that the work remains unresolved and open-ended. Although he wrote during the Stalinist

体和话语社区等多种决定因素组合而成的产物。一个人的话语无法表达其已有的独立的个性；相反，他/她的个性会在对话过程中显现出来，而且这种个性特征是由不同社会语境下的语言构成的。并且，每句话语，不论是现实生活中的，还是文学作品中所描写的，都会因许多场景因素——言语时具体的社会情境、言语者与现场或预期中的听者之间的关系，以及前后应答话语间的照应关系（清晰或模糊）——而具有精确的音调变化和意义。

巴赫金的首要兴趣在于小说，尤其是那种由多重声音构成的从而使得作者单一的声音权威被瓦解的小说文本。在《陀思妥耶夫斯基诗学问题》（1929，1984年卡里尔·爱默生英译版）中，他对比了列夫·托尔斯泰等作家的**独白小说**——即试图使所有人物的声音都从属于作者权威性的话语和操控性的意图——和费奥多·陀思妥耶夫斯基小说的**对话形式**（或"复调形式"），在这种形式里，小说人物能自由表达"一种独立的没有混合的多种声音和意识的多重性，一种完全有效的声音组合成的真正的复调"。但巴赫金认为，一部小说是无法做到完全独白的，因为由叙述者所表述的另一个角色的话语就是一种不可避免的"双重声音"（我们从中可以区分出作者自己的声音和腔调），因此也是对话形式的（其中，作者的话语不断强化、改变或与被表述的话语类型展开论战）。

在《拉伯雷和他的世界》（1984年英译版）中，巴赫金提出了存在于某些文学作品中的**狂欢化**这一被广为引用的概念。这一文学模式等同于许多文化中在狂欢节时允许对权威的蔑视和对社会等级秩序的颠覆。文学作品中的狂欢化是通过引入一个由来自不同社会阶层的多种声音组合成的混合体，自由地嘲弄和颠覆权威，以粗俗的幽默蔑视社会准则，以及通过多种方式亵渎那些通常被认为是神圣而不容侵犯的人与物。巴赫金追溯了出现在古代、中世纪和文艺复兴时期作家（尤其是拉拍雷）的作品中的狂欢化；他也声称，狂欢化也存在于后世的作品中，尤其是在戏谑性戏剧、滑稽模仿作品，以及陀思妥耶夫斯基小说中的颠覆性话语中，它们既属对话型的，又是狂欢化型的。

巴赫金在论文"小说的话语"（1934—1935）中发展了他的观点。他认为，小说是由各种不同而又相互争辩的这样一个多样性的社会声音构成的，这些声音只有在相互间以及与叙述者的声音进行交互对话的过程中才能实现其全部意义。巴赫金的这一理论显然与亚里士多德的《诗学》观点相抵触，亚里士多德认为，构成叙事形式的首要成分是故事情节，在情节从头至尾连贯的发展过程中，任何复杂情况都会得以解决（参见：*情节*）。相反，巴赫金把话语（等同于亚里士多德所说的次要成分*措辞*）提升为叙事作品的首要组成成分；他把话语描述为一个由声音、社会态度和价值观等因素组合而成的集合体，这些因素之间不仅相互对立，而且不可调和，其结果是作品仍然没有结束，其结局是开放的。尽管巴赫金是在斯大林主义政治体制下从事写作，但他的自由主义论和开放的文学叙事概念显

regime in Russia, Bakhtin's libertarian and open concept of the literary narrative is obviously, although tacitly, opposed to the Soviet version of Marxist criticism, which stresses the way a novel either reflects or distorts the true social reality, or expresses only a single dominant ideology, or should exemplify a "social realism" that accords with an authoritarian party line. See *Marxist criticism* and, for a discussion of the complex issue of Bakhtin's relation to Marxism and Soviet literary criticism, see Simon Dentith, *Bakhtinian Thought: An Introductory Reader* (1995), pp. 8–21.

Bakhtin's views have been, in some part and in diverse ways, incorporated by representatives of various types of critical theory and practice, whether traditional or *poststructural*. Among current students of literature, those who are identified specifically as "dialogic critics" follow Bakhtin's example by proposing that the primary component in the constitution of narrative works, or of literature generally—and of general culture as well—is a plurality of contending and mutually qualifying social voices, with no possibility of a decisive resolution into a monologic truth. Self-reflexively, a thoroughgoing dialogic critic, in accordance with Bakhtin's views, considers his or her own critical writings to be simply one voice among many in the contention of critical theories and practices, which coexist in a sustained tension of opposition and mutual definition. As Don Bialostosky, a chief spokesman for dialogic criticism, voiced its rationale and ideal:

> As a self-conscious practice, dialogic criticism turns its inescapable involvement with some other voices into a program of articulating itself with all the other voices of the discipline, the culture, or the world of cultures to which it makes itself responsible.... Neither a live-and-let-live relativism nor a settle-it-once-and-for-all authoritarianism but a strenuous and open-ended dialogism would keep them talking to themselves and to one another, discovering their affinities without resting in them and clarifying their differences without resolving them. ("Dialogic Criticism," in G. Douglas Atkins and Laura Morrow, eds., *Contemporary Literary Theory*, 1989, pp. 223–24)

See the related critical enterprise called *discourse analysis*; and in addition to the writings mentioned above, refer to Mikhail Bakhtin's *The Dialogic Imagination*, ed. Michael Holquist (1981), and *Speech Genres and Other Late Essays*, ed. Caryl Emerson and Michael Holquist (1986). For Bakhtin's life and intellectual views, with attention to the problem of identifying writings that Bakhtin published under the names of various of his colleagues, see Katerina Clark and Michael Holquist, *Mikhail Bakhtin* (1984), and Gary Saul Morson and Caryl Emerson, *Mikhail Bakhtin: Creation of a Poetics* (1990). An influential early exposition that publicized Bakhtin's ideas in the West was Tzvetan Todorov, *Mikhail Bakhtin: The Dialogical Principle* (1984). A later book describing the wide dissemination of these ideas is David Lodge's *After Bakhtin* (1990). For an application of dialogic criticism, see Don H. Bialostosky, *Wordsworth, Dialogics, and the Practice of Criticism* (1992). For a critical view of Bakhtin's claims, see René Wellek, *A History of Modern Criticism, 1750–1950*, Vol. 7 (1991), pp. 354–71.

然——尽管是默默地——与苏联版的马克思主义批评相对立。苏联的马克思主义批评强调小说或者是反映真实的社会现实,或者是歪曲真实的社会现实,或者是仅仅表现一种占统治地位的意识形态,或者是应当成为与专制政党路线相一致的"社会现实主义"的典范。参见:*马克思主义批评*;关于巴赫金与马克思主义和苏联文学批评之间的关系这一复杂问题的讨论,可以参阅:西蒙·登提斯所著的《巴赫金思想:入门读本》(1995)第 8—21 页。

各种不同流派的批评理论和实践——不论是传统的还是*后结构主义*的——都在某些方面和以不同方式吸收了巴赫金的观点。在现今文学研究者中,那些自诩为"对话批评者"的人以巴赫金为榜样,认为叙事作品,或者普遍意义上的文学作品,甚至整个文化,它们的首要构成成分是对立而又相互修正的社会声音组成的多重性,不可能分解为明确的独白的真实性。根据巴赫金自己的观点,彻底的对话批评家在自我反省时,认为在众多的批评理论和实践(这些理论和实践共存于一种对立与相互解释的持续的紧张状态中)的争论中,他/她自己的批评论著只不过是一种声音而已。正如对话批评的主要代言人唐·比亚洛斯托斯基在提出对话批评的基本原理和理想时所陈述的那样:

> 作为一种自觉的实践活动,对话批评不可避免地将与其自身牵连在一起的一些其他声音转变为一个程序,在此程序中,对话批评与其自认为负有责任的学科、文化,或文化世界的其他声音一道清楚地表达它自己……既非和平共存的相对主义,也非一劳永逸地结束争论的独裁主义,而是艰苦的开放的没有结束的对话,能使它们保持和自己以及彼此间展开对话,从而发现它们之间的亲密关系而不必依赖这种关系,澄清它们之间的差异也不必消除这些差异。["对话批评",收入 G. 道格拉斯·阿特金斯与劳拉·莫罗主编的《当代文学理论》(1989),第 223—224 页。]

参见相关批评模式:*话语分析*。除了上述著述,还可参阅:米哈伊尔·巴赫金所著的《对话想象》(1981,迈克尔·霍尔奎斯特主编);《语言类型及其他近期论文》(1986,卡里尔·埃默森与迈克尔·霍尔奎斯特合编)。有关巴赫金的生平和学术观点、涉及鉴别巴赫金以其不同同事名字发表的作品的问题,参阅:凯特琳娜·克拉克与迈克尔·霍尔奎斯特合著的《米哈伊尔·巴赫金》(1984),加里·索尔·莫森与卡里尔·埃默森合著的《米哈伊尔·巴赫金:一种诗学的创建》(1990)。早期向西方世界公开介绍巴赫金学术思想的著名作品是:兹维坦·托多罗夫所著的《米哈伊尔·巴赫金:对话原理》(1984)。后来记叙巴赫金学术思想广为传播的作品是:戴维·洛奇所著的《巴赫金之后》(1990)。运用对话批评的一个例子是:唐·H. 比亚洛斯托斯基所著的《华兹华斯、对话理论与批评实践》(1992)。对巴赫金学术主张的批评,参阅:勒内·韦勒克所著的《现代批评史:1750—1950》(1991)第 7 卷第 354—371 页。

dialogic form: 86.

dialogue: 46; *90*.

diary: 27.

diction: 298; *86*.

didactic literature: The adjective "didactic," which means "intended to give instruction," is applied to works of literature that are designed to expound a branch of knowledge, or else to embody, in imaginative or fictional form, a moral, religious, or philosophical doctrine or *theme*. (See the entry *literature*.) Such works are commonly distinguished from essentially imaginative works (sometimes called "mimetic" or "representational") in which the materials are organized and rendered, not in order to expound and enhance the appeal of the doctrine they embody, but in order to enhance the intrinsic interest of the materials themselves and their capacity to move and give artistic pleasure to an audience. In the first century BC the Roman Lucretius wrote his didactic poem *De Rerum Natura* ("On the Nature of Things") to expound and make persuasive and appealing his naturalistic philosophy and ethics, and in the same era Virgil wrote his *Georgics*, in which the poetic elements add *aesthetic* appeal to a laudation of rural life and information about the practical management of a farm. Most medieval and much Renaissance literature was didactic in intention. In the eighteenth century, a number of poets wrote **georgics** (on the model of Virgil), describing in verse such utilitarian arts as sheepherding, running a sugar plantation, and making cider. Alexander Pope's *Essay on Criticism* and his *Essay on Man* are eighteenth-century didactic poems on the subjects of literary criticism and of moral philosophy.

Such works for the most part directly describe the principles and procedures of a branch of knowledge or a craft, or else argue an explicit doctrine by proofs and examples. Didactic literature, however, may also take on the attributes of imaginative works, by embodying the doctrine in a fictional narrative or dramatic form that is intended to enhance the doctrine's human interest and persuasive force, as well as to add a dimension of pleasure in the artistry of the representation. In the various forms of *allegory*, for example, including Edmund Spenser's *The Faerie Queene* and John Bunyan's *The Pilgrim's Progress*, the purpose of enhancing and adding force to the incorporated doctrines is a primary determinant of the choice and presentation of the allegoric characters, the evolution of the plot, and the invention of fictional details. The diverse types of *satire* are didactic in that they are designed, by various devices of ridicule, to alter the reader's attitudes toward certain types of people, institutions, products, and modes of conduct. Dante's *Letter to Can Grande* tells us that he planned his fourteenth-century *Divine Comedy* to represent, in the mode of a visionary narrative, the major

dialogic form：对话形式　86。

dialogue：对话　46；*90*。

diary：日记　27。

diction：措辞　298；*86*。

Didactic Literature：教诲文学

形容词"教诲的"意为"旨在给予指导"，指旨在阐述某门知识，或以想象或虚构的形式具体表现道德的、宗教的、哲学的学说或*主题*的文学作品。（参见：*文学*。）这类文学作品通常不同于本质上是想象性的作品（有时也称"摹拟性"或"描绘性"作品），因为后者的创作目的不是为了增强其具体表现的学说的吸引力，而是为了增强作品固有的趣味性，强化作品对读者的感染力和给读者以艺术的愉悦。公元前1世纪，罗马作家卢克莱修为了陈述和推行他的自然哲学与伦理观念撰写了教诲诗篇《物性论》，同一时期，维吉尔就田园管理这一实用性题材创作了歌颂田园生活的《农事诗集》，作品中的诗歌成分增强了*审美*感染力。大多数中世纪文学作品和不少文艺复兴时期的作品也表现出教诲性的创作意图。18世纪，许多诗人（效仿维吉尔）创作了诗体**农事篇**作品，以介绍畜牧、蔗园种植经营及果汁制作等实用性生产技术。亚历山大·蒲柏的《批评论》和《人论》也属于18世纪关于文学批评和道德哲学的教诲性诗作。

大多数教诲文学作品都是直截了当地阐述某项知识或技艺的原理和程序，或者通过例证阐述鲜明的哲理，但也可以采用想象性作品的特性，以虚构叙事或戏剧形式体现说教，达到增强作品趣味性和说服力的目的，同时也用以提高作品的艺术魅力。例如，在*寓言*的各种不同形式中，包括埃德蒙·斯宾塞的《仙后》和约翰·班扬的《天路历程》在内，其讽喻人物角色的选择和表现、情节的发展和虚构细节的杜撰，都以增强和提高作品所要呈现的哲理的说服力这一目的为首要决定因素。各类*讽刺*性作品也属教诲性之列，它们采用形形色色的讽刺手法，旨在改变人们对某些类型的人物、风俗惯例、作品和行为方式的态度。但丁在《致坎·格兰德的信》中告诉我们，他在14世纪创作《神曲》的目的在于以梦幻故事的形式

Christian truths and the way to avoid damnation and achieve salvation. And John Milton's *Paradise Lost* (1667) can also be called didactic to the extent that the narrative is in fact organized, as Milton claimed in his opening invocation, around his "great argument" to "assert Eternal Providence, / And justify the ways of God to men."

It will be seen from these examples that "didactic literature," as here defined, is an analytical distinction and not a derogatory term; also that the distinction is not absolute but a matter of relative emphasis on instructing and persuading an audience, as against rendering a subject in such a way as to maximize its power to move and give artistic delight in its own right. The plays of Bernard Shaw and Bertolt Brecht manifest a fine balance of didactic intention, imaginative invention, and artistic enhancement. And some literary masterpieces are primarily didactic, while others (Shakespeare's *King Lear*, Jane Austen's *Emma*, James Joyce's *Ulysses*)—even though their plots involve moral concerns and imply criteria for moral judgments—are primarily, to adopt a phrase by Samuel Taylor Coleridge, works "of pure imagination."

The term **propagandist literature** is sometimes used as the equivalent of didactic literature, but it is more useful to reserve the term for that type of didactic work which is obviously organized and rendered to induce the reader to assume a specific attitude toward, or to take direct action on, a pressing social, political, or religious issue of the time at which the work is written. Prominent and effective examples of such works are Harriet Beecher Stowe's *Uncle Tom's Cabin* (1852, attacking slavery in the South), Upton Sinclair's *The Jungle* (1906, on the horrors of the unregulated slaughtering and meatpacking industry in Chicago), and Clifford Odets' *Waiting for Lefty* (1935, a play directed against the strong-arm tactics used to suppress a taxicab drivers' union). The *socialist realism* that was the official critical doctrine of the former Soviet Union espoused what was essentially a propagandist mode of literature.

See *fiction*, and refer to John Chalker, *The English Georgic: A Study in the Development of a Form* (1969). On a useful way to distinguish between primarily didactic and primarily imaginative, or "mimetic," literature, see R. S. Crane, ed., *Critics and Criticism* (1952), especially pp. 63–68 and 589–94.

différance (dĭf′ äräns″): 78.

difference (in linguistics): **196**; *358*.

dimeter (dĭm′ ĕter): 219.

dirge: 102.

discourse: 312; *86, 245, 306*.

discourse analysis: Traditional linguists and philosophers of language, as well as literary students of *style* and *stylistics*, have typically focused their analyses on isolated units of language—the sentence, or even single words, phrases, and

阐明基督教的主要教理和免入地狱、升入天堂的途径。约翰·弥尔顿的《失乐园》（1667）也可视为教诲性作品，正如作者在开篇乞灵中所申明的那样，全诗情节的安排都围绕着他的"重大论点"："维护永恒的上帝／声辩天公待人之道。"

从以上例子可以看出，这里所说的"教诲文学"指的是作品的特征，并非是含有贬义的术语，并且，对教诲文学的区分也不是绝对的，教诲文学只是相对侧重于对读者的教导和劝说，而不是最大限度地烘托主题的感染力和为读者提供其自身固有的艺术愉悦。萧伯纳和贝尔托尔特·布莱希特的戏剧都很好地平衡了教诲性、虚构性和艺术性三者之间的关系。有些世界名著基本上属于教诲文学之列，而有些（莎士比亚的《李尔王》、简·奥斯丁的《爱玛》、詹姆斯·乔伊斯的《尤利西斯》）尽管也涉及对道德的关注并暗示了道德的衡量标准，但用塞缪尔·泰勒·柯勒律治的话来说，基本上是"纯想象性"作品。

术语**宣教文学**有时被当做教诲文学的代名词，但把那些刻意促使读者对作品所描述的当时迫切的社会、政治或宗教问题采取某种具体的态度或作出直接反应的说教性作品称为"宣教文学"，则更为贴切。这类作品的主要代表作有：哈丽特·比彻·斯托的《汤姆叔叔的小屋》（1852，抨击美国南方的奴隶制）、厄普顿·辛克莱的《屠场》（1906，揭露芝加哥肉类加工厂无节制的屠宰和肉类加工业的恶劣劳动条件）、克利福德·奥德兹的《等待老左》（1935，一部直接抗议对出租车行业工会武装镇压的剧作；又译《等待莱费蒂》）。苏联官方学说社会主义现实主义实质上也是一种宣教文学模式。

参见：*虚构小说*，并参阅：约翰·乔克所著的《英语农事诗演变历程研究》（1969）。关于从本质上区分教诲文学和虚构文学，或"模拟"文学的有益方式，参阅：R. S. 克莱恩主编的《批评家与批评》（1952），尤其是第63—68、589—594页。

différance：异延　78。

difference (in linguistics)：（语言学中的）差异　196；*358*。

dimeter：双音步诗行　219。

dirge：挽歌　102。

discourse：话语　312；*86, 245, 306*。

Discourse Analysis：话语分析

传统的语言学家和语言哲学家，以及文学文体和文体学的学者，都把他们的研究集中在分析摘自某个特定话语语境中单独的语言单位，如句子，甚至单个的词、

figures—in abstraction from the specific circumstances of an utterance. Discourse analysis, on the other hand, as developed in the 1970s, concerns itself with the use of language in a running discourse, continued over a number of sentences, and involving the interaction of speaker (or writer) and auditor (or reader) in a specific situational context, and within a particular framework of social and cultural conventions.

Emphasis on the meaning of a discourse as dependent on specific cultural conditions and particular circumstances derives from a number of investigators and areas of research, including the work of Hans-Georg Gadamer in *hermeneutics*, the concern of Michel Foucault with the institutional conditions and power structures that serve to make given statements accepted as authoritative or true, and the work of Clifford Geertz and other cultural anthropologists on the rootedness of linguistic and other meanings in the social forms and practices specific to a cultural community. (See the above writers, under *interpretation and hermeneutics* and *new historicism*.) The current use of discourse analysis in literary studies was given special impetus by the speech-act philosopher H. P. Grice, who in 1975 coined the term **implicature** to account for indirection in discourse; for example, to explain how we are able to identify the illocutionary force of an utterance that lacks an explicit indicator of its illocutionary intention. (See *speech-act theory*.) Thus, how can we explain the fact that the utterance, "Can you pass the salt?" although it is in the syntactical form of a question of possibility, can be used by the speaker, and correctly understood by the hearer, as a polite form of request? (H. P. Grice, "Logic and Conversation," 1975, reprinted in his *Studies in the Way of Words*, 1989.) Grice proposed that users of a language share a set of implicit expectations which he calls the "communicative presumption"—for example, that an utterance is intended by a speaker to be true, clear, and above all relevant. If an utterance seems purposely to violate these expectations, we seek to make sense of it by transferring it to a context in which it is clearly appropriate. Other language theorists have continued Grice's analysis of the underlying collective assumptions that help to make utterances meaningful and intelligible, and serve also to make a sustained discourse a coherent development of signification instead of a mere collocation of independent sentences. One such assumption is that the hearer shares with the speaker (or the reader shares with the writer) a large body of nonlinguistic knowledge and experience; another is that the speaker is using language in a way that is intentional, purposive, and in accordance with the accepted linguistic and cultural conventions; a third is that there is a shared knowledge of the complex ways in which the meaning of a locution varies with the particular situation, as well as with the type of discourse, in which it is uttered.

Some proponents of stylistics include discourse analysis within their area of investigation. (See *stylistics*.) And since the late 1970s, a number of critics have adapted discourse analysis to the examination of the *dialogue* in novels and dramas. A chief aim is to explain how the characters represented in a

短语和修辞格等上。而发展于 1970 年代的话语分析，关注的是由一系列句子组成的连续性话语中语言的使用情况，而且涉及在特定语境下，以及在社会和文化习俗的框架内，言语者（或作者）和听者（或读者）之间的互动。

对特定文化条件中和特殊环境下话语意义的重视发端于许多研究者和研究领域，包括汉斯－乔治·伽达默尔的*阐释学*著作，米歇尔·福柯对于使得特定的话语表述具有权威性或真实性的制度习俗条件和权力结构的研究，以及克利福德·格尔茨和其他文化人类学者对一特定文化社区内不同的社会形式和实践中的语言及其他意义的植根性的研究著述。（关于以上作家，参见：*释义和阐释、新历史主义*中的相关论述。）言语行为哲学家 H. P. 格赖斯对话语分析应用于目前的文学研究起了特殊的促进作用，他在 1975 年创造了**话语含意**这一新名词，用以解释话语的间接性；例如，对缺少明确的语内表现行为意图指示语的话语，我们该如何识别其语内表现行为功能。（参见：*言语行为理论*。）那么，我们如何解释话语"你能把盐递给我吗？"所蕴涵的含意呢？该话语尽管在句法上属于疑问句，但言语者又是如何能把它作为一种礼貌的请求形式并被听者正确理解呢？[格赖斯所写的文章"逻辑与会话"（1975），收入其所著的《言语方式的研究》（1989 年重印）。]格赖斯指出，一门语言的使用者共有一套含蓄的期望，他称其为"交际预设"——例如，言语者期望话语真实、清晰，但首要的是要具有关联性。如果某一话语似乎故意违反了这些期望，我们就得把该话语移置于与其显然相称的语境中以求理解它的真正含义。其他的语言理论家继承了格赖斯关于隐含的集体预设的分析，集体预设使得话语意义明确可辨，同时也使得连续性的话语的意义连贯发展，而非仅仅是些各自独立的句子的搭配。一种集体预设就是听者和言语者（或者是读者和作者）共同享有的大量非语言的知识和经验；另一种集体预设是言语者是以有意的、有目的的方式使用语言，并且使之与语言和文化的惯例相一致；第三种集体预设是指交际双方对复杂的交际行为都有这样一个共识，认为话语的意义既会随着特定情景的变化而改变，也会随着话语类型的不同而改变。

有些文体学倡导者把话语分析纳入他们的研究领域。（参见：*文体学*。）自从 1970 年代后期以来，许多批评家都在运用话语分析研究小说和戏剧的*对白*。其主要目的是解释文学作品中所描写的角色，也包括其读者在内，是何以常常能够推

literary work, and also the readers of that work, are constantly able to infer correctly meanings that are not asserted or specified in a conversational interchange. The claim is that such inferences are "rule-governed," in that they depend on tacit sets of assumptions, shared by users and interpreters of discourse, that come into play to establish meanings and, furthermore, that these meanings vary systematically, in accordance with whether the rule-guided expectations are fulfilled or intentionally violated. Such explorations of conversational discourse in literature often extend to the reanalysis of *point of view* and other traditional topics in the criticism of literary narratives. (Compare the entry on *dialogic criticism*.)

See Malcolm Coulthard, *An Introduction to Discourse Analysis* (1977); Gillian Brown and George Yule, *Discourse Analysis* (1983); Teun A. van Dijk and Walter Kintsch, *Strategies of Discourse Comprehension* (1983); Dan Sperber and Deirdre Wilson, *Relevance: Communication and Cognition* (1986); Wendell V. Harris, *Interpretive Acts* (1988), chapter 2; Sara Mills, *Discourse* (2d ed., 2009). A relevant collection of writings is Adam Jaworski and Nicholas Coupland, eds., *The Discourse Reader* (1999).

discovery (in a plot): **297**.

discussion play: 318.

disposition (in rhetoric): **343**.

disseminate (in deconstruction): **78**.

dissociation of sensibility: "Dissociation of sensibility" was a phrase introduced by T. S. Eliot in his essay "The Metaphysical Poets" (1921). Eliot's claim was that John Donne and the other *metaphysical poets* of the earlier seventeenth century, like the Elizabethan and Jacobean dramatists, "possessed a mechanism of sensibility which could devour any kind of experience." They manifested "a direct sensuous apprehension of thought," and felt "their thought as immediately as the odour of a rose." But "in the seventeenth century a dissociation of sensibility set in, from which we have never recovered." This dissociation of intellection from emotion and sensuous perception, according to Eliot, was greatly aggravated by the influence of John Milton and John Dryden; and most of the later poets writing in English either thought or felt, but did not think and feel, as an act of unified sensibility.

Eliot's vaguely defined distinction had a great vogue, especially among American *New Critics*. The dissociation of sensibility was said to be the feature that weakened most poetry between Milton and the later writings of W. B. Yeats, and was attributed particularly to the development, in the seventeenth century, of the scientific conception of reality as a material universe stripped of human values and feeling. (See, for example, Basil Willey, *The Seventeenth Century Background*, 1934.) Especially after 1950, however, Eliot's conception

测到会话交际中没有肯定或明确说明的意义的。他们认为这种推测"有章可循",即依赖于一整套话语的使用者和解释者所共享的并使得话语具有特定意义的交际预设,而且,这些话语的意义也会随着有章可循的预设期望的实现或刻意违反而有规则地变化。对文学中会话话语这样的探讨,常常延伸到对*视角*和文学叙事批评中其他传统议题的重新分析。(对比:*对话批评*。)

参阅:马尔科姆·库尔萨德所著的《话语分析入门》(1977);吉利恩·布朗与乔治·尤尔合著的《话语分析》(1983);托伊恩·A. 范·戴克与沃尔特·金特什合著的《话语理解的策略》(1983);丹·斯珀伯与戴尔德丽·威尔逊合著的《关联性:交际与认知》(1986);温德尔·V. 哈里斯所著的《阐释行为》(1988)第2章;萨拉·米尔斯所著的两卷本《话语》(2009)。相关的文章合集是亚当·贾沃斯基与尼古拉斯·库普兰合编的《话语读本》(1999)。

discovery (in a plot):(情节中的) 领悟   297。

discussion play:讨论剧   318。

disposition (in rhetoric):(修辞学中的) 布局   343。

disseminate (in deconstruction):(解构主义中的) 播撒   78。

Dissociation of Sensibility:思想与感受的分裂

思想与感受的分裂是 T. S. 艾略特在"玄学派诗人"(1921)一文中提出的一个概念。艾略特认为约翰·多恩和17世纪初期的其他*玄学派诗人*同伊丽莎白时期和詹姆斯一世时期的戏剧家一样,"具有捕捉任何经验感受的技巧"。他们表现出"对思想的直观感悟",而且感受"他们自己的意念就如同对飘来的玫瑰花香那样能够立即嗅到"。但"在17世纪,思想与感受开始分裂,从此再也没有弥合。"根据艾略特的观点,约翰·弥尔顿和约翰·德莱顿的影响极大地加剧了理智与情感和感知的分裂;而后来的大多数英语诗人无论在思维时还是在感知时,都没有将思维和感知作为一个统一的感受行为。

艾略特这种不甚明确的区分曾经风靡一时,尤其是在美国*新批评家*中广为流行。思想与感受的分裂被认为是自弥尔顿到 W. B. 叶芝后期的作品这一时期内大多数诗歌的一个特征,这一特征削弱了诗歌的艺术感染力,其分裂的原因尤其可归结为17世纪把现实看成是脱离于人的价值与情感的物质世界这一科学观念的发展[参阅巴兹尔·威利所著的《17世纪的背景》(1934)]。然而,尤其是自1950年代

of a sudden but persisting dissociation of sensibility came in for strong criticism, on the ground that it is an invalid historical claim that was contrived to support Eliot's disapproval (as a political and social conservative) of the course of English intellectual, political, and religious history after the Civil War of 1642, as well as to rationalize Eliot's particular poetic preferences.

See T. S. Eliot, "The Metaphysical Poets," in *Selected Essays* (2d ed., 1960), and "Milton II," in *On Poetry and Poets* (1957). Attacks on the validity of the doctrine are Leonard Unger, *Donne's Poetry and Modern Criticism* (1950), and Frank Kermode, *Romantic Image* (1957), chapter 8. For references to *dissociation of sensibility*, see page 360.

dissonance (dĭs′ ŏnans): **115**.

distance and involvement: In his *Critique of Judgment* (1790), Immanuel Kant analyzed the experience of an aesthetic object as an act of "contemplation" which is "disinterested" (that is, independent of one's personal interests and desires) and free from reference to the object's reality, moral effect, or utility. (See *aesthetics* and *aestheticism*.) Various philosophers of art developed this concept into attempts to distinguish "aesthetic experience" from all other kinds of experience, on the basis of the impersonality and disinterestedness with which we contemplate an aesthetic object or work of art. Writing in 1912, Edward Bullough introduced the term "distance" into this type of theory. He points, for example, to the difference between our ordinary experience of a dense fog at sea—with its strains, anxiety, and fear of invisible dangers—and an aesthetic experience, in which we attend with delight to the "objective" features and sensuous qualities of the fog itself. This aesthetic mode of experiencing the fog is, Bullough affirms, the effect of "psychical distance," which "is obtained by separating the object and its appeal from one's own self, by putting it out of gear with practical needs and ends." The degree of this psychical distance varies according to the nature of the artistic object that we contemplate, and also in accordance with an "individual's capacity for maintaining a greater or lesser degree" of such distance.

In recent literary criticism the term **aesthetic distance**, or simply **distance**, is often used not only to define the nature of literary and aesthetic experience in general, but also to analyze the many devices by which authors control the degree of a reader's distance, or "detachment"—which is in inverse relationship to the degree of a reader's **involvement**, or "concern"—with the actions and fortunes of one or another character represented within a work of literature. See, for example, Wayne C. Booth's detailed analysis of the control of distance in Jane Austen's *Emma*, in *The Rhetoric of Fiction* (rev. 1983), chapter 9.

Edward Bullough's innovative essay on "Psychical Distance as a Factor in Art and an Aesthetic Principle," *British Journal of Psychology* 5 (1912), is reprinted in Melvin Rader, ed., *A Modern Book of Aesthetics* (rev. 1952). A useful review of theories of the aesthetic attitude and of aesthetic distance is Jerome Stolnitz, *Aesthetics and Philosophy of Art Criticism* (1960), chapter 2. For the view that such theories are mistaken, see George Dickie, *Art and the Aesthetic* (1974), chapters 4 and 5.

以来，艾略特所谓突发而持续的思想与感受分裂的观点受到强烈批评，批评者认为那是一种不能成立的历史主张，艾略特炮制这一理论是为了支持他（作为一个在政治和社会观念上的保守者）对1642年内战以来英国的思想、政治、宗教历史进程所持的反对观点，同时为自己对特殊诗歌的偏爱进行辩解。

参阅：T. S. 埃利奥特所著的《选集》（1960年第2版）中的"玄学派诗人"和《论诗歌与诗人》（1957）中的"弥尔顿 II"。对这一学说的合理性加以抨击的有：伦纳德·昂格尔所著的《多恩的诗与现代批评》（1950），弗兰克·克莫德所著的《浪漫主义意象》（1957）第8章。其他条目中提及"思想与感受的分裂"的地方，参见第360页。

dissonance：**不和谐** 115。

Distance and Involvement：**心理距离与感情介入**

伊曼纽尔·康德在《判断力批判》（1790）中分析审美客体的审美体验时认为，审美体验是一种"沉思冥想"，是"超功利的"（即超越了个人利益和欲望），独立于审美客体所指的现实、道德效果或实用性。（参见：*美学、唯美主义*。）不同的文艺理论家发展了这一观念，试图把我们公正无私、超越功利地对审美客体或艺术作品的沉思冥想这种"审美体验"与其他各种体验区分开来。爱德华·布洛在其1912年的论著中，把"距离"这一概念引入该理论。他举例说明了一般体验与审美体验两者之间的不同：在海上遇到浓雾时，人们通常的心理体验是紧张、焦虑以及对大雾潜在的危险的恐惧；然而作为一种审美体验，人们面对这种迷雾茫茫的"客观"景致，会感到赏心悦目。布洛把对大雾的这种审美体验方式归因于"心理距离"的作用，该作用是"通过使客体及其感染力与审美主体自我相分离，并使客体与主体的实际需要和目的相脱离而获得的"。心理距离的远近程度既取决于我们沉思冥想的艺术客体的本质，也取决于"个人对这种距离在远近程度上的把握能力"。

在新近的文学批评中，术语**审美距离**，或简称**距离**，不仅常用于从总体上说明文学与审美体验的本质，还用来分析作家所采用的众多手法，作家凭借这些手法控制读者的心理距离或"超然"程度——与读者的**感情介入**，或对文学作品中一位或另一位人物行为和命运的"关注"程度相反。例如：韦恩·C. 布思在《小说修辞学》（1961）第九章中对简·奥斯丁的小说《爱玛》中这种"距离"的控制作了详尽分析。

爱德华·布洛具有创意的文章"作为艺术的一个要素与美学原理的'心理距离'"，载于《英国心理学杂志》1912年第5期上，重印收入梅尔文·雷德主编的《现代美学选》（1952年修订版）。杰罗姆·斯托尼茨在其所著的《美学与艺术批评哲学》（1960）第2章中对审美态度和审美距离理论做了有益的评论。认为该理论属于谬论的观点，参阅乔治·迪基所著的《艺术与美学》（1974）一书第4—5章。

See *empathy and sympathy*.

distancing effect: 7.

documentary drama: 257.

documentary fiction: 257.

doggerel: A term applied to rough, heavy-footed, and jerky *versification*, and also to verses that are monotonously regular in meter and tritely conventional in sentiment. Doggerel is usually the product of ineptitude on the part of the versifier, but is sometimes deliberately employed by poets for satiric, comic, or rollicking effect. John Skelton (1460?–1529) wrote short lines of two or three stresses, intentionally rough and variable in meter, which have come to be called **Skeltonics**; as he both described and exemplified his versification in *Colin Clout:*

> For though my rhyme be ragged,
> Tattered and jagged,
> Rudely rain-beaten,
> Rusty and moth-eaten,
> If ye take well therewith,
> It hath in it some pith.

The tumbling, broken, and comically grotesque *octosyllabic couplet*—often using double, triple, and imperfect rhymes—developed by Samuel Butler for his satiric poem *Hudibras* (1663–78) is a form of deliberate doggerel that has come to be called **Hudibrastic verse**:

> Besides, he was a shrewd philosopher,
> And had read every text and gloss over;
> Whate'er the crabbed'st author hath,
> He understood b'implicit faith.

See *meter*. For references to *doggerel* in other entries, see page *39*.

domestic tragedy: 410.

double plot: 295.

double rhyme: 349.

drama: The form of composition designed for performance in the theater, in which actors take the roles of the characters, perform the indicated actions, and utter the written dialogue. (The common alternative name for a dramatic composition is a **play**.) In **poetic drama** the dialogue is written in verse, which in English is usually *blank verse* and in French is the twelve-syllable

参见：*移情与同情*。

distancing effect：间离效果　7。

documentary drama：纪实戏剧　257。

documentary fiction：纪实小说　257。

Doggerel：打油诗

　　打油诗是指那种韵脚粗俗笨拙、行文拗口的诗文，也指韵律单调、情感陈腐、落入俗套的诗文。它往往出自不才诗人之手，但也时常为高手妙用，以取得讽刺、滑稽、幽默的艺术效果。约翰·斯克尔顿（1460？—1529）写过不少这种打油诗，其诗行仅有两个或三个音步，刻意使得格律粗俗多变，后人称之为**斯克尔顿体短韵诗**。他曾在《科林·克劳特》中这样举例描绘自己的作品：

　　　　尽管我的诗作不完美，
　　　　韵律散乱而参差不齐，
　　　　如狂暴的雨滴溅起的泡沫
　　　　锈迹斑斑又如蛀虫蚕食过
　　　　可你如果细细品读，
　　　　就会发现其中蕴藏着精华

　　塞缪尔·勃特勒在讽刺诗《休迪布拉斯》（1663—1678）中创造出一种零乱破碎、滑稽怪诞的*八音节对句*，该对句常采用双句押韵、三句押韵或不规范的韵式。这种寓意其中的打油诗形式被称作**休迪布拉斯诗体**，例如：

　　　　此外，他是一位精明的哲人
　　　　遍读了每一本书及其注释；
　　　　无论作者的文章多么晦涩，
　　　　他都能明确地理解其主旨。

　　参见：*格律*。其他条目中提及"打油诗"的地方，参见第39页。

domestic tragedy：家庭悲剧　410。

double plot：双重情节　295。

double rhyme：叠韵　349。

Drama：戏剧

　　戏剧是用于舞台演出的一种文学形式，由演员扮演作品中的角色，运用对话与动作表演表现情节（戏剧的另一常用名称是 play）。在*诗剧*中，对话采用诗体，在英语中主要是运用*无韵诗*的形式，在法语中则是被称为*亚历山大体*的

line called an *alexandrine*. Almost all the *heroic dramas* of the English Restoration Period, however, were written in *heroic couplets* (iambic pentameter lines rhyming in pairs). A **closet drama** is written in dramatic form, with dialogue, indicated settings, and stage directions, but is intended by the author to be read rather than to be performed; examples are Milton's *Samson Agonistes* (1671), Byron's *Manfred* (1817), Shelley's *Prometheus Unbound* (1820), and Hardy's *The Dynasts* (1904–08).

For types of drama, see *absurd, literature of the; chronicle plays; comedy; comedy of humours; commedia dell'arte; drama of sensibility; epic theater; expressionism; folk drama; heroic drama; masque; melodrama; miracle plays, morality plays, and interludes; mummer's play; pantomime and dumb show; pastoral; problem play; satire; sentimental comedy; tragedy; tragicomedy.* For features of drama, see *act; atmosphere; character and characterization; deus ex machina; plot; proscenium arch; setting; theater in the round; three unities.*

drama of sensibility: 361.

dramatic irony: 186; *295*.

dramatic lyric: 94.

dramatic monologue: A **monologue** is a lengthy speech by a single person. In a play, when a character utters a monologue that expresses his or her private thoughts, it is called a *soliloquy*. **Dramatic monologue**, however, does not designate a component in a play, but a type of *lyric poem* that was perfected by Robert Browning. In its fullest form, as represented in Browning's "My Last Duchess," "The Bishop Orders His Tomb," "Andrea del Sarto," and many other poems, the dramatic monologue has the following features: (1) A single person, who is patently *not* the poet, utters the speech that makes up the whole of the poem, in a specific situation at a critical moment: the Duke is negotiating with an emissary for a second wife; the Bishop lies dying; Andrea once more attempts wistfully to believe his wife's lies. (2) This person addresses and interacts with one or more other people; but we know of the auditors' presence, and what they say and do, only from clues in the discourse of the single speaker. (3) The main principle controlling the poet's choice and formulation of what the lyric speaker says is to reveal to the reader, in a way that enhances its interest, the speaker's temperament and character.

In monologues such as "Soliloquy of the Spanish Cloister" and "Caliban upon Setebos," Browning omits the second feature, the presence of a silent auditor; but features 1 and 3 are the necessary conditions of a dramatic monologue. The third feature—the focus on self-revelation—serves to distinguish a dramatic monologue from its near relation, the **dramatic lyric**, which is also a monologue uttered in an identifiable situation at a dramatic moment. John Donne's "The Canonization" and "The Flea" (1613), for example, are dramatic lyrics that lack only one feature of the dramatic monologue: the focus of interest is primarily on the speaker's elaborately ingenious argument, rather than on the character he inadvertently reveals in the course of arguing. And although Wordsworth's "Tintern Abbey" (1798) is spoken by one person to a

十二音节形式。王政复辟时期的绝大多数**英雄剧**都是采用**英雄双韵体**的形式（五步抑扬格、双句押韵）。**文房剧**也是一种戏剧形式，剧中有对白、象征性情景和舞台指导，但只供阅读不为演出。例如：弥尔顿的《力士参孙》(1671)、拜伦的《曼弗雷德》(1817)、雪莱的《解放了的普罗米修斯》(1820)和哈代的《列王》(1904—1908)。

关于戏剧的各种类型，参见：*荒诞派文学、编年历史剧、喜剧、风俗喜剧、即兴喜剧、情感戏剧、史诗剧场、表现主义、民间剧、英雄剧、假面歌舞剧、情节剧、奇迹剧、道德剧、插剧、假面剧、哑剧和默剧、牧歌、问题剧、讽刺、感伤喜剧、悲剧、悲喜剧*。关于戏剧的特征，参见：*幕、作品基调、人物与人物塑造、降神、情节、舞台拱顶、场景、圆形剧场、三一律*。

drama of sensibility：情感戏剧　361。

dramatic irony：戏剧性反讽　186；*295*。

dramatic lyric：戏剧抒情诗　94。

Dramatic Monologue：戏剧独白诗

独白是指一个人篇幅冗长的长篇大论。在戏剧中一个角色以独白的形式表达自己私下的思想时，称之为**内心独白**。其实，**戏剧独白诗**并不算戏剧的组成部分，而是属于一种由诗人罗伯特·勃朗宁发展完善起来的*抒情诗*。在这类诗体最成熟的作品中，如勃朗宁的《我那已故的公爵夫人》《圣普拉西德教堂的主教盼咐后事》《萨脱的安德列亚》和许多其他诗作，戏剧独白诗具有以下特点：(1) 全诗由某一他人，显然不是作者本人，在某一特定情境中的关键时刻独白：公爵和使臣商议再娶；主教卧榻临终；安德列亚再次趋于轻信妻子的谎言。(2) 独白人向他人讲话，并和一人或多人形成呼应；我们只是从独白人话语中知道旁听者的存在和他们的所言所行。(3) 诗人选择与组织独白的主要原则是，使抒情诗独白人以更有趣味性的方式向读者展示自己的气质和性格特征。

在像《西班牙修道院里的独白》《卡里班心中的上帝》这些独白诗中，勃朗宁省去了第二个特征，即沉默的听众的出现。但是，第一、三两个特点是构成戏剧独白诗的必要条件。其中第三个特点——自我暴露——用于把戏剧独白诗和与其相近的**戏剧抒情诗**相区别，戏剧抒情诗也是一种在戏剧情节的某个相同情景下的独白。例如，约翰·多恩的《圣徒追封》和《跳蚤》(1613)就是戏剧抒情诗，它们只缺少了独白诗的其中一个特征：这两首诗注重的是独白人的善辩内容，而不是善辩中使他不经意地暴露的个人性格。尽管华兹华斯的《丁登寺》(1798)是

silent auditor (his sister) in a specific situation at a significant moment in his life, it is not a dramatic monologue proper, both because we are invited to identify the speaker with the poet himself, and because the organizing principle and focus of interest is not the revelation of the speaker's distinctive temperament, but the evolution of his observations, memories, and thoughts toward the resolution of an emotional problem.

Tennyson wrote "Ulysses" (1842) and other dramatic monologues, and the form has been used by H. D. (Hilda Doolittle), Amy Lowell, Robert Frost, E. A. Robinson, Ezra Pound, Robert Lowell, and other poets of the twentieth century. The best-known modern instance is T. S. Eliot's "The Love Song of J. Alfred Prufrock" (1915).

See Robert Langbaum, *The Poetry of Experience: The Dramatic Monologue in Modern Literary Tradition* (1957); Adena Rosmarin, *The Power of Genre* (1985), chapter 2, "The Dramatic Monologue"; Elisabeth A. Howe, *The Dramatic Monologue* (1996).

dramatis personae (dräm′ ătĭs pĕrsō′ nē): **286**.

dream allegory: 95.

dream vision: Dream vision (also called **dream allegory**) is a mode of narrative widely employed by medieval poets: the narrator falls asleep, usually in a spring landscape, and dreams the events he goes on to relate; often he is led by a guide, human or animal, and the events which he dreams are at least in part an *allegory*. A very influential example is the thirteenth-century French poem *Roman de la Rose*; the greatest of medieval poems, Dante's *Divine Comedy*, is also a dream vision. In fourteenth-century England, it is the narrative mode of the fine elegy *Pearl*, of Langland's *Piers Plowman*, and of Chaucer's *The Book of the Duchess* and *The House of Fame*. After the Middle Ages the vogue of the dream allegory diminished, but it never died out, as Bunyan's prose narrative *The Pilgrim's Progress* (1678) and Keats' verse narrative *The Fall of Hyperion: A Dream* (1819) bear witness. Lewis Carroll's *Alice's Adventures in Wonderland* (1865) is in the form of a dream vision, and James Joyce's *Finnegans Wake* (1939) consists of an immense cosmic dream on the part of an archetypal dreamer.

See C. S. Lewis, *The Allegory of Love* (1938); and Howard Rollin Patch, *The Other World according to Descriptions in Medieval Literature* (1950, reprinted 1970).

dumb show: 266.

duodecimo (doo′ ŏdĕs″ ĭmō): **34**.

dystopia (dĭstō′ pēā): **417**.

由一个人在特定的情景中及他生活的关键时刻对一个无言听者（他的妹妹）的叙述，但却不能把它列为戏剧独白诗，因为诗人引导我们把诗中独白人与他本人视为同一；再者，这首诗的组织原则和趣味的焦点不是使独白人表现其独特的气质，而是在于叙述他对感情问题的观察、回忆、思考的发展变化过程。

丁尼生创作了《尤利西斯》(1842)和其他戏剧独白诗；20世纪诗人希尔达·杜利特尔、埃米·洛威尔、罗伯特·弗罗斯特、E. A. 罗宾逊、埃兹拉·庞德、罗伯特·洛威尔和其他诗人也采用过这种形式。T. S. 艾略特的《普鲁弗洛克的情歌》(1915)是当代戏剧独白诗的杰出典范。

参阅：罗伯特·兰鲍姆所著的《经验之诗：现代文学传统中的戏剧独白》(1957)；阿登纳·罗斯马林所著的《文类的力量》(1985)第2章"戏剧独白"；伊丽莎白·A. 豪所著的《戏剧独白》(1996)。

dramatis personae：剧中人物　286。

dream allegory：梦幻寓言体　95。

Dream Vision：梦幻体

梦幻体（又译**梦幻寓言体**）是一种叙事形式，曾为中世纪诗人广泛采用。这类作品通常表现叙述者昏然入睡，通常是在一派春色中，并且梦到他将要叙述的事件；他通常是由一位向导（人或动物）引领，他的梦中经历至少在一定程度上是个*寓言*。13世纪法国的寓言诗《玫瑰传奇》是中世纪梦幻体很有影响的范例；中世纪的诗歌之最、但丁的《神曲》也是梦幻体作品。在14世纪的英国，精美的挽歌《珍珠》、朗格兰的《农夫皮尔斯》、乔叟的《公爵夫人的书》和《名望之屋》都是运用这种叙事形式创作的。中世纪后，梦幻寓言体不再流行，但也并没有完全销声匿迹，如班扬的叙事散文《天路历程》(1678)和济慈的叙事诗《海披里昂：梦》(1819)。刘易斯·卡罗尔也用梦幻体形式创作了《艾丽丝漫游奇境记》(1865)，詹姆斯·乔伊斯的《芬尼根的觉醒》(1939)中有一位原型梦幻者在无边的宇宙间经历了一次梦游。

参阅：C. S. 刘易斯所著的《爱情的寓言》(1938)。霍华德·罗林·帕奇所著的《中世纪文学中描述的另一个世界》(1950，1970年重印)。

dumb show：默剧　266。

duodecimo：十二开本　34。

dystopia：反面乌托邦　417。

E

Early Modern (period): 338.

Early National Period (in American literature): 274.

echoism: 264.

eclectic text: 403.

eclogue (ĕk′ lŏg): 268.

ecocentrism: 98.

ecocriticism: Ecocriticism was a term coined in the late 1970s by combining "criticism" with a shortened form of "ecology"—the science that investigates the interrelations of all forms of plant and animal life with each other and with their physical habitats. "Ecocriticism" (or by alternative names, **environmental criticism** and **green studies**) designates the critical writings which explore the relations between literature and the biological and physical environment, conducted with an acute awareness of the damage being wrought on that environment by human activities.

    Representations of the natural environment are as old as recorded literature, and were prominent in the account of the Garden of Eden in the Hebrew Bible, as well as in the *pastoral* form inaugurated by the Greek Theocritus in the third century BC and later imitated by the Roman poet Virgil—an idealized depiction of rural life, viewed as a survival of the simplicity, peace, and harmony that had been lost by a complex and urban society. The nostalgic view of a return to unspoiled nature in order to restore a lost simplicity and concord remained evident in James Thomson's long poem in blank verse *The Seasons* (1726–30), and in the widely practiced *genre* called **nature writing**: the intimate, realistic, and detailed description in prose of the natural environment, rendered as it appears to the distinctive sensibility of the author. This literary form was largely initiated in England by Gilbert White's enormously popular *Natural History and Antiquities of Selborne* (1789)—his close and affectionate observations of wildlife and the natural setting in a particular area of rural England. In America, an early instance of nature writing was William Bertram's *Travels through the Carolinas, Georgia, and Florida* (1791); among its successors was a *classic* of this genre, Henry David Thoreau's *Walden* (1854). By the mid-nineteenth century Thoreau and other writers in America and England were already drawing attention to the threats to the environment by urbanization and industrialization. Later in the century, increasing alarm at the rapidity and extent of the human despoliation of nature led to what came to be called "the environmental movement" to preserve what remained of the American

E

Early Modern (period)：早期现代时期　338。

Early National Period (in American literature)：(美国文学中的) 早期民族文学时期　274。

echoism：回声词　264。

eclectic text：编选的文本　403。

eclogue：牧歌　268。

ecocentrism：生态中心主义　98。

Ecocriticism：生态批评

　　生态批评是 1970 年代后期通过将"批评"与"生态学"的缩写形式相结合创造出的一个术语——生态学是一门研究各种形式动植物生命的相互关系及与其栖息地关系的科学。"生态批评"（又名**环境批评**、**绿色研究**）指探讨文学与生物和物理环境之间关系的批评著作，这些作品对人类活动给环境造成的损害抱有一种敏锐的意识。

　　自从有记载的文献开始就有对自然环境的描述，其中最有名的是希伯来圣经中对伊甸园的描述，和公元前 3 世纪希腊人提奥克里图斯创立后由罗马诗人维吉尔进行模仿的田园*牧歌*式描述——对乡村生活所作的一种理想化描述，被视为复杂的城市社会已经失去的简单、和平、和谐的幸存地。回归未受污染的大自然以恢复丢失的简单与和谐这一怀旧视角，在詹姆斯·汤姆森的无韵长诗《四季》(1726—1730) 和得到广泛实践的*文学类型***自然写作**中仍然可以明显看出，所谓自然写作，就是在散文中对自然环境进行亲密无间的、栩栩如生的、巨细无遗的描述，表达出作者对自然环境的独特感性。这种文学形式在英国主要始于吉尔伯特·怀特广受欢迎的《塞尔彭博物志》(1789)——他对英国乡村一个特定地域野生动物和自然环境进行的近距离的和深情的观察。在美国，自然写作的一个早期实例是威廉·伯特伦漫游卡罗莱纳、乔治亚、佛罗里达三大州后写就的《游记》(1791)；在其后继者中出现了这一文学类型的*经典*之作：亨利·大卫·梭罗的《瓦尔登湖》(1854)。到 19 世纪中叶，梭罗和美国及英国的其他作家，已经让人们开始关注起城市化和工业化对环境的威胁。19 世纪晚些时候，日益增多的对人类掠夺自然的速度和广度的警示信号，促成了后来所称的"环保运动"，为的是保存

wilderness; the most noted advocates were the American writers John Burroughs (1837–1921) and John Muir (1838–1914).

In the twentieth century the warnings by scientists and conservationists increased; two especially influential books were Aldo Leopold's *A Sand County Almanac* (1949), drawing attention to the ominous degradation of the environment, and Rachel Carson's *Silent Spring* (1962), concerning the devastation inflicted by newly developed chemical pesticides on wildlife, both on land and in water. By the latter part of the century there was widespread concern that the earth was in an environmental crisis, brought on by the industrial and chemical pollution of the "biosphere" (the thin layer of earth, water, and air essential to life), the depletion of forests and of natural resources, the relentless extinction of plant and animal species, and the explosion of the human population that threatened to exceed the capacity of the earth to sustain it.

It was in this climate of crisis that ecocriticism was inaugurated. By the 1990s it had become a recognized and rapidly growing field of literary study, with its own organization (ASLE: Association for the Study of Literature and Environment), its own journal (*ISLE: Interdisciplinary Studies in Literature and Environment*), numerous articles in literary and critical periodicals, a proliferation of college courses, and a series of conferences whose concern with the literature of the environment encompassed all continents. As in earlier insurgent modes such as *feminist criticism* and *queer theory*, many ecocritical writings continue to be oriented toward heightening their readers' awareness, and even toward inciting them to social and political action; but while the other movements in criticism are directed toward achieving social and political justice, a number of ecocritics are impelled by the conviction that what is at stake in their enterprise is not only the well-being but, ultimately, the survival of human life.

Ecocritics do not share a single theoretical perspective or procedure; instead, their engagements with environmental literature manifest a wide range of traditional, *poststructural*, and *postcolonial* points of view and modes of analysis. Within this diversity, however, certain issues and concerns are recurrent:

1. It is claimed that the reigning religions and philosophies of Western civilization are deeply **anthropocentric**; that is, they are oriented to the interests of human beings, who are viewed as opposed to and superior to nature, and as free to exploit natural resources and animal species for their own purposes. This viewpoint is grounded in the biblical account of the creation, in which God gave man "dominion over the fish of the sea, and over the birds of the air, and over the cattle, and over all the earth" (*Genesis* 1.26). A similar conception is manifested elsewhere in the Bible, dominated Greek and Roman philosophy, was the prevailing view in Christianity, and underlay the emergence of modern science in the Renaissance, the *humanism* of the eighteenth-century *Enlightenment*, and the triumphs of what has been called "the scientific-technological-industrial complex" in the nineteenth and twentieth centuries. A present-day countermovement, sometimes named "deep ecology," maintains that attempts to reform particular

美国仅剩的荒野；这方面最著名的倡导者是美国作家约翰·巴勒斯（1837—1921）和约翰·缪尔（1838—1914）。

在20世纪，科学家和自然保护主义者发出的警告增多；两本特别有影响力的书是奥尔多·利奥波德的《沙郡年鉴》（1949），提请关注不祥的环境退化，和蕾切尔·卡森的《寂静的春天》（1962），主要关注新开发的化学杀虫剂对地上和水下野生动物造成的破坏。到20世纪后半叶，地球陷入环境危机引发广泛关注，这一危机由以下因素引起：对"生物圈"（生活必不可少的地表薄层、水、空气）的工业和化学污染，森林和自然资源的枯竭，无情的动植物物种灭绝，危及超出地球承载能力的人口爆炸。

正是在这种危机气氛下，生态批评应运而生。到1990年代，它已成为一个公认的和迅速增长的文学研究领域，有它自己的组织（ASLE：文学与环境研究协会），自己的期刊（*ISLE*：《文学与环境跨学科研究》），文学和批评期刊上刊载的大量文章，不断增殖的大学课程，以及一系列关注涵盖所有大洲的环境文献的会议。与*女性主义批评*、*同性恋理论*的早期模式一样，许多生态批评著作的目标也都是持续提高它们的读者意识，甚至煽动读者采取社会和政治行动；不过其他批评主义运动则朝向实现社会正义和政治正义，一些生态批评家也受到这样信念的推动：他们从事的事业不仅攸关人类的福祉，而且最终攸关人类的生死存亡。

生态批评家们并不共享一个单一的理论观点或方法；相反，他们对环境文学的参与，呈现出一个广泛的范围：传统的、*后结构主义的*、*后殖民主义的*视角和分析模式。不过，在这一多样性内，某些问题和关注点也经常出现：

1. 据称，在西方文明中占据主导地位的宗教和哲学带有深深的**人类中心主义**，也就是说，它们以人类利益为目的，人类被视为与自然相对并优于自然，可以为了人类自身目的去开发利用自然资源和动物物种。这种观点基于圣经中对创世的描述，上帝在创世时给了人"管理海里的鱼、空中的鸟、地上的牲畜和全地"（《创世记》1.26）的权力。类似想法在圣经中其他地方也有表现，主导了古希腊罗马哲学，是基督教的普遍看法，是文艺复兴时期现代科学、18世纪启蒙运动里的人文主义、19和20世纪一直被称为"科学－技术－工业情结"的胜利的根基。当今的反向运动，有时名为"深层生态学"，则认为，

instances of the spoliation of the natural world deal with symptoms rather than the root cause, and that the only real hope is to replace anthropocentrism by **ecocentrism**: the view that all living things and their earthly environment, no less than the human species, possess importance, value, and even moral and political rights.

2. Prominent in ecocriticism is a critique of *binaries* such as man/nature or culture/nature, viewed as mutually exclusive oppositions. It is pointed out, instead, that these entities are interconnected, and also mutually constitutive. As Wendell Berry wrote in *The Unsettling of America* (1977), "[W]e and our country create one another, depend upon one another, are literally part of one another.... Our culture and our place are images of each other, and inseparable from each other." Our identities, or sense of self, for example, are informed by the particular place in which we live and in which we feel that we belong and are at home. On the other side, human experience of the natural environment is not a replication of the thing itself, but always mediated by the culture of a particular time and place; and its representation in a work of literature is inescapably shaped by human feelings and the human imagination. A striking example is the radical shift in the conception of the wilderness in America, from the Puritan view of it as a dark and ominous thing, possibly the abode of demons, which needs to be overcome, appropriated, and cultivated by human beings, to the view expressed by Thoreau two centuries later that "[i]n wildness is the preservation of the world" ("Walking," in *Excursions*, 1863). Or as the poet Gerard Manley Hopkins wrote in England some twenty years later, in "Inversnaid":

> What would the world be, once bereft
> Of wet and of wildness? Let them be left,
> O let them be left, wildness and wet;
> Long live the weeds and the wilderness yet.

3. Many ecocritics recommend, and themselves exemplify, the extension of "green reading" (that is, analysis of the implications of a text for environmental concerns and toward political action) to all literary *genres*, including prose fiction and poetry, and also to writings in the natural and social sciences. Within the literary domain, the endeavor is to elevate the status, or to include within the major *canon of literature* the hitherto undervalued forms of nature writing and of *local color* or regional fiction by authors such as Thomas Hardy, Mark Twain, and Sarah Orne Jewett.

4. A conspicuous feature in ecocriticism is the analysis of the differences in attitudes toward the environment that are attributable to a writer's race, ethnicity, social class, and gender. The writings of Annette Kolodny gave impetus to what has come to be called **ecofeminism**—the analysis of the role attributed to women in fantasies of the natural environment by male authors, as well as the study of specifically feminine conceptions of the environment in the neglected nature writings by female authors. In *The*

应该尝试从根源上而不是症状上去改革对自然世界的掠夺，而要做到这一点唯一真正的希望是用**生态中心主义**取代人类中心主义；生态中心主义认为，万物和它们的地球环境，并不低于人类物种，同样有其重要性、价值，甚至是道德和政治权利。

2. 生态批评中引人注目的是对如人/自然、文化/自然这样被视为相互排斥的二元对立的批判。相反，这些实体既相互连接，又相互构成。正如温德尔·贝瑞在《令人不安的美国》(1977)中所写的："[我们]和我们的国家相互创造，彼此依赖，都是彼此的一部分……我们的文化和我们[置身]的地方是彼此的影像，谁也离不开对方。"例如，我们的身份，或自我意识，是由我们生活其中的特定地方告知我们的，在这样的地方，我们认同它并觉得像在家里一样。另一方面，人类对自然环境的体验，并不是事物本身的复制，而总是经由特定时间地点的文化的调节；它在文学作品中的呈现，不可避免地会受到人类情感和人类想象力的塑造。一个突出例子是美国的"旷野"概念出现的根本性转变：从清教认为的它是一个黑暗和不祥之物，可能是恶魔的居留地，需要被人类加以征服、占用和培植，变为两百年后梭罗表达的观点，"世界存乎野性"["散步"，收入其所著的《远足》(1863)]。或如约二十年后诗人杰拉德·曼利·霍普金斯在英格兰所写，在《因弗斯内德》：

> 世界会变成什么，一旦被剥除
> 潮湿与荒野？让它们留住，
> 哦，让它们留住，荒野与潮湿；
> 但愿野草与荒地永存。

3. 许多生态批评家建议并亲身例示了，可以将"绿色阅读"（即，分析文本对环境关注和对政治行动的影响）延伸至所有文学类型，包括散文体小说和诗歌，也延伸至自然科学及社会科学著作。在文学领域，努力提升如托马斯·哈代、马克·吐温、萨拉·奥恩·朱厄特这样的作家所写的迄今被低估的自然写作或地方色彩或地方小说的地位，或将其列入主要的文学经典。

4. 生态批评的一个突出特点是，分析因为作家的种族、民族、社会阶层、性别不同而对环境所持有的不同态度。安妮特·克罗德尼的著作推动了已被称为**生态女性主义**的发展——生态女性主义分析在自然环境的想象中男性作家赋予女性的角色，研究被忽视的女性作家的自然写

Lay of the Land: Metaphor as Experience and History in American Life and Letters (1975), Kolodny stresses, in male-authored literature, the predominant gendering of the land as female, and the accordant tendency to resort to nature for pastoral repose, recuperation, and gratification. She also proposes a parallel between the domination and subjugation of women and the exploitation and spoliation of the land. (For an instance in which the devastation of a natural scene is figured in detail as the rape of a virgin, refer to Wordsworth's autobiographical poem "Nutting," 1800.) In a later book, *The Land before Her: Fantasy and Experiences of the American Frontiers, 1680–1860* (1984), Kolodny details the difference between the traditional representations of the frontier by male authors, and the counterview—domestic, and oriented to gardening and family concerns—in neglected narratives about the frontier by women. Other critics have pointed out that the prominent American form called the **wilderness romance**—represented by such major works as James Fenimore Cooper's Leatherstocking novels, Herman Melville's *Moby Dick*, and Mark Twain's *Huckleberry Finn*—project distinctively male imaginings of escape to an unspoiled natural environment, free of women and of an effete, woman-dominated civilization, in which the protagonist undergoes a test of his character and virility. See for example Nina Baym, "Melodramas of Beset Manhood: How Theories of American Fiction Exclude Women Writers" (1981), in *Feminism and American Literary History* (1992); also Vera Norwood, *Made from This Earth: American Women and Nature* (1993).

5. There is a growing interest in the animistic religions of so-called "primitive" cultures, as well as in Hindu, Buddhist, and other religions and civilizations that lack the Western opposition between humanity and nature, and do not assign to human beings dominion over the nonhuman world. Ecocritics in the United States concern themselves especially with the oral traditions of Native Americans and with the exposition of these cultures by contemporary Native American writers such as N. Scott Momaday and Leslie Marmon Silko. The common view in such traditions, it is pointed out, envisions the natural world as a living, sacred thing, in which each individual feels intimately bonded to a particular physical "place," and where human beings live in interdependence and reciprocity with other living things. See Joni Adamson, *American Indian Literature, Environmental Justice, and Ecocriticism: The Middle Place* (2001), and Donelle N. Dreese, *Ecocriticism: Creating Self and Place in Environmental and American Indian Literatures* (2002). Refer to *primitivism*.

Some radical environmental critics maintain that the ecological crisis can be resolved only by the rejection, in the West, of the Judeo-Christian religion and culture, with its anthropocentric view that human beings, because they possess souls, transcend nature and are inherently masters of the nonhuman world, and by adopting instead an ecocentric religion which promulgates the sacredness of nature and a reverence for all forms of life as intrinsically equivalent. (See for example the influential essay by the intellectual historian

作中特别女性化的环境概念。克罗德尼在《地貌》(1975)中强调指出，在男性撰写的文献中，土地占主导地位的性别角色是女性，一致倾向于从自然那里获得田园般的安宁、休养和满足。她还在支配和征服女性与剥削和掠夺土地之间提出了一种并行。[这方面的一个实例，破坏一处自然景色在细节描述上就像是强奸一个处女，可以参阅华兹华斯的自传体诗《采坚果》(1800)。]在后来的一本书《在她之前的土地：1680—1860年间美国边疆的幻想和体验》(1984)中，克罗德尼详细说明了传统视角下男性作家对边疆的呈现，与被忽视的出自女性作家之手关于边疆的叙事中相反的视角（家庭般、园艺般和家人般的关怀）之间的差异。其他批评家已经指出，一种突出的美国形式叫**荒野传奇**——展现于詹姆斯·费尼莫尔·库珀的皮裹腿小说、赫尔曼·梅尔维尔的《白鲸》和马克·吐温的《哈克贝利·芬历险记》这样的主要作品中——表现了独特的男性想象，逃往一处未受污染的自然环境，远离女性和一种没落的、女性主导的文明，其中主人公要经历对他的性格和男性气概的测试。例见尼娜·贝姆所写的文章"困扰男性气概的情节剧：美国小说理论如何将女性作家排除在外"(1981)，收入其所著的《女性主义与美国文学史》(1992)；亦可参阅维拉·诺伍德所著的《来自这片土地：美国女性与自然》(1993)。

5. 人们对所谓"原始"文化的万物有灵论宗教，以及印度教、佛教、其他宗教和文明，越来越感兴趣，这些宗教和文明没有西方那种人与自然之间的对立，也没有指派人类统治非人类世界。美国的生态批评家尤其关心土著美国人的口述传统和当代美国印第安作家，如N. 斯科特·莫马迪和莱斯利·马蒙·西尔科，对这些文化的阐释/论断。据称，在这样的传统中，普遍的看法是，将自然世界想象为一个有生命力的、神圣的事物，在这个世界中，个体会感到一种与一个特定的自然"地方"紧密联结在一起的纽带关系，在这个地方，人类与其他生物相互依存，互给互惠。参阅：乔尼·亚当森所著的《美国印第安文学、环境正义和生态批评：中间之地》(2001)，唐奈·N. 德里斯所著的《生态批评：环境文学与美国印第安文学中的自我与地域》(2002)。参见：*原始主义*。

一些激进的环境批评家认为，要想解决生态危机，只有拒绝西方的犹太–基督教文化和其人类中心主义观念，该观念认为人类拥有灵魂所以高于自然并理应成为非人类世界的主人，反过来采用生态中心主义的宗教，该宗教传扬自然神圣不可冒犯，应该尊重所有形式的生命，因为它们在本质上都是平等的。(例见下

Lynn White, Jr., "The Historical Roots of Our Ecologic Crisis," in *The Ecocentric Reader*, listed below.) Other environmentalists insist, on the contrary, that the hope for radical reform lies, not in trying to assimilate an outmoded or alien religion, but in identifying and developing those strands in the human-centered religion, philosophy, and ethics of the West which maintain that the human relationship to the nonhuman world is not one of mastery, but of stewardship, and which recognize the deep human need for the natural world as something to be enjoyed for its own sake, as well as the moral responsibility of human beings to maintain and transmit a liveable, diverse, and enjoyable world to their posterity. (See the book by the Australian philosopher John Passmore, *Man's Responsibility for Nature: Ecological Problems and Western Traditions*, 1974. This work includes a useful survey not only of the predominantly anti-environmental religion and metaphysics of the West, but also of the recurrent counterviews that emphasize human responsibility for the natural environment and nonhuman forms of life.) Despite such disagreements, ecocritics concur that science-based knowledge of impending ecological disaster is not enough, because knowledge can lead to effective political and social action only when informed and impelled, as it is in literature, by imagination and feeling.

There are numerous anthologies of nature writing; representative recent ones are *The Norton Book of Nature Writing*, ed. Robert Finch and John Elder (1990); *American Nature Writers*, ed. John Elder (2 vols., 1996); *Literature of Nature: An International Sourcebook* (1998). The *Romantic Period* of the early nineteenth century was the turning point in the long Western tradition of human transcendence and domination over nature. The central view in innovative Romantic literature and philosophy, in England and Germany, was that the root of the modern human malaise is its separation, or "alienation," from its original unity with nature, and that the cure for this disease of civilization lies in a reunion between humanity and nature that will restore concreteness and values to a natural world in which we can once more feel thoroughly at home, in consonance and reciprocity with all living things. (See M. H. Abrams, *Natural Supernaturalism: Tradition and Revolution in Romantic Literature*, 1971, chapters 3–5, 8; also his essay "Coleridge and the Romantic Vision of the World," 1974, included in *The Correspondent Breeze: Essays on English Romanticism*, 1984.) Jonathan Bate, in *Romantic Ecology: Wordsworth and the Environmental Tradition* (1991), details the emergence, in Wordsworth and his English contemporaries and successors, of an environmental consciousness, the result of noting the destruction of forest and farm lands by urban sprawl, and of recognizing what Wordsworth, in the eighth book of *The Excursion* (1814), called "the outrage done to nature" by newly established factories that foul the air and pollute the waterways. See also Karl Kroeber, *Ecological Literary Criticism: Romantic Imagining and the Biology of Mind* (1994); and James C. McKusick, *Green Writing: Romanticism and Ecology* (2000).

Books that were important in the founding and development of ecocriticism, in addition to those already mentioned, include Leo Marx, *The Machine in the Garden: Technology and the Pastoral Ideal in America* (1964); Roderick Frazier Nash,

文提到的《生态中心主义读本》中收录的博学多识的历史学家小林恩·怀特所写的颇有影响力的论文"我们的生态危机的历史根源"。)相反，其他环境主义者则坚持认为，彻底改革的希望所在，不是试着去吸收过时的或外来的宗教，而是确定和发展西方以人为本的宗教、哲学、伦理学中的有益趋向，这些趋向认为：人类与非人类世界之间的关系不是掌控，而是保管；并认识到，人类对自然世界的深层需求是为了自身利益，人类有道德责任去保持和传递给他们的后人一个宜居的、多样的、令人愉快的世界。[参阅：澳大利亚哲学家约翰·帕斯莫尔所著的《人类对自然的责任：生态问题和西方传统》(1974)。这本书既研究了西方占主导地位的反环境的宗教和形而上学，也研究了不断出现的相反观点，即强调人类应负起对自然环境和非人类生命形式的责任。]尽管存在这样的分歧，但是生态批评家们同意，光有关于迫在眉睫的生态灾难的科学知识是不够的，因为知识只有在被了解和推动的情况下，就像在文学中通过想象力和感情，才会转化为有效的政治和社会行动。

有许多关于自然写作的选集，近来较具代表性的有：罗伯特·芬奇与约翰·埃尔德合编的《诺顿自然写作选集》(1990)；约翰·埃尔德主编的两卷本《美国自然作家》(1996)；帕特里克·墨菲主编的《自然文学：一部国际性文献汇编》(1998)。19世纪初的*浪漫主义时期*是人类高于并支配自然这一漫长的西方传统的转折点。在英国和德国，创新的浪漫主义文学和哲学的核心观点是：现代人类萎靡不振的根源在于其与自然之间原初的一体感被分离或"异化"了，治愈文明病的特效药就是，重新将人类与自然结合起来，这样将会恢复具体和有价值的自然世界，在这个世界中，我们可以再次深切地感受到有一种在家的感觉，与世间万物和谐互惠。[参阅 M. H. 艾布拉姆斯所著的《自然的超自然主义：浪漫主义文学中的传统与革新》(1971)第3、4、5、8章；艾布拉姆斯所写的文章"柯勒律治和对世界的浪漫想象"(1974)，收入《相似的微风：英国浪漫主义文学论集》(1984)。]乔纳森·贝特在《浪漫主义生态学：华兹华斯与生态传统》(1991)一书里详细地描述了，在华兹华斯和他的英国同时代人及后来者中环境意识的出现，是注意到城市无序扩张毁坏森林和农田和意识到华兹华斯在其第八本书《远足》(1814)中所说的新建工厂污染空气和河流"对自然所作的暴行"的结果。也可参阅卡尔·克罗伯所著的《生态文学批评：浪漫主义想象与心灵生物学》(1994)；詹姆斯·C.麦库西克所著的《绿色写作：浪漫主义与生态学》(2000)。

对生态批评的创立和发展起到重要作用的书籍，除了上面已经提到的，还包括利奥·马克思所著的《花园里的机器：美国的技术与田园理想》(1964)；

Wilderness and the American Mind (1967; 3d ed., 1982); Donald Worster, *Nature's Economy: A History of Ecological Ideas* (1977); John Elder, *Imagining the Earth: Poetry and the Vision of Nature* (1985); Robert Pogue Harrison, *Forests: The Shadow of Civilization* (1992); Lawrence Buell, *The Environmental Imagination: Thoreau, Nature Writing, and the Formation of American Culture* (1995); Simon Schama, *Landscape and Memory* (1995).

The anthology *The Ecocriticism Reader: Landmarks in Literary Ecology*, ed. Cheryll Glotfelty and Harold Fromm (1996), did much, by its Introduction and selections, to give definition and impetus to the ecocritical movement. The following collections of essays indicate the scope and diversity of ecocritical writings: *Sisters of the Earth: Women's Prose and Poetry about Nature*, ed. Lorraine Anderson (1991); *Being in the World: An Environmental Reader for Writers*, ed. Scott H. Slovic and Terrell F. Dixon (1993); Lawrence Coupe, ed., *The Green Studies Reader: From Romanticism to Ecocriticism* (2000); *The Greening of Literary Scholarship: Literature, Theory, and the Environment*, ed. Steven Rosendale (2002); and Bill McKibben, ed., *American Earth: Environmental Writing since Thoreau* (2008). Greg Garrard outlines the theory and practice of the movement in *Ecocriticism* (2004).

ecofeminism: 98.

écriture (ā′ krĭtyoor″): **400**; *311*.

edition: 33; *32, 34*.

Edwardian Period: 284.

ego: 322.

eiron (ī′ rŏn): **378**; *184*.

elegiac meter (ĕlĕjī′ ăk): **101**.

elegy: In Greek and Roman times, "elegy" denoted any poem written in **elegiac meter** (alternating *hexameter* and *pentameter* lines). The term was also used, however, to refer to the subject matter of change and loss frequently expressed in the elegiac verse form, especially in complaints about love. In accordance with this latter usage, "The Wanderer," "The Seafarer," and other poems in Old English on the transience of all worldly things are even now called elegies. In Europe and England the word continued to have a variable application through the Renaissance. John Donne's elegies, written in the late sixteenth and early seventeenth centuries, are love poems, although they relate to the sense of elegy as lament, in that many of them emphasize mutability and loss. In the seventeenth century the term **elegy** began to be limited to its most common present usage: a formal and sustained lament in verse for the death of a particular person, usually ending in a consolation. Examples are

罗德里克·弗雷泽·纳什所著的《荒野与美国心灵》(1967，1982 年第 3 版）；唐纳德·沃斯特所著的《自然的经济生态思想史》(1977)；约翰·埃尔德所著的《想象地球：诗歌与自然景观》(1985)；罗伯特·波格·哈里森所著的《森林：文明的暗影》(1992)；劳伦斯·比尔所著的《环境的想象：梭罗、自然写作与美国文化的形塑》(1995)；西蒙·沙玛所著的《景观与记忆》(1995)。

谢里尔·格罗特费尔蒂与哈罗德·弗洛姆合编的《生态批评读本：文学生态学的里程碑》(1996) 这本选集，通过其前言和选目，对界定和推动生态文学批评运动起了很大作用。下面的文集表明了生态文学批评作品的范围和多样性：洛林·安德森主编的《地球的姐妹：关于自然的女性散文和诗歌》(1991)；斯科特·H. 斯洛维克与特雷尔·F. 狄克逊合编的《在世存在：写给写作者的环境读本》(1993)；劳伦斯·库普主编的《绿色研究读本：从浪漫主义到生态批评》(2000)；斯蒂芬·罗森代尔主编的《文学研究的绿化：文学、理论与环境》(2002)；比尔·麦吉本主编的《美国大地：梭罗以来的环境书写》(2008)。格雷格·加勒德在其所著的《生态批评》(2004) 中概述了生态批评运动的理论和实践。

ecofeminism：生态女性主义　98。

écriture：书面文字　400；*311*。

edition：版本　33；*32, 34*。

Edwardian Period：爱德华七世时期　284。

ego：自我　322。

eiron：愚人　378；*184*。

elegiac meter：哀歌格律　101。

Elegy：哀歌

在古希腊罗马时代中，"哀歌"指任何采用**哀歌格律**（交替出现的*六音步*诗行与*五音步*诗行）写成的诗作。该术语也常用来指以哀歌诗体表达的关于变故和失去的主题，尤指对爱情的哀怨。根据后一种用法，古英语中的"流浪者""水手"和其他以世俗世界中稍纵即逝的事物为题材的诗作至今仍被称为哀歌。在欧洲和英国文艺复兴时期，哀歌这一术语的用法仍有所不同。例如约翰·多恩作于 16 世纪晚期和 17 世纪初的哀歌属爱情诗，尽管其中有些慨叹人世沧桑和死亡，仍属挽歌悼词。17 世纪时，**哀歌**这一术语才经限制具有目前意义上最常用的用法：为缅怀亡者而写的格式严谨、篇幅较长的悼词，通常以安慰生者为结尾。例如：

the medieval poem *Pearl* and Chaucer's *Book of the Duchess* (elegies in the mode of *dream allegory*); Alfred, Lord Tennyson's *In Memoriam* (1850), on the death of Arthur Hallam; and W. H. Auden's "In Memory of W. B. Yeats" (1940). Occasionally the term is used in its older and broader sense, for somber meditations on mortality such as Thomas Gray's "Elegy Written in a Country Churchyard" (1757), and the *Duino Elegies* (1912–22) of the German poet Rainer Maria Rilke on the transience both of poets and of the earthly objects they write poems about.

The **dirge** is also a versified expression of grief on the occasion of a particular person's death, but differs from the elegy in that it is short, is less formal, and is usually represented as a text to be sung; examples are Shakespeare's "Full Fathom Five Thy Father Lies" and William Collins' "A Song from Shakespeare's *Cymbeline*" (1749). **Threnody** is now used mainly as an equivalent for "dirge," and **monody** for an elegy or dirge which is presented as the utterance of a single person. John Milton describes his "Lycidas" (1638) in the subtitle as a "monody" in which "the Author bewails a learned Friend," and Matthew Arnold called his elegy on A. H. Clough "Thyrsis: A Monody" (1866).

An important subtype is the **pastoral elegy**, which represents both the poet and the one he mourns—who is usually also a poet—as shepherds (the Latin word for shepherd is "pastor"). This poetic form was originated by the Sicilian Greek poet Theocritus, was continued by the Roman Virgil, was developed in various European countries during the Renaissance, and remained current in English poetry through the nineteenth century. Notable English pastoral elegies are Spenser's "Astrophel," on the death of Sir Philip Sidney (1595); Milton's "Lycidas" (1638); Shelley's "Adonais" (1821); and in the Victorian age, Arnold's "Thyrsis." The pastoral elegists, from the Greeks through the Renaissance, developed a set of elaborate *conventions*, which are illustrated here by reference to "Lycidas." In addition to the fictional representation of both mourner and subject as shepherds tending their flocks (lines 23–36 and elsewhere), we often find the following conventional features:

1. The lyric speaker begins by invoking the muses, and goes on to make frequent reference to other figures from classical mythology (lines 15–22, and later).
2. All nature joins in mourning the shepherd's death (lines 37–49). (Recent critics who stress the mythic and ritual origins of poetic genres claim that this feature is a survival from primitive laments for the death of Thammuz, Adonis, or other vegetational deities who died in the autumn to be reborn in the spring. See *myth critics*.)
3. The mourner charges with negligence the nymphs or other guardians of the dead shepherd (lines 50–63).
4. There is a procession of appropriate mourners (lines 88–111).
5. The poet raises questions about the justice of fate, or else of Providence, and adverts to the corrupt conditions of his own times (lines 64–84,

中世纪的诗作《珍珠》、乔叟的《公爵夫人的书》（*梦幻寓言体的哀歌*）、阿尔弗雷德·丁尼生勋爵为阿瑟·哈拉姆之死而写的《悼念》(1850)、W. H. 奥登创作的《悼念叶芝》(1940)。哀歌有时在其古义和广义上也包括对亡者忧郁的沉思，如托马斯·格雷的《墓畔哀歌》(1757)和德国诗人雷纳·马利亚·里尔克的《杜伊诺哀歌》(1912—1922)，里尔克的这部作品主要哀叹诗人及其诗作所描写的世间万物的生命的短暂。

挽歌同样用于表达对亡者离去的悲痛，但与哀歌不同，挽歌篇幅短，不十分拘泥格式，并且一般可以配曲吟唱。例如：莎士比亚的《海下长眠》、威廉·柯林斯的《辛白林里的哀歌》(1749)。**葬歌**现在主要用作"挽歌"的同义词，**独唱挽歌**则是由一人独吟的哀歌或挽歌。约翰·弥尔顿在《利西达斯》(1638)的副标题中把这首诗描述为"作者哀悼博学故友的独唱挽歌"。马修·阿诺德也把他悼念A. H. 克拉夫的哀歌称为《独唱挽歌——色西斯》(1866)。

牧人哀歌是哀歌的一个重要类型，它把哀悼者与亡者——通常也是诗人——都描述为牧羊人（"牧羊人"在拉丁文里为"pastor"）。这种诗歌形式由西西里的古希腊诗人忒奥克里托斯首创，并得到罗马诗人维吉尔的传承，后来在文艺复兴时期在欧洲各国流传发展起来，在整个19世纪仍然是流行的英诗创作形式。蜚声文坛的英国牧人哀歌包括：斯宾塞为缅怀菲利普·锡德尼公爵而作的《爱星者和星星》(1595)、弥尔顿的《利西达斯》(1638)、雪莱的《阿多尼斯》(1821)、维多利亚时期阿诺德的《色西斯》。从古希腊到文艺复兴，牧人哀歌诗人们逐渐形成了这种诗歌形式的严格的*文学惯例*，下面以作品《利西达斯》为例加以说明。除去这首诗把哀悼者与亡者都虚构成放牧羊群的牧羊人外（见原诗23—36行和其他地方），我们还经常发现以下惯例特征：

1. 抒发哀情的悼念者以呼唤乞灵缪斯开始，继而频频提及古代神话里的其他众神（见该诗15—22行及其后）。

2. 自然界的万物都加入到哀悼牧人之死的行列（37—49行）。（强调诗歌类别源于神话与礼仪的当代批评家提出：这一特色是由悼念泰马斯、阿多尼斯或其他秋逝春生的草木之神的原始挽歌所流传下来的。参见：*神话批评家*。）

3. 哀悼者控诉山林女神或死去的牧羊人的其他保护神的失职（50—63行）。

4. 身份相宜的哀悼者列队而至（88—111行）。

5. 诗人质问命运或上苍之公平，叙说当时社会的腐败（64—84, 113—

113–31). Such passages, though sometimes called "digressions," are integral to the evolution of the mourner's thought in "Lycidas."
6. Post-Renaissance elegies often include an elaborate passage in which appropriate flowers are brought to deck the hearse (lines 133–51).
7. There is a closing consolation. In Christian elegies, the lyric reversal from grief and despair to joy and assurance typically occurs when the elegist comes to realize that death in this world is the entry to a higher life (lines 165–85).

In his *Life of Milton* (1779) Samuel Johnson, who disapproved both of pastoralism and mythology in modern poetry, decried "Lycidas" for "its inherent improbability," but in the elegies by Milton and other major poets the ancient rituals provide a structural frame on which they play variations with originality and power. Some of the pastoral conventions, although adapted to an industrial age and a non-Christian worldview, survive still in Walt Whitman's elegy on Lincoln, "When Lilacs Last in the Dooryard Bloom'd" (1866).

In the last two decades of the twentieth century there was a strong revival of the elegy, especially in America, to mourn the devastation and death wrought by AIDS among talented young intellectuals, poets, and artists; see Michael Klein, ed., *Poets for Life: Seventy-six Poets Respond to AIDS* (1989).

See *conventions* and *pastoral*. On the elegy, refer to T. P. Harrison, Jr., and H. J. Leon, eds., *The Pastoral Elegy: An Anthology* (1939); Peter Sacks, *The English Elegy: Studies in the Genre from Spenser to Yeats* (1985). On "Lycidas": C. A. Patrides, ed., *Milton's "Lycidas": The Tradition and the Poem* (rev. 1983), which includes a number of recent critical essays; and Scott Elledge, ed., *Milton's "Lycidas"* (1966), which reprints classical and Renaissance pastoral elegies and other texts as background to Milton's poem. For both traditional and modern forms of elegy, see the introductory materials and the poems reprinted in Sandra M. Gilbert, ed., *Inventions of Farewell: A Book of Elegies* (2001); and for a wide range of analyses and critical discussion, refer to *The Oxford Companion to the Elegy* (2010).

Elizabethan Age: 280.

emblem: 394.

emotive language: 128.

empathy and sympathy: German theorists in the nineteenth century developed the concept of "Einfühlung" ("feeling into"), which has been translated as **empathy**. It signifies an identification of oneself with an observed person or object which is so close that one seems to participate in the posture, motion, and sensations that one observes. Empathy is often described as "an

131 行）。这些诗段有时被视为"离题"，但它们毕竟是《利西达斯》中哀悼者思绪发展的一个组成部分。

6. 文艺复兴以后的哀歌中经常包括一段用适宜的鲜花装饰灵柩的细节描写（133—151 行）。

7. 全诗以慰藉结束。在基督教的哀歌里，随着作者顿悟到与世长辞意味着灵魂的升华，抒情的内容便由悲痛与失望转化为欣慰和确信（165—185 行）。

塞缪尔·约翰逊反对现代诗表现田园风格和神话内容，他在《弥尔顿生平》（1779）中贬斥弥尔顿的《利西达斯》"带着固有的虚假"，但在弥尔顿和其他主要诗人的哀歌作品中，古代礼仪已成为他们创新和力量的一个结构框架。尽管一些牧歌惯例已经掺杂了工业时代的气氛和非基督教观念的色彩，但在沃尔特·惠特曼悼念林肯的哀歌《庭院里的丁香花开放的时候》（1866）中，这些惯例仍然清晰可见。

20 世纪最后二十年中，哀歌，特别是在美国，又空前复兴起来，用以哀悼被艾滋病夺去生命的才华横溢的年轻知识分子、诗人和艺术家。参阅：迈克尔·克莱因主编的《竭尽全力的诗人：76 位诗人对艾滋病的回应》（1989）。

参见：*文学惯例、牧歌*。有关哀歌的参考文献：小 T. P. 哈里森与 H. J. 利昂合编的《牧人哀歌选集》（1939）；彼得·萨克斯所著的《英国的哀歌：从斯宾塞到济慈的哀歌研究》（1985）。关于《利西达斯》参阅：C. A. 帕特里德斯主编的《弥尔顿的〈利西达斯〉：传统与诗歌》（1983 年修订版），里面收录了一些新近的评论文章，斯科特·埃利奇主编的《弥尔顿的〈利西达斯〉》（1966），其中作为弥尔顿诗作的背景资料重印了古典牧人哀歌和文艺复兴时期的牧歌及一些其他文本。关于哀歌的传统和现代形式，参阅桑德拉·M. 吉尔伯特主编的《告别的发明：哀歌选集》（2001）中的导言和重印的诗篇；对哀歌的广泛分析和批判讨论，参阅《牛津哀歌指南》（2010）。

Elizabethan Age：伊丽莎白时期　280。

emblem：象征物　394。

emotive language：传情语言　128。

Empathy and Sympathy：移情与同情

19 世纪德国理论家提出了"移情作用"的概念，英语译为**移情**。"移情作用"表示旁观者自身与眼前的人或物浑然成为一体，以致旁观者似乎切身体验到对

involuntary projection of ourselves into an object," and is commonly explained as the result of an "inner mimicry"; that is, the observation of an object evokes incipient muscular movements which are not experienced as one's own sensations, but as though they were attributes of the outer object. The object may be human, or nonhuman, or even inanimate. In thoroughly absorbed contemplation we seem empathically to pirouette with a ballet dancer, soar with a hawk, bend with the movements of a tree in the wind, and even to participate in the strength, ease, and grace with which a well-proportioned arch appears to support a bridge. When John Keats wrote in a letter that he becomes "a part of all I see," and that "if a sparrow comes before my window I take part in its existence and pick about the gravel," he was describing an habitual experience of his intensely empathic temperament, long before the word was coined.

In literature we call "empathic" a passage which conspicuously evokes from the reader this sense of participation with the pose, movements, and physical sensations of the object that the passage describes. An example is Shakespeare's description, in his narrative poem *Venus and Adonis* (1593), of

> the snail, whose tender horns being hit,
> Shrinks backward in his shelly cave with pain.

Another is the description of the motion of a wave in Keats' *Endymion* (1818),

> when heav'd anew
> Old ocean rolls a lengthen'd wave to the shore,
> Down whose green back the short-liv'd foam, all hoar,
> Bursts gradual, with a wayward indolence.

Also empathic is the description of a wave—experienced from the point of view of Penelope awaiting the long-delayed return of her husband Odysseus—by H. D. (Hilda Doolittle), in her poem, "At Ithaca":

Sympathy, as distinguished from empathy, denotes fellow-feeling; that is, not feeling-into the physical state and sensations, but feeling-along-with the mental state and emotions, of another human being, or of nonhuman beings to whom we attribute human emotions. (See *personification*.) We

方的体态、动作和情感。移情常被描述成"我们的主观感情不自觉地向客体的投射",也常被解释为一种"内模仿"的结果;即对客体的观察引起初发的肌肉牵动,这种牵动并非为观察者自身的知觉所感知,而似乎是由外界事物所引发。客体或为人,或为非人类,甚或为无生命的东西。当我们聚精会神时,面对芭蕾舞演员就会感到要与她旋转同舞,见到苍鹰会觉得要和它一起翱翔,看到劲风中的树木则会产生一同摇曳的感觉,甚至可以分享到造型精巧的桥拱支撑桥梁的那种强劲、自如与优美感。当约翰·济慈在一封信中说他已成为"自己视野中万物的一部分""如果有只麻雀飞临窗前,我会与它同形共存,啄食于沙砾之间"时,他是在"移情"一说产生很久以前,就已在描绘自己反复经历的这种强烈的移情作用。

在文学中,对于明显地引导读者置身于所描绘物的姿态、动作和身体感知的段落,我们称其为"移情篇"。例如莎士比亚在叙事诗《维纳斯与阿多尼》(1593)中有关蜗牛的描写:

> 又像蜗牛,嫩的触角受了打击,
> 苦痛地缩进他那介壳制的窟中。　　　　　　　　(梁实秋译)

又如,济慈在《恩底弥翁》(1818)中对海浪波动的描述

> 有如再次涌起的海洋
> 叫长浪卷向岸边,
> 在绿色的岸沿,倏忽的白沫飞溅,
> 带着任性的慵懒一阵阵迸散。　　　　　　　　(屠岸译)

以下对海浪的描写也是移情——即从珀涅罗珀对自己远航而迟迟不归的丈夫奥德修斯的期待之情出发——希尔达·杜利特尔在她的诗作《在伊萨卡》(版权未授,请参旧版。——译注)中这样描写大海的波浪:

> (略)

同情与移情不同,它表示感情的共鸣,即:不是深入到他人或那些被我们赋予人类感情的非人事物的体内和感知中去体验,而是与其在精神和情感上产生共鸣。

"sympathize," for example, with the emotional experience of a child in his first attempt to recite a piece in public; we may also "empathize" as he falters in his speaking or makes an awkward gesture. Robert Burns' "To a Mouse" (1786) is an engaging expression of his quick sympathy with the terror of the "wee, sleekit, cow'rin, tim'rous beastie" whose nest he has turned up with his plow.

The engagement and control of a reader's sympathy with certain characters, and the establishment of **antipathy** toward others, is essential to the traditional literary artist. In *King Lear*, Shakespeare undertakes to make us sympathize with Cordelia, for example, and progressively with King Lear, but to make us feel horror and antipathy toward his "pelican daughters," Goneril and Regan. Our attitude in the same play toward the villainous Edmund, the bastard son of Gloucester, as managed by Shakespeare, is complex—antipathetic, yet with some element of sympathetic understanding of his distorted personality. (See *distance and involvement*.) Bertolt Brecht's *alienation effect* was designed to inhibit the sympathy of an audience with the protagonists of his plays, in order to encourage a critical attitude to the actions and social and economic realities that the plays represent.

A number of recent critical theorists stress the need to read against one's acquiescence to the sympathetic identification intended by an author. Such feminist critics as Judith Fetterley, for example, in *The Resisting Reader* (1978), propose that women should learn to read in opposition to the sympathy with male protagonists, and the derogation of women characters, that is written into the work of many male authors. (See under *feminist criticism*.) And a tendency in the *new historicism*, as well as in *postcolonial* criticism, is to recommend that the reader, even if against an author's intention, shift his or her sympathy from the dominant to the subversive characters in a literary work—from the magus Prospero, for example, in Shakespeare's *The Tempest*, to his brutish and rebellious slave Caliban, who is taken to represent the natives of the New World who were oppressed and enslaved by English and European invaders. (Some current critics claim that, whatever Shakespeare's intentions, Caliban, as he is represented, is sympathetic, and that Prospero, as he is represented, is not; also that the sympathetic admiration for Prospero in the nineteenth century depended on a willful evasion of certain aspects of the play.)

Refer to H. S. Langfeld, *The Aesthetic Attitude* (1920)—the section on empathy is reprinted in *Problems of Aesthetics* (1963), ed. Eliseo Vivas and Murray Krieger. For detailed analyses of empathic passages in literature, see Richard H. Fogle, *The Imagery of Keats and Shelley* (1949), chapter 4. See also the entry *sensibility, literature of*.

encomiastic (ĕnkō'mĭăs' tĭk): 263.

end (of a plot): 296.

end rhymes: 348.

(参见：拟人。)比如：我们"同情"一位初次当众朗诵的孩子的情感体验；而当孩子言语支吾、呈现窘态时，我们则会产生"移情"。罗伯特·彭斯的《致小鼠》(1786)生动地表达出作者犁坏鼠窝时，对那只受到惊吓的小老鼠即刻产生的同情心："啊，光滑、胆怯、怕事的小东西"。

引发和操纵读者对作品中一些人物的同情而对另一些人物的**反感**是传统文学艺术家的惯用手法。例如在《李尔王》中，莎士比亚引导我们同情考狄莉亚，并对李尔王也逐渐产生恻隐之心；而他的"不孝女儿"高内里尔和里根，则让我们产生一种恐怖和反感之情。在该剧中，在莎士比亚的操控下，我们对"格洛切斯特"的私生子、恶棍埃德蒙的态度显得复杂多变——憎恶中夹杂着几分对他扭曲的性格的怜悯。(参见：*心理距离与感情介入。*)贝尔托尔特·布莱希特创造*间离效果*的目的就是要避免观众对他的剧中人物产生同情，从而使观众以批判的眼光看待戏中描写的行为和社会及经济现实。

近来，许多批评理论家都强调有必要对作者在作品中呈现的同情认同感予以抵制。例如女性主义批评家朱迪思·菲特利在其所著的《抗拒性读者》(1978)中提出，女性在阅读男性作家的作品时应当学会抵制其中所表现的对男性人物的同情，以及许多男性作家在作品中对女性角色的贬抑。(参见：*女性主义批评*中的相关论述。)在*新历史主义*和*后殖民主义*批评中，出现了这样一种趋势，即建议读者在阅读文学作品时，即使有悖作者意图，也应把同情感从正面角色转向反面角色，例如，在莎士比亚的《暴风雨》中，读者的同情心应当从术士普洛斯彼罗转向代表新世界中那些被英国和欧洲人入侵后遭受压迫和奴役的当地土著居民凯列班这个粗野与反叛的奴隶身上（当今有些批评家认为，不论莎士比亚的意图是什么，凯列班和他所代表的群体都是值得同情的，而普洛斯彼罗之类则不值得人们同情；19世纪对普洛斯彼罗的推崇是出于该剧中某些方面有意而为的遁词所致）。

参阅：H. S. 兰菲尔德所著的《审美态度》(1920)；关于移情可以参阅：重版的艾利奥赛·维瓦斯与默里·克莱格合编的《美学的问题》(1963)。关于文学作品中移情段落的详细分析可以参阅：理查德·H. 福格尔所著的《济慈和雪莱的意象》(1949)第四章。也可参见条目：*情感文学*。

encomiastic：赞颂的　263。

end (of a plot)：(情节中的) 结尾　296。

end rhymes：尾韵　348。

end-stopped lines: 221.

English literature, periods of: 278.

English sonnet: 370.

enjambment (ĕnjămb′ mĕnt): 221.

Enlightenment: The name applied to an intellectual movement and cultural ambiance which developed in western Europe during the seventeenth century and reached its height in the eighteenth. The common element was a trust in universal and uniform human reason as adequate to solve the crucial problems and to establish the essential norms in life, together with the belief that the application of such reason was rapidly dissipating the darkness of superstition, prejudice, and barbarity; was freeing humanity from its earlier reliance on mere authority and unexamined tradition; and had opened the prospect of progress toward a life in this world of universal peace and happiness. (See the idea of *progress*.) For some thinkers the model for "reason" was the inductive procedure of science, which proceeds by reasoning from the particular facts of experience to universal laws; for others (especially Descartes and his followers), the model for "reason" was primarily geometrical—the deduction of particular truths from clear and distinct ideas which are universal, and known intuitively by "the light of reason." Many thinkers relied on reason in both these senses.

In England the thought and the world outlook of the Enlightenment are usually traced from Francis Bacon (1561–1626) through John Locke (1632–1704) to late-eighteenth-century thinkers such as William Godwin (1756–1836); in France, from Descartes (1596–1650) through Voltaire (1694–1778) to Diderot and other editors of the great twenty-volume *Encyclopédie* (1751–72); in Germany, from Leibniz (1646–1716) to what is often said to be the highest product of the Enlightenment, the "critical philosophy" of Immanuel Kant (1724–1804). Kant's famous essay "What Is Enlightenment?" written in 1784, defines it as "the liberation of mankind from his self-caused state of minority" and the achievement of a state of maturity which is exemplified in his "determination and courage to use [his understanding] without the assistance of another." On the British enlightenment refer to Roy Porter, *The Enlightenment* (2001).

In America, Benjamin Franklin and Thomas Jefferson represented the principles of the French and English Enlightenment, which also helped shape the founding documents of the United States: the Declaration of Independence and the Constitution.

In recent years, the Enlightenment has been the subject of vigorous reassessment and debate. See Emmanuel Chukwudi Eze, ed., *Race and the Enlightenment: A Reader* (1997), for an anthology of Enlightenment texts, many of them, from the point of view of the present, strikingly unenlightened about race. For a positive assessment of the Enlightenment's contribution to modern

end-stopped lines：行尾停顿式诗行　221。

English literature, periods of：英国文学各时期的划分　278。

English sonnet：英国式十四行诗　370。

enjambment：跨行连续　221。

Enlightenment：启蒙运动

　　启蒙运动是指在 17 世纪兴起于西欧并在 18 世纪发展到顶峰的一次思想文化运动。其基本目标是崇尚普世的、统一的人类理性，认为人类凭借理性能够解决重大难题，并能确立生活的基本准则；同时相信，运用理性可以迅速驱散迷信、偏见及野蛮造成的黑暗，使人解脱早期对权威的单纯依赖和对传统观念的盲从，它打开了人们对于在这个世界上建立通向普遍和平与幸福生活的视野。（参见：*进步论*。）对于一部分思想家来说，"理性"的模式是科学的归纳过程：从特定的经验事实中归纳出一般规律；而其他一些思想家（尤其是法国哲学家笛卡尔及其信徒）则认为，"理性"的模式主要是几何学上的，即从普遍的、被直观地称为"理性之光"的清晰的思想中演绎出特定的真理。很多思想家对理性的认识都是基于以上两层意义。

　　在英国，启蒙运动的思想与世界观可以追溯到弗朗西斯·培根（1561—1626）、约翰·洛克一直到以威廉·葛德文为代表的 18 世纪晚期的思想家；在法国，始于笛卡尔（1596—1650），经过伏尔泰（1694—1778）直至狄德罗和二十卷《大百科全书》（1751—1772）的其他编纂者；在德国，则是从莱布尼兹（1646—1716）直至通常被认为是启蒙运动最辉煌的成就——伊曼纽尔·康德（1724—1804）的"批判哲学"。康德在其写于 1784 年的著名的《论启蒙运动》中，把启蒙运动定义为"将人类从他自己造成的未成年状态中解放出来"和以"不借助外人帮助而运用（他自己的理解力）进行独立思考的决心与勇气"为标志的成熟阶段的到来。关于英国启蒙运动，参阅罗伊·波特所著的《文艺复兴》（2001）。

　　在美国，本杰明·富兰克林和托马斯·杰斐逊提出了体现法国和英国启蒙运动的思想原则，奠定了美国建邦立国的纲领性文件《独立宣言》和《宪法》的制定。

　　近年来，启蒙一直都是热烈的重新评价和辩论的主题。参阅伊曼纽尔·楚库伍迪·埃兹主编的《种族与启蒙读本》（1997），这是文艺复兴文本的一个选集，其中许多文章，从当下视角去看，在种族问题上的看法显得相当愚昧。关于积极评价启蒙运动为现代政治和科学态度的形成作出的贡献，参阅：乔纳森·I.

political and scientific attitudes, see Jonathan I. Israel, *Radical Enlightenment: Philosophy and the Making of Modernity 1650–1750* (2001).

The Enlightenment category of the universal, which was central to eighteenth-century thinkers who sought to transcend national, linguistic, or other divisions, has been both praised as an indispensable tool of a radical social *critique* and derogated as the conceptual means by which local differences such as race, sex, ethnicity, and class are elided in the name of a dubious universality. A crucial text in the latter reassessment was Michel Foucault, "What Is Enlightenment?" in Paul Rabinow, ed., *The Foucault Reader* (1984), pp. 32–50. See also James Schmidt, ed., *What Is Enlightenment?* (1996); Geoffrey Galt Harpham, "So…What *Is* Enlightenment?" in *Shadows of Ethics* (1999), pp. 67–98. For an anthology of Enlightenment writings, see Peter Gay, ed., *The Enlightenment: A Comprehensive Anthology* (1973). Gay has also written *The Enlightenment: An Interpretation* (2 vols., 1995, 1996); see also Ernst Cassirer, *The Philosophy of the Enlightenment* (1968). Refer to the entry *neoclassic and romantic*. For references to Enlightenment in other entries, see pages *283, 341*.

environmental criticism: 96.

envoy (in a poem): **378**.

epic: In its strict sense the term **epic** or **heroic poem** is applied to a work that meets at least the following criteria: it is a long verse narrative on a serious subject, told in a formal and elevated style, and centered on a heroic or quasi-divine figure on whose actions depends the fate of a tribe, a nation, or (in the instance of John Milton's *Paradise Lost*) the human race.

There is a standard distinction between traditional and literary epics. "Traditional epics" (also called "folk epics" or "primary epics") were written versions of what had originally been oral poems about a tribal or national hero during a warlike age. (See *oral poetry*.) Among these are the *Iliad* and *Odyssey* that the Greeks ascribed to Homer; the Anglo-Saxon *Beowulf*; the French *Chanson de Roland* and the Spanish *Poema del Cid* in the twelfth century; and the thirteenth-century German epic *Nibelungenlied*. "Literary epics" were composed by individual poetic craftsmen in deliberate imitation of the traditional form. Of this kind is Virgil's Latin poem the *Aeneid*, which later served as the chief model for Milton's literary epic *Paradise Lost* (1667). *Paradise Lost* in turn became, in the *Romantic Period*, a model for John Keats' fragmentary epic *Hyperion*, as well as for William Blake's several epics, or "prophetic books" (*The Four Zoas, Milton, Jerusalem*), which translated into Blake's own mythic terms the biblical narrative that had been Milton's subject.

The epic was ranked by Aristotle as second only to tragedy, and by many Renaissance critics as the highest of all *genres*. The literary epic is certainly the most ambitious of poetic enterprises, making immense demands on a poet's knowledge, invention, and skill to sustain the scope, grandeur, and authority of a poem that tends to encompass the world of its day and a large portion of its learning. Despite numerous attempts in many languages over nearly three

伊斯雷尔所著的《激进的启蒙运动：哲学与现代性的形成：1650—1750》(2001)。

启蒙这一具有普遍性的分类，是18世纪追求超越国家、语言或其他界限的思想家的核心，一直既被赞扬为一种激进的社会*批判*不可缺少的工具，又被贬低为一种概念工具，通过它，像种族、性别、民族性、阶级等地方性差异，就可以以普世性之名被忽略。近来重新评价中的一个重要文本是米歇尔·福柯所写的文章"什么是启蒙？"收入保罗·拉比诺主编的《福柯读本》(1984)中第32—50页。也可参阅：詹姆斯·施密特主编的《什么是启蒙？》(1996)；杰弗里·高尔特·哈珀姆所写的文章"那么……什么是启蒙？"收入其所著的《道德的阴影》(1999)第67—98页。关于文艺复兴作品的选集，参阅彼得·盖伊主编的《启蒙运动：一个全面的选集》(1973)。盖伊还写有两卷本的《启蒙运动：一种阐释》(1996)；也可参阅厄恩斯特·卡希尔所著的《启蒙哲学》(1968)。参见条目：*新古典主义和浪漫主义*。其他条目中提及"文艺复兴"的地方，参见第283、341页。

environmental criticism：环境批评 96。

envoy (in a poem)：(诗歌中的) 结尾诗行 378。

Epic：史诗

在严格意义上，**史诗**或**英雄诗**指的是至少符合下列标准的作品：长篇叙事体诗歌，主题庄重，风格典雅，集中描写以自身行动决定整个部落、民族或（如约翰·弥尔顿《失乐园》中的例子）人类命运的英雄或近似神明的人物。

传统史诗与文学史诗之间有着标准的区分。传统史诗（又称"民间史诗"或"原始史诗"）往往是由作者根据民间口头流传的关于战争时期部落或民族英雄的故事整理而成的书面形式的史诗。（参见：*口头诗歌*。）此类诗作包括：希腊人认为是荷马所著的《伊利亚特》和《奥德赛》，盎格鲁－撒克逊时期的《贝奥武甫》，法国的《罗兰之歌》，12世纪西班牙的《熙德之歌》，13世纪德国的《尼贝龙根之歌》。"文学史诗"是由擅长诗歌创作的诗人刻意以传统史诗为蓝本创作而成。这类诗作有：维吉尔的拉丁史诗《埃涅阿斯纪》，这首诗后来成为弥尔顿创作文学史诗《失乐园》(1667)的主要蓝本，而《失乐园》又成为浪漫时期约翰·济慈的未完成史诗《海拔里昂》和威廉·布莱克的几首史诗或"预言书"(《四天神》《弥尔顿》《耶路撒冷》)的创作蓝本。布莱克的这些作品旨在把作为弥尔顿创作素材的圣经故事转化为自己的神话形式。

亚里士多德认为史诗仅次于悲剧而居于第二位，文艺复兴时期的许多批评家又把其置于所有文学类型之首。毫无疑问，文学史诗是诗歌的最高形式，它要求作家广见博识，富于创作灵感，善于在那些囊括当时社会及广博学识的诗篇中展现其视野、壮观和权威。在过去近三千年的历史中，尽管各国文人墨客纷纷尝试，

thousand years, we possess no more than a half-dozen such poems of indubitable greatness. Literary epics are highly conventional compositions which usually share the following features, derived by way of the *Aeneid* from the traditional epics of Homer:

1. The hero is a figure of great national or even cosmic importance. In the *Iliad* he is the Greek warrior Achilles, who is the son of the sea nymph Thetis; and Virgil's Aeneas is the son of the goddess Aphrodite. In *Paradise Lost*, Adam and Eve are the progenitors of the entire human race, or if we regard Christ as the protagonist, He is both God and man. Blake's primal figure is "the Universal Man" Albion, who incorporates, before his fall, humanity and God and the cosmos as well.

2. The setting of the poem is ample in scale, and may be worldwide, or even larger. Odysseus wanders over the Mediterranean basin (the whole of the world known at the time), and in Book XI he descends into the underworld (as does Virgil's Aeneas). The scope of *Paradise Lost* is the entire universe, for it takes place in heaven, on earth, in hell, and in the cosmic space between. (See *Ptolemaic universe*.)

3. The action involves extraordinary deeds in battle, such as Achilles' feats in the Trojan War, or a long, arduous, and dangerous journey intrepidly accomplished, such as the wanderings of Odysseus on his way back to his homeland, in the face of opposition by some of the gods. *Paradise Lost* includes the revolt in heaven by the rebel angels against God, the journey of Satan through chaos to discover the newly created world, and his desperately audacious attempt to outwit God by corrupting mankind, in which his success is ultimately frustrated by the sacrificial action of Christ.

4. In these great actions the gods and other supernatural beings take an interest or an active part—the Olympian gods in Homer, and Jehovah, Christ, and the angels in *Paradise Lost*. These supernatural agents were in the *Neoclassic Age* called the **machinery**, in the sense that they were part of the literary contrivances of the epic.

5. An epic poem is a ceremonial performance, and is narrated in a ceremonial style which is deliberately distanced from ordinary speech and proportioned to the grandeur and formality of the heroic subject and architecture. Hence Milton's **grand style**—his formal diction and elaborate and stylized syntax, which are in large part modeled on Latin poetry, his sonorous lists of names and wide-ranging *allusions*, and his imitation of Homer's *epic similes* and *epithets*.

There are also widely used epic *conventions*, or formulas, in the choice and ordering of episodes; prominent among them are these features, as exemplified in *Paradise Lost*:

1. The narrator begins by stating his **argument**, or epic theme, invokes a muse or guiding spirit to inspire him in his great undertaking, then addresses to the muse the **epic question**, the answer to which inaugurates the narrative proper (*Paradise Lost*, I. 1–49).

然而保留至今且为后人交口赞誉的史诗杰作只不过有五、六篇。文学史诗是传统性很强的诗歌作品，通常应具有传承荷马传统史诗的《埃涅阿斯纪》所具有的以下特征：

1. 主人公是一个民族乃至宇宙中举足轻重的伟大人物。《伊利亚特》的主人公是希腊勇士阿喀琉斯——海洋女神忒提斯之子；维吉尔笔下的埃涅阿斯是女神阿佛洛狄忒之子。在《失乐园》中，亚当和夏娃是整个人类的祖先，或者若是把耶稣基督视为主人公的话，那么他所代表的就是上帝和整个人类。布莱克史诗中的主要人物是"宇宙人"阿尔比恩，他在沉沦前把人类、上帝和宇宙融为一体。

2. 史诗具有非常广阔的空间背景，其范围可以是整个世界甚或更大。《奥德赛》中的奥德修斯浪迹整个地中海（当时人们心目中的整个世界）；在该诗第11卷中，他又下到地狱（维吉尔史诗中的埃涅阿斯也有同样的经历）。《失乐园》以整个宇宙为背景，故事发生在天堂、人间、地狱之间和宇宙空间。（参见：*托勒密宇宙观*。）

3. 史诗中描写的战争是一些超乎凡人的行为，如阿喀琉斯在特洛伊战争中的壮举。或者描写英雄经历的漫漫险途，如奥德修斯冲破众神的围堵、历尽艰难的回家之路。《失乐园》描写了天国中天使反叛上帝的斗争，撒旦穿越混沌发现新近创造的人间的旅途及其以腐化人类来智斗上帝的一意孤行，撒旦的得逞最终以耶稣为挫败他而殉难告终。

4. 众神和其他超自然势力对英雄们的壮举表现出兴趣或者采取积极介入的态度——荷马史诗中的奥林匹斯诸神，《失乐园》中的耶和华、耶稣及众天使。这些超自然势力在新古典主义时期被称作**超自然的情节机制**，也就是史诗中文学策略的组成部分。

5. 一首史诗就是一场礼仪的展现，史诗采用礼仪化叙事风格，其行文刻意区别于日常语言，并且与表现英雄主题和篇章结构的壮观与正式相一致。因此，弥尔顿的**宏伟绚丽的文体**——即他常模仿拉丁诗歌而形成的正式的修辞、精致而别具一格的句法、响亮的人物名字和包罗万象的典故，以及对荷马史诗直喻与属性形容词的模拟。

史诗在情节安排与选择方面也有一些广为采用的史诗*惯例*或规则；以《失乐园》为例，有如下一些显著特征：

1. 叙述者以阐明他的**论点**或史诗主题开始，乞求女神或灵魂的引导者激发他大展宏图的勇气，然后向缪斯提出**史诗问题**，其答案便引出全诗的情节内容（例如《失乐园》第1卷，1—49行）。

2. The narrative starts **in medias res** ("in the middle of things"), at a critical point in the action. *Paradise Lost* opens with the fallen angels in hell, gathering their scattered forces and determining on revenge. Not until Books V–VII does the angel Raphael narrate to Adam the events in heaven which led to this situation; while in Books XI–XII, after the fall, Michael foretells to Adam future events up to Christ's second coming. Thus Milton's epic, although its action focuses on the temptation and fall of man, encompasses all time from the creation to the end of the world.
3. There are catalogues of some of the principal characters, introduced in formal detail, as in Milton's description of the procession of fallen angels in Book I of *Paradise Lost*. These characters are often given set speeches that reveal their diverse temperaments and moral attitudes; an example is the debate in Pandemonium, Book II.

The term "epic" is often applied, by extension, to narratives which differ in many respects from this model but manifest the epic spirit and grandeur in the scale, the scope, and the profound human importance of their subjects. In this broad sense Dante's fourteenth-century *Divine Comedy* and Edmund Spenser's late-sixteenth-century *The Faerie Queene* (1590–96) are often called epics, as are conspicuously large-scale and wide-ranging works of prose fiction such as Herman Melville's *Moby-Dick* (1851), Leo Tolstoy's *War and Peace* (1869), and James Joyce's *Ulysses* (1922); this last work achieves epic scope in representing the events of an ordinary day in Dublin (16 June 1904) by modeling them on the episodes of Homer's *Odyssey*. In a still more extended application, the Marxist critic Georg Lukács used the term **bourgeois epic** for all novels which, in his view, reflect the social reality of their capitalist age on a broad scale. In a famed sentence, Lukács said that "the novel is the epic of a world that has been abandoned by God" (*Theory of the Novel*, trans. Anna Bostock, 1971). See Lukács under *Marxist criticism*.

See *mock epic*, and refer to W. W. Lawrence, *Beowulf and Epic Tradition* (1928); C. M. Bowra, *From Vergil to Milton* (1945), and *Heroic Poetry* (1952); C. S. Lewis, *A Preface to "Paradise Lost"* (1942); Brian Wilkie, *Romantic Poets and Epic Tradition* (1965); Paul Merchant, *The Epic* (1971); Michael Murren, *The Allegorical Epic* (1980); David Quint, *Epic and Empire* (1993). In *Epic: Britain's Heroic Muse, 1790–1910* (2008), Herbert F. Tucker reveals how very widely the epic form continued to be composed, long after it was held to have been displaced by the prose novel. For an *archetypal* conception of the epic, see Northrop Frye, *Anatomy of Criticism* (1957), pp. 315–26. For references to *epic* in other entries, see page *159*. See also *heroic drama*.

epic question: 108.

epic similes: Epic similes, also called **Homeric similes**, are formal, sustained similes in which the secondary subject, or *vehicle*, is elaborated far beyond its points of close parallel to the primary subject, or *tenor* (see under *figurative*

2. 史诗以**倒叙**开篇，即从情节发展中的某个紧要关头开始叙述。《失乐园》是从众天使被贬入地狱后联合他们分散的力量并决心报复为开始展开情节的，直到第5—7卷才出现天使拉斐尔向亚当追述导致目前情形的天国往事。第11—12卷描叙被贬入地狱后，天使米迦勒向亚当预言未来直至耶稣基督的复活。所以，尽管弥尔顿的史诗情节集中于撒旦对人的诱惑及人类的沉沦，但它囊括了从创世记到世界末日的全部历程。

3. 对一些主要人物加以分类，并做详细介绍，如弥尔顿《失乐园》第1卷中对被贬的众天使的逐一描写。这些角色常以套式台词展现他们不同的性格和道德原则，如第2卷中在地狱辩论的一节。

从外延上说，"史诗"也常指那些虽与此类作品有许多不同之处，但在描写的程度、范围及突出人物重要性的主题方面也表现出了史诗风采的文学作品。从这一广义上来说，14世纪但丁的《神曲》、16世纪晚期埃德蒙·斯宾塞的《仙后》(1590—1596)都常被称作史诗；另有很多的鸿篇巨制小说也属于此类作品，如赫尔曼·梅尔维尔的《白鲸》(1851)、列夫·托尔斯泰的《战争与和平》(1863—1869)、詹姆斯·乔伊斯的《尤利西斯》(1922)都被誉为史诗，最后一部作品《尤利西斯》模仿荷马史诗《奥德赛》，描写了在一个普通的日子(1904年6月16日)里发生在都柏林的一些事件。在更广义的应用上，马克思主义文学批评家乔治·卢卡奇进一步推广了史诗的范围，他把反映资本主义时期社会现实的所有小说一律称为**市民史诗**。卢卡奇的名言是："小说是这个世界中被上帝抛弃的史诗。"(《小说理论》，1971年安娜·博斯托克英译)参见*马克思主义批评*中有关卢卡奇的叙述。

参见：*模拟史诗*。参阅：W. W. 劳伦斯所著的《贝奥武甫与史诗传统》(1928)；C. M. 鲍勒所著的《从维吉尔到弥尔顿》(1945)和《英雄诗》(1952)；C. S. 刘易斯所著的《"失乐园"的序言》(1942)；布赖恩·威尔基所著的《浪漫主义诗人与史诗传统》(1965)；保罗·麦钱特所著的《史诗》(1971)；迈克尔·穆伦所著的《寓言史诗》(1980)；戴维·奎因特所著的《史诗与帝国》(1993)。在《史诗：不列颠的英雄缪斯，1790—1910》(2008)中，赫伯特·F. 塔克揭示了在认为史诗一直被散文体小说取代很久之后，史诗形式仍在非常广泛的范围被持续创作出来。关于史诗的原型概念，参阅诺斯罗普·弗莱所著的《批评的剖析》(1957)第315—326页。其他条目中提及"史诗"的地方，参见第159页。也可参见：*英雄剧*。

epic question：史诗问题 108。

Epic Similes：史诗明喻

史诗明喻，也叫**荷马式明喻**，是一种形式拘泥、意义稳定的明喻手法，其中对比喻物或称*喻夫*的描写往往远远超乎它和被比喻物或称*喻的*的共性范围(参见：

language). This figure was imitated from Homer by Virgil, Milton, and other writers of literary *epics*, who employed it to enhance the ceremonial quality and wide-ranging reference of the narrative style. In the epic simile in *Paradise Lost* (I. 768ff.), Milton describes his primary subject, the fallen angels thronging toward their new-built palace of Pandemonium, by an elaborate comparison to the swarming of bees:

> As Bees
> In spring time, when the Sun with Taurus rides,
> Pour forth their populous youth about the Hive
> In clusters; they among fresh dews and flowers
> Fly to and fro, or on the smoothèd Plank,
> The suburb of their Straw-built Citadel,
> New rubb'd with Balm, expatiate and confer
> Their State affairs. So thick the aery crowd
> Swarm'd and were strait'n'd; . . .

epic theater: Epic theater is a term that the German playwright Bertolt Brecht, in the 1920s, applied to his plays. By the word "epic," Brecht signified primarily his attempt to emulate on the stage the objectivity of the narration in Homeric *epic*. By employing a detached narrator and other devices to achieve *alienation effects*, Brecht aimed to subvert the sympathy of the audience with the actors, and the identification of the actor with his role, that were features of the theater of bourgeois realism. His hope was to encourage his audience to criticize and oppose, rather than passively to accept, the social conditions and modes of behavior that the plays represent. Brecht's dramatic works continue to be produced frequently, and his epic theater has had an important influence on such playwrights as Edward Bond and Caryl Churchill in England and Tony Kushner in America.

See Bertolt Brecht under *Marxist criticism*, and refer to John Willett, ed., *Brecht on Theatre: The Development of an Aesthetic* (1964); and Janelle Reinelt, *After Brecht: British Epic Theater* (1994).

epideictic oratory: (ĕp˘ıdīk′ tik): **343**.

epigram: The term is now used for a statement, whether in verse or prose, which is terse, pointed, and witty. The epigram may be on any subject and in any mode: amatory, elegiac, meditative, complimentary, anecdotal, or (most often) satiric. Martial, the Roman epigrammatist, established the enduring model for the caustically satiric epigram in verse.

The verse epigram was much cultivated in England in the late sixteenth and seventeenth centuries by such poets as John Donne, Ben Jonson, and Robert Herrick. The form flourished especially in the eighteenth century, the time that Austin Dobson described as the age "of wit, of polish, and of Pope." Matthew Prior is a highly accomplished writer of epigrams, and many closed couplets by Alexander Pope and Lady Mary Wortley Montagu are detachable

比喻语)。维吉尔、弥尔顿及其他文学史诗作家纷纷效仿荷马史诗的这种比喻手法，以加强各自史诗文体的礼仪性和增加叙事风格的多变性。在《失乐园》(第1卷第768行及其后各行)中，弥尔顿用离巢迁徙的蜂阵来比喻沉沦中涌向地狱之都新落成的幽宫的众天使：

> 譬若那春时蜂阵，
> 际太阳已驾金牛乘，
> 出房飞舞结成群；
> 新沐了鲜泽芳芬，
> 在那露点花间，草城廓上，回翔无定，
> 把国事大家商论。
> 彼时那凌空队伍，拥挤纷屯，
> 也得无与此情形等；……
> 　　　　　　　　　　　　　　（傅东华译）

Epic Theater：史诗戏剧

史诗戏剧这一术语，由德国剧作家贝尔托尔特·布莱希特于1920年代首次引用到自己的戏剧中。布莱希特用"史诗"一词主要指他在舞台叙事中模仿荷马*史诗*的客观性的意图。通过利用独立的叙述者和其他手段以取得*异化效果*，布莱希特的目的是解除观众对演员的同情心及对演员与扮演角色之间的等同感，这是资本主义现实主义戏剧的特征。他的愿望是以此鼓励他的观众去批评和反对，而不是被动地接受剧作所呈现的社会环境和行为模式。布莱希特的戏剧作品至今仍在上演，他的史诗戏剧对英国剧作家爱德华·邦德、凯里尔·丘吉尔和美国的托尼·库什纳都产生过重大影响。

参见马克思主义*批评*中关于贝尔托尔特·布莱希特的论述；参阅：约翰·威利特主编的《布莱希特论戏剧：美学的发展》(1964)；贾内尔·赖内尔特所著的《布莱希特之后：英国史诗剧场》(1994)。

epideictic oratory：富于辞藻的雄辩术　　343。

Epigram：警句

该术语现指一种陈述，其形式不论是诗歌还是散文，都显得短小精悍而又机智。警句可以是关于任何主题和任何模式的，如描写恋情、哀悼亡灵、沉思自省、恭维赞赏、趣闻轶事或(往往是)讽刺挖苦。罗马警句诗人马提雅尔为嘲讽辛辣的警句诗树立了不朽的典范。

警句诗经英国16世纪末和17世纪诗人约翰·多恩、本·琼森、罗伯特·赫里克等人之手得以发展完善。警句诗尤其盛行于18世纪，奥斯丁·多布森把这一时期誉为一个"才趣横溢、诗艺圆熟的，也是蒲柏的时代"。马修·普赖尔是杰出的警句作家，亚历山大·蒲柏和玛丽·沃特利·蒙塔古夫人的许多对句也可以

epigrams. In the same century, when the exiled Stuarts were still pretenders to the English throne, John Byrom proposed this epigrammatic toast:

> God bless the King—I mean the Faith's defender!
> God bless (no harm in blessing) the Pretender!
> But who pretender is or who is king—
> God bless us all! that's quite another thing.

And here is one of Samuel Taylor Coleridge's epigrams, to show that Romanticism did not preclude wit:

> *On a Volunteer Singer*
> Swans sing before they die—'twere no bad thing
> Should certain people die before they sing!

Many of the short poems of Walter Savage Landor (1775–1864) were fine examples of the nonsatirical epigram. Boileau and Voltaire excelled in the epigram in France, as did Lessing, Goethe, and Schiller in Germany; and in America, a number of the short poems by Ralph Waldo Emerson and Emily Dickinson may be accounted epigrams. The form continued to be cultivated by Robert Frost, Ezra Pound, Ogden Nash, Phyllis McGinley, Dorothy Parker, A. R. Ammons, Richard Wilbur, Anthony Hecht, and other poets in the twentieth century.

"Epigram" came to be applied, after the eighteenth century, to neat and witty statements in prose as well as verse; an alternative name for the prose epigram is the **apothegm**. (For examples, see *wit, humor, and the comic*.) Such terse and witty prose statements are to be distinguished from the **aphorism**: a pithy and pointed statement of a serious maxim, opinion, or general truth. One of the best known aphorisms is also one of the shortest: *ars longa, vita brevis est*—"art is long, life is short." It occurs first in a work attributed to the Greek physician Hippocrates entitled *Aphorisms*, which consisted of tersely worded precepts on the practice of medicine. (See John Gross, ed., *The Oxford Book of Aphorisms*, 1983.) A related prose form is the *proverb*; see under *allegory*.

Refer to E. B. Osborn, ed., *The Hundred Best Epigrams* (1928); Kingsley Amis, ed., *The New Oxford Book of Light Verse* (1978); Russell Baker, ed., *The Norton Book of Light Verse* (1986). For references to *epigram* in other entries, see page *9*.

epiphany: Epiphany means "a manifestation," or "showing forth," and by Christian thinkers was used to signify a manifestation of God's presence within the created world. In the early draft of *A Portrait of the Artist as a Young Man* entitled *Stephen Hero* (published posthumously in 1944), James Joyce adapted the term to secular experience, to signify the sense of a sudden radiance and revelation that occurs during the perception of a commonplace object. "By an epiphany [Stephen] meant a sudden spiritual manifestation." "Its soul, its whatness, leaps to us from the vestment of its appearance. The soul of the commonest

分解成独立的警句。在同一世纪，流亡的斯图亚特王族觊觎王位之时，约翰·拜罗姆作了如下的祝酒铭词：

> 上帝护佑君王——我指的是信仰的辩护者！
> 上帝护佑（护佑中没有伤害）僭君！
> 但谁为僭君或谁为君王——
> 上帝护佑我们所有人！那完全是另一回事。

下面例举的是塞缪尔·泰勒·柯勒律治的一则警句诗，它表明浪漫主义也不排除机智诙谐的措辞：

> 论一位自告奋勇的歌手
> 天鹅临死前会歌唱——某些人要是
> 唱歌前就死了倒不是坏事！

沃尔特·萨维奇·兰多（1775—1864）的许多短诗是非讽刺性警句的优秀范例。法国诗人布瓦洛和伏尔泰及德国作家莱辛、歌德、席勒也都非常擅长警句创作。在美国，R. W. 爱默生和埃米莉·狄金森的许多短诗都可归为警句诗。警句经20世纪诗人罗伯特·弗罗斯特、埃兹拉·庞德、奥格登·纳什、菲利斯·麦金利、多萝西·帕克、A. R. 阿蒙斯、理查德·威尔伯、安东尼·赫克特和20世纪其他诗人的发展而得以进一步完善。

18世纪以后，"警句"逐渐用于指代散文及诗歌中的精辟之句。散文警句的另一种称谓是**格言**。（相关范例分析参见：*机智、幽默与滑稽*。）这种短小机智的散文警辞与**警语**是有区别的，后者用来表述严肃精辟的格言谚语、观点意见和至理名言。最有名且最短小的警语之一是："艺术长存，生命短暂。"该警语最早见于希腊名医希波克拉底的《箴言》中，书中包括了关于行医的各种简洁精辟的格言警句。[参阅：约翰·格罗斯主编的《牛津格言集》（1983）。]一种相关的散文形式是谚语；参见：*寓言*中的相关阐述。

参阅：E. B. 奥斯本主编的《百佳警句》（1928）；金斯利·阿米斯主编的《新编牛津轻松诗集》（1978）；拉塞尔·贝克主编的《诺顿轻松诗集》（1986）。其他条目中提及"警句"的地方，参见第9页。

Epiphany：灵瞬

该术语的含义是"显灵"，或"显现"，也为基督教思想家用来指上帝在其开创的世界中的显灵。詹姆斯·乔伊斯的《一个青年艺术家的画像》初稿的题名为《英雄斯蒂芬》（作者逝世后于1944年出版），他在该初稿中用此术语指世俗体验，表示在观察普通事物时其灵性的顿悟。"[斯蒂芬]的'灵瞬'指的是他心灵上的顿悟。""事物之灵与实质穿过它的躯壳投向我们。这种普通事物的灵

object . . . seems to us radiant. The object achieves its epiphany." Joyce's short stories and novels include a number of epiphanies; a climactic one is the revelation that Stephen experiences at the sight of the young girl wading on the shore of the sea in *A Portrait of the Artist*, chapter 4. "Epiphany" has become the standard term for the description, recurrent in modern poetry and prose fiction, of the sudden flare into revelation of an ordinary object or scene. Joyce, however, had merely substituted this word for what earlier authors had called the **moment**. Thus Shelley, in his *Defense of Poetry* (1821), described the "best and happiest moments . . . arising unforeseen and departing unbidden," "visitations of the divinity," which poetry "redeems from decay." William Wordsworth was a pre-eminent poet of what he called "moments," or in more elaborate instances, "spots of time." For examples of short poems which represent a moment of revelation, see Wordsworth's "The Two April Mornings" and "The Solitary Reaper." Wordsworth's *Prelude*, like some of Joyce's narratives, is constructed as a sequence of such visionary encounters. Thus in Book VIII, lines 543–54 (1850 ed.), Wordsworth describes the "moment" when he for the first time passed in a stagecoach over the "threshold" of London and the "trivial forms / Of houses, pavement, streets" suddenly assumed a profound power and significance:

> 'twas a moment's pause,—
> All that took place within me came and went
> As in a moment; yet with Time it dwells,
> And grateful memory, as a thing divine.

See Irene H. Chayes, "Joyce's Epiphanies," reprinted in *Joyce's "Portrait": Criticisms and Critiques*, ed. T. E. Connolly (1962); Morris Beja, *Epiphany in the Modern Novel* (1971); Ashton Nichols, *The Poetics of Epiphany: Nineteenth-Century Origins of the Modern Literary Moment* (1987). On the history of the traditional "moment" in sacred writings, beginning with St. Augustine, and its conversion into the modern literary epiphany, see M. H. Abrams, *Natural Supernaturalism: Tradition and Revolution in Romantic Literature* (1971), chapters 7–8.

episodic (plot): **253**; *295*.

epistolary novel (ĕpĭs″ tōlĕr′ ē): **254**.

Epithalamion: Epithalamion, or in the Latin form "epithalamium," is a poem written to celebrate a marriage. Among its classical practitioners were the Greeks Sappho and Theocritus and the Romans Ovid and Catullus. The term in Greek means "at the bridal chamber," since the verses were originally written to be sung outside the bedroom of a newly married couple. The form flourished among the Neo-Latin poets of the Renaissance, who established the model that was followed by writers in the European vernacular languages. Sir Philip Sidney wrote the first English instance in about 1580, and fifteen years later Edmund Spenser wrote his great lyric "Epithalamion," a celebration

魂……在我们眼前显得绚丽夺目。事物获得了其灵感。"乔伊斯的短篇故事和长篇小说中出现过不少这样的灵瞬情节;《一个青年艺术家的画像》第 4 章中,斯蒂芬目击海滩涉水姑娘时的体验则是最典型的范例。在现代诗歌与小说中,"灵瞬"已成为一个标准术语,常用于形容普通事物和平凡场景的灵性的豁然闪现。然而,乔伊斯仅仅是用灵瞬一词取代了以往作家所谓的**黄金瞬息**。雪莱在《诗辩》(1821)中描叙了"令人销魂的黄金瞬息……来无影去无踪",诗歌就是要"从腐败中救赎出""上帝探访人间的时刻"。威廉·华兹华斯是位能卓越地表现"片刻"、或更为详尽的"瞬息"的诗人,如在《四月里的两个早晨》和《孤独的收割者》这两首短诗中对启示的瞬间的呈现。如同乔伊斯的一些叙事小说,华兹华斯的《序曲》是对一系列灵瞬的记述。《序曲》第 8 卷第 543—554 行(1850 年版)描写了这样一些"片刻":他乘公共马车初次进入伦敦大门"门槛","外表平凡的房屋、便道与街巷"顿然显露出无穷的力量和意义:

> 这是瞬间的静止——
> 我心际里闪现的一切来去匆匆
> 皆在片刻;却又与时光并存,
> 销魂的记忆,宛若天赐神授。　　　　　　(丁宏为译)

参阅:艾琳·H. 蔡斯所写的文章"乔伊斯的灵瞬",重印收入 T. E. 康诺利主编的《乔伊斯的"肖像":批评与批判》(1962);莫里斯·贝佳所著的《现代小说中的灵瞬》(1971);阿什顿·尼科尔斯所著的《灵瞬诗学:现代文学瞬息的 19 世纪起源》(1987)。有关始于圣奥古斯丁在宗教作品中对"瞬息"的传统描写及其转化为现代文学的"灵瞬"的历史,参阅:M. H. 艾布拉姆斯所著的《自然的超自然主义:浪漫主义文学中的传统与变革》(1971)一书中第 7—8 章。

episodic (plot):插曲式的(情节)　253;295。

epistolary novel:书信体小说　254。

Epithalamion:喜歌

喜歌(其拉丁文为 epithalamium)是为庆祝婚礼而写的一种诗歌。从事喜歌创作的古代作家主要有希腊的萨福、忒俄克里托斯和罗马的奥维德、卡图鲁斯。"喜歌"在希腊文里的本意是"洞房前",因为喜歌本就是为在新婚夫妇的洞房外吟唱而作。这种诗歌形式盛行于文艺复兴时期的新拉丁语诗人中,他们创造的这种创作模式为后世欧洲的方言作家所仿效。菲利普·锡德尼爵士约在 1580 年创作了英国第一首喜歌。十五年后,埃德蒙·斯宾塞为庆贺自己的婚礼,创作了著

of his own marriage that he composed as a wedding gift to his bride. Spenser's poem follows, in elaborately contrived numbers of stanzas and lines, the sequence of the hours during his wedding day and night and combines, with unfailing ease and dignity, Christian ritual and beliefs, pagan topics and mythology, and the local Irish setting. John Donne, Ben Jonson, Robert Herrick, and many other Renaissance poets composed wedding poems that were solemn or ribald, according to the intended audience and the poet's own temperament.

Sir John Suckling's "A Ballad upon a Wedding" is a good-humored *parody* of this upper-class poetic form, which he applies to a lower-class wedding. The tradition persists. Shelley composed an "Epithalamium"; Tennyson's *In Memoriam*, although it opens with a funeral, closes with an epithalamion; A. E. Housman spoke in the antique idiom of the bridal song in "He Is Here, Urania's Son." Gerard Manley Hopkins wrote an "Epithalamion" in 1888 (published in 1918), as did e. e. cummings in 1923, and W. H. Auden in 1939.

See Robert H. Case, *English Epithalamies* (1896); Virginia J. Tufte, *The Poetry of Marriage* (1970); and (on the elaborate construction of the stanzas and lines in Spenser's "Epithalamion" to correspond with the passage of time on his wedding day) A. Kent Hieatt, *Short Time's Endless Monument* (1960).

epithet: As a term in criticism, **epithet** denotes an adjective or adjectival phrase used to describe a distinctive quality of a person or thing; an example is *"silver snarling* trumpets" in John Keats' *The Eve of St. Agnes*. The term is also applied to an identifying phrase that stands in place of a noun; thus Alexander Pope's "the *glittering forfex"* is an ironically inflated epithet for the scissors with which the Baron performs his heinous act in *The Rape of the Lock* (1714). The frequent use of derogatory adjectives and phrases in *invective* has led to the mistaken notion that an "epithet" is always uncomplimentary.

Homeric epithets are adjectival terms—usually a compound of two words—like those which Homer in his *epic* poems used as recurrent formulas in referring to a distinctive feature of someone or something: *"fleet-footed* Achilles," *"bolthurling* Zeus," "the *wine-dark* sea." Buck Mulligan in James Joyce's *Ulysses parodied* the formula in his reference to "the snot-green sea." We often use "conventional epithets" in identifying historical or legendary figures, as in Charles *the Great*, Lorenzo *the Magnificent*, *Patient* Griselda.

epoché (ĕp′ ŏkē): 289.

epode (ĕ′ pōd): 262.

equivoque (ĕk′ wĭvōk): 326.

Erziehungsroman (ĕrtsē″ ungsrōmän″): 255.

eschatology (ĕs′ kătol″ ōjē): 182.

名的抒情《婚曲》,作为结婚礼物献给新娘。这首喜歌以构思精致的诗节和诗行按时间顺序描写了婚礼的过程及新婚之夜的盛况,将基督教礼仪与信仰、异教题材与神话和爱尔兰的地方风情融为一体,表现出无限的典雅与华贵。约翰·多恩、本·琼森、罗伯特·赫里克和其他许多文艺复兴时期的诗人也创作过婚礼喜歌,根据欣赏者与作者的不同气质情趣,他们的喜歌风格或俗或雅。

约翰·萨克林爵士的《婚礼歌谣》描述了平民的婚礼,是对喜歌这种上流社会诗歌形式的*戏谑模仿*。喜歌这一传统源远流长。雪莱曾创作过一首《喜歌》;丁尼生的《悼念》虽以葬礼开篇,却用喜歌结尾。A. E. 豪斯曼用古代方言创作了新婚喜歌《乌拉尼亚的儿子在这里》。杰勒德·曼利·霍普金斯在1888年写过一首《喜歌》(出版于1918年),e. e. 肯明斯在1923年写过一首《喜歌》,W. H. 奥登在1939年也写过一首《喜歌》。

参阅:罗伯特·H. 凯斯所著的《英国喜歌》(1896);弗吉尼娅·J. 塔夫特所著的《婚姻诗歌》(1970);有关斯宾塞《婚曲》中诗节和诗行与他婚礼的过程相呼应的精致结构,参阅:A. 肯特·海恩特所著的《短暂时刻的永久典范》(1960)。

Epithet 属性形容词

作为文学批评用语,**属性形容词**指用于表明人与物特殊性质的形容词或形容词短语,如约翰·济慈《圣阿格尼斯夜》中的"带有浮凸花纹的银号"。该术语还适用于那种替代名词的识别性短语;亚历山大·蒲柏在《卷发遇劫记》(1714) 中用"闪闪发光的利剪"这一具有嘲讽意味的夸张性属性形容词指代男爵从事罪恶勾当时用的剪刀。由于贬义形容词和形容词短语在漫骂中经常出现,致使人们误认为"属性形容词"总是含有贬义。

荷马属性形容词指的是形容词术语——一般由两个词合成——正如荷马在他的史诗中谈及一些人或事的特定特征时,作为一种反复使用的方式:"飞毛腿阿喀琉斯""雷神爷宙斯""像酒一样绛紫色的大海"。詹姆斯·乔伊斯《尤利西斯》中的巴克·马利根诙谐地模仿荷马的手法,把大海描写成"鼻涕一样青色的大海"。我们常会用"约定俗成的属性形容词"来指代某些历史或传奇人物,如查理大帝、伟大的洛伦佐、善于忍耐的格里塞尔达。

epoché:悬置　289。

epode:后颂部　262。

equivoque:歧义词　326。

Erziehungsroman:末世学　255。

eschatology:教育小说　182。

essay: Any short composition in prose that undertakes to discuss a matter, express a point of view, persuade us to accept a thesis on any subject, or simply entertain. The essay differs from a "treatise" or "dissertation" in its lack of pretension to be a systematic and complete exposition, and in being addressed to a general rather than a specialized audience; as a consequence, the essay discusses its subject in nontechnical fashion, and often with a liberal use of such devices as anecdote, striking illustration, and humor to augment its appeal.

A useful distinction is that between the formal and informal essay. The **formal essay**, or **article**, is relatively impersonal: the author writes as an authority, or at least as highly knowledgeable, and expounds the subject in an orderly way. Examples will be found in scholarly journals, as well as among the serious articles on current topics and issues in any of the magazines addressed to a thoughtful audience—*Harper's*, *Commentary*, *Scientific American*, and so on. In the **informal essay** (or "familiar" or "personal essay"), the author assumes a tone of intimacy with his audience, tends to deal with everyday things rather than with public affairs or specialized topics, and writes in a relaxed, self-revelatory, and sometimes whimsical fashion. Modern examples are to be found in any issue of *The New Yorker*.

The Greeks Theophrastus and Plutarch and the Romans Cicero and Seneca wrote essays long before the genre was given what became its standard name by Montaigne's French *Essais* in 1580. The title signifies "attempts" and was meant to indicate the tentative and unsystematic nature of Montaigne's commentary on topics such as "Of Illness" and "Of Sleeping," in contrast to formal and technical treatises on the same subjects. Francis Bacon, late in the sixteenth century, inaugurated the English use of the term in his own *Essays*; most of them are short discussions such as "Of Truth," "Of Adversity," "Of Marriage and the Single Life." Alexander Pope adopted the term for his expository compositions in verse, the *Essay on Criticism* (1711) and the *Essay on Man* (1733), but the verse essay has had few important exponents after the eighteenth century; the verse essays by the American poet Robert Pinsky are a rare exception. In the early eighteenth century Joseph Addison and Sir Richard Steele's *Tatler* and *Spectator*, with their many successors, gave to the essay written in prose its standard modern vehicle, the literary periodical (earlier essays had been published in books).

In the early nineteenth century the founding of new types of magazines, and their steady proliferation, gave great impetus to the writing of essays and made them a major department of literature. This was the age when William Hazlitt, Thomas De Quincey, Charles Lamb, and, later in the century, Robert Louis Stevenson brought the English essay—and especially the personal essay—to a level that has not been surpassed. Major American essayists in the nineteenth century include Washington Irving, Emerson, Thoreau, James Russell Lowell, and Mark Twain. In our own era the many periodicals pour out scores of essays every week. Most of them are formal in type; Virginia Woolf, George Orwell, E. M. Forster, James Thurber, E. B. White, James Baldwin, Susan Sontag, and Toni Morrison, however, are notable recent practitioners of the informal essay.

Essay：杂文

旨在探讨问题、阐述观点、劝说我们接受关于任一主题的一种观点，或只是怡情的任何散文体短篇作品都属于杂文（又译论说文）。杂文有别于论著或学术论文，其论述说理不够系统完备，其对象只限于一般读者而非专业人士。因此，杂文的论述采用非技术性、灵活多样的方式，往往运用奇闻轶事、鲜明的例证、幽默风趣的说理等手段来加强其感染力。

杂文又有正规与非正规之分，这一区别具有一定实用价值。相对而言，**正规杂文**或**文章**比较客观：作者以权威或至少是博学之士的身份书写，条理清楚、层层深入地阐述论点。这样的例子可见于各种学术期刊，以及面向富有思想性读者的杂志中严肃的时事评论文章中，如《哈珀斯》《评论》《美国科学论坛》等杂志。在**非正规杂文**（或称"通俗的"或"个人随笔"）中，笔者采用亲近于读者的口吻，内容常常涉及生活琐事而非公共事务或专业论题，行文活泼自如、观点直截了当，有时也饶有风趣。杂志《纽约人》中有许多这种现代例子。

杂文体裁是于1580年正式得名于蒙田的法文《随笔》，但在很久之前，古希腊的忒俄弗雷斯托斯、普卢塔克和罗马的西塞罗、塞内加就已开始创作杂文。蒙田以杂文为题名，意味着"尝试"，旨在表明他的论述（如《关于疾病》《关于睡眠》）与主题相同的正规性及学术性论著相对比，表现出的探索性与无系统性。16世纪后期，弗朗西斯·培根的《随笔》开创了英国的杂文创作。他的作品大都篇幅简短，如《论真理》《论逆境》《论婚嫁与独身》等。亚历山大·蒲柏也把杂文一词用于自己的诗体论文，如《批评论》（1711）和《人论》（1733），然而18世纪以后，从事这种诗体杂文创作的有影响力的作者就寥寥无几了；美国诗人罗伯特·平斯基的诗体杂文是一个少有的例外。18世纪早期，约瑟夫·艾迪生和理查德·斯梯尔合办的《闲话者》《旁观者》，以及它们的许多继承者，为杂文开创了以散文形式书写的现代标准途径——文学期刊（此前杂文是汇集成书出版的）。

19世纪初期，新型杂志的问世与稳步发展极大地推动了杂文的创作，并使杂文成为一种主要文学类型。这一时期，威廉·哈兹里特、托马斯·德·昆西、查尔斯·兰姆，以及19世纪后期的罗伯特·路易斯·斯蒂文森将英语杂文，尤其是个人随笔的创作推进到极致。美国19世纪的主要杂文作家有华盛顿·欧文、爱默生、梭罗、詹姆斯·罗素·洛威尔、马克·吐温。当代种类繁多的期刊杂志每周都会刊登大量杂文作品，其中多数都为正规杂文。弗吉尼亚·吴尔夫、乔治·奥威尔、E. M. 福斯特、詹姆斯·瑟伯、E. B. 怀特、詹姆斯·鲍德温、苏珊·桑塔格、托妮·莫里森都是20世纪随笔杂文的杰出作者。

See Robert Scholes and Carl H. Klaus, *Elements of the Essay* (1969); John Gross, ed., *The Oxford Book of Essays* (1991); Wendy Martin, ed., *Essays by Contemporary American Women* (1996). For a suggestive view of the tacit philosophical assumptions underlying the essay form, see Georg Lukács, "On the Nature and Form of the Essay," in *Soul and Form* (1980).

essentialism: 163.

estrange: 139.

estrangement effect: 7.

ethnic writers: 278; *249*.

ethos (ē′ thōs): 270.

euphemism: An inoffensive expression used in place of a blunt one that is felt to be disagreeable or embarrassing. Euphemisms occur frequently with reference to such subjects as religion ("Gosh darn!" for "God damn!"), death ("pass away" instead of "die"), bodily functions ("comfort station" instead of "toilet"), and sex ("to sleep with" instead of "to have sexual intercourse with").

On the extraordinary number and variety of sexual euphemisms in Shakespeare's plays, see Eric Partridge, *Shakespeare's Bawdy* (1960).

euphony and cacophony: **Euphony** is a term applied to language which strikes the ear as smooth, pleasant, and musical, as in these lines from John Keats, *The Eve of St. Agnes* (1820),

> And lucent syrops, tinct with cinnamon;
> Manna and dates, in argosy transferred
> From Fez; and spicèd dainties, every one,
> From silken Samarcand to cedar'd Lebanon.

Analysis of the passage, however, will show that what seems to be a purely auditory agreeableness is due more to the significance of the words, conjoined with the ease and pleasure of the physical act of enunciating the sequence of the speech sounds, than to the inherent melodiousness of the speech sounds themselves. The American critic John Crowe Ransom illustrated the importance of significance to euphony by altering Tennyson's "The murmur of innumerable bees" to "The murder of innumerable beeves"; the euphony is destroyed, not by changing one speech sound and inserting others, but by the change in reference.

Similarly, in **cacophony**, or **dissonance**—language which is perceived as harsh, rough, and unmusical—the discordancy is the effect not only of the sound of the words, but also of their significance, conjoined with the difficulty of enunciating the sequence of the speech sounds. Cacophony may be inadvertent, through a lapse in the writer's attention or skill, as in the unfortunate line of Matthew Arnold's fine poem "Dover Beach" (1867), "Lay

参阅：罗伯特·肖科尔斯与卡尔·H. 克劳斯合著的《杂文的元素》(1969)；约翰·格罗斯主编的《牛津杂文集》(1991)；温迪·马丁主编的《现代美国女性杂文》(1996)。关于散文形式隐含的不言而喻的哲学基础的一种具有启发性的看法，参阅：乔治·卢卡奇所著的《心灵与形式》(1980)中的"论杂文/论说文的本质和形式"。

essentialism：本质主义　163。

estrange：间离　139。

estrangement effect：陌生化效果　7。

ethnic writers：民族作家　278；*249*。

ethos：特质　270。

Euphemism：委婉语

委婉语指的是为了避免因直率而令人不悦或尴尬而采用的含蓄婉转的表达，常用于谈及宗教（"Gosh darn"代替"God damn！"天谴；"Gosh"代替"God"上帝）、死亡（"逝世"而不是"死亡"）、身体功能（如指厕所时用"comfort station"而非"toilet"）、与性有关的话题（如指性交时用"sleep with"而非"have sexual intercourse with"）。

莎士比亚戏剧中有大量关于性的各种委婉语，参阅：埃里克·帕特里奇所著的《莎士比亚的污言秽语》(1960)。

Euphony and Cacophony：谐音与非谐音

谐音指和谐悦耳、富于乐感的语言，如约翰·济慈《圣阿格尼斯夜》(1820)中的诗行：

> 澄明的蜜露，肉桂的香味渗透；
> 仙浆，海枣，鲜美的菜肴和羹汤
> 这些全是用海船运来：桌上有
> 来自非斯、撒马罕、黎巴嫩等地的珍馐　　　　　（屠岸译）

对这段诗文加以分析，就可见悦耳动听之处主要在于词义和诵读时语音如行云流水，清晰怡人，两者珠联璧合、自然流畅，而并非是由于语音固有的乐感。美国批评家约翰·克罗·兰塞姆通过把丁尼生的诗句"无数蜂儿嗡嗡细语"改写成"无数肉牛被杀死"，来说明谐音的重要性；后者的谐音已被破毁，这种破毁不是因为一个语音的改变和插入其他语音所引起，而是含义变化所致。

同样，在**非谐音**或**不和谐**——刺耳、嘈杂、没有乐感——的语言中，音色的不协调不仅是字音发声拗口，也是语义晦涩及语音不畅共同导致的结果。非谐音的出现可能是由于作者的疏忽或措辞的失误所致，如马修·阿诺德的名篇《多弗

like the folds of a bright girdle furled." But cacophony may also be deliberate and functional: for humor, as in Robert Browning's "Pied Piper" (1842),

> Rats!
> They fought the dogs and killed the cats . . .
> Split open the kegs of salted sprats,
> Made nests inside men's Sunday hats;

or else for other purposes, as in Thomas Hardy's attempt, in his poem "In Tenebris I," to mimic, as well as describe, dogged endurance by the difficulty of negotiating the transition in speech sounds from each stressed monosyllable to the next:

> I shall not lose old strength
> In the lone frost's black length.
> Strength long since fled!

For other sound effects see *alliteration* and *onomatopoeia*. Refer to G. R. Stewart, *The Technique of English Verse* (1930), and Northrop Frye, ed., *Sound and Poetry* (1957).

euphuism: A conspicuously formal and elaborate prose style which had a vogue in the 1580s in drama, prose fiction, and probably also in the conversation of English court circles. It takes its name from the moralistic prose romance *Euphues: The Anatomy of Wit*, which John Lyly wrote in 1578. In the dialogues of this work and of *Euphues and His England* (1580), as well as in his stage comedies, Lyly exaggerated and used persistently a stylized prose which other writers had developed earlier. The style is **sententious** (that is, full of moral maxims), relies on syntactical balance and *antithesis*, reinforces the structural parallels by heavy and elaborate patterns of *alliteration* and *assonance*, exploits the *rhetorical question*, and is addicted to long similes and learned allusions which are often drawn from mythology and the supposed characteristics and habits of legendary animals. Here is a brief example from *Euphues*; the character Philautus is speaking:

> I see now that as the fish *Scholopidus* in the flood Araris at the waxing of the Moon is as white as the driven snow, and at the waning as black as the burnt coal, so Euphues, which at the first enceasing of our familiarity, was very zealous, is now at the last cast become most faithless.

Shakespeare good-humoredly *parodied* this self-consciously elegant style in *Love's Labour's Lost* and other plays; nonetheless he, like other authors of the time, profited from Lyly's explorations of the formal and rhetorical possibilities of English prose.

See *style*; also Jonas A. Barish, "The Prose Style of John Lyly," *English Literary History* 23 (1956), and G. K. Hunter, *John Lyly* (1962).

exegesis (ĕxĕjē′ sis): **176**.

exemplum (ĕxĕm′ plŭm): **10**.

滩》(1867)中令人遗憾的诗句:"像一条折拢的明晃晃的腰带堆攒在那里"。然而,作者也可能故意利用非谐音以求得某种艺术效果,如罗伯特·勃朗宁在《吹风笛的人》中以此来增加幽默感:

> 老鼠!
> 它们向狗开战并杀死了猫……
> 捅破了盛着腌制鲱鱼的小桶
> 把窝筑进了绅士的礼帽当中;

或是用于其他目的,如在《在抑郁中》这首诗中,托马斯·哈代利用重读单音节词相连发音上的困难来摹拟和表现一种顽强的耐力:

> 在那孤寂霜夜里
> 我不再丧失体力
> 体力早已衰竭! （刘新民译）

有关其他语音效果,参见:*头韵*、*拟声词*。参阅:G. R. 斯图尔特所著的《英诗的技巧》(1930);诺斯罗普·弗莱主编的《声音与诗歌》(1957)。

Euphuism:尤弗伊斯体

尤弗伊斯体是1580年代盛行于戏剧、小说和宫廷成员间的对话中的一种散文文风,其行文正规、笔触绮丽。该体得名于约翰·黎里创作于1578年的道德说教散文传奇《尤弗伊斯:才智的剖析》。在这部作品与《尤弗伊斯及其英国》(1580)和他的舞台喜剧的对话中,黎里夸张而又持续地沿用了前人倡导的散文风格:行文好*说教*(即充满说教式的道德警句),依靠句式均衡和运用*对偶*,并通过精心设计*头韵*和*半谐音*来强化句型的对仗,采用*修辞性疑问句*,同时热衷于引用神话和传说中动物的所谓特征和习性作为冗长的比喻和博学的典故。以下引自《尤弗伊斯》中菲劳图斯的一番话,就是一个简明的例子:

> 我现在看出,就像阿拉里斯潮水中的鱼儿"斯科洛彼得斯"在满月时洁白如雪而月缺时却黑似墨炭一样,尤弗伊斯起初与我熟悉亲近时热情异常,而如今在这最后一举时却变得不忠不义。

莎士比亚在《爱的徒劳》和其他剧作中风趣地*戏谑模仿*了这种自我感觉良好的文风,但莎士比亚和其他同期作家一样,也从黎里有关英国散文正规化与修辞技巧的探索中受益。

参见:*文体*,参阅:乔纳斯·A. 巴里什所写的文章"约翰·黎里的散文风格",载于《英国文学史》(1956)第23卷;G. K. 亨特所著的《约翰·黎里》(1962)。

exegesis:注释 176。

exemplum:劝谕性故事 10。

existential philosophy: 178; *1.*

explication: 242; *14.*

explication de texte: 243

exposition (in a plot): **296**.

expressionism: A German movement in literature and the other arts (especially the visual arts) which was at its height between 1910 and 1925—that is, in the period just before, during, and after World War I. Its chief precursors were artists and writers who had in various ways departed from realistic depictions of life and the world, by incorporating in their art visionary or powerfully emotional states of mind that are expressed and transmitted by means of distorted representations of the outer world. Among these precursors in painting were Vincent Van Gogh, Paul Gauguin, and the Norwegian Edvard Munch—Munch's lithograph *The Cry* (1894) depicting, against a bleak and stylized background, a tense figure with a contorted face uttering a scream of pure horror, is often taken to epitomize what became the expressionist mode. Prominent among the literary precursors of the movement in the nineteenth century were the French poets Charles Baudelaire and Arthur Rimbaud, the Russian novelist Fyodor Dostoevsky, the German philosopher Friedrich Nietzsche, and above all the Swedish dramatist August Strindberg.

Expressionism itself was not a concerted or well-defined movement. It can be said, however, that its central feature is a revolt against the artistic and literary tradition of *realism*, both in subject matter and in style. The expressionist artist or writer undertakes to express a personal vision—usually a troubled or tensely emotional vision—of human life and human society. This is done by exaggerating and distorting what, according to the norms of artistic realism, are objective features of the world, and by embodying violent extremes of mood and feeling. Often the work implies that what is depicted or described represents the experience of an individual standing alone and afraid in an industrial, technological, and urban society which is disintegrating into chaos. Those expressionists who were radical in their politics also projected utopian views of a future community in a regenerate world.

Expressionist painters tended to use jagged lines to depict contorted objects and forms, as well as to substitute arbitrary, often lurid colors, for natural hues; among these painters were Emil Nolde, Franz Marc, Oskar Kokoschka, and, for a time, Wassily Kandinsky. Expressionist poets (including the Germans Gottfried Benn and Georg Trakl) departed from standard meter, syntax, and poetic structure to organize their works around symbolic images. Expressionist writers of prose narratives (most eminently Franz Kafka) abandoned standard modes of characterization and plot for symbolic figures involved in an obsessive world of nightmarish events.

Drama was a prominent and widely influential form of expressionist writing. Among the better-known German playwrights were Georg Kaiser (*Gas,*

existential philosophy：存在主义哲学　　178；*1*。

explication：解说　　242；*14*。

explication de texte：解说文本　　243。

exposition（in a plot）：（情节中的）交代　　296。

Expressionism：表现主义

　　表现主义是发生在德国的一场文学和其他艺术（尤指视觉艺术）运动，1910—1925年间即第一次世界大战期间及其前后达到高潮。运动的主要先驱是作家和艺术家，他们以不同方式弃离现实主义表现生活和世界的手法，而借用扭曲外部世界的手法表达和传递艺术幻想或充满激情的内心世界。绘画艺术的表现主义先驱有文森特·凡·高、保罗·高更和挪威籍画家爱德华·蒙克。蒙克的版画《呐喊》（1894）表现的是在荒凉惨淡的风格化背景下，一个面部扭曲、躯体痉挛的身影在发出一声惊骇的长嘶。这部作品一向被视作表现主义风格的缩影。表现主义文学先驱主要有19世纪法国诗人查尔斯·波德莱尔、阿尔蒂尔·兰波，俄国小说家费奥多·陀思妥耶夫斯基，德国哲学家弗里德里希·尼采，以及最有代表性的瑞典戏剧家奥古斯特·斯特林堡。

　　表现主义本身从来不是一次协调一致、定义明确的运动。但可断言，其核心特点是在主题与创作风格方面对*现实主义*文学与艺术传统的叛逆。表现主义艺术家、文学家极力表现的是他们对人生与人类社会的自我感受，通常是忧心忡忡、满怀激愤的人生感受。其手法是对现实主义艺术观所谓的客观世界的外部特征加以夸张和扭曲，同时表达出种种极端化的强烈情感。这类作品常通过刻画或描写，塑造出置身于行将溃乱的工业化、技术化、城市化的世界中孤独而又恐慌的个人。那些政见激进的表现主义艺术家也表现关于未来新生世界的乌托邦思想。

　　表现派画家惯用参差不齐的线条刻画扭曲的形象，同时常用强烈的色调任意置换自然色调。这类画家包括埃米尔·诺尔德、弗朗茨·马克、奥斯卡尔·柯柯什卡，在一段时期里还包括瓦西里·康定斯基。表现主义诗人（包括德国的戈特弗里德·贝恩和乔治·特拉克尔）离弃了诗歌标准化的格律、句法和结构，围绕象征性意象来组织他们的作品。表现主义小说家（最杰出的是弗朗兹·卡夫卡）抛弃了对身陷噩梦般境地的象征性人物进行人物刻画和情节安排的传统模式。

　　戏剧是表现主义创作中一种主要的、影响广泛的形式。享有盛名的德国剧作

From Morn to Midnight), Ernst Toller (*Mass Man*), and, in his earlier productions, Bertolt Brecht. Expressionist dramatists often represented anonymous human types instead of individualized characters, replaced plot with episodic renderings of intense and rapidly oscillating emotional states, fragmented the dialogue into exclamatory and seemingly incoherent sentences or phrases, and employed masks and abstract or lopsided and sprawling stage sets. The producer Max Reinhardt, although not himself in the movement, directed a number of plays by Strindberg and by German expressionists; in them he inaugurated such modern devices as the revolving stage and special effects in lighting and sound. This mode of German drama had an important influence on the American theater. Eugene O'Neill's *The Emperor Jones* (1920) projected, in a sequence of symbolic episodes, the individual and racial memories of a terrified African-American protagonist, and Elmer Rice's *The Adding Machine* (1923) used nonrealistic means to represent a mechanical, sterile, and frightening world as experienced by Mr. Zero, a tiny and helpless cog in the impersonal system of big business. The flexible possibilities of the medium made the motion picture an important vehicle of German expressionism. Robert Wiene's early expressionist film *The Cabinet of Dr. Caligari* (1920)—representing, in ominously distorted settings, the machinations of the satanic head of an insane asylum—as well as Friedrich Murnau's *Nosferatu* (1922) and Fritz Lang's *Metropolis* (1926) are often shown in current revivals of films.

Expressionism had begun to flag by 1925 and was finally suppressed in Germany by the Nazis in the early 1930s, but it has continued to exert influence on English and American, as well as European, art and literature. We recognize its effects, direct or indirect, on the writing and staging of such plays as Thornton Wilder's *The Skin of Our Teeth* and Arthur Miller's *Death of a Salesman*, as well as on the *theater of the absurd*; on the poetry of Allen Ginsberg and other *Beat* writers; on the prose fiction of Samuel Beckett, Kurt Vonnegut, Jr., Joseph Heller, and Thomas Pynchon; and on a number of films that exhibit the distorted perceptions and fantasies of disturbed characters, by such directors as Ingmar Bergman, Federico Fellini, and Michelangelo Antonioni.

See Richard Samuel and R. H. Thomas, *Expressionism in German Life, Literature and the Theater, 1910–1924* (1939); Walter H. Sokel, *The Writer in Extremis: Expressionism in Twentieth-Century German Literature* (1959); John Willett, *Expressionism* (1970); Donald E. Gordon, *Expressionism: Art and Idea* (1987); Neil H. Donahue, ed., *A Companion to the Literature of German Expressionism* (2005). On the expressionist cinema: Siegfried Kracauer, *From Caligari to Hitler: A Psychological History of the German Film* (1947); Lotte Eisner, *The Haunted Screen: Expressionism in the German Cinema and the Influence of Max Reinhardt* (1969). For references to *expressionism* in other entries, see pages *1, 258.*

expressive criticism: 69; *290, 344, 382.*

eye rhymes: 349.

家有乔治·凯泽（《煤气》《从清晨到午夜》）、恩斯特·托勒尔（《群众和人》），此外还有当时处于创作初期的贝尔托特·布莱希特。表现主义剧作家惯用毫无个性的人物模式取代个性化的人物角色，通过描写一连串紧张、急剧动荡的情感状态片段来代替传统的戏剧情节，常把对话离析成惊叹性的、近乎语无伦次的只言片语，同时还运用面具伪装以及抽象畸形、拖沓松散的布景道具。马克斯·莱因哈特本人并非表现主义者，但他导演了许多斯特林堡及其他德国表现派剧作家的剧作，并开创了一些现代舞台的表现手法，如旋转舞台、灯光与音响的特殊效果等。德国的这一戏剧模式对美国的戏剧舞台产生了重大影响。尤金·奥尼尔的《琼斯皇》（1920）通过一系列象征性情节片段，展示了一位心怀恐惧的现代美国黑人对自身及种族往事的回忆。埃尔默·赖斯的《加法机》（1923）运用非现实主义手法，通过描写一位弱小无助的零先生这样一位在无情的大商业系统中无足轻重的小人物的亲身经历，呈现出一个机械无效而又令人恐怖的世界。电影作为媒介，其自身的灵活性使它也成为德国表现主义的一个重要工具。罗伯特·韦恩的早期表现主义影片《卡利加里博士的密室》（1920），描写了在险恶变形的场景里一个凶恶的精神病院头目的阴谋。该影片连同弗里德里奇·默诺的《诺斯菲拉图》（1922）、弗里兹·兰格的《都市》（1926）至今仍时常重演。

表现主义运动从 1925 年开始进入低潮，1930 年代初最终在德国被纳粹党镇压下去，但它仍旧对英美和欧洲各国的文学艺术产生着影响。在桑顿·怀尔德的《九死一生》、阿瑟·米勒的《推销员之死》和*荒诞派戏剧*的创作及演出中，在艾伦·金斯堡及其他"垮掉派作家"的诗歌中，在塞缪尔·贝克特、小库尔特·冯内古特、约瑟夫·海勒和托马斯·品钦的小说中，在英格马·伯格曼、费德里科·费利尼和米切朗格洛·安东尼奥尼导演的许多描写变态心理与梦幻空想的影片中，我们都可以直接或间接地感受到表现主义思潮的影响。

参阅：理查德·塞缪尔与 R. H. 托马斯合著的《1910—1924 年间德国生活、文学和戏剧中的表现主义》（1939）；沃尔特·H. 索克尔所著的《走向极端的作家：20 世纪德国文学中的表现主义》（1959）；约翰·威利特所著的《表现主义》（1970）；唐纳德·E. 戈登所著的《表现主义：艺术与观念》（1987）；尼尔·H. 多纳霍主编的《德国表现主义文学指南》（2005）。有关表现主义电影可以参阅：西格弗里德·克拉考尔所著的《从卡利加里到希特勒：德国电影心理史》（1947）；洛特·艾斯纳所著的《群魔乱舞的银幕：德国电影中的表现主义与马克斯·莱因哈特的影响》（1969）。其他条目中提及"表现主义"的地方，参见第 1、258 页。

expressive criticism：表现主义批评　69；*290, 344, 382*。

eye rhymes：视觉韵　349。

F

fable: 9.

fabliau (fab′ lēō): The medieval fabliau was a short comic or satiric tale in verse dealing realistically with middle-class or lower-class characters and delighting in the ribald; one of its favorite themes was the cuckolding of a stupid husband. (Professor Douglas Bush neatly described the type as "a short story broader than it is long.") The fabliau flourished in France in the twelfth and thirteenth centuries and became popular in England during the fourteenth century. Chaucer, who wrote one of the greatest serious short stories in verse, the account of Death and the rioters in "The Pardoner's Tale," also wrote one of the best fabliaux, the hilarious "Miller's Tale."

See Joseph Bédier, *Les Fabliaux* (5th ed., 1928); *Fabliaux: Ribald Tales from the Old French*, trans. Robert Hellman and Richard O'Gorman (1976); Howard Bloch, *The Scandal of the Fabliaux* (1986); John Hines, *The Fabliau in English* (1993).

fabula: 234.

fabulation: 258.

fallible narrator: 305; *185.*

falling action: 296.

false wit: 420.

family resemblances: 150.

fancy and imagination: The distinction between fancy and imagination was a key element in Samuel Taylor Coleridge's theory of poetry, as well as in his general theory of the mental processes. In earlier discussions, "fancy" and "imagination" had for the most part been used synonymously to denote a faculty of the mind which is distinguished from "reason," "judgment," and "memory," in that it receives "images" from the senses and reorders them into new combinations. In the thirteenth chapter of *Biographia Literaria* (1817), Coleridge attributes this reordering function of the sensory images to the lower faculty he calls **fancy**: "Fancy . . . has no other counters to play with, but fixities and definites. The Fancy is indeed no other than a mode of Memory emancipated from the order of time and space." To Coleridge, that is, the fancy is a mechanical process which receives the elementary images—the "fixities and definites" which come to it ready-made from the senses—and, without altering the parts, reassembles them into a different spatial and temporal order from that in which they were originally

F

fable：寓言故事　9。

Fabliau：寓言诗

中世纪的寓言诗是一种滑稽或讽刺性的诗体短篇故事，它形象逼真地描写社会中下层人物，而且以粗俗下流为乐；热衷于描写戴绿帽子的愚蠢的丈夫（道格拉斯·布什教授把这类诗歌的特征简洁地概括为"广度超过长度的短篇故事"）。寓言诗繁荣于12、13世纪的法国，到14世纪又成为英国大众喜闻乐见的文学形式。乔叟不仅写了一篇严肃的短篇叙事诗歌"卖赎罪券者讲的故事"，这是最著名的寓言诗之一，描述死亡和叛乱分子，还写了最为精彩的一部寓言诗：欢快的"磨坊主讲的故事"。

参阅：约瑟夫·贝迪耶所著的《寓言诗》（1928年第5版）；《寓言诗：来自古法语的下流故事》，罗伯特·赫尔曼与理查德·奥戈尔曼1976年英译版；霍华德·布洛克所著的《寓言诗的丑闻》（1986）；约翰·海恩斯所著的《英语中的寓言诗》（1993）。

fabula：故事的组成素材　234。

fabulation：寓言　258。

fallible narrator：容易出错的叙述者　305；*185*。

falling action：下降行动　296。

false wit：假机智　420。

family resemblances：家族类似　150。

Fancy and Imagination：感受力与想象力

区分感受力与想象力是塞缪尔·泰勒·柯勒律治的诗歌理论及其思维过程一般理论中的核心部分。在早期的论述中，人们在很大程度上把"感受力"和"想象力"当做同义词，用以指代大脑的一种官能，这种官能不同于"推理""判断""记忆"，它是通过感官接收到"形象"，整理成新的组合。柯勒律治在《文学传记》（1817）第13章中把这种对感官形象整理加工的功能称为**感受力**的初级官能："感受力……除了固定与明确的形象概念之外没有其他连带关系。感受力实际上不过是一种脱离时空关系的记忆方式。"在柯勒律治看来，感受力是一种机械认识过程，它原封不动地接受感官传导的现成"固定"与"明确"的初级形象，然后再把这些形象按原先被感知的顺序重新组合成不同时空序列。

perceived. The imagination, however, which produces a much higher kind of poetry,

> dissolves, diffuses, dissipates, in order to re-create; or where this process is rendered impossible, yet still at all events it struggles to idealize and unify. It is essentially *vital*, even as all objects (*as* objects) are essentially fixed and dead.

Coleridge's **imagination**, that is, is able to "create" rather than merely reassemble, by dissolving the fixities and definites—the mental pictures, or images, received from the senses—and unifying them into a new whole. And while the fancy is merely mechanical, the imagination is "vital"; that is, it is an organic faculty which operates not like a sorting machine, but like a living and growing plant. As Coleridge says elsewhere, the imagination "generates and produces a form of its own," while its rules are "the very powers of growth and production." And in the fourteenth chapter of the *Biographia*, Coleridge adds his famous statement that the "synthetic" power which is the "imagination . . . reveals itself in the balance or reconciliation of opposite or discordant qualities: of sameness, with difference; of the general, with the concrete; the idea, with the image. . . ." The faculty of imagination, in other words, assimilates and synthesizes the most disparate elements into an organic whole—that is, a newly generated unity, constituted by an interdependence of parts whose identity cannot survive their removal from the whole. (See *organic form*.)

Most critics after Coleridge who distinguished fancy from imagination tended to make fancy simply the faculty that produces a lesser, lighter, or humorous kind of poetry, and to make imagination the faculty that produces a higher, more serious, and more passionate poetry. And the concept of "imagination" itself is as various as the modes of psychology that critics have adopted (associationist, Gestalt, *Freudian, Jungian*), while its processes vary according to the way in which a critic conceives of the nature of a poem (as essentially realistic or essentially visionary, as a verbal construction or as "myth," as "pure poetry" or as a work designed to produce effects on an audience).

See I. A. Richards, *Coleridge on Imagination* (1934); M. H. Abrams, *The Mirror and the Lamp* (1953), chapter 7; Richard H. Fogle, *The Idea of Coleridge's Criticism* (1962).

fantastic literature: 305.

fantasy: 356.

farce: 55; *46.*

feminine ending: 220.

feminine rhyme: 349.

然而，更高级别的诗歌的产娘——想象力

> 会分解、融合、消解（某些形象），以求创新；或是这一过程无法完成，它无论如何也要更加努力地把所有事件加以理想化和一体化。哪怕一切事物（作为事物）在本质上都是定形与呆板的，它在本质上却是*充满活力的*。

柯勒律治所谓的**想象力**是指能够"创造"，而不是单纯地对形象加以重新组合。这种创造是把感官接收到的固定而明确的脑海中的图像或形象加以分解，然后组合成为一个新的统一体。感受力是机械呆板的，想象力却是"充满活力的"；它是人身的一种有机官能，如同一株生机勃勃的植物，而不像一台被驱动的机器。正如柯勒律治在其他论述中谈及的，想象力"蕴育产生出自身的形态"，它的法则正是其"生长与创造的动力"。在《文学传记》第 14 章中，柯勒律治添加了这样一句名言："想象力"这一"综合"能力"在对相同与差异、一般与具体、概念与形象……这些对立或排斥的特性加以平衡调和的过程中，展示了自身的作用"。换言之，想象力的官能把截然不同的各因素同化综合为一个有机整体——即一个重新生成的统一体，这个统一体由各个相互依存的部分构成，其中任一部分一旦脱离这一整体就难以存在。（参见：*有机形式*。）

继柯勒律治之后，大多数文学批评家在区分感受力与想象力时，都趋向于把感受力视为只能创造较低等、肤浅、滑稽的诗歌的一种官能，而把想象力奉为创作更为高雅、严肃、更富有激情的诗歌的一种官能。"想象力"本身的概念因批评家所采用的不同心理模式（如联想主义、格式塔心理学、*弗洛伊德心理学*、*荣格心理分析法*）而不尽相同，想象过程则依据批评家对一首诗的本质的感知方式的不同而不同（如：在本质上是属于现实主义的还是虚幻的，是言语创作的还是"神话"的，是"纯诗歌"的还是用以感染读者的）。

参阅：I. A. 理查兹所著的《柯勒律治论想象》(1934)；M. H. 艾布拉姆斯所著的《镜与灯》(1953) 第 7 章；理查德·H. 福格尔所著的《柯勒律治的批评理念》(1962)。

fantastic literature：怪诞文学　305。

fantasy：幻想小说　356。

farce：闹剧　55；*46*。

feminine ending：弱音尾　220。

feminine rhyme：阴韵　349。

feminist criticism: As a distinctive and concerted approach to literature, feminist criticism was not inaugurated until late in the 1960s. Behind it, however, lie two centuries of struggle for the recognition of women's cultural roles and achievements, and for women's social and political rights, marked by such books as Mary Wollstonecraft's A *Vindication of the Rights of Woman* (1792), John Stuart Mill's *The Subjection of Women* (1869), and the American Margaret Fuller's *Woman in the Nineteenth Century* (1845). Much of feminist literary criticism continues in our time to be interrelated with the movement by political **feminists** for social, legal, and cultural freedom and equality.

An important precursor in feminist criticism was Virginia Woolf, who, in addition to her fiction, wrote *A Room of One's Own* (1929) and numerous other essays on women authors and on the cultural, economic, and educational disabilities within what she called a "patriarchal" society, dominated by men, that have hindered or prevented women from realizing their productive and creative possibilities. (See the collection of her essays, *Women and Writing*, ed. M. Barrett, 1979.) A much more radical critical mode, sometimes called "second-wave feminism," was launched in France by Simone de Beauvoir's *The Second Sex* (1949), a wide-ranging critique of the cultural identification of women as merely the negative object, or "Other," to man as the dominating "Subject" who is assumed to represent humanity in general; the book dealt also with "the great collective myths" of women in the works of many male writers.

In America, modern feminist criticism was inaugurated by Mary Ellmann's deft and witty discussion, in *Thinking about Women* (1968), about the derogatory stereotypes of women in literature written by men, and also about alternative and subversive representations that occur in some writings by women. Even more influential was Kate Millett's hard-hitting *Sexual Politics*, published the following year. By "politics" Millett signifies the mechanisms that express and enforce the relationships of power in society; she analyzes many Western social arrangements and institutions as covert ways of manipulating power so as to establish and perpetuate the dominance of men and the subordination of women. In her book she attacks the male bias in Freud's *psychoanalytic* theory and also analyzes selected passages by D. H. Lawrence, Henry Miller, Norman Mailer, and Jean Genet as revealing the ways in which the authors, in their fictional fantasies, aggrandize their aggressive phallic selves and degrade women as submissive sexual objects.

In the years after 1969 there was an explosion of feminist writings without parallel in previous critical innovations, in a movement that in its earlier stages, as Elaine Showalter remarked, displayed the urgency and excitement of a religious awakening. Current feminist criticism in America, England, France, and other countries is not a unitary theory or procedure. It manifests, among those who practice it, a great variety of critical vantage points and procedures, including adaptations of *psychoanalytic*, *Marxist*, and diverse *poststructuralist* theories, and its vitality is signalized by the vigor (sometimes even rancor) of the debates within the ranks of professed feminists themselves. The various feminisms, however, share certain assumptions and concepts that underlie the

Feminist Criticism：女性主义批评

女性主义批评作为一种特殊而又共同的文学批评模式，是直到 1960 年代后期才发展起来的。然而，在此之前，以玛丽·沃尔斯通克拉夫特的《为女权一辩》(1792)、约翰·斯图尔特·穆勒的《妇女的屈从地位》(1869)、美国作家玛格丽特·富勒的《19 世纪的妇女》(1845) 等著作为标志，女性为争取在文化地位和成就方面的认同，及为争取政治和社会权利而进行的斗争已经持续了两个世纪。如今，许多女性主义文学批评都已与政治上的**女性主义者**为争取社会、法律、文化的自由与平等而进行的女权运动相互结合起来。

女性主义批评的一位重要先驱是弗吉尼亚·吴尔夫，除了小说创作，她在《一间自己的房间》(1929) 和其他大量随笔中论述了在她称之为"父权制"的社会中（男性占据主导地位），女性作家和女性在文化、经济、教育方面所遭受的不公平待遇，从而妨碍或阻止了女性展现其自身才华和创造性的可能（参见她的随笔集《女性与创作》，1979 年 M. 巴雷特主编）。西蒙娜·德·波伏娃的《第二性》(1949) 在法国为女性主义批评开创了更为激进的批评模式，这一模式有时被称为"第二波女性主义"，对相比男性这一被认为是代表了整个人类、占主宰地位的大写的"人"而言女性仅被视为消极的物体或"他者"这种文化认同，进行了范围广泛的批判；该书还论及许多男性作家作品中虚构的女人的"伟大的集体神话"。

美国的现代女性主义批评由玛丽·埃尔曼发起，她在《想想妇女们》(1968) 中敏锐而机智地分析探讨了男性作家作品中把女性描绘成卑劣的、一成不变的形象和女性作家一些作品中标新立异、具有颠覆性的观点。次年，凯特·米利特出版了更为激进的《性政治》，对女性主义批评产生了更为深远的影响。米利特用"政治"指代体现和实施社会权力关系的机制；她通过分析认为，西方的社会组织和社会制度以隐性的手段掌控权力，从而使男性永远处在主宰地位，而使女性永远屈居于从属地位。她在书中抨击了弗洛伊德*精神分析*理论中的男性偏见，并通过分析 D. H. 劳伦斯、亨利·米勒、诺曼·梅勒、让·热内等人作品的部分章节，揭示了在他们的虚幻想象中，是如何夸大阳物崇拜的自我狂热和把女性贬低为顺从的性欲对象的。

1969 年之后，女性主义批评著作大量涌现，这是以前的批评理论创新所无可比拟的，正如伊莱恩·肖瓦尔特所言，这些著作及其所代表的运动，体现了一种宗教式顿悟的迫切和兴奋。当前美国、英国、法国和其他国家女性主义批评的理论或方法并非一致。这表明，在女性主义批评的实践者中，存在着各种不同的批评观点和方法，其中包括对*精神分析*、*马克思主义*和各种不同的*后结构主义*理论的改造，女性主义批评的生命力体现在自称是女性主义者的内部不同流派间公开辩论的活力（有时甚至是白热化）中。不过，不同的女性主义批评也拥有一些共

diverse ways that individual critics explore the factor of sexual difference and privilege in the production, the form and content, the reception, and the critical analysis and evaluation of works of literature:

1. The basic view is that Western civilization is pervasively **patriarchal** (ruled by the father)—that is, it is male-centered and -controlled, and is organized and conducted in such a way as to subordinate women to men in all cultural domains: familial, religious, political, economic, social, legal, and artistic. From the Hebrew Bible and Greek philosophic writings to the present, the female tends to be defined by negative reference to the male as the human norm, hence as an Other, or non-man, by her lack of the identifying male organ, of male capabilities, and of the male character traits that are presumed, in the patriarchal view, to have achieved the most important scientific and technical inventions and the major works of civilization and culture. Women themselves are taught, in the process of being socialized, to internalize the reigning patriarchal *ideology* (that is, the conscious and unconscious presuppositions about male superiority), and so are conditioned to derogate their own sex and to cooperate in their own subordination.

2. It is widely held that while one's sex as a man or woman is determined by anatomy, the prevailing concepts of **gender**—of the traits that are conceived to constitute what is masculine and what is feminine in temperament and behavior—are largely, if not entirely, *social constructs* that were generated by the pervasive patriarchal biases of our civilization. As Simone de Beauvoir put it, "One is not born, but rather becomes, a woman. . . . It is civilization as a whole that produces this creature . . . which is described as feminine." By this cultural process, the masculine in our culture has come to be widely identified as active, dominating, adventurous, rational, creative; the feminine, by systematic opposition to such traits, has come to be identified as passive, acquiescent, timid, emotional, and conventional. (See *gender criticism*.)

3. The further claim is that this patriarchal (or "masculinist," or "androcentric") ideology pervades those writings which have been traditionally considered great literature, and which until recently have been written mainly by men for men. Typically, the most highly regarded literary works focus on male protagonists—Oedipus, Ulysses, Hamlet, Tom Jones, Faust, the Three Musketeers, Captain Ahab, Huck Finn, Leopold Bloom—who embody masculine traits and ways of feeling and pursue masculine interests in masculine fields of action. To these males, the female characters, when they play a role, are marginal and subordinate, and are represented either as complementary and subservient to, or in opposition to, masculine desires and enterprises. Such works, lacking autonomous female role models, and implicitly addressed to male readers, either leave the woman reader an alien outsider or else solicit her to "identify against herself" by taking up the position of the male subject and so assuming male values and ways of perceiving, feeling, and acting.

同的批评假说和概念，这些假说和概念是作为个体的批评家以不同方式探讨文学作品创作中性别的差异和优势、文学作品的形式与内容、读者的接受以及批评分析和文学作品评价的基础：

1. 其基本观点是，**父权制**（受父权统治）是西方文明的普遍特征，即社会是以男性为中心，受男性控制、组织、操纵的，从而使女性在家庭、宗教、政治、经济、社会、法律、艺术等各个文化领域都从属于男性。自希伯来圣经和希腊哲学著作出现至今，相对于男性这一人类标准，女性总是被界定成负面的性别；由于缺乏男性的标志性器官、男性的力量或所谓的男性性格特征这些被父权制社会当做取得重大科学成就和技术发明以及从事主要的文明和文化工作的特征，女性被视为是他者或非男性的类别。女性本身在社会化过程中被灌输占支配地位的父权制意识形态，并被女性接受、内化为自我意识的一部分（即有意识或无意识地认可男性的优越性地位），从而接受女性屈尊于男性并甘愿顺从于男性的社会现实。

2. 人们普遍认为，当一个人的性别决定于解剖学时，那么**性别**这一广为人知的概念，即被理解为构成何为男性和何为女性的身份和行为的性格特征，在很大程度上，如果不是完全的话，就是由我们的文明中盛行的父权制偏见造成的一种社会建构。正如西蒙娜·德·波伏娃所言，"女性与其说是天生的，不如说是转变而成的……正是整体的文明造就了这一产物……被人们描述为女性。"在这一文明过程中，男性在我们的文化中被普遍认为是积极、专横、进取、理性、开拓的代名词；女性则与这些特性完全相反，被认为是消极、顺从、怯懦、感情用事和传统的代名词。（参见：*性别批评*。）

3. 更进一步的观点认为，这种父权制（或"男权主义""男性中心主义"）的意识形态遍布在那些传统上被认为是伟大的文学著作中，而且时至今日以男性为主流的作家仍在为男性读者创作着这样的读物。具有典型意义的是，大多数文学名著集中刻画的都是男性主角：俄狄浦斯、尤利西斯、哈姆雷特、汤姆·琼斯、浮士德、三个火枪手、亚哈船长、哈克·芬、利奥波德·布卢姆，所有这些角色都体现了男性的性格特征和在男性行为领域感受、追求男性志趣的方式。对上述这些男性角色而言，女性角色的作用处于边缘和从属地位，表现为要么是配角，要么与男性的欲望和进取性相悖。这些缺乏自主性的女性角色的作品，含蓄地面向男性读者，要么是使女性读者觉得自己是异类的局外人，要么诱使她放弃自我的性别认同，站在男性主体的立场上接受男性的价值观及其观察、感受、行为的方式。

It is often held, in addition, that the traditional categories and criteria for analyzing and appraising literary works, although represented in standard critical theory as objective, disinterested, and universal, are in fact infused with masculine assumptions, interests, and ways of reasoning, so that the standard selection and rankings, the prevailing *canon*, and the critical treatments of literary works have in fact been tacitly but thoroughly gender-biased.

A major interest of feminist critics in English-speaking countries has been to reconstitute the ways we deal with literature in order to do justice to female points of view, concerns, and values. One emphasis has been to alter the way a woman reads the literature of the past so as to make her not an acquiescent, but (in the title of Judith Fetterley's book published in 1978) *The Resisting Reader*; that is, one who resists the author's intentions and design in order, by a "revisionary rereading," to bring to light and to counter the covert sexual biases written into a literary work. Another prominent procedure has been to identify recurrent and distorting "images of women," especially in novels and poems written by men. These images are often represented as tending to fall into two antithetic patterns. On the one side we find idealized projections of men's desires (the Madonna, the Muses of the arts, Dante's Beatrice, the pure and innocent virgin, the "Angel in the House" that was represented in the writings of the Victorian poet Coventry Patmore). On the other side are demonic projections of men's sexual resentments and terrors (Eve and Pandora as the sources of all evil, destructive sensual temptresses such as Delilah and Circe, the malign witch, the castrating mother). While many feminist critics have decried the literature written by men for its depiction of women as marginal, docile, and subservient to men's interests and emotional needs and fears, some of them have also identified male writers who, in their view, have managed to rise above the sexual prejudices of their time sufficiently to understand and represent the cultural pressures that have shaped the characters of women and forced upon them their negative or subsidiary social roles. The latter class is said to include, in selected works, such authors as Chaucer, Shakespeare, Samuel Richardson, Henrik Ibsen, and George Bernard Shaw.

A number of feminists have concentrated, not on the woman as reader, but on what Elaine Showalter named **gynocriticism**—that is, a criticism which concerns itself with developing a specifically female framework for dealing with works written by women, in all aspects of their production, motivation, analysis, and interpretation, and in all literary forms, including journals and letters. Notable books in this mode include Patricia Meyer Spacks' *The Female Imagination* (1975), on English and American novels of the past three centuries; Ellen Moers' *Literary Women* (1976), on major women novelists and poets in England, America, and France; Elaine Showalter's *A Literature of Their Own: British Women Novelists from Brontë to Lessing* (1977); and Sandra Gilbert and Susan Gubar's *The Madwoman in the Attic* (1979; rev. 2000). This last book stresses especially the psychodynamics of

另外，人们通常认为，用于分析和评价文学作品的传统范畴和标准是客观公允的，而事实上却浸渍着男性的傲慢、志趣、思维方式，以至于对文学作品的标准选择、等级划分、流行的经典和批评，实际上完全陷入了一种以性别偏见为基础而又被默认的境地。

英语国家的女性主义批评家所关注的主要是重新构建看待文学的方式方法，以便公允地对待女性的观点、女性关注的问题、女性的价值观。其中一个重要任务就是改变女性阅读过去文学作品的方式，使她们不要顺从而是成为抗拒性读者（朱迪思·菲特利出版于1978年的书名）；即女性读者应该通过"修正的重读"抗拒作者的写作意图和图谋，进而揭露和驳斥文学作品中隐性的性别偏见。另外一个重要途径是识别文学作品中，尤其是由男性作家创作的小说和诗歌中反复出现的扭曲的"女性形象"。这些形象往往趋向于两种对立模式。一方面，我们发现她们是男性欲望的理想化投射对象（如圣母玛丽亚、缪斯女神、但丁笔下的贝雅特丽齐、纯洁无瑕的处女、维多利亚女王时代的诗人考文垂·帕特莫尔笔下的"家中的天使"）。另一方面，她们则是男性性憎恨和性恐怖的恶魔化投射对象（如邪恶之源的夏娃和潘多拉、色情勾引男性的妖妇迪莱拉和喀耳刻、恶毒的女巫、阉割儿子的母亲）。虽然许多女性主义批评家都谴责男性作家把女性刻画成为边缘化的、温顺的、对男性志趣、情感需求与恐惧俯首帖耳的文学形象，但也有女性主义批评家认为，男性作家以他们自己的视野在极力超越自己所处时代的性别偏见，认识并呈现那些造就女性性格特征和强加于女性身上的反面或附属的社会角色的文化压力。属于后者且其作品出现在各种文选中的作家有乔叟、莎士比亚、塞缪尔·理查逊、亨里克·易卜生、乔治·萧伯纳。

许多女性主义者没有把关注的目光投向作为读者的女性，而是投向伊莱恩·肖瓦尔特所谓的**女性批评**：即建构一种特别针对女性作家作品的批评框架，从她们的创作、动机、分析和阐释的各个方面，以及从包括期刊、书信在内的所有文学形式中研究女性作品。在该批评模式中，著名的著述有帕特里夏·迈耶·斯帕克斯关于过去三百年间英美小说的《女性想象》（1975）；艾伦·莫尔斯关于英美和法国主要女性小说家和诗人的《文学妇女》（1976）；伊莱恩·肖瓦尔特所著的《她们自己的文学：从勃朗特到莱辛的英国女性小说家》（1977）；桑德拉·吉尔伯特与苏珊·格芭合著的《阁楼上的疯女人》（1979，2000年再版），该书着重强调了19世

women writers in the nineteenth century. Its authors propose that the "anxiety of authorship," resulting from the stereotype that literary creativity is an exclusively male prerogative, effected in women writers a psychological duplicity that projected a monstrous counterfigure to the idealized heroine, typified by Bertha Rochester, the madwoman in Charlotte Brontë's *Jane Eyre*; such a figure is "usually in some sense the *author's* double, an image of her own anxiety and rage." (Refer to *influence and the anxiety of influence*.)

One concern of gynocritics is to identify distinctively feminine subject matters in literature written by women—the world of domesticity, for example, or the special experiences of gestation, giving birth, and nurturing, or mother-daughter and woman-woman relations—in which personal and affectional issues, and not external activism, are the primary interest. Another concern is to uncover in literary history a female tradition, incorporated in subcommunities of women writers who were aware of, emulated, and found support in earlier women writers, and who in turn provide models and emotional support to their own readers and successors. A third undertaking is to show that there is a distinctive feminine mode of experience, or "subjectivity," in thinking, feeling, valuing, and perceiving oneself and the outer world. Related to this is the attempt (thus far, without much agreement about details) to specify the traits of a "woman's language," or distinctively feminine *style* of speech and writing, in sentence structure, types of relations between the elements of a discourse, and characteristic figures of speech and imagery. Some feminists have turned their critical attention to the great number of women's domestic and "sentimental" novels, which are noted perfunctorily and in derogatory fashion in standard literary histories, yet which dominated the market for fiction in the nineteenth century and produced most of the best sellers of the time; instances of this last critical enterprise are Elaine Showalter's *A Literature of Their Own* (1977) on British writers, and on American writers, Nina Baym's *Woman's Fiction: A Guide to Novels by and about Women in America, 1820–1870* (1978); and Elaine Showalter, *A Jury of Her Peers: American Women Writers from Anne Bradstreet to Annie Proulx* (2009). Sandra Gilbert and Susan Gubar have described the later history of women's writings in *No Man's Land: The Place of the Woman Writer in the Twentieth Century* (2 vols., 1988–89).

The often-asserted goal of feminist critics has been to enlarge and reorder, or in radical instances entirely to displace, the literary canon—that is, the set of works which, by a cumulative consensus, have come to be considered "major" and to serve as the chief subjects of literary history, criticism, scholarship, and teaching (see *canon of literature*). Feminist studies have succeeded in raising the status of many female authors hitherto more or less scanted by scholars and critics (including Anne Finch, George Sand, Elizabeth Barrett Browning, Elizabeth Gaskell, Christina Rossetti, Harriet Beecher Stowe, and Sidonie-Gabrielle Colette) and to bring into purview other authors who have been largely or entirely overlooked as subjects for serious consideration (among them Margaret Cavendish, Aphra Behn, Lady Mary Wortley Montagu, Joanna Baillie, Kate Chopin, Charlotte Perkins Gilman, and a

纪女性作家的精神动力现象。其作者认为，由那种认为文学创作为男性所特有的陈腐观念引发的"作者身份的焦虑"，给女性作家的心理蒙上一种双重性，从而塑造出了与理想化女主人公相反的恶魔般的女性形象，夏洛蒂·勃朗特《简爱》中的疯女人伯莎·罗彻斯特就是这类女性形象的典型代表，而这种女性形象"在一定意义上往往是作者自己的替身，是她自己焦虑和愤怒的形象"。（参见：*影响和影响的焦虑*。）

女性批评的一个关切点是识别女性作家文学作品中突出的女性题材：如家庭生活，或怀孕的特殊经历、分娩和养育，或母女关系，以及女性彼此间的关系，在这些题材中，关注的首要对象是私人和情感问题，而非表面的激进主义。女性批评关注的另一个焦点是，揭示文学史中体现在女性作家这一亚群体身上的女性传统，她们意识到了这一传统，并模仿早期女性作家且从中得到情感支持，而后又为她们自己的读者和后来的女性作家树立起这种传统模式并提供情感上的支持。女性批评的第三个任务是，展示在思维、情感、价值观、对自我和对外部世界的认识中存在的特有的女性体验模式或"主观性"。与此相关的是尝试（迄今为止，在一些细节上尚未达成共识）具体描述"女性语言"的特征或在句式结构和语篇各组成部分间的关系类型，以及在塑造人物形象和意象的过程中体现出的女性独特的话语和写作*风格*。有些女性主义者已经把批判的眼光投向女性大量的家庭和"感伤"小说上，这些小说貌似闻名一时，在正统的文学史中却声名低下，可是，正是这些著作占据了19世纪的小说市场，且大都成为当时的畅销书；关于女性批评的第三个批评任务的著述，有伊莱恩·肖瓦尔特关于英国作家的《她们自己的文学》（1977）；尼娜·贝姆关于美国作家的《女性小说：1820—1870年美国女作家所创作的小说及有关女性的小说指南》（1978）；伊莱恩·肖瓦尔特的《同命人审案：从安妮·布雷兹特里特到安妮·普鲁的美国女作家》（2009）。桑德拉·吉尔伯特与苏珊·格芭关于女性创作的两卷本《没有男性的领地：20世纪女作家的地位》（1988—1989）。

女性主义批评家常常声称其目标是扩大和重新界定、甚或极端地完全置换文学经典——即人们逐渐公认为"重要"的并成为文学史、文学批评、学术和教学的主要课程科目的作品集（参见：*文学经典*）。女性主义研究已经成功地提升了那些迄今为止仍然或多或少被学者和批评家忽视的许多女性作家的地位（其中包括安妮·芬奇、乔治·桑、伊丽莎白·巴雷特·勃朗宁、伊丽莎白·盖斯凯尔、克里斯蒂娜·罗塞蒂、哈丽特·比彻·斯托、赛多奈-加布里埃尔·科莱特），并把其他那些在很大程度上或完全被忽略的作家纳入认真对待的视野内（其中有玛格丽特·卡文迪什、阿弗拉·贝恩、玛丽·沃特利·蒙塔古夫人、乔安娜·贝利、凯特·肖邦、夏

number of African-American writers such as Zora Neale Hurston). Some feminists have devoted their critical attention especially to the literature written by lesbian writers, or that deals with lesbian relationships in a heterosexual culture. (See *queer theory*.)

American and English critics have for the most part engaged in empirical and thematic studies of writings by and about women. The most prominent feminist critics in France, however, have occupied themselves with the "theory" of the role of gender in writing, conceptualized within various *poststructural* frames of reference, and above all Jacques Lacan's reworkings of Freudian *psychoanalysis* in terms of Saussure's linguistic theory. English-speaking feminists, for example, have drawn attention to demonstrable evidences that a male bias is encoded in our linguistic conventions; instances include the use of "man" or "mankind" for human beings in general, of "chairman" and "spokesman" for people of either sex, and of the pronouns "he" and "his" to refer back to ostensibly gender-neutral nouns such as "God," "human being," "child," "inventor," "author," and "poet." (See Sally McConnell-Ginet, Ruth Borker, and Nelly Furman, eds., *Women and Language in Literature and Society*, 1980; Deborah Cameron, *Feminism and Linguistic Theory* (2d ed., 1992); and Robin Tolmach Lakoff et al., *Language and Woman's Place: Text and Commentaries*, 2004; see also the entry *linguistics in literary criticism*.) The radical claim of some French theorists, on the other hand, is that all Western languages, in all their features, are utterly and irredeemably male-engendered, male-constituted, and male-dominated. Discourse, it is asserted, in a term proposed by Lacan, is **phallogocentric**; that is, it is centered and organized throughout by implicit recourse to the phallus (used in a symbolic sense) both as its supposed "logos," or ground, and as its prime signifier and power source. Phallogocentrism, it is claimed, manifests itself in Western discourse not only in its vocabulary and syntax, but also in its rigorous rules of logic, its proclivity for fixed classifications and oppositions, and its criteria for what is traditionally considered to be valid evidence and objective knowledge. A basic problem for such theorists is to establish the very possibility of a woman's language that will not, when a woman writes, automatically be appropriated into this phallogocentric language, since such appropriation is said to force her into complicity with linguistic features that impose on females a condition of marginality and subservience, or even of linguistic nonentity.

To evade this dilemma, Hélène Cixous posits the existence of an incipient "feminine writing" (écriture féminine) which has its source in the mother, in the stage of the mother-child relation before the child acquires the male-centered verbal language. Thereafter, in her view, this prelinguistic and unconscious potentiality manifests itself in those written texts which, abolishing all repressions, undermine and subvert the fixed signification, the logic, and the "closure" of our phallocentric language, and open out into a joyous freeplay of meanings. Alternatively, Luce Irigaray posits a "woman's writing" which evades the male monopoly and the risk of appropriation into the existing system by establishing as its generative principle, in place of the monolithic phallus, the diversity, fluidity, and multiple possibilities inherent in the

洛特·帕金斯·吉尔曼,及许多非裔美国作家,如佐拉·尼尔·赫斯顿)。有些女性主义者尤其把批评的眼光聚焦在女性同性恋作家,或同性恋文化中涉及女性同性恋关系的文学作品上。(参见:*同性恋理论*。)

美英批评家主要致力于研究女性作家的作品和关于女性的作品中的经验主义和主题。然而法国最负盛名的女性主义批评家则致力于在不同的*后结构主义*理论参照框架中,对作品中的性别作用被概念化了的"理论"进行研究,其中最重要的是雅克·拉康用索绪尔的语言学理论对弗洛伊德*精神分析*的重新诠释。例如,在我们的语言习俗中,一些明确体现男性偏见的现象引起了英语国家女性主义批评家的关注。这样的例子有:用"男人"或"男性"指称全人类,用"男主席"和"男发言人"既指称男性又指称女性,用代词"他"和"他的"公然指代中性名词"上帝""人类""儿童""发明家""作家""诗人"[参见:萨莉·麦康奈尔-吉内特、露丝·伯克尔、内莉·费曼三人合编的《文学与社会中的女性和语言》(1980);德博拉·卡梅伦所著的《女性主义与语言学理论》(1992年第2版);罗宾·托马克·雷柯夫等人合著的《语言和女性的位置:文本与评注》(2004);也可参见:*语言学在文学批评里的应用*。]另一方面,一些法国理论家,不论他们之间有着什么样的分歧,都极端地认为,所有西方语言的一切特征都纯粹是由男性生成、建构和主宰的。用雅克·拉康提出的术语来说,就是话语被认为是**男权主义的**;即话语始终都是含蓄地借助男性生殖器(指象征意义)为中心和组织起来的,作为其"标识语"或基础,并视其为首要能指和权力源泉。西方话语中的男权主义色彩,不仅体现在其词汇和句法中,也体现在严格的逻辑规则、固定的分类和对立面的倾向,以及体现在用以评判什么是传统意义上的有效证据和客观知识的标准中。法国理论家面临的一个基本问题就是,尽一切可能创建一种女性语言,从而使女性作家在写作过程中,不会不由自主地适应于这种男权主义的语言,因为这种适应被认为是有强迫自己与男权主义的语言特征产生共谋之嫌,这种语言特征使得女性处于一种边缘和屈从甚至是语言虚无的情境中。

为了规避这种两难局面,埃莱娜·西苏提出,存在一个"女性书写"的萌芽期,该萌芽期源起于母亲,即在接受男性中心的话语之前的母亲-孩子关系阶段。在西苏看来,这种前语言的、无意识的潜能体现在写作文本中,这样的文本废止一切约束、破坏和颠覆固有的意义、逻辑,"终止"男权主义语言,开创了一个愉悦的意义自由游戏的天地。同时,露丝·伊瑞格瑞提出了"妇女书写"的概念,即通过确立女性性器官和性敏感区的结构与性欲功能以及女性性体验的独特性与生俱来的语言的多样性、流动性和多种可能性,作为其语言生成原则,以取代稳固单一的男性阳物

structure and erotic functioning of the female sexual organs and erogenous zones, and in the distinctive nature of female sexual experiences. Julia Kristeva posits a "chora," or prelinguistic, pre-Oedipal, and unsystematized signifying process, centered on the mother, that she labels "semiotic." This process is repressed as we acquire the father-controlled, syntactically ordered, and logical language that she calls "symbolic." The semiotic process, however, can break out in a revolutionary way—her prime example is avant-garde poetry, whether written by women or by men—as a "heterogeneous destructive causality" that disrupts and disperses the authoritarian "subject" and strikes free of the oppressive order and rationality of our standard discourse which, as the product of the "law of the Father," consigns women to a negative and marginal status.

Since the 1980s a number of feminist critics have used *poststructuralist* positions and techniques to challenge the category of "woman" and other founding concepts of feminism itself. They point out the existence of differences and adversarial strands within the supposedly monolithic history of patriarchal discourse, and emphasize the inherent linguistic instability in the basic conceptions of "woman" or "the feminine," as well as the diversities within these supposedly universal and uniform female identities that result from differences in race, class, nationality, and historical situation. See Barbara Johnson, *A World of Difference* (1987); Rita Felski, *Beyond Feminist Aesthetics: Feminist Literature and Social Change* (1989); and the essays in *Feminism/Postmodernism*, ed. Linda J. Nicholson (1990). Judith Butler, in two influential books, has opposed the notion that the feminist movement requires the concept of a feminine identity; that is, that there exist essential factors that define a woman as a woman. Instead, she elaborates the view that the fundamental features which define gender are social and cultural productions that produce the illusory effect of being natural. Butler proposes also that we consider gender as a "performative"—that to be masculine or feminine or homosexual is not something that one is, but a socially pre-established pattern of behavior that one repeatedly enacts. (For the concept of "the performative," refer to *speech-act theory*.) See Judith Butler, *Gender Trouble: Feminism and the Subversion of Identity* (1990) and *Bodies that Matter* (1993).

Feminist theoretical and critical writings, although recent in origin, expand yearly in volume and range. There exist a number of specialized feminist journals and publishing houses; almost all colleges and universities now have programs in **women's studies**—the investigation of the status and roles of women in history and in diverse institutions and activities—and courses in women's literature and feminist criticism; and ever-increasing place is given to writings by and about women in anthologies, periodicals, and conferences. Of the many critical and theoretical innovations of the past several decades, the concern with the effects of sexual differences in the writing, interpretation, analysis, and assessment of literature seems destined to have the most prominent and enduring effects on literary history, criticism, and academic instruction, when conducted by men as well as by women. See *ecofeminism* and *gender studies*.

象征，避免男性的语言垄断和陷入现有的语言体系中的危险。朱莉娅·克莉丝蒂娃提出了以母亲为中心的被她标示为"符号语言"的"容纳处"，或前语言、前恋母情结和未经系统化的意指过程。当我们在接受由父权控制的被她称之为"象征语言"的句法顺序和逻辑语言时，这一过程受到了压制。但是，符号语言可以通过革命性的手段解脱出来——她的主要例证就是先锋派诗歌，不论是由女性还是男性所创作——作为一种"异质破坏诱因"，颠覆和瓦解独裁"主体"，解放女性在我们规范的话语中受压制的秩序和理性，这是"父权法则"置女性于边缘和负面境地的产物。

1980年代以来，许多女性主义批评家运用*后结构主义*的立场和方法向女性主义自身诸如"妇女"和其他一些基本概念发起挑战。他们指出，在一般认为是稳固单一的父权话语的历史中，存在着差异和对抗性因素，并且强调了"妇女"或"女性"基本观念中固有的语言不稳定性，以及由于不同种族、阶级、民族、历史环境等原因，致使在被认为是普遍同一的女性身份中，也存在着多样性。参阅：芭芭拉·约翰逊所著的《*差异的世界*》(1987)；里塔·费尔斯基所著的《*超越女性主义美学：女性主义文学与社会变革*》(1989)；琳达·J.尼克尔森主编的《*女性主义/后现代主义*》(1990)一书中所收录的文章。朱迪思·巴特勒在其所著的两部颇有影响的著作中，反对认为女性运动需要女性身份认同的观念——即存在着界定妇女成其为妇女的一些基本因素。相反，她论述了这样一种观点，即界定性别的根本要素是社会的和文化的产品，这些产品产生了被认为是理所当然的错觉效果。巴特勒还提出，我们应该把性别视为是"表述行为"的，即其成为男性或女性或同性恋并不是因为自身是男性或女性或同性恋，而是人们往复行事的社会提前确立的行为模式所致（关于"表述行为"的概念参见：*言语行为理论*）。参阅：朱迪思·巴特勒所著的《*性别麻烦：女性主义与身份的颠覆*》(1990)和《*关键的是躯体*》(1993)。

尽管女性主义批评理论刚刚兴起，但其理论和批评著述每年都在大量涌现。有许多专门的女性主义者的期刊和出版社，而今，几乎所有大专院校都有女性研究项目，都开设有女性文学（研究女性在历史中和在多样的制度及行动中的地位和角色）与女性主义批评的课程，而且文集、期刊中越来越多的篇幅，以及会议的发言也越来越多地让位于女性作家的作品和关于女性的作品。过去几十年里的许多批评和理论创新，不论是出自男性还是女性之手，在文学作品的创作、阐释、分析、评价中对性别差异的影响的关注，似乎注定要对文学史、文学批评和学术教育产生最显著、最久远的影响。参见：*生态女性主义*、*性别研究*。

In addition to the books mentioned above, the following works are especially useful. Sandra Gilbert and Susan Gubar, eds., *The Norton Anthology of Literature by Women* (3d ed., 2007)—the editorial materials provide a concise history, as well as biographies and bibliographies, of female authors since the Middle Ages. See also Jane Gallop, *The Daughter's Seduction: Feminism and Psychoanalysis* (1982), and Gayatri Chakravorty Spivak, *In Other Worlds: Essays in Cultural Politics* (1987). Histories and critiques of feminist criticism: K. K. Ruthven, *Feminist Literary Studies: An Introduction* (1984); Toril Moi, *Sexual/Textual Politics: Feminist Literary Theory* (1985)—much of this book is devoted to feminist theorists in France; Mary Evans, *Introducing Contemporary Feminist Thought* (1997); Ruth Robbins, *Literary Feminisms* (2000); Shari Benstock, Suzanne Ferriss, and Susanne Woods, eds., *A Handbook of Literary Feminisms* (2002); Margaret Walters, *Feminism: A Very Short Introduction* (2005); Ellen Rooney, ed., *The Cambridge Companion to Feminist Literary Theory* (2006). Collections of essays in feminist criticism: Elaine Showalter, ed., *The New Feminist Criticism* (1985); Patrocinio P. Schweickart and Elizabeth A. Flynn, eds., *Gender and Reading: Essays on Readers, Texts, and Contexts* (1986); Robyn R. Warhol and Diane Price Herndl, eds., *Feminisms: An Anthology of Literary Theory and Criticism* (2d ed., 1997); Margo Hendricks and Patricia Parker, eds., *Women, "Race," and Writing in the Early Modern Period* (1994). For critiques of some feminist positions and views by women, see Nina Baym, "The Madwoman and Her Languages: Why I Don't Do Feminist Literary Theory," in *Feminist Issues in Literary Scholarship*, ed. Shari Benstock (1987); Elizabeth Fox-Genovese, *Feminism without Illusions: A Critique of Individualism* (1991); Camille Paglia, *Vamps & Tramps* (1994); Susan Gubar, *Critical Condition: Feminism at the Turn of the Century* (2000). Among the books by French feminist theorists available in English are Hélène Cixous and Catherine Clement, *The Newly Born Woman* (1986); Luce Irigaray, *Speculum of the Other Woman* (1985) and *This Sex Which Is Not One* (1985); Julia Kristeva, *Desire in Language: A Semiotic Approach to Literature and Art* (1980); *The Kristeva Reader*, ed. Toril Moi (1986); and Toril Moi, *What Is a Woman? And Other Essays* (2001). On feminist treatments of African-American women: Barbara Christian, *Black Feminist Criticism* (1985); Hazel V. Carby, *Reconstructing Womanhood: The Emergence of the Afro-American Woman Novelist* (1987); Henry L. Gates, Jr., *Reading Black, Reading Feminist: A Critical Anthology* (1990); Joy James and T. Denean Sharpley-Whiting, eds., *The Black Feminist Reader* (2000). Feminist treatments of lesbian and gay literature: Eve Kosofsky Sedgwick, *Between Men: English Literature and Male Homosocial Desire* (1985) and *Epistemology of the Closet* (1990). Feminist theater and film studies: Teresa de Lauretis, *Alice Doesn't: Feminism, Semiotics, Cinema* (1984); Sue-Ellen Case, *Feminism and Theatre* (1987); Constance Penley, *The Future of an Illusion: Film, Feminism, and Psychoanalysis* (1989); Peggy Phelan and Lynda Hart, eds., *Acting Out: Feminist Performances* (1993).

For references to *feminist criticism* in other entries, see pages *97, 146, 248, 287, 323, 419.*

ficelle (fĭ sĕl'): **63**.

除了前面提到过的著作，下述著作也特别有裨益。桑德拉·吉尔伯特与苏珊·格芭合编的《诺顿妇女文学选集》(2007 年第 3 版)，该编著资料提供了自中世纪以来，女性作家精确的创作历史，以及她们的传记和文献目录。也可参阅：简·盖洛普所著的《女儿的诱惑：女性主义与精神分析》(1982)，佳娅特丽·查克拉沃蒂·斯皮瓦克所著的《在他者的世界里：文化政治论文集》(1987)。关于女性主义批评的历史与评论，参阅：K. K. 鲁思文所著的《女性主义文学研究入门》(1984)；陶丽·莫伊所著的《性/文本政治：女性主义文学理论》(1985)，本书大部分内容是关于法国女性主义批评理论家的；玛丽·埃文斯所著的《当代女性主义思想介绍》(1997)；露丝·罗宾斯所著的《文学女性主义》(2000)；莎莉·本斯托克、苏珊娜·费里斯、苏珊妮·伍兹三人合编的《文学女性主义手册》(2002)；玛格丽特·沃尔特斯所著的《女性主义：简介》(2005)；埃伦·鲁尼主编的《剑桥女性主义文学理论指南》(2006)。女性主义批评论文集有：伊莱恩·肖瓦尔特主编的《新女性主义批评》(1985)；帕特罗西尼奥·P. 施韦卡特与伊丽莎白·A. 弗林合编的《性别与阅读：读者、文本和语境论集》(1986)；罗宾·R. 沃霍尔与戴安娜·普赖斯·亨德尔合编的《女性主义：文学理论和批评选集》(1997 年第 2 版)；马戈·亨德里克斯与帕特里夏·帕克合编的《早期现代时期的妇女、"种族"与写作》(1994)。公开对一些女性主义者的观点作出评论的女性主义者有：尼娜·贝姆所写的文章"疯女人和她的语言：为什么我不做女性主义文学理论"，收入莎莉·本斯托克主编的《文学研究中的女性主义主题》(1987)；伊丽莎白·福克斯-吉诺维斯所著的《不抱幻想的女性主义者：个体主义批判》(1991)；卡米尔·佩格利亚所著的《尤物与淫妇》(1994)；苏珊·格芭所著的《危机时刻：世纪之交的女性主义》(2000)。法国女性主义批评理论家著述的英译版有：埃莱娜·西苏与凯瑟琳·克莱门特合著的《新生的女性》(1986)；露丝·伊瑞格瑞所著的《他者女性的反射镜》(1985) 和《非"一"之性》(1985)；朱莉娅·克莉丝蒂娃所著的《语言的欲望：对文学和艺术的符号学分析》(1980)；陶丽·莫伊主编的《克莉丝蒂娃读本》(1986)；陶丽·莫伊所著的《何为女性？及其他论文》(2001)。女性主义者关于美国黑人妇女的论述有：芭芭拉·克里斯琴所著的《黑人女性主义批评》(1985)；哈泽尔·V. 卡比所著的《重构女性特征：美国黑人女性小说家的崛起》(1987)；小亨利·L. 盖茨所著的《解读黑人，解读女性主义：批评文集》(1990)；乔伊·詹姆斯与 T. 黛妮·沙普利-怀廷合编的《黑人女性主义读本》(2000)。女性主义者关于女同性恋文学和男同性恋文学的论述有：伊芙·科索夫斯基·塞奇威克所著的《男人之间：英国文学与男性同性社会性欲望》(1985) 和《衣柜认识论》(1990)。女性主义者关于戏剧和电影的研究有：特雷莎·德·劳拉蒂斯所著的《再见爱丽丝：女性主义、符号学与电影》(1984)；休-埃伦·凯斯所著的《女性主义与剧院》(1987)；康斯坦丝·彭利所著的《幻觉的未来：电影、女性主义与精神分析》(1989)；佩姬·费伦与琳达·哈特合编的《付诸行动：女性主义表演》(1993)。

其他条目中提及"女性批评"的地方，参见第 97、146、248、287、323、419 页。

ficelle：笔偶 63。

fiction and truth: In an inclusive sense, **fiction** is any literary *narrative*, whether in prose or verse, which is invented instead of being an account of events that actually happened. In a narrower sense, however, fiction denotes only narratives that are written in prose (the *novel* and *short story*), and sometimes is used simply as a synonym for the novel. Literary prose narratives in which the fiction is to a prominent degree based on biographical, historical, or contemporary facts are often referred to by compound names such as "fictional biography," the *historical novel*, and the *nonfiction novel*.

Both philosophers and literary critics have concerned themselves with the logical analysis of the types of sentences that constitute a fictional text, and especially with the question of their **truth**, or what is sometimes called their "truth-value"—that is, whether, or in just what way, they are subject to the criterion of truth or falsity. Some thinkers have asserted that "fictional sentences" should be regarded as referring to a special world, "created" by the author, which is analogous to the real world, but possesses its own setting, beings, and mode of coherence. (See M. H. Abrams, *The Mirror and the Lamp*, 1953, pp. 272–85, "The Poem as Heterocosm"; James Phelan, *Worlds from Words: A Theory of Language in Fiction*, 1981.) Others, most notably I. A. Richards, have held that fiction is a form of **emotive language** composed of **pseudostatements**; and that whereas a statement in "referential language" is "justified by its truth, that is, its correspondence . . . with the fact to which it points," a pseudostatement "is justified entirely by its effect in releasing or organizing our attitudes" (I. A. Richards, *Science and Poetry*, 1926). Most current theorists, however, present an elaborated logical version of what Sir Philip Sidney long ago proposed in his *Apology for Poetry* (published 1595), that a poet "nothing affirmes, therefore never lyeth. For, as I take it, to lye is to affirm that to be true which is false." Current versions of this view hold that fictive sentences are meaningful according to the rules of ordinary, nonfictional discourse, but that, in accordance with conventions implicitly shared by the author and reader of a work of fiction, they are not put forward as assertions of fact, and therefore are not subject to the criterion of truth or falsity that applies to sentences in nonfictional discourse. See Margaret MacDonald, "The Language of Fiction" (1954), reprinted in W. E. Kennick, ed., *Art and Philosophy* (rev. 1979).

In *speech-act theory*, a related view takes the form that a writer of fiction only "pretends" to make assertions, or "imitates" the making of assertions, and so suspends the "normal illocutionary commitment" of the writer of such utterances to the claim that what he asserts is true. See John R. Searle, "The Logical Status of Fictional Discourse," in *Expression and Meaning: Studies in the Theory of Speech Acts* (1979, reprinted 1986). We find in a number of other theorists the attempt to extend the concept of "fictive utterances" to include all the genres of literature—poems, narratives, and dramas, as well as novels; all these forms, it is proposed, are imitations, or fictive representations, of some type of "natural" discourse. A novel, for example, not only is made up of fictional utterances, but is itself a fictive utterance, in that it "*represents* the verbal action of a man [that is, the narrator] reporting, describing, and

Fiction and Truth：虚构小说与真实

总体来说，**虚构小说**是指无论是散文体还是诗歌体，只要是虚构的而非描述事实上发生过的事件的任何*叙事*文学作品。然而，狭义上的虚构小说仅指散文体的叙事作品（*小说和短篇小说*），有时也简单地用作小说的同义词。以传记、历史或当代事实为主要素材的文学叙事作品常用合成名词来指称，如"传记小说"、*历史小说*、*非虚构小说*。

哲学家与文学批评家都注重对构成虚构文本的各种句型做逻辑分析，尤其注重其**真实性**的问题，或有时被称为它们的"真实性价值"——也就是说，它们是否能或以何种方法接受真实性或虚构性标准的检验。一些思想家指出：应该把"虚构句子"看成是指代作家"创造"的一个特殊世界，这个特殊世界近似于现实世界，但它有自己的背景、人物及其衔接模式。[参阅：M. H. 艾布拉姆斯所著的《镜与灯》(1953) 中第 272—285 页"诗中的不同世界"；詹姆斯·费伦所著的《词中的世界：小说语言理论》(1981)。] 其他理论家，尤其是颇具声望的 I. A. 理查兹认为：虚构小说是**传情语言**的一种形式，由**模拟陈述**构成；用"所指性语言"表达的陈述是"能被证实的，即与所指事实……相吻合"；而模拟陈述则"完全依靠其宣泄和组织我们的态度时造成的效果来证实其真实性"[I. A. 理查兹《科学与诗》(1926)]。然而，大多数当代理论家则推出了很久以前菲利普·锡德尼爵士在《诗辩》(1595 年出版) 中经过精心构思而提出的极富逻辑性的表述，即：诗人"没有任何东西需要去证实，因此也就无从说谎。因为在我看来，说谎就是证实虚假的东西的真实性。"持这一观点的当代人认为，依据一般非虚构性话语的规则，虚构的语句是有意义的；但是按照作者与读者一致默认的虚构小说惯例来讲，这种语言并非是用作陈述事实而写出来的，因此不宜用判断非虚构话语的真伪标准来衡量它们。参阅：玛格丽特·麦克唐纳所写的文章"虚构小说的语言"(1954)，重印收入 W. E. 肯尼克主编的《艺术与哲学》(1979 年修订版) 中。

言语行为理论中有一种相关的观点认为，虚构小说的作者仅仅是在"佯装"作出表述或者是在"模拟表述"，这样就回避了模拟表述者应该承担的"正常的语内表现行为的义务"，而声称他的表述是真实的。参阅约翰·R. 塞尔《表达和意义：言语行为理论研究》(1979，1986 年重印) 中的"虚构性话语的逻辑情形"一章。我们还发现其他一些理论家试图把"虚构表述"的概念扩展到包括诗歌、叙述作品、戏剧、小说在内的其他一切文学类别中去；他们认为所有这些文学形式都是对"自然"话语的模仿或虚构性再现。例如，一部小说不仅由虚构性表述构成，而且它在"代表一个人 [即叙述者] 报道、描述和指称"时的言语行为本身就

referring." See Barbara Herrnstein Smith, "Poetry as Fiction," in *Margins of Discourse* (1978), and Richard Ohmann, "Speech Acts and the Definition of Literature," *Philosophy and Rhetoric* 4 (1971).

Most modern critics of prose fiction, whatever their persuasion, make an important distinction between the fictional scenes, persons, events, and dialogue that a narrator reports or describes and the narrator's own assertions about the world, about human life, or about the human situation; the central, or controlling, generalizations of the latter sort are said to be the *theme* or **thesis** of a work. These assertions by the narrator may be explicit (for example, Thomas Hardy's statement at the end of *Tess of the D'Urbervilles*, "The President of the immortals had had his sport with Tess"; or Tolstoy's philosophy of history at the end of *War and Peace*). Many such claims, however, are said to be merely "implied," "suggested," or "inferrable" from the narrator's choice and control of the fictional characters and plot of the narrative itself. It is often claimed that such generalizations by the narrator within a fictional work, whether expressed or implied, function as assertions that claim to be true about the world, and that they thereby relate the fictional narrative to the factual and moral world of actual experience. See John Hospers, "Implied Truths in Literature" (1960), reprinted in W. E. Kennick, ed., *Art and Philosophy* (rev. 1979).

A much-discussed topic, related to the question of an author's assertions and truth-claims in narrative fiction, concerns the part played by the **beliefs** of the reader. The problem raised is the extent to which a reader's own moral, religious, and social convictions, as they coincide with or diverge from those asserted or implied in a work, determine the interpretation, acceptability, and evaluation of that work by the reader. For the history and discussions of this problem in literary criticism, see William Joseph Rooney, *The Problem of "Poetry and Belief" in Contemporary Criticism* (1949); M. H. Abrams, editor and contributor, *Literature and Belief* (1957); Walter Benn Michaels, "Saving the Text: Reference and Belief," *Modern Language Notes* 93 (1978). Many discussions of the role of belief in fiction cite S. T. Coleridge's description of the reader's attitude as a "willing suspension of disbelief."

A review of theories concerning the relevance of the criterion of truth to fiction is Monroe C. Beardsley's *Aesthetics: Problems in the Philosophy of Criticism* (1958), pp. 409–19. For an analysis and critique of theories of emotive language see Max Black, "Questions about Emotive Meaning," in *Language and Philosophy* (1949), chapter 9. Gerald Graff defends the claim for propositional truth in poetry in *Poetic Statement and Critical Dogma* (1970), chapter 6. In the writings of Jacques Derrida and his followers in literary criticism, the *binary* opposition truth/falsity is one of the metaphysical presuppositions of Western thought that they put to question; see *deconstruction*. For a detailed treatment of the relationships of fictions to the real world, including a survey of the diverse views about this problem, see Peter Lamarque and Stein Haugom Olsen, *Truth, Fiction and Literature: A Philosophical Perspective* (1994).

figural interpretation: 180.

是一种虚构表述。参阅：巴巴拉·赫恩斯坦·史密斯所著的《话语的边缘》(1978)一书中的"作为虚构的诗歌"和理查德·奥曼所写的文章"言语行为与文学的定义"，载于《哲学与修辞学》(1971)第4期。

多数当代小说批评家，无论他们持何种见解，都对叙述者报告或描述的虚构的场景、人物、事件、对话和叙述者自己对世界、人生或人类境况的认识作了重要的区分；并把后者的核心或主宰的概括性观点视为一部作品的主题或**论点**。叙述者的这些观点可以是明确表述的（如托马斯·哈代在《德伯家的苔丝》结尾的陈述"……那个众神的主宰对于苔丝的戏弄也就完结了"；又如：托尔斯泰在《战争与和平》结尾陈述的历史哲学观）。然而，很多此类观点都是通过叙述者对小说人物与情节本身的选择与安排而"意指""暗示"或"推测"出来的。叙述者在一部虚构性作品中作出的这种概括，无论是明确表述的还是暗示出来的，通常都被认为是对这个世界作出的真实判断，因此它们起到了把虚构性叙事作品和现实经历与道德世界衔接起来的作用。参阅：约翰·霍斯波斯所写的文章"文学暗含的真理"(1960)，重印收入 W. E. 肯尼克主编的《艺术与哲学》(1979年修订版)。

在虚构性叙事作品中，与作者的观点和真实的主张相关的一个常为人们所探讨的议题是读者的**信念**的作用，即读者自己的道德观、宗教信仰、社会观念与一部作品所肯定或暗示的道德观、宗教信仰、社会观念一致或相异的程度决定着他对作品的解释、接受程度和评价。关于该问题在文学批评中的历史沿延和相关论述，参阅威廉·约瑟夫·鲁尼所著的《当代批评中的"诗歌与信念"问题》(1949)；M. H. 艾布拉姆斯主编和撰稿的《文学与信念》(1957)；沃尔特·本·迈克尔斯所写的文章"挽救文本：参考与信念"，载于《现代语言札记》(1978)第93期。许多关于虚构小说中信念问题的讨论，都引用了 S. T. 柯勒律治对读者态度的描述："愿意中止怀疑"。

关于对真实与虚构标准的相关性的理论评述，参阅：门罗·C. 比尔兹利所著的《美学：批评哲学中的问题》(1958)第409—419页。关于传情语言理论的分析和评论，参阅：马克斯·布莱克所著的《语言与哲学》(1949)第9章"关于感情意义的问题"。杰拉尔德·格拉夫在《诗学命题与批评教义》(1970)第6章中为命题的真理作了辩解。在雅克·德里达及其追随者的文学批评著述中，真/假这一二元对立面是他们所质疑的西方思想中形而上学的假说之一；参见：**解构主义**。关于虚构小说与真实世界关系的详尽论述，包括人们对该问题所持不同见解的概述，参阅：彼得·拉马克与斯坦·豪贡·奥尔森合著的《真实、虚构与文学：一种哲学视角》(1994)。

figural interpretation：形象释义　　180。

figurative language: Figurative language is a conspicuous departure from what competent users of a language apprehend as the standard meaning of words, or else the standard order of words, in order to achieve some special meaning or effect. Figures are sometimes described as primarily poetic, but they are integral to the functioning of language and indispensable to all modes of discourse.

Most modern classifications and analyses are based on the treatment of figurative language by Aristotle and later classical rhetoricians; the fullest and most influential treatment is in the Roman Quintilian's *Institutes of Oratory* (first century AD), Books VIII and IX. Since that time, figurative language has often been divided into two classes: (1) **Figures of thought**, or **tropes** (meaning "turns," "conversions"), in which words or phrases are used in a way that effects a conspicuous change in what we take to be their standard meaning. The standard meaning, as opposed to its meaning in the figurative use, is called the **literal meaning**. (2) **Figures of speech**, or "rhetorical figures," or **schemes** (from the Greek word for "form"), in which the departure from standard usage is not primarily in the meaning of the words, but in the order or syntactical pattern of the words. This distinction is not a sharp one, nor do all critics agree on its application. For convenience of exposition, however, the most commonly identified tropes are treated here, and the most commonly identified figures of speech are collected in the article *rhetorical figures*. For recent opposition to the basic distinction between the literal and the figurative, see *metaphor, theories of*.

In a **simile**, a comparison between two distinctly different things is explicitly indicated by the word "like" or "as." A simple example is Robert Burns, "O my love's like a red, red rose." The following simile from Samuel Taylor Coleridge's "The Rime of the Ancient Mariner" also specifies the feature ("green") in which icebergs are similar to emerald:

> And ice, mast-high, came floating by,
> As green as emerald.

For highly elaborated types of simile, see *conceit* and *epic simile*.

In a **metaphor**, a word or expression that in literal usage denotes one kind of thing is applied to a distinctly different kind of thing, without asserting a comparison. For example, if Burns had said "O my love is a red, red rose" he would have uttered, technically speaking, a metaphor instead of a simile. Here is a more complex instance from the poet Stephen Spender, in which he applies several metaphoric terms to the eye as it scans a landscape:

For the distinction between metaphor and symbol, see *symbol*.

It should be noted that in these examples we can distinguish two elements, the metaphorical term and the subject to which it is applied. In a

Figurative Language：比喻语

比喻语是一种明显与有能力的语言使用者对语词标准意义的理解、或与语词常规顺序等相背离的修辞手法，目的是为了取得某种特殊的语义或效果。比喻（或称"修辞格"）有时被认为主要是属于诗歌的修辞手法，但实际上，比喻语已成为语言功能和所有话语模式不可或缺的组成部分。

对比喻语的大多数现代分类和分析，都是以亚里士多德和后来的古典修辞学家对比喻语的论述为基础；罗马修辞学家昆体良（又译：昆提利安）的《雄辩术原理》（公元前1世纪）第8—9卷对比喻修辞作了最充分和最有影响的论述。从那以后，比喻语常被划分为两个类型：(1) **概念性比喻**或称**比喻**（意为"变换""转换"），这类比喻语中的词或短语的用法明显不同于其标准意义。与语词的比喻意义相对立的标准意义被称为**字面意义**。(2) **修辞格**或称**修辞手段**（源自希腊语，意为"形式"），这类比喻中对语言使用标准的偏离，主要不体现在词义上，而是体现在词序或句法上。这种区分并不是绝对的，也不是所有评论家都接受的。为了便于论述，这里只涉及最普通的比喻手法，而把最常见的比喻手法汇集在*修辞格*中论述。关于近期对比喻意义与字面意义这一基本区分持反对观点的论述，参见：*隐喻理论*。

在**明喻**中，用"像"或"如同"对两种明显不同的事物加以明确比较。罗伯特·彭斯的诗句"啊，我的爱人像朵红红的玫瑰"就是此类比喻的一个简单范例。以下明喻引自塞缪尔·泰勒·柯勒律治的《古舟子咏》，其中，用冰山明喻祖母绿，将其特征（"绿"）具体化：

> 如墙的冰山从船旁浮过，
> 晶莹碧绿，色如翡翠。　　　　　　　　　　（顾子欣译）

关于更为复杂的明喻类型，参见：*巧思妙喻*、*史诗明喻*。

在**隐喻**中，通常用指代某事物的词语的字面意义指代另一截然不同的事物，其形式并不构成比较。例如，假如彭斯的诗句是"啊，我的爱人是朵红红的玫瑰"，那么，从修辞技巧上说，这就是隐喻而不是直喻。以下是引自诗人斯蒂芬·斯彭德诗句中更为复杂的一个隐语（版权未授，请参前版。——译注），他以此描写发现美景时的眼神：

> （略）

关于隐喻与象征的区别，参见：*象征*。

应该注意到的是，在这些例子中，我们可以区分出两种成分来，即比喻词和

widely adopted usage, I. A. Richards introduced the name **tenor** for the subject ("my love" in the altered line from Burns, and "eye" in Spender's lines), and the name **vehicle** for the metaphorical term itself ("rose" in Burns, and the three words "gazelle," "wanderer," and "drinker" in Spender). In an **implicit metaphor**, the tenor is not itself specified, but only implied. If one were to say, while discussing someone's death, "That reed was too frail to survive the storm of its sorrows," the situational and verbal context of the term "reed" indicates that it is the vehicle for an implicit tenor, a human being, while "storm" is the vehicle for an aspect of a specified tenor, "sorrows." Those aspects, properties, or common associations of a vehicle which, in a given context, apply to a tenor are called by Richards the **grounds** of a metaphor. (See I. A. Richards, *Philosophy of Rhetoric*, 1936, chapters 5–6.)

All the metaphoric terms, or vehicles, cited so far have been nouns, but other parts of speech may also be used metaphorically. The metaphoric use of a verb occurs in Shakespeare's *Merchant of Venice*, V. i. 54, "How sweet the moonlight *sleeps* upon this bank"; and the metaphoric use of an adjective occurs in Andrew Marvell's "The Garden" (1681):

> Annihilating all that's made
> To a *green* thought in a green shade.

A **mixed metaphor** conjoins two or more obviously diverse metaphoric vehicles. When used inadvertently, without sensitivity to the possible incongruity of the vehicles, the effect can be ludicrous: "Girding up his loins, the chairman plowed through the mountainous agenda." Densely figurative poets such as Shakespeare, however, often mix metaphors in a functional way. One example is Hamlet's expression of his troubled state of mind in his *soliloquy* (III. i. 59–60), "to take arms against a sea of troubles, / And by opposing end them"; another is the complex involvement of vehicle within vehicle, applied to the process of aging, in Shakespeare's Sonnet 65:

> O, how shall summer's honey breath hold out
> Against the wrackful siege of battering days?

A **dead metaphor** is one which, like "the leg of a table" or "the heart of the matter," has been used so long and become so common that we have ceased to be aware of the discrepancy between vehicle and tenor. Many dead metaphors, however, are only moribund and can be brought back to life. Someone asked Groucho Marx, "Are you a man or a mouse?" He answered, "Throw me a piece of cheese and you'll find out." The recorded history of language indicates that a great many words that we now take to be literal were, in the distant past, metaphors.

Metaphors are essential to the functioning of language and have been the subject of copious analyses, and sharp disagreements, by rhetoricians, linguists, literary critics, and philosophers of language. For a discussion of diverse views, see the entry *metaphor, theories of*.

被比喻物。在广为接受的隐喻用法中，I. A. 理查兹提出用**喻的**指代被比喻物（如上述更改后的彭斯诗句中的"我的爱人"及斯彭德诗句中的"眼睛"），用**喻矢**指代比喻词本身（如彭斯诗句中的"玫瑰"和斯彭德诗句中的"小羚羊""漫游者""饮酒者"三个词）。在**含蓄隐喻**中，喻的没有被明确地表示出来，而仅仅是隐含在上下文中。因此，假如在谈及某人的死亡时说"那枝芦苇太纤弱了，经不起凄风苦雨的打击"，那么，从这句话的语境和字里行间可以看出，"芦苇"作为喻矢，指代暗示的喻的——某人，而喻矢"风雨"则指代"忧愁"这一确切喻的的某个属性。在某一特定语境中，喻矢的属性、特征或普通联想意义是可用以表现喻的的，理查兹把喻矢的这些属性特征称为隐喻的**基础**（参阅 I. A. 理查兹《修辞哲学》(1936) 第 5—6 章）。

以上引用的比喻词或喻矢都是名词，其他词类也能用作隐喻。莎士比亚的《威尼斯商人》(第五幕第一场第 54 行)中就有动词用作隐喻的例子："月光是何等甜蜜地沉睡在河岸上"；安德鲁·马韦尔的《花园》(1681)中有用形容词作隐喻的例子：

　　一切虚构的杂念
　　在绿荫下绿色的情怀中都消除殆尽。

并合隐喻兼用两个或更多明显各异的比喻喻矢。采用这种修辞时，如果因大意而忽视各种喻矢之间可能出现的不协调性，很可能会造成荒唐可笑的比喻效果，例如："主席先生紧了紧腰带，便开始穿越议事日程的高山峻岭。"不过，莎士比亚等擅长大量运用比喻的诗人常把并合隐喻运用得恰到好处。例如：哈姆雷特在*内心独白*中（第三幕第一场第 59—60 行）述说自己烦乱心绪时说的这样一句话："挺身反抗无涯的苦难，/ 并通过斗争把它们扫清"；又如莎士比亚十四行诗第 65 首中用以表现衰老过程的一个喻矢复用的例子：

　　呵，夏天甜蜜的芳香怎么能抵挡
　　那一天一天的光阴来猛烈地围攻？　　　　　　　（屠岸译）

亡隐喻指的是如"桌子的一条腿"或"事情的核心"这样一类因长期使用而变得司空见惯，以致我们不会意识到喻矢与喻的之间差异的比喻语。许多亡隐喻行将消亡，但又能起死回生。曾有人问格鲁乔·马克思："你是人是鼠？"他答道："扔给我一块奶酪，你便会知道。"语言的发展历史表明，具有当今字面意义的大多数词在遥远的过去都曾是比喻语。

隐喻对于语言的功能而言至关重要，修辞学家、语言学家、文学批评家和语言哲学家对此作了大量的精心研究，也引发了他们之间的激烈争论。关于隐喻的各种不同论述，参见：*隐喻理论*。

Some tropes, sometimes classified as species of metaphor, are more frequently and usefully given names of their own:

In **metonymy** (Greek for "a change of name") the literal term for one thing is applied to another with which it has become closely associated because of a recurrent relation in common experience. Thus "the crown" or "the scepter" can be used to stand for a king and "Hollywood" for the film industry; "Milton" can signify the writings of Milton ("I have read all of Milton"); and typical attire can signify the male and female sexes: "doublet and hose ought to show itself courageous to petticoat" (Shakespeare, *As You Like It*, II. iv. 6). (For the influential distinction by the linguist Roman Jakobson between the metaphoric, or "vertical," and the metonymic, or "horizontal," dimension, in application to many aspects of the functioning of language, see under *linguistics in literary criticism*.)

In **synecdoche** (Greek for "taking together"), a part of something is used to signify the whole, or (more rarely) the whole is used to signify a part. We use the term "ten *hands*" for ten workers, or "a hundred *sails*" for ships and, in current slang, "wheels" to stand for an automobile. By a bold use of the figure, Milton describes the corrupt and greedy clergy in "Lycidas" as "blind *mouths*."

Another figure related to metaphor is **personification**, or in the Greek term, **prosopopeia**, in which either an inanimate object or an abstract concept is spoken of as though it were endowed with life or with human attributes or feelings (compare *pathetic fallacy*). Milton wrote in *Paradise Lost* (IX. 1002–3), as Adam bit into the fatal apple,

> Sky lowered, and muttering thunder, some sad drops
> Wept at completing of the mortal sin.

The second stanza of Keats' "To Autumn" finely personifies the season, autumn, as a woman carrying on the rural chores of that time of year; and in *Aurora Leigh*, I. 251–52, Elizabeth Barrett Browning wrote:

> Then, land!—then, England! oh, the frosty cliffs
> Looked cold upon me.

The personification of abstract terms was standard in eighteenth-century *poetic diction*, where it sometimes became a thoughtless formula. Coleridge cited an eighteenth-century ode celebrating the invention of inoculation against smallpox that began with this *apostrophe* to the personified subject of the poem:

> Inoculation! heavenly Maid, descend!

See Steven Knapp, *Personification and the Sublime* (1985).

The term **kenning** denotes the recurrent use, in the Anglo-Saxon *Beowulf* and poems written in other Old Germanic languages, of a descriptive phrase in place of the ordinary name for something. This type of *periphrasis*, which at times becomes a stereotyped expression, is an indication of the origin of these poems in oral tradition (see *oral poetry*). Some kennings are instances

有些比喻有时被归属为隐语的范畴，这类比喻时常具有各自的名称：

借喻（源自希腊文，意为"易名"）：用一事物的字面名称指代因在日常生活中与其经常发生联系而关系密切的另一事物。于是，"王冠"或"王杖"成了国王的代名词；"好莱坞"成为电影业的代名词；"弥尔顿"可以用来代表弥尔顿的作品（如"我把弥尔顿读完了"）；典型化的装束也可以指示男女不同性别："穿褐衫紧身裤的总该向穿长裙的显示出勇气来"（莎士比亚，《皆大欢喜》第二幕第四场第6行）。（语言学家罗曼·雅各布森对隐喻或"垂直的"和借喻或"水平的"的区分及其在语言功能各个方面的应用范围作了颇有影响的研究，参见：*语言学在文学批评里的应用*中的有关论述。）

举隅（或提喻，源于希腊文，意为"代全"）：以事物的局部代其整体，或（较为罕见）用整体指代局部。我们用"十把手"指代十位工匠，用"一百挂风帆"指代轮船，在现代俚语中用"车轮"指代汽车。弥尔顿在《利西达斯》中以"烂醉之口"这样粗俗的比喻指代腐化贪婪的教士。

另一种与隐喻相关联的修辞法是**拟人**，希腊文为 **prosopopeia**，它把无生命的事物或抽象的概念描写成似乎具有生命或人的气质或情感（对比：*感伤谬误*）。弥尔顿在《失乐园》（第九卷第1002—1003行）中描述亚当咬那个决定命运的苹果时写道：

> 空中乱云飞渡，闷雷沉吟
> 为人间原罪的成立痛苦而洒泪雨。　　　　（朱维之译）

济慈在《秋颂》第二节中把秋天生动地比拟成在一年的这个时节忙于农活的妇女；伊丽莎白·巴雷特·勃朗宁在《奥罗拉·利》（第一章第251—252行）中写道：

> 接着，大地！——接着，英格兰！喔，结满冰霜的悬崖
> 冰冷地对视着我。

在18世纪的*诗意辞藻*中，抽象概念拟人化是一种普通的修辞手法，但有时也会变成俗套。柯勒律治曾引用一篇18世纪庆贺发明天花疫苗的颂诗，它是以这样的*呼语法*指代诗中拟人化的事物开篇的：

> 疫苗！圣洁的少女，降临了！

参阅：史蒂文·克纳普所著的《拟人与崇高》（1985）。

术语**隐喻表达法**指的是在盎格鲁-撒克逊时期的《贝奥武甫》和其他以古德语创作的诗作中经常出现的用描述性词语取代事物普通名称的手法。这种*迂说*——有时被认为是一种过时陈腐的表达手法——是这些传统口头诗歌的原始形式（参见：*口头诗歌*）。有些隐喻表达法也是*借喻*（用"鲸之路"指代大海，

of *metonymy* ("the whale road" for the sea, and "the ring-giver" for a king); others of *synecdoche* ("the ringed prow" for a ship); still others describe salient or picturesque features of the object referred to ("foamy-necked floater" for a ship under sail, "storm of swords" for a battle).

Other departures from the standard use of words, often classified as tropes, are treated elsewhere in this *Glossary*: *aporia, conceit, epic simile, hyperbole, irony, litotes, paradox, periphrasis, pun, understatement*. Since the mid-twentieth century, especially in the *New Criticism, Russian formalism*, and Harold Bloom's theory of the *anxiety of influence*, there has been a great interest in the analysis and functioning of figurative language, which was once thought to be largely the province of pedantic rhetoricians. In deconstructive criticism, especially in the writings by Jacques Derrida and Paul de Man, the analysis of figurative language is one of the primary ways of establishing what they assert to be the uncertainty and undecidability of meaning; see *deconstruction*.

Summaries of the classification of figures that was inherited from the classical past are Edward P. J. Corbett, *Classical Rhetoric for the Modern Student* (3d ed., 1990); and Richard A. Lanham, *A Handlist of Rhetorical Terms* (2d ed., 1991). Arthur Quinn's lucid and amusing booklet, *Figures of Speech: 60 Ways to Turn a Phrase* (1993), treats mainly what this *Glossary* classifies as *rhetorical figures*. René Wellek and Austin Warren, in *Theory of Literature* (rev. 1970), summarize, with bibliography, diverse treatments of figurative language; and Jonathan Culler, in *The Pursuit of Signs* (1981), discusses the concern with this topic in deconstructive theory.

For references to *figurative language* in other entries, see pages *79, 170, 343*. See also *rhetorical figures; style*. Refer also to the following figures: *allusion; ambiguity; anaphora; antithesis; aporia; conceit; epic simile; epithet; hyperbole and understatement; irony; kenning; litotes; paradox; pathetic fallacy; periphrasis; pun; symbol; synesthesia*. For figures of sound, see *alliteration; onomatopoeia; rhyme*.

figures of speech: 130.

figures of thought: 130.

fin de siècle (făn′ dĕ syĕk′ l): 76.

fine arts: Fine arts in modern usage designates primarily the five arts of *literature*, painting, sculpture, music, and architecture. Individual works of art in all these modes are held to share a defining feature; that is, they are objects that are to be regarded with a close, exclusive, and pleasurable attention.

This grouping of the arts did not appear, in the writings of philosophers and critics, until the latter part of the eighteenth century. During some two thousand years before that time, each of these arts had been treated separately, or else classified with such practical pursuits as agriculture and carpentry. When one of the arts was compared to another, it was only in a limited way; poetry, for example, was sometimes compared to painting,

用"金戒施者"指代国王）；有些隐喻表达法却是*举隅*（如"镶环的船首"指代轮船）；还有一些隐喻表达法则描述所指对象显著或别具一格的特征（如用"泡沫齐颈的漂浮物"指代破浪航行的轮船，用"刀光剑影"指代战争）。

对于其他一些背离词的标准用法而常归类为比喻的修辞格，将在本书中其他条目下逐一论述，如*反逆性、巧思妙喻、史诗明喻、夸张、反讽、反语法、逆说、迂说、双关语、含蓄*。20世纪中期以来，尤其是在*新批评、俄国形式主义、哈罗德·布卢姆的影响的焦虑*等理论流派中，又萌发出研究比喻语功能的极大兴趣，而这类研究曾被认为主要是学究式的修辞分类学学者研究的范畴。在解构主义批评，尤其是在雅克·德里达和保罗·德·曼的著作中，分析比喻语，是确立他们所断言的意义的不确定性和不可判定性的主要方式之一；参见：*解构主义*。

爱德华·P. J.科比特的《古典修辞学今用》（1990年第3版）和理查德·A.拉纳姆的《修辞用语手册》（1991年第2版），对沿承古典时期的比喻分类法作了详尽论述。阿瑟·奎因生动有趣的小册子《修辞：造一个短语的60种方式》（1993），主要讨论的是本书中分类的修辞格。勒内·韦勒克与奥斯汀·沃伦合著的《文学理论》（1970），以文献目录形式总结了对比喻语的各种不同论述；乔纳森·卡勒所著的《符号的追寻》（1981），则论述了近期批评理论对比喻语的关注。

其他条目中提及"比喻语"的地方，参见第79、170、343页。也可参见：*修辞格、文体*。还可参阅下列条目：*典故、歧义、首语重复法、对偶、反逆性、巧思妙喻、史诗明喻、属性形容词、夸张与含蓄、反讽、隐喻表达法、反语法、逆说、感伤谬误、迂说、双关、象征、通感*。关于音型，参见：*头韵、拟声、押韵*。

figures of speech：修辞格　130。

figures of thought：概念性比喻　130。

fin de siècle：世界末日　76。

Fine Arts：美术

美术在现代用法中主要指*文学、绘画、雕塑、音乐、建筑*这五门艺术。所有这些形式中的个人艺术作品都有一个明确的特征，即，它们被视为是一种密切的、排他性的、愉快的关注的对象。

在哲学家和批评家的著作中，这一艺术归类直到18世纪后期才出现。在那之前约两千年的时间里，这五门艺术一直被分别对待，或是归入农业、木工这样的实用性事业中。当这五种艺术中的一种与其他相比时，它只是一种有限的方

but only to make the point that both represented features of the outer world, in different media. The classification of the five arts as "the fine arts" was the result, in the course of the eighteenth century, of a drastic shift in the understructure of art theory. From the ancient Greeks until the eighteenth century, theorists and critics had assumed a maker's perspective toward the product of an art, and had analyzed its attributes in terms of a construction model. That is, they regarded a work of art, such as a poem, as something that an artisan makes according (in the Latin term) to an *ars*—that is, a craft. Each of the five arts, accordingly, was held to require a special kind of skill for manipulating its specific medium—words, or paint, or marble, or musical sounds, or building materials—into a product that its maker designed to have its own kind of use, and to fulfill a particular social function. In discussions of the art of literature—the most highly developed area of art criticism—this assumption of the maker's perspective toward a literary work united such theorists, in other respects very diverse, as Aristotle, Longinus, Horace, and the rhetoricians; all their writings were oriented toward instructing a poet in how to make a good poem, as well as toward helping a reader decide whether, and in what respects, the finished poem is a good poem.

In the course of the eighteenth century, there occurred a radical shift in the treatment of the arts—a shift from a maker's perspective and a construction model to a perceiver's perspective and a contemplation model. Underlying this change was a conspicuous social phenomenon in various major cities of Europe: the establishment and rapid proliferation of institutional arrangements for making each of the five diverse arts available—usually for pay—to a large and rapidly expanding public. In literature, the change from private patronage to the commercial manufacture and public sale of literary books made poems and novels available to a large audience, who bought them to read in isolation, for no purpose other than the interest and pleasure of doing so. That period also saw the founding, for the first time, of great public museums; in each museum, paintings and sculptures from various countries and eras, and of all types, religious and secular, were extracted from their original contexts and put together in one place and for a single purpose: as objects to be contemplated and enjoyed. In that same period, public concerts were inaugurated, where large audiences gathered in order to listen to and enjoy all sorts of musical compositions, vocal and instrumental, sacred and secular. The eighteenth century was also the era in which the phenomenon of tourism developed; in England, for example, many thousands of middle-class tourists visited cathedrals and great country estates, for no other purpose than to inspect and admire their architectural achievements.

Within a single century, then, the standard way of experiencing the hitherto diverse arts had become that of confronting their already-made products as objects of pleasurable attention. In consonance with this large-scale change in the mode of experiencing the arts, theorists shifted from the maker's perspective and a construction model of art to an observer's perspective and a

式；比如以诗歌为例，有时会将其与绘画相比，但这只为说明，两者通过不同的媒介都展现出了外部世界的特征。将这五种艺术归入"美术"这一分类，是在18世纪的历史进程中艺术理论的基础发生巨大转变的结果。从古希腊人直到18世纪，理论家和批评家已经认同了从创造者的视角去看待艺术品的制作，用建筑模型去分析其属性。也就是说，他们认为一件艺术作品，比如一首诗，是艺术家按照（拉丁语）ars，即一种手艺创造出来的一种东西。因此，这五种艺术中的每一种，都需要有一种专门的技艺，操控其特定的介质：词语，或颜料，或大理石，或乐音，或建材，生产出一个产品，它的创造者会事先设计好它自己的用处，去满足特定的社会功能。在讨论文学艺术时，这是艺术批评中高度发达的一个领域，从创造者视角去看文学作品这一假设，将像亚里士多德、朗吉努斯、贺拉斯这样的理论家（他们在其他方面的看法则有很大不同）和修辞学家联合到了一起；他们所有的著作都朝向一个方向：指示诗人如何写出一首好诗，帮助读者判定一首写好的诗是否及在哪些方面是一首好诗。

18世纪时，在对待艺术上发生了一个根本性的转变——从过去的创造者视角和建筑模型，转到了接受者（接受主体）视角和沉思模型。潜藏在这一变化下的是在欧洲各大城市出现的一种突出的社会现象：让这五种不同艺术中的每一个都为大量的和快速扩展的公众可得（通常要付费）的制度安排的确立和迅速扩散。在文学这门艺术中，由私人赞助到商业生产和向公众售卖文学书籍的变化，给诗歌和小说提供了大量读者，后者买回这些书籍独自阅读，除了这样做的兴趣和乐趣外没有别的目的。18世纪也第一次看到了巨大的公共博物馆的落成，在每家博物馆，来自不同国家和时代各种类型（宗教的和世俗的）绘画和雕塑作品，都从它们原来所处的背景下被挑选出来，一块放到同一个地方，只为一个简单的目的：作为思考和欣赏的对象。同一时期，公众音乐会也开始出现，大批观众聚在一起，聆听和欣赏各种音乐作品：声乐和器乐，宗教音乐和世俗音乐。18世纪也是开发旅游业的时代，例如，在英国，成千上万的中产阶级游客参观教堂和伟大的乡村庄园，只为赏鉴和钦佩它们的建筑成就。

因而，在一个世纪中，体验前所未有的多样化的艺术的标准方式已经变成，面对他们已经作出的产品，视作愉悦关注的对象。与这一体验艺术的模式上的大规模变化相一致，理论家也从艺术的创造者视角和建筑模型，转移到观察者视角和

contemplation model. Immanuel Kant, for example, in his immensely influential *Critique of Aesthetic Judgment* (1790), defined the normative judgment of all works of art as "purely contemplative," and as "a pure disinterested delight" in an object that "pleases for its own sake." The result of this paradigm shift was to group together all five arts—patently different in their materials, their required skills, and their social functions—into the single class of "the fine arts," consisting of objects whose reason for being was simply to be read, or looked at, or listened to, for their own sake, simply for the pleasure of doing so.

Refer to the entry *aestheticism*. For the gradual emergence during the eighteenth century of the conception of "the fine arts" as a single class, see Paul Oskar Kristeller, "The Modern System of the Arts: A Study in the History of Aesthetics," *Journal of the History of Ideas*, Vol. 12 (1951), pp. 496–527, and Vol. 13 (1952), pp. 17–46. On the social and institutional developments, and the correlative conceptual changes, that led to this classification, see M. H. Abrams, "Art-as-Such: The Sociology of Modern Aesthetics," in *Doing Things with Texts: Essays in Criticism and Critical Theory* (1989).

first-person narrative: 301.

first-person points of view: 303.

flashback (in a plot): **296**.

flat character: 46; *211*.

focus of character: 302.

focus of narration: 302.

foil: 294.

folio: 34; *22*.

folk ballad: 23.

folk drama: 136.

folk songs: 136; *23*.

folklore: Folklore, since the mid-nineteenth century, has been the collective name applied to sayings, verbal compositions, and social rituals that have been handed down solely, or at least primarily, by word of mouth and example rather than in written form. Folklore developed, and continues even now, in communities where few if any people can read or write. It also continues to flourish among literate populations, in the form of oral jokes, stories, and

沉思模型。例如，康德在其极具影响力的《判断力批判》（1790）中，明确了所有艺术作品的规范性判断为"纯粹静观的"，在一个"因其自身缘故而喜悦的"对象中则为"一种无所为而为的喜悦"。这一范式转型的结果是，将原本合为一体的五种艺术——在它们的材料、所需技能和它们的社会功能上显然有所不同——分为单一的"美术"种类，其存在理由仅仅是被读，或被看，或被听，为自己着想，只为高兴这样做。

参见：*唯美主义*。关于"美术"作为一种单独分类的概念在 18 世纪的逐渐出现，参阅：保罗·奥斯卡·克里斯特勒所写的文章"艺术的现代系统：关于美学历史的研究"，载于《观念史杂志》1952 年第 12 卷第 496—527 页及 1952 年第 13 卷第 17—46 页。关于促成这一分类的社会和制度发展以及相关的概念变化，参阅：M. H. 艾布拉姆斯所著的《以文行事：艾布拉姆斯精选集》（1989）中"像这样的艺术：现代美学社会学"。

first-person narrative：第一人称叙事模式　301。

first-person points of view：第一人称视角　303。

flashback (in a plot)：（情节中的）倒叙　296。

flat character：干瘪的人物形象　46；*211*。

focus of character：人物焦点　302。

focus of narration：叙事焦点　302。

foil：陪衬　294。

folio：对开本　34；*22*。

folk ballad：民间歌谣　23。

folk drama：民间剧　136。

Folklore：民间传说

自 19 世纪中叶以来，民间传说这一集合名称一直用于指代单纯或至少主要是以口头和样板形式而非书面形式流传下来的谚语、口头文学和社会礼仪。民间传说发展流传于几乎目不识丁的社会群体中，时至今日仍在他们中间发展繁荣。民间传说也以口头笑话、故事和各种双关语的形式在文化人中间继续广为流传。

varieties of wordplay; see, for example, the collection of "urban folklore" by Alan Dundes and Carl R. Pagter, *When You're up to Your Ass in Alligators: More Urban Folklore from the Paperwork Empire* (1987). Folklore includes legends, superstitions, songs, tales, proverbs, riddles, spells, and nursery rhymes; pseudoscientific lore about the weather, plants, and animals; customary activities at births, marriages, and deaths; and traditional dances and forms of drama performed on holidays or at communal gatherings. Materials from folklore have at all times been employed in sophisticated written literature. For example, the choice among the three caskets in Shakespeare's *Merchant of Venice* (II. ix.) and the superstition about a maiden's dream which is central to Keats' *Eve of St. Agnes* (1820) are both derived from folklore. Refer to A. H. Krappe, *Science of Folklore* (1930, reprinted 1974); Richard M. Dorson, ed. *Folklore and Folklife: An Introduction* (1972).

The following forms of folklore have been of special importance for later written literature:

Folk drama originated in primitive rites of song and dance, especially in connection with agricultural activities, which centered on vegetational deities and goddesses of fertility. Some scholars maintain that Greek *tragedy* developed from such rites, which celebrated the life, death, and rebirth of the vegetational god Dionysus. Folk dramas survive in England in the forms of the St. George play and the **mummers' play** (a mummer is a masked actor). Thomas Hardy's *The Return of the Native* (Book II, chapter 5) describes the performance of a mummers' play, and a form of this drama is still performed in America in the Kentucky mountains. See Edmund K. Chambers, *The English Folk-Play* (1933).

Folk songs include love songs, Christmas carols, work songs, sea chanties, religious songs, drinking songs, children's game songs, and many other types of lyric, as well as the narrative song, or traditional *ballad*. (See *oral poetry*.) All forms of folk song have been assiduously collected since the late eighteenth century, and have inspired many imitations by writers of lyric poetry, as well as by composers of popular songs in the twentieth century. Robert Burns collected and edited Scottish folk songs, restored or rewrote them, and imitated them in his own lyrics. His "A Red, Red Rose" and "Auld Lang Syne," for example, both derive from one or more folk songs, and his "Green Grow the Rashes, O" is a tidied-up version of a bawdy folk song. See J. C. Dick, *The Songs of Robert Burns* (1903); Cecil J. Sharp, *Folk Songs of England* (5 vols., 1908–12); and Alan Lomax, *The Folk Songs of North America* (1960).

The **folktale**, strictly defined, is a short narrative in prose of unknown authorship which has been transmitted orally; many of these tales eventually achieve written form. The term, however, is often extended to include stories invented by a known author—such as "The Three Bears" by Robert Southey (1774–1843) and Parson Mason L. Weems' story of George Washington and the cherry tree—which have been picked up and repeatedly narrated by word of mouth as well as in written form. Folktales are found among peoples everywhere in the world. They include *myths*, *fables*, tales of heroes (whether

此类例子可以参见阿伦·邓德斯与卡尔·R.帕格特编著的"城市民间传说"选集《当你将自己的臀部塞进鳄鱼群内：更多来自文书帝国的都市传奇》(1987)。民间传说包括神话传说、迷信、民歌、故事、谚语、谜语、符咒和童谣；关于气候与动植物的伪科学传说；生死婚嫁的民俗惯例，以及在节日或公共集会上表演的传统舞蹈和戏剧形式。民间传说的一些成分一直都是成熟的笔头文学的素材来源。例如，莎士比亚的《威尼斯商人》（第二幕第四场）中选择三个首饰匣的情节；济慈《圣阿格尼斯夜》(1820)中的主要情节少女梦事的迷信都来源于民间传说。参阅：A. H. 克拉普所著的《民间传说学》(1930，1974年再版)和理查德·M.多森编选的《民间传说与民间生活介绍》(1972)。

以下几种民间传说的形式，对后来笔头文学的创作有着特殊的重要性。

民间剧源自原始的歌舞礼仪，尤其是与敬奉草木神灵和丰产女神的农业活动有关的礼仪。一些学者认为，希腊*悲剧*就是从庆祝草木神狄俄尼索斯的生死复荣的礼仪中发展而来。在英国，民间剧是以圣·乔治戏剧和**假面剧**（假面剧中的演员头戴面具）的形式保留下来的。在托马斯·哈代的《还乡》（第2卷第5章）中就有关于假面剧表演的描写，这种戏剧形式至今仍流行于美国肯塔基山区。参阅：埃德蒙·K.钱伯斯所著的《英国民间戏剧》(1933)。

民歌包括情歌、圣诞颂歌、劳动号子、水手号子、宗教歌曲、酒歌、儿童游戏小曲，以及许多其他类型的抒情歌谣，也包括叙事歌谣或传统*民谣*。（参见：*口头诗歌*。）18世纪后期以来，所有形式的民歌都得到了精心的收集整理，激发了许多抒情诗人和20世纪流行歌曲作家踊跃模仿。罗伯特·彭斯收集编写了《苏格兰民歌集》，并在自己的抒情诗创作中复原、改写和模拟这些民歌。例如：他的《一朵红红的玫瑰》和《往昔的时光》都源于一首或更多民歌，他的《青春苇子草》是在一首色情民歌的基础上改写而成。参阅：J. C. 迪克所著的《彭斯的歌》(1903)；塞西尔·J.夏普五卷本的《英国民歌》(1908—1912)；阿伦·洛马克斯的《北美民歌》(1960)。

从严格意义上说，**民间故事**是口头流传、作者身份不详的短篇白话故事；不过许多民间故事最终还是以书面形式得以流传。民间故事也往往把范围扩大到包括一些署名的创作故事，如罗伯特·骚塞的《三只熊》(1774—1783)和帕森·梅森·L.威姆斯关于乔治·华盛顿与樱桃树的故事，这些故事都被民众所接受并一直以口传及书面形式流传。世界上各民族的人们都有自己的民间故事，它们包括*神话*、*寓言故事*、英雄故事（无论是历史上散播苹果籽的约翰尼·苹果

historical like Johnny Appleseed or legendary like Paul Bunyan), and fairy tales. Many so-called "fairy tales" (the German word **Märchen** is frequently used for this type of folktale) are not stories of fairies but of various kinds of marvels; examples are "Snow White" and "Jack and the Beanstalk." Another type of folk tale, the set "joke"—that is, the comic (often bawdy) *anecdote*—is the most abundant and persistent of all; new jokes, or new versions of old jokes, continue to be a staple of social exchange, wherever people congregate in a relaxed mood.

The same, or closely similar, oral stories have turned up in Europe, Asia, and Africa, and have been embodied in the narratives of many writers. Chaucer's *Canterbury Tales* includes a number of folktales; "The Pardoner's Tale" of Death and the three rioters, for example, was of Eastern origin. See Benjamin A. Botkin, *A Treasury of American Folklore* (1944); Stith Thompson, *The Folktale* (1974); and Vladimir Propp, *Morphology of the Folktale* (1970). The standard catalogue of recurrent *motifs* in folktales throughout the world is Stith Thompson's *Motif-Index of Folk-Literature* (1932–37).

folktale: 136; *230*.

foot (in meter): **218**.

forced rhyme: 349; *377*.

foregrounding: 139.

forensic oratory (fŏrĕn′ sĭc): **343**.

form and structure: "Form" is one of the most frequent terms in literary criticism, but also one of the most diverse in its meanings. It is often used merely to designate a *genre* or literary type ("the lyric form," "the short story form"), or for patterns of meter, lines, and rhymes ("the verse form," "the stanza form"). It is also, however—in a sense descended from the Latin "forma," which was equivalent to the Greek "idea"—the term for a central critical concept. In this application, the **form** of a work is the principle that determines how a work is ordered and organized; critics, however, differ greatly in their analyses of this principle. All agree that "form" is not simply a fixed container, like a bottle, into which the "content" or "subject matter" of a work is poured; but beyond this, the concept of form varies according to a critic's particular assumptions and theoretical orientation (see *criticism*).

Many *neoclassic* critics, for example, thought of the form of a work as a combination of parts, matched to each other according to the principle of *decorum*, or mutual fittingness. In the early nineteenth century Samuel Taylor Coleridge, following the lead of the German critic A. W. Schlegel, distinguished between **mechanic form**, which is a fixed, pre-existent shape such as we impose on wet clay by a mold, and **organic form**, which, Coleridge

佬，还是如同保罗·班扬式的传奇）和仙女故事。很多所谓的"仙女故事"（德文为 Marchen，常用于指代此类民间故事）并不是关于仙女精灵的故事，而是表现各种奇迹；例如："白雪公主"和"杰克与豆茎"。另外一种民间故事类型是一些"笑话"，即滑稽（往往是色情淫秽的）*轶事*，这类笑话最丰富，生命力也最持久。新笑话或新版本的旧笑话仍是当今各地人们聚集休闲时的谈资。

在欧洲、亚洲和非洲都发现了内容相同或极为近似的口头故事，而且这些故事也体现在许多作家的叙事作品中。乔叟的《坎特伯雷故事集》中收入了不少民间故事；其中描写死神与三个暴徒的"卖赎罪券者讲的故事"就是源自东方的传说。参阅：本雅明·A. 博特金所著的《美国民间传说宝库》（1944）；斯蒂思·汤姆逊所著的《民间故事》（1974）；弗拉基米尔·普洛普所著的《民间故事形态学》（1970）。斯蒂思·汤姆逊所著的《民间文学母题索引》（1932—1937），是世界范围内民间故事中反复出现的题旨的标准目录。

folktale：民间故事　136；*230*。

foot (in meter)：（格律中的）音步　218。

forced rhyme：迫韵　349；*377*。

foregrounding：前景化　139。

forensic oratory：法庭式的雄辩术　343。

Form and Structure：形式与结构

"形式"是文学批评中出现频率最高但也是意义最具争议的术语之一。它常被用来仅指*文学类型*或体裁（如"抒情诗体""短篇小说体"），或指诗歌格律、诗行及韵律的类型（如"诗体""诗节形式"）。"形式"也是文艺理论批评中的一个主要概念，其意义源自拉丁语"forma"，等同于希腊语中的"理念"。在这个意义上，所谓一部作品的**形式**指的是决定一部作品组织和构成的原则；然而，批评家在对这种原则的分析过程中所持的观点却是大相径庭。他们一致认为，"形式"并非仅仅是类似瓶子一样的固定的容器，可以往里面注入作品的"内容"与"题材"；除此之外，批评家对形式这一概念的解释也因其特定的假设和理论取向而众说纷纭（参见：*批评*）。

例如，许多*新古典主义*批评家把作品的形式视为由它的各个组成部分按照仪轨或互相匹配的原则结合而成的组合。19 世纪早期，塞缪尔·泰勒·柯勒律治效仿德国文艺理论家 A. W. 施莱格尔将作品的形式划分为**模具形式**和**有机形式**。前者为一种固定的业已存在的模型，如同我们制作陶器时装入湿黏土的模具；而后者，

says, "is innate; it shapes as it develops itself from within, and the fullness of its development is one and the same with the perfection of its outward form." To Coleridge, in other words, as to other **organicists** in literary criticism, a good poem is like a growing plant which evolves, by an internal energy, into the organic unity that constitutes its achieved form, in which the parts are integral to and interdependent with the whole. (On organic criticism and the concept of organic form, see M. H. Abrams, *The Mirror and the Lamp*, 1953, chapters 7–8; and George Rousseau, *Organic Form*, 1972.) Many *New Critics* use the word **structure** interchangeably with "form," and regard it as primarily an equilibrium, or interaction, or ironic and paradoxical tension, of diverse words and images in an organized totality of "meanings." Various exponents of *archetypal* theory regard the form of a literary work as one of a limited number of plot shapes which it shares with myths, rituals, dreams, and other elemental and recurrent patterns of human experience. And structuralist critics conceive a literary structure on the model of the systematic way that a language is structured; see *structuralist criticism*.

In an influential critical enterprise, R. S. Crane, a leader of the **Chicago School** of criticism, revived and developed the concept of form in Aristotle's *Poetics*, and made a distinction between "form" and "structure." The form of a literary work is (in the Greek term) the "dynamis," the particular "working" or "emotional power" that the composition is designed to effect, which functions as its "shaping principle." This formal principle controls and synthesizes the "structure" of a work—that is, the order, emphasis, and rendering of all its component subject matter and parts—into "a beautiful and effective whole of a determinate kind." See R. S. Crane, *The Languages of Criticism and the Structure of Poetry* (1953), chapters 1 and 4; also Wayne C. Booth, "Between Two Generations: The Heritage of the Chicago School," in *Profession*, Vol. 82 (Modern Language Association, 1982).

See *formalism* and refer to René Wellek, "Concepts of Form and Structure in Twentieth-Century Criticism," in *Concepts of Criticism* (1963); Kenneth Burke, *The Philosophy of Literary Form* (3d ed., 1973); and Eugène Vinaver, *Form and Meaning in Medieval Romance* (1966). See also *plot*.

formal essay: 114.

formal satire: 353.

formalism: A type of literary theory and analysis which originated in Moscow and St. Petersburg in the second decade of the twentieth century. At first, opponents of the movement of **Russian Formalism** applied the term "formalism" derogatorily, because of its focus on the patterns and technical devices of literature to the exclusion of its subject matter and social values; later, however, it became a neutral designation. Among the leading representatives of the movement were Boris Eichenbaum, Victor Shklovsky, and

正如柯勒律治所言："是内在的；随着自身的生发而成型，自我生发到极点便是它外形的最后塑成。"换句话说，在柯勒律治及文艺批评理论的**有机论者**看来，一首好诗好似一棵生长的植株，靠自身内在的活力发育成为表现出其形态的有机整体，其中各组成部分是构成整体所必需的，与整体互相依存。[关于有机批评理论和有机形式的概念，参阅 M. H. 艾布拉姆斯《镜与灯》(1953) 第 7—8 章；乔治·卢梭所著的《有机形式》(1972)。] 很多新批评家用**结构**一词与"形式"替换使用，并认为在"意义"这一组织化的整体内，"结构"首先是不同的词和意象间的一种平衡，或是彼此间的相互作用，或是讽刺与悖论的张力。*原型*理论的不同倡导者则把一部文学作品的形式看做有限的情节形式中的一种形式，它与神话、礼仪、梦幻以及人生阅历中其他基本的和反复显现的各种模式共同具有这些有限的情节形式。结构主义批评家根据语言构成的系统化模式构想出文学结构；参见：*结构主义批评*。

芝加哥学派的领军人物 R. S. 克莱恩在其颇有影响的批评实践中，复兴并发展了亚里士多德《诗学》中关于形式的概念，并对"形式"和"结构"作了区分。一部文学作品的形式是使作品具有感染力的（用希腊术语说）"活力"、特殊的"作用"或"情感'力量'"，是作品"成型的原则"。这条形式原则将作品的"结构"——即对组成作品的题材和各部分的顺序、重点和艺术处理——加以控制和综合，使之成为"一个明确的美丽而又有感染力的整体"。参阅：R. S. 克莱恩所著的《批评的语言与诗歌的结构》(1953) 第 1 章和第 4 章；也可参阅韦恩·C. 布思所写的文章"两代之间：芝加哥学派的遗产"，载于《专业》(现代语言协会，1982年) 第 82 卷。

参见：*形式主义*。参阅：勒内·韦勒克所著的《批评的概念》中的 "20 世纪批评中形式和结构的概念"(1963)；肯尼斯·伯克所著的《文学形式的哲学》(1973 年第 3 版)；尤金·维纳弗所著的《中世纪传奇的形式和意义》(1966)。也可参见：*情节*。

formal essay：正规杂文　114。

formal satire：正规讽刺　353。

Formalism：形式主义

形式主义是 1920 年代发端于莫斯科和圣彼得堡的一种文学分析理论。最初，**俄国形式主义**运动的反对者赋予"形式主义"以贬损之意，因为形式主义关注的只是文学作品的形式模式和技巧手法，而把作品的题材和社会价值排除在外；但后来，形式主义又成为一个中性称谓。俄国形式主义运动的主要代表人物是鲍里斯·艾亨鲍姆、维克托·什克洛夫斯基和罗曼·雅各布森。

Roman Jakobson. When this critical mode was suppressed by the Soviets in the early 1930s, the center of the formalist study of literature moved to Czechoslovakia, where it was continued especially by members of the **Prague Linguistic Circle**, which included Roman Jakobson (who had emigrated from Russia), Jan Mukarovsky, and René Wellek. Beginning in the 1940s both Jakobson and Wellek continued their influential work as professors at American universities.

Formalism views *literature* primarily as a specialized use of language, and proposes a fundamental opposition between the literary (or poetical) use of language and the ordinary, "practical" use of language. It proposes that the central function of ordinary language is to communicate to auditors a message, or information, by references to the world existing outside of language. In contrast, it conceives literary language to be self-focused, in that its function is not to convey information by making extrinsic references, but to offer the reader a special mode of experience by drawing attention to its own "formal" features—that is, to the qualities and internal relations of the linguistic signs themselves. The linguistics of literature differs from the linguistics of practical discourse, because its laws are oriented toward producing the distinctive features that formalists call **literariness**. As Roman Jakobson wrote in 1921: "The object of study in literary science is not literature but 'literariness,' that is, what makes a given work a literary work." (See *linguistics in modern criticism*.)

The literariness of a work, as Jan Mukarovsky, a member of the Prague Circle, described it in the 1920s, consists "in the maximum of **foregrounding** of the utterance," that is, the foregrounding of "the act of expression, the act of speech itself." (To "foreground" is to bring something into prominence, to make it dominant in perception.) By "backgrounding" the referential aspect and the logical connections in language, poetry makes the words themselves "palpable" as phonic signs. The primary aim of literature in thus foregrounding its linguistic medium, as Victor Shklovsky put it in an influential formulation, is to **estrange** or **defamiliarize**; that is, by disrupting the modes of ordinary linguistic discourse, literature "makes strange" the world of everyday perception and renews the reader's lost capacity for fresh sensation. (In the *Biographia Literaria*, 1817, Samuel Taylor Coleridge had long before described the "prime merit" of a literary genius to be the representation of "familiar objects" so as to evoke "freshness of sensation"; but whereas the Romantic critic had stressed the author's ability to express a fresh mode of experiencing the world, the formalist stresses the function of purely literary devices to produce the effect of freshness in the reader's experience of a literary work.) The foregrounded properties, or "artistic devices," which estrange poetic language are often described as "deviations" from ordinary language. Such deviations, which are analyzed most fully in the writings of Roman Jakobson, consist primarily in setting up, and afterward violating, patterns in the sound and syntax of poetic language—including patterns in speech sounds, grammatical constructions, rhythm,

1930 年代早期，这一文艺批评模式受到苏联政府的压制。随后，形式主义文学研究中心迁至捷克斯洛伐克，在那里，特别是在包括雅各布森（从俄国移居捷克）、詹·穆卡诺夫斯基、勒内·韦勒克在内的**布拉格语言学学会**成员的推动下，形式主义文艺理论得以继续发展。从 1940 年代开始，雅各布森和韦勒克都在美国大学担任教授，继续从事他们颇有影响的研究工作。

形式主义把*文学*首先视为一种语言的特殊模式，并指出文学语言（或诗歌语言）与日常"实际"使用的语言之间是根本对立的。形式主义认为，日常语言的主要功能是以存在于语言之外的世界为参照物，向听者传递信息或情报。相反，文学语言则是以自我为中心，其功能并非通过外界参照物传递信息，而是以自身"形式"上的特征吸引注意力，即语言符号自身的品质和内部关系等特征，给读者提供一种特殊的体验模式。文学语言与日常话语是有区别的，因为文学语言规律旨在产生被形式主义者称之为**文学性**的独特效果。正如罗曼·雅各布森 1921 年所言："文学科学的研究对象不是文学，而是'文学性'，也就是使一部特定的作品成为文学作品的东西。"（参见：*语言学在文学批评里的应用*。）

布拉格语言学学会成员詹·穆卡诺夫斯基在 1920 年代指出，一部作品的文学性在于"叙述方式的最大**前景化**"，即"表达方式、话语方式自身"的前景化（"前景化"指的是使某一事物处于最显著的地位，从而能够引人注目，主宰人的感知）。通过使语言的参照方面和逻辑联系"背景化"，诗歌使语言变成了"可感知"的语音符号。文学作品对语言材料进行前景化的首要目的，正如维克托·什克洛夫斯基著名的论断所言，就是为了**间离**或**陌生化**；也就是说，文学作品通过打破普通语言话语的使用模式，使每天人们所感知的世界"变得陌生"起来，从而重新恢复读者已经丧失的新鲜感受的能力。（早在 1817 年，塞缪尔·泰勒·柯勒律治就在《文学传记》中写道，文学大师的"根本优势"在于呈现"熟悉的事物"，从而激发"感受的新鲜性"；但是，浪漫主义批评家强调作家应具有表达体验世界的新鲜模式的能力，形式主义者则强调纯粹的文学手段的功能，认为这种功能可以产生读者体验文学作品的新鲜效果。）用于间离诗歌语言的前景化策略或"艺术手法"常被视为对普通语言的"偏离"。偏离——罗曼·雅各布森在其著述中对这种偏离作了充分的分析——主要在于建立随后则打破诗歌语言的音韵和句法模式（包括语音模式、语法结构、节奏、韵律和诗节形式），

rhyme, and stanza forms—and also in setting up prominent recurrences of key words or images.

Some of the most fruitful work of Jakobson and others, valid outside the formalist perspective, has been in the analysis of *meter* and of the repetitions of sounds in *alliteration* and *rhyme*. These features of poetry they regard not as supplementary adornments of the meaning, but as effecting a reorganization of language on the semantic as well as the phonic and syntactic levels. Formalists have also made influential contributions to the theory of prose fiction. With respect to this genre, the central formalist distinction is that between the "story" (the simple enumeration of a chronological sequence of events) and a plot. An author is said to transform the raw material of a story into a literary *plot* by the use of a variety of devices that violate sequence and that deform and defamiliarize the story elements; the effect is to foreground the narrative medium and devices themselves, and in this way to disrupt and refresh what had been our standard responses to the subject matter. (See *narrative and narratology*.)

The standard treatment of the Russian movement is by Victor Erlich, *Russian Formalism: History, Doctrine* (rev. 1981). See also R. L. Jackson and S. Rudy, eds., *Russian Formalism: A Retrospective Glance* (1985). René Wellek has described Th*e Literary Theory and Aesthetics of the Prague School* (1969). Representative formalist writings are collected in Lee T. Lemon and Marion I. Reese, eds., *Russian Formalist Criticism: Four Essays* (1965); Ladislav Matejka and Krystyna Pomorska, eds., *Readings in Russian Poetics: Formalist and Structuralist Views* (1971); P. L. Garvin, ed., *A Prague School Reader on Esthetics, Literary Structure and Style* (1964); and Peter Steiner, ed., *The Prague School: Selected Writings, 1929–1946* (1982). A comprehensive and influential formalist essay by Roman Jakobson, "Linguistics and Poetics," is included in his *Language in Literature* (1987). Samuel Levin's *Linguistic Structures in Poetry* (1962) represents an American application of formalist principles, and E. M. Thompson has written *Russian Formalism and Anglo-American New Criticism: A Comparative Study* (1971).

American *New Criticism*, although it developed independently, is sometimes called "formalist" because, like European formalism, it stresses the analysis of the literary work as a self-sufficient verbal entity, constituted by internal relations and independent of reference either to the state of mind of the author or to the actualities of the "external" world. It also, like European formalism, conceives poetry as a special mode of language whose distinctive features are defined in terms of their systematic opposition to practical or scientific language. Unlike the European formalists, however, the New Critics did not apply the science of linguistics to poetry, and their emphasis was not on a work as constituted by linguistic devices for achieving specifically literary effects, but on the complex interplay within a work of ironic, paradoxical, and metaphoric meanings around a humanly important "theme." The main influence of Russian and Czech formalism on American criticism has been on the development of *stylistics* and of *narratology*. Roman Jakobson and Tzvetan

同时也在于突出反复再现的一些关键词或意象。

雅各布森和其他学者一些最富有成果的研究工作,是对*格律、头韵、押韵*中声音重复的分析,对此即使在形式主义的视野之外来看也是令人信服的。他们认为诗歌的这些特征不是附加在诗歌意义上的装饰品,而是为了实现对语言在语义及语音和句法等层面的重组。形式主义对散文体小说理论也作出了很大贡献。对于小说这一文学类型,形式主义主要划分了"故事"(对事件按时间顺序所作的简单列举陈述)和情节之间的区别。作者应借用各种文学手段破坏事件原有的顺序,使故事要素变形和陌生化,从而把一则故事的原始素材转变成为一个文学*情节*;目的就是使得叙事方法和手段前景化,以此破坏人们对题材的常规反应。(参见:*叙事和叙事学*。)

维克托·耶里奇在其所著的《俄国形式主义:历史与学说》(1981年修订版)中,对俄国形式主义运动进行了权威论述。参阅:R. L. 杰克逊与 S. 鲁迪合编的《俄国形式主义:回顾性一瞥》(1985)。勒内·韦勒克的述评:《布拉格学派的文学理论和美学》(1969)。形式主义者代表作的汇编有:李·T. 莱蒙与马里恩·I. 里斯合编的《俄国形式主义文论选》(1965);拉迪斯拉夫·马特杰卡与克雷斯蒂娜·泼墨斯卡合编的《俄国诗学读本:形式主义者和结构主义者视角》(1971);P. L. 加文主编的《布拉格学派美学、文学结构和文体学读本》(1964);彼得·斯坦纳主编的《布拉格学派著作精选:1929—1946》(1982)。罗曼·雅各布森所著的全面而著名的形式主义随笔"语言学与诗学",收入其所著的《文学中的语言》(1987)。塞缪尔·莱文在其所著的《诗歌中的语言结构》(1962)中,描述了形式主义原理在美国的应用;E. M. 汤普森则著有《俄国形式主义与英美新批评主义比较研究》(1971)。

尽管美国的新批评是独立发展的,但它有时仍被称为是"形式主义",因为与欧洲的形式主义一样,它也强调把文学作品看成由内部关系构成的、独立于作者的心态和"外部"世界现实所指的自足的语言实体加以分析。新批评也同欧洲的形式主义一样,把诗歌视为语言的一种特殊模式,其显著特征是与实用语言或科学语言截然相反的一种语言形式。但与欧洲形式主义者不同,新批评家没有把语言学科学应用到诗歌中,而且他们研究的重点并不是被视为由语言手段构成的旨在取得特殊文学效果的文学作品,而是作品内部以人类重要"主题"为中心的各种讽刺、逆说、比喻意义之间构成的复杂的相互作用。俄国和捷克形式主义对美国文艺批评的影响,主要表现在*文体学和叙事学*的发展方面。罗曼·雅各布森和

Todorov have also been influential in introducing formalist concepts and methods into French *structuralism*.

Strong opposition to formalism, in both its European and American varieties, has been voiced by some *Marxist critics* (who view it as the product of a reactionary ideology), and more recently by proponents of *reader-response criticism, speech-act theory*, and *new historicism*; these last three types of criticism all reject the view that there is a sharp and definable division between ordinary language and literary language. In the 1990s a number of critics called for a return to a formalist mode of treating a work of literature primarily as literature, instead of with persistent reference to its stand, whether explicit or covert, on political, racial, or sexual issues. A notable instance is Frank Lentricchia's "Last Will and Testament of an Ex-literary Critic" (*Lingua Franca*, Sept./Oct. 1996), renouncing his earlier writings and teachings "about literature as a political instrument," in favor of the view "that literature is pleasurable and important, as literature, and not as an illustration of something else." (Refer to *objective criticism*, under the entry in this *Glossary* on *criticism*.) See also Harold Bloom's advocacy of reading literature not to apply or confirm a political or social theory but for the love of literature, in *The Western Canon* (1994); and the essays in *Aesthetics and Ideology*, ed. George Levine (1994).

Toward the end of the last century, the formalist approach found a number of theoretical advocates. This return to formalism, building on a renewed interest in metrics (see *meter*) and in *aesthetics*, at first was proposed primarily as a reaction against the *new historicism*; but within a few years, what became known as the **new formalism** proposed a positive program, undertaking to connect the formal aspects of literature to the historical, political, and worldly concerns, in opposition to which the formalist movement had earlier defined itself. A number of new formalists argue that the formal integrity of a work of art is what protects it against *ideology*, idealization, and the routinizing effects of everyday experience; others emphasize that the perception of aesthetic or literary form is a necessary condition of critical thought. (The "new formalism" in criticism is to be distinguished from the "new formalism" in the writing of poetry; see the entry *free verse*.)

The first major advocate of new formalism was Susan J. Wolfson in *Formal Charges: The Shaping of Poetry in British Romanticism* (1997). Wolfson and Marshall Brown edited a collection of new-formalist essays, *Reading for Form* (2006). See also W. J. T. Mitchell, "The Commitment to Form," *PMLA*, Vol. 118 (March 2003); and for an appreciative overview of the new-formalist movement, Marjorie Levinson, "What Is New Formalism?" *PMLA*, Vol. 122 (March 2007). The journal *Representations* devoted a special issue to the question of form in 2008. For references to formalism (in literary criticism) in other entries, see pages *52, 168, 290*.

format of a book: 34.

兹维坦·托多罗夫以把形式主义的批评概念和方法引入法国的*结构主义*中而闻名。

形式主义遭到欧洲和美国不同派别的一些*马克思主义批评家*的强烈抨击（认为形式主义是反动意识形态的产物），近来，它又遭到*读者反应批评*、*言语行为理论*、*新历史主义*等倡导者的反对；这后三种批评理论都反对形式主义对普通语言与文学语言之间所作的严格而明确的划分。1980年代，很多批评家呼吁重新回归形式主义批评模式，把文学作品首先当做文学来对待，而非总是针对其不论是明确还是含蓄的政治、种族或性别问题的立场。一个著名的范例是，弗兰克·兰特里夏以"一位批评先辈的最后遗愿和遗嘱"（载于《混合语》1996年9/10月号）声明放弃了自己在先前的著作与学说中关于"文学作为政治工具"的主张，而赞同"文学作为文学而非作为对其他事物的阐述，是令人愉悦而重要的"观点。（参见：*批评*中的*客观批评*。）另可参阅：哈罗德·布卢姆所著的《西方正典》（1994），他在书中主张阅读文学作品不是为了证实一种政治或社会理论，而是出自对文学的热爱；乔治·莱文编著的随笔集《美学和意识形态》（1994）。

临近上个世纪末，形式主义方法找到了一些理论倡导者。这一向形式主义的回归，建立在重新对韵律学（参见：*格律*）和美学感兴趣的基础上，最初主要是计划作为对新历史主义的一种反抗；但经过一些年的发展，后来知名的新形式主义提出了一个积极的计划，决定将文学的形式方面与历史的、政治的、世俗的关注联系到一起，反对形式主义运动早先对其自身的界定。一些新形式主义者认为，一件艺术作品的形式完整，可以保护它抵制*意识形态*、观念化和日常经验的惯例化效应；其他人则强调：对美学或文学形式的认知，是批判思考一个必不可少的条件。（文学批评中的新形式主义，有别于诗歌写作中的新形式主义；参见：*自由诗*。）

新形式主义的第一个主要倡导者是苏珊·J. 沃尔夫森，她著有《形式印章：英国浪漫主义诗歌之塑形》（1997）。沃尔夫森与马歇尔·布朗合编了一本新形式主义文章集《解读形式》（2006）。也可参阅：W. J. T. 米切尔所写的文章"形式的承诺"，载于《美国现代语言学协会会刊》2003年3月第118卷；对新形式主义运动赞赏性的回顾可以参阅：玛乔里·莱文森所写的文章"什么是新形式主义？"载于《美国现代语言学协会会刊》2007年3月第122卷。《表征》在2008年专门就形式问题做了一期专刊。其他条目中提及（文学批评中的）形式主义的地方，参见第52、168、290页。

format of a book：书籍版式　34。

142 FREE VERSE

fourfold meaning: 181.

fourteener: 220.

frame-story: 366.

Frankfurt School: 205.

free indirect discourse: 233; 53.

free verse: Free verse is sometimes referred to as "open form" verse, or by the French term **vers libre**. Like traditional verse, it is printed in short lines instead of in continuous lines of prose, but it differs from such verse by the fact that its rhythmic pattern is not organized into a regular metrical form—that is, into feet, or recurrent units of weak- and strong-stressed syllables. (See *meter*.) Most free verse also has irregular line lengths, and either lacks rhyme or else uses it only sporadically. (*Blank verse* differs from unrhymed free verse in that it is metrically regular.)

Within these broad boundaries, there is a great diversity in the measures that are labeled free verse. An approximation to one modern form occurs in the King James translation of the biblical Psalms and Song of Solomon, which imitates in English prose the parallelism and cadences of Hebrew poetry. In the nineteenth century William Blake, Matthew Arnold, and other poets in England and America experimented with departures from regular meters; and in 1855 Walt Whitman startled the literary world with his *Leaves of Grass* by using verse lines of varying length which depended for rhythmic effects not on recurrent metric feet, but on cadenced units and on the repetition, balance, and variation of words, phrases, clauses, and lines. French *Symbolist* poets in the latter part of the nineteenth century, and American and English poets of the twentieth century, especially after World War I, began the present era of the intensive use of free verse. It has been employed by Rainer Maria Rilke, Jules Laforgue, T. S. Eliot, Ezra Pound, William Carlos Williams, and numberless contemporary poets in all the Western languages. Most of the verse in English that is published today is nonmetrical.

Among the many modes of open versification in English, we can make a broad distinction between the long-lined and often orotund verses of poets like Whitman and Allen Ginsberg, of which a principal origin is the translated poetry of the Hebrew Bible, and the shorter-lined, conversational, often ironic forms employed by the majority of writers in free verse. In the latter type, poets yield up the drive, beat, and song achievable by traditional meters in order to exploit other rhythmic, as well as syntactical possibilities. A poem by e. e. cummings will illustrate the effects that become available when the verse is released from a regular line and reiterative beat. Instead, cummings uses conspicuous visual cues—the variable positioning, spacing, and length of words, phrases, and lines—to control pace, pause, and emphasis in the reading, and also

fourfold meaning：四层含义　181。

fourteener：十四音节诗　220。

frame-story：框形故事　366。

Frankfurt School：法兰克福学派　205。

free indirect discourse：自由式间接话语　233；*53*。

Free Verse：自由诗

　　自由诗有时指"开放形式"的诗行，或为法语中的**自由的诗**。与传统诗歌一样，自由诗按短行的形式书写，而不像散文那样连续起来，但自由诗与传统诗歌的不同之处在于，节奏模式没有形成规律的韵律形式——即音步，或轻重音节单元循环出现。（参见：*格律*。）大多数自由诗的诗行长短不一，除偶有例外，也不讲求押韵。（*无韵诗*不同于不押韵的自由诗，无韵诗的韵律是有规律的。）

　　在这些广义的范围内，用于衡量自由诗的标准多种多样。詹姆斯国王钦定本圣经译文中的《诗篇》和《所罗门之歌》与现代自由诗有相近之处，它们模仿了英语散文的对句法和希伯来诗歌的韵律。19世纪，威廉·布莱克、马修·阿诺德和其他一些英美诗人也做过背离格律诗的创作尝试；1855年，沃尔特·惠特曼在《草叶集》中采用的创作手法曾引起文学界的轰动：其诗行采用长短多变的句式，不依赖音步的重复而借助节奏单元和言词语句和诗行的重复、平行及多变使诗句富于节奏感。19世纪后期法国*象征主义*诗人和20世纪尤其是第一次世界大战后的英美诗人，开创了当代自由诗创作的鼎盛时期。从事自由诗创作的诗人包括赖纳·玛丽亚·里尔克、朱尔斯·拉弗格、T. S. 艾略特、埃兹拉·庞德、威廉·卡洛斯·威廉斯及其他众多用西方语言创作的当代诗人。当今出版的大多数英文诗歌都是非格律诗。

　　在众多的开放式英文诗歌中，我们可以作一广义的区别：既有像惠特曼和艾伦·金斯堡创作的长诗行且遭词往往浮夸的作品，其主要来源是翻译后的希伯来圣经中的诗歌；也有短诗行、口语化、往往富于讽刺意味的作品，这种创作模式为大多数自由诗诗人所采纳。在后一类创作模式中，诗人放弃了传统律诗中的击节、节拍和乐感，以求获得其他韵律及句法效果。下面所引 e. e. 卡明斯的这首诗［指《天真之歌》，版权未授，请参旧版。——译注］可以证明，当诗歌放弃规则诗行和反复节奏的约束后，同样可以取得艺术效果。卡明斯运用明显的视觉暗示：多变的位置、空间，以及词、短语和诗行的长度，来调控阅读过程中的缓急、停顿和重心，

to achieve an alternation of suspension and relief, in accordance as the line endings work against or coincide with the pull toward closure of the units of syntax.

In the following passage from Langston Hughes' free-verse poem "Mother to Son," the second and sixth lines are metrically parallel (in that both fall into fairly regular *iambic pentameter*) in order to enhance their opposition in reference; while the single word "bare," constituting a total verse line, is rhymed with "stair" in the long line to which "bare" contrasts starkly, in meaning as in line-length:

也是为了随着诗行结束与句子单位结束相悖或一致,取得悬停、缓解相应变化的效果。

　　(略)

　　下面一段摘自兰斯顿·休斯的自由诗《母亲对儿子说的一席话》[版权未授,请参旧版。——译注],其中第二行和第六行是押韵的(两行都是规则的*抑扬格五音步诗*行),以此加强彼此间的对比;而自成一行的"光秃秃的"(bare)与长句中的"梯"(stair)押韵,二者在诗行长度和意义上形成了强烈的对比。

　　(略)

A very short poem by A. R. Ammons exemplifies the unobtrusive way in which, even as he departs from them, a free-verse poet can recall and exploit traditional stanza forms and meters:

The visual pattern of the printed poem signals that we are to read it as consisting of four equal lines of three words each, and as divided into two stanzaic *couplets*. The first line of each stanza ends with the same word, "give," not only to achieve tension and release in the suspended syntax of each of the verb phrases, but also, by means of the parallelism, to enhance our surprise at the shift of meaning from "give way" (surrender) to "give . . . away" (reveal, with a suggestion also of yield up). The poet also adapts standard metric feet to his special purposes: the poem is framed by opening and closing with a regular *iambic* foot, yet is free to mimic internally the resistance to the wind in the recurrent strong stresses in the first stanza (The réeds gíve / wáy) and the graceful yielding to the wind in the succession of light iambs in the second stanza (Aňd gíve / thĕ wínd ă wáy).

A number of contemporary poets and critics have called—in a movement sometimes labeled as the **new formalism**—for a return from free verse to the meters, rhyme, and stanza forms of traditional English versification. For discussions see Alan Shapiro, "The New Formalism," *Critical Inquiry*, Vol. 14 (1987); and Dana Gioia, "Notes on the New Formalism," in *Conversant Essays*, ed. James McCorkle (1990). For "new formalism" as applied to a type of literary criticism, see the entry *formalism*.

See Percy Mansell Jones, *The Background of Modern French Poetry* (1951); Donald Wesling, "The Prosodies of Free Verse," in *Twentieth-Century Literature in Retrospect*, ed. Reuben A. Brower (1971); Walter Sutton, *American Free Verse* (1973); Paul Fussell, *Poetic Meter and Poetic Form* (rev. 1979); Charles O. Hartman, *Free Verse: An Essay on Prosody* (1980); H. T. Kirby-Smith, *The Origins of Free Verse* (1996). Timothy Steele's *Missing Measures: Modern Poetry*

A. R. 阿蒙斯这首非常短小的诗 [指《小曲》，版权未授，请参旧版。——译注] 以谨慎的行文，说明了即使自由体诗人背离了传统的诗节形式和韵律，仍能记取并运用传统的诗节形式和韵律。

（略）

这首诗打印后的视觉模式显示，我们将要阅读的是一首每行有三个单词的四行诗，分成两组*对句*诗节。每节的第一行都以同一单词"give"结尾，这样不仅可以在每一个动词词组悬停的句法中造成张力并予以化解，而且通过平行对句，强化了我们对其意义由"give way"（让步、屈服）转换为"give…away"（暴露，也含让步之意）后引起的诧异之情。诗人为了表达特殊意义，也采用了标准的韵脚：诗行在开头和结尾都采用规则的*抑扬格*音步，但在第一节，仍然自由地以重复出现的重音（The réeds gíve / wáy）在诗行中模拟对风的抗拒，在第二节中，又以连续出现的轻抑扬格（Aňd gíve / thě wínd ǎ wáy）模拟对风作出幽雅的让步。

许多当代诗人和批评家都在有时被称为**新形式主义**的运动中，号召从自由诗回归传统英国诗歌的韵律、押韵和诗节形式。相关论述参阅：艾伦·夏皮罗所写的文章"新形式主义"，载于《批评探索》1987 年第 14 卷；达纳·吉奥亚所写的文章"关于新形式主义的注解"，收入詹姆斯·麦克科尔主编的《熟悉的论文集》（1990）。关于"新形式主义"用来指一种文学批评类型，参见条目：*形式主义*。

参阅：珀西·曼塞尔·琼斯所著的《现代法国诗歌的背景》（1951）；唐纳德·韦斯林所写的文章"自由诗的韵律学"，收入鲁本·A. 布劳尔主编的《20 世纪文学回顾》（1971）；沃尔特·萨顿所著的《美国自由诗》（1973）；保罗·富塞尔所著的《诗律与诗歌的形式》（1979 年修订版）；查尔斯·O. 哈特曼所著的《自由诗：一篇关于韵律的论文》（1980）；H. T. 柯比－史密斯所著的《自由诗的起源》（1996）。蒂莫西·斯蒂尔所著的《缺失的韵律：现代诗歌和对格律的反叛》（1990）

and the Revolt against Meter (1990) is a history of free verse by a writer who argues for a return to metrical versification. For references to *free verse* in other entries, see pages *223, 319*.

freestyling: 271.

Freudian criticism: See *psychological and psychoanalytic criticism*.

Freytag's Pyramid: 296.

是一部自由诗史，作者认为应该回归诗律。其他条目中提及"自由诗"的地方，参见第 223、319 页。

freestyling：自由式　271。

Freudian criticism：弗洛伊德批评　　参见：*心理学与精神分析批评*。

Freytag's Pyramid：弗雷泰戈金字塔　296。

G

gangsta rap: 272.

gay studies: 327; *146*.

gender: 122.

gender criticism: Gender criticism, like the **gender studies** of which it is a part, is based on the premise that, while sex (a person's identification as male or female) is determined by anatomy, gender (masculinity or femininity in personality traits and behavior) can be largely independent of anatomy, and is a *social construction* that is diverse, variable, and dependent on historical circumstances. Gender criticism analyzes differing conceptions of gender and their role in the writing, reception, subject matter, and evaluation of literary works.

Gender studies have an obvious (and sometimes contentious) overlap with *feminist criticism, gay studies,* and *lesbian studies*; the distinguishing attribute of gender studies has come to be their special attention to the roles of males, and of varying conceptions of masculinity, in the course of social, political, and artistic history. A field of scholarship known as **men's studies** was established early in the 1980s on the model of the preexisting field of *women's studies*. Proponents of men's studies did not contest the overall fact of *patriarchy*—male privilege and domination over women throughout the social history of the West—but undertook to complicate and subtilize the opposition of oppressors and victims by stressing the variety of male roles, or "masculinities," the internal stresses within each concept of masculinity, and the degree to which patriarchal dominance tended to distort the characters of men as well as women. Early on, a number of feminist scholars decried men's studies as in fact complicit with the patriarchy they ostensibly opposed, and as reinforcing the predominant place of the male in scholarship and the college curriculum. In the course of time, however, tensions have lessened, while a number of courses in women's studies have broadened their scope so as to become, in effect, gender studies. (See Harry Brod, ed., *The Making of Masculinities: The New Men's Studies,* 1987; Alice Jardine and Paul Smith, eds., *Men in Feminism,* 1987; Judith Kegan Gardiner, ed., *Masculinity Studies and Feminist Theory: New Directions,* 2002.)

Gender studies are indebted to the social historian Michel Foucault, who analyzed all sexual identities, whether perceived to be normal or transgressive, as constructed and reconstructed in various eras of social discourses under the impulse of the power-drive and power-competition. In addition, two feminist scholars wrote books that not only were important for gay/lesbian as well as feminist studies, but also helped to give impetus and shape to men's studies and to the analysis of the nature and plurality of masculinities. In 1985 Eve Kosofsky Sedgwick published *Between Men: English Literature and Male*

gangsta rap：匪帮说唱　272。

gay studies：男性同性恋研究　327；*146*。

gender：性别　122。

Gender Criticism：性别批评

　　性别批评，就像它是其中一部分的**性别研究**，也是基于一个前提：性（一个人是男是女的身份）由解剖学确定，性别（个人特质和行为上的男子气概或女性气质）则在很大程度上独立于解剖学，是一种*社会建构*，这种社会建构是多样的、可变的，取决于历史背景。性别批评分析不同的性别概念，和它们在文学作品的写作、接受、题材、评价中所起的作用。

　　性别研究与*女性主义批评*、*男性同性恋研究*、*女性同性恋研究*有一个明显的（有时则是有争议的）重叠；性别研究的本质属性是，它们特别关注社会、政治、艺术历史进程中男性的角色、不同的男性概念的角色。其中一个领域，称为**男性研究**，确立于1980年代早期，以原有的*女性研究*为典范。男性研究的支持者们对*父权制*——在整个西方社会历史进程中与女性相比男性享有特权和主导地位——这一整体事实并没有异议，但是尝试使压迫者和受害者这一对立变得复杂化和精细化，通过强调男性角色或"男子气概"的多样性，强调每一种"男子气概"定义的内部压力，强调父权制主导的程度倾向于既扭曲女性的人格也扭曲男性的人格。在早期，一些女性主义学者谴责男性研究事实上与它们表面上反对的父权制是同谋，并强化了男性在学术界和高校里所占据的主导地位。不过，后来，紧张局面有所缓解，一些女性研究课程，扩大其范围，使之成为事实上的性别研究。[参阅：哈利·布罗德主编的《男子气概的形成：新男性研究》（1987）；艾利斯·贾丁与保罗·史密斯合编的《女性主义视角下的男性》（1987）；朱迪斯·基根·加德纳主编的《男性研究和女性主义理论：新的方向》（2002）。]

　　性别研究要感谢社会历史学家米歇尔·福柯，福柯分析了所有的性别身份，不管是被视为正常的还是违规的，认为它们是权力驱动和权力竞争的动机下不同时代的社会话语的建构和重构。此外，还有两位女性主义学者著书立说，她们的著作不仅对男性同性恋/女性同性恋和女性主义研究很重要，而且也有助于推动和形塑男性研究，及对男子气概的性质和多元化的分析。1985年，伊芙·科索夫斯基·塞奇威克出版了《男人之间：英国文学与男性同性社会性欲望》，

Homosocial Desire, which proposed that there is a large "homosocial spectrum" of male-to-male bondings, ranging from fierce rivalry through a variety of relationships within families, friendships, and all-male societies and organizations, to patently erotic desires and intimacies; she also held that these relationships were crossed, concealed, or distorted by a pervasive homophobia—the fear that one's bondings to other men, whatever its type, should appear to be homosexual, to oneself as well as to other people. In 1990 Judith Butler published *Gender Trouble: Feminism and the Subversion of Identity*. In it she argued that gender is not an innate or essential identity, but a contingent and variable construct that mandates a "performance"—that is, a particular set of practices which an individual acquires from the discourse of his or her social era and strives to enact. (Refer to the comments on Foucault, Sedgwick, and Butler in the entries *feminist criticism* and *queer theory*.)

The predominant emphasis on same-sex desires and on intersexual and intrasexual rivalries in forming masculine and other gender categories has been countered by a number of scholars who insist on the importance of such nonsexual factors as race, ethnicity, economic arrangements, and social class in establishing different types and ideals of manhood. David Leverenz, for example, in *Manhood and the American Renaissance* (1989), attributes the chief influence in fashioning American "ideologies of manhood" to altering economic conditions and class structures. Leverenz stresses the primacy, from the mid-nineteenth century into the present, of the economic era of competitive individualism in establishing middle-class norms of manhood that are based on male rivalry in the working arena, and points out the pervasive effect of the struggle for dominance and status, not of men against women, but of men against other men. James Eli Adams' *Dandies and Desert Saints: Styles of Victorian Masculinity* (1995) analyzes the multiplicity, the multiple determinants, the surprising interrelationships, and the internal strains and instabilities of diverse Victorian masculinities and ideals of "manliness." He identifies shared interests that were dependent on social class, occupation, political allegiance, and religious beliefs, as well as same-sex desires and object-choices, which bonded Victorian men into a diversity of tight-knit groups and sometimes secret communities, and describes the mixed feelings of suspicion, fear, and allure exerted on outsiders by such closed male fellowships, including those that did not have a homosexual component.

Scholars of gender, and particularly of masculinities, focus on eras when rapid changes in social conditions have produced conspicuous strains and alterations in gender-norms. The Victorian period has been a favorite one for these investigations. Another is the present era, in which the vogue of gender studies has itself served to make even more uncertain, precarious, and mutable the gender roles that such studies subject to analytic scrutiny.

Gender studies are interdisciplinary, and are conducted by sociologists, cultural anthropologists, and social historians, as well as by scholars of literature and cinema. The following books indicate the range of these studies: Joseph H. Pleck, *The Myth of Masculinity* (1981); Carroll Smith-Rosenberg, *Disorderly Conduct: Visions of Gender in Victorian America* (1985); Peter G.

书中提出，有一个关于男人间纽带的很大的"同性社会性光谱"，其范围从激烈的角逐，经过家庭、友谊、全是男性的社团和组织等各种关系，直到显然是色情欲望和亲密行为；她也认为，这些关系可以被跨越、掩盖或扭曲，通过一种无处不在的同性恋恐惧症——害怕一个男人与其他男人之间的纽带，无论是什么类型，会在自己和别人眼里看上去显得是同性恋。1990年，朱迪斯·巴特勒出版了《性别麻烦：女性主义与身份的颠覆》。在书中她认为，社会性别并不是一个天生的或基本的身份，而是一个有条件的和可变的结构，规定了"表演"——也就是说，个体从他或她的社会时代的话语中获取并努力践行的一套特定做法。（参见：*女性主义批评*、*同性恋理论*中对福柯、塞奇威克和巴特勒的评述。）

突出强调对同性的欲望和性内及两性间的对抗在形成男性气质和其他性别分类中的作用，一直遭到一些学者的反驳，这些学者坚持强调与性别无关的因素，如种族、民族、经济安排和社会阶层，在建立不同类型和理想的男子汉气概上的重要性。例如，戴维·莱弗伦兹在《男子汉气概与美国文艺复兴》(1989) 中，将塑造美国"男子汉气概的意识形态"的主要影响归因于改变的经济状况和阶级结构。莱弗伦兹强调了，从19世纪中叶到现在，经济时代的竞争性个人主义在确立中产阶级男子汉气概的规范上所处的首要地位，这一规范基于工作舞台上的男性竞争，并指出了争夺主导权和地位（不是男人与女人争夺，而是男人与其他男人争夺）的深远影响。詹姆斯·伊莱·亚当斯的《花花公子和沙漠圣徒：维多利亚时代男性气质的风格》(1995)，分析了维多利亚时代不同的男性气质和理想的"男子气概"的多样性、多重决定因素、令人惊讶的相互关系，以及内部压力和不稳定性。他确认了依赖于社会阶层、职业、政治忠诚和宗教信仰，以及同性欲望和对象选择的共同利益，它们将维多利亚时期的男性结合成一个具有多样性的紧密群体，有时则是秘密会社，描述了这种封闭的男性团体（包括那些没有同性恋成分的）在外人眼里所产生的猜疑、恐惧和诱惑力这些混杂在一起的情感。

研究社会性别，尤其是男性气质的学者，专注于快速变化的社会条件已对性别规范产生了明显的张力和改变的时代。维多利亚时代一直是这些研究最喜欢的时代。另一个则是当今时代，在当今时代，性别研究的潮流使其自身足以让这些研究分析审查的性别角色变得更加不确定、不稳定和易变。

性别研究是一个跨学科领域，社会学家、文化人类学家、社会历史学家，以及文学和电影领域的学者都有人在从事这方面的研究。下列书籍表明了这些研究的范围：约瑟夫·H. 普莱克所著的《男子气概/男性气质的迷思》(1981)；卡罗尔·史密斯－罗森伯格所著的《失调行为：维多利亚时代美国社会性别视界》(1985)；

Filene, *Him/Her/Self: Sex Roles in Modern America* (rev. 1986); Teresa de Lauretis, *Technologies of Gender: Essays on Theory, Film, and Fiction* (1987); Mary Poovey, *Uneven Developments: The Ideological Work of Gender in Mid-Victorian England* (1988); Rita Felski, *The Gender of Modernity* (1995). Consult also the essays collected in Joseph A. Boone and Michael Cadden, eds., *Engendering Men: The Question of Male Feminist Criticism* (1990); Michael Roper and James Tosh, eds., *Manful Assertions: Masculinities in Britain since 1800* (1991); David Glover and Cora Kaplan, eds., *Genders* (2000); Rachel Adams and David Savran, eds., *The Masculinity Studies Reader* (2002). See also Eve Kosofsky Sedgwick, "Gender Criticism: What Isn't Gender," in Stephen Greenblatt and Giles Gunn, eds., *Redrawing the Boundaries: The Transformation of English and American Literary Studies* (1992).

gender studies: 146.

generative linguistics: 198.

Geneva School (of criticism): **290**.

genres: A term, French in origin, that denotes types or classes of *literature*. The genres into which literary works have been grouped at different times are very numerous, and the criteria on which the classifications have been based are highly variable. Since the writings of Plato and Aristotle, however, there has been an enduring division of the overall literary domain into three large classes, in accordance with who speaks in the work: *lyric* (uttered throughout in the first person), *epic* or *narrative* (in which the narrator speaks in the first person, then lets the characters speak for themselves); and *drama* (in which the characters do all the talking). A similar tripartite scheme, elaborated by German critics in the late eighteenth and early nineteenth centuries, was echoed by James Joyce in his *Portrait of the Artist as a Young Man* (1916), chapter 5, and functions still in critical discourse and in the general distinction, in college catalogues, between courses in poetry, prose fiction, and drama.

Within this overarching division, Aristotle and other classical critics identified a number of more specific genres. Many of the ancient names, including *epic, tragedy, comedy,* and *satire,* have remained current to the present day; to them have been added, over the last three centuries, such relative newcomers as *biography, essay,* and *novel*. A glance at the genres in prose and verse listed at the end of this entry will indicate the crisscrossing diversity of the classes and subclasses to which individual works of literature have been assigned.

Through the Renaissance and much of the eighteenth century, the recognized genres—or poetic **kinds** as they were then called—were widely thought to be fixed literary types, somewhat like species in the biological order of nature. Many *neoclassic* critics insisted that each kind must remain "pure" (there must, for example, be no "mixing" of tragedy and comedy), and also proposed *rules* which specified the subject matter, structure, style, and emotional effect proper to each kind. At that time the genres were also commonly ranked in a hierarchy (related to the ranking of social classes, from royalty and the nobility

彼得·G. 法林所著的《他/她/自我：现代美国的性别角色》（1986年修订版）；特蕾莎·德·劳拉提斯所著的《社会性别机制：理论、电影与小说论文集》（1987）；玛丽·普维所著的《非均衡发展：维多利亚中期英国的性别意识形态工作》（1988）；丽塔·费尔斯基所著的《现代性的性别》（1995）。也可参阅文章合集：约瑟夫·A. 布恩与迈克尔·卡登合编的《形成中的男人：男性女性主义批评问题》（1990）；迈克尔·罗珀与詹姆斯·托什合编的《男子气主张：1800年以来英国的男性气质》（1991）；戴维·格洛弗与科拉·卡普兰合编的《性别》（2000）；雷切尔·亚当斯与戴维·萨福兰合编的《男性气质研究读本》（2002）。也可参阅伊芙·科索夫斯基·塞奇威克所写的文章"性别批评：什么不是性别"，收入斯蒂芬·格林布拉特与贾尔斯·冈恩合编的《重划疆界：英美文学研究的变革》（1992）。

gender studies：性别研究　146。

generative linguistics：生成语言学　198。

Geneva School (of criticism)：（批评中的）日内瓦学派　290。

Genres：文学类型

　　术语文学类型源自法语，指*文学*作品的类型、种类。不同时期的文学作品被划分为许多类型，划分标准也是五花八门。但自柏拉图和亚里士多德的著述问世以来，出现了一种持久的划分方法，即根据作品中的叙述者，把所有文学作品划分为三大类型：*抒情诗*（全部由第一人称叙述）；*史诗*或*叙事作品*（其中叙述者采用第一人称，同时让作品中的人物自述）；*戏剧*（全部由剧中人物叙述）。18世纪末与19世纪初，德国文艺批评家阐释了一种与上述分类法类似的三分法，詹姆斯·乔伊斯在《一个青年艺术家的画像》（1916）第5章中也响应了这种分类法，并且一直在文学批评话语和普通分类法中，以及大学课程中对诗歌、小说、戏剧类型的划分中得到沿用。

　　亚里士多德和其他古典批评家在这一包罗万象的划分中，又划分出许多更加具体的文学类型。其中许多类型的旧称一直沿用至今，如*史诗*、*悲剧*、*喜剧*、*讽刺*；过去三个世纪又增添了一些新的类型，如*传记*、*杂文*、*小说*。浏览一下本条目最后附注的其他条目，就会看到文学类型划分交叉的多层次，以及单个文学作品又被划分为众多的亚类。

　　从文艺复兴到18世纪的大部分时间里，人们把公认的文学类型——当时称作诗歌**种类**——普遍视为业已定型的文学类型，就像自然界生物圈中的物种一样。许多*新古典主义*批评家坚持主张每一文学类型必须保持自身的"纯正"（例如悲剧和喜剧切不可"混杂"），同时还为每一文学类型提出了限定其题材、结构、风格及其情感感染力的适当的*规则*。当时所有文学类型还常被分成不同的等级（与当时的社会阶层相关，上起皇家贵族，下至农夫；参见：*仪轨*），

down to peasants—see *decorum*), ranging from epic and tragedy at the top to the pastoral, short lyric, epigram, and other types—then considered to be minor genres—at the bottom. Shakespeare satirized the pedantic classifiers of his era in Polonius' catalogue (*Hamlet*, II. ii.) of types of drama: "tragedy, comedy, history, pastoral, pastoral-comical, historical-pastoral, tragical-historical, tragical-comical-historical-pastoral...."

In the course of the eighteenth century the emergence of new types of literary productions—such as the novel, and the poem combining nature description, philosophy, and narrative (James Thomson's *Seasons*, 1726–30)—helped weaken confidence in the fixity and stability of literary genres. And in the late eighteenth and early nineteenth century, the extraordinary rise in the prominence and prestige of the short lyric poem, and the concurrent shift in the basis of critical theory to an *expressive* orientation (see the entry *criticism*), effected a drastic alteration in both the conception and ranking of literary genres, with the lyric displacing epic and tragedy as the quintessentially poetic type. From the *Romantic Period* on, a decreasing emphasis on the generic conception of literature was indicated by the widespread use of criteria for evaluating literature which—unlike the criteria in *neoclassic* criticism, which tended to be specific to a particular genre—were broadly applicable to all literary works: criteria such as "sincerity," "intensity," "organic unity," and "high seriousness." In the *New Criticism* of the mid-twentieth century, with its ruling concept of the uniqueness of each literary work, genre ceased to play more than a subordinate role in critical analysis and evaluation. For the changes in the nineteenth century in the classification and ranking of the genres, see M. H. Abrams, *The Mirror and the Lamp* (1953), especially chapters 1, 4, and 6; on the continuance, as well as changes, of writings in the traditional genres during the Romantic Period, see Stuart Curran, *Poetic Form and British Romanticism* (1986).

After 1950 or so, an emphasis on generic types was revived by some critical theorists, although on varied principles of classification. R. S. Crane and other Chicago critics have defended the utility for practical criticism of a redefined distinction among genres, based on Aristotle's *Poetics*, in which works are classified in accordance with the similarity in the principles by which they are organized in order to achieve a particular kind of emotional effect; see R. S. Crane, ed., *Critics and Criticism* (1952), pp. 12–24, 546–63, and refer to the *Chicago school* in this *Glossary*. Northrop Frye has proposed an *archetypal* theory in which the four major genres (comedy, romance, tragedy, and satire) are held to manifest the enduring forms bodied forth by the human imagination, as represented in the archetypal myths correlated with the four seasons (*Anatomy of Criticism*, 1957, pp. 158–239). Other current theorists conceive genres as social formations on the model of social institutions, such as the state or church, rather than on the model of biological species. By *structuralist critics* a genre is conceived as a set of constitutive conventions and codes, altering from age to age, but shared by a kind of implicit contract between writer and reader. These codes make possible the writing of a particular literary text, although the writer may play against, as well as

这种等级序列是从上等的史诗、悲剧至下等的田园诗、抒情短诗、讽刺诗和其他类型。莎士比亚通过波洛尼厄斯的剧类目录(《哈姆雷特》第二幕第二场):"悲剧、喜剧、历史剧、田园剧、田园喜剧、田园史剧、历史悲剧、历史田园悲喜剧……"嘲讽了当时那些迂腐的文学类型分析理论家。

18世纪期间,文学创作中出现了一些新的类型,如小说和把自然描写、哲理、叙事融为一体的诗歌[如詹姆斯·汤姆逊的《四季》(1726—1730)],动摇了以往文学类型一成不变的分类标准。18世纪后期及19世纪初期,抒情短诗异军突起、声名大振,同时文艺批评理论开始向*表现主义*方向转化(参见:*批评*),这些因素引起了文学类型概念和文学类型划分的巨大变化,抒情诗取代史诗和悲剧成为诗歌类的精粹。自浪漫主义时期以来,评价文学作品标准的广泛运用,预示着文学类属概念地位的下降。与趋向于局限在某一具体文学类型的*新古典主义*批评标准不同,浪漫主义时期以来的批评标准广泛应用于所有的文学作品;如"真实性""思想感情的强度""有机整体性""高度严肃性"等标准。20世纪中期*新批评*的主导概念是每一部文学作品都具有独特性,文学类型在批评分析和评价作品中只起次要作用。关于19世纪文学类型划分和等级划分的演变,参阅M. H. 艾布拉姆斯所著的《镜与灯》(1953),尤其是书中第1、4、6章;关于浪漫主义时期传统文学类型写作的延续及其演变,参阅:斯图尔特·柯伦所著的《诗歌形式与英国浪漫主义》(1986)。

1950年代前后以来,在一些批评理论家的推动下,尽管划分原则不尽相同,但文学类型理论再次盛行起来。亚里士多德的《诗学》根据作品为取得一种特殊的情感效果,在组织作品时所依循的原则的相似性来划分作品,R. S. 克莱恩和其他芝加哥学派批评家以此为基础,极力主张对文学类型的区分的重新界定应对批评实践具有实用性。参阅R. S. 克莱恩主编的《批评家与批评》(1952)第12—24、546—563页,并参见本书中的条目*芝加哥学派*。诺斯罗普·弗莱提出了一种原型理论,认为四种主要文学类型(喜剧、传奇、悲剧、讽刺作品)代表了人类想象力所体现的永恒形式,这种永恒体现在与四季有关的原型神话中[《批评的剖析》(1957)第158—239页]。其他当代文艺理论家则把文学类型视为以国家或教会等社会机构为模式,而不是以生物种类为模式的社会构成。在*结构主义批评*家看来,每一文学类型都是一套基本的惯例和代码,它们随着时代而变化,但又通过作家与读者之间的默契而被双方接受。尽管作者可能违背或是遵守那些主要的文学类型惯例,但这些代码总是使得某一特殊的文学文本的写作成为可能。

with, the prevailing generic conventions. In the reader, these conventions generate a set of expectations, which may be controverted rather than satisfied, but enable the reader to make the work intelligible—that is, to *naturalize* it, by relating it to the world as defined and ordered by codes in the prevailing culture.

Many current critics regard genres as more or less arbitrary modes of classification, whose justification is their convenience in discussing literature. Some critics have applied to generic classes the philosopher Ludwig Wittgenstein's concept of **family resemblances**. That is, they propose that, in the loosely grouped family of works that make up a genre, there are no essential defining features, but only a set of family resemblances; each member shares some of these resemblances with some, but not all, of the other members of the genre. (For a description and discussion of Wittgenstein's view, see Maurice Mandelbaum, "Family Resemblances and Generalization Concerning the Arts," *American Philosophical Quarterly*, Vol. 2 [1965], pp. 219–28, and Carlo Ginzburg, "Family Resemblances and Family Trees: Two Cognitive Metaphors," *Critical Inquiry*, Vol. 30 [2004], pp. 537–56.) There has also been interest in the role that generic assumptions have played in shaping the work that an author composes, as well as in establishing expectations that alter the way that a reader will interpret and respond to a particular work. Whatever the present skepticism, however, about the old belief that genres constitute inherent species in the realm of literature, the fact that generic distinctions remain indispensable in literary discourse is attested by the unceasing publication of books whose titles announce that they deal with tragedy, the lyric, pastoral, the novel, or another of the many types and subtypes into which literature has over the centuries been classified.

Reviews of traditional theories of genre are René Wellek and Austin Warren, *Theory of Literature* (3d ed., 1973), chapter 17, and the readable short survey by Heather Dubrow, *Genre* (1982). For more recent developments see Paul Hernadi, *Beyond Genre: New Directions in Literary Classification* (1972); Alastair Fowler, *Kinds of Literature: An Introduction to the Theory of Genres and Modes* (1982); Adena Rosmarin, *The Power of Genre* (1985); and David Duff, ed., *Modern Genre Theory* (2000). For a Marxist approach, see Fredric Jameson, "Magical Narratives: On the Dialectical Use of Genre Criticism," chapter 2 of *The Political Unconscious: Narrative as a Socially Symbolic Act* (1981); for a deconstructive approach, see Jacques Derrida, "The Law of Genre," *Critical Inquiry* (Autumn 1980; reprinted in W. J. T. Mitchell, ed., *On Narrative*, 1981); and for an approach indebted to discourse analysis, see John Frow, *Genre* (2006). See the special issue of *PMLA*, Vol. 122:5 (October 2007) on "Remapping Genre."

For references to *genre* in other entries, see pages 17, 27, 37, 45, 96. For prose genres, see *autobiography; biography; the character; drama; essay; exemplum; fable; fantastic literature; nature writing; novel; parable; satire; short story*. For verse genres, see *ballad; chivalric romance; drama; emblem poem; epic; epigram; fable; fabliau; georgic; lai; light verse; lyric; occasional poem; pastoral; rap; satire.*

对读者来说，这些惯例可以使其产生一些期望，这些期望可能是有争议的，不能如愿以偿，但却有助于读者理解作品——即通过把作品与用主流文化中的代码界定和设置的世界相联系，从而使作品*归化*。

当代许多批评家对文学类型划分的模式显得多少有些任意，他们的分类只为谈论文学之便。有些批评家把哲学家路德维希·维特根斯坦提出的**家族类似**概念应用到文学作品的分类中。即：他们提出，在大致划分的构成文学类型的作品族类中，不存在根本的区分特征，只有一些族类的相似之处；同一文学类型中的每一部作品与其他作品并非完全相似，只是部分相似。（关于对维特根斯坦的观点的描述与论述，可以参阅莫里斯·曼德尔鲍姆所写的文章"关于艺术的家族相似性和概化"，载于《美国哲学期刊》1965年第2卷第219—228页；卡洛·金兹伯格所写的文章"家族相似性与家族树：两个认知隐喻"，载于《批评探索》2004年第30卷第537—556页。）文学类型的设想在形成作者所创作的作品中所起的作用，以及在建立使读者改变对某一特定作品的解读和反应方式的期望中所起的作用，使一些批评家也对此产生了兴趣。然而，不论目前对旧有的那种认为在文学领域中文学类型形成固有的类别这一主张持何种怀疑态度，以论述悲剧、抒情诗、田园诗、小说为书名，或者以论述数世纪以来文学作品划分成许多类别及次类别中的任何其他一类别为书名的著作的不断出版，都证明了这样一个事实，即文学类型的区分仍是文学话语中不可或缺的。

对传统文学类型理论的评述，参阅：勒内·韦勒克与奥斯汀·沃伦合著的《文学理论》（1973年第3版）第17章及希瑟·杜布罗所写的简明易懂的短篇概论《文类》（1982）。关于文学类型的近期发展概况，参阅：保罗·赫纳迪所著的《超越文类：文学分类的新方向》（1972）；阿拉斯泰尔·福勒所著的《文学的类型：文类和模式理论简介》（1982）；阿登纳·罗斯马林所著的《文类的力量》（1985）；戴维·达夫主编的《现代文类理论》（2000）。关于马克思主义批评方法，参阅：弗雷德里克·詹姆逊所著的《政治无意识：作为一种社会象征行为的叙事》第2章"魔幻叙述：关于文类批评的辩证运用"（1981）；关于解构主义批评方法，参阅：雅克·德里达所写的文章"文类的法则"，载于《批评探索》1980年秋季卷，重印收入W. J. T. 米切尔主编的《论叙事》（1981）；关于话语分析方法，参阅：约翰·弗劳所著的《文类》（2006）。参阅专题研究：《美国现代语言学协会会刊》2007年10月第122卷第5期"重新定位文类"。

其他条目中提及"文类"的地方，参见第17、27、37、45、96页。关于散文文学类型，参见：*自传、传记、人物素描、戏剧、杂文、劝谕性故事、寓言、怪诞文学、自然写作、小说、寓言、讽刺、短篇小说*。关于诗歌类型，参见：*民谣、骑士传奇、戏剧、寓意诗、史诗、警句、寓言、寓言诗、农事篇、籁歌、轻松诗、抒情诗、应景诗、牧歌、说唱乐、讽刺*。

Georgian period: 284.

Georgian poets: 284.

georgic (jōr′ jik): 88.

golden age: The term derives from the *chronological primitivism* that was propounded in the Greek poet Hesiod's *Works and Days* (eighth century BC), as well as by many later Greek and Roman writers. The earliest period of human history, regarded as a state of perfect felicity, was called "the golden age," and the continuous decline of human well-being through time was expressed by the sequence "the silver age" and "the bronze age," ending with the present sad condition of humanity, "the iron age." See *primitivism and progress* and, for renderings of the golden age in the guise of a carefree rural existence, *pastoral*. Refer to Harry Levin, *The Myth of the Golden Age in the Renaissance* (1969).

Gothic novel: The word **Gothic** originally referred to the Goths, an early Germanic tribe, then came to signify "germanic," then "medieval." "Gothic architecture" now denotes the medieval form of architecture, characterized by the use of the high pointed arch and vault, flying buttresses, and intricate recesses, which spread through western Europe between the twelfth and sixteenth centuries.

The Gothic novel, or in an alternative term, **Gothic romance**, is a type of prose fiction which was inaugurated by Horace Walpole's *The Castle of Otranto: A Gothic Story* (1764)—the subtitle denotes its setting in the Middle Ages—and flourished through the early nineteenth century. Some writers followed Walpole's example by setting their stories in the medieval period; others set them in a Catholic country, especially Italy or Spain. The locale was often a gloomy castle furnished with dungeons, subterranean passages, and sliding panels; the typical story focused on the sufferings imposed on an innocent heroine by a cruel and lustful villain, and made bountiful use of ghosts, mysterious disappearances, and other sensational and supernatural occurrences (which in a number of novels turned out to have natural explanations). The principal aim of such novels was to evoke chilling terror by exploiting mystery and a variety of horrors. Many of them are now read mainly as period pieces, but the best opened up to fiction the realm of the irrational and of the perverse impulses and nightmarish terrors that lie beneath the orderly surface of the civilized mind. Examples of Gothic novels are William Beckford's *Vathek* (1786)—the setting of which is both medieval and Oriental and the subject both erotic and sadistic—Ann Radcliffe's *The Mysteries of Udolpho* (1794) and other highly successful romances, and Matthew Gregory Lewis' *The Monk* (1796), which exploited, with considerable literary skill, the shock effects of a narrative involving rape, incest, murder, and diabolism. Jane Austen made good-humored fun of the more decorous instances of the Gothic vogue in *Northanger Abbey* (written 1798, published 1818).

Georgian period：乔治时期　284。

Georgian poets：乔治时期的诗人　284。

georgic：农事篇　88。

Golden Age：黄金时代

　　该术语源自希腊诗人赫西俄德在《工作与时日》（公元前8世纪）中提出的*年代尚古主义*，对此许多后世的希腊和罗马作家也予以响应。人类历史的远古时期被认为是完美幸福的阶段，故称为"黄金时代"，后来随着时间推移，人类的幸福越来越今不如昔，因而依次称为"白银时代"和"青铜时代"，直至目前人性处于悲惨境地的"黑铁时代"。参见：*尚古主义与进步论*，以及用无忧无虑的乡村生活来描写黄金时代的*田园诗*。参阅：哈里·莱文所著的《文艺复兴时期黄金时代的神话》（1969）。

Gothic Novel：哥特小说

　　哥特一词原指早期日耳曼的哥特部族，后被用于指代"日耳曼"以至"中世纪"。现今所谓的"哥特式建筑"指的是一种中世纪的建筑类型，它以尖拱、穹窿、飞檐和精致的凹壁为造型特征，流行于12—16世纪的西欧。

　　哥特小说或称**哥特式传奇**是霍勒斯·沃波尔以《奥特朗托堡：一个哥特故事》（1764）所开创的一种小说类型（副标题指的是其中世纪的社会背景），盛行于19世纪初期。一些小说家模仿沃波尔，以中世纪为故事背景；有些作家则以天主教国家（尤其是意大利和西班牙）为故事背景。故事场景往往是布满地牢暗道和滑板机关的幽暗城堡；典型的哥特式故事描写的是纯洁的女主人公遭受残忍而淫荡的恶棍的折磨，并且大量运用鬼魂幽灵、神出鬼没和其他恐怖离奇的情节（在许多小说中，作者以自然法则解释这些超自然现象）。这类小说的主要目的是通过描写神秘和各种恐怖现象而渲染一种阴森恐惧的气氛。如今，大多数哥特小说主要作为表现中世纪的作品而为读者所欣赏，它们当中的佳作则为小说创作开创了一个潜藏在文明理性表层下的充满非理性、反常意识冲动和梦魇般恐惧的世界。哥特小说的代表作有威廉·贝克福德的《瓦提克》（1786）——作品以中世纪和东方为背景，表现了色情淫虐的主题；安·拉德克利夫的《尤道弗之谜》（1794）和其他一些杰出的哥特式传奇故事；以及马修·格雷格里·刘易斯的《僧人》（1796），其中运用高超的文学技巧，描述了集奸淫、乱伦、凶杀、妖术于一体的故事情节，取得了令人震惊的叙事效果。简·奥斯丁在《诺桑觉寺》（写于1798年，发表于1818年）中，以诙谐风趣的手法讥笑了风行一时的哥特小说中高雅端庄的举止行为。

The term "Gothic" has also been extended to a type of fiction which lacks the exotic setting of the earlier romances, but develops a brooding *atmosphere* of gloom and terror, represents events that are uncanny or macabre or melodramatically violent, and often deals with aberrant psychological states. In this extended sense the term "Gothic" has been applied to William Godwin's *Caleb Williams* (1794), Mary Shelley's remarkable and influential *Frankenstein* (1818), and the novels and tales of terror by the German E. T. A. Hoffmann. Still more loosely, "Gothic" has been used to describe elements of the macabre and terrifying that are included in such later works as Emily Brontë's *Wuthering Heights*, Charlotte Brontë's *Jane Eyre*, Charles Dickens' *Bleak House* (for example, chapters 11, 16, and 47) and *Great Expectations* (the Miss Havisham episodes). Critics have recently drawn attention to the many women writers of Gothic fiction, and have explained features of the mode as the result of the suppression of female sexuality, or else as a challenge to the gender hierarchy and values of a male-dominated culture. See *feminist criticism* and refer to Sandra Gilbert and Susan Gubar, *The Madwoman in the Attic* (1979), and Juliann E. Fleenor, ed., *The Female Gothic* (1983).

America, especially the American South, has been fertile in Gothic fiction in the extended sense, from the novels of Charles Brockden Brown (1771–1810) and the terror tales of Edgar Allan Poe to William Faulkner's *Sanctuary* and *Absalom, Absalom!* and some of the fiction of Truman Capote. The nightmarish realm of uncanny terror, violence, and cruelty opened by the Gothic novel continued to be explored in novels such as Daphne du Maurier's popular *Rebecca* (1938) and Iris Murdoch's *The Unicorn*; it is also exploited by authors of horror fiction such as H. P. Lovecraft and Stephen King, and by the writers and directors of innumerable horror movies.

See G. R. Thompson, ed., *The Gothic Imagination: Essays in Dark Romanticism* (1974); William Patrick Day, *In the Circles of Fear and Desire* (1985); David Punter, *The Literature of Terror: A History of Gothic Fiction from 1765 to the Present* (1979; 2d ed., 1996); Eugenia DeLamotte, *Perils of the Night* (1990); Anne Williams, *Art of Darkness* (1995); Victor Sage and Allan Lloyd Smith, eds., *Modern Gothic: A Reader* (1996); Fred Botting, *Gothic* (1996); E. J. Clery and Robert Miles, eds., *Gothic Documents: A Sourcebook, 1700–1820* (2000); Fred Botting, *Gothic* (1996). On "American Gothic"—and especially the "southern Gothic"—see Chester E. Eisinger, "The Gothic Spirit in the Forties," *Fiction in the Forties* (1963). For references to *Gothic novel* in other entries, see page *390*, and refer to the *thriller*, in the entry *detective story*.

grammar: **195**; *382*.

grammar of narration: 233.

grand style: 108.

graphic narrative: Graphic narrative, **graphic novel**, and **sequential art** are terms first used in the 1970s to describe works, intended for adults and often

"哥特小说"的范围也已扩展到另一类小说作品，这类作品中没有早期浪漫传奇中的奇异背景，但也渲染一种阴森恐怖的气氛，描写充满离奇神秘、死亡或暴力情节的故事，常常涉及种种变态心理。在这种广延的意义上，威廉·戈德温的《凯勒布·威廉斯》(1794)、玛丽·雪莱杰出而著名的《弗兰肯斯坦》(1817)、德国作家 E. T. A. 霍夫曼的恐怖小说和故事都可列入哥特小说的范畴。在更为宽泛的意义上，"哥特式"也指后来一些作品中对死亡和恐怖情节的描述，如埃米莉·勃朗特的《呼啸山庄》、夏洛蒂·勃朗特的《简爱》、查尔斯·狄更斯的《荒凉山庄》(如第11、16、47章)及《远大前程》(有关女主人公哈维沙姆小姐的情节)。近来，批评家开始关注许多哥特小说的女性作家，认为作品中的模式化特征是女性性压抑的体现，同时也是对性别等级和男权文化价值观的一种挑战。参见：*女性主义批评*，参阅：桑德拉·吉尔伯特与苏珊·格芭合著的《阁楼上的疯女人》(1979)；朱利安·E. 弗利诺主编的《女性哥特小说》(1983)。

　　美国(尤其是其南部地区)也是广义上的哥特小说的多产地区，从查尔斯·布罗克登·布朗(1771—1810)的小说和埃德加·爱伦·坡的恐怖故事到威廉·福克纳的《圣地》《押沙龙，押沙龙！》，以及杜鲁门·卡波特的一些小说，都属广义上的哥特小说。达夫妮·杜·莫里哀在其颇受欢迎的小说《蝴蝶梦》(1938)，以及艾丽斯·默多克在《独角兽》中，都继承了哥特小说开创的噩梦般的离奇恐怖、暴力和残酷的衣钵。另外，H. P. 洛夫克拉夫特和斯蒂芬·金等恐怖小说作家，以及恐怖电影的剧作家和导演，也继承了哥特式的离奇和恐怖。

　　参阅：G. R. 汤普森主编的《哥特式想象：黑暗浪漫主义论文集》(1974)；威廉·帕特里克·戴所著的《在恐惧和欲望的循环中》(1985)；戴维·庞特所著的《恐怖文学：1765年到现在的哥特小说史》(1979；1996年第2版)；尤金尼娅·德拉莫特所著的《危险的黑夜》(1990)；安妮·威廉斯所著的《黑暗艺术》(1995)；维克多·塞奇与艾伦·劳埃德·史密斯合编的《现代哥特小说读本》(1996)；弗雷德·博廷所著的《哥特》(1996)；E. J. 克利里与罗伯特·迈尔斯合编的《哥特文献：1700—1820年间资料汇编》(2000)；弗雷德·博廷所著的《哥特》(1996)(该参考文献重复出现，系原书如此，疑原书有误。——译注)。关于"美国哥特小说"，尤其是美国"南方哥特小说"的论述，参见：切斯特·E. 艾辛格所著的《40年代的小说》(1963)中"40年代的哥特精神"。其他条目中提及"哥特小说"的地方，参见第390页；参见：*侦探故事中的惊险小说*。

grammar：语法　　195；*382*。

grammar of narration：叙事语法　　233。

grand style：宏伟绚丽的文体　　108。

Graphic Narrative：图画叙事

　　图画叙事、**图像小说**、**连环画**是在1970年代首次使用的术语，用来形容那些

nonfiction, in which extended narratives are told through a series of illustrations. The combined use of images with words is, however, much older. Medieval tapestries or woodcut series often told stories, and *illuminated* manuscripts often used pictures to imply, complement, or elaborate on narrative sequences. Both William Hogarth (1697–1764) and William Blake (1757–1826) produced forms of graphic narrative, and Blake's *The Marriage of Heaven and Hell* is often cited as a precursor by contemporary graphic narrative artists. The more direct graphic antecedent was, however, the comic book form as it emerged at the end of the nineteenth century in the United States. In 1930, the American Milt Gross published *He Done Her Wrong*, a three-hundred-page narrative composed entirely of images in comic-book style. Other "wordless novels" followed, and in the 1940s, *Classics Illustrated*, a series that adapted well-known novels to the graphic style of the comic book, began to appear. In 1976, Harvey Pekar began his long-running autobiographical series *American Splendor*, illustrated with framed images by artists such as R. Crumb, whose pictorial style and countercultural sensibility was imitated by many artists who produced graphic narratives.

One of the first works to which the term "graphic novel" was applied was Will Eisner's *A Contract with God, and Other Tenement Stories* (1978), a collection of linked graphic narratives. The most significant graphic narrative of the twentieth century was Art Spiegelman's two-volume *Maus: A Survivor's Tale* (1986, 1991), which recounted in the form of a *fable* the struggle of Spiegelman's father, a Polish Jew, to survive the Holocaust. Other graphic narratives have also focused on traumatic events or episodes in the public realm; see Alan Moore and Dave Gibbons, *Watchmen* (1986), Joe Sacco, *Palestine* (1996); and Marjane Satrapi, *Persepolis: The Story of a Childhood* (2003).

The graphic narratives that began to appear in the 1990s often sought to exploit the appeal of classic novels and popular literary forms by working in the genres of spy fiction, *mysteries*, and autobiography; at the same time, the formal experimentation of many graphic narratives align them with the practices of the artistic *avant-garde*.

One of the first books to develop a theory of graphic narrative was Scott McCloud, *Understanding Comics* (1993). In *Adult Comics: An Introduction* (1993, new ed. 2003), Roger Sabin discusses the history of comics, stressing the British Victorian period, and Japanese and European traditions of graphic narrative; see also Sabin's *Comics, Comix & Graphic Novels* (1996). Stephen Weiner's *Faster than a Speeding Bullet: The Rise of the Graphic Novel* (2003) focuses on comic art in the United States. One of the leading practitioners of graphic narrative, Will Eisner, has written about his craft in *Graphic Storytelling and Visual Narrative* (2008). See also Stephen E. Tabachnick, ed., *Teaching the Graphic Novel* (2009); Hillary Chute, "Comics as Literature? Reading Graphic Narrative," *PMLA* 123.2 (2008); and *Modern Fiction Studies* 2006 (52.4), a special issue devoted to "autographics."

Graveyard Poets: A term applied to eighteenth-century poets who wrote meditative poems, usually set in a graveyard, on the theme of human mortality, in

以成年人为对象经常是非虚构类的作品,在这些作品中,不断扩展的叙事通过一系列插图来讲述。不过,图文结合起来使用的历史则要古老得多。中世纪挂毯或木刻系列经常讲述故事,*彩饰稿本/泥金写本*经常使用图片来暗示、补充或阐述叙事序列(一系列叙事)。威廉·霍加斯(1697—1764)和威廉·布莱克(1757—1826)制作的图画叙事形式,和布莱克的《天国与地狱的联姻》经常被当代图画叙事艺术家们引为先导。然而,更直接的图画祖先是漫画书的形式,它出现在19世纪末期的美国。1930年,美国人米尔特·格罗斯出版了《误会》,全书300页,依照漫画书风格全由图像组成。其他"无字小说"紧随其后,1940年代开始出现《经典故事漫画》,一个将知名小说改编成图画样式的漫画书系列。1976年,哈维·贝克开始了他长期运作的自传体系列《美国荣耀》,里面的插图由R.克拉姆这样的艺术家设计完成,克拉姆的图案风格和反文化的敏感性,为许多生产图像小说的艺术家所模仿。

最早采用"图像小说"这一术语的作品之一是威尔·埃斯纳所著的《神的契约》和《其他佃户的故事》(1978),一部彼此相互联系的图像小说合集。20世纪最重要的图像小说是阿特·施皮格尔曼所著的两卷本《莫斯:一个幸存者的故事》(1986,1991),以寓言的形式讲述了施皮格尔曼的父亲,一个波兰犹太人,如何奋力抗争从大屠杀中幸存下来。其他图像小说也关注公共领域发生的创伤性事件或插曲,参阅:艾伦·摩尔与戴夫·吉本斯合著的《守望者》(1986),乔·萨科所著的《巴勒斯坦》(1996);玛嘉·莎塔碧所著的《我在伊朗长大》(2003)。

1990年代开始出现的图像叙事,通过创作间谍小说、*神秘小说*、自传等文学类型,常常试图利用经典小说和通俗文学形式的吸引力;与此同时,许多图像叙事的正式实验,也将它们自己与前卫艺术实践结合到一起。

最早发展出图像叙事理论的书籍之一是斯科特·麦克劳德所著的《理解漫画》(1993)。罗杰·萨宾在其所著的《成人漫画:简介》(1993,2003年新版)中讨论了漫画的历史,着重强调了图像叙事的英国维多利亚时期、日本、欧洲传统;也可参阅萨宾所著的《漫画、地下漫画及图像小说》(1996)。斯蒂芬·韦纳所著的《比飞驰的子弹还快:图像小说的崛起》(2003)主要关注美国的漫画艺术。图像小说的领军实践者之一威尔·艾斯纳,在其所著的《绘画故事和视觉叙事》(2008)中描写了他的图像叙事手艺。也可参阅:斯蒂芬·E.塔巴齐尼克主编的《讲授图像小说》(2009);希拉里·丘特所写的文章"漫画是一种文学?阅读图像叙事",载于《美国现代语言学协会会刊》2008年(123.2);《现代小说研究》2006年(52.4)专门探讨了"autographics"这一主题。

Graveyard Poets:墓畔诗人

墓畔诗人指的是18世纪从事冥思诗歌创作的诗人,他们的作品通常以墓畔坟

moods which range from elegiac pensiveness to profound gloom. Examples are Thomas Parnell's "Night-Piece on Death" (1721), Edward Young's long *Night Thoughts* (1742), and Robert Blair's "The Grave" (1743). The vogue resulted in one of the best-known English poems, Thomas Gray's "Elegy Written in a Country Churchyard" (1751). The writing of graveyard poems spread from England to Continental literature in the second part of the century and is represented in America by William Cullen Bryant's "Thanatopsis" (1817).

See Amy Louise Reed, *The Background of Gray's Elegy* (1924). Edith M. Sickels, in *The Gloomy Egoist* (1932), follows the evolution of graveyard and other melancholy verse through the Romantic Period. For the vogue in Europe, refer to Paul Von Tieghem, *Le Pré-romantisme* (3 vols., 1924–47).

Great Chain of Being: The conception of the Great Chain of Being is grounded in ideas about the nature of God, or (in metaphysical terms) the First Cause, in the Greek philosophers Plato, Aristotle, and Plotinus, and was developed by later thinkers into a comprehensive philosophy to account for the origin, types, and relationships of all living things in the universe. This worldview was already prevalent in the Renaissance, but was refined and greatly developed by the German philosopher Gottfried Leibniz early in the eighteenth century, and then adopted by a number of thinkers of the *Enlightenment*. In its comprehensive eighteenth-century form, the Great Chain of Being was based on the concept that the essential "excellence" of God consists in His limitless creativity—that is, in an unstinting, unjealous overflow of His own being into the fullest possible variety of other beings. From this premise were deduced three consequences:

1. Plenitude. The universe is absolutely full of every possible kind and variety of life; no conceivable species of being remains unrealized.
2. Continuity. Each species differs from the next by the least possible degree, and so merges all but imperceptibly into the species most nearly related to it.
3. Gradation. The existing species exhibit a hierarchy of status, and so compose a great chain, or ladder, of being, extending from the lowliest condition of the merest existence up to God Himself. In this chain human beings occupy the middle position between the animal kinds and the angels, who are purely spiritual beings.

On these concepts Leibniz and other thinkers also grounded what is called **philosophical optimism**—the view that this is "the best of all possible worlds," but only in the special sense that this is the best world whose existence is logically possible. The reasoning underlying this claim is that, since God's bountifulness consists in His creation of the greatest possible variety of graded beings, aspects of created life that to our limited human point of view seem to be deficient or evil can be recognized, from an overall cosmic viewpoint, to follow necessarily from the very excellence of the divine nature. That is, God's excellence logically entails that there must be a progressive set

地为场景,以哀挽沉思或极度抑郁为基调,表现人之死亡的主题。这类诗作有托马斯·帕内尔的《夜思亡灵》(1721)、爱德华·扬格的长诗《夜思》(1742)、罗伯特·布莱尔的《墓园》(1743)。墓畔诗的流行源自像托马斯·格雷的《墓畔哀歌》(1751)这样广为人知的英诗佳作。18世纪后半期,墓畔诗歌的创作从英国传入欧陆和美国,代表作是美国作家威廉·卡伦·布赖恩特创作的《死亡观》(1817)。

参阅:埃米·路易斯·里德所著的《格雷哀歌的背景》(1924)。伊迪丝·M.西奇尔斯在其所著的《忧伤的自我主义者》(1932)中,仿效演进了的墓畔诗和浪漫主义时期的其他伤感诗歌。关于墓畔诗在欧洲的盛行,参阅:保罗·范第根所著的三卷本《前浪漫主义》(1924—1947)。

Great Chain of Being:伟大的生存(环)链

这一概念以希腊哲学家柏拉图、亚里士多德和柏罗丁关于上帝创造自然万物或(形而上学术语)世界本源的思想为基础,被后世思想家发展成为描述宇宙间一切生命的起源、类属和相互关系的一个综合性哲学命题。这一世界观在文艺复兴时期就已颇为盛行,18世纪初经过德国哲学家戈特弗里德·莱布尼兹的提炼和极大发展,然后为当时许多*启蒙运动*思想家所接受。就其在18世纪时包罗万象的表现形式而言,伟大的生存链的思想基础是,上帝最根本的"卓越之处"在于他无穷尽的创造力,即从他自身慷慨无私地造就出种类繁多的其他万物众生。从这一前提可以推断出以下三个结论:

1. *丰富性*:宇宙间完全充满着各种各样的生命,不存在尚未认识的可想象到的物种。

2. *连合性*:物种与物种间的区别微乎其微,因此它便能以几乎难以觉察的方式与和它最相关的物种相连合。

3. *等级性*:存在中的一切物种体现出不同的地位等级,它们因此组成了一条伟大的生存链或阶梯,从处于最底层的最简单的物种上至上帝自身。在这个环链中,人类介于动物和天使或纯粹的神灵之间。

莱布尼兹和其他思想家在这些观念的基础上又提出所谓的**乐观主义哲学论**。这种哲学观认为,现今世界是"一切可能的世界中的最佳世界";但是,只有当它的存在在逻辑上是可能的这一特殊意义上,这个世界才是最美好的。这种观点所隐含的论据是,既然上帝的慷慨在于他最大限度地创造了种类繁多、不同等级的万物,从我们狭隘的人类视角出发,生命中看似存在着残缺和邪恶,但从整个宇宙视野出发,这些残缺和邪恶必然是神性美德的衍生,神性在逻辑上必然蕴含着一系列递增的缺陷,因此,当我们沿着这条生存链继续向下时,

of limitations, hence increasing "evils," as we move downward along the chain of being. As Voltaire ironically summarized this mode of optimism in his era, "This is the best of all possible worlds, and everything in it is a necessary evil."

With remarkable precision and economy, Alexander Pope compressed the basic concepts that make up the Great Chain of Being into a half-dozen or so *heroic couplets*, in Epistle I of his *Essay on Man* (1732–34):

> Of systems possible, if 'tis confessed
> That Wisdom Infinite must form the best,
> Where all must full or not coherent be,
> And all that rises rise in due degree;
> Then in the scale of reasoning life, 'tis plain,
> There must be, somewhere, such a rank as man....
> See, through this air, this ocean, and this earth,
> All matter quick, and bursting into birth....
> Vast Chain of Being! which from God began,
> Natures ethereal, human, angel, man,
> Beast, bird, fish, insect, what no eye can see,
> No glass can reach! from Infinite to thee,
> From thee to nothing. ...

Philosophical optimism is one type of what is known as a **theodicy**. This term, compounded of the Greek words for "God" and "right," designates any system of thought which sets out to reconcile the assumption that God is perfectly good with the fact that evil exists. Milton's "great argument" in *Paradise Lost*, by which he undertakes to "assert Eternal Providence / And justify the ways of God to men" (I. 24–26) is an example of a traditional Christian theodicy, explaining evil as the result of "man's first disobedience" in Eden to a perfectly just God, which "Brought death into the world, and all our woe."

See A. O. Lovejoy's classic work in the history of ideas, *The Great Chain of Being* (1936); also E. M. W. Tillyard, *The Elizabethan World Picture* (1943), chapters 4–5, which deals with the prevalence of the conception in Shakespeare's lifetime.

green studies: 96.

grotesque: A term originally applied to a style of mosaic and fresco wall paintings first used in ancient Rome and rediscovered in the late fifteenth century during an excavation of the emperor Nero's Golden House, or Domus Aurea. The style combined arabesques with floral, animal, and human elements in a whimsically ornamental mode. Because the rooms of the Golden House were, at the time of excavation, underground and resembled grottoes, the artwork was labeled "grottesca" (Italian for "of a grotto"). The style was adopted and extended by Raphael and other painters of the Italian Renaissance, who used it to fill marginal spaces such as borders of paintings, or to cover ceilings or pilasters.

Facilitated by the rise of printing and the medium of engraving, the dissemination of "grottesca" designs continued throughout Europe from the sixteenth to the eighteenth centuries. The term itself was increasingly used to

就会发现渐增的"邪恶"。伏尔泰曾饶有讽刺意味地把这种乐观主义哲学归纳为"这个世界是一切可能的世界中的最佳世界,其中每一事物都必然是邪恶的"。

亚历山大·蒲柏在他的书信体诗文《人论》(1732—1734)第一章节中,以无比准确和精练的行文,把构成这条伟大的生存链的概念浓缩进几行*英雄对句*中:

> 在一切可能的世界中,如果承认
> 上帝的智慧必定创造出最好的世界,
> 在这个世界里一切都注定是完美的或是不可协同的,
> 一切生发的都在充分地生发;
> 那么在推断生命的级别时,显然,
> 在某种程度上,注定存在着这样一个如同人类一样的序列……
> 从空中,大海,以及地球上,可以观察到,
> 万物在瞬即间皆关联,且在突然间生发……
> 伟大的生存链!其源头始自上帝,
> 天上,人间,天使,人类,
> 走兽,飞禽,鱼类,昆虫,肉眼无法看清的,
> 透镜无法辨识的!自上帝直至你,
> 自你直至微不足道的……

乐观主义哲学论是**神正论**的一种类型。神正论这一术语是希腊词汇"上帝"和"公正"的复合形式,指调和"上帝是完美的"这一假说与"罪恶是存在的"这一事实之间关系的任何思想体系。弥尔顿《失乐园》中用来"阐明永恒的天理/向人类昭示天道的公正"的"伟大的论点"(第一卷第24—26行)就是传统的基督教神正论,它向人们解释罪恶源自在伊甸园"人类违背完美公正的上帝初尝禁果",使"死亡和所有的灾难降临这个世界"。

参阅:A. O. 洛夫乔伊的思想史论著经典《伟大的生存(环)链》(1936);也可参阅:E. M. W. 蒂利亚德所著的《伊丽莎白时代的世界图景》(1943),书中第4—5章探讨了流行于莎士比亚一生中的这一观念。

green studies:绿色研究　96。

Grotesque:奇异艺术风格

奇异艺术风格(又叫怪诞艺术风格)这一术语,起初是指一种马赛克和壁画的风格,最早在古罗马得到使用,15世纪晚期在挖掘尼禄皇帝的金宫(或称黄金剧场)时被重新发现。这一风格以一种异想天开的装饰模式,将阿拉伯式花饰与花卉、动物和人的元素混合到一起。由于金宫的房间在开挖时被埋在地下,类似于石窟,艺术品就被贴上了"奇异艺术风格"(意大利语意为"岩洞")的标签。拉斐尔和意大利文艺复兴时期的其他画家采纳并扩展了这一风格,他们用它来填补边缘空间(如在画作的边缘),或是用来覆盖天花板或壁柱。

在印刷术的兴起和雕刻方法的促进下,奇异艺术风格的设计在16—18世纪一直传遍整个欧洲。这一术语自身被越来越多地用来描述其他艺术形式——

describe other artistic forms that combined incongruous elements; it was applied, for example, to many forms of medieval Christian art and architecture, including depictions of hell, the "temptations" of St. Anthony, the gargoyles and monsters of Romanesque and Gothic church architecture, and the extravagant, even sometimes vulgar and comic designs surrounding devotional texts in illuminated manuscripts. During the nineteenth century, the term was used in discussions of painting, sculpture or stonework, architecture, literature, and even music. In current uses, the concept of the grotesque has been extended to refer to anything unnatural, strange, absurd, ludicrous, distorted, wildly fantastic, or bizarre. In this context, it is worth recalling that the original "grottesca" was intended to be none of these, but simply delightful and diverting.

The grotesque has been identified as a sign of *decadence*—as in the extravagant proliferation of ornamental detail in *baroque* or rococo art—or else as the free expression of primitive exuberance or spontaneity. In an influential discussion of the "Grotesque Renaissance" in *The Stones of Venice* (1981, 2d ed. 2003), John Ruskin distinguished between the "noble" or "terrible grotesque," which expressed "the *repose* or play of a *serious* mind" and the "barbarous" or "ignoble" grotesque, which represented "the *full exertion* of a *frivolous* one," with Dante representing the purest form of the first category and "Hindoos" and "savages" the second.

The term "grotesque" is now widely applied to painters such as Hieronymous Bosch and Pieter Breughel the Elder; to elements in the works of many writers, including Shakespeare (the characters Caliban and Shylock), Dickens (Fagin, and the Miss Havisham episodes in *Great Expectations*), and Franz Kafka ("Metamorphosis"). The term is also used to describe macabre episodes in the films of Alfred Hitchcock (*Psycho* and *Vertigo*).

The first influential academic study of the grotesque was Wolfgang Kayser, *The Grotesque in Art and Literature* (1957, trans. 1981), which stressed the form's darker or demonic attributes of estrangement and alienation. In 1965, a translation of Mikhail Bakhtin's *Rabelais and His World* appeared, offering a completely different view of the grotesque as the expression of an energetic and irreverent popular culture organized around pagan festivals. In *On the Grotesque: Strategies of Contradiction in Art and Literature* (2d ed., 2006), Geoffrey Galt Harpham described the grotesque not as a formal property of particular works but as a feature of the response to those works—an interval of partial comprehension when, confronting an incoherent object, the perceiver senses a hidden principle of unity or intelligibility that he or she does not yet comprehend. For a collection of essays on the grotesque in the work of various literary figures, see Harold Bloom, *The Grotesque* (2009).

grounds (of a metaphor): **131**, *63*.

gull (in drama): **378**.

gynocriticism: **123**.

这种艺术形式将不和谐元素混合到一起；例如，它被用于许多中世纪基督教艺术和建筑形式，包括描绘地狱、"圣安东尼的诱惑"、罗马式和哥特式教堂建筑上的怪兽状滴水嘴，以及有图案装饰的手抄本中环绕虔诚文本四周奢侈的、有时甚至是低俗的和漫画式的设计。在 19 世纪，这一术语被用于讨论绘画、雕塑或石雕、建筑、文学，甚至是音乐。在目前的用法中，奇异艺术风格一直被扩展延伸到指任何非自然的、奇怪的、荒谬的、可笑的、扭曲的、疯狂幻想的或离奇怪诞的。在这一背景下，值得回味：原初的"奇异艺术风格"丝毫无意成为上述这些，而只是简单的愉悦和有趣。

奇异艺术风格一直被认定为是*颓废*的一个标志——就像*巴洛克*或洛可可艺术中夸张奢侈的装饰细节——或是被认定为是原始的生机或自发性的自由表达。在《威尼斯的石头》(1981 年，2003 年第 2 版) 里"怪诞式文艺复兴"一章中颇具影响力的讨论中，约翰·罗斯金将奇异艺术风格区分为"高贵的"或"怪诞可怕的奇异艺术风格"，它表示"一颗严肃心灵的宁静或游戏"，和"野蛮"或"卑鄙"的奇异艺术风格，它代表"一个轻浮的人的充分发挥"，但丁代表第一类最纯粹的形式，"印度人"和"野人"代表第二类最纯粹的形式。

"奇异艺术风格"这一术语现在被广泛用于指像希罗尼穆斯·波希和老彼得·勃鲁盖尔这样的画家；指许多作家作品中的元素，包括莎士比亚（剧中人物卡利班和夏洛克），狄更斯（《远大前程》中费金与郝薇香小姐的一段情节），弗朗兹·卡夫卡（《变形记》）。这个词也被用来描述阿尔弗雷德·希区柯克的电影（《惊魂记》《迷魂记》）里令人毛骨悚然的情节。

对奇异艺术风格进行的最早有影响的学术研究是沃尔夫冈·凯瑟所著的《艺术和文学中的奇异艺术风格》(1957，1981 年英译版)，书中强调了这一形式的隔阂和疏离的阴暗及恶魔属性。1965 年，巴赫金的《拉伯雷和他的世界》英译版问世，提供了一种完全不同的看法：将奇异艺术风格视为一种围绕异教节日组织起来的充满活力和不敬的流行文化的表达。杰弗里·高尔特·哈珀姆在其所著的《论奇异艺术风格：艺术和文学中的矛盾策略》(2006 年第 2 版) 中，将怪诞描述为不是特定作品的一种正式属性，而是对这些作品的回应的一个特征——感知者面对一个支离破碎的对象，感到有一种潜藏的（事物应有的）完整性或（他/她还不理解的）可理解性时一种部分理解的间隔。关于各种文学人物的奇异艺术风格的文章合集，参阅：哈罗德·布鲁姆主编的《怪诞》(2009)。

grounds (of a metaphor)：(隐喻的) 基础　131, *63*。

gull (in drama)：(戏剧中的) 傻子　378。

gynocriticism：女性批评　123。

hagiography (hăg′ ēŏg″ răf ē): **27**.

haiku (sometimes spelled **hokku**): Haiku is a Japanese poetic form that represents—in seventeen syllables that are ordered into three lines of five, seven, and five syllables—the poet's emotional or spiritual response to a natural object, scene, or season of the year. The strict form, which relies on the short, uniform, and unstressed syllabic structure of the Japanese language, is extremely difficult in English; most poets who attempt the haiku loosen the rule for the number and pattern of the syllables. The haiku greatly influenced Ezra Pound and other Imagists, who set out to reproduce both the brevity and the precision of the image in the Japanese original. Ezra Pound's "In a Station of the Metro" is a well-known instance of the haiku in the loosened English form; see this poem under *imagism*.

Earl R. Miner, *The Japanese Tradition in British and American Literature* (1958); R. H. Blyth, *A History of Haiku* (2 vols., 1963–64); Bruce Ross, ed., *Haiku Moment: An Anthology of Contemporary North American Haiku* (1993).

hamartia (hämärtē′ a): **408**.

hard-boiled detective story: 84.

Harlem Renaissance: A period of remarkable creativity in literature, music, dance, painting, and sculpture by African-Americans, from the end of the First World War in 1917 through the 1920s. In the course of the mass migrations to the urban North in order to escape the legal segregation of the American South—and also in order to take advantage of the jobs opened to African-Americans at the beginning of the war—the population of the region of Manhattan known as Harlem became almost exclusively black, and developed into the vital center of African-American culture in America. Distinguished writers who were part of the movement included the poets Countee Cullen, Langston Hughes (who also wrote novels and plays), Claude McKay, and Sterling Brown; the novelists Jean Toomer (whose inventive *Cane*, 1923, included verse and drama as well as prose fiction), Jessie Fauset, and Wallace Thurman; and many essayists, memoirists, and writers in diverse modes such as James Weldon Johnson, Marcus Garvey, and Arna Bontemps.

The Great Depression of 1929 and the early 1930s brought the period of buoyant Harlem culture—which had been fostered by prosperity in the publishing industry and the art world—effectively to an end. Zora Neale Hurston's novel *Their Eyes Were Watching God* (1937), and her other works, however, are widely accounted as late products of the Harlem Renaissance.

See *The New Negro: An Interpretation* (1925), an anthology edited by Alain Locke that did much to define the spirit of the Harlem Renaissance; Arna Bontemps, ed., *The Harlem Renaissance Remembered* (1972); David Levering Lewis, ed., *The Portable Harlem Renaissance Reader* (1994); David Levering Lewis, *When Harlem Was in Vogue* (1997); Steven Watson, *The Harlem*

H

hagiography：圣徒传　27。

Haiku（有时拼写为 hokku）：俳句

俳句是日本的一种十七音节的诗歌形式，由三句分别有五、七、五个音节构成的诗行组成，是诗人吟诵自然景物或四季风光、咏物寄怀、抒发心灵感受的诗歌。日文俳句诗行简短，形式统一，无重音节结构，这种严格的俳句形式在英语中很难做到；大多数俳句诗人并没有严格遵循俳句音节的数量和分布模式。俳句诗歌对埃兹拉·庞德和其他意象派诗人产生过很大影响，他们用日本俳句的形式再现了意象的简洁和独特性。埃兹拉·庞德的《地铁车站》是首著名的结构松散的英文俳句；参见：*意象主义*中的这首诗。

参阅：厄尔·R. 迈纳所著的《英美文学中的日本传统》(1958)；R. H. 布莱思所著的两卷本《俳句史》(1963—1964)；布鲁斯·罗斯主编的《俳句时刻：当代北美俳句选集》(1993)。

hamartia：判断错误　408。

hard-boiled detective story：硬汉派侦探故事　84。

Harlem Renaissance：哈莱姆文艺复兴

哈莱姆文艺复兴指的是自 1917 年第一次世界大战结束后至整个 1920 年代，美国黑人在文学、音乐、舞蹈、绘画、雕塑等方面取得辉煌艺术成就的一段时期。为了逃避南方法定的种族隔离，也为了谋取第一次世界大战开始时对黑人开放的许多工作岗位，美国南部的黑人大批迁移至北方城市中，曼哈顿哈莱姆区居住的几乎是清一色的黑人，哈莱姆区也成了美国黑人最重要的文化中心。参与哈莱姆文艺复兴运动的著名作家有诗人康蒂·卡伦、兰斯顿·休斯（同时既写小说，又从事戏剧创作）、克劳德·麦凯、斯特林·布朗；小说家琼·图默 [著有闻名于世的《甘蔗》(1923)，融诗歌、戏剧、散文体小说于一体]、杰西·福塞特、华莱士·瑟曼；另外还有詹姆士·韦尔登·约翰逊、马库斯·加维、阿纳·邦当普斯等许多杂文作家、回忆录作家和其他各种类型的作家。

1929 年的经济大萧条和 1930 年代早期使得欣欣向荣的哈莱姆文化这一由出版业和文艺界的繁荣所孕育的文艺奇葩完全凋零了。但是，佐拉·尼尔·赫斯顿的小说《他们眼望上苍》(1937) 和其他一些作品则被普遍视作哈莱姆文艺复兴运动后期的成果。

参阅阿兰·洛克主编的选集《新黑人诠释》(1925)，书中大部分内容都是在解释哈莱姆文艺复兴的精神。阿纳·邦当普斯主编的《追忆哈莱姆文艺复兴》(1972)；戴维·利弗林·刘易斯主编的《袖珍哈莱姆文艺复兴读本》(1994)；戴维·利弗林·刘易斯所著的《风靡一时的哈莱姆》(1997)；斯蒂芬·沃森所著的

Renaissance: Hub of African-American Culture, 1920–1930* (1995); Cheryl Wall, *Women of the Harlem Renaissance* (1995); George Hutchinson, *The Harlem Renaissance in Black and White* (1995); William L. Andrews, Frances Smith Foster, and Trudier Harris, eds., *The Concise Oxford Companion to African American Literature* (2001).

hegemony (hĕjĕm′ ŏnē): **207**, *307*.

heptameter (hĕptăm′ ĕter): **220**.

hermeneutic circle (hĕr′ mĕnoo″ tĭk): **176**.

hermeneutics: 176.

hermeneutics of suspicion: 313; *180*.

hero (in a narrative): **294**; *14*.

heroic couplet: Lines of iambic pentameter (see *meter*) which rhyme in pairs: *aa, bb, cc,* and so on. The adjective "heroic" was applied in the later seventeenth century because of the frequent use of such couplets in heroic (that is, *epic*) poems and in *heroic dramas*. This verse form was introduced into English poetry by Geoffrey Chaucer (in *The Legend of Good Women* and most of *The Canterbury Tales*), and has been in constant use ever since. From the age of John Dryden through that of Samuel Johnson, the heroic couplet was the predominant English measure for all the poetic kinds; some poets, including Alexander Pope, used it almost to the exclusion of other meters. In that era, usually called the *Neoclassic Period*, the poets wrote **closed couplets**, in which the end of each pair of lines tends to coincide with the end either of a sentence or of a self-sufficient unit of syntax. The sustained employment of the closed heroic couplet meant that two lines had to serve something of the function of a stanza. In order to maximize the interrelationships of the component parts of the couplet, neoclassic poets often used an end-stopped first line (that is, made the end of the line coincide with a pause in the syntax), and also broke many single lines into subunits by balancing the line around a strong *caesura*, or medial pause in the syntax.

The following passage from John Denham's *Cooper's Hill* (which he added in the version of 1655) is an early instance of the artful management of the closed couplet that fascinated later neoclassic poets; they quoted it and commented upon it again and again, and used it as a model for exploiting the potentialities of this verse form. (See the comment on *Cooper's Hill* under *topographical poetry*.) Note how Denham achieves diversity within the straitness of his couplets by shifts in the position of the caesuras, by the use of rhetorical balance and *antithesis* between the single lines and between the two halves within a single line, and by the variable positioning of the adjectives in the second couplet. Note also the framing and the emphasis gained by inverting

《哈莱姆文艺复兴：1920—1930 年间美国黑人文化的中心》(1995)；谢里尔·沃尔所著的《哈莱姆文艺复兴中的女性》(1995)；乔治·哈钦森所著的《黑人和白人的哈莱姆文艺复兴》(1995)；威廉·L. 安德鲁斯、弗朗西斯·史密斯·福斯特、特鲁迪尔·哈里斯三人合编的《简明牛津美国黑人文学指南》(2001)。

hegemony：霸权主义 **207**，*307*。

heptameter：七音步诗行 **220**。

hermeneutic circle：阐释循环 **176**。

hermeneutics：阐释学 **176**。

hermeneutics of suspicion：怀疑阐释学 **313**；*180*。

hero（**in a narrative**）：（叙事作品中的）男主角 **294**；*14*。

Heroic Couplet：英雄双韵体

英雄双韵体为五步抑扬格诗行（参见：*格律*），对句成韵，形成 aa、bb、cc……的韵律。17 世纪后期，因为对句在英雄诗歌（即*史诗*）和*英雄剧*中的频繁出现，形容词"英雄的"一词便应运而生。这种诗体是经杰弗里·乔叟（在《好女人传说》和大多数《坎特伯雷故事集》中的故事中）引入英国的诗歌创作中的，并且一直流传下来。从约翰·德莱顿直到塞缪尔·约翰逊，在这漫长的时期里，英雄双韵体一直是所有英诗创作的主导形式，包括亚历山大·蒲柏在内的一些诗人对这种韵体的运用几乎到了排斥一切其他格律的地步。在人们通常所谓的*新古典主义时期*，诗人在创作中采用**闭合双韵体**，其中每一对句的结尾往往与一个句子或一个完整的句法单元的结尾相符合。连续使用闭合英雄双韵体意味着一组对句要起到一个"诗节"的作用。为了加强双韵体各组成部分的相互关联，新古典主义诗人们往往运用首句停顿法（即：使首句的结尾刚好形成句法停顿），同时通过明显的*行间停顿*或句法单元的间歇把许多单独的诗行断成若干子单元。

下引约翰·德纳姆《库珀山》中的一段（是他在 1655 年版中增加的），是早期巧妙运用闭合双韵体创作技法的一个例子；后世的新古典主义诗人为之倾倒，他们不断地加以引用和品评，并以此为楷模进行这类诗体的创新。（参见：*风景诗*中对《库珀山》的点评。）注意德纳姆在其对句的有限范围内，是如何通过变换行间停顿的位置、运用每组对句间和单句的两部分间的修辞平衡与*对偶*，以及第二组对句中形容词位置的错落变换而取得多样化的艺术效果的。另外也应注意到，

the iambic foot that begins the first line and the last line, and by manipulating similar and contrasting vowels and consonants. The poet is addressing the River Thames:

> O could I flow like thee, and make thy stream
> My great example, as it is my theme!
> Though deep, yet clear; though gentle, yet not dull;
> Strong without rage, without o'erflowing full.

And here is a passage from Alexander Pope, the greatest master of the metrical, syntactical, and rhetorical possibilities of the closed heroic couplet ("Of the Characters of Women," 1735, lines 243–48):

> See how the world its veterans rewards!
> A youth of frolics, an old age of cards;
> Fair to no purpose, artful to no end,
> Young without lovers, old without a friend;
> A fop their passion, but their prize a sot;
> Alive, ridiculous, and dead, forgot!

These closed neoclassic couplets contrast with the "open" pentameter couplets quoted from Keats' *Endymion* (1818) in the entry on *meter*. In the latter, the pattern of stresses varies often from the iambic norm, the syntax is unsymmetrical, and the couplets run on freely, with the rhyme serving to color rather than to stop the verse.

See George Williamson, "The Rhetorical Pattern of Neoclassical Wit," *Modern Philology*, Vol. 33 (1935); W. K. Wimsatt, "One Relation of Rhyme to Reason (Alexander Pope)," in *The Verbal Icon* (1954); William Bowman Piper, *The Heroic Couplet* (1969). For references to *heroic couplet* in other entries, see page *94*.

heroic drama: Heroic drama was a form mainly specific to the *Restoration Period*, though instances continued to be written in the early eighteenth century. As John Dryden defined it: "An heroic play ought to be an imitation, in little, of an heroic poem; and consequently... love and valour ought to be the subject of it" (Preface to *The Conquest of Granada*, 1672). By "heroic poem" he meant *epic*, and the plays attempted to emulate the epic by employing as protagonist a large-scale warrior whose actions involve the fate of an empire, and by having all the characters speak in an elevated style, usually cast in the epigrammatic form of the closed *heroic couplet*. A noble hero and heroine are typically represented in a situation in which their passionate love conflicts with the demands of honor and with the hero's patriotic duty to his country; if the conflict ends in disaster, the play is called an **heroic tragedy**. Often the central dilemma is patently contrived and the characters seem to modern readers to be statuesque and unconvincing, while the attempt to sustain a high epic style swells sometimes into *bombast*, as in this utterance from Dryden's *Love Triumphant* (1693): "What woods are these? I feel my vital heat / Forsake my limbs, my curdled blood retreat."

第一行和最后一行开头的抑扬格音步的倒用以及对相似或相对的元音和辅音的妙用所形成的衬托和强调的效果。诗人面对泰晤士河咏怀道：

> 噢，我能否像你一样流动，把你的川流
> 当做我伟大的楷模，因为那是我的主旨！
> 尽管深沉，仍却清冽；尽管温柔，但不滞缓，
> 强健而不狂暴，盈满而不泛滥。

以下诗段出自在闭合双韵体韵律、句法与修辞方面最伟大的巨匠亚历山大·蒲柏之笔〔《女人性格论》(1735) 第 243—248 行〕：

> 看看这个世道里的老兵是何以获得酬劳的！
> 一个欢乐的少年，一位年迈的糟老头；
> 美丽而没有意义，狡猾而没有结局，
> 年轻的没有情侣，年老的没有朋友；
> 她们渴望的是花花公子，而获得的却是一个醉鬼；
> 活着时，荒唐可笑，死去后，被人遗忘！

这些新古典闭合双韵体诗句与条目*格律*中引自济慈《恩底弥翁》中的"开放"五音步双韵体诗句形成对照。在后者中，重音模式常与抑扬格的规范相偏离，句法结构不对称，对句自由延伸，其韵式只为诗文增色，而非为了收尾。

参阅：乔治·威廉森所写的文章"新古典机智的修辞模式"，载于《现代语文学》1935 年第 33 卷；W. K. 维姆萨特所著的《语像》一书中的"押韵与理性（亚历山大·蒲柏）的一种关系"(1954)；威廉·鲍曼·派珀所著的《英雄双韵体》(1969)。其他条目中提及"英雄双韵体"的地方，参见第 94 页。

Heroic Drama：英雄剧

英雄剧的创作尽管延续到 18 世纪早期，但它主要是*王政复辟时期*特有的一种戏剧形式。正如约翰·德莱顿所界定的那样："英雄剧应该是对英雄诗歌的小型化模仿，因此……爱情与英雄气概应该是它的主题。"〔《格拉纳达的征服》(1672) 序言〕德莱顿所说的"英雄诗"是指*史诗*，英雄剧试图通过呈现大多是勇士且其行为决定王国命运的主人公，并让所有角色谈吐严肃高雅，往往形成闭合*英雄双韵体*警句诗形式，以此仿效史诗。英雄剧的典型情节是表现高尚的英雄和女主人公之间的热恋，他们之间的炽烈爱情往往与英雄对荣誉的追求、对祖国的爱国使命形成矛盾冲突；如果冲突以灾祸告终，则称为**英雄悲剧**。一般而言，剧情中的主要困境是出于作者的苦心设计，在现代读者看来，剧中人物也显得雕像化，难以令人信服，而过分追求史诗的高雅文体有时则会成为*浮夸之辞*，如德莱顿《爱的胜利》(1693) 中的一段台词："这是什么森林？我感到生命之火／弃离了我的手脚，周身冷固的血液已经退却。"

Dryden is the major writer of this dramatic form; *The Conquest of Granada* is one of the better heroic tragedies, but Dryden's most successful achievement is *All for Love* (1678), which is an adaptation to the heroic formula of Shakespeare's *Antony and Cleopatra*. Other heroic dramatists were Nathaniel Lee (*The Rival Queens*) and Thomas Otway, whose *Venice Preserved* is a fine tragedy that transcends the limitations of the form. We also owe indirectly to heroic tragedy two very amusing *parodies* of the type: the Duke of Buckingham's *The Rehearsal* (1672) and Henry Fielding's *The Tragedy of Tragedies, or the Life and Death of Tom Thumb the Great* (1731).

See Bonamy Dobrée, *Restoration Tragedy* (1929); Allardyce Nicoll, *Restoration Drama* (1955); Arthur C. Kirsch, *Dryden's Heroic Drama* (1965); Derek Hughes, English Drama, 1660–1700 (1996). For references to *heroic drama* in other entries, see page *282*.

heroic poem: 107.

heroic quatrain: 376.

heroic tragedy: 159; *410*.

heroine (in a narrative): 294.

hexameter (hĕxăm′ ĕter): 219.

hieratic style (hī′ ĕrăt″ ĭk): 385.

high burlesque: 38.

high comedy: 56.

high modernism: 226.

high style: 384.

hip-hop: 271.

historical novel: 256.

history play: 50.

hokku: 157.

Homeric epithet: 113.

Homeric simile: 109.

德莱顿是此类剧作的主要创作者；《格拉纳达的征服》是一部比较成功的英雄悲剧，但他最有成就的剧作要数《一切为了爱》(1678)，该剧是他对莎士比亚的《安东尼与克莉奥佩特拉》改写而成的英雄剧。其他英雄剧作家有纳撒尼尔·李(《竞争的皇后们》)和托马斯·奥特韦，他的《被救的威尼斯》是一部打破英雄剧局限性的优秀悲剧作品。不过我们也得承认，英雄悲剧间接地引发了两部对其*戏谑模仿*的趣味横生的剧作：白金汉公爵创作的《排练》(1672)和亨利·菲尔丁的《悲剧中的悲剧，又名大姆指汤姆的生与死》(1731)。

参阅：波纳美·道布雷所著的《王政复辟时期的悲剧》(1929)；阿勒代斯·尼科尔所著的《王政复辟时期的戏剧》(1955)；阿瑟·C.基尔希所著的《德莱顿的英雄剧》(1965)；德里克·休斯所著的《1660—1700年间的英国戏剧》(1996)。其他条目中提及"英雄剧"的地方，参见第282页。

heroic poem：英雄诗　107。

heroic quatrain：英雄体四行诗　376。

heroic tragedy：英雄悲剧　159；*410*。

heroine (in a narrative)：(叙事作品中的) 女主角　294。

hexameter：六音步诗行　219。

hieratic style：神圣文体　385。

high burlesque：上等滑稽讽刺作品　38。

high comedy：高雅喜剧　56。

high modernism：现代主义高潮时期　226。

high style：高雅文体　384。

hip-hop：嘻哈　271。

historical novel：历史小说　256。

history play：历史剧　50。

hokku：俳句　157。

Homeric epithet：荷马属性形容词　113。

Homeric simile：荷马式明喻　109。

homonyms: 325.

homostrophic (hŏ′ mō strō″ fĭk): 263.

Horatian ode: 263.

Horatian satire: 354.

hubris (hyoo′ brĭs): 408.

Hudibrastic poem (hyoo′ dĭbrăs″ tik): 39.

Hudibrastic verse: 93.

humanism: In the sixteenth century the word **humanist** was coined to signify one who taught or wrote in the "studia humanitatis," or "humanities"—that is, grammar, rhetoric, history, poetry, and moral philosophy, as distinguished from fields less concerned with the moral and imaginative aspects and activities of man, such as mathematics, natural philosophy, and theology. At that time, these studies focused on classical, especially Roman, culture; and they put great emphasis on learning to speak and write good Latin. Scholarly humanists recovered, edited, and expounded many ancient texts in Greek and Latin, and so contributed greatly to the store of materials and ideas in the European *Renaissance*. These humanists also wrote many works concerned with educational, moral, and political themes, based largely on classical writers such as Aristotle, Plato, and above all, Cicero. In the nineteenth century a new word, **humanism**, came to be applied to the view of human nature, the general values, and the educational ideas common to many Renaissance humanists, as well as to a number of later writers in the same tradition.

Typically, Renaissance humanism assumed the dignity and central position of human beings in the universe; emphasized the importance in education of studying classical imaginative and philosophical literature, although with emphasis on its moral and practical rather than its aesthetic values; and insisted on the primacy, in ordering human life, of reason (considered the universal and defining human faculty) as opposed to the instinctual appetites and the "animal" passions. Many humanists also stressed the need, in education, for a rounded development of an individual's diverse powers—physical, mental, artistic, and moral—as opposed to a merely technical or specialized kind of training.

In our time the term "humanist" often connotes those thinkers who base truth on human experience and reason and who base values on human nature and culture, as distinguished from those who regard religious revelation as the warrant for basic truth and values. With few exceptions, however, Renaissance humanists were pious Christians who incorporated the concepts and ideals inherited from pagan antiquity into the frame of the Christian creed.

homonyms：同音异义词　325。

homostrophic：同形诗句　263。

Horatian ode：贺拉斯体颂　263。

Horatian satire：贺拉斯式讽刺　354。

hubris：傲睨神明　408。

Hudibrastic poem：休迪布拉斯诗　39。

Hudibrastic verse：休迪布拉斯诗体　93。

Humanism：人文主义

16世纪，人们创造了**人文主义者**这一新词，指代从事人文学科的教学或研究的人员。人文学科包括文法、修辞、历史、诗歌与道德哲学，以区别于数学、自然哲学、神学之类与人类道德和精神活动不那么相关的领域。那时候，人文学科研究着眼于古典文化，首要的是罗马文化；它们非常注重学习很好地掌握拉丁文的读写能力。博学的人文主义者发掘、编辑并详尽地解释了许多古希腊文与拉丁文典籍，从而为欧洲文艺复兴累积了大量资料，奠定了思想基础。他们主要在亚里士多德、柏拉图、尤其是西塞罗等古典作家的思想基础上，撰写了许多有关教育、道德与政治主题的论著。19世纪，人们开始用**人文主义**这一新词来指代许多文艺复兴时期的人文主义者，以及许多承继了同样传统的后世作家在人类本性、普遍价值观及教育理念上所持的共同观点。

文艺复兴时期典型的人文主义通常认为，人是高贵的，在宇宙间占有中心地位；它强调学习研究富于想象与哲理的古典文学作品在教育中的重要性，但侧重于它们的道德与实际价值而非审美价值。人文主义还坚持要将与直觉的欲望和"兽欲"相对的理性（被视为人类普遍具有的官能）放在首位，用来主导人类的生活。许多人文主义者同时强调教育中个人不同能力的全面发展，如体力、脑力、艺术与道德等能力，反对局限于单纯技术性或专业化的培养。

在当代，"人文主义者"通常指代那些把人类经验和理性作为真理的依据，以人性和文化作为价值观基础的思想家，以此与那些把宗教启示视为所有真理及价值观的准则的人区别开来。然而，除个别人外，文艺复兴时的人文主义者都为虔诚的基督徒。他们把从异教徒的古人那里继承下来的观念与理想融入基督教的信条范围里。

The result was that they tended to emphasize the values achievable by human beings in this world rather than in an afterlife, and to minimize the earlier Christian emphasis on the innate corruption of human beings and on the ideals of asceticism and of withdrawal from this world in a preoccupation with the world hereafter. It has become common to refer to this synthesis of classical and Christian views, typical of writers such as Sir Philip Sidney, Edmund Spenser, and John Milton, as **Christian humanism**.

The rapid advance in the achievements and prestige of the natural sciences and technology after the Renaissance sharpened, in later heirs of the humanistic tradition, the need to defend the role of the humanities in a liberal education against the encroachments of the sciences and the practical arts. As Samuel Johnson, the eighteenth-century humanist who had once been a schoolmaster, wrote in his *Life of Milton* (1779):

> The truth is, that the knowledge of external nature, and the sciences which that knowledge requires or includes, are not the great or the frequent business of the human mind.... We are perpetually moralists, but we are geometricians only by chance.... Socrates was rather of opinion that what we had to learn was, how to do good, and avoid evil.

Matthew Arnold, a notable proponent of humanism in the *Victorian Period*, strongly defended the central role of humane studies in general education. Many of Arnold's leading ideas are adaptations of the tenets of the older humanism—his view, for example, that culture is a perfection "of our humanity proper, as distinguished from our animality," and consists of "a harmonious expansion of *all* the powers which make the beauty and worth of human nature"; his emphasis on knowing "the best that is known and thought in the world," with the assumption that much of what is best is in the writings of classical antiquity; and his conception of poetry as essentially "a criticism of life."

In the 1890s the German philosopher Wilhelm Dilthey developed a highly influential distinction between the natural sciences, which aim at an abstract and reductive "explanation" of the world, and the "human sciences" (the humanities), which aim to achieve an "understanding" of the full, concrete world of actual experience—the lived human world, for example, that is represented in works of literature. (See in the entry *interpretation and hermeneutics*.)

In the last century the American movement of 1910–33 known as the **New Humanism**, under the leadership of Irving Babbitt and Paul Elmer More, argued for a return to a primarily humanistic education, and for a very conservative view of moral, political, and literary values that is grounded mainly on classical literature. (See Irving Babbitt, *Literature and the American College*, 1908; Norman Foerster, ed., *Humanism and America*, 1930; and Claes G. Ryn, *Will, Imagination, and Reason: Babbitt, Croce, and the Problem of Reality*, 1997.) But in the present age of proliferating demands for specialists in the sciences, technology, and the practical arts, the broad humanistic base for a general education has been greatly eroded. In most colleges the earlier

结果，他们注重人类能在现世而非来世实现的生活理想，而对早期基督教所强调的人类天性的堕落以及极端禁欲主义和隐退现世专修来世的理想则极不重视。通常把这种古典及基督教思想相综合的观点称为**基督教人文主义**，这类作家尤以菲利普·锡德尼爵士、埃德蒙·斯宾塞、约翰·弥尔顿为代表。

  文艺复兴之后，自然科学、技术的成就与声望迅速扩大，这使得人文主义传统的后继者们捍卫人文学科在自由教育中的作用，反对自然科学与实用艺术侵蚀的需求变得更加强烈。曾出任过校长一职的18世纪人文主义者塞缪尔·约翰逊在《弥尔顿生平》（1779）中写道

> 事实上，有关自然界的知识以及这类知识所需要的或所包括的科学并不是人们头脑中频繁思考的事物……我们永远是道德主义者，而成为几何学家仅仅是出于偶然……苏格拉底认为：我们应该学会的就是怎样行善去恶。

维多利亚时期伟大的人文主义支持者马修·阿诺德极力维护人文学科在普通教育中的核心地位。阿诺德的许多主要观点都起源于早些时期的人文主义思想原则，例如他认为：文化是"我们人性自身区别于兽性"的完美形式，它包含了"形成人性美与价值的全部能力的和谐发展"；他强调认识了解"世界上已知并被视为最美好的事物"，认为这些最美好的事物大多存在于古代的经典作品中。在他看来，从根本上说，诗歌是"对生活的评说"。

  1890年代，德国哲学家威廉·狄尔泰对自然科学和"人文科学"的区分极具影响。他认为自然科学试图抽象地"解释"世界的本来面目，而"人文科学"（人文学科）则试图"理解"一个完整的、具体的实际经验的世界——例如文学作品所展示的那个鲜活的人类世界。（参见：*释义和阐释学*。）

  在上个世纪的1910—1933年间，由欧文·白璧德和保罗·埃尔默·莫尔领导的美国**新人文主义运动**呼吁恢复以人文主义为主体的教育，恢复主要以古典文学为基础的有关道德准则、政治观念与文学标准的极其保守的思想。[参阅欧文·白璧德所著的《文学和美国大学》（1908）；诺曼·福斯特编著的《人文主义与美国》（1930）；克莱·G. 瑞恩所著的《意志、想象和理性：白璧德、克罗斯与实在问题》（1997）。]但是由于当前对科学、技术与实用艺术专门人员的需求日益高涨，普通教育中广泛的人文主义基础已经受到很大程度的侵蚀。在多数大学里，早期

humanistic view of the aims of a liberal education survives mainly in the requirement that all students in the liberal arts must take at least one course in the group called **the humanities**, which comprises literature, philosophy, music, languages, and sometimes history.

It is notable that a number of structuralist and poststructuralist philosophical and critical theories were expressly antihumanistic, not only in the sense that they undertook to subvert many of the values proposed by traditional humanism, but in the more radical sense that they undertook to "decenter," or to eliminate entirely, the focus on the human being, or "subject," as the major object of study and the major agency in effecting scientific, cultural, and literary achievements. "Man," as Michel Foucault put it in a widely quoted affirmation, "is a simple fold in our language" who is destined to "disappear as soon as that knowledge has found a new form." In the realm of literary and critical theory, some *structuralists* conceived of a human author as simply a "space" in which linguistic and cultural codes come together to effect a text; *deconstructionists* tended to reduce the human subject to one of the "effects" engendered by the differential play of language; and a number of *Marxist* and *new-historicist critics* analyzed the subject as a construction that is produced by the ideological "discursive formations," particular to a time and culture, which the author-as-subject acquires and transmits in his or her literary productions. (See subject, under *poststructuralism*.)

Diverse poststructural and other opponents of humanism assert that human-centered systems of norms and values are based on the fallacy of **essentialism**—that is, the view (which antihumanists assume to be mistaken) that there is an essential human nature, or set of defining human features, which is innate, universal, and independent of historical and cultural differences. In response, the philosopher Martha Nussbaum has mounted a defense of essentialism, insisting that we are able to formulate, from within our own historical and cultural situation, a set of basic features, functions, and needs that constitute the specifically human form of life and are shared by human beings across all divisions of time, place, and culture. These common features include the knowledge that we are mortal, and have an instinctual aversion to death; the fact that we live an embodied life, hence have nutritional, sexual, and other needs and desires and a sensibility to pleasure and pain; the cognitive ability to perceive, think, and imagine, together with the practical ability to plan the means to achieve our aims; the capacity to experience emotions such as grief, anger, fear, and love; and a sense of relatedness and affiliation to other human beings. Possessing such capacities, we are able to recognize ourselves in others and to acknowledge our common humanity, whatever our individual and cultural differences. Conversely, if an individual does not have one or more of these features, we consider him to be, to that extent, lacking in humanity. Nussbaum holds that such essentialism provides adequate grounds for establishing basic human norms and values, and also that it is in fact indispensable as a ground for justifying claims for social and political justice on behalf of any oppressed, excluded, or marginalized minority. See Martha Nussbaum, "Social Justice and Universalism: In Defense of an Aristotelian

人文主义教育观念之所以尚能幸存，主要是因为校方规定所有文科学生至少要修读六学时的**人文学科**课程。这些课程包括文学、哲学、音乐、语言，有时还包括历史。

值得注意的是，一些结构主义与后结构主义的哲学和批评理论是明显反人文主义的，这些理论不仅试图颠覆传统人文主义提出的许多价值观，而且更为偏激的是，它们试图对人类"非中心化"，或完全消除对人类或主体的关注，否认人类是研究的主要客体，否认人类在取得科学、文化及文学成就中起着主要作用。正如米歇尔·福柯在其被广泛引用的断言中所说的那样，"人类是我们语言中的简单群体"，注定"在知识一寻求到一种新形式时就消失不见"。在文学和批评理论领域，一些*结构主义者*把人类作家简单地理解为一个语言、文化代码结合在一起以产生文本的"空间"；*解构主义者*则倾向于将人类主体降级到由于语言的差异游戏而产生的"效果"之一；一些*马克思主义及新历史主义批评家*把这一主体描述为一种由特定时间和文化意识形态的"论证组合"产生的结构，作为主体的作者在其自己的文学作品中获得并传达了这种论证组合。（参见：*后结构主义中的主体*。）

人文主义形形色色的后结构主义及其他反对者断言：以人类为中心的行为标准和价值标准体系是以错误的**本质主义**为基础，所谓本质主义就是这一看法：认为存在基本的人性，或是人类特征的一套界定，这是内在的、普遍的，独立于历史及文化差异；反人文主义者则认为这一看法是错误的。作为回应，哲学家玛莎·努斯鲍姆为本质主义进行了辩护，坚持认为我们能够从我们自己的历史文化情境中构想出一套基本的特征、功能和需求，构成具体的人类生活形式，跨越所有时间、空间、文化分离，为人类所共享。这些共同特征包括知道我们总有一死，对死有一种本能的厌恶；明白我们过着一种身体化的生活，因而拥有营养、性及其他需求和欲望，以及感受快乐和痛苦的能力；感受、思考、想象的认知能力，设计办法以实现目的的实践能力；体验悲伤、愤怒、恐惧和爱等情感的能力；对其他人类的亲缘感和接纳感。拥有这样的能力，我们就能在他人中识别出我们自己和承认我们有着共同的人性，不论我们有着什么样的个体和文化差异。反之，若是个体不具备这些特征中的一个或许多，我们便可以在那种程度上认为他缺少人性。努斯鲍姆认为，这样的本质主义为建立基本的人类规范和价值观提供了充足的理由，并认为事实上它也是一个必不可少的理由，可以证明那些代表任何受压迫、被排斥、被边缘化的少数群体争取社会及政治正义的呼声是正当的。参阅：玛莎·努斯鲍姆所写的文章"社会正义与普世主义：捍卫对人类功能的亚里士多

Account of Human Functioning," *Modern Philology*, Vol. 90, supplement, May 1993. In *Women and Human Development: The Capabilities Approach* (2000), Nussbaum proposes a somewhat revised list of human capabilities, in a book oriented toward establishing the ground for freedom and justice for women, across all national and cultural differences; see chapter 1, "In Defense of Universal Values."

The linguist and social philosopher Noam Chomsky also supports human essentialism; not, like Nussbaum, on the basis of shared human capabilities, but on the basis of a biologically determined "universal grammar," fixed in the human brain, which enables the "rule-bound creativity" of the production and understanding of language. (See Chomsky under *linguistics in literary criticism*.) This universal genetic inheritance, in Chomsky's view, constitutes the very core of human nature. He maintains that the anti-essentialist view of poststructural theorists—that all human attitudes, beliefs, and norms are social constructions within particular cultures—abets efforts by dominant social and political groups to shape such attitudes and norms to their own purposes. Only the conviction that human beings have an innate and determinate human nature can provide the grounds on which to resist such impositions on human liberty. (See Chomsky, *Reflections on Language*, 1975, and for evidence drawn from diverse fields to support Chomsky's genetic view of an essential human nature, Steven Pinker, *The Blank Slate: The Modern Denial of Human Nature*, 2002.)

A number of feminists, gay and lesbian critics, and proponents of ethnic *multiculturalism* are adherents of "identity politics," and stake out a position which differs from both the humanistic and poststructural views of the nature and valid role of the human *subject*. Like traditional humanists, **identity theorists** reject the extreme poststructural claims that the human subject is no more than a social construction or textual effect, and reposition the subject—as a particular sexual, gender-specific, or ethnic identity—at the center of the scene of writing, interpretation, and political action. In opposition to traditional humanists, on the other hand, identity theorists emphasize the identity of the subject as a representative of one or another group, rather than as a representative of universal humanity. The term **identity politics** is often used pejoratively, to signify the subordination of objective study to political aims. (On current conflicts about "identity" among advocates of political activism see Jonathan Culler, *Literary Theory: A Very Short Introduction*, 1997, chapter 8; also refer to the entries in this *Glossary* on *feminist criticism*, *postcolonial studies*, and *queer theory*.)

On the concept and history of humanism: Douglas Bush, *The Renaissance and English Humanism* (1939); P. O. Kristeller, *The Classics and Renaissance Thought* (1955); H. I. Marrou, *A History of Education in Antiquity* (1956); R. S. Crane, *The Idea of the Humanities* (2 vols., 1967); Tony Davies, *Humanism* (2d ed., 2008); Tzvetan Todorov, *Imperfect Garden: The Legacy of Humanism* (2002). For antihumanist critiques or deconstruction of the human subject, see the references under *poststructuralism*, *deconstruction*, and *new historicism*. For

德式解释",载于《现代语文学》1993 年 5 月第 90 卷增刊。在《女性与人类发展：能力取向》(2000) 一书中，努斯鲍姆提出了一个略加修订的人类能力清单，这本书的目标是超越所有民族文化差异，确立为女性获得自由和公正的理由；参见该书第 1 章"为普世价值观辩护"。

语言学家和社会哲学家诺姆·乔姆斯基也支持人类本质主义；但不像努斯鲍姆那样是因为共同拥有的人类能力，而是因为生物学上决定的"普遍文法"（又译普遍语法），它存在于人的大脑中，使得生产和理解语言的"规则约束的创造力"成为可能。（参见：*语言学在文学批评里的应用*中关于乔姆斯基的论述。）在乔姆斯基看来，这一普遍的基因遗传，构成人性的核心。他坚称，后结构主义理论家的反本质主义观点，即所有人类的态度、信仰、规范都是特定文化内的社会建构，是占优势的社会和政治群体为了他们自己的目的而去塑造这样的态度和规范的努力促成的。只有坚信人类拥有一种内在的和确定的人性这一信念，才能提供根据去抵制将这样的想法强加于人类自由之上。（参阅：乔姆斯基所著的《语言反思录》(1975)；斯蒂芬·平克所著的《白板：人类本性的当代否认》(2002) 中，则提供了来自不同领域支持乔姆斯基关于基本人性的基因观点的证据。）

一些女性主义者、同性恋主义批评家和民族多元文化主义的支持者拥护"身份政治"，他们提出一种立场，这一立场不同于人文主义和后结构主义关于自然和人类主体的有效作用的观点。像传统人文主义者一样，**身份理论家**反对将人类主体仅仅看成社会结构或文本效用的后结构主义极端思想，取而代之的是将其看成一个具有特定性别、具体性别或民族身份的主体的思想，他们将主体置于写作场景、阐释和政治活动的中心。另一方面，与传统的人文主义者不同，身份理论家重视主体作为这个或那个群体的代表的主体身份，而不是作为共同的人性代表。**身份政治**这一术语常被轻蔑地用来表示从属于政治目的的客观研究。[有关现今政治行动主义倡导者中出现的对"身份"的争论，参阅乔纳森·卡勒所著的《文学理论简介》(1997) 第 8 章；也可参见：*女性主义批评、后殖民主义研究、同性恋理论*。]

有关人文主义的概念和历史，请参阅：道格拉斯·布什所著的《文艺复兴与英国人文主义》(1939)；P. O. 克里斯泰勒所著的《古典和文艺复兴时期的思想》(1955)；H. I. 马卢所著的《古代教育史》(1956)；R. S. 克莱恩所著的两卷本《人文学的理念》(1967)；托尼·戴维斯所著的《人文主义》(2008 年第 2 版)；兹维坦·托多罗夫所著的《不完美的花园：人文主义的遗产》(2002)。对于人类主体的反人文主义批评或解构，参见：*后结构主义、解构主义、新历史主义*中的参考书。

opposition to such views and defenses of the humanist position in authorship, interpretation, and criticism, see Commission on the Humanities, *The Humanities in American Life: Report of the Commission on the Humanities* (1980); Richard Levin, "Bashing the Bourgeois Subject," in *Textual Practice*, Vol. 3 (1989); Clara Claiborne Park, *Rejoining the Common Reader* (1991); M. H. Abrams, "What Is a Humanistic Criticism?" in *The Emperor Redressed: Critiquing Critical Theory*, ed. Dwight Eddins (1995); Richard A. Etlin, *In Defense of Humanism: Value in Arts and Letters* (1996); Alvin Kernan, ed., *What's Happened to the Humanities?* (1997); David A. Hollinger, ed., *The Humanities and the Dynamics of Inclusion since World War II* (2006); Tony Davies, *Humanism* (2d ed., 2008). In *The Humanities and the Dream of America* (2011), Geoffrey Galt Harpham explores recurrent claims of a "crisis in the humanities," and argues that the modern concept of the humanities is a product of the post–World War II system of higher education in America.

For references to *humanism* in other entries, see page *42.*

humanist: 161; *339.*

humanities, the: 163.

humor: 421.

humours character: 57; *46, 421.*

hybridization (in literary cultures): **307**.

hymn: In current usage "hymn" denotes a song that celebrates God or expresses religious feelings and is intended primarily to be sung as part of a religious service. (See *lyric*.) The term derives from the Greek *hymnos*, which originally signified songs of praise that were for the most part addressed to the gods, but in some instances to human heroes or to abstract concepts. The early Christian churches, following classical examples, introduced the singing of hymns as part of the liturgy; some of these consisted of the texts or paraphrases of Old Testament psalms, but others were composed as songs of worship by churchly authors of the time. The writing of religious lyric poems set to music continued through the Middle Ages and into the Protestant Reformation; Martin Luther (1483–1546) himself composed both the German words and the music of hymns, including "A Mighty Fortress Is Our God," which is now sung by most Christian denominations.

The writing of religious hymns, some of them metrical versions of the psalms and others original, continued through the Renaissance and was supplemented by a revival of "literary hymns" on secular or even pagan subjects—a classical type which had been kept alive through the Middle Ages by a number of neo-Latin poets, and was now composed to be read rather than sung.

有关反对这样观点的论述以及对作者身份、阐释和批评的人文主义立场的维护，参阅：人文科学委员会发布的《美国生活中的人文学：人文科学委员会报告》（1980）；理查德·莱文所写的文章"批判布尔乔亚学科"，载于《文本实践》1989年第3卷；克拉拉·克莱本·帕克所著的《重新加入普通读者》（1991）；M.H.艾布拉姆斯所写的文章"什么是人文主义批评？"收入德怀特·埃丁斯主编的《重新穿上衣服的皇帝：对批评理论的批判》（1995）；理查德·A.埃特兰所著的《捍卫人文主义：艺术和文学的价值》（1996）；阿尔文·克南主编的《人文学怎么了？》（1997）；戴维·A.霍林格主编的《人文学与第二次世界大战以来的包含动力学》（2006）；托尼·戴维斯所著的《人文主义》（2008年第2版）。杰弗里·高尔特·哈珀姆在其所著的《人文主义与美国梦》（2011）中探讨了反复出现的"人文主义危机"断言，认为现代的人文主义概念是第二次世界大战后美国高等教育体制的产物。

其他条目中提及"人文主义"的地方，参见第42页。

humanist：人文主义者　　161；*339*。

humanities, the：人文学科　　163。

humor：幽默　　421。

humours character：性格人物　　57；*46, 521*。

hybridization (in literary cultures)：（文学文化中的）混合　　307。

Hymn：赞美诗

　　赞美诗通常用来指赞美上帝或表达宗教情感的歌曲，主要用于在宗教仪式中作为仪式的一部分而被吟唱。（参见：*抒情诗*。）这一术语源于希腊文 hymnos，原指赞美诗歌，大多是献给神明的，但有时也献给人类英雄或抽象思想。早期基督教堂追随古典传统，将吟唱赞美诗作为礼拜仪式的一部分而引入；其中一些赞美诗由《旧约》诗篇中的篇章或韵律译文组成，另一些则是由当时的教会作家所作的敬神歌曲。配上乐曲的宗教抒情诗歌的创作从中世纪延续至宗教改革时期：马丁·路德（1483—1546）本人就创作过赞美诗的德文诗词及乐曲，其中包括《上帝是我们万能的保护者》，至今大部分基督教派仍然吟唱这首赞美诗。

　　宗教赞美诗的创作延续了整个文艺复兴时期，其中一些赞美诗是圣歌的韵律版本，其他一些则是原创。有关世俗乃至异教主题的"文学赞美诗"的复兴，在当时是对宗教赞美诗的补充。"文学赞美诗"属于古典赞美诗类型，在中世纪时期，通过一些新拉丁语诗人保持了生机，而今，人们创作赞美诗的目的是为了阅读而非

Edmund Spenser's *Fowre Hymns* (1596) are distinguished examples of such literary hymns; the first two celebrate earthly love and beauty, and the second two celebrate heavenly (that is, Christian) love and beauty. The tradition of writing hymns on secular subjects continued into the nineteenth century, and produced such examples as James Thomson's "A Hymn on the Seasons" (1730), Keats' "Hymn to Apollo," and Shelley's "Hymn of Apollo" and "Hymn of Pan"; the last three of these hymns, it should be noted, like many of the original Greek hymns, are addressed to pagan gods.

The secular hymns were often long and elaborate compositions that verged closely upon another form of versified praise, the *ode*. These hymns, as well as many religious instances such as the great "Hymn" that constitutes all but the brief introduction of Milton's "On the Morning of Christ's Nativity" (1629), were formal compositions that were intended only to be read. The other type of hymn—the short religious lyric written for public singing—was revived, and developed into its modern form, by the notable eighteenth-century hymnists of personal religious emotions, including Isaac Watts, Charles and John Wesley, and William Cowper; a successor in the next century was John Henry Newman, author of "Lead, Kindly Light." In America the poets John Greenleaf Whittier, Oliver Wendell Holmes, and Henry Wadsworth Longfellow wrote hymns, but the greatest and best-known American devotional songs are the anonymous *African-American* type that we call **spirituals**, such as "Swing Low, Sweet Chariot" and "Go Down, Moses." (James Weldon Johnson and J. Rosamond Johnson, *Book of American Negro Spirituals*, 1925–26.)

See the anthology, *New Oxford Book of Christian Verse*, ed. Donald Davie (1982); and refer to C. S. Phillipe, *Hymnody Past and Present* (1937); Louis F. Benson, *The English Hymn* (1962); P. S. Diehl, *The Medieval European Religious Lyric* (1985); and the article "Hymn" in *The New Princeton Encyclopedia of Poetry and Poetics* (1993).

hyperbole and understatement: The figure of speech, or *trope*, called **hyperbole** (hīpur'bŏlē": Greek for "overshooting") is bold overstatement, or the extravagant exaggeration of fact or of possibility. It may be used either for serious or ironic or comic effect. Iago says gloatingly of Othello (III. iii. 330ff.):

> Not poppy nor mandragora,
> Nor all the drowsy syrups of the world,
> Shall ever medicine thee to that sweet sleep
> Which thou ow'dst yesterday.

Famed examples in the seventeenth century are Ben Jonson's gallantly hyperbolic compliments to his lady in "Drink to me only with thine eyes," and the ironic hyperboles in "To His Coy Mistress," by which Andrew Marvell attests how infinitely slowly his "vegetable love should grow"—if he had "but world enough and time." The "tall talk" or **tall tale** of the American West is a

吟唱。埃德蒙·斯宾塞的《赞美诗四首》(1596)便是这类文学赞美诗的杰出范例；其中前两首赞美了世俗的爱与美，后两首赞美的则是天堂（即基督教）的爱与美。创作世俗主题的赞美诗的传统延续至19世纪，其间出现了像詹姆斯·汤姆逊的《四季颂歌》、济慈的《阿波罗颂》、雪莱的《阿波罗颂》《潘神颂》这样一些杰出范例。值得注意的是，这些赞美诗中的后三首，像原来许多希腊赞美诗一样，都是献给异教神明的。

世俗赞美诗通常篇幅长，结构精巧，与另一种诗体赞美文颂十分接近。这些赞美诗以及诸如构成弥尔顿《圣诞清晨歌》(1629)这一首诗除简短序言之外所有部分的伟大"赞美诗"等许多宗教赞美诗，都是只用于阅读的正式作品。其他形式的赞美诗——专为公众吟唱所作的短篇宗教抒情诗——在18世纪通过一些著名的充满个人宗教热情的赞美诗作者而得以复兴，并发展成为其现代形式，这些作者包括艾萨克·瓦茨、查尔斯和约翰·卫斯理、威廉·柯珀。19世纪的一个继承者是《慈光歌》的作者约翰·亨利·纽曼。美国创作赞美诗的诗人有约翰·格林里夫·惠蒂埃、奥立弗·温德尔·霍姆斯、亨利·华兹沃斯·朗费罗，但最伟大最著名的美国礼拜歌曲是我们称为**灵歌**的佚名非裔美国类型的赞美诗，比如《马车慢慢摇》《去吧，摩西》。[詹姆斯·韦尔登·约翰逊与J.罗莎蒙德合编的《美国黑人灵歌选集》(1925—1926)。]

参阅选集：唐纳德·戴维主编的《新牛津基督教诗歌选集》(1982)；参阅：C.S.菲利皮所著的《过去和现在的赞美诗》(1937)；路易斯·F.本森所著的《英国赞美诗》(1962)；P.S.迪尔所著的《中世纪欧洲宗教抒情诗》(1985)；《新编普林斯顿诗歌与诗学百科全书》(1993)中关于"赞美诗"的论述。

Hyperbole and Understatement：夸张与含蓄

夸张（希腊文"过分"的意思）这种修辞格或*比喻*，指代明显夸大或过度扩大事实或可能性。它可以用来取得或严肃或嘲讽或喜剧的效果。例如莎士比亚《奥赛罗》第三幕第三场里伊阿古幸灾乐祸地道出的几句话：

> 罂粟、曼陀罗
> 或是世上一切使人昏迷的药草，
> 都不能使你得到昨天晚上你还安然享受的酣眠。　　（朱生豪译）

17世纪著名的例子有：本·琼森在《用你的双眸给我祝酒吧》这首抒情诗中对诗中的女主人公过于夸张的殷勤赞美；安德鲁·马韦尔在诗歌《致羞涩的情人》里通过讽刺性的夸张表明他的"爱情之株长得"极其缓慢——但愿自己有"足够的空间和时间"。美国西部的"大话"或**牛皮故事**主要是一种戏谑性夸张的形

form of mainly comic hyperbole. There is the story of a cowboy in an eastern restaurant who ordered a steak well done. "Do you call this well done?" he roared at the server. "I've seen critters hurt worse than that get well!"

The contrary figure is **understatement** (the Greek term is **meiosis**, "lessening"), which deliberately represents something as very much less in magnitude or importance than it really is, or is ordinarily considered to be. The effect is usually ironic. It is savagely (and complexly) ironic in Jonathan Swift's *A Tale of a Tub* (1704), in which the narrator asserts the "superiority" of "that Wisdom, which converses about the surface" to "that pretended Philosophy which enters into the Depth of Things," giving as example that "last week I saw a Woman *flay'd*, and you will hardly believe how much it altered her Person for the worse." The understatement is comically ironic in Mark Twain's comment, "The reports of my death are greatly exaggerated." Some critics extend "meiosis" to the use in literature of a simple, unemphatic statement to enhance the effect of a deeply pathetic or tragic event; an example is the line at the close of the narrative in William Wordsworth's "Michael" (1800): "And never lifted up a single stone."

A special form of understatement is **litotes** (Greek for "plain" or "simple"), the assertion of an affirmative by negating its contrary: "He's not the brightest man in the world" meaning "He is stupid." The figure is frequent in Anglo-Saxon poetry, where the effect is usually one of grim irony. In Beowulf, after Hrothgar has described the ghastly mere where the monster Grendel dwells, he comments, "That is not a pleasant place."

hypermedia: 167.

hypertext: Hypertext designates a nonsequential kind of text, achieved by embedding within it a number of links and references to other texts; the result is to make the experience of reading the hypertext nonlinear, open, and variable. That is, the reader of the hypertext, instead of reading along a single verbal line, branches off into other texts at will. (This *Glossary* can be accounted a form of hypertext, in that the italicized terms invite readers to suspend forward progress while they look ahead or back in order to consult other relevant entries.) The term was coined in the 1960s, and was applied specifically to texts on a computer, in which browsers and hyperlinks enable the reader to move instantly from one document to another. Narratives that use embedded hyperlinks to enable the reader to navigate freely, deviating from the main narrative to explore details of plot, character, or setting, are called **hypertext fiction** or **cyberfiction**. Often, hypertext fiction—like other instances of what are called **hypermedia**—incorporates sound, graphics, and video.

See George P. Landow, ed., *Hyper/Text/Theory* (1994), and *Hypertext 3.0* (2006).

hypotactic style (hī′ pōtăk″ tik): **386**.

式。有这样一个故事：在东部一家餐馆，有个牛仔点了一份烤得很好的牛排（在烹调用语中这是"烤透"或"火候大些"的意思——译者）。牛仔一见牛排就向女侍大声咆哮："你管这叫烤得好吗？比这烧得还焦的牛我都见识过！"

与夸张相反的修辞手法是**含蓄**（希腊文为 meiosis："曲言"），这种手法在形容事物时故意轻描淡写，使其严重性或重要性比实际情况或通常认为的情况要轻得多。它所造成的效果通常是讽刺。在乔纳森·斯威夫特的《一个木桶的故事》（1704）里，叙述者坚称"谈论表面的智慧""优越于""进入事物深处的假装的哲学"，其中有这样一例辛辣（和复合）的讽刺："上周我眼见一个女人被剥光了皮，你真是难以相信这使她看上去更糟到何种地步。"马克·吐温的评论里有句滑稽的讽刺"有关我的死讯的报道有夸大之嫌。"一些评论家把文学作品里以轻描淡写来强化哀怜或悲剧事件之深切效果的手法也划入"曲言"之列。华兹华斯的叙事诗《迈克尔》（1800）的结尾一句"却不曾在那上面垒一块石头"便是一例。

反语法（希腊语意为"平淡"或"简单"）是含蓄手法的一种特殊形式，以否定其反面来表示肯定：用"他不是世界上最聪明的人"来意指"他愚蠢"。这一修辞手法常见于盎格鲁-撒克逊时期的诗歌，其效果往往是严酷的讽刺。在《贝奥武甫》中，赫罗斯加对怪物格伦德尔的栖身之处"那个可怕的沼泽"作了一番描述后评论道："那可不是个好玩的地方。"

hypermedia：超媒体　167。

Hypertext：超文本

超文本是指一种非顺序（不连续）的文本，通过在其内部嵌入对其他文本的许多链接和引用而获得；其结果，使得阅读超文本时会有一种非线性的、开放的、多变的体验。也就是说，超文本的读者，不是按照单一的词语表达去阅读，而是可以自由地岔入其他文本。（本书《文学术语词典》就可视为一种超文本的形式，书中的斜体术语邀请读者暂停前进，他们可以向前或向后查询其他相关条目。）这一术语创造于1960年代，专指电脑上的文本，在电脑上，浏览器和超链接使读者能在瞬间从一个文件移动到另一个文件。使用内置超链接以使读者能自由行进，偏离主要描述去探索情节、人物或背景细节的叙事，称为**超文本小说**或**赛博小说**。通常情况下，超文本小说，就像所谓超媒体中的其他例子，会将声音、图形和视频混合到一起。

参阅：乔治·P. 兰多主编的《超级/文本/理论》（1994）和《超文本3.0版》（2006）。

hypotactic style：从属句文体　386。

I

iambic (īăm′ bik): **218**; *30.*

icon (in semiotics) (ī kŏn): **358**.

iconography (īkŏnŏ′ grăfē): **182**.

id: 322.

Idealism: Idealism is the name for a philosophical doctrine, arising at the end of the eighteenth century, that was transformed over the course of the nineteenth century into an important concept for literature as well. Idealism was founded on the distinction drawn by Immanuel Kant between the realms of freedom (reason, imagination, morality, and aesthetics) and necessity (material objects, nature, the world of science). For subsequent thinkers, including Hölderlin, Schiller, Novalis, Schlegel, Hegel, and, in England, S. T. Coleridge, the idea of freedom was realized most fully in the creation and appreciation of beauty, understood as the unification of truth and goodness. In Schiller's treatise on *Naive and Sentimental Poetry*, Idealism was articulated as a *utopian* program, at the center of which is the image of a harmonious human being perfectly at home in the world.

According to the tenets of Idealism, it was the task of art, and poetry in particular, to help realize this revolutionary vision of freedom and harmony. But by the middle of the nineteenth century, Idealism had hardened into a set of implicit public expectations about the proper moral role of art. The 1857 public trials of Flaubert's *Madame Bovary* for blasphemy and Baudelaire's *Les fleurs du mal* for obscenity demonstrated the consequences for works of art that did not conform to the Idealist aesthetic. Literary *modernism* began, according to Toril Moi, as a series of revolts against an Idealism that had become suffocating rather than liberating. Realism, naturalism, *aestheticism*, and modernist *formalism* all had, she argues, a common enemy in Idealism, whose major tenets were that art should inspire, uplift, and console. See Toril Moi, *Henrik Ibsen and the Birth of Modernism: Art, Theater, Philosophy* (2006). For an important discussion of the French novelist George Sand in the context of Idealism, see Naomi Schor, *Reading in Detail: Aesthetics and the Feminine* (1987).

identity theorists: 164.

ideology (īdēŏl′ ōjē): **203**; *20, 42, 333, 401.*

idyll: 268.

illocutionary act (ĭl′ ōkyoo″ shŭnāry): **372**.

I

iambic：抑扬格　**218**；*30*。

icon (in semiotics)：(符号论中的) 图像　**358**。

iconography：传统性形象　**182**。

id：本我　**322**。

Idealism：唯心主义

　　唯心主义是一种哲学学说的名称，兴起于 18 世纪末，在 19 世纪演变成为一个重要的文学观念。唯心主义建立在伊曼纽尔·康德所作的自由领域（理性，想象力，道德和美学）与需求领域（实物，自然，科学世界）的区分之上。对于其后的思想家来说，包括荷尔德林、席勒、诺瓦利斯、施莱格尔、黑格尔和英国的 S. T. 柯勒律治，自由的理念，在美的创造和欣赏中得到最充分的实现，被理解为真与善的统一。在席勒的论文《论素朴的诗和感伤的诗》中，唯心主义被阐述为一个乌托邦计划，其中心是一个和谐的人的形象，在世界上就像是完全在家一样。

　　根据唯心主义的信条，艺术（尤其是诗歌）的任务是帮助实现这一革命性的自由与和谐景象。但到 19 世纪中期，唯心主义已经变成一组不言自明的公众期望：关于艺术的正确的道德角色。1857 年以亵渎罪名公开审判福楼拜的《包法利夫人》和以淫秽罪名审判波德莱尔的《恶之花》，展示了艺术作品不符合唯心主义美学的后果。根据陶丽·莫伊的看法，文学上的*现代主义*开始对唯心主义进行一系列的反抗，因为唯心主义已经变得令人窒息而非让人解放。她认为，现实主义、自然主义、*唯美主义*和现代主义者的*形式主义*都有一个共同的敌人：唯心主义，它们的主要原则是，艺术应该予人以激励、振奋和安慰。参阅：陶丽·莫伊所著的《易卜生与现代主义的诞生：艺术、戏剧和哲学》(2006)。在唯心主义背景下对法国小说家乔治·桑进行的一个重要讨论，参阅：纳奥米·肖尔所著的《解读细节：美学与女性特质》(1987)。

identity theorists：身份理论家　**164**。

ideology：意识形态　**203**；*20, 42, 333, 401*。

idyll：田园诗　**268**。

illocutionary act：话中行为　**372**。

illuminated (books): **32**, *153*.

image clusters: 170.

Imagery: This term is one of the most common in criticism, and one of the most variable in meaning. Its applications range all the way from the "mental pictures" which, it is sometimes claimed, are experienced by the reader of a poem, to the totality of the components which make up a poem. Examples of this range of usage are the statements by the poet C. Day Lewis, in his *Poetic Image* (1948, pp. 17–18), that an image "is a picture made out of words," and that "a poem may itself be an image composed from a multiplicity of images." Three discriminable uses of the word, however, are especially frequent; in all these senses imagery is said to make poetry *concrete*, as opposed to *abstract*:

1. "Imagery" (that is, "images" taken collectively) is used to signify all the objects and qualities of sense perception referred to in a poem or other work of literature, whether by literal description, by *allusion*, or in the *vehicles* (the secondary references) of its similes and metaphors. In William Wordsworth's "She Dwelt among the Untrodden Ways" (1800), the imagery in this broad sense includes the literal objects the poem refers to (for example, "untrodden ways," "springs," "grave"), as well as the "violet" of the metaphor and the "star" of the simile in the second stanza. The term "image" should not be taken to imply a visual reproduction of the object denoted; some readers of the passage experience visual images and some do not; and among those who do, the explicitness and details of the pictures vary greatly. Also, "imagery" in this usage includes not only visual sense qualities, but also qualities that are auditory, tactile (touch), thermal (heat and cold), olfactory (smell), gustatory (taste), and kinesthetic (sensations of movement). In his *In Memoriam* (1850), No. 101, for example, Tennyson's imagery encompasses not only things that are visible, but also qualities that are smelled, tasted, or heard, together with a suggestion, in the adjective "summer," of warmth:

   > Unloved, that beech will gather brown, …
   > And many a rose-carnation feed
   > With summer spice the humming air.…

2. Imagery is used, more narrowly, to signify only specific descriptions of visible objects and scenes, especially if the description is vivid and particularized, as in this passage from Marianne Moore's "The Steeple-Jack":

illuminated (books)：彩饰（书籍） 32, 153。

image clusters：意象群 170。

Imagery：意象

该术语是文艺评论里最常见而意义又最广泛的术语之一。它的使用范围可以包括有时候所说的读者从一首诗中领悟到的"精神画面"到构成一首诗的全部组成部分。这一系列用法的例子可见 C. 戴·刘易斯在其所著的《诗学意象》（1948）中第 17、18 页里的陈述：意象"是文字组成的画面"，"一首诗本身也可以是多种意象组成的一个意象"。然而意象一词有三种可辨别的用法尤为常见。就这三种用法来说，意象的作用是使诗歌具体而不是抽象：

1. "意象"（即"形象"的总称）用于指代一首诗歌或其他文学作品里通过直叙、暗示，或者明喻及隐喻的喻矢（间接指称），使读者感受到的物体或特性。在威廉·华兹华斯的诗歌《她住在人迹罕至的地方》（1800）中，这种广义上的意象包括诗里提到的直观物体（如"人迹罕至的地方""春天""坟墓"），以及第二段里用于隐喻的"紫罗兰"和用作明喻的"星星"。不能认为"意象"这一术语就是指所描绘的事物的视觉再现。对于一段描写，有些读者能够感觉到段落中的视觉形象而有些读者则不能；即便是对那些能够感受到视觉形象的读者来说，他们所感受到的画面的清晰度和细节也是大有差别。同时，"意象"在这种用法中不仅包括视觉特征，还包括听觉、触觉（触摸）、温度（冷和热）、嗅觉（气味）、味觉（味道）、动觉（运动的感觉）。例如，丁尼生《悼念集》（1850）第 101 首中所包含的意象，不仅包括可见事物，还包括可闻或可听见的事物的特征，并通过"夏日"这一形容词给人以"温暖"：

    > 没人爱，山毛榉依然变黄，……
    > 同众多的玫瑰石竹一样，
    > 把夏香添入嗡嗡的空气…… （飞白译）

2. 意象在较为狭窄的意义上仅用来指对可视客体和场景的具体描绘，尤其是生动细致的描述，正如玛丽安·穆尔在《尖顶》中的诗句（版权未授，请参旧版。——译注）。

    （略）

3. Commonly in recent usage, imagery signifies *figurative language*, especially the *vehicles* of metaphors and similes. Critics after the 1930s, and notably the *New Critics*, went far beyond earlier commentators in stressing imagery, in this sense, as the essential component in poetry, and as a major factor in poetic meaning, structure, and effect.

Using the term in this third sense, Caroline Spurgeon, in *Shakespeare's Imagery and What It Tells Us* (1935), made statistical counts of the referents of the figurative vehicles in Shakespeare, and used the results as clues to Shakespeare's personal experiences, interests, and temperament. Following the lead of several earlier critics, she also pointed out the frequent occurrence in Shakespeare's plays of **image clusters** (recurrent groupings of seemingly unrelated metaphors and similes). She also presented evidence that a number of the individual plays have characteristic image *motifs* (for example, animal imagery in *King Lear*, and the figures of disease, corruption, and death in *Hamlet*); her view was that these elements established the overall tonality or *atmosphere* of a play. Many critics in the next few decades joined Spurgeon in the search for images, image clusters, and "thematic imagery" in works of literature. Some *New Critics* held that the implicit interactions of the imagery—in distinction from explicit statements by the author or the overt speeches and actions of the characters— were the way that the controlling literary subject, or *theme*, worked itself out in many plays, poems, and novels. See, for example, the critical writings of G. Wilson Knight; Cleanth Brooks on *Macbeth* in *The Well Wrought Urn* (1947), chapter 2; and Robert B. Heilman, *This Great Stage: Image and Structure in "King Lear"* (1948).

See also H. W. Wells, *Poetic Imagery* (1924); Richard H. Fogle, *The Imagery of Keats and Shelley* (1949); Norman Friedman, "Imagery: From Sensation to Symbol," *Journal of Aesthetics and Art Criticism* 12 (1953); Frank Kermode, *Romantic Image* (1957). For references to *imagery* in other entries, see page 61.

imaginary (in Lacanian criticism): **324**.

imagination: 120.

Imagism: Imagism was a poetic vogue that flourished in England, and even more vigorously in America, approximately between the years 1912 and 1917. It was planned and exemplified by a group of English and American writers in London, partly under the influence of the poetic theory of T. E. Hulme, as a revolt against what Ezra Pound called the "rather blurry, messy ... sentimentalistic mannerish" poetry at the turn of the century. Pound, the first leader of the movement, was soon succeeded by Amy Lowell; after that Pound sometimes referred to the movement, slightingly, as "Amygism." Other leading participants, for a time, were H. D. (Hilda Doolittle), D. H. Lawrence, William Carlos Williams, John Gould Fletcher, and Richard Aldington. The Imagist proposals, as voiced by Amy Lowell in her preface to the first of three anthologies called *Some Imagist Poets* (1915–17), were for

3. 按照目前最普遍的用法，意象指的是*比喻语*，尤其指隐喻和明喻的喻矢。1930 年代后的批评家，特别是新批评家在强调意象方面已远远超越了早期的评论者，在这个意义上，意象是诗歌的基本成分，是呈现诗歌含义、结构与艺术效果的主要因素。

根据这一术语的第三种含义，卡罗琳·斯珀金在其所著的《莎士比亚的比喻及其意义》(1935) 中，对莎翁作品中用到的比喻喻矢作了统计，并将统计结果用作分析莎士比亚的个人经历、兴趣与气质的线索。她还仿照早先几位批评家的做法，点出了莎剧中频繁出现的**意象群**（即反复出现的看似没有联系的一组组隐喻和明喻）。她同时证明了其中一部分独立的戏剧具有独特的意象*主题*（如《李尔王》里的动物意象，《哈姆雷特》中有关疾病、腐败和死亡的比喻）；斯珀金认为这些元素筑成了一部戏剧的总体*基调*。此后数十年间，许多批评家和她一样探索文学作品里的意象、意象群及"主题意象"。一些*新批评家*认为，很多戏剧、诗歌、小说作品中起主导作用的文学题材或*主题*，并非取决于作品中作者的外在论述或人物公开的言行，而是取决于意象之间暗含的一种相互作用。例如可以参阅：G. 威尔逊·奈特的评论文章；克林斯·布鲁克斯所著的《精制的瓮》(1947) 第 2 章里有关《麦克白》的评论，罗伯特·B. 海尔曼所著的《这个大舞台：〈李尔王〉里的意象与结构》(1948)。

参阅：H. W. 韦尔斯所著的《诗歌意象》(1924)；理查德·H. 福格尔所著的《济慈和雪莱的意象》(1949)；诺曼·弗里德曼所写的文章"意象：从感觉到象征"，载于《美学与艺术批评学刊》1953 年第 12 卷；弗兰克·克莫德所著的《浪漫主义意象》(1957)。其他条目中提及"意象"的地方，参见第 61 页。

imaginary (in Lacanian criticism)：(拉康批评中的) 想象阶段　324。

imagination：想象力　120。

Imagism：意象主义

意象主义是 1912—1917 年间在英国兴起但在美国更为盛行的一个诗歌流派。它由伦敦的一些英美作家发起，在一定程度上受到 T. E. 休姆的诗歌理论的影响，反对世纪之交被庞德称为"模糊、杂乱……感伤造作"的诗歌。庞德是这次运动的首位领头人，不久便由埃米·洛威尔接替，在此之后，这个运动有时便被庞德轻慢地称为"埃米主义"。一段时间内，其他主要参与者有 H. D.（希尔达·杜利特尔）、D. H. 劳伦斯、威廉·卡洛斯·威廉斯、约翰·古尔德·弗莱彻、理查·奥尔丁顿。正如埃米·洛威尔在名为《一些意象主义诗人》(1915—1917) 三卷本诗

a poetry which, abandoning conventional limits on poetic materials and versification, is free to choose any subject and to create its own rhythms, uses common speech, and presents an "image" (vivid sensory description) that is hard, clear, and concentrated. (See *imagery*.)

The typical Imagist poem is written in *free verse* and undertakes to render as precisely, vividly, and tersely as possible, and without comment or generalization, the writer's impression of a visual object or scene; often the impression is rendered by means of metaphor, or by juxtaposing, without indicating a relationship, the description of one object with that of a second and diverse object. This famed example by Ezra Pound exceeds other Imagist poems in the degree of its concentration:

In this poem Pound, like a number of other Imagists, was influenced by the Japanese *haiku*.

Imagism was too restrictive to endure long as a concerted movement, but it served to inaugurate a distinctive feature of *modernist* poetry. Almost every major poet from the 1920s through the middle of the twentieth century, including W. B. Yeats, T. S. Eliot, and Wallace Stevens, manifests some influence by the Imagist experiments with the presentation of precise, clear images that are juxtaposed without specifying their interrelationships.

See T. E. Hulme, *Speculations*, ed. Herbert Read (1924); *The Imagist Poem*, ed. William Pratt (1963); Hugh Kenner, *The Pound Era* (1971); Glenn Hughes, *Imagism and the Imagists: A Study in Modern Poetry* (1973); J. B. Harmer, *Victory in Limbo: Imagism, 1908–1917* (1975); Andrew Thacker, *The Imagist Poets* (2008).

imitation: In literary criticism the word **imitation** has two frequent but diverse applications: (1) to define the nature of literature and the other arts, and (2) to indicate the relationship of one literary work to another literary work which served as its model.

1. In his *Poetics*, Aristotle defines poetry as an imitation (in Greek, **mimesis**) of human actions. (See *criticism*.) By "imitation" he means something like "representation," in its root sense: the poem imitates by taking an instance of human action and re-presenting it in a new "medium"—that of words. By distinguishing differences in the artistic media, in the kind of actions imitated, and in the manner of imitation (for example, dramatic or narrative), Aristotle first distinguishes poetry from other arts, and then makes distinctions between the various poetic kinds, such as drama and epic, tragedy and comedy. From the sixteenth through the eighteenth

选首卷前言中所述，意象派主张诗歌抛弃对诗歌题材与韵律的传统限制，自由选择题材，创造出自己的韵律，采用口语，并要表现出坚实、清晰与凝聚的意象（描写生动的感觉）来。（参见：意象。）

典型的意象派诗歌采用自由诗形式，它不需要任何评注与概括就可以尽可能确切而简洁地反映诗人对可视事物或场景的印象；这种印象常常是通过隐喻或者通过并列描写来表现，在描述一个物体之后，接着描述另一个不同的对象，并不指明一种关联。在下面这个著名的例子（指《地铁车站》，版权未授，请参旧版。——译注）中，埃兹拉·庞德在集中描写方面超过了任何意象派诗歌。

（略）

在这首诗中，庞德与其他意象派诗人一样受到了日本*俳句*的影响。

由于意象主义受到过多限制，以致难以成为一个统一持久的运动，但它却开创了*现代主义*诗歌的特色。从1920年代至20世纪中期，几乎每个主要诗人，包括W. B. 叶芝、T. S. 艾略特和华莱士·史蒂文斯，都显示了并列描述但未指明其间相互关系的准确而清晰的意象尝试对他们的某些影响。

参阅：T. E. 休姆所著的《意度集》（1924，赫伯特·里德主编）和《意象派诗人的诗歌》（1963，威廉·普拉特主编）；休·肯纳所著的《庞德时代》（1971）；格伦·休斯所著的《意象主义与意象派诗人：现代诗歌研究》（1973）；J. B. 哈默所著的《不稳定状态的胜利：1908—1917年间的意象主义》（1975）；安德鲁·撒克所著的《意象派诗人的诗歌》（2008）。

Imitation：摹仿

在文学批评中，**摹仿**一词有两种常见的不同用法：(1) 说明文学或其他艺术形式的性质，(2) 表示一部文学作品和它所仿照的另一部作品之间的关系。

1. 亚里士多德在《诗学》中把诗歌解释为对人类活动的摹仿（希腊文为 **mimesis**）。（参见：*批评*。）他所谓的"摹仿"原意是指某种"再现"，即诗歌通过捕捉人的某一活动再以新的"手段"（即语言）把它再现出来。亚里士多德通过划分不同的艺术手段、所摹仿活动的不同类型、摹仿的不同方式（如戏剧形式或叙事形式），首先把诗歌与其他艺术形式区别开来，继而进一步划分不同的诗歌类型，如戏剧与史诗、悲剧与喜剧。从16世纪一直到18世纪，"摹仿"一向是

century the term "imitation" was a central term in discussing the nature of poetry. Critics differed radically, however, in their concept of the nature of the mimetic relationship, and of the kinds of things in the external world that works of literature imitate, or ought to imitate, so that theories of imitation varied in the kind of art they recommended, from a strict realism to a remote idealism. With the emergence in the early nineteenth century of an *expressive criticism* (the view that poetry is essentially an expression of the poet's feelings or imaginative process), imitation tended to be displaced from its central position in literary theory (see *criticism*). In the last half century, however, the use of the term has been revived, especially by R. S. Crane and other *Chicago critics*, who ground their theory on the analytic method and basic distinctions of Aristotle's *Poetics*. Many *Marxist critics* also propose a view of literature as an imitation, or, in their preferred term, "reflection," of social reality.

2. Greek and Roman rhetoricians and critics often recommended that a poet should "imitate" the established models in a particular literary *genre*. The notion that the proper procedure for poets, with the rare exception of an "original genius," was to imitate the normative forms and styles of the Greek and Roman masters continued to be influential through the eighteenth century. All the major critics, however, also insisted that mere copying was not enough—that a good literary work must imitate the form and spirit rather than the detail of the classic models, and that success can be achieved only by a poet who possesses an innate poetic talent. (See *neoclassic*.)

In a specialized use of the term in this second sense, "imitation" was also used to describe a literary work which deliberately echoed an older work but adapted it to subject matter in the writer's own age, usually in a satirical fashion. In the poems that Alexander Pope called *Imitations of Horace* (1733 and following), for example, an important part of the intended effects depend on the reader's recognition of the resourcefulness and wit with which Pope accommodated to contemporary circumstances the structure, details, and even the wording of one or another of Horace's Roman satires.

On "imitation" as a term used to define literature see R. S. Crane, ed., *Critics and Criticism* (1952); M. H. Abrams, *The Mirror and the Lamp* (1953), chapters 1–2; and Erich Auerbach, *Mimesis* (trans. 1953, reprinted 2003). On Pope's "imitations" of Horace and other ancient masters see R. A. Brower, *Alexander Pope: The Poetry of Allusion* (1959). For denials, on various grounds, that literature can be claimed to be an imitation of reality, see *Russian formalism, structuralist criticism, deconstruction, new historicism,* and *text and writing (écriture)*. Among modern defenses of the view that literature is mimetic, in the broad sense that it has reference beyond the text to the world of human experience, see Gerald Graff, *Literature against Itself* (1979); A. D. Nuttall, *A New Mimesis: Shakespeare and the Representation of Reality* (1983); and Robert Alter, "Mimesis and the Motives for Fiction," in his *Motives for Fiction* (1984).

For references to *imitation* in other entries, see pages *237, 342*.

有关诗歌性质讨论中的关键术语。然而，在关于文学与生活的摹拟关系的实质，以及文学作品所摹仿或应该摹仿的外部世界事物的类型的理念上，批评家们有着极为不同的看法，因此有关摹仿的理论也就根据他们所推崇的艺术类型的变化而不同，从严谨的现实主义到超然的唯心主义都有。随着19世纪早期表现主义批评的兴起（认为诗歌实质上是诗人感情或想象过程的表露），摹仿论在文学理论中的重要位置逐渐被取代（参见：批评）。但在19世纪后半叶，摹仿这一术语再度流行，尤其是得到了R. S. 克莱恩和其他芝加哥批评派成员的青睐，他们将自己的理论建立在亚里士多德《诗学》中的分析方法和各种基本划分的基础之上。此外许多马克思主义批评家也认为文学是一种摹仿，或者用他们偏爱的术语来说，是对社会现实的"反映"。

2. 希腊罗马修辞学家和评论家经常建议诗人去"摹仿"特定文学体裁中业已公认的典范。他们认为除了个别"有独创性的天才"之外，诗人创作的适当途径应该是摹仿希腊罗马名家诗歌作品的规范形式与风格。这种观点一直到18世纪都颇具影响力。然而，所有主要的批评家同时也都坚信：单纯的照搬摹仿是不够的，一部好的文学作品所摹仿的必须是古典典范的形式与精神而非其枝节，而（在这方面）只有那些具备诗歌天赋的诗人才会取得成功。（参见：新经典。）

在这一术语第二个意义上的范畴里还有一种特殊用法："摹仿"还用于描述那种有意仿效某一古典作品，但借以表现作者本人时代题材的文学作品，通常以讽刺形式出现。例如在亚历山大·蒲柏命名为《仿贺拉斯作》的诗集里（1733年及以后），诗人将贺拉斯某些罗马讽刺诗歌的结构、细节乃至措词都融入自己对其所处时代事件的描述中，他所预期的效果主要取决于读者对他的这种机敏与智慧的领会。

关于"摹仿"作为说明文学性质的术语，参阅：R. S. 克莱恩主编的《批评家与批评》(1952)；M. H. 艾布拉姆斯所著的《镜与灯》(1953) 第1—2章；埃利希·奥尔巴赫所著的《摹仿论》(1953年英译版，2003年重印)。论述蒲柏对贺拉斯作品及其他古典名家的"摹仿"，可以参阅：R. A. 布劳尔所著的《亚历山大·蒲柏诗歌的典故》(1959)。从各种不同的理论依据否定"文学是对现实的摹仿"的观点，参见术语：俄国形式主义、结构主义批评、解构主义、新历史主义、文本与书写。现代对于"文学即摹仿"这一观点的辩护，从广义上来说在于文学超越了文本，涉及人类的经验世界，参阅：杰拉尔德·格拉夫所著的《自我作对的文学》(1979)；A. D. 纳托尔所著的《新摹仿论：莎士比亚和现实的再现》(1983)；罗伯特·奥尔特所著的《小说创作动机》(1984) 中的"摹仿与小说创作动机"。

其他条目中提及"摹仿"的地方，参见第237、342页。

imperfect rhyme: 349.

impersonal (narrator): **302**.

implicature: 90.

implicit metaphor: 131.

implied auditor: 287.

implied author: 288.

implied reader: 330.

impressionistic criticism: 68.

in medias res (in mā′ dēäs räs′): **109**; *296*.

incidents (in a plot): **295**.

incremental repetition: 23.

incunabula (ĭn kyoonăb″ yoolă̆): **33**.

index (in semiotics): **358**.

indexicals: 233.

indirect satire: 354.

influence and the anxiety of influence: Critics and historians of literature have for many centuries discussed what was called the **influence** of an author, or of a literary tradition, upon a later author, who was said to adopt, and at the same time to alter, aspects of the subject matter, form, or style of the earlier writer or writers. Among traditional topics for discussion, for example, have been the influence of Homer on Virgil, of Virgil on Milton, of Milton on Wordsworth, or of Wordsworth on Wallace Stevens. The **anxiety of influence** is a phrase used by the influential contemporary critic Harold Bloom to identify his radical revision of this standard theory that influence consists in a direct "borrowing," or assimilation, of the materials and features found in earlier writers. Bloom's own view is that in the composition of any poem, influence is inescapable, but that it evokes in the author an anxiety that compels a drastic distortion of the work of a predecessor. He applies this concept of anxiety to the reading as well as the writing of poetry.

In Bloom's theory a poet (especially since the time of Milton) is motivated to compose when his imagination is seized upon by a poem or poems

imperfect rhyme：不完美韵　349。

impersonal (narrator)：非个人的（叙述者）　302。

implicature：话语含意　90。

implicit metaphor：含蓄隐喻　131。

implied auditor：隐藏的听众　287。

implied author：隐遁的作者　288。

implied reader：隐在读者　330。

impressionistic criticism：印象主义批评　68。

in medias res：倒叙　109；*296*。

incidents (in a plot)：（情节中的）附带事件　295。

incremental repetition：递增的重复　23。

incunabula：古版本　33。

index (in semiotics)：（符号论中的）标示物　358。

indexicals：指示词　233。

indirect satire：间接讽刺　354。

Influence and the Anxiety of Influence：影响与影响的焦虑

很多世纪以来，文学批评家和文学史学家一直在研究某一作家或文学传统对后辈作家的**影响**问题，因为后辈作家被认为在采纳的同时会对前辈的一个或一些作家的题材、形式或风格加以改变。例如，在讨论的传统性议题中，就有关于荷马对维吉尔的影响、维吉尔对弥尔顿的影响、弥尔顿对华兹华斯的影响，或者华兹华斯对华莱士·史蒂文斯的影响。依照权威理论的说法，所谓的影响存在于后世作家对前人之作的素材与特征的直接"借鉴"或吸收上。当代颇有影响的批评家哈罗德·布卢姆用**影响的焦虑**这一说法来表明他对这种权威理论的彻底修正。布卢姆自己的观点是，这种影响在任何诗歌创作中都是不可避免的，但却使作者产生一种心理焦虑，而对前人之作大加歪曲。除了用于诗歌写作，他还把这种心理焦虑的观点引入诗歌阅读中。

根据布卢姆的理论，当诗人（尤其是自弥尔顿以来的诗人）的想象力受到"前辈"诗歌作品的吸引时，他会萌发出一种创作欲望。然而这些"后继"诗人

of a "precursor." The "belated" poet's attitudes to his precursor, like those in Freud's analysis of the Oedipal relationship of son to father, are ambivalent; that is, they are compounded not only of admiration but also (since any strong poet feels a compelling need to be autonomous and original) of hate, envy, and fear of the precursor's preemption of the descendant's imaginative space. The belated poet safeguards his sense of his own freedom and priority by reading a parent poem "defensively," in such a way as to distort it beyond his own conscious recognition. Nonetheless, he cannot avoid embodying the distorted parent poem into his own hopeless attempt to write an unprecedentedly original poem; the most that even the best belated poet can achieve is to write a poem so "strong" that it effects an illusion of "priority"—that is, a double illusion that it has escaped the precursor poem's precedence in time, and that it exceeds it in greatness.

Since Bloom conceives that "every poem is a misinterpretation of a parent poem," he recommends that literary critics boldly practice what he calls **antithetical criticism**—that is, that they learn "to read any poem as its poet's deliberate misinterpretation, *as a poet*, of a precursor poem or of poetry in general." The results of such "strong readings" will be antithetical both to what the poet himself thought he meant and to what standard weak misreadings have made out the poem to mean. In his own powerfully individualistic writings, Bloom applies such antithetical criticism to poets ranging from the eighteenth century through the major Romantics, and Yeats and Stevens, to contemporary poets such as A. R. Ammons and John Ashbery. He is aware that, by the terms of his theory, his own interpretations of both poets and critics are necessarily misreadings. His claim is that his antithetical interpretations are strong, and therefore "interesting," misreadings, and so will take their place in the accumulation of misreadings which constitutes the history both of poetry and of criticism, at least since the seventeenth century—although this history is bound to be tragic, since as time goes on there will be a constant decrease in the area of imaginative possibilities that are left open to poets.

As Bloom points out, a precursor of his views was Walter Jackson Bate's *The Burden of the Past and the English Poet* (1970), which described the struggles by poets, since 1660, to overcome the inhibitive effect of fear that their predecessors might have exhausted all the possibilities of writing great and original poems. Bloom presented his own theory of reading and writing poetry in *The Anxiety of Influence* (1973), then elaborated the theory, and demonstrated its application to diverse poetic texts, in three rapidly successive books, *A Map of Misreading* (1975), *Kabbalah and Criticism* (1975), and *Poetry and Repression* (1976), as well as in a number of writings concerned with individual poets. See also the collection of Bloom's writings, *Poetics of Influence*, ed. John Hollander (1988). For analyses and critiques of this theory of literature see Frank Lentricchia, *After the New Criticism* (1980), chapter 9; David Fite, *Harold Bloom: The Rhetoric of Romantic Vision* (1985); M. H. Abrams, "How to Do Things with Texts," in *Doing Things with Texts* (1989). Bloom proposed his theory, it will have been noted, with respect to male poets; for an application

对"前辈"的态度却是矛盾的，正如弗洛伊德所分析的子与父的俄狄浦斯关系一样；这种感情混和了后继者对先辈的仰慕、敬佩之情，另一方面又夹杂着憎恶、妒忌和担心先辈已经占据了自己的想象天地的心理（因为优秀诗人都会强烈地感受到自主和创新的需要）。后继诗人为了确保自身的自由与优先，便以"防备自卫"的方式阅读先人之作，结果不自觉地歪曲了原作。然而，在他自己想要完成史无前例的原创诗作的绝望尝试里，也不可避免地会体现出先辈作品的扭曲影像；因此大多数后继诗人，即便是最优秀的，他们所能做到的也就是写出一首如此"绝妙"的诗歌，以至于产生"优先"的错觉——即造成在时间上先于前辈诗歌、在质量上比先辈作品更胜一筹的错觉。

由于布卢姆认为"每一首诗都是对前辈诗作的曲解"，他建议文学批评家大胆采用他称为**对立批评**的方法，也就是说学会在"阅读任何一首诗歌作品时都要善于把它视为作者作为一位诗人对前辈诗作或所有诗歌的故意曲解的结果"。这种过激性阅读得出的结果将与诗人自认为所表达的意思形成对立，同时与一般节制型误读解读出的原诗含义也将形成对立。在布卢姆带有强烈个性的文章中，他将这种对立批评法应用于对 18 世纪诗人，从主要浪漫主义诗人到叶芝和史蒂文斯再到像 A. R. 阿蒙斯和约翰·阿什伯里这样的当代诗人的作品的解读中。依据他的理论，布卢姆意识到，他对诗人和批评家的解释也必然是种曲解。他断言，他对作品作出的对立性解释是过激的，因此也是"有趣的"曲解，这些曲解的集聚汇成了至少是 17 世纪以来诗歌与批评的历史长河——尽管这一历史必定是悲剧性的，因为随着时间的流逝，留给诗人们的想象可能性将会逐渐不断减少。

就像布卢姆指出的，他的观点的先驱是沃尔特·杰克逊·巴特所著的《过去的负担和英国诗人》(1970)，巴特在该书中描述了 1660 年以来诗人们为了克服担心先辈们已竭尽了他们创作出原创性伟大诗篇可能性的这种忧虑对他们的抑制性影响而进行的抗争。布卢姆在其所著的《影响的焦虑》(1973) 中提出了自己关于阅读诗歌与诗歌创作的理论，继而又在短时间内连续出版的三部论著《误读的地图》(1975)、《神秘哲学与文学批评》(1975)、《诗与抑制》(1976)，以及一些关于个别诗人的文章中，进一步详尽地阐述了该理论，并说明了它对不同诗歌篇章的适用性。也可参阅布卢姆文集《影响诗学》(1988，约翰·霍兰德主编)；有关对这一文学理论的分析和评论，参阅：弗兰克·兰特里夏所著的《新批评之后》(1980) 第 9 章；戴维·菲特所著的《哈罗德·布鲁姆：浪漫想象的修辞学》(1985)；M. H. 艾布拉姆斯所著的《以文行事》(1989) 中的"如何以文行事"。值得注意的是，布卢姆是就一些男性诗人提出他的理论的；要想了解

of the concept of anxiety of influence to women writers, see Sandra Gilbert and Susan Gubar, *The Madwoman in the Attic* (rev. 2000), discussed in the entry *feminist criticism*.

informal essay: 114.

intention (in interpretation): **177**; *185*.

intention (in phenomenology): **289**.

intentional fallacy: Intentional fallacy signifies what is claimed to be the error of interpreting and evaluating a literary work by reference to evidence, outside the text itself, for the intention—the design and purposes—of its author. The term was proposed by W. K. Wimsatt and Monroe C. Beardsley in "The Intentional Fallacy" (1946), reprinted in Wimsatt's *The Verbal Icon* (1954). They asserted that an author's intended aims and meanings in writing a literary work—whether these are asserted by the author or merely inferred from our knowledge of the author's life and opinions—are irrelevant to the literary critic, because the meaning, structure, and value of a text are inherent within the finished, freestanding, and public work of literature itself. Reference to the author's supposed purposes, or else to the author's personal situation and state of mind in writing a text, is held to be a harmful mistake, because it diverts our attention to such "external" matters as the author's biography, or psychological condition, or creative process, which we substitute for the proper critical concern with the "internal" constitution and inherent value of the literary product. (See *objective criticism*, under *criticism*.)

This claim, which was central in the *New Criticism*, has been strenuously debated, and was reformulated by both of its original proponents. (See Wimsatt, "Genesis: An Argument Resumed," in *Day of the Leopards*, 1976; and Beardsley, *Aesthetics*, 1958, pp. 457–61, and *The Possibility of Criticism*, 1970, pp. 16–37.) A view acceptable to many traditional critics (but not to *structuralist* and *poststructuralist* theorists) is that in the exceptional instances—for example, in Henry James' prefaces to his novels—where we possess an author's express statement about his artistic intentions in a literary work, that statement should constitute evidence for an interpretive hypothesis, but should not in itself be determinative. If the author's stated intentions do not accord with the text, they should be qualified or rejected in favor of an alternative interpretation that conforms more closely to the shared, or "public," linguistic and literary conventions that the text itself incorporates.

Compare *affective fallacy*. For diverse views of the role of authorial intentions in establishing a text and in interpreting the meanings of a text, see *interpretation and hermeneutics* and *textual criticism*. A detailed objection to Wimsatt and Beardsley's original essay is E. D. Hirsch's "Objective Interpretation" (1960), reprinted as an appendix to his *Validity in Interpretation* (1967). An anthology of discussions of this topic in literary criticism is David Newton-De Molina, *On Literary Intention* (1976). Ronald Dworkin discusses parallels

"影响的焦虑"对女性诗人的影响，可以参阅*女性主义批评*中对桑德拉·吉尔伯特与苏珊·格芭合著的《阁楼上的疯女人》(1980) 的论述。

informal essay：非正规杂文　114。

intention (in interpretation)：(释义中的) 意向　177；*185*。

intention (in phenomenology)：(现象学中的) 意向　289。

Intentional Fallacy：意图谬误

　　意图谬误是指那种超越文本之外，参照外在依据，单纯根据作家的意图——即构思和目的——去解释和评价一部文学作品的错误做法。该术语由 W. K. 维姆萨特和门罗·C. 比尔兹利在其合写的文章"意图谬误"(1946) 中提出，重印收入维姆萨特所著的《语像》(1954)。他们宣称，作家创作一部文学作品时的意图和意义，无论是作者自己阐明的还是我们单从自己对作家的生平与见解的了解中推测出来的，都和文学评论家毫不相干，因为文本的意义、结构和价值存在于已经完成的、独立存在于公众面前的文学作品本身。以假想的作家创作文本时的创作意图或当时作者的自身情况及精神状态为依据去评论作品是种有害的错误，这样做会把我们的注意力转向作家的生平、心理状况或其创作过程等"外部"方面，而取代就文学作品的"内部"结构以及内在价值作出恰如其分的批评。(参见：*批评*中的*客观批评*。)

　　意图谬误一说是"新批评"的核心，它引起过激烈的争论，并由两位创始人再次对其进行了系统的论述。[参阅维姆萨特所著的《豹子的日子》(1976) 中的文章"辩论起源：旧论重提"；比尔兹利所著的《美学》(1958) 第457—461页，《批评的可能性》(1970) 第16—37页。] 已为许多传统批评家接受 (但其中不包括*结构主义和后结构主义*理论家) 的一种观点是：在个别我们可以得到作者对其艺术创作意图明确陈述的文学作品里——如亨利·詹姆斯小说的序言——作者的陈述可以成为解释性假设的证据，但这种陈述本身不能起决定性作用。如果作者阐述的创作意图与作品不相吻合，就应予以纠正或否定，并代之以更加符合文本自身所包含的共有的、或"大众化的"语言常规与文学惯例的其他解释。

　　对比：*情感谬误*。有关作者意图在建构文本与解释文本意义中的作用的不同观点，参见：*释义与阐释学*、*文本批评*。 E. N. 赫什在其所写的文章"客观释义" (1960) 中详述了对维姆萨特和比尔兹利原文的反对意见，重印收入《释义的合法性》(1967)，作为书中附录。有关文学批评中这一议题的讨论文集有戴维·牛顿－德莫利纳所著的《论文学意图》(1976)。罗纳德·德沃金在"释义法"一文中 [收

between the role of intention in legal interpretation and literary interpretation, in "Law as Interpretation," *The Politics of Interpretation*, ed. W. J. T. Mitchell (1983). For references to *intentional fallacy* in other entries, see page *179*.

interior monologue: 380.

interlude (in drama): 225.

internal rhyme: 348.

interpellation: 207.

interpretation and hermeneutics: In the narrow sense, to interpret a work of literature is to specify the meanings of its language by analysis, paraphrase, and commentary; usually such **interpretation** focuses on especially obscure, ambiguous, or figurative passages. In a broader sense, to interpret a work of literature is to make clear the artistic features and purport in the overall work of which language serves as the medium. Interpretation in this sense includes the analysis of such matters as the work's *genre*, component elements, form and structure, theme, and effects (see *criticism*).

The term **hermeneutics** originally designated the formulation of principles of interpretation that apply specifically to the Bible; the principles incorporated both the rules governing a valid reading of the biblical text, and **exegesis**, or commentary on the application of the meanings expressed in the text. Since the nineteenth century, however, "hermeneutics" has come to designate the theory of interpretation in general—that is, a formulation of the principles and methods involved in getting at the meaning of all written texts, including legal, historical, and literary, as well as biblical texts.

The German theologian Friedrich Schleiermacher, in a series of lectures in 1819, was the first to frame a theory of "general hermeneutics" as "the art of understanding" texts of every kind. Schleiermacher's views were developed in the 1890s by the influential philosopher Wilhelm Dilthey (1833–1911), who proposed a science of hermeneutics designed to serve as the basis for interpreting all forms of writing in the "human sciences": that is, in the *humanities* and the social sciences, as distinguished from the natural sciences. Dilthey regarded the human sciences as ways of dealing with the temporal, concrete, "lived experience" of human beings. He proposed that whereas the aim of the natural sciences is to achieve "explanation" by means of static, reductive categories, the aim of hermeneutics is to establish a general theory of "understanding." The understanding of a verbal text consists in "the interpretation of *works*, works in which the texture of inner life comes fully to expression." And in literature above all, "the inner life of man finds its complex, exhaustive, and objectively intelligible expression." (See *humanism*.)

In formulating the way in which we come to understand the meaning of a text, Dilthey gave the name the **hermeneutic circle** to a procedure

人 W. J. T. 米切尔主编的《释义政治学》(1983)] 评述了意图角色在法律解释和文学解释中的相似之处。其他条目中提及"意图谬误"的地方，参见第 179 页。

interior monologue：内心独白　380。

interlude (in drama)：(戏剧中的) 插剧　225。

internal rhyme：中间韵　348。

interpellation：质询　207。

Interpretation and Hermeneutics：释义与阐释学

狭义上，解释一部文学作品就是要通过分析、释义、评注来明确说明作品的语言含义；这种**释义**通常特别注重于解释晦涩朦胧、模棱两可、富于比喻的篇章段落。从更广的意义上来说，对文学作品的释义则是弄清以语言为媒介的所有作品的艺术特色和主旨。在这个意义上，释义包括对作品的*类型*、组成成分、结构、主题和效果这些方面的分析（参见：*批评*）。

阐释学一词原指专门用于解释圣经的释义法则；包括正确阅读圣经文本的指导原则和有关圣经文本中所述含义在应用方面的**注释**或评注。然而 19 世纪以来，"阐释学"一词逐渐被用来指代一般释义理论，即对理解包括法律文件、历史文献、文学作品及圣经文本在内的一切文字文本含义的原则和方法的阐述。

德国神学家弗里德里克·施莱尔马赫在 1819 年的一系列讲演里，首先提出了"一般释义原理"，将其作为所有类型文本的"理解技巧"。1890 年代，饶有影响的哲学家威廉·狄尔泰（1833—1911）又进一步发展了施莱尔马赫的理论，提出了一种阐释科学，作为解释所有"人类科学"（即*人文学科*与社会科学）中所有文字形式的基础，以此同自然科学相区别。狄尔泰把人类科学视为研究世间短暂、具体的人类"生活经验"的手段。他指出，鉴于自然科学的目标在于通过固定与简化的范畴方式去"解释"事物，阐释学的目标应该是建立"理解"的一般理论。对文字文本的理解存在于"对充分表现内心生活实质的作品的解释"。最重要的是，在文学中，"人类的内心生活得到了其复杂的、全面而彻底的、客观上可被理解的表述"。（参见：*人文主义*。）

在系统阐述对原文含义的理解方法时，狄尔泰将施莱尔马赫以前描述的阐释

177 INTERPRETATION AND HERMENEUTICS

Schleiermacher had earlier described. That is, in order to understand the determinate meanings of the verbal parts of any linguistic whole, we must approach the parts with a prior sense of the meaning of the whole; yet we can know the meaning of the whole only by knowing the meanings of its constituent parts. This circularity of the interpretive process applies to the interrelations between the single words within any sentence and the sentence as a whole, as well as to interrelations between all the sentences and the work as a whole. Dilthey maintained that the hermeneutic circle is not a vicious circle, in that we can achieve a valid interpretation by a mutually qualifying interplay between our evolving sense of the whole and our retrospective understanding of its component parts.

Interest in the theory of interpretation revived strongly in the 1950s and 1960s, concurrently with the turn of Western philosophy to focus on the uses and meanings of language, and the turn of literary criticism—exemplified by the *New Criticism* in America—to the conception of a literary work as a linguistic object and to the view that the primary task of criticism is to interpret its verbal meanings and their interrelations. There have been two main lines of development in recent hermeneutics:

1. One development, represented notably by the Italian theorist Emilio Betti and the American E. D. Hirsch, takes off from Dilthey's claim that a reader is able to achieve an objective interpretation of an author's expressed meaning. In his *Validity in Interpretation* (1967), followed by *The Aims of Interpretation* (1976), Hirsch asserts that "a text means what its author meant," specifies that this meaning is "the verbal meaning which an author intends," and undertakes to show that such verbal meaning is in principle determinate (even if in some instances determinately ambiguous, or multiply significant), that it remains stable through the passage of time, and that it is in principle reproducible by each competent reader. The author's verbal **intention** is not the author's overall state of consciousness at the time of writing, but only the intention-to-mean something which, by recourse to preexisting linguistic conventions and norms, gets actualized in words, and so may be shared by readers who are competent in the same conventions and norms and know how to apply them in their interpretive practice. If a text is read independently of reference to the author's intentions, Hirsch asserts, it remains indeterminate—that is, capable of an indefinite diversity of meanings. A reader arrives at a determinate interpretation by using an implicit logic of validation (capable of being made explicit by the hermeneutic theorist), which serves to specify the author's intention, by reference not only to the general conventions and norms of a language, but also to all evidence, whether internal or external to the text, concerning "relevant aspects in the author's outlook" or "horizon." Relevant external references include the author's cultural milieu and personal prepossessions, as well as the literary and generic conventions that were available to the author at the time when the work was composed.

过程命名为**阐释循环**。也就是说，要想弄明白任何语言单位整体中各文字部分的确切含义，就必须先领悟该语言单位的总体含义；然而只有理解了各组成部分的含义，我们才能了解作品的整体含义。这种释义过程的循环，既适用于任何语句中的字词与全句之间的关联，也适用于一部作品中所有的句子与作品总体之间的联系。狄尔泰强调，阐释循环并非恶性循环，我们在逐层深入领会全文含义的同时，也在不断地追忆理解其组成部分文字的含义，通过这两个步骤共同的修正性相互作用，我们就能得出正确的释义。

随着西方哲学的关注点向语言的使用及其含义转移，以及以美国*新批评*为代表的文学批评向"文学作品作为语言学的研究对象""文艺批评的基本任务在于解释作品的语义和它们的相互关系"等观念转移，1950、1960年代再度兴起了对阐释理论的极大兴趣。近期阐释学沿着以下两条主线发展：

1. 第一条发展主线以意大利文艺理论家艾米利欧·贝蒂和美国的 E. D. 赫什为主要代表人物，以狄尔泰所说的"读者能够客观地解释作家所表述的含义"的论断为出发点。赫什在《释义的合法性》(1967)和之后的《释义的目的》(1976)里断言："一部作品表达着作者所要表达的意思"，并明确指出作品的含义就是"作者旨在表明的语义"，他还表明这种语义原则上是确定的（即使在某些情形下是含混不清或具多层含义的），它不因时间的推移而变化，原则上能够由每个有能力的读者得以重现。作者的言语**意向**并不是他创作时的意识状态，而仅仅是他借助已存在的语言惯例与规范在字里行间所表达出的想要表达的意向，因此凡是通晓这些语言惯例与规范并知道如何在释义过程中应用这些惯例与规范的读者，都能领悟作者表述的这一层意念。在赫什看来，如果脱离作者的意向孤立地阅读文本，文本就会因为具有多种不定的意义而使其含义难以确定。读者获得作品的确切含义必须借助一种心照不宣的有效的推理（可以被阐释学理论家解释清楚），用这种推理方式确定作者的言语意向，其根据不仅仅是一般语言惯例和规范，还包括涉及"作者观念"或"视野中的相关方面"等文本内、外因素的所有事实证据。相关的外部参考资料包括作者的文化背景、他本人已成型的观念、他在创作时可利用的文学或一般惯例。

Hirsch reformulates Dilthey's concept of the hermeneutic circle as follows: a competent reader forms an "hypothesis" as to the meaning of a part or whole of a text which is "corrigible"—that is, the hypothesis can be either confirmed or disconfirmed by continuing reference to the text; if disconfirmed, it is replaced by an alternative hypothesis which conforms more closely to all the components of the text. Since the interpreted meanings of the components of a text are to some degree constituted by the hypotheses one brings to their interpretation, such a procedure can never achieve absolute certainty as to a text's correct meaning. The most a reader can do is to arrive at the most probable meaning of a text; but this logic of highest probability, Hirsch insists, is adequate to yield objective knowledge, confirmable by other competent readers, concerning the determinate and stable meanings both of the component passages and of the artistic whole in a work of literature.

Hirsch follows traditional hermeneutics in making an essential distinction between verbal meaning and significance. The **significance** of a text to a reader is the relation of its verbal meaning to other matters, such as the personal situation, beliefs, and responses of the individual reader, or the prevailing cultural milieu of the reader's own era, or a particular set of concepts or values, and so on. The **verbal meaning** of a text, Hirsch asserts—the meaning intended by the writer—is determinate and stable; its significance, however—what makes the text alive and resonant for diverse readers in diverse times—is indeterminate and ever-changing. Verbal meaning is the particular concern of hermeneutics; textual significance, in its many aspects, is one of the concerns of literary criticism.

2. The second line of development in recent hermeneutics takes off from Dilthey's view that the genuine understanding of literary and other humanistic texts consists in the reader's re-experience of the "inner life" that the texts express. A primary thinker in this development is Martin Heidegger, whose *Being and Time* (1927, trans. 1962) incorporated the act of interpretation into an **existential philosophy**—that is, a philosophy centered on "Dasein," or what it is to-be-in-the-world. Heidegger's student Hans Georg Gadamer adapted Heidegger's philosophy into an influential theory of textual interpretation, *Truth and Method* (1960, trans. 1975). The philosophical premise is that temporality and historicality—a situation in one's present that looks back to the past and anticipates the future—is inseparably a part of each individual's being; that the process of understanding something, involving an act of interpretation, goes on not only in reading verbal texts but in all aspects of human experience; and that language, like temporality, pervades all aspects of that experience. In applying these philosophical assumptions to the understanding of a literary text, Gadamer translates the traditional hermeneutic circle into the metaphors of dialogue and fusion. Readers bring to a text a "pre-understanding," which is constituted by their own temporal and personal "horizons." They should not, as "subjects," attempt to analyze and dissect the text as an autonomous "object." Instead the reader, as an "I," situated

赫什对狄尔泰的阐释循环概念重新进行了以下系统的表述：有能力的读者就文本某个部分的含义或全文的含义作出一种"假设"，这种假设是可以"修正的"，即可以通过不断参考文本而予以肯定或否定；如果这种假设被否定，就要由与文本所有部分更相吻合的其他假设所代替。由于对文本各部分的释义在某种程度上是由读者在释义过程中的假设所组成，因此这种释义过程永远也不可能对原文的正确含义作出绝对的断定。读者至多也就是获得对原文含义最为可信的理解，然而赫什坚持认为这种准确性最高的推理过程足以使读者客观地领会一部文学作品各组成部分及艺术性整体的明确固定的含义，同时这种认识理解也会被其他善于阅读的读者所肯定。

　　赫什按照传统阐释学原理对语言含义和意义作了重要区分。对一名读者来说，文本的**意义**在于它的语言含义和读者个人的情况、信仰及反应之间的关系，或者是语义和读者所处时期的主要文化背景或特定观念或价值标准等问题之间的关系。赫什断言，文本的**语言含义**，即作者想要表达的含义，是确定不变的；但其意义，也就是使文本在不同时期的不同读者中间经久不衰、引起共鸣的因素，却是永远变幻不定的。语言含义是阐释学的特定关注对象；作品的意义就其很多方面来讲是文学批评所关心的问题之一。

2. 近代阐释学发展的第二条主线源自狄尔泰的观点：对文学及其他人文文本的真正理解在于读者对文本所表达的"内心生活"的再次体验。这一发展的主要思想家是马丁·海德格尔，他所著的《存在与时间》（1927，1962年英译版）把释义行为纳入以"Dasein"（即时空存在论）为核心的**存在哲学**范畴。海德格尔的弟子汉斯－乔治·伽达默尔在其所著的《真理与方法》（1960，1975年英译版）中，把海德格尔的哲学思想运用到他那颇有影响的文本释义理论里。这一理论的哲学前提是：暂存性和历史性，即一种从现在的角度回顾过去和展望未来的立场，是每个人所必有的属性的一部分；涉及释义行为的理解过程，不仅存在于阅读语言文本中，还出现在解读人类经历的所有方面中；语言如同暂存性一样，渗透于人生经历的所有方面。伽达默尔在把这些哲学设想运用到理解文学文本中时，用对话与融合的隐喻来解释传统的阐释循环。读者必然会赋予文本由自己暂时的个人"视野"构成的"预先理解"。但是他们作为"主体"，不应试图把文本当做独立的"客体"加以分析与解剖；而要立足现在，

in his or her present time, addresses questions to the text as a "Thou," but with a receptive openness that simply allows the matter of the text—by means of their shared heritage of language—to speak in responsive dialogue, and to readdress its own questions to the reader. The understood meaning of the text is an event which is always the product of a "fusion of the horizons" that a reader brings to the text and that the text brings to the reader.

Gadamer insists that (unlike most theories of interpretation) this hermeneutics is not an attempt to establish norms or rules for a correct interpretation, but an attempt simply to describe how we in fact succeed in understanding texts. Nonetheless his theory has the consequence that the search for a determinate meaning of a text which remains stable through the passage of time becomes a will-o'-the-wisp. Since the meaning of a text "is always codetermined" by the particular temporal and personal horizon of the individual reader, there cannot be one stable "right interpretation"; the meaning of a text is always to an important extent its meaning that it has here, now, for me. To Gadamer's view that the historical and personal relativity of meaning is inescapable, Hirsch replies that a reader in the present, by reconstructing the linguistic, literary, and cultural conditions of its author, is often able adequately to determine the original and unchanging verbal meaning intended by the writer of a text in the past; and that insofar as Gadamer is right about the unbridgeable gap between the meaning of a text then and its meaning now, he is referring to the ever-alterable "significance" contributed by each reader, in his or her time and personal and social circumstances, to the text's stable verbal meaning.

Traditional literary critics had tacitly assumed that to interpret a text correctly is to approximate the meaning intended by its author, long before theorists such as Hirsch undertook to define and justify this view. Even the *New Critics* took for granted that the meaning of a text is the meaning that the author intended; what some of these critics called the *intentional fallacy* merely designates the supposed error, in interpreting a text, of employing clues concerning an author's intention which are "external" to the "internal" actualization of that intention in the language of the text itself. Most traditional philosophers, including recent "ordinary language philosophers," have also held that to understand an utterance involves reference to the writer's intention, which we infer from our awareness of the writer's linguistic assumptions. H. P. Grice, for example, proposed in the 1950s an influential account of verbal meaning as a speaker's intention in an utterance to produce a specific effect in a hearer, by means of the hearer's recognition of the speaker's intention in making that utterance. (See under *discourse analysis*.) In *Speech Acts* (1970), John Searle accepted this description, with the qualification that the speaker can express, and so enable the hearer to recognize, his or her intention only insofar as the expression conforms to the conventions or rules of their common language. In a later refinement of this view, Searle makes a

作为"我"向作为"你"的文本发问，但还要具备开放性，乐于接受，凭借他们共同的语言传统，只是让文本进行应答对话，再次向读者提出自身的问题。文本被理解的含义，总是读者与文本各自的"视野交流融合"互动的产物。

伽达默尔坚决认为（与大多数释义理论不同），他的阐释理论并不试图为正确的释义方法确立标准或惯例，而只想说明我们事实上是如何成功地理解文本的。不过他的理论实际上造成的则是这样一种结论：对随着时间流逝而文本仍然具有的固定不变的含义的探求，最后要成为泡影。因为文本的含义"总是由"每个读者特定的暂存视野和个人视野"共同确定的"，所以不会存在一种固定的"正确释义"；文本含义在很大程度上总是读者本人在一时一地所领会的。对于伽达默尔关于含义的历史及个人的相对性是不可避免的观点，赫什作出了回应。他认为此时的读者通过重新构建作者的语言、文学及文化条件，常常有足够的能力确定作者在过去通过文本想要表达的固定的语言含义。伽达默尔有关一部作品此时与彼时的含义之间有着不可逾越的鸿沟的说法是正确的，就此而言，他所指的是由于每个读者在其所处的时间、个人及社会环境下对文本固定语言含义的各种理解而形成的永远变化的"意义"。

传统的文学批评家早在赫什等理论家确定并证明这一观点之前就已默认：要正确解释文本就是要粗略估计作者旨在表达的含义。甚至新批评家也认为文本的含义就是作者想要表达的意思；这些批评家中的一些人所谓的*意图谬误*，仅仅是指解释文本过程中的一种假定的错误，即用与文本自身的语言"内在"地实现作者的意图无关的关于作者意图的"外在"线索来解释文本的错误做法。大多数传统哲学家，包括现在的"普通语言哲学家"，也认为要理解一句话语，必然会涉及参照作者的意图，这是我们从自己对作者语言设定的理解中推断出来的。例如，H. P. 格赖斯曾于1950年代提出一项颇具影响的论述，他认为语言含义就是说话人在言谈中通过听者对其说话意图的理解，试图给听者造成一种特殊效果。（参见：*话语分析*中的相关论述。）约翰·塞尔在其所著的《言语行为》(1970) 中接受了这一阐述，并对其加以限定：只有当表述遵循他们双方共同的语言惯例或规范时，言者才能表明自己的意图并使听者理解他/她的意图。在后来对此观点的修正中，

distinction between the speaker's intention which determines the kind and meaning of a *speech act*, and the speaker's intention to communicate that meaning to a hearer; see his *Intentionality* (1983), chapter 6. On this issue in ordinary-language philosophy, see also P. F. Strawson, "Intention and Convention in Speech Acts," in Jay F. Rosenberg and Charles Travis, eds., *Readings in the Philosophy of Language* (1971).

A radical departure from the traditional author-oriented views of a determinate intended meaning occurs in a number of *structural* and *poststructural* theories. (See *author and authorship*.) Some theorists, rejecting any control of interpretation by reference to an author, or *subject*, and his or her intention, insist that the meanings of a text are rendered "undecidable" by the self-conflicting workings of language itself, or alternatively that meanings are entirely relative to the particular interpretive strategy that is brought into play by the reader. (See *deconstruction* and *reader-response criticism*.) Other current theorists, although they may admit that the manifest meanings of a text are specified by the intentions of the author, regard such meanings merely as disguises, or displacements, of the real meanings, which are the unconscious motives and needs of the author, or else the suppressed political realities and power-relationships of the social structure of an historical era. (See *psychoanalytic criticism, Marxist criticism, new historicism*.) Paul Ricoeur has labeled such modes of reading, exemplified by Marx, Nietzsche, and Freud, the *hermeneutics of suspicion*, in that they approach a text as a veiled or mystified set of representations, whose real meaning, or *subtext*, needs to be deciphered by the knowing reader.

In addition to the titles listed above, refer to Richard E. Palmer, *Hermeneutics: Interpretation Theory in Schleiermacher, Dilthey, Heidegger, and Gadamer* (1969), an informative review of the history and conflicting theories of interpretation from the standpoint of an adherent to Gadamer's theory. See also *Literary Criticism and Historical Understanding*, ed. Phillip Damon (1967); *The Conflict of Interpretations: Essays in Hermeneutics* (1974) by the French philosopher Paul Ricoeur; the anthology of essays *Hermeneutics: Questions and Prospects*, ed. Gary Shapiro and Alan Sica (1984); Wendell V. Harris, *Interpretive Acts: In Search of Meaning* (1988); Francis-Noël Thomas, *The Writer Writing* (1992), chapter 2, "'Intentions' and 'Purposes.'" In *Multiple Authorship and the Myth of Solitary Genius* (1991), Jack Stillinger points out that reference to authorial intention in order to determine meaning is complicated by the fact that often a number of persons collaborate in producing a literary or other published text; see under *textual criticism*. John R. Searle distinguishes three different meanings of "intention" in diverse discussions of the interpretation of literary texts, in "Literary Theory and Its Discontents," *The Emperor Redressed*, ed. Dwight Eddins (1995).

interpretation, typological and allegorical: The **typological** (or **figural**) mode of interpreting the Bible was inaugurated by St. Paul and developed by the early Church Fathers as a way of reconciling the history, prophecy,

塞尔对决定一种*言语行为*的类型和含义的说话者意图与言者想要向听者传达那一含义的意图进行了区分；参阅他所著的《意图性》(1983) 第 6 章。有关这一普通语言哲学论题，还可参阅 P. F. 斯特劳逊所写的文章"言语行为的意图与惯例"，收入杰伊·F. 罗森伯格与查尔斯·特拉维斯合编的《语言哲学阅读》(1971)。

　　一些结构主义和后结构主义理论从根本上背弃了传统的作者意图决定含义论。（参见：*作者和作者身份*。）一些理论家反对认为作者，或主体，以及作者意图决定释义的观点，他们坚信文本的含义由于语言自身的矛盾性，或是因为文本含义与读者对其所采用的特定解读策略有着十分密切的关系而变得"不可决定"。（参见：*解构主义、读者反应批评*。）其他当前的理论家尽管可能承认文本的明显含义是由作者意图具体确定的，但他们认为这种含义不过是真正含义的伪装或转移，文本的真正含义在于作者所未意识到的动机和需要，或是一个历史时期社会结构中被压制的政治现实或权力关系。（参见：*精神分析批评、马克思主义批评、新历史主义*。）保罗·利科将以尼采、马克思、弗洛伊德为代表的这样一些阅读方式称为*怀疑阐释学*，因为他们将文本视为一些隐含的或神秘的表述，其真正含义或*潜台词*，需要由能领会其意的读者来破译。

　　除了以上列举的著作，可以参阅：理查德·帕尔默所著的《阐释学：施莱尔马赫、狄尔泰、海德格尔与伽达默尔的释义理论》(1969)，该书从一位伽达默尔理论追随者的视角出发，评述了释义的历史和各种对立的理论，具有资料价值。也可参阅：菲利普·戴蒙主编的《文学批评和历史的理解》(1967)；法国哲学家保罗·利科所著的《解释的冲突：阐释学论文集》(1974)；文选：加里·夏皮罗与艾伦·西卡合编的《阐释学：问题与前景》(1984)；温德尔·V. 哈里斯所著的《阐释行为：追寻意义》(1988)；弗朗西斯－诺埃尔·托马斯所著的《作者书写》(1992) 第 2 章"'意图'与'目的'"。杰克·斯蒂林格在其所著的《多重作者与孤独天才的神话》(1991) 中指出，根据作者意图来确定作品含义是复杂的，因为通常文学文本或其他出版物都是由许多人共同完成的；参见：*文本批评*。约翰·R. 塞尔在其所写的文章"文学理论及其不满"中，在对文学文本的阐释的多样的讨论中，区分了"意图"的三种不同意义，该文收入德怀特·埃丁斯主编的《重新穿上衣服的皇帝》(1995) 中。

Interpretation, Typological and Allegorical: 象征释义和寓意释义

　　象征（或*形象*）释义是圣保罗开创的一种解释圣经的方式，早期基督教会神父将其发展成为融合犹太教《旧约圣经》的历史、预言书、法律和基督教《新

and laws of the Hebrew Scriptures with the narratives and teachings of the Christian Scriptures. As St. Augustine expressed its principle: "In the Old Testament the New Testament is concealed; in the New Testament the Old Testament is revealed." In typological theory, that is, the key persons, actions, and events in the Old Testament are viewed as "figurae" (Latin for "figures") which were historical realities, but also "prefigure" those persons, actions, and events in the New Testament that are similar to them in some aspect, function, or relationship. Often the Old Testament figures are called **types** and their later correlatives in the New Testament are called **antitypes**. The Old Testament figure or type is held to be a prophecy or promise of the higher truth that is "fulfilled" in the New Testament, according to a plan which is eternally present in the mind of God but manifests itself to human beings only in the two scriptural revelations separated by a span of time.

To cite a few of the very many instances of typological interpretation: Adam was said to be a figure (or in alternative terms, a "type," "image," or "shadow") of Christ. One of the analogies cited between prefiguration and fulfillment was that between the creation of Eve from Adam's rib and the flow of blood from the side of the crucified Christ; another was the analogy between the tree that bore the fruit occasioning Adam's original sin and the cross which bore as its fruit Christ, the Redeemer of that sin. In a similar fashion the manna provided the children of Israel in the wilderness (Exodus 16) was held to prefigure the Eucharist, and the relationship between the Egyptian servant girl Hagar and Sarah (Genesis 16) was held to prefigure the relationship between the earthly Jerusalem of the Old Testament and the heavenly Jerusalem of the New Testament. By some interpreters, elements of New Testament history were represented as in their turn prefiguring the events that will come to be fulfilled in "the last days" of Christ's Second Coming and Last Judgment.

The **allegorical interpretation** of the Bible had its roots in Greek and Roman thinkers who treated classical myths as allegorical representations of abstract cosmological, philosophical, or moral truths. The method was applied to narratives in the Hebrew Scriptures by the Jewish philosopher Philo (died AD 50) and was adapted to Christian interpretation by Origen in the third century. The fundamental distinction in the allegorical interpretation of the Bible is between the "literal" (or "historical," or "carnal") meaning of the text—the historical truth that it specifically signifies—and the additional "spiritual" or "mystical" or "allegoric" meaning that it signifies by analogy. (Refer to the entry *allegory*.)

The spiritual aspect of a text's literal meaning was often in turn subdivided into two or more levels; some interpreters specified as many as seven, or even twelve levels. By the twelfth century, however, biblical interpreters widely agreed in finding a **fourfold meaning** in many biblical passages. A typical set of distinctions, as proposed by St. Thomas Aquinas and others, specifies (1) the literal or historical meaning, which is a narrative of what in fact happened; (2) the allegorical meaning proper, which is the New Testament truth, or else the prophetic reference to the Christian Church, that is signified by a passage in

约圣经》的故事和教义的一种方法。圣奥古斯丁把其原理解释为"《旧约》里面蕴含着《新约》,《新约》里面又显露着《旧约》"。象征理论认为,《旧约》里记述的主要人物、情节与事件是历史上的真人真事,他们作为《旧约》里"形象"的同时又"预示"着后来《新约》里出现的在某些方面、作用或关系与之类似的人物、情节与事件。通常,《旧约》里的形象被称为**原型**,此后他们在《新约》中的相应形象则被称为**反原型**。《旧约》的形象或原型被认为是对《新约》里"实现"的更高真理的预示或断言,只不过是在由时间所分隔的两部圣经的启示录中,依据上帝心中的永恒计划,在人类身上得以显现而已。

这里举出许多象征释义例子中的一些:亚当被视为耶稣基督的形象(或者用其他说法是,"原型""形象"或"影像")。亚当的肋骨造就夏娃与耶稣受难时肋部血流如注成为《旧约》的预示与《新约》的应验之间的一个类推;另一个类比推理就是引起亚当原罪的那棵果树和钉着耶稣(即那一罪行的救世主)的十字架。同样,《旧约》里以色列儿童在旷野中获得的神赐食物"吗哪"(《出埃及记》16)预示着《新约》里的圣餐;埃及侍女"夏甲"与"撒拉"的关系(《创世记》16)也预示着《旧约》中人间圣地耶路撒冷与《新约》中天国圣地耶路撒冷之间的关系。按照一些释义者的说法,《新约》里的历史情节继而又预示着耶稣再次降临和最后审判的"最后日子"里将实现的事件。

对圣经的**寓意释义**出自希腊罗马思想家,在他们看来,古代神话是对抽象的宇宙论、哲学或道德真理的寓言化再现。犹太哲学家斐洛(卒于公元50年)曾用这一方法来解释犹太《旧约》故事。公元3世纪奥利金采用了这种方法对基督教进行释义。寓意释义与一般释义解释圣经的主要区别在于:一般释义解释文本的"字面"意思(或者说"历史"或"世俗"的意义),即文本明确表现的历史事实,寓意释义则解释文本通过类推表明的附加"精神"的或"神秘"的或"寓意"的意义。(参见:寓言。)

文本的字面含义的精神层面又常依次划分为两个或更多层次;一些释义者将其含义划分为七个乃至十二个层次。然而,12世纪以前,圣经释义者们普遍认为,圣经的很多章节都有**四层含义**。其中有代表性的一种划分方法由圣·托马斯·阿奎那和其他释义者提出:(1)字面或历史概念上的意思,即记述史实;(2)寓意本身,即《新约》的真理或指《旧约》某一章节对基督教会的预示;

the Old Testament; (3) the tropological meaning, which is the moral truth or doctrine signified by the same passage; and (4) the anagogical meaning, or reference of the passage to Christian **eschatology**, that is, the events that are to come in "the last days" of Christ's judgment and the life after death of individual souls.

We can distinguish between the typological and allegorical mode of interpretation by saying that typology is horizontal, in that it relates items in two texts (the Old and New Testaments) that are separated in time, while allegorical interpretation is vertical, in that it uncovers multiple layers of significance in a single textual item. The two interpretive methods, however, were often applied simultaneously, and in many instances fused, by biblical exegetes. Both methods flourished into the eighteenth century and recur recognizably in later periods. They were employed in sermons and in a great variety of writings on religious matters, and were adapted to **iconography**—that is, representations of biblical and nonbiblical persons and events intended to have allegoric or symbolic significance—in painting and sculpture. Medieval and later poets sometimes adopted the typological and allegorical principles—originally developed for interpreting the Bible—in composing their own writings on religious subjects. Dante, for example, in a letter written in 1319 to his friend and patron Can Grande della Scala, announced that he composed his *Divine Comedy* to signify a double subject, literal and allegorical, and that the allegorical subject can in turn be subdivided into allegorical, moral, and anagogical meanings. Scholars have analyzed the adaptation of typological and allegorical procedures by many later poets who wrote on religious themes, including Edmund Spenser, George Herbert, John Milton, and (in a late and highly individual revival of the mode) William Blake.

The American scholar D. W. Robertson and others have proposed that not only writings on religious subjects but also many seemingly secular poems of the Middle Ages—including the *Roman de la Rose*, the works of Chaucer and Chrétien de Troyes, and medieval love lyrics—were expressly written to incorporate typological and allegorical modes of theological and moral references. The validity, however, of extending these interpretive modes to secular literature is strongly disputed; see the suggested readings below. In *The Genesis of Secrecy: On the Interpretation of Narrative* (1979), the British critic Frank Kermode adapted the ancient interpretive distinction between carnal and spiritual meanings to his analysis of levels of meaning in recent works of prose fiction.

On the various modes of biblical interpretation, see F. W. Farrar, *History of Interpretation* (1886), Beryl Smalley, *The Study of the Bible in the Middle Ages* (rev. 1952), and the notable study by Henri de Lubac, *Exégèse Médiévale: les quatre sens de l'écriture* (4 vols., 1959–74; rev. 1993). A classic discussion of typological, or figural, interpretation is Erich Auerbach's "Figura" in his *Scenes from the Drama of European Literature* (1959). Philip Rollinson, in *Classical Theories of Allegory and Christian Culture* (1981), relates early medieval interpretation of the Bible to modes of literary interpretation in classical times. An American application in the eighteenth century of the old interpretive modes

(3) 道德意义，即同样章节表示出的道德真理与教义；(4) 神秘的含义，或为基督教**末世学**，即耶稣进行审判的"最后日子"里将发生的事件和个人灵魂的来世的引证。

我们可以这样区分象征释义与寓意释义：象征释义是横向的，它把不同时期的两部全书（《旧约》与《新约》）的内容加以联系；寓意释义则是纵向的，它揭示了单一文本的多层意义。然而这两种释义方法往往被圣经解释者同时采用，在许多情况下相互交融。两种方法一直流行到 18 世纪，并在而后的几个时期再度受到重视。它们被用于解释布道及各种宗教题材的作品，还被用于解释**传统性形象**，即绘画与雕刻中具有寓意或象征意义的圣经或非圣经人物及事件。中世纪及以后的诗人有时运用象征和寓意法则（主要随着阐释圣经发展而来）来组织各自关于宗教主题的作品。例如，但丁在 1319 年写给友人及赞助人坎·格兰德·德拉·斯卡拉的一封信中说，他创作的《神曲》包含字面与寓意双重主题，其中寓意性主题又可再分成寓意的、道德的、神秘的多层含义。学者们分析了许多创作宗教主题作品的后世诗人（包括斯宾塞、乔治·赫伯特、约翰·弥尔顿及后来极具个性地复兴了这种方式的威廉·布莱克）对象征和寓意方法的运用。

美国学者 D. W. 罗伯逊及其他一些学者提出，不仅仅是宗教主题的作品，中世纪许多似乎是世俗主题的诗歌，包括《玫瑰传奇》、乔叟和克雷蒂安·德·特鲁瓦的作品、中世纪爱情抒情诗，都明显包含了神学与道德内容表现上的象征与寓意两种方式的结合。然而对这两种方式用于世俗文学的有效性仍有激烈争论；可以参看下面建议的文章。英国文学批评家弗兰克·克莫德在其所著的《神秘的起源：论叙事作品的释义》(1979) 中，把古代对世俗与精神含义的释义划分，应用到他对近期散文体小说作品的意义层次分析中。

有关圣经释义的各种方法，参阅：F. W. 法拉所著的《释义的历史》(1886)，贝丽尔·斯莫利所著的《中世纪的圣经研究》(1952 年修订版)，和亨利·德·吕巴克的四卷本杰作《中世纪的注释》(1959—1974，1993 年修订版)。关于象征或形象释义的经典讨论，可以参阅：埃利希·奥尔巴赫所著的《欧洲文学戏剧场景》(1959) 中的"象喻"。菲利普·罗林森在其所著的《寓言与基督教文化中的经典理论》(1981) 中，将中世纪早期释义圣经的方法与古典时期的文学释义方法联系起来。关于 18 世纪美国采用的旧释义法，可以参阅：乔纳森·爱

is Jonathan Edwards' *Images or Shadows of Divine Things*, ed. Perry Miller (1948). For uses of typological and allegoric materials by various literary authors, see Rosemund Tuve, *A Reading of George Herbert* (1952) and *Allegorical Imagery* (1966); J. H. Hagstrum, *William Blake: Poet and Painter* (1964); P. J. Alpers, *The Poetry of "The Faerie Queene"* (1967); and the essays on a number of authors in Paul Miner, ed., *Literary Uses of Typology* (1977). For the extension of typological and allegoric methods to the analysis of secular medieval poems, see D. W. Robertson, Jr., "Historical Criticism," in *English Institute Essays, 1950*, ed. A. S. Downer (1951), and *A Preface to Chaucer: Studies in Medieval Perspectives* (1962). The validity of such an extension is attacked by several scholars in *Critical Approaches to Medieval Literature*, ed. Dorothy Bethurum (1960), and by R. S. Crane, "On Hypotheses in 'Historical Criticism,'" in *The Idea of the Humanities* (1967, Vol. 2, pp. 236–60). On the application of biblical allegorization to later literary forms see, in addition to Kermode (above), Northrop Frye, *The Great Code: The Bible and Literature* (1982); and Stephen Prickett, ed., *Reading the Text: Biblical Criticism and Literary Theory* (1991).

interpretive communities: 332.

intertextuality: 401; *12*.

intonation: 197.

intrigue: 294.

introspection: 380.

intrusive (narrator): 302.

invective: The denunciation of a person by the use of derogatory *epithets*. Thus Prince Hal, in Shakespeare's *1 Henry IV*, calls the corpulent Falstaff "this sanguine coward, this bedpresser, this horseback-breaker, this huge hill of flesh." (In context, there is in this instance of invective an affectionate undertone, as often when friends, secure in an intimacy that ensures they will not be taken literally, resort to derogatory name-calling in the exuberance of their affection.)

In his *Discourse Concerning Satire* (1693), John Dryden described the difference in efficacy, as a put-down, between the directness of invective and the indirectness of *irony*, in which a speaker maintains the advantage of cool detachment by leaving it to the circumstances to convert bland compliments into insults:

> How easy is it to call rogue and villain, and that wittily! But how hard to make a man appear a fool, a blockhead, or a knave, without using any of those opprobrious terms.... There is ... a vast difference

德华兹所著的《神灵的形影》(1948，佩里·米勒主编)。关于不同文学作家们对象征与寓意题材的运用，可以参阅：罗斯蒙德·图夫所著的《解读乔治·赫伯特》(1952) 和《寓意意象》(1966)；J. H. 哈格斯特鲁姆所著的《威廉·布莱克：诗人和画家》(1964)；P. J. 阿尔珀斯所著的《〈仙后〉的诗歌艺术》(1967)；保罗·迈纳主编的《类型学在文学中的使用》(1977) 里关于一些作家的文章。关于象征与寓意方法在分析中世纪世俗诗歌中的延伸应用，可以参阅：小 D. W. 罗伯逊所写的文章"历史批评"，收入 A. S. 唐纳主编的《英国学院派文选 (1950)》(1951) 和其所著的《中世纪乔叟研究视角介绍》(1962)。有关释义法延伸应用的有效性讨论，可以参阅：多萝西·贝休伦主编的《中世纪文学批评方法》(1960), R. S. 克莱恩所著的《人文学的理念》(1967 年第 2 卷第 236—260 页) 中的"论'历史批评'的假定"。有关圣经寓意法在后来各种文学形式中的应用，除上面提到的克莫德外还有：诺斯罗普·弗莱所著的《伟大的代码：圣经与文学》(1982)；斯蒂芬·普里克特主编的《解读文本：圣经批评与文学理论》(1991)。

interpretive communities：解释群体　332。

intertextuality：互文性　401；*12*。

intonation：语调　197。

intrigue：错综情节　294。

introspection：自我反思　380。

intrusive (narrator)：介入的（叙述者）　302。

Invective：谩骂

　　谩骂是指用贬义的*属性形容词*斥责他人。在莎士比亚《亨利四世》的第一部中，亲王哈尔把又圆又胖的福斯塔夫骂作是"残忍的懦夫，压坏床的坨子，累死好马的驮子，大肉堆……"（在剧中背景下，这个例子里的谩骂尖刻中又略含几分情谊，正像平常密友之间心心相印，互相投几句脏话也不会被当真，不影响感情一样。）

　　约翰·德莱顿在其所著的《论讽刺》(1693) 中，说明了直言不讳的谩骂和曲折隐晦的*反讽*之间的不同效应。运用反讽时，言者可以拥有保持冷静超然态度的优势，让环境将温和的声声赞扬转换成辱骂之意。德莱顿说：

　　　　骂一声无赖、恶棍是多么简易痛快！但是不用任何脏字就叫人露出笨蛋、傻瓜或流氓的本相，这谈何容易……前者把人痛骂得狗血喷头

between the slovenly butchering of a man, and the fineness of a stroke that separates the head from the body, and leaves it standing in its place.

invention (in rhetoric): **65**; *343*.

invocation: 346; *298*.

involuted novel: 258; *187, 305*.

involvement (of a reader): **92**.

Irish Literary Renaissance: 45.

irony: In Greek comedy the character called the *eiron* was a dissembler, who characteristically spoke in understatement and pretended to be less intelligent than he was, yet triumphed over the *alazon*—the self-deceiving and stupid braggart. (See in Northrop Frye, *Anatomy of Criticism*, 1957.) In most modern critical uses of the term "irony," there remains the root sense of dissembling, or of hiding what is actually the case; not, however, in order to deceive, but to achieve special rhetorical or artistic effects.

Verbal irony (which was traditionally classified as one of the *tropes*) is a statement in which the meaning that a speaker implies differs sharply from the meaning that is ostensibly expressed. The ironic statement usually involves the explicit expression of one attitude or evaluation, but with indications in the overall speech-situation that the speaker intends a very different, and often opposite, attitude or evaluation. Thus in Canto IV of Alexander Pope's *The Rape of the Lock* (1714), after Sir Plume, egged on by the ladies, has stammered out his incoherent request for the return of the stolen lock of hair, the Baron answers:

> "It grieves me much," replied the Peer again,
> "Who speaks so well should ever speak in vain."

This is a straightforward case of an ironic reversal of the surface statement (of which one effect is to give pleasure to the reader) because there are patent clues, established by the preceding narrative, that the Peer is not in the least aggrieved and does not think that poor Sir Plume has spoken at all well. A more complex instance of irony is the famed sentence with which Jane Austen opens *Pride and Prejudice* (1813): "It is a truth universally acknowledged that a single man in possession of a good fortune must be in want of a wife"; part of the ironic implication (based on assumptions that Austen assumes the audience shares with her) is that a single woman is in want of a rich husband. Sometimes the use of irony by Pope and other masters is very complicated: the meaning and evaluations may be subtly qualified rather than simply reversed, and the clues to the ironic counter-meanings under the literal statement—or even to the fact that the author intends the statement to be

体无完肤，后者不伤其表却击中要害，两种方法截然不同。

invention (in rhetoric)：(修辞中的) 文学创新，创造　65；*343*。

invocation：祈愿词　346；*298*。

involuted novel：内延小说　258；*187, 305*。

involvement (of a reader)：(读者的) 感情介入　92。

Irish Literary Renaissance：爱尔兰文学复兴　45。

Irony：反讽

在希腊喜剧里，被称作愚人的角色是佯装的，通常都是言辞含蓄，假装比实际上更为愚笨，却击败了*骗子*，即自欺欺人、愚蠢的大话家。[参阅：诺斯罗普·弗莱所著的《批评的剖析》(1957)。]"反讽"一词在大多数现代批评的使用中仍然保留了其原意，即不为欺骗，而是为了达到特殊的修辞或艺术效果而掩盖或隐藏话语的真实含义。

言语反讽（传统习惯上被归类为一种*比喻*），指的是说话人话语的隐含意义和他的表面陈述大相径庭。这类讽刺话语往往表示说话人的某些表面的看法与评价，而实际上在整体话语情境下则说明了一种截然不同通常是相反的态度与评价。在亚历山大·蒲柏的《卷发遇劫记》(1714) 第4章里，普卢姆爵士在太太们的煽动下语无伦次地要求归还被盗的卷发，男爵这样应答：

"这让我深感悲痛，"男爵再次答道，
"话说得如此漂亮之人所说的都是空话。"

这是对表面陈述直截了当的讽刺性反语的例子（它的一个作用在于博得读者一笑），因为根据前文叙述的情况，显然男爵毫无悲痛之意并且认为可怜的普卢姆爵士的一席话毫不中听。另一则更为复杂的有关反讽的例子出自简·奥斯丁《傲慢与偏见》(1813) 的开篇名句："凡是有钱的单身汉，总想娶位太太，这已经成了一条举世公认的真理"，讽刺的部分内涵（建立在奥斯丁认定读者和她共同持有这一观点之上）在于，凡是单身女子都需要一位富有的丈夫。有时蒲柏和其他名家所运用的反讽非常复杂：其含义与评价并非出于直截了当的反语，而是借助微妙的暗示，话语里的讽刺性反义隐藏在字面表述下——或者事实上作者是想要读

understood ironically—may be oblique and unobtrusive. That is why recourse to irony by an author tends to convey an implicit compliment to the intelligence of readers, who are invited to associate themselves with the author and the knowing minority who are not taken in by the ostensible meaning. That is also why many literary ironists are misinterpreted and sometimes (like Daniel Defoe and Jonathan Swift in the eighteenth century) get into serious trouble with the obtuse authorities. Following the intricate and shifting maneuvers of great ironists like Plato, Swift, Voltaire, Austen, or Henry James is a test of skill in reading between the lines.

Some literary works exhibit **structural irony**; that is, the author, instead of using an occasional verbal irony, introduces a structural feature that serves to sustain a duplex meaning and evaluation throughout the work. One common literary device of this sort is the invention of a **naive hero**, or else a naive narrator or spokesman, whose invincible simplicity or obtuseness leads him to persist in putting an interpretation on affairs which the knowing reader—who penetrates to, and shares, the implied point of view of the authorial presence behind the naive *persona*—just as persistently is called on to alter and correct. (Note that verbal irony depends on knowledge of the ironic *intention* of the fictional speaker, which is shared by both the speaker and the reader; structural irony depends on a knowledge of the ironic intention of the author, which is shared by the reader but is not the intention of the fictional speaker.) One example of the naive spokesman is Swift's well-meaning but insanely rational and morally obtuse economist who writes the "Modest Proposal" (1729) to convert the excess children of the oppressed and poverty-stricken Irish into a financial and gastronomical asset. Other examples are Swift's stubbornly credulous Gulliver, the self-deceiving and paranoid monologuist in Browning's "Soliloquy of the Spanish Cloister" (1842), and the insane editor, Kinbote, in Vladimir Nabokov's *Pale Fire* (1962). A related structural device for sustaining ironic qualification is the use of the *fallible narrator*, in which the teller of the story is a participant in it. Although such a narrator may be neither stupid, credulous, nor demented, he nevertheless manifests a failure of insight, by viewing and appraising his own motives, and the motives and actions of other characters, through what the reader is intended to recognize as the distorting perspective of the narrator's own prejudices and interests. (See *point of view*.)

In *A Rhetoric of Irony* (1974) Wayne Booth identifies as **stable irony** that in which the speaker or author makes available to the reader an assertion or position which, whether explicit or implied, serves as a firm ground for ironically qualifying or subverting the surface meaning. **Unstable irony**, on the other hand, offers no fixed standpoint which is not itself undercut by further ironies. The literature of the *absurd* typically presents such a regression of ironies. At an extreme, as in Samuel Beckett's drama *Waiting for Godot* (1955) or his novel *The Unnamable* (1960), there is an endless regress of ironic undercuttings. Such works suggest a denial that there is any secure evaluative standpoint, or even any determinable rationale, in the human situation.

者领会话语的讽刺意义——也是曲折隐晦的。这就是为什么作者借助反讽表达时往往要引导读者站到他的立场上，成为能领会表面意思之下含义的少数人，并且流露出对读者智慧的一丝恭维。这也是为什么许多文学讽刺家遭到曲解，有时还会（像18世纪的丹尼尔·笛福和乔纳森·斯威夫特那样）受到迂腐当局的严厉责难。像柏拉图、斯威夫特、奥斯丁或亨利·詹姆斯这样伟大的讽刺家作品字里行间的讽刺手法错综复杂，变化灵活，是对读者阅读能力的一种考验。

有的文学作品表现出一种**通篇性反讽**，即作者不是偶尔运用讽刺反话，而是采用一种使双关意义和评价通贯全文的特殊篇章结构。这种讽刺类型中常见的一种文学手段是塑造一位**愚偶**，或一个天真单纯的叙述者或代言人，他们天生的单纯或愚钝导致他们对情况的不断误解，而心领神会的读者则能深入并共享那些天真单纯的*第一人称*背后所隐含的作者观点，并在作者的引导下对其加以改变和更正。（应该注意，反话依赖于言者和读者对虚构言者的讽刺*意向*的共同认识；通篇性反讽则依赖于对作者讽刺意向的认知，但这只为读者所知而不被虚构的言者所意识到。）斯威夫特所著的《温和的建议》（1729）里的经济学家，就是这种幼稚的代言人的一个例子，他本意善良，但却具有荒唐的理性和道德上的愚钝，他建议把爱尔兰国内饱受压迫与贫困的多余儿童变成财政资源与美食佳肴。其他例子还有斯威夫特笔下那个固执轻信的格列佛、勃朗宁《西班牙修道院里的独白》（1842）中那个自欺狂妄的"独白人"、弗拉基米尔·纳博科夫《灰火》（1962）里那个失常的编辑金伯特。利用*容易出错的叙述者*是保持讽刺修饰的相关结构手法，其中故事的叙述者也是故事中的一个角色。虽然这样一个叙述者既不愚蠢、轻信也不疯狂，但却通过他对自己的动机和他人的动机与行为的认识和评价而显示出他见识的不足，从中读者可以看出叙述者由于偏见和个人兴趣所形成的扭曲观点。（参见：*视角*。）

韦恩·布思在其所著的《反讽修辞学》（1974）里确定出一种**指令反讽**，即言者或作者使读者获得一种观点或立场，无论这种观点或立场是明显的还是隐含的，都将成为修正或颠覆表面含义、发掘讽刺含义的坚实基础。**非指令反讽**则刚好相反，它不向读者暗示某种特定的不为进一步反讽所削弱的固定观点。*荒诞派*文学突出体现了这种反讽表达手法上的退化。在极端的例子中，如在塞缪尔·贝克特的戏剧《等待戈多》（1955）或小说《无名的人》（1960）中，这种讽刺性削弱退化源源不断。这类作品否定人类处境中任何固定的评估立场，甚至是任何确定的逻辑依据。

Sarcasm in common parlance is sometimes used as an equivalent for irony, but it is far more useful to restrict it only to the crude and taunting use of apparent praise for dispraise: "Oh, you're God's great gift to women, you are!" The difference in application of the two terms is indicated by the difference in their etymologies; whereas "irony" derives from "eiron," a "dissembler," "sarcasm" derives from the Greek verb "sarkazein," "to tear flesh." An added clue to sarcasm is the exaggerated inflection of the speaker's voice.

The term "irony," qualified by an adjective, is used to identify various literary devices and modes of organization:

Socratic irony takes its name from the fact that, as he is represented in Plato's dialogues (fourth century BC), the philosopher Socrates usually dissembles by assuming a pose of ignorance, an eagerness to be instructed, and a modest readiness to entertain opinions proposed by others; although these opinions, upon his continued questioning, turn out to be ill-grounded or to lead to absurd consequences.

Dramatic irony involves a situation in a play or a narrative in which the audience or reader shares with the author knowledge of present or future circumstances of which a character is ignorant; in that situation, the literary character unknowingly acts in a way we recognize to be grossly inappropriate to the actual circumstances, or expects the opposite of what we know that fate holds in store, or says something that anticipates the actual outcome, but not at all in the way that the character intends. Writers of Greek tragedy, who based their plots on legends whose outcome was already known to their audience, made frequent use of this device. Sophocles' *Oedipus the King*, for example, represents a very complex instance of **tragic irony**, for the king ("I, Oedipus, whom all men call great") engages in a hunt for the incestuous father-murderer who has brought a plague upon Thebes; the object of the hunt turns out (as the audience, but not Oedipus, has known right along) to be the hunter himself; and the king, having achieved a vision of the terrible truth, blinds himself. Dramatic irony occurs also in comedy. An example is the scene in Shakespeare's *Twelfth Night* (II. v.) in which Malvolio struts and preens in anticipation of a good fortune that the audience knows is based on a fake letter; the dramatic irony is heightened for the audience by Malvolio's ignorance of the presence of the hidden hoaxers, who gleefully comment on his incongruously complacent speech and actions.

Cosmic irony (or "the irony of fate") is attributed to literary works in which a deity, or else fate, is represented as though deliberately manipulating events so as to lead the protagonist to false hopes, only to frustrate and mock them. This is a favorite structural device of Thomas Hardy. In his *Tess of the D'Urbervilles* (1891) the heroine, having lost her virtue because of her innocence, then loses her happiness because of her honesty, finds it again only by murder, and having been briefly happy, is hanged. Hardy concludes: "The President of the Immortals, in Aeschylean phrase, had ended his sport with Tess."

Romantic irony is a term introduced by Friedrich Schlegel and other German writers of the late eighteenth and early nineteenth centuries to

挖苦按普遍说法，有时可以等同于反讽，但最好把它限定为那种貌似表扬实为贬损的粗鲁嘲弄的做法。例如："哦，你是上帝给女人的最大恩赐，你的确是！"这两个术语的不同词源便说明了它们在使用上的差别；"讽刺"来源于"eiron"，指的是一种"掩盖"；"挖苦"源于希腊语中的动词"sarkazein"，指的是"划伤肉体"。言者的夸张语调也是领会挖苦的另外线索。

"反讽"一词经过某些形容词修饰，可用于指代不同的文学手法和组织模式：

苏格拉底式反讽得名于柏拉图的对话中（公元前4世纪）所呈现的这一事实：哲学家苏格拉底常常故意摆出无知、渴望指导、准备虚心接受他人赐教的姿态；尽管在他不断的询问中，对方说出的观点总是难以成立或导致荒谬结论。

戏剧性反讽涉及戏剧或小说里的这样一种情况：观众或读者与作家共同了解的有关当时或未来的情况不被剧中某个人物所知；在那种情况下，他不是无知地表现出在我们看来与实际情况极其不相适宜的举动，就是作出与我们所知的、等待着的命运相违背的预期，或是人物完全出于无意却又预料出事情的真实结局。希腊悲剧作家取材于结局已被观众熟知的传说，时常采用这样的讽刺手段。索福克勒斯的《俄狄浦斯王》就是一例错综复杂的**悲剧性反讽**，因为俄狄浦斯王（"我，俄狄浦斯，被众人称为伟大的国王"）在寻找给底比斯城邦带来瘟疫的乱伦弑父者，结果所寻找的对象（这一结果观众已经知晓，俄狄浦斯却蒙在鼓里）却是寻找者本人；俄狄浦斯王得到神的启示，弄清了可怕的真相后，弄瞎了自己的双眼以示忏悔。戏剧性反讽也出现在喜剧作品中。例如莎士比亚《第十二夜》的第二幕第五场就是一个戏剧性反讽的例子。在这一场景中，马伏里奥因为预感到要交好运而显得神气活现、洋洋得意，而观众则明白他的预感是由于一封假信造成的错误；在马伏里奥对于隐藏的戏弄者一无所知的同时，这个欺骗者正在幸灾乐祸地评论他那沾沾自喜的言语和行为，这样对观众来说，戏剧性反讽的效果就加强了。

命运反讽是指在一些文学作品里，神灵或命运被描绘成故意左右时事的主宰，他们造成主人公不切实际的愿望，只是为了使之受到挫折或戏弄。这种讽刺形式是托马斯·哈代最喜爱的一种情节组织方式。在他的小说《德伯家的苔丝》(1891) 里，女主人公先是因为天真而失节，后又因为诚实而丧失幸福，通过谋杀再获幸福，但好景不长，她最终被处绞刑。作者最后作出结论："埃斯库罗斯所说的那个众神的主宰对于苔丝的戏弄也就完结了。"

浪漫主义反讽由弗里德里克·施莱格尔和18世纪末19世纪初的其他德国

designate a mode of dramatic or narrative writing in which the author builds up the illusion of representing reality, only to shatter the illusion by revealing that the author, as artist, is the creator and arbitrary manipulator of the characters and their actions. The concept owes much to Laurence Sterne's presentation of a self-conscious and willful narrator in his *Tristram Shandy* (1759–67). Byron's great narrative poem *Don Juan* (1819–24) persistently uses this device for ironic and comic effect, letting the reader into the narrator's confidence, and so revealing the latter to be nothing more than a fabricator of fiction who is often at a loss for matter to sustain his story and undecided about how to continue it. (See Anne Mellor, *English Romantic Irony*, 1980.) This type of irony, involving a self-conscious *narrator*, has become a recurrent mode in the modern form of *involuted fiction*.

A number of writers associated with the *New Criticism* used "irony," although in a greatly extended sense, as a general criterion of literary value. This use is based largely on two literary theorists. T. S. Eliot praised a kind of "wit" (characteristic, in his view, of seventeenth-century *metaphysical poets* but absent in the Romantic poets) which is an "internal equilibrium" that implies the "recognition," in dealing with any one kind of experience, "of other kinds of experience which are possible." ("Andrew Marvell," 1921, in *Selected Essays*, 1960.) And I. A. Richards defined irony in poetry as an equilibrium of opposing attitudes and evaluations *(Principles of Literary Criticism*, 1924, chapter 32):

> Irony in this sense consists in the bringing in of the opposite, the complementary impulses; that is why poetry which is exposed to it is not of the highest order, and why irony itself is so constantly a characteristic of poetry which is.

Such observations were developed by Robert Penn Warren, Cleanth Brooks, and other New Critics into the claim that poems in which the writer commits himself or herself unreservedly to a single attitude or outlook, such as love or admiration or idealism, are of an inferior order because they are vulnerable to the reader's ironic skepticism; the greatest poems, on the other hand, are invulnerable to external irony because they already incorporate the poet's own "ironic" awareness of opposite and complementary attitudes. See Robert Penn Warren, "Pure and Impure Poetry" (1943), in *Critiques and Essays in Criticism*, ed. Robert W. Stallman (1949); Cleanth Brooks, "Irony as a Principle of Structure" (1949), in *Literary Opinion in America*, ed. M. D. Zabel (3d ed., 1962).

See D. C. Muecke, *Irony* (1970); A. E. Dyson, *The Crazy Fabric, Essays in Irony* (1965); Wayne C. Booth, *A Rhetoric of Irony* (1974); Linda Hutcheon, *Irony's Edge: The Theory and Politics of Irony* (1995); Claire Colebrook, *Irony* (2003). A suggestive and wide-ranging earlier exploration of the mode is Søren Kierkegaard's *The Concept of Irony* (1841; trans. Lee M. Capel, 1965). For references to *irony* in other entries, see pages *12, 183*.

irregular ode: 263.

Italian sonnet: 370.

作家提出，以表示戏剧和小说创作的一种手法：作家建立一种展现了现实的幻象，只是为了通过披露作者作为艺术家是在创造与任意操纵笔下的人物角色和他们的行为，从而打破这种幻象。这一手法主要源于劳伦斯·斯特恩在《项狄传》(1759—1767)中所使用的体现自我意识、任性的叙述者。拜伦的伟大叙事诗《唐·璜》(1819—1824)为了求得讽刺和喜剧效果也反复运用了这种手法，诗人向读者泄漏叙述者的隐私，以揭示叙述者是故事的编造者，常常茫然不知该如何延续情节讲完故事。[参阅：安妮·梅勒所著的《英国浪漫体讽刺》(1980)。]这种形式的讽刺涉及一位自我意识的叙述者，已经成为现代*内延小说*中一再出现的模式。

与*新批评*有关的一些作家将"讽刺"——尽管大大扩展了其含义——作为衡量文学价值的一般标准。这种用法主要基于两位文艺理论家T. S.艾略特和I. A.理查兹的思想。T. S.艾略特吹捧一种（在他看来属于17世纪*玄学派诗人*的特征而浪漫主义诗人所不具备的）"心智"，他认为这是一种"内在的均衡"，在说明任何一种经验感受时又包含着"对其他可能经验的认识"。[参阅他所写的文章"安德鲁·马韦尔"(1921)，收入其所著的《论文选》(1960)。]I. A.理查兹把诗歌中的反讽定义为是对立观点和评价的平衡[《文学批评原理》(1924)第32章]：

> 反讽在这个意义上存在于引起对立而又互为补充的刺激作用；正是由于这个道理，那种招致反讽的诗歌不是上乘之作，而反讽却永远是上乘诗歌的特点。

这些论点后来被罗伯特·佩恩·华伦、克林斯·布鲁克斯和其他新批评家发展成一种定论，即在诗歌里，如果诗人自己毫无保留地倾注于单一的态度或观念，如爱、仰慕或理想主义，这样的作品就是劣诗，因为这些诗容易受到读者的讽刺怀疑；最伟大的诗作则因已经综合了诗人自己对于对立与互补态度的"讽刺"认识，因此在外界的讽刺面前是无懈可击的。参阅：罗伯特·佩恩·华伦所写的文章"纯诗歌与非纯诗歌"(1943)，收入R. W.斯托曼主编的《文学批评中的评论与论文》(1949)；克林斯·布鲁克斯所写的文章"讽刺：结构的原则"(1949)，收入M. W.扎贝尔主编的《美国的文学主张》(1962年第3版)。

参阅：D. C.米克所著的《反讽》(1970)；A. E.戴森所著的《疯狂的建构，反讽文选》(1965)；韦恩·C.布思所著的《反讽修辞学》(1974)；琳达·哈琴所著的《反讽的边缘：反讽的理论与政治》(1995)；克莱尔·科尔布鲁克所著的《反讽》(2003)。早期对于这一方法具有启发性的广泛探索，可以参阅：索伦·克尔凯郭尔所著的《论反讽的概念》(1841；1965年李·M.卡佩尔英译版)。其他条目中提及"反讽"的地方，参见第12、183页。

irregular ode：无律颂　263。

Italian sonnet：意大利式十四行诗　370。

ivory tower: A phrase taken from the biblical Song of Songs 7:4, in which the lover says to the beloved woman, "Thy neck is as a tower of ivory." In the 1830s the French critic Sainte-Beuve applied the phrase "tour d'ivoire" to the stance of the poet Alfred de Vigny, to signify his isolation from everyday life and his exaltation of art above all practical concerns. Since then "ivory tower" is often used (usually in a derogatory way) to signify an attitude or a way of life which is isolated from the everyday world and indifferent or hostile to practical affairs; more specifically, it is used to signify a theory and practice of art which insulates it from moral, political, and social concerns or effects. (See *aestheticism*.)

Ivory Tower：象牙塔

　　这一表达来源于《圣经·雅歌》(7：4)，新郎告诉他所爱的新娘，"你的颈项如象牙台"。1830年代，法国批评家圣伯夫用"象牙塔"这一词组来指诗人阿尔弗雷德·德·维尼远离日常生活，认为艺术高于一切实际事物的态度。自那时起，"象牙塔"就常被用来（通常作贬义）指代一种远离日常生活世界、对实际事物漠不关心或充满敌对的态度或生活方式，它更为具体的用法是指代一种与道德、政治、社会的关注或影响相隔绝的艺术理论和行为。（参见：*唯美主义*。）

J

Jacobean Age: 281.

jeremiad: A term derived from the Old Testament prophet Jeremiah, who in the seventh century BC attributed the calamities of Israel to its violation of the covenant with Jehovah and return to pagan idolatry, denounced with gloomy eloquence its religious and moral iniquities, and called on the people to repent and reform in order that Jehovah might restore them to His favor and renew the ancient covenant. As a literary term, **jeremiad** is applied to any work which, with a magniloquence like that of the Old Testament prophet (although it may be in secular rather than religious terms), accounts for the misfortunes of an era as a just penalty for its social and moral wrongdoings, but usually holds open the possibility for reforms that will bring a happier future.

In the *Romantic Period*, powerful passages in William Blake's "prophetic poems" constitute short jeremiads, and the term is often applied to those of Thomas Carlyle's writings in which he uses a resonant biblical idiom to denounce the social and economic misdeeds of the *Victorian Period* and to call for drastic reforms. The jeremiad, in its original religious mode, was a familiar genre in the sermons and writings of the *Colonial Period* in America, at a time when it was a commonplace that the colonies in New England were the "New Israel" with which God had covenanted a glorious future. The misfortunes of the colonists, accordingly, were attributed to deviations from the divine commands and described as punishments inflicted by God on His chosen people for their own ultimate benefit. In the words of Increase Mather, "God does not punish ... other Nations until they have filled up the Measure of their sins, and then he utterly destroyeth them; but if our Nation forsake the God of their Fathers never so little," He punishes us in order "that so he may prevent our destruction" (*The Day of Trouble Is Near*, 1674). Since that era the prophetic stance and denunciatory rhetoric of the jeremiad has been manifested by many orators and writers, religious and secular, into the present time. See Sacvan Bercovitch, *The American Jeremiad* (1978), and George P. Landow, *Elegant Jeremiahs: The Sage from Carlyle to Mailer* (1986).

journal: 27.

judicial criticism: 68.

juncture (in linguistics): **197**.

Jungian criticism: 323.

Juvenalian satire: 354.

J

Jacobean Age：詹姆斯一世时期　281。

Jeremiad：哀史

　　这一术语源自《旧约》里的先知耶利米，他在公元前 7 世纪将以色列的灾难归咎于它违背了与上帝耶和华订下的约定，重新信奉异教，他以其阴郁的言辞谴责了以色列在宗教和道德上的罪孽，号召人们进行忏悔和改革，以便能够重新得到上帝耶和华的眷顾，恢复古代条约。作为一个文学术语，**哀史**用于指代那些带有《旧约》中先知夸张言辞特征（尽管使用的可能是世俗语言而非宗教语言）的任何作品，将一个时代的不幸看成是对社会和道德罪恶的正义惩罚，但通常也都表明了这有可能是会带来一个更为幸福的未来的变革。

　　在*浪漫主义时期*，威廉·布莱克的"预言性诗歌"中强有力的篇章是由短篇哀史组成的；哀史这一术语也常用于托马斯·卡莱尔的一些作品，在这些作品中，他使用了类似于圣经中的成语来谴责*维多利亚时期*的社会和经济弊端，号召进行彻底的变革。由于其原有的宗教内涵，哀史是布道以及美国*殖民地时期*作品的一个常见类别。那时普遍把新英格兰殖民地看成"新以色列"，拥有上帝允诺的美好未来。因此，殖民地人民的苦难被归咎于他们违背了神的指令，上帝为了他所选择的子民自身的最终利益而惩罚他们。按照英克里斯·马瑟的说法，"上帝并不惩罚……其他民族，除非因为他们充满了罪孽，他才彻底毁灭他们；但我们的民族背弃了上帝太多"，他惩罚我们是为了"阻止我们走向毁灭"[《灾难之日近了》(1674)]。从那时起一直到现在，许多世俗及宗教演说家和作家便开始使用哀史中的先知态度和谴责措词。参阅：萨克万·伯罗维奇所著的《美国哀史》(1978)；乔治·P. 兰多所著的《典雅的哀史：从卡莱尔到梅勒的圣人》(1986)。

journal：日志　27。

judicial criticism：分析批评　68。

juncture (in linguistics)：(语言学中的) 连音　197。

Jungian criticism：荣格文学批评　323。

Juvenalian satire：尤维纳利斯式讽刺　354。

kenning: 132.

kinds (of literature): 148.

Künstlerroman (kunst′ lĕrōmän″): 255.

kenning：隐喻表达法　132。

kinds (of literature)：(文学的) 种类　148。

Künstlerroman：艺术家成长小说　255。

Lacanian literary criticism: 324.

lai: A name originally applied to a variety of poems by medieval French writers in the latter part of the twelfth and the thirteenth centuries. Some lais were lyric, but most were short narratives written in *octosyllabic couplets*. Marie de France, who wrote in the French language although probably in England at the court of King Henry II, composed a number of notable poems of this sort; they are called "Breton lais" because most of their narratives are drawn from Arthurian and other Celtic legends. ("Breton" refers to Brittany, which was a Celtic part of France; see *chivalric romance*.) The Anglicized term **Breton lay** was applied in the fourteenth century to English poems written on the model of the narratives of Marie de France; they included *Sir Orfeo*, the *Lay of Launfal*, and Chaucer's "The Franklin's Tale." Later still, **lay** was used by English poets simply as a synonym for song, or as an archaic word for a fairly short narrative poem—for example by Sir Walter Scott in his *Lay of the Last Minstrel*, 1805.

See Roger S. Loomis, ed., *Arthurian Literature in the Middle Ages* (1959); and the Introduction by Charles W. Dunn to *Lays of Courtly Love*, trans. Patricia Terry (1963).

lampoon: 39.

langue (in linguistics) (läng): **194**; *310, 358, 382*.

latent content: 321.

lay (song): **191**.

Lebenswelt: 289.

legend: 230.

leitmotif (līt″ mōtēf′): **229**.

lesbian studies: 327; *146*.

light verse: Light verse is a term applied to a great variety of poems that use an ordinary speaking voice and a relaxed manner to treat their subjects gaily, or playfully, or wittily, or with good-natured *satire*. The subject matter of light verse need not be in itself petty or inconsequential; the defining quality is the *tone* of voice used, and the attitude of the lyric or narrative speaker toward the subject. Thomas Love Peacock's "The War Song of Dinas Vawr" (1829) begins

Lacanian literary criticism：拉康文学批评　324。

Lai：籁歌

籁歌原指 12 世纪末期与 13 世纪期间中世纪法国作家创作的各类诗歌。有些籁歌是抒情诗，但多数都为*八音节对句体*的叙事短诗。法国女诗人玛丽·德·法兰西当时尽管可能生活在英王亨利二世的宫廷，但却用法语创作了一些著名的籁歌；由于她的作品故事大都取材于亚瑟王传说及其他凯尔特传说，故被称为"布列塔尼籁歌"（"Breton"是指布列塔尼，当时是法国的凯尔特部分；参见：*骑士传奇*）。英语化术语**布列塔尼籁歌**指代 14 世纪仿照玛丽·德·法兰西的叙事诗而创作的英国诗歌；其中包括《奥费欧爵士》《朗法尔之歌》和乔叟的《富兰克林的故事》。后来**籁歌**仍被英国诗人仅用作"诗歌"的代名词，或用作表示优美的叙事短诗的古语，例如，沃尔特·司各特爵士的《最后的吟游诗人之歌》（1805）。

参阅：罗杰·S. 卢米斯主编的《中世纪的亚瑟王文学》（1959）；查尔斯·W. 邓恩为《骑士恋之歌》（1963，帕特里夏·特里英译版）所写的简介。

lampoon：讽刺诗　39。

langue (in linguistics)：（语言学中的）语言　194；*310, 358, 382*。

latent content：潜在内容　321。

lay (song)：籁歌（诗歌）　191。

Lebenswelt：现实世界　289。

legend：传说　230。

leitmotif：中心意思　229。

lesbian studies：女性同性恋研究　327；*146*。

Light Verse：轻松诗

轻松诗一词用于指一般采用平常谈话的口吻、轻松自在的方式，主题描写或风趣畅快，或变化离奇，或略含几分温和*讽刺*的各类诗歌。轻松诗的题材并非一定琐细或无关紧要；其关键特征取决于所使用的*语调*及抒情人或叙事人对待主题的态度。例如托马斯·洛夫·皮科克的《黛纳斯·沃的战歌》（1829）的开头部分：

192 LIGHT VERSE

> The mountain sheep are sweeter,
> But the valley sheep are fatter;
> We therefore deemed it meter
> To carry off the latter.

And it ends

> We brought away from battle,
> And much their land bemoaned them,
> Two thousand head of cattle,
> And the head of him who owned them:
> Ednyfed, king of Dyfed,
> His head was borne before us;
> His wine and beasts supplied our feasts,
> And his overthrow, our chorus.

The dispassionate attitude, brisk colloquialism, and pat rhymes convert what could be a matter for epic or tragedy into a comic narrative that qualifies as light verse.

Vers de société (society verse) is the very large subclass of light verse that deals with the relationships, concerns, and doings of polite, upper-class society. It is often satiric, but in the mode of badinage rather than severity; and when it deals with love it does so as a sexual game, or flirtatiously, or in the mode of elegant and witty compliment, rather than with passion or high seriousness. The tone is usually urbane, the style deft, and the form polished and sometimes contrived with technical virtuosity. Most poems using intricate French stanza forms, such as the *villanelle*, are in this form. Many of the lyrics written by Cole Porter for his popular songs qualify as society verse, such as:

> Birds do it, bees do it
> Even educated fleas do it
> Let's do it, let's fall in love.

See Carolyn Wells, ed., *A Vers de Société Anthology*, reprinted 1976.

Nursery rhymes and other children's verses are another type of light verse. Edward Lear ("The Jumblies," "The Owl and the Pussy Cat") and Lewis Carroll ("Jabberwocky," *The Hunting of the Snark*) made children's **nonsense verses** into a Victorian specialty. Lear is also notable for popularizing the **limerick**, which is a largely oral form of light verse that everyone knows and many of us have practiced. (See *oral poetry*.) The name is probably derived from a convivial song with the refrain "Will you come up to Limerick?" (Limerick is a county in Ireland.) It consists of a single five-line stanza in *anapestic* meter, rhyming *aabba*, with the third and fourth lines shortened from three feet to two feet. Some limericks are decorous but many are ribald. Here is a limerick about the limerick by the scholar and humorist Professor Morris Bishop which is itself decorous, but indicates the form's propensity toward the alternative mode:

> 山里的羊儿更甜，
> 谷里的羊儿更肥；
> 因此我们认为
> 带走后者更为适宜。

和这首诗的结尾部分

> 大部分土地为之哀恸，
> 我们从战场带回，
> 两千只牛首，
> 及其拥有者的头颅：
> 埃德尼非德，德韦达郡的国王，
> 他的首级被送到我们面前；
> 他的美酒牲口成为我们的盛宴，
> 他被推翻，我们齐声欢呼。

诗里表现出的公允平和的态度、活泼欢快的口语、节奏轻快的韵律，把原为史诗或悲剧的题材化为一首趣味盎然的轻松诗。

上流社会轻佻诗为轻松诗的一个大分类，主要表现上流社会的关系、人们关心的事情与作为。情调多为讽刺，但语言戏谑而不尖刻；对于爱情的描写不是贯注以激情和庄重格调，而是视之为性的游戏，调情卖俏地加以表现，或是付之以精巧诙谐的赞美。这类诗通常语调文雅，风格洗练，体式完美，有时也过于追求技巧的精湛；多数采用繁杂法式诗节（如*维拉内拉诗体*）的诗歌都属于轻佻诗。科尔·波特为他的流行歌曲写的许多抒情诗也配得上是上流社会轻佻诗，比如：

> 鸟们干这个，蜜蜂干这个
> 甚至知识分子也干这个
> 让我们也来，让我们坠入爱河。

参阅：卡罗琳·威尔斯主编的《上流社会轻佻诗选集》（1976年重印）。

童谣和其他儿歌是轻松诗的另一种类型。爱德华·李尔（《江布利》《猫头鹰与猫咪》）和路易斯·卡罗尔（《捷波瓦奇》《斯纳克的狩猎》）使这类写给儿童的无意义的诗歌成为维多利亚时代的文学特产。李尔还因普及了五行打油诗而知名，这是一种人人皆知的轻松诗形式，并被广为采用。（参见：*口头诗歌*。）这一名字可能来自一首欢快的歌曲，其副歌是"你要来利默里克郡吗？"（利默里克是爱尔兰的一个郡。）它包括简单的五行诗节，*抑抑扬格*格律，押韵 *aabba*，第三、四两行从三音步缩短到二音步。有些五行打油诗比较庄重，但是多数都比较轻佻。下面是一首关于五行打油诗的五行打油诗（版权未授。——译注），出自富有幽默感的学者莫里斯·毕晓普教授之手，这首诗比较庄重，但却展示了这一形式另类模式的倾向：

An accessible collection is *The Penguin Book of Limericks*, ed. E. O. Parrott (1983). For scholarly editions of the ribald variety of the form, largely from oral sources, refer to G. Legman's two volumes, *The Limerick: 1700 Examples, with Notes, Variants, and Index* (1969); and *The New Limerick: 2750 Unpublished Examples, American and British* (1977).

Fine artificers of light and society verse are John Skelton (c. 1460–1529), the *Cavalier poets* of the early seventeenth century, and John Dryden, Matthew Prior, Lady Mary Wortley Montagu, Alexander Pope, W. S. Gilbert, and Austin Dobson. Modern practitioners include Ezra Pound, W. H. Auden, e. e. cummings, Ogden Nash, Marianne Moore, Edna St. Vincent Millay, Dorothy Parker, Phyllis McGinley, Morris Bishop, John Betjeman, A. R. Ammons, Anthony Hecht, John Updike, and Ishmael Reed.

See *epigram*. Refer to *Worldly Muse: An Anthology of Serious Light Verse*, ed. A. J. M. Smith (1951); *The Fireside Book of Humorous Poetry*, ed. W. Cole (1959); *The New Oxford Book of Light Verse*, ed. Kingsley Amis (1978); *The Norton Book of Light Verse*, ed. Russell Baker (1986).

limerick: 192.

limited point of view: 303.

line (of verse): 217.

linguistics in literary criticism: Linguistics is the systematic study of the elements of language and the principles governing their combination and organization. An older term for the scientific study of the constitution and history of language was **philology**—a term that is still sometimes used as synonymous with linguistics. Through the nineteenth century, philology was mainly "comparative" (the analysis of similarities and differences within a family of related languages) and "historical" (the analysis of the evolution of a family of languages, or of changes within a particular language, over a long course of time). This latter study of the changes in language over a span of time has come to be called **diachronic**; the important developments in twentieth-century linguistics came with the shift to the **synchronic** study of the systematic interrelations of the components of a single language at a particular time. A major contributor to modern synchronic linguistics was Ferdinand de Saussure, a French-speaking Swiss whose lectures on language as a self-sufficient

（略）

一本易得的合集是：E. O. 帕罗特主编的《企鹅五行打油诗集》(1983)。关于不同种类轻佻五行打油诗（多来自口述资源）的学术版本，参阅：G. 莱格曼所著的两卷本《五行打油诗：1700 个例子，附带注释、异文和索引》(1969) 和《新五行打油诗：英美 2750 个未发表过的例子》(1977)。

擅长创作轻松诗和上流社会轻佻诗的名家还包括约翰·斯克尔顿（约 1460—1529），17 世纪初期的英国骑士诗人，约翰·德莱顿、马修·普赖尔、玛丽·沃特利·蒙塔古夫人、亚历山大·蒲柏、W. S. 吉尔伯特、奥斯丁·多布森。现代诗人埃兹拉·庞德、W. H. 奥登、e. e. 卡明斯、奥格登·纳什、玛丽安·穆尔、埃德娜·圣·文森特·米莱、多萝西·帕克、菲利斯·麦金利、莫里斯·毕晓普、约翰·贝杰曼、A. R. 阿蒙斯、约翰·厄普代克、伊什梅尔·里德。

参见：警句。参阅：A. J. M. 史密斯主编的《世俗缪斯：严肃轻松诗选集》(1951)；W. 科尔主编的《炉边幽默诗集》(1959)；金斯利·阿米斯主编的《新编牛津轻松诗集》(1978)；拉塞尔·贝克主编的《诺顿轻松诗集》(1986)。

limerick：打油诗　192。

limited point of view：局限性视角　303。

line (of verse)：(韵文的) 诗行　217。

Linguistics in Literary Criticism：语言学在文学批评里的应用

语言学是对语言的各种成分及其组织结合原则的系统研究。指代对语言结构和历史的科学研究更为古老的术语是**语文学**，这一术语有时仍用作语言学的同义词。整个 19 世纪，语文学研究主要是"比较性的"（从事对同一语族内部相关语言之间的共性与差异的分析）和"历史性的"（从历史角度去分析同一语族语言的演变或某种特定语言在一段长时期内的变化）。后面这种对语言在一段时间内变化的研究被称为**历时语言学**；20 世纪语言学的重要发展表现为，向针对特定时期某一种语言内部成分间系统关系的**共时性**研究的转移。瑞士语言学家费迪南·德·索绪尔对现代共时语言学作出了重大贡献，这位讲法语的瑞士语言学家在 1907—1911 年间所作的有关"语言作为自足系统"的讲演，

system, delivered 1907–11, were published from students' notes in 1916, three years after Saussure's death; these lectures have been translated as *Course in General Linguistics* (1916). (See Saussure under *semiotics*.) Important contributions were also made by American "descriptive" or "structural" linguists, notably Edward Sapir and Leonard Bloomfield, who set out to devise a linguistic theory and vocabulary adequate to analyze, as modes of verbal "behavior," various Native American languages. Both Continental and American linguistics have been applied to the analysis of the distinctive uses of language in literary texts (see *Russian formalism* and *stylistics*), and Saussure's concepts and procedures in analyzing a language have been adopted as a model for analyzing the forms and organization of large-scale literary structures (see *structuralist criticism*).

As an empirical, fact-based study of language, philology has often appealed to students of literature who seek to ground their enterprise on hard evidence, rather than what they consider to be *subjective* responses and judgments. Several influential critics, including Paul de Man, Edward Said, and the medievalist Lee Patterson, in articles called a "Return to Philology," argued that literary criticism needed to recover the discipline and rigor of traditional linguistic studies. Such calls for what is often termed a **new philology** have been especially strong in disciplines such as classics and medieval studies, where textual criticism has always been a central concern. In these latter studies, the phrase "new philology" designates a movement to reorient philological study away from its traditional focus on establishing an authoritative text, to a concern with the effect on the reader of the material and verbal particularities of each manuscript text; refer to *book history studies*.

On calls for a return to philology, see Paul de Man, "The Return to Philology," in *The Resistance to Theory* (1986); Edward Said, "The Return to Philology," in *Humanism and Democratic Criticism* (2004); Jan Ziolkowski, *On Philology* (1990); Lee Patterson, "The Return to Philology," in John van Engen, ed., *The Past and Future of Medieval Studies* (1994); and Seth Lerer, ed., *Literary History and the Challenge of Philology: The Legacy of Erich Auerbach* (1996). In "Roots, Races, and the Return to Philology," in *The Humanities and the Dream of America* (2011), Geoffrey Galt Harpham traces the connections between the discipline of philology and racial theorizing in the nineteenth and twentieth centuries. On the new philological movement in medieval studies, see also Stephen Nichols, ed., "The New Philology," a special issue of the journal *Speculum*, Vol. 65 (1990).

The following linguistic terms and concepts are often employed by current critics and theorists of literature:

Saussure introduced an important distinction between langue and parole. A **parole** is any single meaningful utterance, spoken or written. The **langue** is the implicit system of elements, of distinctions and oppositions, and of principles of combination, which make it possible, within a language community, for a speaker to produce and the auditor to understand a particular parole. The linguist's primary concern, in Saussure's view, is to establish the nature of the underlying linguistic system, the langue. The American linguist Noam Chomsky has substituted for Saussure's langue and parole the distinction

在他去世三年后，通过学生笔记整理发表；这些讲演被翻译成《普通语言学教程》(1916)。（参见：*符号论*中有关索绪尔的论述。）著名的美国"描写"或"结构主义"语言学家爱德华·萨丕尔和伦纳德·布龙菲尔德也为现代共时语言学研究作出了重要贡献。他们首创了一套语言学理论和语汇，作为言语"行为"模式，对美国不同的印第安语支的现状进行分析。欧洲大陆和美国的语言学理论已被用于分析文学文本中语言与众不同的用法（参见：*俄国形式主义*、*文体学*），而索绪尔用于语言分析的理论和程序也已被借用于分析文学作品总体结构的形式与组织（参见：*结构主义批评*）。

作为一种实证的、以事实为基础的语言研究，语文学经常会对那些想要将其事业建立在确凿证据之上而非他们所认为的*主体*反应和评判之上的文学学生有很大的吸引力。几位重要批评家，包括保罗·德·曼、爱德华·赛义德、中古史学家李·帕特森，在一篇名为"回归语文学"的文章中认为，文学批评需要恢复传统语言学研究的训练方法和严密性。这一呼声，常被叫做**新语文学**，在像古典和中世纪研究这样的学科中一直表现得尤为强烈，在这样的学科研究中，文本批评始终是一个核心问题。在近来的研究中，"新语文学"这一短语指一场运动，这场运动重新定位语文学研究，远离它的传统关注点：确立一个权威文本，改为关注每一手稿文本的材料和语言特性对读者产生的影响；参见：*书籍史研究*。

关于呼吁回归语文学，参阅：保罗·德·曼所写的文章"回归语文学"，收入其所著的《抗拒理论》(1968)；爱德华·赛义德所写的文章"回归语文学"，收入其所著的《人文主义与民主批评》(2004)；扬·齐奥科夫斯基所著的《论语文学》(1990)；李·帕特森所写的文章"回归语文学"，收入约翰·范恩金主编的《中世纪研究的过去和未来》(1994)；塞思·勒若主编的《文学史和语文学的挑战：埃利希·奥尔巴赫的遗产》(1996)。杰弗里·高尔特·哈珀姆在《人文学与美国梦》(2011)中的"根源、种族和回归语文学"中，描述了语文学这一学科与19、20世纪种族理论化之间的关系。关于中世纪研究领域的新语文学运动，也可参阅：《镜鉴》1990年第65卷斯蒂芬·尼科尔斯主编的"新语文学"专刊。

下面是当代文学批评家与理论家经常使用的一些语言学术语与概念。

索绪尔曾介绍过语言与言语的重要区别。**言语**是指任何口述或书面的具有特定意义的言辞话语。**语言**则是包括各种成分，不同与对立，以及组合原则的内在体系，它们使得在同一语言群体内，言者得以生成、听者得以理解某一特定言语。根据索绪尔的观点，语言学家的基本课题就是要发掘出潜在语言体系，即语言的本质。美国语言学家诺姆·乔姆斯基用**语言能力**（讲母语者对母语系统

between **competence** (the tacit knowledge possessed by native speakers who have mastered, or "internalized," the implicit conventions and rules of a language system that make possible the production and understanding of well-formed and meaningful sentences) and **performance** (the actual utterance of particular sentences). Competent speakers know how to produce such sentences, without being able to specify the conventions and rules that enable them to do so; the function of the linguist is to identify and make explicit the system of linguistic conventions and rules that the speaker unknowingly puts into practice.

Modern linguists commonly distinguish three aspects that together constitute the **grammar**—the components, and the principles of ordering the components—in any "natural language" (English, French, Japanese, and so on): (1) **phonology**, the study of the elementary speech sounds; (2) **morphology**, the study of the ordering of speech sounds into the smallest meaningful groups (*morphemes* and words); and (3) **syntax**, the study of the way that sequences of words are ordered into phrases, clauses, and sentences. Structural linguists usually represent these three aspects as manifesting parallel principles of distinctions and ordering, although on successively higher and more complex levels of organization. A fourth aspect of language sometimes included within the area of linguistics is **semantics**, the study of the meaning of words and of the combination of words in phrases, sentences, and larger linguistic units. In the area of semantics, Saussure introduced the terminology of the *sign* (a single word) as constituted by an inseparable union of **signifier** (the speech sounds or written marks composing the sign) and **signified** (the conceptual meaning of the sign).

1. One branch of phonology is **phonetics**, the physical description of the elementary speech sounds in all known languages and the way they are produced by the vocal apparatus. The "phonetic alphabet" is a standardized set of symbols for representing in written form all these speech sounds. Another branch is "phonemics," which deals with **phonemes**: the smallest units of speech sound which, within any one natural language, are functional—that is, which cannot vary without changing the word of which they are a part into a different word. Thus in the English word represented by the spelling "pin," if we change only the initial speech sound, we get three different words, pin-tin-din; if we change only the medial sound, we get pin-pen-pun; if we change only the final sound, we get pin-pit-pill. From the matrix of such changes, we determine that each of the individual units represented by the spelling p, t, d; i, e, u; and n, t, l function as differentiating phonemes within the English language. Each language has its own system of phonemes which both overlaps with and diverges from the phonemic system of any other language. The imperfect success that a native speaker of one language, such as German or French, manifests in adapting his habitual pronunciations to the phonemic system of a different language, such as English, is a major feature of what we identify as a "foreign accent."

内在惯例与规则的掌握，或"吸收"，这使得说话人得以创造或理解结构完整、富含意义的句子）和**语言运用**（讲母语者实际说出的特定句子）之间的划分，取代了索绪尔有关语言和言语的划分。具有语言运用能力的说话者知晓怎样进行言语表达，他们不会借助语言惯例与规则来指导自己的言语行为。语言学家的任务就在于辨识并揭示说话人非自觉运用的语言惯例和规则体系。

现代语言学家普遍划分出任一"自然语言"（如英语、法语、日语等）的**语法**（语言的组成成分和支配语言成分的原则）的三个组成部分：（一）**音韵学**，研究基本语音；（二）**形态学**，研究语音如何构成最小的语义单位（词素与词）；（三）**句法**，研究一系列词组合成短语、从句和句子的方式。结构主义语言学家通常把这三个方面描述为体现分化与组合的平行原则，尽管它们表现出顺次递升与更为复杂化的结构水平。语言学研究领域有时还包括语言的第四个部分——**语义学**：研究词语、短语、句子和更大语言单位中词语组合的含义。在这方面，索绪尔提出了符号（即"单个词语"）这个术语。符号由不可分割的两个因素组成：**能指**（构成符号的语音与书写标记）和**所指**（符号表示的概念性意义）。

1. 音韵学的一个分支是**语音学**：对一切已知语言的基本语音及其发声器官的发声方法的具体描述。"音标"是记录这些语音的标准化符号系列。音韵学的另一分支是以**音位**为研究对象的"音位学"。音位是任何一种自然语言中起作用的最小语音单位，即在不改变其所在词语的情况下，它们不会变为另一个不同的词。以英语单词"pin"为例：如果我们只变换字头的音，就可得出三个不同的词"pin""tin""din"；如果我们只改变中间一个音，则可引出"pin""pen""pun"；如果我们只变换最后一个音，就会得出"pin""pit""pill"三个词。从这种变化模型里，我们可以断言，由 p, t, d; i, e, u; n, t, l 代表的每一个独立的语音单位，是英语里起着区别词义的音位。每一种语言都有自己的音位体系，同时与其他语言的音位体系有着相同和相异之处。以某种语言（如德语或法语）为母语的人把自己的习惯发音用到另一种不同语言（如英语）的音位体系，这种不足就是我们确认为"外国口音"的主要特征。

Even within a single language, however, a native speaker will vary the pronunciation of a single phonemic unit within different combinations of speech sounds, and will also vary the pronunciation from one utterance to another. Even greater phonetic differences are apparent between two native speakers, especially if they speak the **dialects** of diverse regions, or of diverse social groups. Saussure proposed the principle that what we identify as "the same phoneme" within a language is not determined by the physical features of the speech sound itself, but by its **difference** from all other phonemes in that language—that is, by the differentiability, within a given language, between a particular speech unit and all other functional speech units. Saussure's important claim is that the principle of difference, rather than any "positive" property, functions to establish identity not only for phonemes, but for units on all levels of linguistic organization, including both signs and the concepts that the signs signify. All these types of items, then, are systemic facts that achieve an identity only within a particular language, and vary between one language and another. (This claim, that seeming identities are in fact constituted by networks of differences, has been adopted and generalized as a central feature in *structuralism, semiotics,* and *deconstruction*.)

2. The next level of analysis, after phonology, is morphology—the combination of phonemes into morphemes and into words. A **morpheme** is the smallest meaningful unit of speech sounds within any one language; that is, a morphemic unit, composed of one or more phonemes, is a unit that recurs in a language with the same, or at least similar, meaning. Some morphemes, such as "man," "open," and "run" in English, constitute complete words; others, however, occur only as parts of words. For example the noun "grace" is a word that is a single morpheme. If we prefix to the root element, "grace," the morpheme "dis-," it becomes a different word with a sharply different meaning: "disgrace"; if we add to the root the morphemic suffix "-ful," the noun functions as an adjective, "graceful"; if we add to these two morphemes the further suffix, "-ly," the resulting word functions as an adverb, "gracefully"; if we prefix to this form either the morphemic "dis-" or "un-," we get the adverbial words, each composed of four morphemes, "disgracefully" and "ungracefully."

We find also an interesting set of phoneme combinations which do not constitute specific morphemes, yet are experienced by speakers of English as having a common, though very loose-boundaried, area of meaning. Examples are the initial sounds represented by "fl-" in the set of words "flash, flare, flame, flicker, flimmer," all of which signify a kind of moving light; while in the set "fly, flip, flap, flop, flit, flutter," the same initial sounds all signify a kind of movement in air. The terminal sounds represented by "-ash," as they occur in the set "bash, crash, clash, dash, flash, gash, mash, slash," have an overlapping significance of sudden or violent movement. Such combinations of phonemes are sometimes called **phonetic intensives**, or else instances of **sound-symbolism**; they are important components in the type of words, exploited especially by

然而，即使在同一种语言范围内，讲母语者也会在不同的语音组合里对同一音位发出不同的音，语音也随言语的改变而改变。更大的发音差别则突出地表现在两位讲母语者之间，尤其是在他们讲不同地区或不同社会群体的**方言**时。索绪尔提出一个原理：在一种语言中，我们对"相同的音位"的辨析，并不取决于该语音的自身特征，而是取决于它与同一语言中所有其他音位的**差异**，也即取决于特定语言体系内特定语音单位和其他有效的语音单位的区别。索绪尔的重要主张是，这种差异原则（而非任何"绝对"属性）不仅帮助建立了音位的个性，还确立了各级语言结构，包括符号以及符号的所指概念单位的个性。所有这一切构成了一种语言范围内确立个性的系统实据，而在不同语言之间它们又会有差别变化。（表面上的语言特征实际上是由各种差异组成的，这一论断已被引入并应用于结构主义、符号论、解构主义，成为它们的理论核心。）

2. 音韵学之后的另一分析层为"形态学"，即研究音位结合成词素和结合成词。**词素**为任何一种语言中富有意义的最小语音单位，由一个或更多个音位组成，它在一种语言里以相同或大致相似的意义反复出现。有些词素形成了完整的词，如英语里的"man"（人）、"open"（开）、"run"（跑）；而其他一些词素仅仅作为词的一个部分出现。例如，名词"grace"（优雅）本身是单独的一个词素。如果我们在词根"grace"前加上前缀词素"dis-"（不），它就变成了意义完全不同的另一个词"disgrace"（不优雅）；若我们在词根后加上后缀词素"-ful"（……的），它就从名词变为形容词"graceful"（优雅的）；若我们在这两个词素上再补加一个后缀"-ly"（……地），结果就得出了它的副词"gracefully"（优雅地）；如果在该副词形式前加上词素"dis-"或"un-"（不），就会得出分别由四个词素组成的副词"disgracefully"（不光彩地）和"ungracefully"（不优雅地）。

我们还能发现一些有趣的音位组合，它们并不构成特定词素，但在讲英语者看来则具有某些共同的意义范围，尽管这种共同之处是非常松散的。例如以"fl—"为始音的一组："flash（闪光）、flare（闪亮）、flame（闪耀）、flicker（闪现）、flimmer（发微光）"，它们都表示光的某种动感；而在另一组词"fly（飞）、flip（抛）、flap（扔）、flit（掠过）、flutter（飘）"里，相同的始音都表现了空气中的一种移动。以"-ash"为代表的尾音出现在"bash（猛击）、crash（碰撞）、clash（猛撞）、dash（猛冲）、flash（飞驰）、gash（划开）、mash（捣碎）、slash（猛砍）"这组词里时，大体上都表现出突然或猛烈的动态。这类音位组合有时被称为**语音强意法**或**语音象征**。在那

poets, in which the sounds of the words seem peculiarly appropriate to their significance. See *onomatopoeia*, and refer to Leonard Bloomfield, *Language* (1933), pp. 244–46; I. A. Richards, *The Philosophy of Rhetoric* (1936), pp. 57–65; Leanne Hinton, Johanna Nichols, and John J. Ohala, eds., *Sound Symbolism* (1995).

Phonemes, morphemes, and words are all said to be "segments" of the stream of speech sounds which constitute an utterance. Linguists also distinguish **suprasegmental** features of language, consisting of stress, juncture, and intonation, all of which function morphemically, in that they alter the identity and significance of the segments in an utterance. A shift in **stress**—that is, of relative forcefulness, or loudness, of a component element in an utterance—from the first to the second syllable converts the noun "ínvalid" into the adjective "inválid," and the noun "cónvict" into the verb "convíct." **Juncture** denotes the transition in an utterance between adjacent speech sounds, whether within a word, between words, or between groups of words. Linguists distinguish various functional classes of junctures in English utterances. **Intonation** is the variation of **pitch**, the rise or fall of voice melody, in the course of an utterance. We utter the assertion "He is going home" with a different intonation from that of the question "Is he going home?"; and the use of the question intonation (the rise in pitch), even with the assertive sequence of words "He is going home?" will make the sentence function to an auditor not as an assertion, but as a question. Uttering the following three words so as to alter the relative stress in the ways indicated, and at the same time using a variety of intonational patterns and pauses, will reveal the extent to which suprasegmental features can affect the significance of a sentence constituted by the same words: "Í like you." "I líke you." "I like yóu."

3. The third level of analysis (after the level of phonemes and the level of the combination of phonemes into morphemes and words) is syntax: the combination of words into phrases, clauses, and sentences. Analysis of speech performances (paroles) in any language reveals regularities in such constructions, which are explained by postulating syntactic **rules** that are operative within the linguistic system, or langue, which has been mastered by competent speakers and auditors. (These purely "descriptive" rules, or general regularities of syntax in common speech, are to be distinguished from the "prescriptive" rules of grammar which are presented in school handbooks designed to teach the "correct usage" of upper-class standard English.) A widely used distinction, developed by Roman Jakobson, is that between the rules governing **paradigmatic** relations (the "vertical" relations between any single word in a sentence and other words that are phonologically, syntactically, or semantically similar, and which can be substituted for it), and **syntagmatic** relations (the "horizontal" relations which determine the possibilities of putting words in a sequence so as to make a well-formed syntactic unit). On the phonemic and morphemic levels, a similar distinction is made between

些特意为诗人所采用的、读音似乎与意义格外吻合的词语中,这些音位是重要的组成部分。参见:拟声词;参阅:伦纳德·布龙菲尔德所著的《语言论》(1933)第224—246页和I. A.理查兹所著的《修辞哲学》(1936)第57—65页;利安娜·欣顿、约翰娜·尼古尔斯、约翰·J.奥哈拉三人合编的《语音象征》(1995)。

音位、词素和词都是形成言语的一串发音里的"音段成分"。语言学家还辨析出语言的**超音段**特征,其中包括重音、连音及语调,它们都能作用于词素,从而改变一段话语中音段成分的个性与意义。**重音**(即话语中某一部分的相对重读或高音)从第一音节转移到第二个音节可以把名词"ínvalid"(病弱者)转换成形容词"inválid"(无用的),也可以把名词"cónvict"(罪犯)转化为动词"convíct"(使知罪)。**连音**表示话语里相邻语音的过渡衔接,它可以发生于一词之内,几个词语或几组词之间。语言学家对英语话语里功能性连音的不同类型也加以区分。**语调**是指讲话过程中**音调**(升高或降低)的变化。我们断言"他回家"时所用的语调完全不同于询问"他回家吗?"时的语调;即使是断言的语序"他回家?"若采用疑问语调(音调升高)也会使句子在闻者听来是"问话"而不是"断言"。说出下列由三个同样的词组成的三个语句并按照重读符号的指示变换相对的重读,同时采用不同的语调形式与停顿,就会揭示出超音段特征对由相同词语组成的句子的含义有着何等程度的影响:"Í like you"我(不是他人)喜欢你。"I líke you"我喜欢(非其他感情)你。"I like yóu"我喜欢你(不是喜欢其他人)。

3. 在音位分析及音位组合成词素和词的分析层次之后,第三个分析层次为"句法"分析:研究词组合成短语、分句和句子。对任何语言中语言行为(言语)的分析都将展示这样一些结构的规律,在语言或语言体系内起作用,并为有运用能力的言者和听者所掌握的假定的句法**规则**说明了这些规律。(普通话语中的这些纯"描写性"句法规则或一般句法规律,应与学校手册里为教授上层社会使用标准英语的"正确用法"而"规定的"语法规则区别开。)罗曼·雅各布森提出的对这些规则的聚合关系和组合关系的区分被广为使用。**聚合**关系指的是一个句子中任何一个词与可以取代它的其他词的"纵向关系",这些词与它在语音、句法或语义上相似;**组合**关系指的是限定词的排列顺序以形成完善的句法单元的"横向"关系。在音位分析及词素分析的层

paradigmatic relations among single elements and syntagmatic relations of sequences of elements. This paradigmatic-syntagmatic distinction parallels the distinction made by Jakobson between metaphoric (vertical) and metonymic (horizontal) relations in analyzing *figurative language*.

Noam Chomsky in *Syntactic Structures* (1957) initiated what is known as **transformational-generative grammar**. Chomsky's persistent emphasis is on the central feature he calls "creativity" in language—the fact that a competent native speaker can produce a meaningful sentence which has no exact precedent in the speaker's earlier linguistic experience, as well as the fact that competent auditors can understand the sentence immediately, although it is equally new to them. To explain this "rule-bound creativity" of a language, Chomsky proposed that native speakers' and listeners' competence consists in their mastery of a set of generative and transformational rules. This mode of linguistics is called **generative** in that it undertakes to establish a finite system of rules that will suffice to "generate"—in the sense that it will adequately account for—the totality of syntactically "well-formed" sentences that are possible in a given language. It is **transformational** in that it postulates, in the **deep structure** of a language system, a set of "kernel sentences" (such as "John is building a house") which, in accordance with diverse rules of transformation, serve to produce a great variety of sentences on the **surface structure** of a language system (for example, the passive form "The house is being built by John" and the question form "Is John building a house?" as well as a large number of more complex derivatives from the simple kernel sentence). Debates concerning Chomsky's views are included in Louise M. Antony and Norbert Hornstein, eds., *Chomsky and His Critics* (2003).

For diverse applications of the concepts and methods of modern linguistics to the criticism of literature, see *deconstruction, Russian formalism, semiotics, structuralism,* and *stylistics*. For Saussure's theories refer to Ferdinand de Saussure, *Course in General Linguistics*, trans. Wade Baskin (1966), and the concise analysis by Jonathan Culler, *Ferdinand de Saussure* (rev. 1986). For American linguistics: George L. Trager and Henry Lee Smith, Jr., *An Outline of English Structure* (1957); Zellig S. Harris, *Structural Linguistics* (2d ed., 1960); Leonard Bloomfield, *Language* (1994). On transformational-generative grammar: Noam Chomsky, *Selected Readings*, ed. J. P. B. Allen and Paul Van Buren (1971); *The Structure of Language*, ed. Jerry A. Fodor and Jerrold J. Katz (1964); John Lyons, *Noam Chomsky* (1970). Useful reviews of Continental and American linguistics and of their applications in literary criticism are included in Karl D. Uitti, *Linguistics and Literary Theory* (1969); William H. Youngren, *Semantics, Linguistics, and Criticism* (1972); Jonathan Culler, *The Pursuit of Signs* (1981); Nigel Fabb and others, eds., *The Linguistics of Writing: Arguments between Language and Literature* (1987); Jan Ziolkowski, ed., *On Philology* (1990); Roger Fowler, *Linguistic Criticism* (2d ed., 1996). A comprehensive account of the role of the concept of language in literary theory is Geoffrey Galt Harpham, *Language Alone: The Critical Fetish of Modernity* (2002). See also Roman Jakobson's influential essay "Linguistics and Poetics," in his *Language*

次上，类似地区分了单一语言成分的聚合关系与序列语言成分的组合关系。这种聚合－组合区分和雅各布森在分析比喻语时区分隐喻（纵向）与转喻（横向）之间的关系相类似。

诺姆·乔姆斯基在其所著的《句法结构》(1957)中首创了**转换－生成语法**理论。乔姆斯基一贯强调他称为语言"创造力"的中心特征，即具语言运用能力的讲母语者能够创造出自身语言实践中前所未有的有意义的语句，同时，具语言运用能力的听者能够马上理解这一语句，尽管这一语句对他们来说也是全新的。为了解释这种语言中"限定于语法范围内的语言创造力"，乔姆斯基提出，操母语的言者和听者之所以有这种能力，在于他们掌握了那种语言的生成与转换法则。这种语言学方式被称为是**生成的**，是因为它旨在确立一个限定性的规则系统，这些规则将能有根有据地在某一语言范围内"生成"一切句法上"结构严谨"的句子。它之所以被称为**转换的**，是因为它要在某一语言系统的**深层结构**里假定出一些"核心句"来（如"John is building a house."），根据转换的各种法则，这些核心句可以在该语言体系的**表层结构**上派生出许多不同的句子（例如，从上述陈述句可以派生出被动句式："The house is being built by John."疑问句："Is John building a house？"而且这个简单的核心句还可以派生出许多更为复杂的句型）。有关乔姆斯基观点的争论，收入路易斯·M. 安东尼与诺伯特·霍恩斯坦合编的《乔姆斯基和他的批评》(2003)。

关于现代语言学概念和方法在文学中的各类应用，参见：*解构主义、俄国形式主义、符号论、结构主义、文体学*。关于索绪尔的有关理论，参阅：费迪南·德·索绪尔所著的《普通语言学教程》(1966，韦德·巴什金英译版)；乔纳森·卡勒所著的《费迪南·德·索绪尔》(1986年修订版)中的简明分析。关于美国语言学，参阅：乔治·L. 特拉格与小亨利·李·史密斯合著的《英语结构纲要》(1957)；泽利格·S. 哈里斯所著的《结构语言学》(1960年第2版)；伦纳德·布龙菲尔德所著的《语言论》(1994)。关于生成转换语法参阅：诺姆·乔姆斯基的《乔姆斯基作品选读》(1971, J. P. B. 艾伦与保罗·范布伦合编)；乔姆斯基的《语言结构》(1964，杰里·A. 福多尔与杰罗尔德·J. 卡茨合编)；约翰·莱昂斯所著的《诺姆·乔姆斯基》(1970)。关于对欧美语言学及其在文学批评里的应用的实用评论，参阅：卡尔·D. 尤蒂所著的《语言学和文学理论》(1969)；威廉·H. 杨格伦所著的《语义学、语言学与批评》(1972)；乔纳森·卡勒所著的《符号的追寻》(1981)；奈杰尔·法布等人合编的《书写的语言学：语言与文学之间的论辩》(1987)；扬·齐奥科夫斯基主编的《论语文学》(1990)；罗杰·福勒所著的《语言学批评》(1996年第2版)。杰弗里·高尔特·哈珀曼所著的《只有语言：现代性的批评拜物教》(2002)，对文学理论中语言概念的作用作了全面解释。另请参阅雅各布森颇有影响力的文章"语言学与诗学"，收入其所著的《文学中的语言》

in Literature (1987), and the expansion of Jakobson's basic distinction between the horizontal and vertical dimensions of language in David Lodge, *The Modes of Modern Writing: Metaphor, Metonymy, and the Typology of Modern Literature* (1977).

Issues of gender and language are addressed in Barrie Thorne, Cheris Kramerae, and Nancy Henley, eds., *Language, Gender, and Society* (1983); Dale Spender, *Man Made Language* (2d ed., 1985); Joyce Penfield, ed., *Women and Language in Transition* (1987); Deborah Cameron, *Feminism and Linguistic Theory* (2d ed., 1992); Sally Johnson and Ulrike Hanna Meinhof, eds., *Language and Masculinity* (1997). (Refer to *feminist criticism* and *gender criticism*.) For references to *linguistics* in other entries, see page *358*.

literal meaning: 130; *79, 212*.

literariness: 139.

literary ballad: 24.

literary canon: 41.

literary criticism: 67.

literature (from the Latin *litteraturae*, "writings"): Literature has been commonly used since the eighteenth century, equivalently with the French *belles lettres* ("fine letters"), to designate fictional and imaginative writings—poetry, prose fiction, and drama. (See *genres*.) In an expanded use, it designates also any other writings (including philosophy, history, and even scientific works addressed to a general audience) that are especially distinguished in form, expression, and emotional power. It is in this larger sense of the term that we call "literary" the philosophical writings of Plato and William James, the historical writings of Edward Gibbon, the scientific essays of Thomas Henry Huxley, and the psychoanalytic lectures of Sigmund Freud, and include them in the reading lists of some courses in literature. Confusingly, however, "literature" is sometimes applied also, in a sense close to the Latin original, to all written works, whatever their kind or quality. This all-inclusive use is especially frequent with reference to the sum of works that deal with a particular subject matter. At a major American university that includes a College of Agriculture, the Chairman of the Division of Literature once received this letter: "Dear Sir, Kindly send me all your literature concerning the use of cow manure as a fertilizer."

In its application to imaginative writing, "literature" has an evaluative as well as descriptive function, so that its proper use has become a matter of contention. Modern critical movements, aiming to correct what are seen as historical injustices, stress the strong but covert role played by gender, race, and class in establishing what has, in various eras, been accounted as literature, or in forming the ostensibly timeless criteria of great and *canonical* literature, or

(1987);戴维·洛奇在其所著的《现代创作的式样：隐喻、转喻和现代文学类型学》(1977)中，对雅各布森关于语言横向、纵向的基本区分作了进一步扩展。

巴里·索恩、谢里斯·克雷莫雷、南希·亨利三人合编的《语言、性别与社会》(1983)，戴尔·斯彭德所著的《男性编造/统治的语言》(1985年第2版)，乔伊斯·彭菲尔德主编的《女性和语言转型》(1987)，德博拉·卡梅伦所著的《女性主义与语言学理论》(1992年第2版)，萨莉·约翰逊、乌尔里克·汉娜·迈因霍夫合编的《语言与男性气质》(1997)，论述了性别与语言的问题。(参阅：*女性主义批评*、*性别批评*。)其他条目中提及"语言学"的地方，参见第358页。

literal meaning：字面意义　130；*79, 212*。

literariness：文学性　139。

literary ballad：诗谣　24。

literary canon：文学经典　41。

literary criticism：文学批评　67。

Literature：文学

文学（源自拉丁语 litteraturae，"著作"）：自18世纪以来，文学，等同于法语中的 *belles lettres*（"美文"），一直常被用来指代虚构的和想象的著作：诗歌，散文体小说和戏剧。（参见：*文学类型*。）在其扩展用法中，它也指任何其他著作（包括以普通大众为读者对象的哲学、历史乃至科学作品），尤其是在形式、表达和情感力量上比较出名的著作。正是在这一术语更广泛的意义上，我们称柏拉图和威廉·詹姆斯的哲学著作、爱德华·吉本的历史著作、托马斯·亨利·赫胥黎的科学随笔和弗洛伊德的精神分析讲座为"文学"，并将它们列入一些文学课程的阅读书目。不过，让人困惑的是，"文学"有时也适用于（在接近其拉丁语原意的意义上）所有文字作品，无论其种类或质量。这一无所不包的使用，尤其经常用来指研究特定主题的作品总和。在一所设有农学院的美国主要大学里，文学系主任曾收到这样一封信："亲爱的先生，请把你那里关于使用牛粪作为肥料的所有文学寄给我。"

在用来指富有想象力的写作时，"文学"有一种评价和描述的功能，这使得正确使用"文学"这一术语，已经成为一个有争论的问题。现代批评运动，旨在纠正昔日的历史不公平，强调性别、种族和阶级在确立不同时代什么被视为文学的过程中、在形成伟大和*经典*文学的所谓永恒标准的过程中、或是在区分"高

in distinguishing between "high literature" and the literature addressed to a mass audience. See, for example, the entries on *cultural studies, feminist criticism, gender criticism, Marxist criticism,* and *new historicism*; refer also to Jonathan Culler, *The Literary in Theory* (2007). For the historical development of the concept of a work of literature as a *fine art* that is autonomous, and to be enjoyed for its own sake, see M. H. Abrams, "Art-as-Such: The Sociology of Modern Aesthetics," in *Doing Things with Texts* (1984); and Pierre Bourdieu, *The Rules of Art: Genesis and Structure of the Literary Field* (1995). For references to *literature* in other entries, see page *204*.

literature of fact: 257.

literature of sensibility: 360.

literature of the absurd: 1.

litotes (līˈ tŏtēz): **167**.

local color: The detailed representation in prose fiction of the setting, dialect, customs, dress, and ways of thinking and feeling which are distinctive of a particular region, such as Thomas Hardy's "Wessex" or Rudyard Kipling's India. After the Civil War a number of American writers exploited the literary possibilities of local color in various parts of America; for example, the West (Bret Harte), the Mississippi region (Mark Twain), the South (George Washington Cable), the Midwest (E. W. Howe, Hamlin Garland), and New England (Sarah Orne Jewett and Mary Wilkins Freeman). The term "local color fiction" is often applied to works which, like O. Henry's or Damon Runyon's stories set in New York City, rely for their interest mainly on a sentimental or comic representation of the surface particularities of a region; the term "regional fiction" is then used to distinguish those works which deal with more deep-seated, complex, and general human characteristics and problems. See *regional novel.*

local poetry: 406.

logocentric (lōgō sĕnˈ trik): **77**.

loose sentence: 385.

Lost Generation: 276.

low burlesque: 39.

low comedy: 56.

low style: 384.

雅文学"和面向普通大众的文学的过程中,所起的强劲但隐蔽的作用。例如,可以参见:*文化研究、女性主义批评、性别批评、马克思主义批评、新历史主义*;也可参阅乔纳森·卡勒所著的《文学理论》(2007)。关于一部文学作品作为一件精致的艺术品(它是自主的,可以因其自身而欣赏)这一概念的历史发展,参阅:M. H. 艾布拉姆斯所著的《以文行事》(1984)中的"像这样的艺术:现代美学社会学"和皮埃尔·布迪厄所著的《艺术的法则:文学场的发生和结构》(1995)。其他条目中提及"文学"的地方,参见第 204 页。

literature of fact:事实文学　257。

literature of sensibility:情感文学　360。

literature of the absurd:荒诞派文学　1。

litotes:反语法　167。

Local Color:地方色彩

　　地方色彩是指散文体小说作品中对具有某个地方特色的背景、方言、风俗、服饰、思维方式与情感方式的细致描写,例如托马斯·哈代笔下的英国"威塞克斯地区"或拉迪亚德·吉卜林描写的印度。美国内战后,一些美国作家开拓了文学再现美国不同地域地方色彩的可能性;例如布雷特·哈特描写的西部地区、马克·吐温笔下的密西西比地区、乔治·华盛顿·凯布尔再现的美国南部、E. W. 豪和哈姆林·加兰勾画出的美国中西部地区、萨拉·奥恩·朱厄特和玛丽·威尔金斯·弗里曼描写的新英格兰地区。"带有地方色彩的小说"这一用语通常指的是那种像欧·亨利或达蒙·鲁尼恩以纽约为背景的故事,其兴趣主要在于对地方的表面特色进行感伤或喜剧性的描写;因而,"地方小说"有别于那些揭示更为深入复杂、更为普遍的人物性格特征及问题的作品。参见:*地方小说*。

local poetry:地域诗　406。

logocentric:以理性(词义)为中心(或译"逻各斯中心主义")　77。

loose sentence:松散句　385。

Lost Generation:迷惘的一代　276。

low burlesque:下等滑稽讽刺作品　39。

low comedy:世俗喜剧　56。

low style:低劣文体　384。

lyric: In the most common use of the term, a **lyric** is any fairly short poem, uttered by a single speaker, who expresses a state of mind or a process of perception, thought, and feeling. Many lyric speakers are represented as musing in solitude. In *dramatic lyrics*, however, the lyric speaker is represented as addressing another person in a specific situation; instances are John Donne's "Canonization" and William Wordsworth's "Tintern Abbey."

Although the lyric is uttered in the first person, the "I" in the poem need not be the poet who wrote it. In some lyrics, such as John Milton's sonnet "When I consider how my light is spent" and Samuel Taylor Coleridge's "Frost at Midnight," the references to the known circumstances of the author's life make it clear that we are to read the poem as a personal expression. Even in such **personal lyrics**, however, both the character and utterance of the speaker may be formalized and altered by the author in a way that is conducive to the desired artistic effect. In a number of lyrics, the speaker is a conventional period-figure, such as the long-suffering suitor in the Petrarchan sonnet (see *Petrarchan conceit*), or the courtly, witty lover of the *Cavalier* poems. And in some types of lyrics, the speaker is obviously an invented figure remote from the poet in character and circumstance. (See *persona, confessional poetry*, and *dramatic monologue* for distinctions between personal and invented lyric speakers.)

The lyric genre comprehends a great variety of utterances. Some, like Ben Jonson's "To the Memory of ... William Shakespeare" and Walt Whitman's ode on the death of Abraham Lincoln, "O Captain, My Captain," are ceremonial poems uttered in a public voice on a public occasion. Among the lyrics in a more private mode, some are simply a brief, intense expression of a mood or state of feeling; for example, Shelley's "To Night," or Emily Dickinson's "Wild Nights, Wild Nights," or this fine medieval elegiac song:

> Fowles in the frith,
> The fisshes in the flood,
> And I mon waxe wood:
> Much sorwe I walke with
> For best of bone and blood.

But the genre also includes extended expressions of a complex evolution of feelingful thought, as in the long elegy and the meditative ode. And within a lyric, the process of observation, thought, memory, and feeling is organized in a variety of ways. For example, in "love lyrics" the speaker may simply express an enamored state of mind in an ordered form, as in Robert Burns' "O my love's like a red, red rose," and Elizabeth Barrett Browning's "How do I love thee? Let me count the ways"; or may gallantly elaborate a compliment (Ben Jonson's "Drink to me only with thine eyes"); or may deploy an argument to take advantage of fleeting youth and opportunity (Andrew Marvell's "To His Coy Mistress," or Shakespeare's first seventeen sonnets addressed to a male youth); or may express a cool response to an importunate lover (Christina Rossetti's "No, thank you, John"). In other kinds of lyrics the speaker manifests and celebrates a particular disposition and set of values (John Milton's "L'Allegro" and "Il Penseroso"); or

Lyric：抒情诗

抒情诗一词大多数时候是用来代表由单个抒情人的话语构成的任何短小的诗歌，这一单个抒情人表达了一种思想状态或领悟、思考、感知的过程。许多抒情人被表现为在隐居孤寂中独自沉思冥想。而在*戏剧抒情诗*里，抒情人则被描述为在特定的环境里向他人倾诉衷肠；例如约翰·多恩的《圣徒追封》和威廉·华兹华斯的《丁登寺》。

抒情诗一般采用第一人称，但诗里的"我"不一定就是诗作者。在有些抒情诗里，如约翰·弥尔顿的十四行诗《想到自己失明的时候》和塞缪尔·泰勒·柯勒律治的《霜夜》，诗中涉及的我们已知的有关诗人生活的境况使我们清楚，要把作品作为诗人的个人抒怀来欣赏。然而，即使在这样的**个人抒情诗**中，作者对抒情人角色和话语的安排和塑造也是为了有助于满足一定抒情艺术效果的需要。在一些抒情诗中，抒情人通常是一个时段性人物，比如彼特拉克体十四行诗中那个久受折磨的求婚者（参见：*彼特拉克式巧思妙喻*），或骑士诗歌中典雅机智的情人。而在某些类型的抒情诗里，抒情人明显是一个虚构的角色，其性格和境况与诗作者相去甚远。（参见：*第一人称、自白诗、戏剧独白诗*，以便对作者本人和虚构的抒情人加以区分。）

抒情诗这种文学样式包含许多不同的言语类型。其中一些，像本·琼森的《为了纪念我忠爱的朋友、作者威廉·莎士比亚先生》、沃尔特·惠特曼为林肯之死所作的颂歌《啊，船长！我的船长！》，都属于在公共场合以公众口吻所写的正式诗文。而在一些更具私人性质的抒情诗中，有一些仅仅是对一种心境或情感状态简洁而热烈的描述；例如，雪莱的《致夜晚》、埃米莉·狄金森的《暴风雨夜，暴风雨夜》和下面这首优雅的中世纪抒情诗：

　　河口的飞禽，
　　汪洋中的鱼，
　　我独自给木上蜡：
　　为了最好的骨和血
　　我带着深深的悲伤行走

然而抒情诗这一文学类型还包括那种对充满感情的思想的复杂发展变化进行细腻的延伸描写的作品，如长篇的哀歌和冥想的颂。在抒情诗中，观察、思考、回忆、感知等过程的组织手法多种多样。例如，在"爱情抒情诗"里，抒情人可以平铺直叙地抒发爱恋情怀，像罗伯特·彭斯的《啊，我的爱人像朵红红的玫瑰》，或伊丽莎白·巴雷特·勃朗宁的《我是怎样地爱你？让我逐一细算》；同时抒情人也可能是殷切地倾诉对情人的赞美（如本·琼森的《用你的双眸给我祝酒吧》）；抒情人也可能在进行一场辩论，劝说情人珍惜转瞬即逝的青春和机遇（如安德鲁·马韦尔的《致羞涩的情人》，或莎士比亚献给一名男青年的前十七首十四行诗）；抒情人也有可能表达对纠缠不休的情人的冷酷回应（如克里斯蒂娜·罗塞蒂的《不，谢谢，约翰》）。在其他类型的抒情诗里，抒情人则是在表明和维护特定的意向及价值观念（例如约翰·弥尔顿的《快乐的人》和《沉思的人》）；或者，

expresses a sustained process of observation and meditation in the attempt to resolve an emotional problem (Wordsworth's "Ode: Intimations of Immortality," Arnold's "Dover Beach"); or is exhibited as making and justifying the choice of a way of life (Yeats' "Sailing to Byzantium").

In the original Greek, "lyric" signified a song rendered to the accompaniment of a lyre. In some current usages, lyric still retains the sense of a poem written to be set to music; the *hymn*, for example, is a lyric on a religious subject that is intended to be sung. The adjectival form "lyrical" is sometimes applied to an expressive, song-like passage in a narrative poem, such as Eve's declaration of love to Adam, "With thee conversing I forget all time," in Milton's *Paradise Lost*, IV, 639–56.

See *genre* for the broad distinction between the three major poetic classes of drama, narrative (or epic), and lyric, and also for the sudden elevation of lyric, in the Romantic period, to the status of the quintessentially poetic mode. For subclasses of the lyric, see *aubade, dramatic monologue, elegy, epithalamion, hymn, ode, sonnet*. Refer to Norman Maclean, "From Action to Image: Theories of the Lyric in the 18th Century," in *Critics and Criticism*, ed. R. S. Crane (1952); Maurice Bowra, *Mediaeval Love-Song* (1961); Chaviva Hošek and Patricia Parker, eds., *Lyric Poetry: Beyond New Criticism* (1985); David Lindley, *Lyric* (1985); Helen Vendler, *The Music of What Happens* (1988), and *Invisible Listeners: Lyric Intimacy in Herbert, Whitman, and Ashbery* (2007).

For references to *lyric* in other entries, see pages *8, 94*. For types of lyric, see *aubade; dramatic monologue; elegy; epithalamion; folk song; haiku; ode; sonnet*.

表述自己力求解决某种精神苦恼的漫长的观察体会与沉思冥想的过程（如华兹华斯的《不朽的征兆》和阿诺德的作品《多弗滩》）；或者是表现为正在选择和验证自己的生活道路（如叶芝的《驶往拜占庭》）。

在希腊文中，"抒情诗"原指由里拉琴伴奏吟唱的歌谣。在当前的一些用法中，抒情诗仍可指专为谱曲而作的诗歌；比如*赞美诗*，就是指用于演唱的以宗教为主题的抒情诗。"抒情诗"的形容词形式"抒情诗般的"，有时可以用来指叙事诗中富有表现力的歌曲形式的段落，如弥尔顿《失乐园》第四部分第 639—656 行中夏娃向亚当表达爱慕之情的诗歌《同你的交谈让我忘记时间》。

参见：*文学类型*，以了解三种主要诗歌类型：戏剧、叙事诗（或史诗）、抒情诗的主要区别，同时了解抒情诗如何在浪漫主义时期突然跃居典范诗歌模式地位。要了解抒情诗的分类，参见：*晨歌、戏剧独白诗、哀歌、喜歌、赞美诗、颂、十四行诗*。
参阅：诺曼·麦克莱恩所写的文章"从行动到想象：18 世纪的抒情诗理论"，收入 R. S. 克莱恩主编的《批评家与批评》(1952)；莫里斯·鲍勒所著的《中世纪情歌》(1961)；查维瓦·哈谢克与帕特里夏·帕克合编的《抒情诗：超越新批评》(1985)；戴维·林德利所著的《抒情诗》(1985)；海伦·文德勒所著的《音乐怎么了》(1988)和《看不见的倾听者：赫伯特、惠特曼和阿代伯利诗歌中抒情的亲密感》(2007)。

其他条目中提及"抒情诗"的地方，参见第 8、94 页。关于抒情诗的各种类型，参见：*晨歌、戏剧独白诗、哀歌、喜歌、民歌、俳句、颂、十四行诗*。

machinery (in an epic): **108**.

magazines: **367**.

magic realism: **258**.

malapropism: Malapropism is that type of **solecism** (the conspicuous and unintended violation of standard diction or grammar) which mistakenly uses a word in place of another that it resembles; the effect is usually comic. The term derives from Mrs. Malaprop in Richard Brinsley Sheridan's comedy *The Rivals* (1775), who in the attempt to display a copious vocabulary said things such as "a progeny of learning," "as headstrong as an allegory on the banks of the Nile," and "he is the very pineapple of politeness." In an early radio comedy "The Easy Aces," Jane Ace, an inveterate malapropist, remarked: "He got so excited, he ran around like a chicken with its hat off."

manifest content: **321**.

manifesto: **238**.

manuscripts: **32**; *35*.

Märchen (měr′ shěn): **137**.

Marxist criticism: Marxist criticism, in its diverse forms, grounds its theory and practice on the economic and cultural theory of Karl Marx (1818–83) and his fellow-thinker Friedrich Engels (1820–95), and especially on the following claims:

1. In the last analysis, the evolving history of humankind, of its social groupings and interrelations, of its institutions, and of its ways of thinking are largely determined by the changing mode of its "material production"—that is, of its overall economic organization for producing and distributing material goods.
2. Changes in the fundamental mode of material production effect changes in the class structure of a society, establishing in each era dominant and subordinate classes that engage in a struggle for economic, political, and social advantage.
3. Human consciousness is constituted by an **ideology**—that is, the beliefs, values, and ways of thinking and feeling through which human beings perceive, and by recourse to which they explain, what they take to be reality. An ideology is, in complex ways, the product of the position and interests of a particular class. In any historical era, the dominant

machinery (in an epic)：(史诗中) 超自然的情节机制　108。

magazines：杂志　367。

magic realism：魔幻现实主义　258。

Malapropism：文字误用

文字误用是**语法错误**(即无意中对规范用语或语法的明显违反)的一种形式。它指的是对形近字的误用,其效果通常是喜剧性的。这一术语源自理查德·布林斯利·谢立丹的喜剧《情敌》(1775)。剧中的马拉普罗普太太为了显示她丰富的词汇量而这样说话:"学习的产物";"就像尼罗河里的饿鱼一样顽固";"他真是礼貌的高潮"(周翰译)。在一部早期电台喜剧《讨人喜欢的艾斯》(1930—1945)中,简·艾斯,一个积习难改的文字误用家,评论道:"他激动得像只无头苍蝇似的跑来跑去。"

manifest content：显性内容　321。

manifesto：宣言　238。

manuscripts：手抄稿　32；35。

Märchen：仙女故事　137。

Marxist Criticism：马克思主义批评

马克思主义批评具有多种形式,其理论和实践建立在卡尔·马克思(1818—1883)和他的同伴思想家弗里德里希·恩格斯的经济文化理论上,特别是建立在以下主张上:

1. 归根结底,人类、社会集团和关系、制度、思维方式的发展历史,在很大程度上是由不断变化的"物质生产"即由生产、分配物质财富的整体经济结构所决定的。

2. 物质生产基本方式的变化引起社会阶级结构的变化,确立了每个时期中的统治阶级和被统治阶级。它们为了各自的经济、政治、社会利益而相互斗争。

3. 人类意识由**意识形态**,即信仰、价值观、思维和感觉方式组成,它使人类得以理解和解释他们所认定的现实。综合来看,意识形态就是某一特定阶级地位和利益的产物。在任何历史时期,占统治地位的

ideology embodies, and serves to legitimize and perpetuate, the interests of the dominant economic and social class.

Ideology was not much discussed by Marx and Engels after *The German Ideology*, which they wrote jointly in 1845–46, but it has become a key concept in Marxist criticism of literature and the other arts. Marx inherited the term from French philosophers of the late eighteenth century, who used it to designate the study of the way that all general concepts develop from particular sense perceptions. In the present era, "ideology" is used in a variety of non-Marxist ways, ranging from a derogatory name for any set of political ideas that are held dogmatically and applied inflexibly, to a neutral name for ways of perceiving and thinking that are specific to an individual's race, sex, nationality, education, or ethnic group. In its distinctively Marxist use, the reigning ideology in any era is conceived to be, ultimately, the product of its economic structure and the resulting class relations and class interests. In a famed architectural metaphor, Marx represented ideology as a "superstructure" of which the concurrent socioeconomic system is the "base." Friedrich Engels described ideology as "a false consciousness," and many later Marxists consider it to be constituted largely by unconscious prepossessions that are illusory, in contrast to the "scientific" (that is, Marxist) knowledge of the economic determinants, historical evolution, and present constitution of the social world. A further claim is that, in the era of capitalist economic organization that emerged in the West during the eighteenth century, the reigning ideology incorporates the interests of the dominant and exploitative class, the "bourgeoisie," who own the means of production and distribution, as opposed to the "proletariat," or wage-earning working class. This ideology, it is claimed, to those who live in and with it, seems a natural and inevitable way of seeing, explaining, and dealing with the environing world, but in fact has the hidden function of legitimizing and maintaining the position, power, and economic interests of the ruling class. Bourgeois ideology is regarded as both producing and permeating the social and cultural institutions, beliefs, and practices of the present era—including religion, morality, philosophy, politics, and the legal system, as well as (although in an indirect and complex way) literature and the other arts.

In accordance with some version of the views just outlined, a Marxist critic typically undertakes to explain the *literature* in any historical era, not as works created in accordance with timeless artistic criteria, but as "products" of the economic and ideological determinants specific to that era. What some Marxist critics themselves decried as "vulgar Marxism" analyzed a "bourgeois" literary work as in direct correlation with the present stage of the class struggle, and demanded that such works be replaced by a "social realism" that would represent the true reality and progressive forces of our time; in practice, this usually turned out to be the demand that literature conform to an official party line. More flexible Marxists, on the other hand, building upon scattered comments on literature in Marx and Engels themselves, grant that traditional literary works possess a degree of autonomy that enables some of them to

意识形态都体现了处于统治地位的经济、社会阶级的利益，并会尽力使这种利益合法化并持久延续下去。

在1845—1846年间合作完成《德意志意识形态》后，马克思和恩格斯并未过多探讨意识形态，但意识形态却成为马克思主义批评在文学和其他艺术形式中的主要理论。马克思从18世纪晚期的法国哲学家那里继承了这一术语，用它来指代对形成于特定意识感知的所有一般理论的研究。在当代，"意识形态"被用于许多非马克思主义方面，从用作贬义名词，来表示任何一套教条主义的、被严格推行的政治观点，到用作中性名词，指代跟个人的种族、性别、教育背景或民族相关的特定理解和思维方式。在马克思主义的独特用法中，任何时代占统治地位的意识形态被视为最终是其经济结构，以及随之而产生的阶级关系和阶级利益的产物。马克思用一个著名的建筑学隐喻，将意识形态描述为"上层建筑"，以与其并存的社会经济体系为"基础"。弗里德里希·恩格斯将意识形态描述为"一种虚幻的意识"，许多后来的马克思主义者认为，意识形态很大程度上是由无意中的先入为主的思想所组成，这种先入为主的思想是虚幻的，不同于对经济决定论、历史发展观点和当前社会体制的"科学"（即马克思主义）认识。更进一步的观点认为，在现今这个出现于西方18世纪的资本主义经济体制时代，主要的意识形态体现了统治阶级和剥削阶级即"资产阶级"的利益，他们掌握了生产资料和分配方式，与"无产阶级"或工薪工人阶级形成对立。这种意识形态对那些身处其中并与其共存的人来说，似乎是看待、解释和处理外在世界的一种自然的、不可避免的方式，但事实上，这种意识形态的内在作用却是使统治阶级的地位、权力和经济利益得以合法化并维持下去。马克思主义认为，资产阶级意识形态促成并渗入现今时代的社会文化制度、信仰和实践活动，其中包括宗教、道德、哲学、政治和法制体系，以及（尽管是以一种间接而复杂的方式影响到）文学和其他艺术。

根据上述一些观点，马克思主义批评家在解释任何历史时期的文学作品时，并不把它看做是根据某一不受时代影响的艺术准则所创造出来的作品，而是将其视为是那个时代起决定作用的特定经济、意识形态的"产物"。被一些马克思主义批评家自己所谴责的"庸俗马克思主义"在分析"资产阶级"文学作品时，将其视为与现阶段的阶级斗争直接互相联系，要求用代表我们时代的真实现实和进步力量的"社会现实主义"来取代此类"资产阶级"作品；在实践中，这往往要求文学与某一政党的官方路线方针保持一致。另一方面，更为灵活变通的马克思主义者，以马克思与恩格斯有关文学的零散评论为基础，认为传统文学作品拥有一定程度的自主性，这足以使它们中的一些作品能够完全超越

transcend the prevailing bourgeois ideology sufficiently to represent (or in the frequent Marxist equivalent, to **reflect**) aspects of the "objective" reality of their time. (See *imitation*.)

The Hungarian thinker Georg Lukács, one of the most widely influential of Marxist critics, represents such a flexible view of the role of ideology. He proposed that each great work of literature creates "its own world," which is unique and seemingly distinct from "everyday reality." But masters of realism in the novel such as Balzac or Tolstoy, by "bringing to life the greatest possible richness of the objective conditions of life," and by creating "typical" characters who manifest the essential tendencies and determinants of their epoch, succeed—often "in opposition to [the author's] own conscious ideology"—in producing a fictional world which is a "reflection of life in the greatest concreteness and clarity and with all its motivating contradictions." That is, the fictional world of such great writers accords with the Marxist conception of the real world as constituted by class conflict, economic and social "contradictions," and the alienation of the individual under capitalism. (See *bourgeois epic*, under *epic*, and refer to Georg Lukács, *Writer and Critic and Other Essays*, trans. 1970; the volume also includes Lukács' useful review of the foundational tenets of Marxist criticism, in "Marx and Engels on Aesthetics.")

While lauding nineteenth-century literary realism, Lukács attacked modernist experimental writers as "decadent" instances of concern with the subjectivity of the alienated individual in the fragmented world of our late stage of capitalism. (See *modernism*.) He thereby inaugurated a vigorous debate among Marxist critics about the political standing of formal innovators in twentieth-century literature. In opposition to Lukács, the **Frankfurt School** of German Marxists, especially Theodor Adorno and Max Horkheimer, lauded modernist writers such as James Joyce, Marcel Proust, and Samuel Beckett, proposing that their formal experiments, by the very fact that they fragment and disrupt the life they "reflect," establish a distance and detachment that serve as an implicit critique—or yield a "negative knowledge"—of the dehumanizing institutions and processes of society under capitalism. Adorno and Horkheimer attempted, after World War II, to explain "why humanity, instead of entering into a truly human condition" (as Marxists had predicted) "is sinking into a new kind of barbarism." See the entry *critique*, and refer to *The Essential Frankfurt School Reader*, ed. Andrew Arato and Eike Gebhardt (1982), and for an authoritative history of the Frankfurt School, Martin Jay, *The Dialectical Imagination* (1996).

Two rather maverick German Marxists, Bertolt Brecht and Walter Benjamin, who supported modernist and nonrealistic art, have had considerable influence on non-Marxist as well as Marxist criticism. In his critical theory, and in his own dramatic writings (see *epic theater*), Bertolt Brecht rejected what he called the "Aristotelian" concept that a tragic play is an imitation of reality, with a unified plot and a universal theme that establishes an identification of the audience with the hero and produces a catharsis of the spectator's emotions. (See Aristotle, under *tragedy* and *plot*.) Brecht proposes instead that the illusion of reality should be deliberately shattered by an episodic plot, by

占优势的资产阶级意识形态，展现（或用马克思主义常用的类似说法，**反映**）它们所处时代的"客观"现实的方方面面。（参见：*摹仿*。）

具有最广泛影响力的马克思主义批评家、匈牙利思想家乔治·卢卡奇，提出了关于意识形态作用的一种变通观点。他提出，每一部伟大的文学作品都创造了"它自己的世界"，这一世界是独特的，似乎不同于"日常现实"。但现实主义大师如巴尔扎克或托尔斯泰在小说中，通过"将客观生活环境中最丰富多彩的方方面面描绘得栩栩如生"，以及通过塑造"典型"人物（这些人物最大限度地展现了他们所处时代的必然趋势和决定因素），成功地创造出一个"最具体最清晰地反映了生活及其所激发的各种矛盾"的虚构世界——这通常"与[作者]自己意识中的意识形态相悖"。也就是说，这些作家所虚构的世界与马克思主义认为现实世界是由阶级冲突、经济、社会"矛盾"所构成的观点相一致，也与马克思主义认为资本主义制度下个人异化的观点相符。[参见：*史诗*中的*市民史诗*；参阅：乔治·卢卡奇所著的《作家、批评家和其他论文》（1970年英译版），该书也收录了卢卡奇在其所著的《马克思和恩格斯的美学思想》中对马克思主义批评基本原则的有用评论。]

在赞扬19世纪现实主义文学的同时，卢卡奇将现代实验主义作家视为"堕落颓废"的例子加以抨击，认为他们关注资本主义后期这个破碎的世界中陌生化个人的主体性。（参见：*现代主义*。）因此，他在马克思主义批评家中引发了对20世纪文学形式的革新者的政治立场的激烈争论。与卢卡奇相反，德国马克思主义者的**法兰克福学派**，特别是西奥多·阿多诺和马克斯·霍克海姆则盛赞现代主义作家，如詹姆斯·乔伊斯、马塞尔·普鲁斯特和塞缪尔·贝克特，认为这些作家的形式实验，通过打碎和瓦解他们所"反映"的生活，取得了一种距离和超脱的艺术效果，或者说产生了一种"否定认知"，从而含蓄地批判了资本主义制度下的非人性制度和社会进程。阿多诺和霍尔海默在二战后试图解释"为什么人性的演进不是进入一种真正人的境况"（就像马克思主义者所预期的那样）"反而坠入一种新的野蛮主义之内"。参见：*批判*；参阅：安德鲁·阿拉托与艾克·格布哈特合编的《法兰克福学派基础读本》（1982），马丁·杰伊所著的权威的法兰克福学派史《辩证的想象》（1996）。

其他两位标新立异的德国马克思主义者：贝尔托尔特·布莱希特和沃尔特·本雅明，也支持现代主义和非现实主义艺术，他们对马克思主义批评和非马克思主义批评具有巨大影响。贝尔托尔特·布莱希特在他的批评理论和戏剧作品中（参见：*史诗剧*），摒弃他所谓的"亚里士多德"理论，这种理论认为悲剧作品是对现实的摹仿，具有统一的情节和普遍的主题，引发观众对主角的认同，净化观众的情感。（参见：*悲剧*、*情节*中关于亚里士多德的论述。）布莱希特提出，必须通过情节片段，

protagonists who do not attract the audience's sympathy, by a striking theatricality in staging and acting, and by other ways of baring the artifice of drama so as to produce an "alienation effect" (see under *distance and involvement*). The result of such alienation, Brecht asserts, will be to jar audiences out of their passive acceptance of modern capitalist society as a natural way of life, into an attitude not only (as in Adorno) of critical understanding of capitalist shortcomings, but of active cooperation with the forces of change.

Another notable critic, Walter Benjamin, was both an admirer of Brecht and briefly an associate of the Frankfurt School. Particularly influential was Benjamin's attention to the effects of changing material conditions in the production of the arts, especially the recent developments of the mass media that have promoted, he said, "a revolutionary criticism of traditional concepts of art." In his essay "The Work of Art in the Age of Mechanical Reproduction," Benjamin proposes that modern technical innovations such as photography, the phonograph, the radio, and especially the cinema, have transformed the very concept and status of a work of art. Formerly an artist or author produced a work which was a single object, regarded as the special preserve of the bourgeois elite, around which developed a quasi-religious "aura" of uniqueness, autonomy, and aesthetic value independent of any social function—an aura which invited in the spectator a passive attitude of absorbed contemplation in the object itself. (See *aestheticism* and *fine arts*.) The new media not only make possible the infinite and precise reproducibility of the objects of art, but effect the production of works which, like the motion pictures, are specifically designed to be reproduced in multiple copies. Such modes of art, Benjamin argues, by destroying the mystique of the unique work of art as a subject for pure contemplation, make possible a radical role for works of art by opening the way to "the formulation of revolutionary demands in the politics of art." (Benjamin's writings are available in Walter Benjamin, *Selected Writings*, 4 vols., 2002–4. Useful collections of essays by the Marxist critics Lukács, Brecht, Adorno, and Horkheimer are R. Taylor, ed., *Aesthetics and Politics*, 1977; and Roger S. Gottlieb, ed., *An Anthology of Western Marxism: From Lukács and Gramsci to Socialist-Feminism*, 1989.)

The second half of the twentieth century witnessed a resurgence of Marxist criticism, marked by an openness, on some level of literary analysis, to other current critical perspectives; a degree of flexibility which acknowledges that Marxist critical theory is itself, at least in some part, an evolving historical process; a subtilizing of the concept of ideology as applied to literary content; and a tendency to grant an increased role to nonideological and distinctively artistic determinants of literary structures and values.

In the 1960s the influential French Marxist Louis Althusser assimilated the *structuralism* then current into his view that the structure of society is not a monolithic whole, but is constituted by a diversity of "nonsynchronous" social formations, or "ideological state apparatuses," including religious, legal, political, and literary institutions. Each of these possesses a "relative autonomy"; only "in the last instance" is the ideology of a particular institution determined by its material base in contemporary economic production.

通过不会引发观众同情的主人公，通过在舞台和演出中令人印象深刻的戏剧性表现，通过其他展现戏剧技巧的方式，有意击碎现实的幻象，以此产生"异化效果"（参见：*心理距离与感情介入*中的相关论述）。布莱希特强调，这种异化的结果将使观众不再被动地将现代资本主义社会看成是自然的生活方式，从而不仅会形成一种对资本主义的缺陷进行批判的理解态度（就像阿多诺一样），而且会积极参与到谋求变化的力量中去。

另一位著名批评家沃尔特·本雅明是布莱希特的信奉者，而且在一段短暂的时间内还曾是法兰克福学派的成员。本雅明尤其具有影响的是他对艺术生产过程中不断变化的物质环境，尤其是对新近大众传媒技术发展所产生的作用的关注。他说，这些变化和发展促进了"一种对传统艺术观念的革命性批评"的产生。本雅明在其所写的文章"机械复制时代的艺术作品"中提出，现代技术的革新，如摄影、留声机、收音机，尤其是电影，已经转变了艺术作品的概念和地位。从前，一个艺术家或作家创造了作为单一物的作品，它被视为是资产阶级精英特有的领域，由此形成了一种独立于任何社会作用的独特性、自主性和审美价值的半宗教式"氛围"，即诱发了观众对作品本身深思熟虑的被动态度的氛围。（参见：*唯美主义、美术*。）新的媒介不仅使艺术作品无限的、精确的再生产成为可能，还实现了专门为成批再生产而设计的作品（如电影）的生产。本雅明坚称这样的艺术形式打破了独特艺术作品作为纯粹思考主体的神秘感，通过为"制订艺术政治中的革命要求"开辟道路，使艺术作品有可能发挥激进的作用。[本雅明的著作见于四卷本《本雅明著作精选》（2002—2004）。关于马克思主义批评家卢卡奇、布莱希特、本雅明、阿多诺主要文章的实用合集是 R. 泰勒编选的《美学与政治》（1977）和罗杰·S. 戈特利布编选的《西方马克思主义选集：从卢卡奇到葛兰西到社会－女性主义》（1989）。]

20世纪下中叶见证了马克思主义批评的复兴，它以在某一文学分析层面上，对于其他现今批评观点的开明态度为标志；出现了一种变通的观点，它承认马克思主义批评理论本身至少在某一限度上是一种不断发展的历史进程；出现了一种淡化将意识形态运用到文学内容的观念；出现了一种承认文学结构和价值观中非意识形态和独特的艺术决定因素起更多作用的趋势。

1960年代，颇具影响力的法国马克思主义者路易斯·阿尔都塞借鉴当时流行的结构主义理论并将其融入他的观点，认为社会结构并非铁板一块的整体，而是由各种各样"非同步"社会形式或"意识形态国家机器"构成，其中包括宗教、法律、政治和文学制度。其中每一种形式都拥有"相对的自主性"；只有某种特定制度的意识形态，才是由当时的经济生产方式的物质基础"最终"决定的。

In an influential reconsideration of the general nature of ideology, Althusser opposes its definition as simply "false consciousness." He declares instead that the ideology of each mode of state apparatus is different, and operates by means of a discourse which **interpellates** (calls upon) the individual to take up a pre-established "subject position"—that is, a position as a person with certain views and values, which, however, in every instance serve the ultimate interests of the ruling class. (See *discourse*, and *subject* under *poststructuralism*.) Althusser affirms, furthermore, that a great work of literature is not a mere product of ideology, because its fiction establishes for the reader a distance from which to recognize, hence expose, "the ideology from which it is born ... from which it detaches itself as art, and to which it alludes." Pierre Macherey, in *A Theory of Literary Production* (1966, trans. 1978), stressed the supplementary claim that a literary text not only distances itself from its ideology by its fiction and form, but also exposes the "contradictions" that are inherent in that ideology by its "silences" or "gaps"—that is, by what the text fails to say because its inherent ideology makes it impossible to say it. Combining Marxism and *Freudianism*, Macherey asserts that such textual "absences" are symptoms of ideological repressions of the contents in the text's own "unconscious." The aim of Marxist criticism, Macherey asserts, is to make these silences "speak" and so to reveal, behind what an author consciously intended to say, the text's unconscious content—that is, its repressed awareness of the flaws, stresses, and incoherence in the very ideology that it incorporates. (See *hermeneutics of suspicion*.)

Between 1929 and 1935 the Italian Communist Antonio Gramsci, while imprisoned by the fascist government, wrote approximately thirty documents on political, social, and cultural subjects, known as the "prison notebooks." Gramsci maintains the original Marxist distinction between the economic base and the cultural superstructure, but replaces the claim that culture is a disguised "reflection" of the material base with the concept that the relationship between the two is one of "reciprocity," or interactive influence. Gramsci places special emphasis on the popular, as opposed to the elite elements of culture, ranging from *folklore* and popular music to the cinema. Gramsci's most widely echoed concept is that of **hegemony**: that a social class achieves a predominant influence and power, not by direct and overt means, but by succeeding in making its ideological views so pervasive that the subordinate classes unwittingly accept and participate in their own oppression. The concept of hegemony, unlike the classical Marxist conception of ideology, implies an openness to negotiation and exchange, as well as conflict, between classes, and so refashions Marxist categories to fit a modern, post-industrial society in which diverse concepts and ideas, apart from "modes of production," play a leading role. Another appealing feature of Gramsci's thought to recent theorists is his emphasis on the role of intellectuals and opinion makers in helping people understand how they can effect their own transformation. Especially since Gramsci's prison writings began to be translated into English in 1971, they have had a strong influence on literary and social critics such as Terry Eagleton in England and Fredric Jameson and Edward Said in America,

在其对意识形态本质颇有影响的重新思考中,阿尔都塞反对将意识形态简单定义为"虚幻的意识";他认为意识形态随着各种模式的国家机器的形式和实践的变化而改变,每种意识形态模式通过一种类型的话语运作,**质询**(号召)个人采取某种预先确立的"主观立场",即作为具有某种观点和价值观的个人的立场,这种观点和价值观在任何情况下都是为统治阶级的最终利益服务的。(参见:*后结构主义*中的*话语*、*主体*。)进一步说,在特定的社会文学结构中,一部伟大的作品不仅仅是意识形态的产物,因为它的虚构为读者确立了一个距离,从这个距离,读者们可以认识,进而揭示"产生这部作品……使之作为艺术分离出来,并且反映出来的意识形态。"彼埃尔·马舍雷在其所著的《文学生产理论》(1966,1978 年英译版)中强调补充说,文学文本不仅通过虚构和形式远离其意识形态,同时也通过"沉默"或"脱漏"揭示了那种意识形态内在的"矛盾",这里所说的"沉默"与"脱漏"指的是因为意识形态本身之故而使文本不能表达出来的内容。这种文本的"空缺"是文本本身"无意识"中意识形态压制内容的征候。马舍雷坚称,马克思主义批评的目的是为了让这些沉默"说话",以此揭示暗藏在作者意识中想要表达的内容背后的文本的无意识内容——即,文本对其所包含的意识形态中的缺陷、强调和不一致的被压制的认识。(参见:*怀疑阐释学*。)

1929—1935 年间,意大利共产主义者安东尼奥·葛兰西在被法西斯政府囚禁期间,写了约三十篇有关政治、社会和文化主题的文献,这些文献被称为"狱中笔记"。葛兰西坚持马克思原来对经济基础和文化上层建筑的区分,但是他对马克思主义原来认为文化是对物质基础的别样"反映"这一观点则代之以另一种理念,即文化上层建筑和物质基础之间是"相互依存"或相互影响的关系。葛兰西特别强调与文化中的精英成分相对立的大众流行文化,从*民间传说*和流行音乐到电影。葛兰西得到最广泛响应的理论是**领导权理论**(又译霸权理论):即一个社会阶级取得占主宰地位的影响和权力,不是通过直接公开的手段,而是通过成功地使它的社会意识形态观念广泛流传,以至于被统治阶级不知不觉地在他们自身被压迫之中接受并参与到统治阶级的意识形态中。领导权这一概念,不像意识形态这一经典的马克思主义概念,暗含了一种开放性,不同阶级之间可以协商和交换,当然也有冲突;从而重塑了马克思主义分类,去适应一个现代的、后工业主义的社会,在这个社会中,形形色色的概念和观念("生产模式"除外)在发挥主导作用。葛兰西思想另一个吸引近代理论家的特点是,他对知识分子和舆论引导者在帮助人们理解他们如何能够影响他们自己的转变上所起的作用的强调。尤其是自从葛兰西的狱中文章在 1971 年开始译为英文以来,对文学和社会批评家产生了强大的影响,如英国的特里·伊格尔顿、美国的弗雷德里克·詹姆逊和爱德华·赛义德,

who argue for the power of literary culture to intervene in and transform existing economic and political arrangements and activities. (See Gramsci, *Selections from Cultural Writings*, trans. William Boelhower, 1985; David Forgacs, ed., *The Antonio Gramsci Reader: Selected Writings 1916–1935*, 2000; Chantal Mouffe, ed., *Gramsci and Marxist Theory*, 1979.)

Gramsci's writings also inspired a number of **post-Marxist** thinkers, who sought to adapt Marxism to *poststructural* discourse. Among these was a leader of the British Cultural Studies movement, Stuart Hall. (See *cultural studies*, also *cultural materialism* under the entry *new historicism*.) Hall insisted that ideology must not be considered a "false consciousness" or kind of concealment, but rather as a multifaceted force in the struggle for cultural power, carried on in the mode of the production of meaning. All "meaning," Hall said, "is always a social production, a practice. The world has to be *made to mean*." (See Hall, "The Recovery of 'Ideology,'" in Michael Gurevitch and others, eds., *Culture, Society and the Media*, 1982.)

Also strongly influenced by Gramsci were Ernesto Laclau and Chantal Mouffe, who in *Hegemony and Socialist Strategy* (1985) argued for an understanding of society grounded, not in economic determinism, but in the nature of language. Adapting the linguistic view of Ferdinand de Saussure that the identity of a sign and of its significance was not intrinsic, but determined by its position in a differential system, they argued that such "unfixity" was "the condition of every social identity," so that the place of power in a society can be legitimately occupied by anyone or any group. With the aid of Sausserian language theory, Laclau and Mouffe propose a view of society that, instead of being strictly determined by modes of production and the laws of economics, is open to innovation, transformation, and self-invention. (For Saussure's linguistic theory, see under *linguistics in literary criticism* and *semiotics*. For post-Marxist theory in general, refer to Geoffrey Galt Harpham, *Language Alone: The Critical Fetish of Modernity*, 2002, pp. 70–141.)

In England the many social and critical writings of Raymond Williams manifest an adaptation of Marxist concepts to his humanistic concern with the overall texture of an individual's "lived experience." A leading theorist of Marxist criticism in England is Terry Eagleton, who expanded and elaborated the concepts of Althusser and Macherey into his view that a literary text is a special kind of production in which ideological discourse—described as any system of mental representations of lived experience—is reworked into a specifically literary discourse. In his later writings Eagleton became increasingly hospitable to the tactical use, for dealing with ideology in literature, of concepts derived from *deconstruction* and from Lacan's version of Freudian *psychoanalysis*. Eagleton views such poststructuralist analyses as useful to Marxist critics of literary texts insofar as they serve to undermine reigning beliefs and certainties, but solely as preliminary to the properly Marxist enterprise of exposing their ideological motivation and to the application of the criticism of literature toward politically desirable ends.

The most prominent American theorist, Fredric Jameson, is also the most eclectic of Marxist critics. In *The Political Unconscious: Narrative as a Socially*

他们重视的是文学文化在干预和改变现有经济、政治体制和活动中的力量。[参阅：葛兰西的《文化作品选集》(1985，威廉·博尔豪尔英译版)；戴维·福加克斯主编的《安东尼奥·葛兰西读本：1916—1935年间作品选》(2000)；查特尔·墨菲主编的《葛兰西和马克思主义理论》(1979)。]

葛兰西的著作也激发了一些**后马克思主义**思想家，他们竭力想要让马克思主义适应*后结构主义*话语。其中就有英国文化研究运动的领军人物斯图尔特·霍尔。(参见：*文化研究*，也可参见：*新历史主义中的文化物质主义*。)霍尔坚持认为，没有必要把意识形态视为一种"虚假的意识"或是一种遮蔽，而是可以将其视为在争取文化权力的斗争中一种多层面的力量，按照生产意义的模式运作。霍尔说："所有的意义总是一种社会生产，一种实践。世界必须由意义组成。"[参见霍尔所写的文章"还原'意识形态'"，收入迈克尔·古雷维奇等人主编的《文化、社会与媒介》(1982)。]

欧内斯托·拉克劳和查特尔·墨菲同样受到葛兰西的强烈影响，他们两个人在其合著的《领导权与社会主义的策略》(1985)中争辩道：理解社会的根基不在经济决定论，而在语言的本质上。他们改编了费迪南·德·索绪尔的语言学观点，一个符号及其意义的特征并非天生就有，而是决定于它在不同体系中所处的位置，认为这一"不稳定性"是"每种社会认同的情况"，所以社会中的权力位置可被任何人或任何群体合理地占有。在索绪尔语言学理论的帮助下，拉克劳和墨菲提出了一种看法，认为社会并非是被生产模式和经济规律所严格决定，而是对变革、转型、自我创造开放的。[关于索绪尔的语言学理论，参见：*语言学在文学批评里的应用*、*语义学*中的论述。关于后马克思主义理论的概述，参阅：杰弗里·高尔特·哈珀姆所著的《只有语言：现代性的拜物教批评》(2002) 第70—141页。]

在英国，雷蒙德·威廉斯的许多有关社会和批评的论著表明，他在自己对于个体"生活经验"的整体结构的人文主义关怀中引入了马克思主义思想观念。马克思主义批评在英国的主要理论家是特里·伊格尔顿，他在自己的观点中扩展并详尽地阐述了阿尔都塞和马舍雷的理论。他认为文学文本是一种特殊的生产，在这种生产中，被描述为思想上再现了生活经验的系统的意识形态话语，被重新加工为一种特殊的文学话语。近年来，伊格尔顿在论述文学中的意识形态方面，越来越愿意变通地采用源自*解构主义*和拉康的弗洛伊德精神分析的观念。伊格尔顿认为，此类后解构主义分析对马克思主义文学文本批评家是有益的，因为这些分析有助于削弱占统治地位的信仰和确定性，但这仅仅是有助于马克思主义正确揭示文本的意识动机的任务及将文学批评运用于政治上有利的目的。

美国最杰出的理论家，同时也是当代最兼收并蓄的马克思主义批评家是弗雷德里克·詹姆逊。在其所著的《政治无意识：叙事的社会象征行为》(1981)中，

Symbolic Act (1981), Jameson expressly adapts to his critical enterprise such seemingly incompatible viewpoints as the medieval theory of fourfold levels of meaning in the *allegorical interpretation* of the Bible, the *archetypal criticism* of Northrop Frye, *structuralist criticism*, Lacan's reinterpretations of Freud, *semiotics*, and *deconstruction*. These modes of criticism, Jameson asserts, are applicable at various stages of the critical interpretation of a literary work; but Marxist criticism, he contends, "subsumes" all the other "interpretive modes," by retaining their positive findings within a "political interpretation of literary texts" which stands as the "final" or "absolute horizon of all reading and all interpretation." This last-analysis "political interpretation" of a literary text involves an exposure of the hidden role of the "political unconscious"—a concept which Jameson describes as his "collective," or "political," adaptation of the Freudian concept that each individual's unconscious is a repository of repressed desires. (See *psychological and psychoanalytic criticism*.) In a mode similar to Macherey, Jameson affirms that in any literary product of our late capitalist era, the "rifts and discontinuities" in the text, and especially those elements which, in the French phrase, are its "non-dit" (its not-said), are symptoms of the repression by a predominant ideology of the contradictions of "History" into the depths of the political unconscious; and the content of this repressed History, Jameson asserts, is the revolutionary process of "the collective struggle to wrest a realm of Freedom from a realm of Necessity." In the final stage, or last analysis, of an interpretation, Jameson holds, the Marxist critic "rewrites," in the mode of "allegory," the literary text "in such a way that the [text] may be seen as the ... reconstruction of a prior historical or ideological *subtext*"—that is, of the text's unspoken, because repressed and unconscious, awareness of the ways it is determined not only by current ideology, but also by the long-term process of true "History." (See *allegory*.)

Refer to *sociology of literature*, and for the Marxist wing of the new historicism, see *cultural materialism* under the entry *new historicism*. Useful introductions to Marxist criticism in general are the essays in Maynard Solomon, ed., *Marxism and Art: Essays Classic and Contemporary* (1979); Terry Eagleton and Drew Milne, eds., *Marxist Literary Theory: A Reader* (1996). In addition to the writings listed above, refer to Georg Lukács, *Studies in European Realism* (1950); Raymond Williams, *Culture and Society, 1780–1950* (1960) and *Marxism and Literature* (1977); Peter Demetz, *Marx, Engels and the Poets: Origins of Marxist Literary Criticism* (1967); Walter Benjamin, *Illuminations* (trans. 1968); Louis Althusser, *Lenin and Philosophy, and Other Essays* (1969, trans. 1971), and *For Marx* (1996); Fredric Jameson, *Marxism and Form* (1971), and *Late Marxism: Adorno, or the Persistence of the Dialectic* (1996); Lee Baxandall and Stefan Morawski, eds., *Marx and Engels on Literature and Art* (1973); Terry Eagleton, *Criticism and Ideology* (1976) and *Marxism and Literary Criticism* (1976); Chris Bullock and David Peck, eds., *Guide to Marxist Literary Criticism* (1980); Michael Ryan, *Marxism and Deconstruction* (1982); J. J. McGann, *The Romantic Ideology* (1983); J. G. Merquior, *Western Marxism* (1986). Various essays by Gayatri Chakravorty Spivak assimilate Marxist concepts both to *deconstruction* and to the viewpoint of *feminist criticism*; see, for example, her

詹姆逊明显地把那些看似互不相容的观点：如对圣经的*寓意释义*中四层含义的中世纪理论，诺斯罗普·弗莱的*原型批评*，*结构主义批评*，拉康对弗洛伊德的再解释，*符号论和解构主义*，加以修正并引用到其批评实践中。詹姆逊坚称，这些批评模式可以用在对一部文学作品不同阶段的批评解释中；然而他认为，马克思主义批评"包含"了其他所有"诠释模式"，"在对文学文本政治性的诠释中"保留了这些诠释模式的所有建设性发现，这种诠释代表了对"所有阅读、所有诠释的'最后'或'绝对'的认识"。这种对文学文本"政治性诠释"的最后分析，包括了对"政治潜意识"的隐含作用的揭示——詹姆逊把这一理论描述为把弗洛伊德理论（即认为每一个体的潜意识都是被压制欲望的贮存器）改写为"集体的"或"政治的"潜意识。（参见：*心理学与精神分析批评*。）詹姆逊以一种与马舍雷相似的方式指出，资本主义时代后期所有文学作品中存在于文本中的那些"空隙与断裂"，尤其是在法语中被称为"non-dit"的成分（即文本中未说出来的部分），是占主宰地位的意识形态将"历史"的各种矛盾压制到政治潜意识深层的征候；詹姆逊坚持认为，这一被压制的历史的内容，是"从必然王国争夺自由王国的集体抗争"的革命过程。在阐释的最后阶段或最后分析中，詹姆逊认为，马克思主义批评家以"喻意"的方式"重写"了文学文本，"这样的方式使 [文本] 可被视为……是对先前历史或意识形态的次文本的重建"，即对文本中未说出部分的重建，因为在被压制的潜意识中认识到，文本的表述方式不仅是由当前的意识形态所决定的，而且是由真正"历史"的长期过程所决定的。（参见：*寓言*。）

参见：*文学社会学*，有关新历史主义的马克思主义派别，参见*新历史主义*中的*文化唯物主义*。实用的马克思主义批评概览入门是梅纳德·所罗门主编的《马克思主义和艺术：经典及当代文章》；特里·伊格尔顿与德鲁·米尔恩合编的《马克思主义文学理论读本》(1996)。除了上举篇章，还可参阅：乔治·卢卡奇所著的《欧洲现实主义研究》(1950)；雷蒙德·威廉斯所著的《1780—1950年间的文化与社会》(1960) 和《马克思主义与文学》(1977)；彼得·德梅茨所著的《马克思、恩格斯和诗人：马克思主义文学批评的起源》(1967)；沃尔特·本雅明所著的《启迪》(1968年英译版)；路易斯·阿尔都塞所著的《列宁与哲学及其他论文选》(1969, 1971年英译版) 和《保卫马克思》(1996)；弗雷德里克·詹姆逊所著的《马克思主义与形式》(1971) 和《晚期马克思主义：阿多诺或辩证法的坚持》(1996)；李·巴克森德尔与斯蒂芬·莫拉夫斯基合编的《马克思和恩格斯论文学与艺术》(1973)；特里·伊格尔顿所著的《批评与意识形态》(1976) 和《马克思主义与文学批评》(1976)；克里斯·布洛克与戴维·佩克合编的《马克思主义文学批评指南》(1980)；迈克尔·瑞安所著的《马克思主义与解构主义》(1982)；J.J.麦根所著的《浪漫主义意识形态》(1983)；J. G. 莫奎尔所著的《西方马克思主义》(1986)。佳娅特丽·查克拉沃蒂·斯皮瓦克的不同文章将马克思主义理论与解构主义和女性主义批评的观点结合到了一起，可以参阅她所著的

"Displacement and the Discourse of Women," in *Displacement: Derrida and After*, ed. Mark Krupnick (1983). For Derrida's "reading" of Marx, see his *Specters of Marx: The State of the Debt, the Work of Mourning, and the New International* (1994). For a sharp critique of recent theorists of Marxist criticism, see Frederick Crews, "Dialectical Immaterialism," in *Skeptical Engagements* (1986); also Richard Levin, "The New Interdisciplinarity in Literary Criticism," in Nancy Easterlin and Barbara Riebling, eds., *After Poststructuralism: Interdisciplinarity and Literary Theory*, 1993. Marxist concerns also serve to form the *new formalism* in literary criticism; see Robert Kaufman, "Red Kant, or The Persistence of the Third Critique in Adorno and Jameson," *Critical Inquiry*, Vol. 26 (2000).

For references to *Marxist criticism* in other entries, see pages *163, 172, 246, 311.*

masculine ending: 220.

masculine rhyme: 349.

masque: The masque (a variant spelling of "mask") was inaugurated in Renaissance Italy and flourished in England during the reigns of Elizabeth I, James I, and Charles I. In its full development, it was an elaborate form of court entertainment that combined poetic drama, music, song, dance, splendid costuming, and stage spectacle. A plot—often slight, and mainly mythological and allegorical—served to hold together these diverse elements. The speaking characters, who wore masks (hence the title), were often played by amateurs who belonged to courtly society. The play concluded with a dance in which the players doffed their masks and were joined by the audience.

In the early seventeenth century in England the masque drew upon the finest artistic talents of the day, including Ben Jonson for the poetic script (for example, *The Masque of Blacknesse* and *The Masque of Queens*) and Inigo Jones, the architect, for the elaborate sets, costumes, and stage machinery. Each lavish production cost a fortune; it was literally the sport of kings and queens, until both court and drama were abruptly ended by the Puritan triumph of 1642. The two examples best known to modern readers are the masque-within-a-play in the fourth act of Shakespeare's *The Tempest*, and Milton's sage and serious revival of the form, *Comus*, with songs by the composer Henry Lawes, which was presented at Ludlow Castle in 1634. The jubilant fourth act which Shelley added to his poetic drama *Prometheus Unbound* (1819) was modeled on the Renaissance masque, as are two dramas by the American poet Robert Frost, *A Masque of Reason* (1945) and *A Masque of Mercy* (1947). Edgar Allen Poe's lurid tale, "The Masque of the Red Death," depicts not a dramatic masque, but a masquerade ball, conducted by a medieval prince and his courtiers in defiance of a lethal plague that was ravishing the land. At this ball, a ghastly masked intruder turns out to be the Red Death itself.

The **antimasque** was a form developed by Ben Jonson. In it the characters were *grotesque* and unruly, the action ludicrous, and the humor broad; it

《置换：德里达与后来者》(1983)中的"置换与女性话语"。德里达对马克思的"解读"，参见他所著的《马克思的幽灵：债务国家、哀悼活动和新国际》(1994)。有关新近马克思主义批评理论家的尖锐批评，可以参阅：弗雷德里克·克鲁斯所著的《怀疑主义的交战》中的"辩证唯心论"；也可参阅理查德·莱文所写的文章"文学批评中新的跨学科性"，收入南希·伊斯特林与巴巴拉·里布林合编的《后结构主义之后：跨学科性与文学理论》(1993)。马克思主义视角也有助于促成文学批评中的新形式主义，参阅：罗伯特·考夫曼所写的文章"红色/激进的康德，或阿多诺与詹姆逊对第三批判的坚持"，载于《批评探索》2000年第26卷。

其他条目中提及"马克思主义批评"的地方，参见第163、172、246、311页。

masculine ending：强音尾　220。

masculine rhyme：阳韵　349。

Masque：假面歌舞剧

假面歌舞剧(masque为"mask"的另一种拼写方法)起源于意大利文艺复兴时期，在英国盛行于伊丽莎白一世、詹姆斯一世与查理一世统治时期。在其全面发展时期，作为一种精巧的宫廷娱乐形式，假面歌舞剧融合了诗剧、音乐、歌舞、华丽的服饰和舞台场景，其情节——通常微不足道，主要以神话和寓言为内容——把这些不同表现形式结合在一起。剧中有台词的角色都戴着面具(这正是其名称由来)，通常由贵族阶层中的戏剧爱好者所扮演。剧终，演员脱下面具，观众加入，共同起舞。

在17世纪初期的英国，假面歌舞剧从当时最杰出的艺术天才手中汲取了营养，其中包括选用本·琼森的诗剧剧本(如《黑色假面剧》《王后假面剧》)，同时求助于建筑师伊尼戈·琼斯的技艺设计精致复杂的背景、服饰和舞台装置。这样每次演出都要挥霍大笔钱财；在1642年英国清教徒成功推翻王朝并废止宫廷和戏剧演出之前，这种戏剧形式实际上是国王和王后的一种娱乐游戏。现在人所共知的两出假面歌舞剧包括莎士比亚《暴风雨》第四幕的假面剧中剧，和弥尔顿创作的《科玛斯》，后者巧妙而严肃地复兴了假面歌舞剧这种形式，剧中音乐由作曲家亨利·劳斯所作，于1634年在拉德洛城堡上演。雪莱为他的诗剧《解放了的普罗米修斯》(1819)增添的喜气洋洋的第四幕，模仿的是文艺复兴假面歌舞剧，它自身则为美国诗人罗伯特·弗罗斯特的《理性假面剧》(1945)和《仁慈假面剧》(1947)所模仿。埃德加·爱伦·坡骇人的故事《红死病的假面舞会》，描绘的并不是一个假面歌舞剧，而是一个化装舞会，该舞会由一位中世纪的王子和他的廷臣们举办，他们不顾一场致命的瘟疫正在侵犯人类。在这场舞会上，一个可怕的蒙面入侵者原来正是红死病自身。

滑稽穿插戏是本·琼森发展出的一种形式。它的人物角色*奇形怪状*、放荡不

served as a foil and countertype to the elegance, order, and ceremony of the masque proper, which preceded it in a performance.

See Allardyce Nicoll, *Stuart Masques and the Renaissance Stage* (1937); Stephen Orgel, *The Illusion of Power* (1975). Stephen Orgel and Roy Strong, in *Inigo Jones: The Theatre of the Stuart Court* (2 vols., 1973), discuss Jones' contributions to the masque, with copious illustrations.

mechanic form: 137.

medieval romance: 48.

medieval tragedy: 409.

meiosis (mīō′ sĭs): **167.**

melodrama: "Melos" is Greek for song, and the term "melodrama" was originally applied to all musical plays, including opera. In early-nineteenth-century London, many plays were produced with a musical accompaniment that (as in modern motion pictures) served simply to fortify the emotional tone of the various scenes; the procedure was developed in part to circumvent the Licensing Act (1737), which allowed "legitimate" plays only as a monopoly of the Drury Lane and Covent Garden theaters, but permitted musical entertainments elsewhere. The term "melodrama" is now often applied to some of the typical plays, especially during the *Victorian Period*, that were written to be produced to musical accompaniment.

The Victorian melodrama can be said to bear the relation to tragedy that *farce* does to comedy. Typically, the protagonists are *flat* types: the hero is greathearted, the heroine pure, and the villain a monster of malignity. (The sharply contrasted good guys and bad guys of the movie western and some television dramas are modern derivatives from standard types in the old melodramas.) The plot revolves around malevolent intrigue and violent action, while the credibility of both character and plot is often sacrificed for violent effect and emotional opportunism. Nineteenth-century melodramas such as *Under the Gaslight* (1867) and the temperance play *Ten Nights in a Barroom* (1858) are still sometimes produced—less for thrills, however, than for laughs. Recently, the composer Stephen Sondheim converted George Dibdin Pitt's Victorian thriller *Sweeney Todd, The Barber of Fleet Street* (1842) into a highly effective musical drama.

The terms "melodrama" and "melodramatic" are also, in an extended sense, applied to any literary work or episode, whether in drama or prose fiction, that relies on implausible events and sensational action. Melodrama, in this sense, was standard fare in cowboy-and-Indian and cops-and-robber types of silent films, and remains alive and flourishing in current cinematic and television productions.

See M. W. Disher, *Blood and Thunder: Mid-Victorian Melodrama and Its Origins* (1949) and *Plots That Thrilled* (1954); Frank Rahill, *The World of*

羁，情节荒唐滑稽，插科打诨也较粗俗；在假面剧的幕间安插这种滑稽戏的目的在于，衬托出假面歌舞剧本身的优雅、有序及其礼仪。

参阅：阿勒代斯·尼科尔所著的《斯图亚特时期的假面歌舞剧与文艺复兴时期的舞台》(1937)；斯蒂芬·奥格尔所著的《权力的幻觉》(1975)。斯蒂芬·奥格尔与罗伊·斯特朗合著的两卷本《伊尼戈·琼斯：斯图亚特时代宫廷戏剧》(1973)，详细地说明并讨论了琼斯对假面歌舞剧的贡献。

mechanic form：模具形式　137。

medieval romance：中世纪传奇　48。

medieval tragedy：中世纪悲剧　409。

meiosis：曲言　167。

Melodrama：情节剧

"melos"是希腊文"歌"的意思，"情节剧"这一术语原指包括歌剧在内的一切音乐剧。19世纪早期伦敦上演的许多剧目里都有音乐伴奏，其目的（正如在现代电影中一样）仅仅是为了加强各种场景的感情色彩；这种做法在一定程度上是为了巧妙地躲避当时的戏剧检查法的限制（检查法只准许所谓"合法"剧目独占特鲁里戏剧街和科文特加登剧院的戏剧舞台，但却允许音乐剧在舞台上演）。"情节剧"一词现在常用来指一些特定的配乐戏剧，尤其是*维多利亚时期*的这类戏剧。

维多利亚时期的情节剧和悲剧之间的关系正像闹剧和喜剧的关系一样。情节剧的特点是：主要角色通常是些*干瘪的*人物模式：男主角勇敢豪爽，女主角纯洁无瑕，反面角色则被刻画成十恶不赦的魔鬼。（西部电影和一些电视剧里好汉与恶棍的强烈对比，正是这些老式情节剧标准人物模式的现代变种。）其情节主要围绕恶毒的阴谋与暴力的行为展开，但由于过分追求暴力效果和扣人心弦的情感效果，致使人物和情节都失去了可信度。19世纪的一些情节剧如今仍然时有上演，如《煤气灯下》(1867)和用于戒酒宣传的剧目《酒吧十宵》(1858)，但重演这些剧目已经不是为了刺激而是为了引笑观众。最近，作曲家斯蒂芬·桑德海姆将维多利亚时期乔治·迪布丁·皮特的惊悚剧《斯维尼·托德：舰队街的理发师》(1842)改编成音乐剧，给人留下了深刻的印象。

广义上来说，"情节剧"和"情节剧的"这两个术语也用于指代戏剧或散文体小说中一味追求难以置信的事件或耸人听闻的行动的文学作品或片段。在这个意义上，情节剧通常出现在"牛仔与印第安人"和"警察与强盗"类型的无声电影中，并在如今的电影或电视作品中仍然欣欣向荣。

参阅：M. W. 迪舍所著的《鲜血与惊雷：维多利亚中期的情节剧及其起源》(1949)和《让人刺激的情节》(1954)；弗兰克·拉希尔所著的《情节剧的世界》

Melodrama (1967); R. B. Heilman, *Tragedy and Melodrama* (1968); David Thorburn, "Television Melodrama," *Television as a Cultural Force*, ed. Douglass Cater (1976); Bruce McConachie, *Melodramatic Formations: American Theatre and Society, 1820–1870* (1992).

memoir: 27.

Menippean satire (mĕnĭp′ ēăn): 354.

men's studies: 146.

metafiction: 258.

metaphor: 130; *63*.

metaphor, theories of: When someone says, discussing John's eating habits, "John is a pig," and when Coleridge writes in "The Ancient Mariner"

> The moonlight steeped in silentness
> The steady weathercock,

we recognize that the noun "pig" and the verb "steeped" are metaphors, and have no trouble understanding them. (See *metaphor* under *figurative language*.) But after twenty-five centuries of discussions of metaphor by rhetoricians, grammarians, and literary critics—in which during the second half of the twentieth century they were joined by many philosophers—there is no general agreement about the way we identify metaphors, how we are able to understand them, and what (if anything) they serve to tell us. Following is a brief summary of the most prominent among competing theories of metaphor:

1. The similarity view. This was the traditional way of analyzing metaphors, from the time that Aristotle introduced it in the fourth century BC until the recent past. It holds that a metaphor is a departure from the *literal* (that is, what a competent speaker experiences as the standard) use of language which serves as a condensed or elliptical *simile*, in that it involves an implicit comparison between two disparate things. (The two things in the examples cited above are John's eating habits and those of a pig, and the event of something being steeped—soaked in a liquid—and the appearance of the moonlit landscape.) This view usually assumes that the features being compared pre-existed the use of the metaphor; that the metaphor can be translated into a statement of literal similarity without loss of cognitive content (that is, of the information it conveys); and also that a metaphor serves mainly to enhance the rhetorical force and stylistic vividness and pleasantness of a discourse.
2. The interaction view. In *The Philosophy of Rhetoric* (1936) I. A. Richards introduced the terms *vehicle* for the metaphorical word (in the two

(1967)；R. B. 海尔曼所著的《悲剧与情节剧》(1968)；戴维·索伯恩所写的文章"电视情节剧"，收入道格拉斯·凯特主编的《电视作为一种文化力量》(1976)；布鲁斯·麦康纳基所著的《情节剧的形成：1820—1870年间美国的剧院与社会》(1992)。

memoir：回忆录　27。

Menippean satire：梅尼普斯式讽刺　354。

men's studies：男性研究　146。

metafiction：元小说　258。

metaphor：隐喻／暗喻　130；*63*。

Metaphor, Theories of：隐喻理论

当某人在谈论约翰的饮食习惯时说"约翰是只猪"，当柯勒律治在《古舟子咏》中写道：

> 月色如水，高高的风标
> 在寂静中沐浴着月光，　　　　　　　　　　　　　　　（顾子欣译）

我们都能意识到，名词"猪"和动词"沐浴"是隐喻手法，而且我们不难理解这两个隐喻。（参见：*比喻语中的隐喻*。）但在修辞家、语法学家、文学批评家讨论隐喻二十五个世纪之后——其中在20世纪下半个世纪，许多哲学家也加入其中——我们定义隐喻、理解隐喻的方式、隐喻向我们揭示的含义（如果有的话）并无定论。以下是有关隐喻最主要观点的简要概述：

1. 相似观点。从亚里士多德在公元前4世纪引入这种观点直到近期，这都是分析隐喻的传统方法。该观点认为隐喻偏离语言的字面（即标准）用法，是一种简洁的或省略而晦涩的明喻形式，其中包含了对两种根本不同事物的含蓄比较（上面所举两例中的两个事物，例一中是约翰的饮食习惯和猪的饮食习惯，例二中是某物沐浴这一事件——浸在液体中——与月光照耀下所呈现的景色）。这种观点通常认为，被比较的特征在使用隐喻之前业已存在；可以在不失去认知内容（即其所传达的信息）的情况下将隐喻转变为字面上相似的陈述，而且隐喻的主要目的是为了加强修辞力量、文体生动、话语活泼。

2. 相互作用观点。I. A. 理查兹在其所著的《修辞哲学》(1936)中介绍了一些术语：如，用来指代隐喻词的喻矢（在上面两个例子中，

examples, "pig" and "steeped") and *tenor* for the subject to which the metaphorical word is applied (John's eating habits and the moonlit landscape). In place of the similarity view, he proposed that a metaphor works by bringing together the disparate "thoughts" of the vehicle and tenor so as to effect a meaning that "is a resultant of their interaction" and that cannot be duplicated by literal assertions of a similarity between the two elements. He also asserted that metaphor cannot be viewed simply as a rhetorical or poetic departure from ordinary usage, in that it permeates all language and affects the ways we perceive and conceive the world. Almost twenty years later, in an influential essay entitled "Metaphor" (1954–55), the philosopher Max Black refined and greatly expanded Richards' treatment. Black proposed that each of the two elements in a metaphor has a "system of associated commonplaces," consisting of the properties and relations that we commonly attach to the object, person, or event. When we understand a metaphor, the system of commonplaces associated with the "subsidiary subject" (equivalent to I. A. Richards' "vehicle") interacts with the system associated with the "principal subject" (Richards' "tenor") so as to "filter" or "screen" that system, and thus effects a new way of perceiving and conceiving the principal subject. This process, by which one complex set of associations serves to select and reorganize a second set, Black claims, is a "distinctive *intellectual* operation." He also claims that, in place of saying that metaphors simply formulate a pre-existing similarity between the two subjects, "it would be more illuminating in some of these cases to say that the metaphor *creates* the similarity."

Before Max Black's essay, philosophers had paid only passing attention to metaphor. The reigning assumption had been that the main function of language is to communicate truths, and that truths can be clearly communicated only in literal language. For the most part, accordingly, philosophers had adverted to metaphor only to warn against its intrusion into rational discourse, as opposed to poetry and oratory, on the ground that figurative language, as John Locke had said in his *Essay Concerning Human Understanding* (1690), serves only "to insinuate wrong ideas, move the passions, and thereby mislead the judgment." Black's essay, however, helped inaugurate a philosophical concern with metaphor which, since the 1960s, has resulted in a flood of publications. Many of these writings restate, with various qualifications, refinements, and expansions, either the similarity or interaction views of metaphor. Within these contributions, however, one can identify two additional views, both of which have been influential in literary theory as well as in philosophy:

3. The pragmatic view. In an essay entitled "What Metaphors Mean" (1978), Donald Davidson mounted a challenge to the standard assumption that there is a metaphorical meaning as distinct from a literal meaning. "Metaphors," he claims, "mean what the words, in their most literal interpretation, mean, and nothing more." The question of metaphor is

"猪"和"沐浴"就是喻矢）；用来表示隐喻词所指代的主体的喻的（"约翰的饮食习惯"和"月光照耀下的景色"就是主体）。他提出了另一种理论来取代相似观点。他认为隐喻通过将喻的、喻矢根本不同的"想法"结合在一起，以此实现一种意义，这一意义是"两者相互作用的结果"，不能通过对两个成分之间相似性字面上的肯定得以复制。他还坚称，不能仅仅将隐喻视为是修辞或诗歌偏离语言的普通用法，因为隐喻在所有的语言中比比皆是，并影响了我们感知和理解世界的方式。差不多二十年后，在一篇颇具影响、名为"隐喻"（1954—1955）的文章中，哲学家马克斯·布莱克完善并大大扩展了理查兹的论述。布莱克提出，隐喻两个组成部分中的任何一个都具有一种"相关的常见事物体系"，由我们通常赋予一类物体、人物或事件的属性和亲属关系组成。当我们理解一则隐喻时，这一与"副体"（等同于理查兹提出的"喻矢"）相关的常见事物体系，同与"主体"（即理查兹提出的"喻的"）相关的常见事物体系产生相互作用，以此"过滤"或"筛选"本体体系，实现一种新的感知和理解主体的方式。布莱克宣称，这一过程是一种"独特的智力活动"，在这一过程中，一组复杂的相关事物选择并重组了第二组相关事物。他还称，与其说隐喻仅仅构想出两个主体之间预先存在的相似之处，"在一些这样的例子中，倒不如说隐喻创造了这种相似更具有启发性"。

在马克斯·布莱克的文章之前，哲学家们对隐喻的关注仅是顺便提及。其主要观点认为，语言的主要作用是交流真理，这种真理只能靠文字语言清楚地得以交流。因此，大部分时候，哲学家们关注隐喻只是为了提防它进入理性话语，这与诗歌和演说不同。这种观点以约翰·洛克在其所著的《人类理解论》（1690）中的理论为依据：比喻语仅仅"产生错误的观点，引发激情，由此误导判断"。然而，布莱克的文章引发了对隐喻的哲学关注，其结果是自1960年代起出版了大量相关论著。许多论著通过各种各样的描述、深入细腻的论述和延伸，重申了隐喻的相似观点和相互作用观点。然而在这些成果中还可发现另外两种观点，这两种观点无论在哲学还是文学理论方面都产生了影响：

3. 语用观点。在"隐喻的意义"（1978）一文中，唐纳德·戴维森对普遍的假定提出挑战，普遍的假定认为存在一种不同于字面意义的隐喻意义。他声称："隐喻指的是词语在其最表面的字面释义中所表示的意义，除此之外，别无他意。"隐喻的问题属于语用问题而非

pragmatic, not semantic; that is, it is the use of a literal statement in such a way as to "suggest," or "intimate," or "lead us to notice" what we might otherwise overlook. In a chapter on "Metaphor" in *Expression and Meaning* (1979), John Searle also rejected the similarity and interaction views, on the grounds that at best they serve to explain, and that only in part and in a misleading way, how some metaphors come to be used and understood. In consonance with his overall *speech-act theory*, Searle proposed that to explain metaphor we must distinguish between "word, or sentence meaning" (what the word or sentence means literally) and a particular speaker's "utterance meaning" (the metaphorical meaning that a speaker uses the literal word or sentence meaning to express). Searle goes on to propose a set of implicit principles, shared by the speaker and interpreter, to explain how a speaker can use a sentence with a literal meaning to say something with a very different metaphorical meaning, as well as to clarify how a hearer recognizes and proceeds to interpret a literal sentence that is used metaphorically.

4. The cognitive (or conceptual) view. This treatment of metaphor, prominent since about 1980, begins by rejecting the assumption in many earlier theories that the ordinary, normal use of language is literal, from which metaphor is a deviation for special rhetorical and poetic purposes. Instead it claims that the ordinary use of language is pervasively and indispensably metaphorical, and that metaphor persistently and profoundly structures the ways human beings perceive, what they know, and how they think.

George Lakoff and Mark Turner in *More than Cool Reason* (1979) provide a short and accessible introduction to this cognitive view, with special attention to its relevance for the analysis of metaphors in poetry. They conceive metaphor to be a projection and mapping across what they call "conceptual domains"; that is, its use is basically a cognitive mental process, of which the metaphorical word, phrase, or sentence is only the linguistic aspect and expression. To identify the two elements that compose a metaphor, the authors replace "vehicle" and "tenor," or "primary" and "secondary," with the terms "source domain" and "target domain." In using and understanding a metaphor, part of the conceptual structure of the source domain is "mapped" onto the conceptual structure of the target domain, in a one-way "transaction" (as distinct from an "interaction") which may alter and reorganize the way we perceive or think about the latter element.

A distinctive procedure in this view is to identify a number of "basic conceptual metaphors" that pervade discourse in our Western culture, but are so common and operate so automatically that for the most part we use them without noticing them. Some of the most common basic metaphors are Purposes Are Destinations; Time Moves; Time Is A Reaper; Life Is A Journey; Life Is A Play; People Are Plants. Such metaphors establish cross-conceptual mappings that manifest themselves in our ordinary speech as well as in the greatest poetry. People Are Plants, for example, is a type of cognitive mapping that underlies such everyday expressions as

语义问题；即以这种方式使用字面陈述以"暗示"或"提示"或"引导我们注意"我们否则可能会忽略的意义。在《表达和意义》(1979)中有关"隐喻"的章节里，约翰·塞尔也摒弃了相似观点和相互作用观点，他的理由是这两种观点至多解释了（而且只是部分地且是以误导的方式）一些隐喻的使用和理解方法。和他在言语行为理论中的总体观点一样，塞尔提出，要解释隐喻，我们必须区别"词或句子的含义"（即词或句子的字面意义）与特定说话者的"话语含义"（即一个说话者利用词或句子的字面意义来表达的隐喻意义）。塞尔进一步提出一套说话者与释义者共享的隐含原则，用来解释一个说话者如何使用句子的字面意义来表达一种完全不同的隐喻含义，以及说明听者是如何理解、进而解释用作隐喻的字面句子的含义。

4. 认知（或概念）观点。有关隐喻的这种观点，大约从1980年以来异军突起，它首先摒弃了许多早先的隐喻理论，那些隐喻理论认为语言普遍标准的用法就是字面用法，隐喻是为了特殊的修辞和诗歌目的而对语言普遍标准用法的偏离。与其相反，认知观点提出语言的普通标准用法是无所不在、不可或缺的隐喻用法，隐喻持续而深刻地建构了人类理解他们所知事物的方式以及他们的思维方式。

乔治·雷柯夫和马克·特纳在其合著的《并非只是冰冷的理论》(1979)中，简洁明了地介绍了这种认知观点，并特别关注了认知观点与分析诗歌中的隐喻的关系。他们将隐喻视为是跨越了他们所谓的"概念领域"的推测与映射；即隐喻的使用本质上是一个认知的精神过程，在这个过程中，隐喻的词、词组或句子仅仅是语言成分和表述。为了识别组成一个隐喻的两个部分，作者用"源领域""目标领域"来代替"喻矢"和"喻的"，或"主体"和"副体"。在对隐喻的使用和理解中，部分源领域的概念结构在一个单向"处理"中（不同于"相互作用"）被"映射"到目标领域的概念结构中。这种单向"处理"可能改变并重组我们理解或思考后一部分（即目标领域）的方式。

对这种观点的独特应用就是识别一些遍及西方文化话语中的"基本的概念隐喻"，但这些隐喻是如此常见，使用得如此自然，大多数时候，我们不知不觉中就使用了这些隐喻。一些最常见的基本隐喻有：目的是终点；时光飞逝；时间是一个收获者；人生是段旅程；人生是出戏剧；人是草木。这些隐喻建立起一种跨概念映射，不仅出现在伟大的诗篇里，还出现在我们的日常用语中。例如，"人是草木"是一种认知映射，派生出这样一些日常表达，比如

"She's in the flower of youth," "She's a late bloomer," and "He's withering fast," no less than it does King Lear's "Ripeness is all." The difference between trivially conventional and innovatively poetic uses of a basic metaphor, by this analysis, is a difference not in cognitive kind, but in the range and diversity of application, and in the skill manifested in its verbal expression. And in all uses (including in the language of the sciences) cross-domain metaphors play an ineradicable part in determining what we know, how we reason, what values we assign, and the ways we conduct our lives.

Vigorous debates about metaphor continue apace. A plausible conclusion is that the diverse accounts of metaphor listed above need not be mutually exclusive, in that each is directed especially to a particular one of many kinds of metaphor or functions of metaphor, or focuses on a different moment in the process of recognizing and understanding a metaphor, or is adapted to the perspective of a preferred mode of philosophy.

Mark Johnson, ed., *Philosophical Perspectives on Metaphor* (1981), includes, among others, the writings on metaphor (mentioned above) by Richards, Black, Davidson, and Searle; Sheldon Sacks, ed., *On Metaphor* (1987), contains essays by both philosophers and literary critics; and Andrew Ortony, ed., *Metaphor and Thought* (2d ed., 1993), includes an essay by George Lakoff that summarizes the cognitive treatments of metaphor. On the cognitive view, see also George Lakoff and Mark Johnson, *Metaphors We Live By* (1980); and Mark Turner, *Death Is the Mother of Beauty* (1987). For earlier treatments of the pervasive cognitive function of metaphors, see Stephen C. Pepper, *World Hypotheses* (1942), on the "root metaphors" that generate the major philosophical worldviews; and M. H. Abrams, *The Mirror and the Lamp* (1953), on the diverse "constitutive metaphors" that provide the structure and categories of divergent theories of literature and the other arts. See also Paul Ricoeur, *The Rule of Metaphor* (1977), and for an influential essay on metaphor by a *deconstructive* theorist, Jacques Derrida, "White Mythology," in *Margins of Discourse* (1982).

metaphysical conceit: 59; *64*.

metaphysical poets: John Dryden said in his *Discourse Concerning Satire* (1693) that John Donne in his poetry "affects the metaphysics," meaning that Donne employs the terminology and abstruse arguments of the medieval Scholastic philosophers. In 1779 Samuel Johnson extended the term "metaphysical" from Donne to a school of poets, in the acute and balanced critique which he incorporated in his "Life of Cowley." The name is now applied to a group of seventeenth-century poets who, whether or not directly influenced by Donne, employ similar poetic procedures and imagery, both in secular poetry (Cleveland, Marvell, and Cowley) and in religious poetry (Herbert, Vaughan, Crashaw, and Traherne).

"她正处在花样的青春年华""她是朵迟开的花儿""他迅速枯萎",以及李尔王的"成熟就是一切"。通过这样的分析可以得知,基本隐喻在琐碎的日常言谈中的使用和它在诗歌中的创新性使用的不同之处不在于认知形式,而在于使用的范围和多样性,以及其文字表达所体现出的技巧上。在隐喻的所有使用(包括科学语言)中,跨领域隐喻在决定我们的所知、推理方式、价值观和生活方式上起着不可抹杀的作用。

现今有关隐喻的各种争论仍在飞速发展。一个合理的结论是,对隐喻的不同解释无须彼此排斥,因为每种解释都是专门针对许多种隐喻中特定的某一种隐喻而言,或者是针对隐喻的许多功能中特定的某一种功能而言,或者是关注认知和理解隐喻过程中不同的时刻,或者是为了适应某种偏好的哲学形式的观点。

马克·约翰逊主编的《有关隐喻的哲学观点》(1981),收录了(前面提及的)理查兹、布莱克、戴维森、塞尔等人有关隐喻的文章以及其他人的论述;谢尔登·萨克斯主编的《有关隐喻》(1987),包含了哲学家和文学批评家的文章;安德鲁·奥特尼主编的《惑喻与思维》(1993年第2版),收录了乔治·雷柯夫概述有关对隐喻的认知叙述的文章。有关认知观点,也可参阅:乔治·雷柯夫与马克·约翰逊合著的《我们赖以生存的隐喻》(1980);马克·特纳所著的《死是美之母》(1987)。有关对隐喻认知功能的早期分析,参阅:斯蒂芬·C.佩珀所著的《世界假说》(1942),该书论述了产生主要哲学世界观的"根源隐喻";M. H. 艾布拉姆斯所著的《镜与灯》(1953),本书论述了提供给文学和其他艺术各种不同理论的结构和分类的"构成隐喻"。同时也可参阅利科所著的《隐喻规则》(1977);以及解构主义理论家雅克·德里达有关隐喻的颇具影响的文章"白色的神话",收入《话语边界》(1982)。

metaphysical conceit:玄学派巧思妙喻 59;*64*。

Metaphysical Poets:玄学派诗人

约翰·德莱顿在《讽刺对话》(1693)里指出,约翰·多恩在他的诗歌作品中"爱用玄学",也就是说多恩喜欢采用中世纪经院哲学学者们的术语及其晦涩难解的论点。1779年,塞缪尔·约翰逊在"考利传"这篇尖锐而又力求平衡的批评论著里把源于多恩的"玄学"扩展到泛指一派诗人。现在,"玄学派诗人"就是指17世纪的一群诗人,无论是否直接受到多恩的影响,他们在非宗教诗歌(以克利夫兰、马韦尔、考利为代表)或宗教诗歌(以赫伯特、沃恩、克拉肖、特拉赫恩为首)中都采用了相似的诗歌创作手法及意象描写。

Attempts have been made to demonstrate that these poets had in common a philosophical worldview. The term "metaphysical," however, fits these very diverse writers only if it is used, as Johnson used it, to indicate a common poetic style, use of figurative language, and way of organizing the meditative process or the poetic argument. Donne set the metaphysical mode by writing poems which are sharply opposed to the rich mellifluousness and the idealized view of human nature and of sexual love which had constituted a central tradition in Elizabethan poetry, especially in Spenser and the writers of *Petrarchan sonnets*; Donne's poems are opposed also to the fluid, regular versification of Donne's contemporaries, the *Cavalier poets*. Instead, Donne wrote in a diction and meter modeled on the rough give-and-take of actual speech, and often organized his poems as an urgent or heated argument—with a reluctant mistress, or an intruding friend, or God, or death, or with himself. He employed a subtle and often deliberately outrageous logic; he was realistic, ironic, and sometimes cynical in his treatment of the complexity of human motives, especially in the sexual relationship; and whether playful or serious, and whether writing the poetry of love or of intense religious experience, he was above all "witty," making ingenious use of *paradox*, *pun*, and startling parallels in simile and metaphor (see *metaphysical conceit* and *wit*). The beginnings of four of Donne's poems will illustrate the shock tactic, the dramatic form of direct address, the rough idiom, and the rhythms of the living voice that are characteristic of his metaphysical style:

> Go and catch a falling star,
> Get with child a mandrake root ...
>
> For God's sake hold your tongue, and let me love.
>
> Busy old fool, unruly sun ...
>
> Batter my heart, three-personed God....

Some, not all, of Donne's poetic procedures have parallels in each of his contemporaries and successors whom literary historians usually group as metaphysical poets.

These poets have had admirers in every age, but beginning with the *Neoclassic Period* of the later seventeenth century, they were by most critics and readers regarded as interesting but perversely ingenious and obscure exponents of *false wit*, until a drastic revaluation after World War I elevated Donne, and to a lesser extent Herbert and Marvell, high in the hierarchy of English poets (see *canon of literature*). This reversal owed much to H. J. C. Grierson's Introduction to *Metaphysical Lyrics and Poems of the Seventeenth Century* (1912), was given strong impetus by T. S. Eliot's essays "The Metaphysical Poets" and "Andrew Marvell" (1921), and was continued by a great number of commentators, including F. R. Leavis in England and especially the American *New Critics*, who tended to elevate the metaphysical style into the model of their ideal poetry of irony, paradox, and "unified sensibility." (See *dissociation of sensibility*.)

一直有人试图证明玄学派诗人有着共同的哲学世界观。然而只有像约翰逊那样用"玄学的"这一字眼指代一种共同的诗歌风格、修辞语言的使用以及思想过程、或诗歌论点表现方式的组织,把这些特性互异的诗人统称为"玄学派"才会适当。流畅的文体、理想化的人性观和性爱观构成了伊丽莎白时代的主要诗歌创作传统,这些特征尤其体现在斯宾塞的作品和创作*彼特拉克式十四行诗*的那些作家的作品中;多恩通过创造这些与传统截然对立的作品创立了玄学派诗歌的模式。他的诗歌也与和他同时代*骑士诗人*作品流畅规范的诗律截然相反。在创作中,他效仿言来语去、不加修饰的日常实际谈话的措词与韵律,常常把作品组织成一种与不情愿的情人、强加于人的朋友、上帝、死亡或自己进行激烈争辩的形式。他使用的逻辑推理精细微妙,但也时常故意表现出肆无忌惮。多恩以现实的、讽刺的,有时则是玩世不恭的态度来表现人们动机的复杂性,尤其是在性关系方面;无论是以戏谑的还是严肃的笔触,无论是创作爱情诗还是表现强烈宗教体验的诗歌,多恩的"机智巧思"都无与伦比。他运用的*逆说*、双关机智巧妙,笔下的明喻、隐喻也是令人叫绝(参见:*玄学派巧思妙喻、机智*)。这里例举多恩四首诗的开头几句,它们体现了作者玄学派风格的特色:惊人的笔法、富于戏剧性的直接对白、粗犷的方言习语、逼真的言语节奏:

  去吧,跑去抓一颗流星,
  去叫何首乌肚子里也有喜……　　　　　　　　(卞之琳译)
  看上帝面上请住嘴,让我爱　　　　　　　　　(飞　白译)
  忙碌的老傻瓜,任性的太阳……　　　　　　　(汪剑钊译)
  粉碎我的心,三位一体的上帝　　　　　　　　(汪剑钊译)

一些(而非所有)与多恩同时代或后世的诗人,有着与多恩类似的诗歌创作过程,这些诗人通常被文学史学家归类为玄学派诗人。

  玄学派诗人在每个时代都有不少崇拜者,但从17世纪后期的*新古典主义时期*开始,他们开始被大多数批评家和读者视为饶有趣味但又晦涩怪异的*假机智*。直到第一次世界大战之后出现的一次爆炸性的重新评价,多恩才得以在英国诗人的行列中跃居高位,比赫伯特和马韦尔略胜一筹(参见:*文学经典*)。这一转折主要应归功于 H. J. C. 格里尔森对《17 世纪玄学派抒情诗与诗歌》(1912)的介绍及 T.S.艾略特的两篇文章"玄学派诗人"和"安德鲁·马韦尔"(1921)的巨大促进作用。包括英国的 F. R. 利维斯,尤其是美国的新批评家在内的一大批批评家都继承了对玄学派诗人的重新评估,他们极力要把玄学派的诗歌风格推崇为兼具讽刺、逆说、"感受化一"的完美诗歌典范。(参见:*思想与感受的分裂*。)

More recently, Donne has lost this exemplary status, but continues to occupy a firm position as a prominent poet in the English canon.

See F. R. Leavis, *Revaluation: Tradition and Development in English Poetry* (1936); Cleanth Brooks, *Modern Poetry and the Tradition* (1939); Rosemund Tuve, *Elizabethan and Metaphysical Imagery* (1947); J. E. Duncan, *The Revival of Metaphysical Poetry* (1959); Helen Gardner, ed., *John Donne: A Collection of Critical Essays* (1962). F. J. Warnke, *European Metaphysical Poetry* (1961), treats the Continental vogue of this style. For references to *metaphysical poets* in other entries, see page *420*.

meter: Meter is the recurrence, in regular units, of a prominent feature in the sequence of speech sounds of a language. There are four main types of meter in European languages: (1) In classical Greek and Latin, the meter was **quantitative**; that is, it was established by the relative duration of the utterance of a syllable, and consisted of recurrent patterns of long and short syllables. (2) In French and many other Romance languages, the meter is **syllabic**, depending on the number of syllables within a line of verse, without regard to the fall of the stresses. (3) In the older Germanic languages, including Old English, the meter is **accentual**, depending on the number of stressed syllables within a line, without regard to the number of intervening unstressed syllables. (4) The fourth type of meter, combining the features of the two preceding types, is **accentual-syllabic**, in which the metric units consist of a recurrent pattern of stresses on a recurrent number of syllables. The stress-and-syllable type has been the predominant meter of English poetry since the fourteenth century.

The study of the theory and practice of meter is called **metrics**. There is considerable dispute about the most valid or useful way to analyze and classify English meters. This entry will begin by presenting a traditional accentual-syllabic analysis which has the virtues of being simple, widely used, and applicable to by far the greater part of English poetry from Chaucer to the present. Major departures from this stress-and-syllable meter will be described in the latter part of the entry.

In all sustained spoken English we sense a **rhythm**; that is, a recognizable although varying pattern in the beat of the **stresses**, or **accents** (the more forcefully uttered, hence louder syllables) in the stream of speech sounds. In meter, this rhythm is structured into a recurrence of regular—that is, approximately equivalent—units of stress pattern. Compositions written in meter are also known as **verse**.

We attend, in reading verse, to the individual **line**, which is a sequence of words printed as a separate entity on the page. The meter is determined by the pattern of stronger and weaker stresses on the syllables composing the words in the verse line; the stronger is called the "stressed" syllable and all the weaker ones the "unstressed" syllables. (What the ear perceives as a strong stress is not an absolute quantity, but is relative to the degree of stress in the adjacent syllables.) Three major factors determine where the stresses (in the sense of the relatively stronger stresses or accents) will fall in a line of verse: (1) Most important is the "word accent" in words of more than one syllable;

近来，多恩已经失去了他的楷模地位，但他作为英语文学经典中的一名杰出诗人，仍然占有稳固的地位。

参阅：F. R. 利维斯所著的《再评价：英国诗歌的传统与发展》(1936)；克林斯·布鲁克斯所著的《现代诗歌与传统》(1939)；罗斯蒙德·图夫所著的《伊丽莎白时期与玄学派意象》(1947)；J. E. 邓肯所著的《玄学派诗歌的复兴》(1959)；海伦·加德纳主编的《约翰·多恩：批评文集》(1962)。F. J. 沃恩克所著的《欧洲玄学派诗歌》(1961)，论述了欧陆的玄学派诗歌时尚。其他条目中提及"玄学派诗人"的地方，参见第 420 页。

Meter：格律

格律就是一种语言里一系列语音中的主要特征以有规律的单元复现。欧洲语言中有四种主要格律：(1) 在古典希腊文和拉丁文中，格律依据**音长**划分；即它建立在一个音节发音的相对持续长度的基础上，由长短音节的复现形式组成。(2) 在法语和许多其他罗曼语中，格律按照**音节**划分，由一句诗行中的音节数目所决定，无需考虑重音。(3) 在更古老的日耳曼语言中，包括古英语，格律依**重音**所定，取决于一句诗行中重音音节的数目，不考虑中间插入的非重读音节数量。(4) 第四种格律，包含了前两种格律的特征，叫做**音强－音节**格律，即格律单元由复现音节数量中的重音复现形式组成。这种重音－音节格律自从 14 世纪以来一直是英语诗歌中的主要格律形式。

研究格律的理论及其运用叫**韵律学**。对于如何最准确有效地分析、划分英语格律，存在很大争议。本条目将从介绍传统的"重音－音节"分析法入手。这种方法简单明了，使用广泛，迄今为止适用于自乔叟以来的大部分英诗。本条目末尾部分将对与重音－音节格律分析法不同的其他主要分析法作出说明。

我们从所有持续的英语口语中都能感觉出**一种韵律**，即连续发音时形成的富于变化又可辨析的**重读**或**重音节拍**（发音越强，音节越重）。在格律中，这种节奏形成重音形式单元的规律性（即大约等量）的重复。依照格律写成的作品也叫**韵文**。

我们读诗时所注意的是书页上一连串分开印刷的词语，即单独的**诗行**。韵行的格律取决于构成韵行的词的音节的重读与弱读方式，其中较强的音节称为"重读"音节，所有较弱的音节称为"非重读"音节（我们听出的重音不是绝对的音量，而只是与相邻音节的音强程度相比较而言）。在一个韵行里，重音（指相对更强的重音）应该落到何处取决于三个主要因素：(1) 最重要的是多音节词中

in the noun "áccent" itself, for example, the stress falls on the first syllable. (2) There are also many monosyllabic words in the language, and on which of these—in a sentence or a phrase—the stress will fall depends on the grammatical function of the word (we normally put stronger stress on nouns, verbs, and adjectives, for example, than on articles or prepositions), and depends also on the "rhetorical accent," or the emphasis we give a word because we want to enhance its importance in a particular utterance. (3) Another determinant of perceived stress is the prevailing "metrical accent," which is the beat that we have come to expect, in accordance with the stress pattern that was established earlier in the metrical composition.

If the prevailing stress pattern enforces a drastic alteration of the normal word accent, we get a **wrenched accent**. Wrenching may be the result of a lack of metrical skill; it was, however, conventional in the *folk ballad* (for example, "fair ladíe," "far countrée"), and is sometimes deliberately used for comic effects, as in Lord Byron's *Don Juan* (1819–24) and in the verses of Ogden Nash.

It is possible to distinguish a number of degrees of syllabic stress in English speech, but the most common and generally useful fashion of analyzing and classifying the standard English meters is "binary." That is, we distinguish only two categories—strong stress and weak stress—and group the syllables into metric feet according to the patterning of these two degrees. A **foot** is the combination of a strong stress and the associated weak stress or stresses which make up the recurrent metric unit of a line. The relatively stronger-stressed syllable is called, for short, "stressed"; the relatively weaker-stressed syllables are called "light," or most commonly, "unstressed."

The four standard feet distinguished in English are:

1. **Iambic** (the noun is "iamb"): an unstressed syllable followed by a stressed syllable.

    Thĕ cúr | fĕw tólls | thĕ knéll | ŏf pár | tĭng dáy. |

    (Thomas Gray, "Elegy Written in a Country Churchyard")

2. **Anapestic** (the noun is "anapest"): two unstressed syllables followed by a stressed syllable.

    Thĕ Ăs sýr | ĭan cămĕ dówn | lĭke ă wólf | ŏn thĕ fóld. |

    (Lord Byron, "The Destruction of Sennacherib")

3. **Trochaic** (the noun is "trochee"): a stressed followed by an unstressed syllable.

    Thére thĕy | áre, mў | fíf tў | mén ănd | wó mĕn. |

    (Robert Browning, "One Word More")

    Most trochaic lines lack the final unstressed syllable—in the technical term, such lines, or any verse lines that lack the final syllable, are **catalectic**. So in Blake's "The Tiger":

的"重音布局",例如,"áccent"(重音)这个名词本身的重音落在第一个音节上;(2)语言里还有许多单音节词汇,它们所在句子或词组里的重音落于何处取决于该词的语法作用(例如,一般来说,名词、动词、形容词的发音要比冠词、介词重一些),同时还取决于"修辞重音"的需要或者是由于我们在特定话语中想要增强某个词的重要性而对它的强调。(3)第三个辨别重音的决定因素是与韵文里早已确立的重音形式相一致的主要的"格律重音",即我们所期待的诗歌节拍。

如果主要的重音形式迫使单词大大改变其正常的重音位置,那么就形成了**误加重音**。这往往是因韵律技法不佳所致;然而,这却是*民间歌谣*的惯用技法[例如:"fair ladíe"(美丽的女士)、"far countrée"(遥远的国度)],有时,诗人为了造成喜剧效果也会故意运用误加重音,例如拜伦的《唐·璜》和奥格登·纳什的诗歌作品。

对于英语言语里一些音节重读的程度是能够加以区别的,但分析、划分标准英语格律最常见、总体来说最有效的方法是"二分法"。即我们只区分"强重音"与"弱重音",同时按照这两级重音的划分形式将音节分组成音步。**音步**由组成诗行里重复的韵律单元的强重音和相连的弱读音组合而成。相对强重音节简称为"重读",相对弱读音节简称为"弱读",更常见的称法是"非重读"。

英语诗歌里的四种标准音步划分如下:

1. **抑扬格**(名词形式为"iamb"):一个弱读音节后跟一个重读音节,如:

   Thĕ cúr | fĕw tólls | thĕ knéll | ŏf pár | tĭng dáy. |

   (托马斯·格雷,《墓畔哀歌》)

2. **抑抑扬格**(名词形式为"anapest"):两个弱读音节后接一个重读音节,例如:

   Thĕ Ăs sýr | ĭăn cămĕ dówn | lĭkĕ ă wólf | ŏn thĕ fóld. |

   (拜伦,《塞纳切里布的毁灭》)

3. **扬抑格**(名词形式为"trochee"):一个重读音节后接一个弱读音节,如:

   Thére thĕy | áre, mў | fíf tў | mén ănd | wó mĕn. |

   (罗伯特·勃朗宁,《再进一言》)

多数扬抑格诗行缺少最后一个弱读音节,诗律术语将这样的诗行称为异体扬抑格。如布莱克的作品《虎》里面的例子:

> Tí gĕr! | tí gĕr! | búrn ĭng | bríght |
> Ín thĕ | fó rĕst | óf thĕ | níght. |

4. **Dactylic** (the noun is "dactyl"): a stressed syllable followed by two unstressed syllables.

> Éve, wĭth hĕr | bás kĕt, wăs |
> Déep ĭn thĕ | bélls ănd grăss. |

(Ralph Hodgson, "Eve")

Iambs and anapests, since the strong stress is at the end, are called "rising meter"; trochees and dactyls, with the strong stress at the beginning, are called "falling meter." Iambs and trochees, having two syllables, are called "duple meter"; anapests and dactyls, having three syllables, are called "triple meter." It should be noted that the iamb is by far the commonest English foot; some metric theorists treat other types of stress patterns as variants of the iamb. (For the development of the iambic line in English, see John Thompson, *The Founding of English Metre*, 1961.)

Two other feet are often distinguished by special names, although they occur in English meter only as occasional variants from standard feet:

Spondaic (the noun is "spondee"): two successive syllables with approximately equal strong stresses, as in each of the first two feet of this line:

> Góod stróng | thíck stú | pĕ fý | ĭng ín | cĕnse smóke. |

(Browning, "The Bishop Orders His Tomb")

Pyrrhic (the noun is also "pyrrhic"): a foot composed of two successive syllables with approximately equal light stresses, as in the second and fourth feet in this line:

> Mý wăy | ĭs tŏ | bĕ gín | wĭth thĕ | bĕ gín nĭng |

(Byron, *Don Juan*)

This latter term is used only infrequently. Some traditional metrists deny the existence of a true pyrrhic, on the grounds that the prevailing metrical accent—in the above instance, iambic—always imposes a slightly stronger stress on one of the two syllables.

A metric line is named according to the number of feet composing it:

monometer: one foot

dimeter: two feet

trimeter: three feet

tetrameter: four feet

pentameter: five feet

hexameter: six feet (an **Alexandrine** is a line of six iambic feet)

Tí gĕr! | tí gĕr! | búrn ĭng | bríght |
Ín thĕ | fó rĕst | óf thĕ | níght. |

4. **扬抑抑格**（名词形式为"dactyl"）：一个重读音节后接两个弱读音节，如：

Éve, wĭth hĕr | bás kĕt, wăs |
Déep ĭn thĕ | bélls ănd grăss. |

（拉尔夫·霍奇森，《伊夫》）

抑扬格和抑抑扬格由于重读在后，被称为"升韵"；扬抑格和扬抑抑格因重读在前，被称为"降韵"。抑扬格与扬抑格只有两个音节，故称"双拍韵"；抑抑扬格和扬抑抑格各有三个音节，故称"三拍韵"。应注意的是，抑扬格是迄今英语中最常见的音步；一些格律理论家把其他类型的重音模式视作抑扬格的变体。[关于英语中抑扬格诗行的发展，可以参阅：约翰·汤姆逊所著的《英语格律的确立》（1961）。]

另外两种音步通常由专门的名称加以区分，尽管在英文格律中它们只是作为标准音步的变体出现：

扬扬格（名词为"spondee"）：连续两个音节大体同样重读，例如以下诗行的前两个音步：

Góod stróng | thíck stú | pĕ fý | ĭng ín | cĕnse smóke. |

（勃朗宁，《圣普拉西德教堂的主教吩咐后事》）

抑抑格（名词也是"pyrrhic"）：一个音步由相连的两个大体同样弱读的音节组成，见以下诗行的第二、四音步：

Mý wăy | ĭs tŏ | bĕ gín | wĭth thĕ | bĕ gín nĭng |

（拜伦，《唐·璜》）

后一种音步只是偶尔使用。有些传统的韵律学家否认有真正的抑抑格存在，他们的根据是，在上述例子中主要的韵律重音形式，即抑扬格，总要在两个音节中间强选一个重读一些的音节。

韵行的名称依据其所含音步的数目而定：

单音步诗行：一个音步
二音步诗行：两个音步
三音步诗行：三个音步
四音步诗行：四个音步
五音步诗行：五个音步
六音步诗行：六个音步（**亚历山大体**为六步抑扬格韵行）

heptameter: seven feet (a **fourteener** is another term for a line of seven iambic feet—hence, of fourteen syllables; it tends to break into a unit of four feet followed by a unit of three feet)
octameter: eight feet

To describe the meter of a line we name (1) the predominant foot and (2) the number of feet it contains. In the illustrations above, for example, the line from Gray's "Elegy" is "iambic pentameter," and the line from Byron's "The Destruction of Sennacherib" is "anapestic tetrameter."

To **scan** a passage of verse is to go through it line by line, analyzing the component feet, and also indicating where any major pauses in the phrasing fall within a line. Here is a **scansion**, signified by conventional symbols, of the first five lines from John Keats' *Endymion* (1818). The passage was chosen because it exemplifies a flexible and variable rather than a highly regular metrical pattern.

1. Ă thíng | ŏf béau | tў ís | ă jóy | fŏr é vĕr: |
2. Ĭts lóve | lĭ nĕss | ĭn créas | ĕs; // ít | wĭll név ĕr |
3. Páss ĭn | tŏ nóth | ĭng nĕss, | // bŭt stíll | wĭll kéep |
4. Ă bów | ĕr quí | ĕt fŏr | ŭs, // ánd | ă sléep |
5. Fúll ŏf | swĕet dréams, | ănd héalth, | ănd quí | ĕt bréath ĭng. |

The prevailing meter is iambic pentameter. As in all fluent verse, however, there are many variations upon the basic iambic foot; these are sometimes called "substitutions." Thus:

1. The closing feet of lines 1, 2, and 5 end with an extra unstressed syllable, and are said to have a **feminine ending**. In lines 3 and 4, the closing feet, because they are standard iambs, end with a stressed syllable and are said to have **masculine endings**.
2. In lines 3 and 5, the opening iambic feet have been "inverted" to form trochees. (This initial position is the most common place for inversions in iambic verse.)
3. I have marked the second foot in line 2, and the third foot of line 3 and line 4, as pyrrhics (two unstressed syllables); these help to give Keats' verses their rapid movement. This is a procedure in scansion about which metric analysts disagree: some will feel enough of a metric beat to mark all these feet as iambs; others will mark still other feet (for example, the third foot of line 1) as pyrrhics also. And some metrists prefer to use symbols measuring two degrees of strong stress, and will indicate a difference in the feet, as follows:

Ĭts lőve | lĭ néss | ĭn crĕ́ás | ĕs.

Notice, however, that these are differences only in nuance; analysts agree that the prevailing pulse of Keats' versification is iambic throughout, and

七音步诗行：七个音步（**十四音节诗**是七步抑扬格诗行的另一种名称——顾名思义，它包括14个音节；常分为前四步与紧接着的后三步）

八音步诗行：八个音步

要描述一行诗的格律，我们要说明：(1) 诗行内的主导音步和 (2) 它所包括音步的数目。例如，在上述例子中，格雷《墓畔哀歌》里的那行诗就是"五步抑扬格"，拜伦《塞纳切里布的毁灭》里的那行诗则是"四步抑抑扬格"。

给一段诗歌**标示格律**就是要逐行分析音步构成，同时注明韵行内的主要停顿点。以下是采用传统符号为约翰·济慈的《恩底弥翁》(1818) 前五行诗所作的**格律标示**。由于这段诗文代表了一种格律形式的灵活多变而不属于格律非常整齐的诗文，所以选为示例：

1. Ă thíng | ŏf béau | ty ís | a jóy | fŏr é vĕr: |
2. Its lóve | lĭ nĕss | ĭn créas | ĕs; //ít | wĭll név ĕr |
3. páss ĭn | tŏ nóth | ĭng nĕss, | // bŭt stíll | wĭll kéep |
4. Ă bów | ĕr quí | ĕt fŏr | ŭs, //ánd | ă sléep |
5. Fúll ŏf | swĕet dréams, | ănd héalth, | ănd quí | ĕt bréath ĭng. |

这五行诗的主导格律是五步抑扬格。然而，与所有流畅的诗文一样，它们的格律在抑扬格的基础上也有许多变换；有时称这种现象为"替代"，例如：

1. 其中第1、2、5行，以行尾附加的一个弱读音节结束，通常称其为**弱音尾**。而第3、4两行的行尾音步是标准的抑扬格，以重读音节结尾，因而称其为**强音尾**。
2. 第3、5两行每行开头的抑扬格音步被"转换"成扬抑格（抑扬格韵文里，韵行的开头位置最常出现这种变换）。
3. 我将第2行的第二个音步、第3及第4两行每行的第三个音步标示成抑抑格（两个弱读音节）；这样可以加快济慈诗句的推进速度。格律分析者对这种格律标示方法常常会有异议，有人还会觉得诗行里的格律节拍足以把它们标为抑扬格，而另一些人则还可能把别的音步（如第1行里的第三音步）也划归为抑抑格。有些诗律分析家喜欢使用两级重音符号，对于音步的不同作如下标示：

Ĭts lŏve | lĭ néss | ĭn créas | ĕs.

然而，应该看到这些不同只是极其细微的；分析者们一致认为济慈诗律的主要节拍始终是抑扬格；尽管有许多变化，韵行中所能感受

that despite many variations, the felt norm is of five stresses in the verse line.

Two other elements are important in the metric movement of Keats' passage: (1) In lines 1 and 5, the pause in the reading—which occurs naturally at the end of a sentence, clause, or other syntactic unit—coincides with the end of the line; such lines are called **end-stopped**. Lines 2 through 4, on the other hand, are called **run-on lines** (or in a term derived from the French, they exhibit **enjambment**—"a striding-over"), because the pressure of the incompleted syntactic unit toward closure carries on over the end of the verse line. (2) When a strong phrasal pause falls within a line, as in lines 2, 3, and 4, it is called a **caesura**—indicated in the quoted passage by the conventional symbol //. The management of these internal pauses is important for giving variety and for providing expressive emphases in the long pentameter line.

To understand the use and limitations of an analysis such as this, we must realize that a prevailing metric pattern (iambic pentameter, in the passage from Keats) establishes itself as a perceived norm which controls the reader's expectations, even though the number of lines that deviate from the norm may exceed the number that fit the norm exactly. In addition, scansion is an abstract scheme which deliberately omits notation of many aspects of the actual reading of a poem that contribute importantly to its pace, rhythm, and total impression. It does not specify, for example, whether the component words in a metric line are short words or long words, or whether the strong stresses fall on short vowels or long vowels; it does not give any indication of the *intonation*—the overall rise and fall in the pitch and loudness of the voice, and the rhetorical emphases—which we use to bring out the meaning and effect of these poetic lines. It also does not indicate the interplay of the metric stresses with the **phrasal rhythms**—the anticipation, suspension, and closure of the syntactic and semantic phrases—within a sustained verse passage. Such details are omitted in order to lay bare the essential metric skeleton; that is, the pattern of the stronger and weaker stresses in the syllabic sequence of a verse line. Moreover, an actual reading of a poem, if it is a skillful reading, will not accord mechanically with the scansion. There is a marked difference between the scansion, as an abstract metrical norm, and a skilled and expressive oral reading, or **performance**, of a poem; and no two competent readers will perform the same lines in precisely the same way. But in a performance, the metric norm indicated by the scansion is sensed as an implicit understructure of pulses; in fact, the interplay of an expressive performance, with its intonational and phrasal patterns operating sometimes with and sometimes against this underlying metric pulse, gives tension and vitality to our experience of verse.

We need to note, finally, that some kinds of versification which occur in English poetry differ from the syllable-and-stress type already described:

1. **Strong-stress meters** or **accentual verse**. In this meter, native to English and other Germanic languages, only the beat of the strong stresses counts in the scanning, while the number of intervening light syllables is

到的规范还是五个重音。

济慈这段诗的格律变化里还有另外两个重要因素：(1) 第 1 行与第 5 行里，句子、分句或其他句法单位结尾自然形成的朗读停顿刚好出现在韵行的结尾，这类韵行被称为**行尾停顿式**。而第 2 到第 4 行里，因为句法结构到行尾处尚不完整而不得不延续到下一诗行结尾处，所以被称为**跨行连句式诗行**（或用源于法文中的一个术语来说，它们表现出**跨行连续**）。(2) 当较强的片语停顿出现在一句诗行中间时，如示例中的第 2、3、4 行，这种情况叫做**行间停顿**，在示例中以惯用的符号"//"表明。运用这种行内停顿对于丰富韵文的格律变化并加强长五音步诗行的语气强调十分重要。

为了理解这种格律标示分析法的作用和局限，我们必须认识到，即使背离了规范的诗行数量可能超过完全符合规范的诗行数量，一种主导格律形式（如济慈诗段中的抑扬格五音步）是作为一种可被感知的规范而存在的，它主导了读者的期望。此外，格律标示是一种抽象系统，它有意省略了实际诗歌朗读中对如何掌握节奏、韵律的起伏变化和整体印象十分重要的许多方面的标示符号。比如，它没有具体说明组成韵行的词是长是短，重读音应该落到短元音上还是长元音上；对于我们用来赋予这些诗行含义和修辞效果的**语调**，即整体语音的高低起伏与音强和修辞强调，标示中也未做任何说明；此外，连续的诗段中格律重音与不同片语、分句结构中韵律的相互作用也未标明。它也没有表明在一个持续的诗段中诗体重音与**短语韵律**（句法及语义短语的预期、悬浮和闭合）的相互影响。省略这些细节的目的在于突出基本的格律轮廓，即诗行音节序列里强弱重音的形式。此外，在实际的诗歌朗读中，有技巧的朗读并非机械地与这类格律标示保持一致。作为抽象的格律规范的格律标示与富于技巧、充满表现力的实际诗歌口头吟诵或**表现**之间存在着差别；两个有能力的读者也不可能以完全一致的方法表现同样的诗句。但在诗歌朗诵中，格律标示表明的格律规范被理解为暗含的格律节奏的基础；事实上，饱含感情的吟诵及其操控的语调模式和片语模式，有时符合、有时则违背了这种暗含的格律节奏，但都给我们的诗歌体验带来了张力和生机。

最后我们还应注意到，英诗中的几种诗律形式不同于已经描述过的"音节－重音"形式：

1. 重音体格律或**强音诗歌**。在这种英语和其他日耳曼语的本土格律中，格律标示只表明强重音的节拍，其间的弱读音节的数目则变化

highly variable. Usually there are four strong-stressed syllables in a line, whose beat is emphasized by *alliteration*. This was the meter of Old English poetry and continued to be the meter of many Middle English poems, until Chaucer and others popularized the syllable-and-stress meter. In the opening passage, for example, of *Piers Plowman* (later fourteenth century) the four strong stresses (always divided by a medial caesura) are for the most part reinforced by alliteration (see *alliterative meter*); the light syllables, which vary in number, are recessive and do not assert their individual presence:

> In a sómer séson, // whan sóft was the sónne,
> I shópe me in shróudes, // as Í a shépe were,
> In hábits like an héremite, // unhóly of wórkes,
> Went wýde in this wórld, // wónders to hére.

Strong-stress meter survives in some *folk* poetry and in traditional children's rhymes such as "Hickory, dickory, dock." It was revived as an artful literary meter by Samuel Taylor Coleridge in *Christabel* (1816), in which each line has four strong stresses but the number of syllables within a line varies from four to twelve. Strong-stress meter, with four stresses to a line, is also the basic metric structure in the modern types of performance poetry called *rap*.

What G. M. Hopkins in the later nineteenth century called his **sprung rhythm** is a variant of strong-stress meter: each foot, as he describes it, begins with a stressed syllable, which may either stand alone or be associated with from one to three (occasionally even more) light syllables. Two six-stress lines from Hopkins' "The Wreck of the *Deutschland*" indicate the variety of the rhythms in this meter, and also exemplify its most striking feature: the great weight of the strong stresses, and the frequent juxtaposition of strong stresses (*spondees*) at any point in the line. The stresses in the second line were marked in a manuscript by Hopkins himself; they indicate that in complex instances, his metric decisions may seem arbitrary:

> The | sóur | scythe | crínge, and the | bléar | sháre | cóme. |
> Our | héarts' chárity's | héarth's | fire, our | thóughts' chivalry's | thróng's | Lórd. |

(See Marcella M. Holloway, *The Prosodic Theory of Gerard Manley Hopkins*, 1947.) A number of modern metrists, including T. S. Eliot and Ezra Pound, skillfully interweave both strong-stress and syllable-and-stress meters in some of their versification.

2. *Quantitative meters* in English are written in imitation of classical Greek and Latin versification, in which the metrical pattern is not determined by the stress but by the "quantity" (duration of pronunciation) of a syllable, and the foot consists of a combination of "long" and "short" syllables. Sir Philip Sidney, Edmund Spenser, Thomas Campion, and

多端。每行诗一般包括四个强重音音节，其节拍通过头韵来强调。在乔叟和其他诗人推广音节-重音体格律以前，这是古英诗及后来许多中世纪英诗的格律。例如《农夫皮尔斯》（14世纪后期的诗歌）的开始部分里，每行的四个强重音（总是由中间节律的行间停顿断开）大多通过头韵来强化（参见：*头韵格律*）；而数目不等的弱读音节则更不明显，并不独立存在。示例如下：

> In a sómer séson, // whan sóft was the sónne,
> I shópe me in shróudes, // as Í a shépe were,
> In hábits like an héremite, // unhóly of wórkes,
> Went wýde in this wórld, //wónders to hére.

至今民间诗歌和传统的儿歌里还保存着这种强重音格律形式，如《滴答，滴答，钟声响》。塞缪尔·泰勒·柯勒律治曾把它作为一种文学格律技巧用到诗歌《克利斯托贝尔》（1816）的创作里。这首诗每行包括四个强重音，但每行的音节从四到十二数量不等。重音体格律，一行四个重音，也是表演诗歌的现代类型说唱最基本的格律结构。

  G. M. 霍普金斯在19世纪晚期称他的**弹性节奏**是强重音格律的一种变体：正如他所描述的那样，其中每个音步都是由一个重读音节开头，该重音节或独立存在或是伴有一至三个（偶尔更多的）弱读音节。霍普金斯《德意志号的沉没》中的两句六次重音诗行，就说明了这种格律节奏的多样性，也代表了其最显著的特征：强重音的压倒优势和强重音（*扬扬格*）在韵行内任意处的频繁并列。下面第二行的重音标示出自霍普金斯本人的手稿，说明在复杂的情况下，他对格律的决定看上去也可能是相当武断的：

> The | sóur | scythe | crínge, and the | bléar | sháre | cóme. |
>   Our | héarts' chárity's | héarth's | fíre, our | thóughts' chivalry's | thróng's | Lórd. |

[参阅：马塞拉·M. 霍洛韦所著的《霍普金斯诗法理论》（1947）。] 一些现代诗律学家，其中包括 T. S. 艾略特和埃兹拉·庞德，在他们的一些诗律作品中把"强重音"和"音节-重音"格律巧妙地结合成一体。

2. **音长格律**：英诗的这种格律体式是对古希腊罗马古典诗律的模仿，它的韵律形式不取决于重音而在于音节的"音长"（即发音的持续时间），音步由"长"音节和"短"音节合成。菲利普·锡德尼爵士、埃德蒙·斯宾塞、托马斯·坎皮恩和其他一些伊丽莎白时期的

other Elizabethan poets experimented with this meter in English, as did Coleridge, Tennyson, Henry Wadsworth Longfellow, and Robert Bridges later on. The strong accentual character of English, however, as well as the indeterminateness of the duration of a syllable in the English language, makes it impossible to sustain a quantitative meter for any length. See Derek Attridge, *Well-Weighted Syllables: Elizabethan Verse in Classical Meters* (1974).
3. In *free verse* (discussed in a separate entry), the component lines have no (or only occasional) metric feet, or uniform stress patterns.

George Saintsbury, *Historical Manual of English Prosody* (1910), is a well-illustrated treatment of traditional syllable-and-stress metrics. For later discussions of this and alternative metric theories see Seymour Chatman, *A Theory of Meter* (1965); and W. K. Wimsatt and Monroe C. Beardsley, "The Concept of Meter" (1959). This last essay is reprinted in W. K. Wimsatt, *Hateful Contraries* (1965), and in Harvey Gross, ed., *The Structure of Verse* (1966)—an anthology that reprints other useful essays, including Northrop Frye, "The Rhythm of Recurrence," and Yvor Winters, "The Audible Reading of Poetry." See also W. K. Wimsatt, ed., *Versification: Major Language Types* (1972); Paul Fussell, *Poetic Meter and Poetic Form* (rev. 1979); John Hollander, *Rhyme's Reason: A Guide to English Verse* (1981); T. V. F. Brogan, *English Versification, 1570–1980* (1981); Robert Pinsky, *The Sounds of Poetry: A Brief Guide* (1998); Amittai Aviram, *Telling Rhythm: Body and Meaning in Poetry* (1994); Derek Attridge, *Poetic Rhythm: An Introduction* (1995); Thomas Carper and Derek Attridge, *Meter and Meaning: An Introduction to Rhythm in Poetry* (2003). For responses by contemporary poets to David Baker's contention that there are only iambic feet in English, see David Baker, ed., *Meter in English: A Critical Engagement* (1996). For references to *meter* in other entries, see page 140. See also *alliterative meter; blank verse; doggerel; free verse*.

metonymy (mĕtŏn′ ĭmē): **132**.

metrical romance: 49.

middle (of a plot): **296**.

Middle English: 280.

Middle English period: 280.

middle style: 384.

miles gloriosus (mē′ lās glŏrēō′ sŭs): **379**.

mime (mīm): **266**.

诗人，以及后世诗人柯勒律治、丁尼生、亨利·华兹沃斯·朗费罗、罗伯特·布里奇斯等，都尝试过英文中的这种音长格律。但是由于英语的强重音特点和音节长短的不定性，英诗里很难维持纯正的音长格律。参阅：德里克·阿特瑞治所著的《加权音节：伊丽莎白时期的古典格律诗歌》(1974)。

3. *自由诗*（前面已讨论过）的诗行里不存在（或只是偶尔出现）韵脚，或一致的重音形式。

乔治·塞恩斯伯里所著的《英文韵律学历史手册》(1910)对传统的音节-音强体格律作了充分论述。后来对音节-音强体及其他不同格律理论的讨论参阅：西摩尔·查特曼所著的《格律理论》(1965)；W. K. 维姆萨特与门罗·C. 比尔兹利合写的文章"格律概念"(1959)。"格律概念"一文重印于 W. K. 维姆萨特的《恶意的对立》(1965)并被收入哈维·格罗斯主编的《韵文结构》(1966)，这本选集还重印了其他一些比较有用的文章，包括诺斯罗普·弗莱所写的"复现的节奏"与伊弗·温特斯所写的"听得见的诗歌阅读"。也可参阅：W. K. 维姆萨特主编的《诗律：主要语言类型》(1972)；保罗·福塞尔所著的《诗律与诗歌形式》(1979年修订版)；约翰·霍兰德所著的《押韵的理由：英诗指南》(1981)；T. V. F. 布罗根所著的《1570—1980年间英语诗律》(1981)；罗伯特·平斯基所著的《诗歌的声音：一个简要的指南》(1998)；阿米泰·阿维拉姆所著的《谈谈押韵：诗歌的形体与意义》(1994)；德里克·阿特里奇所著的《诗歌押韵入门》(1995)；托马斯·卡珀与德里克·阿特里奇合著的《格律与意义：诗歌押韵入门》(2003)。关于当代诗人对戴维·贝克认为英语中只有抑扬格音步这一看法的回应，参阅：戴维·贝克主编的《英语中的格律：一种批评式参与》(1996)。其他条目中提及"格律"的地方，参见第 140 页。也可参见：*头韵格律、无韵诗、打油诗、自由诗*。

metonymy：借喻　132。

metrical romance：格律传奇　49。

middle (of a plot)：(情节中的) 中部　296。

Middle English：中古英语　280。

Middle English period：中古英语时期　280。

middle style：平庸文体　384。

miles gloriosus：满口大话的士兵　379。

mime：摹仿　266。

mimesis (mĭmē′ sĭs): **171**.

mimetic criticism (mĭmĕt′ ĭk): **69**; *382*.

miracle plays, morality plays, and interludes: These are all types of late-medieval drama, written in a variety of verse forms.

The **miracle play** had as its subject either a story from the Bible, or else the life and martyrdom of a saint. In the usage of some historians, however, "miracle play" denotes only dramas based on saints' lives, and the term **mystery play** is applied to dramas based on the Bible. "Mystery" is used in the archaic sense (probably derived from the Latin *ministerium*, "work," "occupation") of the "trade" conducted by each of the medieval guilds which sponsored these plays.

The plays representing biblical narratives originated within the church in about the tenth century, in dramatizations of brief parts of the Latin liturgical service, called **tropes**, especially the "Quem quaeritis" ("Whom are you seeking") trope portraying the visit of the three Marys to the tomb of Christ. Gradually these evolved into complete plays which were written in English instead of in Latin, produced under the auspices of the various trade guilds, and acted on stages set outside the church. The miracle plays written in England are of unknown authorship. In the fourteenth century there developed in cities such as York and Chester the practice, on the feast of Corpus Christi (sixty days after Easter), of putting on great "cycles" of such plays, representing crucial events in the biblical history of mankind from the Creation and Fall of man, through the Nativity, Crucifixion, and Resurrection of Christ, to the Last Judgment. The precise way that the plays were staged is a matter of scholarly debate, but it is widely agreed that each scene was played on a separate "pageant wagon" which was drawn, in sequence, to one after another fixed station in a city, at each of which some parts of the cycle were enacted. The biblical texts were greatly expanded in these plays, and the unknown authors added scenes, comic as well as serious, of their own invention. For examples of the variety, vitality, and power of these dramas, see the Wakefield "Noah" and "Second Shepherd's Play," and the Brome "Abraham and Isaac."

Morality plays were dramatized *allegories* of a representative Christian life in the plot form of a quest for salvation, in which the crucial events are temptations, sinning, and the climactic confrontation with death. The usual protagonist represents Mankind, or Everyman; among the other characters are personifications of virtues, vices, and Death, as well as angels and demons who contest for the prize of the soul of Mankind. A character known as the **Vice** often played the role of the tempter in a fashion both sinister and comic; he is regarded by some literary historians as a precursor both of the cynical, ironic villain and of some of the comic figures in Elizabethan drama, including Shakespeare's Falstaff. The best-known morality play is the fifteenth-century *Everyman*, which is still given an occasional performance; other notable examples, written in the same century, are *The Castle of Perseverance* and *Mankind*.

mimesis：摹仿　　171。

mimetic criticism：摹仿式文学批评　　69；*382*。

Miracle Plays, Morality Plays, and Interludes：奇迹剧、道德剧和插剧

奇迹剧、道德剧和插剧是中世纪后期用不同的韵文体形式写成的戏剧模式。

奇迹剧的主题取材于圣经故事，或圣徒的生活和殉教的事迹。某些历史学家将"奇迹剧"仅仅用来表示那些以圣徒生活为题材的戏剧，而将术语**神秘剧**用来表示那些以圣经为题材的戏剧。"神秘"的古意（可能源于拉丁文 ministerium，"工作""职业"）指的是资助这些戏剧的各个中世纪同业工会进行的"贸易"。

这种表现圣经故事的戏剧大约 10 世纪时起源于教堂，戏剧化地表现罗马天主教堂礼拜仪式上的主要部分，被称为**圣歌对白**，尤其是一种叫做"复活问答"（"你们在寻觅谁"）的圣歌对白描述了三位玛丽拜访耶稣坟墓的故事。这些戏剧逐渐发展成为用英语而非拉丁文写成的完整戏剧，它们由不同的贸易同业公会赞助制作，在教堂外的戏台上公演。在英国，奇迹剧的作者身份不为人知。到 14 世纪时，在约克和切斯特等城市兴起了这样一种活动：在圣体节（复活节后六十天）演出大"套"这种奇迹剧，表演从上帝创世到人的堕落、耶稣诞生、蒙难、复活，直至最后的审判等圣经中记载的人类历史上的重要事件。关于这些剧目演出的确切方式是专家学者们讨论的问题，但大部分人都认为每一个场景都是在单独的"活动露天舞台车"上表演。舞台车按照恰当的顺序用马匹拉到市镇上一个又一个固定的"站"。在每一站上演整套奇迹剧中的某些部分。在这些奇迹剧里，圣经主题得到极大发挥，不知名的剧作者还在其中加入自己创造的喜剧或严肃情节。关于奇迹剧的各种形式、活力和影响力的范例，参阅：威克菲尔德所著的《挪亚》《牧人剧之二》和布罗姆所著的《亚伯拉罕和以撒》。

道德剧是表现基督教生活的种种戏剧化寓言，其情节形式是对拯救的探索，其中的主要事件包括人受诱惑、犯下罪孽和与死亡对抗。一般来说，剧中主人公象征人类，或任何一个普通人。其他角色有天使和恶魔，围绕着对占有人的灵魂展开争夺；也有拟人化的德行、恶习和死亡。被称为**丑角**的人物往往以邪恶可笑的诱惑者的面目出现；一些文学史学家认为这一人物是伊丽莎白时期戏剧中愤世嫉俗、冷嘲热讽的反派角色和包括莎士比亚笔下的福斯塔夫在内的滑稽人物的前身。最著名的道德剧是 15 世纪的《每人》，这一剧目至今仍在不时上演。写于同一世纪的其他著名道德剧有《坚固的城堡》和《人类》。

Interlude (Latin, "between the play") is a term applied to a variety of short stage entertainments, such as secular *farces* and witty dialogues with a religious or political point. In the late fifteenth and early sixteenth centuries, these little dramas were performed by bands of professional actors; it is believed that they were often put on between the courses of a feast or between the acts of a longer play. Among the better-known interludes are John Heywood's farces of the first half of the sixteenth century, especially *The Four PP* (that is, the Palmer, the Pardoner, the 'Pothecary, and the Peddler, who engage in a lying contest), and *Johan Johan the Husband, Tyb His Wife, and Sir John the Priest*.

Until the middle of the twentieth century, concern with medieval drama was scholarly rather than critical. Since that time a number of studies have dealt with the relationships of the texts to the religious and secular culture of medieval Europe, and have stressed the artistic excellence and power of the plays themselves. See Karl Young, *The Drama of the Medieval Church* (2 vols., 1933); Arnold Williams, *The Drama of Medieval England* (1961); T. W. Craik, *The Tudor Interlude* (1962); David M. Bevington, *From Mankind to Marlowe* (1962); V. A. Kolve, *The Play Called Corpus Christi* (1966); Rosemary Woolf, *The English Mystery Plays* (1972); Jerome Taylor and Alar Nelson, eds., *Medieval English Drama: Essays Critical and Contextual* (1972); Robert Potter, *The English Morality Play* (1975). For references to *miracle play* in other entries, see pages *409, 411*.

mirror stage: 324.

mise en scène (mē' zän sěn'): **364**.

mixed metaphor: 131.

mock epic: 38.

mock heroic: 38; *26, 39*.

Modern Period: 285.

modernism and postmodernism: The term **modernism** is widely used to identify new and distinctive features in the subjects, forms, concepts, and styles of literature and the other arts in the early decades of the twentieth century, but especially after World War I (1914–18). The specific features signified by "modernism" (or by the adjective **modernist**) vary with the user, but many critics agree that it involves a deliberate and radical break with some of the traditional bases not only of Western art, but of Western culture in general. Important intellectual precursors of modernism, in this sense, are thinkers who had questioned the certainties that had supported traditional modes of social organization, religion, and morality, and also traditional ways of conceiving the human self—thinkers such as Friedrich Nietzsche (1844–1900), Karl

插剧（拉丁文，意思是"剧之间"）一词用来指代各种简短的舞台娱乐活动，包括世俗*闹剧*和带有宗教色彩或政治见解的机智对白。15 世纪后期和 16 世纪早期，这些小型戏剧由职业演员剧团演出。据信，这些短剧时常穿插在宴席的上菜之间，或在较长戏剧的各幕之间演出。较著名的插剧有 16 世纪上半叶约翰·海伍德的闹剧，尤其是《四 PP》[即托钵僧（Palmer）、赦罪僧（Pardoner）、药剂师（Pothecary）和小贩（Peddler），他们卷入了一场说谎竞赛] 和《约翰、他的妻子蒂卜和牧师约翰爵士》。

到 20 世纪中期为止，对中世纪戏剧的关注多来自学者而非评论家。自那时起，一些研究开始着眼于中世纪欧洲戏剧文本与当时欧洲宗教和非宗教文化间的关系，并强调了这些戏剧的艺术成就和影响力。参阅：卡尔·扬所著的两卷本《中世纪教堂剧》(1933)；阿诺德·威廉斯所著的《中世纪英国戏剧》(1961)；T. W. 克雷克所著的《都铎王朝时期的插剧》(1962)；戴维·M. 贝文顿所著的《从〈人类〉到马洛》(1962)；V. A. 科尔夫所著的《基督圣体节戏剧》(1966)；罗斯玛丽·伍尔夫所著的《英国神秘剧》(1972)；杰尔姆·泰勒与阿拉·纳尔逊合编的《中世纪英国戏剧：批评及背景论文集》(1972)；罗伯特·波特所著的《英国道德剧》(1975)。其他条目中提及"奇迹剧"的地方，参见第 409、411 页。

mirror stage：镜子阶段 / 镜像阶段　324。

mise en scène：放置在舞台上　364。

mixed metaphor：并合隐喻　131。

mock epic：模拟史诗　38。

mock heroic：仿英雄体诗　38；26，39。

Modern Period：现代时期　285。

Modernism and Postmodernism：现代主义和后现代主义

现代主义这个术语被广泛用于表示在 20 世纪初期几十年，尤其是第一次世界大战（1914—1918）后，具有新颖独特的主题、形式、理念、风格的文学和其他艺术作品。对"现代主义"（或其形容词形式：**现代主义的**）特征的定义因使用者不同而不尽相同；但许多批评家都认为，现代主义不但有意识地与一些西方文化艺术的传统基础彻底决裂，还与整个西方文化彻底决裂。从这种意义上看，现代主义的重要文化先驱是对支撑社会结构的传统模式、宗教、道德和理解人类自身的传统方式的确定性提出质疑的思想家。这些思想家包括：弗里德里希·尼采（1844—1900）、

Marx, Sigmund Freud, and James G. Frazer, whose twelve-volume *The Golden Bough* (1890–1915) stressed the correspondence between central Christian tenets and pagan, often barbaric, myths and rituals.

Some literary historians locate the beginning of the modernist revolt as far back as the 1890s, but most agree that what is called **high modernism**, marked by an unexampled scope and rapidity of change, came after the First World War. The year 1922 alone was signalized by the appearance of such monuments of modernist innovation as James Joyce's *Ulysses*, T. S. Eliot's *The Waste Land*, and Virginia Woolf's *Jacob's Room*, as well as many other experimental works of literature. The catastrophe of the war had shaken faith in the moral basis, coherence, and durability of Western civilization and raised doubts about the adequacy of traditional literary modes to represent the harsh and dissonant realities of the postwar world.

T. S. Eliot wrote in a review of Joyce's *Ulysses* in 1923 that the inherited mode of ordering a literary work, which assumed a relatively coherent and stable social order, could not accord with "the immense panorama of futility and anarchy which is contemporary history." Like Joyce and like Ezra Pound in his *Cantos*, Eliot experimented with new forms and a new style that would render contemporary disorder, often contrasting it to a lost order and integration that, he claimed, had been based on the religion and myths of the cultural past. In *The Waste Land* (1922), for example, Eliot replaced the standard syntactic flow of poetic language by fragmented utterances, and substituted for the traditional type of coherent poetic structure a deliberate dislocation of parts, in which very diverse components are related by connections that are left to the reader to discover, or invent. Major works of modernist fiction, following Joyce's *Ulysses* and his even more radical *Finnegans Wake* (1939), subvert the basic conventions of earlier prose fiction by breaking up the narrative continuity, departing from the standard ways of representing characters, and violating the traditional syntax and coherence of narrative language by the use of *stream of consciousness* and other innovative modes of narration. Gertrude Stein—often linked with Joyce, Pound, Eliot, and Woolf as a trail-blazing modernist—experimented with **automatic writing** (writing that has been freed from control by the conscious, purposive mind) and other modes of language that achieved their effects by violating the norms of standard English syntax and sentence structure. Among other European and American writers who are central representatives of modernism are the novelists Marcel Proust, Thomas Mann, André Gide, Franz Kafka, Dorothy Richardson, and William Faulkner; the poets Stéphane Mallarmé, William Butler Yeats, Rainer Maria Rilke, Marianne Moore, William Carlos Williams, and Wallace Stevens; and the dramatists August Strindberg, Luigi Pirandello, Eugene O'Neill, and Bertolt Brecht. Their new forms of literary construction and rendering had obvious parallels in the break away from representational conventions in the artistic movements of *expressionism* and *surrealism*, in the modernist paintings and sculpture of Cubism, Futurism, and Abstract Expressionism, and in the violations of standard conventions of melody, harmony, and rhythm by the modernist musical composers Stravinsky, Schoenberg, and their radical followers.

卡尔·马克思、西格蒙德·弗洛伊德、詹姆斯·G.弗雷泽。弗雷泽十二卷的《金枝》(1890—1915)，着重论述基督教的主要教义与异教（通常是未开化民族）的神话和仪典之间的相互对应关系。

一些文学史学家将现代主义反叛的开始时间追溯到1890年代，但他们中的大多数都认为，以空前的广泛性和快速变化为标志的**现代主义高潮时期**始于第一次世界大战后。仅1922年一年就出现了现代主义创新文学的几座丰碑，如詹姆斯·乔伊斯的《尤利西斯》、T. S.艾略特的《荒原》、弗吉尼亚·吴尔夫的《雅各布的房间》及许多其他文学实验作品。第一次世界大战的浩劫动摇了人们对西方文明道德基础、连贯性、持久性的信念，引发了对传统文学模式能否充分再现战后世界严酷和不和谐的现实的怀疑。

T. S.艾略特在1923年评论乔伊斯的《尤利西斯》的文章中指出：用以组织文学作品的传统模式假定社会秩序是相对连贯和稳定的，它已不能适应"当代历史中大规模的无效和无政府状态"。像乔伊斯，也像埃兹拉·庞德在其长诗《诗章》中一样，艾略特追求在形式和文体上的创新实验，以表现当代社会的动乱不安，并常常把当代社会的混沌动乱与已经成为过去的、建立在旧文化宗教和神话基础上的秩序和融合相对照。例如在《荒原》(1922)这首诗里，艾略特用支离破碎的话语替代诗歌语言的规范化句法节奏并有意打乱诗歌各部分的顺序以取代传统诗歌的前后连贯结构。打乱后的诗歌的不同部分靠连接来联系，但这些连接留给读者自己去发现或创造。现代主义小说家的重要作品仿效乔伊斯的《尤利西斯》(1922)和他更为激进的小说《芬尼根的觉醒》(1939)，通过分解叙事的连续性、摒弃表现人物的标准方式、以*意识流*和其他创新叙事形式来打破传统的句法结构和叙事语言的连贯性，破坏了早期散文体小说创作的基本规范。格特鲁德·斯泰因通常作为现代主义先驱与乔伊斯、庞德、艾略特、吴尔夫联系在一起。他对**自动写作**（即不受意识、目的性思想控制的作品）和其他通过违反标准英语句法和句子结构规则来取得效果的写作模式进行了实验。其他作为现代主义主要代表的欧洲和美国作家包括小说家马塞尔·普鲁斯特、托马斯·曼、安德烈·纪德、弗朗兹·卡夫卡、多萝西·理查森、威廉·福克纳；诗人斯蒂芬·马拉梅、威廉·巴特勒·叶芝、赖纳·玛丽亚·里尔克、玛丽安·穆尔、威廉·卡洛斯·威廉斯、华莱士·史蒂文斯；剧作家奥古斯特·斯特林堡、路易吉·皮兰德娄、尤金·奥尼尔、贝尔托尔特·布莱希特。他们在文学结构和表现手法的新形式中对惯例的违反，类似于*表现主义*、*超现实主义*艺术运动对表现性传统的违反，类似于现代主义绘画、立体主义、未来主义和抽象表现主义雕塑中对写实规则的背离，也类似于现代主义音乐作曲家斯特拉文斯基、勋伯格和他们的激进追随者们对旋律、和弦和节奏的标准常规的违反。

A prominent feature of modernism is the phenomenon called the **avant-garde** (a French military metaphor: "advance-guard"); that is, a small, self-conscious group of artists and authors who deliberately undertake, in Ezra Pound's phrase, to "make it new." By violating the accepted conventions and proprieties, not only of art but of social discourse, they set out to create ever-new artistic forms and styles and to introduce hitherto neglected, and sometimes forbidden, subject matter. Frequently, avant-garde artists represent themselves as "alienated" from the established order, against which they assert their own autonomy; a prominent aim is to shock the sensibilities of the conventional reader and to challenge the norms and pieties of the dominant bourgeois culture. See Renato Poggioli, *The Theory of the Avant-Garde* (1968). Peter Bürger's *Theory of the Avant-Garde* (1984) is a neo-Marxist analysis both of modernism and of its distinctive cultural formation, the avant-garde.

The term **postmodernism** is often applied to the literature and art after World War II (1939–45), when the effects on Western morale of the First World War were greatly exacerbated by the experience of Nazi totalitarianism and mass extermination, the threat of total destruction by the atomic bomb, the progressive devastation of the natural environment, and the ominous fact of overpopulation. Postmodernism involves not only a continuation, sometimes carried to an extreme, of the countertraditional experiments of modernism, but also diverse attempts to break away from modernist forms which had, inevitably, become in their turn conventional, as well as to overthrow the elitism of modernist "high art" by recourse for models to the "mass culture" in film, television, newspaper cartoons, and popular music. Many of the works of postmodern literature—by Jorge Luis Borges, Samuel Beckett, Vladimir Nabokov, Thomas Pynchon, Roland Barthes, and many others—so blend literary genres, cultural and stylistic levels, the serious and the playful, that they resist classification according to traditional literary rubrics. And these literary anomalies are paralleled in other arts by phenomena like pop art, op art, the musical compositions of John Cage, and the films of Jean-Luc Godard and other directors.

An undertaking in some postmodernist writings—prominently in Samuel Beckett and other authors of the literature of the *absurd*—is to subvert the foundations of our accepted modes of thought and experience so as to reveal the meaninglessness of existence and the underlying "abyss," or "void," or "nothingness" on which any supposed security is conceived to be precariously suspended. Postmodernism in literature and the arts has parallels with the movement known as poststructuralism in linguistic and literary theory; poststructuralists undertake to subvert the foundations of language in order to demonstrate that its seeming meaningfulness dissipates, for a rigorous inquirer, into a play of conflicting indeterminacies, or else undertake to show that all forms of cultural discourse are manifestations of the reigning ideology, or of the relations and constructions of power, in contemporary society. See *poststructuralism*.

For some postmodernist developments in literature, see literature of the *absurd, antihero, antinovel, Beat writers, concrete poetry, metafiction, new novel, performance poetry*. On modernism, refer to Richard Ellmann and Charles Feidelson, eds., *The Modern Tradition: Backgrounds of Modern Literature* (1965); Irving

现代主义显著的特征之一是**先锋派**("avant-garde"是军事上用的比喻，意思是"前进－卫士")这一现象。一小群自我意识强烈的艺术家和作家有意从事埃兹拉·庞德称为"创新"的活动：他们破坏艺术和社会话语中已被人们接受的规范与繁文缛节，创造不断更新的艺术形式和风格，描绘迄今为止无人问津、有时遭忌讳的题材。前卫派艺术家往往表现为对现存秩序的"异化"。他们主张自成一统，想达到的主要目的是让墨守成规的读者从情感上受到震动，并向占据主导地位的资产阶级文化准则和正统性挑战。参阅：雷纳托·波吉奥利所著的《先锋派艺术理论》(1968)。彼得·伯格所著的《先锋派理论》(1984)是对现代主义及其突出的文化形式——先锋派的新马克思主义分析。

后现代主义通常用于指第二次世界大战(1939—1945)以后的文学艺术作品。在这一时期，纳粹的极权主义、大规模的人种灭绝、原子弹毁灭世界的威胁、对自然环境愈来愈严重的摧残、人口过剩所造成的不祥后果，大大地加重了第一次世界大战对西方道德准则的灾难性影响。后现代主义不仅是对现代主义反传统尝试的继续(有时趋于极端)，而且也是抛弃其现代主义形式的不同尝试，因为现代主义形式在其发展过程中不可避免地也变得日益陈旧。后现代主义还通过依靠"大众文化"中的电影、电视、报纸卡通和流行音乐等模式，颠覆了现代主义"高雅艺术"中的精英主义。豪尔赫·路易斯·博尔赫斯、塞缪尔·贝克特、弗拉基米尔·纳博科夫、托马斯·品钦、罗兰·巴尔特和许多其他作家的很多后现代主义文学作品，融合了许多文学体裁、文化和文体层面，既有严肃的也有戏谑的，无法根据传统文学类目对它们进行分类。这些文学异类在表现上跟其他艺术，如流行艺术、欧普艺术、约翰·凯奇的音乐作品、让－吕克·戈达尔和其他导演的电影相类似。

一些后现代主义作品，尤其是塞缪尔·贝克特和其他*荒诞派*文学作家的作品，是要颠覆我们已接受的思想和经验模式的基础，以此揭示存在的无意义和潜在的"深渊"或"空虚""虚无"，任何假定的安全都是危险地悬浮在这些潜在的"深渊"或"空虚"或"虚无"之上。文学和艺术中的后现代主义与语言学和文学理论中的后结构主义运动类似；后结构主义者想要颠覆语言的基础来证明语言表面上的意义对缜密的探索者来说消散成为一场相互矛盾、无法确定的游戏，或者为了表明所有形式的文化话语都是意识形态的表现，或是当代社会中权力关系和结构的表现。参见：*后结构主义*。

有关后现代主义在文学中的一些发展，参见：*荒诞派、反英雄、反小说、垮掉派作家、具像诗、元小说、新小说、表演诗歌*。关于现代主义和后现代主义，参阅：理查德·埃尔曼与查尔斯·费德尔森合编的《现代传统：现代文学的背景》(1965)；

Howe, ed., *The Idea of the Modern in Literature and the Arts* (1967); Lionel Trilling, *Beyond Culture* (1968); Paul de Man, "Literary History and Literary Modernity," in *Blindness and Insight* (1971); Hugh Kenner, *The Pound Era* (1971); David Perkins, *A History of Modern Poetry: From the 1890s to the High Modernist Mode* (1976); Peter Nicholls, *Modernisms: A Literary Guide* (1995); Christopher Butler, *Early Modernism: Literature, Music, and Painting in Europe, 1900–1916* (1994); Malcolm Bradbury and James McFarlane, eds., *Modernism: 1890–1930/A Guide to European Literature* (1991); Michael North, *The Dialect of Modernism: Race, Language, and Twentieth-Century Literature* (1998); Michael Levenson, ed., *The Cambridge Companion to Modernism* (1999). See also the journal *Modernism/Modernity*.

On postmodernism, see Clement Greenberg, *The Notion of Post-Modern* (1980); J. F. Lyotard, *The Postmodern Condition* (trans. 1984); Andreas Huyssen, *After the Great Divide: Modernism, Mass Culture, Postmodernism* (1986); David Harvey, *The Condition of Postmodernity: An Enquiry into the Origins of Cultural Change* (1989); John McGowan, *Postmodernism and Its Critics* (1991); Fredric Jameson, *Postmodernism* (1991); Ingeborg Hoesterey, ed., *Zeitgeist in Babel: The Postmodernist Controversy* (1991); Stuart Sim, ed., *The Routledge Companion to Postmodernism* (2001); Victor E. Taylor and Charles E. Winquist, eds., *Encyclopedia of Postmodernism* (2003).

On the massive impact on culture and literature of the two World Wars, see Paul Fussell, *Wartime: Understanding and Behavior in the Second World War* (1989), and *The Great War and Modern Memory* (2000).

On modern and postmodern drama: Austin Quigley, *The Modern Stage and Other Worlds* (1985); William B. Worthen, *Modern Drama and the Rhetoric of Theater* (1992); Debora Geis, *Postmodern Theatric(k)s* (1993). For references to *modernism* in other entries, see page *168*.

modernist: 225; *171*.

moment, the: 112.

monody: 102.

monologic: 86.

monologue: 94.

monometer (mŏnŏm' ĕ ter): 219.

mood: 19.

morality play: 224; *8, 379, 409, 411*.

morpheme: 196.

欧文·豪主编的《文学与艺术中的现代观念》(1967);莱昂内尔·特里林所著的《超越文化》(1968);保罗·德·曼所著的《盲目与洞见》(1971)中的"文学史与文学现代性";休·肯纳所著的《庞德时代》(1971);戴维·珀金斯所著的《现代诗歌史:从1890年代到极端现代主义者模式》(1976);彼得·尼古尔斯所著的《现代主义:文学指南》(1995);克里斯托弗·巴特勒所著的《早期现代主义:1900—1916年间欧洲的文学、音乐和绘画》(1994);马尔科姆·布拉德伯里与詹姆斯·麦克法兰合编的《现代主义:1890—1930年间欧洲文学指南》(1991);迈克尔·诺思所著的《现代主义的辩证法:种族、语言与20世纪文学》(1998);迈克尔·莱文森主编的《剑桥现代主义指南》(1999)。也可参阅期刊《现代主义/现代性》。

关于后现代主义,可以参阅:克莱门特·格林伯格所著的《后现代观念》(1980);J. F. 利奥塔所著的《后现代状况》(1984年英译版);安德烈亚斯·胡伊森所著的《大分野之后:现代主义、大众文化、后现代主义》(1986);戴维·哈维所著的《后现代的状况:对文化变迁之缘起的探究》(1989);约翰·麦高恩所著的《后现代主义和它的批评》(1991);弗雷德里克·詹姆逊所著的《后现代主义》(1991);英格堡·霍斯特雷主编的《巴别塔的时代精神:后现代主义者的论战》(1991);斯图尔特·西姆主编的《劳特里奇后现代主义指南》(2001);维克托·E. 泰勒与查尔斯·E. 文奎斯特合编的《后现代主义大百科》(2003)。

关于对二战时的文化和文学的巨大影响,可以参阅:保罗·福塞尔所著的《战时:第二次世界大战中的理解和行为》(1989)、《大战和现代的记忆》(2000)。

关于现代和后现代戏剧,可以参阅:奥斯汀·奎格利所著的《现代舞台和其他世界》(1985);威廉·B. 沃森所著的《现代戏剧和剧院修辞学》(1992);戴博拉·盖斯所著的《后现代戏剧演出》(1993)。其他条目中提及"现代主义"的地方,参见第168页。

modernist:现代主义的　**225**;*171*。

moment, the:黄金瞬息　**112**。

monody:独唱挽歌　**102**。

monologic:独白(小说)　**86**。

monologue:独白(诗)　**94**。

monometer:单音步韵行　**219**。

mood:氛围　**19**。

morality play:道德剧　**224**;*8, 379, 409, 411*。

morpheme:词素,语素　**196**。

morphology: 195.

motif and theme: A **motif** is a conspicuous element, such as a type of event, device, reference, or formula, which occurs frequently in works of literature. The "loathly lady" who turns out to be a beautiful princess is a common motif in *folklore*, and the man fatally bewitched by a fairy lady is a motif adopted from folklore in Keats' "La Belle Dame sans Merci" (1820). Common in lyric poems is the **ubi sunt motif**, the "where-are" formula for lamenting the vanished past ("Where are the snows of yesteryear?"), and also the *carpe diem* motif, whose nature is sufficiently indicated by Robert Herrick's title "To the Virgins, to Make Much of Time." An **aubade**—from the Old French "alba," meaning dawn—is an early-morning song whose usual motif is an urgent request to a beloved to wake up. A familiar example is Shakespeare's "Hark, hark, the lark at heaven's gate sings." An older term for recurrent poetic concepts or formulas is the **topos** (Greek for "a commonplace"); Ernst R. Curtius, *European Literature and the Latin Middle Ages* (trans. 1953), treats many of the ancient literary topoi. The term "motif," or else the German **leitmotif** (a guiding motif), is also applied to the frequent repetition, within a single work, of a significant verbal or musical phrase, or set description, or complex of images, as in the operas of Richard Wagner or in novels by Thomas Mann, James Joyce, Virginia Woolf, and William Faulkner. See *imagery*; and for a *deconstructive* treatment of recurrent elements or motifs in prose fiction, see J. Hillis Miller, *Fiction and Repetition* (1982).

Theme is sometimes used interchangeably with "motif," but the term is more usefully applied to a general concept or doctrine, whether implicit or asserted, which an imaginative work is designed to involve and make persuasive to the reader. John Milton states as the explicit theme of *Paradise Lost* to "assert Eternal Providence, / And justify the ways of God to men"; see *didactic literature* and *fiction and truth*. Some critics have claimed that all nontrivial works of literature, including lyric poems, involve an implicit theme which is embodied and dramatized in the evolving meanings and imagery; see, for example, Cleanth Brooks, *The Well Wrought Urn* (1947). And *archetypal critics* trace such recurrent themes as that of the scapegoat, or the journey underground, through myths and social rituals, as well as literature. For a discussion of the overlapping applications of the critical terms "subject," "theme," and "thesis" see Monroe C. Beardsley, *Aesthetics* (1958, pp. 401–11).

motivation: 46.

movements in recent criticism: 405.

multiculturalism: 43.

multiple authorship: 404.

multiple meaning: 13.

morphology：形态学　195。

Motif and Theme：题旨与主题

题旨是文学作品中经常出现的一个值得注意的成分，它可以是一类事件、一种手段、一项关联或一个程式。"令人生厌的女子"最后竟然是一位美丽的公主——这是*民间传说*里一个常见的题旨，济慈的诗歌《无情的美人》(1820) 里那位让仙女弄得神魂颠倒的男子，也是从民间传说里借用的题旨。抒情诗里常见的题旨是 **ubi sunt motif**，即悲叹消逝的岁月"在哪里"的程式（"去年的雪都到哪儿去了？"），另一常见的题旨是 Carpe diem，即*及时行乐*题旨。罗伯特·赫里克一首诗的题目《致处女：及时行乐》足以说明及时行乐这一题旨的本质。**晨歌**源自古法语"alba"（意思是拂晓），是一种清晨歌曲，其通常的题旨是殷切地呼唤爱人醒来，大家熟悉的一个例子是莎士比亚的《听！听！云雀在天堂之门歌唱》。表示反复出现的诗歌概念或程式的一个较古老的词是**常用主题**（**topos** 是希腊文，意为"日常琐事"）。厄恩斯特·R. 库齐乌斯所著的《欧洲文学和拉丁中世纪》(1953) 中就谈到了许多古代文学的常用主题。"题旨"或德文里的**中心意思**（引导性题旨）也用于表示在一部作品中重复出现的某个重要的文字短句、乐句、固定的描写或意象的复合体，正如在理查德·瓦格纳的歌剧，托马斯·曼、詹姆斯·乔伊斯、弗吉尼亚·吴尔夫、威廉·福克纳的小说里都有这样的用法。参见：*意象*；有关对散文体小说中循环元素或题旨的*解构主义*论述，可以参阅：J. 希利斯·米勒所著的《重复与小说》(1982)。

主题有时可与"题旨"互换使用，不过，这个词更常用来表示一般的概念或信条。这种概念或信条既可以是含蓄的，也可以是明确的。一部虚构的作品总是包含一个抽象概念或信条，并使其对读者具有说服力。约翰·弥尔顿阐明《失乐园》明确的主题就是："发扬那无疆的造化功程，/ 使人间得把天心悟领"；参见：*教诲文学、虚构小说与真实*。一些批评家宣称：所有重要的文学作品，包括抒情诗在内，都有内在的主题，这个主题在作品不断展开的意思和意象中被具体地、戏剧性地表现出来，比如可以参阅克林斯·布鲁克斯所著的《精制的瓮》(1947)。原型批评家从神话和社会礼仪以及文学中寻找这样一些反复再现的主题，如替罪羊和地狱之旅。有关对批评术语"论题""主题""命题"重复应用的讨论，可以参阅：比尔兹利所著的《美学》(1958) 第 401—411 页。

motivation：动机　46。

movements in recent criticism：当代批评理论和运动　405。

multiculturalism：多元文化主义　43。

multiple authorship：多重作者身份 / 多重作者署名　404。

multiple meaning：语义重叠　13。

mummers' play: 136.

mystery novels: 84.

mystery play: 224.

myth: In classical Greek, "mythos" signified any story or plot, whether true or invented. In its central modern significance, however, a myth is one story in a **mythology**—a system of hereditary stories of ancient origin which were once believed to be true by a particular cultural group, and which served to explain (in terms of the intentions and actions of deities and other supernatural beings) why the world is as it is and things happen as they do, to provide a rationale for social customs and observances, and to establish the sanctions for the rules by which people conduct their lives. Most myths are related to social **rituals**—set forms and procedures in sacred ceremonies—but anthropologists disagree as to whether rituals generated myths or myths generated rituals. If the protagonist is a human being rather than a supernatural being, the traditional story is usually called not a myth but a **legend**. If the hereditary story concerns supernatural beings who are not gods, and the story is not part of a systematic mythology, it is usually classified as a *folktale*.

The French structuralist Claude Lévi-Strauss departed from the traditional views just described, to treat the myths within each culture as signifying systems whose true meanings are unknown to their proponents. He analyzes the myths of a particular culture as composed of signs which are to be identified and interpreted by the cultural anthropologist on the model of the linguistic theory of Ferdinand de Saussure. See Lévi-Strauss, "The Structural Study of Myth," in *Structural Anthropology* (1968), and refer to *structuralist criticism* and *semiotics*. Another influential contribution to the theory of myths is the German intellectual historian Hans Blumenberg's *Work on Myth* (1979, trans. 1985). Among other things, Blumenberg proposes that the function of myth is to help human beings cope with the inexorability of reality and the course of events—a need that is not outmoded by scientific advances and rationality; that myths evolve according to a "Darwinism of words," in which those forms and variations survive that cope most effectively with the changing social environment; and that myth is best conceived not as a collection of fixed and final stories, but as "a work"—an ongoing and ever-changing process that is expressed in oral and written narratives and involves the diverse ways in which these narratives are received and appropriated.

It can be said that a mythology is a religion which we do not believe. Poets, however, after having ceased to believe them, have persisted in using the myths of Jupiter, Venus, Prometheus, Wotan, Adam and Eve, and Jonah for their plots, episodes, or allusions; as Coleridge said, "Still doth the old instinct bring back the old names." The term "myth" has also been extended to denote supernatural tales that are deliberately invented by their authors. Plato in the fourth century BC used such invented myths in order to project philosophical speculation beyond the point at which certain knowledge is

mummers' play：假面剧　136。

mystery novels：神秘小说　84。

mystery play：神秘剧　224。

Myth：神话

在古希腊语里，"神话"表示任何真实的或虚构的故事或情节。然而在其主要的现代意义上，一篇神话是**神话学**里的一则故事。神话学是曾被特定的文化群落认为是真实的并流传下来的故事体系，它（从神明及其他超自然人物的意向和行为的角度）解释了世界为什么是这个样子和事物为什么以这样的方式存在，以此为社会习俗惯例提供依据，建立人们生活所应遵循的规则。大部分神话都与社会**仪式**——祭典中固定的形式和程序——有关。但社会人类学者在究竟是宗教礼仪产生了神话，还是神话催生了宗教礼仪这一问题上还未达成一致。如果故事里的主人公是人，而不是超自然的神，这类故事就不叫神话，而叫**传说**。如果传承下来的故事与非神的超自然人物有关而又不属于系统神话体系的一部分，这类故事通常就被称为*民间故事*。

法国结构主义学者克劳德·列维－斯特劳斯抛弃了上述传统观念，认为每种文化中的神话都是符号指向系统，其真正含义不为神话的支持者所知晓。他经分析认为，特定文化中的神话由符号组成，文化人类学家必须用费迪南·德·索绪尔的语言学理论模式来识别和解释这些符号。参阅列维－斯特劳斯所著的《结构人类学》(1968)中的"神话的结构研究"，参见：*结构主义批评*、*符号论*。德国文化历史学家汉斯·布鲁门贝格所著的《神话》(1979，1985年英译版)，是对神话学说另一具有影响力的贡献。除了其他观点，他提出神话的功能就是帮助人们应对现实的无情，这种需要不因科学的进步与理性的发展而过时；他还提出，根据"达尔文主义的言论"，神话不断发展，它的形式和变体保留下来能最有效地适应变化的社会环境；最好不要把神话理解为固定不变的故事集，而应将其看做一部"作品"——一个用口头及书面叙述表达的不断向前、不断变化的过程，在这个过程中，这些故事以各种不同的方式得以接受和完善。

可以说，神话是我们不再相信的一种宗教。尽管诗人们早就不再相信神话，可他们仍在用朱比特、维纳斯、普罗米修斯、沃坦、亚当和夏娃、约拿等神话故事作为他们诗歌的情节、插曲和典喻。正如柯勒律治所说："根深蒂固的本能依然使古老的名字复现。""神话"这个词也被引申用来形容作家刻意虚构的超自然故事。柏拉图在公元前4世纪就用过这样有意虚构的神话，把富于哲理的思索臆测运用于某种可能的知识范围以外；例如，《理想国》第十卷里的"原始的神话"。德国

possible; see, for example, his "Myth of Er" in Book X of *The Republic*. The German *Romantic* authors F. W. J. Schelling and Friedrich Schlegel proposed that to write great literature, modern poets must develop a new unifying mythology which will synthesize the insights of the myths of the Western past with the new discoveries of philosophy and the physical sciences. In the same period in England William Blake, who felt "I must create a system or be enslaved by another man's," incorporated in his poems a system of mythology he had himself created by fusing hereditary myths, biblical history and prophecy, and his own intuitions, visions, and intellection. A number of modern writers have also asserted that an integrative mythology, whether inherited or invented, is essential to literature. James Joyce in *Ulysses* and *Finnegans Wake*, T. S. Eliot in *The Waste Land*, Eugene O'Neill in *Mourning Becomes Electra*, and many other writers have deliberately woven their modern materials on the pattern of ancient myths, while W. B. Yeats, like his admired predecessor Blake, undertook to construct his own systematic mythology, which he expounded in *A Vision* (1926) and embodied in a number of remarkable lyric poems such as "The Second Coming" and "Byzantium."

Around the middle of the twentieth century, "myth" became a prominent term in literary analysis. A large group of writers, the **myth critics**—including Robert Graves, Francis Fergusson, Maud Bodkin, Richard Chase, and (the most influential) Northrop Frye—viewed the genres and individual plot patterns of many works of literature, including what on the surface are highly sophisticated and realistic works, as recurrences of basic mythic formulas. As Northrop Frye put it, "[T]he typical forms of myth become the conventions and genres of literature." According to Frye's theory, there are four main narrative genres—comedy, romance, tragedy, and irony (satire)—and these are "displaced" modes of the four elemental forms of myth that are associated with the seasonal cycle of spring, summer, autumn, and winter. (See *archetypal criticism* and *genre*.)

A reader needs to be alert to the bewildering variety of applications of the term "myth" in contemporary criticism. In addition to those already described, its uses range all the way from signifying any widely held fallacy ("the myth of progress," "the American success myth") to denoting the solidly and detailedly imagined realm within which a fictional narrative is enacted ("Faulkner's myth of Yoknapatawpha County," "the mythical world of *Moby-Dick*").

For classical mythology see H. J. Rose, *A Handbook of Greek Mythology* (1939), and on the use of classical myths in English literature, Douglas Bush, *Mythology and the Renaissance Tradition in English Poetry* (rev. 1963) and *Mythology and the Romantic Tradition in English Poetry* (rev. 1969). Among studies of myths especially influential for modern literature and criticism are James G. Frazer, *The Golden Bough* (rev. 1911); Jessie L. Weston, *From Ritual to Romance* (1920); Jane E. Harrison, *Themis* (2d ed., 1927). On "myth critics" see William Righter, *Myth and Literature* (1975); and for instances of the theory and practice of myth criticism, Richard Chase, *Quest for Myth* (1949); Leslie Fiedler, *Love and Death in the American Novel* (1960); John B. Vickery, ed., *Myth and Literature* (1966); Northrop Frye, *Anatomy of Criticism* (1957) and "Literature and Myth"

浪漫主义作家 F. W. J. 谢林和弗里德里克·施莱格尔提出：现代诗人要想写出伟大的文学作品，就必须建立一个全新的、囊括一切的神话体系，这一体系要能把以往西方神话的深刻见解和人类在哲学、自然科学方面的新发现综合在一起。同一时期英国的威廉·布莱克感到，"我必须创建一个自己的神话体系，否则我将会受到他人的神话体系支配"。他将自己的直觉、想象、观念与因袭的神话和圣经历史以及预言相融合，创造了他自己的神话体系，并将这种体系与他的诗歌结合在一起。一些现代作家也声称：一个综合的神话体系，不管它是因袭而来的或是创造出来的，对文学来说都必不可少。詹姆斯·乔伊斯在《尤利西斯》和《芬尼根的觉醒》中、T. S. 艾略特在《荒原》中、尤金·奥尼尔在《哀悼》中，以及许多其他作家在他们的作品里，都有意识地把现代题材编织进古代神话的模式里，而 W. B. 叶芝则像他所敬仰的前辈布莱克一样，创建了他自己系统的神话体系。他在其所著的《一种见解》（1926）中，详细阐述了这一神话体系，并在其许多卓越的抒情诗，如《第二次到来》《拜占庭》里展现了这一神话体系。

大约在 20 世纪中期，"神话"已经成为文学分析中的一个重要术语。许多作家和包括罗伯特·格莱弗斯、弗朗西斯·弗格森、莫德·博德金、理查德·蔡斯、（最有影响的）诺斯罗普·弗莱在内的**神话批评家**都认为，许多文学作品中的各种体裁和独立情节格式，包括表面看来非常复杂和写实的作品，都是基本神话程式的再现。正如诺斯罗普·弗莱所说："神话的典型形式成为文学的惯例和文学体裁。"弗莱的理论指出，存在四种主要叙事型文学体裁：喜剧、传奇、悲剧和嘲讽（讽刺）。这是与春夏秋冬四季更迭有关的神话的四种基本形式的"替代"模式。（参见：*原型批评、文学类型*。）

读者应当注意到当代文学批评中对"神话"这个词的种种混乱的用法。这个词除了具有上述意思，它的用法多种多样：从表示广为流传的谬误（"发展的神话""美国式成功的神话"）到指代一部小说里叙述的确切可信的虚构世界（如"福克纳的约克纳帕塔法郡的神话""《白鲸》里的神话世界"）。

关于古典神话，可以参阅：H. J. 罗斯所著的《希腊神话手册》（1939）；关于古典神话在英语文学中的应用，可以参阅：道格拉斯·布什所著的《神话与英语诗歌中的文艺复兴传统》（1963 年修订版）和《神话与英语诗歌中的浪漫主义传统》（1969 年修订版）；在有关神话的研究中，对现代文学和文学批评特别有影响的著作是：詹姆斯·G. 弗雷泽所著的《金枝》（1911 年修订版）；杰西·韦斯顿所著的《从仪式到传奇》（1920）；简·E. 哈里森所著的《忒弥斯》（1927 年第 2 版）。关于神话批评，可以参阅：威廉·赖特所著的《神话与文学》（1975）；关于神话批评中理论和实践的例子，可以参阅：理查德·蔡斯所著的《神话追踪》（1949）；莱斯利·菲德勒所著的《美国小说里的爱与死》（1960）；约翰·B. 维克里主编的《神话与文学》（1966）；诺斯罗普·弗莱所著的《批评的原型》（1957）和其所写的文

in *Relations of Literary Study*, ed. James Thorpe (1967). This last essay has a useful bibliography of the theory and history of myths, as well as of major exponents of myth criticism. See *archetypal criticism*; *folklore*.

myth critics: 231; *323*.

mythoi (mĭth′ oy): **17**.

mythology: 230.

mythos: 293.

章"文学与神话",收入詹姆斯·索普主编的《文学关系研究》(1967)。最后这篇文章的参考书目对于了解神话的理论、历史以及神话批评的主要倡导者十分有益。参见:*原型批评、民间传说*。

myth critics:神话批评家　231;*323*。

mythoi:主题　17。

mythology:神话学　230。

mythos:神话　293。

naive hero: 185.

narratee: 234.

narration, grammar of: The **grammar of narration** is the analysis of special and distinctive grammatical usages that occur in fictional *narratives*. Its systematic study was begun by Käte Hamburger in *The Logic of Literature* (1957, trans. 1973). One focus of such analysis is the special play of **deictics**, also known as **indexicals** or **shifters**—that is, words and phrases such as "now," "then," "here," "there," "today," "last week," as well as personal pronouns ("I," "you") and some tenses of verbs—whose reference depends on the particular speaker and his or her position in place and time. In many narratives, usually in a way not explicitly noticed by the reader, the references of such terms constantly shift or merge, as the narration moves from the narrator, by whom the events are told in the past tense (for example, then and there), to a character in the narration, for whom the action is present (for example, here and now). Another notable grammatical usage in narration has been called **free indirect discourse** (equivalent to the French "style indirect libre"), or "represented speech and thought." These terms refer to the way, in many narratives, that the reports of what a character says and thinks shift in pronouns, adverbs, tense, and grammatical mode, as we move—or sometimes hover—between the direct narrated representation of these events as they occur to the character and the indirect representation of such events by the narrator of the story. Thus, a direct representation, "He thought, 'I will see her home now, and may then stop at my mother's,'" might shift, in an "indirect representation," to "He thought that he would see her home and then maybe stop at his mother's." In a further shift to "free indirect representation" the sentence might change to "He would see her home, and might afterward stop at his mother's." Refer to *narrative and narratology*, and see Roy Pascal, *The Dual Voice: Free Indirect Speech and Its Functioning in the Nineteenth-Century European Novel* (1977); Dorrit Cohn, *Transparent Minds: Narrative Modes for Presenting Consciousness in Fiction* (1978); Ann Banfield, *Unspeakable Sentences: Narration and Representation in the Language of Fiction* (1982).

narrative and narratology: A **narrative** is a story, whether told in prose or verse, involving events, characters, and what the characters say and do. Some literary forms such as the novel and short story in prose, and the epic and romance in verse, are explicit narratives that are told by a *narrator*. In drama, the narrative is not told, but evolves by means of the direct presentation on stage of the actions and speeches of the characters. (Refer to *genres*.) It should be noted that there is an implicit narrative element even in many *lyric* poems. In William Wordsworth's "The Solitary Reaper," for example, we infer from

N

naive hero：愚偶 185。

narratee：叙事对象 234。

Narration, Grammar of：叙事语法

  叙事语法指的是对小说*叙事*特有的特殊语法用法的分析。凯特·汉伯格所著的《文学的逻辑》(1957, 1973 年英译版)，开创了系统分析叙事语法的先河。这类分析的关注之一是**指示词**，也叫**指示**或**代替**——即一些像"现在""那时""这儿""那儿""今天""上个月"、人称代词这样的词语和动词的某些时态——的特殊作用，这些词的所指取决于特定的说话者以及他/她所处的时间地点。在许多叙事文中，通常以一种并不为读者所明确注意到的方式使这些词语指代的事物随着叙事从叙述者向叙事中某一人物的转移而不断变化或融为一体。在这一过程中，叙述者用过去时态来讲述事件（如，那时候和那儿），而对叙事中的人物来说，这一行动则是用现在时态来表现的（如，这儿和现在）。另一种著名的语法用法被称为**自由间接引语**（等同于法语中的"style indirect libre"）或"描述的话语和思想"。在许多叙事文中，这些术语指的是叙事方式，即当我们在直接叙事再现发生在人物身上的这些事件与故事叙述者间接描述这些事件之间来回转换，或者有时处在两者之间的边缘时，对人物的言语和思想的叙事方式在代词、副词、时态和语法形式上的变化。因此，直接描述"他想：'我现在将送她回家，然后可能去我妈妈家待上一会儿'"可能转变成为"间接描述"："他想他将送她回家，然后可能去他妈妈家待上一会儿"。而在"自由直接描述"中，这句话则可以变成："他那时将送她回家，然后可能在他妈妈家待上一会儿"。参见：*叙事和叙事学*，并参阅：罗伊·帕斯卡尔所著的《双重声音：19 世纪欧洲小说中的自由间接引语及其功用》(1977)；多里特·科恩所著的《透明的思想：小说中展现意识的叙事模式》(1978)；安娜·班菲尔德所著的《没有说出的句子：小说语言中的叙事和再现》(1982)。

Narrative and Narratology：叙事和叙事学

  叙事就是指散文体或诗体的故事，其内容包括事件、人物及人物的言行。一些文学形式，比如散文体小说和短篇故事，诗体的史诗和传奇，都是由*叙述者*讲述的明显的叙事故事。在戏剧中，故事并不是由叙述者讲述的，而是通过在舞台上直接表现人物的言语和行为的方式来展开。（参见：*文学类型*。）应该注意的是，即使在许多*抒情诗*中，也存在隐含的叙事成分。例如，在威廉·华兹华

what the lyric speaker says that, coming unexpectedly in the Scottish Highlands upon a girl reaping and singing, he stops, attends, meditates, and then resumes his climb up the hill.

Narratology denotes a concern, which became prominent in the mid-twentieth century, with the general theory and practice of narrative in all literary forms. It deals especially with types of narrators, the identification of structural elements in narratives and their diverse modes of combination, recurrent narrative devices, and the analysis of the kinds of *discourse* by which a narrative gets told, as well as with the **narratee**—that is, the explicit or implied person or audience to whom the narrator addresses the narrative. Recent narratological theory picks up and elaborates upon many topics in traditional treatments of fictional narratives, from Aristotle's *Poetics*, in the fourth century BC, to Wayne Booth's *The Rhetoric of Fiction* (rev. 1983); this modern theory, however, deals with such topics in terms of concepts and analytic procedures that derive from developments in *Russian formalism* and especially in French *structuralism*. Narratologists, accordingly, do not treat a narrative in the traditional way, as a fictional representation of life and the world, but as a systematic and purely formal construction. A primary interest of structural narratologists is in the way that narrative discourse fashions a **story**—a mere sequence of events in time—into the organized and meaningful structure of a literary *plot*. (The Russian formalists had made a parallel distinction between the **fabula**—the elemental materials of a story—and the **syuzhet**, the concrete representation used to convey the story.) The general undertaking is to determine the rules, or codes of composition, that are manifested by the diverse forms of plot, and also to formulate the "grammar" of narrative in terms of structures and narrative formulas that recur in many stories, whatever the differences in the narrated subject matters. In *Narrative Discourse* (1980), followed by *Figures of Literary Discourse* (1982), the French structuralist critic Gérard Genette presented influential analyses of the complex interrelationships between a story and the types of discourse in which the story is narrated, and greatly subtilized the treatment of *point of view* in narrative fiction.

In the 1970s the historian Hayden White set out to demonstrate that the narratives written by historians are not simple representations of a sequence of facts, nor the revelation of a design inherent in events themselves. Instead, White analyzes historical narratives as shaped by the imposition on events of cultural patterns similar to the narratological, *archetypal*, and other structural concepts that had been applied in the criticism of literature; see his *Metahistory* (1973) and *The Content of the Form: Narrative Discourse and Historical Representation* (1987). The philosopher W. B. Gallie wrote an influential book on the kind of explanation and understanding that, in the writing of history, is achieved by narration instead of propositional statements and logical arguments; see W. B. Gallie, *Philosophy and the Historical Understanding* (1964); also Arthur C. Danto, *Narration and Knowledge* (1985).

A book which did much to inaugurate modern narratology was *The Morphology of the Folktale* by the Russian formalist Vladimir Propp (trans. 1970). For later developments in narrative theory see, in addition to Genette

斯的《孤独的收割者》中，我们可以从抒情者的话语中推测出，在苏格兰高地上，他邂逅了一位姑娘，一边收割一边歌唱；他停下脚步，聆听，思索，而后继续爬山。

叙事学在20世纪中期名噪一时，表现了在所有文学形式中对叙事的一般理论和实践的关注。它主要研究叙述者类型、结构成分的辨别以及它们的不同组成模式、反复出现的叙事手段、对各种叙事*话语*的分析，以及**叙事对象**（即叙述者向其叙述故事的明显的或隐含的人或观众）。近代的叙事学理论选取并详细阐述了对虚构故事的传统论述中的许多论题，从公元前4世纪亚里士多德的《诗学》到韦恩·布思的《小说修辞学》（1983年修订版）；近期的理论适用于来源于*俄国形式主义*，尤其是在法国结构主义中新近发展起来的论题、概念和分析方法此类论题。因此，叙事学家并不用传统的方式来对待叙事，并不把它当做对生活和世界的虚构式再现，而是将其视为系统化的形式结构。结构叙事学家的主要兴趣在于，叙事话语将**故事**（即仅仅是按时间先后顺序发生的事件）编排成为文学*情节*上有组织有意义的结构的方式。[俄国形式主义者对 **fabula**（故事的组成素材）和 **syuzhet**（用于表述故事的具体描述）作了同样的区分。] 一般的做法是确定规则或写作规范，这由不同的情节形式表现出来；同时，在许多故事（无论叙事题材有何不同）里反复出现的结构和叙事惯例方面，规定叙事"语法"。法国结构主义批评家杰勒德·热奈特在其所著的《叙事话语》（1980）及其后的《文学话语特征》（1982）中，对故事和叙述故事的不同话语类型间的复杂关系作了颇有影响的分析，并详细阐述了叙事小说中对视角的处理。

1970年代，历史学家海登·怀特首先说明了，由历史学家所写的叙事故事并非只是对一系列事实的简单再现，也不是揭示事件中的内在构思。相反，怀特分析历史叙事故事时，认为它是由作用于事件的文化模式强制力所形成的，这些文化模式强制力类似于运用于文学批评中的叙事学、*原型*和其他结构主义的概念；参阅他所著的《史元》（1973）和《形式的内容：叙事话语和历史再现》（1987）。哲学家W. B. 加利写了一部重要论著，说明了对历史篇章的解释和理解是通过叙事，而不是通过命题的阐述和逻辑的论证取得的；参阅：W. B. 加利所著的《哲学与历史的理解》（1964）和阿瑟·C. 丹托所著的《叙事与学问》（1985）。

对开创现代叙事学具有重要意义的著作是俄国形式主义家弗拉基米尔·普洛普所著的《民间故事形态学》（1970年英译版）。有关叙事学理论后来的发展，

(above), Tzvetan Todorov, *The Poetics of Prose* (trans. 1977); Seymour Chatman, *Story and Discourse: Narrative Structure in Fiction and Film* (1978); Robert Alter, *The Art of Biblical Narrative* (1981); Wallace Martin, *Recent Theories of Narrative* (1986); Gerald Prince, *A Dictionary of Narratology* (1987); Paul Ricoeur, *Time and Narrative* (3 vols., 1984–88); Peter Brooks, *Reading for the Plot: Design and Intention in Narrative* (1992); Mieke Bal, *Narratology: Introduction to the Theory of Narrative* (rev. 1997); Seymour Chatman, *Coming to Terms: The Rhetoric of Narration in Fiction and Film* (1990); David Herman, ed., *Narratologies: New Perspectives on Narrative Analysis* (1999). Some cognitive psychologists and literary theorists have proposed that narrative, or the telling of diverse "stories" about how one thing leads to another, is the basic means by which we make sense of the world, provide meaning to our experiences, and organize our lives. See Jerome Bruner, *Acts of Meaning* (1990), and *Actual Worlds, Possible Minds* (1986); and Mark Turner, *The Literary Mind* (1996). For some narratological contributions to older analyses of how a story gets told, see *point of view*.

narratology: 234.

narrator: 301.

natural geniuses: 237.

naturalism: 335.

Naturalistic Period: 275.

naturalize (in reading): **401**; *247, 258, 296*.

nature writing: 96.

negative capability: The poet John Keats introduced this term in a letter written in December 1817 to define a literary quality "which Shakespeare possessed so enormously—I mean *Negative Capability*, that is, when man is capable of being in uncertainties, mysteries, doubts, without any irritable reaching after fact and reason." Keats contrasted to this quality the writings of Coleridge, who "would let go by a fine isolated verisimilitude ... from being incapable of remaining content with half knowledge," and went on to express the general principle "that with a great poet the sense of beauty overcomes every other consideration, or rather obliterates all consideration." The elusive term has entered critical circulation and has accumulated a large body of commentary. When conjoined with observations in other letters by Keats, "negative capability" can be taken (1) to characterize an impersonal, or objective, author who maintains *aesthetic distance*, as opposed to a subjective author who is personally involved with the characters and actions represented in a work of literature, and as opposed also to an author who uses a literary

除了上面提到过的热奈特，还可参阅：兹维坦·托多罗夫所著的《散文的诗学》（1977年英译版）；西摩尔·查特曼所著的《故事与话语：小说和电影里的叙事结构》（1978）；罗伯特·奥尔特所著的《圣经叙事的艺术》（1981）；华莱士·马丁所著的《当代叙事学》（1986）；杰拉尔德·普林斯所著的《叙事学词典》（1987）；保罗·利科所著的三卷本《时间与叙事》（1984—1988）；彼得·布鲁克斯所著的《解读情节：叙事的设计与意图》（1992）；米尔克·巴尔所著的《叙事学：叙事理论入门》（1997年修订版）；西摩尔·查特曼所著的《叙事术语评论：小说和电影的叙事修辞学》（1990）；戴维·赫尔曼主编的《叙述学：叙事分析的新视野》（1999）。一些认知心理学家、文学和文化理论家提出，叙事，或讲述一件事情引发另一件事情的不同"故事"，是我们认识世界的基本手段，也赋予我们的经历以意义，使我们的生活井井有条。参阅：杰尔姆·布鲁纳所著的《行为的意义》（1990）和《真实的心灵，可能的世界》（1986；此处英文书名原书有误。——译注）；马克·特纳所著的《文学思想》（1996）。有关叙事学对老式分析故事叙述方式方面的贡献，参见：*视角*。

narratology：叙事学　234。

narrator：叙述者　301。

natural geniuses：天才　237。

naturalism：自然主义　335。

Naturalistic Period：自然主义时期　275。

naturalize (in reading)：(阅读中的) 归化　401；*247, 258, 296*。

nature writing：自然写作　96。

Negative Capability：否定能力

　　诗人约翰·济慈在1817年12月的一封书信中提出了这一术语，用以定义一种文学特质，"莎士比亚在很大程度上具有这种特质——我指的是*否定能力*，即人类有能力处于一种不确定、神秘、怀疑状态，却不急于谋求事实和理性"。济慈用柯勒律治的作品来对比这种特性，柯勒律治"通过一种绝佳的孤立的貌似逼真的事物……来摆脱这种对于一知半解的不满状态"，济慈接着表达了一种普遍原则："对一位伟大诗人来说，美感超越了任何其他思考，或打消了所有的思考。"这一难以捉摸的术语进入批评领域后，引发了大量的评论。同济慈在其他书信中的评论联系起来，"否定能力"可以用于：(1) 描述保持一种*审美距离*、不受个人喜好影响的或客观的作者，不同于本人介入文学作品中所表现的人物和行为的主观的作者，

work to present and to make persuasive his or her personal beliefs; and (2) to suggest that, when embodied in a beautiful artistic form, the literary subject matter, concepts, and characters are not subject to the ordinary standards of evidence, truth, and morality, as we apply these standards in the course of our everyday experience. Refer to *distance and involvement* and *objective and subjective*. On the diverse interpretations of Keats' "negative capability," see W. J. Bate, *John Keats* (1963).

neoclassic and romantic: The simplest use of these extremely variable terms is as noncommittal names for periods of literature. In this application, the "Neoclassic Period" in England spans the 140 years or so after the Restoration (1660), and the "Romantic Period" is usually taken to extend approximately from the outbreak of the French Revolution in 1789—or alternatively, from the publication of *Lyrical Ballads* in 1798—through the first three decades of the nineteenth century. With reference to American literature, the term "neoclassic" is rarely applied to eighteenth-century writers; on the other hand, 1830–65, the era of Emerson, Thoreau, Poe, Melville, and Hawthorne, is sometimes called "the American Romantic Period." (See *periods of English literature* and *periods of American literature*.) "Neoclassic" and "romantic" are frequently applied also to periods of German, French, and other Continental literatures, but with differences in the historical spans they identify.

Historians have often tried to "define" neoclassicism or romanticism, as though each term denoted an essential feature which was shared, to varying degrees, by all the major writings of an age. But the multiplex course of literary events has not formed itself around such simple entities, and the numerous and conflicting single definitions of neoclassicism and romanticism are either so vague as to be next to meaningless or so specific as to fall far short of equating with the great range and variety of the literary phenomena. A more useful undertaking is simply to specify some salient attributes of literary theory and practice that were shared by a number of prominent writers in the Neoclassic Period in England, and that serve to distinguish them from many outstanding writers of the Romantic Period. The following list of ideas and characteristics that were shared, between 1660 and the late 1700s, by authors such as John Dryden, Alexander Pope, Joseph Addison, Jonathan Swift, Samuel Johnson, Oliver Goldsmith, and Edmund Burke, may serve as an introductory sketch of some prominent features of **neoclassic** literature:

1. These authors exhibited a strong traditionalism, which was often joined to a distrust of radical innovation and was evidenced above all in their great respect for **classical** writers—that is, the writers of ancient Greece and Rome—who were thought to have achieved excellence, and established the enduring models, in all the major literary *genres*. Hence the term "neoclassic." (It is from this high estimate of the literary achievements of classical antiquity that the term "**a classic**" has come to be applied to any later literary work that is widely agreed to have achieved excellence and to have set a standard in its kind. Refer to the entry *canon*

也不同于通过文学作品提出和宣扬个人信仰的作者;(2)表明被体现在优美的艺术形式中的文学的题材、概念和人物,并不像我们将例证、事实和道德的普遍标准运用于我们的现实经历中那样,受到这些普遍标准的支配。参见:*心理距离与感情介入*、*客观的与主观的*。有关济慈"否定能力"的不同释义,参阅:W. J. 贝特所著的《约翰·济慈》(1963)。

Neoclassic and Romantic:新古典主义和浪漫主义

这两个意思极为多变的词,在最一般的用法上被用作区分文学时期的不明确的名称。根据这一用法,英国的"新古典主义时期"指的是王政复辟时期(1660)之后的一百四十余年,"浪漫主义时期"则通常被认为大约从1789年法国大革命爆发(或根据另一种说法,从1798年《抒情歌谣集》出版)开始,延续至19世纪的最初三十年。在美国文学中,"新古典主义"一词很少被用在18世纪的作家身上;另一方面,1830—1865年被称为爱默生、梭罗、坡、梅尔维尔和霍桑的时代,这个时期有时也被称为"美国的浪漫主义时期"(参见:*英国文学各时期的划分*、*美国文学各时期的划分*)。"新古典主义"和"浪漫主义"也常适用于德国、法国和其他欧陆国家的文学时期,但所确定的历史时期则不尽相同。

历史学家常常试图"定义"新古典主义和浪漫主义,似乎这两个词都具有在一个时代所有重要作品里都有不同程度反映的单一的基本特征。然而,文学事件的发展过程本身并非是围绕这种简单的基本特征而形成的。无数互相矛盾的新古典主义和浪漫主义的定义,或者是模糊不清以致几乎毫无意义,或者是太过专门化而与包罗广泛的各类文学现象不相符合。较实用的办法是具体阐明英国新古典主义时期一些重要作家在文学理论和实践中所共有的显著特征,这些特征能把他们与浪漫主义时期的杰出作家区别开来。下面列举的思想和特征是1660年至18世纪晚期作家,如约翰·德莱顿、亚历山大·蒲柏、约瑟夫·艾迪生、乔纳森·斯威夫特、塞缪尔·约翰逊、奥利弗·哥尔德斯密斯、埃德蒙·伯克共同所有的,可权当是**新古典主义**文学一些显著特点的入门概要:

1. 这些作家表现出强烈的传统主义,其中往往夹杂着对激进的文学创新的怀疑,而且首先明显地表现在他们对**古典**作家(即古希腊罗马作家)的无限敬佩上,他们认为这些作家取得了卓越的成就,为所有重要的文学类型创立了永久的范本。"新古典主义"一词即由此而来。[正是出于对古典作品所取得的文学成就的高度评价,**经典**一词被用来指代任何被公认为取得了杰出成就并为其所属的文学类型树立典范的后世文学作品。参见:*文学经典*和 T. S. 艾

of literature, and see T. S. Eliot, *What Is a Classic?* (1945), and Frank Kermode, *The Classic* 1975.)

2. Literature was conceived to be primarily an "art"; that is, a set of skills which, although it requires innate talents, must be perfected by long study and practice and consists mainly in the deliberate adaptation of known and tested means to the achievement of foreseen ends upon the audience of readers. (See *pragmatic criticism,* under *criticism.*) The neoclassic ideal, founded especially on Horace's Roman *Ars Poetica* (first century BC), is the craftsman's ideal, demanding finish, correction, and attention to detail. Special allowances were often made for the unerring and innovative freedom of what were called **natural geniuses,** and also for felicitous strokes, available even to some less gifted poets, which occur without premeditation and achieve, as Alexander Pope said (in his deft and comprehensive summary of neoclassic principles *An Essay on Criticism,* 1711), "a grace beyond the reach of art." But the prevailing view was that a natural genius such as Homer or Shakespeare is extremely rare, and probably a thing of the past, and that to even the best of artful poets, literary "graces" come only occasionally. The representative neoclassic writer commonly strove, therefore, for "correctness," was careful to observe the complex demands of stylistic *decorum,* and for the most part respected the established "rules" of his art. The neoclassic **rules of poetry** were, in theory, the essential properties of the various *genres* (such as epic, tragedy, comedy, pastoral) that have been abstracted from classical works whose long survival has proved their excellence. Such properties, many critics believed, must be embodied in modern works if these too are to be excellent and to survive through the ages. In England, however, many critics were dubious about some of the rules accepted by Italian and French critics, and opposed the strict application of rules such as the *three unities* in drama.

3. Human beings, and especially human beings as an integral part of a social organization, were regarded as the primary subject matter of the major forms of *literature.* Poetry was held to be an *imitation* of human life—in a common phrase, "a mirror held up to nature." And by the human actions it imitates, and the artistic form it gives to the imitation, poetry is designed to yield both instruction and pleasure to the people who read it. Not art for art's sake, but art for humanity's sake, was a central ideal of neoclassic *humanism.*

4. In both the subject matter and the appeal of art, emphasis was placed on what human beings possess in common—representative characteristics and widely shared experiences, thoughts, feelings, and tastes. "True wit," Pope said in a much-quoted passage of his *Essay on Criticism,* is "what oft was thought but ne'er so well expressed." That is, a primary aim of poetry is to give new and consummate expression to the great commonplaces of human wisdom, whose universal acceptance and durability are the best warrant of their importance and truth. Some critics also insisted, it should be noted, on the need to balance or enhance the

略特所著的《什么是经典？》(1945)、弗兰克·克莫德所著的《经典》(1975)。]

2. 将文学视为主要是"艺术"；即一套固然需要天赋的才能，但必须经过长期的钻研和实践使之完美的技能。这主要是靠有意识地采用已知的和已被证明是行之有效的文学手法，在读者身上达到预期的效果。(参见：*批评中的实用主义批评*。)新古典主义的理想主要是在古罗马贺拉斯的《诗艺》(公元前 1 世纪)上建立起来的，这是一种技匠的理想，即追求最大限度的完美、准确和对细节的重视。**天才**只要不超越规范，通常就享有可以痛快运笔的特殊自由，甚至一些不那么具有天赋的诗人也常常享有这样的自由，他们可以不经预先深思熟虑而达到亚历山大·蒲柏[在《批评论》(1711)中对新古典主义理论睿智而全面的概括中]所说的"一种超越艺术范畴的优雅"。但是，普遍的观点认为，像荷马、莎士比亚这样的天才难得出现，或许可以说他们只是属于过去的人物。即使对那些技艺最为高超的诗人来说，他们也只能偶尔达到文学上的"优雅"。所以新古典主义代表作家通常竭力追求"准确性"，谨小慎微地遵从文体仪轨的复杂要求，并在很大程度上尊重他所从事的艺术业已确立的"法则"。新古典主义**诗歌法则**从理论上来说，是各类文学类型(如史诗、悲剧、喜剧、牧歌)的基本特质。这些特质是从那些久为流传并被证明为不朽之作的古典作品中概括出来的。许多批评家认为，如果现代作品也要成为传世经典，就必须在作品中体现出这些特质。然而，在英国，许多评论家都对意大利和法国批评家所接受的某些规则存有疑问，并且反对严格遵守某些规则，如戏剧中的三一律。

3. 人，尤其是作为社会结构不可分割的一分子的人，被认为是主要的文学题材。诗歌被视为是对人生的一种摹仿——通俗地说，"是一面展示人生的镜子"。诗歌通过摹仿人的行动并给予这一摹仿以艺术形式使读者受到教诲，同时也给读者带来审美的愉悦。新古典人文主义的主要理想"不是为艺术而艺术，而是为人类而艺术"。

4. 不论是在题材上，还是在艺术魅力上，新古典主义都强调人类所共有的，具有代表性的特征和广为接受的经验、思想、感情、情趣。蒲柏在他的《批评论》中说过一句常被引用的话："真正的机智是那种人们常常想到但却从来无法完美表达的机智。"换言之，诗歌的一个重要目的是以新颖、完美的手法来表现人类智慧所能想象到的最平凡的事物。这些平凡事物的普遍性和持久性，是它们重要性和真实性的最佳证明。应该提到的是，有些批评家也要求

general, typical, and familiar with the opposing qualities of novelty, particularity, and invention. Samuel Johnson substituted for Pope's definition of true wit the statement that wit "is at once natural and new" and praised Shakespeare because, while his characters are species, they are all "discriminated" and "distinct." But there was wide agreement that the general nature and the shared values of humanity are the basic source and test of art, and also that the fact of universal human agreement, everywhere and always, is the best test of moral and religious truths, as well as of artistic values. (Compare *deism*.)

5. Neoclassic writers, like the major philosophers of the time, viewed human beings as limited agents who ought to set themselves only accessible goals. Many of the great works of the period, satiric and didactic, attack human "pride"—interpreted as presumption beyond the natural limits of the species—and enforce the lesson of the golden mean (the avoidance of extremes) and of humanity's need to submit to its restricted position in the cosmic order—an order sometimes envisioned as a natural hierarchy, or *Great Chain of Being*. In art, as in life, what was for the most part praised was the law of measure and the acceptance of limits upon one's freedom. The poets admired extremely the great genres of epic and tragedy, but wrote their own masterpieces in admittedly lesser and less demanding forms such as the essay in verse and prose, the comedy of manners, and especially satire, in which they felt they had more chance to equal or surpass their classical and English predecessors. They submitted to at least some "rules" and other limiting conventions in literary subjects, structure, and diction. Typical was their choice, in many poems, to write within the extremely tight limits of the *closed couplet*. But a distinctive quality of the urbane poetry of the Neoclassic Period was, in the phrase often quoted from Horace, "the art that hides art"; that is, the seeming freedom and ease with which, at its best, it meets the challenge set by traditional and highly restrictive patterns.

Here are some aspects in which **romantic** aims and achievements, as manifested by many prominent and innovative writers during the late eighteenth and early nineteenth centuries, differ most conspicuously from their neoclassic precursors:

1. The prevailing attitude favored innovation over traditionalism in the materials, forms, and style of literature. Wordsworth's preface to the second edition of *Lyrical Ballads* in 1800 was written as a poetic **manifesto**, or statement of revolutionary aims, in which he denounced the upper-class subjects and the *poetic diction* of the preceding century and proposed to deal with materials from "common life" in "a selection of language really used by men." Wordsworth's serious or tragic treatment of lowly subjects in common language violated the neoclassic rule of *decorum*, which asserted that the serious genres should deal only with the momentous actions of royal or aristocratic characters in an appropriately elevated style. Other innovations in the period were the exploitation by Samuel

在普遍、典型、熟悉的特性和与之对立的新颖、独特、创新的特性之间保持均衡或促成这种均衡。塞缪尔·约翰逊用另一种说法来取代蒲柏对真正的机智所下的定义,即"机智既是天生的,也是独具一格的"。他称赞莎士比亚,因为莎士比亚笔下的人物虽然各式各样,但他们都"不尽相同""各有特色"。但普遍认为,人类的一般品性和共有的价值观是艺术的基本源泉和试金石,并且认为被人们普遍赞同的事实,不论在什么地方什么时代,既是对审美价值,也是对道德和宗教真理的最好检验。(对比:*自然神论*。)

5. 新古典主义作家与当时的主要哲学家一样,认为个人能力有限,只应设定自己所能达到的目标。这一时期的许多伟大作品都具有讽刺、说教性质,它们抨击人类企图超越物种自然能力范围之外的目标的"傲慢",或放肆,极力推崇中庸之道(避免走极端),认为人类必须服从自己在宇宙万物秩序中的受限定地位。这一秩序有时被想象成一个自然的等级制度,即所谓的伟大的生存链。艺术和生活一样,很大程度上最值得称道的是衡量一切的法则和接受在自由基础上的限制。虽然新古典主义诗人极为赏识史诗和悲剧这两种伟大的文学类型,但他们的杰作却是以公认的较为下乘的文学体裁,如韵文体和散文体写成的论说文、风俗喜剧,尤其是讽刺作品。他们认为在这些形式上他们更有可能与古典作家和英国前辈作家并驾齐驱乃至超出。他们在文学题材、结构和措辞方面遵循了至少一些"规范"和其他限制性惯例。具有典型意义的是,他们选择极端严格的闭合双韵体的格式来创作许多诗歌。不过,新古典主义时期温文尔雅的诗歌的独到特点,用贺拉斯常被引用的话来说就是"掩饰其技艺的艺术";也就是说,这类诗歌看似自由和轻松自如,却在最大限度上受到传统的和异常严谨的文体格式所设定的挑战。

以下是 18 世纪晚期和 19 世纪早期许多杰出的具有创新精神的作家在**浪漫主义**目标和成就方面同新古典主义前辈大相径庭的一些方面:

1. 在文学素材、形式和风格上,普遍支持革新、反对传统主义。华兹华斯 1800 年出版的《抒情歌谣集》第二版的序言是诗歌的**宣言**,或者说是诗歌革命目标的声明。他在文中抨击了 18 世纪诗歌所表现的上流社会题材和诗意辞藻,提出要"选择人们真正使用的语言"来表现"平凡生活"中的题材。华兹华斯这种用大众语言在诗歌中严肃地或悲剧式地描述低劣题材的观点,违背了新古典主义的仪轨原则,即认为严肃的文学类型只能以一种恰当的、高尚的文体风格来描述王室或贵族人物的重要行动。这一时期文学上的其他创新包括

Taylor Coleridge, John Keats, and others of the realm of the supernatural and of "the far away and the long ago"; the assumption by William Blake, William Wordsworth, and Percy Bysshe Shelley of the persona of a poet-prophet who writes a visionary mode of poetry; and the use of poetic *symbolism* (especially by Blake and Shelley) deriving from a worldview in which objects are charged with a significance beyond their physical qualities. "I always seek in what I see," as Shelley said, "the likeness of something beyond the present and tangible object."

2. In his preface to *Lyrical Ballads*, Wordsworth repeatedly declared that good poetry is "the spontaneous overflow of powerful feelings." According to this view, poetry is not primarily a mirror of men in action; on the contrary, its essential component is the poet's own feelings, while the process of composition, since it is "spontaneous," is the opposite of the artful manipulation of means to foreseen ends stressed by the neoclassic critics. (See *expressive criticism*.) Wordsworth carefully qualified this radical doctrine by describing his poetry as "emotion recollected in tranquility," by specifying that a poet's spontaneity is the result of a prior process of deep reflection, and by granting that it may be followed by second thoughts and revisions. But the immediate act of composition, if a poem is to be genuine, must be spontaneous—that is, unforced, and free of what Wordsworth decried as the "artificial" rules and conventions of his neoclassic predecessors. "If poetry comes not as naturally as the leaves to a tree," Keats wrote, "it had better not come at all." The philosophical-minded Coleridge substituted for neoclassic "rules," which he describes as imposed on the poem from without, the concept of inherent organic "laws"; that is, he conceives that each poetic work, like a growing plant, evolves according to its own internal principles into its final *organic form*.

3. To a remarkable degree external nature—the landscape, together with its flora and fauna—became a persistent subject of poetry, and was described with an accuracy and sensuous nuance unprecedented in earlier writers. It is a mistake, however, to describe the romantic poets as simply "nature poets." (See *nature writing*, under *ecocriticism*.) While many major poems by Wordsworth and Coleridge—and to a great extent by Shelley and Keats—set out from and return to an aspect or change of aspect in the landscape, the outer scene is not presented for its own sake but as a stimulus for the poet to engage in the most characteristic human activity, that of thinking. Representative Romantic works are in fact poems of feelingful meditation which, although often stimulated by a natural phenomenon, are concerned with central human experiences and problems. Wordsworth asserted, in what he called a "Prospectus" to his major poems, that it is "the Mind of Man" which is "my haunt, and the main region of my song."

4. Neoclassic poetry was about other people, but many Romantic poems, long and short, invited the reader to identify the protagonists with the poets themselves, either directly, as in Wordsworth's *Prelude* (1805, rev.

塞缪尔·泰勒·柯勒律治、约翰·济慈和其他作家对超自然的和"遥远的年代和地方"题材的利用;威廉·布莱克、威廉·华兹华斯、珀西·比希·雪莱用"诗人-先知"第一人称来创作他们的冥想诗;而诗歌象征主义的使用(尤其是布莱克和雪莱)则来自这样一种世界观,认为事物充满了超越其自身物质特性的意义。正如雪莱所说:"我总是在我所见的事物中找寻超越物体的现状和实体的相似之物。"

2. 在《抒情歌谣集》的序文中,华兹华斯再三论述了他的观点:优秀诗歌是"强烈情感的自然流露"。依据这种观点,诗歌并不像镜子那样主要是映现行动中的人们;相反,诗歌的根本要素是诗人自己的情感。创作诗歌的过程是"自然而然的",因此与新古典主义批评家所强调的用巧妙的筹划操纵来达到预期目的的方式截然不同。(参见:*表现主义批评*。)华兹华斯对这一激进的学说进行了缜密的论述,将自己的诗歌描述为"在冷静中追忆的情感",明确指出诗人的自发情感是先前深思熟虑的结果,也可能伴随着以后进一步的思索和修正。然而,一首诗若要写得真实,这种即兴写作行为就必须是自发的。这就是说,既不受制约,也不受华兹华斯所谴责的新古典主义前辈们所采用的"人为的"法则和规范的束缚。济慈写道:"倘若诗歌不能像树上的叶子那样自然地出现,那就最好别出现了。"具有哲学思想的柯勒律治反对从外部强加给诗人的新古典主义"法则",以诗人想象力固有的有机"法规"这一概念取而代之:他认为每一篇诗文就像正在生长的植物一样,是依据其自身内在法则最终发展成为一个有机形式。

3. 外在的大自然,即包括动植物在内的自然景色,在很大程度上成为诗歌的一个不变主题。浪漫主义作家以先前作家所没有的精确和感觉上的微妙差异对大自然加以描述。不过,仅仅将浪漫主义诗人描述为"自然诗人"是错误的。(参见:*生态批评中的自然写作*。)虽然华兹华斯和柯勒律治的许多重要诗篇,以及雪莱和济慈的诗歌很大程度上都是从自然风光的某一景色或景色的变换出发,然后又回到这一景色,但外界景色入诗并不是为其自身的缘故,而是激发诗人去从事一项最有特色的人类活动:思维活动。许多浪漫主义诗歌代表作实际上都是充满了感情的沉思默想,尽管这些诗歌都是由自然现象所激发,但它们关注的却是人类的主要体验和问题。华兹华斯在他称之为对他主要诗歌的"说明"中提出:"人的思维"是"我常常寻觅之物,也是我咏歌的主要范畴"。

4. 新古典主义诗歌描写的是其他人,但是许多浪漫主义诗歌(长篇和短篇)则是引导读者将作品中的主人公与诗人本人等同起来,或是像华兹华斯的《序曲》(1805;1850年修订版)和其他一些浪漫

1850) and a number of lyric poems (see *lyric*), or in altered but recognizable form, as in Lord Byron's *Childe Harold* (1812–18). In prose we find a parallel vogue in the revealingly personal essays of Charles Lamb and William Hazlitt and in a number of spiritual and intellectual autobiographies: Thomas De Quincey's *Confessions of an English Opium Eater* (1822), Coleridge's *Biographia Literaria* (1817), and Thomas Carlyle's fictionalized self-representation in *Sartor Resartus* (1833–34). And whether Romantic subjects were the poets themselves or other people, they were no longer represented as part of an organized society but, typically, as solitary figures engaged in a long, and sometimes infinitely elusive, quest; often they were also social nonconformists or outcasts. Many important Romantic works had as protagonist the isolated rebel, whether for good or ill: Prometheus, Cain, the Wandering Jew, the Satanic hero-villain, or the great outlaw.

5. What seemed to a number of political liberals the infinite social promise of the French Revolution in the early 1790s fostered the sense in Romantic writers that theirs was a great age of new beginnings and high possibilities. Many writers viewed a human being as endowed with limitless aspiration toward an infinite good envisioned by the faculty of imagination. "Our destiny," Wordsworth says in a visionary moment in *The Prelude*, "our being's heart and home, / Is with infinitude, and only there," and our desire is for "something evermore about to be." "Less than everything," Blake announced, "cannot satisfy man." Humanity's undaunted aspirations beyond its assigned limits, which to the neoclassic moralist had been its tragic error of generic "pride," now became humanity's glory and a mode of triumph, even in failure, over the pettiness of circumstance. In a parallel way, the typical neoclassic judgment that the highest art is the perfect achievement of limited aims gave way to dissatisfaction with rules and inherited restrictions. According to a number of Romantic writers, the highest art consists in an endeavor beyond finite human possibility; as a result, neoclassical satisfaction in the perfectly accomplished, because limited, enterprise was replaced in writers such as Blake, Wordsworth, Coleridge, and Shelley, by a preference for the glory of the imperfect, in which the artist's very failure attests the grandeur of his aim. Also, Romantic writers once more entered into competition with their greatest predecessors in audacious long poems in the most exacting genres: Wordsworth's *Prelude* (a rerendering, at epic length and in the form of a spiritual autobiography, of central themes of John Milton's *Paradise Lost*); Blake's visionary and prophetic epics; Shelley's *Prometheus Unbound* (emulating Greek drama); Keats' Miltonic epic *Hyperion*; and Byron's ironic conspectus of contemporary European civilization, *Don Juan*.

See *Enlightenment*, and refer to R. S. Crane, "Neoclassical Criticism," in *Dictionary of World Literature*, ed. Joseph T. Shipley (rev. 1970); A. O. Lovejoy, *Essays in the History of Ideas* (1948); James Sutherland, *A Preface to Eighteenth*

主义抒情诗（参见：抒情诗）那样直接抒发诗人的胸怀，或是像拜伦勋爵用《恰尔德·哈罗德游记》（1812—1818）那样改头换面、但依然能够辨认出来的形式来表现诗人自己。在散文方面，我们在查尔斯·兰姆、威廉·黑兹利特自我表露的文章和一些宗教性的睿智的自传，如托马斯·德·昆西的《一个英国鸦片服用者的自白》（1822）、柯勒律治的《文学传记》（1817）和托马斯·卡莱尔的虚构体自传《旧衣新裁》（1833—1834）中也能发现这种自我抒怀同样风行。不论浪漫主义所表现的主体是诗人自己或其他人，他们都已不再是一个有组织的社会的一分子，而是被典型地描述成孤独的人物；他们从事漫长的、有时甚至是难以捉摸的探求；他们通常都不循规蹈矩或是被社会遗弃。许多重要的浪漫主义作品都是用孤独的叛逆者作为主人公，这些叛逆者有好有坏。例如，普罗米修斯、该隐、流浪的犹太人、撒旦式的英雄－恶棍或了不起的歹徒。

5. 发生在 1790 年代早期的法国大革命，在一些政治自由主义者看来具有无限的社会前途。它使浪漫主义作家们认为，他们所处的时代是一个万象更新、大有作为的伟大时代。许多作家都认为个人具有无限的抱负，能够达到诗人凭借想象力所憧憬的无限美好的境界。华兹华斯在《序曲》中凭借一时的洞察力预言："我们的命运，我们生存的中心和归宿，/ 是和无限连在一起的，仅此而已"；我们向往"永远都将要发生的事物"。布莱克宣称："少于任一事物都不能使人满足。"人类这种不受限制、无畏的渴望，对新古典主义道学家来说是一种"傲慢"的通病式的悲剧性错误，现在却成了人类的荣耀，即使失败了，也是人类克服琐碎现状的一种成功。同样，典型的新古典主义断言最高形式的艺术是最完美地达到有限目的的观点，也被对各种规制和因袭的束缚的不满所取代。一些浪漫主义作家认为，最高形式的艺术存在于人们为了超越人类有限的可能而作出的努力中；由此导致的结果是：新古典主义对完美无缺（这种完美无缺之所以有可能达到是因为它们范围有限）津津乐道，而布莱克、华兹华斯、柯勒律治、雪莱等作家却代之以对不完美事物的赞美和青睐，因为艺术家的失败证明了其目标的宏伟壮观。浪漫主义作家同时也创作最苛刻严谨的文学体裁，以篇幅巨大的诗文来和他们最伟大的前辈进行较量：比如华兹华斯的《序曲》（这是以史诗的篇幅和宗教自传体形式重新表现约翰·弥尔顿《失乐园》主题的一首长诗）；布莱克带有预言性的梦幻史诗；雪莱的《解放了的普罗米修斯》（摹仿古希腊戏剧）；济慈的弥尔顿式史诗《海披里昂》，以及拜伦对所有现代欧洲文明的概观性嘲讽长诗《唐·璜》。

参见：启蒙运动；参阅：R. S. 克莱恩所写的词条"新古典批评"，收入约瑟夫·T. 希普利主编的《世界文学词典》（1970 年修订版）；A. O. 洛夫乔伊所著的《观念史论文集》（1948）；詹姆斯·萨瑟兰所著的《18 世纪诗歌导言》（1948）；

Century Poetry (1948); W. J. Bate, *From Classic to Romantic* (1948); Harold Bloom, *The Visionary Company: A Reading of English Romantic Poetry* (1961); René Wellek, "The Concept of Romanticism in Literary History" and "Romanticism Re-examined," in *Concepts of Criticism* (1963); Northrop Frye, ed., *Romanticism Reconsidered* (1963), and *A Study of English Romanticism* (1968); M. H. Abrams, *The Mirror and the Lamp: Romantic Theory and the Critical Tradition* (1953), and *Natural Supernaturalism: Tradition and Revolution in Romantic Literature* (1971); Thomas McFarland, *Romanticism and the Forms of Ruin* (1981); Marilyn Butler, *Romantics, Rebels and Reactionaries: English Literature and Its Background 1760–1830* (1982); Jerome McGann, *The Romantic Ideology* (1983); Marilyn Gaull, *English Romanticism: The Human Context* (1988); Philippe Lacoue-Labarthe and Jean-Luc Nancy, *The Literary Absolute: The Theory of Literature in German Romanticism* (trans. 1988); Isaiah Berlin, *The Crooked Timber of Humanity: Chapters in the History of Ideas* (1990); Stuart Curran, ed., *The Cambridge Companion to British Romanticism* (1993). Hugh Honour, in his books on *Neo-classicism* (1969) and on *Romanticism* (1979), stresses the visual arts. A collection of essays that define or discuss Romanticism is Robert F. Gleckner and Gerald E. Enscoe, eds., *Romanticism: Points of View* (rev. 1975); see also *An Oxford Companion to the Romantic Age: British Culture 1776–1832* (2001). In *Poetic Form and British Romanticism* (1986), Stuart Curran stresses the relationship of innovative Romantic forms to the traditional poetic genres.

See also *closed couplet; decorum; deism; Enlightenment; Great Chain of Being; humanism; primitivism; satire.*

Neoclassic Period: 282.

neoclassic poetic diction: 298.

Neoplatonism (nēōplāt′ ŏnism): **292.**

New Comedy: 55.

New Criticism: This term, made current by the publication of John Crowe Ransom's *The New Criticism* in 1941, came to be applied to a theory and practice that remained prominent in American literary criticism until late in the 1960s. The movement derived in considerable part from elements in I. A. Richards' *Principles of Literary Criticism* (1924) and *Practical Criticism* (1929) and from the critical essays of T. S. Eliot. It opposed a prevailing interest of scholars, critics, and teachers of that era in the biographies of authors, in the social context of literature, and in literary history by insisting that the proper concern of literary criticism is not with the external circumstances or effects or historical position of a work, but with a detailed consideration of the work itself as an independent entity. Notable critics in this mode were the southerners Cleanth Brooks and Robert Penn Warren, whose textbooks

W. J. 贝特所著的《从古典到浪漫》(1948)；哈罗德·布鲁姆所著的《虚构导读：英国浪漫主义诗歌的阅读》(1961)；勒内·韦勒克所著的《批评的概念》(1963)中的"文学史上的浪漫主义概念"和"浪漫主义的再考察"；诺斯罗普·弗莱主编的《重新思考浪漫主义》(1963)和《英国浪漫主义研究》(1968)；M. H. 艾布拉姆斯所著的《镜与灯：浪漫主义文论及批评传统》(1953)和《自然的超自然主义：浪漫主义文学中的传统与革新》(1971)；托马斯·麦克法兰所著的《浪漫主义与形式的废墟》(1981)；玛丽莲·巴特勒所著的《浪漫派·叛逆者·反动派：论18、19世纪英国文学》(1982)；杰尔姆·麦根所著的《浪漫主义意识形态》；玛丽莲·高尔所著的《英国浪漫主义：人类语境》(1988)；菲利普·拉古-拉巴特与让-吕克·南希合著的《文学的绝对：德国浪漫主义文学理论》(1988年英译版)；以赛亚·伯林所著的《扭曲的人性之材：思想史篇章》(1990)；斯图尔特·柯伦主编的《剑桥英国浪漫主义指南》(1993)。休·昂纳在《新古典主义》(1969)和《关于浪漫主义》(1979)中强调了视觉艺术。定义或讨论了浪漫主义的文集有：罗伯特·F. 格莱克纳与杰拉尔德·E. 恩斯科合编的《浪漫主义：观点》(1975年修订版)；也可参阅：《牛津浪漫主义时代指南：1776—1832年间的英国文化》(2001)。在《诗歌形式和英国浪漫主义》(1986)中，斯图尔特·卡伦强调了浪漫主义创新形式与传统诗歌体裁的关系。

也可参见：闭合双韵体、仪轨、自然神论、启蒙运动、伟大的生存(环)链、尚古主义、讽刺。

Neoclassic Period：新古典主义时期　282。

neoclassic poetic diction：新古典主义诗意辞藻　298。

Neoplatonism：新柏拉图主义　292。

New Comedy：新喜剧　55。

New Criticism：新批评

自从约翰·克罗·兰塞姆的《新批评》在1941年出版后，"新批评"这个术语就流行开来，并在截至1960年代晚期以前被用来指代美国文学批评中一派重要的理论与实践。这一运动在很大程度上源起于I. A. 理查兹所著的《文学批评原理》(1924)、《实用批评》(1929)和T. S. 艾略特的文学批评论文。新批评反对那个时期在学者、批评家、教师中风行的只对作者的传记、文学的社会背景以及文学史感兴趣的现象，坚信文学批评正确的关注对象不是一部作品的外在情况、影响或历史地位，而是应该仔细考虑作品本身作为一个独立实体的地位。著名的新批评家有南方作家克林斯·布鲁克斯和罗伯特·佩恩·华伦，他们合著的教科

Understanding Poetry (1938) and *Understanding Fiction* (1943) did much to make the New Criticism the predominant method of teaching literature in American colleges, and even in high schools, for the next two or three decades. Other prominent writers of that time—in addition to Ransom, Brooks, and Warren—who are often identified as New Critics are Allen Tate, R. P. Blackmur, and William K. Wimsatt.

An influential English critic, F. R. Leavis, in turning his attention from background, sources, and biography to the detailed analysis of "literary texts themselves," shared some of the concepts of the New Critics and their analytic focus on what he called "the words on the page." He differed from his American counterparts, however, in his insistence that great literary works are a concrete and life-affirming enactment of moral and cultural values; he stressed also the essential role in education of what he called "the Great Tradition" of English literature in advancing the values of culture and "civilization" against the antagonistic forces in modern life. See F. R. Leavis, *Revaluation: Tradition and Development in English Poetry* (1936); *Education and the University* (1943, 2d ed. 1948); *The Great Tradition: George Eliot, Henry James, Joseph Conrad* (1948); also Anne Sampson, *F. R. Leavis* (1992).

The New Critics differed from one another in many ways, but the following points of view and procedures were shared by many of them:

1. A poem, it is held, should be treated as such—in Eliot's words, "primarily as poetry and not another thing"—and should therefore be regarded as an independent and self-sufficient verbal object. The first law of criticism, John Crowe Ransom said, "is that it shall be objective, shall cite the nature of the object" and shall recognize "the autonomy of the work itself as existing for its own sake." (See *objective criticism*.) New Critics warn the reader against critical practices which divert attention from the poem itself (see *intentional fallacy* and *affective fallacy*). In analyzing and evaluating a particular work, they eschew reference to the biography and temperament and personal experiences of the author, to the social conditions at the time of its production, or to its psychological and moral effects on the reader; they also tend to minimize recourse to the place of the work in the history of literary forms and subject matter. Because of its focus on the literary work in isolation from its attendant circumstances and effects, the New Criticism is often classified as a type of critical *formalism*.

2. The principles of the New Criticism are basically verbal. That is, literature is conceived to be a special kind of language whose attributes are defined by systematic opposition to the language of science and of practical and logical discourse, and the explicative procedure is to analyze the meanings and interactions of words, *figures of speech*, and *symbols*. The emphasis is on the "organic unity," in a successful literary work, of its overall structure with its verbal meanings, and we are warned against separating the two by what Cleanth Brooks called "the heresy of paraphrase."

3. The distinctive procedure for a New Critic is **explication**, or **close reading**: the detailed analysis of the complex interrelationships and *ambiguities* (multiple meanings) of the verbal and figurative components

书《理解诗歌》(1938)和《理解小说》(1943)在后来二三十年间使新批评在美国大学,甚至中学里成为文学教学的主要方法。除了兰塞姆、布鲁克斯和沃伦,其他同时期常被划归为新批评家的主要作家还包括艾伦·泰特、R. P. 布莱克默和威廉·K. 维姆萨特。

F. R. 利维斯是一位很有影响力的英国批评家,当他把注意力从背景、来源和传记转向对"文学文本自身"的详尽分析时,他对新批评家的一些概念和他们在分析中关注他所谓的"纸面上的文字"持有类似的看法。然而,与他的美国同行不同,他强调把伟大的文学作品视为是对道德与文化价值观具体的、肯定人生的展现;同时他也强调教育在他称之为英国文学在推进文化价值观和文明、反对现代生活中的对抗力量的"伟大传统"中所发挥的重要作用。参阅:F. R. 利维斯所著的《革命:英诗的传统与发展》(1936);《教育和大学》(1943,1948年第二版);《伟大的传统:乔治·艾略特、亨利·詹姆斯、约瑟夫·康拉德》(1948);安·桑普森所著的《F. R. 利维斯》(1992)。

新批评家在许多方面都各持己见,但许多新批评家在以下观点和做法上却有其共同之处:

1. 认为应该这样对待一首诗歌——用艾略特的话来说就是:"主要是作为诗,而不是其他东西";必须把诗看做是独立自足的文字对象。约翰·克罗·兰塞姆说过,文学批评的首要法则是"它必须是客观的,必须引用对象的实质",必须辨认出"作品自身的自主性,只为本身的存在而存在"。(参见:客观批评。)新批评家告诫读者反对那些脱离对诗歌自身的关注的文学批评实践(参见:意图谬误、情感谬误)。在分析和评价某一特定作品时,新批评家避免求助于作者传记、性情、作品成文的年代的社会背景,或作品对读者心理上和道德上的影响;他们也倾向于尽量不求助作品在文学形式和文学题材历史上的地位。由于新批评脱离作品所处的环境和影响,批评的焦点在文学作品本身,因此它常被归于形式主义批评的一个种类。

2. 新批评的原理基本上都是有关言辞方面的。也就是说,新批评认为文学是语言的一种特殊形式,其属性特征是由系统地违反科学的语言和实际的、逻辑的话语决定的,其解释过程在于分析词汇、修辞格和象征的意义,以及它们之间的相互作用。新批评强调的是一部成功的文学作品中整体结构和文字含义的"有机统一性",并警告读者不要用克林斯·布鲁克斯所谓的"解释的异说"把这两者分隔开来。

3. 新批评家独特的批评方式是**解说**,或称为**细读**,即对一部作品中文字和修辞成分间复杂的相互关系和歧义(多种含义)作细致的分析。

within a work. **Explication de texte** (stressing all kinds of information, whether internal or external, relevant to the full understanding of a word or passage) had long been a formal procedure for teaching literature in French schools, but the explicative analysis of internal verbal interactions characteristic of the New Criticism derives from such books as I. A. Richards' *Practical Criticism* (1929) and William Empson's *Seven Types of Ambiguity* (1930).

4. The distinction between literary *genres*, although acknowledged, does not play an essential role in the New Criticism. The essential components of any work of literature, whether lyric, narrative, or dramatic, are conceived to be words, images, and symbols rather than character, thought, and plot. These linguistic elements, whatever the genre, are often said to be organized around a central and humanly significant *theme*, and to manifest high literary value to the degree that they manifest *"tension," "irony,"* and *"paradox"* in achieving a "reconciliation of diverse impulses" or an "equilibrium of opposed forces." The form of a work, whether or not it has characters and plot, is said to be primarily a "structure of meanings," which evolve into an integral and freestanding unity mainly through a play and counterplay of "thematic imagery" and "symbolic action."

The basic orientation and modes of analysis in the New Criticism were adapted to the **contextual criticism** of Eliseo Vivas and Murray Krieger. Krieger defined contextualism as "the claim that the poem is a tight, compelling, finally closed context," which prevents "our escape to the world of reference and action beyond," and requires that we "judge the work's efficacy as an aesthetic object." (See Murray Krieger, *The New Apologists for Poetry*, 1956, and *Theory of Criticism*, 1976.) The revolutionary thrust of the mode had lost much of its force by the 1960s, when it gave way to various newer theories of criticism, but it has left a deep and enduring mark on the criticism and teaching of literature, in its primary emphasis on the individual work and in the variety and subtlety of the devices that it made available for analyzing its internal relations. *Lyric Poetry: Beyond New Criticism*, eds. Chaviva Hošek and Patricia Parker (1985), is a collection of *structuralist, poststructuralist,* and other essays which—often in express opposition to the New Criticism—exemplify the diverse newer modes of "close reading"; some of these essays claim that competing forces within the language of a lyric poem preclude the possibility of the unified meaning that was a central tenet of the New Critics.

Central instances of the theory and practice of New Criticism are Cleanth Brooks, *The Well Wrought Urn* (1947), and W. K. Wimsatt, *The Verbal Icon* (1954). The enterprises of New Criticism are privileged over alternative approaches to literature in René Wellek and Austin Warren, *Theory of Literature* (3d ed., 1964), which became a standard reference book in the graduate study of literature. Robert W. Stallman's *Critiques and Essays in Criticism, 1920–1948* (1949) is a convenient collection of essays in this critical mode; the literary journal *The Explicator* (1942ff.), devoted to the close reading of single poems, was a characteristic product of its approach to literary texts, as are

解说文本（强调与完全理解文字或段落相关的所有信息，不论是内在的还是外在的）长期以来一直是法国学校里教授文学的正规程序。然而，新批评对文字相互作用独特的解释性分析方法却是源自诸如 I. A. 理查兹的《实用批评》(1929) 和威廉·燕卜荪的《晦涩的七种类型》(1930) 之类的论著。

4. 文学类型之间的区别尽管已经得到承认，但在新批评中并不重要。在新批评看来，任何一部文学作品的基本要素——不论这部作品是抒情的、叙事的或戏剧式的——都是词汇、意象和象征，而不是人物、思想和情节。新批评认为，无论在什么体裁中，这些语言学要素常常是围绕着某个中心或从人类角度来看具有意义的主题而组织的，用来显示崇高的文学价值，表现出"张力""讽刺""逆说"，以取得"各种冲动的调和"或"相互排斥力量的均衡"。一部作品，不管它是否有人物和情节，其形式基本上都是"多层意义的结构"，该结构主要是通过"主题意象"和"象征性行动"的作用和反作用，发展成为一个完整、独立的统一体。

新批评分析的基本方向和方式，也适合套用于埃利西厄·维瓦斯和默里·克里格创建的**语境批评**。克里格将语境主义定义为："宣称诗歌是一种结构严谨、强制，最终封闭式的前后关系"，这就阻止"我们逃到所涉及的世界和行动之外"，它要求我们"把一部作品的效用当做一个审美对象来加以评价"。[参阅：克里格所著的《诗歌的新辩护者》(1956) 和《批评理论》(1976)。] 不过，这种文学批评模式的革命性冲击，到了 1960 年代就失去了其大部分影响力，让步于各种更新的批评理论，但它侧重分析具体的作品，在分析内部关系时所采用的多样化而又细腻微妙的方式，对文学批评和教学仍具有深远长久的影响。查维拉·霍塞克与帕特里夏·帕克合编的《新批评之外的抒情诗歌》(1985)，汇集了*结构主义、后结构主义*和其他一些文章——通常在表述上与新批评截然不同——代表了更为新颖、不同的"细读"模式；其中一些文章宣称，一首抒情诗的语言里的竞争力量排除了统一含义的可能性，这是新批评的核心原则。

新批评理论和实践的主要作品有：克林斯·布鲁克斯所著的《精制的瓮》(1947)；W. K. 维姆萨特所著的《语像》(1954)；勒内·韦勒克与奥斯汀·沃伦合著的《文学理论》(1964 年第 3 版)，阐释了新批评体系优于其他文学方法的地方，它已成为文学研究生学习中的权威参考著作。罗伯特·W. 斯托尔曼所著的《文学批评论文随笔，1920—1948》(1949)，是运用这一批评模式的论文集，便于研究使用。1942 年创刊的文学刊物《释义者》，专门从事诗歌的细读研究，是运用新批评方法分析文学文本的典型产物；约瑟夫·M. 孔茨主编的《诗歌解说：1924 年

the items listed in *Poetry Explication: A Checklist of Interpretation since 1924 of British and American Poems Past and Present*, ed. Joseph M. Kuntz (3d ed., 1980). See also W. K. Wimsatt, ed., *Explication as Criticism* (1963); the review of the movement by René Wellek, *A History of Modern Criticism*, Vol. 6 (1986); and the spirited retrospective defense of New Criticism by its chief exponent, Cleanth Brooks, "In Search of the New Criticism" (1983), reprinted in Brooks, *Community, Religion, and Literature* (1995). For critiques of the theory and methods of the New Criticism, see R. S. Crane, ed., *Critics and Criticism, Ancient and Modern* (1952), and *The Languages of Criticism and the Structure of Poetry* (1953); Gerald Graff, *Poetic Statement and Critical Dogma* (1970); Terry Eagleton, *Literary Theory: An Introduction* (1993); Susan Wolfson, *Formal Charges* (1997). For references to *New Criticism* in other entries, see pages *42, 52, 140, 170, 262, 267*. See also *affective fallacy; ambiguity; form and structure; intentional fallacy; tension.*

new formalism (in literary criticism): **141**.

new formalism (in writing poetry): **144**.

new historicism: New historicism, since the early 1980s, has been the accepted name for a mode of literary study that its proponents oppose to the *formalism* they attribute both to the *New Criticism* and to the critical *deconstruction* that followed it. In place of dealing with a text in isolation from its historical context, new historicists attend primarily to the historical and cultural conditions of its production, its meanings, its effects, and also of its later critical interpretations and evaluations. This is not simply a return to an earlier kind of literary scholarship, for the views and practices of the new historicists differ markedly from those of earlier scholars who had adverted to social and intellectual history as a "background" against which to set a work of literature as an independent entity, or had viewed literature as a "reflection" of the worldview characteristic of a period. Instead, new historicists conceive of a literary text as "situated" within the totality of the institutions, social practices, and discourses that constitute the culture of a particular time and place, and with which the literary text interacts as both a product and a producer of cultural energies and codes.

What is most distinctive in this mode of historical study is mainly the result of concepts and practices of literary analysis and interpretation that have been assimilated from various recent poststructural theorists (see *poststructuralism*). Especially prominent are: (1) The views of the revisionist Marxist thinker Louis Althusser that ideology manifests itself in different ways in the discourse of each of the semi-autonomous institutions of an era, including literature, and also that ideology operates covertly to form and position the users of language as the "subjects" in a discourse, in a way that in fact "subjects" them—that is, subordinates them—to the interests of the ruling classes; see *ideology* under *Marxist criticism*, and *subject* under *poststructuralism*. (2) Michel

至今新旧英美诗歌释义目录》（1980 年第 3 版）一书所列举的书目也是这种分析方法的产物。也请参阅：W. K. 维姆萨特主编的《作为批评法的解释》（1963）；勒内·韦勒克所著的《现代批评史》（1986 年第 6 卷），评论了这一文学运动。新批评的主要倡导者克林斯·布鲁克斯在其所写的文章"寻找新批评"（1983）[重印收入布鲁克斯所著的《团体、宗教和文学》（1995）] 中对新批评进行了充满激情的回顾式辩护。对新批评理论和方法的批判，可以参阅：R. S. 克莱恩主编的《古代和现代的批评家与批评》（1952）和《批评的语言与诗歌的结构》（1953）；杰拉尔德·格拉夫所著的《诗学命题与批评教义》（1970）；特里·伊格尔顿所著的《文学理论导论》（1993）；苏珊·沃尔夫森所著的《形式印章》（1997）。其他条目中提及"新批评"的地方，参见第 42、52、140、170、262、267 页。也请参见：*情感谬误、歧义、形式与结构、意图谬误、（诗歌中的）张力*。

new formalism（in literary criticism）：（文学批评中的）新形式主义　141。

new formalism（in writing poetry）：（诗歌写作中的）新形式主义　144。

New Historicism：新历史主义

自 1980 年代初以来，新历史主义这一名称就已被人们接受，用来指称一种文学研究模式。其支持者反对*形式主义*，把形式主义归因于*新批评*及其后产生的批评性*解构主义*。新历史主义者不再将文本孤立于其历史背景之外进行研究，而是将注意力主要投向文本产生时的历史、文化背景，文本的意义所在，其影响力，以及后世批评家对它的理解与评价。这并非是对早期学术成就的简单回归，因为新历史主义者的观点与实践都与从前的学者有显著不同：从前的学者或者把社会与知识历史看做"背景"，而将文学作品视为是此背景下的独立实体，或者把文学视为某一时期特定世界观的"反映"。与其相反，新历史主义者认为文学文本"处于"构成某一特定时间、地点的整体文化的制度、社会实践和话语之内，而文学文本与文化相互作用，同时扮演了文化活力与文化代码的产物和生产者的角色。

这种新的历史研究模式最具特色之处主要在于它是吸取了近期不同的后结构主义理论家（参见：*后结构主义*）的文学分析与释义的概念和实践的产物。特别显著的是：(1) 修正主义的马克思主义思想家路易斯·阿尔都塞的观点认为：意识形态在某一时期每一种半自主的制度的话语中（包括文学在内）以不同形式展示自身；同时，意识形态也暗中起作用，形成和确定了语言运用者在话语中的"主体"地位，事实上是"支配"他们，也就是使他们从属于统治阶级的利益；参见：*马克思主义批评*中的*意识形态、后结构主义中的主体*。(2) 米歇尔·福柯

Foucault's view that the *discourse* of an era, instead of reflecting pre-existing entities and orders, brings into being the concepts, oppositions, and hierarchies of which it speaks; that these elements are both products and propagators of "power," or social forces; and that as a result, the particular discursive formations of an era determine what is at the time accounted to be "knowledge" and "truth," as well as what is considered to be humanly normal as against what is considered to be criminal, or insane, or sexually deviant; see Foucault under *poststructuralism*. (3) The central concept in *deconstructive* criticism that all texts involve modes of signification that war against each other, merged with Mikhail Bakhtin's concept of the dialogic nature of many literary texts, in the sense that they incorporate a number of conflicting voices that represent diverse social classes and interests; see *dialogic criticism*. (4) Developments in cultural anthropology, especially Clifford Geertz's view that a culture is constituted by distinctive sets of signifying systems, and his use of what he calls **thick descriptions**—the close analysis, or "reading," of a particular social production or event so as to recover the meanings it has for the people involved in it, as well as to discover, within the overall cultural system, the network of conventions, codes, and modes of thinking with which the particular item is implicated, and which invest the item with those meanings.

In an oft-quoted phrase, Louis Montrose described the new historicism as "a reciprocal concern with the historicity of texts and the textuality of history." That is, history is conceived to be not a set of fixed, objective facts but, like the literature with which it interacts, a text that itself needs to be interpreted. Any text, on the other hand, is conceived as a discourse which, although it may seem to present, or reflect, an external reality, in fact consists of what are called **representations**—that is, verbal formations which are the "ideological products" or **cultural constructs** of the historical conditions specific to an era. A number of historicists claim also that these cultural and ideological representations in texts serve mainly to reproduce, confirm, and propagate the complex power structures of domination and subordination which characterize a given society.

Despite their common perspective on literary writings as mutually implicative with all other components of a culture, we find considerable diversity and disagreements among individual exponents of the new historicism. The following proposals, however, occur frequently in their writings, sometimes in an extreme and sometimes in a qualified form. All of them are formulated in opposition to views that, according to new historicists, were central ideological constructs in traditional literary criticism. Many historicists assign the formative period of some basic constructs to the early era of capitalism in the seventeenth and eighteenth centuries.

1. Literature does not occupy a "trans-historical" *aesthetic* realm which is independent of the economic, social, and political conditions specific to an era, nor is literature subject to timeless criteria of artistic value. Instead, a literary text is simply one of many kinds of texts—religious, philosophical, legal, scientific, and so on—all of which are formed and structured by the

的观点认为，某一时期的*话语*并非是对先前存在的实体和秩序的反映，而是促成了其所谈论的概念、对抗与等级制度的产生；这些要素是"权力"，或者说是社会力量的产物和传播者；其结果是，一个时期特定的论证结构决定了什么在当时被视为是"知识"与"真理"，什么被视为是人类正常的行为，以及与此相反，什么被视为是犯罪的、或是精神失常的、或是性变态的；参见：*后结构主义*中关于福柯的论述。(3) *解构主义*批评的中心观点认为，所有文本都包含相互对抗的含义模式，从这些模式融合了代表不同社会阶级相互冲突的声音这个意义上来说，这种观点与米哈伊尔·巴赫金关于诸多文学文本具有对话体性质的概念相融合；参见：*对话批评*。(4) 文化人类学近期的发展，尤其是克利福德·格尔茨认为，文化由种种各不相同的能指系统构成；他还使用他所称的**深描**，即对特定社会产物或事件的细致分析或"解读"，以便重新发现其对所涉及人群所具有的意义，并在文化系统内部发现给某一事物注入这些意义的普遍惯例、法规和特定项目涉及的思维模式的一般形式。

路易斯·蒙特罗斯在其常被引用的一句话中，把新历史主义描述为"对文本史实性和史实文本性的交互关注"。其意思是：历史不应被视为一套固定、客观的事实，而是如同它与之互相影响的文学一样，是本身需要得到解释的文本。另一方面，任何文本都被认为是一种话语，尽管它看起来像是在表现或反映一种外在的现实，事实上它是由我们所说的**陈述**——这种陈述是特定时代历史条件下的"**意识形态产物**"或"**文化观念**"(/ **文化建构**)的文字——构成。一些历史主义者也经常宣称，文本中这些文化和意识形态的陈述，主要是用来再现、肯定和宣传具有某一特定社会特色的统治和被统治的权力结构。

尽管对文学作品与其他文化组成成分的背景主义看法相同，但是我们在新历史主义的个别解释者中发现了大量不同和分歧。然而，下面的提法却经常出现在新历史主义者的文章中，有时以极端的形式出现，有时以有所保留的形式出现。这些提法的形成都是为了反对在许多新历史主义者看来属于传统文学批评中的中心意识形态结构的观念。许多历史主义者把这些传统观点的形成时期划归到17、18世纪的资本主义早期。

1. 文学不能占据独立于某个时期特定的经济、社会和政治条件之外的"跨历史"的审美领域，也不从属于永恒的艺术价值标准。相反，文学文本仅仅是多种文本——宗教、哲学、法律、科学等中的一种，所有这些文本都是由某一时间和地点的特定条件所形成和建构的，

particular conditions of a time and place, and among which the literary text has neither unique status nor special privilege. A related fallacy of mainstream criticism, according to new historicists, was to view a literary text as an autonomous body of fixed meanings that cohere to form an organic whole in which all conflicts are artistically resolved. (See, for example, *New Criticism*.) On the contrary, it is claimed, many literary texts consist of a diversity of dissonant voices, and these voices express not only the orthodox, but also the subordinated and subversive forces of the era in which the text was produced. Furthermore, what may seem to be the artistic resolution of a literary plot, yielding pleasure to the reader, is in fact deceptive, for it is an effect that serves to cover over the unresolved conflicts of power, class, gender, and diverse social groups that make up the tensions that underlie the surface meanings of a literary text.

Some new historicists nonetheless maintain the distinction between literary and nonliterary works, as well as between major and lesser works of literary artistry. As Stephen Greenblatt has said, "Major works of art remain centrally important, but they are jostled now by an array of other texts and images." The confrontation of such works with minor or nonliterary works, he claims, in fact serves to explain what it means to be major, and indicate why it is that works that are major have outlasted the others.

2. History is not a homogeneous and stable pattern of facts and events which serve as the "background" to the literature of an era, or which literature can be said simply to reflect, or which can be adverted to (as in early *Marxist criticism*) as the "material" conditions that, in a unilateral way, determine the particularities of a literary text. In contrast to such views, a literary text is said by new historicists to be thoroughly "embedded" in its context, and in a constant interaction and interchange with other components inside the network of institutions, beliefs, and cultural power relationships, practices, and products that, in their ensemble, constitute what we call history. New historicists commonly regard even the conceptual "boundaries" by which we currently discriminate between *literature* and nonliterary texts to be a construct of post-Renaissance ideological formations. They continue to make use of such discriminations, but only for tactical convenience in conducting critical discussion, and stress that one must view all boundaries between types of discourse as entirely permeable to interchanges of diverse elements and forces. Favored terms for such interchanges—whether among the modes of discourse within a single literary text, or among diverse kinds of texts, or between a text and its institutional and cultural context—are "negotiation," "commerce," "exchange," "transaction," and "circulation." Such metaphors are intended not only to denote the two-way, oscillatory relationships among literary and other components of a culture, but also to indicate, by their obvious origin in the monetary discourse of the marketplace, the degree to which the operations and values of modern consumer capitalism saturate the literary and aesthetic, as well as all other institutions and relations. As Stephen Greenblatt expressed such a view, the "negotiation" that

文学文本在这些文本中既没有独特的地位,也不享有什么特权。在新历史主义者看来,与主流批评相关的一个谬误就是把文学文本视为具有固定意义的自主实体,这些固定意义凝聚在一起形成一个有机整体,这一整体中的所有冲突都通过艺术手段得到解决。(例如可以参见:*新批评*。)实际上,恰恰与之相反,新历史主义宣称,许多文学文本都是由各种各样不和谐的声音构成,这些声音不仅表达了正统的思想,也表达了文本产生的时代中那些从属的和具有颠覆性的力量。而且,那些看似文学情节的艺术化解决并且给读者带来愉悦的东西事实上是具有欺骗性的,因为其功用只是掩盖未曾解决的权力、阶级、性别和各种社会群体的矛盾冲突,而正是这些矛盾冲突构成了潜藏在文学文本表面意义下的真正张力。

尽管如此,一些新历史主义者仍然维持文学作品与非文学作品,以及重要文学艺术作品与次要文学艺术作品这一区分。就像斯蒂芬·格林布拉特说过的,"重要的作品依然相当重要,但是它们现在受到了大量其他文本和图像的竞争"。他认为,与这样的次要作品或非文学作品的对抗,实际上可以用来解释成为重要作品意味着什么,并可说明为什么那些重要作品的流传时间会超过其他作品的流传时间。

2. 历史不是可被用作一个时代文学"背景"的事实与事件的相似而稳定的模式,不是文学简单的反映,不是(如早期的马克思主义批评)只被视为是单向决定文学文本特性的"物质"条件。与这些观点相反,新历史主义者都认为文学文本"嵌入"背景本身,不断与制度、信仰、文化的权力关系、实践和产品交织成的网络中的其他组成部分互相作用和交替,这些元素的总和构成了我们所称的历史。新历史主义者普遍认为,甚至我们现在用来区分文学文本与非文学文本的概念性"分界线",也是后文艺复兴时期意识形态结构的观念。他们继续利用这种区分,但只是为了进行批评讨论时便于操作,而且他们强调必须把所有这样的分界线看成具有可完全渗透不同元素和力量相互交替的能力。新历史主义者喜欢用来描述这种相互交替的术语——不管是用于单个文学文本的话语模式中、各种不同类型的文本中,还是用于文本与其所处的制度和文化背景之间——有"谈判""商业""交换""交易""流通"等。这些隐喻不仅意在表示文学与文化中其他元素之间双向、摇摆的关系,还通过它们在市场货币话语中的明显原意来表明现代消费者资本主义的运作和价值观充斥文学、审美和其他社会制度和关系的程度。斯蒂芬·格林布拉特曾表达过这样的观

results in the production and circulation of a work of art involves a "mutually profitable exchange"—including "a return normally measured in pleasure and interest"—in which "the society's dominant currencies, money and prestige, are invariably involved." ("Toward a Poetics of Culture," in *The New Historicism*, ed. H. Aram Veeser, 1989.)

3. The humanistic concept of an essential human nature that is shared by the author of a literary work, the characters within the work, and the audience the author writes for, is another of the widely held ideological illusions that, according to many new historicists, were generated primarily by a capitalist culture. They also attribute to this "bourgeois" and "essentialist humanism" the view that a literary work is the imaginative creation of a free, or "autonomous," author who possesses a unified, unique, and enduring personal identity. (See *essentialism* in the entry *humanism*, also *author and authorship*.) In the epilogue to *Renaissance Self-Fashioning* (1980) Stephen Greenblatt says that, in the course of writing the book, he lost his initial confidence in "the role of human autonomy," for "the human subject itself began to seem remarkably unfree, the ideological product of the relations of power in a particular society." An area of contest among new historicists is the extent to which an author, despite being a *subject* who is constructed and positioned by the play of power and ideology within the discourse of a particular era, may retain some scope for individual initiative and "agency." A number of historicists who ascribe a degree of freedom and initiative to an individual author do so, however, not as in traditional criticism, in order to account for an author's literary invention and distinctive artistry, but in order to keep open the theoretical possibility that an individual author can intervene so as to inaugurate radical changes in the social power structure of which that individual's own "subjectivity" and function are themselves a product.

4. Like the authors who produce literary texts, their readers are *subjects* who are constructed and positioned by the conditions and ideological formations of their own era. All claims, therefore, for the possibility of a disinterested and objective interpretation and evaluation of a literary text—such as Matthew Arnold's behest that we see a work "as in itself it really is"—are among the illusions of a humanistic idealism. Insofar as the ideology of readers conforms to the ideology of the writer of a literary text, the readers will tend to *naturalize* the text—that is, interpret its culture-specific and time-bound representations as though they were the features of universal and permanent human nature and experience. On the other hand, insofar as the readers' ideology differs from that of the writer, they will tend to **appropriate** the text—that is, interpret it so as to make it conform to their own cultural prepossessions.

New historicists acknowledge that they themselves, like all authors, are "subjectivities" that have been shaped and informed by the circumstances and discourses specific to their era, hence that their own critical writings in great part construct, rather than discover ready-made, the textual meanings they describe and the literary and cultural histories

点,艺术作品的生产和流通所带来的"谈判"涉及"互利互惠的交换"——这种交换包括"一般以愉悦和利益来衡量的回报"——其中不可避免地总是要涉及"主导社会的通货、钱币和声望"。[参阅格林布拉特所写的文章"走向文化诗学",收入 H. 阿拉姆·维瑟主编的《新历史主义》(1989)。]

3. 文学作品作者、作品中的人物、作者所针对的读者所共有的关于人类本质的人文主义概念,是另一个被广泛采纳的意识形态的错误观念,许多新历史主义者都认为这些错误观念主要是由资本主义文化所造成的。他们也认为"文学作品是一位自由或'独立'的,具有统一、独特和永恒的个人个性的作者的想象性创作"这一观点具有"资产阶级"和"本质主义的人文主义"属性。(参见:人文主义中的本质主义,也可参见:作者与作者身份。)斯蒂芬·格林布拉特在《文艺复兴的自我形成》(1980) 的结尾部分说到,在写作本书的过程中,他丧失了最初对"人类自主角色"的信心,因为"人类主体本身,即某一特定社会中权力关系的意识形态产物,开始显得如此不自由"。新历史主义者们争论的一个领域是,作者可以在何种程度上保留发挥个人主动性和"能动作用"的余地,尽管作者是某一特定时期话语内部由权力和意识形态的作用构筑和定位的主体。不过,那些认为作者个人具有一定程度的自由和主动性的新历史主义者,与传统批评借此解释作者的文学创造和特殊艺术性不同,为的是有可能从理论上说明,作者个人能够干预社会权力结构从而引发社会权力结构发生激烈变革的"主体性"和作用本身就是社会权力结构的产物。

4. 与文学文本的作者一样,他们的读者也是他们所属时代的环境和意识形态结构所构筑与定位的主体。因此,所有认为有可能对文本进行公正客观的解释与评价的说法,都只是人文主义的理想主义幻想而已,马修·阿诺德要求我们将作品视为"其本身就是真实的"观点也在此之列。当读者的意识形态与某一文学文本的作者的意识形态相一致时,读者往往会归化文本,即将文本中具有文化特色和受时间限制的描述解释为似乎是普遍的、永恒的人类体验的特征。另一方面,当读者的意识形态与作者的意识形态不一致时,读者往往会**挪用**文本,即作出与自己先入为主的文化观念相一致的解释。

新历史主义者承认他们自己与所有作者一样,都是由所属时代特定环境与话语所塑造并受到其影响的"主观性",因此,他们自己的批评论著在很大程度上都是在构建他们所描述的文本意义以及他们所叙述的文学与文化历史,而不是去发现那些现成的文本意义和

they narrate. To mitigate the risk that they will unquestioningly appropriate texts that were written in the past, they stress that the course of history between the past and present is not coherent, but exhibits discontinuities, breaks, and ruptures; by doing so, they hope to "distance" and "estrange" an earlier text and so sharpen their ability to detect its differences from their present ideological assumptions. Some historicists present their readings of texts written in the past as (in their favored metaphor) "negotiations" between past and present. In this two-way relationship, the features of a cultural product, which are identifiable only relative to their differences from the historicist's subject-position, in return make possible some degree of insight into the forces and configurations of power—especially with respect to class, gender, race, and ethnicity—that prevail in the historicist's present culture and serve to shape the historicist's own ideology and interpretations.

The concepts, themes, and procedures of new historicist criticism took shape in the late 1970s and early 1980s, most prominently in writings by scholars of the English Renaissance. They directed their attention especially to literary forms such as the pastoral and masque, and above all drama; emphasized the role in shaping a text of social and economic conditions such as literary patronage, censorship, and the control of access to printing; analyzed texts as discursive "sites" which enacted and reproduced the interests and power of the Tudor monarchy; but were alert to detect within such texts the voices of the oppressed, the marginalized, and the dispossessed. At almost the same time, students of the English Romantic period developed parallel conceptions of the intertextuality of literature and history, and similar views that the "representations" in literary texts are not reflectors of reality but "concretized" forms of ideology. Historicists of Romantic literature, however, in distinction from most Renaissance historicists, often name their critical procedures **political readings** of a literary text—readings in which they stress quasi-Freudian mechanisms such as "suppression," "displacement," and "substitution" by which, they assert, a writer's political ideology (in a process of which the writer remains largely or entirely unaware) inevitably disguises, or entirely elides into silence and "absence," the circumstances and contradictions of contemporary history. The primary aim of a political reader of a literary text is to undo these ideological disguises and suppressions in order to uncover its *subtext* of historical and political conflicts and oppressions which are the text's true, although covert or unmentioned, subject matter. (On such textual "silences," see Pierre Macherey and Fredric Jameson, under *Marxist criticism*.)

In the course of the 1980s, the characteristic viewpoints and practices of new historicism spread rapidly to all periods of literary study, and were increasingly represented, described, and debated in conferences, books, and periodical essays. The interpretive procedures of this critical mode have interacted with the earlier concern of *feminist* critics, who stressed the role of male power structures in forming dominant ideological and cultural constructs. New historicist

文学与文化历史。为了降低盲目挪用过去所创作的文本所带来的风险，他们强调历史进程中的过去与现在之间并非连贯一致，而是表现出间断、停顿和割裂；他们希望通过这样的强调来"疏远"和"间离"早先的文本并以此加强他们发现该文本与他们目前的意识形态假定的不同之处的能力。一些历史主义者将他们对前人所写的文本的解读描述为（用他们喜欢采用的隐喻来说就是）过去与现在之间的"谈判"。在这种双向关系中，某一文化产品的特征，只是因为它们与历史主义者的主体立场的不同之处才得以辨认，反过来又有可能在某种程度上洞察到权力的各种力量和结构——尤其是在阶级、性别、人种和种族地位等方面——这些权力的力量和结构盛行于历史主义者现在所处的文化中并促进历史主义者自身意识形态和理解的形成。

新历史主义批评的概念、主题和方法在 1970 年代后期与 1980 年代前期形成，在英国文艺复兴时期学者的著作中表现最为显著。他们的兴趣主要指向诸如田园诗和假面歌舞剧等文学形式，尤以戏剧为甚；他们强调诸如文学赞助、文学审查制度和印刷控制等社会、经济条件在形成文本中所起的作用；他们将文本分析为颁布与再现都铎王朝的利益和权力的论证"场所"；但他们却特别注意发掘这类文本中被压迫者、被边缘化者、被剥削者的声音。几乎与此同时，英国浪漫主义时期的学者提出了关于文学和历史的互文性的类似概念，以及文学文本中的"描述"不是现实的反映，而是意识形态的"具体化"形式的类似观点。然而与大多数文艺复兴时期的历史主义者不同，浪漫主义文学的历史主义者经常将他们的批评方法命名为文学文本的**政治解读**——在这种解读中，他们强调如"抑制""移位""取代"等类似弗洛伊德的心理机制术语；他们宣称作者的政治意识形态（在作者大体上或完全无意识的过程中），不可避免地会掩盖其同时代的历史环境与矛盾，或完全归于沉寂和"不存在"。政治解读某一文学文本的主要目的是，除去所有这些意识形态的伪装和抑制，揭示文本真正的、尽管被掩盖或者未曾提及的题材，即*潜在的*历史的和政治的冲突和压迫。（关于这样的文本"沉寂"，可以参见：*马克思主义批评*中关于彼埃尔·马舍雷和弗雷德里克·詹姆逊的论述。）

1980 年代期间，新历史主义的代表性观点和实践，很快传播到文学研究的各个时期，并越来越多地在会议、论著、期刊论文中得到阐述、描绘和辩论。这种批评模式的解释方法与早期*女性主义*批评家的关注点互相影响，女性主义批评家强调男性的权力结构在形成占据主导地位的意识形态与文化观念中所起的作用。

procedures also have parallels in the critics of *African-American* and other *ethnic* literatures, who stress the role of culture formations dominated by white Europeans in suppressing, marginalizing, or distorting the achievements of non-white and non-European peoples. In the 1990s, various forms of new historicism, and related types of criticism that stress the embeddedness of literature in historical circumstances, replaced deconstruction as the reigning mode of *avant-garde* critical theory and practice.

Stephen Greenblatt inaugurated the currency of the label "new historicism" in his Introduction to a special issue of *Genre*, Vol. 15 (1982). He prefers, however, to call his own critical enterprise **cultural poetics**, in order to highlight his concern with literature and the arts as integral with other social practices that, in their complex interactions, make up the general culture of an era. Greenblatt's essay entitled "Invisible Bullets" in *Shakespearean Negotiations* (1988) serves to exemplify the interpretive procedures of the leading exponent of this mode of criticism, who often inaugurates a commentary on a work of literature with an unexpected historical anecdote, or with a "luminous" interpretive detail in a marginal literary text, or in a nonliterary text. In this essay, Greenblatt begins by reading a selection from Thomas Harriot's *A Brief and True Report of the New Found Land of Virginia*, written in 1588, as a representative discourse of the English colonizers of America which, without its author's awareness, serves to confirm "the Machiavellian hypothesis of the origin of princely power in force and fraud," but nonetheless draws its "audience irresistibly toward the celebration of that power." Greenblatt also asserts that Harriot tests the English power structure that he attests by recording in his *Report* the countervoices of the Native Americans who are being appropriated and oppressed by that power. Greenblatt then identifies parallel modes of power discourse and counterdiscourse in the dialogues in Shakespeare's *Tempest* between Prospero the imperialist appropriator and Caliban the expropriated native of his island, and goes on to find similar discursive configurations in the texts of Shakespeare's *Henry IV, 1 and 2*, and *Henry V*. In Greenblatt's reading, the dialogue and events of the Henry plays reveal the degree to which princely power is based on predation, calculation, deceit, and hypocrisy; at the same time, the plays do not scruple to record the dissonant and subversive voices of Falstaff and various other representatives of Elizabethan subcultures. These counterestablishment discourses in Shakespeare's plays, however, in fact are so managed as to maneuver their audience to accept and even glorify the power structure to which that audience is itself subordinated. Greenblatt applies to these plays a conceptual pattern, the **subversion-containment dialectic**, which has been a central concern of new historicist critics of Renaissance literature. The thesis is that, in order to sustain its power, any durable political and cultural order not only to some degree allows, but also actively fosters "subversive" elements and forces, yet in such a way as more effectively to "contain" such challenges to the existing order. (Foucault had established such a conception by his claim that, under a dominating "regimen of truth," all attempts at opposition to power cannot help but be "complicitous" with it.) This view of the general triumph of

新历史主义的批评方法与**美国黑人**文学和其他**民族**文学的批评家的批评方式也有类似之处，后者强调欧洲白种人在文化形成过程中所扮演的抑制、边缘化或歪曲非白种人和非欧洲人所取得成就的主导角色。到1980年代，新历史主义的各种形式及其他强调文学植根于历史环境中的相关批评类型，已经明显地取代解构主义而成为先锋派批评理论和实践的主要模式。

斯蒂芬·格林布拉特在他为《文类》特刊第15卷（1982）所写的导言中，开创了"新历史主义"一词的流行时期。但他却更喜欢将自己的批评方式称为**文化诗学**，为的是强调他所关注的文学和艺术是其他社会实践不可缺少的一个组成部分，在它们复杂的相互作用中，构成了一个时代的整体文化。格林布拉特《莎士比亚的谈判》（1988）中题为"看不见的子弹"一文，可以视为这一批评模式主要倡导者阐释方法的典型代表，他经常用一个意想不到的历史掌故，或是用非主流文学文本或非文学文本中一个"明亮的"详细细节，来开启对一部文学作品的评述。在这篇文章中，格林布拉特从解读托马斯·哈里奥特写于1588年的《新发现的弗吉尼亚简要真实的报道》一书的选段开始，将它作为美国的英国殖民者的代表话语，在作者没有意识到的情况下，该书证实了"马基雅维利关于王侯的权力源于力量和骗局的假设"，但同时却又使"读者不可抗拒地赞美这种权力"。格林布拉特还声称哈里奥特检验了他通过记录在《报道》一书中美国印第安人的反对声音所证实的英国权力结构，这些美国印第安人都被英国权力所侵吞和压迫。格林布拉特接着在莎士比亚《暴风雨》中的两位人物：皇室专权者普洛斯彼罗和被剥夺了自己居住岛屿的当地人卡利班的对话中，确认了权力话语与反话语的类似模式；继而还在莎士比亚《亨利四世》第一、第二部和《亨利五世》的文本中找到了类似的论证结构。从格林布拉特的解读来看，亨利系列剧中的对话和事件都揭露了以掠夺、算计、欺诈和虚伪为基础的王侯权力达到了何种程度；同时，这些系列剧也毫无顾忌地记录了伊丽莎白时代亚文化群体中福斯塔夫和其他各种代表人物不和谐、颠覆性的声音。然而，事实上莎剧中对这些反对现存体系的揭示安排得如此天衣无缝，以至于诱使观众接受甚至美化他们自己所从属的权力结构。格林布拉特将一个概念模式，即**颠覆遏制对立**，应用于这些戏剧，这一概念模式也成为研究文艺复兴时期文学的新历史主义批评家的主要关注点。他的论点是，为了维持其权力，任何持久的政治文化秩序不仅要在某种程度上允许，而且积极鼓励这种"颠覆性"元素和力量，这样才能更有效地"遏制"对现存秩序的挑战。（福柯通过宣称：在占据主导地位的"真理制度"下，所有反对权力的尝试都会不由自主地与它"串通一气"，已经确立了这样一个概念。）这种遏制策略总体上战

containment over the forces of subversion has been criticized as "pessimistic" and "quietist" by the group of new historicists known as "cultural materialists," who insist on the capacity of subversive ideas and practices—such as those manifested in their own critical writings—to effect drastic social changes.

Cultural materialism is a term, employed by the British neo-Marxist critic Raymond Williams, which has been adopted by a number of other British scholars, especially those concerned with the literature of the Renaissance, to indicate the Marxist orientation of their mode of new historicism—Marxist in that they retain a version of Marx's view of cultural phenomena as a "superstructure" which, in the last analysis, is determined by the "material" (that is, economic) "base." (See *Marxist criticism*.) They insist that, whatever the "textuality" of history, a culture and its literary products are always to an important degree conditioned by the true, material forces and relations of production in their historical era. They are particularly interested in the political significance, and especially the subversive aspects and effects, of a literary text, not only in its own time, but also in later versions that have been revised for the theater and the cinema. Cultural materialists stress that their criticism is itself oriented toward political "intervention" in their own era, in an express "commitment," as Jonathan Dollimore and Alan Sinfield have put it, "to the transformation of a social order which exploits people on grounds of race, gender, and class." (Foreword to *Political Shakespeare: New Essays in Cultural Materialism*, 1985. See also the comment on Stuart Hall, in the entry *Marxist criticism*.) Similar views are expressed by those American exponents of the new literary history who are political activists; indeed, some of them claim that if new historicists limit themselves to analyzing examples of class dominance and exploitation in literary texts, but stop short of a commitment to reform the present social order, they have been co-opted into "complicity" with the *formalist* literary criticism that they set out to displace. For the connections between North American forms of historicism and British cultural materialism, see Kiernan Ryan, ed., *New Historicism and Cultural Materialism: A Reader* (1996), and John Brannigan, *New Historicism and Cultural Materialism* (1998).

See *cultural studies*, which are closely related to the new historicism. For writers especially influential in forming the concepts and practices of the new historicism, see Louis Althusser, *Lenin and Philosophy, and Other Essays* (1969, trans. 1971); Louis McKay, *Foucault: A Critical Introduction* (1994); and Clifford Geertz, "Thick Description: Toward an Interpretive Theory of Culture," in *The Interpretation of Cultures* (1973). *The New Historicism*, ed. H. Aram Veeser (1989), is a useful collection of essays by Louis Montrose, Stephen Greenblatt, and other prominent historicists who focus on the Renaissance; see also Veeser's *The New Historicism Reader* (1994); the essays in Jeffrey N. Cox and Larry J. Reynolds, eds., *New Historical Literary Study* (1993); Stephen Greenblatt, ed., *Representing the English Renaissance* (1988), and his *Learning to Curse: Essays in Early Modern Culture* (1990); the survey in Paul Hamilton, *Historicism: The New Critical Idiom* (1996); and Peter C. Herman, ed., *Historicizing Theory* (2004). See also Catherine Gallagher and Stephen Greenblatt, *Practicing New*

胜了颠覆性力量的观点，被一些新历史主义者团体批评为"悲观主义"和"寂静主义"，这些新历史主义者被称为"文化唯物主义者"，他们坚持认为颠覆性的观点和实践——包括他们自己批评性论著中所体现的那些观点和实践——具有引发激烈社会变革的能力。

文化唯物主义是英国新马克思主义批评家雷蒙德·威廉斯所使用的一个术语，这一术语被英国其他一些学者，尤其是那些关注文艺复兴时期文学的学者所采用，用来表明其新历史主义模式的马克思主义取向——之所以说是"马克思主义的"，是因为他们保留了马克思主义把文化现象视为归根到底是由"物质"（即经济）"基础"所决定的"上层建筑"这一观点。（参见：*马克思主义批评*。）他们坚称，不管历史的"文本性"如何，文化及其文学产品总在很重要的程度上取决于其所处历史时期真实的物质力量和生产关系。他们对文学文本的政治意义，尤其是对其颠覆性的方面和作用特别感兴趣。这种兴趣并不局限于文学文本所处的时代，而是还关注后世改编的戏剧和电影版本。文化唯物主义者强调，他们的批评以对他们所处时代的政治"干预"为取向，用乔纳森·多利莫尔和艾伦·辛菲尔德明确的话说就是"介入改革以人种、性别和阶级为基础剥削人民的社会秩序"[《政治的莎士比亚：文化唯物主义新论》（1985）前言。也可参见：*马克思主义批评*中对斯图尔特·霍尔的评论]。美国一些政治上很激进的新文学历史倡导者也表达了类似的观点；事实上，他们中的一些人宣称，如果新历史主义者将自己局限于对文学文本中阶级统治和剥削的描述而不介入重建现行社会秩序，那么他们就已经被同化，就已与他们所想要取代的文学批评类型中的*形式主义*"同流合污"了。关于北美历史主义的各种形式与英国文化唯物主义之间的关系，可以参阅：基尔南·瑞安主编的《新历史主义与文化唯物主义读本》（1996）；约翰·布兰尼根所著的《新历史主义与文化唯物主义》（1998）。

参见与新历史主义概念及实践密切相关的条目：*文化研究*。有关那些对新历史主义概念与实践的形成具有特殊影响的作家，可以参阅：路易斯·阿尔都塞所著的《列宁与哲学及其他论文选》（1969，1971年英译版）；路易斯·麦凯所著的《福柯：批判介绍》（1994）；克利福德·格尔茨所著的《文化的阐释》（1973）中的"深描：迈向文化的阐释理论"。H. 阿拉姆·维泽主编的《新历史主义》（1989）是一本收录了路易斯·蒙特罗斯、斯蒂芬·格林布拉特和其他关注文艺复兴的著名历史主义者所写文章的有用文集。也可参阅：杰弗里·N. 考克斯与拉里·J. 雷诺兹合编的《新历史文学研究》中的文章；斯蒂芬·格林布拉特主编的《再现英国的文艺复兴》（1988）和他所著的《学会诅咒：早期现代文化散论》（1990）。概论：保罗·汉密尔顿所著的《历史主义：新的批评习语》（1996）；彼得·C. 赫尔曼主编的《理论的历史化》（2004）。也可参阅凯瑟琳·加拉格尔与斯蒂芬·格林布拉

Historicism (2000). For a *feminist* application of new historicism, refer to Margaret W. Ferguson, Maureen Quilligan, and Nancy J. Vickers, eds., *Rewriting the Renaissance: The Discourses of Sexual Difference in Early Modern Europe* (1986). Treatments of Romantic literature that exemplify a new historicist orientation include Jerome J. McGann, *The Romantic Ideology: A Critical Investigation* (1983); Marjorie Levinson, *Wordsworth's Great Period Poems* (1986); Clifford Siskin, *The Historicity of Romantic Discourse* (1988); Alan Liu, *Wordsworth: The Sense of History* (1989); and Marjorie Levinson and others, *Rethinking Historicism: Critical Readings in Romantic History* (1989). For new historicist criticism focused on literature after the Romantic period, see Catherine Gallagher, *The Industrial Reformation of English Fiction: Social Discourse and Narrative Form, 1832–1867* (1985), and Walter Benn Michaels, *The Gold Standard and the Logic of Naturalism: American Literature at the Turn of the Century* (1987). Refer also to the journal *Representations*. In "What Is New Formalism?" (*PMLA*, Vol. 122, 2007), Marjorie Levinson stresses the connection between new historicism and the revival of critical interest in questions of literary form; see *new formalism*.

Jonathan Dollimore and Alan Sinfield present writings by British cultural materialists in *Political Shakespeare: New Essays in Cultural Materialism* (1985), as does John Drakakis in *Alternative Shakespeares* (1985); see also Raymond Williams, *Marxism and Literature* (1977), and Terry Eagleton, *Marxism and Literary Criticism* (1976). Walter Cohen, "Political Criticism of Shakespeare," in Jean E. Howard and Marion F. O'Connor, eds., *Shakespeare Reproduced: The Text in History and Ideology* (1987), interrogates new historicism from a Marxist point of view; while J. Hillis Miller, in his presidential address to the Modern Language Association on "The Triumph of Theory" (*PMLA*, Vol. 102, 1987, pp. 281–91), does so from the point of view of deconstructive criticism. Feminist critiques of new historicism are Lynda Boose, "The Family in Shakespeare Studies," *Renaissance Quarterly*, Vol. 40 (1987); and Carol Thomas Neely, "Constructing the Subject: Feminist Practice and the New Renaissance Discourse" (*English Literary Renaissance*, Vol. 18, 1988). Critiques of some forms of new historicism from more traditional critical positions are Edward Pechter, "The New Historicism and Its Discontents," *PMLA*, Vol. 102 (1987); M. H. Abrams, "On Political Readings of *Lyrical Ballads*," in *Doing Things with Texts: Essays in Criticism and Critical Theory* (1989); Richard Levin, "Unthinkable Thoughts in the New Historicizing of English Renaissance Drama," *New Literary History*, Vol. 21 (1989–90), pp. 433–47; and Brook Thomas, *The New Historicism and Other Old-Fashioned Topics* (1991). For tendencies in the writing of general history closely parallel to the new historicism in literary studies, see Dominick La Capra, *History and Criticism* (1985); and Lynn Hunt, ed., *The New Cultural History* (1989). For references to *new historicism* in other entries, see pages *52, 163, 311.*

New Humanism: 162.

new novel: 258; 47.

特合著的《新历史主义实践》(2000)。关于新历史主义在女性主义中的应用,可以参阅:玛格丽特·W. 弗格森、莫琳·奎利根、南茜·J. 维克斯三人合编的《重写文艺复兴:早期现代欧洲性别差异的话语》(1986)。论述浪漫主义文学体现了新历史主义取向的论著包括:杰尔姆·J. 麦根所著的《浪漫主义意识形态:批判探究》(1983);玛乔里·莱文森所著的《华兹华斯重大时期的诗歌》(1986);克利福德·西斯金所著的《浪漫主义话语的历史性》(1988);艾伦·刘所著的《华兹华斯:历史的意义》(1989);玛乔里·莱文森等人合著的《反思历史主义:浪漫史的批判读法》(1989)。关于关注浪漫主义时期之后文学的新历史主义批评,可以参阅:凯瑟琳·加拉格尔所著的《英国小说中的工业变革:1832—1867年间的社会话语与叙事形式》(1985)和沃尔特·本·迈克尔斯所著的《黄金标准与自然主义逻辑:世纪之交的美国文学》(1987)。也可参阅期刊《再现》。在"什么是新形式主义?"(载于《美国现代语言学协会会刊》2007年第122卷)这篇文章中,玛乔里·莱文森强调指出了新历史主义与对文学形式问题批评兴趣的复兴之间的关系;参见:*新形式主义*。

乔纳森·多利莫尔与艾伦·辛菲尔德合编的《政治的莎士比亚》(1985)及约翰·德拉卡基斯主编的《标新立异的莎士比亚》(1985)中都收录了英国文化唯物主义者的文章。也可参阅:雷蒙德·威廉斯所著的《马克思主义与文学》(1977)和伊格尔顿所著的《马克思主义与文学批评》(1976)。沃尔特·科恩所写的文章"莎士比亚的政治批评",收入吉恩·E. 霍华德与马里恩·F. 奥康纳合编的《重温莎士比亚:历史和意识形态的文本》(1987),从马克思主义的观点质疑了新历史主义。J. 希利斯·米勒在对现代语言学会所作的题为"理论的胜利"(《美国现代语言学会季刊》1987年第102卷第281—291页)的主席发言中,则从解构主义观点对新历史主义提出了质疑。女性主义对新历史主义的评论,可以参阅:琳达·布斯所写的文章"莎士比亚研究中的家庭",载于《文艺复兴季刊》1987年第40卷;卡罗尔·托马斯·尼利所写的文章"建构主体:女性主义实践与新文艺复兴话语"(《文艺复兴时期的英国文学》1988年第18卷)。从更传统的立场对新历史主义所作的评论有:爱德华·佩克特所写的文章"新历史主义和它的不满",载于《美国现代语言学协会会刊》1987年第102卷;M. H. 艾布拉姆斯所著的《以文行事:艾布拉姆斯精选集》(1989)中的"论抒情民谣的政治解读";理查德·莱文所写的文章"英国文艺复兴时期戏剧新历史化中难以想象的思想",载于《新文学史》第21卷(1989—1990)第433—447页;布鲁克·托马斯所著的《新历史主义及其他一些老话题》(1991)。有关文学研究中与新历史主义极为相似的撰写一般性历史作品的趋势,可以参阅:多米尼克·拉·卡普拉所著的《历史与批评》(1985);林恩·亨特主编的《新文化史》(1989)。其他条目中提及"新历史主义"的地方,参见第52、163、311页。

New Humanism:新人文主义运动 162。

new novel:新小说 258;47。

new philology: 194.

new philosophy: 340.

new pragmatism: 314.

new science, the: 341.

New York Intellectuals: 277.

New York Poets: 277.

Noble Savage: 316.

nonfiction novel: 257.

nonperiodic sentence: 385.

nonsense verses: 192.

nouveau roman (noovō′ rōmän′): **258.**

novel: The term "novel" is applied to a great variety of writings that have in common only the attribute of being extended works of *fiction* written in prose. As an extended narrative, the novel is distinguished from the *short story* and from the work of middle length called the *novelette*; its magnitude permits a greater variety of characters, greater complication of plot (or plots), ampler development of milieu, and more sustained exploration of character and motives than do the shorter, more concentrated modes. As a narrative written in prose, the novel is distinguished from the long narratives in verse of Geoffrey Chaucer, Edmund Spenser, and John Milton which, beginning with the eighteenth century, the novel has increasingly supplanted. Within these limits the novel includes such diverse works as Samuel Richardson's *Pamela* and Laurence Sterne's *Tristram Shandy*; Jane Austen's *Emma* and Virginia Woolf's *Orlando*; Charles Dickens' *Pickwick Papers* and Henry James' *The Wings of the Dove*; Leo Tolstoy's *War and Peace* and Franz Kafka's *The Trial*; Ernest Hemingway's *The Sun Also Rises* and James Joyce's *Finnegans Wake*; Doris Lessing's *The Golden Notebook* and Vladimir Nabokov's *Lolita*.

The term for the novel in most European languages is **roman**, which is derived from the medieval term, the *romance*. The English name for the form, on the other hand, is derived from the Italian **novella** (literally, "a little new thing"), which was a short tale in prose. In fourteenth-century Italy there was a vogue for collections of such tales, some serious and some scandalous; the best known of these collections is Boccaccio's *Decameron*, which is still available in English translation at any well-stocked bookstore. Currently the term "novella" (or in the German form, *Novelle*) is often used as an equivalent for

new philology：新语文学　194。

new philosophy：新哲学　340。

new pragmatism：新实用主义　314。

new science, the：新科学　341。

New York Intellectuals：纽约文人　277。

New York Poets：纽约诗人　277。

Noble Savage：高贵的野蛮人　316。

nonfiction novel：非虚构小说　257。

nonperiodic sentence：疏置句　385。

nonsense verses：无意义的诗歌　192。

nouveau roman：新小说　258。

Novel：小说

"小说"这一术语现被用来表示种类繁多的作品，其唯一的共同特性是它们都是延伸了的、用散文体写成的*虚构*小说。作为延伸的叙事文，小说既不同于*短篇小说*，也异于篇幅中等的*中篇小说*。它的庞大篇幅使它比那些短小精悍的文学形式具有更多的人物、更复杂的情节、更广阔的环境展现、对人物性格及其动机更持续的探究。作为散文体写就的叙事文，小说不同于杰弗里·乔叟、埃德蒙·斯宾塞、约翰·弥尔顿用韵文体写成的长篇叙事文。小说从18世纪开始逐渐取代了韵文体叙事文。在这些范围内，小说的模式多种多样，包括塞缪尔·理查逊的《帕美勒》和劳伦斯·斯特恩的《项狄传》；简·奥斯丁的《爱玛》和弗吉尼亚·吴尔夫的《奥兰多》；查尔斯·狄更斯的《匹克威克外传》和亨利·詹姆斯的《鸽翼》；列夫·托尔斯泰的《战争与和平》和弗朗兹·卡夫卡的《审判》；欧内斯特·海明威的《太阳照样升起》和詹姆斯·乔伊斯的《芬尼根的觉醒》；多丽丝·莱辛的《金色笔记本》和弗拉基米尔·纳博科夫的《洛丽塔》。

在大多数欧洲语言里，表示小说的术语都是"roman"，该词源自中世纪的*传奇*。另一方面，其英文名称则衍生于意大利语"novella"（字面意思是"小巧新颖之物"）：一种用散文体写成的小故事。在14世纪的意大利，这类故事集十分流行。故事的题材时而严肃，时而中伤。这些故事集中最著名的是薄伽丘的《十日谈》。这本书的英译版在任何一家藏书丰富的书店里都仍可买到。现在"novella"（或德文 Novelle）常用作"novelette"（中篇小说）的同义词：指一部

novelette: a prose fiction of middle length, such as Joseph Conrad's *Heart of Darkness* or Thomas Mann's *Death in Venice*. (See under *short story*.)

Long narrative romances in prose were written by Greek writers as early as the second and third centuries AD. Typically they dealt with separated lovers who, after perilous adventures and hairbreadth escapes, are happily reunited at the end. The best known of these Greek romances, influential in later European literature, were the *Aethiopica* by Heliodorus and the charming pastoral narrative *Daphnis and Chloe* by Longus. Thomas Lodge's *Rosalynde* (the model for Shakespeare's *As You Like It*) and Sir Philip Sidney's *Arcadia* were Elizabethan continuations of the pastoral romance of the ancient Greeks. See *romance* and *pastoral*.

Another important predecessor of the novel was the **picaresque narrative**, which emerged in sixteenth-century Spain; see Michael Alpert, trans., *Lazarillo de Tormes* and *The Swindler* (2003), and Giancarlo Maiorino, *At the Margins of the Renaissance: Lazarillo de Tormes and the Picaresque Art of Survival* (2003). The most popular instance, however, *Gil Blas* (1715), was written by the Frenchman Le Sage. "Picaro" is Spanish for "rogue," and a typical story concerns the escapades of an insouciant rascal who lives by his wits and shows little if any alteration of character through a long succession of adventures. Picaresque fiction is realistic in manner, **episodic** in structure (that is, composed of a sequence of events held together largely because they happened to one person), and often satiric in aim. The first, and very lively, English example was Thomas Nashe's *The Unfortunate Traveller* (1594). We recognize the survival of the picaresque type in many later novels such as Mark Twain's *The Adventures of Tom Sawyer* (1876), Thomas Mann's *The Confessions of Felix Krull* (1954), and Saul Bellow's *The Adventures of Augie March* (1953). The development of the novel owes much to prose works which, like the picaresque story, were written to deflate romantic or idealized fictional forms. Cervantes' great quasi-picaresque narrative *Don Quixote* (1605) was the single most important progenitor of the modern novel; in it, an engaging madman who tries to live by the ideals of chivalric romance in the everyday world is used to explore the relationships of illusion and reality in human life.

After these precedents and many others—including the seventeenth-century *character* (a brief sketch of a typical personality or way of life) and Madame de La Fayette's psychologically complex study of character, *La Princesse de Clèves* (1678)—what is recognizably the novel as we now think of it appeared in England in the early eighteenth century. In 1719 Daniel Defoe wrote *Robinson Crusoe* and in 1722, *Moll Flanders*. Both of these are still picaresque in type, in the sense that their structure is episodic rather than in the organized form of a *plot*; while Moll is herself a colorful female version of the old picaro—"twelve Year a Whore, five times a Wife (whereof once to her own Brother), Twelve Year a Thief, Eight Year a Transported Felon in Virginia," as the title page resoundingly informs us. But *Robinson Crusoe* is given an enforced unity of action by its focus on the problem of surviving on an uninhabited island, and both stories present so convincing a central

篇幅适中的散文体小说，譬如，约瑟夫·康拉德的《黑暗的心脏》和托马斯·曼的《死在威尼斯》。（参见：*短篇小说*中的相关论述。）

早在公元2、3世纪，希腊作家就开始创作散文体长篇叙事传奇。他们的一大特色是描述一对分离的恋人经历重重危难最终死里逃生、快乐重聚的故事。这些希腊传奇中最著名、对后世欧洲文学影响最大的是赫里奥多鲁斯的《伊西奥皮卡》和朗格斯所著的迷人田园叙事诗《达芙妮与克罗埃》。托马斯·洛奇的《罗莎琳德》（莎士比亚《皆大欢喜》的原型）和菲利普·锡德尼爵士的《阿卡迪亚》是伊丽莎白时代对古希腊田园传奇的延续。参见：*传奇、牧歌*。

小说的另一个重要前身是兴起于16世纪的西班牙的**流浪汉叙事文**；参阅：迈克尔·阿尔珀特翻译的《小癞子》和《诈骗犯》（2003），詹卡洛·迈奥里诺所著的《在文艺复兴的边缘：〈小癞子〉与流浪汉小说艺术的幸存》（2003）。不过，流浪汉叙事文最受欢迎的作品却是法国人勒萨日所著的《吉尔·布拉斯》（1715）。"picaro"是西班牙语，意思是"流氓"，典型的流浪汉叙事文的主题是一个自在逍遥的"流氓"的胡作非为。他靠自己的机智度日，其性格在其漫长的冒险生涯里几乎毫无改变。流浪汉叙事文的手法是写实的，结构是**插曲式的**（即由大体上相连的一系列事件组成，这些事件之所以有关系，是因为它们都发生在同一人身上），往往还带有嘲讽的目的。第一部生动的英国流浪汉叙事文是托马斯·纳什的《倒霉的旅行家》（1594）。流浪汉叙事文在许多后来的小说里依然可以见到。譬如，马克·吐温的《汤姆·索亚历险记》（1876）、托马斯·曼的《费利克斯·克鲁尔》（1954）、索尔·贝娄的《奥吉·玛琪历险记》（1953）。小说的发展主要归功于像流浪汉故事那样浓缩了浪漫的或理想化的虚构形式的散文作品。塞万提斯的半流浪汉叙事文杰作《堂吉诃德》（1605），是现代小说独一无二的最重要先驱；小说中叙述了一位可爱的疯子，试图以骑士传奇的理想方式生活在日常世界的故事，主要用来探索幻觉和现实在人类生活中的关系。

继小说的这些和其他许多雏形模式之后——其中包括17世纪的*人物素描*（对一种典型个性或生活方式的简短素描）和拉法耶特夫人对人物复杂心理研究的作品《克莱芙公主》（1678）——我们现在所定义的小说是18世纪早期在英国出现的。1719年丹尼尔·笛福的《鲁滨逊漂流记》问世，1722年他的《摩尔·弗兰德斯》出版。这两部小说仍属于流浪汉叙事文的类型，因为它们的结构都是插曲式的而不是以有组织的*情节*形式出现。摩尔本人是一位富有特色的流氓原型的女性翻版。小说的扉页上这样赫然醒目地告知读者："从妓12年，为人妻5次（其中一次是和亲兄弟），行窃12年，在弗吉尼亚州服刑役8年"。《鲁滨逊漂流记》则是靠侧重于在荒无人迹的海岛上如何生存的问题，使小说带有行动上的完整性。这两部小说里都有令人信服的主要人物，

character, set in so solid and detailedly realized a world, that Defoe is often credited with writing the first **novel of incident**.

The credit for having written the first English **novel of character**, or "psychological novel," is almost unanimously given to Samuel Richardson for his *Pamela; or, Virtue Rewarded* (1740). Pamela is the story of a sentimental but shrewd young woman who, by prudently safeguarding her beleaguered chastity, succeeds in becoming the wife of a wild young gentleman instead of his debauched servant girl. The distinction between the novel of incident and the novel of character cannot be drawn sharply; but in the novel of incident the greater interest is in what the *protagonist* will do next and on how the story will turn out; in the novel of character, it is on the protagonist's motives for what he or she does, and on how the protagonist as a person will turn out. On twentieth-century developments in the novel of character see Leon Edel, *The Modern Psychological Novel* (rev. 1965). For an account, in the mode of *cultural studies*, of the genesis of the conception of character in the novel, see Deidre S. Lynch, *The Economy of Character: Novels, Market Culture, and the Business of Inner Meaning* (1998).

Pamela, like its greater and tragic successor, Richardson's *Clarissa* (1747–48), is an **epistolary novel**; that is, the narrative is conveyed entirely by an exchange of letters. Later novelists have preferred alternative devices for limiting the narrative *point of view* to one or another single character, but the epistolary technique is still occasionally revived—for example, in Mark Harris' hilarious novel *Wake Up, Stupid* (1959) and Alice Walker's *The Color Purple* (1982). See Linda Kauffman, *Special Delivery: Epistolary Modes in Modern Fiction* (1992).

Novels may have any kind of plot form—tragic, comic, satiric, or romantic. A common distinction—which was described by Hawthorne, in his preface to *The House of the Seven Gables* (1851) and elsewhere, and has been adopted and expanded by a number of recent critics—is that between two basic types of prose fiction: the realistic novel (which is the novel proper) and the romance. The **realistic novel** can be described as the fictional attempt to give the effect of realism, by representing complex characters with mixed motives who are rooted in a social class, operate in a developed social structure, interact with many other characters, and undergo plausible, everyday modes of experience. This novelistic mode, rooted in such eighteenth-century writers as Defoe and Fielding, achieved a high development in the master novelists of the nineteenth century, including Jane Austen, George Eliot, Anthony Trollope, William Dean Howells, and Henry James in England and America; Stendhal, George Sand, Balzac, and Flaubert in France; and Turgenev and Tolstoy in Russia. If, as in the writings of Jane Austen, Edith Wharton, and John P. Marquand, a realistic novel focuses on the customs, conversation, and ways of thinking and valuing of the upper social class, it is often called a **novel of manners**. The **prose romance**, on the other hand, has as its precursors the *chivalric romance* of the Middle Ages and the *Gothic novel* of the later eighteenth century. It usually deploys characters who are sharply discriminated as heroes or villains, masters or victims; its protagonist is often solitary, and relatively isolated from a social context; it tends

都发生在如此可靠、复杂现实的人世间,因此笛福常被誉为是写出第一部**事件小说**的作家。

英国第一部**性格小说**或"心理小说"的作者,几乎毫无异议地被认为是创作了《帕美勒》(又名《美德受到了奖赏》)(1740)的塞缪尔·理查逊。《帕美勒》描写的是一位多愁善感但聪敏伶俐的年轻女子的故事。她谨慎地护卫了自己的贞操,最终成为一位放荡的年轻绅士的妻子,而不是成为受他诱惑而堕落的女仆。事件小说和性格小说的区别不易辨别清楚。但在事件小说里,较多的篇幅是用在*主人公*下一步将会做些什么和故事将如何结束上;而在性格小说里,作者侧重描写主人公行为的动机和主人公作为一个人,最终结局将会怎样。有关 20 世纪性格小说的发展,可以参阅利昂·埃德尔所著的《现代心理小说》(1965 年修订版)。关于依照文化研究模式对小说中性格这一概念的起源所作的解释,可以参阅:戴德丽·S.林奇所著的《性格经济学:小说、市场文化与内在意义的经营》(1998)。

《帕美勒》和它后来更为杰出的悲剧式姐妹篇、理查逊的《克拉丽莎》(1747—1748)一样,都是**书信体小说**;也就是说,叙述内容完全是靠信件的交流来传达的。后世的小说家较喜欢采用其他叙述方法将叙述*视角*限制在某个单独的人物身上。然而书信体小说的技巧还是偶尔会被重新采用——譬如,马克·哈里斯令人忍俊不禁的小说《醒来,蠢家伙》(1959)和艾丽斯·沃克的《紫色》(1982)。参阅:琳达·考夫曼所著的《特殊风格:现代小说中的书信体模式》(1992)。

小说可以采用任何一种情节形式:悲剧的、喜剧的、嘲讽的,或浪漫传奇的。霍桑在其小说《七个尖角阁的房子》(1851)的序文里和其他一些地方描述了两种基本的散文体小说类型:**现实主义小说**(即严格意义上的小说)与传奇之间最普遍的区别,并被近代许多批评家采纳和发展。现实主义小说可被描述为:用虚构手段表现动机复杂的各类人物,他们植根于社会的某一阶层,在某个高度发达的社会结构中处事度日,与许多其他人物打交道,体验貌似真实的日常经历的种种形式,以此营造小说的现实主义效果。这种文学形式源于 18 世纪的一些作家,如笛福、菲尔丁,并在 19 世纪一些大师级小说家手中得到高度发展,这些大师包括英国和美国的作家:简·奥斯丁、乔治·艾略特、安东尼·特罗洛普、威廉·迪安·豪威尔斯和亨利·詹姆斯;法国的司汤达、乔治·桑、巴尔扎克和福楼拜;俄国的屠格涅夫和托尔斯泰。如果一部现实主义小说,像简·奥斯丁、伊迪丝·华顿和约翰·P.马昆德的作品那样,注重上流社会阶层的习俗、对话、思维方式和价值观念,这部小说通常就被称为**生活方式小说**。另一方面,**散文体传奇**的最初模式是中世纪的*骑士传奇*和 18 世纪后期出现的*哥特小说*。它所设置的人物通常一目了然地区分成英雄或恶人,占有者或受害者;小说主人公通常是独自一人,相对来说,孤立于社会环境;

to be set in the historical past, and the *atmosphere* is such as to suspend the reader's expectations that are based on everyday experience. The plot of the prose romance emphasizes adventure, and is frequently cast in the form of the *quest* for an ideal, or the pursuit of an enemy; and the nonrealistic and occasionally melodramatic events are claimed by some critics to project in symbolic form the primal desires, hopes, and terrors in the depths of the human mind, and to be therefore analogous to the materials of dream, myth, ritual, and folklore. Examples of romance novels are Walter Scott's *Rob Roy* (1817), Alexandre Dumas' *The Three Musketeers* (1844–45), Emily Brontë's *Wuthering Heights* (1847), and an important line of American narratives which extends from Edgar Allan Poe, James Fenimore Cooper, Nathaniel Hawthorne, and Herman Melville to recent writings of William Faulkner and Saul Bellow. Martin Green, in *Dreams of Adventure, Deeds of Empire* (1979), distinguishes a special type of romance, "the adventure novel," which deals with masculine adventures in the newly colonized non-European world. Defoe's *Robinson Crusoe* (1719) is an early prototype; some later instances are H. Rider Haggard's *King Solomon's Mines* (1886), Robert Louis Stevenson's *Treasure Island* (1883), and Rudyard Kipling's *Kim* (1901).

Refer to Laurie Langbauer, *Women and Romance: The Consolations of Gender in the English Novel* (1990); Deborah Ross, *The Excellence of Falsehood: Romance, Realism, and Women's Contribution to the Novel* (1991). On the realistic novel in the nineteenth century see Harry Levin, *The Gates of Horn: A Study of Five French Realists* (1963); Ioan Williams, *The Realist Novel in England* (1975); G. J. Becker, *Master European Realists* (1982). On the prose romance in America, see Richard Chase, *The American Novel and Its Tradition* (1957); Northrop Frye, "The Mythos of Summer: Romance," in *Anatomy of Criticism* (1957); Joel Porte, *The Romance in America* (1969); Michael D. Bell, *The Development of American Romance* (1980); and for a skeptical view of the usual division between novel and romance, Nina Baym, *Novels, Readers, and Reviewers: Responses to Fiction in Antebellum America* (1984).

Other often identified subclasses of the novel are based on differences in subject matter, emphasis, and artistic purpose:

Bildungsroman and **Erziehungsroman** are German terms signifying "novel of formation" or "novel of education." The subject of these novels is the development of the protagonist's mind and character, in the passage from childhood through varied experiences—and often through a spiritual crisis—into maturity; this process usually involves recognition of one's identity and role in the world. The mode began in Germany with K. P. Moritz's *Anton Reiser* (1785–90) and Goethe's *Wilhelm Meister's Apprenticeship* (1795–96); it includes Charlotte Brontë's *Jane Eyre* (1847), George Eliot's *The Mill on the Floss* (1860), Charles Dickens' *Great Expectations* (1861), Somerset Maugham's *Of Human Bondage* (1915), and Thomas Mann's *The Magic Mountain* (1924). An important subtype of the Bildungsroman is the **Künstlerroman** ("artist-novel"), which represents the development of a novelist or other artist from childhood into the stage of maturity that signalizes the recognition of the protagonist's artistic destiny and mastery of an artistic craft. Dickens' *David*

故事通常发生在过去的历史背景下，作品*基调*是悬置读者建立在日常经验上的期望。散文体传奇的情节强调冒险，常以*追求*某一理想，或追踪某一敌人的形式表现出来；一些批评家认为，非现实的和偶尔夸张的戏剧性事件以象征方式折射出人们心灵深处的原始欲望、期待和恐惧，因此，它们与梦幻、神话、祭仪和民间传说的素材相似。传奇小说的范例有：沃尔特·司各特的《罗伯·罗伊》(1817)、亚历山德拉·大仲马的《三个火枪手》(1844—1845)、埃米莉·勃朗特的《呼啸山庄》(1847)及一系列美国重要小说，从埃德加·爱伦·坡、詹姆斯·费尼莫尔·库珀、纳撒尼尔·霍桑、赫尔曼·梅尔维尔的作品到威廉·福克纳、索尔·贝娄最近的作品。马丁·格林在《冒险之梦，帝国的功绩》(1979)中区分出一种特殊的传奇小说："冒险小说"，这类小说描述的是欧洲以外新殖民世界的男性冒险。笛福的《鲁滨逊漂流记》(1719)是这类小说的早期原型；后期的一些例子有 H. 里德·哈格德的《所罗门王的宝藏》(1886)、罗伯特·路易斯·斯蒂文森的《金银岛》(1883)和拉迪亚德·吉卜林的《吉姆》(1901)。

参阅：劳里·朗鲍尔所著的《女性与传奇：英语小说中的性别慰藉》(1990)；德博拉·罗斯所著的《卓越的谎言：传奇、现实主义与女性对小说的贡献》(1991)。有关19世纪的现实主义小说，可以参阅：哈里·莱文所著的《角门：对五位法国现实主义者的研究》；约安·威廉斯所著的《英国的现实主义小说》(1975)；G. J. 贝克尔所著的《欧洲现实主义大师》(1982)。关于美国的散文体传奇，可以参阅：理查德·蔡斯所著的《美国小说及其传统》(1957)；诺斯罗普·弗莱所著的《批评的剖析》(1957)中的"夏天的神话：传奇"；乔尔·波特所著的《美国的传奇》(1969)；迈克尔·D. 贝尔所著的《美国传奇的发展》(1980)。对小说和传奇通常的划分所持的怀疑观点，可以参阅：尼娜·贝姆所著的《小说、读者和评论家：对内战前美国小说的回应》(1984)。

其他常见的小说分类，是以题材、侧重点和艺术目的的不同而定的：

Bildungsroman 和 **Erziehungsroman** 这两个德语术语表示"主人公成长小说"或"教育小说"。这类小说的主题是主人公思想和性格的发展，叙述主人公从童年开始所经历的各种遭遇——通常都要经历一场精神危机——然后长大成熟，认识到自己在世间的位置和作用。这类小说模式始于 K. P. 莫里茨的《安东·赖绥》(1785—1790)和歌德的《威廉·迈斯特的学徒生涯》(1795—1796)；还包括夏洛蒂·勃朗特的《简爱》(1847)、乔治·艾略特的《弗洛斯河上的磨坊》(1860)、查尔斯·狄更斯的《远大前程》(1861)、萨默塞特·毛姆的《人生的桎梏》(1915)和托马斯·曼的《魔山》(1924)。"教育小说"的一个重要分支是**艺术家成长小说**（"艺术家小说"），艺术家小说再现了小说家或其他艺术家从儿时到步入成熟，认识到自己的艺术使命，并掌握他的艺术技巧这一阶段的成长经历。

Copperfield (1849–50) can be considered an early instance of this type; later and more developed examples include some major novels of the twentieth century: Marcel Proust's *Remembrance of Things Past* (1913–27), James Joyce's *A Portrait of the Artist as a Young Man* (1914–15), Thomas Mann's *Tonio Kröger* (1903) and *Dr. Faustus* (1947), and André Gide's *The Counterfeiters* (1926). See Lionel Trilling, "The Princess Casamassima," in *The Liberal Imagination* (1950); Maurice Beebe, *Ivory Towers and Sacred Founts: The Artist as Hero in Fiction* (1964); Jerome H. Buckley, *Season of Youth: The Bildungsroman from Dickens to Golding* (1974); Martin Swales, *The German Bildungsroman from Wieland to Hesse* (1978); Thomas L. Jeffers, *Apprenticeships: The Bildungsroman from Goethe to Santayana* (2005). In *Unbecoming Women: British Women Writers and the Novel of Development* (1993), Susan Fraiman analyzes novels about "growing up female"; she proposes that they put to question the "enabling fiction" that the *Bildungsroman* is a "progressive development" toward "masterful selfhood."

The **social novel** emphasizes the influence of the social and economic conditions of an era on shaping characters and determining events; if it also embodies an implicit or explicit thesis recommending political and social reform, it is often called a **sociological novel**. Examples of social novels are Harriet Beecher Stowe's *Uncle Tom's Cabin* (1852); Upton Sinclair's *The Jungle* (1906); John Steinbeck's *The Grapes of Wrath* (1939); Nadine Gordimer's *Burger's Daughter* (1979). A Marxist version of the social novel, representing the hardships suffered by the oppressed working class, and usually written to incite the reader to radical political action, is called the **proletarian novel** (see *Marxist criticism*). Proletarian fiction flourished especially during the great economic depression of the 1930s. An English example is Walter Greenwood's *Love on the Dole* (1933); American examples are Grace Lumpkin's *To Make My Bread* (1932), about a mill strike in North Carolina, and Robert Cantwell's *Laugh and Lie Down* (1931), about the harshness of life in a lumber mill city in the Northwest.

Some realistic novels, including George Eliot's *Middlemarch* and Tolstoy's *War and Peace*, make use of events and personages from the historical past to add interest and credibility to the narrative, but in them, the principal focus is on the fictional protagonists. What we usually specify as the **historical novel** proper began in the nineteenth century with Sir Walter Scott. The historical novel not only takes its setting and some characters and events from history, but makes the historical events and issues crucial for the central characters (who may themselves be historical personages) and for the course of the narrative. Some of the greatest historical novels also use the protagonists and actions to reveal what the author regards as the deep forces that impel the historical process. Examples of historical novels are Scott's *Ivanhoe* (1819), set in the period of Norman domination of the Saxons at the time of Richard I; Dickens' *A Tale of Two Cities* (1859), set in Paris and London during the French Revolution; George Eliot's *Romola* (1863), in Florence during the Renaissance; and Margaret Mitchell's *Gone with the Wind* (1936), in Georgia during the Civil War and Reconstruction. An influential treatment of the form was by the Marxist scholar and critic Georg Lukács, *The Historical Novel*

狄更斯的《大卫·科波菲尔》(1849—1850)可以视为这一类型的一个早期例子；后来更成熟的例子包括20世纪的一些主要小说：马塞尔·普鲁斯特的《追忆逝水年华》(1913—1927)、詹姆斯·乔伊斯的《一个青年艺术家的画像》(1914—1915)、托马斯·曼的《托尼奥·克略格尔》(1903)和《浮士德博士》(1947)、安德烈·纪德的《伪币制造者》(1926)。参阅：莱昂内尔·特里林所著的《自由主义的想象力》中的"卡萨玛西玛公主"(1950)；莫里斯·毕比所著的《象牙塔与圣洗池：小说中作为英雄的艺术家》(1964)；杰尔姆·H. 巴克利所著的《青春的季节：从狄更斯到戈尔丁的成长小说》(1974)；马丁·斯韦尔斯所著的《从维兰到黑塞的德国成长小说》(1978)；托马斯·L. 杰弗斯所著的《学徒：从歌德到桑塔亚纳的成长小说》(2005)。苏珊·弗雷曼在《形成中的女性：英国女性作家与小说的发展》(1993)这本书中分析了描写"成长中的女性"的小说；提出了"成长中的女性"的小说，对认为主人公成长小说是描写"逐步发展"成为"出色的自我"的"能力小说"这一观点提出了质疑。

社会小说强调一个时期的社会状况和经济条件对塑造人物和决定事件的影响；如果它也体现了赞成政治和社会变革的或含蓄或明确的主题，它常被叫做**社会学小说**。社会小说的例子有：哈丽特·比彻·斯托的《汤姆叔叔的小屋》(1852)、厄普顿·辛克莱的《屠场》(1906)、约翰·斯坦贝克的《愤怒的葡萄》(1939)、内丁·戈迪默的《伯格的女儿》(1979)。马克思主义者描述的社会小说，再现了受压迫的工人阶级所遭受的苦难，通常带有鼓动读者采取激进政治行动的写作目的，叫做**无产阶级小说**。(参见：*马克思主义批评*。)无产阶级小说的繁盛期出现在1930年代的经济大萧条中。一个英国的例子是沃尔特·格林伍德的《靠施舍的爱情》(1933)；美国的例子有：格蕾丝·伦普金的《给我我的面包》(1932)，讲述了北卡罗来纳州爆发的一次煤矿大罢工；罗伯特·坎特韦尔的《笑着倒下》(1931)，讲述了西北一个木材厂城的艰辛生活。

一些现实主义小说，包括乔治·艾略特的《米德尔马契》和托尔斯泰的《战争与和平》，以历史上的事件、人物为素材，以增加叙事的趣味性和生动性，但在这些小说中，主要关注的是虚构的主人公。我们通常定义的**历史小说**始于19世纪沃尔特·司各特爵士的作品。历史小说不仅以历史为背景，以历史上的一些人物及事件为素材，而且使历史事件和问题对主要人物（他们自己可能是历史名人）和叙述具有重大意义。一些最著名的历史小说还利用主人公和行为来揭示在作者看来是推动历史进程的深层力量。历史小说的例子有司各特的《艾凡赫》(1819)，以理查一世时诺曼人统治撒克逊人的时期为背景；狄更斯的《双城记》(1859)的故事发生在法国大革命时期的巴黎和伦敦；乔治·艾略特的《罗马拉》(1863)以文艺复兴时期的佛罗伦萨为背景；托尔斯泰的《战争与和平》(1869)的故事发生在拿破仑入侵俄国期间；玛格丽特·米切尔的《飘》(1936)的故事发生在美国内战和南部重建时期的乔治亚州。马克思主义学者和批评家乔治·卢卡奇所著的《历史小说》

(1937, trans. 1962); a comprehensive later commentary is by Harry E. Shaw, *The Forms of Historical Fiction: Sir Walter Scott and His Successors* (1983).

One twentieth-century variant of the historical novel is known as **documentary fiction**, which not only incorporates historical characters and events, but also reports of everyday happenings in contemporary newspapers: John Dos Passos, *USA* (1938); E. L. Doctorow, *Ragtime* (1975) and *Billy Bathgate* (1989). Another recent offshoot is the form that one of its innovators, Truman Capote, named the **nonfiction novel**. This uses a variety of novelistic techniques, such as deviations from the temporal sequence of events and descriptions of a participant's state of mind, to give a graphic rendering of recent people and happenings, and is based not only on historical records but often on personal interviews with the chief agents. Truman Capote's *In Cold Blood* (1965) and Norman Mailer's *The Executioner's Song* (1979) are instances of this mode; both offer a detailed rendering of the life, personality, and actions of murderers, based on a sustained series of prison interviews with the protagonists themselves. Other examples of this form are the writings of John McPhee, which the author calls **literature of fact**; see his *Levels of the Game* (1969) and *The Deltoid Pumpkin Seed* (1973). A third variant is the *fabulative* historical novel that interweaves history with fantasized, even fantastic events: John Barth, *The Sot-Weed Factor* (1960, rev. 1967); Thomas Pynchon, *Gravity's Rainbow* (1973). See John Hollowell, *Fact and Fiction: The New Journalism and the Nonfiction Novel* (1977); Barbara Foley, *Telling the Truth: The Theory and Practice of Documentary Fiction* (1986); and Barbara Lounsberry, *The Art of Fact: Contemporary Artistic Nonfiction* (1990). Cushing Strout, in *The Veracious Imagination* (1981), studies such developments in recent novels, as well as the related form called **documentary drama** in theater, film, and television, which combines fiction with history, journalistic reports, and biography.

The **regional novel** emphasizes the setting, speech, and social structure and customs of a particular locality, not merely as *local color*, but as important conditions affecting the temperament of the characters and their ways of thinking, feeling, and interacting. Instances of such localities are "Wessex" in Thomas Hardy's novels, and "Yoknapatawpha County," Mississippi, in Faulkner's. Stella Gibbons wrote a witty *parody* of the regional novel in *Cold Comfort Farm* (1936). For a discussion of regionalism centered on the Maine author Sarah Orne Jewett, see chapter 4 in Bill Brown, *A Sense of Things* (2003).

Beginning with the second half of the nineteenth century, the novel displaced all other literary forms in popularity. The theory as well as the practice of the novelistic art has received the devoted attention of some of the greatest masters of modern literature—Flaubert, Henry James, Proust, Mann, Joyce, and Virginia Woolf. (Henry James' prefaces, gathered into one volume as *The Art of the Novel*, ed. R. P. Blackmur, 1934, exemplify the care and subtlety that have been lavished on this craft.) There has been constant experimentation with new fictional methods, such as management of the *point of view* to minimize or eliminate the apparent role of the author-narrator or, at

(1937，1962年英译版）是论述这一文学形式的颇有影响的论著；后来的综合评论有哈里·E. 肖所著的《历史小说的形式：司各特和他的后继者们》（1983）。

20世纪历史小说的一种变体被称为**纪实小说**，它不仅包含了历史人物和事件，还结合了当代报纸关于日常事件的报导。约翰·多斯·帕索斯的《美国》(1938)、E. L. 多克特罗的《爵士乐》(1975)和《比利·巴斯盖特》(1989)是此类小说的代表。历史小说的另一近代分支是被其创始人杜鲁门·卡波特称为**非虚构小说**的小说形式。这类小说采用多种小说技巧，例如违背事件发生的时间顺序，描述事件参与者的精神状态等，以此生动地刻画出近代人物和事件。它不仅建立在历史记录之上，也常常建立在作者与小说中主要人物的私下访谈上。杜鲁门·卡波特的《冷血》(1965)和诺曼·梅勒的《刽子手之歌》(1979)是这类小说形式的范例，这两部小说以叙述者与主人公本人在监狱里的一系列持续访谈为基础，对杀人犯的生活、性格和行为进行了详细描述。这一小说形式的其他例子还包括约翰·麦克菲的作品，这些作品被作者称为**事实文学**；参阅他所著的《游戏的层面》(1969)和《三角形的南瓜子》(1973)。第三种变体是*寓言性*历史小说，将历史与幻想化的乃至虚幻的事件编织在一起：如约翰·巴思的《烟草代理商》(1960，1967年修订版）；托马斯·品钦的《万有引力之虹》(1973)；参阅：约翰·霍洛韦尔所著的《事实与小说：新新闻学和非虚构小说》(1977)；芭芭拉·福里所著的《讲述真实：文献小说的理论与实践》(1986)；芭芭拉·劳恩斯伯里所著的《事实的艺术：当代艺术性纪实小说》(1990)；库欣·斯特劳特在其所著的《真实的想象》(1981)里，研究了近代小说的发展及其相关形式：在戏剧、电影和电视中被称作**纪实戏剧**，它将小说与历史、新闻报道和传记结合到了一起。

地方小说强调某一特定地区的背景、言谈、社会结构和习俗，这不仅是*地方色彩*，而且是影响人物的气质、他们的思维方式、感情和相互作用的重要条件。这类地区有托马斯·哈代小说里的"威塞克斯"和福克纳小说里的密西西比州的"约克纳帕塔法郡"。斯特拉·吉本斯在其《寒冷舒适的农庄》(1936)中对地方小说作了诙谐的*戏谑模仿*描写。对主要关注缅因州的作家萨拉·奥恩·朱厄特的地区主义的讨论，可以参阅：比尔·布朗所著的《事物的意义》(2003)第4章。

小说是从19世纪后半叶开始比所有其他文学形式更受欢迎。小说艺术的理论与实践受到现代文学一些最卓越大师的青睐，如福楼拜、亨利·詹姆斯、普鲁斯特、曼、乔伊斯和弗吉尼亚·吴尔夫。[亨利·詹姆士所写的一些序言，被收入一本名为《小说的艺术》(1934，R. P. 布莱克默主编）的集子，这些序言举例论述了为这一文学类型所付出的大量心血和所取得的许多精益求精的精妙技法。]现代作家不断地试验新型小说写作技巧，例如通过对*视角*的支配来尽量减少或消除作者－叙述者在小说里的明显作用，或正好极端相反，以此来突出作者作为小说

the opposite extreme, to foreground the role of the author as the inventor and controller of the fiction; the use of *symbolist* and *expressionist* techniques and of devices adopted from the art of the cinema; the dislocation of time sequence; the adaptation of forms and motifs from myths and dreams; and the exploitation of *stream of consciousness* narration in a way that converts the story of outer action and events into a drama of the life of the mind.

Such experimentation reached a radical extreme in the second half of the twentieth century (see *postmodernism*). Vladimir Nabokov was a supreme technician who wrote **involuted novels** (a work whose subject incorporates an account of its own genesis and development—for example, his *Pale Fire*); employed multilingual puns and jokes; incorporated esoteric data about butterflies (a subject in which he was an accomplished scientist); adopted strategies from chess, crossword puzzles, and other games; parodied other novels (and his own as well); and set elaborate traps for the unwary reader. This was also the era of what is sometimes called the **antinovel**—that is, a work which is deliberately constructed in a negative fashion, relying for its effects on the deletion of standard elements, on violating traditional norms, and on playing against the expectations established in the reader by the novelistic methods and conventions of the past. Thus Alain Robbe-Grillet, a leader among the exponents of the **nouveau roman** (the **new novel**) in France, wrote *Jealousy* (1957), in which he left out such standard elements as plot, characterization, descriptions of states of mind, locations in time and space, and frame of reference to the world in which the work is set. We are simply presented in this novel with a sequence of perceptions, mainly visual, which we may *naturalize* (that is, make intelligible in the mode of standard narrative procedures) by postulating that we are occupying the physical space and sharing the hyperacute observations of a jealous husband, from which we may infer also the tortured state of his disintegrating mind. Other new novelists are Nathalie Sarraute and Philippe Sollers. See Roland Barthes, *Writing Degree Zero* (trans. 1967), and Stephen Heath, *The Nouveau Roman: A Study in the Practice of Writing* (1972).

The term **magic realism**, originally applied in the 1920s to a school of surrealist German painters, was later used to describe the prose fiction of Jorge Luis Borges in Argentina, as well as the work of writers such as Gabriel García Márquez in Colombia, Isabel Allende in Chile, Günter Grass in Germany, Italo Calvino in Italy, and John Fowles and Salman Rushdie in England. These writers weave, in an ever-shifting pattern, a sharply etched *realism* in representing ordinary events and details together with fantastic and dreamlike elements, as well as with materials derived from myth and fairy tales. See, for example, Gabriel García Márquez's *One Hundred Years of Solitude* (1967). Robert Scholes popularized **metafiction** (an alternative is **surfiction**) as an overall term for the growing class of novels which depart from realism and foreground the roles of the author in inventing the fiction and of the reader in receiving the fiction. Scholes has also popularized the term **fabulation** for a current mode of freewheeling narrative invention. Fabulative novels violate, in various ways, standard novelistic expectations by drastic—and sometimes

创作者和掌控者的作用；运用*象征主义*、*表现主义*的技巧和从电影艺术里借鉴的手法；打乱时间顺序；从神话和梦幻中获取文学的形式和主题；运用*意识流*叙述手法将外部的行动和事件转换成心理活动剧。

20世纪下半叶，这种小说技巧上的试验走向了极端（参见：*后现代主义*）。技艺精湛的弗拉基米尔·纳博科夫创作了**内延小说**（一种把小说的构思形成和发展记载都纳入其主题之内的作品，如他的《灰火》），他采用多种语言的双关语和笑料，把有关蝴蝶的难以理解的资料（在这方面，他可是位有造诣的科学家）、下棋、字谜及其他游戏策略、对其他小说（包括他自己的小说）的戏谑摹仿，统统合并在一起，给粗疏的读者设下精心布置的圈套。这也是个有时被冠之为**反小说**的时代。"反小说"是这样一种作品：它们在结构上有意背离常理，删除传统小说的标准要素，违反传统文学创作的基本标准，打破过去的小说表现手法和惯例使读者产生的种种臆测，从而取得艺术效果。法国**新小说**代表人物的领头人阿兰·罗布-格里耶写有一部题为《嫉妒》(1957)的小说。这部小说摒弃了传统小说的标准要素，如情节、人物刻画、心理状态描写、正常的时空设置、作品中故事背景的外部参照框架。在这部小说里，作品向我们提供的只是主要用视觉表现出来的一连串概念。这些概念的归化（即用标准的叙事步骤模式使这些概念能被理解）取决于我们臆想自己占据着一位嫉妒成性的丈夫的物理空间位置，有着和他同样过于敏锐的观察力，这使我们也能推测出他那正在崩溃的心理所处的痛苦状态。其他新小说家还有纳撒利·萨洛特和菲利普·索勒尔斯。参阅：罗兰·巴尔特所著的《零度写作》(1967年英译版)；斯蒂芬·希思所著的《新小说：写作实践研究》(1972)。

魔幻现实主义这一术语在1920年代原本用来指代超现实主义德国画派的画家，后来用于指阿根廷的豪尔赫·路易斯·博尔赫斯的散文体小说，以及其他一些作家，如哥伦比亚的加布里埃尔·加西亚·马尔克斯、智利的伊莎贝尔·阿连德、德国的君特·格拉斯、意大利的伊塔洛·卡尔维诺、英国的约翰·福尔斯和萨尔曼·拉什迪的作品。这些作家在一种不断转换的模式中，将再现寻常事件和描述性细节的深刻的*现实主义*与奇异的、梦境般的成分以及来自神话、童话故事中的素材天衣无缝地结合在一起。例如，参阅加布里埃尔·加西亚·马尔克斯的《百年孤独》(1967)。罗伯特·斯科尔斯使**元小说**（另一种表达为超小说）作为指代一种不断发展的小说门类的术语而流传开来，这类小说背离现实主义，突出了作者和读者在创造和接受小说中的作用。斯科尔斯也使**寓言**一词作为指代现今一种随心所欲的小说创作模式而广为流传。寓言式小说在许多方面通过对作品题材、形式、文体、时间顺序极端

highly effective—experiments with subject matter, form, style, temporal sequence, and fusions of the everyday, the fantastic, the mythical, and the nightmarish, in renderings that blur traditional distinctions between what is serious or trivial, horrible or ludicrous, tragic or comic. Recent fabulators include Thomas Pynchon, John Barth, Donald Barthelme, William Gass, Robert Coover, and Ishmael Reed. See Raymond Federman, *Surfiction* (1975); Robert Scholes, *Fabulation and Metafiction* (1979)—an expansion of his *The Fabulators* (1967); James M. Mellard, *The Exploded Form: The Modernist Novel in America* (1980); and Patricia Waugh, *Metafiction* (1984). For an account of metafiction from a *feminist* viewpoint, see Joan Douglas Peters, *Feminist Metafiction and the Evolution of the British Novel* (2002). Refer also to the entries in this *Glossary* on the literature of the *absurd* and *black humor*.

See *fiction* and *narrative and narratology*. Histories of the novel: E. A. Baker, *History of the English Novel* (12 vols., 1924ff.); Arnold Kettle's Marxist survey, *An Introduction to the English Novel* (2 vols., 1951); Dorothy Van Ghent, *The English Novel: Form and Function* (1953); Ian Watt, *The Rise of the Novel* (1957); Michael McKeon, *The Origins of the English Novel 1600–1740* (1987; 2d ed., 2002); J. Paul Hunter, *Before Novels: The Cultural Contexts of Eighteenth-Century English Fiction* (1990); Nancy Armstrong, *Desire and Domestic Fiction: A Political History of the Novel* (1990); *The Columbia History of the British Novel*, ed. John Richetti (1994); and *The Columbia History of the American Novel*, ed. Emory Elliott (1991). *The Novel*, ed. Franco Moretti (2 vols., 2006), consists of essays by many critics on the history, forms, and themes of the novel as an international literary type. Michael McKeon, ed., *Theory of the Novel: A Historical Approach* (2000), gathers essays in literary criticism of the novel, from its beginnings to the present. On the art of the novel: Percy Lubbock, *The Craft of Fiction* (1921); E. M. Forster, *Aspects of the Novel* (1927); and three later influential books—Wayne C. Booth, *The Rhetoric of Fiction* (rev. 1983); Frank Kermode, *The Sense of an Ending* (1968); and David Lodge, *The Art of Fiction* (1992). Philip Stevick, ed., *The Theory of the Novel* (1967) is a collection of influential essays by various critics; J. Hillis Miller applies a deconstructive mode of criticism in *Fiction and Repetition* (1982); and Daniel Schwarz, *The Humanistic Heritage* (1986), reviews theories of prose fiction from 1900 to the present. The Czech émigré writer Milan Kundera has written three notable meditations on the novel in Europe: *The Art of the Novel* (2003), *Testaments Betrayed: An Essay in Nine Parts* (1995), and *The Curtain: An Essay in Seven Parts* (2006).

For additional types of the novel, see *absurd, literature of the; detective story; fantastic literature; Gothic novel; magic realism; novel of sensibility; novelette; realism and naturalism; romance novel; science fiction; utopias and dystopias*. For features of the novel, see *atmosphere; character and characterization; confidant; distance and involvement; frame story; local color; narration, grammar of; persona, tone, and voice; plot; point of view; realism and naturalism; setting; stock character; stock situations; stream of consciousness*.

novel of character: 254.

novel of incident: 254.

的——有时是卓有成效的——实验，以及在描写中融合了日常生活、想象世界、神话传说和噩梦体验，从而打破传统小说的期望，使小说或严肃或琐碎、或恐怖或荒谬、或悲或喜之间的传统区别变得模糊不清。近代寓言家包括托马斯·品钦、约翰·巴思、唐纳德·巴西尔默、威廉·加斯、罗伯特·库弗、伊什梅尔·里德。参阅：雷蒙德·费德曼所著的《超小说》（1975），罗伯特·斯科尔斯所著的《寓言和元小说》（1979），该书是对他的《寓言家》（1967）的扩充；詹姆斯·M.梅拉德所著的《被打破的形式：美国现代派小说》（1980）和帕特里夏·沃所著的《元小说》（1984）。从女性主义视角去解读元小说，可以参阅：琼·道格拉斯·彼得斯所著的《女性主义元小说和英国文学的发展》（2002）。也可参阅本书中有关*荒诞派文学*和*黑色幽默文学*的词条。

参见：*虚构小说、叙事和叙事学*。有关小说的历史，可以参阅：E. A. 贝克所著的十二卷《英国小说史》（1924年及其后）；阿诺德·凯特尔采用马克思主义研究方法所著的两卷本《英国小说概论》（1951）；多萝西·范根特所著的《英国小说：形式与功能》（1953）；伊恩·沃特所著的《小说的兴起》（1957）；迈克尔·麦基翁所著的《英国小说的起源：1600—1740》（1987，2002年第2版）；J. 保罗·亨特所著的《小说出现之前：18世纪英国小说的文化背景》（1990）；南希·阿姆斯特朗所著的《欲求与家庭小说：小说的政治史》（1990）；约翰·里查蒂主编的《哥伦比亚英国小说史》（1994）；埃默里·埃利奥特主编的《哥伦比亚美国小说史》（1991）。佛朗哥·莫雷蒂编选的两卷本《小说》（2006），包含了许多批评家将小说视为一种国际文学类型就小说的历史、形式、主题写成的文章。迈克尔·麦基翁主编的《小说理论：一种历史方法》（2000），汇集了从小说的开始一直到现在关于小说的文学批评的文章。关于小说艺术，可以参阅：珀西·卢伯克所著的《小说的技艺》（1921）；E. M. 福斯特所著的《小说面面观》（1927）；后来三部具有影响的著作：韦恩·C. 布思所著的《小说修辞学》（1983年修订版）；弗兰克·克莫德所著的《结尾的意义》（1968）；戴维·洛奇所著的《小说的艺术》（1992）。菲利普·斯特维克主编的《小说理论》（1967）收录了不同批评家的重要论文；J. 希利斯·米勒在其所著的《小说与重复》（1982）中采用了解构主义批评模式；丹尼尔·史瓦兹在其所著的《人文传统》（1986）中，回顾了1900年至今有关散文体小说的理论。捷克流亡作家米兰·昆德拉就欧洲小说写有三本重要的沉思录：《小说的艺术》（2003），《被背叛的遗嘱：一篇分为九部分的论文》（1995）和《帷幕：一篇分为七部分的论文》（2006）。

关于小说的类型，参见：*荒诞派文学、侦探故事、怪诞文学、哥特小说、魔幻现实主义、情感小说、中篇小说、现实主义和自然主义、爱情小说、科幻小说、乌托邦和反面乌托邦*。关于小说的特征，参见：*作品基调、人物与人物塑造、心腹、心理距离与感情介入、框形故事、地方色彩、叙事语法；第一人称、基调和信念；情节、视角、现实主义和自然主义、背景、定型人物、定型情景、意识流*。

novel of character：性格小说　254。
novel of incident：事件小说　254。

novel of manners: 254.

novel of sensibility: 361.

novelette: 366; *253*.

novella (nōvĕl′ ă): 252.

Novelle (nōvĕl′ ĕ): 366.

novel of manners：生活方式小说　254。

novel of sensibility：情感小说　361。

novelette：中篇小说　366；*253*。

novella：中篇小说　252。

Novelle：中篇小说　366。

objective and subjective: John Ruskin complained in 1856 that "German dullness and English affectation have of late much multiplied among us the use of two of the most objectionable words that were ever coined by the troublesomeness of metaphysicians—namely, 'objective' and 'subjective.'" Ruskin was at least in part right: the words were imported into English criticism from the post-Kantian German critics of the late eighteenth and early nineteenth centuries, and they have certainly been troublesome. Amid the great variety of ways in which the opposition has been applied to literature, one is sufficiently widespread to be worth specifying. A **subjective** work is one in which the author incorporates personal experiences, or projects into the narrative his or her personal disposition, judgments, values, and feelings. An **objective** work is one in which the author presents the invented situation or the fictional characters and their thoughts, feelings, and actions and undertakes to remain detached and noncommittal. Thus a subjective *lyric* is one in which we are invited to associate the "I," or lyric speaker, with the poet (Coleridge's "Frost at Midnight," Wordsworth's "Tintern Abbey," Shelley's "Ode to the West Wind," Sylvia Plath's "Daddy"); in an objective lyric the speaker is obviously an invented character, or else is simply a lyric voice without specific characteristics (Robert Browning's "My Last Duchess," T. S. Eliot's "The Love Song of J. Alfred Prufrock," Wallace Stevens' "Sunday Morning"). A subjective novel is one in which the author (or at any rate the narrator) intervenes to comment and deliver judgments about the characters and actions represented; an objective novel is one in which the author is self-effacing and tries to create the effect that the story tells itself. Critics agree, however, that the difference between a subjective and objective literary work is not absolute, but a matter of degree. See *confessional poetry, distance and involvement, negative capability, persona,* and *point of view.*

On the introduction of the terms "objective" and "subjective" into English criticism and the variousness of their application, see M. H. Abrams, *The Mirror and the Lamp* (1953), pp. 235–44. For their uses in modern criticism of the novel, see Wayne C. Booth, *The Rhetoric of Fiction* (rev. 1983), chapter 3.

objective correlative: This term, which had been coined by the American painter and poet Washington Allston (1779–1843), was introduced by T. S. Eliot, rather casually, into his essay "Hamlet and His Problems" (1919); its subsequent vogue in literary criticism, Eliot said, astonished him. "The only way of expressing emotion," Eliot wrote, "is by finding an 'objective correlative'; in other words, a set of objects, a situation, a chain of events which shall be the formula of that *particular* emotion," and which will evoke the same emotion from the reader. Eliot's formulation has been often criticized for falsifying the way a poet actually composes, on the ground that no object or situation is in itself a "formula" for an emotion, but depends for its emotional significance and effect on the way it is rendered and used by a particular poet.

O

Objective and Subjective：客观的与主观的

约翰·罗斯金在 1856 年抱怨说："德国人的无聊和英国人的热情近来使我们愈多地采用了爱找麻烦的玄学家们迄今为止所创造的两个最有争议的词——也就是'客观的'和'主观的'。"罗斯金至少说对了一部分：这两个词是在 18 世纪晚期和 19 世纪早期，从属于后康德派的德国批评家那里引入英国文学批评里的。这两个词的确一直令人头疼。这两个意思完全相反的词在文学上的用法多种多样，不过有一种广为流传的用法倒是值得一提：在**主观的**作品里，作家把自己的亲身经历跟作品合为一体，或是把自己的性情、判断、价值观和感情投射到作品中去。在**客观的**作品里，作者展现了他创造出来的场景或虚构的人物，以及他们的思想、感情和行动，作者本人保持不介入的姿态，并不表明自己的见解。譬如，一首主观的*抒情诗*引导我们把"我"，或抒情人与诗人联系在一起（如柯勒律治的《霜夜》、华兹华斯的《丁登寺》、雪莱的《西风颂》、西尔维亚·普拉斯的《父亲》）；在一首客观的抒情诗里，说话人很显然是一个虚构的人物，或者仅仅是一个没有具体特征的抒情的声音（如罗伯特·勃朗宁的《我那已故的公爵夫人》、T. S. 艾略特的《普鲁弗洛克的情歌》、华莱士·史蒂文斯的《礼拜日之晨》）。在一部主观的小说里，作者（或者是叙述者）对他所描述的人物和行动加以评论和判断；而在一部客观的小说里，作者却遁隐起来，试图造成故事是在自然发展的效果。然而，评论家们一致认为，主观的文学作品与客观的文学作品之间的区别并不绝对，而只是一个程度问题。参见：*自白诗*、*心理距离与感情介入*、*否定能力*、*第一人称*、*视角*。

关于"客观的"和"主观的"这两个术语如何进入英国文学批评以及它们不同的应用范畴，参阅：M. H. 艾布拉姆斯所著的《镜与灯》(1953) 第 235—244 页。关于这两个词在现代小说批评方法上的应用，参阅：韦恩·C. 布思所著的《小说修辞学》(1983 年修订版) 第 3 章。

Objective Correlative：客观对应物

这个术语是由美国画家和诗人华盛顿·奥尔斯顿 (1779—1843) 创造的，T. S. 艾略特在他所写的文章"哈姆雷特和他的疑难"(1919) 中漫不经心地引入了这一术语；艾略特说，这一术语后来在文学批评界变得如此时髦，让他感到惊讶。他写道："表达情感的唯一的方法是找出一个'客观对应物'；换言之，也就是找出一组事物、一个场景、一连串事件，它们是体现那种*特定*情感的固定形式"，在读者心里唤起同样的情感。艾略特的这一表述时常遭到批评，认为它曲解了诗人作诗的确切方法，因为没有任何事物或场景本身可以成为体现一种情感的"固定形式"，事物或场景在情感上的重要性和影响力，取决于特定诗人表现和使用它们的方式。

The vogue of Eliot's concept of an outer correlative for inner feelings was due in part to its accord with the campaign of the *New Criticism* against vagueness of description and the direct statement of feelings in poetry—an oft-cited example was Shelley's "Indian Serenade": "I die, I faint, I fail"—and in favor of definiteness, impersonality, and descriptive concreteness. See Eliseo Vivas, "The Objective Correlative of T. S. Eliot," reprinted in *Critiques and Essays in Criticism*, ed. Robert W. Stallman (1949).

objective criticism: **70**; *6*.

objective (narrator): **302**.

occasional poems: Occasional poems are written to celebrate or memorialize a particular occasion, such as a birthday, a marriage, a death, a military engagement or victory, the dedication of a public building, or the opening performance of a play. Edmund Spenser's "Epithalamion," on the occasion of his own marriage; John Milton's "Lycidas," on the death of the young poet Edward King; Andrew Marvell's "An Horatian Ode upon Cromwell's Return from Ireland"; and Alfred, Lord Tennyson's "The Charge of the Light Brigade" are all poems that have long survived their original occasions, and W. B. Yeats' "Easter, 1916" and W. H. Auden's "September 1, 1939" are notable later examples. England's poet laureate is often called on to meet the emergency of royal anniversaries and important public events with an appropriate occasional poem.

octameter (ŏktăm' ĕter): **220**.

octave (ŏk' tāv): **370**.

octavo (ŏktāv' ō): **34**.

octosyllabic couplet (ŏk' tō sĭlăb" ik): **375**; *191*.

ode: In its traditional application, "ode" denotes a long lyric poem that is serious in subject and treatment, elevated in style, and elaborate in its stanzaic structure. Norman Maclean said that the term now calls to mind a *lyric* which is "massive, public in its proclamations, and Pindaric in its classical prototype" ("From Action to Image," in *Critics and Criticism*, ed. R. S. Crane, 1952). The prototype was established by the Greek poet Pindar, whose odes were modeled on the songs by the *chorus* in Greek drama. His complex stanzas were patterned in sets of three: moving in a dance rhythm to the left, the chorus chanted the **strophe**; moving to the right, the **antistrophe**; then, standing still, the **epode**.

The **regular** or **Pindaric ode** in English is a close imitation of Pindar's form, with all the strophes and antistrophes written in one *stanza* pattern, and all the epodes in another. This form was introduced into England by Ben Jonson's ode "To the Immortal Memory and Friendship of That Noble Pair,

艾略特的这种用外在物体对应内在情感的概念之所以流行，部分因为它符合*新批评*反对诗歌描述的朦胧性和在诗歌中直接陈述感情的态度——一个常被引用的例子是雪莱的诗歌《印度小夜曲》里的一行诗："我完了！我昏迷，倒下！"——而赞同用直截了当、非人格化和描述性的具体感来抒发诗人胸臆的手法。参阅：埃利塞奥·维瓦斯所写的文章"T. S. 艾略特的客观对应物"，重印收入罗伯特·W. 斯托尔曼主编的《批判与批评文集》(1949)。

objective criticism：客观批评　70；6。

objective (narrator)：客观的（叙述者）　302。

Occasional Poems：应景诗

应景诗是为庆祝或纪念某一特殊活动，如诞辰、婚礼、死亡、军事交战、凯旋、公共建筑物的落成，或一场戏的首演而作。埃德蒙·斯宾塞的《婚曲》是为他自己的婚礼而作；约翰·弥尔顿的《利西达斯》是为悼念年轻诗人爱德华·金之死而作；安德鲁·马韦尔的《贺拉斯体颂：为克伦威尔从爱尔兰归来而作》和阿尔弗雷德·丁尼生勋爵的《轻骑兵旅的进击》等诗歌尽管为之而作的活动早已过去，但也都流传下来。W. B. 叶芝的《1916年复活节》和 W. H. 奥登的《1939年9月1日》，是现代应景诗的著名代表作。英国的桂冠诗人时常应召为皇家的周年庆典和重大的公众事件创作合适的应景诗。

octameter：八音步诗行　220。

octave：前八行　370。

octavo：八开本　34。

octosyllabic couplet：八音节对句　375；191。

Ode：颂

在其传统用法上，颂是一种抒情长诗，主题和写作方式严肃，风格高雅，诗节结构细腻精巧。诺曼·迈克利恩说："颂"这个词使人想到一首抒情诗，"其内容广泛且大众化，其古典的原型属于品达诗体"["从行动到意象"，收入 R. S. 克莱恩主编的《批评家与批评》(1952)]。这种原型由古希腊诗人品达创立，他的颂模仿了古希腊戏剧中的合唱部。他的复杂诗节仿效了戏剧里合唱的三段式：以舞蹈的节奏自右向左移动，合唱队吟唱**诗句**；然后从左移至右，吟唱**相衬诗句**；而后静静站在原地，吟唱**后颂部**。

英文中的**律颂**，或**品达体颂**，是对品达颂诗形式的细致摹仿——所有的诗句和相衬诗句都在一个*诗节*里完成；所有的后颂部诗句在另一个诗节里完成。这一形式经过本·琼森的颂文《为了那一对高贵朋友卢修斯·卡里爵士和 H. 莫里森

Sir Lucius Cary and Sir H. Morison" (1629); the typical construction can be conveniently studied in this poem or in Thomas Gray's "The Progress of Poesy" (1757). The **irregular ode**, also called the **Cowleyan Ode**, was introduced in 1656 by Abraham Cowley, who imitated the Pindaric style and matter but disregarded the recurrent stanzaic pattern in each strophic triad; instead, he allowed each stanza to establish its own pattern of varying line lengths, number of lines, and rhyme scheme. This type of irregular stanzaic structure, which is free to alter in accordance with shifts in subject and mood, has been the most common for the English ode ever since; Wordsworth's "Ode: Intimations of Immortality" (1807) is representative.

Pindar's odes were **encomiastic**; that is, they were written to praise and glorify someone—in the instance of Pindar, the ode celebrated a victorious athlete in the Olympic games. (See *epideictic*, under *rhetoric*.) The earlier English odes, and many later ones, were also written to eulogize something, such as a person (John Dryden's "Anne Killigrew"), or the arts of music or poetry (Dryden's "Alexander's Feast"), or a time of day (Collins' "Ode to Evening"), or abstract concepts (Gray's "Hymn to Adversity" and Wordsworth's "Ode to Duty"). Romantic poets perfected the personal ode of description and passionate meditation, which is stimulated by (and sometimes at its close reverts to) an aspect of the outer scene and turns on the attempt to solve either a personal emotional problem or a generally human one (Wordsworth's "Intimations" ode, Coleridge's "Dejection: An Ode," Shelley's "Ode to the West Wind"). Recent examples of this latter type are Allen Tate's "Ode to the Confederate Dead" and Wallace Stevens' "The Idea of Order at Key West." (See *descriptive-meditative lyric*, in the entry *topographical poetry*.)

The **Horatian ode** was originally modeled on the matter, tone, and form of the odes of the Roman Horace. In contrast to the passion, visionary boldness, and formal language of Pindar's odes, many Horatian odes are calm, meditative, and colloquial; they are also usually **homostrophic** (that is, written in a single repeated stanza form), and shorter than the Pindaric ode. Examples are Marvell's "An Horatian Ode upon Cromwell's Return from Ireland" (1650) and Keats' ode "To Autumn" (1820).

See Robert Shafer, *The English Ode to 1660* (1918); G. N. Shuster, *The English Ode from Milton to Keats* (1940, reprinted 1964); Carol Maddison, *Apollo and the Nine: A History of the Ode* (1960)—this book includes a discussion of the odes of Pindar and Horace (chapter 2); John Heath-Stubbs, *The Ode* (1969); Paul H. Fry, *The Poet's Calling in the English Ode* (1980).

Oedipus complex: 322.

Old Comedy: 55.

Old English Period: 279.

omniscient point of view: 301.

爵士的永恒记忆和友谊》(1629)传入英国；我们可以在这首诗或托马斯·格雷的《灵感的进程》(1757)中十分便利地研究这种形式的典型结构。**无律颂**，又叫**考利体颂**，于1656年由亚伯拉罕·考利引入英国诗坛，他摹仿品达体的风格和题材，但不注意每一分节三段式中反复出现的诗节形式，而让每一诗节形成自己不同的长短、行数和韵律设置模式。这种无规律诗节结构随着主题和情绪的变化而自由改变，从此成为英语中最常见的一种颂体诗；华兹华斯的《不朽的征兆》(1807)就是其中的代表作。

品达的颂诗都是**赞颂的**，即为称赞或颂扬某人而作——拿品达来说，他的颂诗赞颂的是奥林匹克运动会上获胜的运动员。（参见：*修辞学*中的*富于辞藻的*。）英国早期的颂诗和许多后来的颂诗也是为颂扬而作，比如说，赞扬的对象可以是人（如约翰·德莱顿的《安妮·齐利格如》），可以是音乐或诗歌艺术（如德莱顿的《亚历山大的盛宴》），可以是一天的某个时辰（如柯林斯的《黄昏颂》），也可以是某种抽象概念（如格雷的《逆境颂》和华兹华斯的《责任颂》）。浪漫主义诗人使描绘性和表达热烈沉思的个人颂诗达到完美的程度，这类颂诗触发于外界情景的某个方面（有时是对外界情景的忠实复现），而后转向试图解决个人的情感问题，或普遍的人类问题（譬如华兹华斯的《不朽的征兆》、柯勒律治的《沮丧颂》、雪莱的《西风颂》）。近代的后一种颂体诗有艾伦·泰特的《南军死难将士颂》和华莱士·史蒂文斯的《基·韦斯特的秩序观念》（又译《西屿的秩序感》）。（参见：*风景诗*中的*描述－沉思式抒情诗*。）

贺拉斯体颂原是仿照古罗马人贺拉斯的颂诗的题材、格调和形式。与品达体颂诗奔放的感情、驰骋的想象、正式的语言相反，许多贺拉斯体颂冷静、沉思，使用口语；常用**同形诗句**（即单一重复的诗节形式），且比品达体颂诗要短。此类例子有马韦尔的《贺拉斯体颂：为克伦威尔从爱尔兰归来而作》(1650)和济慈的《秋颂》(1820)。

参阅：罗伯特·谢弗所著的《1660年前的英国颂诗》(1918)；G. N. 舒斯特所著的《从弥尔顿到济慈的英国颂诗》(1940，1964年再版)；卡罗尔·麦迪逊所著的《阿波罗与第九位缪斯：颂诗的历史》(1960)第2章收录了一篇关于品达的颂诗和贺拉斯的颂诗的讨论；约翰·希思－斯塔布斯所著的《颂诗》(1969)；保罗·H. 弗赖伊所著的《英语颂诗中诗人的使命》(1980)。

Oedipus complex：俄狄浦斯情结　322。

Old Comedy：旧喜剧　55。

Old English Period：古英语时期　279。

omniscient point of view：全知全能视角　301。

onomatopoeia: Onomatopoeia, sometimes called **echoism**, is used both in a narrow and in a broad sense.

1. In the narrow and most common use, onomatopoeia designates a word, or a combination of words, whose sound seems to duplicate the sound it denotes: "hiss," "buzz," "rattle," "bang." There is no exact duplication, however, of nonverbal by verbal sounds; the perceived similarity is due as much to the meaning, and to the sensation of articulating the words, as to their sounds. Two lines of Alfred, Lord Tennyson's "Come Down, O Maid" (1847) are often cited as a skillful instance of onomatopoeia:

   > The moan of doves in immemorial elms,
   > And murmuring of innumerable bees.

   The American critic John Crowe Ransom remarked that by making only two changes in the speech sounds of the last line, we lose the echoic effect because we change the meaning drastically: "And murdering of innumerable beeves."

   The sounds seemingly mimicked by onomatopoeic words need not be pleasant ones. Robert Browning liked to represent squishy and scratchy sounds, as in "Meeting at Night" (1845):

   > As I gain the cove with pushing prow,
   > And quench its speed i' the slushy sand.
   > A tap at the pane, the quick sharp scratch
   > And blue spurt of a lighted match....

   Compare *euphony and cacophony*.

2. In the broad sense, "onomatopoeia" is applied to words or passages which seem to correspond to, or to strongly suggest, what they denote in any way whatever—in size, movement, tactile feel, duration, or force, as well as sound (see *sound symbolism*). Alexander Pope recommends such extended verbal mimicry in his *Essay on Criticism* (1711) when he says that "the sound should seem an echo of the sense," and goes on to illustrate his maxim by mimicking two different kinds of action or motion by the metrical movement and by the difficulty or ease of utterance, in conjunction with the signification, of the poetic lines that describe them:

   > When Ajax strives some rock's vast weight to throw,
   > The line too labors, and the words move slow;
   > Not so when swift Camilla scours the plain,
   > Flies o'er th' unbending corn, and skims along the main.

opsis (ŏp′ sĭs): **364**.

oral poetry: Oral poetry, or "oral formulaic poetry," is composed and transmitted by singers or reciters; in its older instances, the recitations were often accompanied by a harp or a drum, or by other musical instruments. Its origins

Onomatopoeia：拟声词

拟声词，有时也叫**回声词**，有广义和狭义两种用法：

1. 在狭义的和最普遍的意思上，拟声词指的是一个词或几个词的组合，其发音似乎要复制它所要表示的声音：如"嘶嘶""嗡嗡""嘎嘎""砰砰"。然而，非言辞的声音不可能被言辞模拟得完美无缺；人们所感知到的词与音的相似主要是由词的意思、发音时的感觉、词本身的发音造成的。阿尔弗雷德·丁尼生勋爵的《下来吧，少女》（1847）里的两行诗常被用来作为高超的拟声手法的例证：

   > 古老的榆树上鸽子咕咕呻吟，
   > 夹杂着无数的蜜蜂嗡嗡细语。

   美国批评家约翰·克罗·兰塞姆评论道：我们只要在第二句诗行里改变两个辅音，整个诗行的回声效果就会消失，因为我们也完全改变了诗行的意思："夹杂着对无数肉牛的宰杀。"
   　　拟声词所摹拟的不一定都是悦耳动听的声音。罗伯特·勃朗宁就喜爱用能够产生挤压、刺耳声响效果的词，就像他的《夜半相会》（1845）里的四行诗：

   > 我驾小船驶入小小的海湾，
   > 就在泥泞的海涂稳稳刹住。
   > 窗玻璃上轻弹，嗤的一声摩擦，
   > 擦燃的火柴喷出一朵蓝花……　　（飞白译）

   对比：*谐音与非谐音*。

2. 广义上，"拟声词"指的似乎是与其所表现的事物在任何方面（不仅在声音，而且在大小、运动、触感或力量方面）都相互对应，或能强烈引发类似联想的词或一段文字（参见：*语音象征*）。亚历山大·蒲柏在他的《批评论》（1711）中推荐了这种文辞上扩展延伸的模仿，他说："语言应当像是感觉的回声。"蒲柏还通过韵律的变动或诗行话语的难易，连同对其描述的诗行的意义来模拟两种不同的行为或运动，以此来进一步说明他所描述的准则：

   > 当埃阿斯奋力抛出千钧巨石，
   > 诗行和词句也变得沉重缓慢；
   > 不如卡米拉奔跑过旷野，
   > 越过麦田掠过大陆那般迅捷。

opsis：场景 364。

Oral Poetry：口头诗歌

　　口头诗歌，又叫口头程式诗歌，是由歌唱者或朗诵者创作并传播的诗歌；在其古老的例子中，朗诵经常伴着竖琴或鼓或其他乐器进行。这种诗歌的起源可以

are prehistoric, yet it continues to flourish even now among populations which for the most part cannot read or write. Oral poetry includes both narrative forms (see *epic* and *ballad*) and lyric forms (see *folk songs*). There is no fixed version of an oral composition, since each performer tends to render it differently, and sometimes introduces differences between one performance and the next. Such poems, however, typically incorporate verbal formulas—set words, word patterns, refrains, and set-pieces of description—which help a performer to improvise a narrative or song on a given theme, and also to recall and repeat, although often with variations, a poem that has been learned from someone else. (For examples of such formulas, see *ballad*, *epic*, and *refrain*.)

Oral ballads and songs have been collected and published ever since the eighteenth century. The systematic analysis of oral formulaic poetry in its origins and early renderings, however, was begun in the 1930s by the American scholar Milman Parry on field trips to Yugoslavia, the last place in Europe where the custom of composing and transmitting oral poetry, especially heroic narratives of warfare, still survived. Albert B. Lord and other successors continued Parry's work, and also applied the principles of this contemporary oral poetry retrospectively to an analysis of the constitution of the Homeric epics, the Anglo-Saxon *Beowulf*, the Old French *Chanson de Roland*, and other epic poems which, although they survive only in a written form, had originated and evolved as oral formulaic poetry. Research into oral literary performances is also being carried on in Africa, Asia, and other parts of the world where the ancient tradition maintains its vitality. Walter J. Ong, *Orality and Literacy: The Technologizing of the Word* (1982), analyzes the effects on literary compositions of the shift from an oral to a print culture. For current modes of primarily oral poetry within a print culture, see *limerick* (under *light verse*) and *rap poetry* (under *performance poetry*).

A description of Milman Parry's work is in *Serbocroatian Heroic Songs*, ed. Albert B. Lord, Vol. 1; see also Albert B. Lord, *The Singer of Tales* (1960, 2d ed., 2000); Adam Parry, ed., *The Making of Homeric Verse: The Collected Papers of Milman Parry* (1971); Ruth Finnegan, *Oral Poetry: Its Nature, Significance and Social Context* (1977); and J. M. Foley, *Oral Traditional Literature* (1981). For references to *oral poetry* in other entries, see pages *19, 22, 97, 121, 243*.

organic form: 137.

organicist: 138; *4*.

orientalism: 306.

originality: 65.

ottava rima (ŏtäv′ ă rē′ mă): 377.

over-reading: 14.

oxymoron (ŏxĭmō′ rŏn): **267**.

追溯到史前，但至今仍在绝大多数不具备读写能力的人群中盛行。口头诗歌包括叙事形式（参见：*史诗*、*民谣*）和抒情形式（参见：*民歌*）两种。由于每个表演者的表现方法各不相同，有时在前后两次表演之间就会有所不同，所以口头诗歌没有固定的形式。然而，这类诗歌一般都采用了言辞上的惯用语句——固定的单词、词语模式、叠句和事先精心设计的说明——这些固定程式既可以帮助表演者即兴按照某一特定主题叙事或歌唱，也可以帮助他们记忆和重复从旁人处学来的诗歌，尽管往往会有所变异。（这种惯用词语的例子，参见：*民谣*、*史诗*、*叠句*。）

自从 18 世纪以来，已有人收集出版了一些口头民谣和歌曲。然而对口头程式诗歌起源及其早期艺术表现的系统分析却始于 1930 年代，当时美国学者米尔曼·帕里去南斯拉夫作旅行考察，那时的南斯拉夫是欧洲最后一个仍然留存着创作和传播口头诗歌，尤其是创作和传播关于战争的英雄叙事文的习俗的地方。艾伯特·B. 洛德和其他后继者继续从事帕里的工作并回顾性地把这种当代口头诗歌的原则应用于分析荷马史诗、盎格鲁－撒克逊人的《贝奥武甫》、古法语诗《罗兰之歌》和其他一些史诗的构成，尽管这些史诗只是以文字形式留传下来但却是由它们起源并演变成为口头程式诗歌。在这一古老传统依然保持着活力的非洲、亚洲及世界上其他地方，也正在开展对口头文学表现的研究。沃尔特·J. 翁格在其所著的《口头和文字：文字的技术化》(1982) 中，也分析了口头文化向印刷文化的转变对文学创作的影响。关于印刷文化中口头诗歌的现代主要模式，参见：*五行打油诗*（在轻松诗中）、*说唱诗*（在表演诗歌中）。

对米尔曼·帕里著作的描述，参阅：艾伯特·B. 洛德主编的《塞波克罗地亚英雄短歌》（第 1 卷）；也可参阅：艾伯特·B. 洛德所著的《故事的歌手》(1960, 2000 年第 2 版)；亚当·帕里主编的《荷马史诗的形成：米尔曼·帕里论文选》(1971)；鲁斯·芬尼根所著的《口头诗歌：其本质、重要性及社会语景》(1977)；J. M. 福利所著的《口述传统文学》(1981)。其他条目中提及"口头诗歌"的地方，参见第 19、22、97、121、243 页。

organic form：有机形式　137。

organicist：有机论者　138；*4*。

orientalism：东方学　306。

originality：创造性　65。

ottava rima：八行诗　377。

over-reading：过度解读　14。

oxymoron：逆喻，矛盾修辞法　267。

P

palimpsest: 32.

palinode: Palinode, from the Greek for "song again," is a poem or poetic passage in which the poet renounces or retracts an earlier poem, or an earlier type of subject matter. An elaborate and charming example is the Prologue to *The Legend of Good Women* in which Geoffrey Chaucer, contrite after being charged by the God of Love with having slandered women lovers in *Troilus and Criseyde* and in his translation of the *Romance of the Rose*, does penance by writing this poem on women who were saints in their fidelity to the creed of love. (Refer to *courtly love*.) Palinodes are especially common in love poetry. The Elizabethan sonnet by Sir Philip Sidney, "Leave me, O love which reachest but to dust," is a palinode renouncing the poetry of sexual love for that of heavenly love.

panegyric: 343.

pantomime and dumb show: Pantomime is acting on the stage without speech, using only posture, gesture, bodily movement, and exaggerated facial expression to **mime** ("mimic") a character's actions and to express a character's feelings. Elaborate pantomimes, halfway between drama and dance, were put on in ancient Greece and Rome, and the form was revived, often for comic effect, in Renaissance Europe. Mimed dramas enjoyed a vogue in eighteenth-century England, and in the twentieth century the silent movies encouraged a brief revival of the art and produced a superlative pantomimist in Charlie Chaplin. Miming survived into the recent past with French masters such as Marcel Marceau in the theater and Jacques Tati in the cinema. England still retains the institution of the Christmas pantomime, which enacts children's nursery rhymes, or familiar children's stories such as "Puss in Boots," in a blend of miming, music, and dialogue. In America and many other countries, circus clowns are expert pantomimists, and miming has recently been revived in the theater for the deaf.

A **dumb show** is an episode of pantomime introduced into a spoken play. It was a common device in Elizabethan drama, in imitation of its use by Seneca, the Roman writer of tragedies. Two well-known dumb shows are the preliminary episode, summarizing the action to come, of the play-within-a-play in *Hamlet* (III. ii.), and the miming of the banishment of the Duchess and her family in John Webster's *The Duchess of Malfi* (III. iv.).

See R. J. Broadbent, *A History of Pantomime* (1901).

papyrus: 32.

parable: 9.

P

palimpsest：重写羊皮纸卷　32。

Palinode：翻案诗

　　翻案诗，源于希腊语，意为"重唱"，是诗人摒弃或取消早先的诗歌或某类题材形式的诗歌或诗歌段落。一个精巧、吸引人的范例就是《好女人传说》的序言。在序言中，杰弗里·乔叟被爱神指控在《特洛伊罗斯与克丽西德》和译作《玫瑰传奇》中诽谤了女性恋人之后深感懊悔，于是通过创作这首诗歌描述了忠于爱情信条的圣女来悔罪。（参见：*骑士恋*。）翻案诗在情诗中尤为常见。比如菲利普·锡德尼爵士创作的伊丽莎白时期的十四行诗《离开我吧，那最轻易就能得到的爱轻如尘埃》就是一首翻案诗，它摒弃了性爱诗歌而去称颂神圣的爱情。

panegyric：颂词　343。

Pantomime and Dumb Show：哑剧和默剧

　　哑剧是无言语的舞台表演，只用姿势、手势、身体的移动和夸张的面部表情来**摹仿**人物的行动，表达人物的感情。介于戏剧和舞剧之间的精巧别致的哑剧，在古希腊罗马时期就已上演过。这一形式在文艺复兴时期的欧洲再度流行，但通常只是为了达到喜剧效果。在18世纪的英国，哑剧十分流行。20世纪的无声电影促进了这一艺术形式的短暂复兴，并造就出一位最杰出的哑剧演员查理·卓别林。法国大师们使哑剧保存至今，比如，戏剧方面有马塞尔·马索，电影方面有雅克·泰蒂。英国仍然保持着圣诞哑剧的习俗，上演孩子们的童谣或大家熟悉的儿童故事，如《穿长筒靴的猫》，其中融合了摹仿、音乐和对话。在美国和其他许多国家，马戏团小丑都是精湛的哑剧演员，哑剧近来在为聋人开设的剧院里得到了复兴。

　　默剧是在话剧里插入的一个哑剧片断。这是伊丽莎白时期戏剧中一种常见的表现手法。默剧仿效古罗马悲剧作家塞内加的剧作。两出著名默剧是：《哈姆雷特》第三幕第二场序曲部分的戏中戏，它扼要地表现了将要发生的事情；约翰·韦伯斯特《马尔菲公爵夫人》第三幕第四场里，用默剧表现公爵夫人和她的家人被流放的情景。

　　参阅：R. J. 布罗德本特所著的《哑剧史》(1901)。

papyrus：纸莎草　32。

parable：醒世寓言　9。

paradigmatic (in linguistics): **197**.

paradox: A paradox is a statement which seems on its face to be logically contradictory or absurd, yet turns out to be interpretable in a way that makes sense. An instance is the conclusion to John Donne's sonnet "Death, Be Not Proud":

> One short sleep past, we wake eternally
> And death shall be no more; *Death, thou shalt die.*

The paradox is used occasionally by almost all poets, but was a persistent and central device in seventeenth-century *metaphysical poetry*, in both its religious and secular forms. Donne, who wrote a prose collection titled *Problems and Paradoxes*, exploited the figure constantly in his poetry. "The Canonization," for example, is organized as an extended proof, full of local paradoxes, of the paradoxical thesis that sexual lovers are saints. Paradox is also a frequent component in verbal *wit*.

If the paradoxical utterance conjoins two terms that in ordinary usage are contraries, it is called an **oxymoron**; an example is Alfred, Lord Tennyson's "*O Death in life,* the days that are no more." The oxymoron was a familiar type of *Petrarchan conceit* in Elizabethan love poetry, in phrases like "pleasing pains," "I burn and freeze," "loving hate." It is also a frequent figure in devotional prose and religious poetry as a way of expressing the Christian mysteries, which transcend human sense and logic. So John Milton describes the appearance of God, in *Paradise Lost* (III, 380):

> Dark with excessive bright thy skirts appear.

Paradox was a prominent concern of many *New Critics*, who extended the term from its limited application to a type of *figurative language* so as to encompass all surprising deviations from, or qualifications of, common perceptions or commonplace opinions. It is in this expanded sense that Cleanth Brooks is able to claim, with some plausibility, that "the language of poetry is the language of paradox," in *The Well Wrought Urn* (1947). See also *deconstruction* for the claim that all uses of language disseminate themselves into the unresolvable paradox called an *aporia*.

paralipsis (părălĭp′ sĭs): **347**.

parallelism: 15.

paranomasia (părănōmā′ zya): **325**.

pararhyme: 349.

paratactic style: 385.

paradigmatic (in linguistics)：(语言学中的) 聚合　197。

Paradox：逆说

逆说是一种表面上看来逻辑矛盾、荒诞不经，但最后却能被合情合理解读的陈述。约翰·多恩在他的十四行诗《死神，别那么得意》的结尾部分就用了逆说：

> 人们小憩一会儿，精神便得以永远清朗，
> 便再不会有死亡；死神你自己将死亡。　　　　　（汪剑钊译）

几乎所有诗人都会时常用到逆说，但逆说是17世纪*玄学派诗歌*长期以来在宗教和非宗教形式上一贯的主要表现手法。多恩写了一本散文集，题为《疑难与逆说》，探讨他的诗歌里经常采用的这种修辞格。譬如，他的《圣徒追封》这首诗被处理成充满了褊狭的逆说和矛盾的主题，旨在进一步证实性欲上的情人是圣人。逆说也常是言辞机智的组成部分。

如果自相矛盾的言语是将日常使用中意思相反的两个词结合在一起，那它就叫**逆喻**。如阿尔弗雷德·丁尼生勋爵的诗句："啊，生命里的死亡，不复返的岁月。"逆喻是伊丽莎白时期情诗里所表现的*彼特拉克式巧思妙喻*的一种常见类型，如短语"甜蜜的伤悲""我冻得火辣辣的""深情的仇恨"等。逆喻也是虔诚的散文和宗教诗歌中常见的修辞格，用来表示超越人类感知和逻辑思维的基督教之奥秘。约翰·弥尔顿在《失乐园》第三卷第380行里这样描绘上帝的出现：

> 从异常的光中露出黑的衣裾　　　　　　　　　　（朱维之译）

逆说是许多*新批评家*的关注焦点。他们将这个术语从其有限的使用中扩展成为*比喻语*的一种，使其包含从常识概念或陈腐见解中衍生出的各种令人吃惊的用法。在这一术语的延伸意义上，克林斯·布鲁克斯才能似有道理地在《精制的瓮》(1947)里宣称"诗歌的语言是逆说的语言"。也可参阅*解构主义*中的一个说法，即所有语言的使用都将自身引入无法解析的逆说中，这被称为反逆性。

paralipsis：假省笔法　347。

parallelism：对仗，平行结构　15。

paranomasia：谐音双关　325。

pararhyme：平行韵　349。

paratactic style：并列句文体　385。

parchment: 32.

parody: 38; *25, 59*.

parole (in linguistics): **194**; *310, 358*.

partial rhyme: 349.

pastoral: The originator of the pastoral was the Greek poet Theocritus, who in the third century BC wrote poems representing the life of Sicilian shepherds. ("Pastor" is Latin for "shepherd.") Virgil later imitated Theocritus in his Latin *Eclogues*, and in doing so established the enduring model for the traditional **pastoral** (păs′ tŏrăl): a deliberately conventional poem expressing an urban poet's nostalgic image of the supposed peace and simplicity of the life of shepherds and other rural folk in an idealized natural setting. The *conventions* that hundreds of later poets imitated from Virgil's imitations of Theocritus include a shepherd reclining under a spreading beech tree and meditating on the rural muse, or piping as though he would ne'er grow old, or engaging in a friendly singing contest, or expressing his good or bad fortune in a love affair, or grieving over the death of a fellow shepherd. From this last type developed the *pastoral elegy*, which persisted long after the other traditional types had lost their popularity. Other terms often used synonymously with pastoral are **idyll**, from the title of Theocritus' pastorals; **eclogue** (literally, "a selection"), from the title of Virgil's pastorals; and **bucolic poetry**, from the Greek word for "herdsman."

Classical poets often described the pastoral life as possessing features of the mythical *golden age*. Christian pastoralists conjoined the golden age of pagan fable with the Garden of Eden in the Bible, and also exploited the religious symbolism of "shepherd" (applied to the ecclesiastical or parish "pastor," and to the figure of Christ as the Good Shepherd) to give many pastoral poems a Christian range of reference. In the Renaissance the traditional pastoral was also adapted to diverse satirical and allegorical uses. Edmund Spenser's *Shepherd's Calendar* (1579), which popularized the mode in English poetry, included most of the varieties of pastoral poems current in that period.

Such was the attraction of the pastoral dream that Renaissance writers incorporated it into various other literary forms. Sir Philip Sidney's *Arcadia* (1581–84) was a long pastoral *romance* written in an elaborately artful prose. (**Arcadia** was a mountainous region of Greece which Virgil substituted for Theocritus' Sicily as his idealized pastoral milieu.) There was also the pastoral lyric (Christopher Marlowe's "The Passionate Shepherd to His Love"), and the pastoral drama. John Fletcher's *The Faithful Shepherdess* is an example of this last type, and Shakespeare's *As You Like It*, based on the contemporary pastoral romance *Rosalynde* by Thomas Lodge, is set in the forest of Arden, a green refuge from the troubles and complications of ordinary life where enmities are reconciled, problems resolved, and the course of true love made to run smooth.

The last important series of traditional pastorals, and an extreme instance of their calculated and graceful display of high artifice, was Alexander Pope's

parchment：羊皮纸　**32**。

parody：戏谑模仿　**38**；*25，59*。

parole（in linguistics）：（语言学中的）言语　**194**；*310，358*。

partial rhyme：半韵　**349**

Pastoral：牧歌

　　牧歌的创始者是古希腊诗人忒奥克里托斯，他在公元前3世纪写过描绘西西里岛牧羊人生活的诗歌。（拉丁文"pastor"的意思是"牧羊人"。）而后维吉尔在用拉丁文写的《牧歌》里摹仿忒奥克里托斯，这样就建立了传统**牧歌**的永久模式：它是一种精美的传统诗歌，表达了都市诗人对在理想化的自然环境里的牧羊人和其他农人生活中所谓的纯朴恬静充满怀旧气息的描绘。数以百计的后世诗人效法维吉尔在摹仿忒奥克里托斯的牧歌时所制定的*文学惯例*：一位牧羊人斜倚在茂密的山毛榉下冥思默想着乡村诗魂，他或是吹着牧笛，好像永远不会变老，或是加入友善的歌咏竞赛，或是倾诉自己幸运或不幸的爱情故事，或是悲悼自己牧羊伙伴的夭逝。从最后一种牧歌的类型里发展形成了*牧人哀歌*，这一类型的牧歌在其他传统类型的牧歌不再盛行后依然保存。和牧歌意思往往相同的词有：idyll（田园诗），出自忒奥克里托斯的牧歌标题；eclogue（**牧歌**）（其字面意思是"选择"），出自维吉尔的牧歌标题；bucolicpoetry（田园诗），源自希腊词"牧人"。

　　古典诗人常将田园生活描绘为具有神话中*黄金时代*的主要特征。基督教田园诗人把异教神话里的黄金时代和圣经中的伊甸乐园结合在一起，还利用了"牧羊人"这个词的宗教象征意义（"牧羊人"可以指代教会或教区的"牧师"；在修辞用法上，"好牧羊人"象征耶稣基督的形象），赋予许多牧歌基督教的意义。在文艺复兴时期，传统牧歌也用于各种嘲讽和寓意用法。埃德蒙·斯宾塞的《牧人月历》（1579）囊括了那个时期流行的大部分不同牧歌类型，使牧歌这种形式在英诗里广为流行。

　　牧歌式梦想是如此引人入胜，文艺复兴时期的作家们甚至将它纳入其他各种文学形式。菲利普·锡德尼爵士的《阿卡迪亚》（1581—1584）是一部用精美绮丽的散文写成的长篇牧歌式*传奇*（**阿卡迪亚**是希腊的一个山区，维吉尔用它来替代忒奥克里托斯笔下的西西里岛，作为他心目中理想化的田园环境）。此外还有田园抒情诗（如克里斯托弗·马洛的《热情的牧人致情人》）和田园剧。约翰·弗莱彻的《忠实的牧羊女》就是田园剧的一个例子，莎士比亚的《皆大欢喜》取材于托马斯·洛奇的一部同时代的田园传奇《罗莎琳德》，其故事发生在亚登森林，这是个逃离日常生活中烦恼纠纷的绿色避难所，在那里，所有的憎恨敌意都烟消云散，所有的疑难都获得解决，真挚的爱情也得以顺利发展。

　　传统牧歌的最后一部重要诗集、精心得体地展现了牧歌高超技巧的最典型范例是亚历山大·蒲柏的《牧歌集》（1709）。五年后，约翰·盖伊在《牧人一

Pastorals (1709). Five years later John Gay, in his *Shepherd's Week*, wrote a parody of the type by applying its elegant formulas to the crudity of actual rustic manners and language; by doing so, he inadvertently showed later poets the way to the seriously realistic treatment of rural life. In 1783 George Crabbe published *The Village* specifically in order to

> paint the cot
> As Truth will paint it and as bards will not.

How far the term then lost its traditional application to a poetry of aristocratic artifice is indicated by Wordsworth's title for his realistic rendering of a rural tragedy in 1800: "Michael, A Pastoral Poem."

In recent decades the term "pastoral" has been expanded in various ways. William Empson, in *Some Versions of Pastoral* (1935), identified as pastoral any work which opposes simple to complicated life, to the advantage of the former: the simple life may be that of the shepherd, the child, or the working man. In Empson's view this literary mode serves as an oblique way to criticize the values and hierarchical class structure of the society of its time. Empson accordingly applies the term to works ranging from Andrew Marvell's seventeenth-century poem "The Garden" to Lewis Carroll's *Alice in Wonderland* and the modern *proletarian novel*. Other critics apply the term "pastoral" to any work which represents a withdrawal to a place apart that is close to the elemental rhythms of nature, where the protagonist gains a new perspective on the complexities, frustrations, and conflicts of the social world. On the continuation of the pastoral strain in "nature writers," see *ecocriticism*.

W. W. Greg, *Pastoral Poetry and Pastoral Drama: A Literary Inquiry, with Special Reference to the Pre-Restoration Stage in England* (1906); the Introduction to *English Pastoral Poetry from the Beginnings to Marvell*, ed. Frank Kermode (1952); Thomas G. Rosenmeyer, *The Green Cabinet: Theocritus and the European Pastoral Lyric* (1969); Andrew V. Ettin, *Literature and the Pastoral* (1985); Annabel Patterson, *Pastoral and Ideology, Virgil to Valéry* (1987); Paul Alpers, *What Is Pastoral?* (1996); Terry Gifford, *Pastoral* (2008).

pastoral elegy: 102; 65, 268.

pathetic fallacy: A phrase invented by John Ruskin in 1856 to signify any representation of inanimate natural objects that ascribes to them human capabilities, sensations, and emotions (*Modern Painters*, Vol. 3, chapter 12); see *pathos*. As used by Ruskin—for whom "truth" was a primary criterion of art—the term was derogatory; for, he claimed, such descriptions do not represent the "true appearances of things to us" but "the extraordinary, or false appearances, when we are under the influence of emotion, or contemplative fancy." Two of Ruskin's examples are the lines

> The spendthrift crocus, bursting through the mould
> Naked and shivering, with his cup of gold,

and Coleridge's description in "Christabel" of

周》中戏谑模仿了这一典范,用牧歌的优雅形式来表现农夫在现实中粗鲁的举止谈吐,通过这种方式,他无意中向后世诗人展示了严肃地描绘乡村生活的写实方法。1783年乔治·克雷布出版了题为《乡村》的诗集,旨在:

> 像上帝那样真实地描绘村舍
> 而吟游诗人却不然。

牧歌这个用于指代具有高雅技法的诗歌的术语当时到底失去了多少传统含义,可以在华兹华斯1800年以写实手法创作的一部乡村悲剧《迈克尔,一首田园诗》的标题中看出。

近几十年来,"牧歌"这个词又有了不同方面的引申含义。譬如,威廉·燕卜荪在《牧歌的一些形式》(1935)中,把任何将简朴与繁琐的生活方式相比较而偏向于简朴生活的作品都定义为牧歌式作品。他认为简朴的生活应该是牧人、孩童或劳动者的生活。在燕卜荪看来,这一文学类型是用来批判它所处时代的社会价值观和等级结构的间接手段。燕卜荪就是这样把从安德鲁·马韦尔在17世纪所作的诗歌《花园》到刘易斯·卡罗尔的《艾丽丝漫游奇境记》以及现代*无产阶级小说*,统统归类为牧歌式作品。其他批评家将"牧歌"这个词用于某类特殊作品,这类作品描写主人公脱离凡俗生活,到贴近大自然原始节奏的边远地区,在那里得以从一种新的角度去看待社会中的错综复杂、浮沉挫折和矛盾冲突。关于"自然作家"中牧歌风格的持续存在,参见:*生态批评*。

参阅:W. W. 格雷格所著的《田园诗与田园剧:一项文学研究,附带英国王政复辟时期之前舞台特别指南》(1906);格雷格为弗兰克·克莫德主编的《英国田园诗:从起始到马维尔》(1952)所写的序言;托马斯·G. 罗森迈耶所著的《绿色庇护所:忒奥克里托斯与欧洲田园抒情诗》(1969);安德鲁·埃廷所著的《文学与牧歌》(1985);安娜贝尔·帕特森所著的《牧歌与意识形态:从维吉尔到瓦莱里》(1987);保罗·阿尔珀斯所著的《什么是牧歌?》(1996);特里·吉福德所著的《牧歌》(2008)。

pastoral elegy:牧人哀歌   102;*65, 268*。

Pathetic Fallacy:感伤谬误

感伤谬误是约翰·罗斯金1856年创造的词组,用来指代将人类的能力、感觉和情感赋予无生命的自然物体的一种表现手法(《现代画家》第3卷第12章);参见:*悲伤感*。从罗斯金的用法上看——对他来说"真实"是一条基本的艺术准则——这一术语带有贬义性质;因为他宣称这样的描述不能代表"事物向我们展示的真实面貌",而是"我们在情感或冥想的影响下,事物在我们眼中异常的、非真实的呈现"。以下是他的两个例证

> 挥霍的番红花,从松软沃土中绽开
> 捧着金杯,赤裸裸地颤动着。

和柯勒律治在《克利斯托贝尔》一诗中的描写:

> The one red leaf, the last of its clan,
> That dances as often as dance it can.

These passages, Ruskin says, however beautiful, are false and "morbid." Only in the greatest poets is the use of the pathetic fallacy valid, and then only at those rare times when it would be inhuman to resist the pressure of powerful feelings to humanize the perceived fact. Ruskin's contention would make just about all poets, including Shakespeare, "morbid." "Pathetic fallacy" is now used mainly as a neutral name for a procedure in which human traits are ascribed to natural objects in a way that is less formal and more indirect than in the figure called *personification*.

See Josephine Miles, *Pathetic Fallacy in the Nineteenth Century* (1942); Harold Bloom, ed., *The Literary Criticism of John Ruskin* (1965), Introduction and pp. 62–78.

pathos: Pathos in Greek meant the passions, or suffering, or deep feeling generally, as distinguished from **ethos**, a person's overall disposition or character. In modern criticism, however, pathos is applied in a much more limited way to a scene or passage that is designed to evoke the feelings of tenderness, pity, or sympathetic sorrow from the audience. In the *Victorian* era some prominent writers exploited pathos beyond the endurance of many readers today—examples are the rendering of the death of Little Nell in Charles Dickens' *The Old Curiosity Shop* and of the death of Little Eva in Harriet Beecher Stowe's *Uncle Tom's Cabin*. (See *sentimentalism*.) To many modern readers, the greatest passages of pathos do not dwell on the details of suffering but achieve their effect by understatement and suggestion. Examples are the speech of King Lear when he is briefly reunited with Cordelia (IV. vii. 59ff.), beginning

> Pray, do not mock me.
> I am a very foolish fond old man,

and William Wordsworth's terse and indirect revelation of the grief of the old father for the loss of his son in *Michael* (1800), ll. 465–66:

> Many and many a day he thither went,
> And never lifted up a single stone.

patriarchal: 122; *42, 146*.

pattern poem: 61.

pentameter (pĕntăm' ĕter): 219.

perfect rhyme: 349.

performance (in linguistics): **195**.

> 那片红红的叶子，剩下的最后一片，
>
> 尽情地舞蹈着回旋着。

罗斯金指出：这几句诗行尽管优美，却是虚妄和"病态"的。只有最杰出的诗人所采用的"感伤谬误"才能取得逻辑上真实的效果，而且只有在如果极力遏制想把所看见的事物人格化的强烈感情将会显得不近情理的那些极为罕见的情形下，才会取得这样的艺术效果。罗斯金的论点使得几乎所有诗人，包括莎士比亚在内，都显得"病态"。"感伤谬误"现在在大多数情况下作为一个中性名词来使用，指把人的特征赋予无生命的事物，与被称为*拟人*的修辞手法相比，这种手法显得不那么正式和不那么直接。

参阅：约瑟芬·迈尔斯所著的《19 世纪的感伤谬误》(1942)；哈罗德·布卢姆主编的《约翰·罗斯金的文学批评》(1965) 一书的序言和书中第 62—78 页。

Pathos：悲伤感

悲伤感在希腊语中通常是指激情、痛苦或深沉的感情，与代表一个人整体性情或个性的**特质**不同。但在现代文学批评里，感伤一词的使用范围要狭窄得多，它是指有意设计出来的、使观众产生心软、怜悯、同情的悲叹等感情的一个情景或一段文字。*维多利亚时代*的一些著名作家对悲伤感这种手法的使用超出了当今大多数读者的忍受范围——譬如，查尔斯·狄更斯在《老古玩店》里对小耐儿之死和哈丽特·比彻·斯托在《汤姆叔叔的小屋》里对小夏娃之死的描写。（参见：*感伤主义*。）对许多现代读者来说，文学上最著名的悲伤感段落，并不是对痛苦的细致描写，而是以含蓄和暗示的表现手法来获得悲伤效果。譬如，李尔王和女儿考狄利娅短促相会时说的一番话（《李尔王》第四幕第七场第 59—60 行）是这样开始的：

> 请你不咎既往，宽赦我的过失。
> 我是个年老糊涂的人，

以及威廉·华兹华斯在《迈克尔》(1800) 一诗里，简洁概述那位老父亲失去儿子的悲伤的两行诗句（第二卷第 465—466 行）：

> 有好些，好些日子，尽管这老汉到了羊栏工地，
> 却不曾在那上面垒一块石头。　　　　　　（杨德豫译）

patriarchal：父权制　122；*42, 146*。

pattern poem：图案诗　61。

pentameter：五音步诗行　219。

perfect rhyme：完美韵　349。

performance (in linguistics)：(语言学中的) 语言运用　195。

performance (of a poem): 221.

performance poetry: Since the seventeenth century, poetry—like other forms of literature—has been composed primarily for printing. In recent years, however, the ancient tradition of composing poetry specifically for oral performance before an audience has been revived in a number of modes, some of which involve extemporizing the poem during the performance itself. Taken together, these compositions can be accounted the first widespread and sustained revival of oral poetry since the beginning of the print culture in the fifteenth century. (See *oral poetry*; also *printing*, under *Renaissance*.) During the rebellious 1960s, for example, **poetry happenings** (public recitations, often to musical accompaniment) were an integral part of the countercultural scene. Later, other marginalized groups produced similar performances, usually in urban settings and before audiences who regarded poetry in print as academic and elitist. The **poetry slam** emerged in the 1980s as competitions in which rival poets were set a time limit, then scored for their oral productions by members of the audience; the poetry at such events was marked by emphatic rhythms, succinctness, clarity, and hipness. For essays by various inquirers about the public performance of printed poems, as well as about contemporary poems composed for public performance, see Charles Bernstein, ed., *Close Listening: Poetry and the Performed Word* (1998). The anthology *Poetry Nation*, ed. Regie Cabico, Todd Swift, and Bob Holman (1998), traces the genealogy of various modes of "alternative" poetry that fuse oral and printed traditions to the performances of the Beat Generation, especially Allen Ginsberg. (See under *Beat Writers*.)

The most widely known and practiced performance poetry is **rap**, an element in **hip-hop**; the latter term since the 1980s has come to designate a cultural movement among urban African-American youths that originated in New York and was marked by distinctive clothing, graffiti, break dancing, and music, especially rap. Both the music and verse form of rap had complex origins in African, *African-American*, and West Indian musical traditions. The verbal component, technically speaking, consists of a hard-driving four-stress line, with a variable number of intervening syllables and a varying number of mainly sequential rhymes, in which there is a frequent use of *partial* and *forced rhymes* (see *meter* and *rhyme*). "To rap" is slang for "to talk," and rap verse is spoken, in a heavily stressed beat, over an accompaniment of bass, percussion, and sometimes other musical instruments. (There is an interesting parallel between rap and the strong-stress meter and the performance of Old English poetry; see under *meter*.) Often in rap the accompaniment is punctuated by "scratching" (the sounds made by rotating a phonograph record to and fro on a turntable so that the needle moves back and forth in the groove) and by "sampling" (the insertion of fragments of recorded music). In the mode known as **freestyling**, or **battle-rapping**, rap verses are improvised during performance, often in competitions between rival rappers. A rapper's distinctive style, in versification, pace, and voice quality, is called his or her "flow."

In its early years rap usually conveyed a self-aggrandizing, contentious, and anti-establishment message, and in the 1980s the genre came to be

performance (of a poem)：(诗歌中的) 表现　221。

Performance Poetry：表演诗歌

　　自从 17 世纪以来，就像其他文学形式一样，诗歌的写作一直主要用于印刷。不过，近些年来，写诗专为在观众面前进行口头表演这一古老传统，通过多种模式得到了复活，其中就包括在表演现场即席赋诗。综合起来看，这些创作可被算作 15 世纪印刷文化出现以来，口头诗歌第一次广泛而持续的复兴。（参见：*口头诗歌*；*文艺复兴中的印刷术*。）例如，在反叛的 1960 年代，**诗歌即兴艺术表演**（经常有音乐伴奏的公开朗诵），是反文化活动中必不可少的一部分。后来，其他边缘群体进行了相似的表演，通常是在城市背景下，在那些认为印刷出来的诗歌带有学院味和精英气的观众面前。**咏诗擂台赛**（又译现场诗歌）作为一种比赛出现于 1980 年代，参赛诗人在规定时限内表演，由一定数量的观众根据他们的口语表现进行打分；这种比赛现场诗歌的特点是强烈的韵律、简明、易懂、时髦。关于不同研究者针对印刷诗歌的公开表演和当前写来用于公开表演的诗歌的论述文章，可以参阅：查尔斯·伯恩斯坦主编的《近距离倾听：诗歌和表演的词语》(1998)。雷吉·卡比克、托德·斯威夫特、鲍勃·霍尔曼三人合编的《诗国》，追溯了不同样式的"另类"诗歌的谱系，包括从口头和印刷传统到垮掉的一代的表演，尤其是金斯堡。（参见：*垮掉派作家*。）

　　最广为人知和最常见的表演诗歌是**说唱**，它是**嘻哈**中的一个元素；嘻哈自从 1980 年代以来，逐渐用来指在都市非裔美国年轻人中间出现的一种文化运动，这一运动源起于纽约，其特点是与众不同的衣着打扮、涂鸦、霹雳舞和音乐，尤其是说唱。说唱的音乐和诗歌形式都有复杂的起源，源于非洲、非裔美国人和西印度音乐传统。从技术上来讲，言语成分由以下部分组成：咄咄逼人的四重音诗行、数量可变的插入音节、不同数量的主要是顺序押韵，其中经常会用到*半韵*和*迫韵*。（参见：*格律*、*韵律*。）"rap"是俚语，意思是"谈话"，说唱诗歌在贝斯、打击乐器，有时则是其他乐器的伴奏下，在猛烈而紧张的节奏下进行。（说唱与重音体格律和古英语诗歌的表现之间有一种有趣的类比；参见：*格律*。）在说唱中，伴奏经常被"擦刮"（通过在一张唱盘上来回旋转唱片以便唱针在沟槽中来回移动发出的声音）和"节录"（插入唱片音乐的碎片）打断。在**自由式说唱**或**战斗说唱**中，说唱诗歌是在表演中即兴创作，经常是在相互竞争的说唱歌手的竞赛中。说唱歌手在诗律、节奏、音色上的独特风格被叫做他／她的"流"。

　　早期说唱通常传达出一种自我扩张的、引起争议的、反正统的信息，进入 1980

dominated by the highly aggressive form, originating on the West Coast, called **gangsta rap** ("gangster rap"), which flaunted (sometimes in a self-mocking way) its transgressive stance against propriety, law, and conventional morality by celebrating violence, misogyny, homophobia, and a candid desire for material goods and sex. Soon, however, rap became less iconoclastic, although much of it continued to express defiance and challenge, as in this passage from "Poetry," by the rapper KRS-One, recorded in 1987.

Increasingly, women rappers and white rappers entered the field that was originally the preserve of urban African-American males, and it became common for rap to voice moderate and even mainstream values. In 1989, for example, Queen Latifah recorded a moral warning, "The Evil That Men Do"; this is an excerpt:

Rap has achieved a remarkable and wide-ranging popularity. The lyrics are composed in many languages, and the form attracts enthusiastic audiences—in personal, recorded, and televised performances—in most countries of the world.

See Gregory Nagy, *Poetry as Performance: Homer and Beyond* (1996); Nelson George, *Hip Hop America* (2d ed., 1999); Michael Eric Dyson, *Know What I Mean? Reflections on Hip Hop* (2007); Lesley Wheeler, *Voicing American Poetry: Sound and Performance from the 1920s to the Present* (2008). For a discussion of rap in relation to other African-American modes of expression, refer to Tricia Rose, *Black Noise: Rap Music and Black Culture in Contemporary America* (1994). The online encyclopedia Wikipedia has informative articles

年代，说唱逐渐被一种源起于西岸的具有高度攻击性的形式**匪帮说唱**所主导，它标榜（有时以一种自嘲的方式）它的违法立场，通过欢庆暴力、厌恶女性、憎恶同性恋、坦承渴求物质和性，来反对规矩、法律、习俗道德。不过，说唱很快就变得较少打破旧习，尽管其中多数仍在表达蔑视和挑战，就像说唱歌手 KRS-One1987 年录制的"Poetry"中的一段（版权未授。——译注）。

（略）

渐渐地，女性说唱歌手和白人说唱歌手开始进入这一此前一直为都市非裔美国男性所专有的圈子；对说唱来说，表达温和的乃至主流的价值观也变得比较常见起来。例如，1989 年，奎因·拉蒂法录制了一首道德忠告歌曲《人之罪》，下面是其中一段（版权未授。——译注）：

（略）

说唱已经赢得了显著而广泛的声望。歌词用多种语言写成，这一形式通过广告、唱片、电视表演，吸引了世界上许多国家热情的观众。

参阅：格雷戈里·纳吉所著的《诗歌作为表演：荷马及超越》（1996）；纳尔逊·乔治所著的《嘻哈美国》（1999 年第 2 版）；迈克尔·埃里克·戴森所著的《知道我什么意思吗？反思嘻哈》（2007）；莱斯利·惠勒所著的《唱出美国诗歌：1920 年代到现在的声音与表演》（2008）。关于说唱与其他非裔美国人的表达模式之间关系的讨论，参阅：特里西娅·罗斯所著的《黑噪音：当代美国的说唱乐和黑人文化》（1994）。在线百科全书维基上有关于表演诗歌、嘻哈、说唱及相关

on performance poetry, hip-hop, rap, and related topics. For references to *performance poetry* in other entries, see page *26*.

performative (in speech-act theory): **373**; *328*.

performative (in constructionist/deconstructionist theory): **373**; *328*.

periodic sentence: 385.

periods of American literature: The division of American literature into convenient historical segments, or "periods," lacks the consensus among literary scholars that we find with reference to English literature; see *Periods of English Literature*. The many syllabi of college surveys reprinted in *Reconstructing American Literature*, ed. Paul Lauter (1983), and the essays in *Redefining American Literary History*, ed. A. LaVonne Brown Ruoff and Jerry W. Ward (1990), demonstrate how variable are the temporal divisions and their names, especially since the beginning of efforts to do justice to literature written by women and by ethnic minorities. Some recent historians, anthologists, and teachers of American literature simply divide their survey into dated sections, without affixing period names. A prominent tendency, however, is to recognize the importance of major wars in marking significant changes in literature. This tendency, as the scholar Cushing Strout has remarked, "suggests that there is an order in American political history more visible and compelling than that indicated by specifically literary or intellectual categories."

The following divisions of American literary history recognize the importance assigned by many literary historians to the Revolutionary War (1775–81), the Civil War (1861–65), World War I (1914–18), and World War II (1939–45). Under these broad divisions are listed some of the more widely used terms to distinguish periods and subperiods of American literature. These terms, it will be noted, are diverse in kind; they may signify a span of time, or a type of political organization, or a prominent intellectual or imaginative mode, or a predominant literary form.

1607–1775. This era, from the founding of the first settlement at Jamestown to the outbreak of the American Revolution, is often called the **Colonial Period**. Writings were for the most part religious, practical, or historical. Notable among the seventeenth-century writers of journals and narratives about the founding and early history of some of the colonies were William Bradford, John Winthrop, and the theologian Cotton Mather. In the following century Jonathan Edwards was a major philosopher as well as theologian, and Benjamin Franklin an early American master of lucid and cogent prose. Not until 1937, when Edward Taylor's writings were first published from manuscript, was Taylor discovered to have been an able religious poet in the *metaphysical* style of the English devotional poets Herbert and Crashaw. Anne Bradstreet was the chief Colonial poet of secular and domestic as well as religious subjects.

美国文学各时期的划分 **273**

主题的信息丰富的文章。其他条目中提及"表演诗歌"的地方,参见第 26 页。

performative (in speech-act theory):(言语行为理论中的) 施为句 373;*328*。

performative (in constructionist/deconstructionist theory):(建构主义/解构主义理论中的) 施为句 373;*328*。

periodic sentence:尾重句 385。

Periods of American Literature:美国文学各时期的划分

将美国文学分成便于讨论的历史片段或"时期",不像划分英国文学时期那样能够获得文学学者们的共识;参见:*英国文学各时期的划分*。保罗·劳特编写的《重建美国文学》(1983) 中的许多大学教学大纲调查和 A. 拉冯内·布朗·鲁奥夫与杰里·W. 沃德合写的文章"重新界定美国文学史"(1990),证明了(尤其是为公正对待女性和少数民族作者的作品所作的努力以来)文学时期时间的划分及其名称具有多么大的可变性。近来,一些历史学家、人类学家和教授美国文学的教师,只是简单地把他们的研究按日期分段而没有附上各阶段的名称。但是一个显著的趋势是,承认重大战争在标志文学重大变革中的重要性。正如学者库欣·斯特劳特所评论的那样,这种趋势"表明在美国的政治史中存在着比具体的文学或文化类别中更明显、更为人信服的顺序"。

以下对美国文学史的划分认可了许多文学史学家赋予独立战争(1775—1781)、南北战争(1861—1865)、第一次世界大战(1914—1918)、第二次世界大战(1939—1945)的重要性。在这些粗略的划分下列举了一些被更广泛应用的术语,以区分美国文学的时期和其中的细分时期。必须注意的是,这些术语种类繁多;它们可能代表一段时间、一种政治组织形式、一种显著的文化或想象模式,或是一种占支配地位的文学形式。

1607—1775 年。从在詹姆斯敦建立第一个殖民地到美国独立战争爆发这一时期,经常被称为**殖民地时期**。这一时期的作品大都是宗教性、实用性或历史性的。17 世纪以一些殖民地的创建和早期历史为写作题材的期刊和叙事作家中著名的有威廉·布雷德福、约翰·温思罗普和神学家科顿·马瑟。接下去一个世纪中,乔纳森·爱德华兹是主要的哲学家和神学家,本杰明·富兰克林则是早期美国写作清晰易懂且极具说服力的散文大师。直到 1937 年爱德华·泰勒的手稿首次出版,他才被发现是一位具有英国虔诚的诗人赫伯特和克拉肖*玄学派*风格的出色的宗教诗人。安·布拉兹特里特是采用世俗、家庭和宗教主题的殖民地时期的主要诗人。

The publication in 1773 of *Poems on Various Subjects* by Phillis Wheatley, then a nineteen-year-old slave who had been born in Africa, inaugurated the long and distinguished, but until recently neglected, line of **black writers** (or by what has come to be the preferred name, **African-American writers**) in America. The complexity and diversity of the African-American cultural heritage—both Western and African, oral and written, slave and free, Judeo-Christian and pagan, plantation and urban, integrationist and black nationalist—have effected tensions and fusions that, over the course of time, have produced a highly innovative and distinctive literature, as well as musical forms that have come to be considered America's most important contribution to the Western musical tradition. See J. Saunders Redding, *To Make a Poet Black* (1939; reissued 1986); Houston A. Baker, Jr., *Black Literature in America* (1971); Bernard W. Bell, *The Afro-American Novel and Its Tradition* (1987); Henry L. Gates, Jr., *Figures in Black* (1987), and ed., *Black Literature and Literary Theory* (1984); also Henry L. Gates, Jr., Nellie Y. McKay, and others, eds., *The Norton Anthology of African-American Literature* (1997).

The period between the Stamp Act of 1765 and 1790 is sometimes distinguished as the **Revolutionary Age**. It was the time of Thomas Paine's influential revolutionary tracts; of Thomas Jefferson's "Statute of Virginia for Religious Freedom," "Declaration of Independence," and many other writings; of *The Federalist Papers* in support of the Constitution, most notably those by Alexander Hamilton and James Madison; and of the patriotic and satiric poems by Philip Freneau and Joel Barlow.

1775–1865. The years 1775–1828, the **Early National Period** ending with the triumph of Jacksonian democracy in 1828, signalized the emergence of a national imaginative literature, including the first American stage comedy (Royall Tyler's *The Contrast*, 1787), the earliest American novel (William Hill Brown's *The Power of Sympathy*, 1789), and the establishment in 1815 of the first enduring American magazine, *The North American Review*. Washington Irving achieved international fame with his essays and stories; Charles Brockden Brown wrote distinctively American versions of the *Gothic novel* of mystery and terror; the career of James Fenimore Cooper, the first major American novelist, was well launched; and William Cullen Bryant and Edgar Allan Poe wrote poetry that was relatively independent of English precursors. In the year 1760 was published the first of a long series of **slave narratives** and autobiographies written by *African-American* slaves who had escaped or been freed. Most of these were published between 1830 and 1865, including Frederick Douglass' *Narrative of the Life of Frederick Douglass* (1845) and Harriet Jacobs' *Incidents in the Life of a Slave Girl* (1861).

The span 1828–65 from the Jacksonian era to the Civil War, often identified as the **Romantic Period in America** (see *neoclassic and romantic*), marks the full coming of age of a distinctively American literature. This period is sometimes known as the **American Renaissance**, the title of F. O. Matthiessen's influential book (1941) about its outstanding writers, Ralph Waldo Emerson, Henry David Thoreau, Edgar Allan Poe, Herman Melville, and Nathaniel Hawthorne (see also *symbolism*); it is also sometimes called the

1773年菲利斯·惠特利——当时他还是一个出生于非洲的19岁奴隶——出版的《论各种主题的诗歌》，宣告了一大批杰出**黑人作家**（或者用一个后来更易为人接受的称谓，**非裔美国作家**）的产生，但直到最近他们仍被忽视。美国的非洲文化传统十分复杂，种类繁多——既是西方的又是非洲的，既有口头的又有书面的，既有奴隶的又有自由人的，既是犹太基督教的又是异教徒的，既有种植园的又有城市的，既是主张取消种族隔离的又是黑人民族主义的——这种文化传统产生了张力和融合力，在历史的长河中创造了高度创新和极具特色的文学，以及被视为美国对西方音乐传统重要贡献的音乐形式。参阅：J. 桑德斯·雷丁所著的《造出黑肤色诗人》（1939，1986年再版）；小休斯顿·A. 贝克所著的《美国黑人文学》（1971）；伯纳德·W. 贝尔所著的《美国黑人小说和它的传统》（1987）；小亨利·L. 盖茨所著的《黑人形象》（1987）及其主编的《黑人文学与文学理论》（1984）；小亨利·L. 盖茨、内利·Y. 麦凯等人合编的《诺顿美国黑人文学选集》（1997）。

1765年印花税法和1790年之间的这一阶段有时被区分为**独立战争时期**。这是托马斯·潘恩颇具影响的革命宣传短文的时代；是托马斯·杰斐逊的《弗吉尼亚宗教自由法令》和《独立宣言》以及其他许多作品的时代；是《联邦党人文集》（那些最知名的文章是由亚历山大·汉密尔顿和詹姆斯·麦迪逊撰写的）支持宪法的时代；是菲利普·弗瑞诺和乔·巴洛创作爱国讽刺诗歌的时代。

1775—1865年。1775—1828年被称为**早期民族文学时期**，它以1828年杰克逊民主的获胜为结束，标志着富有想象力的民族文学的出现，这一时期的作品包括首部美国舞台喜剧［罗耶尔·泰勒的《对比》（1787）］，最早的美国小说［威廉·希尔·布朗的《同情的力量》（1789）］和1815年创办的第一家长盛不衰的美国杂志《北美评论》。华盛顿·欧文的散文和故事获得了国际声誉；查尔斯·布罗克登·布朗写出了具有美国特色的神秘和恐怖的*哥特小说*；美国第一位重要小说家，詹姆斯·费尼莫尔·库珀，成功地开始了他的创作生涯；威廉·卡伦·布赖恩特和埃德加·爱伦·坡写出了相对独立于其英国前辈的诗歌。1760年出版了一大批**奴隶故事**和自传中的首批作品，作者是逃跑的或获得自由的*非裔美国*奴隶，这些作品大都出版于1830—1865年间，其中包括弗雷德里克·道格拉斯的《弗雷德里克·道格拉斯的生平与时代》（1845）和哈丽特·雅各布斯的《一个女奴的生平事件》（1861）。

1828—1865年，从杰克逊时代至美国内战这一阶段常被视为**美国的浪漫主义时期**（参见：*新古典主义和浪漫主义*），标志着独特的美国文学时代完全来临。这一时期有时也叫**美国的文艺复兴时期**，这一名称来自 F. O. 麦西森颇有影响的同名著作（1941），该书评介了这一时期的著名作家拉尔夫·沃尔多·爱默生、亨利·戴维·梭罗、埃德加·爱伦·坡、赫尔曼·梅尔维尔和纳撒尼尔·霍桑（也可参见：*象*

Age of Transcendentalism, after the philosophical and literary movement, centered on Emerson, that was dominant in New England (see *Transcendentalism*). In all the major genres except drama, writers produced works of an originality and excellence not exceeded in later American literature. Emerson, Thoreau, and the early feminist Margaret Fuller shaped the ideas, ideals, and literary aims of many contemporary and later American writers. It was the age not only of continuing writings by William Cullen Bryant, Washington Irving, and James Fenimore Cooper, but also of the novels and short stories of Poe, Hawthorne, Melville, Harriet Beecher Stowe, and the southern novelist William Gilmore Simms; of the poetry of Poe, John Greenleaf Whittier, Emerson, Henry Wadsworth Longfellow, and the most innovative and influential of all American poets, Walt Whitman; and of the beginning of distinguished American criticism in the essays of Poe, Simms, and James Russell Lowell. The tradition of *African-American* poetry by women was continued by Francis Ellen Watkins Harper, and the African-American novel was inaugurated by William Wells Brown's *Clotel* (1853) and by Harriet E. Wilson's *Our Nig* (1859).

1865–1914. The cataclysm of the bloody Civil War and Reconstruction, followed by a burgeoning industrialism and urbanization in the North, profoundly altered American self-awareness, and also American literary modes. The years 1865–1900 are often known as the **Realistic Period**, by reference to the novels by Mark Twain, William Dean Howells, and Henry James, as well as by John W. DeForest, Harold Frederic, and the *African-American* novelist Charles W. Chesnutt. These works, though diverse, are often labeled "realistic" in contrast to the "romances" of their predecessors in prose fiction: Poe, Hawthorne, and Melville (see *prose romance* and *realism*). Some realistic authors grounded their fiction in a regional milieu; these include (in addition to Mark Twain's novels on the Mississippi River region) Bret Harte in California, Sarah Orne Jewett in Maine, Mary Wilkins Freeman in Massachusetts, and George W. Cable and Kate Chopin in Louisiana. (See *regional novel*.) Chopin has become prominent as an early and major *feminist* novelist. Whitman continued writing poetry up to the last decade of the century, and (unknown to him and almost everyone else) was joined by Emily Dickinson; although only seven of Dickinson's more than a thousand short poems were published in her lifetime, she is now recognized as one of the most distinctive and eminent of American poets. Sidney Lanier published his experiments in versification based on the meters of music; the *African-American* author Paul Laurence Dunbar wrote both poems and novels between 1893 and 1905; and in the 1890s Stephen Crane, although he was only twenty-nine when he died, published short poems in free verse that anticipate the experiments of Ezra Pound and the *Imagists*, and wrote also the brilliantly innovative short stories and short novels that look forward to two later narrative modes: naturalism and impressionism. The years 1900–1914—although James, Howells, and Mark Twain were still writing, and Edith Wharton was publishing her earlier novels—are sometimes discriminated as the **Naturalistic Period**, in recognition of the powerful although sometimes crudely wrought novels by

征主义);这一阶段有时也被称为**超验主义时期**,以爱默生为中心,始于在新英格兰占统治地位的哲学和文学运动之后(参见:*超验主义*)。在除戏剧外的所有文学体裁中,这一时期的作家们所创作的作品的原创性和高度的艺术成就都是后世美国文学所无法超越的。爱默生、梭罗和早期女性主义者玛格丽特·福勒在思想、理想、文学目的方面影响了那一时代和后世的许多美国作家。这不仅仅是威廉·卡伦·布赖恩特、华盛顿·欧文、詹姆斯·费尼莫尔·库珀不断有新作问世的年代,还是坡、霍桑、梅尔维尔、哈丽特·比彻·斯托和南部小说家威廉·吉尔摩·西姆斯创作小说和短篇故事的年代;是坡、约翰·格林里夫·惠蒂埃、爱默生、亨利·华兹沃斯·朗费罗和所有美国诗人中最具创新意识和影响力的沃尔特·惠特曼创作诗歌的时代;也是坡、西姆斯和詹姆斯·拉塞尔·洛威尔开始在散文中展现杰出的美国式文学批评的时代。弗朗西斯·埃伦·沃特金斯·哈珀延续了*非裔美国*女性诗人的诗歌创作传统,非裔美国小说则由威廉·韦尔斯·布朗的《克洛代尔》(1853)和哈丽特·E.威尔逊的《我们黑人》(1859)拉开了序幕。

1865—1914 年。血腥的美国内战带来的大变革与战后南部重建及随后北部工业化和城市化的迅速发展,深刻地改变了美国对自身的认识,也改变了美国的文学模式。1865—1900 年间经常被称为**现实主义时期**,指的是包括马克·吐温、威廉·迪安·豪威尔斯、亨利·詹姆斯、约翰·W.德福雷斯特、哈罗德·弗雷德里克和*非裔美国*小说家查尔斯·W.切斯纳特的作品。这些作品尽管各有不同,但都被归为"现实主义的",以区别于其散文体小说的前辈坡、霍桑和梅尔维尔的"传奇"作品(参见:*散文体传奇*、*现实主义*)。一些现实主义作家以地域为小说的创作背景;这些作家(除了马克·吐温描绘密西西比河流域地区的小说外)包括加利福尼亚的布雷特·哈特、缅因州的萨拉·奥恩·朱厄特、马萨诸塞州的玛丽·威尔金斯·弗里曼、路易斯安那州的乔治·W.卡布尔和凯特·肖邦。(参见:*地方小说*。)肖邦现已作为早期主要*女性主义*作家而闻名。惠特曼直到 19 世纪最后十年还在继续他的诗歌创作,随后埃米莉·狄金森加入了诗歌创作的行列(这是惠特曼和几乎其他所有人所不了解的)。尽管狄金森创作的 1000 多首短诗在她生前只发表了七首,但她今天已被视为美国最独特、最杰出的诗人之一。西德尼·拉尼尔出版了以音乐节拍为基础的诗律实验诗作;*非裔美国*作家保罗·劳伦斯·邓巴在 1893—1905 年间出版了诗歌和小说;1890 年代,斯蒂芬·克莱恩(尽管他去世时年仅 29 岁)先于埃兹拉·庞德和*意象主义者*的实验性作品出版了自由体短篇诗歌,与此同时,他还创作了才华横溢充满新意的短篇故事和短篇小说,这些作品预示了后来出现的两种叙事模式:自然主义和印象主义。1900—1914 年间,尽管詹姆斯、豪威尔斯和马克·吐温仍在继续创作,伊迪丝·华顿也出版了她的早期小说,但为了表示对弗兰克·诺里斯、

Frank Norris, Jack London, and Theodore Dreiser, which typically represent characters who are joint victims of their instinctual drives and of external sociological forces; see *naturalism*, under *realism and naturalism*.

1914–1939. The era between the two world wars, marked by the trauma of the great economic depression beginning in 1929, was that of the emergence of what is still known as "modern literature," which in America reached an eminence rivaling that of the American Renaissance of the mid-nineteenth century; unlike most of the authors of that earlier period, however, the American modernists also achieved widespread international recognition and influence. (See *modernism*.) *Poetry* magazine, founded in Chicago by Harriet Monroe in 1912, published many innovative authors. Among the notable poets were Edgar Lee Masters, Edwin Arlington Robinson, Robert Frost, Carl Sandburg, Wallace Stevens, William Carlos Williams, Ezra Pound, Robinson Jeffers, Marianne Moore, T. S. Eliot, Edna St. Vincent Millay, and e. e. cummings—authors who wrote in an unexampled variety of poetic modes. These included the *Imagism* of Amy Lowell, H. D. (Hilda Doolittle), and others; the metric poems by Frost and the free-verse poems by Williams in the American vernacular; the formal and typographic experiments of cummings; the poetic naturalism of Jeffers; and the assimilation to their own distinctive uses by Pound and Eliot of the forms and procedures of French *symbolism*, merged with the intellectual and figurative methods of the English *metaphysical poets*. Among the major writers of prose fiction were Edith Wharton, Sinclair Lewis, Ellen Glasgow, Willa Cather, Gertrude Stein, Sherwood Anderson, John Dos Passos, F. Scott Fitzgerald, William Faulkner, Ernest Hemingway, Thomas Wolfe, and John Steinbeck. America produced in this period its first great dramatist in Eugene O'Neill, as well as a group of distinguished literary critics that included Van Wyck Brooks, Malcolm Cowley, T. S. Eliot, Edmund Wilson, and the irreverent and caustic H. L. Mencken.

The literary productions of this era are often subclassified in a variety of ways. The flamboyant and pleasure-seeking 1920s are sometimes referred to as "the Jazz Age," a title popularized by F. Scott Fitzgerald's *Tales of the Jazz Age* (1922). The same decade was also the period of the Harlem Renaissance, which produced major writings in all the literary forms by Countee Cullen, Langston Hughes, Claude McKay, Jean Toomer, Zora Neale Hurston, and many other *African-American* writers. (See *Harlem Renaissance*.)

Many prominent American writers of the decade following the end of World War I, disillusioned by their war experiences and alienated by what they perceived as the crassness of American culture and its "puritanical" repressions, are often tagged (in a term first applied by Gertrude Stein to young Frenchmen of the time) as the **Lost Generation**. A number of these writers became expatriates, moving either to London or to Paris in their quest for a richer literary and artistic milieu and a freer way of life. Ezra Pound, Gertrude Stein, and T. S. Eliot lived out their lives abroad, but most of the younger "exiles," as Malcolm Cowley called them (*Exile's Return*, 1934), came back to America in the 1930s. Hemingway's *The Sun Also Rises* and Fitzgerald's *Tender Is the Night* are novels that represent the mood and way of life of two

杰克·伦敦和西奥多·德莱塞那些尽管有时显得粗糙但却具有强大感染力的小说（这些作品对成为那些本能欲望与外界社会力量共同作用下的牺牲品的人物形象进行了典型的描写）的认可，这一时期被区别为**自然主义时期**；参见：*现实主义与自然主义*中的*自然主义*。

1914—1939 年。这一时期介于两次世界大战之间，以始于 1929 年的经济大萧条带来的创伤为标志，这是出现了现在仍然称为"现代文学"的时期，其在美国的卓越成就达到了足以与 19 世纪中期美国文艺复兴时期比肩的高度；但与早期大多数作家不同，美国的现代主义作家也享有广泛的国际声誉和影响力。（参见：*现代主义*。）哈丽特·门罗 1912 年创办于芝加哥的《诗歌》杂志，发表了许多具有创新性的作家的作品。这些著名诗人中有埃德加·李·马斯特斯、埃德温·阿林顿·罗宾逊、罗伯特·弗罗斯特、卡尔·桑德堡、华莱士·史蒂文斯、威廉·卡洛斯·威廉斯、埃兹拉·庞德、鲁宾逊·杰弗斯、玛丽安·穆尔、T. S. 艾略特、埃德娜·圣·文森特·米莱和 e. e. 卡明斯。这些诗人采用了史无前例种类繁多的诗歌创作模式，其中包括埃米·洛威尔、H. D.（希尔达·杜利特尔）和其他诗人的*意象主义*，弗罗斯特的韵律诗，威廉斯用美国方言创作的自由体诗，卡明斯在形式和排版上的实验，杰弗斯的诗体自然主义，庞德与艾略特将法国的*象征主义*形式和传统方式与英国*玄学派诗人*的智慧和比喻手法融会贯通、消化吸收，运用于他们各自别具一格的诗歌创作。散文体小说的主要作家有伊迪丝·华顿、辛克莱·刘易斯、埃伦·格拉斯哥、威拉·凯瑟、格特鲁德·斯泰因、舍伍德·安德森、约翰·多斯·帕索斯、F. 司各特·菲茨杰拉德、威廉·福克纳、欧内斯特·海明威、托马斯·乌尔夫和约翰·斯坦贝克。这一时期，美国产生了第一位杰出的剧作家尤金·奥尼尔和一大群著名的文学批评家，他们包括范·威克·布鲁克斯、马尔科姆·考利、T. S. 艾略特、埃德蒙·威尔逊和傲慢而刻薄的 H. L. 门肯。

这一时期的文学作品经常以多种方式再度细分。奢华浮夸、追求享乐的 1920 年代有时被称为"爵士时代"，这个名称因为 F. 司各特·菲茨杰拉德的《爵士时代的故事》(1922) 而流行。这十年也是哈莱姆文艺复兴时期，康蒂·卡伦、兰斯顿·休斯、克劳德·麦凯、琼·图默、佐拉·尼尔·赫斯顿和其他许多非裔美国作家用各种文学形式创作了哈莱姆文艺复兴时期的主要作品。（参见：*哈莱姆文艺复兴*。）

这十年间的许多杰出美国作家在第一次世界大战结束后因其自身的战争经历而深感幻灭，因他们所感悟到的美国文化的愚钝无知与其"清教徒式"的压抑而异化，经常被冠以**迷惘的一代**（格特鲁德·斯泰因最先用这一术语来指那时法国的年轻人）。为了追求更加丰富多彩的文学艺术环境和更为自由的生活方式，这些作家中的一部分移居国外，他们或者去了伦敦，或者去了巴黎。埃兹拉·庞德、格特鲁德·斯泰因和 T. S. 艾略特终老国外，但大部分较年轻的"流亡者"，正如马尔科姆·考利称呼他们的那样[《流亡者归来》(1934)]，都在 1930 年代回到了美国。海明威的《太阳照样升起》和菲茨杰拉德的《夜未央》是描绘了两种美国流亡者心

groups of American expatriates. In "the radical '30s," the period of the Great Depression and of the economic and social reforms in the New Deal inaugurated by President Franklin Delano Roosevelt, some authors joined radical political movements, and many others dealt in their literary works with pressing social issues of the time—including, in the novel, William Faulkner, John Dos Passos, James T. Farrell, Thomas Wolfe, and John Steinbeck, and in the drama, Eugene O'Neill, Clifford Odets, and Maxwell Anderson. See Peter Conn, *The American 1930s: A Literary History* (2009), and Morris Dickstein, *Dancing in the Dark: A Cultural History of the Great Depression* (2009).

1939 to the Present, the **contemporary period.** World War II, and especially the disillusionment with Soviet Communism consequent upon the Moscow trials for alleged treason and Stalin's signing of the Russo-German pact with Hitler in 1939, largely ended the literary radicalism of the 1930s. A final blow to the very few writers who had maintained intellectual allegiance to Soviet Russia came in 1991 with the collapse of Russian Communism and the dissolution of the Soviet Union. For several decades the *New Criticism*—dominated by conservative southern writers, the **Agrarians**, who in the 1930s had championed a return from an industrial to an agricultural economy—typified the prevailing critical tendency to isolate literature from the life of the author and from society and to conceive a work of literature, in formal terms, as an organic and autonomous entity. (See John L. Stewart, *The Burden of Time: The Fugitives and Agrarians*, 1965.) The eminent and influential critics Edmund Wilson and Lionel Trilling, however—as well as other critics grouped with them as the **New York Intellectuals**, including Philip Rahv, Alfred Kazin, Dwight McDonald, and Irving Howe—continued through the 1960s to deal with a work of literature humanistically and historically, in the context of its author's life, temperament, and social milieu, and in terms of the work's moral and imaginative qualities and its consequences for society. See Alexander Bloom, *Prodigal Sons: The New York Intellectuals & Their World* (1986); V. B. Leitch, *American Literary Criticism from the Thirties to the Eighties*, 1988, chapter 4. For a discussion of radically new developments in American literary theory and criticism in the 1970s and later, see *poststructuralism*.

The 1950s, while often regarded in retrospect as a period of cultural conformity and complacency, was marked by the emergence of vigorous antiestablishment and antitraditional literary movements: the *Beat writers* such as Allen Ginsberg and Jack Kerouac; the American exemplars of the literature of the *absurd*; the **Black Mountain Poets**, Charles Olson, Robert Creeley, and Robert Duncan; and the **New York Poets**, Frank O'Hara, Kenneth Koch, and John Ashbery. It was also a time of *confessional poetry* and the literature of extreme sexual candor, marked by the emergence of Henry Miller as a notable author (his autobiographical and fictional works, begun in the 1930s, had earlier been available only under the counter) and the writings of Norman Mailer, William Burroughs, and Vladimir Nabokov (*Lolita* was published in 1955). The **counterculture** of the 1960s and early 1970s continued some of these modes, but in a fashion made extreme and fevered by the rebellious youth movement and the vehement and sometimes violent

态和生活方式的小说。在"激进的 30 年代",即美国经济大萧条和富兰克林·德拉诺·罗斯福总统推行新政带来经济、社会变革的时期,一些作家投身于激进的政治运动,其他许多作家则在其文学作品中触及当时亟须解决的社会问题,其中包括威廉·福克纳、约翰·多斯·帕索斯、詹姆斯·T. 法雷尔、托马斯·乌尔夫、约翰·斯坦贝克的小说和尤金·奥尼尔、克利福德·奥德兹、马克斯韦尔·安德森的剧作。参见:彼得·康恩所著的《美国 1930 年代:文学史》(2009);莫里斯·迪克斯坦所著的《在黑暗中舞蹈:大萧条的文化史》(2009)。

1939 年至今,当代时期。第二次世界大战,尤其是因为随之而来的对所谓叛国罪的莫斯科审判,以及 1939 年斯大林与希特勒签订苏德条约而导致对苏联共产主义的幻灭,在很大程度上给 1930 年代的文学激进主义画上了句号。1991 年苏联解体给那些极少数依然在文化上效忠于苏联的作家以最后一击。接下去数十年间,那些在 1930 年代积极支持从工业经济回归农业经济的南部保守派作家,即**平均地权论者**,主宰了*新批评*,代表了将文学与作者生平及社会隔离开的普遍批评趋势,用正式术语来说,就是将文学作品视为有机的和自主的实体。[参阅:约翰·L. 斯图尔特所著的《时间的重负:逃亡者与平均地权论者》(1965)。] 然而,颇具声望和影响力的批评家埃德蒙·威尔逊和莱昂内尔·特里林——以及包括菲利普·拉夫、艾尔弗雷特·卡辛、德怀特·麦克唐纳和欧文·豪在内被归为**纽约文人**的其他批评家——在 1960 年代依然用人性和历史的观点来对待文学作品,以作者的生平、气质和社会环境为评述背景,以作品的道德、想象力品质和对社会的影响作为评价标准。参阅:亚历山大·布鲁姆所著的《浪子回头:纽约文人和他们的世界》(1986);V. B. 利奇所著的《20 世纪 30 年代到 80 年代的美国文学批评》(1988)第 4 章。有关美国文学理论和批评在 1970 年代及之后的激进新发展的讨论,参见:*后结构主义*。

回顾过去,尽管 1950 年代经常被视为是一个文化一致和满足现状的时期,但这一时期的标志却是涌现了反现存社会体制和反传统的各种充满活力的文学运动:艾伦·金斯堡和杰克·凯鲁亚克等*垮掉派作家*;*荒诞派文学的美国典范*;**黑山诗人**查尔斯·奥尔森、罗伯特·克瑞莱和罗伯特·邓肯;**纽约诗人**弗兰克·奥哈拉、肯尼斯·科赫和约翰·阿什伯利。这也是一个*自白诗*盛行的时期,文学上对性持极端坦率开放的态度,这个时期以著名作家亨利·米勒(他 1930 年代开始创作自传体和虚构作品,但在 1950 年代之前只在私下流通)的出现,以及诺曼·梅勒、威廉·巴罗斯和弗拉基米尔·纳博科夫(《洛丽塔》出版于 1955 年)等人的著作为标志。1960 年代和 1970 年代初期的**反文化**运动,继承了前期的一些创作模式,但是叛逆的青年运动和对越战激烈的、有时甚至是猛烈的反对却将其推向了

opposition to the war in Vietnam; for an approving treatment of this movement, see Theodore Roszak, *The Making of a Counter Culture* (1969), and for a later retrospective, Morris Dickstein, *Gates of Eden: American Culture in the Sixties* (1978). See *modernism and postmodernism*, and for radical developments of this era in African-American literature, see *Black Arts Movement*.

Important American writers after World War II include, in prose fiction, Vladimir Nabokov (who emigrated to America in 1940), Eudora Welty, Robert Penn Warren, Bernard Malamud, James Gould Cozzens, Saul Bellow, Mary McCarthy, Norman Mailer, John Updike, Kurt Vonnegut, Jr., Thomas Pynchon, John Barth, Donald Barthelme, E. L. Doctorow, Cynthia Ozick, and Joyce Carol Oates; in poetry, Marianne Moore, Robert Penn Warren, Theodore Roethke, Elizabeth Bishop, Richard Wilbur, Robert Lowell, Allen Ginsberg, Adrienne Rich, Sylvia Plath, A. R. Ammons, and John Ashbery; and in drama, Thornton Wilder, Lillian Hellman, Arthur Miller, Tennessee Williams, Edward Albee, and a number of more recent playwrights, including Sam Shepard, David Mamet, Tony Kushner, and Wendy Wasserstein. Many of the most innovative and distinguished literary works of the later decades of the twentieth century have been written by writers who are often identified as belonging to one or another "minority," or **ethnic** literary group. (An "ethnic group" consists of individuals who are distinguishable, within a majority cultural and social system, by shared characteristics such as race, religion, language, cultural modes, and national origin.) There is, however, much contention, both within and outside these groups, whether it is more just and enlightening to consider such writers simply as part of the American mainstream or to stress what is called the identity of each writer as a participant in an ethnic culture with its distinctive subject matter, themes, and formal features. (See *identity theorists*, under *humanism*.) This is the era of the notable *African-American* novelists and essayists Ralph Ellison, James Baldwin, Richard Wright, Albert Murray, Gloria Naylor, Alice Walker, and Toni Morrison; the poets Amiri Baraka (LeRoi Jones), Gwendolyn Brooks, Maya Angelou, and Rita Dove; and the dramatists Lorraine Hansberry and August Wilson. (For some developments in popular modes of versification, see *performance poetry*.) It is also the era of the emergence of such prominent minority novelists as Leslie Marmon Silko (Native American); Oscar Hijuelos and Sandra Cisneros (Hispanic); Jhumpa Lahiri (East Indian); and Maxine Hong Kingston and Amy Tan (Chinese-American). See Houston A. Baker, ed., *Three American Literatures: Essays in Chicano, Native American, and Asian-American Literature for Teachers of American Literature* (1982).

The contemporary literary scene in America is crowded and varied, and these lists could readily be expanded. We must await the passage of time to determine which writers now active will emerge as enduringly major figures in the *canon* of American literature.

periods of English literature: For convenience of discussion, historians divide the continuity of English literature into segments of time that are called "periods." The exact number, dates, and names of these periods vary, but

极端和狂热；对这一运动持赞成态度的论述，参阅：西奥多·罗斯扎克所著的《反文化的形成》(1969)；后来对这一运动的回顾，参阅：莫里斯·迪克斯坦所著的《伊甸园之门：60年代的美国文化》(1978)。参见：*现代主义和后现代主义*，有关非裔美国文学作品在此阶段的激进发展，参见：*黑人艺术运动*。

  二战后美国散文体小说的重要作家包括：弗拉基米尔·纳博科夫(1940年移居美国)、尤多拉·韦尔蒂、罗伯特·佩恩·华伦、伯纳德·马拉默德、詹姆斯·库尔德·科森斯、索尔·贝娄、玛丽·麦卡锡、诺曼·梅勒、约翰·厄普代克、小库特·冯尼戈特、托马斯·品钦、约翰·巴思、唐纳德·巴塞尔姆、E. L. 多克特罗、辛西娅·奥兹克和乔伊斯·卡罗尔·奥茨；诗歌创作方面的主要代表包括：玛丽安·穆尔、罗伯特·佩恩·华伦、西奥多·罗特克、伊丽莎白·毕肖普、理查德·威尔伯、罗伯特·洛威尔、艾伦·金斯堡、阿德里安娜·里奇、西尔维亚·普拉斯、A. R. 阿蒙斯和约翰·阿什伯利；戏剧方面包括：桑顿·怀尔德、莉莲·海尔曼、阿瑟·米勒、田纳西·威廉斯、爱德华·阿尔比，以及包括萨姆·谢泼德、戴维·马梅特、托尼·库什纳和温迪·沃瑟斯坦在内的一些其后出现的剧作家。20世纪后几十年很多最具创新意识、最杰出的文学作品，往往都是那些被归于某一"少数群体"或某一**民族**的文学群体的作家所创作的（"民族群体"由处于主体文化和社会体系中、明显具有共同的种族、宗教、语言、文化模式和民族根源等特性的个人组成）。但在这些群体的内部与外部却存在许多争议，争议的焦点是：到底是只把这类作家视为美国主流文学的组成部分更为公正准确，还是强调每个作家作为某一民族文化的参与者身份，具有其所属文化独特的题材、主题和形式特征更为公正准确。(参见：*人文主义中的身份理论家*。)这是杰出非裔美国小说家和散文家拉尔夫·埃里森、詹姆斯·鲍德温、理查德·赖特、艾伯特·默里、格洛丽亚·内勒、艾丽斯·沃克和托尼·莫里森的时代，是诗人阿米里·巴拉卡（莱罗伊·琼斯）、格温德林·布鲁克斯、玛亚·安杰洛和丽塔·达芙的时代；是剧作家洛兰·汉斯伯里和奥古斯特·威尔逊的时代。(关于大众化的诗律模式的一些发展，参见：*表演诗歌*。)这也是涌现了莱斯利·马蒙·席尔科（美国印第安人）、奥斯卡·胡罗斯和桑德拉·西斯内罗斯（西班牙裔美国人）、茱帕·拉希里（东印度人）、玛克辛·汉·金斯敦（即汤婷婷）和谭恩美（华裔美国人）等杰出少数民族小说家的时代。参阅：休斯敦·A. 贝克主编的《三种美国文学：奇卡诺人文学、美国本土文学与亚裔美国文学文丛：美国文学教师手册》(1982)。

  当代美国的文学场景繁复多样，以上所列随时都可能得到进一步扩展。我们需要等待时间来决定究竟哪一位目前活跃的作家可以成为美国文学经典中长盛不衰的重要人物。

Periods of English Literature：英国文学各时期的划分

  为了便于讨论，历史学家把延续至今的英国文学划分成时间段，称为"时期"。这些时期的确切数目、日期和名称的规定各有不同，但下表符合广为流行

the list below conforms to widespread practice. The list is followed by a brief comment on each period, in chronological order.

 450–1066 Old English (or Anglo-Saxon) Period
 1066–1500 Middle English Period
 1500–1660 The Renaissance (or Early Modern)
  1558–1603 Elizabethan Age
  1603–1625 Jacobean Age
  1625–1649 Caroline Age
  1649–1660 Commonwealth Period (or Puritan Interregnum)
 1600–1785 The Neoclassical Period
  1660–1700 The Restoration
  1700–1745 The Augustan Age
  1745–1785 The Age of Sensibility (or Age of Johnson)
 1785–1832 The Romantic Period
 1832–1901 The Victorian Period
  1848–1860 The Pre-Raphaelites
  1880–1901 Aestheticism and Decadence
 1901–1914 The Edwardian Period
 1910–1936 The Georgian Period
 1914– The Modern Period
 1945–   Postmodernism

 The **Old English Period**, or the **Anglo-Saxon Period**, extended from the invasion of Celtic England by Germanic tribes (the Angles, Saxons, and Jutes) in the first half of the fifth century to the conquest of England in 1066 by the Norman French under the leadership of William the Conqueror. Only after they had been converted to Christianity in the seventh century did the Anglo-Saxons, whose earlier literature had been oral, begin to develop a written literature. (See *oral poetry*.) A high level of culture and learning was soon achieved in various monasteries; the eighth-century churchmen Bede and Alcuin were major scholars who wrote in Latin, the standard language of international scholarship. The poetry written in the vernacular Anglo-Saxon, known also as Old English, included *Beowulf* (eighth century), the greatest of Germanic epic poems, and such lyric laments as "The Wanderer," "The Seafarer," and "Deor," all of which, although composed by Christian writers, reflect the conditions of life in the pagan past. Caedmon and Cynewulf were poets who wrote on biblical and religious themes, and there survive a number of Old English lives of saints, sermons, and paraphrases of books of the Bible. Alfred the Great, a West Saxon king (871–99) who for a time united all the kingdoms of southern England against a new wave of Germanic invaders, the Vikings, was no less important as a patron of literature than as a warrior.

的区分方法。每一时期都附有一篇简短的评述，按年代顺序排列。

450—1066 年	古英语（或盎格鲁－撒克逊）时期
1066—1500 年	中古英语时期
1500—1660 年	文艺复兴时期（或早期现代时期）
1558—1603 年	伊丽莎白时期
1603—1625 年	詹姆斯一世时期
1625—1649 年	查理时期
1649—1660 年	共和国时期（或清教徒执政期）
1660—1785 年	新古典主义时期
1660—1700 年	王政复辟时期
1700—1745 年	奥古斯都文学盛世（或蒲柏时代）
1745—1785 年	情感时期（或约翰逊时代）
1785—1830 年	浪漫主义时期
1832—1901 年	维多利亚时期
1848—1860 年	前拉斐尔时期
1880—1901 年	唯美主义和颓废派文艺
1901—1914 年	爱德华七世时期
1910—1936 年	乔治五世时期
1914—	现代时期
1945—	后现代主义时期

古英语时期，或**盎格鲁－撒克逊时期**，从 5 世纪前半叶日耳曼部落（盎格鲁人、撒克逊人和朱特人）入侵凯尔特人的英格兰开始，到 1066 年诺曼法国在征服者威廉领导下征服英国。直到 7 世纪皈依基督教后，早先一直采用口头形式文学的盎格鲁－撒克逊人才开始发展书面文学。（参见：*口头诗歌*。）各个修道院中的文化与学识很快都达到了很高水平；8 世纪的传教士比德和阿尔昆是用国际学术界标准语言拉丁文写作的重要学者。用盎格鲁－撒克逊方言（亦称古英语）创作的诗歌包括日耳曼英雄史诗中最伟大的作品《贝奥武甫》（8 世纪），以及抒情哀歌，如《流浪者》《航海家》《狄奥尔》。这些诗歌尽管都是由信奉基督教的作者所写，但却反映了过去异教徒的生活状况。凯德蒙和基涅武甫就是根据圣经和宗教主题进行创作的诗人，保存下来的有用古英语写就的关于圣徒生活、布道诗篇和圣经的韵律译文的书籍。威塞克斯王国国王，阿尔弗烈德大王（871—899）联合英格兰南部的所有王国对抗日耳曼侵略者即维京人的新一轮侵略；他既是一名武士，也是一位重要的文学资助者。

He himself translated into Old English various books of Latin prose, supervised translations by other hands, and instituted the Anglo-Saxon Chronicle, a continuous record, year by year, of important events in England.

See S. B. Greenfield, *A Critical History of Old English Literature* (1965); C. L. Wrenn, *A Study of Old English Literature* (1966).

Middle English Period. The four and a half centuries between the Norman Conquest in 1066, which effected radical changes in the language, life, and culture of England, and about 1500, when the standard literary language (deriving from the dialect of the London area) had become recognizably "modern English"—that is, close enough to the language we speak and write to be intelligible to a present-day reader.

The span from 1100 to 1350 is sometimes discriminated as the **Anglo-Norman Period**, because the non-Latin literature of that time was written mainly in Anglo-Norman, the French dialect spoken by the invaders, who had established themselves as the ruling class of England, and who shared a literary culture with French-speaking areas of mainland Europe. Among the important and influential works from this period are Marie de France's *Lais* (c. 1180—which may have been written while Marie was at the royal court in England), Guillaume de Lorris' and Jean de Meun's *Roman de la Rose* (1225?–75?), and Chrétien de Troyes' *Erec et Enide* (the first Arthurian romance, c. 1165) and *Yvain* (c. 1177–81). When the native vernacular—descended from Anglo-Saxon, but with extensive lexical and syntactic elements assimilated from Anglo-Norman, and known as **Middle English**—came into general literary use, it was at first mainly the vehicle for religious and homiletic writings. The first great age of primarily secular literature—rooted in the Anglo-Norman, French, Irish, and Welsh, as well as the native English literature—was the second half of the fourteenth century. This was the age of Chaucer and John Gower, of William Langland's great religious and satirical poem *Piers Plowman*, and of the anonymous master who wrote four major poems in complex *alliterative meter*, including *Pearl* (an elegy) and *Sir Gawain and the Green Knight*. This last work is the most accomplished of the English *chivalric romances* in verse; the most notable prose romance was Thomas Malory's *Morte d'Arthur*, written a century later. The outstanding poets of the fifteenth century were the "Scottish Chaucerians," who included King James I of Scotland and Robert Henryson. The fifteenth century was more important for popular literature than for the artful literature addressed to the upper classes: it was the age of many excellent songs, secular and religious, and of diverse *folk ballads*, as well as the flowering time of the *miracle* and *morality plays*, which were written and produced for the general public.

See W. L. Renwick and H. Orton, *The Beginnings of English Literature to Skelton* (rev. 1952); H. S. Bennett, *Chaucer and the Fifteenth Century* (1947); Edward Vasta, ed., *Middle English Survey: Critical Essays* (1965).

The **Renaissance**, 1500–1660. See the entry *Renaissance*. There is an increasing use by historians of the term *early modern* to denote this era.

Elizabethan Age. Strictly speaking, the period of the reign of Elizabeth I (1558–1603); the term "Elizabethan," however, is often used loosely to refer

他亲自将各种拉丁语散文的书籍译成古英语,指导其他人的翻译,并编订《盎格鲁-撒克逊编年史》,将英格兰发生的重要事件逐年记录下来。

参阅:S. B. 格林菲尔德所著的《古英语文学批评史》(1965);C. L. 雷恩所著的《古英语文学研究》(1966)。

中古英语时期。这一时期指的是从1066年到约1500年间的四个半世纪。1066年的诺曼征服给英格兰语言、生活和文化造成了根本变化,1500年左右标准的文学语言(源于伦敦地区的方言)被公认为"现代英语"——它与我们今天所说所写的语言大同小异,足以被当今读者所理解。

1100—1350年这段时间有时被区别为**盎格鲁-诺曼时期**,因为当时的非拉丁语文学主要是用盎格鲁-诺曼语创作的。盎格鲁-诺曼语是一种法语方言,是那些在英国确立了统治阶级地位并与欧洲大陆本土法语区具有共同文学文化的入侵者所使用的语言。这一时期具有影响的重要作品有玛丽·德·法兰西的《籁歌》(约1180年,这部作品可能是玛丽在英格兰皇家宫廷时写成的),纪尧姆·德·洛里斯和吉恩·德·莫恩的《玫瑰传奇》(1225?—1275?),克里蒂安·德·特鲁瓦的《艾赫克与艾妮德》(这是第一部关于亚瑟王的传奇故事,约1165年)和《伊万》(约1177—1181)。当本族语言——即源自盎格鲁-撒克逊语,但吸收了盎格鲁-诺曼语的大量词汇和句法成分,被称为**中古英语**——被普遍用于文学写作时,最初主要是作为宗教和说教作品的手段。植根于盎格鲁-诺曼文学、法国文学、爱尔兰文学、威尔士文学和本土英国文学、以世俗文学为主的第一个盛世出现在14世纪后五十年。这是乔叟和约翰·高尔的时代,是威廉·朗格兰创作伟大的宗教与讽刺诗《农夫皮尔斯》的时代,是无名巨匠以*押头韵*的复杂方式创作了包括《珍珠》(挽歌)、《高文爵士与绿衣骑士》在内的四部重要诗作的时代。《高文爵士与绿衣骑士》是英国诗体骑士传奇成就最高的一部作品;最著名的散文体传奇则是一个世纪后托马斯·马洛礼的作品《亚瑟王之死》。15世纪的杰出诗人则是"苏格兰的乔叟们",包括苏格兰国王詹姆斯一世和罗伯特·汉里森。15世纪的大众文学比针对上流阶层所创作的精致文学更重要;这是许多世俗与宗教的优秀诗歌的时代,是多种多样*民间歌谣*的时代,也是*奇迹剧*、*道德剧*欣欣向荣的时期,这些作品都是为大众而创作的。

参阅:W. L. 伦威克与H. 奥顿合著的《从英国文学发端到斯克尔顿》(1952年修订版);H. S. 贝纳特所著的《乔叟与15世纪》(1947);爱德华·瓦斯塔主编的《中古英语概况:批评文集》(1965)。

文艺复兴时期,1500—1660年。参见条目:*文艺复兴时期*。历史学家越来越多地采用*早期现代时期*这一术语来指称这个时代。

伊丽莎白时期。严格地说,这是指伊丽莎白一世执政时期(1558—1603);但"伊丽莎白一世的"这一术语却常被用来泛指16世纪晚期和17世纪初期,甚

to the late sixteenth and early seventeenth centuries, even after the death of Elizabeth. This was a time of rapid development in English commerce, maritime power, and nationalist feeling—the defeat of the Spanish Armada occurred in 1588. It was a great (in drama the greatest) age of English literature—the age of Sir Philip Sidney, Christopher Marlowe, Edmund Spenser, William Shakespeare, Sir Walter Raleigh, Francis Bacon, Ben Jonson, and many other extraordinary writers of prose and of dramatic, lyric, and narrative poetry. A number of scholars have looked back on this era as one of intellectual coherence and social order; an influential example was E. M. W. Tillyard's *The Elizabethan World Picture* (1943). Recent historical critics, however, have emphasized its intellectual uncertainties and political and social conflicts; see *new historicism*.

Jacobean Age. The reign of James I (in Latin, "Jacobus"), 1603–25, which followed that of Queen Elizabeth. This was the period in prose writings of Bacon, John Donne's sermons, Robert Burton's *Anatomy of Melancholy*, and the King James translation of the Bible. It was also the time of Shakespeare's greatest tragedies and tragicomedies, and of major writings by other notable poets and playwrights including Donne, Ben Jonson, Michael Drayton, Lady Mary Wroth, Sir Francis Beaumont and John Fletcher, John Webster, George Chapman, Thomas Middleton, Philip Massinger, and Elizabeth Cary, whose notable biblical drama *The Tragedy of Mariam, the Faire Queene of Jewry* was the first long play by an Englishwoman to be published.

See Basil Willey, *The Seventeenth Century Background* (1934); Douglas Bush, *English Literature in the Earlier Seventeenth Century* (1945); C. V. Wedgwood, *Seventeenth Century English Literature* (1950).

Caroline Age. The reign of Charles I, 1625–49; the name is derived from "Carolus," the Latin version of "Charles." This was the time of the English Civil War fought between the supporters of the king (known as "Cavaliers") and the supporters of Parliament (known as "Roundheads," from their custom of wearing their hair cut short). John Milton began his writing during this period; it was the time also of the religious poet George Herbert and of the prose writers Robert Burton and Sir Thomas Browne.

Associated with the court were the **Cavalier poets**, writers of witty and polished lyrics of courtship and gallantry. The group included Richard Lovelace, Sir John Suckling, and Thomas Carew. Robert Herrick, although a country parson, is often classified with the Cavalier poets because, like them, he was a **Son of Ben**—that is, an admirer and follower of Ben Jonson—in many of his lyrics of love and gallant compliment.

See Robin Skelton, *Cavalier Poets* (1960).

The **Commonwealth Period**, also known as the **Puritan Interregnum**, extends from the end of the Civil War and the execution of Charles I in 1649 to the restoration of the Stuart monarchy under Charles II in 1660. In this period England was ruled by Parliament under the Puritan leader Oliver Cromwell; his death in 1658 marked the dissolution of the Commonwealth. Drama almost disappeared for eighteen years after the Puritans closed the public theaters in September 1642, not only on moral and religious grounds, but

至是伊丽莎白女王去世后的时期。这是英国商业快速发展、海上力量迅速加强、民族感情飞快提升的时代——1588 年英国击败了西班牙无敌舰队。这是英国文学的一个伟大时代（就戏剧而言则是最伟大的时代）——这是菲利普·锡德尼爵士、克里斯托弗·马洛、埃德蒙·斯宾塞、莎士比亚、沃尔特·罗利爵士、弗朗西斯·培根、本·琼森和其他许多出色的散文、戏剧、抒情和叙事诗歌作家的时代。一些学者回顾这个时代时将其视为心智统一、社会有序的时代，E. M. W. 蒂利亚德的《伊丽莎白时代尘世图》(1943) 是一个具有影响的例子。但近来的历史批评家则强调其心智上的不确定性及政治、社会冲突；参见：*新历史主义*。

詹姆斯一世时期。詹姆斯时期（James 的拉丁文为"Jacobus"）是指 1603—1625 年，伊丽莎白女王之后詹姆斯一世统治时期。这是培根的散文著作、约翰·多恩的布道、罗伯特·伯顿的《忧郁的剖析》和英皇钦定英译版圣经诞生的时代。这也是莎士比亚最伟大的悲剧与悲喜剧和包括多恩、本·琼森、迈克尔·德雷顿、玛丽·罗思夫人、弗朗西斯·博蒙特爵士、约翰·弗莱彻、约翰·韦伯斯特、乔治·查普曼、托马斯·米德尔顿、菲利普·马辛杰和伊丽莎白·卡里在内的其他著名诗人和剧作家的重要著作问世的时代，其中伊丽莎白·卡里的著名圣经戏剧《玛丽安的悲剧，犹太仙后》是出版的第一部英国女性创作的长篇戏剧。

参阅：巴兹尔·韦利所著的《17 世纪背景》(1934)；道格拉斯·布什所著的《17 世纪早期的英国文学》(1945)；C. V. 韦奇伍德所著的《17 世纪英国文学》(1950)。

查理时期。指 1625—1649 年查理一世统治期间；这个名称来自"Carolus"，即"查理"的对应拉丁文。这是英国拥护国王者（被称为"骑士党"）与拥护议会者（被称为"圆颅党"，因其理短发的传统而得名）展开内战的时期。约翰·弥尔顿在此期间开始写作；这也是宗教诗人乔治·赫伯特及散文作家罗伯特·伯顿和托马斯·布朗爵士的时代。

与宫廷相关的**骑士诗人**，用机智诙谐、华美优雅的抒情诗来描写爱情与勇气。这一群体包括理查德·洛夫莱斯、约翰·萨克林爵士和托马斯·卡鲁。罗伯特·赫里克尽管是个乡村牧师，却经常被归入骑士诗人之列，因为和其他骑士诗人一样，他也是**本之子**，即本·琼森的仰慕者和追随者，这有他的许多赞美爱情和勇气的抒情诗为证。

参阅：罗宾·斯克尔顿所著的《骑士诗人》(1960)。

共和国时期。亦称**清教徒执政期**，始于 1649 年内战结束、查理一世被处以极刑，直至 1660 年查理二世在位的斯图亚特王朝复辟。在此期间，英国处于清教徒领袖奥立弗·克伦威尔领导下的议会统治之下；1658 年克伦威尔去世标志着共和国的解体。自清教徒出于道德和宗教的考虑，同时为了防止可能导致社会骚乱的公众聚会，在 1642 年 9 月关闭了公共剧院后，整整十八

also to prevent public assemblies that might foment civil disorder. It was the age of Milton's political pamphlets, of Hobbes' political treatise *Leviathan* (1651), of the prose writers Sir Thomas Browne, Thomas Fuller, Jeremy Taylor, and Izaak Walton, and of the poets Henry Vaughan, Edmund Waller, Abraham Cowley, Sir William Davenant, and Andrew Marvell.

The **Neoclassical Period**, 1660–1785; see the entry *neoclassic and romantic*.

Restoration. This period takes its name from the restoration of the Stuart line (Charles II) to the English throne in 1660, at the end of the Commonwealth; it is specified as lasting until 1700. The urbanity, wit, and licentiousness of the life centering on the court, in sharp contrast to the seriousness and sobriety of the earlier Puritan regime, is reflected in much of the literature of this age. The theaters came back to vigorous life after the revocation of the ban placed on them by the Puritans in 1642, although they became more exclusively oriented toward the aristocratic classes than they had been earlier. Sir George Etherege, William Wycherley, William Congreve, and John Dryden developed the distinctive comedy of manners called *Restoration comedy*, and Dryden, Thomas Otway, and other playwrights developed the distinctive form of tragedy called *heroic drama*. Dryden was the major poet and critic, as well as one of the major dramatists. Other poets were the satirists Samuel Butler and the Earl of Rochester; notable writers in prose, in addition to the masterly Dryden, were Samuel Pepys, Sir William Temple, the religious writer in vernacular English John Bunyan, and the philosopher John Locke. Aphra Behn, the first Englishwoman to earn her living by her pen and one of the most inventive and versatile authors of the age, wrote poems, highly successful plays, and *Oroonoko*, the tragic story of a noble African slave, an important precursor of the novel.

See Basil Willey, *The Seventeenth Century Background* (1934); L. I. Bredvold, *The Intellectual Milieu of John Dryden* (1932).

Augustan Age. The original Augustan Age was the brilliant literary period of Virgil, Horace, and Ovid under the Roman emperor Augustus (27 BC–AD 14). In the eighteenth century and later, however, the term was frequently applied also to the literary period in England from approximately 1700 to 1745. The leading writers of the time (such as Alexander Pope, Jonathan Swift, and Joseph Addison) themselves drew the parallel to the Roman Augustans, and deliberately imitated their literary forms and subjects, their emphasis on social concerns, and their ideals of moderation, decorum, and urbanity. (See *neoclassicism*.) A major representative of popular, rather than classical, writing in this period was the novelist, journalist, and pamphleteer Daniel Defoe. Lady Mary Wortley Montagu was a brilliant letter writer in a great era of letter writing; she also wrote poems of wit and candor that violated the conventional moral and intellectual roles assigned to women in the Augustan era.

Age of Sensibility. The period between the death of Alexander Pope in 1744, and 1785, which was one year after the death of Samuel Johnson and one year before Robert Burns' *Poems, Chiefly in Scottish Dialect*. (Alternative dates frequently proposed for the end of this period are 1789 and 1798; see *Romantic Period*.) An older name for this half century, the **Age of Johnson**,

年间戏剧几乎完全消失。这是弥尔顿的政治小册子、霍布斯的政治专题论文《利维坦》(1651)的时代，是散文作家托马斯·布朗爵士、托马斯·富勒、杰里米·泰勒和艾萨克·沃尔顿的时代，也是诗人亨利·沃恩、埃德蒙·沃勒、亚伯拉罕·考利、威廉·戴夫南特爵士和安德鲁·马韦尔的时代。

新古典主义时期。1660—1785 年，参见：*新古典主义和浪漫主义*。

王政复辟时期。这个时期的名字从共和国末期斯图亚特王朝（查理二世）1660 年复辟重掌英国王权而来，确切来说，一直延续到 1700 年。以宫廷为中心的温文尔雅、聪慧机智、淫乱放荡的生活与先前清教徒统治下的严肃节制形成鲜明对比，这在这个时期的许多文学中都得到了反映。在撤销了 1642 年清教徒对戏院的禁令后，剧院重获活力，尽管与早先相比，它们变得更加单一地为贵族阶层服务。乔治·埃思里奇爵士、威廉·威彻利、威廉·康格里夫和约翰·德莱顿创造了一种被称为*王政复辟时期的喜剧*的独特的风俗喜剧形式，德莱顿、托马斯·奥特韦和其他剧作家还创造了一种独特的悲剧形式，称为*英雄剧*。德莱顿是当时重要的诗人和批评家，也是重要的剧作家之一。其他诗人还有讽刺作家塞缪尔·勃特勒和罗切斯特公爵；除了散文大师德莱顿之外，著名散文作家还包括塞缪尔·佩皮斯、威廉·坦普尔爵士、用英语方言创作的宗教作家约翰·班扬以及哲学家约翰·洛克。阿弗拉·贝恩是第一位以写作为生的英国女性，也是这一时期最有创造力和最多才多艺的作家之一。她创作了诗歌和大获成功的戏剧，还创作了描写一个著名的非洲奴隶的悲剧故事《奥鲁挪克》，成为小说的一个重要先驱。

参阅：巴兹尔·韦利所著的《17 世纪背景》(1934)；L. I. 布雷德沃尔德所著的《约翰·德莱顿的心智环境》(1932)。

奥古斯都文学盛世。最初的奥古斯都时代是罗马皇帝奥古斯都（公元前 27 年至公元 14 年）统治下的拥有维吉尔、贺拉斯和奥维德的文学辉煌时期。然而，18 世纪及以后，这个术语也被频繁用于指称大约从 1700 年到 1745 年的英国文学时期。这时的主要作家（如亚历山大·蒲柏、乔纳森·斯威夫特和约瑟夫·艾迪生）都将自己与罗马奥古斯都时代的作家相比拟，刻意模仿他们的文学形式与主题，强调对社会的关注，以及他们所向往的中庸、正派与礼仪的理想。（参见：*新古典主义*。）小说家、报刊撰稿人、政论小册子作者丹尼尔·笛福是当时流行文学而非古典文学的主要代表。玛丽·沃特利·蒙塔古夫人是书信写作繁盛时期的一位杰出书信作者；她打破了奥古斯都时代赋予女性的传统道德和才智角色的限制，创作了充满智慧与真诚的诗篇。

情感时期。从亚历山大·蒲柏去世的 1744 年至 1785 年（即塞缪尔·约翰逊去世的后一年、罗伯特·彭斯的《苏格兰方言诗集》出版的前一年）这一时期被称为情感时期。（关于这一时期结束的时间，通常有两种其他提法：1789 年和 1798 年；参见：*浪漫主义时期*。）这半个世纪有一个较为陈旧的名称，即**约翰逊时代**，

stresses the dominant position of Samuel Johnson (1709–84) and his literary and intellectual circle, which included Oliver Goldsmith, Edmund Burke, James Boswell, Edward Gibbon, and Hester Lynch Thrale. These authors on the whole represented a culmination of the literary and critical modes of *neoclassicism* and the worldview of the *Enlightenment*. The more recent name, "Age of Sensibility," puts its stress on the emergence, in other writers of the 1740s and later, of new cultural attitudes, theories of literature, and types of poetry; we find in this period, for example, a growing sympathy for the Middle Ages, a vogue of *cultural primitivism*, an awakening interest in ballads and other folk literature, a turn from neoclassic "correctness" and its emphasis on judgment and restraint to an emphasis on instinct and feeling, the development of a *literature of sensibility*, and above all the exaltation by some critics of "original genius" and a "bardic" poetry of the sublime and visionary imagination. Thomas Gray expressed this anti-neoclassic sensibility and set of values in his "Stanzas to Mr. Bentley" (1752):

> But not to one in this benighted age
> Is that diviner inspiration given,
> That burns in Shakespeare's or in Milton's page,
> The pomp and prodigality of Heaven.

Other poets who showed similar shifts in thought and taste were William Collins and Joseph and Thomas Warton (poets who, together with Gray, began in the 1740s the vogue for what Samuel Johnson slightingly referred to as "ode, and elegy, and sonnet"), Christopher Smart, and William Cowper. Thomas Percy published his influential *Reliques of Ancient English Poetry* (1765), which included many *folk ballads* and a few medieval metrical romances, and James Macpherson in the same decade published his greatly altered (and in considerable part fabricated) versions of the poems of the Gaelic bard Ossian (Oisin) which were enormously popular throughout Europe. This was also the period of the great novelists, some realistic and satiric and some "sentimental": Samuel Richardson, Henry Fielding, Tobias Smollett, and Laurence Sterne.

See Northrop Frye, "Toward Defining an Age of Sensibility," in *Fables of Identity* (1963), and ed., *Romanticism Reconsidered* (1965); F. W. Hilles and Harold Bloom, eds., *From Sensibility to Romanticism* (1965).

Romantic Period. The Romantic Period in English literature is dated as beginning in 1785 (see *Age of Sensibility*)—or alternatively in 1789 (the outbreak of the French Revolution), or in 1798 (the publication of William Wordsworth's and Samuel Taylor Coleridge's *Lyrical Ballads*)—and as ending either in 1830 or else in 1832, the year in which Sir Walter Scott died and the passage of the Reform Bill signaled the political preoccupations of the Victorian era. For some prominent characteristics of the thought and writings of this remarkable and diverse literary period, as well as for a list of suggested readings, see *neoclassic and romantic*. The term is often applied also to literary movements in European countries and America; see *periods of American literature*. Romantic characteristics are usually said to have been manifested first in

这一名称强调了塞缪尔·约翰逊(1709—1784)以及他的文学和文人圈的主导地位,这个文学和文人圈包括奥利弗·哥尔德斯密斯、埃德蒙·伯克、詹姆斯·鲍斯韦尔、爱德华·吉本和赫斯特·林奇·斯雷尔。这些作家作为一个整体代表了新古典主义文学和批评模式的最高成就以及*启蒙运动*的世界观。"主情时期"这一较新的名称则重在强调1740年代及其后出现的其他作家的新文化态度、文学理论和诗歌类型;例如,我们发现这一时期越来越移情于中世纪、*文化尚古主义*风行、对民谣和其他民间文学的兴趣复苏、从新古典主义要求"准确"和强调判断与克制转向强调直觉与情感、*情感文学*得以发展,最重要的是,一些评论家大力推崇"独创性的天才"和崇高而富于虚幻想象的"吟游式"诗歌。托马斯·格雷在他的《献给本特利先生的诗》(1752)中表现了这种反对新古典主义的情感和价值观:

在这愚昧的年代
没有任何一个人拥有天才的灵感,
上苍的庄严慷慨
只在莎翁与弥尔顿的篇章中闪现。

在思想和品味上有相似转变的诗人还有威廉·科林斯、约瑟夫和托马斯·沃顿(这些诗人与格雷一起在1740年代开风气之先,却被约翰逊讥为"颂、哀歌与十四行诗")、克里斯托弗·司马特和威廉·柯珀。托马斯·珀西出版了影响颇大的《英国古诗拾遗》(1765),其中包括许多*民间歌谣*和一些中世纪诗体传奇;同期,詹姆斯·麦克弗森出版了经过重大修改(大部分都是虚构)的盖耳语吟游诗人奥西恩的诗歌,这些诗歌在欧洲各国大受欢迎。这也是塞缪尔·理查逊、亨利·菲尔丁、托拜厄斯·斯摩莱特和劳伦斯·斯特恩等伟大小说家的时代,他们的作品或现实,或嘲讽,或"感伤"。

参阅:诺斯罗普·弗莱所著的《本体寓言》(1963)中的"为主情时代定性"及其主编的《浪漫主义再思考》(1965);F. W. 希尔斯与哈罗德·布卢姆合编的《从主情主义到浪漫主义》(1965)。

浪漫主义时期。英国文学中的浪漫主义时期始于1785年(参见:*情感时期*),另有两种说法分别始于1789年(法国大革命爆发)或1798年(威廉·华兹华斯和塞缪尔·泰勒·柯勒律治的《抒情歌谣集》出版),到1830年或1832年结束,在这一年(1832年)沃尔特·司各特爵士去世和《选举法修正法案》的通过标志着维多利亚时代对政治的极端关注。这一辉煌而多元的文学时期的一些思想与写作特色和建议阅读书目参见:*新古典主义和浪漫主义*。这一术语也常用来指称发生在欧洲各国和美国的文学运动;参见:*美国文学各时期的划分*。论者通常认为,

Germany and England in the 1790s, and not to have become prominent in France and America until two or three decades after that time. Major English writers of the period, in addition to Wordsworth and Coleridge, were the poets Robert Burns, William Blake, Lord Byron, Percy Bysshe Shelley, John Keats, and Walter Savage Landor; the prose writers Charles Lamb, William Hazlitt, Thomas De Quincey, Mary Wollstonecraft, and Leigh Hunt; and the novelists Jane Austen, Sir Walter Scott, and Mary Shelley. The span between 1786 and the close of the eighteenth century was that of the *Gothic romances* by William Beckford, Matthew Gregory Lewis, William Godwin, and, above all, Ann Radcliffe.

Victorian Period. The beginning of the Victorian Period is frequently dated 1830, or alternatively 1832 (the passage of the first Reform Bill), and sometimes 1837 (the accession of Queen Victoria); it extends to the death of Victoria in 1901. Historians often subdivide the long period into three phases: Early Victorian (to 1848), Mid-Victorian (1848–70), and Late Victorian (1870–1901). Much writing of the period, whether imaginative or didactic, in verse or in prose, dealt with or reflected the pressing social, economic, religious, and intellectual issues and problems of that era. (For a summary of these issues, and also for the derogatory use of the term "Victorian," see *Victorian and Victorianism*.) Among the notable poets were Alfred, Lord Tennyson, Robert Browning, Elizabeth Barrett Browning, Christina Rossetti, Matthew Arnold, and Gerard Manley Hopkins (whose remarkably innovative poems, however, did not become known until they were published, long after his death, in 1918). The most prominent essayists were Thomas Carlyle, John Ruskin, Arnold, and Walter Pater; the most distinguished of many excellent novelists (this was a great age of English prose fiction) were Charlotte and Emily Brontë, Charles Dickens, William Makepeace Thackeray, Elizabeth Gaskell, George Eliot, George Meredith, Anthony Trollope, Thomas Hardy, and Samuel Butler.

For prominent literary movements during the Victorian era, see the entries on *Pre-Raphaelites, Aestheticism,* and *Decadence*.

Edwardian Period. The span between the death of Victoria (1901) and the beginning of World War I (1914) is named for King Edward VII, who reigned from 1901 to 1910. Poets writing at the time included Thomas Hardy (who gave up novels for poetry at the beginning of the century), Alfred Noyes, William Butler Yeats, and Rudyard Kipling; dramatists included Henry Arthur Jones, Arthur Wing Pinero, James Barrie, John Galsworthy, George Bernard Shaw, and the playwrights of the *Celtic Revival* such as Lady Gregory, Yeats, and John M. Synge. Many of the major achievements were in prose fiction—works by Thomas Hardy, Joseph Conrad, Ford Madox Ford, John Galsworthy, H. G. Wells, Rudyard Kipling, and Henry James, who published his major final novels, *The Wings of the Dove, The Ambassadors,* and *The Golden Bowl,* between 1902 and 1904.

Georgian Period is a term applied both to the reigns in England of the four successive Georges (1714–1830) and (more frequently) to the reign of George V (1910–36). The term **Georgian poets** usually designates a group of writers in the latter era who loomed large in four anthologies entitled

浪漫主义的特征最初是1790年代在德国和英国显现出来的，直到此后二三十年才在法国和美国为人瞩目。除了华兹华斯和柯勒律治，这一时期其他重要的英国作家有诗人罗伯特·彭斯、威廉·布莱克、拜伦勋爵、珀西·比希·雪莱、约翰·济慈、沃尔特·萨维奇·兰多；散文作家查尔斯·兰姆、威廉·黑兹利特、托马斯·德·昆西、玛丽·沃斯通克拉夫特、利·亨特，小说家简·奥斯汀、沃尔特·司各特爵士、玛丽·雪莱。1786年到18世纪末期是威廉·贝克福德、马修·格雷戈里·刘易斯、威廉·戈德温，尤其是安·拉德克利夫创作*哥特式传奇*的时期。

维多利亚时期。一般都认为维多利亚时期始于1830年或1832年（第一部《选举法修正法案》通过），有时也认为是1837年（维多利亚女王登基）；一直持续到1901年维多利亚女王去世这一年。历史学家经常把这一漫长时期细分为三个阶段：维多利亚时代早期（到1848年为止）、维多利亚时代中期（1848—1870）和维多利亚时代晚期（1870—1901）。这个时期的许多作品，无论是想象的还是说教的、诗体还是散文体，都涉及或反映了当时紧迫的社会、经济、宗教、思想议题和问题。（有关这些议题的简要介绍和对"维多利亚时代的"一词的贬义使用，参见：*维多利亚时期与维多利亚时期的特点*。）这一时代的著名诗人有阿尔弗雷德·丁尼生勋爵、罗伯特·勃朗宁、伊丽莎白·巴雷特·勃朗宁、克里斯蒂娜·罗塞蒂、马修·阿诺德和杰勒德·曼利·霍普金斯（不过他极富创造性的诗作直到1918年出版后才为人所知，此时他已去世许久）。著名的随笔作家有托马斯·卡莱尔、约翰·罗斯金、阿诺德和沃尔特·佩特；在诸多杰出小说家（这是英国散文体小说的盛世）中，最优秀的有夏洛蒂·勃朗特、埃米莉·勃朗特、查尔斯·狄更斯、威廉·梅克皮斯·萨克雷、伊丽莎白·盖斯凯尔、乔治·艾略特、乔治·梅瑞狄斯、安东尼·特罗洛普、托马斯·哈代和塞缪尔·勃特勒。

有关维多利亚时代重要的文学运动，参见：*前拉斐尔派画家和诗人、唯美主义、颓废派文艺*。

爱德华七世时期。维多利亚女王去世（1901）到一战开始（1914）这段时期以1901—1910年在位的爱德华七世命名。这个时期的诗人包括哈代（他从20世纪初就开始放弃小说创作而专写诗歌）、阿尔弗雷德·诺伊斯、威廉·巴特勒·叶芝、拉迪亚德·吉卜林；剧作家包括亨利·阿瑟·琼斯、阿瑟·温·平内罗、詹姆斯·巴里、约翰·高尔斯华绥、乔治·萧伯纳和诸如格雷戈里夫人、叶芝、约翰·M. 辛格等*凯尔特文艺复兴*的剧作者。这一时期许多主要成就都集中在散文体小说上——如托马斯·哈代、约瑟夫·康拉德、福特·马多克斯·福特、约翰·高尔斯华绥、H. G. 威尔斯、拉迪亚德·吉卜林和在1902—1904年间出版了最后几部重要小说《鸽翼》《大使》《金碗》的亨利·詹姆斯的作品。

乔治时期。这一术语既用于指称连续四位乔治国王统治英国的时期(1714—1830)，也（更常）用来指称乔治五世的统治时期（1910—1936）。**乔治时期的诗人**一般是指这一时期后半段在四卷名为《乔治时期的诗歌》的选集中凸现出

Georgian Poetry, which were published by Edward Marsh between 1912 and 1922. Marsh favored writers we now tend to regard as relatively minor poets such as Rupert Brooke, Walter de la Mare, Ralph Hodgson, W. H. Davies, and John Masefield. "Georgian poetry" has come to connote verse which is mainly rural in subject matter, deft and delicate rather than bold and passionate in manner, and traditional rather than experimental in technique and form.

Modern Period. The application of the term "modern," of course, varies with the passage of time, but it is frequently applied specifically to the literature written since the beginning of World War I in 1914; see *modernism and postmodernism*. This period has been marked by persistent and multidimensioned experiments in subject matter, form, and style, and has produced major achievements in all the literary genres. Among the notable writers are the poets W. B. Yeats, Wilfred Owen, T. S. Eliot, W. H. Auden, Robert Graves, Dylan Thomas, and Seamus Heaney; the novelists Joseph Conrad, James Joyce, D. H. Lawrence, Dorothy Richardson, Virginia Woolf, E. M. Forster, Aldous Huxley, Graham Greene, Doris Lessing, and Nadine Gordimer; the dramatists G. B. Shaw, Sean O'Casey, Noel Coward, Samuel Beckett, Harold Pinter, Caryl Churchill, Brendan Behan, Frank McGuinness, and Tom Stoppard. The modern age was also an important era for literary criticism; among the innovative and influential English critics were T. S. Eliot, I. A. Richards, Virginia Woolf, F. R. Leavis, and William Empson. (See *New Criticism*.)

This entry has followed what has been the widespread practice of including under "English literature" the works of **anglophone authors**—that is, authors who speak and write in the English language—in all the British Isles. A number of the writers listed above were in fact natives of Ireland, Scotland, and Wales. Of the Modern Period especially it can be said that much of the greatest "English" literature was written by the Irish writers Yeats, Shaw, Joyce, O'Casey, Beckett, Iris Murdoch, and Seamus Heaney. And in recent decades, some of the most notable achievements in the English language have been written by authors who are natives or residents of recently liberated English colonies. They are often referred to as **postcolonial authors**, and include Doris Lessing in Rhodesia; the South Africans Nadine Gordimer, Athol Fugard, and J. M. Coetzee; the West Indians V. S. Naipaul and Derek Walcott; the Nigerians Chinua Achebe and Wole Soyinka; and the Indian novelists R. K. Narayan, Anita Desai, and Salman Rushdie. See Terry Eagleton, *Exiles and Emigrés* (1975), and refer to *postcolonial studies*.

The **Postmodern Period** is applied to the era from the end of World War II (1945) to approximately 1990. See *modernism and postmodernism* and, for innovations during the postmodern period in critical theory and practice, *poststructuralism*. Refer also to *periods of American literature*.

peripety (pĕrĭp′ ĕtē): **297**; *409*.

periphrasis (pĕrĭf′ răsĭs): **298**.

perlocutionary act: 373.

来的诗人；这部诗集在 1912—1922 年间由爱德华·马什出版。鲁珀特·布鲁克、沃尔特·德·拉·梅尔、拉尔夫·霍奇森、W. H. 戴维斯和约翰·梅斯菲尔德等马什喜欢的作家，在我们现在看来只能算是相对不那么重要的诗人。"乔治时期的诗歌"现已被用来暗指主要以田园生活为题材、创作态度灵巧精致而非大胆激情、技巧与形式上较为传统而不是实验性质的诗文。

现代时期。"现代"这一术语的运用当然随着时间的改变而改变，但它通常被用于特指 1914 年第一次世界大战开始以来所创作的文学；参见：*现代主义与后现代主义*。这一时期以在文学题材、形式和风格上多方面坚持不懈的实验为标志，在所有文学体裁上都取得了重要成就。著名作家有诗人 W. B. 叶芝、威尔弗雷德·欧文、T. S. 艾略特、W. H. 奥登、罗伯特·格雷夫斯、迪伦·托马斯和西默斯·希尼；小说家有约瑟夫·康拉德、詹姆斯·乔伊斯、D. H. 劳伦斯、多萝西·理查森、弗吉尼亚·吴尔夫、E. M. 福斯特、奥尔德斯·赫胥黎、格雷厄姆·格林、多丽丝·莱辛和内丁·戈迪默；剧作家有萧伯纳、肖恩·奥凯西、诺埃尔·科沃德、塞缪尔·贝克特、哈罗德·品特、卡里尔·丘吉尔、布伦丹·贝汉、弗兰克·麦吉尼斯和汤姆·斯托帕德。现代时期对文学批评来说也是一个重要时期；具有创新意识和影响力的英国批评家包括 T. S. 艾略特、I. A. 理查兹、弗吉尼亚·吴尔夫、F. R. 利维斯和威廉·燕卜荪。（参见：*新批评*。）

本条目遵循的是普遍的做法，即把所有不列颠群岛上用英语写作的作家都纳入"英国文学"范畴，这样的作家又叫**英语作家**。事实上，上面列举的一些作家是爱尔兰、苏格兰和威尔士人。尤其是现代时期，可以说许多最伟大的"英国"文学作品都是由爱尔兰作家叶芝、萧伯纳、乔伊斯、奥凯西、贝克特、艾丽斯·默多克和西默斯·希尼创作的。近几十年来，英语中一些最著名的文学成就则是由解放不久的英属殖民地本土作家或是长期居住此地的作家取得的。他们通常被称为**后殖民主义作家**，其中有罗德西亚的多丽丝·莱辛，南非的内丁·戈迪默、阿索尔·富加德和 J. M. 库切，西印度群岛的 V. S. 奈保尔和德里克·沃尔科特，尼日利亚的奇努阿·阿奇贝和沃利·索因卡，以及印度小说家 R. K. 纳拉扬和萨尔曼·拉什迪。参阅：特里·伊格尔顿所著的《流放与流亡者》(1975)；参见：*后殖民主义研究*。

后现代主义时期用来指称第二次世界大战结束 (1945) 到约 1990 年这一时期。参见：*现代主义和后现代主义*；有关后现代时期批评理论与实践的革新，参见：*后结构主义*。也可参阅：*美国文学各时期的划分*。

peripety：突变　297；*409*。

periphrasis：迂说　298。

perlocutionary act：话后行为　373。

persona, tone, and voice: These terms reflect the tendency in recent criticism to think of narrative and lyric works of literature as a mode of speech, or in what is now a favored term, as *discourse*. To conceive a work as an utterance suggests that there is a speaker who has determinate personal qualities, and who expresses attitudes both toward the characters and materials within the work and toward the audience to whom the work is addressed. In his *Rhetoric* (fourth century BC), Aristotle, followed by other Greek and Roman rhetoricians, pointed out that an orator projects in the course of his oration an *ethos*, that is, a personal character, which itself functions as a means of persuasion. For example, if the impression a speaker projects is that of a person of rectitude, intelligence, and goodwill, the audience is instinctively inclined to give credence to such a speaker's arguments. The current concern with the nature and function of the author's presence in a work of imaginative literature is related to this traditional concept, and is part of the rhetorical emphasis in modern criticism. (See *rhetoric, rhetorical criticism*, and *speech-act theory*.) Specific applications of the terms "persona," "tone," and "voice" vary greatly and involve difficult concepts in philosophy and social psychology—concepts such as "the self," "personal identity," "role-playing," and "sincerity." This essay will merely sketch some central uses of these terms that have proved helpful in analyzing diverse works of literature.

Persona was the Latin word for the mask worn by actors in the classical theater, from which was derived the term **dramatis personae** for the list of characters who play a role in a drama, and ultimately the English word "person," a particular individual. In recent literary discussion "persona" is often applied to the first-person speaker who tells the story in a narrative poem or novel, or whose voice we hear in a lyric poem. Examples of personae, in this broad application, are the visionary first-person narrator of John Milton's *Paradise Lost* (who in the opening passages of various books of that epic discourses at some length about himself); the Gulliver who tells us about his misadventures in *Gulliver's Travels*; the "I" who carries on most of the conversation in Alexander Pope's satiric dialogue *Epistle to Dr. Arbuthnot*; the genial narrator of Henry Fielding's *Tom Jones*, who pauses frequently for leisurely discourse with his reader; the speaker who talks first to himself, then to his sister, in William Wordsworth's "Tintern Abbey"; the Duke who tells the emissary about his former wife in Robert Browning's "My Last Duchess"; and the fantastic "biographer" who narrates Virginia Woolf's *Orlando*. Calling such diverse speakers "personae" indicates that they are all, to some degree, adapted to the generic and formal requirements and the artistic aims of a particular literary work. We need, however, to go on to make distinctions between such speakers as Jonathan Swift's Gulliver and Browning's Duke, who are entirely fictional characters very different from their authors; the narrators in Pope's *Epistle* and Fielding's *Tom Jones*, who are presented as closer to their authors, although clearly shaped to fit the roles they are designed to play in those works; and the speakers in the autobiographical passages in *Paradise Lost*, in "Tintern Abbey," and in "Ode to a Nightingale," where we are invited to attribute the voice we hear, and the sentiments it utters, to the poet in his own person.

Persona, Tone, and Voice：第一人称、基调和言念

这三个术语反映了当代文学批评中把叙事和抒情的文学作品都视为一种言语模式的倾向，或者用现今流行的一个术语来说，就是*话语*。把文学作品视为言语的表达，就暗示了作品内有一位具有鲜明个人特性的说话人，他同时对作品中的人物、素材及对这部作品的读者阐明自己的态度。亚里士多德在他的《修辞学》（公元前4世纪）中指出：演说家在他的演说过程中呈现出一种特质，即个人的特点，这一理念本身就是说服听众的手段，这一观点得到了其他希腊罗马修辞学家的支持。譬如，要是演说家投射出来的个人形象是一个正直、智慧、善良的人，听众就会不由自主地倾向于相信他的论点。当前对作者在想象性文学作品中所处位置的性质和功用的关注与这一传统概念有关，这也是现代文学批评里十分强调修辞重要性的部分原因。（参见：*修辞学、修辞学批评、言语行为理论*。）"第一人称""基调""言念"这三个术语的具体应用大不相同，涉及哲学和社会心理学中一些复杂的概念，如"自我""个人认同""角色扮演""诚挚性"等。本文仅能粗略地讨论已被证明对分析不同文学作品有用的这三个术语的一些主要用法。

第一人称是拉丁词汇，原指古代剧场中演员们所戴的面具。从这个词衍生出**剧中人物**这一术语，用来指代在剧中出演角色的一系列演员，最后派生出英文单词"人"——某一特殊的个人。在近代文学的探讨里，"第一人称"常用于指在一首叙事诗或一部小说里讲述故事的第一人称叙述者，或一首抒情诗里的说话人。从这一广义用法上看，第一人称的例子有：弥尔顿《失乐园》里想象中的第一人称叙述者（他在这部史诗作品各卷的头几段诗行中详细地论述了自己）；《格列佛游记》里对我们叙述他不幸历险遭遇的格列佛；亚历山大·蒲柏的讽刺作品《致阿布斯纳博士书》里言谈最多的"我"；亨利·菲尔丁《汤姆·琼斯》里时不时停笔与读者惬意交谈的温文尔雅的叙述者；威廉·华兹华斯《丁登寺》一诗中先是自言自语然后对姐姐说话的讲述者；罗伯特·勃朗宁《我那已故的公爵夫人》里向使者讲述自己亡妻的公爵；弗吉尼亚·吴尔夫《奥兰多》中想象出来的叙述故事的"传记作者"。将所有这些不同的发言者称为"第一人称"，说明他们的存在在某种程度上都是为了适应某一特定文学作品的一般形式上的要求和艺术意旨。但是我们需要对这些发言者加以区分：乔纳森·斯威夫特作品中的格列佛和勃朗宁作品中的公爵是完全虚构的人物，与作者截然不同；蒲柏《致阿布斯纳博士书》和菲尔丁《汤姆·琼斯》中的叙述者尽管明显经过刻画使之符合作品中的角色，但他们仍与作者较为接近；而在《失乐园》《丁登寺》《夜莺颂》这些带有自传性质的篇章中，叙述者则使我们不由自主地将听到的声音和声音中表露出的情感与作者本人的声音和情感等同起来。

In an influential discussion, I. A. Richards defined **tone** as the expression of a literary speaker's "attitude to his listener." "The tone of his utterance reflects ... his sense of how he stands toward those he is addressing" (*Practical Criticism*, 1929, chapters 1 and 3). In a more complex definition, the Soviet critic Mikhail Bakhtin said that tone, or "intonation," is "oriented *in two directions*: with respect to the listener as ally or witness and with respect to the object of the utterance as the third, living participant whom the intonation scolds or caresses, denigrates or magnifies." ("Discourse in Life and Discourse in Art," in Bakhtin's *Freudianism: A Marxist Critique*, trans. 1976.) The sense in which the term is used in recent criticism is suggested by the phrase "tone of voice," as applied to nonliterary speech. The way we speak reveals, by subtle clues, our conception of, and attitude toward, the things we are talking about, our personal relationship to our auditor, and also our assumptions about the social level, intelligence, and sensitivity of that auditor. The tone of a speech can be described as critical or approving, formal or intimate, outspoken or reticent, solemn or playful, arrogant or prayerful, angry or loving, serious or ironic, condescending or obsequious, and so on through numberless possible nuances of relationship and attitude both to object and to auditor. In a literary narrative, the *narratee* (the person or persons to whom the narrator addresses the story) is sometimes explicitly identified, but at other times remains an **implied auditor**, revealed only by what the narrator implicitly takes for granted as needing or not needing explanation or justification, and by the tone of the narrator's address. *Feminist critics*, for example, point out that much of the literature by male authors assumes a readership of males who share the narrator's views, interests, and values. See Judith Fetterley, *The Resisting Reader* (1978).

Some current critical uses of "tone" are broader, and coincide in reference with what other critics prefer to call "voice."

Voice, in a recently evolved usage, signifies the equivalent in imaginative literature to Aristotle's "ethos" in a speech of persuasive rhetoric, and suggests also the traditional rhetorician's concern with the importance of the physical voice in an oration. The term in criticism points to the fact that we are aware of a voice beyond the fictional voices that speak in a work, and of a persona behind all the dramatic personae, and behind even the first-person narrator. We have the sense, that is, of a pervasive authorial presence, a determinate intelligence and moral sensibility, who has invented, ordered, and rendered all these literary characters and materials in just this way. The particular qualities of the author's ethos, or voice, in Henry Fielding's novel *Tom Jones* (1749) manifest themselves, among other things, in the fact that he has chosen to create the wise, ironic, and worldly persona who ostensibly tells the story and talks to the reader about it. The sense of a distinctive authorial presence is no less evident in the work of recent writers who, unlike Fielding, pursue a strict policy of authorial noninterference and, by effacing themselves, try to give the impression that the story tells itself (see *point of view*). There is great diversity in the quality of the authorial mind, temperament, and sensibility which, by inventing, controlling, and rendering the particular fiction, pervades works—all of them "objective" or impersonal in narrative technique—such as

I. A. 理查兹在一次颇具影响的讨论中，将**基调**定义为文学叙述者表达他"对听众的态度"。"叙述者话语的基调反映了……他意识到他是如何对听众说话的。"[《实用批评》(1929)第一、三章] 俄国批评家米哈伊尔·巴赫金在一条更为复杂的定义中提出，基调，或"语调"指向两个方面：将听者看做同盟或目击者，以及将说话对象看做活生生的第三方参与者，语调对其或责备或景仰或贬低或称颂（"生活中的话语和艺术中的话语"，引自巴赫金所著的《弗洛伊德主义：马克思主义批评》，1976年英译版）。"说话的基调"一语说明了这一术语在当代文学批评中的用法意义，如同在非文学语言中的用法一样。我们的话语方式微妙地显示出我们对所谈论事物的观念和态度、我们个人与听者的关系，以及我们对听者社会阶层、才智和感受力的假定。由于说话人与描述对象及听众的关系和对他们的态度可能存在无穷多的微妙差异，言语的格调可以是批判的或称许的、一本正经的或亲昵的、直率的或寡言的、庄严的或戏谑的、傲慢的或诚恳的、愤怒的或慈爱的、严肃的或讽刺的、谦卑的或谄媚的。在文学叙事作品中，*叙事对象*（即听叙述者讲述故事的一个或几个人）有时候是明确的、确定的，但其他时候却是一个**隐藏的听众**，只有通过叙述者暗示是否需要加以解释或判断，以及通过叙述者的话语基调才会得以揭示。例如*女性主义批评家*指出，男性作家的大部分作品都想当然地认为男性读者与叙述者拥有共同的观点、兴趣和价值观。参阅：朱迪思·菲特利所著的《抗拒性读者》(1978)。

如今"基调"一词在文学批评中的使用更为广泛，与其他批评家更喜欢用的"言念"意义一致。

言念在其近代扩展了的用法里，表示在虚构的文学作品中，等同于亚里士多德在一篇关于说服性修辞的演说中所说的"理念"这种概念，也显示了传统修辞学家对演说中自然语调重要性的关注。在文学批评里，这一术语表明我们意识到一部作品内除了虚构的各种声音外还有某种言念：在所有的剧中人物（甚至包括第一人称的叙述者）背后存在的一个人物。我们感觉到作者无所不在，凭借一种确定的睿智和道德上的敏感力以一种方式创造、编排、描写这些文学角色和题材。在亨利·菲尔丁的小说《汤姆·琼斯》(1749)里，作者的理念或言念的独特性质，表现在他选择创造一个足智多谋、嘲弄讥讽、有处世才能的"第一人称"，这个"第一人称"对读者详细地讲述和谈论汤姆·琼斯的故事。对作者这一独特存在的感知，在近代作家的作品中也不少见，但与菲尔丁不同，这些作家追求严格的作者不干预策略。作者将自己隐遁起来，企图给读者造成是故事本身在叙述的感觉（参见：*视角*）。作者的思想、气质和感受力在性质上存在显著差异，这种差异由于作者编造、支配和表现特定故事方法的不同，自始至终地体现于不同的作品中。这些作品都是采用"客观的"或"不受个人感情影响的"叙事技巧的作品。譬如，

James Joyce's *Ulysses*, Virginia Woolf's *Mrs. Dalloway*, Ernest Hemingway's "The Killers," and William Faulkner's *The Sound and the Fury*. For a particular emphasis on the importance of the author's implicit presence as this is sustained from work to work, see *critics of consciousness*. For a discussion of the relation between a poet's speaking voice in real life and the qualities of his or her poem, refer to Francis Berry, *Poetry and the Physical Voice* (1962).

Of the critics listed below who deal with this concept, Wayne C. Booth prefers the term **implied author** over "voice," in order better to indicate that the reader of a work of fiction has the sense not only of the timbre and tone of a supervisory speaking voice, but of a total human presence. Booth's view is that this implied author is "an ideal, literary, created version of the real man"—that is, the implied author, although related to the actual author, is nonetheless part of the total fiction, whom the author gradually brings into being in the course of his composition, and who plays an important role in the overall effect of a work on the reader. Critics such as Walter J. Ong, on the other hand, distinguish between the author's "false voice" and his "true voice," and regard the latter as the expression of the author's genuine self or identity; as they see it, to discover one's true "voice" is to discover oneself. All of these critics agree, however, that the overall sense of a convincing authorial voice and presence, whose values, beliefs, and moral vision serve implicitly as controlling forces throughout a work, helps to sway the reader to yield the imaginative consent without which a poem or novel would remain an elaborate verbal game.

Refer to Bakhtin's view of the multiplex voices in narrative fiction, in the entry *dialogic criticism*. See Richard Ellmann, *Yeats: The Man and the Masks* (1948), which discusses Yeats' theory of a poet's "masks" or "personae," in both his life and his art; Reuben Brower, "The Speaking Voice," in *Fields of Light* (1951); Wayne C. Booth, *The Rhetoric of Fiction* (rev. 1983), chapter 3; W. J. Ong, *The Barbarian Within* (1962); J. O. Perry, ed., *Approaches to the Poem* (1965)—in which section 3, "Tone, Voice, Sensibility," includes selections from I. A. Richards, Reuben Brower, and W. J. Ong; Walter J. Slatoff, *With Respect to Readers* (1970); Lionel Trilling, *Sincerity and Authenticity* (1972); and Robert C. Elliott, *The Literary Persona* (1982).

personal lyrics: 201.

personification: 132; *7, 298*. See also *invocation*; *pathetic fallacy*.

Petrarchan conceit (pĕträr′ kan): 58; *64*.

Petrarchan sonnet: 370.

phallogocentric (fălŏg′ ōsĕn″ trik): 125.

phenomenological criticism: 290.

詹姆斯·乔伊斯的《尤利西斯》、弗吉尼亚·吴尔夫的《黛洛维夫人》、欧内斯特·海明威的《杀人者》和威廉·福克纳的《喧哗与骚动》。有关对不同作品内作者隐性存在的重要性的特别强调，参见：*意识批评家*。有关诗人在现实生活中的言语言念与其诗歌特性的关系，参阅：弗朗西斯·贝里所著的《诗歌与自然言念》（1962）。

以下列出的探讨"言念"这一概念的批评家中，韦恩·C. 布思认为用**隐遁的作者**要比用"言念"恰当，因为它可以更好地表明，一部虚构作品的读者不仅感知到某种监督的正在陈述的声音的音色和基调，也感知到了一个整体的人的存在。布思的论点是：这个隐遁的作者是"一种创造出来的理想化的、文学化了的真实的人"。也就是说，这位隐遁的作者虽然与真实的作者相关，却是虚构整体不可分割的一部分；作者在其创作过程中把他逐渐勾勒出来，他在作品对读者所产生的整体效果中发挥了重要的作用。另一方面，像沃尔特·J. 翁格等批评家则区分了作者的"假言念"和"真言念"，并把"真言念"视为作者真实自我或身份的表达；他们认为，发现他的真正"言念"，也就是发现他自己。不过，所有这些批评家都承认，总体上令人信服的作者言念和存在的感觉，其价值观、信仰和道德理念是贯穿整部作品的内在支配力，有助于读者在想象上与作品产生共鸣，倘若没有这种共鸣，一首诗或一部小说只能是一场精致的文字游戏。

参见：*对话批评*中巴赫金有关叙事小说中多重声音的观点。参阅：理查德·埃尔曼所著的《叶芝：人和面具》（1948），该书讨论了叶芝有关诗人在生活和艺术中的"面具"或"第一人称"的理论；鲁本·布劳尔所著的《思想之光》（1951）中的"言语言念"；韦恩·C. 布思所著的《小说修辞学》（1983 年修订版）第 3 章；W. J. 翁格所著的《内心里的野蛮人》（1962）；J. O. 佩里主编的《理解诗歌》（1965）第三部分"基调、言念与敏感"，选录了 I. A. 理查兹、鲁本·布劳尔和 W. J. 翁格的文章；沃尔特·J. 斯莱托夫所著的《尊重读者》（1970）；莱昂内尔·特里林所著的《诚与真》（1972）；罗伯特·C. 埃利奥特所著的《文学形象》（1982）。

personal lyrics：个人抒情诗　201。

personification：拟人　132；*7, 298*。也可参见：*祈愿词、感伤谬误*。

Petrarchan conceit：彼特拉克式巧思妙喻　58；*64*。

Petrarchan sonnet：彼特拉克式十四行诗　370。

phallogocentric：男权主义　125。

phenomenological criticism：现象学批评　290。

phenomenology and criticism: The philosophical perspective and method called **phenomenology** was established by the German thinker Edmund Husserl (1859–1938). Husserl set out to analyze human consciousness—that is, to describe the concrete **Lebenswelt** (lived world), as this is experienced independently of any prior suppositions, whether these suppositions come from philosophy or from common sense. He proposes that consciousness is a unified **intentional** act. By "intentional" he does not mean that it is deliberately willed, but that it is always directed to an "object"; in other words, to be conscious is always to be conscious of something. Husserl's claim is that in this unitary act of consciousness, the thinking subject and the object it "intends," or is aware of, are interinvolved and reciprocally implicative. In order to free itself of prior conceptions, the phenomenological analysis of consciousness begins with an **epoché** (suspension) of all presuppositions about the nature of experience, and this suspension involves "bracketing" (holding in abeyance) the question whether or not the object of consciousness is real—that is, whether or not the object exists outside the consciousness which "intends" it.

Phenomenology had widespread philosophical influence after it was put forward by Husserl in 1900 and later, and was diversely developed by Martin Heidegger in Germany and Maurice Merleau-Ponty in France. It greatly influenced Hans-Georg Gadamer and other theorists concerned with analyzing the conscious activity of understanding language (see *interpretation and hermeneutics*), and, directly or indirectly, affected the way in which many critics analyze the experience of literature. In the 1930s the Polish theorist Roman Ingarden (1893–1970), who wrote his books in both Polish and German, adapted the phenomenological viewpoint and concepts to an innovative formulation of the way we understand and respond to a work of literature.

In Ingarden's analysis, a literary work originates in the intentional acts of consciousness of its author—"intentional" in the phenomenological sense that the acts are directed toward an object. These acts, as recorded in a text, make it possible for a reader to re-experience the work in his or her own consciousness. The recorded text contains many elements which are potential rather than fully realized, as well as many "places of indeterminacy" in what it sets forth. An "active reading" responds to the sequence of the printed words by a temporal process of consciousness which "fills out" these potential and indeterminate aspects of the text, and in so doing, in Ingarden's term, the reading **concretizes** the schematic literary work. Such a reading is said to be "co-creative" with the conscious processes recorded by the author, and to result in an actualized "aesthetic object" within the reader's consciousness which does not depict a reality that exists independently of the work, but instead constitutes a "quasi-reality"—that is to say, its own fictional world. See Roman Ingarden, *The Literary Work of Art* (1931, trans. 1973), and *The Cognition of the Literary Work of Art* (1937, trans. 1973); also, the exposition in Eugene Falk, *The Poetics of Roman Ingarden* (1981). For German critics strongly influenced by Ingarden, see Wolfgang Iser under *reader-response criticism*, and Hans Robert Jauss under *reception theory*.

Phenomenology and Criticism：现象学与文学批评

被称为**现象学**的哲学观点和方法，是由德国思想家埃德蒙·胡塞尔（1859—1938）创立的。胡塞尔试图分析人的意识，他把具体的**现实世界**（存在的世界）描述为不带任何先决假设的经验世界——不论这些假设是来自哲学还是来自常识。他提出意识是统一的**意向性**行为。他所说的意向性并不是指人为的意志支配着意识，而是说意识总是指向某一"客体"；换言之，"有意识"总是指对某一事物的"有意识"。胡塞尔宣称：在意识的这种统一行为下，思维的主体和它所"意指"的客体或它所察觉到的客体是相互关联、相互包含的。为了摆脱所有先前的概念，对意识的现象学分析，从**悬置**一切关于经验之本质的预先假定开始。这种悬置包括"排除"（即中止）任何关于意识的客体是否真实的判断。也就是说，要放弃对意识的"意指"之外的客体是否存在这一问题的思考。

自胡塞尔在 1900 年及其后提出现象学理论以来，它的哲学影响极为广泛。德国的马丁·海德格尔和法国的莫里斯·梅洛－庞蒂各自独立地从不同的方面发展了这一理论。现象学还极大地影响了汉斯－乔治·伽达默尔和其他理论家对理解语言这一意识行为的分析（参见：*释义和阐释学*），也直接或间接地影响了许多批评家分析文学体验的方法。1930 年代，用波兰文和德文进行写作的波兰理论家罗曼·英加登（1893—1970）把现象学的观点和概念运用到我们理解文学作品并作出反应的理论里。

根据英加登的分析，一部文学作品产生于作者意识的意向性行为——从现象学的意义上来说，"意向性"是指行为是指向某一客体的。这些行为被记录在文本中，使读者有可能在自己的意识里重新体验作品。记录下来的文本里带有许多陈述过程中的"未确定之处"和许多潜在的、没有完全被意识到的因素。"积极的阅读"是用短暂的意识程序对一连串的印刷字句作出反应，它"填补"了文本中潜在的和未确定的方面。用英加登的术语来说，这样做阅读也使得概略的文学作品**具体化**了。"积极的阅读"是读者与作者记录下的意识过程进行"共同创造"，结果是在读者意识中建立了一个具体的"审美客体"。审美客体所描绘的不是独立存在于作品之外的现实，而是"拟现实"，即一个虚构的世界。参阅：罗曼·英加登所著的《艺术的文学作品》（1931，1973 年英译版）和《艺术的文学作品之认知》（1937，1973 年英译版）；也可参阅尤金·福尔克在其所著的《罗曼·英加登诗论》（1981）中的阐述。有关深受英加登影响的德国文学批评家的论述，参见：*读者反应批评*中的沃尔夫冈·伊塞尔和*接受理论*中的汉斯·罗伯特·姚斯。

The term **phenomenological criticism** is often applied specifically to the theory and practice of the **Geneva School** of critics, most of whose members taught at the University of Geneva, and all of whom were joined by friendship, interinfluence, and their general approach to literature. The older members of the Geneva School were Marcel Raymond and Albert Beguin; later members were Jean Rousset, Jean-Pierre Richard, and, most prominently, Georges Poulet. J. Hillis Miller, who for six years was a colleague of Poulet's at Johns Hopkins University, was in his earlier career (before turning to *deconstructive criticism*) the leading American representative of the Geneva School of criticism, and applied this critical mode to the analysis of a variety of American and English authors.

Geneva critics regard each work of literature as a fictional world that is created out of the *Lebenswelt* of its author and embodies the author's unique mode of consciousness. In its approach to literature as primarily subjective, this criticism is opposed to the objective approach of *formalism*, both in its European variety and in American *New Criticism*. Its roots instead go back through the nineteenth century to that type of romantic *expressive criticism* which regarded a literary work as the revelation of the personality of its author, and also proposed that the awareness of this personality is the chief aim and value of reading literature. (As early as 1778, for example, the German critic Johann Gottfried Herder wrote: "This *living reading*, this divination into the soul of the author, is the sole mode of reading, and the most profound means of self-development.") In the course of time, however, Geneva critics assimilated a number of the concepts and methods of Husserl, Heidegger, and other phenomenologists. In the view of the Geneva critics the **cogito**, or distinctive formations of consciousness, of the individual author—related to, but not identical with, the author's "empirical," or biographical, self—pervades a work of literature, manifesting itself as the subjective correlate of the "contents" of the work; that is, of the objects, characters, imagery, and style into which the author's personal mode of awareness and feeling imaginatively projects itself. (For a related critical concept see *voice*; refer also to *objective and subjective*.) By "bracketing" their own prepossessions and particularities, the readers of a literary work make themselves purely and passively receptive, and so are capable of achieving participation, or even identity, with the immanent consciousness of its author. Their undertaking to read a work so as to experience the mode of consciousness of its author, and then to reproject this consciousness in their own critical writing about that work, underlies the frequent application to the Geneva School of the term **critics of consciousness**, and the description of their aim in a critical reading of works of literature as "consciousness of the consciousness of another." As Georges Poulet put it in "Phenomenology of Reading" (1969): "When I read as I ought ... with the total commitment required of any reader," then "I am thinking the thoughts of another.... But I think it as my very own.... My consciousness behaves as though it were the consciousness of another." (It should be noted that whereas the philosopher Husserl's aim in phenomenology was to describe the essential features of consciousness which are shared by all human beings, the Geneva

现象学批评这一术语常用于特指**日内瓦学派**批评家的理论和实践，这一学派的大多数成员在日内瓦大学任教，他们都是出于友情、相互影响和对文学的一般研究方法的相同看法才聚集到一起的。日内瓦学派老资格的成员有：马塞尔·雷蒙和艾伯特·贝金。后期成员有：让·罗塞特、让－皮埃尔·理查德，以及这一学派最著名的人物乔治·普莱和J.希利斯·米勒。米勒在约翰·霍普金斯大学与普莱共事六年，早期（在转向*解构主义批评*前）曾是日内瓦批评学派的主要美国代言人，是米勒首先将现象学批评应用于分析英美许多作家的作品。

日内瓦学派的批评家认为，每一部文学作品都是其作者根据现实世界创作出来的一个虚构世界，体现了作者独特的意识模式。这一批评学派研究文学的方法基本上是主观的，它反对*形式主义*在欧洲的种种变化，以及在美国*新批评*中客观研究文学作品的方法。它的根源可以追溯到19世纪浪漫主义的*表现主义批评*，这种批评把文学作品看成是作者个性的展现，认为对作者个性的认知是阅读文学作品的主要目的和价值所在。（譬如，早在1778年，德国批评家约翰·戈特弗里德·赫尔德就写道："这种*活阅读*，这种深入作者灵魂的预知，是阅读的'唯一'方式，也是自我发展最深奥的手段。"）然而，在其发展过程中，日内瓦学派的批评家从胡塞尔、海德格尔和其他现象学家那里汲取了一些概念和方法。在日内瓦学派的批评家看来，**自我**思想活动过程，或作者个人独特的意识构造——与他的"经验的"或传记的自我有关，但并非完全一致——渗透整部文学作品，并显示为这部作品"内容"的主观对应物，即作为客体、人物、意象和风格的主观对应物，它们在虚构作品中折射出作者的个人意识模式和感情。（相关的批评概念可以参阅：*言念*；也可参阅：*客观的与主观的*。）当一部文学作品的读者"排除"了其内心成见和个人看法之后，他的感受力就会变得非常敏锐，因而他也就能够获得与作者的内在意识相沟通甚至相一致的感受。日内瓦学派通过阅读文学作品来体验作者的意识形式，而后又将这一意识再次反映到他们自己对文学作品的批评论著里，因此常被称为**意识批评家**，他们阅读文学作品的批评宗旨被描述为："他人意识的意识"。就像乔治·普莱在其所写的文章"现象学的阅读"（1969）中所说的那样："当我需要阅读时……阅读中我完全承诺了作品对读者的要求"，于是"我思考他人的想法……但我把他人的想法当做就是我自己的想法……我的意识似乎是按照他人的意识在活动。"（应当指出的是，哲学家胡塞尔的现象学理论的目的是描述人类所共有的意识的本质特征，

critics' quite different aim is to identify—and also to identify oneself with—the unique consciousness of each individual author.)

Within this framework, critics of consciousness differ in the extent to which they attend to specific elements in the "external" contents, formal structure, and style of a text, on their way toward isolating its author's "interior" mode of consciousness. A conspicuous tendency of most of these critics is to put together widely separated passages within a single work, on the principle, as J. Hillis Miller says in his book *Charles Dickens*, that since all these passages "reveal the persistence of certain obsessions, problems, and attitudes," the critic may, by analyzing them, "glimpse the original unity of a creative mind." Furthermore the critics of consciousness often treat a single work not as an individual entity, but as part of the collective body of an author's writings, in order, as Miller said of Dickens, "to identify what persists through all the swarming multiplicity of his novels as a view of the world which is unique and the same." Georges Poulet has also undertaken, in a number of books, to tell the history of the varying imaginative treatments of the topic of time throughout the course of Western literature, regarding these treatments as correlative with diverse modes of lived experience. In these histories Poulet sets out to identify "for each epoch a consciousness common to all contemporary minds"; he claims, however, that within this shared period-consciousness, the consciousness of each author also manifests its own uniqueness. The influence of the criticism of consciousness reached its height in the 1950s and 1960s, then gave way to the explicitly opposed critical modes of *structuralism* and *deconstruction*. Many of its concepts and procedures, however, survive in some forms of *reader-response criticism* and *reception aesthetic*.

Robert R. Magliola, *Phenomenology and Literature* (1977), deals with various types of phenomenological poetics and criticism in the context of an exposition of Husserl, Heidegger, and other phenomenological philosophers. Brief introductions to the Geneva School of criticism are Georges Poulet, "Phenomenology of Reading," *New Literary History* 1 (1969–70), and J. Hillis Miller, "The Geneva School ... ," in *Modern French Criticism*, ed. J. K. Simon (1972). In "Geneva or Paris? The Recent Work of Georges Poulet," *University of Toronto Quarterly*, Vol. 39 (1970), Miller indicates his own transition from the criticism of consciousness to the very different critical mode of deconstruction. A detailed study of the Geneva School is Sarah Lawall's *Critics of Consciousness: The Existential Structures of Literature* (1968); see also Michael Murray, *Modern Critical Theory: A Phenomenological Introduction* (1976). Among the writings of Geneva critics and other critics of consciousness available in English are Georges Poulet, *Studies in Human Time* (1949), *The Interior Distance* (1952), and *The Metamorphoses of the Circle* (1961); Jean Starobinski, *The Invention of Liberty, 1700–1789* (1964); Gaston Bachelard, *Subversive Humanist: Texts and Reading*, ed. Mary M. Jones (1991); J. Hillis Miller, *Charles Dickens: The World of His Novels* (1959), *The Disappearance of God* (1963), and *Poets of Reality* (1965). Other critical works influenced by phenomenology are Paul Brodtkorb, *Ishmael's White World: A Phenomenological Reading of Moby Dick* (1965); David Halliburton, *Edgar Allan Poe: A Phenomenological View* (1973);

而日内瓦学派迥然不同的目的却是认同——也是使自己认同于——每一位作者个人独特的意识。）

在现象学这一批评理论体系内，意识批评家们的相异点在于：当他们分离作者的"内部"意识形式时，他们对作品的"外在"内容、形式结构和文本风格具体的组成因素的注重程度各不相同。在大多数日内瓦学派批评家中有一种很明显的倾向：即依据 J. 希利斯·米勒在《查尔斯·狄更斯》一书中所阐明的原则，把一部文学作品里支离分隔的段落组合起来，因为这些段落"揭示了某些持续存在的困扰、难题和态度"，批评家也许可以通过分析它们来"管窥一个富有创造力的心智原有的统一性"。此外，意识批评家们常常不把一部作品视为一个独立的实体，而是将其视为作家所有作品的集合体的一部分，正如米勒在讨论狄更斯的小说时所指出的，目的是为了"找出在作者浩瀚的小说里某种一贯的、独特的、一成不变的对世界的看法"。乔治·普莱还在他的许多论著中探讨了整个西方文学对时间这一主题的种种富有想象力的表现手法的历史，认为这些表现手段与不同的生活经验有关。在这些史实里，普莱找寻"每个时代中同代人所共有的意识"；但他宣称，在这一大家所共有的时代意识内，每一位作家的意识也体现出其独特性。意识批评的影响力在 1950、1960 年代达到顶峰，而后让位于结构主义和解构主义这两种与其完全对立的批评模式。然而，它的许多概念和传统做法仍然存在于*读者反应批评*和*接受美学*的某些形式中。

罗伯特·R. 马格利奥拉所著的《现象学与文学》(1977)，在阐述胡塞尔、海德格尔和其他现象学哲学家的理论的同时，讨论了现象学诗学和现象学文学批评的各种类型。对日内瓦学派文学批评的简介有：乔治·普莱所写的文章"现象学的阅读"，载于《新文学史》第 1 期 (1969—1970)，J. 希利斯·米勒所写的文章"日内瓦学派……"，收入 J. K. 西蒙主编的《现代法国批评》(1972)。在《多伦多大学季刊》1970 年第 39 期上刊登的论文"日内瓦或巴黎？乔治·普莱的近期作品"里，米勒说明了自己在文学批评上的转变——从意识批评转变到一种完全不同的文学批评模式解构主义。莎拉·洛华尔所著的《意识批评家：文学的存在结构》(1968)，详细研究了日内瓦学派。也可参阅：迈克尔·默里所著的《现代批评理论：现象学的介绍》(1976)。已被译成英文的日内瓦学派批评家和其他意识批评家的著作有：乔治·普莱所著的《人类时代研究》(1949)，《内在的距离》(1952)；《变形的圆环》(1961)；让·斯塔罗宾斯基所著的《自由的发明：1700—1789》(1964)；加斯东·巴什拉所著的《颠覆性的人文主义者：文本与解读》(1991，玛丽·M. 琼斯主编）；J. 希利斯·米勒所著的《查尔斯·狄更斯：他的小说世界》(1959)、《上帝的消失》(1963)、《现实的诗人》(1965)。其他受到现象学影响的批评作品还有：保罗·布罗德科伯所著的《伊希梅尔的白色世界：对〈白鲸〉的一种现象学解读》(1965)；戴维·哈利伯顿所著的《埃德加·爱伦·坡：一种现象学观点》(1973)；

and Bruce Johnson, *True Correspondence: A Phenomenology of Thomas Hardy's Novels* (1983).

philology: 193.

philosophical optimism: 154.

phoneme (fō′ nēm): 195.

phonetic intensives: 196.

phonetics (fōnĕt′ ĭks): 195.

phonocentric (fōnōsĕn′ trĭk): 77.

phonology: 195.

phrasal rhythms (in verse): 221.

picaresque narrative (pĭk′ ărĕsk″): 253; *15, 295*.

Pindaric ode: 262.

pitch: 197.

Platonic love: In Plato's *Symposium* 210–12, Socrates recounts the doctrine about Eros (love) that, he modestly says, has been imparted to him by the wise woman Diotima. She bids us not to linger in the love evoked by the beauty in a single human body, but to mount up as by a stair, "from one going on to two, and from two to all fair forms," then up from the beauty of the body to the beauty of the mind, until we arrive at a final contemplation of the Idea, or Form, of "beauty absolute, separate, simple, and everlasting." From this beauty, existing in its own realm of Ideas, the human soul is in exile; and of this ideal beauty, the beauties of the body and of the world perceived by the senses are only distant, distorted, and impermanent reflections. Plotinus and other **Neoplatonists** (the "new Platonists," a school of Platonic philosophers of the third to the fifth century) developed the view that all beauty in the sensible world—as well as all goodness and truth—is an "emanation" (radiation) from the One or Absolute, which is the essence and source of all being and all value. Christian thinkers of the Italian Renaissance, merging this impersonal Absolute with the personal God of the Bible, developed the theory that genuine beauty of the body is only the outer manifestation of a moral and spiritual beauty of the soul, which in turn is rayed out from the absolute beauty of the one God Himself. The Platonic lover is irresistibly attracted to the bodily beauty of a beloved person, but reveres it as a sign of the spiritual beauty that it shares with all other beautiful bodies, and at the same time regards it as merely the lowest rung on a ladder that leads up from sensual desire to the pure contemplation of Heavenly Beauty in God.

布鲁斯·约翰逊所著的《真正的相似：托马斯·哈代小说现象学》(1983)。

philology：语文学　193。

philosophical optimism：乐观主义哲学论　154。

phoneme：音素，音位　195。

phonetic intensives：语音强义法　196。

phonetics：语音学　195。

phonocentric：语音中心　77。

phonology：音韵学　195。

phrasal rhythms (in verse)：(诗歌中的)短语韵体　221。

picaresque narrative：流浪汉叙事文　253；*15*，*295*。

Pindaric ode：品达体颂　262。

pitch：音调　197。

Platonic Love：柏拉图式恋爱

　　在柏拉图《会饮篇》第210—212行的对话里，苏格拉底详述了厄洛斯(爱神)的教义，他谦逊地表示，这是由智慧的妇人狄俄蒂玛传授给他的。她告诫我们，不要对一个人身上的美所激起的爱恋之情留连忘返，而要像登梯子那样，"从一个美好形态到达第二个美好形态，接着从第二个美好形态到达所有美好的形态"；然后从对人体美的追求转移到对心智美的追求，直至我们达到对"绝对、独立、质朴和永恒美"这一理念和形态的最终沉思。从这种美学观来看(存在于它自己的理念领域)，人类灵魂远离这种理念世界；对这一理念美来说，肉体美和感观世界的美都是渺茫的、歪曲的、暂时的影像。柏罗丁和其他**新柏拉图主义者**("新柏拉图主义者"指3—5世纪柏拉图主义哲学家的一个学派)发展了这一观点，他们认为在感觉世界里，所有的美，包括善与真，都是从"太一"或"绝对"这一所有生命和价值的本质和本源里"放射"出来的。意大利文艺复兴时期的基督教思想家，将这一客观的"绝对"与圣经中的位格上帝融合起来，形成了这样的理论：肉体上的纯美只是灵魂上的道德美和精神美的外部表现，这种灵魂上的美又是从唯一上帝的绝对美里放射出来的。柏拉图式的情人不可抗拒地被他所爱之人的肉体美吸引，但同时也将肉体美敬奉为它与其他所有美好的躯体所共有的精神美的标志，同时，也把这种肉体美视为是始于性感官欲望，通往对上帝神圣之美的纯洁冥思的阶梯的最低一级。

Highly elaborated versions of this conception of Platonic love are to be found in Dante, Petrarch, and other writers of the thirteenth and fourteenth centuries, and in many Italian, French, and English authors of sonnets and other love poems during the Renaissance. See, for example, the exposition in Book IV of Castiglione's *The Courtier* (1528), and in Edmund Spenser's "An Hymn in Honor of Beauty." As Spenser wrote in one of the sonnets he called *Amoretti* (1595):

> Men call you fayre, and you doe credit it....
> But only that is permanent and free
> From frayle corruption, that doth flesh ensew.
> That is true beautie: that doth argue you
> To be divine and borne of heavenly seed:
> Derived from that fayre spirit, from whom al true
> And perfect beauty did at first proceed.

From this complex religious and philosophical doctrine, the modern notion that Platonic love is simply love that stops short of sexual gratification is a drastic reduction.

The concept of Platonic love fascinated many later poets, especially Shelley; an example is his poem "Epipsychidion" (1821). But his friend Byron took a skeptical view of such lofty claims for the human Eros-impulse. "Oh Plato! Plato!" Byron sighed,

> you have paved the way,
> With your confounded fantasies, to more
> Immoral conduct by the fancied sway
> Your system feigns o'er the controlless core
> Of human hearts, than all the long array
> Of poets and romancers....

(*Don Juan*, I. cxvi)

See Plato's *Symposium* and *Phaedrus*, and the exposition of Plato's doctrine of Eros (which Plato applied to male/male relationships) in G. M. A. Grube, *Plato's Thought* (1935), chapter 3. For a cognitive and moral assessment of Plato's doctrines of love and desire, see Martha Craven Nussbaum, *Love's Knowledge: Essays on Philosophy and Literature* (1990), especially chapter 3. Refer to Paul Shorey, *Platonism Ancient and Modern* (1938); George Santayana, "Platonic Love in Some Italian Poets," in *Selected Critical Writings*, ed. Norman Henfrey (2 vols., 1968), I, pp. 41–59. See *courtly love*.

play (drama): 93.

plot: The plot (which Aristotle termed the **mythos**) in a dramatic or narrative work is constituted by its events and actions, as these are rendered and ordered toward achieving particular artistic and emotional effects. This description is deceptively simple, because the actions (including verbal discourse as well as physical actions) are performed by particular characters in a work,

柏拉图式恋爱这一观念极其复杂的变体既体现在但丁、彼特拉克和其他13、14世纪作家的作品中，也体现在文艺复兴时期许多意大利、法国、英国作家的十四行诗和其他爱情诗里。例如，可以参阅卡斯底格朗所著的《宫廷人物》(1528) 第四卷和埃德蒙·斯宾塞所著的《美颂》。斯宾塞在他的十四行诗《爱情小诗》(1595) 中写道：

> 人们说你美，你也相信是如此，……
> 只有心智的美才能够避免
> 那伴随肉体的腐坏而永存不朽。
> 这是真正的美：它证明你本来就
> 萌生于天国的种子，十分神圣：
> 发源于那位美的仙灵，而所有
> 真纯的美最初都从他产生。 （胡家峦译）

从柏拉图式恋爱复杂的宗教和哲学信条上看，那种认为它只是不带性满足的爱情的现代观点，是一种极度简化的观念。

柏拉图式恋爱这一观念使后世一些诗人大为着迷，尤其是雪莱，这方面的一个例子就是他的诗《厄皮塞乞迪翁》(1821)。不过，他的朋友拜伦却对这种将人的"厄洛斯冲动"升华的概念持怀疑态度。拜伦在他的长诗《唐·璜》（第一章第116节）中叹道："柏拉图啊！柏拉图！"

> 你硬说你那一直胡诌的哲学
> 可以对人不驯的心灵发号施令
> 你那可憎的奇想
> 比历代无数的诗人和传奇家
> 更甚地铺平了
> 引到不道德行为去的路 （朱维基译）

参阅：柏拉图所著的《会饮篇》和《斐德罗》，G. M. A. 格鲁布所著的《柏拉图的思想》(1935) 第3章阐述了柏拉图的厄洛斯学说（柏拉图用这一学说来解释同性之爱恋）。关于对柏拉图的爱欲学说所作的认知和道德评价，可以参阅：玛莎·克雷文·努斯鲍姆所著的《爱的知识：哲学与文学文集》(1990)，尤其是书中第3章。也可参阅：保罗·肖里所著的《古代和现代的柏拉图主义》(1938)；乔治·桑塔亚纳所写的文章"一些意大利诗歌中的柏拉图之爱"，收入诺曼·亨弗利编选的两卷本《批评作品选》(1968) 第一卷第41—59页。参见：**骑士恋**。

play (drama)：戏剧 93。

Plot：情节

戏剧或叙事作品中的情节（亚里士多德称之为**神话**）是由事件和行动组成的，它们经过作者的描述和安排，以获得艺术上和情感上的特别效果。这一定义简单得令人觉得有诈，因为行动（既包括口头话语，也包括身体行动）是由作品中的特定

and are the means by which they exhibit their moral and dispositional qualities. Plot and character are therefore interdependent critical concepts—as Henry James has said, "What is character but the determination of incident? What is incident but the illustration of character?" (See *character and characterization*.) Notice also that a plot is distinguishable from the *story*—that is, a bare synopsis of the temporal order of what happens. When we summarize the story in a literary work, we say that first this happens, then that, then that.... It is only when we specify how this is related to that, by causes and motivations, and in what ways all these matters are rendered, ordered, and organized so as to achieve their particular effects, that a synopsis begins to be adequate to the plot. (On the distinction between story and plot see *narrative and narratology*.)

There are a great variety of plot forms. For example, some plots are designed to achieve tragic effects, and others to achieve the effects of comedy, romance, satire, or of some other *genre*. Each of these types in turn exhibits diverse plot patterns, and may be represented in the mode either of drama or of narrative, and either in verse or in prose. The following terms, widely current in traditional criticism, are useful in distinguishing the component elements of plots and in helping to discriminate types of plots, and of the characters appropriate to them, in both narrative and dramatic literature.

The chief character in a plot, on whom our interest centers, is called the **protagonist** (or alternatively, the **hero** or **heroine**), and if the plot is such that he or she is pitted against an important opponent, that character is called the **antagonist**. Elizabeth Bennet is the protagonist, or heroine, of Jane Austen's *Pride and Prejudice* (1813); Hamlet is the protagonist and King Claudius the antagonist in Shakespeare's play, and the relation between them is one of **conflict**. If the antagonist is evil, or capable of cruel and criminal actions, he or she is called the **villain**. Many, but far from all, plots deal with a conflict; Thornton Wilder's play *Our Town* (1938), for example, does not. In addition to the conflict between individuals, there may be the conflict of a protagonist against fate, or against the circumstances that stand between him and a goal he has set himself; and in some works (as in Henry James' *Portrait of a Lady*) the chief conflict is between opposing desires or values in the protagonist's own temperament. For the recent employment of an anti-traditional protagonist, see *antihero*.

A character in a work who, by sharp contrast, serves to stress and highlight the distinctive temperament of the protagonist is termed a **foil**. Thus Laertes the man of action is a foil to the dilatory Hamlet; the firebrand Hotspur is a foil to the cool and calculating Prince Hal in Shakespeare's *1 Henry IV*; and in *Pride and Prejudice*, the gentle and compliant Jane Bennet serves as a foil to her strong-willed sister Elizabeth. ("Foil" originally signified "leaf," and came to be applied to the thin sheet of bright metal placed under a jewel to enhance its brilliance.)

If a character initiates a scheme which depends for its success on the ignorance or gullibility of the person or persons against whom it is directed, it is called an **intrigue**. Iago is a villain who intrigues against Othello and Cassio in Shakespeare's tragedy *Othello*. A number of comedies, including

人物表现出来的，也是他们表现自己的道德和性格特质的方式。因此，情节和人物是相互依赖的两个文学批评概念——正如亨利·詹姆斯所说："人物不就是事件的确定，而事件不就是人物的说明吗？"（参见：*人物和人物塑造*。）我们也应注意，情节和故事不同——故事只是按时序发生的事件的概要。在概述一部文学作品里的故事时我们说：首先这事件发生了，接着那事件发生了，然后另一事件发生了……只有当我们在阐明这事件在原因和动机上如何与那事件相互关联，以及用什么方式描写、安排和组织所有这些事件以便获得特殊的效果时，概要才足以等同于情节。（有关故事与情节的区别，参见：*叙事和叙事学*。）

情节有多种多样的形式。譬如，一些情节是为了获得悲剧效果，而其他情节则用来获得喜剧、传奇、嘲讽或其他文学类型的效果。反过来，这些类型也显示了各种情节模式，可以用戏剧或叙事文、韵文体或散文体的形式表现出来。下面列举的在传统文学批评里极为常见的术语，有助于区分情节的组成因素，也有助于辨别叙事文和戏剧里不同的情节类型，以及适合这些情节的人物。

一个情节中我们最感兴趣的主要人物叫**主人公**（或**男主角/女主角**），而如果情节设置主人公与一个重要的对手相抗衡，那个对手就叫**对立角色**。简·奥斯丁《傲慢与偏见》（1813）中的伊丽莎白·贝内特就是主人公或者说女主角。在莎剧《哈姆雷特》里，哈姆雷特是主人公，克劳狄斯国王是对立角色。他们两人之间的关系是**冲突**关系。如果对立角色品性邪恶、行事冷酷、作恶多端，他/她就被称为**反面人物**。许多情节，但也并非所有情节，都涉及冲突，比如桑顿·怀尔德的戏剧《小城风光》（1938）里就没有冲突。除人物与人物之间的冲突外，冲突也可以发生在主人公与命运之间，或在主人公与阻碍他实现既定目标的环境之间。在一些作品里（如亨利·詹姆斯的《贵妇人的画像》中），主要冲突产生于人物内心世界里对立的欲望或价值观之间。有关近期对反传统主人公的探索，参见：*反英雄*。

作品中与主人公形成鲜明对比，起着加强或突出主人公独特性情作用的人物被称为**陪衬**。因此，善于行动的雷欧提斯就衬托了哈姆雷特的拖沓；莎士比亚《亨利四世》第一部中狂热的豪斯伯就反衬出哈尔王子的冷静和审慎；而在《傲慢与偏见》中，温和柔顺的珍妮·贝内特则衬托（foil）出她妹妹伊丽莎白的意志坚强。（"foil"原指"叶片"，后来用于指置于珠宝下用来增强其光彩的闪亮薄金属片。）

如果某一人物策划出一个计谋，计谋的成功取决于它所针对的人物的无知和易受欺骗，这就叫**错综情节**。譬如，在莎士比亚的悲剧《奥赛罗》里，伊阿古是设计陷害奥赛罗和凯西奥的反面人物。一些喜剧，包括本·琼森的《狐狸》

Ben Jonson's *Volpone* (1607) and many *Restoration* plays (for example, William Congreve's *The Way of the World* and William Wycherley's *The Country Wife*), have plots which turn largely on the success or failure of an intrigue.

As a plot evolves it arouses expectations in the audience or reader about the future course of events and actions and how characters will respond to them. A lack of certainty on the part of a concerned reader about what is going to happen, especially to characters with whom the reader has established a bond of sympathy, is known as **suspense**. If what in fact happens violates the expectations we have formed, it is known as **surprise**. The interplay of suspense and surprise is a prime source of vitality in a traditional plot. The most effective surprise, especially in realistic narratives, is one which turns out, in retrospect, to have been grounded in what has gone before, even though we have hitherto made the wrong inference from the given facts of circumstance and character. As E. M. Forster put it, the shock of the unexpected, "followed by the feeling, 'oh, that's all right' is a sign that all is well with the plot." A "surprise ending," in the pejorative sense, is one in which the author resolves the plot without adequate earlier grounds in characterization or events, often by the use of highly unlikely coincidence; there are numerous examples in the short stories of O. Henry. (For one type of manipulated ending, see *deus ex machina*.) *Dramatic irony* is a special kind of suspenseful expectation, when the audience or readers foresee the oncoming disaster or triumph but the character does not.

A plot is commonly said to have **unity of action** (or to be "an artistic whole") if it is apprehended by the reader or auditor as a complete and ordered structure of actions, directed toward the intended effect, in which none of the prominent component parts, or **incidents**, is nonfunctional; as Aristotle put this concept (*Poetics*, section 8), all the parts are "so closely connected that the transposal or withdrawal of any one of them will disjoint and dislocate the whole." Aristotle claimed that it does not constitute a unified plot to present a series of episodes which are strung together simply because they happen to a single character. Many *picaresque narratives*, nevertheless, such as Daniel Defoe's *Moll Flanders* (1722), have held the interest of readers for centuries with such an *episodic* plot structure; while even so tightly integrated a plot as that of Henry Fielding's *Tom Jones* (1749) introduces, for variety's sake, a long story by the Man of the Hill, which is related to the main plot only by parallels and contrasts.

A successful later development which Aristotle did not foresee is the type of structural unity that can be achieved with **double plots**, familiar in *Elizabethan* drama. In this form, a **subplot**—a second story that is complete and interesting in its own right—is introduced into the play; when skillfully invented and managed, the subplot serves to broaden our perspective on the main plot and to enhance rather than diffuse the overall effect. The integral subplot may have the relation of analogy to the main plot (the Gloucester story in *King Lear*), or else of counterpoint against it (the comic subplot involving Falstaff in *1 Henry IV*).

Edmund Spenser's *The Faerie Queene* (1590–96) is an instance of a narrative romance which interweaves main plot and a multiplicity of subplots into

(1607)和许多王政复辟时期的戏剧（如威廉·康格里夫的《如此世道》和威廉·威彻利的《乡下夫人》），都有以计谋的成败来展开的错综情节。

随着情节的展开，它引发了观众或读者对事件和行动的将来进程以及人物如何应付这些事件的期待。对于关注故事的读者来说，将会发生何事，尤其是对那些读者已经抱有怜悯之心的人物命运的不确定感叫做**悬念**。如果实际发生的事件出乎我们意料，就叫做**意外**。悬念和意外的相互作用是传统情节充满活力的一个重要来源。最有效的意外（尤其是在现实主义叙事作品中），是我们在回顾中发现的、在之前已发生的事件的基础上建立起来的意外，尽管此前我们从情境和人物的既定事实里得出了错误的推论。正如 E. M. 福斯特所说，在出乎意料的震惊之后，"伴随着一种感觉'哦，没错'是情节完美的一个标志"。从贬义上来看，"意外结局"指的是作者在前期的人物塑造或事件描写缺乏足够依据的情况下就了结了情节，他们经常采用可能性非常小的巧合来造成意外结局。欧·亨利的短篇小说里有无数这样的例证。（关于巧妙处理结局的一种形式，参见：*降神*。）*戏剧性反讽*是充满悬念期待的一种特殊的表现方式：观众或读者预见到将要到来的灾难或胜利，但剧中人物自己却对此一无所知。

只有在读者或听众发现情节是完整和有次序的行动结构，行动结构导向预定的效果，并且其中所有的主要组成部分或**附带事件**都发挥作用时，我们通常才认为情节具有**行动一致律**（或成为"一个艺术整体"）；正如亚里士多德所说：情节的所有组成部分"如此紧密地联系在一起，以致任何部分的变换或抽离，都会使整体分解混乱"（《诗学》第八部分）。亚里士多德声称：将仅仅是因为发生在同一个人物身上而串连在一起的一系列事件呈现出来，并不能构成完整的情节。然而，许多*流浪汉叙事文*，如丹尼尔·笛福的《摩尔·弗兰德斯》(1722)，就是由于有这种插曲式的情节结构而使读者对这部小说的兴趣几个世纪以来经久不衰。甚至亨利·菲尔丁的情节紧凑、完整的小说《汤姆·琼斯》(1749)，为了要显得多样化也引入了山里人讲述的冗长的故事，这一故事与主要情节通过并列和对比的形式相联系。

亚里士多德所没有预见到的、后来情节上一个成功的发展是：用**双重情节**来获得结构上的完整统一。这种情节类型在*伊丽莎白时期*的戏剧中很常见。在这种情节结构形式里，**次情节**——第二个自身完整并且有趣的故事——被纳入剧情。对次情节的娴熟创造和运用可以扩大我们对主要情节的认识，并加强而不是分散故事的整体效果。作为整体一部分的次情节与主情节可以有相似的关系（如《李尔王》里的葛罗斯特故事），也可以有完全对立的关系（如《亨利四世》第一部里有关福斯塔夫的喜剧式次情节）。

埃德蒙·斯宾塞的《仙后》(1590—1596)是一个叙事体传奇的例子，它把主

an intricately interrelated structure, in a way that the critic C. S. Lewis compares to the **polyphonic** art of contemporary Elizabethan music, in which two or more diverse melodies are carried on simultaneously.

The order of a unified plot, Aristotle pointed out, is a continuous sequence of beginning, middle, and end. The **beginning** initiates the main action in a way which makes us look forward to something more; the **middle** presumes what has gone before and requires something to follow; and the **end** follows from what has gone before but requires nothing more; we feel satisfied that the plot is complete. The structural beginning (sometimes also called the "initiating action," or "point of attack") need not be the initial stage of the action that is brought to a climax in the narrative or play. The epic, for example, plunges *in medias res*, "in the middle of things" (see *epic*), many short stories begin at the point of the climax itself, and the writer of a drama often captures our attention in the opening scene with a representative incident, related to and closely preceding the event which precipitates the central situation or conflict. Thus Shakespeare's *Romeo and Juliet* opens with a street fight between the servants of two great houses, and his *Hamlet* with the apparition of a ghost; the **exposition** of essential prior matters—the feud between the Capulets and Montagues, or the posture of affairs in the Royal House of Denmark—Shakespeare weaves rapidly and skillfully into the dialogue of these startling initial scenes. In the novel, the modern drama, and especially the motion picture, such exposition is sometimes managed by **flashbacks**: interpolated narratives or scenes (often justified, or *naturalized*, as a memory, a reverie, or a confession by one of the characters) which represent events that happened before the time at which the work opened. Arthur Miller's play *Death of a Salesman* (1949) and Ingmar Bergman's film *Wild Strawberries* (1957) make persistent and skillful use of this device.

The German critic Gustav Freytag, in *Technique of the Drama* (1863), introduced an analysis of plot that is known as **Freytag's Pyramid**. He described the typical plot of a five-act play as a pyramidal shape, consisting of a rising action, climax, and falling action. Although the total pattern that Freytag described applies to only a limited number of plays, various of his terms are frequently echoed by critics of prose fiction as well as drama. As applied to *Hamlet*, for example, the **rising action** (a section that Aristotle had called the **complication**) begins, after the opening scene and exposition, with the ghost's telling Hamlet that he has been murdered by his brother Claudius; it continues with the developing conflict between Hamlet and Claudius, in which Hamlet, despite setbacks, succeeds in controlling the course of events. The rising action reaches the **climax** of the hero's fortunes with his proof of the King's guilt by the device of the play within a play (III. ii.). Then comes the **crisis**, the reversal or "turning point" of the fortunes of the protagonist, in his failure to kill the King while he is at prayer. This inaugurates the **falling action**; from now on the antagonist, Claudius, largely controls the course of events, until the **catastrophe**, or outcome, which is decided by the death of the hero, as well as of Claudius, the Queen, and Laertes. "Catastrophe" is usually applied to tragedy only; a more general

情节和许多次情节交织成一个复杂精巧相互关联的结构。批评家 C. S. 刘易斯把这种叙事手法比作伊丽莎白时期音乐中同时采用两个或两个以上不同旋律的**多声部艺术**。

亚里士多德指出：一个完整情节的顺序是一个具有开始、中部、结尾的连续系列。**开始**引发主要行动，使我们期待更多的行动；**中部**认定先前发生的事件并要求行动继续下去；**结尾**继续先前发生的事件但不再要求任何进展。这样的情节是完整的，我们也感到满足。结构上的开始（有时也叫"激发行动"或"着手点"）不一定非得是行动的最初阶段并随着叙事或剧情的发展达到高潮。譬如，史诗是以"倒叙"（"in medias res"）开篇（参见：*史诗*）；许多短篇小说是从高潮那一点开始。剧作家常常在第一幕里用一个具有代表性的事件来抓住我们的注意力，这一事件刚好发生在促成主要剧情或冲突的事件之前并与之相联系。譬如，莎士比亚的《罗密欧与朱丽叶》是以两大家族仆人间的街战开始的；《哈姆雷特》则是以鬼魂的出现开始。莎士比亚迅速而娴熟地把这些对先前发生的事件的必要**交代**——凯普莱特和蒙太古这两大家族之间的世仇，或丹麦皇室里的事态发展——编织进这些令人震惊的开始场景里的对白中。在小说和现代戏剧里，尤其是在电影里，这种情节交代有时是靠**倒叙**来实现的。倒叙是指插入的叙述或情境（通常以回忆、幻想或某一人物的表白等形式出现，以显得*自然而不突兀*），它被用来交代作品叙述开始以前所发生的事件。阿瑟·米勒的剧作《推销员之死》（1949）和英格马·伯格曼的电影《野草莓》都熟练地反复运用了倒叙。

德国文学批评家古斯塔夫·弗雷泰戈在他所著的《戏剧的技巧》（1863）中，介绍了一种名为**弗雷泰戈金字塔**的情节分析方法。他将一出五幕剧的典型情节描绘成一个由起始行动、高潮和下降行动构成的金字塔。尽管弗雷泰戈所描绘的整体情节模式只能应用于有限的一些戏剧，但他的许多术语却时常引起散文体小说及戏剧批评家们的共鸣。譬如，《哈姆雷特》一剧在开场戏和情节交代之后，**起始行动**（亚里士多德称为**纠葛**的部分）以鬼魂告知哈姆雷特他是被自己的叔父克劳狄斯杀害为始端，以哈姆雷特与克劳狄斯之间逐渐加剧的冲突继续发展。在冲突中，哈姆雷特尽管遇到一些挫折却还是成功地控制住事态的发展。起始行动在主角利用戏中戏的策略（第三幕第二场）证实国王有罪时达到了主角命运的**高潮**。随之而来的是哈姆雷特在国王祈祷时刺杀他失败，从而导致主人公命运的**逆转或转折**——**关子**。此后便开始了情节的**下降行动**，从这时起，对立角色克劳狄斯在**结局**（或收场）之前在很大程度上控制着事态的发展。这一悲剧是以克劳狄斯、皇后、雷欧提斯和主角的死为尾声的。"结局"通常仅用于悲剧；一个用来指迅速

term for this precipitating final scene, which is applied to both comedy and tragedy, is the **dénouement** (French for "unknotting"): the action or intrigue ends in success or failure for the protagonist, the conflicts are settled, the mystery is solved, or the misunderstanding cleared away. A frequently used alternative term for the outcome of a plot is the **resolution**.

In many plots the dénouement involves a **reversal**, or in Aristotle's Greek term, **peripety**, in the protagonist's fortunes, whether to the protagonist's failure or destruction, as in tragedy, or success, as in comic plots. The reversal frequently depends on a **discovery** (in Aristotle's term, **anagnorisis**). This is the recognition by the protagonist of something of great importance hitherto unknown to him or to her: Cesario reveals to the Duke at the end of Shakespeare's *Twelfth Night* that he is really Viola; the fact of Iago's lying treachery dawns upon Othello; Fielding's Joseph Andrews, in his comic novel by that name (1742), discovers on the evidence of a birthmark—"as fine a strawberry as ever grew in a garden"—that he is in reality the son of Mr. and Mrs. Wilson.

Since the 1920s, a number of writers of prose fiction and drama—building on the example of Laurence Sterne's *Tristram Shandy*, as early as 1759–67—have deliberately designed their works to frustrate the expectations of chronological order, coherence, reliable narration, and resolution that the reader or auditor has formed by habituation to traditional plots; some writers have even attempted to dispense altogether with a recognizable plot. (See, for example, literature of the *absurd*, *modernism and postmodernism*, *antinovel*, the *new novel*.) Also, various types of critical theory have altered or supplemented many traditional concepts in the classification and analysis of plots. The *archetypal critic* Northrop Frye reduced all plots to four types that, he claims, reflect the myths corresponding to the four seasons of the year. Structuralist critics, who conceive diverse plots as sets of alternative conventions and codes for constructing a fictional narrative, analyze and classify these conventional plot forms on the model of linguistic theory. (See *structuralist criticism* and *narratology*, and the discussion of plots in Jonathan Culler, *Structuralist Poetics*, 1975, pp. 205–24.) And some *poststructuralist* critical theorists have undertaken to explode entirely the traditional treatments of plots, on the ground that any notion of the "unity" of a plot and its "teleological" progress toward a resolution are illusory, or else that the resolution itself is only a façade to mask the irreconcilable conflicts and contradictions (whether psychological or social) that are the basic components of any literary text. See under *poststructuralism*.

For recent developments in the concept of plot, see *narrative and narratology*. Refer to Aristotle, *Poetics*; E. M. Forster, *Aspects of the Novel* (1927); R. S. Crane, "The Concept of Plot and the Plot of *Tom Jones*," in Crane, ed., *Critics and Criticism* (1952); Wayne C. Booth, *The Rhetoric of Fiction* (rev. 1983); Elder Olson, *Tragedy and the Theory of Drama* (1966); Robert Scholes and Robert Kellogg, *The Nature of Narrative* (1966); Frank Kermode, *The Sense of an Ending: Studies in the Theory of Fiction* (1967); Eric S. Rabkin, *Narrative Suspense* (1974); Tzvetan Todorov, *The Poetics of Prose* (trans. 1977); Seymour

发展的最后一幕的较普遍的术语（可用于喜剧和悲剧）是**结局**（法文意为"解开纠结"）——即行动或阴谋以主人公的成功或失败而告终，冲突解决了，秘密解开了，或误会消除了。另一个经常用来表示情节收场的术语是**冲突解开**。

在许多情节里，结局都包含着主人公命运的**逆转**，用亚里士多德的希腊术语表示就是**突变**。这种逆转在悲剧情节中导致主人公的失败或毁灭；在喜剧情节中将主人公引向成功。逆转往往依赖**领悟**（用亚里士多德的术语表示就是**发现**）。这是指主人公对原先他/她不知道的某件具有重要意义的事情的认识。在莎士比亚《第十二夜》的结尾，西萨里奥向公爵显露他其实就是薇奥拉；奥赛罗突然发现伊阿古的谎言背叛行径；菲尔丁笔下的约瑟夫·安德鲁斯在同名喜剧性小说（1742）中，发现了一个胎记"像花园里长得最好的草莓一样"，证实了他实际上就是威尔逊夫妇的儿子。

自 1920 年代起，一些散文体小说和戏剧作家，以劳伦斯·斯特恩早在 1759—1767 年的作品《项狄传》为范例，有意在作品中打破那些习惯了传统情节的读者或听众对作品情节的先后顺序、连贯、可靠叙述、冲突解决方式的期待；一些作家甚至试图完全摒弃可辨认的情节。（例如，可以参见：*荒诞派*、*现代主义和后现代主义*、*反小说*、*新小说*中的文学作品。）同样，近代各种类型的文学批评理论也改变或补充了情节分类和情节分析的传统概念。原型批评家诺斯罗普·弗莱将所有情节归纳为四种类型，他宣称这四种类型反映了与一年四个季节相对应的神话。结构主义批评家们把不同情节看成是构建虚构故事的成套可替换的规范与代码，他们用语言学理论模式来分析、划分这些传统情节形式。[参见：*结构主义批评*、*叙事学*，以及乔纳森·卡勒所著的《结构主义诗学》（1975）第 205—224 页有关情节的探讨。] 一些*后现代主义*批评理论家以完全破除传统的情节论述方式为己任。他们的理由是，任何关于情节"统一"和情节向冲突解决"有目的"的发展的看法都是虚幻的，或者说冲突的解决本身只是为了掩盖不可调和的冲突和矛盾（无论是心理矛盾还是社会矛盾）的表面假象，这些矛盾才是所有文学文本的基本组成部分。参见：*后结构主义*中的相关论述。

有关情节理论的新近发展，参见：*叙事和叙事学*。也可参阅：亚里士多德所著的《诗学》；E. M. 福斯特所著的《小说面面观》（1927）；R. S. 克莱恩所写的文章"情节概念与〈汤姆·琼斯〉的情节"，收入克莱恩主编的《批评家与批评》（1952）；韦恩·C. 布思所著的《小说修辞学》（1961）；埃尔德·奥尔索所著的《悲剧和戏剧理论》（1966）；罗伯特·肖科尔斯与罗伯特·凯洛格合著的《叙事的本质》（1966）；弗兰克·克莫德所著的《终结的意义——虚构理论研究》（1967）；埃里克·S. 拉布金所著的《叙事中的悬念》（1974）；兹维坦·托多罗夫所著的《散文诗学》（1977 年英译版）；西摩尔·查特曼所著的《故事和

Chatman, *Story and Discourse: Narrative Structure in Fiction and Film* (1980); Peter Brooks, *Reading for the Plot: Design and Invention in Narrative* (1984). For references to *plot* in other entries, see pages *54, 234.*

plurisignation: 13.

poetaster (pō″ ĕtăs′ tĕr): 52.

poetic diction: The term **diction** signifies the kinds of words, phrases, and sentence structures, and sometimes also of figurative language, that constitute any work of literature. A writer's diction can be analyzed under a great variety of categories, such as the degree to which the vocabulary and phrasing is abstract or concrete, Latin or Anglo-Saxon in origin, colloquial or formal, technical or common. See *style.*

Many poets in all ages have used a distinctive language, a "poetic diction," which includes words, phrasing, and figures not current in the ordinary discourse of the time. (See *poetic license.*) In modern discussion, however, the term **poetic diction** is applied especially to poets who, like Edmund Spenser in the Elizabethan age or G. M. Hopkins in the Victorian age, deliberately employed a diction that deviated markedly not only from common speech, but even from the writings of other poets of their era. And in a frequent use, "poetic diction" is narrowed to specify the special style developed by *neoclassic* writers of the eighteenth century who, like Thomas Gray, believed that "the language of the age is never the language of poetry" (letter to Richard West, 1742). This **neoclassic poetic diction** was in large part derived from the characteristic usage of admired earlier poets such as the Roman Virgil, Edmund Spenser, and John Milton, and was based primarily on the reigning principle of *decorum*, according to which a poet must adapt the "level" and type of his diction to the mode and status of a particular genre (see *style*). Formal satire, such as Alexander Pope's "Epistle to Dr. Arbuthnot" (1735), because it represented a poet's direct commentary on everyday matters, permitted—indeed required—the use of language really spoken by urbane and cultivated people of the time. But what were ranked as the higher genres, such as epic, tragedy, and ode, required a refined and elevated poetic diction to raise the style to the level of the form. On the other hand, pastoral and descriptive poems, which involved references to lowly materials, used a special diction to invest such materials with the dignity and elegance that were considered appropriate to poetry.

Prominent characteristics of this eighteenth-century poetic diction were its *archaism* and its use of recurrent *epithets*; its preference for resounding words derived from Latin ("refulgent," "irriguous," "umbrageous"); the frequent *invocations* to, and *personifications* of, abstractions and inanimate objects; and above all, the persistent use of **periphrasis** (a roundabout, elaborate way of saying something) to avoid what were regarded as low, technical, or commonplace terms by means of a substitute phrase that was thought to be of higher dignity and decorum. Among the many periphrases in James Thomson's *The Seasons*

话语：小说与电影中的叙事结构》(1980)；彼得·布鲁克斯所著的《解读情节：叙事中的设计和意图》(1984)。其他条目中提及"情节"的地方，参见第54、234页。

plurisignation：复义 **13**。

poetaster：冒牌诗人 **52**。

Poetic Diction：诗意辞藻

措辞是指构成任何一部文学作品的字词、短语、句子结构类型，有时还包括比喻用语。我们可以从许多不同的范畴来分析一个作家的措辞，比如词汇和组词是抽象还是具体，是拉丁词源还是盎格鲁-撒克逊词源，是俗语还是正式语，属于技术用语还是一般用语。参见：*文体*。

所有时代的许多诗人都使用一种特殊的语言，即"诗意辞藻"，它包括在特定时代一般话语中不常用的字词、组词和比喻。（参见：*诗的破格*。）但在现代文学批评的讨论里，**诗意辞藻**这一术语通常是专指像伊丽莎白时期的埃德蒙·斯宾塞或维多利亚时期的 G. M. 霍普金斯这样的诗人所用的措辞。他们故意采用与一般言谈，甚至与他们同时代的诗人作品中的措辞都大不相同的措辞。"诗意辞藻"狭义上常用来表示由18世纪的*新古典主义*作家发展起来的特殊文体。这些诗人和托马斯·格雷一样，相信"时代的语言从来就不是诗的语言"（1742年致理查德·韦斯特信中语）。这种**新古典主义诗意辞藻**大部分出自备受赞美的早期诗人，如古罗马诗人维吉尔、埃德蒙·斯宾塞、约翰·弥尔顿颇有特色的遣字用词；它以占主导地位的*仪轨*原则为基础，根据这一原则，诗人必须使自己措辞的"水平"和类型顺应某一特殊文学类型的模式和地位（参见：*文体*）。正规的嘲讽文体，如亚历山大·蒲柏的《致阿布斯纳博士书》(1735)，由于表现的是诗人对日常琐事的直接评论，允许——事实上是需要——诗人使用那个时代里温文尔雅、有教养的人士实际上所说的语言。然而其他更高层次的文学类型，如史诗、悲剧、颂等，则要求诗人用优雅别致的诗意辞藻将文体升华到那一特殊文学形式的高度。而在另一方面，以卑微题材为内容的田园诗和描述性诗歌，则采用特殊措辞来赋予诗歌恰到好处的典雅庄重。

18世纪诗意辞藻的显著特点是仿古和使用反复出现的*属性形容词*；喜欢使用响亮的拉丁词源的字词 [如"光辉的"(refulgent)、"湿润的"(irriguous)、"成荫的"(umbrageous)]；经常对抽象的概念和无生命的物体使用*祈愿词*，并使其*拟人化*和不断使用**迂说**（用拐弯抹角、精巧的方式来诉说某事），用较为高雅、得体的词句来替代低贱、专门或平庸的词句。詹姆斯·汤姆逊的《四季》

(1726–30) are "the finny tribe" for "fish," "the bleating kind" for "sheep," and "from the snowy leg ... the inverted silk she drew" instead of "she took off her silk stocking." The following stanza from Thomas Gray's excellent period piece, "Ode on a Distant Prospect of Eton College" (1747), manifests all these devices of neoclassic poetic diction. Contemporary readers took special pleasure in the ingenuity of the periphrases by which Gray, to achieve the stylistic elevation appropriate to an ode, managed to describe schoolboys at play while evading the use of common—hence what were considered to be unpoetic—words such as "swim," "cage," "boys," "hoop," and "bat":

> Say, Father Thames, for thou hast seen
> Full many a sprightly race
> Disporting on thy margent green
> The paths of pleasure trace;
> Who foremost now delight to cleave
> With pliant arm thy glassy wave?
> The captive linnet which enthrall?
> What idle progeny succeed
> To chase the rolling circle's speed,
> Or urge the flying ball?

In William Wordsworth's famed attack on the neoclassic doctrine of a special language for poetry, in his preface of 1800 to *Lyrical Ballads*, he claimed that there is no "*essential* difference between the language of prose and metrical composition"; decried the poetic diction of eighteenth-century writers as "artificial," "vicious," and "unnatural"; set up as the criterion for a valid poetic language that it be, not a matter of artful contrivance, but the "spontaneous overflow of powerful feelings"; and, by a drastic reversal of the class hierarchy of linguistic decorum, claimed that the best model for the natural expression of feeling is not an idealized version of upper-class speech, but the actual speech of "humble and rustic life."

See Thomas Quayle, *Poetic Diction: A Study of Eighteenth-Century Verse* (1924); Geoffrey Tillotson, "Eighteenth-Century Poetic Diction" (1942), reprinted in *Eighteenth-Century English Literature*, ed. James L. Clifford (1959); J. Arthos, *The Language of Natural Description in Eighteenth-Century Poetry* (1949); M. H. Abrams, "Wordsworth and Coleridge on Diction and Figures," in *The Correspondent Breeze* (1984). For general treatments of the diverse vocabularies of poets, refer to Owen Barfield, *Poetic Diction* (rev. 1973); Winifred Novotny, *The Language Poets Use* (1962); Emerson R. Marks, *Taming the Chaos: English Poetic Diction Theory since the Renaissance* (1998). For references to *poetic diction* in other entries, see page 8.

poetic drama: 93.

poetic justice: Poetic justice was a term coined by Thomas Rymer, an English critic of the later seventeenth century, to signify the distribution, at the end of a literary work, of earthly rewards and punishments in proportion to the

(1726—1730)一诗里有许多迂说词组,如用"有鳍的俦辈"代替"鱼",用"咩咩叫唤的物类"代替"羊",用"她从被雪覆盖的腿上摘去倒置的丝绸",而不用"她脱下长丝袜"。以下是选自托马斯·格雷在他创作最佳时期的名作《伊顿公学远眺》(1747)里的一节诗,新古典主义诗意辞藻的所有技巧都在这些诗行里展现出来。当时的读者尤为喜爱格雷用匠心独具的迂说所创作的、适合于颂诗体这一高雅文学体裁标准的诗歌。格雷描述了玩耍的学童,同时也成功地避免了使用因为常见而缺乏诗意的词,如"游泳""笼子""男孩""铁环""环拍":

  啊,泰晤士河——我的父亲,你曾看见,
  多少次欢愉的追逐嬉戏,
  在你绿流的岸边留下了,
  一道道快乐的行踪径迹,
  请告诉我:如今是谁最先快活地,
  轻舒他温柔的手臂,
  分开你草绿的波澜?
  是谁在把捕获的红雀戏玩,
  谁个年轻贪闲,
  继承了滚环的游戏,
  或是教圆球飞旋在运动场间? (周式中译)

  在1800年出版的《抒情歌谣集》的序言里,威廉·华兹华斯对新古典主义关于诗歌有其特殊语言的理论进行了著名的驳斥。他声称:"散文与韵文语言之间并无本质区别";他指责18世纪作家的诗意辞藻是"矫揉造作的""邪恶的""不自然的"。华兹华斯奠定了判断有效的诗歌语言的标准:诗歌语言不是玩弄技巧的词语组合,而是"强烈感情的自然流露"。他还推翻了语言仪轨的阶级等级原则,宣称感情自然表露的最好模式不是来自上层阶级的谈吐,而是源于"卑微乡野生活"的真实言语。

  参阅:托马斯·奎尔所著的《诗意辞藻:18世纪诗歌研究》(1924);杰弗里·蒂洛森所写的文章"18世纪的诗意辞藻"(1942),重印收入詹姆斯·L.克利福德主编的《18世纪英国文学》(1959);J.阿瑟斯所著的《18世纪诗歌中自然描述的语言》(1949);M.H.艾布拉姆斯所著的《相似的微风》(1984)中的"华兹华斯和柯勒律治论辞藻与形象"。有关不同诗人使用的不同词汇的概述,参阅:欧文·巴菲尔德所著的《诗意辞藻》(1973年修订版);威妮弗雷德·诺沃特尼所著的《诗人用的语言》(1962);埃默森·R.马克斯所著的《驯服混乱:文艺复兴以来英语诗意辞藻理论》(1998)。其他条目中提及"诗意辞藻"的地方,参见第8页。

poetic drama:诗剧 93。

Poetic Justice:诗的正义

  这是17世纪后期英国批评家托马斯·赖默创造的术语,表示在一部文学作品

virtue or vice of the various characters. Rymer's view was that a poem (in a sense that includes dramatic tragedy) is an ideal realm of its own, and should be governed by ideal principles of *decorum* and morality and not by the random way things often work out in the actual world. No important critics or literary writers since Rymer's day have acceded, in any but a highly qualified way, to his rigid recommendation of poetic justice; it would, for example, destroy the possibility of tragic suffering, which exceeds what the protagonist has deserved because of his or her *tragic flaw*, or error of judgment.

See "Introduction" to *The Critical Works of Thomas Rymer*, ed. Curt A. Zimansky (1956); M. A. Quinlan, *Poetic Justice in the Drama* (1912); Martha C. Nussbaum, *Poetic Justice: The Literary Imagination and Public Life* (1995).

poetic license: John Dryden in the late seventeenth century defined poetic license as "the liberty which poets have assumed to themselves, in all ages, of speaking things in verse which are beyond the severity of prose." In its most common use the term is confined to *poetic diction* alone, to justify the poet's departure from the rules and conventions of standard spoken and written prose in matters such as syntax, word order, the use of archaic or newly coined words, and the conventional use of *eye-rhymes* (wind-bind, daughter-laughter). The degree and kinds of linguistic freedom assumed by poets have varied according to the conventions of each age, but in every case the justification of the freedom lies in the success of the effect. The sustained opening sentence of Milton's *Paradise Lost* (1667), for example, departs radically, but with eminent success, from the colloquial language of his time in the choice and order of words, in idiom and figurative construction, and in syntax, to achieve a distinction of language and grandeur of announcement commensurate with Milton's high subject and the tradition of the epic form.

In a broader sense "poetic license" is applied not only to diction, but to all the ways in which poets and other literary authors are held to be free to violate, for special effects, the ordinary norms not only of common discourse but also of literal and historical truth, including the devices of meter and rhyme, the recourse to literary *conventions*, and the representation of fictional characters and events. In *1 Henry IV*, for example, Shakespeare follows Samuel Daniel's history in verse of the Wars of the Roses by making the valiant Hotspur much younger than he was in fact, in order to serve as a more effective *foil* to the apparently dissolute Prince Hal. A special case is **anachronism**—the placing of an event or person or thing outside of its historical era. Shakespeare described his Cleopatra as wearing Elizabethan corsets; and in *Julius Caesar*, which is set in ancient Rome, he introduced a clock that strikes the hour. The term "poetic license" is sometimes extended to a poet's violation of fact from ignorance, as well as by design. It need not diminish our enjoyment of the work that Shakespeare attributed a seacoast to landlocked Bohemia in *The Winter's Tale*, or that Keats, in writing "On First Looking into Chapman's Homer" (1816), mistakenly made Cortez instead of Balboa the discoverer of the Pacific Ocean.

See Geoffrey N. Leech, *A Linguistic Guide to English Poetry* (1969), chapter 3, "Varieties of Poetic License." For the view by *Russian Formalists*

的结尾依据各类人物的善恶程度给予现世的奖惩。赖默认为一首诗（某种意义上也包括戏剧形式的悲剧）有其自身的理想范畴，应当受其自身的*仪轨*和道德的理想准则的支配，而不是受现实世界里人们随机解决问题的方法的支配。从赖默的时代到现在，极少有重要的文学批评家或作家接受他对诗的正义这种严格而死板的推崇，除非是经过对它进行大幅度的修正；这是因为"诗的正义"可能会毁掉悲剧性苦难的可能性，这种悲剧程度远远超过主人公由于悲剧性缺陷所应遭受的苦难。

参阅：克特·A. 齐格曼斯基主编的《托马斯·赖默评著》(1956) 的序言；M.A. 昆兰所著的《戏剧中的诗的正义》(1912)。玛莎·C. 努斯鲍姆所著的《诗的正义：文学想象与公共生活》(1995)。

Poetic License：诗的破格

17 世纪晚期，约翰·德莱顿给诗的破格下的定义是："在所有的时代里，诗人赋予自己的那种不受散文的严谨限制、用韵文表达意思的自由。"在其最一般的意义上，这个术语仅用于*诗意辞藻*，指的是诗人在句法、词序、使用古词或新近杜撰词，以及使用传统*视觉韵*（如 wind-bind, daughter-laughter）等方面，有权背离标准的口语或书面散文的语言规则和惯例。诗人运用这种语言的自由程度和类别，随着每个时代文学规范的变迁而异。但在任何情况下，这种自由的正当性都取决于其运用效果成功与否。例如，弥尔顿《失乐园》(1667) 开篇第一句就在遣词造句、习惯用语、比喻组合和句法上，与他所处时代盛行的口语体语言大相径庭，但还是取得了巨大的成功，以此创造出一种独特的语言表现方式和与他那伟大的主题和史诗形式的传统相对衬的宏伟篇章。

在其较广泛的意义上，"诗的破格"不仅指语言，还用来表示诗人和其他文学作家为了取得特殊的效果，拥有从各方面违反日常话语的一般规范和文字、历史上的真实性的自由，这也包括韵律和韵脚的使用，以及求助于文学*惯例*和再现虚构人物和事件的自由。例如，在《亨利四世》第一部中，莎士比亚依据塞缪尔·丹尼尔有关玫瑰战争的诗体历史，让勇敢的豪斯伯比其实际年龄年轻许多，其目的是为了更有效地*陪衬*出放荡的哈尔王子。"诗的破格"的一个特殊用法是**时代错误**——将某一事件、人物或事物置于其时代之外。莎士比亚让他的克莉奥佩特拉穿上伊丽莎白时代的束腹衣裙；在《尤利乌斯·恺撒》里，故事发生在古罗马，但他却引入了报时的时钟。"诗的破格"这一术语有时被引申为指诗人出于无知、或有意违反事实。莎士比亚在《冬天的故事》里，给处于内陆的波西米亚添了一道海岸线，但这并未减少我们对这一戏剧的喜爱；济慈在写《初读查普曼译荷马有感》一诗时，误把科尔特斯而不是巴尔博厄当做太平洋的发现者。

参阅：杰弗里·N. 利奇所著的《英诗学习指南：语言学的分析方法》(1969) 第 3 章"不同种类的诗的破格"；有关俄国形式主义者认为不同的诗的破格可

that varieties of poetic license are used to freshen our perceptions both of literary language and of the world it represents, see Victor Erlich, *Russian Formalism* (1965).

poetry happenings: 271.

poetry slam: 271.

point of view: Point of view signifies the way a story gets told—the mode (or modes) established by an author by means of which the reader is presented with the characters, dialogue, actions, setting, and events which constitute the *narrative* in a work of fiction. The question of point of view has always been a practical concern of the novelist, and there have been scattered observations on the matter in critical writings since the emergence of the modern *novel* in the eighteenth century. Henry James' prefaces to his various novels, however—collected as *The Art of the Novel* in 1934—and Percy Lubbock's *The Craft of Fiction* (1926), which codified and expanded upon James' comments, made point of view one of the most prominent and persistent concerns in modern treatments of the art of prose fiction.

Authors have developed many different ways to present a story, and many single works exhibit a diversity of methods. The simplified classification below, however, is widely recognized and can serve as a preliminary frame of reference for analyzing traditional types of narration and for determining the predominant type in mixed narrative modes. It deals first with by far the most widely used modes, first-person and third-person narration. It establishes a broad distinction between these two modes, then divides third-person narratives into subclasses according to the degree and kind of freedom or limitation which the author assumes in getting the story across to the reader. It then goes on to deal briefly with the rarely used mode of second-person narration.

In a **third-person narrative**, the **narrator** is someone outside the story proper who refers to all the characters in the story by name, or as "he," "she," "they." Thus Jane Austen's *Emma* begins: "Emma Woodhouse, handsome, clever, and rich, with a comfortable home and happy disposition, seemed to unite some of the best blessings of existence; and had lived nearly twenty-one years in the world with very little to distress or vex her." In a **first-person narrative**, the narrator speaks as "I," and is to a greater or lesser degree a participant in the story, or else is the *protagonist* of the story. J. D. Salinger's *The Catcher in the Rye* (1951), an instance of the latter type, begins: "If you really want to hear about it, the first thing you'll really want to know is where I was born, and what my lousy childhood was like, and how my parents were occupied and all before they had me, and all that David Copperfield kind of crap...."

I. **Third-person points of view**

    A. **The omniscient point of view.** This is a common term for the many and varied works of fiction written in accord with the *convention* that the narrator knows everything that needs to be known

以用来更新我们对文学语言及其所表现的世界的看法的观点，参阅：维克托·厄利克所著的《俄国形式主义》(1965)。

poetry happenings：诗歌即兴艺术表演　271。

poetry slam：咏诗擂台赛（又译现场诗歌）　271。

Point of View：视角

　　视角表示讲述故事的方式——作者通过建立一种（或多种）模式向读者展示构成虚构作品*叙事*部分的人物、对白、行为、背景和事件。视角是小说家们在实践中一直关注的问题，自从18世纪出现了现代*小说*，文学批评论著就对此作出了各种零散的评论。但是，视角成为现代散文体小说艺术研究中最常受到关注的最显著问题之一，这还得归功于亨利·詹姆斯为自己的各类小说所写的序言——收入1934年出版的《小说的艺术》——以及珀西·卢伯克所著的《小说的技艺》(1926)。《小说的技艺》对詹姆斯的评论进行了整理和扩充。

　　作家们已经发展出许多不同的方式来讲述故事，许多作品在单一的叙事文体形式里呈现出各种不同的叙述方式。以下的简要分类得到了广泛认同，可以作为基本的参照框架，用来分析传统的叙事类型，确定混合叙事模式中占主要地位的叙事类型。以下分类首先论述了迄今为止使用最广泛的两种模式：第一人称叙事与第三人称叙事，并对这两种模式进行了广义区分，然后根据作者在向读者讲述故事的过程中所能运用的自由或所受的限制的类型与程度，对第三人称叙事作了进一步划分。接着简要论述了极少使用的第二人称叙事模式。

　　在**第三人称叙事模式**中，**叙述者**是处于故事本身之外的某个人，讲述故事中的人物，称呼他们的姓名或称之为"他""她""他（她）们"。例如，简·奥斯丁的《爱玛》是这样开篇的："爱玛·伍德豪斯漂亮，聪明，富裕，家庭舒适，性情快乐，似乎同时有了生活中的几种最大幸福，已经无忧无虑地在世上过了差不多二十一个年头了。"在**第一人称叙事模式**中，叙述者以"我"的口吻讲述故事，或多或少是故事的*参与者*，或者是故事的*主人公*。J. D. 塞林格的小说《麦田里的守望者》(1951)是这样开头的："假如你真的想听这个故事，你真想知道的头一件事是我是在哪儿出生的，我倒霉的童年是怎么过的，父母生我之前都干了些什么，以及诸如此类大卫·科波菲尔式的废话……"

I 第三人称视角

1. **全知全能视角**。这个常用术语指的是按文学惯例所创作的许多纷繁各异的虚构作品。这一文学惯例就是，叙述者通晓有关人物、行为与事件的所有需要被认知的方面。他不仅能够优先得知人物的思想、

about the agents, actions, and events, and has privileged access to the characters' thoughts, feelings, and motives; also that the narrator is free to move at will in time and place, to shift from character to character, and to report (or conceal) their speech, doings, and states of consciousness.

Within this mode, the **intrusive narrator** is one who not only reports, but also comments on and evaluates the actions and motives of the characters, and sometimes expresses personal views about human life. Most works are written according to the convention that the omniscient narrator's reports and judgments are to be taken as **authoritative** by the reader, and so serve to establish what counts as the true facts and values within the fictional world. This is the fashion in which many of the greatest novelists have written, including Henry Fielding, Jane Austen, Charles Dickens, William Makepeace Thackeray, George Eliot, Thomas Hardy, Fyodor Dostoevsky, and Leo Tolstoy. (In Fielding's *Tom Jones* and Tolstoy's *War and Peace*, 1869, the intrusive narrator goes so far as to interpolate commentary, or short essays suggested by the subject matter of the novels.) On the other hand, the omniscient narrator may choose to be **unintrusive** (alternative terms are **impersonal** or **objective**). Flaubert in *Madame Bovary* (1857), for example, for the most part describes, reports, or "shows" the action in dramatic scenes without introducing his own comments or judgments. More radical instances of the unintrusive narrator, who gives up even the privilege of access to inner feelings and motives, are to be found in a number of Ernest Hemingway's short stories; for example, "The Killers" and "A Clean, Well-Lighted Place." (See *showing and telling*, under *character*.) For an extreme use of impersonal representation, see the comment on Robbe-Grillet's *Jealousy*, under *novel*.

Gérard Genette subtilized in various ways the analysis of third-person point of view. For example, he distinguishes between **focus of narration** (who tells the story) and **focus of character** (who perceives what is narrated in one or another section of the story). In Henry James' *What Maisie Knew*, for example, the focus of narration is an adult who tells the story, but his focus is on events as they are perceived and interpreted by the character Maisie, a child. Both the focus of narration and the focus of character (that is, of perception) in a single story may shift rapidly from the narrator to a character in the story, and from one character to another. In *To the Lighthouse*, Virginia Woolf shifts the focus of character in turn to each of the principal participants in the story; and Hemingway's *short story*, "The Short Happy Life of Francis Macomber," is a third-person narrative in which the focus of perception is, in various passages, the narrator, the hunter Wilson, Mrs. Macomber, Mr. Macomber, and even, briefly, the hunted lion. See Gérard Genette, *Narrative Discourse: An Essay in Method* (1972, trans. 1980). For an analysis of the grammatical shift in pronouns, indicators of time and place, and the tenses of verbs as the

情感与动机，而且可以随心所欲地超越时空，从一个人物转到另一个人物，报道（或掩饰）人物的言语、行为和意识状态。

在这种叙事模式中，**介入的叙述者**不仅描述人物的行为与动机，而且对此作出评价，有时还会表达对人生的个人看法。全知全能叙述者的描述和判断通常被读者视为**权威**，因此有助于在虚构的小说世界里建立人们所认为的真实与价值观。许多作品的创作都遵循了这种惯例。许多伟大的小说家也按照这种方式进行创作，包括菲尔丁、简·奥斯丁、查尔斯·狄更斯、威廉·梅克匹斯·萨克雷、乔治·艾略特、托马斯·哈代、费奥多·陀思妥耶夫斯基和列夫·托尔斯泰。[在菲尔丁的《汤姆·琼斯》和托尔斯泰的《战争与和平》(1863—1869)里，介入的叙述者甚至就小说表达的主题插入评论或简短的论说文。] 另一方面，全知全能的叙述者也可以是**非介人的叙述者**（也可称为**非个人的**或**客观的**叙述者）。例如，在《包法利夫人》(1857)里，福楼拜主要是在描绘、讲述或"展示"戏剧性情景里的人物行为，而没有添加自己的评论或判断。更加极端的非介入叙述者甚至放弃进入人物内心情感和动机的特权。欧内斯特·海明威的许多短篇故事都有这样的叙述者，如《杀人者》和《一个干净明亮的地方》。（参见：人物中的展示手法和讲述手法。）关于客观表现这一极端的用法，参见：小说中对罗布·格里耶的《嫉妒》的评论。

热拉尔·热奈特以多种方式详细地分析了第三人称视角。例如，他区分了**叙事焦点**（讲述故事的人）与**人物焦点**（在故事的任何部分都能感知到所叙述的事）。以亨利·詹姆斯的《梅西知道的》为例，叙事焦点是讲述故事的成年人，但他的焦点则是梅西这个孩子所感知、所领会的事件。在一个单一故事中，叙事焦点和人物焦点（即感知焦点）可以迅速地从叙述者转向故事中的某个人物，从某个人物转向另一人物。在弗吉尼亚·吴尔夫的《到灯塔去》这部小说中，吴尔夫就让人物焦点随着故事的主要参与者依次转移；海明威的短篇小说《弗朗西斯·麦康博的短暂幸福生活》采用第三人称叙事方式，在不同的段落，感知焦点依次为叙述者、猎人威尔逊、麦康博夫人、麦康博先生，甚至短暂地转向了被捕猎的狮子。参阅热拉尔·热奈特所著的《叙事话语：方法论随笔》(1972, 1980年英译版)。对作为故事内叙事转换焦点和模式的代词、时间地点指示物和动词时态

focus and the mode of narration shifts within a story, see *free indirect discourse*, under *narration, grammar of*.

B. **The limited point of view.** The narrator tells the story in the third person, but stays inside the confines of what is perceived, thought, remembered, and felt by a single character (or at most by very few characters) within the story. Henry James, who refined this narrative mode, described such a selected character as his "focus," or "mirror," or "center of consciousness." In a number of James' later works all the events and actions are represented as they unfold before, and filter to the reader through, the particular perceptions, awareness, and responses of only one character; for example, Strether in *The Ambassadors* (1903). A short and artfully sustained example of this limited point of view in narration is Katherine Mansfield's story "Bliss" (1920). Later writers developed this technique into *stream-of-consciousness narration*, in which we are presented with outer perceptions only as they impinge on the continuous current of thought, memory, feelings, and associations which constitute a particular observer's total awareness. The limitation of point of view represented both by James' "center of consciousness" narration and by the "stream-of-consciousness" narration sometimes used by James Joyce, Virginia Woolf, William Faulkner, and others, is often said to exemplify the "self-effacing author," or "objective narration," more effectively than does the use of an unintrusive but omniscient narrator. In the latter instance, it is said, the reader remains aware that someone, or some outside voice, is telling us about what is going on; the alternative mode, in which the point of view is limited to the consciousness of a character within the story itself, gives readers the illusion of experiencing events that evolve before their own eyes. For a revealing analysis, however, of the way even an author who restricts the narrative center of consciousness to a single character nonetheless communicates authorial judgments on people and events, and also controls the judgments evoked from the reader, see Ian Watt, "The First Paragraph of *The Ambassadors*: An Explication," reprinted in David Lodge, ed., *Twentieth Century Literary Criticism: A Reader* (1972). See also *persona, tone, and voice*.

II. **First-person points of view**
This mode, insofar as it is consistently carried out, limits the matter of the narrative to what the first-person narrator knows, experiences, infers, or finds out by talking to other characters. We distinguish between the narrative "I" who is only a fortuitous witness and auditor of the matters he relates (Marlow in *Heart of Darkness* and other works by Joseph Conrad); or who is a participant, but only a minor or peripheral one, in the story (Ishmael in Herman Melville's *Moby-Dick*, Nick in F. Scott Fitzgerald's *The Great Gatsby*); or who is himself or herself the central character in the story (Daniel Defoe's *Moll Flanders*, Charlotte Brontë's *Jane Eyre* and *Villette*, Charles Dickens' *Great Expectations*, Mark Twain's *The Adventures of Huckleberry Finn*, J. D. Salinger's *The Catcher in the Rye*).

的语法转换的分析，参见：*叙事语法中的自由式间接话语*。

2. **局限性视角**。叙述者用第三人称讲述故事，但局限于故事中某个人物（或至多是极少的几个人物）的感知、思想、记忆、情感中。亨利·詹姆斯完善了这一叙事方式，他把这种选择出来的人物称为他的"焦点""镜子"或"意识中心"。在詹姆斯后期的一些作品中，所有的事件与行为都按其之前发展的样子呈现出来，并仅仅通过一位人物特有的感知、意识和反应透露给读者，例如，《大使》(1903)中的斯特西尔。凯瑟琳·曼斯菲尔德的故事《幸福》(1920)就是这种局限性视角叙事方式的典范。这篇故事短小精悍，艺术性经久不衰。稍后的作家将这种技巧发展成意识流叙事方法。在这种叙事方法里，呈现给我们的只是与构成观察者整个意识的思想、回忆和感情流动有关的外部观测。詹姆斯采用的"意识中心"叙事，以及詹姆斯·乔伊斯、弗吉尼亚·吴尔夫、威廉·福克纳和其他作家有时采用的"意识流"叙事，都体现了这种视角局限。一般认为，这种视角局限与全知全能的非介入叙述者相比，更为有效地体现了"自我隐遁的作者"或"客观叙事"。在全知全能的非介入叙事方法中，读者一直意识到，某人或某种外部声音在向我们讲述正在发生的事情；在局限性视角模式中，视角局限于故事本身的某个人物的意识，使读者产生幻觉，仿佛自己正在经历展现在他们自己眼前的事情。然而，即使作者将叙事的意识中心局限于某一人物，他也会表现出自己对人物与事件的判断，并控制读者的判断。有关这点的详尽分析，参阅：伊恩·瓦特所写的文章"《大使》中第一段的解说"，重印收入戴维·洛奇主编的《20世纪文学批评读本》(1972)。也可参见：*第一人称、基调与言念*。

II 第一人称视角

如果在故事中自始至终都运用这种叙事方式，那么叙事的内容将局限于第一人称叙述者所了解、经历和推断的事情，或是叙述者与其他人物交谈中发现的事情。叙述故事的"我"，或是所叙述事件的偶然目击者或听众（如《黑暗的心脏》中的马洛和约瑟夫·康拉德其他作品中的叙述者）；或是故事里次要的、无足轻重的参与者（赫尔曼·梅尔维尔《白鲸》中的伊什梅尔和司各特·菲茨杰拉德《了不起的盖茨比》中的尼克）；或是故事的中心人物（丹尼尔·笛福的《摩尔·弗兰德斯》，夏洛蒂·勃朗特的《简爱》《维莱特》，查尔斯·狄更斯的《远大前程》，马克·吐温的《哈克贝利·芬历险记》，J. D. 塞林格的《麦田里的守望者》）。

Ralph Ellison's *Invisible Man* manifests a complex narrative mode in which the protagonist is the first-person narrator, whose *focus of character* is on the perceptions of a third party—white America—to whose eyes the protagonist, because he is black, is "invisible." For a special type of first-person narrative, see *epistolary novel*, under *novel*.

III. **Second-person points of view**

This name has been given to a mode in which the story gets told solely, or at least primarily, as an address by the narrator to someone he calls by the second-person pronoun "you," who is represented as experiencing that which is narrated. This form of narration occurred in occasional passages of traditional fiction, but has been exploited in a sustained way only since the latter part of the twentieth century and then only rarely; the effect is of a virtuoso performance. The French novelist Michel Butor in *La Modification* (1957, trans. as *Second Thoughts* in 1981), the Italian novelist Italo Calvino in *If on a Winter's Night a Traveler* (trans. 1981), and the American novelist Jay McInerney in *Bright Lights, Big City* (1984), all tell their story with "you" as the *narratee*. McInerney's *Bright Lights, Big City*, for example, begins:

> You are not the kind of guy who would be at a place like this at this time of the morning. But here you are, and you cannot say that the terrain is entirely unfamiliar, though the details are fuzzy. You are at a nightclub talking to a girl with a shaved head. The club is either Heartbreak or the Lizard Lounge.

This second person may turn out to be a specific fictional character, or the reader of the story, or even the narrator himself or herself, or not clearly or consistently the one or the other; and the story may unfold by shifting between telling the narratee what he or she is now doing, has done in the past, or will or is commanded to do in the future. Italo Calvino uses the form to achieve a complex and comic form of *involuted fiction*, by involving "you," the reader, in the fabrication of the narrative itself. His novel opens:

> You are about to begin reading Italo Calvino's new novel, *If on a winter's night a traveler*. Relax. Concentrate.... Best to close the door, the TV is always on in the next room. Tell the others right away, "No, I don't want to watch TV!" ... Or if you prefer, don't say anything; just hope they'll leave you alone.

Refer to Bruce Morrissette, "Narrative 'You' in Contemporary Literature," *Comparative Literature Studies*, Vol. 2 (1965); Brian Richardson, "The Poetics and Politics of Second-Person Narrative," *Genre*, Vol. 24 (1991); Monika Fludernick, "Second-Person Narrative as a Test Case for Narratology," *Style*, Vol. 28 (1994); and "Second-Person Narrative: A Bibliography," *Style*, Vol. 28 (1994).

Two other frequently discussed narrative tactics are relevant to a consideration of points of view:

The **self-conscious narrator** shatters any illusion that he or she is telling something that has actually happened by revealing to the reader that the narration

拉尔夫·埃里森的《隐身人》就展现了复杂的叙事模式。故事中的主人公是第一人称叙述者，人物焦点却是第三方——美国白人——的感知。在白人眼里，因为主人公是黑人，所以他是"隐身的"。有关第一人称叙事的特殊类型，参见：小说中的书信体小说。

III 第二人称视角

在这种叙事模式里，叙述者仅仅或主要向他称之为"你"的第二人称讲述故事，"你"将体验到所叙述的一切。这种叙事模式偶尔会出现在传统小说的某些篇章里，但以持续的方式运用这一叙事模式只出现在20世纪后半叶，此后便鲜有人用；它往往会带来类似于精湛表演的效果。法国小说家迈克尔·布托尔的《政变》(1957, 1981年英译版为《三思之后》)，意大利小说家伊塔洛·卡尔维诺的《如果在冬夜，一个旅人》(1981年英译版)，以及美国小说家杰伊·麦金纳尼的《明亮的灯火，伟大的城市》(1984)都以"你"为叙事对象来讲述故事。例如，麦金纳尼在《明亮的灯火，伟大的城市》中是这样开头的：

> 你这种家伙不会在早晨的这个时候出现在这种地方。但现在你的确在这儿。而且，尽管具体事物有些模糊，但你不能说这一带你不熟悉。你正在夜总会和一位理光头的女孩聊天。这家夜总会可能叫心碎夜总会也可能是蜥蜴酒吧。

第二人称可能是某个具体的虚构人物、故事的读者，甚至是叙述者本人，或是模糊不清或者从头到尾不是同一个人或另一个人；故事可能向叙事对象讲述他或她现在正在做的事、过去已经做过的事，或将来要做的或被命令做的事。故事在这之间进行转化，并由此得到发展。伊塔洛·卡尔维诺采用这种形式在建构叙述本身时创造了一种复杂的、喜剧性的*内延小说*形式。这种小说包含了"你"，即读者。他的小说是这样开头的：

> 你即将读到伊塔洛·卡尔维诺的新小说，《如果在冬夜，一个旅人》。放松。集中注意力……最好把门关上，因为隔壁房间的电视总是开着。立刻告诉其他人："不，我不想看电视！"……或者，假如你愿意的话，你也可以一言不发；只希望他们能让你单独待着。

参阅：布鲁斯·莫瑞塞特所写的文章"当代文学中的叙事'你'"，载于《比较文学研究》1965年第2期；布赖恩·理查森所写的文章"第二人称叙事的诗学和政治学"，载于《文类》1991年第24卷；莫尼卡·弗拉德米克所写的文章"第二人称叙事：书目"，载于《文体》1994年第28卷。

此外，还有两种文学家经常讨论的与视角有关的叙事策略：

自我意识的叙述者向读者透露，叙事是一种虚构艺术作品，或夸大叙事明显

is a work of fictional art, or by flaunting the discrepancies between its patent fictionality and the reality it seems to represent. This can be done either seriously (Henry Fielding's narrator in *Tom Jones* and Marcel in Marcel Proust's *Remembrance of Things Past*, 1913–27) or for primarily comic purposes (Tristram in Laurence Sterne's *Tristram Shandy*, 1759–67, and the narrator of Lord Byron's versified *Don Juan*, 1819–24), or for purposes which are both serious and comic (Thomas Carlyle's *Sartor Resartus*, 1833–34). See Robert Alter, *Partial Magic: The Novel as a Self-Conscious Genre* (1975), and refer to *romantic irony*, under the entry *irony*.

One variety of self-conscious narrative exploited in recent prose fiction is called the **self-reflexive novel**, or the *involuted novel*, which incorporates into its narration reference to the process of composing the fictional story itself. An early modern version, André Gide's *The Counterfeiters* (1926), is also one of the most intricate. As the critic Harry Levin summarized its self-involution: it is "the diary of a novelist who is writing a novel [to be called *The Counterfeiters*] about a novelist who is keeping a diary about the novel he is writing"; the nest of Chinese boxes was further multiplied by Gide's publication, also in 1926, of his own *Journal of The Counterfeiters*, kept while he was composing the novel. Vladimir Nabokov is an ingenious exploiter of involuted fiction; for example, in *Pale Fire* (1962). See *metafiction* under the entry *novel*.

We ordinarily accept what a narrator tells us as authoritative. The **fallible** or **unreliable narrator**, on the other hand, is one whose perception, interpretation, and evaluation of the matters he or she narrates do not coincide with the opinions and norms implied by the author, which the author expects the alert reader to share. (See the commentary on reliable and unreliable narrators in Wayne C. Booth, *The Rhetoric of Fiction*, rev. 1983.) Henry James made repeated use of the narrator whose excessive innocence, or oversophistication, or moral obtuseness, makes him a flawed and distorting "center of consciousness" in the work; the result is an elaborate structure of ironies. (See *irony*.) Examples of James' use of a fallible narrator are his short stories "The Aspern Papers" and "The Liar." *The Sacred Fount* and *The Turn of the Screw* are works by James in which, according to some critics, the clues for correcting the views of the fallible narrator are inadequate, so that what we are meant to take as factual within the story, and the evaluations intended by the author, remain problematic. See, for example, the remarkably diverse critical interpretations collected in *A Casebook on Henry James' "The Turn of the Screw,"* ed. Gerald Willen (1960), and in *The Turn of the Screw*, ed. Deborah Esch and Jonathan Warren (2d ed., 1999). The critic Tzvetan Todorov, on the other hand, has classified *The Turn of the Screw* as an instance of **fantastic literature**, which he defines as deliberately designed by the author to leave the reader in a state of uncertainty whether the events are to be explained by reference to natural causes (as hallucinations caused by the protagonist's repressed sexuality) or to supernatural causes. See Todorov's *The Fantastic: A Structural Approach to a Literary Genre* (trans. Richard Howard, 1973); also Eric S. Rabkin, *The Fantastic in Literature* (1976).

的虚构性与它看似反映出的现实性之间的差异，从而打破了认为他或她正在讲述某件真实发生的事情的幻觉。这可以通过严肃的方法得以实现 [亨利·菲尔丁《汤姆·琼斯》中的叙述者，马塞尔·普鲁斯特《追忆逝水年华》（1913—1927）中的马塞尔]，或主要是为了取得滑稽的效果 [劳伦斯·斯特恩《项狄传》（1759—1767）中的项狄，拜伦勋爵《唐·璜》（1819—1824）中的叙述者]，或是为了达到既严肃又滑稽的目的 [托马斯·卡莱尔的《旧衣新裁》（1833—1834）]。参阅：罗伯特·奥尔特所著的《部分魔术：作为自我意识体裁的小说》（1975）；参见：*反讽*中的*浪漫体反讽*。

近代的散文体小说中采用的另一种自我意识的叙事被称为**自省小说**或*内延小说*。这类小说在叙事中融合了虚构故事本身的创作过程。安德烈·纪德的《伪币制造者》（1926）是这类小说的早期现代作品，也是最复杂的一部。正如哈里·莱文对这部小说自我还原性的概括：它是"小说家的日记。这位小说家正在创作一部小说 [这部小说将起名为《伪币制造者》]，小说描写了小说家所记录的与他正在创作的小说有关的日记"；纪德在 1926 年又出版的《伪币制造者日志》中进一步增加了这组套盒的套数。《日志》是作者在构思小说的过程中记录下来的。弗拉基米尔·纳博科夫是内延小说卓有成就的开拓者，如他创作的《灰火》（1962）。参见：*小说*中的*元小说*。

我们通常都会接受叙述者告诉我们的事并将其视为权威。但是，**容易出错或不可信任的叙述者**对他或她所述事件的感知、解释和评价却与作者暗示的见解和准则并不一致，而作者则希望警觉的读者能够分享这些见解和准则。[参阅：韦恩·C.布思所著的《小说修辞学》（1961）中对可信任的叙述者与不可信任的叙述者的评论。] 亨利·詹姆斯一再采用的叙述者往往因为过于单纯无知，或过于世故，或道德上的迟钝，而成为作品中有瑕疵、扭曲变形的"意识中心"，结果形成了一种精心安排的多种反讽结构。（参见：*反讽*。）詹姆斯采用容易出错的叙述者的例子可在他的短篇故事集《阿斯朋遗稿》和《说谎者》中找到。一些批评家认为，在詹姆斯的作品《圣泉》和《螺丝在拧紧》中，矫正容易出错的叙述者观点的依据并不充分，这使得在故事中我们本应认定的事实以及作者的评价都令人困惑。例如，参阅：杰拉德·维伦主编的《有关亨利·詹姆斯〈螺丝在拧紧〉的资料汇编》（1960），德博拉·埃施与乔纳森·沃伦主编的《螺丝在拧紧》（1999 年第 2 版）中搜集的、对容易出错的叙述者视角各种迥然不同的批评解释。但批评家兹维坦·托多罗夫则将《螺丝在拧紧》归入**怪诞文学**。他对怪诞文学的定义是，作者有意进行设计，使读者处于一种不确定的状态：这些事件究竟是该用自然原因（如主人公受压抑的性欲引起的幻觉）还是该用超自然原因来解释。参阅：托多罗夫所著的《怪诞：一种文学类型的结构主义分析》（1973，理查德·霍华德英译版）；也可参阅：埃里克·S.拉伯金所著的《文学中的怪诞》（1976）。

Drastic experimentation in recent prose fiction has complicated in many ways traditional renderings of point of view, not only in second-person, but also in first- and third-person narratives; see *fiction*; *persona, tone, and voice*; and *postmodernism*. On point of view, in addition to the writings mentioned above, refer to Norman Friedman, "Point of View in Fiction," *PMLA*, Vol. 70 (1955); Leon Edel, *The Modern Psychological Novel* (rev. 1964), chapters 3–4; Wayne C. Booth, *The Rhetoric of Fiction* (rev. 1983); Franz Stanzel, *A Theory of Narrative* (1979, trans. 1984); Susan Lanser, *The Narrative Act: Point of View in Fiction* (1981); Wallace Martin, *Recent Theories of Narrative* (1986). For references to *point of view* in other entries, see pages *57, 82, 209, 228, 231, 259*.

political readings: 248.

polyphonic: 296.

popular ballad: 23.

portmanteau word (pŏrtmăn tō′): **13**; *78*.

positivism: 419.

postcolonial studies: The critical analysis of the history, culture, literature, and modes of discourse that are specific to the former colonies of England, Spain, France, and other European imperial powers. These studies have focused especially on the Third World countries in Africa, Asia, the Caribbean islands, and South America. Some scholars, however, extend the scope of such analyses also to the discourse and cultural productions of countries such as Australia, Canada, and New Zealand, which achieved independence much earlier than the Third World countries. Postcolonial studies sometimes also encompass aspects of British literature in the eighteenth and nineteenth centuries, viewed through a perspective that reveals the ways in which the social and economic life represented in that literature was tacitly underwritten by colonial exploitation.

An important text in establishing the theory and practice in this field of study was *Orientalism* (1978) by the Palestinian-American scholar Edward Said, which applied a revised form of Michel Foucault's historicist critique of discourse (see under *new historicism*) to analyze what he called "cultural imperialism." This mode of imperialism imposed its power not by force, but by the effective means of disseminating in subjugated colonies a Eurocentric *discourse* that assumed the normality and pre-eminence of everything "occidental," correlatively with its representations of the "oriental" as an exotic and inferior other. The term **orientalism** is now sometimes applied to cultural imperialism by means of the control of discourse, not only in the orient, but anywhere in the world.

Since the 1980s, such analysis has been supplemented by other theoretical principles and procedures, including Althusser's redefinition of the Marxist

近代散文体小说进行了重大的实验,在许多方面都使得对视角的传统理解变得复杂化,不仅是在第二人称叙事中,也包括第一、第三人称叙事;参见:*虚构小说*、*第一人称*、*基调与言念*;*后现代主义*。除了上面提到的著作,有关视角的讨论还可参阅:诺曼·弗里德曼所写的文章"小说中的视角",载于《美国现代语言学协会会刊》1955 年第 70 卷;利昂·埃德尔所著的《现代心理小说》(1964 年修订版)第 3—4 章;韦恩·C. 布思所著的《小说修辞学》(1983 年修订版);弗朗兹·斯坦泽尔所著的《叙事理论》(1979,1984 年英译版);苏珊·兰泽所著的《叙事行为:小说中的视角》(1981);华莱士·马丁所著的《当代叙事理论》(1986)。其他条目中提及"视角"的地方,参见第 57、82、209、228、231、259 页。

political readings:政治解读　248。

polyphonic:多声部　296

popular ballad:流行民谣　23。

portmanteau word:合并词　13;78。

positivism:实证主义　419。

Postcolonial Studies:后殖民主义研究

　　该术语是指对英国、西班牙、法国和其他欧洲帝国的前殖民地所特有的历史、文化、文学和话语模式的批评分析。这类研究尤其关注非洲、亚洲、加勒比海诸岛及南美洲的第三世界国家。但有些学者也把分析范围扩展到澳大利亚、加拿大、新西兰等国家的话语与文化产物,这些国家比第三世界国家更早取得了独立。有时后殖民主义研究还包括对 18、19 世纪英国文学中某些方面的分析,其审视角度旨在揭示殖民剥削对文学作品所表现的社会、经济生活产生无形影响的方式。

　　建立这一研究领域的理论与实践的重要文本是美籍巴勒斯坦裔学者爱德华·赛义德所著的《东方主义》(1978),该书更改了米歇尔·福柯对话语的历史主义批评方式(参见:*新历史主义*中的相关论述),用来分析他所谓的"文化帝国主义"。这种帝国主义形式并不是通过武力来施加影响,而是在被征服的殖民地中有效地散播欧洲中心论的话语。欧洲中心论的话语认为,任何"西方的"事物都具有规范性与卓越地位;与之相对应,"东方的"事物则被描绘为怪异的、次等的他者。**东方主义**这一术语现在有时也用来指通过话语控制进行的文化帝国主义,不仅是在东方,而且是在世界上任何地方。

　　1980 年代以来,这种分析得到了其他理论原则与方法的补充,包括阿尔都塞对马克思主义*意识形态*理论的重新定义和德里达的*解构主义*理论,这使得后

theory of *ideology* and the *deconstructive* theory of Derrida. The rapidly expanding field of postcolonial studies, as a result, is not a unified movement with a distinctive methodology. One can, however, identify several central and recurrent issues:

1. The rejection of the "master narrative" of Western imperialism—in which the colonial "other" is not only subordinated and marginalized, but in effect deleted as a cultural agency—and its replacement by a counter-narrative in which the colonial cultures fight their way back into a world history written by Europeans. In the influential book *The Empire Writes Back: Theory and Practice in Post-Colonial Literatures* (2d ed., 2002), Bill Ashcroft, Gareth Griffiths, and Helen Tiffin stress what they term the **hybridization** of colonial languages and cultures, in which imperialist importations are superimposed on indigenous traditions; they also draw attention to a number of postcolonial countertexts to the *hegemonic* texts that present a Eurocentric version of colonial history.

2. An abiding concern with the construction, within Western discursive practices, of the colonial and postcolonial "subject," as well as of the categories by means of which this subject conceives itself and perceives the world within which it lives and acts. (See *social constructs* and *subject*, under *poststructuralism*.) The **subaltern** has become a standard way to designate the colonial subject that has been constructed by European discourse and internalized by colonial peoples who employ this discourse; "subaltern" is a British word for someone of inferior military rank, and combines the Latin terms for "under" (*sub*) and "other" (*alter*). A recurrent topic of debate is how, and to what extent, a subaltern subject, writing in a European language, can manage to serve as an agent of resistance against, rather than of compliance with, the very discourse that has created its subordinate identity.

3. A major element in the postcolonial agenda is to disestablish Eurocentric norms of literary and artistic values, and to expand the literary *canon* to include colonial and postcolonial writers. In the United States and Britain, there is an increasingly successful movement to include, in the standard academic curricula, the brilliant and innovative novels, poems, and plays by such postcolonial writers in the English language as the Africans Chinua Achebe and Wole Soyinka, the Caribbean islanders V. S. Naipaul and Derek Walcott, and the authors from the Indian subcontinent G. V. Desani and Salman Rushdie. Compare *ethnic writers* under *periods of American literature*, and see Homi Bhabha, *The Location of Culture* (1994). For a survey of the large and growing body of *anglophone* literature by postcolonial writers throughout the world, see Martin Coyle and others, *Encyclopedia of Literature and Criticism* (1990), pp. 1113–1236; and Gaurav Desai and Supriya Nair, *Postcolonialisms: An Anthology of Cultural Theory and Criticism* (2005).

Postcolonial scholarship also studies forms of imperialism other than European, including the domination of some southern-hemisphere groups or

殖民主义的研究领域迅速扩大，并使之成为一场没有显著方法论的、并非统一的运动。尽管如此，我们仍可确定其反复讨论的几个中心议题。

1. 摒弃西方帝国主义的主体－叙述——在这种叙述中，殖民地"他者"不仅处于从属地位和被边缘化，而且实质上它的文化主体身份已经消失殆尽——并用反叙述来取代这种主体－叙述。在反叙述中，殖民地文化力争重返欧洲人撰写的世界历史中。比尔·阿什克洛夫特、加勒思·格里菲思、海伦·蒂芬斯在他们合编的产生了深远影响的论文集《帝国反击：后殖民主义文学理论与实践》(1989)中，强调了殖民地语言与文化的**混合**，在这种混合中，帝国主义输出的文化强加于本土传统之上；他们也关注了一些针对反映了殖民历史中欧洲中心论的霸权主义文本的后殖民主义反文本。

2. 始终关注在西方推理实践中殖民主义与后殖民主义"主体"的形成、这一主体借以认识自己的各种表现方式类别的形成，以及这一主体对自身所生存和活动的世界的各种认知方式的形成。（参见：后结构主义中的社会建构、主体。）**低等**一词已经成为用来指代欧洲话语所建构的殖民地主体的标准方式，而且被采用欧洲话语的殖民地各民族在意识中"内在化"了。"低等"（subaltern）是一个英国英语单词，意为下等人，是拉丁文中的 sub（"下等"）和 alter（"另一个"）两个词的合成。后殖民主义反复争论的一个话题是，用欧洲语言书写的低等主体如何能够，又是在何种程度上能够成为一种反抗主体，抵制建立其从属身份的话语，而不是遵从这种话语。

3. 后殖民主义一项重要的研究议程在于废除以欧洲为中心的文学规范与艺术价值，将殖民地作家与后殖民主义作家扩充到文学经典里。在英美两国发起了一场日益成功的运动，将一些后殖民主义作家用英语创作的新颖出众的小说、诗歌、戏剧列入正规的学术课程中。这些作家包括非洲的奇努阿·阿奇贝与沃什·索因卡，加勒比海岛的 V. S. 奈保尔与德里克·沃尔科特，印度次大陆的 G. V. 德塞尼与萨曼·拉什迪。对比：美国文学各时期的划分中的民族作家；参阅：霍米·巴巴所著的《文化的定位》(1994)。世界各地的后殖民主义作家用英语创作了大量且日益增加的英语文学作品，有关这方面的研究可以参阅：马丁·科伊尔等人合编的《文学与批评百科全书》(1990)第 1113—1236 页；高拉夫·德赛与苏普利亚·奈尔合编的《后殖民主义：文化理论与批评选集》(2005)。

后殖民主义学术也研究欧洲以外的帝国主义形式，包括一些南半球群体或国

nations by other southern-hemisphere groups or nations. This rethinking of empire has brought the United States into focus as an object of postcolonial scholarship, both as a contemporary empire and as itself a postcolonial nation. See Amy Kaplan and Donald E. Pease, eds., *Cultures of United States Imperialism* (1993). In recent years, scholars in postcolonial studies have turned their attention to identities in a globalized world where large groups of people have, for various reasons, left their homelands, producing diasporas, population flows, and émigré groups. See Rey Chow, *Writing Diaspora: Tactics of Intervention in Contemporary Cultural Studies* (1993) and *The Protestant Ethnic and the Spirit of Capitalism* (2002); and Arjun Appadurai, *Modernity at Large: Cultural Dimensions of Globalization* (1996). Ania Loomba provides an overview of the field in *Colonialism/Postcolonialism* (2d ed., 2008).

Comprehensive anthologies: Henry Schwarz and Sangeeta Ray, eds., *A Companion to Postcolonial Studies* (2000); David Theo Goldberg and Ato Quayson, eds., *Relocating Postcolonialism* (2002); and Bill Ashcroft and others, eds., *The Post-Colonial Studies Reader* (2d ed., 2006). In addition to titles listed above, refer also to Frantz Fanon, *The Wretched of the Earth* (trans. 1963), and *Black Skin, White Masks* (trans. 1967); Gayatri Chakravorty Spivak, *In Other Worlds* (1987), and Ranajit Guha and Gayatri Chakravorty Spivak, eds., *Selected Subaltern Studies* (1988); Christopher L. Miller, *Theories of Africans: Francophone Literature and Anthropology in Africa* (1990); Homi K. Bhabha, ed., *Nation and Narration* (1990); Aijaz Ahmad, *In Theory: Classes, Nations, Literatures* (1992); Edward W. Said, *Culture and Imperialism* (1993); Chris Weedon, *Feminist Practice and Poststructuralist Theory* (2d ed., 1997); Robert J. C. Young, *Postcolonialism: An Historical Introduction* (2001); and Neil Lazarus, ed., *The Cambridge Companion to Postcolonial Literary Studies* (2004). For a useful introduction, see Bill Ashcroft, Gareth Griffiths, and Helen Tiffin, *Post-Colonial Studies: The Key Concepts* (2d ed., 2008).

Anne McClintock, Aamir Mufti, Ella Shohat, eds., *Dangerous Liaisons: Gender, Nation, and Postcolonial Perspectives* (1997), stress the convergence of postcolonial studies and *feminism*. Much postcolonial inquiry takes its point of departure from theories of nationalism; often cited are Benedict Anderson, *Imagined Communities: Reflections on the Origin and Spread of Nationalism* (rev. 1991), and Partha Chatterjee, *Nationalist Thought and the Colonial World* (1993). See also *Interventions: International Journal of Postcolonial Studies*. For references to *postcolonial studies* in other entries, see page **72**.

post-Marxism: 208.

postmodern period: 285.

postmodernism: 227.

poststructuralism: Poststructuralism designates a broad variety of critical perspectives and procedures that in the 1970s displaced structuralism from its prominence as the radically innovative way of dealing with language and

家控制其他南半球群体或国家的方式。对帝国的这一反思，使得美国成为后殖民主义学术关注的一个对象，既是作为一个当代帝国，同时其本身也是作为一个后殖民主义国家。参阅：埃米·卡普兰与唐纳德·E. 皮斯合编的《美国帝国主义的文化》(1993)。近年来，后殖民主义研究的学者已经将他们的注意力转向全球化世界里的身份认同，在这个全球化世界，大量人群出于各种各样的原因，离开他们的祖国，产生了离散者、人口流动和流亡群体。参阅：周蕾所著的《写在家国以外：当代文化研究的干涉策略》(1993) 和《新教民族与资本主义精神》(2002)；阿尔君·阿帕杜莱所著的《消失的现代性：全球化的文化向度》(1996)。对这一领域的综述，参阅：艾妮亚·鲁巴主编的《殖民主义/后殖民主义》(2008 年第 2 版)。

综合性选集：亨利·施瓦茨与桑吉他·雷合编的《后殖民主义研究指南》(2000)；戴维·西奥·戈德堡与奥托·奎伊森合编的《重新安置后殖民主义》(2002)；比尔·阿什克罗夫特等人合编的《后殖民主义研究读本》(2006 年第 2 版)。除了上举书目，也可参阅：弗朗茨·法农所著的《全世界受苦的人》(1963 年英译版) 和《黑皮肤，白面具》(1967 年英译版)；佳娅特丽·查克拉沃蒂·斯皮瓦克所著的《在他者的世界里》(1987)；拉纳吉特·古哈与佳娅特丽·查克拉沃蒂·斯皮瓦克合编的《属下研究选集》(1988)；克里斯托弗·L. 米勒所著的《非洲人的理论：非洲的法属文学及人类学》(1990)；霍米·K. 巴巴主编的《国族与叙事》(1990)；艾贾兹·阿赫迈德所著的《在理论中：阶级、民族与文学》(1992)；爱德华·W. 赛义德所著的《文化与帝国主义》(1993)；克里斯·威登所著的《女性主义实践与后殖民主义理论》(1997 年第 2 版)；罗伯特·J. C. 扬所著的《后殖民主义：历史导引》(2001)；尼尔·拉扎鲁斯主编的《剑桥后殖民主义文学研究指南》(2004)。关于实用的介绍，参阅：比尔阿什·克罗夫特、加勒思·格里菲斯、海伦·蒂芬三人合编的《后殖民主义研究关键词》(2008 年第 2 版)。

安妮·麦克林托克、阿米尔·穆夫提、艾拉·肖哈特三人合编的《危险的关系：性别、国族与后殖民主义视角》(1997)，强调了后殖民主义研究与女性主义的交合。许多后殖民主义研究都远离了国家主义理论的视角，常被引述的两本书是：本尼迪克特·安德森的《想象的共同体：民族主义的起源与散布》(1991 年修订版) 和帕沙·查特吉的《民族思想与殖民世界》(1993)。也可参阅：《干预：国际后殖民主义研究期刊》。其他条目中提及"后殖民主义研究"的地方，参见第 72 页。

post-Marxism：后马克思主义　208。

postmodern period：后现代主义时期　285。

postmodernism：后现代主义　227。

Poststructuralism：后结构主义

后结构主义是指 1970 年代出现的内容广泛的各种批评角度与方法，它们取代了以极其新颖的方式论述语言及其他符号系统的结构主义的显著地位。

other signifying systems. A conspicuous announcement to American scholars of the poststructural point of view was Jacques Derrida's paper on "Structure, Sign and Play in the Discourse of the Human Sciences," delivered in 1966 to an International Colloquium at Johns Hopkins University. (The paper is included in Derrida's *Writing and Difference*, 1978.) Derrida attacked the systematic, quasi-scientific pretensions of the strict form of structuralism—derived from Saussure's concept of the structure of language and represented by the cultural anthropologist Claude Lévi-Strauss—by asserting that the notion of a systemic structure, whether linguistic or other, presupposes a fixed "center" that serves to organize and regulate the structure yet itself "escapes structurality." In Saussure's theory of language, for example, this center is assigned the function of controlling the endless differential play of internal relationships, while remaining itself outside of, and immune from, that play. (See *structuralism*.) As Derrida's other writings made clear, he regarded this incoherent and unrealizable notion of an ever-active yet always absent center as only one of the many ways in which all of Western thinking is "logocentric," or dependent on the notion of a self-certifying foundation, or absolute, or essence, or ground, which is ever-needed but never present. See *deconstruction*.

Other contemporary thinkers, including Michel Foucault, Jacques Lacan, and (in his later phase) Roland Barthes, although in diverse ways, also undertook to "decenter" or "undermine" or "subvert" traditional claims for the existence of self-evident foundations that guarantee the validity of all knowledge and truth, and establish the possibility of determinate communication. This **antifoundationalism** in philosophy, conjoined with skepticism about traditional conceptions of meaning, knowledge, truth, value, and the subject or "self," is evident in some (although not all) current exponents of diverse modes of literary studies, including *feminist*, *new historicist*, and *reader-response* criticism. In its extreme forms, the poststructural claim is that the workings of language inescapably undermine meanings in the very process of making such meanings possible, or else that every mode of discourse "constructs," or constitutes, the very facts or truths or knowledge that it claims to discover.

"Postmodern" is sometimes used in place of, or interchangeably with, "poststructural." It is more useful, however, to follow the example of those who apply "postmodern" to developments in literature and other arts, and reserve "poststructural" for theories of criticism and of intellectual inquiries in general. (See *modernism and postmodernism*.)

Salient features or themes that are shared by diverse types of poststructural thought and criticism include the following:

1. The primacy of theory. Since Plato and Aristotle, discourse about poetry or literature has involved a "theory," in the traditional sense of a conceptual scheme, or set of principles, distinctions, and categories—sometimes explicit, but often only implied in critical practice—for identifying, classifying, analyzing, and evaluating works of literature. (See *criticism*.) In poststructural criticism what is called "theory" came to be foregrounded, so that many critics felt it incumbent to "theorize" their individual positions and practices. The nature of theory, however, was conceived in a new

1966年，雅克·德里达向约翰·霍普金斯大学举办的国际学术报告会提交了"结构、符号、人类科学话语中的游戏"一文 [该文收入德里达所著的《写作与差异》(1978)]。这篇论文明确地向美国学者宣告了后结构主义的观点。德里达抨击了结构主义严格形式的系统性、类似科学的假象——源于索绪尔的语言结构概念，其典型代表是文化人类学家列维-斯特劳斯——德里达坚持认为，语言或其他系统结构的概念预先设定了一个"中心"，这个"中心"有助于结构的组织调节，但中心本身又"逃离了结构性"。例如，在索绪尔的语言理论中，这个中心被赋予了控制内在关系无穷无尽的差异游戏的功能，但中心本身却一直处于这种差异游戏之外，不受它的影响。(参见：*结构主义*。)德里达在其他文章中阐明，这个中心永远活跃着，但又总是不在场。他将这种不甚连贯、不可实现的中心概念视为只是众多西方思维方式中的一种。所有的西方思维都是"以理性为中心的"，或是依赖于必需的但又从不在场的自我证明的基础概念或绝对本质或理由。参见：*解构主义*。

传统观点宣称，自我证明基础的存在确保了所有知识与真理的有效性，并建立了明确交流的可能性，但与德里达同时期的其他思想家，如米歇尔·福柯、雅克·拉康、罗兰·巴尔特（在他的后期研究中）等，则以不同的方式力图"消除中心"或"破坏"或"颠覆"这种传统观点。哲学中的这种**反基础论**，及对意义、知识、真理、主体或"自我"等传统概念的怀疑主义，在文学研究的各种模式包括*女性主义*、*新历史主义*、*读者反应批评*的一些（虽然不是全部）当代倡导者中明显地表现出来。最极端的后结构主义模式宣称，语言活动就在使意义成为可能的过程中又不可避免地破坏了意义，或者，每种话语模式都"建构"或构成了它声称要发现的事实或真理或知识。

"后现代"有时也用来代替"后结构主义"一词，或与它交替使用。但更有效的做法是仿效那些将"后现代"用于指代文学及其他艺术新近发展的用法，用"后结构主义"特指新近批评理论与一般的思想探索理论。(参见：*现代主义与后现代主义*。)

各种后结构主义思想及批评类型共有的显著特征或主题包括以下几个方面：

1. 理论的首要地位。自柏拉图和亚里士多德以来，诗歌或文学话语就涉及"理论"，即传统意义上的概念系统，或一系列的原理、特征和范畴——有时是明确的，但通常隐含在批评实践中——用于文学作品的鉴定、划分、分析和评价。(参见：*批评*。)在后结构主义批评中，所谓的"理论"被置于突出地位，因此，许多批评家认为必须将自己的立场与实践"理论化"。但他们对**理论**的本质有了一种新的、

and very inclusive way; for the word **theory**, standing without qualification, often designated an account of the general conditions of signification that determine meaning and interpretation in all domains of human action, production, and intellection. In most cases, this account was held to apply not only to verbal language, but also to psychosexual and sociocultural "signifying systems." As a consequence, the pursuit of literary criticism was conceived to be integral with all the other pursuits traditionally classified as the "human sciences," and to be inseparable from consideration of the general nature of human "subjectivity," and also from reference to all forms of social and cultural phenomena. Often the theory of signification was granted primacy in the additional sense that, when common experience in the use or interpretation of language does not accord with what the theory entails, such experience is rejected as unjustified and illusory, or else is accounted an ideologically imposed concealment of the actual operation of the signifying system.

A prominent aspect of poststructural theories is that they are posed in opposition to inherited ways of thinking in all provinces of knowledge. That is, they expressly "challenge" and undertake to "destabilize," and in many instances to "undermine" and "subvert," what they identify as the foundational assumptions, concepts, procedures, and findings in traditional modes of discourse in Western civilization (including literary criticism). In a number of politically oriented critics, this questioning of established ways of thinking and of formulating knowledge is joined to an adversarial stance toward established institutions, class structures, and practices of economic and political power and social organization.

2. The decentering of the **subject**. The oppositional stance of many poststructural critics is manifested in a sharp critique of what they call "humanism"; that is, of the traditional view that the human being or human author is a coherent identity, endowed with purpose and initiative, whose design and intentions effectuate the form and meaning of a literary or other product. (See *humanism*.) For such traditional terms as "human being" or "individual" or "self" poststructuralists tend to substitute "subject," because this word is divested of the connotation that it has originating or controlling power, and instead suggests that the human being is "subjected to" the play of external forces; and also because the word suggests the grammatical term, the "subject" of a sentence, which is an empty slot, to be filled by whoever happens to be speaking at a particular time and place. *Structuralism* had already tended to divest the subject of operative initiative and control, evacuating the purposive human agent into a mere location, or "space," wherein the differential elements and codes of a systematic *langue* precipitate into a particular *parole*, or signifying product. Derrida, however, by deleting the structural linguistic "center," had thereby also eliminated the possibility of a controlling agency in language, leaving the use of language an unregulatable and undecidable play of purely relational elements. In the view of many deconstructive critics, the subject or author or narrator of a text becomes itself a purely linguistic

很有包容性的理解方式；因为理论一词没有任何限定，通常表示对一般指代条件的描述。这些指代条件决定着人类行为、生产及思想所有领域的意义与阐释。大多数情况下，这种描述不仅适用于文字语言，也适用于性心理学和社会文化学的"符号指向系统"。其结果是，文学批评的探索被视为与其他所有传统意义上被区别为"人类科学"的探索密不可分，既不能脱离对人类"主观性"一般本质的考虑，也不能脱离对所有社会、文化现象形式的参照。此外，指代理论通常被赋予的首要地位还体现在，当语言使用或阐释的普通经验与理论蕴含的内容不相符合时，这种经验往往被视为无法解释、不切实际的经验而被摒弃；或者被视为意识形态对符号指向系统的实际运作所造成的掩盖。

后结构主义理论的一个显著方面在于，它们反对所有知识领域承袭的思维方式，即对西方文明（包括文学批评）中它们确认为传统话语模式的基础假设、概念、方式及研究结果提出了明确的"挑战"，试图"动摇其稳定性"，并在许多情况下力图对其予以"破坏"和"颠覆"。一些具有政治倾向的批评家，将这种对业已确立的思维方式、知识阐述方式的质疑，与对现有制度、阶级结构、经济和政治权力及社会组织实践的敌对态度结合在一起。

2. 消除**主体**的中心地位。许多后结构主义批评家的反对观点体现在他们对所谓的"人文主义"的尖锐批评上；即传统观点认为，人类主体或作者是一个连贯的本体，被赋予了目的性与主动性。主体的构思与意图实现了文学或其他产物的形式与意义。（参见：人文主义。）对"人类"或"个体"或"自我"这样的传统术语，后结构主义者倾向于用"主体"予以替代，因为这个词摆脱了它有创造或控制力量这层含义，代之以人类受制于外力活动的支配，也因为这个词暗示了语法术语，一个句子的"主体"，是一个空槽，等待被在某一特定时间和地点言说的不拘什么人所填充。结构主义总是倾向于解除主体的有效主动性与控制，消除具有目的性的人类主体，仅仅将其视为一种位置或"空间"。在这个空间里，系统性语言的各种差异因素与代码促成了特定的言语，或指向性的产物。但是，德里达消除了结构主义的语言"中心"，也因此取消了语言中支配主体的可能性，使语言的使用成了纯粹相关因素之间不可约束和不可判定的游戏。在许多解构主义批评家看来，文本的主体或作者或叙述者本身成了纯语

product—as Paul DeMan has put it in *Allegories of Reading* (1979), we "rightfully reduce" the subject "to the status of a mere grammatical pronoun." Alternatively, the subject-author is granted at most the function of trying (although always vainly) to "master" the incessant freeplay of the decentered signifiers. For a collection of essays on "the subject" in writings on politics, philosophy, psychoanalysis, and history, see Eduardo Cadava, Peter Connor, Jean-Luc Nancy, eds., *Who Comes After the Subject?* (1991).

Michel Foucault and Roland Barthes both signaled the evacuation of the traditional conception of the subject who is an author by announcing the "disappearance of the author," or even more melodramatically, "the **death of the author**." (Foucault, "What Is an Author," 1969, in *Language, Counter-Memory, Practice*, 1977; Barthes, "The Death of the Author," 1968, in *Image, Music, Text*, 1977.) They did not mean to deny that a human individual is a necessary link in the chain of events that results in a parole or text. What they denied was the validity of the "function," or "role" hitherto assigned in Western discourse to a uniquely individual and purposive author, who is conceived as the *cogito*, or origin of all knowledge; as the initiator, purposive planner, and (by his or her intentions) the determiner of the form and meanings of a text; and as the "center," or organizing principle, of the matters treated in traditional literary criticism and literary history. In addition, a number of current forms of *psychoanalytic, Marxist,* and *new historicist* criticism manifest a similar tendency to decenter, and in extreme cases to delete, what is often called the "agency" of the author as a self-coherent, purposive, and determinative human being. Instead, the human agent is said to be a disunified subject that is the product of diverse psychosexual conditions, and subjected to the uncontrollable workings of unconscious compulsions. Alternatively, the subject is held to be no more than a "construction" by current forms of ideology; or a "site" traversed by the *cultural constructs* and the discursive formations engendered by the conceptual and power configurations in a given era. (See *author and authorship*.)

3. Reading, texts, and writing. The decentering or deletion of the author leaves the reader, or interpreter, as the focal figure in poststructural accounts of signifying practices. This figure, however, like the author, is stripped of the traditional attributes of purposiveness and initiative and converted into an impersonal process called "reading." What this reading engages is no longer called a literary "work" (since this traditional term implies a purposive human maker of the product); instead, reading engages a "text"—that is, a structure of signifiers regarded merely as a given for the reading process. Texts in their turn (especially in deconstructive criticism) lose their individuality, and are often represented as manifestations of *écriture*—that is, of an all-inclusive "textuality," or writing-in-general, in which the traditional "boundaries" between literary, philosophical, historical, legal, and other classes of texts are considered to be both artificial and superficial. See *text and writing (écriture)*.

A distinctive poststructural view is that no text can mean what it seems to say. To a deconstructive critic, for example, a text is a chain of

言产物——例如，保罗·德·曼在其所著的《阅读的寓言》(1979)中指出，我们"适如其分地"将主体"降低到仅仅是语法代词的地位"。或者，主体-作者至多被赋予了这样的功能，即试图（但总是徒劳无功）"控制"非中心的能指持续不断的自由游戏。关于政治、哲学、心理分析和历史著述中"主体"的文章合集，可以参阅：爱德华·多卡达瓦、彼得·康纳、让-吕克·南希三人合编的《谁在主体之后到来？》(1991)。

米歇尔·福柯与罗兰·巴尔特通过宣称"作者的消失"，或更为耸人听闻地宣告**"作者的死亡"**，表明了对传统作者概念的消除。[福柯所写的文章"作者是什么？"(1969)，收入其所著的《语言，反记忆，实践》(1977)；巴尔特所写的文章"作者的死亡"(1968)，收入其所著的《意象-音乐-文本》(1977)。] 他们并不否认在构成言语或文本的一连串事件中，人类个体是其中的一个必要环节。他们否认的是迄今为止西方思想中赋予具有独特个性及目的性的作者的"功能"或"作用"的有效性——具有独特个体及目的性的作者被视为"我思"，或所有知识的源泉；被视为创始者、具有目的性的计划者及（通过他或她的意图成为）文本形式与意义的决定者；并被当做传统文学批评与文学史中所探讨的问题的"中心"，或组织原则。此外，精神分析批评、马克思主义批评和新历史主义批评的一些当代形式，也表现出对作为自我连贯、具有目的性、决定性人类个体的作者所具有的"施动性"消除中心，在一些极端的情况下加以取消的类似的倾向。这些批评形式认为，人类是一种四分五裂的自我，是各种不同的性心理状态的产物，受无意识冲动不可控制的作用的支配。也可以这么说，主体是当代意识形态的"建构物"，或是文化建构与话语结构相互交叉的"地方"。这种文化建构与话语结构产生于特定时代的概念构型与权力构型。（参见：*作者与作者身份*。）

3. 阅读、文本与书写。消除或取消作者中心地位，使得读者或阐释者在后结构主义对指代实践的描述中成为焦点人物。但与作者一样，这类人物被剥夺了目的性、主动性等传统属性，并被转化为一种被称为"阅读"的非个人过程。这种阅读涉及的对象不再被称为文学"作品"（因为这一传统术语暗指，作品具有目的性的人类作者）；相反，阅读涉及的是"文本"，即被视为仅仅是给予阅读过程的一种能指结构。文本自身（尤其是在解构主义批评中）失去了个性，通常被描述为书面文字的表现形式，即包含一切"文本性"的表现形式，或一般书写的表现形式。在这种书写中，文学、哲学、历史、法律及其他种类文本之间的传统"界线"被视为人为的和肤浅的。参见：*文本与书写/书面文字*。

典型的后结构主义观点认为，没有文本能够表达出它似乎想要表达的意思。例如，对解构主义批评家来说，文本是一连串的能指；

signifiers whose seeming determinacy of meaning, and seeming reference to an extra-textual world, are no more than "effects" produced by the differential play of conflicting internal forces which, on closer analysis, turn out to deconstruct the text into an undecidable scatter of opposed significations. In the representation of Roland Barthes, the "death" of the author frees the reader to enter the literary text in whatever way he or she chooses, and the intensity of pleasure yielded by the text becomes proportionate to the reader's abandonment of limits on its signifying possibilities. In Stanley Fish's version of *reader-response criticism*, all the meanings and formal features seemingly found in a text are projected into the printed marks by each individual reader; any agreement about meaning between two individuals is contingent upon their happening to belong to a single one among many diverse "interpretive communities."

4. The concept of discourse. Literary critics had long made casual use of the term "discourse," especially in application to passages representing conversations between characters in a literary work, and in the 1970s there developed a critical practice called *discourse analysis* which focuses on such conversational exchanges. This type of criticism (as well as the *dialogic criticism* inaugurated by Mikhail Bakhtin) deals with literary discourse as conducted by human characters whose voices engage in a dynamic interchange of beliefs, attitudes, sentiments, and other expressions of states of consciousness.

In poststructural criticism, **discourse** has become a very prominent term, supplementing (and in some cases displacing) "text" as the name for the verbal material which is the primary concern of literary criticism. In poststructural usage, however, the term is not confined to conversational passages but, like "writing," designates all verbal constructions and implies the superficiality of the boundaries between literary and nonliterary modes of signification. Most conspicuously, discourse has become the focal term among critics who oppose the deconstructive concept of a "general text" that functions independently of particular historical conditions. Instead, they conceive of discourse as social parlance, or language-in-use, and consider it to be both the product and manifestation not of a timeless linguistic system, but of particular social conditions, class structures, and power relationships that alter drastically in the course of history. In Michel Foucault, discourse-as-such is the central subject of analytic concern. Foucault conceives that "discourse" is to be analyzed as totally anonymous, in that it is simply "situated at the level of the 'it is said' (*on dit*)." (*The Archaeology of Knowledge*, 1972, pp. 55, 122.) For example, *new historicists* (for whom, in this respect, Foucault serves as a model) may attend to all Renaissance references to usury as part of an anonymous "discourse," which circulates through legal, religious, philosophical, and economic writings of the era; it circulates also through those literary writings, such as Shakespeare's sonnets or *The Merchant of Venice*, in which usury is alluded to, whether literally or figuratively. Any allusion to usury is conceived to be better understood if it is referred to the total body of

这些能指意义的表面确定性和对文本外部世界的表面所指,都是相互冲突的内在力量的差异游戏所产生的"效果",在更仔细的分析下,其结果是将文本解构成无法确定、支离破碎的对立意义。在罗兰·巴尔特看来,作者的"死亡"使读者能以他或她选择的任何方式自由地进入文学文本,文本所产生的愉悦强度与读者抛弃指代可能性限制的程度成比例。斯坦利·费什的*读者反应批评*观点认为,似乎是在文本中发现的所有意义与形式特征,都由每位读者个人投射到印刷符号中。两个个体对意义的一致看法取决于他们是否碰巧属于同一个"解释群体"。

4. **话语概念**。文学批评家长期以来都在随意使用"话语"这一术语,尤其是用它来指代文学作品中表现人物对话的篇章;1970年代形成了一种主要研究对话交谈的*话语分析*批评实践。这种批评类型(以及米哈伊尔·巴赫金创立的*对话批评*)认为文学话语是人物角色——其言念进行了信念、态度、情感及其他意识状态表达的动态交流——的行为。

在后结构主义批评中,**话语**成了一个十分显著的术语。它对"文本"作为文学批评主要关注的言辞材料的名称作了补充说明(有时则取而代之)。但后结构主义并没有将这一术语局限于会话篇章,而是像"书写"一样,用该词来指代所有的文字建构,暗示了文学意义模式与非文学意义模式之间界限的表面性。最显著的是,解构主义观点认为,"一般文本"的功能不依赖于特定的历史条件,而话语则成了反对这种观点的批评家们特别关注的术语。这些批评家们将话语视为一种社会说法或用语,它并非是永恒的语言系统的产物和表现,而是随着历史进程而急剧改变的特定的社会条件、阶级结构及权力关系的产物与表现。在米歇尔·福柯看来,这种话语是分析关注的中心主体。福柯认为应该将"话语"分析为来源完全不明的东西,因为它只是"位于'据说'这一层次上"[《语言考古学》(1972)第55、122页]。例如,*新历史主义*批评家(对他们来说,福柯在这方面是个典范)可能会将文艺复兴时期的所有参考资料都视为来源不明的"话语"带来的部分好处。这种话语通过这一时期的法律、宗教、哲学与经济作品得以传播,它也通过文学作品进行传播,如莎士比亚的十四行诗或《威尼斯商人》。这些作品间接提到了这种好处,不论是字面上的还是比喻的。如果对这种好处的暗示指

discourse on that topic, as well as to the social forces and institutions that have produced the conception of usury at that time and in that place.

5. Many socially oriented analysts of discourse share with other poststructuralists the conviction (or at any rate the strong suspicion) that no text means what it seems to say, or what its writer intended to say. But whereas deconstructive critics attribute the subversion of the apparent meaning to the unstable and self-conflicting nature of language itself, social analysts of discourse—and also *psychoanalytic critics*—view the surface, or "manifest" meanings of a text as a disguise, or substitution, for underlying meanings which cannot be overtly said, because they are suppressed by psychic, or ideological, or discursive necessities. By some critics, the covert meanings are regarded as having been suppressed by all three of these forces together. Both the social and psychoanalytic critics of discourse therefore interpret the manifest meanings of a text as a distortion, displacement, or total "occlusion" of its real meanings; and these real meanings, in accordance with a particular critic's theoretical orientation, turn out to be either the writer's psychic and psycholinguistic compulsions, or the material realities of history, or the social power structures of domination, subordination, and marginalization that obtained when the text was written. The widespread poststructural view that the surface or overt meanings of a literary or other text serve as a "disguise" or "mask" of its real meanings, or **subtext**, has been called, in a phrase taken from the French philosopher of language Paul Ricoeur, a **hermeneutics of suspicion**.

6. Many poststructural theorists propose or assume an extreme form of both cognitive and evaluative **relativism.** The claim is that, in the absence of an absolute and atemporal standard or foundation or center, all asserted truths and values and cultural norms are relative to the predominant culture at a given time and place; or else to the *ideology* of a particular economic, social, ethnic, or interpretive class; or else to the subjective conditions of a particular individual or type of individuals. A general relativism is affirmed even by some theorists who are also political activists, and advocate (by explicit or implicit appeal to social justice as a fundamental and universal value) emancipation and equality for sexual, racial, ethnic, or other oppressed, marginalized, or excluded minorities.

The primacy of "theory" in poststructural criticism has evoked countertheoretical challenges, most prominently in an essay "Against Theory" by Steven Knapp and Walter Benn Michaels (1982). Defining theory (in consonance with the widespread poststructural use of the term) as "the attempt to govern interpretations of particular texts by appealing to an account of interpretation in general," the two authors claim that this is an impossible endeavor "to stand outside practice in order to govern practice from without," assert that accounts of interpretation in general entail no consequences for the actual practice of interpretation, and conclude that all theory "should therefore come to an end." Such a conclusion is supported by a number of writers, including Stanley Fish and the influential philosophical pragmatist

的是该话题的整体话语，指的是当时当地产生这种好处概念的社会力量与制度，这种暗示就能被更好地理解。

5. 与后结构主义批评家一样，许多具有社会化倾向的话语分析家坚信（或强烈怀疑）没有文本能够表达出它似乎想要表达的意思，或它的作者想要表达的意思。但解构主义批评家将表面意义的颠覆归因于语言自身不稳定、自我冲突的本质，而社会话语分析家——及精神分析批评家——则认为，文本的表面或"显而易见的"意义掩盖或替代了潜在的意义。这些潜在的意义不可能公开地表达，因为它们受到精神或意识形态或推理需要的压制。有些批评家认为，隐藏的意义受到了这三种力量的共同压制。因此，话语的社会批评家及精神分析批评家都将文本显而易见的意义阐释为对其真实意义的歪曲、取代或完全的"阻挡"。这些真实意义，根据批评家的理论取向，应该是作者的精神冲动和心理-语言冲动，或是历史的物质现实，或是文本创作时期所包含的支配、从属、边缘化的社会权力结构。后结构主义广泛认为，文学或其他文本的表面或显而易见的意义是真实意义的"掩饰"或"面具"，或**次文本**，用法国语言哲学家保罗·利科的话来说，可以称为**怀疑阐释学**。

6. 许多后结构主义理论家提出或假定了一种认知和评价的极端形式：**相对主义**。这一说法是，在缺失一种绝对的和不受时间影响的标准或基础或中心的情况下，所有宣称的真理和价值观及文化模式，都与特定时间和地点的主流文化相关；或是与特定经济、社会、民族或解释（拥有解释话语权的）阶级的意识形态相关；或是与特定个体或个体类型的主体状况相关。一种宽泛的相对主义，甚至得到一些理论家的认可，这些理论家也是政治活动家，他们倡导（通过直接或间接地呼吁社会正义，将其视为一种基本的和普世的价值观）性别、种族、民族或是其他受压迫、被边缘化或被排除在外的少数民族群体的解放和平等。

后结构主义批评中的"理论"的首要地位激起了反理论的挑战。斯蒂文·纳普与沃尔特·贝恩·迈克尔斯1982年共同发表的"反理论"一文最为显著地体现了这一点。这两位作者把理论定义为（与后结构主义对理论这一术语的广泛使用相一致）"试图借助对释义的一般描述来支配对特定文本的释义"，他们认为这是一种"为了从外部支配实践而立于实践之外"的徒劳无益的努力，断言对释义的一般描述没有蕴含实际的释义实践的结果，并进而得出结论，所有的理论都"应当结束"。一些作者，如斯坦利·费什及具有影响的哲学实用主义者

Richard Rorty, who (despite disagreements in their supporting arguments) agree that no general account of interpretation entails particular consequences for the actual practice of literary interpretation and criticism. (See W. J. T. Mitchell, ed., *Against Theory: Literary Studies and the New Pragmatism*, 1985, which includes the initiating essay plus a supplementary essay by Knapp and Michaels, together with essays and critiques by Fish, Rorty, E. D. Hirsch, and others.) The French philosopher Jean-François Lyotard has also mounted an influential attack against "theory," which he regards as an attempt to impose a common vocabulary and set of principles in order illegitimately to control and constrain the many independent "language-games" that constitute discourse; see his *The Postmodern Condition* (1984). One response to this skepticism about the efficacy of theory on practice (a skepticism that is often labeled the **new pragmatism**) is that, while no general theory of meaning entails consequences for the practice of interpretation (in the strict logical sense of "entails"), it is a matter of common observation that diverse current theories have in actual fact served both to foster and to corroborate diverse and novel interpretive practices by literary critics. For a view of both the inescapability and practical functioning of literary and artistic theory in traditional criticism, see M. H. Abrams, "What's the Use of Theorizing about the Arts?" (1972, reprinted in *Doing Things with Texts*, 1989).

Jonathan Culler's *Literary Theory: A Very Short Introduction* (1997) analyzes the issues and debates that cut across the boundaries of diverse poststructural theories. See also Richard Harland, *Superstructuralism: The Philosophy of Structuralism and Post-Structuralism* (1987); Anthony Easthope, *British Poststructuralism since 1968* (1988). Anthologies that include important poststructural essays and selections: David Lodge, ed., *Modern Criticism and Theory* (1988); K. M. Newton, ed., *20th-Century Literary Theory* (1988); Robert Con Davis and Ronald Schleifer, eds., *Contemporary Literary Criticism* (rev. 1989). The most inclusive collection, with extensive bibliographies, is Vincent Leitch, ed., *The Norton Anthology of Theory and Criticism* (2001). For discussions and critiques of poststructuralist theories and practices from diverse points of view: Fredric Jameson, *Poststructuralism; or The Cultural Logic of Late Capitalism* (1991); John McGowan, *Postmodernism and Its Critics* (1991); Jonathan Arac and Barbara Johnson, eds., *Consequences of Theory* (1991); Dwight Eddin, ed., *The Emperor Redressed: Critiquing Critical Theory* (1995); James Battersby, *Reason and the Nature of Texts* (1996); Wendell V. Harris, ed., *Beyond Structuralism* (1996); Daphne Patai and Will H. Corral, eds., *Theory's Empire: An Anthology of Dissent* (2005).

For references to *poststructuralism* in other entries, see pages 74, 87.

practical criticism: 68.

pragmatic criticism: 69; *344*.

Prague Linguistic Circle: 139.

理查德·罗蒂，都赞同这样的结论。这些作者一致认为（尽管他们支持的论点有所不同），对释义的一般描述并没有包含实际的文学释义与批评实践的特殊结果。[参阅：W. J. T. 米切尔主编的《反理论：文学研究与新实用主义》（1985），该书收录了纳普与迈克尔斯最初的论文及增补论文，以及费什、罗蒂、E. D. 赫兹和其他人的论文与评论文章。] 法国哲学家让－弗朗索瓦·利奥塔也对"理论"发起了颇具影响的抨击。他认为，"理论"试图强行建立通用的词汇和一组准则，以非法控制和限制构成话语的许多独立的"语言游戏"；参阅其所著的《后现代条件》（1984）。对理论对于实践功效的怀疑（这种怀疑通常被称为**新实用主义**）作出的一种反应是，一般的意义理论没有蕴含释义实践的结果（从"蕴含"一词严格的逻辑意义上说），但显然，当代的各种理论实际上都有助于鼓励、支持文学批评家各不相同而新颖的释义实践。有关传统批评中文学与艺术理论的不可避免性及其实际功能，可以参阅：M. H. 艾布拉姆斯所写的文章"艺术的理论化有何用处？"（1972），重印收入其所著的《以文行事》（1989）。

乔纳森·卡勒所著的《文学理论简介》（1997），分析了跨越当前各种理论界限且反复出现的议题与争论。也可参阅：理查德·哈兰所著的《超结构主义：结构主义和后结构主义哲学》（1987）；安东尼·伊斯特霍普所著的《1968年以来英国的结构主义》（1988）。关于后结构主义的重要论文集及作品选集，可以参阅：戴维·洛奇主编的《现代批评与理论》（1988）；K. M. 牛顿主编的《20世纪文学理论》（1988）；罗伯特·康·戴维斯与罗纳德·施莱弗合编的《当代文学批评》（1989年修订版）。包罗最广并有大量参考书目的合集是文森特·利奇主编的《诺顿理论与批评文选》（2001）。从各种角度讨论、评论后结构主义理论与实践的著作包括：弗雷德里克·詹姆逊所著的《后结构主义；或晚期资本主义的文化逻辑》（1991）；约翰·麦高恩所著的《后现代主义及其批评家》（1991）；乔纳森·阿拉克与芭芭拉·约翰逊合编的《理论的后果》（1991）；德怀特·埃丁主编的《重新穿上衣服的皇帝：对批评理论的批判》（1995）；詹姆斯·巴特斯比所著的《理性与文本的本质》（1996）；温德尔·V. 哈里斯主编的《超越结构主义》（1996）；达芙妮·帕泰与威尔·H. 克拉尔合编的《理论帝国：不同观点选集》（2005）。

其他条目中提及"后结构主义"的地方，参见第74、87页。

practical criticism：实用批评　　68。

pragmatic criticism：实用主义批评　　69；*344*。

Prague Linguistic Circle：布拉格语言学学会　　139。

Pre-Raphaelites: In 1848 a group of English artists, including Dante Gabriel Rossetti, William Holman Hunt, and John Millais, organized the "Pre-Raphaelite Brotherhood." Their aim was to replace the reigning academic style of painting by a return to the truthfulness, simplicity, and spirit of devotion which they attributed to Italian painting before the time of Raphael (1483–1520) and the other painters of the high Italian *Renaissance*. The ideals of this group of painters were taken over by a literary movement which included Dante Gabriel Rossetti himself (who was a poet as well as a painter), his sister Christina Rossetti, William Morris, and Algernon Swinburne. Dante Gabriel Rossetti's poem "The Blessed Damozel" typifies the medievalism, the pictorial realism with symbolic overtones, and the union of flesh and spirit, sensuousness and religiousness, associated with the earlier writings of this school. Other examples are Christina Rossetti's remarkable poem "Goblin Market" (1862) and William Morris' narrative in verse *The Earthly Paradise* (1868–70). See Graham Hough, *The Last Romantics* (1949); T. J. Barringer, *Reading the Pre-Raphaelites* (1999); Jan Marsh and Pamela Gerrish Nun, *Pre-Raphaelite Women Artists* (1999); Christopher Wood, *The Pre-Raphaelites* (2d ed., 2001); Elizabeth Helsinger, *Poetry and the Pre-Raphaelite Arts: William Morris and Dante Gabriel Rossetti* (2007).

presence (in deconstruction): 77.

primitivism and progress: A **primitivist** is someone who prefers what is "natural" (in the sense of that which exists prior to or independently of human culture, reasoning, and contrivance) to what is "artificial" (in the sense of what human beings achieve by thought, activities, laws and conventions, and the complex arrangements of a civilized society). A useful, although not mutually exclusive, distinction has been made between two manifestations of primitivism:

1. **Cultural primitivism** is the preference for what is conceived to be "nature" and "the natural" over "art" and "the artificial" in any area of human culture and values. As the intellectual historian A. O. Lovejoy has neatly summarized it, the "natural" is "a thing you reach by going back and leaving out." For example, in ethics a cultural primitivist lauds the natural (that is, the innate) instincts and passions over the dictates of reason and prudential forethought. In social philosophy, the ideal is the simple and natural forms of social and political order in place of the anxieties and frustrations engendered by a complex and highly developed social organization. In milieu, a primitivist prefers outdoor "nature," unmodified by human intervention, to cities or artful gardens. And in literature and the other arts, the primitivist lauds spontaneity, the free expression of emotion, and the intuitive productions of "natural genius," as against a calculated adaptation of artistic means to foreseen ends and a conformity to "artificial" forms, rules, and conventions. Typically, the cultural primitivist asserts that in the modern world, the life, activities, and products of "primitive" people—who are considered to live in a way more accordant

Pre-Raphaelites：前拉斐尔派画家和诗人

1848年，一群英国艺术家，包括但丁·加布里埃尔·罗塞蒂、威廉·霍曼·亨特和约翰·密莱司，组成了"前拉斐尔派兄弟会"。他们的目标是回归拉斐尔（1483—1520）及意大利文艺复兴全盛时期其他画家之前意大利绘画所具有的真实、简朴和对艺术的奉献精神，以此取代当时占据统治地位的学院派绘画风格。随后，但丁·加布里埃尔·罗塞蒂（他本人既是画家又是诗人）、罗塞蒂的妹妹克里斯蒂娜·罗塞蒂、威廉·莫里斯和阿尔杰农·斯温伯恩等人接受了这群画家的理想，将其发展成为一场文学运动。罗塞蒂的诗歌《天女》突出表现了该学派早期作品的特征：中世纪信仰，生动的写实中暗含象征，并体现了肉体与灵魂、世俗与宗教的结合。其他例子有克里斯蒂娜·罗塞蒂的名诗《精灵集市》（1862）和威廉·莫里斯的叙事诗歌《人间天堂》（1868—1870）。参阅：格雷厄姆·霍夫所著的《最后的浪漫主义者》（1949）；T. J. 巴林杰所著的《阅读前拉斐尔派画家》（1999）；简·马什与帕梅拉·格里什·努恩合著的《前拉斐尔派女性艺术家》（1999）；克里斯托弗·伍德所著的《前拉斐尔派画家和诗人》（2001年第2版）；伊丽莎白·赫尔辛格所著的《诗歌与前拉斐尔派艺术：威廉·莫里斯和但丁·加布里埃尔·罗塞蒂》（2007）。

presence (in deconstruction)：(解构主义中的) 在场　77。

Primitivism and Progress：尚古主义与进步论

　　尚古主义者是指那些与"人为"事物（人类依据思想、行为、法律、惯例和文明社会复杂的制度安排所获得的事物）相比更喜欢"自然"事物（独立存在于人类文化、推理与谋划之外或之前的事物）的人。下面是对两种尚古主义表现形式实用但并不相互排斥的区分：

1. **文化尚古主义**是指在任何人类文化和价值领域里，都偏爱"自然"或"自然事物"，而非"艺术"或"人为事物"。文化史学家A. O. 洛夫乔伊将"自然事物"精辟地概括为"回到过去、遗留在露天而获得的东西"。例如，在伦理学上，文化尚古主义者崇尚自然的（即天生的）本能和激情，而不赞成受理性与谨慎的三思而后行的支配。在社会哲学上，其理想是简单自然的社会政治秩序，而不是高度发展的复杂社会结构所引起的焦虑和沮丧。在环境方面，尚古主义者更倾向于人类尚未涉足、未经修饰的户外"自然"，而不是城市或人工花园。在文学和其他艺术上，尚古主义者赞美自发性、情绪的自由表露以及"自然天赋"的本能产物，反对为达到预期效果而精心改编的艺术手段，反对遵循"人为的"形式、规则与惯例。典型的文化尚古主义者宣称，在现代世界中，"原始"人类——由于远离文明，因此他们的生活方式与"自然"更加和谐——的生活、活动和

to "nature" because they are isolated from civilization—are at least in some ways preferable to the life, activities, and products of people living in a highly developed society, especially in cities. The eighteenth-century cult of the **Noble Savage**—who was conceived to be "naturally" intelligent, moral, and possessed of high dignity in thought and deed—and the concurrent vogue of "natural" poetry written by supposedly uneducated peasants or working folk, were both aspects of primitivism. Cultural primitivism has played an especially prominent and persistent role in American thought and literature, where the "new world" was early conceived in terms of both the classical *golden age* of the distant past and the Christian millennium of the future. The American Indian was sometimes identified with the legendary Noble Savage, and the American pioneer was often represented as a new Adam who had cut free from the artifice and corruptions of European civilization in order to reassume a "natural" life of freedom, innocence, and simplicity. See Henry Nash Smith, *Virgin Land* (1950), and R. W. B. Lewis, *The American Adam* (1955).

2. **Chronological primitivism** designates the belief that the ideal era of humanity's way of life lay in the very distant past, when men and women lived naturally, simply, and freely, and that the process of history has been a gradual "decline" from that happy stage into an increasing degree of artifice, complexity, inhibitions, prohibitions, and consequent anxieties and discontents in the psychological, social, and cultural realms. In its extreme form, the ideal era is postulated as having existed in "the state of nature," before social organization and civilization had even begun; more commonly, it is placed at some later stage of development, and sometimes as late as the era of classical Greece. Many, but not all, cultural primitivists are also chronological primitivists.

A historical concept that is antithetic to chronological primitivism emerged in the seventeenth century and reached its height in the nineteenth century. This is the idea of **progress**: the doctrine that—by virtue of the development and exploitation of art, science, and technology, and by the application of human rationality—the course of history represents an overall improvement in the life, morality, and happiness of human beings from early barbarity to the present stage of civilization. Sometimes it is also claimed that this historical progress of humanity will continue indefinitely, possibly to end in a final stage of social, rational, and moral perfection. (See *Enlightenment* and *utopia*.)

Primitivism is as old as humanity's recorded intellection and imaginings, and is reflected in myths of a vanished age of gold and a lost Garden of Eden. It achieved a special vogue, however, in the eighteenth century, by way of reaction to the prevailing stress on artfulness and the refinements of civilization during the *Neoclassic Period*, in a European movement in which Jean-Jacques Rousseau (1712–78) was a central figure. D. H. Lawrence (1885–1930) is a later example of a broadly primitivistic thinker, in his laudation of the spontaneous instinctual life, his belief in an ancient, vanished condition of humanity's personal and social wholeness, his high regard for "primitive"

产品至少在某些方面，要比居住在高度发达的社会，尤其是城市中人们的生活、活动和产品更加可取。18世纪对**高贵的野蛮人**——这些人"天生"聪明睿智、品德高尚，具有高雅、尊严的思想与行为——的狂热崇尚，及同时流行的对未受教育的农民或劳动者所创作的"自然"诗歌的崇尚，是尚古主义表现的两个方面。文化尚古主义者在美国的思想和文学中发挥了特别显著、持续的作用。尚古主义早期认为"新世界"既是遥远过去的经典黄金时代，又是未来基督教千禧年的经典黄金时代。美国的印第安人有时被当做传说中的高贵的野蛮人；美国的拓荒者常被视为新亚当，他们从欧洲文明的尔虞我诈和腐败堕落中挣脱出来，为的是重新获得一种自由、单纯、简朴的"自然"生活。参阅：亨利·纳什·史密斯所著的《处女地》(1950)和R. W. B.刘易斯所著的《美国式亚当》(1955)。

2. **年代尚古主义**相信，人类生活方式的理想阶段出现在非常遥远的过去，那时男人与女人自然、简朴、自由地生活。年代尚古主义还相信，历史的进程逐渐从幸福阶段"衰落"到心理、社会与文化秩序中与日俱增的虚伪、复杂、压制、禁止以及随之而来的焦虑与不满。就其极端形式而言，他们假定这个理想的时代存在于社会组织和文明出现之前的"自然状态"中。他们更常将这一理想时代定位于稍后的发展阶段——有时被推后到古希腊时期。许多文化尚古主义者，但并非全部，也是年代尚古主义者。

  17世纪出现了一种与年代尚古主义相对立的历史观念，并在19世纪达到了顶峰。这就是**进步论**。进步论认为，历史进程表明，由于对艺术、科学、技术与人类理性的发展和利用，人类的生活、道德与幸福方面呈现出全面进步，从早期的野蛮状态发展到现在的文明阶段。进步论有时也宣称，这种人类的历史进步将会永无止境地继续下去——最终可能达到社会、理性与道德的完美阶段。(参见：启蒙运动、乌托邦。)

  尚古主义和人类有史记载的思想与想象一样历史悠久，并在消逝了的黄金时代和失去了的伊甸园等神话中得到反映。不过，18世纪欧洲的一场文学运动使得尚古主义风行一时。这场运动以让-雅克·卢梭(1712—1778)为中心人物，反对*新古典主义时期*对非自然的艺术性和文明的各种教养的普遍推崇。D. H.劳伦斯(1885—1930)是后来的一位毫无拘束的、典型的尚古主义思想家。他赞美自发本能的生活，相信远古曾经有过一种已经消失了的人类自身与社会完整统一的状态；

modes of life that still survive outside the bounds of sophisticated societies, and his attacks on the disintegrative effects of modern science and technology and on the economy and culture that science and technology have generated. There are also strains of cultural primitivism in, for example, James Fenimore Cooper's *Leather-Stocking Tales*, in Mark Twain's *Huckleberry Finn*, and in the outlook and lifestyle of dropouts and various kinds of subcultures in our own time, as well as in the establishment of communes whose ideal is a radically simplified individual and social life close to the soil. (Refer to *ecocriticism*.) But most men and women, and many writers of literature, are primitivists in some moods, longing to escape from the complexities, fever, anxieties, and "alienation" of modern civilization into what are taken to be the elemental simplicities of a lost natural life. That imagined life may be identified with the individual's own childhood, or with the prehistoric or classical or medieval past, or may be conceived as existing still in some primitive, carefree, faraway place on earth.

See H. N. Fairchild, *The Noble Savage* (1928); J. B. Bury, *The Idea of Progress* (1932); Lois Whitney, *Primitivism and the Idea of Progress* (1934); A. O. Lovejoy and George Boas, *Primitivism and Related Ideas in Antiquity* (1948); A. O. Lovejoy, *Essays in the History of Ideas* (1948); Clifford Geertz, *Local Knowledge* (1983). Marianna Torgovnick's *Gone Primitive: Savage Intellects, Modern Lives* (1990) argues that modern Western culture has been formed in dialectical opposition to presumably nonmodern or premodern cultures. Friedrich Nietzsche's *The Genealogy of Morals* (1887) and Sigmund Freud's *Civilization and Its Discontents* (1949; see *psychoanalysis*) involve aspects of cultural primitivism, in their stress on the compelling needs of the body and of the natural human instincts, especially sexuality, which require a complex and perhaps impossible reconciliation with the repressions and inhibitions that are inescapable in a civilized society. A work of radical cultural primitivism that was influential on the rebellious youth movements of the 1960s and 1970s is Norman O. Brown's *Life against Death* (1959); refer to *Beat writers*, and to the *contemporary period*, under *periods of American literature*.

printing: 339.

problem play: A type of drama that was popularized by the Norwegian playwright Henrik Ibsen. In problem plays, the situation faced by the protagonist is put forward by the author as a representative instance of a contemporary social problem; often the dramatist manages—by the use of a character who speaks for the author, or by the evolution of the plot, or both—to propose a solution to the problem which is at odds with prevailing opinion. The issue may be the inadequate autonomy, scope, and dignity allotted to women in the middle-class nineteenth-century family (Ibsen's *A Doll's House*, 1879); or the morality of prostitution, regarded as a typical product of the economic system in a capitalist society (George Bernard Shaw's *Mrs. Warren's Profession*, 1898); or the crisis in racial and ethnic relations in present-day America (in numerous current dramas and films). Compare *social novel*.

他极为钟情于仍然幸存于世故的社会限制范围之外的"原始"生活方式,抨击现代科技所造成的分崩离析以及现代科技发展所产生的经济和文化。詹姆斯·费尼莫尔·费珀的《皮袜子的故事》,马克·吐温的《哈克贝利·芬历险记》,我们当代的逃避现实者、"嬉皮士"与相关的亚文化的世界观和生活方式,以及为实现极其简朴的个人和社会生活、接近土地的理想而建立的公社,都带有尚古主义的特征。(参阅:*生态批评*。)不过,多数人和许多文学家只有在某些情绪下才是尚古主义者:他们渴望逃脱现代文明的错综复杂、狂热、焦虑和"异化",向往已经遗失的自然生活所固有的简朴。这种想象中的生活可以设想是个人的孩提时代,或者是史前的岁月、古代或中世纪,也可以设想仍存在于地球上某个原始、无忧无虑和遥远的地方。

参阅:H. N. 费尔柴尔德所著的《高贵的野蛮人》(1928);J. B. 伯里所著的《进步的观念》(1932);洛伊斯·惠特尼所著的《尚古主义与进步的观念》(1934);A. O. 洛夫乔伊与乔治·博厄斯合著的《古代的尚古主义及相关诸观念》(1948);A. O. 洛夫乔伊所著的《观念史散论》(1948);克利福德·格尔茨所著的《地方性知识》(1983)。弗里德里希·尼采所著的《道德的谱系》(1887)与西格蒙德·弗洛伊德所著的《文明与它的不满》(1949;参见:*精神分析*)涉及了文化尚古主义的诸多方面。他们强调肉体及自然的人类本能,尤其是性本能的强制性需求。这些需求必须与文明社会中不可逃避的抑制和压制形成复杂的,也许是不可能实现的调和。诺曼·O. 布朗所著的《生与死》(1959)是一部激进的文化尚古主义作品,对1960、1970年代青年的反抗运动颇具影响。参见:*垮掉派作家、美国文学各时期的划分中的当代时期*。

printing:印刷术 339。

Problem Play:问题剧

一种经挪威剧作家亨里克·易卜生之手而深受欢迎的戏剧类型。在问题剧里,作者将主人公面临的处境展示为代表当时社会问题的缩影;剧作家往往通过剧中代表作者发言的人物,或情节的展开,或两者兼用,从而提出一种与盛行的舆论相悖的解决问题的方法。问题可能是19世纪中产阶级家庭中女性享有的自主权、活动范围和尊严极为不够[亨里克·易卜生的《玩偶之家》(1879)];也可能是被视为资本主义社会中经济制度的典型产物——卖淫——的道德问题[乔治·萧伯纳的《华伦夫人的职业》(1898)];或者是当今美国种族关系和民族关系中存在的危机(当代许多戏剧和电影都表现了这一问题)。对比:*社会小说*。

A subtype of the modern problem play is the **discussion play**, in which the social issue is not incorporated into a plot but expounded in the give-and-take of a sustained debate among the characters. See Shaw's *Getting Married*, and Act III of his *Man and Superman*; also his book on Ibsen's plays, *The Quintessence of Ibsenism* (1891).

In a specialized application, the term **problem plays** is sometimes applied to a group of Shakespeare's plays, also called "bitter comedies"—especially *Troilus and Cressida*, *Measure for Measure*, and *All's Well That Ends Well*—which explore ignoble aspects of human nature, and in which the resolution of the plot seems to some readers to be problematic, in that it does not settle or solve, except superficially, the moral problems raised in the play. By extension, the term came to be applied also to other Shakespearean plays which explore the dark side of human nature, or which seem to leave unresolved the issues that arise in the course of the action. See A. P. Rossiter, "The Problem Plays," in *Shakespeare: Modern Essays in Criticism*, ed. Leonard F. Dean (rev. 1967).

progress, idea of: 316.

proletarian novel: 256.

propagandist literature: 89.

properties (stage): 364.

proscenium arch (prōsēn' ēŭm): **3**; *64*.

prose: Prose is an inclusive term for all discourse, spoken or written, which is not patterned into the lines either of metric verse or of free verse. (See *meter*.) It is possible to discriminate a great variety of nonmetric types of discourse, which can be placed along a spectrum according to the degree to which they exploit, and make prominent, modes of formal organization. At one end is the irregular, and only occasionally formal, prose of ordinary conversation. Distinguished written discourse, in what John Dryden called "that other harmony of prose," is no less an art than distinguished verse; in all literatures, in fact, artfully written prose seems to have developed later than written verse. As written prose gets more "literary"—whether its function is descriptive, expository, narrative, or expressive—it exhibits more patent, though highly diverse, modes of rhythm and other formal features. The prose translations of the poetic books of the Old Testament in the King James Bible, for example, have a repetition, balance, and contrast of clauses which approximate the form that in the nineteenth century was named "the prose poem." **Prose poems** are compact, rhythmic, and usually sonorous compositions which exploit the poetic resources of language for poetic ends, but are written as a continuous sequence of sentences without line breaks. Early examples of prose poems are, in French, Charles Baudelaire's *Little Poems in Prose* (1869) and

讨论剧是现代问题剧的一种类型。在讨论剧里，社会问题并不融入情节，而是通过角色之间持续辩论中的意见交流加以阐述。参阅：萧伯纳的《结婚》和《人与超人》的第三幕，以及他评论易卜生戏剧的著作《易卜生主义的精华》（1891）。

问题剧有时特指莎士比亚的一些戏剧，也叫"痛苦喜剧"——尤其是《特洛伊罗斯与克瑞西达》《一报还一报》《终成眷属》——这类戏剧探讨人类本性中可耻的各个方面。剧中情节的结局对许多观众来说似乎难以琢磨，因为它除了表面上的解决，实际上并没有处理或解决剧中提出的道德问题。广义而言，这个术语也可用来指代莎士比亚创作的其他探讨人类本性黑暗面的剧作，或是行为发展过程中出现的问题悬而未决的莎翁戏剧。参阅：A. P. 罗西特所写的文章"问题剧"，收入伦纳德·F. 迪安主编的《莎士比亚：现代批评文集》（1967年修订版）。

progress, idea of：进步论 316。

proletarian novel：无产阶级小说 256。

propagandist literature：宣教文学 89。

properties (stage)：(舞台)道具 364。

proscenium arch：拱形舞台 3；*64*。

Prose：散文

这一包容性术语指代所有口头的或书面的话语，这些话语没有形成诗韵行或自由诗行模式。（参见：*格律*。）我们有可能区分出许多各式各样非韵律的话语类型，并可根据这些语言对形式组织模式的使用程度和突出程度，将它们按某种范畴排列。该范畴的一端是无规则的、偶尔是正式的日常话语散文。优美的书面话语同优美的韵文一样也是一门艺术，正如约翰·德莱顿所说的"散文的另一种和谐"；事实上，在所有文学形式中，艺术性的书面散文似乎比书面韵文发展得更晚。当书面散文越来越富有"文学"味时——无论其功能是描绘、说明、叙述或表现性的——它都会显示出更加独特但迥然不同的节奏模式和其他形式特征。譬如，钦定本圣经对《旧约》中的诗篇进行的散文体翻译，就采用了重复、均衡和对比句的表现形式，从而使译文的形式近似于19世纪出现的一种被称为"散文诗"的形式。**散文诗**结构紧凑，富有节奏感，通常铿锵有力，借用语言的诗意资源达到诗意收尾的目的，诗中往往包含一连串的句子，但各行之间没有停顿。早期的散文诗包括法国查尔斯·波德莱尔的《散文小诗》（1869）与

Arthur Rimbaud's *Illuminations* (1886), and in English, excerptible passages in Walter Pater's prose essays, such as his famous meditation on Leonardo da Vinci's painting the *Mona Lisa*, in *The Renaissance* (1873). John Ashbery's *Three Poems* (1972) are prose poems, in that they are printed continuously, without broken lines. Farther still along the formal spectrum, we leave the domain of prose, by the use of line breaks and the controlled rhythms, pauses, syntactical suspensions, and cadences that identify *free verse*. At the far end of the spectrum we get the regular, recurrent units of weaker and stronger stressed syllables that constitute the meters of English verse.

See *style* (including the list of readings), and for a special form of elaborately formal prose, *euphuism*. Refer to George Saintsbury, *A History of English Prose Rhythm* (1912); George L. Trager and Henry Lee Smith, Jr., *An Outline of English Structure* (1951); Robert Adolphe, *The Rise of Modern Prose Style* (1968). E. D. Hirsch discusses the development of English prose in *The Philosophy of Composition* (1977), pp. 51–72. See also Richard A. Lanham, *Analyzing Prose* (2d ed., 2003). On the prose poem, refer to Jonathan Monroe, *A Poverty of Objects: The Prose Poem and the Politics of Genre* (1987); and David Lehman, ed., *Great American Prose Poems: From Poe to the Present* (2003). For forms of literature written in prose, see the references under *genre*.

prose poem: 318.

prose romance: 254; *54*.

prosody: Prosody signifies the systematic study of **versification** in poetry; that is, the principles and practice of *meter*, *rhyme*, and *stanza* forms. Sometimes the term "prosody" is extended to include also the study of speech-sound patterns and effects such as *alliteration*, *assonance*, *euphony*, and *onomatopoeia*.

prosopopoeia (prŏsō′ pŏpē″ a): 132.

prospect poem: 406.

protagonist: 294; *254, 301*.

proverbs: 10.

pseudostatements: 128.

psychoanalytic criticism: 320; *311, 313*.

psychobiography: 322.

psychological and psychoanalytic criticism: **Psychological** criticism deals with a work of literature primarily as an expression, in an indirect and fictional form, of the state of mind and the structure of personality of the individual

阿尔蒂尔·兰波的《灵光篇》(1886)，英国沃尔特·佩特的散文随笔中一些可摘录的段落，如在《文艺复兴史研究》(1873)这部论著中，他对列奥纳多·达芬奇的油画《蒙娜丽莎》进行思索的著名篇章。约翰·亚斯比利的《三首诗》(1972)也是散文诗，因为在它们的印刷体中行与行之间没有停顿，而是一直继续下去。在散文的形式范畴上走得更远的是自由诗。自由诗采用诗行间的停顿，而且诗中的节奏、停顿、句法中止与节拍都有所约束。形式范畴的另一个极端是英语格律诗。英语格律诗的韵律由富有规律且反复出现的轻重音节单位构成。

参见：*文体*（包括参考书目）。形式精巧的特殊散文类型，参见：*尤弗伊斯体*。参阅：乔治·圣茨伯里所著的《英国散文韵律史》(1912)；乔治·L.特拉格与小亨利·李·史密斯合著的《英语结构纲要》(1951)；罗伯特·阿道夫所著的《现代散文风格的兴起》(1968)。E. D. 赫兹在其所著的《写作的哲理》(1977)第 51—72 页中讨论了英语散文的发展。也可参阅：理查德·A. 拉纳姆所著的《散文诗分析》(2003 年第 2 版)。有关散文诗的讨论，参阅：乔纳森·门罗所著的《客体的匮乏：散文诗与体裁策略》(1987)；戴维·莱曼主编的《伟大的美国散文诗篇：从坡到当下》(2003)。关于用散文写成的各种文学类型，参见*文类*中的参考书目。

prose poem：散文诗　**318**。

prose romance：散文体传奇　**254**；*54*。

Prosody：韵律学

指对诗歌**韵律**的系统研究，即对格律、押韵和诗节的形式原理及其运用的研究。这一术语有时也包括对*头韵*、*半谐音*、*谐音*、*拟声词*等语音模式及其效果的研究。

prosopopoeia：拟人　**132**。

prospect poem：展望诗　**406**。

protagonist：主人公　**294**；*254, 301*。

proverbs：谚语　**10**。

pseudostatements：模拟描述　**128**。

psychoanalytic criticism：精神分析批评　**320**；*311, 313*。

psychobiography：心理传记　**322**。

Psychological and Psychoanalytic Criticism：心理学与精神分析批评

心理学批评主要论述文学作品以间接和虚构的形式表现了作者个人的心理

author. This approach emerged in the early decades of the nineteenth century, as part of the romantic replacement of earlier mimetic and pragmatic views by an *expressive* view of the nature of literature; see *criticism*. By 1827 Thomas Carlyle could say that the usual question "with the best of our own critics at present" is one "mainly of a psychological sort, to be answered by discovering and delineating the peculiar nature of the poet from his poetry." During the *Romantic Period*, we find widely practiced all three types of the critical procedures (still current today) that are based on the assumption that the details and form of a work of literature are correlated with its author's distinctive mental and emotional traits: (1) reference to the author's personality in order to explain and interpret a literary work; (2) reference to literary works in order to establish, biographically, the personality of the author; and (3) the mode of reading a literary work specifically in order to experience the distinctive subjectivity, or consciousness, of its author (see *critics of consciousness*). We even find that John Keble, in a series of Latin lectures *On the Healing Power of Poetry*—published in 1844, but delivered more than ten years earlier—proposed a thoroughgoing proto-Freudian literary theory. "Poetry," Keble claimed, "is the indirect expression ... of some overpowering emotion, or ruling taste, or feeling, the direct indulgence whereof is somehow repressed." This repression is imposed by the author's sentiments of "reticence" and "shame"; the conflict between the need for expression and the compulsion to repress such self-revelation is resolved by the poet's ability to give "healing relief to secret mental emotion, yet without detriment to modest reserve" by a literary "art which under certain veils and disguises ... reveals the fervent emotions of the mind." This disguised mode of self-expression, Keble also asserts, serves as "a safety valve, preserving men from madness." (The emergence and the varieties of romantic psychological criticism are described in M. H. Abrams, *The Mirror and the Lamp*, 1953, chapters 6 and 9.) In the present era many critics make at least passing references to the psychology of an author in discussing works of literature, with the notable exception of those whose critical premises invalidate such reference; mainly proponents of *formalism*, *New Criticism*, *structuralism*, and *deconstruction*.

Since the 1920s, a widespread type of psychological literary criticism has come to be **psychoanalytic criticism**, whose premises and procedures were established by Sigmund Freud (1856–1939). Freud had developed the dynamic form of psychology that he called "psychoanalysis" as a procedure for the analysis and therapy of neuroses, but soon expanded it to account for many developments and practices in the history of civilization, including warfare, mythology, and religion, as well as literature and the other arts. Freud's brief comment on the workings of the artist's imagination at the end of the twenty-third lecture of his *Introduction to Psychoanalysis* (1920), supplemented by relevant passages in the other lectures in that book, set forth the theoretical framework of what is sometimes called "classical" psychoanalytic criticism. Freud proposes that *literature* and the other arts, like dreams and neurotic symptoms, consist of the imagined, or fantasied, fulfillment of wishes that are either denied by reality or prohibited by the social standards of morality and propriety. The forbidden, mainly sexual ("libidinal") wishes come into conflict with the "censor" (the internalized representative within each individual of

状态与人格结构。这种批评方法出现于19世纪初的前几十年，作为浪漫主义的一部分，取代了早先表现主义认为文学的本质是模仿和实用的观点；参见：*文学批评*。托马斯·卡莱尔在1827年就曾说过，"我们当代最优秀的批评家"通常面临的问题"主要是心理方面的，要回答此类问题，需要从诗人的诗歌来发现并描述他独特的本质"。我们发现，浪漫主义时期广为使用的三种不同的批评方法（至今仍很流行）都是建立在这样的假设之上，即文学作品的细节和形式与作者独特的精神特征和情绪特征相联系：(1) 参照作者的个性，以此来说明和阐释文学作品；(2) 参照文学作品，从生平角度确定作者的人格；(3) 具体阅读文学作品以体验作者独特的主观性或意识的解读方式（参见：*意识批评*）。我们甚至发现，约翰·基布尔在系列拉丁文讲稿《论诗歌的治疗功能》（1844年出版，但是在十多年前演讲的）中就已提出了彻头彻尾的原始弗洛伊德文学理论。基布尔宣称，"诗歌间接地表达了……某种难以抑制的情感，或主导的品味，或感受，直接的放纵则受到了某种方式的压抑"；这种压抑是作者的"节制"与"羞愧"情感造成的；表达的需求与压抑自我表露的冲动形成了冲突，但诗人能够通过文学艺术"为隐秘的精神情绪提供有效的缓解，但又不损害谨慎的矜持"，从而解决这种冲突。文学"艺术在某种面纱和掩饰下……揭示了思想上的炽热情绪"。基布尔也强调指出，这种自我表达的掩饰模式起到了"安全阀门的作用，防止人们发疯"。[M. H. 艾布拉姆斯所著的《镜与灯》（1953）第6、9两章描述了浪漫主义心理批评的出现及其各种不同形式。]当代许多批评家在讨论文学作品时至少还会粗略地参照一下作者的心理，但也有明显的例外：一些批评学派的批评前提否认这种参照；这些学派主要有*形式主义*、*新批评*、*结构主义*、*解构主义*。

　　1920年代以来，**精神分析批评**成为一种广为流传的心理文学批评。西格蒙德·弗洛伊德（1856—1939）创立了这种批评的前提和方法。他发展了动态心理学模式，并称其为"精神分析"，作为分析和治疗神经机能病的一种手段，但他很快就将其扩展到用于描述文明史的许多发展与实践，包括战争、神话、宗教、文学及其他艺术形式。弗洛伊德在《精神分析引论》（1920）第23讲的最后部分简要地评论了艺术家想象的作用，并在该书其他讲义的相关章节中对此作了补充论述，建立了被称为"经典的"精神分析批评的理论框架。弗洛伊德提出，*文学与其他艺术形式，就像梦和神经病症一样，由想象的或幻想的愿望的实现构成*。这些愿望受到现实的否定，或遭到社会道德标准与礼节标准的禁止。遭到禁止的愿望，主要是性欲（"利比多"欲望）与"审查者"（社会道德礼教标准在个人身上的内在化代表）相冲突。

a society's standards of morality and propriety) and are repressed by the censor into the unconscious realm of the artist's mind, but are permitted to achieve a fantasied satisfaction in distorted forms that serve to disguise their real motives and objects from the conscious mind. The chief mechanisms that effect these disguises of unconscious wishes are (1) "condensation" (the omission of parts of the unconscious material and the fusion of several unconscious elements into a single entity); (2) "displacement" (the substitution for an unconscious object of desire by one that is acceptable to the conscious mind); and (3) "symbolism" (the representation of repressed, mainly sexual, objects of desire by nonsexual objects which resemble them or are associated with them in prior experience). The disguised fantasies that are available to consciousness are called by Freud the **manifest content** of a dream or work of literature; the unconscious wishes that find a semblance of satisfaction in this disguised expression he calls the **latent content**.

Also present in the unconscious of every individual, according to Freud, are residual traces of prior stages of psychosexual development, from earliest infancy onward, which have been outgrown, but remain as "fixations" in the unconscious of the adult. When triggered by some later event in adult life, a repressed wish is revived and motivates a fantasy, in disguised form, of a satisfaction that is modeled on the way that the wish had been gratified in infancy or early childhood. The chief enterprise of the psychoanalytic critic, in a way that parallels the enterprise of the psychoanalyst as a therapist, is to decipher the true content, and thereby to explain the emotional effects on the reader, of a literary work by translating its manifest elements into the latent, unconscious determinants and fixations that constitute their real but suppressed meanings.

Freud also asserts, however, that artists possess special abilities that differentiate them radically from the patently neurotic type of personality. The artistic person, for example, possesses to an especially high degree the power to **sublimate** (that is, to shift the instinctual drives from their original sexual goals to nonsexual "higher" goals, including the goal of becoming proficient as an artist); the ability to elaborate fantasied wish fulfillments into the manifest features of a work of art in a way that conceals or deletes their merely personal elements, and so makes them capable of satisfying the unconscious desires that other people share with the individual artist; and the "puzzling" ability—which Freud elsewhere says is a power of "genius" that psychoanalysis cannot explain—to mold an artistic medium into "a faithful image of the creatures of his imagination," as well as into a satisfying artistic form. The result is a fantasied wish fulfillment of a complex and artfully shaped sort that not only allows the artist to overcome, at least partially and temporarily, personal conflicts and repressions, but also makes it possible for the artist's audience "to obtain solace and consolation from their own unconscious sources of gratification which had become inaccessible" to them. Literature and art, therefore, unlike dreams and neuroses, may serve the artist as a mode of fantasy that opens "the way back to reality."

This outline of Freud's theory of art in 1920 was elaborated and refined, but not radically altered, by later developments in his theory of mental structures, dynamics, and processes. Prominent among these developments was

"审查者"将这些愿望压抑在艺术家思想的潜意识领域内，但允许这些愿望以变相的形式来实现幻想的性满足，这些变相的形式掩盖了来自意识的真正动机和对象。实现对潜意识愿望掩饰的主要机制包括：(1)"凝聚"（排除部分潜意识素材，将几种潜意识因素融合成单一实体）；(2)"移置"（用意识思想可以接受的欲望对象替代潜意识的欲望对象）；(3)"象征"（用非性欲对象表现被压抑的欲望对象，主要是性欲对象。这些非性欲对象类似于性欲对象，或在先前的经验中与之相联系）。弗洛伊德将意识能够明显感觉到的、被伪装的幻想称为梦或文学作品的**显性内容**；在变相的形式中找到类似满足感的潜意识愿望则被他称为**潜在内容**。

根据弗洛伊德的理论，每个人的潜意识中都存在心理性欲发展各个前期阶段的残留痕迹。最初的阶段始于婴儿时期。这些痕迹随着个人的成长而不再适用，但仍以"固恋"的形式存留在成人的潜意识中。当受到成人生活中某一事件的激发时，受压抑的欲望就会重新复苏，并以伪装的形式引发对欲望满足的幻想。这种满足是以婴儿时期或童年早期愿望得到满足的方式出现的。精神分析批评家的主要任务与精神分析治疗专家的任务相类似，就是将文学作品的显性因素转化为潜在的、潜意识的决定因素和情结，这些决定因素和情结构成了其受压制的意义，从而可以揭示文学作品的真正内容，并解释作品对读者造成的效果。

但是，弗洛伊德也断言说，艺术家具有特殊的能力，使他们与明显的神经病人的人格截然不同。例如，从事艺术的人都具有特别高层次的**升华**能力（即将源自于他们最初性欲目标的本能冲动转化为"更高的"非性欲目标，包括精通作为艺术家的行为准则）；并且具有将幻想的愿望实现精心制作为艺术作品的显现特征的能力。这种精心制作的方式掩盖或消除了幻想的愿望实现的个人因素，从而使其能够满足艺术家个人之外的其他人的潜意识愿望；此外，从事艺术的人还具有"令人迷惑"的能力，即弗洛伊德所说的精神分析无法解释的"天赋"能力，能将艺术素材塑造成"其想象产物的如实意象"，以及令人满意的艺术形式。其结果是一种复杂的、艺术加工而成的幻想性愿望实现，不仅能让艺术家克服——至少是部分克服或暂时克服——个人的冲突与压抑，而且使得艺术家的观众有可能"从他们自身潜意识未曾获得过的满足来源中获得慰藉"。因此，与梦和神经症不同，文学和艺术可能以幻想的形式帮助艺术家开启"返回现实的道路"。

弗洛伊德关于精神结构、精神动力及精神过程理论的后期发展，进一步阐述并完善了他在1920年提出的艺术理论框架，但并未彻底改变这一框架。这些理论最

Freud's model of the mind as having three functional aspects: the **id** (which incorporates libidinal and other innate desires), the **superego** (the internalization of social standards of morality and propriety), and the **ego** (which tries as best it can to negotiate the conflicts between the insatiable demands of the id, the impossibly stringent requirements of the superego, and the limited possibilities of gratification offered by reality). Freud has himself summarized for a general audience his later theoretical innovations, with his notable power for clear and dramatic exposition, in *New Introductory Lectures on Psychoanalysis* (1933) and *An Outline of Psychoanalysis* (1939).

Freud asserted that many of his views had been anticipated by insightful authors in Western literature, and he himself applied psychoanalysis to brief discussions of the latent content in the manifest characters or events of literary works, including Shakespeare's *Hamlet, Macbeth, A Midsummer Night's Dream,* and *King Lear*. He also wrote a brilliant analysis of Fyodor Dostoevsky's *The Brothers Karamazov* and a full-length psychoanalytic study, *Delusion and Dream* (1917), of the novel *Gradiva* by the Danish writer Wilhelm Jensen. Especially after the 1930s, a number of writers produced critical analyses, modeled on classical Freudian theory, of the lives of authors and of the content of their literary works. One of the best-known books in this mode is *Hamlet and Oedipus* (1949) by the psychoanalyst Ernest Jones. Building on earlier suggestions by Freud himself, Jones explained Hamlet's inability to make up his mind to kill his uncle by reference to his **Oedipus complex**—that is, the repressed but continuing presence in the adult's unconscious of the male infant's desire to possess his mother and to have his rival, the father, out of the way. (Freud derived the term from Sophocles' Greek tragedy *Oedipus the King*, whose protagonist has unknowingly killed his father and married his mother.) Jones proposes that Hamlet's conflict is "an echo of a similar one in Shakespeare himself," and goes on to account for the audience's powerful and continued response to the play, over many centuries, as a result of the repressed Oedipal conflict that is shared by all men.

In more recent decades there has been increasing emphasis by Freudian critics, in a mode suggested by Freud's later writings, on the role of "ego psychology" in elaborating the manifest content and artistic form of a work of literature; that is, on the way that the ego, in contriving the work, consciously manages to mediate between the conflicting demands of the id, the superego, and the limits imposed by reality. On such developments see Frederick C. Crews, "Literature and Psychology," in *Relations of Literary Study*, ed. James Thorpe (1967), and the issue on "Psychology and Literature: Some Contemporary Directions," in *New Literary History*, Vol. 12 (1980). Norman Holland is a leading exponent of the application of psychoanalytic concepts not (as in most earlier criticism) to the relation of the author to the work, but to the relation of the reader to the work, explaining each reader's individual response as the product of a "transactive" engagement between his or her unconscious desires and defenses and the fantasies that the author has projected in the literary text; see under *reader-response criticism*.

The term **psychobiography** designates an account of the life of an author (see *biography*) that focuses on the subject's psychological development,

显著的发展是弗洛伊德将精神模式分为三个功能方面：**本我**（包括性欲和其他欲望），**超我**（道德与礼仪标准的内在化），**自我**（尽其所能地调节本我无法满足的愿望、超我异乎严格的要求、"现实"世界给予满足的有限可能性这三者间的冲突）。在《精神分析新引论讲义》（1933）和《精神分析概要》（1939）中，弗洛伊德以其清晰明了、引人注目的杰出阐释能力，为一般读者概述了自己后期的理论创新。

弗洛伊德声称，西方文学中富有洞察力的作者在他之前就已体现了他的许多观点，他自己也运用精神分析简要地探讨了文学作品中显现的人物与事件的潜在内容，这些作品包括莎士比亚的《哈姆雷特》《麦克白》《仲夏夜之梦》《李尔王》。他还撰文精湛地分析了费奥多·陀思妥耶夫斯基的《卡拉马佐夫兄弟》，并在《错觉与梦》（1917）中详尽地研究了丹麦作家威廉·詹森的小说《格拉迪沃》。尤其是在1930年代之后，许多作家都根据经典的弗洛伊德理论，撰写了批评分析作者的生平及其文学作品内容的论著。其中最著名的论著之一就是精神分析学家欧内斯特·琼斯以这种方式撰写的《哈姆雷特与俄狄浦斯》（1949）。受弗洛伊德先前理论的启发，琼斯参照弗洛伊德所谓的**俄狄浦斯情结**——即男性婴儿对母亲拥有占有欲而把父亲视为竞争对手予以排斥，这是一种被压抑的但不断出现于成年人的潜意识中的情结——来解释哈姆雷特为什么不能下定杀死其叔父的决心。（弗洛伊德的这个术语源于索福克勒斯的希腊悲剧《俄狄浦斯王》。该剧的主人公在不知情的状况下弑父娶母。）琼斯认为，哈姆雷特的内心冲突是"莎士比亚自身类似冲突的回应"，而且进一步说明，许多世纪以来，观众对该剧持续而强烈的反应源于所有男人所共有的、受到压抑的俄狄浦斯式冲突。

近几十年来，弗洛伊德精神分析法的批评家们依据弗洛伊德在其后期论著中提出的模式，愈加强调"自我心理"在阐述文学作品的显现内容与艺术形式中的作用。也就是说，在构思作品时，"自我"有意识地设法调解本我的要求、超我及现实强加的限制之间的相互冲突。有关这方面的发展情况，可以参阅：弗雷德里克·C. 克鲁斯所写的文章"文学与心理学"[收入詹姆斯·索普主编的《文学研究的关系》(1967)]、"心理学与文学：当代发展的若干方向"（载于《新文学历史》1980年第12期）。诺曼·霍兰不是将精神分析概念运用于分析作者与作品的关系（如大部分的早期批评）、而是将其运用于分析读者与作品关系的主要倡导者。霍兰把每一个读者个人的反应解释为是读者的潜意识欲望及保护与作者投射到文学文本中的幻想之间"相互作用的"密切关系的产物。参见：*读者反应批评*中的论述。

心理传记这一术语是指对作者生平的一种描述（参见：*传记*），这种描述

relying for evidence both on external sources and on the author's own writings. It stresses the role of unconscious and disguised motives in forming the author's personality, and is usually written in accordance with a version, or a revision, of the Freudian theory of the stages of psychosexual development. A major exemplar of the mode was Erik H. Erikson's *Young Man Luther* (1958), in which Erikson stressed the importance of Luther's adolescent "identity crisis." Other notable instances of literary psychobiography are Leon Edel, *Henry James* (5 vols., 1953–72); Justin Kaplan, *Mark Twain and His World* (1974); and Bernard C. Meyer, *Joseph Conrad: A Psychoanalytic Biography* (1967). Prominent and diverse examples of Freudian literary criticism can be found in the collections listed below. It should be noted, in addition, that many modern literary critics, like many modern authors, owe some debt to Freud; such major critics, for example, as Kenneth Burke, Edmund Wilson, and Lionel Trilling assimilated central Freudian concepts into their overall critical views and procedures.

Carl G. Jung is sometimes called a psychoanalyst, but although he began as a disciple of Freud, his mature version of depth psychology is very different from that of his predecessor, and what we call **Jungian criticism** of literature departs radically from psychoanalytic criticism. Jung's emphasis is not on the individual unconscious, but on what he calls the **collective unconscious**, shared by all individuals in all cultures, which he regards as the repository of "racial memories" and of primordial images and patterns of experience that he calls *archetypes*. He does not, like Freud, view literature as a disguised form of libidinal wish fulfillment that to a large extent parallels the fantasies of a neurotic personality. Instead, Jung regards great literature as, like the *myths* whose patterns recur in diverse cultures, an expression of the archetypes of the collective racial unconscious. A great author possesses, and provides for readers, access to the archetypal images buried in the racial memory, and so succeeds in revitalizing aspects of the psyche which are essential both to individual self-integration and to the mental and emotional well-being of the human race. Jung's theory of literature has been a cardinal formative influence on *archetypal criticism* and *myth criticism*. See Jung, *Contributions to Analytic Psychology* (1928) and *Modern Man in Search of a Soul* (1933); also Edward Glover, *Freud or Jung* (1950).

Since the development of *structural* and *poststructural* theories in the latter half of the twentieth century, there has been a strong revival of Freudian theories, although in diverse reformulations of the classical Freudian scheme. Close attention to Freud's writings, and frequently the assimilation of some version of Freud's ideas to their own views and procedures, are features of the criticism of many current writers, whether they are Marxist, Foucauldian, or Derridean in theoretical commitment or primary focus. Harold Bloom's theory of the *anxiety of influence* specifically adapts to the composition and reading of poetry Freud's concepts of the Oedipus complex and of the distorting operation of defense mechanisms in dreams. A number of *feminist critics* have attacked the male-centered nature of Freud's theory—especially evident in such crucial conceptions as the Oedipus complex and the notion of "penis envy" on the part of the female child; but many feminists have also adapted a

依靠来自外部来源及作者自身作品中的证据，集中描写作者主体的心理发展。它强调潜意识与伪装的动机对形成作者的人格所起的作用，通常依据弗洛伊德提出的精神性欲发展阶段论的模式或其修改模式进行创作。这种模式的主要代表作是埃里克·H. 埃里克森的《年轻人路德》(1958)。埃里克森在书中强调了路德青春期的"性格认同危机"的重要性。其他著名文学心理传记作品有：利昂·埃德尔的五卷本《亨利·詹姆斯》(1953—1972)，查斯丁·卡普兰的《马克·吐温与他的世界》(1974)；伯纳德·C. 迈耶的《约瑟夫·康拉德：一部心理分析传记》(1967)。形形色色的弗洛伊德精神分析法的文学批评的知名论著，收录在本条目最后所列的参考书目中。此外应该指出的是，与许多现代作家一样，许多现代文学批评家也都受到弗洛伊德的某些影响；例如，像肯尼思·伯克、埃德蒙·威尔逊、莱昂内尔·特里林这样重要的批评家，在其各自的总体批评观点与方法中都吸收了弗洛伊德的主要概念。

卡尔·G. 荣格有时也被称作精神分析学家。尽管他最初是弗洛伊德的追随者，但他成熟的深层心理学理论却与他的前辈截然不同。我们所说的**荣格文学批评**与精神分析批评大相径庭。荣格强调的不是个人潜意识，而是他所谓的所有文化的所有个人共有的**集体潜意识**。荣格认为，集体潜意识是"种族记忆"、原始意象及他称之为*原型*的经验模式的贮藏室。弗洛伊德将文学视为实现性欲的伪装形式，在很大程度上类似于神经病人人格的幻想，但荣格并不这么认为。荣格将伟大的文学视为集体潜意识原型的表现，类似于各种文化中反复出现的*神话*模式。伟大的作者拥有种族记忆中埋藏的原型意象，并为读者提供这些原型意象。这样就成功地为对个人的自我完善和人类精神与情绪的健康而言都是必不可少的某些精神方面注入活力。荣格的文学理论对原型批评及神话批评的形成产生了重要影响。参阅：荣格所著的《分析心理学文集》(1928)和《追寻灵魂的现代人》(1933)；也可参阅：爱德华·格洛弗所著的《弗洛伊德或荣格》(1950)。

自20世纪下半叶*结构主义*与*后结构主义*理论获得发展以来，弗洛伊德理论得到了极大的复兴，尽管是对经典的弗洛伊德理论系统进行了形形色色的重新阐述。密切关注弗洛伊德的论著，不断地将弗洛伊德的某些观点吸收到自己的观点和方法中，这是许多现代作者在批评上的特点，不论他们的理论信仰或主要观点是马克思主义、福柯主义还是德里达主义。哈罗德·布卢姆提出的*影响的焦虑*理论，就具体地借用了弗洛伊德关于俄狄浦斯情结和梦中保护机制的变相作用等概念，将这些概念运用到诗歌的创作与阅读中。一些*女性主义批评家*抨击了弗洛伊德理论的男性中心本质——在俄狄浦斯情结和女性儿童的"阴茎妒忌"等关键概念中表现得尤为明显，但许多女性主义者也对弗洛伊德的概念及精神

revised version of Freudian concepts and mental mechanisms to their analyses of the writing and reading of literary texts. See Juliet Mitchell, *Psychoanalysis and Feminism* (1975); Mary Jacobus, *Reading Woman* (1986); Nancy Chodorow, *Feminism and Psychoanalytic Theory* (1990); Elisabeth Young-Bruehl, *Freud on Women: A Reader* (1992); Rosalind Minsky, ed., *Psychoanalysis and Gender: An Introductory Reader* (1996).

Jacques Lacan, "the French Freud," developed a *semiotic* version of Freud, converting the basic concepts of psychoanalysis into formulations derived from the linguistic theory of Ferdinand de Saussure, and applying these concepts not to the mental processes of human individuals, but to the operations of the process of signification. (See under *linguistics in literary criticism*.) Typical is Lacan's oft-quoted dictum, "The unconscious is structured like a language." His procedure is to recast Freud's key concepts and mechanisms into the linguistic mode, viewing the human mind not as pre-existent to, but as constituted by, the language we use. In Lacan's revision, for example, both *gender* and desire are not producers, but products of the signifying system. Especially important in **Lacanian literary criticism** is Lacan's reformulation of Freud's concepts of the early stages of psychosexual development, and of the formation of the Oedipus complex, into the distinction between a prelinguistic stage of development that he calls the **imaginary** and the stage after the acquisition of language that he calls the **symbolic**. In the imaginary stage, there is no clear distinction between the subject and an object, or between the individual self and other selves. Intervening between these two stages is what Lacan calls the **mirror stage**, the moment when the infant learns to identify with his or her image in a mirror, and so begins to develop a sense of a separate self, and an (illusory) understanding of oneself as an autonomous subject, that is later enhanced by what is reflected back to it from encounters with other people. When it enters the symbolic, or linguistic, stage, the infant subject assimilates the inherited system of linguistic differences, hence is constituted by the symbolic, as it learns to accept its predetermined "position" in such linguistic oppositions as male/female, father/son, mother/daughter. This symbolic realm of language, in Lacan's theory, is the realm of the law of the father, in which the "phallus" (used in a symbolic sense to stand for male privilege and authority) is "the privileged signifier" that serves to establish the mode for all other signifiers. In a parallel fashion, Lacan translates Freud's views of the mental workings of dream formation into textual terms of the play of *signifiers*, converting Freud's distorting defense mechanisms into linguistic figures of speech. And according to Lacan, all processes of linguistic expression and interpretation, driven by "desire" for a lost and unachievable object, move incessantly (as in Derrida's theory of *deconstruction*) along a chain of unstable signifiers, without any possibility of coming to rest on a fixed signified, or presence. (See Jacques Lacan, *Ecrits: A Selection*, 1977; *The Four Fundamental Concepts of Psychoanalysis*, 1998; and *The Seminar of Jacques Lacan: The Ethics of Psychoanalysis, 1959–60*, 1997. See also Lacan's much discussed reading of Edgar Allan Poe's short story *The Purloined Letter* as an allegory of the workings of the linguistic signifier, in *Yale French Studies*, Vol. 48, 1972; and Malcolm Bowie, *Lacan*, 1991.) Lacan's notions of

机制进行了修改，并用其来分析文学文本创作与阅读。参阅：朱丽叶·米切尔所著的《精神分析与女性主义》(1975)；玛丽·雅各布斯所著的《解读女性》(1986)；南希·乔多罗所著的《女性主义与精神分析理论》(1990)；伊丽莎白·扬-布鲁尔主编的《弗洛伊德论女性读本》(1992)；罗萨林德·明斯基主编的《精神分析与性别：导论读本》(1996)。

"法国的弗洛伊德"雅克·拉康，建立了一种弗洛伊德的*符号*论理论，将精神分析的基本概念转化为源自费迪南·德·索绪尔语言学理论的表述模式。他并没有将这些概念运用于人类个体的心理过程，而是运用于指代过程的活动。（参见：*语言学在文学批评里的应用*。）拉康最常被引用的名言就是"潜意识就像语言一样构建起来"。他的批评方法是，将弗洛伊德的关键概念与机制重新塑造成语言学的模式。他认为，人类思想并非先于语言而存在，而是由我们使用的语言所构成。例如，在拉康看来，*性别*和欲望都不是生产者，而是意指系统的产物。**拉康文学批评**中尤为重要的一点在于，他重新阐述了弗洛伊德关于精神性欲发展的早期阶段和俄狄浦斯情结形成的概念，将其区别为前语言发展阶段与语言习得之后阶段。拉康把前语言发展阶段称为**想象**阶段，语言习得之后阶段称为**符号**阶段。在想象阶段，主体与客体间，或个体自我与其他自我之间并没有显著区别。介于这两个阶段之间的是拉康所谓的**镜子阶段／镜像阶段**。在这一期间，婴儿开始学会辨认自己在镜子中的映像，并开始形成独立自我的意识，以及一种（虚假的）将自我理解为一个能动的主体。此后，与他人意外接触反射给自我的影响又增强了这种独立自我意识。进入符号阶段，婴儿主体吸收了承袭的语言差异系统，因此符号构成了婴儿的主体，因为婴儿学会接受它在诸如男性／女性，父／子，母／女等语言对立中预先确定的"位置"。在拉康的理论中，这一语言的符号领域就是父亲法则的领域。在该领域，"阴茎"（就象征意义而言代表男性特权和权威）是"特权能指"，用来建立其他所有能指模式。拉康用类似方式将弗洛伊德提出的形成梦的精神作用转化为*能指游戏*的文本术语，并将弗洛伊德的变相保护机制转化为语言的修辞格。在拉康看来，所有的语言表达及阐释过程都受到寻求失去的、无法实现的目标这一"欲望"的驱使，沿着一连串不稳定的能指持续运动（就像在德里达的*解构*理论中那样），绝不可能停止于某一固定的所指或存在。[参阅：雅克·拉康的《作品选集》(1977)、《精神分析的四个基本概念》(1998)、《雅克拉康研讨会：精神分析伦理(1959—1960)》(1997)。也可参阅：拉康对埃德加·爱伦·坡的短篇故事《失窃的信》的解读文章（载于1972年第48期《耶鲁法语研究》），拉康将其视为能指运作的象征，引发众多讨论；马尔科姆·鲍伊的《拉康》，1991。]

the inalienable split, or "difference," that inhabits the self, and of the endless chain of displacements in the quest for meaning, have made him a prominent reference in *poststructural theorists*. And his distinction between the pre-Oedipal, maternal stage of the prelinguistic imaginary and the "phallocentric" stage of symbolic language has been exploited at length by a number of French feminists; see Hélène Cixous, Luce Irigaray, and Julia Kristeva under *feminist criticism*.

See Jerome Neu, ed., *The Cambridge Companion to Freud* (1991). Many of Freud's psychoanalytic writings on literature and the arts have been collected by Benjamin Nelson, ed., *Sigmund Freud on Creativity and the Unconscious* (1958). Anthologies of psychoanalytic criticism by various authors are William Phillips, ed., *Art and Psychoanalysis* (1957), and Leonard and Eleanor Manheim, eds., *Hidden Patterns: Studies in Psychoanalytic Literary Criticism* (1966). Useful discussions and developments of Freudian literary theory are Frederick J. Hoffman, *Freudianism and the Literary Mind* (rev. 1957), which also describes Freud's wide influence on writers and critics; Norman N. Holland, *Holland's Guide to Psychoanalytic Psychology and Literature-and-Psychology* (1990); and Peter Brooks, *Psychoanalysis and Storytelling* (1994). Elizabeth Wright, *Psychoanalytic Criticism: Theory in Practice* (1984), reviews various developments in psychoanalytic theories and their applications to literary criticism. For two major traditional critics who have to an important extent adapted Freudian concepts to their general enterprise, see Edmund Wilson, *The Wound and the Bow* (1941), and Lionel Trilling, "Freud and Literature," in *The Liberal Imagination* (1950). Frederick C. Crews, who in 1966 wrote an exemplary Freudian critical study, *The Sins of the Fathers: Hawthorne's Psychological Themes*, later retracted his Freudian commitment; see his *Skeptical Engagements* (1986). For *feminist* views and adaptations of Jacques Lacan, see Jane Gallop, *Reading Lacan* (1985); Shoshana Felman, *Jacques Lacan and the Adventure of Insight* (1987); and Elizabeth Grosz, *Jacques Lacan: A Feminist Introduction* (1990). The psychoanalytically trained philosopher Slavoj Žižek has argued for the primacy of Lacan as an ethical and political thinker. See *The Sublime Object of Ideology* (1989) and *Looking Awry: An Introduction to Jacques Lacan through Popular Culture* (1991).

Ptolemaic universe (tŏl′ ĕmā″ ik): **340**.

pun: Pun (which traditional rhetoricians call **paranomasia**) denotes a play on words that are either identical in sound (**homonyms**) or very similar in sound, but are sharply diverse in significance; an example is the last word in the title of Oscar Wilde's comedy, *The Importance of Being Earnest* (1895). Puns have often had serious literary uses. The authority of the Pope in Roman Catholicism goes back to the Greek pun uttered by Jesus in Matthew 16:18, "Thou art Peter [Petros] and upon this rock [petra] I will build my church." Shakespeare and other writers used puns seriously as well as for comic purposes. In *Romeo and Juliet* (III. i. 101) Mercutio, bleeding to death, says grimly, "Ask for me tomorrow and you shall find me a grave man"; and John Donne's solemn "Hymn to God the Father" (1633) puns throughout on his own name and the past participle "done." Milton was an inveterate inventor

拉康提出了存在于自我之中不可分割的分裂或"差异",以及在探寻意义中永无止境的一连串取代等概念,使其成为*后结构主义理论家*的重要参照。许多法国女性主义批评家详尽地运用了拉康对前俄狄浦斯阶段、前语言想象的母性阶段、符号语言的"阴茎中心"阶段之间的区分;参见:*女性主义批评*中的埃莱娜·西苏、露丝·伊瑞格瑞、朱莉娅·克莉丝蒂娃。

参阅:杰洛米·诺伊主编的《剑桥哲学指南:弗洛伊德》(1991)。本杰明·纳尔逊主编的《西格蒙德·弗洛伊德论创造性与潜意识》(1958)收录了许多弗洛伊德有关文学艺术的精神分析论著。不同作家的精神分析批评文集还包括:威廉·菲利普斯主编的《艺术与精神分析》(1957);伦纳德与埃莉诺·曼海姆夫妇合编的《隐藏的模式:精神分析文学批评研究》(1966)。弗雷德里克·J. 霍夫曼所著的《弗洛伊德主义与文学思想》(1957 年修订版)有效地讨论并发展了弗洛伊德的文学理论,该书也描述了弗洛伊德对作者与批评家产生的广泛影响;诺曼·N. 霍兰所著的《霍兰精神分析心理学及文学与心理学指南》(1990);彼得·布鲁克斯所著的《精神分析和讲故事》(1994)。伊丽莎白·赖特所著的《精神分析批评:实践中的理论》(1984),回顾了精神分析理论新近的各种发展及其在文学批评中的运用。埃德蒙·威尔逊与莱昂内尔·特里林这两位重要的传统批评家的总体理论,在很大程度上修改并借用了弗洛伊德的概念,参阅:埃德蒙·威尔逊所著的《伤与弓》(1941);莱昂内尔·特里林所写的文章"弗洛伊德与文学",收入其所著的《自由主义的想象力》(1950);1966 年弗雷德里克·C. 克鲁斯撰写了弗洛伊德批评研究的代表作《父亲的罪恶:霍桑的心理主题》,但后来他放弃了自己的弗洛伊德信念;参阅:他所著的《心存怀疑的信奉》(1986)。女性主义对雅克·拉康理论的看法与修正,参阅:简·盖洛普所著的《阅读拉康》(1985);肖珊娜·费尔曼所著的《雅克·拉康和冒险的洞察力》(1987);伊丽莎白·格罗斯所著的《雅克·拉康:一种女性主义介绍》(1990)。接受过精神分析训练的哲学家斯拉沃热·齐泽克认为拉康主要是位伦理和政治思想家。参阅:齐泽克所著的《意识形态的崇高客体》(1989)和《斜目而视:透过通俗文化看拉康》(1991)。

Ptolemaic universe:托勒密宇宙观　340。
Pun:双关

双关(传统修辞学家称其为**谐音双关**)是利用发音相同(**同音异义词**)或发音相似但意义截然不同的词进行的文字游戏。例如,奥斯卡·王尔德创作的喜剧《认真的重要性》(1895)剧名中的最后一个词。双关语常常具有严肃的文学用途。罗马天主教中大主教的权威可以追溯到《马太福音》16:18 中基督所说的希腊文双关语:"你是彼得,我要把我的教会建造在这磐石上。"莎士比亚和其他作家使用双关语既用来达到滑稽的目的,也用来获得严肃的效果。在《罗密欧与朱丽叶》第三幕第一场第 101 行里,即将血流身亡的茂丘西奥严肃地说道:"明天来找我就会发现我是个严肃的人(grave 既指'坟墓'又指'严肃')。"约翰·多恩在庄严肃穆的《上帝天父颂》(1633)中通篇采用了他自己的名字(Donne)与过去分词"done"的双关语。弥尔顿在《失乐园》中锲而不舍地创造

of serious puns in *Paradise Lost*. In the eighteenth century and thereafter, however, the literary use of the pun has been almost exclusively comic. A major exception is James Joyce's *Finnegans Wake* (1939), which exploits puns throughout in order to help sustain its complex effect, at once serious and comic, of multiple levels of meaning; see *portmanteau word*.

A special type of pun, known as the **equivoque**, is the use of a single word or phrase which has two disparate meanings, in a context which makes both meanings equally relevant. An example is the phrase "come to dust" in a song from Shakespeare's *Cymbeline*: "Golden lads and girls all must, / As chimney sweepers, come to dust." An epitaph suggested for a bank teller contains a series of equivocal phrases:

> He checked his cash, cashed in his checks,
> And left his window. Who is next?

And an *epigram* by Hilaire Belloc (1870–1953) ends in an equivoque:

> When I am done, I hope it can be said:
> His sins were scarlet, but his books were read.

Refer to Jonathan Culler, ed., *On Puns: The Foundation of Letters* (1988).

Puritan Interregnum: 281.

purple patch: A translation of Horace's Latin phrase "purpureus ... pannus" in his versified *Ars Poetica* (first century BC). It signifies a marked heightening of style in rhythm, diction, repetitions, and figurative language that makes a passage of verse or prose—especially a descriptive passage—stand out from its context. The term is sometimes applied without derogation to a set piece, separable and quotable, in which an author rises to an occasion. An example is the eulogy of England by the dying John of Gaunt in Shakespeare's *Richard II* (II. i. 40ff.), beginning:

> This royal throne of kings, this scept'red isle,
> This earth of majesty, this seat of Mars,
> This other Eden, demi-paradise....

Other famed examples are Lord Byron's depiction of the Duchess of Richmond's ball on the eve of Waterloo in *Childe Harold's Pilgrimage*, Canto III, xxi–xxviii (1816), and Walter Pater's prose description of the *Mona Lisa* in his essay on Leonardo da Vinci in *The Renaissance* (1873). Usually, however, "purple passage" connotes disparagement, implying that one has self-consciously girded oneself to perform a piece of fine writing. In Stella Gibbons' satiric novel, *Cold Comfort Farm*, the fictional narrator is proud of her purple descriptive passages, and follows the example of Baedeker's guidebooks by marking them with varying numbers of asterisks: "Dawn crept over the Downs like a sinister white animal, followed by the snarling cries of the wind eating its way between the black boughs of the thorns."

pyrrhic (pĭr′ ĭk): **219.**

了严肃的双关语。然而，自 18 世纪开始及其后，双关语在文学上的运用几乎全是为了获得喜剧效果。主要的例外是詹姆斯·乔伊斯的《芬尼根的觉醒》(1939)。这部小说通篇利用双关语来维持既严肃又滑稽、含多层意义的复杂效果；参见：合并词。

歧义词是一种特殊的双关语，它利用了某个词或短语两种截然不同的意义，使这两种意义在语境中都同样恰当。如"归入尘土"这个例子，莎士比亚《辛白林》中的一首歌含有这样的对句：尊贵的小伙与姑娘都必须／像扫烟囱的人一样，归入尘土（dust 既指"尘土"又指"遗骸"）。某个银行出纳员的碑文上也含有歧义短语：

> 他核对了他支票中存入的现金，
> 离开了他的窗口。谁会是下一个？

希拉里·贝洛克（1870—1953）的一个警句以一个双关语结束：

> 当我死的时候，我希望他们会说：
> 他罪孽深重，但他的书有人读过。

参阅：乔纳森·卡勒主编的《论双关：文学的基础》(1988)。

Puritan Interregnum：清教徒执政期　281。

Purple Patch：辞藻华丽的章节

辞藻华丽的章节是贺拉斯的韵文体作品《诗艺》（公元前 1 世纪）一书中的拉丁文短语"purpureus...pannus"的英文译名，表示节奏、措词、重复和修辞性语言在文体上的突然提升，使得韵文或散文的某个段落，尤其是描述性段落，在上下文中突显出来。这个术语有时也不带贬义，用于指代某一确定的段落，可以分离、可以引用，作者用这种段落来应付某种场面。例如，在莎士比亚的《理查二世》（第二幕第一场第 40—42 行）中，弥留之际的冈特伯爵约翰在颂扬英格兰时说道：

> 这一个君王们的御座，这一个统于一尊的岛屿，
> 这一片庄严的土地，这一个战神的别邸，
> 这一个新的伊甸——地上的天堂……　　　　　（朱生豪译）

其他著名例子包括，拜伦勋爵在《恰尔德·哈罗德游记》(1816) 第 3 章第 21—28 行里，对里奇蒙德公爵夫人在滑铁卢战役前夕举办的舞会的描述，以及沃尔特·佩特在《文艺复兴史研究》(1873) 里评论列奥纳多·达芬奇的文章中对油画《蒙娜丽莎》的散文体描述。不过，"辞藻华丽的章节"通常带有贬义，暗指那些有意识地准备刻意写出精美之作的人。斯特拉·吉本斯的讽刺小说《寒冷舒适的农庄》中，虚构的叙述者对华丽辞藻的描述性章节自豪不已，并模仿贝德克尔旅游指南的例子，用各种不同的星号加以标记："拂晓如同邪恶的白兽爬上了道恩斯，风的咆哮声随之而来，一路吞噬，穿越在黑色的荆棘树枝之间。"

pyrrhic：抑抑格　219。

quantitative meter: 217; *222*.

quarto: 34.

quatrain: 376, *23*.

queer reading: 328.

queer theory: Queer theory is often used to designate the combined area of gay and lesbian studies, together with the theoretical and critical writings about all modes of variance—such as cross-dressing, bisexuality, and transsexuality—from society's normative model of sexual identity, orientation, and activities. The term "queer" was originally derogatory, used to stigmatize male and female same-sex love as deviant and unnatural; since the early 1990s, however, it has been adopted by gays and lesbians themselves as a noninvidious term to identify a way of life and an area for scholarly inquiry. See Teresa de Lauretis, *Queer Theory: Lesbian and Gay Sexualities*, 1991; and Annamarie Jagose, *Queer Theory: An Introduction*, 1996.

Both **lesbian studies** and **gay studies** began as "liberation movements"—in parallel with the movements for *African-American* and *feminist* liberation—during the anti-Vietnam War, anti-establishment, and countercultural ferment of the late 1960s and 1970s. Since that time these studies have maintained a close relation to the activists who strive to achieve, for gays and lesbians, political, legal, and economic rights equal to those of the heterosexual majority. Through the 1970s, the two movements were primarily separatist: gays often thought of themselves as quintessentially male, while many lesbians, aligning themselves with the feminist movement, characterized the gay movement as sharing the anti-female attitudes of the reigning patriarchal culture. There has, however, been a growing recognition (signalized by the adoption of the joint term "queer") of the degree to which the two groups share a history as a suppressed minority and possess common political and social aims.

In the 1970s, researchers for the most part assumed that there was a fixed, unitary identity as a gay man or as a lesbian that has remained stable through human history. A major endeavor was to identify and reclaim the works of nonheterosexual writers from Plato to Walt Whitman, Oscar Wilde, Marcel Proust, Andre Gide, W. H. Auden, and James Baldwin, and from the Greek poet Sappho of Lesbos to Virginia Woolf, Adrienne Rich, and Audre Lorde. The list included writers (William Shakespeare and Christina Rossetti are examples) who represented in their literary works homoerotic subject matter, but whose own sexuality the available biographical evidence leaves uncertain. (See Claude J. Summers, *The Gay and Lesbian Literary Heritage: A Reader's Companion to the Writers and Their Works, from Antiquity to the Present*, 1995.) In the 1980s and 1990s, however—in large part because of the assimilation of the viewpoints and analytic methods of Derrida, Foucault, and other *poststructuralists*—the earlier assumptions about a unitary and stable gay or lesbian

quantitative meter：音长格律　217；*222*。

quarto：四开本　34。

quatrain：四行诗　376，*23*。

queer reading：酷儿解读　328。

Queer Theory：同性恋理论（又译酷儿理论）

　　同性恋理论常用来指代男女同性恋研究的混合领域，也用来指代有关性别认同、性取向与性行为合乎规范模式的所有变异模式（如身着异性服饰、双性恋、易性癖）的理论和批评论著。"同性恋"这一术语最初带有贬义，用来指责男性和女性同性相爱的变态和异常现象；但自 1990 年代初以来，男女同性恋者自己越来越将这一术语用作不易让人反感的术语，指代一种生活方式和学术探索的一个领域。参阅：特雷莎·德·劳伦蒂斯所著的《同性恋理论：男女同性恋的性行为》(1991)；安娜玛丽·杰格斯所著的《同性恋理论引论》(1996)。

　　女性同性恋研究和**男性同性恋研究**都始于 1960 年代末及 1970 年代反越战、反正统、反文化动乱期间的"解放运动"——类似于*非裔美国人解放运动*和*女性主义解放运动*。自那时起，男女同性恋研究始终与政治活动有密切联系，以便为男女同性恋者取得与异性恋大多数人平等的政治、法律与经济权利。在 1970 年代，这两场运动在本质上是分离主义的：男性同性恋者常常认为自己的本质是男性，而许多女性同性恋者则与女性主义运动结盟，认为男性同性恋运动的特征与占统治地位的父权文化一样，都持反对女性的态度。但近来，人们日益认识到（其标志就是采用了"同性恋"这一共同的词汇）其地位，即这两个群体在历史上都是受压制的少数派，拥有共同的政治目标与社会目标。

　　1970 年代的研究者大都认为，男性同性恋者或女性同性恋者都具有固定、统一的身份，这种身份在人类历史中保持稳定不变。他们的主要任务是力图确认和挖掘非异性恋作家的作品，从柏拉图到沃尔特·惠特曼、奥斯卡·王尔德、马塞尔·普鲁斯特、安德烈·纪德、W. H. 奥登与詹姆斯·鲍德温，以及从古希腊诗人女性同性恋的莱斯博斯岛的萨福到弗吉尼亚·吴尔夫、阿德瑞尼·里奇和奥德·洛德。这份名单还包括那些在作品中表现同性恋题材的作家（如威廉·莎士比亚和克里斯蒂娜·罗塞蒂），但可获得的传记证据并不能确定他们自己的性行为。[参阅：克劳迪·J. 塞默斯所著的《男女同性恋文学遗产：作者及其作品读本，从古至今》(1995)。] 但在 1980、1990 年代——大部分是由于吸收了德里达、福柯及其他后结构主义批评家的观点与分析方法——早先有关统一和稳定的男女同性恋身

identity were frequently put to question, and historical and critical analyses of sexual differences became increasingly subtle and complex.

A number of queer theorists, for example, adopted the deconstructive mode of dismantling the key *binary oppositions* of Western culture, such as male/female, heterosexual/homosexual, and natural/unnatural, by which a spectrum of diverse things is forced into only two categories, and in which the first category is assigned privilege, power, and centrality, while the second is derogated, subordinated, and marginalized. (See under *deconstruction*.) In an important essay of 1980, "Compulsive Heterosexuality and Lesbian Existence," Adrienne Rich posited what she called the "lesbian continuum" as a way of stressing how far-ranging and diverse is the spectrum of love and bonding among women, including female friendship, the family relationship between mother and daughter, and women's partnerships and social groups, as well as overtly physical same-sex relations. Later theorists such as Eve Sedgwick and Judith Butler undertook to invert the standard hierarchical opposition by which homosexuality is marginalized and made unnatural, by stressing the extent to which the ostensible normativity of heterosexuality is based on the suppression and denial of same-sex desires and relationships. **Queer reading** has become the term for interpretive activities that undertake to subvert and confound the established verbal and cultural oppositions and boundaries between male/female, homosexual/heterosexual, and normal/abnormal.

Another prominent theoretical procedure has been to undo the "essentialist" assumption that heterosexual and homosexual are universal and transhistorical types of human subjects, or identities, by historicizing these categories—that is, by proposing that they are *cultural constructs* that emerged under special ideological conditions in a particular culture at a particular time. (See *essentialism* under *humanism*.) A central text is the first volume of Michel Foucault's *History of Sexuality* (1976), which claims that, while there had long been a social category of sodomy as a transgressive human act, the "homosexual," as a special type of human *subject* or identity, was a construction by the medical and legal discourse that developed in the latter part of the nineteenth century. In a further expansion of cultural-constructionist theory, Judith Butler, in *Gender Trouble: Feminism and the Subversion of Identity* (1990), described the categories of gender and of sexuality as *performative*, in the sense that the features which a cultural discourse institutes as masculine or feminine, heterosexual or homosexual, the discourse also makes happen, by establishing an identity that the socialized individual assimilates and the patterns of behavior that he or she proceeds to enact. Homosexuality, by this view, is not a particular identity that effects a pattern of action, but a socially pre-established pattern of action that produces the effect of originating in a particular identity. A fundamental constructionist text, frequently cited in the arguments against essentialism, is "One Is Not Born a Woman" (1981) by Monique Wittig, in *The Straight Mind and Other Essays* (1992).

The constructionist view has been elaborated by considering the cross-influences of race and of economic class in producing the identities and modes of behavior of gender and sexuality. (See, for example, Barbara Smith,

份的假设不断受到质疑，关于性差异的历史分析与批评分析变得越来越细致缜密和错综复杂。

例如，许多同性恋理论家采用了消解西方文化中关键的*二元对立*（如男性/女性，异性恋/同性恋，自然/非自然）这一解构主义模式。二元对立把纷繁各异的事物强行分成两类，第一类被赋予特权、权力与中心地位，第二类则被贬低、处于从属和边缘化的地位。（参见：*解构主义*中的相关论述。）阿德瑞尼·里奇在其一篇重要文章"强制的异性恋与女同性恋之存在"（1980）中，将她所谓的"女同性恋连续体"设想为一种强调女性之间范围广泛、形式各异的爱与联系的方式，包括女性友谊、家庭中母女的关系、女性的伙伴关系与社会群体，以及生理上明显的同性关系。规范的等级对立使同性恋处于边缘化地位，并将其视为异常现象，稍后的理论家，如伊芙·塞奇威克与朱迪思·巴特勒，颠覆了这种规范的等级对立，她们强调，异性恋表面上的规范性是建立在压制和否定同性欲望及同性关系的基础之上。**酷儿解读**已经成为一个术语，用来指决意颠覆和混淆男/女、同性恋/异性恋、正常/异常之间既有的语言和文化对立及边界的阐释活动。

早期的理论认为，异性恋与同性恋是人类主体或身份固有的、普通的、超越历史的两种类型，但另一种显著的理论方法则将这些类别历史化——即提出异性恋与同性恋是在特定时期特定文化中特殊的意识条件下出现的*文化建构*——从而消解了这一早期"本质主义者"的假设。（参见：*人文主义*中的*本质主义*。）米歇尔·福柯的《性史》（1976）第一卷是这一理论的重要文本。作者在文中指出，长期以来口交都被列入违反道德准则的人类行为这一社会范畴，而"同性恋"作为人类主体或身份的一种特殊类型，则是19世纪下半叶发展出来的医学话语与法律话语建构的产物。朱迪思·巴特勒在《性别麻烦：女性主义与身份的颠覆》（1990）中进一步发展了文化建构理论。她将性别分类与性行为分类描述为*施为性*的行为，即文化话语形成了男性特征与女性特征、异性恋特征与同性恋特征；建立一种社会化个人认同的身份，建立他或她实行的行为模式，也可以构成这些特征。按照这种观点，同性恋并非是一种产生行为模式的特定身份，而是一种社会预先确立的并产生了源于某一特定身份的影响的行为模式。在常被引用来反对本质主义的论据中，一个重要的建构主义者文本是莫妮卡·威蒂格所写的文章"女人并非生来就是女人"，收入其所著的《异性恋思维和其他文章》（1992）。

建构主义的这一观点，由于考虑到了种族与经济阶级对产生性别身份、性别行为模式和性行为的交叉影响，而得到了进一步的阐释。[例如，可以参阅：芭芭

"Toward a Black Feminist Criticism," 1977, reprinted in *Within the Circle: An Anthology of African-American Literary Criticism from the Harlem Renaissance to the Present*, ed. Angelyn Mitchell, 1994; and Ann Allen Stickley, "The Black Lesbian in American Literature: An Overview," in *Conditions: Five Two*, 1979.) Sustained debate among queer theorists concerns the risk of a radical constructionism, which would dissolve a lesbian or gay identity into a linguistic and discursive product specific to a particular culture, as against the need to affirm a special and enduring type of human identity, in order to signalize and celebrate it, as well as to establish a basis for concerted political action.

A number of journals are now devoted to queer theory and to lesbian, gay, and transgender studies and criticism; the field has also become the subject of regularly scheduled learned conferences, and has been established in the curriculum of the humanities and social sciences in a great many colleges and universities. Anthologies: Karla Jay and Joanne Glasgow, eds., *Lesbian Texts and Contexts: Radical Revisions* (1990); Diana Fuss, ed., *Inside/Out: Lesbian Theories, Gay Theories* (1991); and Henry Abelove, Michèle Aina Barale, and David M. Halperin, eds., *The Lesbian and Gay Studies Reader* (1993), which includes selections by almost all the theorists and critics mentioned in this entry. *Out Takes: Essays on Queer Theory and Film*, ed. Ellis Hanson (1999), is a collection of essays in queer criticism devoted to a variety of motion pictures. There is a large and rapidly growing body of books on these subjects. In addition to the texts listed above, see Eve Kosofsky Sedgwick, *Between Men: English Literature and Male Homosocial Desire* (1985) and *Epistemology of the Closet* (1990); Diana Fuss, *Essentially Speaking: Feminism, Nature, and Difference* (1989); Richard Dyer, *Now You See It: Studies on Lesbian and Gay Film* (1990); Gregory W. Bredbeck, *Sodomy and Interpretation, Marlowe to Milton* (1991); Susan J. Wolfe and Julia Penelope, eds., *New Lesbian Criticism: Literary and Cultural Readings* (1992); Judith Butler, *Bodies That Matter* (1993); Michael Warner, ed., *Fear of a Queer Planet* (1993); Lee Edelman, *Homographesis: Essays in Gay Literary and Cultural Theory* (1994); Gregory Woods, *A History of Gay Literature: The Male Tradition* (1998). See also the readings listed under *feminist criticism* and *gender studies*. For references to *queer theory* in other entries, see page 97.

quest (romance): 48; *255*.

拉·史密斯所写的文章"走向黑人女性主义批评"(1977),重印收入安格林·米切尔主编的《圈内:从哈莱姆文艺复兴到当代的美国黑人文学批评选集》(1994);安·爱伦·斯蒂克雷所写的文章"美国文学中的黑人同性恋概述",载于《形势:5》(1979)第2期。]同性恋理论家之间一直就激进建构主义的危险性问题进行论战:激进建构主义把男女同性恋身份消解为特定文化中预言和推论的产物,这与为了表明并突出男女同性恋身份以建立一致的政治行动基础,需要确认一种特殊而持久的身份的观点是相对立的。

  一些期刊现在专门刊登同性恋理论、男女同性恋、跨性恋研究与批评;该领域也成为定期学术会议的主题,并出现在许多学院和大学设立的人文社科课程中。理论选集包括:卡拉·杰伊与乔安娜·格拉斯哥合编的《女性同性恋文本和语境:激进的修正》(1990);戴安娜·法斯主编的《内／外:女性同性恋理论,男性同性恋理论》(1991);亨利·阿贝拉夫、米歇尔·艾娜·巴拉尔、戴维·M.霍尔珀林三人合编的《女性同性恋和男性同性恋研究读本》(1993),该书收录了本条目中提到的几乎所有理论家与批评家的文章。埃利斯·汉森主编的《弃用镜头／剪辑:同性恋理论与电影论文集》(1999),是以各种各样的电影为研究对象的同性恋批评文章合集。与这些主题有关的书籍日益迅速增长,数量繁多。除了以上所列的文本,还可参阅:伊芙·科索夫斯基·塞奇威克所著的《男人之间:英国文学与男性同性社会性欲望》(1985)和《衣柜认识论》(1990);戴安娜·法斯所著的《从本质上讲:女性主义、自然与区隔》(1989);理查德·戴尔所著的《现在你看到它了:女性同性恋和男性同性恋电影研究》(1990);格雷戈里·W.布雷德贝克所著的《鸡奸和阐释:从马洛到弥尔顿》(1991);苏珊·J.沃尔夫与朱利亚·佩内洛普合编的《新同性恋批评:文学和文化读本》(1992);朱迪斯·巴特勒所著的《身体之重》(1993);迈克尔·沃纳主编的《恐惧一个同性恋星球》(1993);李·埃德尔曼所著的《同形异构:同性恋文学和文化理论散论》(1994);格雷戈里·伍兹所著的《同性恋文学史:男性传统》(1998)。也可参见:*女性主义批评、性别研究*中所列的参考书目。其他条目中提及"同性恋理论"的地方,参见第97页。

quest (romance):(骑士传奇中的)追求   48;255。

rap: **271**; 72.

reader-response criticism: Reader-response criticism does not designate any one critical *theory*, but rather a focus on the process of reading a literary text that is shared by many of the critical modes, American and European, which have come into prominence since the 1960s. Reader-response critics turn from the traditional conception that a text embodies an achieved set of meanings, and focus instead on the ongoing mental operations and responses of readers as their eyes follow a text on the page before them. In the more drastic forms of such criticism, matters that had been considered by critics to be objective features of the literary work itself (including narrator, plot, characters, style, and structure, as well as meanings) are dissolved into an evolving process, consisting primarily of diverse expectations, and the violations, deferments, satisfactions, and restructurings of expectations, in the flow of a reader's experience. Reader-response critics of all theoretical persuasions agree that, at least to some considerable degree, the meanings of a text are the "production" or "creation" of the individual reader, hence that there is no one correct meaning for all readers either of the linguistic parts or of the artistic whole of a text. Where these critics importantly differ is (1) in their view of the primary factors that shape a reader's responses; (2) in the place at which they draw the line between what is "objectively" given in a text and the "subjective" responses of an individual reader; and as a result of this difference, (3) in their conclusion about the extent, if any, to which a text controls, or at least "constrains," a reader's responses, so as to justify the rejection of at least some readings as misreadings, even if, as most reader-response critics assert, we are unable to demonstrate that any single reading is the correct reading.

The following is a brief survey of the more prominent forms of reader-response criticism:

The German critic Wolfgang Iser developed the phenomenological analysis of the reading process proposed by Roman Ingarden, but whereas Ingarden had limited himself to a description of reading in general, Iser applied his theory to the analysis of many individual works of literature, especially prose fiction. (For a discussion of Ingarden's views, see *phenomenology and criticism*.) In Iser's view the literary text, as a product of the writer's intentional acts, in part controls the reader's responses, but always contains (to a degree that has greatly increased in many modern literary texts) a number of "gaps" or "indeterminate elements." These the reader must fill in by a creative participation with what is given in the text before him. The experience of reading is an evolving process of anticipation, frustration, retrospection, reconstruction, and satisfaction. Iser distinguishes between the **implied reader**, who is established by a particular text itself as someone who is expected to respond in specific ways to the "response-inviting structures" of the text, and the "actual reader," whose responses are inevitably colored by his or her accumulated

R

rap：说唱 **271**；*72*。

Reader-Response Criticism：读者反应批评

读者反应批评并非指代任何一种批评*理论*，而是注重于文学文本的阅读过程，并被许多欧美文学批评模式所采用。从1960年代开始，读者反应批评逐渐占据显著地位。传统批评将文本理解为意义的完整结构，但读者反应批评家认为，作品是读者浏览他们眼前的文本书页时持续进行的精神活动与反应。更加激进的读者反应批评则把批评家所考虑的作品本身的特征（包括叙述者、情节、人物、文体、结构和意义）分解成一种逐渐演变的过程。这一过程主要由读者经验流动过程中不同的期待及对期待的违背、推延、满足和重建所构成。所有理论流派的读者反应批评家或多或少都承认，一部文本的意义是读者个人的"产物"或"创造物"。因此，不论是在语言方面还是在文本整体的艺术性方面，一部文本都没有对所有读者而言是唯一正确的意义。这些批评家重要的不同观点是：(1) 他们对形成读者反应的主要因素的看法；(2) 他们如何划分文本中"客观地"表现的事物和读者个人"主观的"反应之间的界限；由于这一不同，进而导致 (3) 他们关于文本能在何种程度上控制、或至少是"限制"读者反应的不同结论。虽然几乎所有的读者反应批评家都断定，即使我们无法论证任何一种阅读是正确的解读，但文本对读者反应的控制，至少可以使我们有理由将某些解读作为误读加以摒弃。

下面简要概述了一些较为重要的读者反应批评形式：

德国批评家沃尔夫冈·伊塞尔拓展了罗曼·英加登提出的运用现象学原理分析阅读过程的方法。不过，英加登局限于对一般阅读的描述，而伊塞尔则将他的理论应用到许多具体文学作品的分析中，尤其是对散文体小说的分析。（有关对英加登观点的讨论，参见：*现象学与文学批评*。）伊塞尔认为，文学文本是作者意图行为的产物，或多或少控制着读者的反应，但文本总会包含许多"空隙"或"不确定因素"（在许多现代文学文本中，这些空隙与不确定因素在某种程度上已经大大增加）。读者必须利用眼前的文本提供给他的信息，创造性地参与其中，填补这些空隙。阅读的经历是一个逐步演变的过程，充满了期待、失望、追忆、重建与满足。伊塞尔区分了**隐在读者**与"真实读者"：特定文本自身确定了隐在读者，预计他们会以具体的方式对文本中"吸引反应的结构"作出反应，而"真实读者"的反应则不可避免地具有他或她累积的个人经验的色彩。

private experiences. In both cases, however, the process of the reader's consciousness serves to constitute both the partial patterns (which we ordinarily attribute to objective features of the work itself) and the coherence, or unity, of the work as a whole. As a consequence, literary texts always permit a varied range of possible meanings. The fact, however, that the author's intentional acts establish limits, as well as incentives, to the reader's creative additions to a text allows us to reject some readings as misreadings. (For an application of phenomenological analysis to the history, from era to era, of ever-altering reader responses to a given text, see *reception theory*.)

French *structuralist criticism*, as Jonathan Culler said in *Structuralist Poetics* (1975), "is essentially a theory of reading" which aims to "specify how we go about making sense of texts" (pp. viii, 128). As practiced by critics such as Culler in the course of his book, this mode of criticism stresses literary conventions, codes, and rules which, having been assimilated by competent readers, serve to structure their reading experience and so make possible, at the same time as they impose constraints on, the partially creative activity of interpretation. The structuralist Roland Barthes, however, in his later theory encouraged a mode of reading that opens the text to an endless play of alternative meanings. And the poststructuralist movement of *deconstruction* is a theory of reading that specifically subverts the structuralist view that interpretation is in some part controlled by linguistic and literary codes, and instead proposes a "creative" reading of any text as a play of "differences" that generate innumerable, mutually contradictory, and "undecidable" meanings.

American proponents of reader-response types of interpretive theory often begin by rejecting the claim of the American *New Criticism* that a literary work is a self-sufficient object invested with publicly available meanings, whose internal features and structure should be analyzed without "external" reference to the responses of its readers (see *affective fallacy*). In radical opposition to this view, these newer critics turn their attention exclusively from the verbal text to the reader's responses; they differ greatly, however, in the factors to which they attribute the formation of these responses.

David Bleich, in *Subjective Criticism* (1978), undertakes to show, on the basis of classroom experiments, that any purportedly "objective" reading of a text, if it is more than an empty derivation from theoretical formulas, turns out to be based on a response that is not determined by the text, but is instead a "subjective process" determined by the distinctive personality of the individual reader. In an alternative analysis of reading, Norman Holland accounts for the responses of a reader to a text by recourse to Freudian concepts (see *psychoanalytic criticism*). The subject matter of a work of literature is a projection of the fantasies—engendered by the interplay of unconscious needs and defenses—that constitute the particular "identity" of its author. The individual reader's "subjective" response to a text is a "transactive" encounter between the fantasies projected by its author and the particular defenses, expectations, and wish-fulfilling fantasies that make up the reader's own identity. In this transactive process the reader transforms the fantasy content, "which he has created from the materials of the story his defenses admitted," into a unity,

但在这两种情况中,读者的意识活动过程都有助于构成部分模式(我们通常将其归入作品本身的客观特征)以及作品作为总体的连贯或统一。因此,文学文本总是含有一系列不同的可能意义。然而,作者的意图行为不仅刺激了读者对文本的创造性补充,而且也对此加以限制,这使得我们能够剔除一些误读的解读。(关于用现象学分析去解读对某一特定文本的读者反应总是在不断改变的历史,参见:*接受理论*。)

乔纳森·卡勒在《结构主义诗学》(1975)中指出,法国的*结构主义批评*"实质上是一种阅读理论",其宗旨在于"具体说明我们是如何理解文本的"(序言第8页,正文第128页)。正如卡勒在书中所述,这类批评强调文学的惯例、符号与规则。这些惯例、符号与规则被有能力的读者吸纳,有助于读者建构他们的阅读经历;它们在限制阅读的同时,也使得读者阐释作品的半创造性行为成为可能。但结构主义者罗兰·巴尔特在其后期理论中鼓励一种新的阅读模式,这种模式使文本成为一种开放的、各种可供选择的意义的无穷无尽的游戏。结构主义认为,阐释在某种程度上受到语言符号和文学符号的控制。后结构主义中的*解构主义*运动是一种颠覆了结构主义这一观点的阅读理论,它取而代之地提出:对任何文本"富有创造性的"阅读都是"差异"的游戏,这些"差异"产生了无数相互矛盾却又"无法确定的"意义。

美国阐释理论中各类读者反应的倡导者,通常都从批驳美国*新批评*的观点入手——新批评认为,一部文学作品是一个自足的客体,其本身赋予大众可读取的意义,分析这些意义的内部特征与结构无需参照"外部"的读者反应(参见:*情感谬误*)。这些读者反应批评者强烈反对这种观点,他们把注意力从词语文本上全部集中到读者的反应上,但对这些反应构成因素的看法则大相径庭。

戴维·布莱奇在《主观性批评》(1978)中力图以课堂试验为基础来说明,如果文本阅读不仅仅是理论模式的空洞衍生,那么任何声称是"客观的"文本阅读其实都是以不受文本制约的反应为基础,是一种由读者个人显著的性格特征所决定的"主观过程"。诺曼·霍兰另辟蹊径,对阅读进行分析;他借助弗洛伊德的概念(参见:*精神分析批评*)来描述读者对文本作出的反应。一部文学作品的题材是幻想的投射——这些幻想由潜意识需求和保护的相互作用所产生——这些幻想构成了其作者的特定"身份"。读者个人对文本的"主观"反应,是作者投射的幻想与构成读者自己身份的特定防卫、期待以及满足愿望的幻想之间的"相互作用的"遭遇。在这种相互作用的过程中,读者"将从其自身保护所接受的故事素材创造的"幻想内容转化成一个统一体,或"有意义的整体",这个

or "meaningful totality," that constitutes the reader's particular interpretation of the text. There is no universally determinate meaning of a work; two readers will agree in their interpretation only insofar as their "identity themes" are sufficiently alike to enable each to fit the other's re-creation of a text to his or her own distinctive pattern of responses.

In his theory of reading, Harold Bloom also employs psychoanalytic concepts; in particular, he adapts Freud's concept of the mind's mechanisms of defense against the revelation to consciousness of repressed desires to his own view of the process of reading as the application of "defense mechanisms" against the "influence," or threat to the reader's imaginative autonomy, of the poet whose text is being read. Bloom applies Freudian concepts in a much more complex way than Holland; he arrives, however, at a parallel conclusion that there can be no determinate or correct meaning of a text. All "reading is ... misreading"; the only difference is that between a "strong" misreading and a "weak" misreading. (See *anxiety of influence*.)

Stanley Fish is the proponent of what he calls **affective stylistics**. In his earlier writings Fish represented the activity of reading as one that converts the spatial sequence of printed words on a page into a temporal flow of experience in a reader who has acquired a "literary competence." In following the printed text with his eye, the reader makes sense of what he has so far read by anticipating what is still to come. These anticipations may be fulfilled by what follows in the text; often, however, they will turn out to have been mistaken. But since, according to Fish, "the meaning of an utterance" is the reader's "experience—all of it," and the reader's mistakes are "part of the experience provided by the author's language," these mistakes are an integral part of the meaning of a text. (See "Literature in the Reader: Affective Stylistics," published in 1970 and reprinted with slight changes in *Self-Consuming Artifacts: The Experience of Seventeenth Century Literature*, 1974, and in *Is There a Text in This Class?* 1980.) Fish's analyses of large-scale literary works were designed to show a coherence in the kinds of mistakes, constitutive of specific types of meaning-experience, which are effected in the reader by the text of John Milton's *Paradise Lost*, and by various essayists and poets of the seventeenth century.

Fish's early claim was that he was describing a universal process in all competent readings of literary texts. In later publications, however, he introduced the concept of **interpretive communities**, each of which is composed of members who share a particular reading "strategy," or "set of community assumptions." Fish, in consequence, now presented his own affective stylistics as only one of many alternative modes of interpretation, which his earlier writings were covertly attempting to persuade his readers to adopt. He also proposed that each communal strategy in effect "creates" all the seemingly objective features of the text itself, as well as the "intentions, speakers, and authors" that we may infer from the text. The result is that there can be no universal "right reading" of any text; the validity of any reading, however obvious it may seem to a reader, will always depend on the assumptions and strategy of reading that he or she happens to share with

整体构成了读者对文本的特定阐释。一部作品没有普遍确定的意义；两位读者只有在他们的"身份主题"极为相似时，才能各自使对方对文本的再创作符合自己特有的反应；只有在这时，他们才会对一部作品的阐释有一致的看法。

哈罗德·布卢姆在其阅读理论中也使用了精神分析的概念；特别是他将弗洛伊德提出的保护机制概念加以改动并运用到他自己有关阅读过程的观点中。弗洛伊德的"保护机制"抵制的是受压抑欲望的意识流露，而布卢姆的"保护机制"抵抗的是所读文本的诗人对读者的想象自主权产生的"影响"或威胁。与霍兰相比，布卢姆更加复杂地运用了弗洛伊德的概念，但他得出了类似的结论，即文本没有确定的或正确的意义。所有的"阅读"都是"……误读"，唯一的不同在于"严重"误读与"轻微"误读之分。（参见：*影响的焦虑*。）

斯坦利·费什是他所称**感受文体学**的倡导者。在其早期论著中，费什把阅读活动描写成一种将印刷文字的空间顺序变换成有"文学能力的"读者经验的瞬息流动。读者的视线跟随着印刷文本，并对之后的内容进行预测，据此来理解他已读过的部分。这些预测可能会在文本随后的部分中得到证实，不过它们更常被证明是错误的。但在费什看来，既然"言语的意义"是读者的"全部经验"，读者的错误是"作者的语言提供的部分经验"，那么这些错误也是文本意义不可缺少的一部分。[参见1970年发表的文章"读者中的文学：感受文体学"，该文稍作改动后重印收入《自我消耗的艺术品：17世纪文学的经验》（1974）和《这堂课有文本吗？》（1980）。] 费什分析了许多长篇文学作品，目的是为了说明各种错误的前后一致性。这些错误由意义–经验的具体类型构成，它们对读者的影响源于弥尔顿的《失乐园》和17世纪的许多散文随笔作家与诗人。

费什在早期曾声称，他描述的是有能力的读者阅读文学文本的普遍过程。但在其稍后的论著中，他引入了**解释群体**这一概念。每个解释群体的组成成员都具有共同的特定阅读"策略"，或一系列"群体设想"。费什因此将自己的感受文体学描述为只是众多可选择的解释模式之一，而在早期论著中，费什曾试图婉转地劝说读者采用自己的模式。他还提出，每种群体策略实际上都"创造"了我们从文本中推断出来的"意图、说话者和作者"以及文本自身所有看似客观的特征。其结果就是，任何文本都没有普遍"正确的阅读"；即使任何阅读的正确性对某位读者来说似乎是显而易见的，但它总是取决于读者刚好与其特定解释群体内其他

other members of a particular interpretive community. Fish's claim is that all values, as well as meanings, of a text are *relative* to the concept or scheme of a particular interpretive community; furthermore, that such conceptual schemes are "incommensurable," in that there is no available standpoint, outside of all interpretive communities, for translating the discourse of one community into that of another, or for mediating between them. (See Fish, *Is There a Text in This Class? The Authority of Interpretive Communities*, 1980; and for a concise exposition of philosophical critiques of Fish's claims for interpretive and evaluative relativism and incommensurability, see James Battersby, *Reason and the Nature of Texts*, 1996.) In a later book, *Doing What Comes Naturally: Change, Rhetoric, and the Practice of Theory in Literary and Legal Studies* (1989), Fish analyzes, and defends, the role of the professional "interpretive community" of academic critics in literary studies; he also extends his views of literary interpretation into the domain of legal interpretation.

Since the early 1980s, as part of a widespread tendency to stress changing cultural and political factors in the study of literature, reader-response critics have increasingly undertaken to "situate" a particular reading of a text in its historical setting, in the attempt to show the extent to which the responses that constitute both the interpretation and evaluation of literature have been determined by a reader's *ideology* and by built-in biases about race, class, or gender. See Peter J. Rabinowitz, *Before Reading: Narrative Conventions and the Politics of Interpretation*, 1987; and for *feminist* emphasis on the male biases that affect the responses of readers, Judith Fetterley, *The Resisting Reader* (1978); and Elizabeth A. Flynn and Patrocinio Schweikart, eds., *Gender and Reading: Essays on Readers, Texts, and Contexts* (1986).

A survey of a number of reader-response theories of criticism is included in Steven Mailloux's own contribution to this mode in *Interpretive Conventions* (1982); a different survey, from the point of view of deconstructive theory, is Elizabeth Freund, *The Return of the Reader: Reader-Response Criticism* (1987). Anthologies of diverse reader-response essays: Susan Suleiman and Inge Crossman, eds., *The Reader in the Text* (1980); Jane P. Tompkins, ed., *Reader-Response Criticism* (1980). Important early instances of a criticism that is focused on the reader: Walter J. Slatoff, *With Respect to Readers* (1970); Louise Rosenblatt, *The Reader, the Text, the Poem* (1978); Umberto Eco, *The Role of the Reader* (trans. 1979).

In addition to the titles mentioned in this essay, the following are prominent exemplars of reader-response criticism: Stanley Fish, *Surprised by Sin: The Reader in "Paradise Lost"* (1967); Norman Holland, *The Dynamics of Literary Response* (1968) and *Five Readers Reading* (1975); Wolfgang Iser, *The Implied Reader* (1974) and *The Act of Reading: A Theory of Aesthetic Response* (1978). For critiques of Fish's "affective stylistics": Jonathan Culler, *The Pursuit of Signs* (1981); Eugene Goodheart, *The Skeptic Disposition in Contemporary Criticism* (1984); M. H. Abrams, "How to Do Things with Texts," in *Doing Things with Texts* (1989). For references to *reader-response criticism* in other entries, see page *336*.

成员具有共同的设想和阅读策略。费什声称，文本所有的价值与意义都与特定解释群体的概念或计划*有关*。而且，这种概念计划是"无法测量的"，因为在任何解释群体之外都不存在群体间话语的转换或斡旋的立足点。[参见：费什所著的《这堂课有文本吗？解释群体的权威》(1980)；对费什的"解释及评价都是相对的和不可测量的"这一看法的哲学批评的简要阐述，参阅：詹姆斯·巴特斯比所著的《文本的原因与本质》(1996)。]费什在其后所著的《做自然的事：改变、修辞以及文学研究和法律研究的理论实践》(1989)里，对文学研究中学术批评家作为职业"解释群体"的角色作了分析与辩护；他还将自己的文学阐释观点扩展到法律解释领域。

1980年代初以来，作为文学研究强调文化与政治因素这一普遍倾向的一部分，读者反应批评学家越来越多地尝试将对文本的特定阅读"置于"其历史背景中，试图说明读者的*意识形态*及固有的种族、阶级或性别偏见在多大程度上决定了构成文学解释及文学评价的反应。参阅：彼得·J.拉比诺维茨所著的《阅读之前：叙事惯例与阐释策略》(1987)；女性主义强调影响读者反应的男性偏见，有关这方面的内容，可以参阅：朱迪思·菲特利所著的《抗拒性读者》(1978)；伊丽莎白·A.弗林与普特洛西尼奥·施威卡特合编的《性别与阅读：有关读者、文本与语境的论文》(1986)。

斯蒂文·梅洛克斯在其所著的《阐释惯例》(1982)中概述了许多读者反应批评理论，并对这种模式进行了自己的阐述；伊丽莎白·弗罗因德所著的《读者回归：读者反应批评》(1987)则用解构主义观点概述了读者反应理论。各种有关读者反应的论文集包括：苏珊·苏莱曼与英奇·克罗斯曼合编的《文本里的读者》(1980)；简·P.汤普金斯主编的《读者反应批评》(1980)。早期强调读者批评的重要论著包括：沃尔特·J.斯拉托夫所著的《尊重读者》(1970)；路易斯·罗森布拉特所著的《读者，文本，诗歌》(1978)；翁贝托·艾柯所著的《读者的角色》(1979年英译版)。

除了上面文中提到的书目，有关读者反应批评的重要著作还包括：斯坦利·费什所著的《为罪恶所震惊：〈失乐园〉中的读者》(1967)；诺曼·霍兰所著的《文学反应动力学》(1968)和《五种读者阅读》(1975)；沃尔夫冈·伊塞尔所著的《隐含读者》(1974)和《阅读活动：审美反应理论》(1978)。有关对费什的"感受文体学"的批评，参阅：乔纳森·卡勒所著的《符号的追寻》(1981)；尤金·古德哈特所著的《当代批评的怀疑论倾向》(1984)；M. H.艾布拉姆斯所著的《以文行事》(1989)中的"如何以文行事"。其他条目中提及"读者反应批评"的地方，参见第36页。

realism and naturalism: **Realism** is applied by literary critics in two diverse ways: (1) to identify a movement in the writing of novels during the nineteenth century that included Honoré de Balzac in France, George Eliot in England, and William Dean Howells in America (see *realistic novel*, under *novel*), and (2) to designate a recurrent mode, in various eras and literary forms, of representing human life and experience in literature.

Realistic fiction is often opposed to romantic fiction. The *romance* is said to present life as we would have it be—more picturesque, fantastic, adventurous, or heroic than actuality; realism, on the other hand, is said to represent life as it really is. This distinction in terms solely of subject matter, while relevant, is clearly inadequate. Casanova, T. E. Lawrence, and Winston Churchill were people in real life, but their biographies demonstrate that truth can be stranger than literary realism. It is more useful to identify realism in terms of the intended effect on the reader: realistic fiction is written to give the effect that it represents life and the social world as it seems to the common reader, evoking the sense that its characters might in fact exist, and that such things might well happen. To achieve such effects, the novelists we identify as realists may or may not be selective in subject matter—although most of them prefer the commonplace and the everyday, represented in minute detail, over rarer aspects of life—but they must render their materials in ways that make them seem to their readers the very stuff of ordinary experience. For example, Daniel Defoe in the early eighteenth century dealt with the extraordinary adventures of a shipwrecked mariner named Robinson Crusoe and with the extraordinary misadventures of a woman named Moll Flanders; but he made his novels seem to readers a mirror held up to reality by his reportorial manner of rendering all the events, whether ordinary or extraordinary, in the same circumstantial, matter-of-fact, and seemingly unselective way. Both the fictions of Franz Kafka and the present-day novels of *magic realism* achieve their effects in large part by exploiting a realistic manner in rendering events that are in themselves fantastic, absurd, or flatly impossible.

Russian formalists, followed more systematically by *structuralist critics*, proposed that both the selection of subject matter and the techniques of rendering in a realistic novel depend on their accordance with literary *convention* and codes which the reader has learned to interpret, or *naturalize*, in a way that makes the text seem a reflection of everyday reality. (See Roland Barthes, "The Reality Effect," in *French Literary Theory Today*, ed. Tzvetan Todorov, 1982; and Jonathan Culler, *Structuralist Poetics*, 1975, chapter 7, "Convention and Naturalization.") Some theorists draw the conclusion that, since all literary representations are constituted by arbitrary conventions, there is no valid ground for holding any one kind of fiction to be more realistic than any other. It is a matter of common experience, however, that some novels in fact produce on the reader the effect of representing the ordinary course of events. Skepticism about the possibility of fictional realism is not an empirical doctrine which is based on the widespread experience of readers of literature, but a metaphysical doctrine that denies the existence of any objective reality that is independent of altering human conventions and cultural formations.

Realism and Naturalism：现实主义与自然主义

　　文学批评家对**现实主义**有两种不同的用法：(1) 表示 19 世纪的一场小说创作运动，包括法国的奥诺雷·德·巴尔扎克、英国的乔治·艾略特和美国的威廉·迪安·豪威尔斯（参见：*小说中的现实主义小说*）；(2) 表示各个时期或各类文学样式中反复使用的、在文学中表现人类生活与经验的一种模式。

　　现实主义小说往往与传奇小说大相径庭。一般认为*传奇*表现了我们所向往的那种生活——比实际生活更加风景秀丽、奇异怪诞、更具冒险精神或者更为英勇无畏；而现实主义则是真实地展现生活。这种区分仅仅考虑到题材方面，而从其他相关方面来说显然不够完善。卡萨诺瓦、T. E. 劳伦斯、温斯顿·丘吉尔都是真实生活中的人物，但他们的传记却表明，真实可以比文学现实主义更为奇特。从小说有意对读者产生的效果来确定现实主义更为有效：现实主义小说的创作目的在于表现普通读者眼中的生活和社会环境，引导读者产生这样的意识，即小说中的人物可能真的存在，小说中的事情可能真的会发生。为了取得这样的效果，我们称为现实主义者的小说家可能会也可能不会在题材方面进行选择——虽然大多数人都偏爱对普通、平凡、日常的事物，而非生活中罕见的方面，加以细腻的描述——但他们必须对创作素材进行处理，使读者感到它们似乎就是日常经验中的事物。例如，18 世纪早期，丹尼尔·笛福在小说中描述了一位名叫鲁滨逊·克鲁索的水手在船只失事后非同寻常的冒险经历，以及一位名叫摩尔·弗兰德斯的女子不同寻常的不幸遭遇。然而，笛福以新闻报道式的手法描写了所有的事件，不论这些事件本身是否非同寻常，都以同样详尽的、切合实际的和似乎是不加选择的方式加以描述，从而使读者觉得，他的小说如同一面展现现实的镜子。弗朗兹·卡夫卡的小说和当代的*魔幻现实主义*小说在描述荒诞、离奇、绝不可能发生的事件时，大都采用了现实主义手法而取得了小说的效果。

　　俄国形式主义批评家提出——*结构主义批评家*则更为系统地提出——现实主义小说中对题材和写作技巧的选择，都取决于它们与读者已经学会对其进行阐释或*归化*的文学惯例及文学符号的一致性，从而使文本成为似乎是对日常现实生活的反映。[参见：罗兰·巴尔特所写的文章"现实效果"，收入兹维坦·托多罗夫主编的《法国今日文学理论》(1982)；乔纳森·卡勒所著的《结构主义诗学》(1975) 第七章"惯例与归化"。] 有些理论家得出这样的结论，由于所有的文学表现都是由任意的惯例构成的，所以没有确凿的理由认为某种小说比其他小说更为现实。但是，依据普通经验，有些小说的确对读者产生了这样的效果，使读者认为它们表现了日常事件。对小说现实主义可能性的怀疑论并非基于文学读者普遍经验之上的经验主义论，而是一种形而上学论，它否认有独立于不断变化的人类惯例与文化形式之外的任何客观现实的存在。

(For philosophical discussions of conventionality and reality, see the essays by Hilary Putnam, Nelson Goodman, and Menachem Brinker in *New Literary History*, Vol. 13, 1981, and Vol. 14, 1983.)

Naturalism is sometimes claimed to give an even more accurate depiction of life than realism. But naturalism is not only, like realism, a special selection of subject matter and a special way of rendering those materials; it is a mode of fiction that was developed by a school of writers in accordance with a particular philosophical thesis. This thesis, a product of post-Darwinian biology in the nineteenth century, held that a human being exists entirely in the order of nature and does not have a soul nor any access to a religious or spiritual world beyond the natural world; and therefore, that such a being is merely a higher-order animal whose character and behavior are entirely determined by two kinds of forces: heredity and environment. Each person inherits compulsive instincts—especially hunger, the drive to accumulate possessions, and sexuality—and is then subjected to the social and economic forces in the family, the class, and the milieu into which that person is born. The French novelist Émile Zola, beginning in the 1870s, did much to develop this theory in what he called "le roman expérimental" (that is, the novel organized in the mode of a scientific experiment on the behavior, under given conditions, of the characters it depicts). Zola and later naturalistic writers, such as the Americans Frank Norris, Stephen Crane, and Theodore Dreiser, try to present their subjects with scientific objectivity and with elaborate documentation, sometimes including an almost medical frankness about activities and bodily functions usually unmentioned in earlier literature. They tend to choose characters who exhibit strong animal drives such as greed and sexual desire, and who are helpless victims both of glandular secretions within and of sociological pressures without. The end of the naturalistic novel is usually "tragic," but not, as in classical and Elizabethan *tragedy*, because of a heroic but losing struggle of the individual mind and will against gods, enemies, and circumstances. Instead the protagonist of the naturalistic plot, a pawn to multiple compulsions, usually disintegrates, or is wiped out.

Aspects of the naturalistic selection and management of subject matter and its austere or harsh manner of rendering its materials are apparent in many modern novels and dramas, such as Hardy's *Jude the Obscure*, 1895 (although Hardy largely substituted a cosmic determinism for biological and environmental determinism), various plays by Eugene O'Neill in the 1920s, and Norman Mailer's novel of World War II, *The Naked and the Dead*. An enlightening exercise is to distinguish the diverse ways in which the relationship between the sexes is represented in a romance (Richard Blackmore's *Lorna Doone*, 1869), an ironic comedy of manners (Jane Austen's *Pride and Prejudice*, 1813), a realistic novel (William Dean Howells' *A Modern Instance*, 1882), and a naturalistic novel (Émile Zola's *Nana*, 1880, or Theodore Dreiser's *An American Tragedy*, 1925). Movements originally opposed to both nineteenth-century realism and naturalism (although some modern works, such as Joyce's *Ulysses*, 1922, combine aspects of these and other novelistic modes) are *expressionism* and *symbolism* (see *Symbolist Movement*).

（有关惯例与现实的哲学讨论，可以参阅：《新文学史》1981 年第 13 卷、1983 年第 14 卷上希拉里·普特南、纳尔逊·古德曼、蒙纳切姆·布瑞恩克所写的文章。）

自然主义与现实主义相比有时被认为更加准确地描绘了生活。但与现实主义一样，自然主义不单要对题材加以特别的选择，并要采用特殊的方式艺术地处理这些素材。自然主义这种小说类型是由一个流派的作家根据特殊的哲学观点发展起来的。这种哲学观点是 19 世纪后达尔文生物学的产物，认为人完全存在于自然法则中；人没有灵魂，也没有进入超出自然世界之外的宗教或精神世界的任何方式。因此，人仅仅是更为高级的动物，他的品性与行为完全是由遗传和环境两种力量所决定。每个人都继承了不由自主的本能——尤其是饥饿、聚敛财富的欲望和性欲——所以他便受制于他出生的家庭、阶级和环境的社会动力与经济动力。法国小说家埃米尔·左拉从 1870 年代开始，就在他所谓的"实验小说"（即以对小说中所描绘的人物的行为举止进行科学实验的模式组织起来的小说）中大大发展了这一理论。左拉和后来的自然主义作家，如美国的弗兰克·诺里斯、史蒂芬·克莱恩、西奥多·德莱塞，都曾尝试过用科学的客观性和详尽的实证材料来表现他们所描述的对象，有时甚至对行为与身体功能进行医学上不加掩饰的描述，这在之前的文学作品中是罕见的。这些作家倾向于选择能够展现强烈的兽性本能（如贪婪和性欲）的人物，而这些人物既是自身内腺分泌的牺牲品，又是外部社会压力的牺牲品。自然主义小说的结局往往是"悲剧性"的。但是，这种悲剧与古典悲剧和伊丽莎白时期的*悲剧*又有所不同。在古典悲剧和伊丽莎白时期的悲剧中，是由于个人的理性和意志英勇地反抗神灵、仇敌与环境但以失败告终，从而导致悲剧；自然主义小说情节中的主人公只是多种冲动的一个卒子，通常走向崩溃或最终消亡。

自然主义对题材的选择与安排及其对素材不加掩饰或冷峻的表现方式，在许多现代小说和戏剧中都有明显的体现，如哈代的《无名的裘德》(1895)（尽管在这部小说里哈代用宇宙决定论代替了生物和环境决定论）、尤金·奥尼尔在 1920 年代创作的各种剧作、诺曼·梅勒有关第二次世界大战的小说《裸者与死者》。富有启迪性的做法是区别各类小说中如何描写两性之间的关系，如在传奇小说中[理查德·布莱克莫尔的《洛娜·杜恩》(1869)]，在反讽性风俗喜剧中[简·奥斯丁的《傲慢与偏见》(1813)]，在现实主义小说中[威廉·迪恩·豪威尔斯的《一个现代的例证》(1882)]，在自然主义小说中[左拉的《娜娜》(1880)或西奥多·德莱塞的《美国悲剧》(1925)]。最初反对 19 世纪现实主义和自然主义[但像乔伊斯的《尤利西斯》(1922)等一些现代作品则运用了所有这些小说模式的某些方面]的文学运动是表现主义和象征主义（参见：*象征主义运动*）。

See *socialist realism*, and refer to Erich Auerbach, *Mimesis: The Representation of Reality in Western Literature* (reprinted 2003); Ian Watt, *The Rise of the Novel* (1957); Ernst Gombrich, *Art and Illusion* (1960); Harry Levin, *The Gates of Horn: A Study of Five French Realists* (1963); René Wellek, "The Concept of Realism in Literary Scholarship," in *Concepts of Criticism* (1963); J. P. Stern, *On Realism* (1973); Ioan Williams, *The Realist Novel in England* (1975); Donald Pizer, *Realism and Naturalism in Nineteenth-Century American Literature* (rev. 1984); Walter Benn Michaels, *The Gold Standard and the Logic of Naturalism* (1987); James Nagel and Thomas Quirk, eds., *The Portable American Realism Reader* (1997); Harry E. Shaw, *Narrating Reality: Austen, Scott, Eliot* (1999); Pam Morris, *Realism* (2003).

realistic novel: 254.

Realistic Period (in American literature): **275.**

reception aesthetic: 336.

reception history: 337.

reception theory: Reception theory is the application to literary history of a form of *reader-response* theory that was proposed by Hans Robert Jauss in "Literary History as a Challenge to Literary Theory" (in *New Literary History*, Vol. 2, 1970–71). Like other reader-response criticism, it focuses on the reader's reception of a text; its prime interest, however, is not on the response of a single reader at a given time, but on the altering responses, interpretive and evaluative, of the general reading public over the course of time. Jauss proposes that although a text has no "objective meaning," it does contain a variety of objectively describable features. The response of a particular reader, which constitutes for that reader the meaning and aesthetic qualities of a text, is the joint product of the reader's own "horizon of expectations" and the confirmations, disappointments, refutations, and reformulations of these expectations when they are "challenged" by the features of the text itself. Since the linguistic and aesthetic expectations of the general population of readers change over the course of time, and since later readers and critics have access not only to the literary text but also to the published responses of earlier readers, there develops an evolving historical "tradition" of critical interpretations and evaluations of a given literary work. Following concepts proposed by Hans-Georg Gadamer (see under *interpretation and hermeneutics*), Jauss represents this tradition as a continuing "dialectic," or "dialogue," between a text and the ever-altering horizons of successive readers; in itself, a literary text possesses no fixed and final meanings or value.

This mode of studying literary reception as a dialogue, or "fusion" of horizons, has a double aspect. As a **reception aesthetic**, it "defines" the meaning and aesthetic qualities of any individual text as a set of implicit

参见：*社会主义现实主义*；参阅：埃利希·奥尔巴赫所著的《摹仿论：西方文学中现实的再现》(2003年重印版)；伊恩·沃特所著的《小说的兴起》(1957)；厄恩斯特·贡布里希所著的《艺术与错觉》(1960)；哈里·莱文所著的《角门：五位法国现实主义者研究》(1963)；勒内·韦勒克所著的《批评的概念》(1963)中的"文学研究中的现实主义概念"；J. P. 斯特恩所著的《论现实主义》(1973)；约安·威廉斯所著的《英国的现实主义小说》(1975)；唐纳德·皮泽所著的《19世纪美国文学中的现实主义和自然主义》(1984年修订版)；沃尔特·本·迈克尔斯所著的《黄金标准与自然主义逻辑》(1987)；詹姆斯·内格尔与托马斯·奎克合编的《袖珍美国现实主义读本》(1997)；哈里·E. 肖所著的《叙述现实：奥斯汀、斯科特、艾略特》(1999)；帕姆·莫里斯所著的《现实主义》(2003)。

realistic novel：现实主义小说　254。

Realistic Period (in American literature)：(美国文学中的) 现实主义时期　275。

reception aesthetic：接受美学　336。

reception history：接受历史　337。

Reception Theory：接受理论

接受理是*读者反应理论*应用到文学历史中的一种形式，这一理论最早由汉斯·罗伯特·姚斯在其所写的文章"作为向文学理论挑战的文学史"（载于《新文学史》1970—1971年第2卷）中提出。与其他读者反应批评一样，这一理论也注重读者对文学文本的接受；但它的主要兴趣不是某位读者在某个特定年代的反应，而是普遍的阅读大众在一段时期内不断变化的阐释性反应和评价性反应。姚斯认为，尽管一部作品没有"客观的意义"，但却的确含有许多可以客观描述出来的特征。特定读者的反应为这个读者构成了一部文本的意义和美学品质，是读者自己的"期待视野"与这些期待在受到文本自身特征的"挑战"时所得到证实、落空、否定或是重新阐释的共同产物。由于读者母体的语言期待与审美期待随时间而改变，也由于后世的读者和批评家不仅能够读到文本而且能够得到已出版的先前读者对作品的反应，于是，对特定文学作品进行批判性阐释与评价的历史"传统"也就逐渐发展起来。姚斯沿袭了汉斯–乔治·伽达默尔（参见：*释义与阐释学*）提出的概念，把这种传统描述为文本与连绵不断的读者不断改变的视野之间持续的"辩证"或"对话"；文学文本自身并不具有任何固定的最终意义或价值。

这种把文学接受视为对话或视野"融合"的研究模式具有双重意义。一方面，作为**接受美学**，它把任何一部文本的意义和美学品质"定义"为一系列暗含的语

semantic and aesthetic "potentialities" which become manifest only as they are realized by the cumulative responses of readers over the course of time. In its other aspect as a **reception history**, this mode of study also transforms the history of literature—traditionally conceived as an account of the successive production of a variety of works with relatively fixed meanings and values—by making it a history that requires an "ever-necessary retelling," since it narrates the changing yet cumulative way that selected texts are interpreted and assessed, as the horizons of successive generations of readers alter over the passage of time.

See Hans Robert Jauss, *Towards an Aesthetic of Reception* (1982), and *The Aesthetic Experience and Literary Hermeneutics* (1982); and for a history and discussion of this viewpoint, Robert C. Holub, *Reception Theory: A Critical Introduction* (1984).

recto: 34.

recuperation (in reading): **401**.

reflection (in Marxist criticism): **205**.

Reformation: 339.

refrain: A line, or part of a line, or a group of lines, which is repeated in the course of a poem, sometimes with slight changes, and usually at the end of each *stanza*. The refrain occurs in many *ballads* and work poems, and is a frequent element in Elizabethan songs, where it may be merely a nonverbal carrier of the melodic line, as in Shakespeare's "It Was a Lover and His Lass": "With a hey, and a ho, and a hey nonino." A famous refrain is that which closes each stanza in Edmund Spenser's "Epithalamion" (1594)—"The woods shall to me answer, and my echo ring"—in which sequential changes indicate the altering sounds during the successive hours of the poet's wedding day. The refrain in Spenser's "Prothalamion"—"Sweet Thames, run softly, till I end my song"—is echoed ironically in Part III of T. S. Eliot's *The Waste Land* (1922), where it is applied to the Thames in the modern age of polluted rivers.

A refrain may consist of only a single word—"Nevermore," as in Poe's "The Raven" (1845)—or of an entire stanza. If the stanza refrain occurs in a song, which all the auditors join in singing, it is called the **chorus**; for, example, in "Auld Lang Syne" and many other songs by Robert Burns in the late eighteenth century.

regional novel: 257.

regular ode: 262.

relativism: 331.

义及美学的"潜在可能",这些"潜在可能"只有通过随时代逐渐累积起来的读者反应才能得以体现。另一方面,作为**接受历史**,这种研究模式通过把文学历史看成需要"必要重述"的历史改变了文学史——文学史在传统意义上一直被视为对历史上相继产生的各类具有固定含义和价值的作品所进行的叙事——由于历代读者的视野随时间而变,所以文学史描述了对精选的文本进行不断变化、逐渐累积的阐述方式与评价方式。

参阅:汉斯·罗伯特·姚斯所著的《论接受美学》(1982)和《美学经验与文学阐释学》(1982);关于这种观点的历史与讨论,参阅:罗伯特·C.霍勒布所著的《接受理论:批判介绍》(1984)。

recto:正页　34。

recuperation (in reading):(阅读中的)复原　401。

reflection (in Marxist criticism):(马克思主义批评中的)反映　205。

Reformation:宗教改革　339。

Refrain:叠句

叠句是指一首诗歌中重复出现的一行、一行的部分或一组诗句,有时也会稍加变动,通常出现在每一诗节的结尾。在许多*民谣*和劳动诗歌中都能找到叠句。叠句也是伊丽莎白时期的歌曲里常见的一个组成因素。在这些歌曲中,叠句有时没有任何意义,仅仅是音调优美的歌行的载体。例如,莎士比亚的《那是一个情人和他的姑娘》一诗中有这么一句"唱着嘿,嗬,嘿,哝呢哝"。著名的叠句出现在埃德蒙·斯宾塞的《婚曲》(1594)里。诗中每一诗节都以叠句"森林将向我回应,我的回声响彻森林"结束——在这首诗中,有规律的一连串变化显示了诗人结婚那天接连好几个小时里声音的不断变化。T. S.艾略特在《荒原》(1922)一诗的第3章中,戏谑地附和斯宾塞《婚前曲》中的叠句("迷人的泰晤士河,轻柔地流淌,直到我停止歌唱"),以此来描绘现在这个河流污染时代中的泰晤士河。

叠句也可能仅由一个词构成,如坡的诗歌《乌鸦》(1845)中的单词"永不"(Nevermore),也可能由一整段诗节构成。如果整个叠句诗节作为所有观众都参与演唱的一个部分出现在歌曲中,这部分就叫**合唱部**;例如,罗伯特·彭斯在18世纪末创作的《往昔的时光》及其他许多歌曲中都运用了合唱部。

regional novel:地方小说　257。

regular ode:律颂　262。

relativism:相对主义　331。

Renaissance: Renaissance ("rebirth") is the name commonly applied to the period of European history following the Middle Ages; it is usually said to have begun in Italy in the late fourteenth century and to have continued, in Italy and other countries of Western Europe, through the fifteenth and sixteenth centuries. In this period the European arts of painting, sculpture, architecture, and literature reached an eminence not exceeded in any age. The development came late to England in the sixteenth century, and did not have its flowering until the Elizabethan and Jacobean periods; sometimes, in fact, John Milton (1608–74) is described as the last great Renaissance poet. (See *periods of English literature*.)

Many attempts have been made to define "the Renaissance" in a brief statement, as though a single essence underlay the complex features of the intellectual and cultural life of a great variety of European countries over several hundred years. It has, for example, been described as the birth of the modern world out of the ashes of the Dark Ages; as the discovery of the world and the discovery of man; and as the era of the emergence of untrammeled individualism in life, thought, religion, and art. Recently some historians, finding that attributes similar to these were present in various people and places in the Middle Ages, and also that many elements long held to be medieval survived into the Renaissance, have denied that the Renaissance ever existed. This skeptical opinion serves as a reminder that history is a continuous process, and that "periods" are not intrinsic in history, but invented by historians. Nonetheless, the division of the temporal continuum into named segments is an all but indispensable convenience in discussing history. Furthermore, during the span of time called "the Renaissance," it is possible to identify a number of events and discoveries which, beginning approximately in the fifteenth century, clearly effected distinctive changes in the beliefs, productions, and manner of life of many people in various countries, especially those in the upper and the intellectual classes.

Beginning in the 1940s, a number of historians have replaced (or else supplemented) the term "Renaissance" with **early modern** to designate the span from the end of the Middle Ages until late in the seventeenth century. The latter term looks forward rather than back, emphasizing the degree to which the time, instead of being mainly a rebirth of the classical past, can be viewed, in its innovations and intellectual concerns, as a precursor of our present time. (See Leah S. Marcus, "Renaissance/Early Modern Studies," in *Redrawing the Boundaries*, ed. Stephen Greenblatt and Giles Gunn, 1992.)

The innovations during this period may be regarded as putting a strain on the relatively closed and stable world of the great civilization of the later Middle Ages, when most of the essential and permanent truths about God, man, and the universe were considered to be adequately known. The full impact of many developments in the Renaissance did not make itself felt until the Enlightenment in the later seventeenth and the eighteenth centuries, but the fact that they occurred in this period indicates the vitality, the restless curiosity, and the imaginative audacity of many people of the era, whether

Renaissance：文艺复兴

文艺复兴（"rebirth"）是指中世纪之后的那段欧洲历史时期。人们通常认为文艺复兴始于14世纪后期的意大利，15、16世纪在意大利和其他西欧国家继续得到发展。在这一时期，欧洲的绘画、雕塑、建筑和文学艺术达到了任何时代都无法超越的辉煌。文艺复兴在16世纪传到英国，直到伊丽莎白时期和詹姆斯一世时期才达到全盛。实际上，约翰·弥尔顿（1608—1674）有时被视为文艺复兴时期最后一位伟大诗人。（参见：*英国文学各时期的划分*。）

许多人都尝试用简短的表述给"文艺复兴"下定义，就像几百年来在许多欧洲国家的思想、文化生活的复杂特征中潜藏着某种单一的本质。例如，文艺复兴被描述为从黑暗时代的灰烬中诞生的现代世界；被描述为发现世界和人类；被描述为在生活、思想、宗教和艺术中出现无拘无束的个人主义的时代。最近一些历史学家发现，类似特征也可在中世纪不同的风土人情中找到，而且许多长期以来一直被认为是中世纪的因素在文艺复兴时期依然可见。因此，这些历史学家否认文艺复兴曾经存在过。这种怀疑观点提醒人们，历史是一个延续的过程，"历史时期"不是历史赋予的，而是历史学家创造的。尽管如此，将时间连续体划分成拥有各自名称的片断，还是为讨论历史带来了必不可少的方便。而且，在所谓的"文艺复兴"这段时期里，我们有可能确认出许多大致始于15世纪的事件与发现。这些事件与发现显然给不同国家的许多民族的信仰、生产及生活方式，尤其是上层阶级与知识阶级，带来了显著而彻底的变化。

从1940年代开始，许多历史学家用**早期现代时期**替代（或补充）了"文艺复兴"这一术语，用来指代从中世纪末到17世纪末这段时间。早期现代时期立足于未来而非过去，强调就其创新实践与思想观念而言，这个时期可被视为我们当前这个世纪的先驱，而不仅仅是经典历史的再生。[参阅：利厄·S. 马库斯所写的文章"文艺复兴/早期现代时期研究"，收入斯蒂芬·格林布拉特与贾尔斯·冈恩合编的《重新划定界限》（1992）。]

这一时期的创新都可视为对中世纪后期相对封闭、稳定的伟大文明世界所施加的压力。中世纪后期，人们认为大部分有关上帝、人类、宇宙的根本性、永久性真理已被充分了解。直到17世纪后期和18世纪的启蒙运动时期，文艺复兴时期许多发展的全面影响才充分体现出来。不过，这些发展都产生于文艺复兴时期这一事实表明，文艺复兴时期的许多人，无论是学者、思想家、艺术家还

scholars, thinkers, artists, or adventurers. Prominent among these developments were:

1. The new learning. Renaissance scholars of the classics, called *humanists*, revived the knowledge of the Greek language, discovered and disseminated a great number of Greek manuscripts, and added considerably to the number of Roman authors and works which had been known during the Middle Ages. The result was to open up a sense of the vastness of the historical past, as well as to enlarge immensely the stock of ideas, materials, literary forms, and styles available to Renaissance writers. In the mid-fifteenth century the invention of **printing** on paper from movable type (for which Johann Gutenberg of Mainz, Germany, is usually given credit, although the Chinese had developed a similar mode of printing several centuries earlier) made books for the first time cheap and plentiful, and floods of publications, ancient and modern, poured from the presses of Europe to satisfy the demands of the expanding population who had learned to read. The rapidity and range of the spread of ideas, discoveries, and types of literature in the Renaissance was made possible by this new technology of printing. (See *book* and *book history studies*.) The technology reached England in 1476, when William Caxton set up a press at Westminster, where he published, among many other books, Chaucer's *Canterbury Tales* and Malory's *Le Morte D'Arthur*.

    The humanistic revival sometimes resulted in pedantic scholarship, sterile imitations of ancient works and styles, and a rigidly authoritarian rhetoric and literary criticism. It also bred, however, the gracious and tolerant humanity of an Erasmus, and the high concept of a cultivated Renaissance aristocracy expressed in Baldassare Castiglione's *Il Cortegiano* ("The Courtier"), published in 1528. This was the most admired and widely translated of the many Renaissance **courtesy books**, or books on the character, obligations, and training of the man of the court. It sets up the ideal of the completely rounded or **Renaissance man**, developed in all his faculties and skills—physical, intellectual, and artistic. He is especially trained to be a warrior and statesman, but is capable also as athlete, philosopher, artist, conversationalist, and man of society. The courtier's relationships to women, and women's to men, are represented in accordance with the quasi-religious code of *Platonic love,* and his activities and productions are crowned by the grace of **sprezzatura**—the Italian term for the seeming spontaneity and casual ease with which a trained person may meet the requirements of complex and exacting rules. Leonardo da Vinci in Italy and Sir Philip Sidney in England are often represented as embodying the many aspects of the courtly ideal.

2. The new religion. The **Reformation** led by Martin Luther (1483–1546) was a successful heresy which struck at the very foundations of the institutionalism of the Roman Catholic Church. This early Protestantism was grounded on each individual's inner experience of spiritual struggle and salvation. Faith (based on the word of the Bible) alone was thought sufficient to save, and salvation itself was regarded as a direct transaction

是冒险家，都充满活力，具有无尽的好奇心和大胆的想象。这一时期显著的发展包括：

1. 新学问。文艺复兴时期的古典主义学者被称为人文主义者。他们复兴了希腊语知识，发现并传播了大量的古希腊手稿，并在中世纪已经了解的基础上大大扩充了大量的古罗马作家及作品，结果是展现了逝去历史的广博，极大地丰富了文艺复兴时期的作者所能获得的思想、素材、文学形式与风格。15世纪中叶活字**印刷术**的发明（人们通常将活字印刷归功于德国美因兹的约翰·谷登堡，但中国人早在几个世纪前就已发展出类似的印刷方法）第一次使得书籍数量丰富、价格便宜。古代和现代的出版物从欧洲印刷作坊中涌出，以满足日益扩大的、学会了阅读的人群的需求。正是这项新的印刷技术，使得文艺复兴时期的种种思想、发现与文学类型得以迅速传播。（参见：书籍、书籍史研究。）1476年这项技术传到英国，同年，威廉·卡克斯顿在威斯敏斯特成立了一家印刷社，并出版了许多作品，其中有乔叟的《坎特伯雷故事集》和马洛礼的《亚瑟王之死》。

   人文主义的复兴有时也会导致迂腐的学术风气、对古代作品和风格呆板的模仿，以及刻板专制的修辞学与文学批评。但它也孕育了伊拉斯谟那样仁慈宽容的人性，培育了巴尔达萨雷·卡斯底格朗1528年出版的《宫廷人物》中所表现的高度文明的文艺复兴贵族理念。《宫廷人物》是文艺复兴时期的许多**礼仪书籍**（即论宫廷人物的性格、义务和训练的书籍）中最受推崇、译文最多的一部作品。它树立了尽善尽美的理想人物或**文艺复兴人**；这种人物在体力、智力、艺术上的才能与技巧得到了全面的发展。他接受特别训练，以成为一名武士和政治家，但他也能成为运动家、哲学家、艺术家、健谈者和社交高手。宫廷人物与女性的关系，或女性与男性的关系，与柏拉图式恋爱这一类似宗教的准则相一致。他的行为与作品被冠以一种**自然**（sprezzatura，这是一个意大利词语，指的是使人感到自然的举止或轻松自如）的优雅。一些经过训练的人能够以此应付复杂、严厉规定的要求。意大利的列奥纳多·达芬奇和英国的菲利普·锡德尼爵士身上都体现了这种宫廷理想的许多方面。

2. 新宗教。马丁·路德（1483—1546）领导的**宗教改革**是一次成功的异教改革，它打击了罗马天主教现存制度优越论的基础。早期的新教以个人精神斗争和救赎的内心经验为基础。新教徒们认为，只要有信念（建立在圣经教义的基础上）就能得到拯救。拯救本身被视

with God in the theater of the individual soul, without the need of intermediation by church, priest, or sacrament. For this reason Protestantism is sometimes said to have been an extreme manifestation of "Renaissance individualism" in northern Europe; it soon, however, developed its own type of institutionalism in the theocracy proposed by John Calvin (1509–64) and his Puritan followers. Although England officially broke with the Catholic Church during the reign of Henry VIII, the new religious establishment (the Anglican Church), headed by the monarch, retained many of the characteristics of the old church while embracing selected Protestant theological principles. The result was a political and theological compromise that remained the subject of heated debate for centuries.

3. The new world. In 1492 Christopher Columbus, acting on the persisting and widespread belief in the old Greek idea that the world is a globe, sailed west to find a new commercial route to the East, only to be frustrated by the unexpected barrier of a new continent. The succeeding explorations of this continent and its native populations, and its settlement by Europeans, gave new materials to the literary imagination. The magic world of Shakespeare's *The Tempest*, for example, as well as the treatment of its native inhabitants by Prospero and others, is based on a contemporary account of a shipwreck on Bermuda and other writings about voyages to the New World. More important for English literature, however, was the fact that economic exploitation of the new world—often cruel, oppressive, and devastating to the native peoples—put England at the center, rather than as heretofore at the edge, of the chief trade routes, and so helped establish the commercial prosperity that in England, as in Italy earlier, was a necessary though not sufficient condition for the development of a vigorous intellectual and artistic life.

4. The new cosmos. The cosmos of medieval astronomy and of medieval Christian theology was **Ptolemaic** (that is, based on the Greek astronomer Ptolemy, second century) and pictured a stationary earth around which rotated the successive spheres of the moon, the various planets, and then the fixed stars. Heaven, or the Empyrean, was thought to be situated above the spheres, and Hell to be situated either at the center of the earth (as in Dante's *Inferno*) or else below the system of the spheres (as in John Milton's *Paradise Lost*). In 1543 Copernicus published his new hypothesis concerning the astronomic system; this gave a much simpler and more coherent explanation of accumulating observations of the actual movements of the heavenly bodies, which had led to ever greater complications within the scheme of the Ptolemaic world picture. The **Copernican theory** proposed a system in which the center is the sun, not the earth, and in which the earth is not stationary, but only one planet among many planets, all of which revolve around the sun.

5. Investigations have not borne out the earlier assumption by historians that the world picture of Copernicus and of the scientists who followed him (sometimes referred to as the **new philosophy**) delivered an immediate and profound shock to the theological and secular beliefs of thinking

为个人灵魂中与上帝的直接交流，无需教会、牧师或圣礼的调解。由于这个原因，新教有时被视为是北欧"文艺复兴个人主义"的极端表现。但新教很快就形成了自己的现存制度优越论，这体现在约翰·加尔文（1509—1564）及其清教徒追随者所提出的神权政治中。尽管英国在亨利八世统治时期正式脱离了天主教，但君王领导下的新宗教机构（英国国教）仍然保留了旧教会的许多特征，同时也包含了一些精选出的新教神学原理。结果，政治与神学间的妥协几个世纪以来一直是激烈争论的问题。

3. 新世界。古希腊观点认为世界是一个球形的物体。根据这种持续且广为流传的信念，1492年克里斯托弗·哥伦布向西航行，希望找到通往东方的新贸易航线，但意想不到的新大陆阻扰了这次航行，使他受挫。对这一新大陆和当地居民随后的探索，以及欧洲人对其殖民地的开拓，给文学想象带来了新的素材。例如，莎士比亚的《暴风雨》描绘了一个神奇的世界，以及普洛斯彼罗等人对当地居民的描述都取材于当时对在百慕大一只沉船的描述以及其他有关新世界航行的作品。但对英国文学更重要的一点在于，对新世界的经济剥削——对当地民族来说，这种剥削通常是残忍的、压迫的、毁灭性的——将英国置于主要贸易航线的中心，而非此前的边缘地位，因此有助于建立英国的商业繁荣。同早先的意大利一样，英国商业上的繁荣为发展生机勃勃的思想及艺术生活提供了必要条件，虽然这种条件并不充分。

4. 新宇宙。中世纪的天文学与基督教神学信奉**托勒密宇宙观**（建立在公元2世纪的托勒密天文学基础之上），描述了一个静止不动的地球。月球、各种行星、恒星依次绕着地球转。他们认为天（或曰天堂）位于星球之上，地狱则位于地球中心（如但丁的《地狱篇》）或星系之下（如约翰·弥尔顿在《失乐园》中所述）。1543年，哥白尼发表了有关天文学体系的新假说。这一假说更为简单、连贯地解释了对天体实际运动的一系列观察，导致托勒密世界观的结构变得更加复杂。**哥白尼理论**提出了以太阳为中心而不是以地球为中心的体系。在这个体系中，地球并非静止不动，它只是众多行星中的一个，所有的行星都绕着太阳转。

5. 历史学家在早期曾提出，哥白尼及其追随他的科学家们所描绘的世界（有时称为**新哲学**），迅速而深刻地震动了思想家的神学信仰与世俗信念，但这种假设并没有得到调查研究的证实。例如，

people. For example in 1611, when Donne wrote in "The First Anniversary" that "new Philosophy calls all in doubt," for "the Sun is lost, and th' earth," he did so only to support the ancient theme, or literary *topos*, of the world's decay, and to enforce a traditional Christian "contemptus mundi" (contempt for the worldly). Still later, Milton in *Paradise Lost* (1667) expressed a suspension of judgment between the Ptolemaic and Copernican theories; he adopted, however, the older Ptolemaic scheme as the cosmic setting for his poem, because it was more firmly traditional and better adapted to his narrative purposes.

6. Much more important, in the long run, was the effect on opinion of the general principles and methods of the **new science** developed by the great successors of Copernicus in the late sixteenth and early seventeenth centuries, such as the physicists Johannes Kepler and Galileo and the English physician and physiologist William Harvey. Even after Copernicus, the cosmos of many writers in the Elizabethan era (exemplified in a number of Shakespeare's plays) not only remained Ptolemaic, it also remained an animate cosmos that was invested with occult powers and inhabited by demons and spirits, and was widely believed to control men's lives by stellar influences and to be itself subject to control by the powers of witchcraft and of magic. The universe that emerged in the course of the seventeenth century, as a product of the scientific procedure of posing hypotheses that could be tested by precisely measured observations, was the physical one propounded by the French philosopher René Descartes (1596–1650). "Give me extension and motion," Descartes wrote, "and I will construct the universe." The universe of Descartes and the new science consisted of extended particles of matter which moved in space according to fixed mathematical laws, free from interference by angels, demons, human prayer, or occult magical powers. This universe was, however, subject to the manipulations of experimental scientists who set out in this way to discover the laws of nature, and who, in the phrase of the English thinker Francis Bacon, had learned to obey nature in order to be her master. In Descartes and other philosophers, the working hypotheses of the scientists about the physical world were converted into a philosophical worldview, which was made current by popular expositions, and—together with the methodological principle that a controlled observation is the criterion of truth in many areas of knowledge—helped constitute the climate of eighteenth-century opinion known as the *Enlightenment*.

Joan Kelly inaugurated a spirited debate among *feminist* and other scholars with her essay, published in 1977, "Did Women Have a Renaissance?" (in *Women, History and Theory*, 1984). Her own answer to the question, based primarily on evidence from central Italy, was that women did not. For a book by a feminist scholar who counters this claim, by reference to women's changing roles in the family, in the church, and in positions of political and cultural power, see Margaret L. King, *Women of the Renaissance* (1991).

1611年，多恩在《第一周年》中写道："新哲学对一切都产生了怀疑"，因为"太阳消失了，地球也不见了。"他这么说只是为了支持世界衰败这一古代主题，或文学常用主题，强调基督教"蔑视世俗"的传统信念。随后，弥尔顿在《失乐园》(1667) 中对托勒密理论与哥白尼理论的判断显得举棋不定，但他采用了更古老的托勒密假想作为自己诗歌的宇宙背景，因为它更加传统，更适合作者的叙述目的。

6. 16世纪末17世纪初哥白尼的伟大继承者，如物理学家约翰尼斯·开普勒与伽利略，英国医师与生理学家威廉·哈维发展了**新科学**。从长远观点来看，更重要的一点在于新科学的普遍原理与方法对观念的影响。即使在哥白尼之后，伊丽莎白时期的许多作家不仅仍然保持托勒密的宇宙观（如莎士比亚的许多戏剧所示），而且这些作家保持的宇宙是一个生机勃勃的宇宙，充满了超自然力量，居住着恶魔与神灵。人们普遍相信，这个宇宙通过星球的影响来控制人们的生活，宇宙自身又受到巫术与魔法力量的控制。17世纪出现的宇宙观是勒内·笛卡尔（1596—1650）提出的物质宇宙观，它是科学方法的产物，这种科学方法建构的假说能够经受精确测量观察的检验。笛卡尔写道："给我广延性和运动"，"我就能建构宇宙"。笛卡尔和新科学提出的宇宙由广泛的物质微粒构成。这些物质微粒根据固定的数学规则在太空中运动，不受天使、恶魔、人类祷告或超自然魔力的干涉。但这个宇宙受到实验科学家有限的支配。这些科学家们试图以这种方式来发现自然法则。用弗朗西斯·培根的话来说，他们已经学会服从自然，其目的在于成为自然的主人。在笛卡尔等哲学家的身上，科学家有关物质世界的运作假说被转换成一种哲学世界观。大众化的阐述使得这种哲学世界观广为流传，而且这种世界观——与控制观察是许多知识领域的真理标准这一方法论原理——帮助建构了18世纪启蒙运动的思想氛围。

琼·凯莉1977年发表的文章"女性有过文艺复兴吗？"[收入其所著的《女性、历史与理论》(1984)]，在*女性主义*学者及其他学者中间引发了一场激烈的讨论。凯莉自己对这一问题的回答是，女性不曾有过文艺复兴。这一回答主要以从意大利中部收集的证据为依据。女性主义学者玛格丽特·L. 金参照女性在家庭、教会、政治地位、文化权力中角色的改变，对上述观点提出了反驳；参阅其所著的《文艺复兴时期的女性》(1991)。

Refer to J. Burckhardt, *Civilization of the Renaissance in Italy* (first published in 1860); E. A. Burtt, *The Metaphysical Foundations of Modern Science* (rev. 1932); C. S. Lewis, *English Literature in the 16th Century* (1954); Marjorie Nicolson, *Science and Imagination* (1956); Thomas S. Kuhn, *The Copernican Revolution* (1957); Paul O. Kristeller, *Renaissance Thought: The Classic, Scholastic, and Humanistic Strains* (rev. 1961); John R. Hale, *The Civilization of Europe in the Renaissance* (1993); Jerry Brotton, *The Renaissance* (2006).

Renaissance (historical period): **280**; *24, 161*.

Renaissance, American: 274.

Renaissance, Harlem: 157.

Renaissance, Irish Literary: 45.

Renaissance man: 339.

repartee (rĕp′ ärtē″): **421**; *55*.

representation (in new historicism): **245**.

resolution (of a plot): **297**.

Restoration: 282.

Restoration comedy: 55; *282, 421*.

revenge tragedy: 409.

reversal (in a plot): **297**; *365*.

Revolutionary Age (in American literature): **274**.

rhetoric: In his *Poetics* the Greek philosopher Aristotle defined poetry as a mode of *imitation*—a fictional representation in a verbal medium of human beings thinking, feeling, acting, and interacting—and focused his discussion on elements such as plot, character, thought, and diction within the work itself. In his *Rhetoric*, on the other hand, Aristotle defined rhetorical discourse as the art of "discovering all the available means of persuasion in any given case," and focused his discussion on the means and devices that an orator uses in order to achieve the intellectual and emotional effects on an audience that will persuade them to accede to the orator's point of view. Most of the later rhetoricians of the classical era concurred in the view that the concern of rhetoric is with the type of discourse whose chief aim is to persuade an audience to

参阅：J. 布克哈特所著的《意大利文艺复兴时期的文化》(1860 年第一版)；E. A. 伯特所著的《近代物理科学的形而上学基础》(1932 年修订版)；C. S. 刘易斯所著的《16 世纪英国文学》(1954)；玛乔丽·尼科尔森所著的《科学与想象力》(1956)；托马斯·库恩所著的《哥白尼革命》(1957)；保罗·O. 克里斯泰勒所著的《文艺复兴思想：古典的、经院的和人文主义的风格》(1961 年修订版)；约翰·R. 黑尔所著的《文艺复兴时期的欧洲文明》(1993)；杰里·布罗顿所著的《文艺复兴》(2006)。

Renaissance (historical period)：文艺复兴（历史时期）　280；*24, 161*。

Renaissance, American：美国的文艺复兴时期　274。

Renaissance, Harlem：哈莱姆文艺复兴　157。

Renaissance, Irish Literary：爱尔兰文学复兴　45。

Renaissance man：文艺复兴人　339。

repartee：机智应答　421；*55*。

representation (in new historicism)：(新历史主义中的) 陈述　245。

resolution (of a plot)：(情节中的) 冲突解开　297。

Restoration：王政复辟时期　282。

Restoration comedy：王政复辟时期的喜剧　55；*282, 421*。

revenge tragedy：复仇悲剧　409。

reversal (in a plot)：(情节中的) 逆转　297；*365*。

Revolutionary Age (in American literature)：(美国文学中的) 独立战争时期　274。

Rhetoric：修辞学

　　古希腊哲学家亚里士多德在《诗学》中将诗歌定义为一种摹仿形式——诗歌以文字为媒介虚构地表现了人们的思想、情感、行为和相互作用——并着重讨论了作品本身的情节、人物、思想和措辞等因素。另一方面，亚里士多德又在《修辞学》中把修辞话语定义为一种艺术，这种艺术能"在任何特定情况下发现所有可以获得的劝说手段"。他还着重论述了演说家为了对听众造成理智与情感上的效果而采用的手段策略，这种理智与情感上的效果将会说服听众接受演说家的观点。后来古典时期的大部分修辞学家们一致认为，修辞学关注的是那种旨在

think and feel or act in a particular way. (A notable exception is the major Roman rhetorician Quintilian who, in the first century, gave rhetoric a moral basis by defining it as the art "of a good man skilled in speaking.") In a broad sense, then, rhetoric can be described as the study of language in its practical uses, focusing on the persuasive and other effects of language, and on the means by which one can achieve those effects on auditors or readers.

Following Aristotle's lead, classical theorists analyzed an effective rhetorical discourse as consisting of three components: *invention* (the finding of arguments or proofs), **disposition** (the arrangement of such materials), and *style* (the choice of words, verbal patterns, and rhythms that will most effectively express and convey these materials). This last topic of "style" came to include extensive classifications and analyses of *figurative language*. Rhetoricians also discriminated three main classes of oratory, each of which uses characteristic devices to achieve its distinctive type of persuasive effect:

1. **Deliberative**—to persuade an audience (such as a legislative assembly) to approve or disapprove of a matter of public policy, and to act accordingly.
2. **Forensic**—to achieve (for example, in a judicial trial) either the condemnation or approval of some person's actions.
3. **Epideictic**—"display rhetoric," used on appropriate, usually ceremonial, occasions to enlarge upon the praiseworthiness (or sometimes, the blameworthiness) of a person or group of persons, and in so doing, to display the orator's own talents and skill in rising to the rhetorical demands of the occasion. Abraham Lincoln's "Gettysburg Address" is a famed instance of epideictic oratory. In America, it remains traditional for a chosen speaker to meet the challenge of the Fourth of July or other dates of national significance by appropriately ceremonious oratory. The *ode* is a poetic form often used for epideictic purposes. A composition in prose or a public speech in sustained and elaborate praise of a person, group, or deed is called a **panegyric**.

Figurative language, although dealt with at length in classical and later traditional rhetorics, had been considered as only one element of style and, often, as subordinated to the overall aim of persuasion. Within the past century, however, the analysis of the types and functions of figurative language has been increasingly excerpted from this rhetorical context and made an independent and central concern, not only by critics of literature but also by language theorists and by philosophers. (See *metaphor, theories of*.) Some recent theorists regard all modes of discourse to be constituted by "rhetorical" and figurative elements which are inherently nonreferential and counterlogical, and therefore subvert attempts to speak or write in ways that have decidable meanings, or logical coherence, or reference to a world beyond language. (See *deconstruction*.) Other theorists undertake to develop a **cognitive rhetoric**, from the viewpoint of "cognitive science"—that is, representations of the most general operations of the mind and brain (based in part on the workings of high-level computers), which cut across the standard distinctions between literary and nonliterary, and between rhetorical and nonrhetorical mental and

劝说听众以独特方式思维、感觉和行动的话语类型（古罗马著名修辞学家昆体良是个值得注意的例外。公元 1 世纪，昆体良将修辞学定义为"擅长演说的善良人士的"艺术，从而赋予修辞学以道德基础）。广义上，修辞学是对语言实际运用的研究，侧重于研究语言的说服性和其他效果，以及能对听众或读者产生这些效果的策略。

古典理论家在亚里士多德的引导下，将有效的修辞话语分析为由三个部分组成：文学创新（发现论点和论据），**布局**（论点和论据在行文上的安排）与文体（选择能够最有效地表达这些论点、论据的词语、言语模式与节奏）。最后这一部分，"文体"，包含了对*修辞性语言*进行的广泛分类与分析。修辞学家们还将雄辩术分成三大类，每一类都有其特殊策略以取得其独特说服效果：

1. **审议性的**——用于说服听众（如立法会议等）赞同或反对某项公共政策，并要求听众采取相应的行动。

2. **法庭式的**——用于谴责或赞同某人的行为（如法庭审理）。

3. **富于辞藻的**——"展示修辞的"，通常用于合适的礼仪场合，详细论述某个人或某类人的可钦佩之处（有时也可能是应受责备之处），并以此来展现演说者迎合该场合修辞需求的才华与技巧。亚伯拉罕·林肯的《葛底斯堡演说》就是著名的富于辞藻的范例。在美国，为迎接 7 月 4 日或其他国家性的节日而选择某位演说者发表合乎礼仪的演说，仍然是一项传统。颂是经常用于富于辞藻的目的的一种诗歌形式。持续而精心地赞美一个人、群体或事迹的散文形式的诗篇或公开演讲叫做**颂词**。

尽管古典修辞学与后来的传统修辞学都长篇大论地探讨*比喻语*，但它被视为只是文体的要素之一，通常从属于劝说这一总体目标。然而，在 20 世纪，有关修辞性语言的类型和功能的分析已经逐渐脱离了这种修辞语境，文学批评家、语言理论家与哲学家都将其视为独立的和关注的中心。（参见：*隐喻理论*。）当代一些理论家认为，所有的话语模式都由"修辞的"和比喻的因素组成，这些因素本身不具有指代性而且是反逻辑的，因此颠覆了那种试图按照确定意义、逻辑连贯、或指代语言外部世界的方式说话或书写的努力。（参见：*解构主义*。）其他理论家正从"认知科学"——即对思维与大脑最普遍的运作的描述（部分以发展高层次计算机所面临的问题为基础）——的角度出发，形成一种**认知修辞学**。这种修辞学跨越了文学与非文学、修辞与非修辞的思维和语言过程之间的一般界限。

linguistic processes. See Mark Turner, *Reading Minds: The Study of English in the Age of Cognitive Science* (1991) and *The Literary Mind* (1996).

Refer to *ethos* (the rhetorical concept of a speaker's projected character that functions as a means of persuasion) under *persona, tone, and voice*; also *rhetorical criticism*. See Aristotle's *Rhetoric*, ed. Lane Cooper (1932), and George A. Kennedy, ed., *Aristotle on Rhetoric* (1991); Quintilian, *Institutes of Oratory* (4 vols., Loeb Classical Library, 1920–22); M. L. Clarke, *Rhetoric at Rome: A Historical Survey* (1953); George Kennedy, *The Art of Persuasion in Greece* (1963); Edward P. J. Corbett, *Classical Rhetoric for the Modern Student* (4th ed., 1998); Thomas O. Sloane, ed., *Encyclopedia of Rhetoric* (2001). For a brief history of rhetoric, from the Greeks to the revived interest among contemporary theorists, see Renato Barilli, *Rhetoric* (trans. 1989). Walter J. Ong, in *Orality and Literacy: The Technologizing of the Word* (1982), discusses the central and pervasive role of rhetoric in Western education through the eighteenth century, and the attendant view that the oral rather than the written mode is the paradigmatic use of language.

For references to *rhetoric* in other entries, see page 65.

rhetorical criticism: The Roman Horace in his versified *Art of Poetry* (first century BC) declared that the aim of a poet is to either instruct or delight a reader, and preferably to do both. This view, by making poetry a calculated means to achieve effects on its audience, breaks down Aristotle's distinction between imitative poetry and persuasive rhetoric (see *rhetoric*). Such *pragmatic criticism* became the dominant form of literary theory from late classical times through the eighteenth century. Discussions of poetry in that long span of time absorbed and expanded upon the analytic terms that had been developed in traditional rhetoric, and represented a poem mainly as a deployment of established artistic means for achieving foreseen effects upon its readers. The triumph in the early nineteenth century of *expressive* theories of literature (which conceive a work primarily as the expression of the feelings, temperament, and mental powers of the author), followed by the prominence, beginning in the 1920s, of *objective* theories of literature (which maintain that a work should be considered as an object in itself, independently of the attributes and intentions of the author and the responses of a reader), served to diminish, and sometimes to eliminate, rhetorical considerations in literary criticism. See under *criticism*.

Since the late 1950s, however, there has been a strong revival of interest in literature as a mode of communication from author to reader, and this has led to the development of a **rhetorical criticism** which, without departing from a primary focus on the literary work itself, undertakes to identify and analyze those elements within a poem or a prose narrative which are there primarily in order to effect certain responses in a reader. As Wayne Booth said in the preface to his influential book *The Rhetoric of Fiction* (rev. 1983), his subject is "the rhetorical resources available to the writer of epic, novel, or short story as he tries, consciously or unconsciously, to impose his fictional

参阅：马克·特纳所著的《阅读思维：在认知科学时代学习英语》(1991)和《文学思想》(1996)。

参见：*第一人称*、*基调*和*言念*中的特质（这是一个修辞学概念，表示说话者投射出的、作为劝说手段起作用的个性）；也可参见：*修辞学批评*。参阅：亚里士多德所著的《修辞学》(1932，莱恩·库珀主编)和乔治·A. 肯尼迪主编的《亚里士多德论修辞学》(1991)；昆体良所著的四卷本《雄辩术原理》(洛布古典丛书，1920—1922)；M. L. 克拉克所著的《古罗马修辞学：历史考察》(1953)；乔治·肯尼迪所著的《古希腊说服艺术》(1963)；爱德华·P. J. 科比特所著的《写给现代学生的古典修辞学》(1998 年第 4 版)；托马斯·O. 斯隆主编的《修辞学百科全书》(2001)。有关修辞学的简短历史，从古希腊时期到当代理论家的重新关注，参阅：雷纳多·巴里利所著的《修辞学》(1989 年英译版)。沃尔特·J. 翁格在其所著的《口头表达和读写能力：文字科技化》(1982) 中，讨论了修辞学在整个 18 世纪西方教育中所起的核心和普遍作用，以及相伴而生的观点：口头表达而非书写模式是使用语言的范式。

其他条目中提及"修辞学"的地方，参见第 65 页。

Rhetorical Criticism：修辞学批评

古罗马的贺拉斯在他的韵文体著作《诗艺》（公元前 1 世纪）中声称，诗人的目的或是为了对读者说教，或是让读者得到乐趣，最好是二者兼有。这种观点将诗歌视为经过精心构思并对读者产生影响的一种手段，从而打破了亚里士多德对摹仿性诗歌与劝说性修辞（参见：*修辞学*）之间的区别。这种*实用主义批评*自古典时代后期开始直到 18 世纪，一直是占据统治地位的文学理论类型。在漫长的时期里，有关诗歌的讨论，吸收扩展了传统修辞学所形成的分析术语，并认为诗歌主要是利用了已有的艺术手段，对读者产生预见的效果。19 世纪早期*表现主义*文学理论的胜利（将作品视为是表达作者的情感、性情和智力）以及从 1920 年代起占据统治地位的*客观*文学理论（认为必须把作品自身视为一个客体，不受作者品质、意图和读者反应的制约），都削弱了有时甚至消除了文学批评对修辞法的考虑。参见：*文学批评*。

然而，从 1950 年代后期开始，文学界重又强烈地把文学看做是从作者到读者的一种交流模式，这导致**修辞学批评**的发展。修辞学批评主要关注的仍是文学作品本身，力图辨认并分析诗歌或散文叙事中主要是为了引起读者某些反应的那些因素。韦恩·布思在其影响深远的《小说修辞学》(1983 年修订版) 的序言中指出，他的主旨是分析"史诗作者、小说家或短篇小说家在试图将自己虚构的世界强加于读者时有意或无意地选用的修辞手法"。近代许多散文体小说和叙

world upon the reader." A number of recent critics of prose fiction and of narrative and non-narrative poems have emphasized the author's use of a variety of means—including the authorial presence or "voice" that he or she projects—in order to engage the interest and guide the imaginative and emotional responses of the readers to whom, whether consciously or not, the literary work is addressed. (See *persona, tone, and voice*.) Since the 1960s there has also emerged a reader-response criticism which focuses upon a reader's interpretive responses to the sequence of words in a literary text; most of its representatives, however, either ignore or reject the rhetorical view that such responses are effected by devices that, for the most part, are contrived for that purpose by the author. See *reader-response criticism*.

For recent examples of the rhetorical criticism of poetry and fiction see (in addition to Wayne Booth) Kenneth Burke, *A Rhetoric of Motives* (1955); M. H. Nichols, *Rhetoric and Criticism* (1963); Donald C. Bryant, ed., *Papers in Rhetoric and Poetic* (1965); Edward P. J. Corbett, ed., *Rhetorical Analyses of Literary Works* (1969); Brian Vickers, *Classical Rhetoric in English Poetry* (2d ed., 1989).

rhetorical figures: It is convenient to list under this heading some common "figures of speech" which depart from what is experienced by competent users as the standard, or "literal," use of language mainly by the arrangement of their words to achieve special effects, and not, like metaphors and other *tropes*, by a radical change in the meaning of the words themselves. (See *figurative language*.) A number of current theorists, however, reject the distinction between figures of speech and tropes; some reject even the general distinction between literal and figurative language. (See *metaphor, theories of*.)

Anaphora (Greek for "repetition") is the deliberate repetition of a word or phrase at the beginning of each one of a sequence of sentences, paragraphs, lines of verse, or *stanzas*. "A Song" by the seventeenth-century English poet Thomas Carew begins:

> Ask me no more where Jove bestows,
> When June is past the fading rose....

Each of the remaining four stanzas also begins with the words: "Ask me no more." Anaphora is frequent in the Bible and in verse or prose strongly influenced by the Bible, such as Walt Whitman's poems, or sermons by eloquent black preachers. In the powerful address to Civil Rights marchers by the Reverend Martin Luther King, Jr., in front of the Lincoln Memorial in 1963, five successive sentences begin, "I have a dream," and six later sentences begin, "Let freedom ring."

An **apostrophe** is a direct and explicit address either to an absent person or to an abstract or nonhuman entity. Often the effect is of high formality, or else of a sudden emotional impetus. Many *odes* are constituted throughout in the mode of such an address to a listener who is not literally able to listen. So John Keats begins his "Ode on a Grecian Urn" (1820) by apostrophizing the

事体或非叙事体诗歌的批评家强调，作家使用的各种手法——包括他或她投射到作品中的作家存在或"言念"——旨在唤起读者的兴趣，引导读者的想象反应与情感反应——文学作品总是有意无意地面向读者。（参见：*第一人称、基调和言念*。）1960年代以来出现了读者反应批评，重点关注读者对文学文本中一系列词语的阐释性反应。不过，读者反应批评的大多数代表，要么忽视、要么拒绝承认这样的修辞学观点，即读者的这些反应主要是作者为了达到此目的而有意运用的修辞手段所造成的。参见：*读者反应批评*。

有关对诗歌与小说的修辞学批评的近代论著（除了韦恩·布思的作品）还可参阅：肯尼斯·伯克所著的《动机修辞学》（1955）；M. H. 尼科尔斯所著的《修辞学与批评》（1963）；唐纳德·C. 布赖恩特主编的《修辞学与诗学论文选》（1965）；爱德华·P. J. 科比特主编的《文学作品的修辞学分析》（1969）；布莱恩·维克斯所著的《英语诗歌中的古典修辞》（1989年第2版）。

Rhetorical Figures：修辞格

在这一条目下，可以很顺当地列出一些普通的"修辞格"，它们经过排列组合便能产生特殊效果，从而有别于有能力的使用者感知为寻常的语言使用或"字面上的"语言使用；普通的修辞格不会彻底改变词语自身的意义，这一点与隐喻及其他比喻不同。（参见：*比喻语*。）但是，当代许多理论家都反对修辞格与比喻之间的区别，有些理论家甚至反对字面语言与比喻语之间的一般区分。（参见：*隐喻理论*。）

首语重复法（希腊语意为"重复"）是指有意在每个句子、段落、诗行或*诗节*的开始重复一个词或短语。17世纪英国诗人托马斯·卡鲁的《不要再问我》这样开头：

> 不要再问我，爱神在哪里，
> 当六月过去，玫瑰凋残……

余下四个诗节的每一个都以"不要再问我"开始。首语重复法在圣经及受到圣经很大影响的诗歌或散文中很常见，比如沃尔特·惠特曼的诗，或者是雄辩的黑人牧师的布道词。在1963年牧师小马丁·路德·金对民权运动游行者和在林肯纪念碑前所发表的有力的演说中，五个相连的句子都始于"我有一个梦想"，六个随后的句子都始于"让自由之声响彻"。

呼语法直接明了地针对一位不在场的人物或一个抽象的、非人类的实体发话。呼语法往往具有十分拘谨的效果，或引起突然的感情冲动。这种呼语法模式贯穿于许多*颂*中，面对的是原本无法聆听的听者。约翰·济慈在《希腊古瓮颂》（1820）一诗的开头就对古瓮采用了呼语法——"你，尚未失身的恬静的新

Urn—"Thou still unravished bride of quietness"—and directs the entirety of the poem to the Urn and to the figures represented on it. Samuel Taylor Coleridge's fine lyric "Recollections of Love" (1817) is an apostrophe addressed to an absent woman; at the end of the poem, Coleridge, while speaking still to his beloved, turns by a sudden impulse to apostrophize also the River Greta:

> But when those meek eyes first did seem
> To tell me, Love within you wrought—
> O Greta, dear domestic stream!
> Has not, since then, Love's prompture deep,
> Has not Love's whisper evermore
> Been ceaseless, as thy gentle roar?
> Sole voice, when other voices sleep,
> Dear under-song in clamor's hour.

Many apostrophes, as in these examples from Keats and Coleridge, imply a *personification* of the nonhuman object that is addressed. (See Jonathan Culler, "Apostrophe," in *The Pursuit of Signs*, 1981.)

If such an address is to a god or muse or other supernatural being to assist the poet in his composition, it is called an **invocation**. An invocation often serves to establish the authoritative or prophetic identity of the poetic *voice*; thus John Milton invokes divine guidance at the opening of *Paradise Lost*:

> And chiefly Thou, O Spirit, that dost prefer
> Before all temples th' upright heart and pure,
> Instruct me....

Chiasmus (derived from the Greek term for the letter X, or for a crossover) is a sequence of two phrases or clauses which are parallel in syntax, but which reverse the order of the corresponding words. So in this line from Pope, the verb first precedes, then follows, the adverbial phrase:

> *Works* without show, and without pomp *presides*.

The crossover is sometimes reinforced by alliteration and other similarities in the length and component sounds of words, as in Pope's summary of the common fate of coquettes after marriage:

> A *fop* their *passion*, but their *prize* a *sot*.

In Yeats' "An Irish Airman Foresees His Death" (1919), the chiasmus consists in a reversal of the position of an entire phrase:

> The years to come seemed *waste of breath*,
> A *waste of breath* the years behind.[13]

---

[13] Lines from "An Irish Airman Foresees His Death" reprinted with permission of Scribner, an imprint of Simon and Schuster Adult Publishing, from *The Poems of W. B. Yeats: A New Edition*, edited by Richard J. Finneran. Copyright © 1919 by Macmillan Publishing Company, renewed 1947 by Bertha Georgie Yeats.

娘"——并将诗歌的整体指向古瓮及古瓮上呈现的图形。塞缪尔·泰勒·柯勒律治优美的抒情诗《爱的回忆》(1817)就是面对一位不在场的女士的呼语；在诗歌结尾处，柯勒律治仍在向他心爱的人倾诉，但在突然的冲动下转向了对格里塔河的呼唤：

> 但是那温顺的目光第一次似乎就在
> 告诉我，你内心激荡着爱——
> 噢，格里塔河，亲爱的温顺的河流！
> 难道，自那时起，爱的内心深处，
> 难道爱的私语就已经永远
> 不再停息，正如你温和的呼喊？
> 当其他声音沉寂时，
> 你孤独的声音成了喧嚣时刻亲切的衬腔。

正如以上济慈与柯勒律治的例子所示，许多呼语都暗含着对聆听话语的非人类物体的拟人。[参阅：乔纳森·卡勒所著的《符号的追寻》(1981)中的"呼语法"。]

如果呼语法是为了祈求神灵、缪斯或其他超自然力量在诗人创作时助其一臂之力，这种呼语法就叫祈愿词。祈愿词通常有助于树立诗歌言念的权威性或预言性的特征。弥尔顿在《失乐园》的开篇处就祈求神灵的引导：

> 啊，天神，你更喜欢一颗
> 正直纯洁的心，胜于一切寺庙，
> 教导我吧……　　　　　　　　　　　　　　（顾子欣译）

交错配列法（源自希腊文，表示字母X或交叉形状的名称），是指句法平行的一对短语或短句，其对应词的顺序正好相反。在以下蒲柏的这一诗句中，动词最初位于副词短语之前，随后又出现在副词短语之后：

> 工作毫不炫耀，也不受炫耀主宰。

有时，头韵及单词长度和语音的其他相似之处也会加强交错配列的效果。譬如，蒲柏在以下诗行中概述了卖弄风情的女子婚后的普遍命运：

> 她们热恋纨绔子弟，但捕获的却是酒鬼。

在叶芝的《爱尔兰飞行员预见自己的死亡》(1919)一诗中，交错配列法构成了整个短语的位置倒转：

> 未来的日子是一句空话，
> 过去的岁月已年华虚耗。　　　　　　　　　（顾子欣译）

And as a reminder that all figures of speech occur in prose as well as in verse, here is an instance of chiasmus in the position of the two adjectives in Shelley's *Defence of Poetry* (1821): "Poetry is the record of the best and happiest moments of the happiest and best minds."

In **paralipsis** someone says that he need not, or will not, say something, then proceeds to do so. The most familiar use of the figure is on public occasions in which an introducer says that a speaker needs no introduction, then goes on to introduce him or her, often at considerable length. The classic literary example is Mark Antony's funeral oration, in the third act of Shakespeare's *Julius Caesar*, which is constructed around the repeated and devastatingly ironic use of this figure. The speech begins, for example, with the statement "I came to bury Caesar, not to praise him," then proceeds to eulogize Caesar and to incite his auditors against the "honorable men" who have assassinated him.

A **rhetorical question** is a sentence in the grammatical form of a question which is not asked in order to request information or to invite a reply, but to achieve a greater expressive force than a direct assertion. In everyday discourse, for example, if we utter the rhetorical question "Isn't it a shame?" it functions as a forceful alternative to the assertion "It's a shame." (In terms of modern *speech-act theory*, its "illocutionary force" is not to question but to assert.) The figure is often used in persuasive discourse, and tends to impart an oratorical tone to an utterance, whether in prose or verse. When "fierce Thalestris" in Alexander Pope's *The Rape of the Lock* (1714) asks Belinda,

> Gods! Shall the ravisher display your hair,
> While the fops envy, and the ladies stare?

she does not stay for an answer, which she obviously thinks should be "No!" (A common form of rhetorical question is one that won't take "Yes" for an answer.) Shelley's "Ode to the West Wind" (1820) closes with the most famous rhetorical question in English:

> O, Wind,
> If Winter comes, can Spring be far behind?

This figure was a favorite of W. B. Yeats. A well-known instance is "Among School Children," which ends with the rhetorical question, "How can we know the dancer from the dance?" In this instance the poetic context indicates that the question is left hanging because it is unanswerable, posing a problem for which there is no certain solution. In a *deconstructive* reading of this and other examples in his *Allegories of Reading* (1979), Paul de Man proposed that it is impossible to decide, not only what the answer is to the question, but also whether it is or is not a question.

Zeugma in Greek means "yoking"; in the most common present usage, it is applied to expressions in which a single word stands in the same grammatical relation to two or more other words, but with an obvious shift in its

值得一提的是，所有的修辞格不但出现在诗歌中，也出现在散文里。下面这个句子摘自雪莱的《诗辩》(1821)。这句话中出现了两个形容词位置的交错配列："诗歌是最愉快、最优秀的思想对最美好、最幸福时刻的记录。"

在**假省笔法**中，某人说他不需要或者不会说出某些事，然后就这样做了。它最熟悉的用法是在公共场合，介绍人说这位发言人无需介绍，然后开始介绍他/她，经常比较冗长。文学中的经典例子是莎士比亚《尤利乌斯·恺撒》中第三幕马克·安东尼的祭文，围绕对这一修辞格的重复和极具反讽性的使用构思而成。例如，开篇始于这一声明："我来是为了埋葬恺撒而不是赞颂他"，然后开始颂扬恺撒，鼓动听众起来反对那些暗杀了恺撒的"贵人"。

修辞性疑问句在语法结构上是问句的形式，但这种问句并不是为了获取信息或请求回答，而是为了达到比直接陈述更富表现力的效果。例如，在日常话语中，如果我们说"难道这不是件丢脸的事吗？"这个修辞性疑问句就更为有力地表达了陈述句"这是件丢脸的事"这一断言。（用现代*言语行为理论*中的术语来说，修辞性疑问句的"言外作用"在于断言而非提问。）修辞性疑问句常用于劝说性的话语里，不论是在散文还是在诗歌中，这种修辞手法往往会给言语注入雄辩的基调。在亚历山大·蒲柏的《卷发遇劫记》(1714) 一诗中，"暴怒的泰勒斯忒瑞斯"质问贝琳达：

> 天哪！劫掠者会展示你的头发，
> 让纨绔子弟羡慕、女士凝视吗？

她并不期待回答，她显然认为答案只是"不！"（最常见的修辞性疑问句是答案绝不会是"是的"的问题。）雪莱的《西风颂》(1820) 以最著名的英语修辞性疑问句结尾：

> 西风啊，
> 假如冬天已到，春天还会远吗？

修辞性疑问句是 W. B. 叶芝最喜欢采用的修辞手法。著名的例子是《在学童中间》一诗的结尾处出现的"我们怎能区分舞蹈与跳舞的人呢？"这一修辞性疑问句。在这个例子中，诗歌的语境很可能表明，这一问句悬而未决，因为该句提出了一个没有确定答案的问题，从而使得问题无法回答。在他的《阅读的寓言》(1979) 中对这一例子和其他例子进行的*解构主义*阐释中，保罗·德·曼认为：不仅这个问题的答案是不可能决定的，就连它是不是一个问题都是无法决定的。

轭式搭配法这个词的希腊文原意是"上轭"，现在最常用于指代这样的表达方式，即一个词与其他两个或两个以上词语之间具有相同的语法关系，但其意义

significance. Sometimes the word is literal in one relation and metaphorical in the other. Here are two examples of zeugma in Pope:

> Or *stain* her honour, or her new brocade.

> *Obliged* by hunger, and request of friends.

Byron uses zeugma for grimly comic effects in his description of a shipwreck in *Don Juan* (1819–24), Canto 2:

> And the waves oozing through the port-hole *made*
> His berth a little damp, and him afraid.

> The loud tempests *raise*
> The waters, and repentance for past sinning.

To achieve the maximum of concentrated verbal effects within the tight limits of the *closed couplet*, Pope in the early eighteenth century exploited all the language patterns described in this entry with supreme virtuosity. He is an English master of the rhetorical figures, as Shakespeare is of tropes.

Other linguistic patterns or "schemes" that are sometimes classified as rhetorical figures are treated elsewhere in this *Glossary*; see *antithesis, alliteration, assonance*, rhetorical *climax* (under *bathos*), and *parallelism*. For concise definitions and examples of additional figures of speech which are less commonly referred to in literary analyses, refer to Richard A. Lanham, *A Handlist of Rhetorical Terms* (2d ed., 1991); Edward P. J. Corbett, *Classical Rhetoric for the Modern Student* (4th ed., 1998); and Arthur Quinn's entertaining and informative *Figures of Speech: Sixty Ways to Turn a Phrase* (1993). See references under "*figurative language.*"

rhetorical question: 347.

rhyme: In English versification, standard rhyme consists of the repetition, in the rhyming words, of the last stressed vowel and of all the speech sounds following that vowel: láte-fáte; fóllow-hóllow.

End rhymes, by far the most frequent type, occur at the end of a verse line. **Internal rhymes** occur within a verse line, as in the Victorian poet Algernon Swinburne's

> Sister, my sister, O *fleet sweet* swallow.

A stanza from Coleridge's "The Rime of the Ancient Mariner" illustrates the patterned use both of internal rhymes (within lines 1 and 3) and of an end rhyme (lines 2 and 4):

> In mist or *cloud*, on mast or *shroud*,
> It perched for vespers *nine*;
> Whiles all the *night*, through fog-smoke *white*,
> Glimmered the white moon-*shine*.

却有明显的转化。有时，这个词与其中一个词搭配的是字面意思，与另一个词搭配的却是比喻义。在下面两个例子中，蒲柏就使用了轭式搭配法：

> 或玷污她的声誉，或她的新锦缎。

> 受到饥饿与朋友要求的胁迫。

拜伦采用轭式搭配法来营造冷嘲的滑稽效果。例如，在《唐·璜》(1819—1824) 第二章中关于海难的描写：

> 从舷窗渗进的海水把他的床
> 弄得有些湿，也使他的心发慌。
> 咆哮的暴风雨激起
> 海浪，激起对过去罪孽的忏悔。　　　　　　　　　（查良铮译）

为了在*闭合双韵体*的严格约束下获得最大限度的文字集中效果，蒲柏在 18 世纪初以其精妙绝伦的技艺，采用了本条目中描述的所有语言模式。正如莎士比亚是英语比喻用法的大师，蒲柏是英语修辞格用法的巨匠。

　　本书还讨论了其他一些常被列入修辞格范围的语言模式或"手法"，参见：*对偶、头韵、半谐音、修辞层进法（突降法中）、对仗*等。有关文学分析中其他较为罕见的修辞格的简要定义和例子，参阅：理查德·A.拉纳姆所著的《修辞用语手册》(1991 年第 2 版)；爱德华·P. J.科比特所著的《适用于现代学者的古典修辞学》(1998 年第 4 版)；阿瑟·奎因所著的既有趣味又长见识的《修辞：造一个短语的 60 种方式》(1993)。参见"比喻语"中的参考书目。

rhetorical question：修辞性疑问句　　**347**。

Rhyme：押韵

　　在英语韵律中，标准的押韵重复了押韵词的最后一个重读元音之后的所有语音，如 late-fate、follow-hollow。

　　尾韵是目前最常见的一种韵律类型，出现在诗行的结尾处。**中间韵**出现在诗行内，例如，在维多利亚时期诗人阿尔杰农·斯温伯恩以下的诗句中：

> 姐妹，我的姐妹，哦轻盈温柔的燕子。

选自柯勒律治《古舟子咏》中的这一诗节展现了中间韵（第一、三行）与尾韵（第二、四行）的典型用法：

> 它在桅索上栖息了九夜，
> 无论是雾夜或满天阴云；
> 而一轮皎月透过白雾，
> 迷离闪烁，朦朦胧胧。　　　　　　　　　　　　　（顾子欣译）

The numbered lines in the following stanza of Wordsworth's "The Solitary Reaper" (1807) are followed by a column which, in the conventional way, marks the terminal rhyme elements by a corresponding sequence and repetition of the letters of the alphabet:

1. Whate'er her theme, the maiden sang	*a*
2. As if her song could have no *ending*;	*b*
3. I saw her singing at her work	*c*
4. And o'er the sickle *bending*—	*b*
5. I listened, motionless and *still*;	*d*
6. And as I mounted up the *hill*,	*d*
7. The music in my heart I *bore*,	*e*
8. Long after it was heard no *more*.	*e*

Lines 1 and 3 do not rhyme with any other line. Both in lines 5 and 6 and in lines 7 and 8 the rhyme consists of a single stressed syllable, and is called a **masculine rhyme**: stíll–híll, bóre–móre. In lines 2 and 4, the rhyme consists of a stressed syllable followed by an unstressed syllable, and is called a **feminine rhyme**: éndĭng–béndĭng.

A feminine rhyme, since it involves the repetition of two syllables, is also known as a **double rhyme**. A rhyme involving three syllables is called a **triple rhyme**; such rhymes, since they coincide with surprising patness, usually have a comic quality. In *Don Juan* (1819–24) Byron often uses triple rhymes such as comparison–garrison, and sometimes intensifies the comic effect by permitting the pressure of the rhyme to force a distortion of the pronunciation. This maltreatment of words, called **forced rhyme**, in which the poet gives the effect of seeming to surrender helplessly to the exigencies of a difficult rhyme, has been comically exploited by the poet Ogden Nash:

If the correspondence of the rhymed sounds is exact, it is called **perfect rhyme**, or else "full" or "true rhyme." Until recently almost all English writers of serious poems have limited themselves to perfect rhymes, except for an occasional *poetic license* such as **eye-rhymes**: words whose endings are spelled alike, and in most instances were once pronounced alike, but have in the course of time acquired a different pronunciation: prove–love, daughter–laughter. Many modern poets, however, deliberately supplement perfect rhyme with **imperfect rhyme** (also known as **partial rhyme**, or else as **approximate rhyme, slant rhyme**, or **pararhyme**). This effect is fairly

以下标有数字的诗行选自华兹华斯的《孤独的收割者》(1807)，在诗行随后的一栏中，依据传统惯例，按照字母的相应顺序以及重复模式，标出了押尾韵的韵律要素：

(1) 不管唱的内容是什么，那姑娘　　　　a
(2) 唱的歌儿仿佛没有尽头；　　　　　　b
(3) 她一面干活，一面歌唱　　　　　　　c
(4) 手握着镰刀深深低着头——　　　　　b
(5) 我静静地站着默默地听；　　　　　　d
(6) 好久以后，当我爬上山顶，　　　　　d
(7) 歌声依然在我的耳畔回响，　　　　　e
(8) 虽然我早已听不到她歌唱。　　　　　e　　　（何功杰译）

第 1、3 行不和其他任何一行押韵。第 5、6 行和第 7、8 行的押韵都含有单个重读音节，这叫做**阳韵**：still-hill, bore-more。第 2、4 行的押韵格式是由一个重读音节加上一个非重读音节构成，这称为**阴韵**：ending-bending。

　　由于阴韵包含了两个音节的重复，因此也叫**叠韵**。由三个音节构成的韵律称为**三重韵**。三重韵与令人吃惊的轻拍感相似，所以通常带有滑稽的成分。在《唐·璜》(1819—1824) 中，拜伦常使用三重韵，如 comparison-garrison。诗人有时也强加上押韵，迫使发音发生歪曲，从而增强了滑稽的效果。这种滥用字词的押韵手法叫做**迫韵**。迫韵让人觉得诗人面对难度较大的押韵时似乎束手无策。奥格登·纳什在下面两行诗句（版权未授，请参旧版。——译注）中使用了迫韵，从而产生了滑稽的效果：

　　　　（略）

　　如果押韵的语音完全一致就叫**完美韵**，也可称为"全韵"或"真韵"。直至近代，几乎所有创作严肃诗歌的英语诗人都局限于使用完美韵。他们偶尔才会使用*诗的破格*，如**视觉韵**：押韵词的词尾拼写相同，大多数情况下发音也相同，但随着时间推移有了不同的发音，如 prove—love, daughter—laughter。但是，许多现代诗人有意采用**不完美韵**（也叫**半韵**、"近似韵""偏韵"或"平行韵"）来增补完美韵。这

common in *folk songs* such as children's verses, and it was employed occasionally by various writers of art lyrics such as Henry Vaughan in the seventeenth, William Blake in the late eighteenth, and very frequently by Emily Dickinson in the nineteenth century. Later, Gerard Manley Hopkins, W. B. Yeats, Wilfred Owen, and other poets systematically exploited partial rhymes, in which the vowels are only approximate or else quite different, and occasionally even the rhymed consonants are similar rather than identical. Wilfred Owen, in 1917–18, wrote the following six-line stanza using only two sets of partial rhymes, established at the ends of the first two lines:

In his poem "The Force That Through the Green Fuse Drives the Flower" (1933), Dylan Thomas uses, very effectively, such distantly approximate rhymes as (with masculine endings) trees–rose, rocks–wax, tomb–worm, and (with feminine endings) flower–destroyer–fever.

Rime riche (French for "rich rhyme") is the repetition of the consonant that precedes, as well as the one that follows, the last stressed vowel; the resulting pair of words are pronounced alike but have different meanings: stare-stair, night-knight. The device is common in French poetry and was adopted by Geoffrey Chaucer. Early in the General Prologue to *The Canterbury Tales*, for example, he rhymes "seke," which has two diverse meanings, "seek" and "sick." The pilgrims go to Canterbury

> the holy blissful martyr for to seke
> That hem hath holpen when they were seke.

The use of rime riche is very rare in English poetry after Chaucer.

The passages quoted above will illustrate some of the many effects that can be achieved by the device that has been called "making ends meet in verse"—the pleasure of the expected yet varying chime; the reinforcement of syntax and rhetorical emphasis when a strong masculine rhyme concurs with the end of a clause, sentence, or stanza; the sudden grace of movement that may be lent by a feminine rhyme; the broadening of the comic by a pat coincidence of sound; the haunting effect of the limited *consonance* in partial rhymes. Cunning artificers in verse make rhyme more than an auxiliary sound effect; they use it to enhance, or contribute to, or counterpoint the significance of the words. When Pope in the early eighteenth century satirized two contemporary pedants in the lines

种押韵效果在*民俗诗歌*（如童谣）中相当常见。17 世纪的亨利·沃恩、18 世纪末的威廉·布莱克等艺术抒情诗人偶尔也会采用这种押韵方法，而 19 世纪的埃米莉·狄金森则经常使用不完美韵。更近代的杰勒德·曼利·霍普金斯、W. B. 叶芝、威尔弗雷德·欧文等诗人都系统地利用了半韵。在他们的不完美韵中，元音只是相似或完全不同，有时连押韵的辅音也只是近似相同而非完全相同。威尔弗雷德·欧文在 1917—1918 年间创作了以下六行诗节。诗人仅仅在头两行诗句（版权未授，请参旧版。——译注）的结尾处采用了两组半韵：

（略）

迪兰·托马斯在其诗歌《那通过绿色的茎催放花朵的力》（1933）中十分有效地采用了（强音尾）trees-rose，rocks-wax，tomb-worm 和（弱音尾）flower-destroyer-fever 等模糊近似的押韵方式。

（完）全韵（法语中指"博韵"）是指重复协调一致的音节，这一音节先于或后接最后一个重读的元音；由此形成的两个词，发音相似，意思却完全不同，如：凝视 – 楼梯（stare-stair），夜晚 – 骑士（night-knight）。这一技巧在法语诗歌中比较常见并为杰弗里·乔叟所采用。例如，在《坎特伯雷故事集》总序（开场白）开始不久，他押韵"seke"，这个词有两个不同意思："寻找"和"生病"。朝圣者前往坎特伯雷

去朝谢医病救世的恩主，

以缅怀大恩大德的圣徒。

乔叟之后的英语诗歌中使用（完）全韵的情况非常少见。

以上引用的诗句说明了所谓的"诗歌中的将就凑合"这一手法的某些效果——意料之中却又不尽相同的声韵带来的愉悦；在短语、句子或诗节的结尾，重读阳韵同时出现增强了句法和修辞重点；借用阴韵使得行文突然变得高雅；语音与轻快节拍的重合扩大了滑稽效果；半韵中有限的*辅音韵*带来了萦绕于心的效果。诗歌的能工巧匠不仅把押韵当成辅助的语音效果，也用它来增强或补充字词的含义。蒲柏在 18 世纪初创作的以下诗行中，嘲讽了当时两位卖弄学问的人：

> Yet ne'er one sprig of laurel graced these ribalds,
> From slashing Bentley down to piddling Tibalds,

the rhyme of "Tibalds," as W. K. Wimsatt has said, demonstrates "what it means to have a name like that," with its implication that the scholar is as graceless as his appellation. And in one of its important functions, rhyme ties individual lines into the larger pattern of a *stanza*.

See George Saintsbury, *History of English Prosody* (3 vols., 1906–10); W. K. Wimsatt, "One Relation of Rhyme to Reason," in *The Verbal Icon* (1954); Donald Wesling, *The Chances of Rhyme: Device and Modernity* (1980); John Hollander, *Rhyme's Reason: A Guide to English Verse* (1981). For an analysis of the complex interrelations between sound repetitions and meaning, see Roman Jakobson, "Linguistics and Poetics," in his *Language and Literature* (1987). For references to *rhyme* in other entries, see page *140*.

rhythm: 217.

rime riche: 350.

rime royal: 376.

rising action: 296.

rituals: 230.

roman (the genre) (rōmän′): **252**.

roman à clef (French for "novel with a key"): A work of prose fiction in which the author expects the knowing reader to identify, despite their altered names, actual people of the time. The mode was begun in seventeenth-century France with novels such as Madeleine de Scudéry's *Le Grand Cyrus* (1649–53). An English example is Thomas Love Peacock's *Nightmare Abbey* (1818), whose characters are entertaining *caricatures* of such contemporary literary figures as Coleridge, Byron, and Shelley. A later instance is Aldous Huxley's *Point Counter Point* (1928), which represents, under fictional names, well-known English personages of the 1920s such as the novelist D. H. Lawrence, the critic Middleton Murry, and the right-wing political extremist Oswald Mosely.

romance, the: **48**; *8*. See also *prose romance*; *chivalric romance*; *Gothic romance*; *romantic comedy*; *wilderness romance*.

romance novels: Love stories that focus on the heroine rather than the hero, in which, after diverse obstacles have been overcome, the plots end happily with the betrothal or marriage of the lovers. This narrative form was exemplified early in such classic novels as Samuel Richardson's *Pamela* (1740) and in all six of Jane Austen's novels, published between 1811 and 1818. The term

> 但是月桂枝叶从来不会眷顾这些言谈粗俗者，
> 从尖锐的本特利一直到微不足道的蒂巴尔兹，

正如 W. K. 维姆萨特指出的那样，"Tibalds"上的押韵显示了"拥有那样的名字意味着什么"。言外之意，这位学者和他的名称一样不雅。另外，押韵的重要功能之一在于把单句诗行组成*诗节*这一更大的单位。

参阅：乔治·圣茨伯里所著的三卷本《英语韵律史》(1906—1910)；W. K. 维姆萨特所著的《语像》中的"押韵与理性的一种关系"(1954)；唐纳德·韦斯林所著的《押韵的时机：技巧与现代性》(1980)；约翰·霍兰德所著的《押韵的理由：英诗指南》(1981)。有关语音重复与意义之间复杂联系的分析，参阅：罗曼·雅各布森所写的文章"语言学和诗学"，收入其所著的《语言和文学》(1987)。其他条目中提及"押韵"的地方，参见第 140 页。

rhythm：韵律　217。

rime riche：(完)全韵　350。

rime royal：皇家韵律　376。

rising action：起始行动　296。

rituals：仪式　230。

roman（the genre）：小说（文学类型）　252。

Roman à Clef：影射小说（法语，意为"带有答案的小说"）

指一类散文体小说作品。这类小说的作者希望精明的读者能在小说中辨认出当时的真实人物，尽管人物的名字在小说中有所改变。这种模式始于17世纪的法国，如玛德琳·德·斯古德瑞的小说《居鲁士大帝》(1649—1653)。这类小说的英文代表作是托马斯·洛夫·皮科克的小说《噩梦隐修院》(1818)。小说中的人物是当时一些文人有趣的*讽刺漫画*，如柯勒律治、拜伦和雪莱。稍后的例子是奥尔德斯·赫胥黎的《针锋相对》(1928)。在这部小说中，我们可以找到以虚构名字出现的英国1920年代的著名人物，如小说家 D. H. 劳伦斯、文学批评家米德尔顿·默里、右翼政治极端分子奥斯瓦德·莫塞利。

romance, the：传奇　48；8。也可参见：*散文体传奇、骑士传奇、哥特式传奇、爱情喜剧、荒野传奇*。

Romance Novels：浪漫小说

更多关注女主角而非男主角的爱情故事，在故事中，在克服重重阻碍之后，结局圆满，有情人订下婚约或终成眷属。这种叙事形式的早期例子有塞缪尔·理查逊的《帕美勒》(1740)这样的经典小说和简·奥斯丁 1811—1818 年间出版的六本小说。

"romance novel," however, is usually applied specifically to works published since the 1950s and aimed at a mass market. Chief among them are the **Harlequin romances** published by Harlequin Enterprises, which is headquartered in Canada and employs over thirteen hundred authors, most of them women, who produce thousands of new titles each year in twenty-nine languages and on six continents. Such novels are sold in supermarkets and newsstands, rather than in traditional bookstores, and in annual sales far exceed all other novelistic types, including *detective stories* and *science fiction*.

The history and analysis of this novelistic form has increasingly become the subject of scholarly investigation; it now has its own literary periodical, the *Journal of Popular Romance Studies*, begun in 2010. Refer to Carol Thurston, *The Romance Revolution* (1987); and Pamela Regis, *A Natural History of the Romance Novel* (2003).

romantic (ideas and aims): **238**.

romantic comedy: 54.

romantic irony: 186.

Romantic Period: 283; *21, 30, 189*.

Romantic Period in America: 274.

round character: 46.

rules (linguistic): **197**.

rules (neoclassic): **237**.

run-on lines: 221.

Russian formalism: 138; 7. See also *formalism*.

不过,"浪漫小说"这一术语通常用来专门指1950年代以来出版的面向大众市场的作品。其中最主要的是禾林(Harlequin Enterprises)出版的**禾林罗曼司**,公司总部设在加拿大,雇有一千三百多名作者,其中大多数都是女性,每年在六大洲以二十九种语言生产上千种新作品。这样的小说主要在超市和报摊出售,而不是在传统书店,其年销售额远远超过其他所有小说类型,包括*侦探故事*和*科幻小说*。

这种小说形式的历史和分析已经越来越多地成为学术研究的主题;它现在有自己的文学期刊:《通俗罗曼司研究期刊》,创刊于2010年。参阅:卡罗尔·瑟斯顿所著的《浪漫的革命》(1987)和帕梅拉·里吉斯所著的《浪漫小说的自然史》(2003)。

romantic (ideas and aims):浪漫主义(观念和目标)　238。

romantic comedy:爱情喜剧　54。

romantic irony:浪漫主义反讽　186。

Romantic Period:浪漫主义时期　283;*21, 30, 189*。

Romantic Period in America:美国的浪漫主义时期　274。

round character:丰满的人物形象　46。

rules (linguistic):规则(语言学)　197。

rules (neoclassic):法则(新古典主义)　237。

run-on lines:跨行连句体诗行　221。

Russian formalism:俄国形式主义　138;*7*。也可参见:*形式主义*。

S

sarcasm: 186.

satire: Satire can be described as the literary art of diminishing or derogating a subject by making it ridiculous and evoking toward it attitudes of amusement, contempt, scorn, or indignation. It differs from the *comic* in that comedy evokes laughter mainly as an end in itself, while satire derides; that is, it uses laughter as a weapon, and against a butt that exists outside the work itself. That butt may be an individual (in "personal satire"), or a type of person, a class, an institution, a nation, or even (as in the Earl of Rochester's "A Satyr against Mankind," 1675, and much of Jonathan Swift's *Gulliver's Travels*, 1726, especially Book IV) the entire human race. The distinction between the comic and the satiric, however, is sharp only at its extremes. Shakespeare's Falstaff is mainly a comic creation, presented primarily for our enjoyment; the puritanical Malvolio in Shakespeare's *Twelfth Night* is for the most part comic but has aspects of satire directed against the type of the fatuous and hypocritical Puritan; Ben Jonson's *Volpone* (1607) clearly satirizes the type of person whose cleverness—or stupidity—is put at the service of his cupidity; and John Dryden's *MacFlecknoe* (1682), while representing a permanent type of the pretentious *poetaster*, satirized specifically the living author Thomas Shadwell.

Satire has usually been justified, by those who practice it, as a corrective of human vice and folly; Alexander Pope, for example, remarked that "those who are ashamed of nothing else are so of being ridiculous." Its frequent claim (not always borne out in the practice) has been to ridicule the failing rather than the individual, and to limit its ridicule to corrigible faults, excluding those for which a person is not responsible. As Swift said, speaking of himself in his *ironic* "Verses on the Death of Dr. Swift" (1739):

> Yet malice never was his aim;
> He lashed the vice, but spared the name....
> His satire points at no defect,
> But what all mortals may correct....
> He spared a hump, or crooked nose,
> Whose owners set not up for beaux.

Satire occurs as an incidental element within many works whose overall mode is not satiric—in a certain character or situation, or in an interpolated passage of ironic commentary on some aspect of the human condition or of contemporary society. But for some literary writings, verse or prose, the attempt to diminish a subject by ridicule is the organizing principle of the whole, and these works constitute the formal *genre* labeled "satires." In discussing such writings the following distinctions are useful:

1. Critics make a broad division between formal (or "direct") satire and indirect satire. In **formal satire** the satiric *persona* speaks out in the first

S

sarcasm：挖苦　186。

Satire：讽刺

讽刺可以称为一门文学艺术，用来使某一主体显得荒谬可笑，引起读者对这一主体产生乐趣、鄙夷、愤慨或蔑视的态度，并以此来贬低这一主体。讽刺与喜剧中的*滑稽*有所不同。滑稽把逗人发笑作为自身的主要目的，讽刺的目的则在于嘲笑，即把笑作为武器，抨击存在于作品之外的某个嘲讽对象。这个对象可以是某个人（在"个人讽刺"中），也可以是某种类型的人、某个阶级、某个机构、某一国家乃至整个人类 [如罗彻斯特伯爵的文章"对人类的讽刺"（1675）和乔纳森·斯威夫特《格列佛游记》（1726）中的大部分章节，尤其是第四卷]。不过，讽刺与滑稽之间的区别只有在极端的例子中才是明显的。莎士比亚笔下的福斯塔夫大体上是个滑稽人物，对他的描写主要是为了取悦观众。在《第十二夜》里，清教徒式的马伏里奥可算是个滑稽人物，但他身上也具有讽刺的方面，嘲讽了那些愚昧伪善的清教徒。本·琼森的《狐狸》（1607）显然是在讽刺那些将自己的聪明——或愚蠢——用于贪婪上的人。约翰·德莱顿的《迈克弗列诺》（1682）在描写自命不凡的*冒牌诗人*这一永恒类型时，具体讽刺了当时一位在世的作家：托马斯·沙德威尔。

用讽刺来矫正人类罪孽与愚蠢的人常常为讽刺辩护。例如，亚历山大·蒲柏曾评论道，"那些恬不知耻的人显得如此可笑"。作家经常讽刺的对象（并非总是来源于实践）通常是人类的弱点，而不是某个人；讽刺只用于可以改正的过失上，而不包含那些人们无法负责的过错。正如斯威夫特在《悼斯威夫特博士》（1739）这首*讽刺*诗中谈及自己时说道：

　　但恶意绝非他的目的；
　　他抨击罪恶，但隐去姓名……
　　他的讽刺不是针对缺陷，
　　而是针对所有凡人都可以改正的过失……
　　他不会抨击驼背，或歪鼻子，
　　它们的主人不是用来做情郎的。

在许多整体模式并非是讽刺的作品中偶尔也会出现讽刺要素——出现在某一人物、某一情景，或插入在某段评论人类现状和当时社会某一方面的讽刺篇章中。不过，在一些文学作品中，无论是韵文体还是散文体，利用嘲笑来贬低某一主体是整部作品的主要组织原则，这些作品也因此构成了"讽刺作品"这一文学形式的*类型*。在讨论这类文学作品时，以下区别颇有益处。

1. 文学批评家大体上区分了正规（或"直接"）讽刺和间接讽刺。**在正规讽刺中**，讽刺第一人称以第一人称的身份进行表述。

person. This "I" may address either the reader (as in Pope's *Moral Essays*, 1731–35), or else a character within the work itself, who is called the **adversarius** and whose major artistic function is to elicit and add credibility to the satiric speaker's comments. (In Pope's "Epistle to Dr. Arbuthnot," 1735, Arbuthnot serves as adversarius.) Two types of formal satire are commonly distinguished, taking their names from the great Roman satirists Horace and Juvenal. The types are defined by the character of the persona whom the author presents as the first-person satiric speaker, and also by the attitude and *tone* that such a persona manifests toward both the subject matter and the readers of the work.

In **Horatian satire** the speaker is an urbane, witty, and tolerant man of the world, who is moved more to wry amusement than to indignation at the spectacle of human folly, pretentiousness, and hypocrisy, and who uses a relaxed and informal language to evoke from readers a wry smile at human failings and absurdities—sometimes including his own. Horace himself described his aim as "to laugh people out of their vices and follies." Pope's *Moral Essays* and other formal satires for the most part sustain an Horatian stance.

In **Juvenalian satire** the speaker is a serious moralist who uses a dignified and public utterance to decry modes of vice and error which are no less dangerous because they are ridiculous, and who undertakes to evoke from readers contempt, moral indignation, or an unillusioned sadness at the aberrations of humanity. Samuel Johnson's "London" (1738) and "The Vanity of Human Wishes" (1749) are distinguished instances of Juvenalian satire. In its most denunciatory instances, this mode of satire resembles the *jeremiad*, whose model is not Roman but Hebraic.

2. **Indirect satire** is cast in some other literary form than that of direct address to the reader. The most common indirect form is that of a fictional narrative, in which the objects of the satire are characters who make themselves and their opinions ridiculous or obnoxious by what they think, say, and do, and are sometimes made even more ridiculous by the author's comments and narrative style.

One type of indirect satire is **Menippean satire**, modeled on a Greek form developed by the Cynic philosopher Menippus. It is sometimes called **Varronian satire**, after a Roman imitator, Varro; Northrop Frye, in *Anatomy of Criticism*, pp. 308–12, suggests an alternative name, the **anatomy**, after a major English instance of the type, Burton's *Anatomy of Melancholy* (1621). Such satires are written in prose, usually with interpolations of verse, and constitute a miscellaneous form often held together by a loosely constructed narrative. A prominent feature is a series of extended dialogues and debates (often conducted at a banquet or party) in which a group of loquacious eccentrics, pedants, literary people, and representatives of various professions or philosophical points of view serve to make ludicrous the attitudes and viewpoints they typify by the arguments they urge in their support. Examples are Rabelais' *Gargantua and Pantagruel* (1564), Voltaire's *Candide* (1759), Thomas Love

这个"我"可以与读者攀谈[如蒲柏的《道德论》(1731—1735)],或与作品内的某个人物进行交谈。这个人物叫做**对立者**,他在艺术上的主要作用在于引导讽刺表述者的评论或增加其评论的可信度。[在蒲柏的《致阿布斯纳博士书》(1735)中,阿布斯纳就起着对立者的作用。]正规讽刺通常分为两种,它们的名称源于两位伟大的古罗马讽刺作家贺拉斯与尤维纳利斯。这两种讽刺类型是依据作者指定的第一人称讽刺表述者来界定的,也可根据该讽刺表述者对作品的题材和作品读者所表达的态度与基调来界定。

在**贺拉斯式讽刺**中,讽刺的表述者是一个温文尔雅、机智诙谐和通情达理的人,他常为人类的愚蠢、自负和虚伪感到一种辛酸的快乐,而不是感到愤慨。他运用轻松随便的语言,并以此让读者对人类的愚昧荒唐——有时甚至包括表述者自身的愚昧荒唐——抱以辛酸的微笑。贺拉斯把自己的目标描述成"用笑声让人们摆脱自身的罪恶与愚蠢"。蒲柏创作的《道德论》等正规讽刺作品大都具有贺拉斯式讽刺风格。

在**尤维纳利斯式讽刺**中,讽刺的表述者是一个严肃的道德家,他运用庄严公开的表述风格来谴责罪行与过失的种种表现形式。这些罪责与过失并不因其荒唐可笑而降低危害。表述者竭力引起读者对人类过错的鄙夷、道德感上的愤慨或发自内心的悲哀。塞缪尔·约翰逊的《伦敦》(1738)和《人类愿望的虚荣》(1749)都是典型的尤维纳利斯式讽刺类型。尤维纳利斯式讽刺最具谴责性的模式类似于哀史,但哀史这一模式源于希伯来文化而非古罗马。

2. **间接讽刺**反映在另一种文学形式中,并没有直接面向读者表述。最普通的间接讽刺形式是虚构叙事形式。在这一形式里,讽刺的对象是某类人物。他们的言语思想、所作所为使他们自身和他们的见解显得滑稽可笑、惹人憎恶。有时作者夹叙夹议的风格会使这些人物显得更为可笑。

梅尼普斯式讽刺是间接讽刺的一种。这种间接讽刺类型以古希腊犬儒主义哲学家梅尼普斯建立的模式为基础。有时也叫**瓦罗式讽刺**,得名于古罗马的一位仿效者:瓦罗。诺斯罗普·弗莱在《批评的剖析》第308—312页中提出另外一种名称:**剖析**,这是以间接讽刺的一个重要英语范例——伯顿的《忧郁的剖析》(1621)——命名的。这些讽刺作品采用了散文体,常穿插一些诗文,形式混杂,常由结构松散的叙述构成。其突出特征在于一连串扩展的对话和辩论(通常发生在宴席或聚会上):一群夸夸其谈的怪人、学究、文人和各类职业或各种哲学观点的代表人物,竭力陈述有利于自己论点的观点和态度,结果却使得他们所代表的观点与态度显得更为荒谬可笑。拉伯雷的《巨人传》(1564)、伏尔泰的《老实人》(1759)、托马

Peacock's *Nightmare Abbey* (1818) and other satiric fiction, and Aldous Huxley's *Point Counter Point* (1928); in this last novel, as in those of Peacock, the central satiric scenes are discussions and disputes during a weekend at an English country manor. Frye also classifies Lewis Carroll's two books about Alice in Wonderland as "perfect Menippean satires."

It should be noted that any narrative or other literary vehicle can be adapted to the purposes of indirect satire. John Dryden's *Absalom and Achitophel* turns Old Testament history into a satiric allegory on *Restoration* political maneuverings. In *Gulliver's Travels* Swift converts to satiric use the early eighteenth-century accounts of voyage and discovery, and his *Modest Proposal* is written in the form of a project in political economy. Many of Joseph Addison's *Spectator* papers are satiric essays; Byron's *Don Juan* is a versified satiric form of the old episodic *picaresque* fiction; Ben Jonson's *The Alchemist*, Molière's *The Misanthrope*, Wycherley's *The Country Wife*, and Shaw's *Arms and the Man* are satiric plays; and Gilbert and Sullivan's *Patience*, and other works such as John Gay's eighteenth-century *Beggar's Opera* and its modern adaptation by Bertolt Brecht, *The Threepenny Opera* (1928), are satiric operettas. T. S. Eliot's *The Waste Land* (1922) employs motifs from myth in a work which can be considered by and large as a verse satire directed against what Eliot perceives as the spiritual dearth in twentieth-century life. The greatest number of modern satires, however, are written in prose, and especially in novelistic form; for example Evelyn Waugh's *The Loved One*, Joseph Heller's *Catch-22*, and Kurt Vonnegut, Jr.'s *Player Piano* and *Cat's Cradle*. Charlie Chaplin's *Modern Times* (1936) and *The Great Dictator* (1940) are classic instances of dramatic satire in the cinema. Much of the satiric thrust in current *black humor* is directed against what the author conceives to be the widespread contemporary condition of social cruelty, inanity, or chaos.

Effective English satire has been written in every period beginning with the Middle Ages. Pieces in the English *Punch* and the American *New Yorker* demonstrate that formal essayistic satire, like satiric novels, plays, and cinema, still commands a wide audience; and W. H. Auden is a twentieth-century author who wrote superb satiric poems. The proportioning of the examples in this article, however, indicates how large the Restoration and eighteenth century loom in satiric achievement: the century and a half that included Dryden, the Earl of Rochester, Samuel Butler, Wycherley, Aphra Behn, Addison, Pope, Lady Mary Wortley Montagu, Swift, Gay, Fielding, Johnson, Oliver Goldsmith, and late in the period (it should not be overlooked) the Robert Burns of "The Holy Fair" and "Holy Willie's Prayer" and the William Blake of *The Marriage of Heaven and Hell*. This same span of time was also in France the period of such major satirists as Boileau, La Fontaine, and Voltaire, as well as Molière, the most eminent of all satirists in drama. In the nineteenth century, American satire broke free of English domination with the light satiric touch of Washington Irving's *Sketch Book*, the deft satiric essays of Oliver Wendell Holmes (*The Autocrat of the Breakfast Table*), and above all the satiric essays and novels of Mark Twain.

斯·洛夫·皮科克创作的《噩梦隐修院》(1818) 等讽刺小说和奥尔德斯·赫胥黎的《针锋相对》(1928) 就是其范例。与皮科克的小说一样，《针锋相对》这部小说的主要讽刺场景出现在某个乡间庄园的周末讨论与争议中。弗莱把路易斯·卡罗尔的两部有关艾丽丝仙境漫游的小说也归入"完美的梅尼普斯式讽刺作品"。

应当指出的是，任何一种叙事文体或其他文学手段都可以用来达到间接讽刺的目的。约翰·德莱顿的《押沙龙与阿奇托菲尔》将《旧约》历史转换成一则针砭王政复辟时期政治花招的讽刺寓言。在《格列佛游记》中，斯威夫特把18世纪早期有关航海和地理新发现的描述加以转化，使之具有讽刺作用，而他的《温和的建议》则采用了政治经济实施项目的形式。约瑟夫·艾迪生在《旁观者》杂志上发表的许多文章都是讽刺性的随笔；拜伦的《唐·璜》将结构松散的流浪汉小说这一传统形式转换成讽刺诗文体形式；本·琼森的《炼金术士》，莫里哀的《愤世嫉俗》，威彻利的《乡下女人》和萧伯纳的《武器与人》都是讽刺戏剧；吉尔伯特与沙利文的《耐心》，约翰·盖伊18世纪创作的《乞丐的歌剧》，贝尔托尔特·布莱希特改编的现代剧《三分钱歌剧》(1928) 等都是讽刺性轻歌剧。T. S. 艾略特的《荒原》(1922) 从神话中汲取其主旨，这首诗可以看做是一部讽刺诗歌，抨击了艾略特所感知的20世纪生活中的精神匮乏。不过，现代讽刺作品绝大多数都采用了散文体，尤其是小说形式，如，伊弗林·沃的《被爱的人》，约瑟夫·海勒的《第二十二条军规》，小库特·冯尼戈特的《自动钢琴》和《猫的摇篮》。查尔斯·卓别林的《摩登时代》(1936) 和《大独裁者》(1940) 是电影里戏剧性反讽的经典例子。当今流行的黑色幽默大都出现在讽刺作品中，讽刺的对象是作者认为社会现状中普遍存在的残暴、空虚与混乱。

从中世纪开始，每个时期都产生了优秀的英国讽刺作品。英国的《笨拙周报》和美国的《纽约人》这两家杂志上刊登的文章表明，正规讽刺散文与讽刺小说和讽刺戏剧、电影一样，仍然拥有广泛的读者。20世纪作家 W. H. 奥登就创作有极为出色的讽刺诗歌。但从比例上说，这里列举的大量作品说明了王政复辟时期和18世纪在讽刺作品方面取得了多么辉煌卓越的成就：在这一个半世纪内，孕育了德莱顿、罗彻斯特伯爵、塞缪尔·勃特勒、威彻利、阿弗拉·贝恩、艾迪生、蒲柏、玛丽·沃特利·蒙塔古夫人、斯威夫特、盖伊、菲尔丁、约翰逊、奥利弗·哥尔德斯密斯，以及该时期末期（不应被忽略的）罗伯特·彭斯的《圣女》《圣威利的祷告》和威廉·布莱克的《天堂与地狱的婚礼》。这一个半世纪也是法国杰出的讽刺作家布瓦洛、拉封丹、伏尔泰和最伟大的讽刺剧作家莫里哀的创作时期。19世纪，美国的讽刺文学脱离英国的影响，这期间的作品包括：华盛顿·欧文的轻讽刺作品《见闻札记》，奥利弗·温德尔·霍姆斯技巧娴熟的讽刺短文（《早餐桌上的霸主》)，以及马克·吐温的讽刺短文与小说。

See also *light verse*. The articles on *burlesque*, on *irony*, and on *wit, humor, and the comic* describe some of the derogatory modes and devices available to satirists. Consult James Sutherland, *English Satire* (1958); Gilbert Highet, *The Anatomy of Satire* (1962); Alvin B. Kernan, *The Plot of Satire* (1965); Matthew Hodgart, *Satire* (1969); Charles Sanders, *The Scope of Satire* (1971); Michael Seidel, *Satiric Inheritance, Rabelais to Sterne* (1979); Dustin Griffin, *Satire: A Critical Reintroduction* (1994); Fredric V. Bogel, *The Difference Satire Makes: Rhetoric and Reading from Jonson to Byron* (2001). Anthologies: Ronald Paulson, ed., *Satire: Modern Essays in Criticism* (1971); Ashley Brown and John L. Kimmey, eds., *Satire: An Anthology* (1977), which includes both satiric writings and critical essays on satire; Ruben Quintero, ed., *A Companion to Satire* (2006). For references to *satire* in other entries, see pages 8, 37.

satiric comedy: 55.

scan: 220.

scansion (skăn′ shŭn): **220**.

scenario: 58.

scene (in drama): **3**.

schemes (figures of speech): **130**.

science fiction and fantasy: These terms encompass novels and short stories that represent an imagined reality that is radically different in its nature and functioning from the world of our ordinary experience. Often the setting is another planet, or this earth projected into the future, or an imagined parallel universe. The two terms are not sharply discriminated, but by and large the term **science fiction** is applied to those narratives in which—unlike in pure **fantasy**—an explicit attempt is made to render plausible the fictional world by reference to known or imagined scientific principles, or to a projected advance in technology, or to a drastic change in the organization of society.

Mary Shelley's remarkable *Frankenstein* (1818) is often considered a precursor of science fiction, but the basing of fictional worlds on explicit and coherently developed scientific principles did not occur until later in the nineteenth century, in such writings as Jules Verne's *Journey to the Center of the Earth* and H. G. Wells' *The War of the Worlds*. More recent important authors of science fiction include Isaac Asimov, Arthur Clarke, Ray Bradbury, J. G. Ballard, and Doris Lessing. Science fiction is also frequently represented in television and film; a notable and immensely popular instance is the *Star Trek* series.

Fantasy is as old as the fictional *utopias*, and its *satiric* forms have an important precursor in the extraordinary countries portrayed in Jonathan Swift's *Gulliver's Travels* (1726). Among the notable twentieth-century writers of

也可参见：*轻松诗。滑稽讽刺作品，反讽，机智、幽默与滑稽*三个条目描述了讽刺作家选用的一些贬低性模式与手法。参阅：詹姆斯·萨瑟兰所著的《英国的讽刺》(1958)；吉尔伯特·海特所著的《讽刺的剖析》(1962)；阿尔文·B.克南所著的《讽刺的情节》(1965)；马修·霍加特所著的《讽刺》(1969)；查尔斯·桑德斯所著的《讽刺的范围》(1971)；迈克尔·塞德尔所著的《讽刺的传统：从拉伯雷到斯特恩》(1979)；达斯廷·格里芬所著的《讽刺：批评重介》(1994)；弗雷德里克·V.博格尔所著的《讽刺造成的不同：从琼生到拜伦的修辞学和解读》(2001)。文集有：罗纳德·鲍尔森主编的《讽刺：现代批评文选》(1971)；阿什利·布朗与约翰·L.基梅合编的《讽刺文选》(1977)，该书既收录了一些讽刺作品，也收集了一些有关讽刺的批评文章；鲁本·昆特罗主编的《讽刺指南》(2006)。其他条目中提及"讽刺"的地方，参见第8、37页。

satiric comedy：讽刺喜剧　55。

scan：标示格律　220。

scansion：格律标示　220。

scenario：剧情说明　58。

scene (in drama)：(戏剧中的) 场　3。

schemes (figures of speech)：(修辞格中的) 修辞手段　130。

Science Fiction and Fantasy：科幻小说与幻想作品

　　这两个术语包括那些表现和想象在本质与功能上都与我们日常经验的世界截然不同的现实生活的小说与短篇小说。小说背景通常是另一星球，或者投射在未来的地球，或是同时存在的另一个想象的宇宙。这两个术语没有明确的区别，但一般来说，**科幻小说**指的是那样一些故事——与纯粹的**幻想小说**不同——这些故事通过涉及已知或想象的科学原理，或是设计好的技术进步，或是社会结构发生巨变，试图使其虚构的世界显得合情合理。

　　玛丽·雪莱非凡的《弗兰肯斯坦》(1818)常被视为科幻小说的先驱，但直到19世纪后期，科幻世界才开始以明确且连贯发展的科学原理为基础，如儒勒·凡尔纳的《地心游记》和H. G. 威尔斯的《星球大战》。近代重要的科幻小说家包括艾萨克·阿西莫夫、阿瑟·克拉克、雷·布雷德伯里、J. G. 巴拉德和多丽丝·莱辛。科幻小说也常在电视、电影中得到体现，一个极受欢迎的著名例子就是《星际迷航》系列。

　　幻想小说与虚构的*乌托邦*一样历史悠久，其讽刺形式的重要先驱是乔纳森·斯威夫特《格列佛游记》(1726)中描述的奇异国度。20世纪著名的幻想小

fantasy are C. S. Lewis and J. R. R. Tolkien (*The Hobbit, The Lord of the Rings*), whose works incorporate materials from classical, biblical, and medieval sources. Ursula Le Guin is a major author of both science fiction and works of fantasy.

Some instances of science fiction and fantasy project a future utopia (Le Guin's *The Dispossessed*), or else attack an aspect of current science or society by imagining their dystopian conclusion (George Orwell's *Nineteen Eighty-Four*, 1949, and Margaret Atwood's *The Handmaid's Tale*, 1986); and many writers use their imaginary settings, as Swift had in *Gulliver's Travels*, for political and social satire (Aldous Huxley's *Brave New World* and much of Kurt Vonnegut's prose fiction). See *utopia and dystopia* and *satire*.

Cyberpunk emerged in the early 1980s as a *postmodern* form of science fiction in which the events take place partially or entirely within the "virtual reality" formed by computers or computer networks, in which the characters may be humans, or aliens, or artificial intelligences. Well-known instances are William Gibson's novel *Neuromancer* (1984), and the *Matrix* films (1999, 2003). See the essays in *Fiction 2000: Cyberpunk and the Future of Narrative*, eds. George Slusser and Tom Shippey (1992), and Larry McCaffery, ed., *Storming the Reality Studio* (1991).

For other novelistic forms that depart radically from the world of ordinary experience, see *magic realism* and *metafiction*, under *novel*. Refer to Kingsley Amis, *New Maps of Hell: A Survey of Science Fiction* (1960); H. Bruce Franklin, *Future Perfect: American Science Fiction of the Nineteenth Century* (rev. 1978); Robert Scholes and Eric S. Rabkin, *Science Fiction: History, Science, Vision* (1977); Ursula K. Le Guin, *The Language of the Night: Essays on Fantasy and Science Fiction* (1979); Gary K. Wolfe, *Critical Terms for Science Fiction and Fantasy* (1986); Jane Donawerth, *Frankenstein's Daughters: Women Writing Science Fiction* (1997); Adam Roberts, *Science Fiction* (2d ed., 2006).

scriptoria: 32.

second-person points of view: 304.

self-conscious narrator: 304.

self-reflexive novel: 305.

semantics: 195.

semiology: 357.

semiotics: At the end of the nineteenth century Charles Sanders Peirce, the American philosopher, proposed and described a study that he called "semiotic," and in his *Course in General Linguistics* (1915) the Swiss linguist Ferdinand de Saussure independently proposed a science that he called "semiology." Since then **semiotics** and **semiology** have become alternative

说作家包括 C. S. 刘易斯、J. R. R. 托尔金(《霍比特人》《魔戒》),他们的作品融入了源自古典的、圣经的与中世纪时期的素材。厄休拉·列·吉恩既是一位重要的科幻小说家,也是一位幻想小说家。

一些科幻小说与幻想作品反映了未来的乌托邦(列·吉恩的《一无所有》),或是想象一种反面乌托邦的结局,以此来抨击当代科学或社会的某一方面[乔治·奥威尔的《1984》,玛格丽特·阿特伍德的《使女的故事》(1986)];许多作家用想象的背景,如在斯威夫特的《格列佛游记》中,来讽刺社会与政治(奥尔德斯·赫胥黎的《美丽新世界》、冯尼戈特大部分的散文体小说)。参见:*乌托邦与反面乌托邦、讽刺*。

电脑朋客(又叫赛博朋克)出现于 1980 年代早期,是一种科幻小说的*后现代主义*形式。小说中部分或全部的事件发生在电脑或电脑网络建立的"虚拟现实"中,书中人物可能是人,也可能是人工智能。著名的例子有威廉·吉布森的《神经漫游者》(1984)和电影《黑客帝国》(1999,2003)。参阅:乔治·斯拉瑟与汤姆·什贝合编的《小说 2000:电脑朋客与叙事的未来》(1992),拉里·麦卡弗里主编的《现实工作室风暴:赛博朋克和后现代小说资料汇编》(1991)中的文章。

与日常经验的世界截然不同的其他小说形式,参见:*小说中的魔幻现实主义、元小说*。参阅:金斯利·埃米斯所著的《地狱新图:科幻小说概观》(1960);H. 布鲁斯·富兰克林所著的《未来的理想生产方式:美国 19 世纪科幻小说》(1978 年修订版);罗伯特·斯科尔斯与埃里克·S. 拉伯金合著的《科幻小说:历史、科学、视觉》(1977);厄休拉·K. 列·吉恩所著的《黑夜的语言:奇幻与科幻小说论文集》(1979);加里·K. 沃尔夫所著的《科幻和奇幻批评术语》(1986);简·多纳沃斯所著的《弗兰肯斯坦的女儿们:女性写作科幻小说》(1997);亚当·罗伯茨所著的《科幻小说》(2006 年第 2 版)。

scriptoria:缮写室　32。
second-person points of view:第二人称视角　304。
self-conscious narrator:自我意识的叙述者　304。
self-reflexive novel:自省小说　305。
semantics:语义学　195。
semiology:符号学　357。
Semiotics:符号论

19 世纪末,美国哲学家查尔斯·桑德斯·皮尔斯提出并描述了他称为"符号"的研究。在《普通语言学教程》(1915)一书中,瑞士语言学家费迪南·德·索绪尔独自提出了他命名为"符号学"的科学。自那时起,**符号论**和**符号学**就成为两

names for the systematic study of signs, as these function in all areas of human experience. The consideration of **signs** (conveyors of meaning) is not limited to the realm of language. The Morse code, traffic signs and signals, and a great diversity of other human activities and productions—our bodily postures and gestures, the social rituals we perform, the kinds of clothes we wear, the meals we serve, the buildings we inhabit, the objects we deal with—also convey common meanings to members who participate in a particular culture, and so can be analyzed as signs which function in diverse modes of signifying systems. Although the study of language (the use of specifically verbal signs) is technically regarded as only one branch of the general science of semiotics, *linguistics*, the highly developed science of language, in fact has for the most part supplied the basic concepts and methods that a semiotician applies to the study of non-linguistic sign systems.

C. S. Peirce distinguished three classes of signs, defined in terms of the kind of relation that exists between a signifying item and that which it signifies: (1) An **icon** functions as a sign by means of inherent similarities, or shared features, with what it signifies; examples are the similarity of a portrait to the person it depicts, or the similarity of a map to the geographical area it stands for. (2) An **index** is a sign which bears a natural relation of cause or of effect to what it signifies; thus, smoke is a sign indicating fire, and a pointing weathervane indicates the direction of the wind. (3) In the **symbol** (or in a less ambiguous term, the "**sign proper**"), the relation between the signifying item and what it signifies is not a natural one, but entirely a matter of social convention. The gesture of shaking hands, for example, in some cultures is a conventional sign of greeting or parting, and a red traffic light conventionally signifies "Stop!" The major and most complex examples of this third type of purely conventional sign, however, are the words that constitute a language.

Ferdinand de Saussure introduced many of the terms and concepts exploited by current semioticians; see Saussure under *linguistics in modern criticism*. Most important are the following: (1) A sign consists of two inseparable components or aspects, the *signifier* (in language, a set of speech sounds, or of marks on a page) and the *signified* (the concept, or idea, which is the meaning of the sign). (2) A verbal sign, in Saussure's term, is "arbitrary." That is, with the minor exception of *onomatopoeia* (words which we perceive as similar to the sounds they signify), there is no inherent, or natural, connection between a verbal signifier and what it signifies. (3) The identity of all elements of a language, including its words, their component speech sounds, and the concepts the words signify, are not determined by "positive qualities," or objective features in these elements themselves, but by *differences*, or a network of relationships, consisting of distinctions and oppositions from other speech sounds, other words, and other signifieds that obtain only within a particular linguistic system. (4) The aim of linguistics, or of any other semiotic enterprise, is to regard the *parole* (a single verbal utterance, or a particular use of a sign or set of signs) as only a manifestation of the *langue* (that is, the general system of implicit differentiations and rules of combination which underlie and make possible a particular use of signs). The focus of semiotic interest,

个可以互相替换使用的名称，指代系统研究符号及其在人类经验的各个领域所起作用的科学。对**符号**（意义的传送者）的研究并不局限于语言领域。莫尔斯代码、交通标志与交通信号等明确的交流系统，许多种类繁多的人类行为和产物——我们的身体姿态和手势，我们遵循的社会礼节，我们穿戴的衣着服饰，我们安排的便餐宴席，我们居住的房屋建筑，我们打交道的客观对象——都向参与某一特定文化的成员传递了共同的意义，因此可以将它们分析为作用于各种形式的符号指向系统中的符号。尽管语言的研究（特殊的文字符号的使用）严格来说被视为只是普通符号科学的一个分支，但*语言学*这门高度发展的语言科学，实际上提供了符号学家应用于非语言的符号系统研究中的大部分基本概念和方法。

　　C. S. 皮尔斯根据能指物体与所指物体之间的关系，区分了三类符号：(1) **图像**。图像作为一种符号，通过与所指物体之间固有的相似之处或共有的特征发挥作用。如肖像画与所画人物之间的相似性，或一幅地图与它所表示的地理区域之间的相似性。(2) **标示物**，是与它所指物体有自然因果关系的符号；因此，烟是标示火的符号，指向风标是标示风向的符号。(3) **象征**（或用更清晰明了的术语，"**适当的符号**"）。在象征中，能指物体与所指物体之间的关系不是自然的关系，而是完全依从于社会习俗。例如，握手这一姿势在一些文化中是问候或分别的习惯性符号；红色交通灯在惯例上表示"停止！"不过，第三种纯惯例类型的符号最主要也最为复杂的例子是构成语言的字词。

　　费迪南·德·索绪尔介绍了当前符号学家采用的许多术语和概念。参见：*语言学在文学批评里的应用*中有关索绪尔的内容。以下是一些最重要的符号学术语与概念：(1) 符号由两个不可分割的要素或部分构成：*能指*（即语言中的一套语音或书页上的一组标记）与*所指*（即作为符号意义的概念或意义）。(2) 用索绪尔的术语来说，文字符号是"任意的"。除了语言中很少的*拟声词*（我们所感知的这些词与其所指的声音相似），在文字的能指与所指之间没有固定或自然的联系。(3) 对一种语言所有组成因素的辨认，包括对其字词、字词的语音以及字词所指概念的辨认，都不是由"确切的特征"所决定的，或是由这些因素自身的客观特征所决定的，而是由*差异*，或是由与仅仅存在于某一特定语言系统中的其他语音、字词和所指构成区别与对立的关系网所决定的。(4) 语言学的主旨，或其他任何一门符号学的主旨是将*言语*（单一的口头表述，或一个符号、一组符号的特殊用法）仅仅看成是*语言*（即潜在变异与组合规则的总体系统，这些变异与组合规则是符号的特殊用法的基础，并使符号的特殊用法成为可能）的一种表现形式。因

accordingly, is not in interpreting a particular instance of signification but in establishing the general signifying system that each particular instance relies upon.

Modern semiotics, like structuralism, has developed in France under the aegis of Saussure, so that many semioticians are also structuralists. They deal with any set of social phenomena or social productions as *texts*; that is, as constituted by self-sufficient, self-ordering, hierarchical structures of differentially determined signs, codes, and rules of combination and transformation which make significant materials "meaningful" to members of a particular society who are competent in that signifying system. (See *structuralist criticism*.) Claude Lévi-Strauss, in the 1960s and later, inaugurated the application of semiotics to cultural anthropology, and also established the foundations of French structuralism in general, by using Saussure's linguistics as a model for analyzing, in primitive societies, a great variety of phenomena and practices, which he treated as quasi-languages that manifest the structures of an underlying signifying system. These include kinship systems, totemic systems, ways of preparing food, myths, and prelogical modes of interpreting the world. Jacques Lacan has applied semiotics to Freudian psychoanalysis—interpreting the unconscious, for example, as (like language) a structure of signs (see Lacan under *psychological and psychoanalytic criticism*). Michel Foucault developed a mode of semiotic analysis to deal with the changing medical interpretations of symptoms of disease; the diverse ways of identifying, classifying, and treating insanity; and the altering conceptions of human sexuality (see under *poststructuralism*). Roland Barthes, explicitly applying Saussurean principles and methods, has written semiotic analyses of the constituents and codes of the sign systems in advertisements which describe and promote women's fashions, as well as analyses of many "bourgeois myths" about the world which, he claims, are exemplified in such social sign systems as professional wrestling matches, children's toys, cookery, and the striptease. (See his *Mythologies*, trans. 1972.) In his earlier writings Barthes was also a major exponent of *structuralist criticism*, which deals with a literary text as "a second-order semiotic system"; that is, it views a literary text as employing the first-order semiotic system of language to form a secondary semiotic structure, in accordance with a specifically literary system of conventions and codes.

For a related field of study, which can be characterized as the semiotics of culture, see *cultural studies*. Introductions to the elements of semiotic theory are included in Terence Hawkes, *Structuralism and Semiotics* (1977); Jonathan Culler, *The Pursuit of Signs* (1981); Robert Scholes, *Semiotics and Interpretation* (1982); also in the anthologies, Thomas A. Sebeok, ed., *The Tell-Tale Sign: A Survey of Semiotics* (1975); and Robert E. Innis, ed., *Semiotics: An Introductory Anthology* (1985). See also Umberto Eco, *A Theory of Semiotics* (1976); Roland Barthes, *Elements of Semiology* (trans. 1967); Thomas A. Sebeok, *Semiotics in the United States* (1991). Among the semiotic analyses of diverse social phenomena available in English are Claude Lévi-Strauss, *Structural Anthropology* (1968) and *The Raw and the Cooked* (1966); Roland Barthes, *Selected Writings*, ed. Susan Sontag (1983); Jacques Lacan, *The Language of the Self: The Function of Language*

此，符号学侧重于建立各个特例所依赖的一般符号指向系统，而不在于阐述某个指代的特例。

现代符号学与结构主义一样，主要是在法国由索绪尔倡导发展起来的，因此许多符号学家也是结构主义者。他们把任何一组社会现象或社会产物都视为"文本"，即当做由差异分明的符号、代码、组合转化规则的自足自律的层次结构构成的文本；对特定社会符号指向系统中有能力的成员来说，这些符号、代码与规则使得重要的事物"具有意义"。（参见：*结构主义批评*。）自 1960 年代以来，克劳德·列维-斯特劳斯首次将符号学应用于文化人类学，并建立了法国结构主义的一般基础。他用索绪尔的语言学作为分析原始社会中形形色色现象和习俗的模式，把这些现象和习俗看成体现了潜在符号指向系统结构的拟语言。这些拟语言包括亲族系统、图腾系统、食物的准备方式、神话和解释世界的前逻辑方式。雅克·拉康将符号学运用到弗洛伊德的精神分析学中，如把潜意识解释为一种（像语言一样的）符号结构（参见：*心理学与精神分析批评*中有关拉康的内容）。米歇尔·福柯将符号学的分析模式扩展到对疾病症状所作的不断变化的医学解释上，扩展到确诊、分类和治疗精神病的各种方式上，扩展到改变中的人类性观念上（参见：*后结构主义*）。罗兰·巴尔特运用索绪尔的原则和方法，从符号学角度详尽地分析了描绘和促销女性时装的广告中符号系统的组成因素和代码，分析了许多关于世界的"资产阶级的神话"；他宣称，这些组成因素和代码在职业拳击比赛、儿童玩具、烹调和脱衣舞等社会符号系统中都有所体现。[参阅：巴尔特所著的《神话学》(1972 年英译版)。] 巴尔特在其早期论著中也是*结构主义批评*的一位主要倡导者。结构主义批评把文学文本作为"一种第二层次的符号系统"进行研究；即结构主义认为，文学文本利用了语言这种第一层次符号系统，再根据具体的文学惯例和代码的系统组成了一个第二层次的符号结构。

有关以文化符号学为特征的相关领域的研究，参见：*文化研究*。有关符号学理论要素的介绍，可以参阅：托伦斯·豪克斯所著的《结构主义与符号学》(1977)；乔纳森·卡勒所著的《符号的追寻》(1981)；罗伯特·斯科尔斯所著的《符号学与阐释》(1982)；也可参阅选集：托马斯·A. 西比奥克主编的《指示信号：符号学概述》(1975)；罗伯特·E. 英尼斯主编的《符号学入门文选》(1985)。也可参阅：翁贝托·艾柯所著的《符号学理论》(1976)；罗兰·巴尔特所著的《符号学原理》(1967 年英译版)；托马斯·A. 西比奥克所著的《美国的符号学》(1991)。对形形色色的社会现象的符号学分析，可参阅的英文论著包括：克劳德·列维-斯特劳斯所著的《结构人类学》(1968) 和《生食与熟食》(1966)；罗兰·巴尔特所著的《作品选集》(1983，苏珊·桑塔格主编)；雅克·拉康所著的《自我的语言：

in Psychoanalysis (1968); and Michel Foucault, *Madness and Civilization* (1965), *The Archaeology of Knowledge* (1972), and *The Birth of the Clinic* (1973). On semiotics and literary analysis, see Maria Corti, *An Introduction to Literary Semiotics* (1978); Michael Riffaterre, *Semiotics of Poetry* (1978); and, in application to dramatic literature, Marvin Carlson, *Theatre Semiotics: Signs of Life* (1990). For a critical view of semiotics, see J. G. Merquior, *From Prague to Paris* (1986).

For references to *semiotics* in other entries, see pages *196, 324*.

Senecan tragedy: 403.

sensibility: 360.

Sensibility, Age of: 282.

sensibility, drama of: 361.

sensibility, literature of: When a contemporary critic talks of a poet's **sensibility**, the reference is to a characteristic way of responding, in perception, thought, and feeling, to experience; and when T. S. Eliot claimed that a *dissociation of sensibility* set in with the poetry of John Milton and John Dryden, he signified that there occurred at that time a division between a poet's sensuous, intellectual, and emotional modes of experience. When a literary historian, however, talks of the **literature of sensibility**, the reference is to a particular cultural phenomenon of the eighteenth century. This type of literature was fostered by the moral philosophy that had developed as a reaction against seventeenth-century Stoicism (which emphasized reason and the unemotional will as the sole motives to virtue), and even more importantly, as a reaction against Thomas Hobbes' claims, in *Leviathan* (1651), that a human being is innately selfish and that the mainsprings of human behavior are self-interest and the drive for power and status. In opposition to such views, many sermons, philosophical writings, and popular tracts and essays proclaimed that "benevolence"—wishing other persons well—is an innate human sentiment and motive, and that the central elements in all morality are the feelings of sympathy and "sensibility"—that is, a hair-trigger responsiveness to another person's distresses and joys. (See *empathy and sympathy*.) "Sensibility" also connoted, in the eighteenth century, an intense emotional responsiveness to beauty and *sublimity*, whether in nature or in art, and such responsiveness was often represented as an index to a person's gentility—that is, to one's upper-class status.

Emphasis on the human capability for sympathy and wishing others well—an important contribution was Adam Smith's *The Theory of Moral Sentiments* (1759)—helped to develop social consciousness and a sense of communal responsibility in an era of expanding commercialism and of a market economy based on self-interest. (For a recent application of Smith's *Theory of the Moral Sentiments* to literature, see Martha Craven Nussbaum, *Love's Knowledge*, 1990,

语言在精神分析中的作用》(1968)；米歇尔·福柯所著的《疯癫与文明》(1965)、《知识考古学》(1972)和《临床医学的诞生》(1973)；有关符号学与文学分析，参阅：玛丽亚·科蒂所著的《文学符号学入门》(1978)；米歇尔·里法泰尔所著的《诗歌符号学》(1978)；有关符号学在戏剧文学中的运用，参阅：马尔文·卡尔森所著的《戏剧符号学：人生的标记》(1990)。批判性的观点可以参阅：J. G. 莫奎尔所著的《从布拉格到巴黎》(1986)。

其他条目中提及"符号论"的地方，参见第 196、324 页。

Senecan tragedy：塞内加式悲剧　403。

sensibility：情感　360。

Sensibility, Age of：情感时期　282。

sensibility, drama of：情感戏剧　361。

Sensibility, Literature of：情感文学

现代文学批评家在谈论诗人的**情感**时，指的是诗人在感知、思维和感情上对经验的独特反应方式；当 T. S. 艾略特宣称，*情感的分裂*源于约翰·弥尔顿和约翰·德莱顿的诗歌时，他指的是在诗人的感观、智力和情绪的体验模式之间在当时出现的分裂。然而，文史学家在谈论**情感文学**时，指的是 18 世纪的一种特殊文化现象。这一文学类型的导因是道德哲学。道德哲学是对 17 世纪的斯多葛哲学（斯多葛哲学强调，理性和非情感意愿是美德的唯一动力）的反动而发展起来的，更重要的是反对托马斯·霍布斯在《利维坦》(1651)中提出的观点。霍布斯在《利维坦》中宣称，人生来自私，人类行为的原动力是利己主义和对权势、地位的追求。许多宗教布道文、哲理文和通俗的短文随笔都对霍布斯的观点提出异议，公开宣称"善"（祝福他人）是人类固有的情感与动机；所有道德的核心要素在于同情心和"情感"，即对他人的悲伤和欢乐具有一触即发的反应。（参见：*移情与同情*。）"情感"在 18 世纪也意味着对自然界或艺术上的美与崇高具有一种强烈的情感反应。这种反应显示了个人的高贵，即显示了其上层阶级的地位。

对人类同情心和祝福他人的强调——亚当·斯密在《道德情操论》(1795)中对这一观点作出了重要贡献——在日益扩展的商业主义时代和以利己为基础的经济时代，有助于增强社会意识及公共责任感。[近来将斯密的《道德情操论》应用于文学的一个例子，可以参阅：玛莎·克雷文·努斯鲍姆所著的《爱的知识》

chapter 14.) Highly exaggerated forms of sympathy and manifestations of benevolence, however, became prominent in eighteenth-century culture and literature. It was a commonplace in widespread views of morality that readiness to shed a sympathetic tear, quite apart from moral actions, is the sign both of polite breeding and a virtuous heart; and such a view was often accompanied by the observation that sympathy with another's grief, unlike personal grief, is a pleasurable emotion, hence to be sought as a value in itself. Common phrases in the cult of sensibility were the *oxymorons* "the luxury of grief," "pleasurable sorrows," and "the sadly pleasing tear." A late eighteenth-century mortuary inscription in Dorchester Abbey reads:

> Reader! If thou hast a Heart fam'd for Tenderness and Pity, Contemplate this Spot. In which are deposited the Remains of a Young Lady.... When Nerves were too delicately spun to bear the rude Shakes and Jostlings which we meet with in this transitory world, Nature gave way; She sunk and died a Martyr to Excessive Sensibility.

It is clear that much of what in that age was called, with approval, "sensibility" we now call, with disapproval, *sentimentalism*.

In literature these ideas and tendencies were reflected in the **drama of sensibility**, or **sentimental comedy**, which were representations of middle-class life that replaced the tough amorality and the comic or satiric representation of aristocratic sexual license in *Restoration comedy*. In the contemporary plays of sensibility, Oliver Goldsmith remarked in his "Comparison between Sentimental and Laughing Comedy" (1773), "the virtues of private life are exhibited rather than the vices exposed, and the distresses rather than the faults of mankind make our interest in the piece"; the characters, "though they want humor, have abundance of sentiment and feeling"; with the result, he added, that the audience "sit at a play as gloomy as at the tabernacle." Plays such as Richard Steele's *The Conscious Lovers* (1722) and Richard Cumberland's *The West Indian* (1771) present monumentally benevolent heroes and heroines of the middle class, whose dialogue abounds with elevated moral sentiments and who, prior to the manipulated happy ending, suffer tribulations designed to evoke from the audience the maximum of pleasurable tears.

The **novel of sensibility**, or **sentimental novel**, of the latter part of the eighteenth century similarly emphasized the tearful distresses of the virtuous, either at their own sorrows or at those of their friends; some of them represented in addition a sensitivity to beauty or sublimity in natural phenomena which also expressed itself in tears. Samuel Richardson's *Pamela; or, Virtue Rewarded* (1740) exploits sensibility in some of its scenes; and Laurence Sterne, in *Tristram Shandy* and *A Sentimental Journey*, published in the 1760s, gives us his own inimitable compound of sensibility, self-irony, and innuendo. The vogue of sensibility was international. Jean-Jacques Rousseau's novel *Julie, or the New Héloise* (1761) dealt with lovers who manifest sensibility, and in his autobiography, *The Confessions* (written 1764–70), Rousseau represented himself, in

(1990)第14章。]但是,同情与仁慈的各种过于夸张的形式在18世纪的文化与文学中变得日益突出。在大众道德观里,总是挥洒同情之泪(经常与道德行为相伴随)便是良好的教养与贤德之心的标志。而且,人们同时还发现,与自己的悲伤不同,对他人的悲伤所产生的同情本身也是一种十分愉快的情感,因此应当作为一种本身就具有价值的东西加以追求。在这种情感狂热中,文学作品中常常出现"悲伤的欢快""怡人的哀愁""悲喜交加的泪水"等*逆喻*。18世纪后期,多尔切斯特寺院里矗立的一块墓碑上有这样一段碑文:

> 读者!您若是有一颗以温柔和怜悯而闻名的心,请凝视这块土地吧!这里埋葬着一位年青淑女的遗骸……当柔弱的神经再也忍受不住我们在这个转瞬即逝的世界里所面对的粗野震动和碰撞时,连大自然也无能为力;她日趋衰弱,像一位为过于伤感而殉教的人那样死去了。

显然,那个时代赞许的"情感",就是我们如今反对的*感伤主义*。

在文学上,这些感伤观念和倾向在**情感戏剧**或**感伤喜剧**里得到了反映。它们表现了中产阶级的生活,在戏剧舞台上取代了*王政复辟时期的喜剧*中冷酷无情的超道德观和对贵族社会纵情恣欲的喜剧式或讽刺式的表现。奥利弗·哥尔德斯密斯在其所写的文章"感伤喜剧与消遣喜剧的对比"(1773)中提出,当时的感伤戏剧揭示了"个人生活中的美德而不是邪恶。人类的悲伤而不是人类的过错使我们对这些戏剧感兴趣"。剧中人物"尽管缺乏幽默感,但却多愁善感,具有丰富的情感"。结果,观众"观看这类戏剧的心情和他们在犹太圣堂里的心情一样凄凉抑郁"。理查德·斯梯尔的《自觉的情人》(1722)与理查德·坎伯兰的《西印度人》(1771)等剧作,都表现了极其仁慈的中产阶级男女主人公,他们的对话充分体现出其高尚的道德情感;为了最大限度地赢得观众充满喜悦的泪水,主人公在受尽磨难之后才得到幸福的结局。

18世纪后期的**情感小说**或**感伤小说**也类似地渲染贤德之人对自己的悲伤或朋友的悲伤产生的催人泪下的哀痛;此外,书中人物对自然现象之美或崇高表现出的敏感性也是用泪水表达的。塞缪尔·理查逊的《帕美勒;或善有善报》(1740)在一些情景中宣扬多愁善感;劳伦斯·斯特恩在1760年代出版的《项狄传》《感伤旅行》中,呈现给我们他那独具一格的感伤、自嘲和影射的综合情结。情感热在当时是国际性的。让-雅克·卢梭的小说《朱莉,或新爱洛绮斯》(1761)描写的是多愁善感的情人,而在其自传《忏悔录》(1764—1770)中,卢梭在某些环境

some circumstances and moods, as a man of extravagant sensibility. Goethe's novel *The Sorrows of Young Werther* (1774) was an enormously popular presentation of the aesthetic sensitivities and finespun emotional tribulations of a young man who, frustrated in his love for a woman betrothed to another, and in general unable to adapt his sensibility to the demands of ordinary life, finally shoots himself.

An extreme English instance of the sentimental novel is Henry Mackenzie's *The Man of Feeling* (1771), which represents a hero of such exquisite sensibility that he goes into a decline from excess of pent-up tenderness toward a young lady, and dies in the perturbation of finally declaring to her his emotion. "If all his tears had been tears of blood," declares an editor of the novel, Hamish Miles, "the poor man could hardly have been more debile." Jane Austen's gently satiric treatment of a young woman of sensibility in *Sense and Sensibility* (begun 1797, published 1811) marks the decline of the fashion; but the exploitation of the mode of literary sensibility survives in such later novelistic episodes as the death of Little Nell in Charles Dickens' *Old Curiosity Shop* (1841) and the death of Little Eva in Harriet Beecher Stowe's *Uncle Tom's Cabin* (1852). Sentimentality was exploited also in Victorian *melodramas*, as well as in many movies that Hollywood labeled "tearjerkers."

In *The Politics of Sensibility* (1996), Markman Ellis departs from the usual derogatory treatment of the sentimental novels of the later eighteenth century, by arguing that they contributed to movements for social reform, including opposition to slavery, criticism of the questionable morality involved in some commercial and business practices, and the movement for the reformation and relief of prostitutes.

In America, sentimental novels were referred to as "woman's fiction" or "domestic novels," and often involved the story of a young girl who must make her way in the world unprotected. See Nina Baym, *Woman's Fiction: A Guide to Novels by and about Women in America, 1820–70* (2d ed., 1993). According to Jane Tompkins, many novels denigrated by sophisticated readers as overly sentimental or merely popular in fact represented attempts to reorganize culture from the women's point of view, and in some cases achieved devastating critiques of American society. See "Sentimental Power: *Uncle Tom's Cabin* and the Politics of Literary History," chapter 5 in *Sensational Designs: The Cultural Work of American Fiction, 1790–1860* (1985).

See *Age of Sensibility* under *periods of English literature*. Refer to Arthur Sherbo, *English Sentimental Drama* (1957); R. P. Utter and G. B. Needham, *Pamela's Daughters* (1963); R. S. Crane, "Suggestions toward a Genealogy of the 'Man of Feeling,'" in *The Idea of the Humanities* (2 vols., 1967); Janet Todd, *Sensibility: An Introduction* (1986); John Mullan, *Sentiment and Sociability: The Language of Feeling in the Eighteenth Century* (1988); G. J. Barker-Benfield, *The Culture of Sensibility: Sex and Society in Eighteenth-Century Britain* (1992); Claude Rawson, *Satire and Sentiment 1660–1830* (1994); Jerome McGann, *The Poetics of Sensibility* (1996); Paul Goring, *Rhetoric of Sensibility in Eighteenth-Century Culture* (2005).

与心境下把自己描写成一位极度多愁善感之人。歌德极为流行的小说《少年维特之烦恼》(1774)，出色地描写了一位年青人对美的敏感及其细腻的情感忧伤；这位年青人爱上了一位许配给他人的女子，这使他深感沮丧。他无法使自己的情感顺应平凡生活的要求，最终开枪自杀。

亨利·麦肯齐的《情感男人》(1771)是一部典型的英国感伤小说。这部小说描写了一位异常多愁善感的主人公，由于他对一位年青女士过分痴迷而日渐衰弱；最后，他在向这位女士表达自己的感情时心烦意乱地死去。这部小说的编辑哈米什·迈尔斯认为："即便他所有的眼泪都是血泪，这个可怜人也不会更虚弱了。"简·奥斯丁在《理智与情感》（写于1797年，1811年出版）中，温和地讽刺了一位多愁善感的年轻女子，这标志着情感热的消退。但是，文学情感模式的表现手法仍然存在于后来小说的片段中，如查尔斯·狄更斯《老古玩店》(1841)里的小耐儿之死、斯托夫人《汤姆叔叔的小屋》(1852)里的小夏娃之死、维多利亚时期的一些*情节剧*，以及好莱坞许多标榜为"催泪弹"的电影等。

在《情感策略》(1996)中，马克曼·埃利斯提出观点有别于对18世纪后期感伤小说的一般贬义看法。他认为，18世纪后期的感伤小说对社会改革运动作出了贡献，包括反对奴隶制、对商业行为涉及的道德性的讨论，以及对卖淫改革救助运动的参与。

在美国，感伤小说用来指"女性小说"或"家庭小说"，经常包括一个年轻女孩的故事，她必须在一个不受保护的世界上想尽办法打拼谋生。参见：尼娜·贝姆主编的《女性小说：美国1820—1870年间女性所写及关于女性的小说指南》(1993年第2版)。按照简·汤普金斯的看法，许多被高档次读者贬低为过于感伤或通俗的小说，事实上展现了从女性视角重组文化这一努力，并在某些情况下成功地对美国社会进行了猛烈的批判。参阅：《杰出的设计：1790—1860年间美国小说的文化成果》(1985)第五章"感伤的力量：《汤姆叔叔的小屋》与文学政治史"。

参见：*英国文学各时期的划分中的情感时期*。参阅：阿瑟·舍伯所著的《英国情感戏剧》(1957)；R. P. 厄特与G. B. 尼达姆合著的《帕美勒的女儿们》(1963)；R. S. 克莱恩所写的文章"走向'情感男人'谱系学的建议"，收入其所著的两卷本《人文学的理念》(1967)；珍妮特·托德所著的《情感时期：入门》(1986)；约翰·马伦所著的《感伤与社交：18世纪的情感语言》(1988)；G. J. 巴克-本菲尔德所著的《感伤主义文化：18世纪英国的性与社会》(1992)；克劳德·劳森所著的《讽刺与感伤：1660—1830》(1994)；杰尔姆·麦根所著的《感伤主义诗学》(1996)；保罗·戈林所著的《18世纪文化中的感伤主义修辞学》(2005)。

sentimental comedy: 361.

sentimental novel: 361.

sentimentalism: Sentimentalism is now a derogatory term applied to what is perceived to be an excess of emotion to an occasion, and especially to an overindulgence in the "tender" emotions of pathos and sympathy. Since what constitutes emotional excess or overindulgence is relative both to the judgment of the individual and to large-scale historical changes in culture and in literary fashion, what to the common reader of one age is a normal and laudable expression of humane feeling may seem sentimental to many later readers. The emotional responses of a lover that Shelley expresses and tries to evoke from the reader in his "Epipsychidion" (1821) seemed sentimental to the *New Critics* of the 1930s and later, who insisted on the need for an ironic counterpoise to intense feeling in poetry. Most readers now find both the *drama of sensibility* and the *novel of sensibility* of the eighteenth century ludicrously sentimental, and respond with jeers instead of tears to once celebrated episodes of pathos, such as many of the death scenes, especially those of children, in some Victorian novels and dramas. A staple in current anthologies of bad poetry are sentimental poems which were doubtless written, and by some people read, with deep and sincere feeling. A useful distinction between sentimental and nonsentimental is one which does not depend on the intensity and type of the feeling expressed or evoked, but labels as sentimental a work or passage in which the feeling is rendered in commonplaces and *clichés*, instead of being freshly verbalized and sharply realized in the details of the representation.

See *pathos*, and *sensibility, literature of*, and refer to I. A. Richards, *Practical Criticism* (1929), chapter 6; and the discussion of sentimentality by Monroe C. Beardsley, "Bad Poetry," in *The Possibility of Criticism* (1970). Suzanne Clark has written a *feminist* reconsideration of sentimentalism in literature, *Sentimental Modernism and the Revolution of the Word* (1991), and Shirley Samuels has edited a collection of essays on *Culture of Sentiment: Race, Gender, and Sentimentality in Nineteenth-Century America* (1992).

sequential art: 152.

sestet: 370.

sestina (sĕstē′ na): 378.

setting: The overall setting of a narrative or dramatic work is the general locale, historical time, and social circumstances in which its action occurs; the setting of a single episode or scene within the work is the particular physical location in which it takes place. The overall setting of *Macbeth*, for example, is medieval Scotland, and the setting for the particular scene in which Macbeth comes upon the witches is a blasted heath. The overall setting of James Joyce's *Ulysses* is Dublin on June 16, 1904, and its opening episode is set in the

sentimental comedy：感伤喜剧　361。

sentimental novel：感伤小说　361。

Sentimentalism：感伤主义

感伤主义一词现在带有贬义，特指对某一场合流露出过多的情感，尤其是对怜悯、同情等"多愁善感的"情感放纵。由于情感过多或情感放纵的构成因素与个人的判断和文化、文学领域里发生的巨大历史变化有关，所以，对某个时代的普通读者而言是人类情感的正常表露，在后世的许多读者看来也许就显得多愁善感。雪莱在他的《厄皮塞乞迪翁》(1821)里表达了一位情人的情感反应并试图唤起读者的情感共鸣，在 1930 年代的*新批评家*看来就显得多愁善感；但后来新批评派又坚持认为，诗歌中需要一种反讽式的平衡，以加强诗歌中的情感。当今大多数读者认为 18 世纪的*情感戏剧*与*情感小说*都表现出荒唐可笑的感伤主义。曾经相当出名的悲伤片段，如维多利亚时期的小说和戏剧中的许多死亡场景，尤其是孩童死亡的场景，都引起现代读者的嘲笑而不是唤起他们的眼泪。当前许多劣诗选的主要题材也属于感伤主义诗歌，但毫无疑问，写诗的和一些读诗的却怀有深挚真诚的情感。如何有效区别感伤作品与非感伤作品，并不取决于作品表达或唤起的情感是否强烈或属于何种类型，只有在作品或篇章平淡无奇、用*陈词滥调*来表达情感、而不是用新颖的文字和极其具体的方式进行细节描述时，我们才称其为感伤主义作品。

参见：*悲伤感*、*情感文学*；参阅：I. A. 理查兹所著的《实用批评》(1929) 第 6 章；门罗·C. 比尔兹利所著的《批评的可能性》(1970) 中"劣等诗歌"部分关于多愁善感的讨论。苏珊娜·克拉克在《感伤现代主义与词语革命》(1991) 中，从女性主义视角重新思考了文学中的感伤主义；雪利·塞缪尔斯则编选了一部文章合集：《感伤文化：19 世纪美国的种族、性别和感伤情调》(1992)。

sequential art：连环画　152。

sestet：最后六行　370。

sestina：六节诗　378。

Setting：背景

叙事作品或戏剧作品的总体背景指的是作品情节发生的总体场所、历史时代和社会环境；一部作品中某一事件或场景的背景指的是该事件或场景发生的特定地理位置。如《麦克白》的总背景是中世纪的苏格兰；然而，麦克白遇见女巫这一特定场景的背景却是一片石南丛生的荒野。詹姆斯·乔伊斯的《尤利西斯》的总背景是 1904 年 6 月 16 日的都柏林，而其开篇事件的背景却是在俯瞰都柏林海

Martello Tower overlooking Dublin Bay. In works by writers such as Edgar Allan Poe, Thomas Hardy, and William Faulkner, both the overall and individual settings are important elements in generating the *atmosphere* of their works. The Greek term **opsis** ("scene," or "spectacle") is now occasionally used to denote a particular visible or picturable setting in any work of literature, including a lyric poem.

When applied to a theatrical production, "setting" is synonymous with **décor**, which is a French term denoting both the scenery and the **properties**, or movable pieces of furniture, on the stage. The French **mise en scène** ("placing on stage") is sometimes used in English as another synonym for "setting"; it is more useful, however, to apply the term more broadly, as the French do, to signify a director's overall conception, staging, and directing of a theatrical performance.

seven cardinal virtues: 364.

seven deadly sins: In medieval and later Christian theology these sins were usually identified as Pride, Covetousness, Lust, Envy, Gluttony, Anger, and Sloth. They were called "deadly" because they were considered to put the soul of anyone manifesting them in peril of eternal perdition; such sins could be expiated only by absolute penitence. Among them, Pride was often considered primary, since it was believed to have motivated the original fall of Satan in heaven. **Sloth** was accounted a deadly sin because it signified not simply laziness, but a torpid and despondent spiritual condition that threatened to make a person despair of any chance of achieving divine Grace. Alternative names for sloth were **accidie**, "dejection," and "spiritual dryness"; it was probably a condition close to that which present-day psychiatrists diagnose as acute depression.

The seven deadly sins (or in an alternative term, **cardinal sins**) were defined and discussed at length by such major theologians as Gregory the Great and Thomas Aquinas, and served as the topic of countless sermons. They also played an important role in many works of medieval and Renaissance literature—sometimes in elaborately developed *personifications*—including William Langland's *Piers Plowman* (B, Passus 5), Geoffrey Chaucer's "Parson's Tale," William Dunbar's "The Dance of the Sevin Deidly Synnis," and Edmund Spenser's *Faerie Queene* (Book I, Canto 4). See Morton W. Bloomfield, *The Seven Deadly Sins* (1952).

The seven deadly or cardinal sins were balanced by the **seven cardinal virtues**. Three of these, called the "theological virtues" because they were stressed in the New Testament, were Faith, Hope, and Charity (that is, Love)—see St. Paul's *I Corinthians* 13:13: "And now abideth faith, hope, and charity, these three." The other four, the "natural virtues," were derived from the moral philosophy of the ancient Greeks: justice, prudence, temperance, and fortitude.

Refer to Robert W. Ackerman, *Backgrounds to Medieval English Literature* (1966). For essays on the seven deadly sins written in 1962 by eminent

湾的马泰楼碉堡。在埃德加·爱伦·坡、托马斯·哈代和威廉·福克纳等作家的作品中，总体背景与单独背景都是构成*作品基调*的重要因素。希腊词 opsis（意为"场景"或"场面"）现在偶尔也用来表示任何一部文学作品（包括抒情诗）中可见的或可描绘的特定背景。

当用于戏剧作品时，"背景"与**布景**（decpr）同义。布景是一个法语术语，指舞台布景与**道具**，也指舞台上可移动的家具。法语中的 mise en scene（意为"放置在舞台上"）有时也与英语中的"背景"同义，但是，该术语更有用之处是像法国人那样用它来更广泛地指代戏剧表演中导演的整体构思、舞台布置和导演方式。

seven cardinal virtues：七项基本美德　364。

Seven Deadly Sins：七大罪

在中世纪及后来的基督教神学中，这七大罪通常指的是骄傲、贪婪、淫邪、嫉妒、贪食、愤怒与懒惰。它们之所以被称为"大罪"，是因为任何流露出这些罪过的灵魂都将被打入万劫不复之地；只有全心忏悔才能抵偿这些罪过。在这七大罪里，骄傲经常被视为最主要的罪过，因为人们相信撒旦在天堂中最初的堕落正是受到骄傲的驱使。**懒惰**也被列入七大罪，因为它不仅代表懒散，而且表示一种麻木、沮丧的精神状态；这种状态将会使人对获得神圣的天恩感到绝望。懒惰也可称为**倦怠**、"沮丧""精神萎靡"；这种状态近似于当今精神病学家诊断的深度抑郁症。

一些重要神学家，如格列高利一世、托马斯·阿奎那等，都详尽讨论、定义过这七大罪（或称**基本罪过**），无数布道都以这些罪过为主题。它们也在中世纪及文艺复兴时期的许多文学作品中发挥了重要作用——有时以精心雕琢而成的拟人形式出现——包括威廉·朗格兰的《农夫皮尔斯》（B 文本第 5 节），杰弗里·乔叟的"牧师讲的故事"，威廉·邓巴的《七大罪的舞蹈》和埃德蒙·斯宾塞的《仙后》（第 1 卷第 4 章）。参阅：莫顿·W. 布卢姆菲尔德所著的《七大罪》（1952）。

七大罪与**七项基本美德**相对称。这七项美德中有三项被称为"神学三德"，因为它们在《新约》中得到了强调。这三德指的是信、望、善（即爱）——见圣保罗的《哥林多前书》13：13："如今常存的有信、有望、有爱。"其他四德称为"自然美德"，源自古希腊人的道德哲学：公正、审慎、节制与坚毅。

参阅：罗伯特·W. 阿克曼所著的《中世纪英语文学背景》（1966）。1962 年

English authors, see W. H. Auden, Cyril Connolly, Patrick Leigh-Fermor, Edith Sitwell, Christopher Sykes, Evelyn Waugh, and Angus Wilson, *Seven Deadly Sins: Common Reader Edition* (2002).

Shakespearean sonnet: 370.

shaped verse: 61.

shifters (in grammar): 233.

short short story: 366.

short story: A short story is a brief work of prose fiction, and most of the terms for analyzing the component elements, the types, and the narrative techniques of the *novel* are applicable to the short story as well. The short story differs from the **anecdote**—the unelaborated narration of a single incident—in that, like the novel, it organizes the action, thought, and dialogue of its characters into the artful pattern of a plot, directed toward particular effects on an audience. (See *narrative and narratology*.) And as in the novel, the plot form may be comic, tragic, romantic, or satiric; the story is presented to us from one of many available *points of view*; and it may be written in the mode of fantasy, realism, or naturalism.

In the **tale**, or "story of incident," the focus of interest is primarily on the course and outcome of the events, as in Edgar Allan Poe's *The Gold Bug* (1843) and other tales of detection, in many of the stories of O. Henry (1862–1910), and in the stock but sometimes well-contrived western, *detective*, and adventure stories in popular magazines. "Stories of character" focus instead on the state of mind and motivation, or on the psychological and moral qualities, of the protagonists. In some of the stories of character by Anton Chekhov (1860–1904), the Russian master of the form, nothing more happens than an encounter and conversation between two people. Ernest Hemingway's classic "A Clean, Well-Lighted Place" consists only of a curt dialogue between two waiters about an old man who each day gets drunk and stays on in the café until it closes, followed by a brief meditation on the part of one of the waiters. In some stories there is a balance of interest between external action and character. Hemingway's "The Short Happy Life of Francis Macomber" is as violent in its packed events as any sensational adventure tale, but every particular of the action and dialogue is contrived to test and reveal, with a surprising set of *reversals*, the moral quality of all three protagonists.

The short story differs from the novel in the dimension that Aristotle called "magnitude," and this limitation of length imposes differences both in the effects that the story can achieve and in the choice and elaboration of the elements to achieve those effects. Edgar Allan Poe, who is sometimes called the originator of the short story as an established *genre*, was at any rate its first critical theorist. He defined what he called "the prose tale" as a narrative which can be read at one sitting of from half an hour to two hours, and is

杰出英语作家写的关于七大罪的文章，参见：W. H. 奥登、西里尔·康诺利、帕特里克·利－弗莫尔、伊迪丝·西特韦尔、克里斯托弗·赛克斯、伊夫林·休和安格斯·威尔逊合著的《七大罪：大众读者版》(2002)。

Shakespearean sonnet：莎士比亚式十四行诗　370。

shaped verse：形状诗/拟形诗　61。

shifters（**in grammar**）：（语法中的）代替　233。

short short story：小小说　366。

Short Story：短篇小说

短篇小说是一种简短的散文体虚构作品。绝大多数用来分析*小说*组成部分、类型和叙事技巧的术语也都适用于短篇小说。短篇小说不同于**轶事**——对单个事件粗略的叙述——因为短篇小说像小说那样把人物的行动、思想和对话组成了巧妙的情节模式，直接对读者产生特定的影响。（参见：*叙事和叙事学*。）和小说情节一样，短篇小说的情节形式可以是喜剧性的、悲剧性的、传奇性的或讽刺性的；作家可以从许多*视角*中选用一种来陈述故事，故事的创作模式可以是幻想的、现实主义的或自然主义的模式。

故事，或"事件故事"，关注的中心在于事件的发展过程和最终结局，如埃德加·爱伦·坡的《金甲虫》(1843) 和其他侦探故事，欧·亨利 (1862—1910) 创作的许多故事，以及大众杂志上刊登的陈腐但偶尔构思巧妙的西部故事或*侦探故事*或冒险故事。"人物故事"则侧重于主人公的心理和动机，或侧重于主人公的心理特征或道德品质。俄国短篇小说大师安东·契诃夫 (1860—1904) 的一些人物小说仅仅陈述了两个人物之间的邂逅和交谈。欧内斯特·海明威的经典之作《一个干净明亮的地方》仅仅描述了两位侍者间简短的交谈。这两位侍者谈论了一位每天喝得酩酊大醉，一直待到咖啡馆关门的老人。作者接着描写了其中一位侍者简短的沉思。有些故事对外部行动和人物性格的侧重不偏不倚。海明威的《弗朗西斯·麦康博的短暂幸福生活》，与任何骇人听闻的冒险故事一样，充满了曲折的暴力事件。不过，故事中每一个行为和对话的细节都以令人惊异的一系列*逆转*检验并揭示了三位主人公的道德品质。

短篇小说在亚里士多德所谓的"篇幅规模"方面与小说有所不同。篇幅长短的限制导致故事效果的差别，也使得作者对故事要素作出不同的选择、阐述和安排以取得故事的这些效果。有时被称为短篇小说之父确立了短篇小说这一*文学类型*的埃德加·爱伦·坡也是第一位短篇小说批评理论家。他把所谓的"散文故事"定义为能在半小时至两小时内一口气读完的叙事文，这种叙事文

limited to "a certain unique or single effect" to which every detail is subordinate (review of Nathaniel Hawthorne's *Twice Told Tales*, 1842). Poe's comment applies to many short stories, and points to the economy of management which the tightness of the form always imposes in some degree. We can say that, by and large, the short story writer introduces a limited number of persons, cannot afford the space for a leisurely analysis and sustained development of character, and cannot develop as dense and detailed a social milieu as does the novelist. The author often begins the story close to, or even on the verge of, the climax, minimizes both prior exposition and the details of the *setting*, keeps the complications down, and clears up the *dénouement* quickly—sometimes in a few sentences. (See *plot*.) The central incident is often selected to manifest as much as possible of the protagonist's life and character, and the details are devised to carry maximum import for the development of the plot. This spareness in the narrative often gives the artistry in a good short story higher visibility than the artistry in the more capacious and loosely structured novel.

Many distinguished short stories depart from this paradigm in various ways. It must be remembered that the name covers a great diversity of prose fiction, all the way from the **short short story**, which is a slightly elaborated anecdote of perhaps five hundred words, to such long and complex forms as Herman Melville's *Billy Budd* (c. 1890), Henry James' *The Turn of the Screw* (1898), Joseph Conrad's *Heart of Darkness* (1902), and Thomas Mann's *Mario and the Magician* (1930). In such works, the status of middle length between the tautness of the short story and the expansiveness of the novel is sometimes indicated by the name **novelette**, or *novella*. This form has been especially exploited in Germany (where it is called the **Novelle**) after it was introduced by Goethe in 1795 and carried on by Heinrich von Kleist and many other writers; it has been the subject of special critical attention by German theorists.

The short narrative, in both verse and prose, is one of the oldest and most widespread of literary forms; the Hebrew Bible, for example, includes the stories of Jonah, Ruth, and Esther. Some of the narrative types which preceded the modern short story, treated elsewhere in this *Glossary*, are the *fable*, the *exemplum*, the *folktale*, the *fabliau*, and the *parable*. Early in its history, there developed the device of the **frame-story**: a preliminary narrative within which one or more of the characters proceeds to tell a series of short narratives. This device was widespread in the oral and written literature of the East and Middle East, as in the collection of stories called *The Arabian Nights* (see the Introduction to *The Arabian Nights*, trans. Husain Haddawy, 1990). This device was used by a number of other writers, including Boccaccio for his prose *Decameron* (1353) and by Chaucer for his versified *Canterbury Tales* (c. 1387). In the latter instance, Chaucer developed the frame-story of the journey, dialogue, and interactions of the Canterbury pilgrims to such a degree that the frame itself approximated the form of an organized plot. Within Chaucer's frame-plot, each story constitutes a complete and rounded narrative, yet functions also both as a means of characterizing the teller and as a

只是为了达到"某个特定的或单一的效果",而文内的所有细节都是次要的(对纳撒尼尔·霍桑《旧事重述》的评论,1842)。坡的评论适用于许多短篇小说,揭示了短篇小说形式上的严谨紧凑必然在某种程度上造成布局安排上的经济简洁。我们不妨这么说,短篇小说家塑造的人物数量有限,他没有足够的篇幅来从容地分析人物和持续发展人物个性;他也无法像长篇小说家那样,详尽细致地描绘某一社会环境。作者往往在临近或接近情节的高潮处开始讲述故事,尽量减少事前的交代或*背景*的细节。他压缩情节的纠葛,干净利落地结束故事——有时只需几句话便可结束故事。(参见:*情节*。)选取的中心事件是为了尽最大限度展现主人公的生活和性格,而设计的细节则用来最大限度地传递情节的发展。与篇幅冗长、结构松散的小说相比,优秀短篇小说在叙事手法上的简朴更加突显了它的艺术性。

许多杰出的短篇小说都以各种各样的方式偏离这一范式。需要记住的是,"短篇小说"这一名称包含大量纷繁各异的散文体虚构作品,短至五百字左右,简单描述某件轶事的**小小说**;长而复杂的形式则如赫尔曼·梅尔维尔的《比利·巴德》(约1890)、亨利·詹姆斯的《螺丝在拧紧》(1898)、约瑟夫·康拉德的《黑暗的心脏》(1902)、托马斯·曼的《魔术师马里奥》(1930)等。这些故事篇幅中等,地位介于紧凑的短篇小说与卷幅浩瀚的小说之间,因此有时也被称作**中篇小说**(novelette/novella)。自从1795年歌德将中篇小说这一术语引入德国文学(在德国,中篇小说用 **novelle** 表示),这种形式便在德国得到运用,海因里希·冯·克莱斯特等许多作家都采用了这一文学体裁。这种文学体裁也是德国文学理论家特别关注的批评主题。

短篇的韵文或散文体叙事文,是最古老也是最广泛的文学形式之一。例如,希伯来圣经就包括约拿、路德和以斯帖的故事。现代短篇小说产生之前的一些叙事类型在本书其他地方也曾描述过,如*寓言故事*、*劝谕性故事*、*民间故事*、*寓言诗*、*醒世寓言*。在短篇小说历史发展的早期曾出现过一种**框形故事**的叙事手法:在一个开场的故事中,一位或多位人物连续讲述一系列简短的故事。这种叙事手法在东方及中东的口头文学或书面文学中十分常见,如《一千零一夜》故事集(参阅:侯赛因·哈达维1990年翻译的《一千零一夜》的引言)。许多作家也采用过这种叙事方式,如薄伽丘的散文体《十日谈》(1353)和乔叟韵文体的《坎特伯雷故事集》(约1387)。在《坎特伯雷故事集》里,乔叟在讲述坎特伯雷的朝圣者们结伴旅行、互相交谈和交往的过程中,逐渐发展了框形故事,使之近似于有组织的情节模式。在乔叟的框形情节中,每个故事都构成一篇自成一统的完整叙事文,既是塑造讲述者性格的一种方法,又是朝圣者途中争吵与

vehicle for the quarrels and topics of argument en route. In its more recent forms, the frame-story may enclose either a single narrative (Henry James' *The Turn of the Screw*) or a sequence of narratives (Joel Chandler Harris' stories as told by Uncle Remus, 1881 and later; see under *beast fable*).

The type of prose narrative which approximates the present concept of the short story was developed, beginning in the early nineteenth century, in order to satisfy the need for short fiction by the many **magazines** (periodical collections of diverse materials, including essays, reviews, verses, and prose stories) that were inaugurated at that time. Among the early practitioners were Washington Irving, Hawthorne, and Poe in America, Sir Walter Scott and Mary Shelley in England, E. T. A. Hoffmann in Germany, Balzac in France, and Gogol, Pushkin, and Turgenev in Russia. Since then, almost all the major novelists in all the European languages have also written notable short stories. The form has flourished especially in America; Frank O'Connor has called it "the national art form," and its American masters include (in addition to the writers mentioned above) Mark Twain, William Faulkner, Katherine Anne Porter, Eudora Welty, Flannery O'Connor, John O'Hara, J. F. Powers, John Cheever, and J. D. Salinger.

See Sean O'Faolain, *The Short Story* (1948, reprinted 1964); Frank O'Connor, *The Lonely Voice: A Study of the Short Story* (1962); R. L. Pattee, *The Development of the American Short Story* (rev. 1966); Ian Reid, *The Short Story* (1977); Malcolm Bradbury, ed., *The Penguin Book of Modern British Short Stories* (1987); Julie Brown, ed., *American Women Short Story Writers* (1995); John Updike, ed., *The Best American Short Stories of the Century* (1999). On the novella: Ronald Paulson, *The Novelette Before 1900* (1968); Mary Doyle Springer, *Forms of the Modern Novella* (1976); Martin Swales, *The German Novelle* (1977).

showing (in narrative): **47**.

sign: **358**.

sign proper (in semiotics): **358**.

significance (in interpretation): **178**.

signified (in linguistics): **195**; *358*.

signifier: **195**; *358*.

simile (sĭm′ ĭ lē): **130**; *212*.

Skeltonics: **93**.

slam (poetry): **271**.

议论话题的载体。框形故事的近代形式既包括单一的故事（如亨利·詹姆斯的《螺丝在拧紧》），也包括一系列的故事（如乔·钱德勒·哈里斯1881年以来创作的雷默斯大叔讲述的故事；参见：*动物寓言故事*）。

近似于当代短篇小说概念的散文体叙事形式始于19世纪早期，为的是满足当时创办的许多**杂志**（收集各式各样材料的期刊，包括随笔、评论、诗歌、散文体故事等）对短篇小说的需求。早期的实践者包括美国的华盛顿·欧文、霍桑和坡；英国的沃尔特·司各特爵士和玛丽·雪莱；德国的 E. T. A. 霍夫曼；法国的巴尔扎克；俄国的果戈理、普希金和屠格涅夫。自那时起，几乎所有欧洲语系的主要小说家都创作了著名的短篇小说。这种形式在美国尤为繁盛，弗兰克·奥康纳称其为"美国的国家艺术形式"。美国短篇小说大师（除了上面提到的）还包括：马克·吐温、威廉·福克纳、凯瑟琳·安妮·波特、尤多拉·韦尔蒂、弗兰纳里·奥康纳、约翰·欧哈拉、J. F. 鲍尔斯、约翰·契弗和 J. D. 塞林格。

参阅：肖恩·奥法莱恩所著的《短篇小说》(1948，1964年重印)；弗兰克·奥康纳所著的《寂寞之声：短篇小说研究》(1962)；R. L. 帕蒂所著的《美国短篇小说的发展》(1966年修订版)；伊恩·里德所著的《短篇小说》(1977)；马尔科姆·布拉德伯里主编的《企鹅现代英国短篇小说选》(1987)；朱莉·布朗主编的《美国短篇小说女作家》(1995)；约翰·厄普代克主编的《美国20世纪最佳短篇小说》(1999)。关于中篇小说，可以参阅：罗纳德·保尔森所著的《1900年以前的中篇小说》(1968)；玛丽·多伊尔·斯普林格所著的《现代中篇小说的形式》(1976)；马丁·斯韦尔斯所著的《德国中篇小说》(1977)。

showing (in narrative)：(叙事中的) 展示手法　47。

sign：符号　358。

sign proper (in semiotics)：(符号论中) 适当的符号　358。

significance (in interpretation)：(释义中的) 意义　178。

signified (in linguistics)：(语言学中的) 所指　195；*358*。

signifier：能指　195；*358*。

simile：直喻，明喻　130；*212*。

Skeltonics：斯克尔顿体短韵诗　93。

slam (poetry)：咏诗擂台赛（又译 现场诗歌）　271。

slant rhyme: 349.

slave narratives: 274.

sloth: 364.

social novel: 256.

social theory of textual criticism: 403.

Socialist Realism: Socialist Realism was a term used by Marxist critics for novels which, they claimed, reflected social reality—that is, novels that accorded with the Marxist view that the struggle between economic classes is the essential dynamic of society. After the 1930s "Socialist Realism" was the officially sanctioned artistic mode for communist writers until the dissolution of the Soviet Union in 1991. In its crude version, it served as a term of approval for novels that adhered to the party line by stressing the oppression of workers by bourgeois capitalists, the virtues of the proletariat, and the felicities of life under a communist regime. A flexible Marxist critic such as Georg Lukács, on the other hand, applied complex criteria of narrative realism to analyze and laud the traditional classics of European realistic fiction.

See *Marxist criticism, proletarian novel,* and *realism,* and refer to Georg Lukács, *Studies in European Realism* (trans. 1964); Mark Slonim, *Soviet Russian Literature* (1967); and George Bisztray, *Marxist Models of Literary Realism* (1978).

society verse: 192.

sociological novel: 256.

sociology of literature: Most literary historians and critics have taken some account of the relation of individual authors to the circumstances of the social and cultural era in which they live and write, as well as of the relation of a literary work to the segment of society that its fiction represents or to the audience toward which the work is addressed. (For major exceptions in recent types of criticism see *Russian formalism, New Criticism, structuralism, deconstruction.*) The term "sociology of literature," however, is applied only to the writings of those historians and critics whose primary, and sometimes exclusive, interest is in the ways that the subject matter and form of a literary work are affected by such circumstances as its author's class status, gender, and political and other interests; the ways of thinking and feeling characteristic of its era; the economic conditions of the writer's profession and of the publication and distribution of books; and the social class, conceptions, and values of the audience to which an author addresses the literary product. Sociological critics treat a work of literature as inescapably conditioned—in the choice and development of its subject matter, the ways of thinking it incorporates, its

slant rhyme：偏韵　349。

slave narratives：奴隶故事　274。

sloth：懒惰　364。

social novel：社会小说　256。

social theory of textual criticism：文本批评社会理论　403。

Socialist Realism：社会主义现实主义

马克思主义批评学家用这个术语指代他们认为反映了社会现实的小说，即这些小说与马克思主义观点相一致，认为经济阶级间的斗争是社会最根本的动力。1930 年代后，"社会主义现实主义"是官方鼓励共产主义作家采用的一种艺术模式，这种状况一直持续到 1991 年苏联解体。粗略来说，这一官方认可的术语指代遵循苏联共产党路线的小说，这类小说强调资产阶级资本家对工人的压迫、无产阶级的美德，以及共产主义政权领导下生活的快乐与幸福。另一方面，乔治·卢卡奇等灵活的马克思主义批评家，则运用复杂的叙事现实主义标准，来分析和称赞欧洲现实主义小说中的传统经典之作。

参见：马克思主义批评、无产阶级小说、现实主义；参阅：乔治·卢卡奇所著的《欧洲现实主义研究》（1964 年英译版）；马克·斯隆尼姆所著的《苏俄文学》（1967）；乔治·比兹特瑞所著的《文学现实主义的马克思主义模式》（1978）。

society verse：上流社会轻佻诗　192。

sociological novel：社会学小说　256。

Sociology of Literature：文学社会学

大多数文学史学家和批评家都注重作者个人与其生活、创作其中的社会及文化时代环境之间的关系，也注重文学作品与其所反映或针对的社会层面之间的关系。（近代的一些批评学派是主要的例外，参见：俄国形式主义、新批评、结构主义、解构主义。）不过，"文学社会学"这一术语只用来指这样一些史学家和批评家的作品，这些史学家和批评家主要关注（或有时只是关注）文学作品的主题与形式如何受到作者的阶级地位、性别、政治或其他利益等环境的影响；如何受到其创作时代特有的思想情感方式的影响；如何受到作者的职业经济状况与书籍出版销售的影响；如何受到文学作品所针对的读者的社会阶层、思想观念与价值观的影响。社会学派的批评家认为，文学作品——题材的选择与形成，作品体现的

evaluations of the modes of life it renders, and even in its formal qualities—by the social, political, and economic organization and forces of its age. Such critics also tend to view the interpretation and assessment of a literary work by a reading public as shaped by the circumstances specific to that public's time and place. The French historian Hippolyte Taine is sometimes considered the first modern sociologist of literature in his *History of English Literature* (1863), which analyzed a work as determined by three factors: its author's "race," its geographical and social "milieu," and its historical "moment."

For prominent sociological emphases in recent critical writings, see *feminist criticism*—which emphasizes the role of male interests and assumptions as determinants of the content, values, and interpretations of the standard literary *canon*—and also *Marxist criticism*. For an influential Marxist version, see Lucien Goldmann, *Essays on Method in the Sociology of Literature*, 1980. For approaches by the *Frankfurt School* of Marxist criticism, see two essays by Leo Lowenthal, both titled "On Sociology of Literature," 1932, 1948, reprinted in *Literature and Mass Culture*, 1984. It should be noted that Marx's views of the economic basis of social organization, class *ideologies*, and class conflict have influenced the work of many critics who, although not committed to Marxist doctrine, stress the sociological context and content of works of literature. The most thoroughgoing treatments of literary works as cultural products that are embedded in the circumstances and discourses of a time and place are by advocates of the current modes of criticism called the *new historicism*. For late developments in the sociology of literary texts, see *book history studies*.

See the readings listed under *authors and authorship, book history studies, feminist criticism, Marxist criticism,* and *new historicism*. Refer also to the pioneering study by Alexandre Beljame, *Men of Letters and the English Public*—that is, in the eighteenth century (1883, trans. 1948); Levin Schücking, *The Sociology of Literary Taste* (rev. 1941); Hugh Dalziel Duncan, *Language and Literature in Society, with a Bibliographical Guide to the Sociology of Literature* (1953); Pierre Bourdieu, *The Field of Cultural Production: Essays in Art and Literature* (1996). Bourdieu's views have been applied to the formation of the canon of literature by John Guillory in *Cultural Capital* (1995). See also two books on the sociology of the production of popular literature and its audience by Janice Radway, *A Feeling for Books: The Book-of-the-Month Club, Literary Taste, and Middle-Class Desire* (1997), and *Reading the Romance: Women, Patriarchy, and Popular Literature* (1991). Collections of essays in sociological criticism include Joseph P. Strelka, ed., *Literary Criticism and Sociology* (1973); Elizabeth and Tom Burns, eds., *Sociology of Literature and Drama: Selected Readings* (1973); and the issue of *Critical Inquiry* devoted to the sociology of literature, Vol. 14 (Spring 1988).

Socratic irony: 186.

solecism (sŏl′ ĕsĭsm): **203.**

思维方式,作品对其表现的生活方式的评价,甚至作品的形式特征——不可避免地受制于其特定时代的社会、政治、经济力量及结构。社会学派的批评家也认为,阅读大众所处的时代与地点所特有的环境,决定了阅读大众对文学作品的阐释和评价。法国史学家伊波莱特·泰纳有时被视为第一位现代文学社会学批评家,他在其所著的《英国文学史》(1863)中提出,一部作品大致可用三个因素来分析,即作者的"种族"、地理与社会"环境"、历史"时代"。

当代批评论著中明显强调社会学分析的,可以参见:*女性主义批评*(女性主义批评强调男性利益及设想对标准的文学经典的内容、形式、阐释所起的决定作用)和*马克思主义批评*。关于一种有影响的马克思主义版本,参阅:吕西安·戈德曼所著的《文学社会学方法论》(1980)。关于马克思主义批评的*法兰克福学派*方法,参阅:利奥·洛温塔尔所写的两篇文章,两篇文章的名字都叫"论文学社会学"(1932,1948),重印收入其所著的《文学与大众文化》(1984)。值得一提的是,马克思认为经济是社会结构、阶级*意识形态*和阶级冲突的基础,这一观点影响了许多批评家的研究。尽管这些批评家并不信奉马克思主义的学说,但是他们同样强调社会背景与文学作品的内容。当代批评学派*新历史主义*的追随者将文学作品完全视为文化的产物,认为文学作品完全扎根于时代、地点的背景环境中。关于文学文本社会学近来的发展,参见:*书籍史研究*。

参见:*作者与作者身份*、*女性主义批评*、*马克思主义批评*、*新历史主义*中所列的参考书目。也可参阅:亚历山大·贝尔杰姆在18世纪进行的开拓性研究《作家与英国公众》(1883,1948年英译版);莱文·许京所著的《文学趣味社会学》(1941年修订版);休·达尔齐尔·邓肯所著的《社会中的语言与文学:附带文学社会学书目指南》(1953);皮埃尔·布迪厄所著的《文化生产场:论艺术与文学》(1996)。约翰·杰洛瑞在《文化资本》(1995)中用布迪厄的观点来解释文学经典的形成。也可参阅两本关于大众文学及其受众的生产的社会学的书籍:贾尼丝·拉德维所著的《书的感觉:每月一书俱乐部、文学趣味与中产阶级欲念》(1997)和《阅读浪漫:女性、父权制与大众文化》(1991)。社会学派批评的论文集包括:约瑟夫·P. 斯特雷尔卡主编的《文学批评与社会学》(1973);伊丽莎白和汤姆·伯恩斯夫妇合编的《文学和戏剧社会学选读》(1973);以及《批评探索》第14卷(1988年春)中有关文学社会学的内容。

Socratic irony:苏格拉底式反讽　186。

solecism:语法错误　203。

soliloquy: Soliloquy is the act of talking to oneself, whether silently or aloud. In drama it denotes the *convention* by which a character, alone on the stage, utters his or her thoughts aloud. Playwrights have used this device as a convenient way to convey information about a character's motives and state of mind, or for purposes of exposition, and sometimes in order to guide the judgments and responses of the audience. Christopher Marlowe's *Dr. Faustus* (first performed in 1594) opens with a long expository soliloquy, and concludes with another which expresses Faustus' frantic mental and emotional state during his belated attempts to evade damnation. The best-known of dramatic soliloquies is Hamlet's speech which begins "To be or not to be." Compare *monologue*.

A related stage device is the **aside**, in which a character expresses to the audience his or her thought or intention in a short speech which, by convention, is inaudible to the other characters on the stage. Both devices, common in Elizabethan and later drama, were largely rejected by dramatists in the later nineteenth century, when the increasing requirement that plays convey the illusion of real life impelled writers to exploit indirect means for revealing a character's state of mind, and for conveying exposition and guidance to the audience. Eugene O'Neill, however, revived and extended the soliloquy and aside and made them basic devices throughout his play *Strange Interlude* (1928). For references to *soliloquy* in other entries, see pages *63, 64, 94*.

Son of Ben: 281.

sonnet: A *lyric* poem consisting of a single *stanza* of fourteen iambic pentameter lines linked by an intricate rhyme scheme. (Refer to *meter* and *rhyme*.) There are two major patterns of rhyme in sonnets written in the English language:

1. The **Italian** or **Petrarchan sonnet** (named after the fourteenth-century Italian poet Petrarch) falls into two main parts: an **octave** (eight lines) rhyming *abbaabba* followed by a **sestet** (six lines) rhyming *cdecde* or some variant, such as *cdccdc*. Petrarch's sonnets were first imitated in England, in both their stanza form and their standard subject—the hopes and pains of an adoring male lover—by Sir Thomas Wyatt in the early sixteenth century. (See *Petrarchan conceit*.) The Petrarchan form was later used, for a great variety of subjects, by Milton, Wordsworth, Christina Rossetti, D. G. Rossetti, and other sonneteers, who sometimes made it technically easier in English (which does not have as many rhyming possibilities as Italian) by introducing a new pair of rhymes in the second four lines of the octave.
2. The Earl of Surrey and other English experimenters in the sixteenth century also developed a stanza form called the **English sonnet**, or else the **Shakespearean sonnet**, after its greatest practitioner. This sonnet falls into three *quatrains* and a concluding *couplet*: *abab cdcd efef gg*. There was a notable variant, the **Spenserian sonnet**, in which Spenser linked each quatrain to the next by a continuing rhyme: *abab bcbc cdcd ee*.

Soliloquy：内心独白

内心独白是一种默默地或大声地自言自语的行为。在戏剧中，内心独白表示某一人物遵循*文学惯例*，独自在戏剧舞台上大声说出他或她的想法。剧作家采用内心独白这种手法作为便于传达某个人物动机和心理状态信息的一种方式，或用这一手法来达到解说的目的；他们有时也用内心独白来引导观众的判断与反应。克里斯托弗·马洛的《浮士德博士》（1594 年首次上演）以一段长篇的解说性内心独白开场，并以另一段内心独白结尾；结尾那段内心独白表现了浮士德为时已晚地想要逃脱惩罚时疯狂的精神状态与情感状态。最著名的戏剧内心独白首推哈姆雷特以"生存还是毁灭"这句话开头的一段言语。对比：*独白*。

旁白是另一种与内心独白有关的舞台手法；在这种手法中，某个人物用简短的言语向观众表达他或她的思想或意图。依照惯例，舞台上的其他角色是听不见旁白言语的。内心独白与旁白这两种手法在伊丽莎白时期及稍后的戏剧中经常出现，但到 19 世纪后期，人们日益要求戏剧表现出对现实生活的幻想，这迫使戏剧家们采用间接方式进行解说、引导观众，所以内心独白与旁白便渐渐不再使用。但尤金·奥尼尔在《奇妙的插曲》(1928) 一剧中重新使用并扩展了旁白这一手法，使其成为贯穿该剧的主要手法。其他条目中提及"独白"的地方，参见第 63、64、94 页。

Son of Ben：本之子　281。

Sonnet：十四行诗

十四行诗（又译商籁诗）是由单个*诗节*构成的*抒情诗*，全诗共十四行，每行都为抑扬格五音步诗句，每行诗句之间的连接遵循精心安排的押韵格式。（参见：*格律、押韵*。）用英语创作的十四行诗主要有两种押韵模式：

1. **意大利式十四行诗**，或称**彼特拉克式十四行诗**（以 14 世纪意大利诗人彼特拉克的名字命名），分为两部分：**前八行**的韵脚格式为 abbaabba，紧接着的**最后六行**的韵脚格式为 cdecde，有时也会有所变化，如 cdccdc。16 世纪初期，英国的托马斯·怀亚特爵士最早模仿了彼特拉克的十四行诗，不仅模仿其诗节形式，也模仿了诗歌的主题——痴情男子的希望与痛苦。（参见：*彼特拉克式巧思妙喻*。）弥尔顿、华兹华斯、克里斯蒂娜·罗塞蒂、D. G. 罗塞蒂和其他后来的十四行诗诗人，用彼特拉克十四行诗的形式来表现多种多样的主题，有时还在第 5、6、7、8 行中引入一对新的韵脚，从而在技巧上简化了英语十四行诗（英语中的押韵可能性比意大利语小）。

2. 16 世纪的萨里伯爵等英国创新诗人也发展了一种诗节形式，称为**英国式十四行诗**，又称**莎士比亚式十四行诗**，这得名于这一诗节形式最杰出的实践者莎士比亚。这种十四行诗分为三组四行诗和结尾的一组对句：abab cdcd efef gg。该诗体形式有一种重要的变体，即**斯宾塞式十四行诗**。斯宾塞用连续的韵脚将每组四行诗一一相连：abab bcbc cdcd ee。

John Donne shifted from the hitherto primary subject, sexual love, to a variety of religious themes in his *Holy Sonnets*, written early in the seventeenth century; and Milton, in the latter part of that century, expanded the range of the sonnet to other matters of serious concern. Except for a lapse in the English *Neoclassic Period*, the sonnet has remained a popular form to the present day and includes among its distinguished practitioners, in the nineteenth century, Wordsworth, Keats, Elizabeth Barrett Browning, Christina Rossetti, and Dante Gabriel Rossetti, and in the twentieth century, Edwin Arlington Robinson, Edna St. Vincent Millay, W. B. Yeats, Robert Frost, W. H. Auden, and Dylan Thomas. The stanza is just long enough to permit a fairly complex lyric development, yet so short, and so exigent in its rhymes, as to pose a standing challenge to the ingenuity and artistry of the poet. The rhyme pattern of the Petrarchan sonnet has on the whole favored a statement of a problem, situation, or incident in the octave, with a resolution in the sestet. The English form sometimes uses a similar division of material, but often presents instead a repetition-with-variation of a statement in each of the three quatrains; in either case, the final couplet in the English sonnet usually imposes an *epigrammatic* turn at the end. In Drayton's fine Elizabethan sonnet in the English form "Since there's no help, come let us kiss and part," the lover brusquely declares in the first quatrain, then reiterates in the second, that he is glad that the affair is cleanly ended, then hesitates at the finality of the parting in the third quatrain, and in the concluding couplet suddenly drops his swagger to make one last plea. Here are the third quatrain and couplet:

> Now at the last gasp of love's latest breath,
> When, his pulse failing, passion speechless lies,
> When faith is kneeling by his bed of death,
> And innocence is closing up his eyes;
> > Now if thou wouldst, when all have given him over,
> > From death to life thou mightst him yet recover.

Following Petrarch's early example, a number of Elizabethan authors arranged their poems into **sonnet sequences**, or **sonnet cycles**, in which a series of sonnets are linked together by exploring the varied aspects of a relationship between lovers, or else by indicating a development in the relationship that constitutes a kind of implicit plot. Shakespeare ordered his sonnets in a sequence, as did Sidney in *Astrophel and Stella* (1580) and Spenser in *Amoretti* (1595). Later examples of the sonnet sequence on various subjects are Wordsworth's *The River Duddon*, D. G. Rossetti's *House of Life*, Elizabeth Barrett Browning's *Sonnets from the Portuguese*, and the American poet William Ellery Leonard's *Two Lives*. Dylan Thomas' *Altarwise by Owl-light* (1936) is a sequence of ten sonnets which are abstruse meditations on the poet's own life. George Meredith's *Modern Love* (1862), which concerns a bitterly unhappy marriage, is sometimes called a sonnet sequence, even though its component poems consist not of fourteen but of sixteen lines.

On the early history of the sonnet and its development in England through Milton, see Michael R. G. Spiller, *The Development of the Sonnet: An*

约翰·多恩在17世纪初创作了《神圣十四行诗》；诗歌的主题从当时流行的主题，即两性间的爱情，转向各种宗教主题。17世纪后期，弥尔顿又把十四行诗的主题范围扩展到人们关注的其他严肃问题上。在英国*新古典主义时期*，十四行诗曾一度衰落。除此时期之外，十四行诗一直是从古至今的一种流行形式。19世纪杰出的十四行诗实践者包括华兹华斯、济慈、伊丽莎白·巴雷特·勃朗宁、克里斯蒂娜·罗塞蒂、但丁·加布里埃尔·罗塞蒂，以及更近代的埃德温·阿林顿·罗宾逊、埃德娜·圣文森特·米莱、W. B. 叶芝、罗伯特·弗洛斯特、W. H. 奥登和迪伦·托马斯。十四行诗的长度正好适合表达相对复杂的情感发展，但诗歌短促、急迫的韵脚又对诗人的艺术技巧形成永恒的挑战。彼特拉克式十四行诗的押韵格式一般倾向于在前八行诗句中陈述某一问题、情景或事件，而在后六行诗句里提出解决方法。英国式十四行诗有时也对题材进行类似分配，但常在三组的四行诗句中，对某一陈述采用带有变化的重复形式。不过，英国十四行诗最后的一组对句通常会在结尾加入*警句*式的转折。德雷顿在伊丽莎白时期创作了《既然毫无指望，就让我们吻别吧》这首优美的英国式十四行诗。在这首诗里，情人在第一组四行诗句中，生硬无礼地宣称他十分高兴他们的恋情干净利落地结束了，接着又在第二组四行诗中加以重申；在结尾的对句中，他突然抛弃先前妄自尊大的态度，转而提出最后的请求。下面是这首诗最后一组四行诗句和结尾的对句：

> 现在爱的临终呼吸发出最后的喘息，
> 他的脉搏衰弱，热情安卧无语，
> 信仰跪在他的死榻一隅，
> 无辜在将他的双眼合起；
> 假如你愿，在一切抛弃他的瞬间，
> 你仍然可以使他从死里生还。 （李霁野译）

伊丽莎白时期的许多作家仿效彼特拉克早期的模式，将诗歌布局成**十四行组诗**或称**十四行诗序列集**。这种十四行组诗或序列集将一系列十四行诗联结在一起，探讨恋人关系中的各种方面，或表现构成某种内在情节的恋人关系的发展。莎士比亚就曾把十四行诗排列成十四行组诗，锡德尼的《爱星者和星星》（1580）与斯宾塞的《爱情小诗》（1595）也都是用十四行组诗的格式写成的。后来的十四行组诗描写了各种主题，如华兹华斯的《杜冬河》、D. G. 罗塞蒂的《生命之家》、伊丽莎白·巴雷特·勃朗宁的《葡萄牙人的十四行诗》、美国诗人威廉·艾勒里·伦纳德的《两条生命》。迪伦·托马斯的《祭坛黄昏》（1936）是一首由十首十四行诗组成的十四行组诗，表现了诗人对自己一生的思索。乔治·梅瑞狄斯的《摩登爱情》（1862）关注的是一桩极为不幸的婚姻，尽管其中的诗歌由十六行而非十四行诗句组成，但人们有时还是称其为十四行组诗。

关于十四行诗的早期历史，以及十四行诗自弥尔顿以来在英国的发展，参阅：迈克尔·R. G. 斯皮勒所著的《十四行诗的发展：导论》（1992）。也可

Introduction (1992). See also L. G. Sterner, *The Sonnet in American Literature* (1930); J. B. Leishman, *Themes and Variations in Shakespeare's Sonnets* (1963); Michael R. G. Spiller, *The Sonnet Sequence: A Study of the Strategies* (1997); Helen Vendler, *The Art of Shakespeare's Sonnets* (1997); Stephen Burt and David Mikics, *The Art of the Sonnet* (2010).

sonnet cycle: 371.

sonnet sequence: 371.

sound symbolism: 196.

speech-act theory: Speech-act theory, developed by the philosopher John Austin, was described most fully in his posthumous book *How to Do Things with Words* (1962), and was explored and expanded by other "ordinary-language philosophers," including John Searle and H. P. Grice. Austin's theory is directed against traditional tendencies of philosophers (1) to analyze the meaning of isolated sentences, abstracted from the context of a discourse and from the attendant circumstances in which a sentence is uttered; and (2) to assume, in what Austin calls a "logical obsession," that the standard sentence—of which other types are merely variants—is a statement that describes a situation or asserts a fact, and is to be judged as either true or false. John Searle's adoption and elaboration of Austin's speech-act theory opposes to these views the claim that when we attend to the overall linguistic and situational context—including the institutional conditions that govern many uses of language—we find that in speaking or writing we perform simultaneously three, and sometimes four, distinguishable kinds of **speech acts**: (1) We utter a sentence; Austin called this act a "locution." (2) We refer to an object, and predicate something about that object. (3) We perform an illocutionary act. (4) Often, we also perform a perlocutionary act.

The **illocutionary act** performed by a locution may indeed be the one stressed by traditional philosophy and logic, to assert that something is true; but it may instead be one of very many other possible speech acts, such as questioning, commanding, promising, warning, praising, thanking, and so on. A sentence consisting of the same words in the same grammatical form, such as "I will leave you tomorrow," may in a particular verbal and situational context turn out to have the "illocutionary force" either of an assertion, or of a promise, or of a threat. In an illocutionary act that is not an assertion, the prime criterion (although the utterance makes reference to some state of affairs) is not its truth or falsity, but whether or not the act has been performed successfully, or in Austin's term, "felicitously." A felicitous performance of a particular illocutionary act depends on its meeting "appropriateness conditions" which obtain for that type of act; these conditions are tacit linguistic and social (or institutional) conventions, or rules, that are shared by competent speakers and interpreters of a language. For example, the "felicitous," or successful, performance of an illocutionary act of promising, such as "I will come

参阅：L.G.斯特纳所著的《美国文学中的十四行诗》(1930)；J.B.利什曼所著的《莎士比亚十四行诗的主题与变化》(1963)；迈克尔·R.G.斯皮勒所著的《十四行诗序列：策略研究》(1997)；海伦·温德勒所著的《莎士比亚十四行诗的艺术》(1997)；斯蒂芬·伯特与戴维·米基克斯合著的《十四行诗的艺术》(2010)。

sonnet cycle：十四行诗序列集　　371。

sonnet sequence：十四行组诗　　371。

sound symbolism：语音象征　　196。

Speech-Act Theory：言语行为理论

　　言语行为理论是由哲学家约翰·奥斯汀发展起来的一种理论。该理论在奥斯汀的遗作《如何以言行事》(1962)中得到了详尽的描述。约翰·塞尔、H. P. 格赖斯等"普通语言哲学家"探讨并扩展了言语行为理论。奥斯汀的这种理论反对哲学家的一些传统倾向：(1)分析孤立句子的意义。这些孤立的句子脱离了话语的语篇，脱离了表述句子时的相应环境；(2)认为标准的句子——其他类型的句子都只是变体——是一种陈述，它或描述某一情景，或断言某一事实，并可用真或假来判断，奥斯汀将这种观点称为逻辑执迷。约翰·塞尔采用并详尽地阐述了奥斯汀的言语行为理论，对上述观点提出质疑。他提出，当我们侧重于整体的语言语境或情景语境时——包括制约许多语言用法的既定条件——我们会发现，在说或书的过程中，我们同时进行三种，有时是四种不同的**言语行为**：(1)我们说出一句话；奥斯汀称这种行为为"发话行为"；(2)我们指某一事物，并对该事物进行描述；(3)我们表达一种话中行为；(4)我们也常表达一种话后行为。

　　发话行为表达的**话中行为**可能的确是传统哲学与逻辑学强调的那样，断言某事物具有真值，但它也可能是其他许多可能的言语行为中的一种，如询问、命令、承诺、警告、赞扬、感谢等。同样词语组成且语法形式相同的句子，如"我明天将离开你"，在特定文字语境和情景语境中可能会有不同的"言外作用"，可能是断言、许诺或威胁。在非断言性的话中行为中，主要判断标准（尽管这些语言可能指某些事物的状态）不在于真值或假值，而在于是否成功地，或用奥斯汀的话说，"有效地"执行了这一行为。是否有效地执行某一特殊的话中行为，取决于这一行为是否符合该种行为具有的"适宜条件"。这些条件是有某种语言能力的说话者和解说者共同的默契语言、社会（或组织）惯例或规则。例如，能否"恰当"或

to see you tomorrow," depends on its meeting its special set of appropriateness conditions: the speaker must be capable of fulfilling his promise, must intend to do so, and must believe that the listener wants him to do so. Failing the last condition, for example, the same verbal utterance might have the illocutionary force of a threat.

In *How to Do Things with Words*, John Austin established an initial distinction between two broad types of locutions: **constatives** (sentences that assert something about a fact or state of affairs and are adjudged to be true or false) and **performatives** (sentences that are speech acts that accomplish something, such as questioning, promising, praising, and so on). As he continued his subtle analysis, however, Austin showed that this initial division of utterances into two sharply exclusive classes does not hold, in that many performatives also involve reference to a state of affairs, while constatives also perform an illocutionary act. Austin, however, drew special attention to the "explicit performative," which is a sentence whose utterance itself, when executed under appropriate institutional and other conditions, brings about the state of affairs that it signifies. Examples are "I name this ship the Queen Elizabeth"; "I apologize"; "I call this meeting to order"; "Let spades be trumps."

If an illocutionary act has an effect on the actions or state of mind of the hearer which goes beyond merely understanding what has been said, it is also a **perlocutionary** act. Thus, the utterance "I am going to leave you," with the illocutionary force of a warning, not only may be understood as such, but may have (or fail to have) the additional perlocutionary effect of frightening the hearer. Similarly, by the illocutionary act of promising to do something, one may please (or else anger) the hearer; and by asserting something, one may have the effect either of enlightening, or of inspiring, or of intimidating the hearer. Some perlocutionary effects are intended by the speaker; others occur without the speaker's intention, and even against that intention. For a useful exploration of the relations, in diverse cases, of illocutionary and perlocutionary speech acts, see Ted Cohen, "Illocutions and Perlocutions," in *Foundations of Language*, Vol. 9 (1973).

A number of deconstructive theorists have proposed that the use of language in fictional literature (which Austin had excluded from his consideration of what he called "seriously" intended speech acts) is in fact a prime instance of the **performative**, in that it does not refer to a pre-existing state of affairs, but brings about, or brings into being, the characters, action, and world that it describes. On the other hand, since performative linguistic acts can't avoid recourse to statement and assertion, some deconstructive theorists convert Austin's constative/performative distinction into an undecidable deadlock, or oscillation, of irreconcilable oppositions. See deconstruction and refer to Barbara Johnson, "Poetry and Performative Language: Mallarmé and Austin," in *The Critical Difference* (1980); Sandra Petrey, *Speech Acts and Literary Theory* (1990); Jonathan Culler, *Literary Theory: A Very Short Introduction* (1997), chapter 7, "Performative Language." Judith Butler has proposed that the terms we use to identify a person's gender and sexuality are modes of performative language, in that the reiterated application of such terms to persons,

成功执行许诺，如"我明天来看你"的话中行为，取决于是否符合其特有的适宜条件：说话者必须有能力履行他的诺言，必须有意去履行他的诺言，必须相信听者希望他这么做。倘若不符合最后一个条件，同样的言语或许就会带有威胁的言外作用。

约翰·奥斯汀在《如何以言行事》中初步区分了两种广义上的言表行为：**表述句**（这类句子对某个事实或事物的状态进行断言，可以用真或假来判断）与**施为句**（这类句子是完成了某些事情的行为，如询问、许诺、赞扬等）。但奥斯汀在对此继续进行详细分析后表示，将言语初步区分成两种完全相互排斥的类型是站不住脚的，因为许多施为句也涉及指事物的状态，而表述句也会执行话中行为。然而，奥斯汀尤为关注"显性施为句"，在适宜的组织条件或其他条件下，这种句子的言语本身得到执行时，其言语本身会随之带来句子所指事物的状态，如"我把这艘船命名为伊丽莎白女王号""我道歉""我宣布会议开始""让黑桃当王牌"等。

如果话中行为对听者的行动或心理状态产生的效果超过了对所说言语的理解，这就叫**话后行为**。因此，带有警告言外作用的言语"我要离开你"，不仅被理解成一种警告，而且会对听者造成（或没有造成）一种恐吓听者的额外话后效果。与此同理，我们可以通过许诺做某事的话中行为取悦（或激怒）听者；我们可以断言某事，从而获得启发、激励或恐吓听者的效果。一些话后行为的效果是说话者有意造成的；另一些则与说话人的意图无关，甚至与说话人的本意相反。有关对话中言语行为与话后言语行为在各种情况下相互关系的有益探讨，参阅：泰德·科恩所写的文章"话中行为与话后行为"，载于《语言基础》1973年第9期。

许多解构主义理论家提出，虚构文学中语言的使用（奥斯汀将其排除在他认为是意图"严肃"的言语行为之外）事实上是**施为句**的一种重要例子，因为它并非指先前存在的事物状态，而是带来了或创造了它所描绘的人物、行为与世界。另一方面，由于施为句的语言行为不可避免地借助于陈述语言和断言性语言，所以解构主义理论家将奥斯汀有关表述句／施为句的区分转化成不可调和的对立中无法确定的僵局，或是摆动。参见：*解构主义*；参阅：芭芭拉·约翰逊所著的《批评的差异》（1980）中的"诗歌和述行语言：马拉美与奥斯汀"；桑德拉·佩特雷所著的《言语行为与文学理论》（1990）；乔纳森·卡勒所著的《文学理论简介》（1997）第7章"述行语言"。朱迪思·巴特勒提出，我们用来描述性别与性的术语都是语言施为句的应用模式，因为这些术语的反复运用

in accordance with the linguistic conventions that govern their use, in fact bring about (or cause persons to "perform") the identities and the modes of behavior that they purport to describe. See Judith Butler, *Gender Trouble: Feminism and the Subversion of Identity* (1990) and *Excitable Speech* (1997); refer also to *queer theory*.

Since 1970 speech-act theory has influenced in conspicuous and varied ways the practice of literary criticism. When applied to the analysis of direct discourse by a character within a literary work, it provides a systematic but sometimes cumbersome framework for identifying the unspoken presuppositions, implications, and effects of speech acts which competent readers and critics have always taken into account, subtly though unsystematically. (See *discourse analysis*.) Speech-act theory has also been used in a more radical way, however, as a model on which to recast the theory of literature in general, and especially the theory of prose narratives (see *fiction and truth*). What the author of a fictional work—or else what the author's invented narrator—narrates is held to constitute a "pretended" set of assertions, which are intended by the author, and understood by the competent reader, to be free from a speaker's ordinary commitment to the truth of what he or she asserts. Within the frame of the fictional world that the narrative thus establishes, however, the utterances of the fictional characters—whether these are assertions or promises or marital vows—are held to be responsible to ordinary illocutionary commitments. Alternatively, some speech-act theorists propose a new version of mimetic theory (see *imitation*). Traditional mimetic critics had claimed that *literature* imitates reality by representing in a verbal medium the setting, actions, utterances, and interactions of human beings. Some speech-act theorists, on the other hand, propose that all literature is simply "mimetic discourse." A lyric, for example, is said to be an imitation of that form of ordinary discourse in which we express our feelings about something, and a novel is an imitation of a particular form of written discourse, such as biography (Henry Fielding's *The History of Tom Jones*, 1749), or autobiography (Charles Dickens' *David Copperfield*, 1849–50), or even a scholar's annotated edition of a poetic text (Nabokov's *Pale Fire*, 1962). See Barbara Herrnstein Smith, *On the Margins of Discourse: The Relation of Literature to Language* (1978).

For basic philosophical treatments of speech acts see John Austin, *How to Do Things with Words* (1962); John R. Searle, *Speech Acts: An Essay in the Philosophy of Language* (1970); and H. P. Grice, "Logic and Conversation," in *Syntax and Semantics*, Vol. 3 (1975). On the application of speech-act theory to metaphor and to literary dialogue, see *metaphor, theories of*, and *discourse analysis*. Among the attempts to model the general theory of literature, or at least of prose fiction, on the theory of speech acts are Richard Ohmann, "Speech Acts and the Definition of Literature," *Philosophy and Rhetoric*, Vol. 4 (1971); John R. Searle, "The Logical Status of Fictional Discourse," in his *Expression and Meaning* (1979), chapter 3; refer also to the entry *fiction and truth*. A detailed application to literary theory is Mary Louise Pratt's *Toward a Speech Act Theory of Literary Discourse* (1977). For views of the limitations of speech-act theory when applied in literary criticism, see Stanley Fish, "How to Do

符合制约它们使用的惯例，事实上带来了（或让人"执行"）它们意欲描绘的身份与行为模式。参阅：朱迪思·巴特勒所著的《性别麻烦：女性主义与身份的颠覆》(1990) 和《易激动的言语》(1997)；也可参见：*同性恋理论*。

1970 年代以来，言语行为理论以各种显著的方式影响了文学批评实践。用这一理论分析文学作品中某位人物的直接话语时，它提供了一种系统但有时累赘的框架，用以识别未说出口的预设、暗示和言语行为效果。有能力的读者和文学批评家虽然非系统地但却是细致入微地考虑了这些因素。(参见：*话语分析*。) 不过，更激进的做法则是将言语行为理论用作一种模式，用来改写一般的文学理论，尤其是散文体叙事理论（参见：*虚构小说与真实*）。虚构作品的作者——或作者臆造出的叙述者——所叙述的事情被视为构成了一套"虚假"的说法；这套说法是有能力的读者所理解的，而作者则希望这套说法能够摆脱说话人对所说言语真实性的惯常承诺。然而，在叙事建立的虚构世界框架中，虚构人物的言语——不论是断言、承诺或婚姻誓言——被认为必须服从惯常的话中承诺。一些言语行为理论家也提倡一种新的摹仿理论学说（参见：*摹仿*）。传统的摹仿批评学家曾提出，文学通过文字媒介表现人类的情景、行动、言谈和相互作用，以此来摹仿现实。另一方面，一些言语行为理论家认为，所有的文学都只不过是"摹仿式的话语"。例如，认为抒情诗摹仿了我们对某物抒发感情的惯常话语形式，小说摹仿了一种特殊的书写话语模式，如传记 [亨利·菲尔丁的《汤姆·琼斯》(1749)]、自传 [查尔斯·狄更斯的《大卫·科波菲尔》(1849—1850)]、甚或是某一学者对诗歌文本所作的注释版本 [纳博科夫的《灰火》(1962)]。参阅：芭芭拉·赫恩斯坦·史密斯所著的《话语的边缘：文学与语言的关系》(1978)。

对言语行为基本的哲学论述，参阅：约翰·奥斯汀所著的《如何以言行事》(1962)；约翰·R. 塞尔所著的《言语行为：论语言哲学》(1970)；H. P. 格赖斯所写的文章"逻辑与会话"，载于《语法与语义》(1975) 第 3 卷。关于将言语行为理论应用于隐喻/暗喻和文学对话，参见：*隐喻/暗喻理论*、*话语分析*。尝试用言语行为理论构建一般文学理论，至少是散文体小说的一般理论，参阅：理查德·奥曼所写的文章"言语行为与文学的定义"，载于《哲学与修辞》1971 年第 4 卷；约翰·R. 塞尔所写的文章"虚构话语的逻辑地位"，收入其所著的《表达式和意义》(1979) 第 3 章；也可参阅条目：*虚构小说与真实*。该理论在文学理论中的具体运用，参阅：玛丽·露易丝·普拉特所著的《文学语篇的言语行为理论》(1977)。有关言语行为理论在文学批评运用中的局限，参阅：斯坦利·费什所写的文章"如

Things with Austin and Searle: Speech-Act Theory and Literary Criticism," in *Is There a Text in This Class?* (1980); and Joseph Margolis, "Literature and Speech Acts," *Philosophy and Literature*, Vol. 3 (1979). For Jacques Derrida's deconstructive analysis of Austin's views, and John Searle's reply, see under *deconstruction*. For references to *speech-act theory* in other entries, see pages 128, 347.

Spenserian sonnet: 370.

Spenserian stanza: 377.

spiritual autobiography: 27; *62*.

spirituals (African-American): **166**.

spondaic (spŏndā′ ĭk): **219**.

sprezzatura (sprēts′ ătoo″ rä): **339**.

sprung rhythm: 222.

stable irony: 185.

stanza: A stanza (Italian for "stopping place") is a grouping of the verse lines in a poem, often set off by a space in the printed text. Usually the stanzas of a given poem are marked by a recurrent pattern of rhyme and are also uniform in the number and lengths of the component lines. Some unrhymed poems, however, are divided into stanzaic units (for example, William Collins' "Ode to Evening," 1747), and some rhymed poems are composed of stanzas that vary in their component lines (for example, the *irregular ode*).

Of the great diversity of English stanza forms, many lack specific names and must be described by describing the number of lines, the type and number of metric *feet* in each line, and the pattern of the *rhyme*. Certain stanzas, however, are used so often that they have been given the convenience of a name.

A **couplet** is a pair of rhymed lines that are equal in length. The **octosyllabic couplet** has lines of eight syllables, usually consisting of four iambic feet, as in Andrew Marvell's "To His Coy Mistress" (1681):

> The grave's a fine and private place,
> But none, I think, do there embrace.

Iambic pentameter lines rhyming in pairs are called **decasyllabic** ("ten-syllable") **couplets** or "heroic couplets." (For examples, see the entry *heroic couplet*.)

The **tercet**, or **triplet**, is a stanza of three lines, usually with a single rhyme. The lines may be the same length (as in Robert Herrick's "Upon Julia's Clothes," 1648, written in tercets of iambic tetrameter), or else of

何用奥斯汀和塞尔的理论做事：言语行为理论和文学批评"，收入其所著的《这堂课有文本吗？》(1980)；约瑟夫·马戈利斯所写的文章"文学与言语行为"，载于《哲学与文学》1979年第3卷。雅克·德里达对奥斯汀观点的解构主义分析，以及约翰·塞尔的回应，参见：*解构主义*中的相关论述。其他条目中提及"言语行为理论"的地方，参见第128、347页。

Spenserian sonnet：斯宾塞式十四行诗　370。

Spenserian stanza：斯宾塞式诗节　377。

spiritual autobiography：精神自传　27；*62*。

spirituals (African-American)：(非裔美国人的) 灵歌　166。

spondaic：扬扬格　219。

sprezzatura：自然　339。

sprung rhythm：弹性节奏　222。

stable irony：指令反讽　185。

Stanza：诗节

　　诗节（意大利语，意为"停顿处"）是指诗歌中的诗行群，在印刷文本中常用空行隔开。某一特定诗歌的诗节通常以反复出现的押韵格式为特征，各诗节中的诗行行数相同、长度一致。不过，一些非格律诗也以诗节为单位 [如威廉·柯林斯的《黄昏颂》(1747)]，而在一些格律诗中，组成诗节的一些诗句长短也不尽相同（如*无律颂*）。

　　英语诗节的形式种类极为繁多，许多都缺少专属名称，只能具体按诗行数的多少、每行诗句*音步*的类型和数目，以及*押韵*格式来描述。但因一些诗节经常出现，故为方便起见，赋予了它们名称。

　　对句是指长度相等、相互押韵的一对诗行。**八音节对句**中的每行诗句有八个音节，通常由四个抑扬格音步构成。如安德鲁·马韦尔的《致羞涩的情人》(1681) 里的八音节对句：

　　　　坟墓可以隐私，固然很好，
　　　　但我想，绝没有人在那里拥抱。　　　　　　　　（何功杰译）

互相押韵含抑扬格五音步诗行的两行诗句叫**十音节对句**或"英雄双韵体"（例见*英雄双韵体*）。

　　同韵三行诗节或**三行联句**指的是含三行诗句的诗节，通常所有诗句押同一个韵。诗行可能长度相同 [如罗伯特·赫里克的《赞茱莉叶的衣裳》(1648) 就采用了抑扬格四音步同韵三行诗节]，也可能长短不一。理查德·克拉肖的《祝愿意中

varying lengths. In Richard Crashaw's "Wishes to His Supposed Mistress" (1646), the lines of each tercet are successively in *iambic dimeter, trimeter,* and *tetrameter*:

> Who e'er she be
> That not impossible she
> That shall command my heart and me.

Terza rima is composed of tercets which are interlinked, in that each is joined to the one following by a common rhyme: *aba, bcb, cdc,* and so on. Dante composed his *Divine Comedy* (early fourteenth century) in terza rima; but although Sir Thomas Wyatt introduced the form early in the sixteenth century, it has not been a common meter in English, in which rhymes are much harder to find than in Italian. Shelley, however, used it brilliantly in "Ode to the West Wind" (1820), and it occurs also in the poetry of Milton, Browning, and T. S. Eliot.

The **quatrain**, or four-line stanza, is the most common in English versification, and is employed with various meters and rhyme schemes. The *ballad stanza* (in alternating four- and three-foot lines rhyming *abcb,* or less frequently *abab*) is one common quatrain; when this same stanza occurs in *hymns,* it is called **common measure**. Emily Dickinson is the most subtle, varied, and persistent of all users of this type of quatrain; her frequent resort to *partial rhyme* prevents monotony:

> Purple—is fashionable twice—
> This season of the year,
> And when a soul perceives itself
> To be an Emperor.

The **heroic quatrain**, in iambic pentameter rhyming *abab,* is the stanza of Gray's "Elegy Written in a Country Churchyard" (1751):

> The curfew tolls the knell of parting day,
>   The lowing herd winds slowly o'er the lea,
> The plowman homeward plods his weary way,
>   And leaves the world to darkness, and to me.

Rime royal was introduced by Chaucer in *Troilus and Criseyde* (the latter 1380s) and other narrative poems; it is believed to take its name, however, from its later use by "the Scottish Chaucerian," King James I of Scotland, in his poem *The Kingis Quair* ("The King's Book"), written about 1424. It is a seven-line, iambic pentameter stanza rhyming *ababbcc*. This form was quite widely used by Elizabethan poets, including by Shakespeare in "A Lover's Complaint" and *The Rape of Lucrece,* which begins:

> From the besieged Ardea all in post
> Borne by the trustless wings of false desire,
> Lust-breathèd Tarquin leaves the Roman host
> And to Collatium bears the lightless fire

人》(1646) 中，同韵三行诗节的诗句分别采用了**抑扬格双音步诗行、三音步诗行和四音步诗行**：

> 不论她是谁
> 她不是不可能
> 将会控制我的心与我。

三行诗节隔句押韵法由相互衔接的同韵三行诗节组成，每一连句与之后的另一连句依靠一个共同的韵脚格式彼此衔接：aba, bcb, cdc 等。但丁的《神曲》(14 世纪初) 就采用了三行诗节隔句押韵法。虽然托马斯·怀亚特爵士早在 16 世纪就将三行诗节隔句押韵法引入英诗，但这一诗体在英诗中的运用并不普遍，因为英语中的押韵词比意大利语中的押韵词难找。不过，雪莱却在《西风颂》(1820) 里娴熟地运用了这一诗体形式。弥尔顿、勃朗宁和 T. S. 艾略特的诗歌中也曾出现过三行诗节隔句押韵法。

四行诗或四行诗节是英语律诗中最常见的一种诗体，可与各种音步和押韵格式一起使用。*民谣体诗节*（四音步和三音步诗行交替出现，押韵格式为 abcb，或较为罕见的 abab）是一种常见的四行诗。当同样的诗节出现在*赞美诗*中，它被称为*普通韵律*。在所有使用这种四行诗节的诗人中，埃米莉·狄金森的技巧最为精湛，富于变化且孜孜以求。她常用*偏韵*，以免行文单调：

> 紫色——两度流行——
> 一年的这个季节，
> 当心灵把自身看做
> 一位君王时。

下面摘自格雷《墓畔哀歌》(1751) 中的诗节采用了**英雄体四行诗**，由抑扬格五音步组成，押韵格式为 abab：

> 晚钟殷殷响，夕阳已西沉，
> 群牛呼叫归，迂回走草径。
> 农夫荷锄犁，倦倦回家门。
> 唯我立旷野，独自对黄昏。
> 　　　　　　　　　　　　　　（丰华瞻译）

乔叟在《特洛伊罗斯与克丽西德》(1380 年代后期) 和其他叙事诗中引入了**皇家韵律**。不过，人们相信这一诗体得名于被称为"苏格兰的乔叟"的苏格兰国王詹姆斯一世。他在大约 1424 年创作的《国王书》中采用了这一诗体。皇家韵律由七行抑扬格五音步诗节组成，押韵格式为 ababbcc。伊丽莎白时期的诗人普遍采用这一诗体形式，如莎士比亚的《情人的抱怨》与《鲁克丽丝受辱记》。《鲁克丽丝受辱记》是这样开篇的：

> 情欲熏心的塔昆，离开了罗马军营
> 从那被围的阿狄亚，向柯拉廷急行
> 他振着不可凭藉的淫邪欲念的双翼，
> 把那无光之火暂时隐藏于心

> Which, in pale embers hid, lurks to aspire
> And girdle with embracing flames the waist
> Of Collatine's fair love, Lucrece the chaste.

Ottava rima, as the Italian name indicates, has eight lines; it rhymes *abababcc*. Like terza rima and the sonnet, it was brought from Italian into English by Sir Thomas Wyatt in the first half of the sixteenth century. Although employed by a number of earlier poets, it is notable especially as the stanza which helped Byron discover what he was born to write, the satiric poem *Don Juan* (1819–24). Note the comic effect of the *forced rhyme* in the concluding couplet:

> Juan was taught from out the best edition,
> Expurgated by learned men, who place,
> Judiciously, from out the schoolboy's vision,
> The grosser parts; but, fearful to deface
> Too much their modest bard by this omission,
> And pitying sore his mutilated case,
> They only add them all in an appendix,
> Which saves, in fact, the trouble of an index.

Spenserian stanza is a still longer form devised by Edmund Spenser for *The Faerie Queene* (1590–96)—nine lines, in which the first eight lines are iambic pentameter and the last iambic hexameter (an *Alexandrine*), rhyming *ababbcbcc*. Enchanted by Spenser's gracious movement and music, many poets have attempted this stanza in spite of its difficulties. Its greatest successes have been in poems which, like *The Faerie Queene*, evolve in a leisurely way, with ample time for unrolling the richly textured stanzas; for example, James Thomson's "The Castle of Indolence" (1748), John Keats' "The Eve of St. Agnes" (1820), Percy Bysshe Shelley's "Adonais" (1821), and the narrative section of Alfred, Lord Tennyson's "The Lotos-Eaters" (1832). The following is a stanza from Spenser's *Faerie Queene* 1.1.41:

> And more, to lulle him in his slumber soft,
>   A trickling streame from high rocke tumbling downe
>   And ever-drizling raine upon the loft
>   Mixt with a murmuring winde, much like the sowne
>   Of swarming Bees, did cast him in a swowne:
>   No other noyse, nor peoples troublous cryes,
>   As still are wont t'annoy the wallèd towne,
>   Might there be heard: but carelesse Quiet lyes,
> Wrapt in eternall silence farre from enemyes.

There are also various elaborate stanza forms imported from France, such as the rondeau, the villanelle, and the triolet, containing intricate repetitions, at set intervals, both of rhymes and of entire lines; these stanzas have been used mainly, but not exclusively, for *light verse*. Their revival by W. H. Auden, William Empson, and other mid-twentieth-century poets was a sign of

> 这火恰似埋在灰白余烬中的火星
> 　只等化作烈焰熊熊的火环，去紧紧
> 　　把柯拉廷贞淑的妻子——鲁克丽丝抱定。　　（杨德豫译）

八行诗体，正如其意大利名所示，含有八行诗句，押韵格式为ababacc。与三行诗节隔句押韵法和十四行诗一样，八行诗体是在16世纪前半叶由托马斯·怀亚特爵士从意大利引入英语诗歌中的。虽然早期也有许多诗人采用这种诗体，但因这种诗体使得拜伦发现了自己就是为诗而生而尤其引人注目；他采用八行诗体创作了讽刺诗《唐·璜》(1819—1824)。请留意《唐·璜》结尾对句中*迫韵*造成的滑稽效果：

> 唐璜读过的书都是最佳的版本，
> 而且经过了饱学之士的删节，
> 他们正当地抹去碍眼的部分，
> 以保护青年学子的天真无邪，
> 可是唯恐诗人被涂得面目全非，
> 而且痛惜于它们如此受肢解，
> 于是编了附录把那一切收进，
> 事实上，也省得老师再添索引。　　（查良铮译）

斯宾塞式诗节是埃德蒙·斯宾塞为《仙后》(1590—1596)所设计的比八行诗体更长的诗歌形式——斯宾塞式诗节有九行诗句，前八行是抑扬格五音步，最后一行是抑扬格六音步（称为*亚历山大体*），押韵格式为ababbcbcc。许多诗人都为斯宾塞优美流畅的诗行及其音乐效果所吸引，他们不顾这种诗体的难度而竞相采用。在这些诗歌中，如最成功的例子《仙后》，诗人行文自如，有充裕的时间铺展神韵丰富的诗节。这类诗歌的例子还包括詹姆斯·汤姆逊的《懒散的城堡》(1748)，约翰·济慈的《圣阿格尼斯节前夕》(1820)，珀西·比什·雪莱的《阿多尼斯》(1821)，阿尔弗雷德·丁尼生的《食落拓枣的人》(1832)中的叙事部分。下面是选自斯宾塞《仙后》（第一卷第一章第41节）中的一个诗节：

> 而且，使他在安稳的睡眠中舒缓下来，
> 　从高耸的岩石上倾泻而下的涓涓细流
> 　落在阁楼上淅淅沥沥的绵绵细雨
> 　和着沙沙的风声，仿佛蜂群的
> 　嗡嗡声，这的确使他陷入酣睡中；
> 　没有别的声响，也没有人们躁动不安的哭喊，
> 　安静得不会去惊扰城墙围绕着的城镇，
> 　能听到的：只有自然随意的安静，
> 陷入永恒的沉寂中，远离敌人。

英语诗歌还从法国引入了各种精巧优美的诗节形式，如四旋诗体、维拉内拉诗体、八行两韵诗体。这些诗体具有复杂的韵律重复（每隔一定间隔）和整句诗行重复，主要用于但并非完全用于*轻松诗*。W. H. 奥登、威廉·燕卜荪和20世纪中期的其他诗人再次采用了这些诗体形式，表明诗人重新对高层次的韵律

renewed interest in high metrical artifice. Dylan Thomas' "Do not go gentle into that good night" is a **villanelle**; that is, it consists of five *tercets* and a *quatrain*, all on two rhymes, and with systematic later repetitions of lines 1 and 3 of the first tercet.

One of the most intricate of poetic forms is the **sestina**: a poem of six six-line stanzas in which the end words in the lines of the first stanza are repeated, in a set order of variation, as the end words of the stanzas that follow. The sestina concludes with a three-line envoy which incorporates, in the middle and at the end of the lines, all six of these end words. (An **envoy**, or "send-off," is a short formal stanza which is appended to a poem by way of conclusion.) This form, introduced in the twelfth century, was cultivated by Italian, Spanish, and French poets. Despite its extreme difficulty, the sestina has also been managed with success by the Elizabethan Sir Philip Sidney, the Victorian Algernon Swinburne, and the modern poets W. H. Auden and John Ashbery.

See *meter*. Poetic stanzas and nonstanzaic forms of verse discussed elsewhere in the *Glossary* are *ballad stanza, blank verse, free verse, heroic couplet, limerick,* and *sonnet*. The pattern and history of the various stanzas are described and exemplified in R. M. Alden, *English Verse* (1903), and in Paul Fussell, *Poetic Meter and Poetic Form* (rev. 1979). For references to *stanza* in other entries, see page *351*.

stock characters: Stock characters are types of persons that occur repeatedly in a particular literary genre, and so are recognizable as part of the *conventions* of the form. The *Old Comedy* of the Greeks had three stock characters whose interactions constituted the standard plot: the **alazon**, or impostor and self-deceiving braggart; the **eiron**, or self-derogatory and understating character, whose contest with the alazon is central to the comic plot; and the **bomolochos**, or buffoon, whose antics add an extra comic element. (See Lane Cooper, *An Aristotelian Theory of Comedy*, 1922.) In his *Anatomy of Criticism* (1957), Northrop Frye revived these old terms, added a fourth, the **agroikos**—the rustic or easily deceived character—and identified the persistence of these types (very broadly defined) in comic plots up to our own time. The Italian commedia dell'arte revolved around such stock characters as Pulcinella and Pantaloon; see *commedia dell'arte*.

The plot of an Elizabethan *romantic comedy*, such as Shakespeare's *As You Like It* and *Twelfth Night*, often turned on a heroine disguised as a handsome young man; and a stock figure in the Elizabethan comedy of intrigue was the clever servant who, like Mosca in Ben Jonson's *Volpone*, connives with his master to fleece another stock character, the stupid **gull**. Nineteenth-century comedy, on stage and in fiction, exploited the stock Englishman with a monocle, an exaggerated Oxford accent, and a defective sense of humor. Western stories and films generated the tight-lipped sheriff who lets his gun do the talking; while a familiar figure in the fiction of the recent past was the stoical Hemingway hero, unillusioned but faithful to his primal code of honor and loyalty in a civilization grown effete and corrupt. The *Beat* or hipster or

技巧产生了兴趣。迪伦·托马斯的《别轻柔地走进那美好的夜晚》就是一首**维拉内拉诗**,即它包含五个同韵*三行诗节*和一个*四行诗*,押两种韵。第一个同韵三行诗节中的第一行和第三行系统地重复。

最复杂的诗歌形式之一当数**六节诗**:诗歌由六个诗节组成,每个诗节包含六句诗句。后五个诗节中每句诗的最后一个字按固定的变化顺序重复了第一个诗节中每行诗句的最后一个字。六节诗的结尾诗节包含三行诗句。结尾诗节的中间与结尾部分包含了所有六个末尾词(**结尾诗节**,或"送别诗节",是一种简短正式的诗节,以总结的方式附于诗歌的结尾处)。这种形式自 12 世纪引入之后,得到意大利、西班牙与法国诗人的完善。尽管六节诗的运用极其困难,但伊丽莎白时期的菲利普·锡德尼爵士、维多利亚时期的阿尔杰农·斯温伯恩,以及现代诗人 W. H. 奥登与约翰·亚斯比利,都成功地运用了这一诗体。

参见:*格律*。本书在其他地方还探讨了诗节及非诗节形式的诗歌,如*民谣体诗节、无韵诗、自由诗、英雄双韵体、五行打油诗、十四行诗*。有关各种诗节形式及其历史的描述与例子,参阅:R. M. 奥尔登所著的《英语诗节》(1903);保罗·富塞尔所著的《诗律与诗歌的形式》(1979 年修订版)。其他条目中提及"诗节"的地方,参见第 351 页。

Stock Characters:定型人物

定型人物是指在某一特定文学体裁内反复出现的人物类型,因此被视为这一文学体裁惯例的组成部分。古希腊的旧喜剧中有三种定型人物,他们相互作用构成了标准的情节:**骗子**或冒名顶替者和自欺欺人的吹牛者;**愚人**或自我诋毁、贬低者,愚人与骗子之间的争斗是喜剧剧情的中心;**丑角**,他的滑稽举止增添了额外的喜剧成分。[参阅:莱恩·库珀所著的《亚里士多德式的喜剧理论》(1922)。] 诺斯罗普·弗莱在《批评的剖析》(1957) 中重新使用了这些旧术语,并添加了第四种人物**乡巴佬**——土里土气的或易受骗者——弗莱也确认了这些人物类型在当今喜剧情节中的延续(广义而言)。意大利的即兴喜剧也围绕一些定型人物展开,如傻老头等;参见:*即兴喜剧*。

伊丽莎白时期的*爱情喜剧*,如莎士比亚的《皆大欢喜》和《第十二夜》,往往以一位女主人公假扮成英俊少年为主要情节。钩心斗角、情节复杂的伊丽莎白喜剧中的定型人物是聪明的仆人,如本·琼森的《狐狸》中的莫斯卡,他与主人共谋去欺诈另一位定型人物:愚蠢的**傻子**。19 世纪的喜剧,不论在戏剧舞台上还是在小说中,都会固定出现一位戴着单片眼镜的英国人,说话时带有夸大了的牛津腔调和怪模怪样的幽默感。美国的西部故事和电影里则出现了用枪代替自己说话、双唇紧闭的警长;近代小说里为人熟知的人物是恬淡寡欲的海明威式英雄,在日益腐朽衰败的文明社会中不抱任何幻想,但忠实于自己所信奉的头条法规,即荣誉和忠诚。

alienated protagonist who, with or without the help of drugs, has opted out of the Establishment is a more recent stock character.

In some literary forms, such as the *morality play* and Ben Jonson's *comedy of humours*, the artistic aim does not require more than type characters. (See also *flat character*, under *character and characterization*.) But even in realistic literary forms, the artistic success of a protagonist does not depend on whether or not an author incorporates an established type, but on how well the type is re-created as a convincing individual who fulfills his or her function in the overall plot. Two of Shakespeare's greatest characters are patently conventional. Falstaff is in part a re-rendering of the *Vice*, the comic tempter of the medieval morality play, and in part of the familiar braggart soldier, or **miles gloriosus**, of Roman and Renaissance comedy, whose ancestry goes back to the Greek *alazon*; and Hamlet combines some stock attributes of the hero of Elizabethan *revenge tragedies* with those of the Elizabethan melancholic man. Jane Austen's delightful Elizabeth Bennet in *Pride and Prejudice* (1813) can be traced back through Restoration comedy to the type of intelligent, witty, and dauntless heroines that enliven Shakespeare's romantic comedies.

For references to *stock character* in other entries, see pages *55, 58*.

stock response: A derogatory term for a reader's reaction that is considered to be habitual and stereotyped, in place of one which is genuinely and aptly responsive to a given literary passage or text. The term is sometimes applied to the response of authors themselves to characters, situations, or topics that they set forth in a work; usually, however, it is used to describe standard and inadequate responses of the readers of the work. I. A. Richards, in his *Practical Criticism* (1929), chapter 5, gave currency to this term by citing and analyzing stock responses by students and other respondents who wrote critiques of unidentified poems presented for their interpretation and evaluation.

stock situations: Stock situations are the counterparts to *stock characters*; that is, they are recurrent types of incidents or of sequences of actions in a drama or narrative. Instances range from single situations or events—the eavesdropper who is hidden behind a bush or in a closet, or the suddenly discovered will or birthmark—to the overall pattern of a plot. The Horatio Alger books for boys, in mid-nineteenth-century America, were all variations on the stock plot of rags-to-riches-by-pluck-and-luck, and we recognize the standard boy-meets-girl incident in the opening episode of much popular fiction and in many motion pictures.

Some recent critics distinguish certain recurrent character types and elements of plot, such as the sexually irresistible but fatal enchantress, the sacrificial scapegoat, and the underground journey, as "archetypal" components which are held to recur, not simply because they are functional literary conventions, but because, like dreams and myths, they express and appeal to universal human impulses, anxieties, and needs. See *archetype*, and for structuralist analyses of recurrent plot types, *narrative and narratology*.

更为现代的定型人物是*垮掉的一代*、赶时髦的人或异化了的主人公——这类人物不论是否借助毒品的帮助都已退出现存的社会体制。

在一些文学形式如*道德剧*、本·琼森的*性格喜剧*等中，艺术目标仅仅在于表现类型人物。(参见：*人物与人物塑造*中干瘪的人物形象。)但即使在现实主义文学形式中，主人公在艺术上的成功也并不取决于作者是否吸纳了某种定型人物类型，而是取决于作者如何重新塑造这一类型的人物，使之成为在全部情节中发挥其作用的、令人信服的个体。莎士比亚创作的两个著名人物显然就承袭了惯例。福斯塔夫既是中世纪道德剧中改头换面的*丑角*——喜剧的诱发者，也是古罗马和文艺复兴时期喜剧中为人熟知的吹牛士兵，或**满口大话的士兵**这一角色的再现。这一人物原型可以追溯到古希腊的骗子角色。哈姆雷特这一人物综合了伊丽莎白时期*复仇悲剧*里的英雄所具有的某些固定特质和这一时期忧郁者的固有特征。简·奥斯丁在《傲慢与偏见》(1813)中塑造了讨人喜欢的伊丽莎白·贝内特，这一角色可以追溯到王政复辟时期的喜剧，甚至可以追溯到莎士比亚爱情喜剧中聪明睿智、勇敢无畏的女主人公类型。

其他条目中提及"定型人物"的地方，参见第55、58页。

Stock Response：定型反应

该术语带有贬义，指的是读者的一种习惯性的刻板反应，而不是对特定的文学篇章或文本作出的真实而恰当的反应。这个术语有时指作者本人对作品中描绘的人物、情景或主题所作出的反应；但通常则是用来描述作品的读者作出的中规中矩、不恰当的反应。I. A. 理查兹在其所著的《实用批评》(1929)第五章中，引用并分析了对指定给他们诠释和评价无署名诗歌写评论的学生的定型反应，从而使这一术语广为流传。

Stock Situations：定型情景

定型情景与*定型人物*相对应，指的是戏剧或叙事文中常用的事件类型或行动的顺序类型。定型情景可能是单个情景或事件——藏在灌木丛后或柜橱中的窃听者，或是突然发现的遗嘱或胎记——也可能是情节的整体模式。在19世纪中期的美国，霍拉旭·阿尔杰为男孩子创作的书籍，都是有关穷小子如何凭借胆量与运气发迹这一定型情节的种种变体。我们也常会在畅销小说的开篇部分和电影的开场事件中发现少男遇上少女的定型故事。

近代一些批评家将某些反复出现的人物类型和情节要素当成"原型的"要素，如性感十足却又能致人于死地的迷人女子、替罪羊和地狱之旅等；这些要素的反复出现并非仅仅因为它们是起作用的文学惯例，而是因为它们像梦幻和神话一样，表达并迎合了人类普遍的冲动、焦虑和需求。参见：*原型*；关于结构主义对反复出现的情节类型所作的分析，参见：*叙事和叙事学*。

story: **234**; *294*.

stream of consciousness: A phrase used by William James in his *Principles of Psychology* (1890) to describe the unbroken flow of perceptions, memories, thoughts, and feelings in the waking mind; it has since been adopted to describe a narrative method in modern fiction. Long passages of **introspection**, in which the narrator records in detail what passes through a character's awareness, are found in novelists from Samuel Richardson, through William James' brother Henry James, to many novelists of the present era. The long chapter 42 of James' *Portrait of a Lady*, for example, is entirely given over to the narrator's description of the sustained process of Isabel's memories, thoughts, and varying feelings. As early as 1888 a minor French writer, Edouard Dujardin, wrote a short novel *Les Lauriers sont coupés* ("The Laurels Have Been Cut") which undertakes to represent the scenes and events of the story solely as they impinge upon the consciousness of the central character. As it has been refined since the 1920s, "stream of consciousness" is the name applied specifically to a mode of narration that undertakes to reproduce the full spectrum and continuous flow of a character's mental process, in which sense perceptions mingle with conscious and half-conscious thoughts, memories, expectations, feelings, and random associations.

Some critics use "stream of consciousness" interchangeably with the term **interior monologue**. It is useful, however, to follow the usage of critics who use the former as the inclusive term, denoting all the diverse means employed by authors to communicate the total state and process of consciousness in a character. "Interior monologue" is then reserved for that species of stream of consciousness which undertakes to present to the reader the course and rhythm of consciousness precisely as it occurs in a character's mind. In interior monologue the author does not intervene, or at any rate intervenes minimally, as describer, guide, or commentator, and does not tidy the vagaries of the mental process into grammatical sentences or into a logical or coherent order. The interior monologue, in its radical form, is sometimes described as the exact presentation of the process of consciousness; but because sense perceptions, mental images, feelings, and some aspects of thought itself are nonverbal, it is clear that the author can present these elements only by converting them into some sort of verbal equivalent. Much of this conversion is a matter of narrative *conventions* rather than of unedited, point-for-point reproduction, and each author puts his or her own imprint on the interior monologues that are attributed to characters in the narrative. For the linguistic techniques that have been used to render the states and flow of consciousness, see Dorrit Cohn, *Transparent Minds: Narrative Modes for Presenting Consciousness in Fiction* (1978).

James Joyce developed a variety of devices for stream-of-consciousness narrative in *Ulysses* (1922). Here is a passage of interior monologue from the "Lestrygonians" episode, in which Leopold Bloom saunters through Dublin, observing and musing:

> Pineapple rock, lemon platt, butter scotch. A sugar-sticky girl shoveling scoopfuls of creams for a christian brother. Some school treat.

story：故事　**234**；*294*。

Stream of Consciousness：意识流

　　这是威廉·詹姆斯在其所著的《心理学原理》(1890)中使用的一个短语，用来描述清醒的头脑中源源不断地流动着的感知、记忆、思想与情感；自此之后，"意识流"就被用来描述现代小说中的一种叙事手法。从塞缪尔·理查逊开始，到威廉·詹姆斯的弟弟亨利·詹姆斯，直至当今的众多小说家，都有描写**自我反思**的长篇段落，在这些段落中，叙述者详细记录了人物的意识流动。例如，在亨利·詹姆斯的《贵妇人的画像》中，叙述者用了整个第42章的长篇篇幅来描述伊莎贝尔持续不断的记忆过程、思维过程和情感过程。早在1888年，名不见经传的法国作家艾都瓦·杜雅丹便创作了短篇小说《月桂树砍倒了》，作者一直力求按照中心人物意识上受到的影响来展现故事中的情景与事件。自1920年代开始，意识流这一手法得到了完善；**意识流**一词用来特指一种叙事模式。这种模式再现人物心理活动过程的整个轨迹与持续流动。在这一流动过程中，人的感觉认知与意识的或半意识的思想、回忆、期望、感情及琐碎的联想融合在一起。

　　一些批评家时常交替使用"意识流"和**内心独白**这两个术语。不过，也有批评家将"意识流"作为一个包罗万象的术语来使用，指作家用来传达人物的意识状态和意识过程的各种技巧，这种用法更实用。而"内心独白"只是用来指意识流的一种类别，它力图向读者准确地展现人物思想中出现的意识过程与律动。在内心独白里，作者不以描述者、向导或评论者的身份介入，或者说介入程度微乎其微，也不把离奇古怪的心理活动过程加以整理，使之成为语法正确的句子或合乎逻辑、前后连贯的顺序。极端的内心独白形式有时被视为意识过程的准确再现；不过，由于感觉认知、精神意象、情感和思维本体的某些方面是非文字性的，所以显而易见，作者想要展现这些要素，就只能把它们转化成某种文字对等物。这种转换大体上是一种叙事*惯例*，而不是不加剪辑、逐点逐条的复制；而每位作者都会在所述的人物内心独白里加入自己的印迹。如何利用语言技巧去创造意识状态和意识流动，可以参阅：多里特·科恩所著的《透明的思想：小说中展现意识的叙事模式》(1978)。

　　詹姆斯·乔伊斯在《尤利西斯》(1922)中发展了许多不同的意识流叙事技巧。以下是"莱斯特里戈尼厄"插曲中的一段内心独白。在这段摘录中，利奥波德·布卢姆在都柏林里闲逛，一边观察，一边思索：

　　　　椰子糖，柠檬鞭，黄油球。一个棒糖似的姑娘，正在为一位公修弟
　　　　兄会的修士舀着一勺勺的奶油。什么学校的招待会吧。对胃不好。国王

Bad for their tummies. Lozenge and comfit manufacturer to His Majesty the King. God. Save. Our. Sitting on his throne, sucking red jujubes white.

Dorothy Richardson sustains a stream-of-consciousness mode of narrative, focused exclusively on the mind and perceptions of her heroine, throughout the twelve volumes of her novel *Pilgrimage* (1915–38); Virginia Woolf employs the procedure as a prominent, although not exclusive, narrative mode in several novels, including *Mrs. Dalloway* (1925) and *To the Lighthouse* (1927); and William Faulkner exploits it in the first three of the four parts of *The Sound and the Fury* (1929).

Refer to *narratology* and *point of view*, and see Leon Edel, *The Modern Psychological Novel* (1955, rev. 1964); Robert Humphrey, *Stream of Consciousness in the Modern Novel* (1954); Melvin Friedman, *Stream of Consciousness: A Study in Literary Method* (1955). For a review of early and more recent scientific writings on the stream of consciousness, see Oliver Sachs, "In the River of Consciousness," *New York Review of Books*, 15 Jan. 2004.

stress (in linguistics): **197**.

stress (in meter): **197**.

strong-stress meter: 221.

strophe (strō′ fē): **262**.

structural irony: 185.

structuralism: 381; *196, 310*.

structuralist criticism: Almost all literary theorists beginning with Aristotle have emphasized the importance of *structure*, conceived in diverse ways, in analyzing a work of literature. (See *form and structure*.) "Structuralist criticism," however, now designates the practice of critics who analyze literature on the explicit model of structuralist linguistics. The class includes a number of *Russian formalists*, especially Roman Jakobson, but consists most prominently of a group of writers, with their headquarters in Paris, who applied to literature the concepts and analytic distinctions developed by Ferdinand de Saussure in his *Course in General Linguistics* (1915). This mode of criticism is part of a larger movement, French **structuralism**, inaugurated in the 1950s by the cultural anthropologist Claude Lévi-Strauss, who analyzed, on the model of Saussure's linguistics, such cultural phenomena as mythology, kinship relations, and modes of preparing food. See *linguistics in literary criticism*.

In its early form, as employed by Lévi-Strauss and other writers in the 1950s and 1960s, structuralism cuts across the traditional disciplinary areas within and between the humanities and social sciences by undertaking to provide an objective account of all social and cultural practices, in a range that

陛下御用糖果蜜饯公司。上帝。保佑。我们的。[典出英国国歌第一句：上帝保佑我们的仁慈国王。]高踞宝座嚼糖锭，把红色的糖锭都嚼白了。

(金隄译)

在小说《朝圣》(1915—1938)的所有十二卷中，多萝西·理查森一直采用意识流的叙事模式。她无一例外地集中表现女主人公的心理和感知。弗吉尼亚·吴尔夫在她的几部小说里，也将意识流手法作为主要的叙事模式，但不是唯一的模式。她的这些小说包括《黛洛维夫人》(1925)和《到灯塔去》(1927)等。威廉·福克纳在《喧哗与骚动》(1929)的前三个部分里也精湛地运用了这种叙事手法。

参见：*叙事学、视角*。参阅：利昂·埃德尔所著的《现代心理小说》(1955，1964年修订版)；罗伯特·汉弗莱所著的《现代小说中的意识流》(1954)；梅尔文·弗里德曼所著的《意识流：文学方法研究》(1955)。对早期和近来关于意识流的科学著作的综述，参阅：奥利弗·萨克斯所写的文章"在意识的河流中"，载于《纽约书评》2004年1月15日。

stress (in linguistics)：(语言学中的) 重音　197。

stress (in meter)：(格律中的) 重读　197。

strong-stress meter：重音体格律　221。

strophe：诗句　262。

structural irony：通篇性反讽　185。

structuralism：结构主义　381；*196, 310*。

Structuralist Criticism：结构主义批评

从亚里士多德开始，几乎所有的文学理论家在分析文学作品时都以不同的方式强调*结构*的重要性。(参见：*形式与结构*。)不过，"结构主义批评"这一术语现在则被用来表示批评家运用明显的结构主义语言学模式来分析文学的做法。这一批评学派包括一些*俄国形式主义*批评家，尤其是罗曼·雅各布森，但其主要成员是以巴黎为中心的一群作家。这些作家把费迪南·德·索绪尔在《普通语言学教程》(1915)中发展的概念和分析特点应用到文学中。这种文学批评模式是一场更大的文学运动法国**结构主义**的一部分。法国结构主义由文化人类学家克劳德·列维-斯特劳斯于1950年代创立，他用索绪尔的语言学模式来分析神话、亲族关系、食物的准备方式等文化现象。参见：*语言学在文学批评里的应用*。

正如列维-斯特劳斯和其他作家在1950、1960年代所展示的那样，早期的结构主义试图客观地描述所有的社会与文化实践，内容包括神话叙事、文学文本、

includes mythical narratives, literary texts, advertisements, fashions in clothes, and patterns of social decorum. It views these practices as combinations of *signs* that have a set significance for the members of a particular culture, and undertakes to make explicit the rules and procedures by which the practices have achieved their cultural significance, and to specify what that significance is, by reference to an underlying system (analogous to Saussure's *langue*, the implicit system of a particular language) of the relationships among signifying elements and their rules of combination. The elementary cultural phenomena, like the elements of language in Saussure's exposition, are not objective facts identifiable by their inherent properties, but purely "relational" entities; that is, their identity as signs is given to them by their relationships of differences from, and binary oppositions to, other elements within the cultural system. This system of internal relationships, and of "codes" that determine significant combinations, has been mastered by each person competent within a given culture, although he or she remains largely unaware of its nature and operations. The primary interest of the structuralist, like that of Saussure, is not in the cultural *parole* but in the *langue*; that is, not in any particular cultural phenomenon or event except as it provides access to the structure, features, and rules of the general system that engenders its significance.

As applied in literary studies, **structuralist criticism** conceives *literature* to be a second-order signifying system that uses the first-order structural system of language as its medium, and is itself to be analyzed primarily on the model of linguistic theory. Structuralist critics often apply a variety of linguistic concepts to the analysis of a literary text, such as the distinction between *phonemic* and *morphemic* levels of organization, or between *paradigmatic* and *syntagmatic* relationships; and some critics analyze the structure of a literary text on the model of the *syntax* in a well-formed sentence. The undertaking of a thoroughgoing literary structuralism, however, is to explain how it is that a competent reader is able to make sense of a particular literary text by specifying the underlying system of literary conventions and rules of combination that has been unconsciously mastered by such a reader. The aim of classic literary structuralism, accordingly, is not (as in *New Criticism*) to provide the interpretation of single texts, but to make explicit, in a quasi-scientific way, the tacit *grammar* (the system of rules and codes) that governs the forms and meanings of all literary productions. As Jonathan Culler put it in his lucid exposition, the aim of structuralist criticism is "to construct a poetics which stands to literature as linguistics stands to language" (*Structuralist Poetics*, 1975, p. 257). Roland Barthes, Gérard Genette, Julia Kristeva, and Tzvetan Todorov were, at least in some part of their careers, prominent structuralist critics of literature.

Structuralism is in explicit opposition to *mimetic criticism* (the view that literature is primarily an imitation of reality), to *expressive criticism* (the view that literature primarily expresses the feelings or temperament or creative imagination of its author), and to any form of the view that literature is a mode of communication between author and readers. More generally, in its attempt to develop a science of literature and in many of its salient concepts,

广告、流行服饰、社会礼仪方式等,从而跨越了人文学科和社会科学的传统学科领域。结构主义认为这些实践是一种符号组合,这些符号对特定文化的成员来说具有特定的意义。结构主义试图清晰地说明这些实践在实现其文化意义的过程中所遵循的规则与步骤,并试图通过符号指示要素间的关系及其组合规则的基本系统(类似于索绪尔的语言,即某一特定语言的内含系统)来具体说明这种文化的意义是什么。基本的文化现象就像索绪尔分析的语言要素一样,不是通过其内在属性能辨别的客观事实,而是纯粹的"相关"实体;即它们的符号身份是通过它们与文化系统内其他要素的区别与二元对立被赋予的。特定文化中每一个有能力的人都精通这种内在的关系系统和这种决定有意义的组合的"代码"系统,但他或她大都没有意识到这种系统的本质与作用方式。结构主义者的主要兴趣,与索绪尔一样,不在于文化的*言语*而在于文化的*语言*;即他们感兴趣的不是某种特定的文化现象或文化事件,除非这种文化现象或文化事件能够使人了解形成其意义的总体系统的结构、特征和规则。

运用到文学研究中时,**结构主义批评**认为,文学是利用语言这种第一层次结构系统作为自己媒介的第二层次符号指示系统。文学本身主要得依靠语言学理论的模式来分析。结构主义批评家经常把各种语言学概念应用到文学文本的分析中,如*音素*与*语素*之间结构层次的区别,或*聚合关系*与*组合关系*之间的区别。有些结构主义批评家还依据结构完整的句子中的*句法*模式来分析文学文本的结构。但是,彻底的文学结构主义试图解释:有能力的读者如何能够具体说明无意识地掌握的文学惯例与组合规则的基本系统,并以此理解某部特定文学文本的意义。所以,典型的文学结构主义的目标(与新批评不同)不是阐释某部单一的文本,而是以类似科学的方式,明确指出支配所有文学产物的形式与意义的潜在*语法*(规则与代码系统)。正如乔纳森·卡勒在其简明论述中所说的那样,结构主义批评的目标是"建立一种支撑文学的诗学,就像语言学支撑语言一样"[《结构主义诗学》(1975)第257页]。罗兰·巴尔特、热拉尔·热奈特、朱莉娅·克莉丝蒂娃、兹维坦·托多罗夫,至少在他们职业生涯的某些时期,都是杰出的结构主义文学批评家。

结构主义明确反对*摹仿式批评*(认为文学主要是对现实的摹仿),反对*表现主义批评*(认为文学主要表现了作者的情感、气质或创作想象),反对其他任何将文学视为作者与读者之间交流模式的观点。总体来说,就其试图建立文学科学的

the radical forms of structuralism depart from the assumptions and ruling ideas of traditional humanistic criticism. (See *humanism*.) For example:

1. In the structuralist view, what had been called a literary "work" becomes a *text*; that is, a mode of writing constituted by a play of internal elements according to specifically literary conventions and codes. These factors may generate an illusion of reality, but have no truth-value, nor even any reference to a reality existing outside the literary system itself.
2. The individual author, or *subject*, is not assigned any initiative, expressive intentions, or design as the "origin" or producer of a work. Instead the conscious "self" is declared to be a construct that is itself the product of the workings of the linguistic system, and the mind of an author is described as an imputed "space" within which the impersonal, "always-already" existing system of literary language, conventions, codes, and rules of combination gets precipitated into a particular text. Roland Barthes expressed, dramatically, this subversion of the traditional humanistic view, "as institution, the author is dead" ("The Death of the Author," in *Image-Music-Text*, trans. 1977). See *author and authorship* and the *subject*, under *poststructuralism*.
3. Structuralism replaces the author with the reader as the central agency in criticism; but the traditional reader, as a conscious, purposeful, and feeling individual, is replaced by the impersonal activity of "reading," and what is read is not a work imbued with meanings, but *écriture*, writing. The focus of structuralist criticism, accordingly, is not on the sensibility of the reader, but on the impersonal process of reading which, by bringing into play the requisite conventions, codes, and expectations, makes literary sense of the sequence of words, phrases, and sentences that constitute a text. See *text and writing (écriture)*.

In the late 1960s, the structuralist enterprise, in its rigorous form and inclusive pretensions, ceded its central position to deconstruction and other modes of poststructural theories, which subverted the scientific claims of structuralism and its view that literary meanings are made determinate by a system of invariant conventions and codes. (See *poststructuralism*.) This shift in the prevailing point of view is exemplified by the changing emphases in the lively and influential writings of the French critic and man of letters, Roland Barthes (1915–80). His early work developed the structuralist theory that was based on the linguistics of Saussure—a theory that Barthes applied not only to literature but also to decoding, by reference to an underlying signifying system, many aspects of popular culture. (See Barthes' *Mythologies*, 1957, trans. 1972, and refer to *cultural studies*.) In his later writings, Barthes abandoned the scientific aspiration of structuralism, and distinguished between the "readerly" text such as the realistic novel that tries to "close" interpretation by insisting on specific meanings, and the "writerly" text that aims at the ideal of "a galaxy of signifiers," and so encourages the reader to be a producer of his or her own meanings according not to one code but to a multiplicity of codes. And in *The Pleasure of the Text* (1973) Barthes lauds, in contrast to the

尝试及其显著概念而言，结构主义的激进方式与传统人文主义批评（参见：人文主义）的假说和主导观念分道扬镳。例如：

1. 结构主义认为，所谓的文学"作品"其实成了"文本"，即根据特定的文学惯例与代码，由组成要素相互作用构成的一种书写模式。这些因素可能会引起对现实的幻觉，但不具备真值，甚至不指代存在于文学系统本身之外的现实。
2. 作者个人或主体并不具有主动性、表现的意图或是作为作品"本源"或生产者的任何构思。相反，意识"自身"被视为一个抽象概念，其本身是语言系统作用的产物；作者的头脑被描述成一个归纳的"空间"；在这个空间里，由文学语言、惯例、代码和组合规则组成的客观的、"始终已经"存在的系统凝结成某一特定文本。罗兰·巴尔特明确地表达了这种对传统人文主义观点的颠覆，"作为基本原理，作者已经死亡"["作者的死亡"，收入其所著的《意象-音乐-文本》(1977年英译版)]。参见：*作者与作者身份、后结构主义中的主体*。
3. 结构主义把读者，而非作者，视为批评的中心力量；但是，传统的读者，作为有意义、有目的和有情感的个人，已经被非个人化的"阅读"行为所取代；他们阅读的不是充满意义的作品，而是书面文字，书写。所以，结构主义批评关注的焦点不是读者的感受力，而是非个人化的阅读过程；通过利用必要的惯例、代码与期待，非个人化的阅读过程使得构成文本的一系列单词、短语和句子具有文学意义。
参见：*文本与书写（书面文字）*。

到了1960年代后期，拥有缜密形式、自命为包罗万象的整个结构主义流派，将其中心地位转让给解构主义和其他后结构主义理论模式；这些后结构主义颠覆了结构主义的科学主张，也颠覆了文学意义由恒定的惯例与代码系统所确定这一结构主义观点。（参见：*后结构主义*。）这一主要观点的转变在法国批评家和学者罗兰·巴尔特（1915—1980）充满活力、颇具影响的论著中得到了体现；巴尔特在其论著中改变了批评的侧重点。他的早期论著发展了以索绪尔语言学为基础的结构主义理论——巴尔特不仅将索绪尔的语言学理论应用到文学中，还参照其基本的符号指示系统，将其运用到对大众文化许多方面的解码中。[参阅：巴尔特所著的《神话学》(1957, 1972年英译版)；参见：*文化研究*。] 在他的后期论著中，巴尔特放弃了结构主义的科学理想，区分了"读者性"文本与"作者性"文本。"读者性"文本坚持明确的意义，力图"终止"阐释，如现实主义小说；而"作者性"文本的目标则在于实现找出"一批能指"的理想。所以，"作者性"文本鼓励读者根据多种多样的代码，而不是一种代码，创作出属于他或她自己的意义。巴尔特在《文本的乐趣》(1973)中称赞了快乐地放纵其能指

comfortable pleasure offered by a traditional text that accords with cultural codes and conventions, the "jouissance" (or orgasmic bliss) evoked by a text that incites a hedonistic abandon to the uncontrolled play of its signifiers. See Roland Barthes, in the entry *text and writing (écriture)*.

Structuralist premises and procedures, however, continue to be deployed in a number of current enterprises, and especially in the semiotic analysis of cultural phenomena, in stylistics, and in the investigation of the formal structures that, in their combinations and variations, constitute the plots in novels. See *semiotics, cultural studies, stylistics*, and *narrative and narratology*.

A clear and comprehensive survey of the program and accomplishments of structuralist literary criticism, in poetry as well as narrative prose, is Jonathan Culler, *Structuralist Poetics* (1975); also Robert Scholes, *Structuralism in Literature: An Introduction* (1974). For an introduction to the general movement of structuralism see Peter Caws, *Structuralism: The Art of the Intelligible* (1960); Philip Pettit, *The Concept of Structuralism: A Critical Analysis* (1975); and Terence Hawkes, *Structuralism and Semiotics* (1977). For critical views of structuralism see Gerald Graff, *Literature against Itself* (1979); Frank Lentricchia, *After the New Criticism* (1980), chapters 4–5; J. G. Merquior, *From Prague to Paris: A Critique of Structuralist and Post-Structuralist Thought* (1986); Leonard Jackson, *The Poverty of Structuralism: Literature and Structuralist Theory* (1991). Some collections of structuralist writings: Richard T. De George and M. Fernande, eds., *The Structuralists: From Marx to Lévi-Strauss* (1972); David Robey, ed., *Structuralism: An Introduction* (1973); see also Richard Macksey and Eugenio Donato, eds., *The Structuralist Controversy: The Languages of Criticism and the Sciences of Man* (1970). Among the books of structuralist literary criticism available in English translations are Roland Barthes, *Critical Essays* (1964); Stephen Heath, *The Nouveau Roman: A Study in the Practice of Writing* (1972); Tzvetan Todorov, *The Poetics of Prose* (trans. 1977) and *Introduction to Poetics* (trans. 1981); Gérard Genette, *Figures of Literary Discourse* (trans. 1984). Structuralist treatments of cinema are Peter Wollen, *Signs and Meaning in the Cinema* (1969), and Christian Metz, *Language of Film* (1973).

For references to *structuralist criticism* in other entries, see pages *149, 163, 331, 400*.

structure: 138. See also *structuralism*.

style: Style has traditionally been defined as the manner of linguistic expression in prose or verse—as *how* speakers or writers say whatever it is that they say. The style specific to a particular work or writer, or else distinctive of a type of writings, has been analyzed in such diverse terms as the rhetorical situation and aim (see *rhetoric*); the characteristic *diction*, or choice of words; the type of sentence structure and *syntax*; and the density and kinds of *figurative language*.

In standard theories based on Cicero and other classical rhetoricians, styles were usually classified into three main levels: the **high** (or "grand"), the **middle** (or "mean"), and the **low** (or "plain") **style**. The doctrine of

毫无节制的游戏的文本所引起的"狂喜"（或极度兴奋），这种狂喜与符合文化惯例的传统文本所提供的舒适性愉悦截然不同。参见：*文本与书写（书面文字）*中关于罗兰·巴尔特的部分。

不过，结构主义的理论假设与分析方法在当前的一些批评方法中仍然得到体现，尤其是在文化现象的符号学分析、文体学，以及对在组合与变异中构成小说情节的形式结构的调查分析中。参见：*符号论、文化研究、文体学、叙事和叙事学*。

以下作品清晰而全面地概述了结构主义文学批评在诗歌和叙事散文中的应用及取得的成就：乔纳森·卡勒所著的《结构主义诗学》（1975）；罗伯特·斯科尔斯所著的《文学结构主义导引》（1974）。有关结构主义整体运动的介绍，参阅：彼得·考斯所著的《结构主义：理解的艺术》（1960）；菲利普·佩蒂特所著的《结构主义概念批评分析》（1975）；特伦斯·豪克斯所著的《结构主义与符号学》（1977）。有关结构主义的批评观点，参阅：杰拉尔德·格拉夫所著的《自我作对的文学》（1979）；弗兰克·兰特里夏所著的《新批评之后》（1980）第 4—5 章；J. G. 莫奎尔所著的《从布拉格到巴黎：结构主义与后结构主义思想批判》（1986）；伦纳德·杰克逊所著的《结构主义的贫困：文学与结构主义理论》（1991）。结构主义文集包括：理查德·T. 德·乔治与 M. 费尔南德合编的《结构主义者：从马克思到列维－斯特劳斯》（1972）；戴维·罗比主编的《结构主义入门》（1973）；也可参阅：理查德·麦克希与尤吉尼奥·多纳托合编的《结构主义的论战：批评的语言与人的科学》（1970）。译成英文的结构主义文学批评论著包括：罗兰·巴尔特所著的《批评文选》（1964）；斯蒂芬·希思所著的《新小说：写作实践研究》（1972）；兹维坦·托多罗夫所著的《散文的诗学》（1977 年英译版）和《诗学概论》（1981 年英译版）；热拉尔·热奈特所著的《文学话语的修辞》（1984 年英译版）。有关结构主义对电影的论述，参阅：彼得·沃伦所著的《电影中的符号和意义》（1969）；克里斯琴·梅茨所著的《电影语言》（1973）。

其他条目中提及"结构主义批评"的地方，参见第 149、163、331、400 页。

structure：结构　138。也可参见：*结构主义*。

Style：文体

就传统意义而言，文体指的是散文和韵文中语言的表达方式——说话者或作者如何说话，不论他们说的是什么。修辞情景与目的（参见：*修辞学*），有特点的*措词*或言词的选择，句子结构类型和*句法*，*比喻语*的数量与种类等术语，都能用于分析某部特定作品、某位作家或某类作品特有的风格。

根据西塞罗和其他古典修辞学家的标准理论，文体通常分为三个层次：**高雅**（或"高贵的"）**文体**、**平庸**（或"中等"）**文体**和**低劣**（或"平淡"）**文体**。18 世纪

decorum, which was influential through the eighteenth century, required that the level of style in a work be appropriate to the social class of the speaker, to the occasion on which it is spoken, and to the dignity of its literary genre (see *poetic diction*). The critic Northrop Frye introduced a variant of this long-persisting analysis of stylistic levels in literature. He made a primary differentiation between the **demotic style** (which is modeled on the language, rhythms, and associations of ordinary speech) and the **hieratic style** (which employs a variety of formal elaborations that separate the literary language from ordinary speech). Frye then proceeded to distinguish a high, middle, and low level in each of these classes. See *The Well-Tempered Critic* (1963), chapter 2.

In analyzing style, two types of sentence structure are often distinguished: The **periodic sentence** is one in which the component parts, or "members," are so composed that the close of its syntactic structure remains suspended until the end of the sentence; the effect tends to be formal or oratorical. An example is the eloquent opening sentence of James Boswell's *Life of Samuel Johnson* (1791), in which the structure of the syntax is not concluded until we reach the final noun, "task":

> To write the life of him who excelled all mankind in writing the lives of others, and who, whether we consider his extraordinary endowments, or his various works, has been equaled by few in any age, is an arduous, and may be reckoned in me a presumptuous task.

In the **nonperiodic** (or **loose**) **sentence**—more relaxed and conversational in its effect—the component members are continuous, but so loosely joined that the sentence would have been syntactically complete if a period had been inserted at one or more places before the actual close. So the two sentences in Joseph Addison's *Spectator 105*, describing the limited topics in the conversation of a "man-about-town," or dilettante, could each have closed at several points in the sequence of their component clauses:

> He will tell you the names of the principal favourites, repeat the shrewd sayings of a man of quality, whisper an intrigue that is not yet blown upon by common fame; or, if the sphere of his observations is a little larger than ordinary, will perhaps enter into all the incidents, turns, and revolutions in a game of ombre. When he has gone thus far he has shown you the whole circle of his accomplishments, his parts are drained, and he is disabled from any farther conversation.

Another distinction often made in discussing prose style is that between parataxis and hypotaxis:

A **paratactic style** is one in which the members within a sentence, or else a sequence of complete sentences, are put one after the other without any expression of their connection or relations except (at most) the noncommittal connective "and." An example is the passage just quoted from Addison's *Spectator*. Ernest Hemingway's style is characteristically paratactic. The members in this sentence from his novel *The Sun Also Rises* (1926) are

颇具影响的**仪轨**准则要求作品的文体层次要与说话者的社会阶层、说话场合及其所属文学体裁的地位相称（参见：*诗意辞藻*）。批评家诺斯罗普·弗莱提出了文学上这种经久不衰的文体层次分析的一种变体。他从本质上区分了**通俗文体**（以普通言谈的语言、节奏和相互关联为模式）与**神圣文体**（这类文体采用了把文学语言与普通言谈分离的各种正式阐述）。弗莱还进一步划分了这两类文体里的高、中、低水准。参阅：《好脾气的批评家》（1963）第 2 章。

分析文体时，常区分两种句子结构类型：

尾重句，这种句子的组成部分或"成员"一直处于悬而未决的状态，全句结束时句法结构才结束；其效果倾向于正式的或雄辩的风格。如詹姆斯·鲍斯韦尔的《约翰逊传》(1791) 以一句雄辩性的句子开篇。直到我们读完该句的最后一个名词"任务"(task)，句法结构才结束：

> 在描写他人生平方面超越了所有人，无论是他非凡的天赋，还是他纷繁各异的作品，在任何时代都鲜有匹敌者，要书写这么一位人物的生平是一件可能我要为我的冒昧付出代价的艰巨任务。

在**非尾重句**（或**松散句**）——效果上更为轻松、更加口语化——中，组成部分彼此延续但联结松散，在句子真正结束前的某一处或多处添加句号，也能获得句法上的完整。约瑟夫·艾迪生在《旁观者》第 105 期中描写了一位附庸风雅的"花花公子"贫乏的交谈话题；在这两个句子组成分句的多个地方都可以结句：

> 他会告诉你他最喜爱的人的名字，重复上等人精明的言论，窃窃私语一般谣言还未提到的私情；或者，假如他的评论范围比一般时候稍微广泛些，他可能会讨论奥伯尔牌戏中的事件、轮次与循环。他若是告诉你他所有的技能，他的交谈部分已经枯竭了，再也无法进行进一步的交谈了。

在分析散文文体时，也常区分并列句文体与从属句文体。

并列句文体指的是一个句子或一连串完整句子中的成分一个紧接着一个，而句中没有任何连接或关联的表达法，（至多）除了含糊连词"and"（和）。这方面的一个例子就是上引艾迪生《旁观者》上描写的例子。欧内斯特·海明威的文体是典型的并列句文体。在下面这一引自海明威的小说《太阳照样升起》(1926) 的句子中，

joined merely by "ands": "It was dim and dark and the pillars went high up, and there were people praying, and it smelt of incense, and there were some wonderful big buildings." The curt paratactic sentences in his short story "Indian Camp" omit all connectives: "The sun was coming over the hills. A bass jumped, making a circle in the water. Nick trailed his hand in the water. It felt warm in the sharp chill of the morning."

A **hypotactic style** is one in which the temporal, causal, logical, and syntactic relations between members and sentences are specified by words (such as "when," "then," "because," "therefore") or by phrases (such as "in order to," "as a result") or by the use of subordinate phrases and clauses. The style in this *Glossary* is mainly hypotactic.

A very large number of loosely descriptive terms have been used to characterize kinds of style, such as "pure," "ornate," "florid," "gay," "sober," "simple," "elaborate," and so on. Styles are also classified according to a literary period or tradition ("the *metaphysical* style," "Restoration prose style"); according to an influential text ("biblical style," *euphuism*); according to an institutional use ("a scientific style," "journalese"); or according to the distinctive practice of an individual author (the "Shakespearean" or "Miltonic style"; "Johnsonese"). Historians of English prose style, especially in the seventeenth and eighteenth centuries, have distinguished between the vogue of the "Ciceronian style" (named after the characteristic practice of the Roman writer Cicero), which is elaborately constructed, highly periodic, and typically builds to a climax, and the opposing vogue of the clipped, concise, pointed, and uniformly stressed sentences in the "Attic" or "Senecan" styles (named after the practice of the Roman Seneca). See J. M. Patrick and others, eds., *Style, Rhetoric, and Rhythm: Essays by Morris W. Croll* (1966), and George Williamson, *The Senecan Amble: A Study in Prose Form from Bacon to Collier* (1951).

Francis-Noël Thomas and Mark Turner, in *Clear and Simple as the Truth* (1994), claim that standard treatments of style such as those described above deal only with the surface features of writing. They propose instead a basic analysis of style in terms of a set of fundamental decisions or assumptions by an author concerning "a series of relationships: What can be known? What can be put into words? What is the relationship between thought and language? Who is the writer addressing and why? What is the implied relationship between writer and reader? What are the implied conditions of discourse?" An analysis based on all these elements yields an indefinite number of types, or "families," of styles, each with its own criteria of excellence. The authors focus on what they call "the classic style" exemplified in writings like René Descartes' *Discourse on Method* (1637) or Thomas Jefferson's "Declaration of Independence" (1776), but identify and discuss briefly a number of other styles such as "plain style," "practical style," "contemplative style," and "prophetic style."

For some recent developments in the analysis of style based on modern linguistic theory and philosophy of language, see *stylistics* and *discourse analysis*. Among the more traditional theorists and analysts of style are Herbert Read,

句子的主要成分仅仅靠许多 and 来衔接:"里面阴沉而幽暗,几根柱子高高耸起,有人在做祷告,堂里散发着香火味,有几扇精彩的大花玻璃窗。"以下这些句子选自他的短篇小说《印第安人营地》;这些简短的并列句省略了所有的连接词。"太阳正从山那边升起。一条鲈鱼跳出水面,在水面上弄出一个水圈。尼克把手伸进水里,让手在水里滑过。清早,真是冷飕飕的,水里倒是很温暖。"

从属句文体是指用词(如"当……的时候""然后""因为""所以"等)、短语(如"为了……""结果"等)或从属的词组与句子来明确说明句子成分之间和句子之间的时间顺序、因果关系、逻辑关系及句法关系。本书的文体主要是从属句文体。

一直用来大致区别各种文体类型的描述性术语非常多,如"平铺直叙""辞藻华丽""言词绚丽""轻松明快""肃穆凝重""朴实无华""精心雕琢"等。也可依据文学时期或文学传统(如"*玄学派*文体""王政复辟时期的散文文体"等),某部影响深远的文本(如"圣经文体"、*尤弗伊斯体*等),某种组织机构的用语(如"科学文体""新闻文体"等),或某一作家的独特实践(如"莎士比亚文体""弥尔顿文体""约翰逊文体"等)来对文体进行分类。研究英国散文文体的史学家,尤其是研究 17、18 世纪英国散文文体的史学家,还区分了当时流行的"西塞罗式文体"(因古罗马作家西塞罗的独特实践而得名)和与之对峙的"阿提卡"或"塞内加式"文体(因古罗马作家塞内加的实践而得名)。"西塞罗式"文体布局结构精巧,多用尾重句,其典型特点在于渐次达到高潮。"塞内加式"文体则采用省略、简洁、准确、重音一致的句式。参阅:J. M. 帕特里克等主编的《文体、修辞与节奏:莫里斯·W. 克罗尔论文集》(1996),乔治·威廉森所著的《塞内加式漫步:从培根到柯里尔的散文形式研究》(1951)。

弗朗西斯-诺埃尔·托马斯与马克·特纳在其合著的《像真理一样简单明了》(1994)中提出,诸如上面提及的标准文体区分,只论述了作品的表面特征。他们认为,基本的文体分析应当遵循作者对"一系列关系所作的基本决定和假设:什么能够为人所知?什么能放入文字中?思想和语言是什么关系?作者在对谁说话,为什么?作者与读者之间隐含的关系是什么?话语隐含的条件是什么?"建立在这些基本要素之上的分析,带来了无穷无尽的文体类型,或文体"派别";每种文体类型都有自己优点的评判标准。弗朗西斯-诺埃尔与特纳强调了勒内·笛卡尔《方法谈》(1637)或托马斯·杰斐逊《独立宣言》(1776)中展示的"古典文体",但也简明地讨论、定义了许多其他文体,如"朴实的文体""实用文体""深思的文体""预言性文体"等。

关于建立在现代语言学理论和现代语言哲学基础上的文体论述近年来的发展,参见:*文体学*、*话语分析*。更加传统的文体理论家和分析家的论著,参阅:

English Prose Style (1928); Bonamy Dobree, *Modern Prose Style* (1934); W. K. Wimsatt, *The Prose Style of Samuel Johnson* (1941); P. F. Baum, *The Other Harmony of Prose* (1952); Erich Auerbach, *Mimesis: The Representation of Reality in Western Literature* (trans. 1953, reissued 2003); Josephine Miles, *Eras and Modes in English Poetry* (1957); Louis T. Milic, ed., *Stylists on Style: A Handbook with Selections for Analysis* (1969).

See also *connotation and denotation; decorum; stream of consciousness*. For features of style, see *ambiguity; antithesis; archaism; bathos and anticlimax; bombast; cliché; conceit; concrete and abstract; epithet; euphemism; euphony and cacophony; euphuism; figurative language; grand style; imagery; purple patch*.

stylistics: Since the 1950s the term **stylistics** has been applied to critical procedures which undertake to replace what is claimed to be the subjectivity and impressionism of standard analyses with an "objective" or "scientific" analysis of the style of literary texts. Much of the impetus toward these analytic methods, as well as models for their practical application, was provided by the writings of Roman Jakobson and other *Russian formalists*, as well as by European *structuralists*.

We can distinguish two main modes of stylistics, which differ both in conception and in the scope of their application:

1. In the narrower mode of formal stylistics, style is identified, in the traditional way, by the distinction between what is said and how it is said, or between the content and the form of a text. (See *style*.) The content is now often denoted, however, by terms such as "information," "message," or "propositional meaning," while the style is defined as variations in the presentation of this information that serve to alter its "aesthetic quality" or the reader's emotional response. The concepts of modern *linguistics* are used to identify the stylistic features, or "formal properties," which are held to be distinctive of a particular work, or else of an author, or a literary tradition, or an era. These stylistic features may be phonological (patterns of speech sounds, meter, or rhyme), or syntactic (types of sentence structure), or lexical (*abstract* vs. *concrete* words, the relative frequency of nouns, verbs, adjectives), or rhetorical (the characteristic use of *figurative language, imagery*, and so on). A basic problem, acknowledged by a number of stylisticians, is to distinguish between the innumerable features and patterns of a text which can be isolated by linguistic analysis, and those features which are functionally stylistic—that is, features which make an actual difference in the aesthetic and other effects on a competent reader. See, for example, Michael Riffaterre's objection to the elaborate stylistic analysis of Charles Baudelaire's sonnet "Les Chats" (The Cats) by Roman Jakobson and Claude Lévi-Strauss, in *Structuralism*, ed. Jacques Ehrmann (1966).

    Stylisticians who aim to either replace or supplement the qualitative judgments of literary scholars by objectively determinable methods of research exploit the ever-increasing technological resources of computers in

赫伯特·里德所著的《英语散文文体》(1928)；博纳米·多布里所著的《现代散文文体》(1934)；W. K. 维姆萨特所著的《塞缪尔·约翰逊的散文风格》(1941)；P. F. 鲍姆所著的《散文的不同和谐》(1952)；埃利希·奥尔巴赫所著的《摹仿论：西方文学中现实的再现》(1953 年英译版，2003 年再版)；约瑟芬·迈尔斯所著的《英语诗歌中的时期和模式》(1957)；路易斯·T. 米利克主编的《文体学家论文体：选择分析手册》(1969)。

也可参见：*涵义和表意、仪轨、意识流*。关于文体的特征，参见：*歧义、对偶、仿古、突降与突降法、浮夸之辞、陈词滥调、巧思妙喻、具体与抽象、属性形容词、委婉语、谐音与非谐音、尤弗伊斯体、比喻语、宏伟绚丽的文体、意象、辞藻华丽的章节*。

Stylistics：文体学

1950 年代以来，**文体学**这一术语便被用来指代一种文学批评方法。这种批评方法试图"客观"或"科学"地分析文学文本的文体，以此取代标准的文学分析中的主观性与印象主义。罗曼·雅各布森和其他*俄国形式主义者*及*欧洲结构主义者*的论著，推动了这些分析方法及其实际运用的模式。

我们可以区分出两种主要的文体学模式，这两种模式在其概念及应用范围上都有所不同：

1. 第一种是形式文体学较为狭义的模式。在这种模式中，是以通过区分所说的与如何说，或区分文本的内容与形式的传统方式来辨别文体的。(参见：*文体*。) 不过，内容现在常用"信息""主旨"或"主题意义"等术语表示，而文体则被定义为信息表达方式的各种变体；这些变体有助于改变信息的"审美特性"及读者的情感反应。现代语言学的概念被用来辨认某一特定作品、或者某位作者、某种文学传统或某个年代有特色的文体特征或"形式上的特性"。这些文体特征可以是语音上的（即语音模式、韵律或节奏），或句法上的（即句子结构类型），或词汇上的（即抽象词还是具体词，以及名词、动词、形容词出现的相对频率），或修辞上的（即比喻语、意象等的独特用法）。许多文体学家承认的一个基本问题是区分通过语言学分析能分离出来的无数的文本特征和模式与那些在功能上具有文体效果的特征——即对有能力的读者的审美和其他效果造成实质差别的特征。如迈克尔·里法泰尔反对罗曼·雅各布森和克劳德·列维－斯特劳斯对查尔斯·波德莱尔的十四行诗《猫》所作的详尽文体分析，文章收入雅克·厄尔曼主编的《结构主义》(1966)。

   一些文体学家试图通过客观的可确定的研究方法来取代或补充文学学者的定性判断；他们把日益发展的计算机技术资源应用于

the service of what has come to be called **stylometry**: the quantitative measurement of the features of an individual writer's style. *Literary and Linguistic Computing* is a journal devoted to the use of computers in literary studies. See also B. H. Rudall and T. N. Corns, *Computers and Literature: A Practical Guide* (1987). Other analysts of style who use non-quantitative methods adopt concepts derived from language theory, such as the distinction between *paradigmatic* and *syntagmatic* relations, or the distinction between surface structure and deep structure in *transformational linguistics*, or the distinction between the propositional content and the *illocutionary force* of an utterance in *speech-act theory*. For a stylistic analysis of the ways a character's speech and thought are represented in narratives, refer to *free indirect discourse*, under *point of view*.

Sometimes the stylistic enterprise stops with the qualitative or quantitative determination, or "fingerprinting," of the style of a single text or class of texts. Often, however, the analyst tries also to relate distinctive stylistic features to traits in an author's psyche; or to an author's characteristic ways of perceiving the world and organizing experience (see Leo Spitzer, *Linguistics and Literary History*, 1948); or to the typical conceptual frame and the attitude toward reality in an historical era (Erich Auerbach, *Mimesis: The Representation of Reality in Western Literature*, reissued 2003); or else to semantic, aesthetic, and emotional functions and effects in a particular literary text (Michael Riffaterre and others).

Stanley Fish wrote a sharp critique of the scientific pretensions of formal stylistics; he proposed that since, in his view, the meaning of a text consists of a reader's total response to it, there is no valid way to make a distinction in this spectrum of response between style and content ("What Is Stylistics and Why Are They Saying Such Terrible Things about It?" in *Is There a Text in This Class?* 1980; see also *reader-response criticism*). For extended critiques both of traditional analyses of style, and of modern stylistics, based on the thesis that style is not a separable feature of language, see Bennison Gray, *Style: The Problem and Its Solution* (1969), and "Stylistics: The End of a Tradition," *Journal of Aesthetics and Art Criticism*, Vol. 31 (1973). In *Clear and Simple as the Truth* (1994), Francis-Nöel Thomas and Mark Turner claim that standard stylistic analyses concern merely the surface features of writing, and propose a set of more basic features by which to define styles of writing; see under *style*. On the other side, the validity of distinguishing between style and propositional meaning—not absolutely, but on an appropriate level of analysis—is defended by E. D. Hirsch, "Stylistics and Synonymity," in *The Aims of Interpretation* (1976).

2. In the second mode of stylistics, which has been prominent since the mid-1960s, proponents greatly expand the conception and scope of their inquiry by defining stylistics as, in the words of one theorist, "the study of the use of language in literature," involving the entire range of the "general characteristics of language … as a medium of literary expression."

所谓的**文体测量学**：对某个作家的文体特征进行定量测量。《文学与语言学计算》是一本专门介绍文学研究中运用计算机的期刊。也可参阅：B. H. 卢达与 T. N. 科恩斯合著的《电脑与文学：实用指南》(1987)。其他采用非定量方法的文体分析家则利用了源于语言理论的概念，如聚合关系与组合关系的区分、转换语言学中表层结构与深层结构的区分、言语行为理论中言语的主题内容与言外作用的区分。叙事中的人物言语和思想的文体分析方法，可以参见：*视角*中的*自由式间接话语*。

有时文体学研究会止于某一文本或某一类文本文体的定性和定量确定或"指纹式测定"。不过，文体分析者也试图把独特的文体特征与作者的精神特征相联系，或与作者感知世界和组织其经历的独特方式相联系 [参阅：利奥·斯皮泽尔所著的《语言学与文学史》(1948)]；或与某一历史时期特有的观念框架及对现实的态度相联系 [埃利希·奥尔巴赫所著的《摹仿论》(2003年再版)]；或与某一特定文学文本的语义、审美、情感功能与效果相联系（迈克尔·里法泰尔和其他批评家的论著）。

斯坦利·费什对形式文体学自命科学的做法作出了尖锐的评论；他认为，由于文本的意义是由读者对该文本的总体反应组成的，因此在反应范围内不存在区分文体与内容的有效方法 [参阅：《这堂课有文本吗？》(1980)中的"何谓文体学？为什么他们如此讨厌它？"也可参见：*读者反应批评*]。认为文体并非是语言一个可以分割的特征，并以此论点对传统的文体分析和现代文体学展开广泛评论，可以参阅：本尼森·格雷所著的《文体：问题及其解决方法》(1969)和他写的文章"文体学：传统的终结"，载于《美学与艺术批评期刊》1973年第31期。弗朗西斯－诺埃尔·托马斯与马克·特纳在其合著的《像真理一样简单明了》(1994)中指出，标准文体分析只考虑作品的表面特征；他们提出了一套更为基本的特征，以此来定义作品的文体；参见：*文体*。相反，E. D. 赫兹在其所著的《释义的目的》(1976)中的"文体学与同义性"标题下，则对有效区分文体与主题意义——不是绝对的，而是在合适的分析层次上的区分——加以辩护。

2. 第二种文体学模式自1960年代中期以来异军突起，其倡导者极大地扩展了他们探讨的概念与范围，他们把文体学定义为，用一位理论家的话来说，"研究文学中的语言使用"，涉及"作为文学表达媒介的……语言的一般特征"整个领域。[参阅：杰弗里·N. 里奇所

(Geoffrey N. Leech, *A Linguistic Guide to English Poetry*, 1969; see also Mick Short, "Literature and Language," in *Encyclopedia of Literature and Criticism*, ed. Martin Coyle and others, 1990.) By this definition, stylistics is expanded so as to incorporate most of the concerns of both traditional literary *criticism* and traditional *rhetoric*; its distinction from these earlier pursuits is that it insists on the need to be objective by focusing sharply on the text itself and by setting out to discover the "rules" governing the process by which linguistic elements and patterns in a text accomplish their meanings and literary effects. The historian of criticism René Wellek has described this tendency of stylistic analysis to enlarge its territorial domain as "the imperialism of modern stylistics."

A comprehensive anthology is *The Stylistics Reader from Roman Jakobson to the Present*, ed. Jean Jacques Weber (1996). On formal stylistics see Thomas A. Sebeok, ed., *Style in Language* (1960); Seymour Chatman, ed., *Literary Style: A Symposium* (1971); Howard S. Babb, ed., *Essays in Stylistic Analysis* (1972); Richard Bradford, *Stylistics* (1997). For an exhaustive stylistic analysis of a twelve-line poem, see Roman Jakobson and Stephen Rudy, *Yeats's "Sorrow of Love" Through the Years* (1977).

In the practice of some critics, stylistics includes the area of study known as *discourse analysis*, which is treated in a separate entry in this *Glossary*. For inclusive views of the realm of stylistics, see M. A. K. Halliday, *Explorations in the Functions of Language* (1973); G. N. Leech and M. H. Short, *Style in Fiction* (1981); Roger Fowler, *Linguistic Criticism* (1986); Ronald Carter and Paul Simpson, eds., *Language, Discourse and Literature: An Introductory Reader in Discourse Stylistics* (1989).

stylometry (stī lŏ′ mĕtrē): **388**.

subaltern: 307.

subject, the (in poststructural criticism): **310**; *19, 383*.

subjective: 261.

sublimate: 321.

sublime: The concept was introduced into the criticism of literature and art by a Greek treatise *Peri hupsous* ("On the sublime"), attributed in the manuscript to Longinus and probably written in the first century AD. As defined by Longinus, the sublime is a quality that can occur in any type of discourse, whether poetry or prose. Whereas the effect of *rhetoric* on the hearer or reader of a discourse is persuasion, the effect of the sublime is "transport" (*ekstasis*)—it is that quality of a passage which "shatters the hearer's composure," exercises irresistible "domination" over him, and "scatters the subjects like a bolt of

著的《英语诗歌的语言学指南》(1969)；也可参阅：马丁·科伊尔等主编的《文学与批评百科全书》(1990)中米克·肖特编写的词条"文学与语言"。]依据这一定义，文体学得到了扩展，包含了传统文学批评与传统修辞学所关注的大多数问题。它与先前研究的区别在于：它明显地将关注的焦点集中在文本本身，力图发掘支配文本的语言要素与模式实现其意义与文学效果的过程的"规则"，坚持必须力求客观。文学批评史学家勒内·韦勒克把这种扩大其研究疆域的文体学分析趋势描述为"现代文体学的帝国主义"。

参阅综合性文集：让·雅克·韦伯主编的《文体学读本：从罗曼·雅各布森到现在》(1996)。有关形式文体学的内容，参阅：托马斯·A.西比奥克主编的《语体》(1960)；西摩尔·查特曼主编的《文体文论集》(1971)；霍华德·S.芭布主编的《文体分析论文选》(1972)；理查德·布拉德福德所著的《文体学》(1997)。对一首十二行的诗歌进行透彻的文体分析，参阅：罗曼·雅各布森与斯蒂芬·鲁迪合著的《历年来叶芝的〈爱的忧伤〉》(1977)。

在一些批评家的实践中，文体学包含了*话语分析*这一研究领域，本书将话语分析单列为一个条目。有关文体学领域的综合性观点，参阅：M. A. K.哈利迪所著的《语言功能研究》(1973)；G. N.利奇与M. H.肖特合著的《小说文体论》(1981)；罗杰·福勒所著的《语言批评》(1986)；罗纳德·卡特与保罗·辛普森合编的《语言、话语与文学：话语文体学入门读本》(1989)。

stylometry：文体测量学　388。

subaltern：低等　307。

subject, the (in poststructural criticism)：(后结构主义批评中的)主体　310；19，383。

subjective：主观的　261。

sublimate：升华　321。

Sublime：崇高

希腊论文"论崇高"最早将这一概念引入文学艺术批评中。根据该文手稿，文章作者是朗吉努斯，很可能写于公元1世纪。朗吉努斯认为，崇高是任何类型的话语中，不论是在诗歌还是在散文中，都可能出现的一种品质。*修辞*对话语的听者或读者产生的是劝说性的效果，而崇高的效果却是"激情"——即文章"打破听者镇静心态"，不可抵抗地"支配"读者并"如同一道闪电似的撒播主题"的

lightning." The source of the sublime, according to Longinus, lies in the capabilities of the speaker or writer. Three of these—the use of figurative language, nobility of expression, and elevated composition—are matters of art that can be acquired by practice; but two other, and more important, capabilities, are largely innate: "loftiness of thought" and "strong and inspired passion." The ability to achieve sublimity is in itself enough to prove the transcendent genius of a writer, and expresses the nobility of the writer's character: "sublimity is the ring of greatness in the soul." Longinus' examples of sublime passages in poems range from the epics of Homer through the tragedies of Aeschylus to a love lyric by Sappho; his examples in prose are taken from the writings of the philosopher Plato, the orator Demosthenes, and the historian Herodotus. Especially notable is his quotation, as a prime instance of sublimity, of the passage in the Book of Genesis written, he says, by "the lawgiver of the Jews": "And God said, 'Let there be light,' and there was light, 'Let there be land,' and there was land."

Longinus' innovative treatise exerted a strong and persistent effect on literary criticism after it became widely known by way of a French translation by Boileau in 1674; eventually, it helped establish the *expressive* theory of poetry, and also *impressionistic criticism* (see under *criticism*). In the eighteenth century an important tendency in critical theory was to shift the application of the term, "the sublime," from a quality of linguistic discourse that originates in the powers of a writer's mind, to a quality inherent in external objects, and above all in the scenes and occurrences of the natural world. Thus Edmund Burke's highly influential *Philosophical Enquiry into the Origin of Our Ideas of the Sublime and Beautiful,* published in 1757, attributes the source of the sublime to those things which are "in any sort terrible"—that is, to whatever is "fitted in any sort to excite the ideas of pain, and danger"— provided that the observer is in a situation of safety from danger, and so is able to experience what would otherwise be a painful terror as a "delightful horror." (Compare *distance and involvement.*) The features of objects which evoke sublime horror are obscurity, immense power, and vastness in dimension or quantity. Burke's examples of the sublime include vast architectural structures, Milton's description of Satan in *Paradise Lost*, the description of the king's army in Shakespeare's *1 Henry IV*, and natural phenomena; a sublime passion, he says, may be produced by "the noise of vast cataracts, raging storms, thunder or artillery," all of which evoke "a great and awful sensation in the mind."

During the eighteenth century, tourists and landscape painters traveled to the English Lake Country and to the Alps in search of sublime scenery that was thrillingly vast, dark, wild, stormy, and ominous. Writers of what was called "the sublime ode," such as Thomas Gray and William Collins, sought to achieve effects of wildness and obscurity in their descriptive style and abrupt transitions, as well as to render the wildness, vastness, and obscurity of the sublime objects they described. (See *ode*.) Authors of *Gothic novels* exploited the sublimity of delightful horror in both the natural and architectural settings of their narratives and in the actions and events that they

那种品质。按照朗吉努斯的看法，崇高来源于说话人或作者的能力。其中的三种能力：比喻语的使用、表达的崇高性格、高尚的构思，是能够通过实践获得的艺术能力；但另外两种更重要的能力则大多是与生俱来的："思想的高尚"和"强烈的灵感激情"。实现崇高的能力本身就足以证明作家的卓越天赋，表现作者性格的崇高："崇高是灵魂的伟大光环。"朗吉努斯在诗歌中选取的崇高篇章的范例从荷马史诗、埃斯库罗斯的悲剧到萨福的爱情抒情诗。他选取的散文范例则来源于哲学家柏拉图、雄辩家狄摩西尼、历史学家希罗多德的作品。尤其值得注意的是，他援引了"犹太人立法者"创作的《创世记》中的一段篇章作为崇高的主要例子："神说：'要有光'，就有了光；'要有地'，就有了地。"

　　1674年，布瓦洛将朗吉努斯的论著译成法语使其广为人知，此后便对文学批评产生了强烈而持久的影响；它最终促进了诗歌的*表现主义*理论和*印象主义批评*方法的建立（参见：*批评*中的相关论述）。18世纪批评理论中出现的一个重要趋势是崇高定位的转变，从源自作家心灵影响力的语言话语品质转向外部客体，特别是自然世界的情景与事件所固有的品质。1757年，埃德蒙·伯克出版了影响极为深远的《崇高与美的理念之起源的哲学探索》，认为崇高起源于任何"可怕类"的事物，即"存在于能激起痛苦、危险这类想法"的任何一种事物中，只要观察者处于远离危险的安全情境下，他就能将其他情境下是痛苦的惊骇体验为"愉快的恐惧"。（对比：*心理距离与感情介入*。）引起崇高恐惧的客体具有晦涩黑暗、力量巨大、数量规模庞大等特性。伯克选取的崇高范例包括庞大的建筑结构、弥尔顿《失乐园》中对撒旦的描写、莎士比亚《亨利四世》上部中对国王军队的描写，以及自然现象；他说，"巨大的瀑布、狂风暴雨、雷鸣或大炮发出的声响"可能会引发崇高的激情；所有这些事物都会激发起"心灵中伟大与敬畏的感觉"。

　　18世纪，旅行者与风景画家游览了英国的湖泊地区和阿尔卑斯山脉，寻找极其广阔、黑暗、狂野、狂暴、不祥等令人震颤的崇高风景。所谓"崇高颂"的作家，如托马斯·格雷和威廉·柯林斯，在其描述性的文体与突然转折中，力求取得狂野与黑暗的效果，并力图使他们描述的崇高物体呈现出狂野、广袤、黑暗的特点。（参见：*颂*。）*哥特小说*的作者在他们故事中的自然与建筑背景，及其所描述的行为动作和事件中，都运用了愉快的恐惧感的崇高性。塞缪尔·H.蒙克

narrated. Samuel H. Monk, a pioneer historian of the concept of the sublime in the eighteenth century, cites as the "apotheosis" of the natural sublime the description of Simplon Pass in Wordsworth's *The Prelude* (1805), 4.554ff.:

> The immeasurable height
> Of woods decaying, never to be decayed,
> The stationary blasts of waterfalls,
> And everywhere along the hollow rent
> Winds thwarting winds, bewildered and forlorn,
> The torrents shooting from the clear blue sky,
> The rocks that muttered close upon our ears—
> Black drizzling crags that spake by the wayside
> As if a voice were in them—the sick sight
> And giddy prospect of the raving stream,
> Tumult and peace, the darkness and the light....

(Samuel H. Monk, *The Sublime: A Study of Critical Theories in Eighteenth-Century England*, 1935)

In an extended analysis of the sublime in his *Critique of Judgment* (1790), the German philosopher Immanuel Kant divided the sublime objects specified by Burke and other earlier theorists into two kinds: (1) the "mathematical sublime" encompasses the sublime of magnitude—of vastness in size or seeming limitlessness or infinitude in number. (2) The "dynamic sublime" encompasses the objects conducive to terror at our seeming helplessness before the overwhelming power of nature, provided that the terror is rendered pleasurable by the safe situation of the observer. All of Kant's examples of sublimity are scenes and events in the natural world: "the immeasurable host" of starry systems such as the Milky Way, "shapeless mountain masses towering one above the other in wild disorder," "volcanoes in all their violence of destruction, hurricanes leaving desolation in their track, the boundless ocean rising with rebellious force, the high waterfall of some mighty river." Kant maintains, however, that the sublimity resides "not in the Object of nature" itself, but "only in the mind of the judging Subject" who contemplates the object. In a noted passage he describes the experience of sublimity as a rapid sequence of painful blockage and pleasurable release—"the feeling of a momentary check to the vital forces followed at once by a discharge all the more powerful." In the mathematical sublime, the mind is checked by its inadequacy to comprehend as a totality the boundlessness or seeming infinity of natural magnitudes, and in the dynamic sublime, it is checked by its helplessness before the seeming irresistibility of natural powers. But the mind then goes on to feel exultation at the recognition of its inherent capacity to think a totality in a way that transcends "every standard of sense," or else at its discovery within itself of a capacity for resistance which "gives us courage to be able to measure ourselves against the seeming omnipotence of nature." In Kant's view, the experience of the sublime manifests on the one hand the limitations and weakness of finite humanity, but on the other hand its "pre-eminence over nature," even

是18世纪最早研究崇高概念的历史学家,他引用了华兹华斯《序曲》(1805)(第四卷第554行及其下)中有关辛普朗山口的描述,并将其视为自然的崇高的"完美典范":

正在腐烂,却永不腐朽的森林

高耸入云,

静静流动的瀑布,

沿着空旷的峡谷随处流淌

呼啸而过的风,困惑而荒凉,

激流从清澈蔚蓝的天空奔腾而下,

岩石贴近我们的耳边轻声细语——

幽暗而潮湿的险崖在路旁轰轰作响

仿佛在它们之中有个声音——令人害怕

而头晕目眩、湍急的河流景象,

喧闹与宁静,黑暗与光明……

(塞缪尔·H.蒙克,《崇高:18世纪英国批评理论研究》,1935)

德国哲学家伊曼纽尔·康德在《判断力批判》(1790)中扩展了对崇高的分析,他将伯克和其他先前理论家具体说明的崇高物体分为两类:(1)"数学上的崇高"包括数量巨大的崇高,或者说规模庞大或数量上似乎是无限度的或无穷无尽的崇高;(2)"动态的崇高"包括那些我们在强大的自然力量面前似乎显得无能为力而产生恐惧的客体,假如观察者处于安全情境,就会把这种恐惧描述得令人愉悦。康德选取的崇高例子,全都是自然世界中的风景与事件:如银河这类多不可测的星系,"形状各异、竞相矗立、杂乱无章的群山","具有强烈破坏性的火山,沿途留下一片废墟的飓风,桀骜不驯、辽阔无垠的海洋,强大的河流飞流直下而形成的高悬瀑布"。但康德坚持认为,崇高并不存在于"自然的客体"本身,而"只存在于"那些对自然客体进行思索的"判断主体的心灵中"。在一个著名段落中,康德将崇高的体验描述成一连串快速的痛苦的阻塞与愉悦的释放:"感觉到生命力受到瞬间的抑制,但立刻又得以更加强烈的发泄。"在数学上的崇高中,心灵无法将自然巨大的无边无际或表面上的无穷大理解为一个整体而受到抑制;在动态的崇高中,心灵对自然力量表面上的不可抗拒性感到束手无策而受到压抑。但心灵一旦超越了"各种感觉的标准",并因此认识到自身整体思考的固有能力,或是在自我身上发现抵抗的能力,这能"使我们勇于抗衡自然表面上的无所不能",心灵就能继续感觉一种狂喜。在康德看来,体验崇高一方面说明了有限的人类具有的局限与缺陷,但另一方面也表明,

when confronted by the "immeasurability" of nature's magnitude and the "irresistibility" of its might.

In *The Romantic Sublime: Studies in the Structure and Psychology of Transcendence* (1976), Thomas Weiskel undertook to translate Kant's theory of the sublime, and especially his analysis of blockage and release, into terms both of *semiotic* theory and of *psychoanalytic* theory. See also the development of Kant's views by Neil Hertz, *The End of the Line: Essays on Psychoanalysis and the Sublime* (1985). Slavoj Žižek applied the concept of the sublime to a Lacanian interpretation of *ideology* (see under *Marxist criticism*) in *The Sublime Object of Ideology* (1989). For the argument that eighteenth-century debates about the sublime illuminate some debates in recent literary theory, see Frances Ferguson, *Solitude and the Sublime: Romanticism and the Aesthetics of Individuation* (1992).

Refer to Elder Olson, "The Argument of Longinus' *On the Sublime*," in *Critics and Criticism, Ancient and Modern*, ed. R. S. Crane (1952); W. J. Hipple, *The Beautiful, the Sublime, and the Picturesque in Eighteenth-Century British Aesthetic Theory* (1957); Marjorie Nicholson, *Mountain Gloom and Mountain Glory* (1959); Steven Knapp, *Personification and the Sublime: Milton to Coleridge* (1985); Philip Shaw, *The Sublime* (2005).

subplot: 295.

subtext: 313.

subversion-containment dialectic: 249.

superego: 322.

suprasegmental (in linguistics): **197**.

surface structure (in linguistics): **198**.

surfiction: 258.

surprise (in a plot): **295**.

surrealism ("superrealism"): Surrealism was launched as a concerted artistic movement in France by André Breton's *Manifesto on Surrealism* (1924). It was a successor to the brief movement known as **Dadaism**, which emerged in 1916 out of disgust with the brutality and destructiveness of the First World War, and set out, according to its manifestos, to engender a negative art and literature that would shock and bewilder observers and serve to destroy the false values of modern bourgeois society, including its rationality and the kind of art and literature that rationality had fostered. Among the exponents of Dadaism were, for a time, artists and writers such as Tristan Tzara, Marcel Duchamp, Man Ray, and Max Ernst.

即使人类面对着"不可估量"的自然之庞大以及"不可抗拒"的自然力量,"人类也比自然更卓越"。

托马斯·魏斯克尔在其所著的《浪漫的崇高:超验结构与心理学之研究》(1976)中,致力于将康德的崇高理论,尤其是康德对抑制与释放的分析,转化成近代符号论理论的术语和*精神分析理论*的术语。也可参阅:尼尔·赫兹在其所著的《界线的末端:心理分析与崇高论文集》(1985)中对康德观点的发展。斯拉沃热·齐泽克在其所著的《意识形态的崇高客体》(1989)中,用崇高这一概念对意识形态(参见:*马克思主义批评*)做了拉康式解读。有关18世纪对崇高的辩论阐明了近来文学理论中一些辩论的论据,可以参阅:弗朗西斯·弗格森所著的《孤独与崇高:浪漫主义与个体化美学》(1992)。

参阅:埃尔德·奥尔森所写的文章"朗吉努斯'论崇高'的论据",收入 R. S. 克莱恩主编的《古代和现代的批评家与批评》(1952);W. J. 希佩尔所著的《18世纪英国美学理论中的优美、崇高和风景》(1957);玛乔里·尼科尔森所著的《阴郁的山和壮丽的山》(1959);史蒂文·纳普所著的《拟人化与崇高:从弥尔顿到柯勒律治》(1985);菲利普·肖所著的《崇高》(2005)。

subplot:次情节　295。

subtext:次文本　313。

subversion-containment dialectic:颠覆遏制对立　249。

superego:超我　322。

suprasegmental (in linguistics):(语言学中的) 超音段　197。

surface structure (in linguistics):(语言学中的) 表层结构　198。

surfiction:超小说　258。

surprise (in a plot):(情节中的) 意外　295。

Surrealism/Superrealism:超现实主义

超现实主义是由安德烈·布雷东的《超现实主义宣言》(1924)在法国引发的一场协调一致的艺术运动。超现实主义继承了被称为**达达主义**的短暂运动。出于对第一次世界大战的野蛮及其毁灭性的厌恶,达达主义兴起于1916年。根据达达主义的宣言,这场运动试图形成一种否定性的艺术与文学。这种艺术与文学将会让旁观者感到震撼和混乱,目的是摧毁现代资产阶级社会虚伪的价值观,包括其理性以及它培育的文学艺术。达达主义的倡导者一度曾包括特里斯坦·查拉、马塞尔·杜尚、曼·雷、马克斯·恩斯特等艺术家和诗人。

The expressed aim of surrealism was a revolt against all restraints on free creativity, including logical reason, standard morality, social and artistic conventions and norms, and all control over the artistic process by forethought and intention. To ensure the unhampered operation of the "deep mind," which they regarded as the only source of valid knowledge as well as art, surrealists turned to *automatic writing* (writing delivered over to the promptings of the unconscious mind), and to exploiting the material of dreams, of states of mind between sleep and waking, and of natural or drug-induced hallucinations.

Surrealism was a revolutionary movement in painting, sculpture, and the other arts, as well as literature; and it often joined forces, although briefly, with one or another revolutionary movement in the political and social realm. The effects of surrealism extended far beyond the small group of its professed adherents such as André Breton, Louis Aragon, and the painter Salvador Dali. The influence, direct or indirect, of surrealist innovations can be found in many modern writers of prose and verse who have broken with conventional modes of artistic organization to experiment with free association, a broken syntax, nonlogical and non-chronological order, dreamlike and nightmarish sequences, and the juxtaposition of bizarre, shocking, or seemingly unrelated images. In England and America such effects can be found in a wide range of writings, from the poetry of Dylan Thomas to the flights of fantasy, hallucinative writing, startling inconsequences, and *black humor* in the novels of Henry Miller, William Burroughs, and Thomas Pynchon.

For a precursor of some aspects of surrealism, see *decadence*; for later developments that continued some of the surrealist innovations, see literature of the *absurd, antinovel, magic realism,* and *postmodernism*. Refer to David Gascoyne, *A Short Survey of Surrealism* (1935); A. E. Balakian, *Literary Origins of Surrealism* (1947); Maurice Nadeau, *History of Surrealism* (trans. 1989); Mary Ann Caws, *The Poetry of Dada and Surrealism* (1970); Mary Ann Caws, ed., *Surrealist Painters and Poets: An Anthology* (2001); Paul C. Ray, *The Surrealist Movement in England* (1971); David Hopkins, *Dada and Surrealism* (2004). In *Dada Turns Red* (1990), Helena Lewis explores the relations between Surrealists and Communists from the 1920s to the 1950s. In *Automatic Woman: The Representation of Women in Surrealism* (1996), Katharine Conley writes a *feminist* analysis of the obsessive and complex concern of male surrealists with the female body, which they often represented in a distorted or dissected form; she also discusses the work of two female surrealists, Unica Zürn and Leonora Carrington.

suspense (in a plot): **295**.

syllabic meter: 217.

symbol: In the broadest sense a symbol is anything which signifies something else; in this sense all words are symbols. In discussing literature, however, the

超现实主义所表达的宗旨是反抗对自由创造的一切限制,包括逻辑推理、标准的道德规范、社会与艺术的惯例和准则,以及一切预先筹划与意图对艺术创作过程的制约。超现实主义者将"深层意识"视为艺术与正确知识的唯一源泉;为了确保"深层意识"的自由运作,他们求助于*自动写作*(无意识思想刺激下产生的书写),并运用梦、半梦半醒间的心理状态,以及自然或药物造成的幻觉等素材。

超现实主义是一场文学、绘画、雕塑和其他艺术形式的革命运动。这一运动往往与某些政治、社会领域内的革命运动相呼应,尽管时间很短暂。超现实主义的影响范围远远超越了一小群自诩为超现实主义倡导者如安德烈·布雷东、路易斯·阿拉贡和画家萨尔瓦多·达利的影响。在许多现代散文作家或诗人身上都可以找到超现实主义创新思想的直接或间接影响;这些作家和诗人打破了艺术构思的传统方式,大胆地尝试自由联想、支离破碎的句法、不合逻辑和不合时间顺序的次序、梦幻式的或梦魇般的片段,以及离奇古怪、令人震惊、似乎毫不相关的意象的并列等等手法。英美受此影响的作品比比皆是,从迪伦·托马斯的诗歌到亨利·米勒、威廉·巴罗斯、托马斯·品钦的小说中体现的幻想飞跃、幻想式的描写、不合逻辑的怪异事件和*黑色幽默*。

关于超现实主义某些方面的先驱,参见:*颓废派文艺*;关于超现实主义创新后续的发展,参见:*荒诞派文学*、*反小说*、*魔幻现实主义*、*后现代主义*。参阅:戴维·加斯科因所著的《超现实主义概述》(1935);A. E. 巴拉基安所著的《超现实主义文学》(1947);莫里斯·纳多所著的《超现实主义史》(1967年英译版);玛丽·安·考斯所著的《达达主义诗歌与超现实主义》(1970);保罗·C. 雷所著的《英国的超现实主义运动》(1971)。凯瑟琳·康利在其所著的《机械的女性:超现实主义中的女性描写》(1996)中,从女性主义者立场出发,分析了男性超现实主义者对女性过分的、情结式的关注,他们往往以歪曲或解剖的形式来描写女性的身体;她还讨论了两位超现实主义女性作家尤妮卡·苏朗与利奥诺拉·卡林顿的作品。

suspense (in a plot):(情节中的)悬念 295。

syllabic meter:音节格律 217。

Symbol:象征

从最广泛的意义上说,象征是指任何能够指代某事物的事物;就此意义而言,所有的词都是象征。不过,在讨论文学时,"象征"这个术语仅用来表示指代某一

term "symbol" is applied only to a word or phrase that signifies an object or event which in its turn signifies something, or suggests a range of reference, beyond itself. Some symbols are "conventional" or "public": thus "the Cross," "the Red, White, and Blue," and "the Good Shepherd" are terms that refer to symbolic objects of which the further significance is determinate within a particular culture. Poets, like all of us, use such conventional symbols; many poets, however, also use "private" or "personal symbols." Often they do so by exploiting widely shared associations between an object or event or action and a particular concept; for example, the general association of a peacock with pride and of an eagle with heroic endeavor, or the rising sun with birth and the setting sun with death, or climbing with effort or progress and descent with surrender or failure. Some poets, however, repeatedly use symbols whose significance they largely generate themselves, and these pose a more difficult problem in interpretation.

Take as an example the word "rose," which in its literal use signifies a species of flower. In Robert Burns' line "O my love's like a red, red rose," the word "rose" is used as a *simile*; and in the lines by Winthrop Mackworth Praed (1802-39),

> She was our queen, our rose, our star;
> And then she danced—O Heaven, her dancing!

the word "rose" is used as a *metaphor*. In *The Romance of the Rose*, a long medieval *dream vision*, we read about a half-opened rose to which the dreamer's access is aided by a character called "Fair Welcome," but impeded or forbidden by other characters called "Reason," "Shame," and "Jealousy." We readily recognize that the whole narrative is a sustained *allegory* about an elaborate courtship, in which most of the agents are personified abstractions and the rose itself functions as an allegorical **emblem** (that is, an object whose significance is made determinate by its qualities and by the role it plays in the narrative) which represents both the lady's love and her lovely body. Then we read William Blake's poem "The Sick Rose."

> O Rose, thou art sick.
> The invisible worm
> That flies in the night
> In the howling storm
> Has found out thy bed
> Of crimson joy,
> And his dark secret love
> Does thy life destroy.

This rose is not the *vehicle* for a simile or metaphor, because it lacks the paired subject—"my love," or the girl referred to as "she," in the examples just cited—which is an identifying feature of these figures. And it is not an allegorical rose, since, unlike the flower in *The Romance of the Rose*, it is not part of an obvious double order of correlated references, one literal and the second allegorical, in which the allegorical or emblematic reference of the

事物或事件的词或短语，被指代的事物或事件本身又指代了另一事物，或具有超越自身的参照范围。一些象征是"约定俗成的"或"公众的"，如"十字架""红、白、蓝""好牧羊人"等都是指象征性事物的术语，这些事物的深远意义受到某一特定文化的制约。诗人和我们大家一样也会采用这些约定俗成的象征；但许多诗人也会采用"私人的"或"个人的"象征。他们往往利用了某一事物、事件或行动与某一特定概念之间人们广泛共有的联想。例如，人们常把孔雀与高傲、老鹰与英勇、朝阳与诞生、落日与死亡、登山与努力前进、下山与投降或失败联想到一起。但有些诗人一再使用他们自己赋予意义的象征，这使得解释这些象征的意义成为一个更加困难的问题。

就拿"玫瑰"一词为例，其字面意思代表一种花。在罗伯特·彭斯的诗句"我的爱人像朵红红的玫瑰"里，"玫瑰"一词被用作**明喻**；但在温思罗普·麦克沃思·普里德（1802—1818）的诗句中，

> 她是我们的女王，我们的玫瑰，我们的星辰；
> 随后她翩翩起舞——噢，天哪，她的舞蹈！

"玫瑰"一词用作**隐喻**。在中世纪的长篇梦幻体诗歌《玫瑰传奇》中，我们读到这样一个故事，梦幻者想要得到一朵含苞欲放的玫瑰，一位名叫"美好迎接"的角色帮了他的忙，但却遇到名为"理智""廉耻""嫉妒"等角色的阻拦或禁止。我们很容易就能辨认出，整篇叙事诗自始至终都是一则精心构思的求爱寓言，其中的大多数角色都是拟人化的抽象概念，而玫瑰本身则是含有寓意的**象征物**（即这一事物的意义由其自身特质及其在叙事中所发挥的作用来决定）；玫瑰既代表这位淑女的爱情，也代表她窈窕的身材。让我们再来看看威廉·布莱克的《病玫瑰》这首诗：

> 玫瑰啊，你病了！
> 那看不见的飞虫
> 出现在黑夜里
> 在怒号的暴风雨中
> 他找到了你的床
> 陶醉于红色的欢欣，
> 他黑暗而隐秘的爱
> 断送了你的生命。
>
> （宋雪亭译）

玫瑰在这里不是明喻或隐喻的喻失，因为它缺少相对应的主体——"我的爱"，或是前面引用的例子中被称为"她"的少女——而主体则是这些修辞格的辨认特征。这也不是一朵带有寓言意义的玫瑰，因为它与《玫瑰传奇》中的玫瑰不同，它并不是相应意指中明显的双重语序的一部分，第一层是字面的，第二层是寓意的；

rose is made determinate by its role within the literal narrative. Blake's rose *is* a rose—yet it is patently also something more than a rose: words such as "bed," "joy," "love," which do not comport literally with an actual flower, together with the sinister tone, and the intensity of the lyric speaker's feeling, press the reader to infer that the described object has a further range of suggested but unspecified reference which makes it a symbol. But Blake's rose is a personal symbol and not—like the symbolic rose in the closing cantos of Dante's fourteenth-century *Paradiso* and other Christian poems—an element in a set of conventional and widely known (hence "public") religious symbols, in which concrete objects of this passing world are used to signify, in a relatively determinate way, the objects and truths of a higher and eternal realm. (See Barbara Seward, *The Symbolic Rose*, 1960.) Only from the implicit suggestions in Blake's poem itself—the sexual connotations, in the realm of human experience, of "bed" and "love," especially in conjunction with "joy" and "worm"—supplemented by our knowledge of similar elements and topics in his other poems, are we led to infer that Blake's lament for a crimson rose which has been entered and sickened unto death by a dark and secret worm symbolizes, in the human realm, the destruction wrought by furtiveness, deceit, and hypocrisy in what should be a frank and joyous relationship of physical love. Various critics of the poem, however, have proposed alternative interpretations of its symbolic significance. It is an attribute of many private symbols—the White Whale in Melville's *Moby-Dick* (1851) is another famed example—as well as a reason why they are an irreplaceable literary device, that they suggest a direction or a broad area of significance rather than, like an emblem in an allegorical narrative, a relatively determinate reference.

In the copious modern literature on the nature of the literary symbol, reference is often made to two seminal passages, written early in the nineteenth century by Coleridge in England and Goethe in Germany, concerning the difference between an allegory and a symbol. Coleridge is in fact describing what he believes to be the uniquely symbolic nature of the Bible as a sacred text, but later commentators have assumed that he intended his comment to apply also to the symbol in secular literature:

> Now an allegory is but a translation of abstract notions into a picture-language, which is itself nothing but an abstraction from objects of the senses.... On the other hand a symbol ... is characterized by a translucence of the special [i.e., of the species] in the individual, or of the general [i.e., of the genus] in the special, or of the universal in the general; above all by the translucence of the eternal through and in the temporal. It always partakes of the reality which it renders intelligible; and while it enunciates the whole, abides itself as a living part in that unity of which it is the representative. [Allegories] are but empty echoes which the fancy arbitrarily associates with apparitions of matter....

(Coleridge, *The Statesman's Manual*, 1816)

玫瑰的寓意或象征义是由它在文字叙述中的功能确定的。布莱克的玫瑰的确是玫瑰——但它显然又不仅仅是玫瑰:"床""欢欣""爱"这些词的字面意思与真正的花朵毫不相称,再加上邪恶的语调和抒情者强烈的情感,这都迫使读者推断诗中描述的物体或许有着更深一层的暗示但又没有明说的意指,从而使它成为一种象征。不过,布莱克的玫瑰是一种个人的象征,不是——如同14世纪但丁《天国篇》结尾诗篇和其他基督教诗歌中具有象征意义的玫瑰——遵循惯例的、众所周知的(所以是"公众的")宗教象征中的某个因素;在宗教象征中,这个短暂世界内的具体事物是以一种相对确定的方式来指代更高层的永恒国度里的事物与真理。[参阅:芭芭拉·苏厄德所著的《象征性的玫瑰》(1960)。]只有从布莱克的诗歌本身隐隐约约的暗示里——在人类经验领域中,"床"和"爱"带有性欲的含义,尤其当这两个词与"欢欣"和"虫子"连用时——再加上我们对布莱克其他诗歌中类似的元素与话题的了解,我们才会推断出,布莱克在哀叹一朵被黑暗、隐秘的虫子所侵犯而患病至死的红玫瑰;在人类世界中,诗人的悲伤象征着被诡秘、欺骗、虚伪摧毁的人伦之爱的关系;这种关系原本应该是坦然、欢愉的。但是,许多批评家则对这首诗的象征意义提出了其他解释。这是许多私人象征的特点——梅尔维尔的小说《白鲸》(1851)中的白鲸是另一个著名例子——这也说明私人象征是一种不可替代的文学手法,它们暗示了某个方向或某个广阔的意义范围,而不像寓言叙事中的象征物那样具有相对确定的意指。

当今众多有关文学象征本质的文献,常常提到19世纪早期英国的柯勒律治和德国的歌德的两段开创性的论述;这两段文字都论述了寓言与象征的区别。柯勒律治事实上所描述的是,他相信作为宗教文本的圣经具有独特的象征本质,但后世的评论家却认为他的本意也想将这段评论运用于世俗文学中的象征:

> 如今一则寓言只不过是把抽象的意念转换成象形语言,而这一语言本身仅仅是感觉客体的抽象概念……另一方面,象征……是以个体内的特殊(即种的)半透明性,或以特殊里的一般(即属的)半透明性,或以一般里的普遍半透明性为其特征,尤其以穿越现世和在现世内达到永恒的半透明性为特征。象征总是参与现实,并使现实显得清晰易懂;尽管象征启示整体,但它也是作为代表整体的有机部分。[寓言]只不过是空洞的回声,而幻想力则随意地把这些回声与物体的幻影联想在一起……
>
> (柯勒律治,《政治家手册》,1816)

Goethe had been meditating about the nature of the literary symbol in secular writings since the 1790s, but gave his concept its most specific formulation in 1824:

> There is a great difference, whether the poet seeks the particular for the sake of the general or sees the general in the particular. From the former procedure there ensues allegory, in which the particular serves only as illustration, as example of the general. The latter procedure, however, is genuinely the nature of poetry; it expresses something particular, without thinking of the general or pointing to it.
>
> Allegory transforms the phenomenon into a concept, the concept into an image, but in such a way that the concept always remains bounded in the image, and is entirely to be kept and held in it, and to be expressed by it.
>
> Symbolism [however] transforms the phenomenon into idea, the idea into an image, and in such a way that the idea remains always infinitely active and unapproachable in the image, and even if expressed in all languages, still would remain inexpressible.

(Goethe, *Maxims and Reflections*, Nos. 279, 1112, 1113)

It will be noted that, whatever the differences between these two cryptic passages, both Coleridge and Goethe stress that an allegory presents a pair of subjects (an image and a concept) but a symbol only one (the image alone); that the allegory is relatively specific in its reference, while the symbol remains indefinite, but richly—even boundlessly—suggestive in its significance; and also that for this very reason, a symbol is the higher mode of expression. To these claims, characteristic in the *Romantic Period*, critics until the recent past have for the most part agreed. In express opposition to romantic theory, however, Paul de Man has elevated allegory over symbol because, he claims, it is less "mystified" (confused and deceived) about its status as a purely rhetorical device. See de Man, "The Rhetoric of Temporality," in *Interpretation: Theory and Practice*, ed. C. S. Singleton (1969), and *Allegories of Reading* (1979).

See also W. B. Yeats, "The Symbolism of Poetry" (1900), in *Essays and Introductions* (1961); H. Flanders Dunbar, *Symbolism in Medieval Thought* (1929); C. S. Lewis, *The Allegory of Love: A Study in Medieval Tradition* (1936); Elder Olson, "A Dialogue on Symbolism," in R. S. Crane, ed., *Critics and Criticism* (1952); W. Y. Tindall, *The Literary Symbol* (1955); Harry Levin, "Symbolism and Fiction," in *Contexts of Criticism* (1957); Isabel C. Hungerland, *Poetic Discourse* (1958), chapter 5; Maurice Beebe, ed., *Literary Symbolism* (1960); Michael Ferber, *A Dictionary of Literary Symbols* (1999). See *Symbolist Movement*, and for references to a literary *symbol* in other entries, see page 9.

symbol (in semiotics): **358**.

自 1790 年代起，歌德就开始思索世俗作品中文学象征的本质，但直到 1824 年他才对这一概念作出最明确的表述：

> 诗人是为了普遍性才寻找特殊性，还是为了在特殊性里发现普遍性，这是大不一样的。前一种做法产生了寓言。在寓言中，特殊性只用做说明，是普遍性的范例。然而，后一种做法却纯粹是诗歌的本质；它表达了某种特殊的东西，而不考虑普遍性或不倾向于普遍性。
>
> 寓言把现象转换成某一概念，又把这一概念转换成某一意象，但这个概念始终受制于该意象，完全被意象左右，也被意象表达出来。
>
> [不过] 象征却是把现象转换成观念，又把观念转化成某一意象；这个观念始终保持其无限的活跃性，在意象内难以捕捉，即使作家采用各种语言来表达它，也无法表达清楚。
>
> （歌德，《格言和感想集》，第 279、1112、1113 条）

值得一提的是，不管这两段晦涩的段落之间有着什么样的区别，两个人都强调：寓言体现了一对主体（一个意象和一个概念），而象征只表现了一个主体（只有意象）。寓言的意指相对明确，象征的意指则是不确定的，但却具有丰富乃至无限的暗含意义；而也正是出于这一原因，象征也是更高级的表达模式。时至近代，文学批评家大都同意这些*浪漫主义*时期所特有的评论。但是，保罗·德·曼却反对浪漫主义的理论，把寓言提到象征之上，他认为，这是因为寓言对自己作为一种纯粹修辞手法的地位不会感到"费解"（被困惑和被误导）。参阅：德·曼所写的文章"短暂的修辞"，收入 C. S. 辛格顿主编的《阐释：理论与实践》(1969)；德·曼所著的《阅读的寓言》(1979)。

参阅：W. B. 叶芝所写的文章"诗歌的象征主义"(1900)，收入其所著的《文集与介绍》(1961)；H. 弗兰德斯·邓巴所著的《中世纪思想中的象征主义》(1929)；C. S. 刘易斯所著的《爱情的寓言：中世纪传统研究》(1936)；埃尔德·奥尔森所写的文章"关于象征主义的对话"，收入 R. S. 克莱恩主编的《批评家与批评》(1952)；W. Y. 廷德尔所著的《文学象征》(1955)；哈里·莱文所写的文章"象征主义与小说"，收入其所著的《批评的语境》(1957)；伊莎贝尔·C. 亨格兰所著的《诗学篇章》(1958) 第 5 章；莫里斯·毕比主编的《文学象征主义》(1960)；迈克尔·费伯所著的《文学符号词典》(1999)。参见：*象征主义运动*，其他条目中提及"象征"的地方，参见第 9 页。

symbol (in semiotics)：(符号论中的) 符号　358。

symbolic (in Lacanian criticism): **324**.

symbolism: 397.

Symbolist Movement: Various poets of the *Romantic Period*, including Novalis and Hölderlin in Germany and Shelley in England, often used private symbols in their poetry (see *symbol*). Shelley, for example, repeatedly made symbolic use of objects such as the morning and evening star, a boat moving upstream, winding caves, and the conflict between a serpent and an eagle. William Blake, however, exceeded all his romantic contemporaries in his recourse to a persistent and sustained **symbolism**—that is, a coherent system composed of a number of symbolic elements—in both his lyric poems and his long "prophetic," or epic poems. (See, for example, Northrop Frye, *Fearful Symmetry: A Study of William Blake*, 1947.) In nineteenth-century America, a symbolist procedure was a prominent element in the novels of Nathaniel Hawthorne and Herman Melville, the prose of Emerson and Thoreau, and the poetic theory and practice of Poe. (See Charles Feidelson, Jr., *Symbolism and American Literature*, 1953.) These writers derived the mode in large part from the native Puritan tradition of divine typology (see *interpretation: typological and allegorical*), and also from the theory of "correspondences" of the Swedish theologian Emanuel Swedenborg (1688–1772).

In the usage of literary historians, however, **Symbolist Movement** designates specifically a group of French writers beginning with Charles Baudelaire (*Fleurs du mal*, 1857) and including such later poets as Arthur Rimbaud, Paul Verlaine, Stéphane Mallarmé, and Paul Valéry. Baudelaire based the symbolic mode of his poems in part on the example of the American Edgar Allan Poe, but especially on the ancient belief in **correspondences** —the doctrine that there exist inherent and systematic analogies between the human mind and the outer world, and also between the material and the spiritual worlds. As Baudelaire put this doctrine: "Everything, form, movement, number, color, perfume, in the *spiritual* as in the *natural* world, is significative, reciprocal, converse, *correspondent*." The techniques of the French **Symbolists**, who exploited an order of private symbols in a poetry of rich suggestiveness rather than explicit signification, had an immense influence throughout Europe, and (especially in the 1890s and later) in England and America on poets such as Arthur Symons and Ernest Dowson (see *Decadence*) as well as W. B. Yeats, Ezra Pound, Dylan Thomas, Hart Crane, e. e. cummings, and Wallace Stevens. Major symbolist poets in Germany are Stefan George and Rainer Maria Rilke.

The *Modern Period*, in the decades after World War I, was a notable era of symbolism in literature. Many of the major writers of the period exploit symbols which are in part drawn from religious and esoteric traditions and in part invented. Some of the works of the age are symbolist in their settings, their agents, and their actions, as well as in the objects they refer to. Instances of a persistently symbolic procedure occur in lyrics (Yeats' "Byzantium" poems, Dylan Thomas' series of sonnets *Altarwise by Owl-light*), in longer poems

symbolic (in Lacanian criticism)：(拉康批评中的) 符号阶段　324。

symbolism：象征主义　397。

Symbolist Movement：象征主义运动

　　浪漫主义时期的许多诗人，如德国的诺瓦利斯、荷尔德林和英国的雪莱，经常在他们的诗歌中使用私人象征（参见：*象征*）。例如，雪莱一再运用象征手法描写晨星与昏星、逆流行驶的船只、迂回的山洞、蛇鹰之斗等。然而，威廉·布莱克在他的抒情诗和长篇预言诗或史诗中则自始至终地采用**象征主义**，即由许多象征元素构成的连贯系统。在这一点上，布莱克远胜于同时代的所有浪漫主义诗人。[例如可以参阅：诺斯罗普·弗莱所著的《可怖的对称：威廉·布莱克研究》(1947)。]在19世纪的美国，象征主义手法在纳撒尼尔·霍桑和赫尔曼·梅尔维尔的小说中、爱默生和梭罗的散文中、坡的诗歌理论与实践中运用得也十分显著。[参阅：小查尔斯·费德尔森所著的《象征主义与美国文学》(1953)。]这些作家的象征主义表现手法主要来自美国本土的清教徒象征传统（参见：*象征释义和寓意释义*），以及瑞典神学家伊曼纽尔·斯维登堡（1688—1772）的"对应"理论。

　　不过，在文学史学家的用法中，**象征主义运动**这一术语是特指自查尔斯·波德莱尔[《恶之花》(1857)]以来的一群法国作家，包括后来的阿尔蒂尔·兰波、保罗·魏尔兰、斯蒂芬·马拉梅、保罗·瓦莱里等诗人。波德莱尔诗中的象征模式，部分建立在美国作家埃德加·爱伦·坡论著的基础上，尤其是建立在对应这一古代信仰的基础上——即在人类思想与外部世界之间，在自然世界与精神世界之间，存在着内在的、系统的相似性这一学说。波德莱尔对这一学说是这样解释的："在精神世界就像在自然世界里一样，每种事物、形式、运动、数量、色彩、香气都意义深远，相辅相成，彼此相对，相互对应。"法国**象征主义者**在其寓意丰富而非意义明确的诗歌里，娴熟地运用一种私人象征的表现手法，对整个欧洲都产生了巨大影响，(特别是从1890年代开始)对英美诗人也产生了深远影响，如阿瑟·西蒙斯、欧内斯特·道森等（参见：*颓废派文艺*），以及W. B. 叶芝、埃兹拉·庞德、迪伦·托马斯、哈特·克莱恩、e. e. 卡明斯和华莱士·史蒂文斯。德国主要的象征主义诗人有施特凡·格奥尔格与赖纳·玛丽亚·里尔克。

　　现代时期，即第一次世界大战之后的几十年，是象征主义在文学中占据显著地位的时期。这一时期的许多重要作家都采用了象征。这种象征部分源自宗教和神秘教义的传统，部分来自创新。这一时期的部分作品在背景、人物及其行动，以及所提及的物体上都采用了象征主义。抒情诗（如叶芝的《拜占庭》诗集，迪伦·托马斯的十四行诗系列《祭坛黄昏》），长篇诗歌（如哈特·克莱恩的《桥》，

(Hart Crane's *The Bridge*, T. S. Eliot's *The Waste Land*, Wallace Stevens' "The Comedian as the Letter C"), and in novels (James Joyce's *Finnegans Wake*, William Faulkner's *The Sound and the Fury*).

See Arthur Symons, *The Symbolist Movement in Literature* (1899, reprinted 1958); Edmund Wilson, *Axel's Castle* (1936); C. M. Bowra, *The Heritage of Symbolism* (1943); Edward Engelberg, ed., *The Symbolist Poem* (1967); Anna Balakian, ed., *The Symbolist Movement in the Literature of European Languages* (1982); and René Taupin, *The Influence of French Symbolism on Modern American Poetry* (1920, trans. 1985).

Symbolists: 397; *142, 258*.

sympathy: 104.

synchronic (sĭnkrŏn′ ĭk): **193**.

synecdoche (sĭněk′ dŏkē): **132**.

synesthesia: Synesthesia, in psychology, signifies the experience of two or more modes of sensation when only one sense is being stimulated. In literature the term is applied to descriptions of one mode of sensation in terms of another; color is attributed to sounds, odor to colors, sound to odors, and so on. We often, for example, speak of loud colors, bright sounds, and sweet music. A complex literary instance of synesthesia (which is sometimes also called "sense transference" or "sense analogy") is this passage from Shelley's "The Sensitive Plant" (1820):

> And the hyacinth purple, and white, and blue,
> Which flung from its bells a sweet peal anew
> Of music so delicate, soft, and intense,
> It was felt like an odor within the sense.

The varicolored, bell-shaped flowers of the hyacinth send out a peal of music which effects a sensation as though it were (what in fact it is) the scent of the flowers. Keats, in the "Ode to a Nightingale" (1819), calls for a draught of wine

> Tasting of Flora and the country green,
> Dance, and Provençal song, and sunburnt mirth;

that is, he calls for a drink tasting of sight, color, motion, sound, and heat.

Occasional uses of synesthetic imagery have been made by poets ever since Homer. Such imagery became much more frequent in the *Romantic Period*, and was especially exploited by the French *Symbolists* of the middle and later nineteenth century; see Baudelaire's sonnet "Correspondences," and Rimbaud's sonnet on the color of vowel sounds "A black, E white, I red, U green, O blue."

T.S.艾略特的《荒原》，华莱士·史蒂文斯的《喜剧家字母C》，以及小说（如詹姆斯·乔伊斯的《芬尼根的觉醒》，威廉·福克纳的《喧哗与骚动》）都是自始至终采用象征手法的范例。

参阅：阿瑟·西蒙斯所著的《象征主义文学运动》（1899，1958 年再版）；埃德蒙·威尔逊所著的《阿克塞尔的城堡》（1936）；C.M.鲍勒所著的《象征主义的遗产》（1943）；爱德华·恩格尔伯格主编的《象征主义诗歌》（1967）；安娜·巴拉基安主编的《欧洲语言文学中的象征主义运动》（1982）；雷纳·泰冰所著的《法国象征主义对美国现代诗歌的影响》（1920，1985 年英译版）。

Symbolists：象征主义者　397；*142, 258*。

sympathy：同情　104。

synchronic：共时性　193。

synecdoche：举隅　132。

Synesthesia：通感

通感在心理学中是指某一感观在受到刺激时产生的两种或两种以上的感觉经验。在文学上，这一术语表示用一种感觉来描述另一种感觉，如用色彩描绘声音、用气味描绘色彩、用声音描绘气味等。例如，我们常常提到喧闹的色彩、明亮的声音、甜美的音乐等。下面这段诗选自雪莱的《敏感的植物》（1820）。这是一个文学中采用复杂的通感（有时也叫"移情"或"感觉类同"）的例子：

> 还有紫色、白色、蓝色的风信子，
> 从花铃中发出甜蜜的乐曲
> 这般浓郁、优雅、热烈、温柔，
> 仿佛一股芳香飘荡在心头。　　　　　　　（吴笛译）

色彩丰富、形似钟铃的风信子花释放出当当的音乐声，这乐声触动了感觉，似乎变成（事实上就是）风信子花的芬芳。济慈在《夜莺颂》（1819）里希望能一饮美酒：

> 它有乡村的花香和绿野的风光，
> 普罗旺斯的阳光、舞蹈和歌声悠悠；

诗人希望品尝景致、色彩、舞姿、乐声与阳光。

自荷马开始，诗人们就已在偶尔运用通感的意象。在*浪漫主义时期*，这种意象的运用变得愈加频繁，尤其是 19 世纪中后期法国的*象征主义者*更是经常运用；参阅：波德莱尔的十四行诗《感应》和兰波描述元音色彩的十四行诗《A 黑色，E 白色，I 红色，U 绿色，O 蓝色》。

Refer to the detailed analyses of literary synesthesia in Richard H. Fogel, *The Imagery of Keats and Shelley* (1949), chapter 3; also Simon Baron-Cohen, *Synaesthesia: Classic and Contemporary Readings* (1996); and John E. Harrison, *Synaesthesia: The Strangest Thing* (2001).

syntagmatic (sĭn′ tăgmăt″ ĭk): **197**.

syntax: 195.

syuzhet (in Russian formalism): **234**.

参阅：理查德·H. 福格尔在其所著的《济慈和雪莱的意象》(1949) 第 3 章里对文学作品中通感的详细分析；也可参阅：西蒙·巴伦－科恩主编的《通感：经典与当代读本》(1996)；约翰·E. 哈里森所著的《通感：最奇怪的事情》(2001)。

syntagmatic：组合　197。

syntax：句法　195。

syuzhet（in Russian formalism）：(俄国形式主义中) 用于表述故事的具体描述　234。

T

tale: 365.

tall tale: 166.

telling (in narrative): 47.

tenor (of a metaphor): 131; *213*.

tension: Tension became a common descriptive and evaluative word in the criticism of the 1930s and later, especially after Allen Tate, one of the *New Critics*, proposed it as a term to be made by "lopping the prefixes off the logical terms *ex*tension and *in*tension." In technical logic the "intension" of a word is the set of abstract attributes which must be possessed by any object to which the word can be literally applied, and the "extension" of a word is the class of concrete objects to which the word applies. The meaning of good poetry, according to Tate, "is its 'tension,' the full organized body of all the extension and intension that we can find in it." ("Tension in Poetry," 1938, in *On the Limits of Poetry*, 1948.) It would seem that by this statement Tate meant that a good poem incorporates both the abstract and the concrete, the general idea and the particular image, in an integral whole. See *concrete and abstract*.

Other critics use "tension" to characterize poetry that manifests an equilibrium of the serious and the ironic, or "a pattern of resolved stresses," or a harmony of opponent tendencies, or any other mode of that stability-in-opposition which was the favorite way in the *New Criticism* for conceiving the organization of a good poem. And some critics, dubious perhaps about the validity of Tate's logical derivation of the term, simply apply "tension" to any poem in which the elements seem tightly rather than loosely interrelated.

tercet (tŭr′ sĕt): 375.

terza rima (tĕr′ tsă rē″ mă): 376.

tetrameter (tĕtrăm′ ĕtĕr): 219.

text and writing (écriture): Traditional critics conceived the object of their critical concern to be a literary "work"; that is, a human product whose form is achieved by its author's design and its meanings by the author's intentional uses of the verbal medium. French *structuralist* critics, on the other hand, depersonalized a literary product by conceiving it to be not a "work," but an impersonal **text**, a manifestation of the social institution called **écriture** (writing). The author is regarded as only an intermediary in whom the action of writing precipitates the elements and codes of the preexisting linguistic and literary system

T

tale：故事　365。

tall tale：牛皮故事　166。

telling (in narrative)：(叙事中的) 讲述手法　47。

tenor (of a metaphor)：(隐喻中的) 喻的　131；*213*。

Tension：张力

　　张力是自 1930 年代以来在文学批评中常见的一个描述性和评价性术语，尤其是在新批评家艾伦·泰特提出"把逻辑术语'外延'(extension) 和'内涵'(intension) 的前缀删去"之后便形成了"张力"这个术语以来。按照严格的逻辑意义，某个词的"内涵"是任何物体所必然具备的一些抽象特质，这个词可以按其字面意义用来指这一物体，而某个词的"外延"则是该词指代的一类具体事物。根据泰特的理论，优秀诗歌的意义"是它的'张力'，即我们在诗歌中能够发现的所有外延与内涵的有机整体"。[参阅：泰特所写的文章"诗歌的张力"(1938)，收入其所著的《论诗歌的局限》(1948)。] 从这一论述来看，泰特似乎认为一首优秀的诗歌能够把抽象和具体、普遍观念和特殊意象都纳入一个完整的总体内。参见：*具体与抽象*。

　　其他批评家则用"张力"来概括展现严肃与讽刺均衡的诗歌，或是"一种消除压力的模式"，或互相对抗的趋势的调和，或任何其他对立中的稳定的模式，这是*新批评*在评价优秀诗歌结构时最喜欢采用的一种方式。有些批评家可能对泰特这个术语的逻辑衍生的正确性心存怀疑，因此他们仅用"张力"来指代任何一首组成元素看似紧密联系而非松散连接的诗歌。

tercet：同韵三行诗节　375。

terza rima：三行诗节隔句押韵法　376。

tetrameter：四音步诗行　219。

Text and Writing (Écriture)：文本与书写 (书面文字)

　　传统的批评家认为，批评主要关注的对象是文学"作品"；即一件人工制品，作品的形式是作者设计的，作品的意义则通过作者对文字媒介的刻意使用而体现出来。但是，法国*结构主义*批评家却把文学产品非个人化，认为文学产品不是"作品"，而是一种非个人的**文本**，是社会惯例的一种体现，称为**书面文字**（书写）。作者被视为只是一种媒介，其写作行为把先前存在的语言体系与文学体系

into a particular text. The interpretation of this writing is effected by "lecture" (in French, the process of reading) which, by bringing to bear expectations formed by earlier exposure to the functioning of the linguistic system, invests the marks on the page with what merely seem to be their inherent meanings and references to an outer world. Structuralists differ about the degree to which the activity of reading a text is constrained by the literary conventions and codes that went into the writing; many *deconstructive critics*, however, propose that all writing, by the internal play of opposing forces, necessarily disseminates into an indefinite array of diverse and opposed meanings.

The system of linguistic and literary conventions that constitute a literary text are said by structuralist and *poststructuralist* critics to be "naturalized" in the activity of reading, in that the artifices of a nonreferential "textuality" are made to seem **vraisemblable** (credible)—that is, made to give the illusion of referring to reality—by being brought into accord with modes of discourse and cultural stereotypes that are so familiar and habitual as to seem natural. **Naturalization** (an alternative term is **recuperation**) takes place through such habitual procedures in reading as assigning the text to a specific *genre*, or taking a fictional text to be the speech of a credibly human narrator, or interpreting its artifices as signifying characters, actions, and values that represent, or accord with, those in an extratextual world. To a thoroughgoing structuralist or poststructuralist critic, however, not only is the text's representation of the world no more than an illusory "effect" generated by the process of reading, but the world is itself held to be in its turn a text; that is, simply a structure of *signs* whose significance is constituted by the cultural conventions, codes, and *ideology* that happen to be shared by members of a cultural community. The term **intertextuality**, popularized especially by Julia Kristeva, is used to signify the multiple ways in which any one literary text is in fact made up of other texts, by means of its open or covert citations and *allusions*, its repetitions and transformations of the formal and substantive features of earlier texts, or simply its unavoidable participation in the common stock of linguistic and literary conventions and procedures that are "always-already" in place and constitute the discourses into which we are born. In Kristeva's formulation, accordingly, any text is in fact an "intertext"—the site of an intersection of numberless other texts, and existing only through its relations to other texts.

Roland Barthes in *S/Z* (1970) proposed a distinction between a text which is "lisible" (readable) and one which, although "scriptible" (writable) is "illisible" (unreadable). Readable texts are traditional or "classical" ones—such as the realistic novels by Honoré Balzac and other nineteenth-century authors—which for the most part conform to the prevailing codes and conventions, literary and social, and so are readily and comfortably interpretable and naturalizable in the process of reading. An "unreadable" text (such as James Joyce's *Finnegans Wake*, or the French *new novel*, or a poem by a highly experimental poet) is one which largely violates, parodies, or innovates upon prevailing conventions, and thus persistently shocks, baffles, and frustrates standard expectations. In Barthes' view an unreadable text, by drawing attention in this way to the pure conventionality and artifice of literature, laudably

中的元素和代码凝结成某一特定的文本。对这种书写的阐释受到"阅读过程"（相当于法语中的 lecture 一词）的影响，由于这一阅读过程具有先前对语言体系功能的了解所形成的期望，从而赋予书页上的符号似乎只是其固有的意义及其所指的外部世界。结构主义批评家在进入书写中的文学惯例与代码会对阅读文本的活动产生多大程度的制约这一问题上看法各异；但许多*解构主义批评家*都提出，由于相对立的力量的内部游戏，所有的书写都必然散布为一系列各种各样互相对立的意义。

结构主义批评家及*后结构主义*批评家认为，构成文学文本的语言及文学惯例体系，在阅读活动中被"归化"了，因为当某种非意指性的"文本化"手法与读者所熟悉和习以为常因而似乎是自然的话语模式及文化原型保持一致时，这些手法似乎就变得**貌似真实的**（可信的）了——即造成了一种意指现实的假象。**归化**（或称**复原**）是通过阅读中的一些习惯性做法得以实现的，例如，把文本归入某一具体文学类型，或把虚构文本当做某一令人信服的人类叙述者的言谈，或将文本的表现手法解释为描述了与文本之外的世界相吻合的人物、行动和价值观。然而，对彻底的结构主义或后结构主义批评家来说，文本对世界的反映只不过是阅读过程产生的一种虚幻的"效果"，而且世界本身也是一种文本；即仅仅是*符号*的一种结构，而这些符号的意义是由某个文化群体的成员恰巧共有的文化惯例、代码和*意识形态*构成的。朱莉娅·克莉丝蒂娃推广了**互文性**这一术语。该术语指的是，任何一部文学文本事实上都是由其他文本以多种方式组合而成，比如这一文本中公开的或隐秘的引用与典故，对先前文本形式特征及本质特征的重复与改造，或仅仅是文本对共同累积的语言、文学惯例与手法不可避免的参与等方式。这些惯例与手法"总是已经"处在合适的"位置"，从而构成了我们生而享有的话语。因此，克莉丝蒂娃认为，任何文本事实上都是"互文"——无数文本交叉的地方，只有通过自身与其他文本的联系才能得以存在。

罗兰·巴尔特在其所著的《S/Z》(1970) 中区分了"可读性"文本与"可写"但"不可读性"文本。可读性文本是传统的或"经典的"文本，如奥诺雷·巴尔扎克和其他 19 世纪作家创作的现实主义小说，它们大致顺应了盛行的文学及社会代码与惯例，因此在阅读过程中能够轻松自如地得到解释与归化。"不可读性"文本（如詹姆斯·乔伊斯的《芬尼根的觉醒》、法国的*新小说*，或某个勇于创新的诗人所写的诗歌）在很大程度上是对盛行惯例的违背、滑稽模仿或标新立异，因此它总是使标准的期望准则感到震惊、困惑和失望。巴尔特认为，"不可读性"文本通过以这种方式去注意文学纯粹的因循守旧和故弄玄虚，从而令人赞许地摧毁

destroys any illusion that it represents reality. In *The Pleasure of the Text* (published 1973), Barthes assigns to the readable text the response of mere "plaisir" (quasi-erotic pleasure), but to the unreadable text the response of "jouissance" (orgasmic ecstasy); as Jonathan Culler has put Barthes' view, jouissance is "a rapture of dislocation produced by ruptures or violations of intelligibility" (*Structuralist Poetics*, p. 192).

For related matters and relevant bibliographic references, see *structuralist criticism*, *poststructuralism*, and *semiotics*.

textual criticism: Textual criticism expounds the principles and procedures that will establish and validate the text of a literary or other work that an editor prepares and publishes. The theory and practice of textual criticism goes back many centuries. It was applied at first to biblical and classical texts, of which all the surviving manuscripts had been written (and often altered, deliberately or inadvertently) by scribes long after the death of the original writers. Later, textual criticism was adapted to apply to the early era of the printed book, then to later times when editors had access to diverse *editions* of a printed text, and sometimes to differing manuscripts written by the authors themselves, as well as differing transcripts of such manuscripts by various people. (See *book editions* and *book format*.) Until recently the ruling principle, whether explicit or tacit, was that the invariable task of a scholarly editor is to establish, from all the available evidences in manuscript and print, the text that as nearly as possible conforms to the text originally composed by its author.

In the mid-twentieth century, most scholarly editors subscribed to the principles of the **copy-text**, as propounded in a highly influential paper by the English bibliographer W. W. Greg. Greg formulated his views mainly with reference to editing Shakespeare and other Renaissance authors, but the principles he proposed were soon expanded and modified by Fredson Bowers and others to apply also to later authors and modes of publication and transmission. The Greg-Bowers theory (as it is often called) proposed, as the goal of a scholarly edition, to establish a single "authoritative" or "definitive" text that represented the "final intentions" of the author at the conclusion of his or her process of composing and revising a work. Editors choose, as the "copy-text," that one of the existing texts judged to be closest to what the author wrote or intended to write; usually the copy-text is the earliest printed edition of a work (or in some cases, the author's written manuscript of a work), since this is considered to be closest to the author's own intentions. This base-text is emended by the editor to eliminate what are judged to be inadvertent errors made by the author in writing out his composition, and also to delete intrusive "substantive" changes (changes in wording) that are judged to have been introduced by other people without the author's "authorization." (Such nonauthorial intrusions and changes in the words of a text, by copy editors, printers, and others, are often labeled "corruptions" or "contaminations" of the original text.) The copy-text is further emended to include any later deletions or additions that the editor judges, from the available evidence, to have been introduced or authorized by the author himself or

了所谓文学反映社会现实的任何假象。在《文本的乐趣》(1973)中，巴尔特认为，阅读可读性文本仅仅是可以获得"类似性欲快感"的反应，阅读不可读性文本则可以获得"性高潮狂喜"的反应。乔纳森·卡勒这样解释巴尔特的观点：性高潮的狂喜是"对可理解性的决裂或破坏而产生的一种无所适从的狂喜"(《结构主义诗学》第192页)。

相关问题与参考书目，参见：*结构主义批评*、*后结构主义*、*符号论*。

Textual Criticism：文本批评

文本批评阐释了能够证明学术性编辑为公众阅读而准备的文学文本或其他文本是符合要求的原则与方法。文本批评的理论与实践可以追溯到许多世纪之前。它最初运用于圣经文本与经典文本，这些文本尚存的手稿都是在原作者去世许久之后由抄写员记录(经常有意或无意地有所改动)而成。后来，文本批评有所改变，用于印刷书本的早期阶段；之后，编辑能够获得印刷文本的不同版本，有时还能获得作者自己书写的不同手稿，以及许多人对这些手稿所作的不同誊写；这时，文本批评仍然适用。(参见：*书籍版本*、*书籍版式*。)时至近代，文本批评明确或暗含的主要原则是：学术性编辑的任务是，利用从手稿或印刷作品中可以获得的所有证据，来确定文本是尽可能与作者最初创作的文本相一致的。

英国目录学家 W. W. 格雷格在一篇影响极为深远的文章中提出了**复制－文本**的原则，20世纪中期的学术性编辑大都赞同这一原则。格雷格提出这些观点主要是针对编辑莎士比亚和其他文艺复兴时期作者的作品而言，但是，弗雷德森·鲍尔斯等人不久便扩展、修订了格雷格提出的原则，将其用于后世作家及出版和传播模式中。(就像常说的那样)格雷格－鲍尔斯理论的提出，是作为学术性版本的目标，即确定一部"权威性的"或"最可靠的"文本，这一文本代表了作者在创作和修改作品过程最后阶段的"最终意图"。编辑在现有文本中选择一部被认为是最接近作者创作或想要创作的文本，作为"复制－文本"；复制－文本通常是一部作品最早的印刷版本(有时是作者某部作品的书写手稿)，因为这被认为最接近作者自己的意图。编辑对这种基础文本进行修订，消除被认为是作者在书写文本时因疏忽而犯的错误，删去被认为是其他人未经作者"授权"而加入的侵入性"本质"改变(措词的改变)(文字编辑、印刷者和其他人这种非作者本人对文本词语的侵入和改变，常被称为对原创文本的"讹误"或"混杂")。进一步修订复制－文本包括编辑从获得的证据中判断是经作者本人后来加入或授权的任何增

herself, and that therefore may be assumed to embody the author's "final intentions." The resulting published document (often with copious editorial footnotes and other materials to identify all these emendations and to record the textual "variants" that the editor has rejected) is known as an **eclectic text**, in that it accords with no single existing model, but is constructed by fitting together materials from a variety of texts—materials that are sometimes supplemented by the editor's own conjectures.

Beginning in the late 1920s, two developments helped to bring the copy-text theory under increasing scrutiny and objection. One was the appearance of scholarly publications that made available a multitude of diverse forms of a single literary work, in drafts, manuscripts, transcriptions (sometimes with changes and insertions) by family and friends, and corrected proof sheets, even before the poem was originally published. The many volumes of the *Cornell Wordsworth*, for example, begun in 1975 under the general editorship of Stephen Parrish, record all such variants; for a number of Wordsworth's writings, they also print "reading copies" of the full text at sequential stages in the author's composition and revision of a single work. There are being printed also a number of texts from manuscripts that are versions of works by novelists that were rejected by the author, or radically revised before the final text was published. An early example was *Stephen Hero*, published in 1944, part of the first draft of *A Portrait of the Artist*, which James Joyce had published thirty years earlier; other examples are uncut versions from manuscript of F. Scott Fitzgerald's *The Great Gatsby*, Thomas Wolfe's *Look Homeward, Angel*, and Richard Wright's *Native Son*. Another development was the poststructural climate of critical opinion, which brought into radical question the centrality of the "subject," or author, and denied the validity of appealing to the intention of a writer as determinative of text or meaning. A number of poststructural theorists also stressed the role of social factors in "constructing" the meanings of a text, or emphasized the variability in the reception and interpretation of a text over time. (See *author and authorship*, *poststructuralism*, and *reception theory*.)

Scholarly endeavors at a single, eclectic, and definitive text of a literary work are now often derogated as resulting in an "ideal" text that never in fact existed, and is apt to incorporate the inclinations of the editor, labeled as the intentions of the author. In a *Critique of Modern Textual Criticism* (1983, reissued 1992), Jerome McGann expounded his **social theory of textual criticism**, in which he attributes "textual authority" to the cumulative social history of the work, including the contributions not only of the author, but also of the editor, publisher, printer, and all others who have cooperated in bringing into being and producing a book that is made available to the public; all these components, in McGann's view, are valid determinants of a text and its meanings, considered as social constructions. (See *social constructs*, under *new historicism*, and *book history studies*.) In later writings, McGann has stressed also the material features of a book—including its typography, paper, format, and even pricing and advertising—as cooperative with its verbal element in generating its total cultural significance. (See McGann, *The Textual Condition*, 1991; refer also to D. F. McKenzie, *Bibliography and Sociology of Texts*, 1986.) Attempts to edit by

减，因此可以认为体现了作者的"最终意图"。经过进一步修订而最终出版的文献（常有大量编者脚注和其他资料，以辨认校订的内容和记录已被编辑剔除的版本"变体"）被称为**编选的文本**，虽然它与现有的模式不相符合，但它是容纳了来自各种现存版本的素材构建而成的——编辑自己的揣摩有时也补充了这些素材。

自 1920 年代末开始，两种发展趋势有助于复制－文本理论经受审视与反对。其中一种发展趋势是学术性出版物的出现，这些出版物为一首诗提供了多种不同形式，如草稿、手稿、家人或朋友的抄本（有时会有所改动、增添）等形式，甚至还有这首诗第一次出版前经过校订的校样。例如，斯蒂芬·帕里什 1975 年主编的《康奈尔·华兹华斯》多卷本诗集，就记录了所有这些不同的形式；他们也为华兹华斯的一些作品出版了单部作品在作者的创作和修改各个连续的不同阶段完整的文本的"阅读副本"。被出版的也有一些最终文本出版前被作者否定或进行彻底修改的作家作品不同版本的手稿文本。一个早期例子是 1941 年出版的《斯蒂芬英雄》，它是詹姆斯·乔伊斯三十年前出版的《一个青年艺术家的肖像》初稿的一部分；其他例子是 F. 斯科特·菲茨杰拉德的《了不起的盖茨比》、托马斯·沃尔夫的《天使望故乡》和理查德·赖特的《私生子》手稿的未删节版。另一种发展趋势是批评观点的后结构主义风气，后结构主义强烈质疑"主体"或作者的中心地位，否定把作者意图视为意义决定因素的正确性。许多后结构主义理论家转而关注社会因素在"建构"文本意义时的作用，或强调文本的接受与阐释随时间而变化。（参见：*作者与作者身份*、*后结构主义*、*接受理论*。）

力图获得某部文学作品单一、兼容并蓄且最可靠的文本的学术性努力，现在经常遭到贬低，认为这种努力的结果只能是一种事实上永远不会存在的理想文本。而且，它易于将编辑的倾向，而非作者的意图收入其中。杰尔姆·麦根在其所著的《现代文本批评之评论》(1983，1992 年再版) 中，介绍了自己提出的**文本批评社会理论**。他将"文本的权威性"归因于作品累积的社会历史，这不仅包括作者的贡献，还包括编辑、出版商、印刷者和其他人的贡献，他们共同合作，创造、生产了提供给公众的书。在麦根看来，所有这些组成部分都是文本及其意义的有效决定因素，被视为社会的构成因素。（参见：*新历史主义*中的*社会建构*、*书籍史研究*。）在后来的论著中，麦根强调了书籍的物质特征——包括排版、纸张、版式、甚至定价与广告——与文本的文字元素共同产生了文本整体的文化意义。[参阅：麦根所著的《文本的条件》(1991)；D. F. 麦肯齐所著的《书目学与文本社会学》(1986)。]

reference to an author's final intentions have been brought into further question by the view that most published works are in fact products of **multiple authorship**. See Jack Stillinger's *Multiple Authorship and the Myth of Solitary Genius* (1991), which demonstrates by many examples that the printed text of a work is typically the joint product of a number of participants, including friends, family members, transcribers, literary agents, editors, and printers, in addition to the person who is ordinarily considered to be its sole author.

Despite such critiques, the Greg-Bowers copy-text theory has continued to be defended and applied, although with various modifications, by a number of scholars, most prominently by G. Thomas Tanselle (see his *A Rationale of Textual Criticism*, 1989). Many editors now subscribe to some form of a theory of textual **versions**, of which an early exponent was James Thorpe in *Principles of Textual Criticism* (1972). The growing consensus is that the composition of a literary work is a continuous process without a fixed terminus or perfected state, and that each existing stage, or "version," of the process, whether in manuscript or print, has an equal right to be regarded as a product intended by the author at its particular time. A scholarly editor ought, therefore, to give up the hopeless aim to achieve a single definitive master text of a literary work. Instead, the editor should select and edit that textual "version" of a work that accords with the circumstances of the particular case, and also according to whether the editor's purpose is to approximate what the author wrote, or else to reproduce the printed text, however it came about, as it existed for its readers when it was first published.

For a concise survey of the history of textual theory and criticism, see D. C. Greetham, *Textual Scholarship: An Introduction* (1992). Greetham has also edited, for the Modern Language Association of America, *Scholarly Editing: A Guide to Research* (1995), which includes a survey, written by specialists, of the history and types of scholarly editing applied to classical literature, the Bible, and a number of foreign literatures, as well as to the various periods of English literature. See also, in addition to works cited above: W. W. Greg, "The Rationale for Copy-Text," reprinted in his *Collected Papers*, ed. J. C. Maxwell (1966); Fredson Bowers, *Bibliography and Textual Criticism* (1964); and for subsequent developments, Gary Taylor and Michael Warren, eds., *The Division of the Kingdoms: Shakespeare's Two Versions of "King Lear"* (1983); Donald H. Reiman, *Romantic Texts and Contexts* (1982); George Bornstein and Ralph G. Williams, eds., *Palimpsest: Editorial Theory in the Humanities* (1993). Walter Gabler describes briefly current modes of German and French textual theory and procedures in *The Johns Hopkins Guide to Literary Theory and Criticism*, ed. Michael Groden and Martin Kreiswirth (1994).

theater in the round: 64.

theater of the absurd: 2.

theme: 229; *129*.

试图根据作者的最终意图进行编辑的做法,一直受到一种观点的质疑,这种观点认为,多数出版的作品事实上都是**多重作者身份**的产物。参阅:杰克·斯蒂林格所著的《多重作者与孤独天才的神话》(1991),该书通过许多例子来说明,一部作品的印刷文本通常是许多参与者的共同产物,除了人们通常视为其唯一作者的人之外,还包括朋友、家人、誊写人、文稿代理人、编辑、出版商等。

尽管有这样一些评论,格雷格-鲍尔斯的复制-文本理论仍在被维护和运用,不过一些学者也对这一理论进行了各种修正,其中最突出的是 G.托马斯·坦塞尔[参阅他所著的《文本批评的原理》(1989)]。现在许多编辑都赞成文本**版本**理论的某种形式。这一理论最初的倡导者是著有《文本批评原理》(1972)的詹姆斯·索普。日趋一致的观点是,文学作品的创造是一个持续的过程,并没有终点或完美的状态;这个过程中存在的每个阶段或"版本",不论是手稿还是印刷本,都同样有权被视为作者在某一特定时间意图创造的产品。因此,学术性编辑应当放弃追求文学作品最可靠的唯一原版-文本这一毫无希望的目标。相反,编辑应该根据特定情况下的环境,同时也根据编辑的目的是要接近作者所写的内容,还是要复制文本第一次出版时读者所看到的印刷文本,不管它是怎样出现的,以此来选择或编辑一部作品的文本"版本"。

关于文本理论与批评历史的简要概述,参阅:D. C. 格里瑟姆所著的《文本研究入门》(1992)。格里瑟姆还为美国现代语言学协会编辑了《学术性编辑:研究指南》(1995),里面收录了专家们所著的概述,这些概述回顾了运用于经典文学、圣经、一些外国文学作品及英国文学不同时期的学术性编辑的历史与类型。除了上列作品,还可参阅:W. W. 格雷格所写的文章"复制-文本的基本原理",重印收入其所著的《论文集》(1996,J. C. 马克斯韦尔主编);弗雷德森·鲍尔斯所著的《书目学与文本批评》(1964);这一理论在当代的发展,可以参阅:加里·泰勒与迈克尔·沃伦合编的《分裂的王国:莎士比亚〈李尔王〉的两个版本》(1983);唐纳德·H. 赖曼所著的《浪漫主义文本与语境》(1982);乔治·伯恩斯坦与拉尔夫·G. 威廉斯合编的《重写本:人文学中的编辑理论》(1993)。在迈克尔·格罗登与马丁·克里斯沃思合编的《约翰·霍普金斯文学理论与批评指南》(1994)中,沃尔特·盖布勒简要地描述了德国及法国当前的文本理论与方法模式。

theater in the round:圆形剧场 64。

theater of the absurd:荒诞戏剧 2。

theme:主题 229;*129*。

theodicy (thē·ŏd' ĭ·sē): **155**.

theoretical criticism: 67.

theories and movements in recent criticism: The entry in this *Glossary* on *criticism* describes traditional types of literary theory and of applied criticism from Aristotle through the early twentieth century. Since World War I, and especially since the 1960s, there have appeared a large number of innovative literary theories and methods of critical analysis, including revised and amplified versions of the earlier forms of *Marxist criticism* and *psychoanalytic criticism*. An entry on each of these latter-day critical modes is included in the *Glossary*, according to the alphabetic order of its title. Following is a table of the approximate time when these modes became prominent in literary criticism:

1920s–1930s	*Russian Formalism*
1930s–1940s	*archetypal criticism*
1940s–1950s	*New Criticism*; *phenomenological criticism*
1960s	modern forms of *feminist criticism*; *structuralist criticism*; *stylistics*
1970s	theory of the *anxiety of influence*; *deconstruction*; *discourse analysis*; various forms of *reader-response criticism*; *reception theory*; *semiotics*; *speech-act theory*
1980s	*cultural studies*; *dialogic criticism*; *gender criticism*; *new historicism*; *queer theory*
1990s	*Darwinian literary studies*; *ecocriticism*; *postcolonial studies*
2000ff	*cognitive literary studies*

See the entry *poststructuralism* for current uses of the term "theory," as well as for a description of some critical perspectives and practices shared by a number of the theories that have appeared after the 1960s.

theory (in poststructuralism): **310**.

theory (in traditional criticism): **67**.

thesis (of a literary work): **129**.

thick descriptions: 245.

third-person narrative: 301.

third-person point of view: 301.

three unities: In the sixteenth and seventeenth centuries, critics of the drama in Italy and France added to Aristotle's *unity of action*, which he describes in his

theodicy：神正论　155。

theoretical criticism：理论批评　67。

Theories and Movements in Recent Criticism：当代批评理论和运动

本书中有关*文学批评*的条目描述了从亚里士多德到 20 世纪初期传统的文学理论类型与应用批评类型。第一次世界大战以来，尤其自 1960 年代开始，出现了大量创新的文学理论和批评分析方法，包括对马克思主义批评、精神分析批评的早期形式进行的修正和进一步阐述发挥的各种版本。本书收录的这些新批评模式按各模式名称的字母顺序排列。下面列出了这些模式在文学批评中占据显著地位的大致时间：

1920—1930 年代	俄国形式主义
1930—1940 年代	原型批评
1940—1950 年代	新批评；现象学批评
1960 年代	女性主义批评的现代形式；结构主义批评；文体学
1970 年代	影响的焦虑理论；解构主义；话语分析；读者反应批评的各种形式；接受理论；符号论；言语行为理论
1980 年代	文化研究；对话批评；性别批评；新历史主义；同性恋理论
1990 年代	达尔文主义文学研究；生态批评；后殖民主义研究
21 世纪以来	认知文学研究

有关"理论"这一术语的当代意义，及对 1960 年代后出现的许多（但是并非全部）理论共有的一些批评角度与实践的描述，参见：*后结构主义*。

theory (in poststructuralism)：(后结构主义中的) 理论　310。

theory (in traditional criticism)：(传统批评中的) 理论　67。

thesis (of a literary work)：(文学作品中的) 论点　129。

thick descriptions：深描　245。

third-person narrative：第三人称叙事模式　301。

third-person point of view：第三人称视角　301。

Three Unities：三一律

在 16、17 世纪，意大利和法国的戏剧评论家对亚里士多德在其《诗学》中提到

Poetics, two other unities, to constitute one of the so-called *rules* of drama known as "the three unities." On the assumption that **verisimilitude**—the achievement of an illusion of reality in the audience of a stage play—requires that the action represented by a play approximate the actual conditions of the staging of the play, these critics imposed the requirement of the "unity of place" (that the action represented be limited to a single location) and the requirement of the "unity of time" (that the time represented be limited to the two or three hours it takes to act the play, or at most to a single day of either twelve or twenty-four hours). In large part because of the potent example of Shakespeare, many of whose plays represent frequent changes of place and the passage of many years, the unities of place and time never dominated English *neoclassicism* as they did criticism in Italy and France. A final blow was the famous attack against them, and against the principle of dramatic verisimilitude on which they were based, in Samuel Johnson's "Preface to Shakespeare" (1765). Since then in England, the unities of place and time (as distinguished from the unity of action) have been regarded as optional devices, available as needed by the playwright to achieve special effects of dramatic concentration.

See René Wellek, *A History of Modern Criticism*, Vol. 1, *The Later Eighteenth Century* (1955); Bernard Weinberg, *A History of Literary Criticism in the Italian Renaissance* (1961).

threnody (thrĕn′ ŏdē): **102**.

thrillers: 85.

tone: 287.

topographical poetry: Topographical poetry, also called **local poetry**, combines the description of a specific natural scene with historical, political, or moral reflections that are associated with the scene or are suggested by its details. Samuel Johnson, in his "Life of John Denham" (1779), attributed its origin to Denham's fine poem *Cooper's Hill*, first written in 1642; as Johnson defines the *genre*, "local poetry" is a species "of which the fundamental subject is some particular landscape to be poetically described, with the addition of such embellishments as may be supplied by historical retrospection or incidental meditation." See the analysis of a passage from *Cooper's Hill*, under *heroic couplet*.

This poetic type had an enormous vogue through the eighteenth century; Robert Aubin, in *Topographical Poetry in XVIII-Century England* (1936), lists some two thousand examples. Many of these, like "Cooper's Hill," are **prospect poems** that describe the landscape that is visible from a high point of vantage; notable examples are John Dyer's "Grongar Hill" (1726) and Thomas Gray's "Ode on a Distant Prospect of Eton College" (1747). Local poems were later developed into a major Romantic form, the **descriptive-meditative lyric**, which is characterized by a sustained flow of consciousness;

的*行动一致律*加以发展，增加了另外两个一致定律，从而构成了戏剧的*规则*之一，即所谓的"三一律"。他们假定，**逼真**——造成观众产生舞台上的戏剧是现实的错觉——这一艺术准则，要求剧中展示的行动必须接近戏剧舞台上的实际条件。基于这样的假定，他们提出了"地点一致律"（展现的行动必须局限在同一地点）和"时间一致律"（表现的时间被限制在演出一场戏剧所需要的两三个小时里，至多在一天内的十二或二十四个小时里）的要求。莎士比亚在他的许多戏剧里时常变换地点，时间穿越许多年。很大程度上由于他的强烈影响，地点与时间一致律从未像在意大利和法国的批评界那样在英国*新古典主义*中占主导地位。塞缪尔·约翰逊在"莎士比亚绪论"（1765）中，给予地点和时间一致律著名的最后一击，抨击了这两个定律的理论基础，即戏剧性逼真这一准则。从那时起，在英国，地点与时间一致律（有别于行动一致律）就被视为剧作家为取得戏剧性集中的特殊效果时可以采用的策略。

参阅：勒内·韦勒克所著的《近代文学批评史》第一卷"18世纪后期"（1955）；伯纳德·温伯格所著的《意大利文艺复兴时期的文学批评史》（1961）。

threnody：葬歌　102。

thrillers：惊险小说　85。

tone：基调　287。

Topographical Poetry：风景诗

风景诗，也叫**地域诗/乡土诗**，将对某一特定自然风光的描述，和与这一风光相联系或是其中的细节所暗示的历史、政治或道德思考融合到一起。塞缪尔·约翰逊在其"约翰·德纳姆小传"（1779）中，将风景诗的起源归功于德纳姆1642年写出的精美诗作《库珀山》；就像约翰逊定义这一*文类*的那样，"地域诗"的"基本主题是对某一特定风景进行诗意的描写，通过历史回顾或附带冥想对其加以润色"。参见：*英雄双韵体*中对《库珀山》中一段诗句的分析。

这一诗歌类型在18世纪广为流行。罗伯特·奥宾在《18世纪英国的风景诗》（1936）中列出了约两千个例子。其中许多都像《库珀山》一样属于**展望诗**，从一高点俯视，描述可见的景观；这方面有名的例子有约翰·戴尔的《格伦哥山》（1726）和托马斯·格雷的《伊顿公学远眺》（1747）。地域诗后来发展成为一种主要的浪漫形式：**描述–沉思式抒情诗**，它的特点是持续不断的意识流；感知、思考

a subtle interweaving of perceptions, thoughts, and feelings; and an integrated design. Early examples are Coleridge's "The Eolian Harp" (1796) and "Frost at Midnight" (1798), and Wordsworth's "Tintern Abbey" (1798); formal variants of the mode include Coleridge's "Dejection: An Ode" (1802) and Wordsworth's "Ode: Intimations of Immortality" (1807). See M. H. Abrams, "Structure and Style in the Greater Romantic Lyric," in *The Correspondent Breeze: Essays on English Romanticism*, 1984.

Related to the topographical poem is the **country house poem**, which had a brief vogue in the seventeenth century. This form describes and praises a rural estate and its grounds, and uses the occasion, by sometimes ingenious connections, to extol also its owner and the owner's family and family history. It was inaugurated by Aemilia Lanyer's "The Description of Cooke-ham" (1611) and Ben Jonson's "To Penshurst" (1616). Andrew Marvell's "Upon Appleton House" (1651) is the longest (776 lines), the most intricately wrought, and the wittiest of the country house poems.

topos (tŏp′ ŏs): **229**.

touchstone: A touchstone is a hard stone used to determine, by the streak left on it when rubbed by a piece of gold, whether the metal is pure gold, and if not, the degree to which it contains an alloy. The word was introduced into literary criticism by Matthew Arnold in "The Study of Poetry" (1880) to denote short but distinctive passages, selected from the writings of the greatest poets, which he used to determine the relative value of passages or poems which are compared to them. Arnold proposed this method of evaluation as a corrective for what he called the "fallacious" estimates of poems according to their "historic" importance in the development of literature, or else according to their "personal" appeal to an individual critic. As Arnold put it:

> There can be no more useful help for discovering what poetry belongs to the class of the truly excellent ... than to have always in one's mind lines and expressions of the great masters, and to apply them as a touchstone to other poetry.... If we have any tact we shall find them ... an infallible touchstone for detecting the presence or absence of high poetic quality, and also the degree of this quality, in all other poetry which we may place beside them.

The touchstones he proposed are passages from Homer, Dante, Shakespeare, and Milton, ranging in length from one to four lines. Two of his best-known touchstones are also the shortest: Dante's "In la sua volontade è nostra pace" ("In His will is our peace"; *Paradiso*, III. 85), and the close of Milton's description in *Paradise Lost*, IV, 271–2, of the loss to Ceres of her daughter Proserpine, "... which cost Ceres all that pain / To seek her through the world."

trace (in deconstruction): **78**.

和感情的微妙交织；一个合为一体的设计。这方面早期的例子是柯勒律治的《伊俄勒斯之琴》(1796)、《霜夜》(1798) 和华兹华斯的《丁登寺》(1798)；这一模式的正式变体包括柯勒律治的《忧郁颂》(1802) 和华兹华斯的《不朽颂》(1807)。参阅：M. H. 艾布拉姆斯所著的《相似的微风：英国浪漫主义文学论集》(1984) 中的"优秀浪漫主义抒情诗中的结构和风格"。

与风景诗相关的是**乡村诗**，17 世纪曾有一段时间比较流行。这种形式描述和歌颂郊区房屋及其院子，利用时机，有时则是巧妙的连接，也歌颂它的主人和主人的家庭和家族史。它创始于艾米利亚·兰叶的《库克姆即景》(1611) 和本·琼森的《致遍所食》(1616)。安德鲁·马韦尔的《在阿普尔顿的庄园上》(1651) 是最长的 (776 行)、最错综复杂的、最妙趣横生的乡村诗。

topos：常用主题　229。

Touchstone：试金石

试金石是一种坚硬的石块。人们从金子留在这种石块上的擦痕来判断这种金属是不是纯金，如果不是，它的含金量是多少。马修·阿诺德在其所写的文章"诗歌研究"(1880) 中首次将该词引入文学批评，用来指代选自伟大诗人作品中的简短但独具特色的篇章。阿诺德将这些篇章与其他篇章或诗歌进行比较，以此来确定其他篇章或诗歌的优秀之处。他提出，可以根据诗歌在文学发展中的"历史"重要性或根据诗歌对某一评论家的"个人"吸引力，将这一评价方法当做一种矫正物，用于矫正他所说的对诗歌作出的"谬误"评价。他指出：

> 判断诗歌是否属于佳作的最有效方法莫过于……自始至终牢记伟大诗人们的诗句及其表达法，并把它们当做检验其他诗歌的试金石……只要我们机敏，就会发现它们……是检验所有与之相比较的其他诗歌是否具备高雅诗歌的特质和检验这种特质的程度的准确无误的试金石。

阿诺德提议的试金石包括选自荷马、但丁、莎士比亚和弥尔顿创作的篇章。篇章长度从一行到四行不等。他提出的两个最著名也是篇幅最短的试金石是：但丁的"我们的宁静蕴藏于您的意愿"(《天堂篇》第三歌第 85 行) 和弥尔顿在《失乐园》第四卷第 271—272 行中描述刻瑞斯失去女儿普罗塞耳皮娜诗句的结尾"……使刻瑞斯耗尽心血/在世上将她寻找。"

trace (in deconstruction)：(解构主义中的) 踪迹　78。

traditional ballad: 23.

tragedy: The term is broadly applied to literary, and especially to dramatic, representations of serious actions which eventuate in a disastrous conclusion for the *protagonist* (the chief character). More precise and detailed discussions of the tragic form properly begin—although they should not end—with Aristotle's classic analysis in the *Poetics* (fourth century BC). Aristotle based his theory by reference to the only examples available to him, the tragedies of Greek dramatists such as Aeschylus, Sophocles, and Euripides. In the subsequent two thousand years and more, various new types of serious plots ending in a catastrophe have been developed—types that Aristotle had no way of foreseeing. The many attempts to stretch Aristotle's analysis to apply to later tragic forms serve merely to blur his critical categories and to obscure important differences among a diversity of plays, all of which have proved to be dramatically effective. When flexibly managed, however, Aristotle's discussions apply in some part to many tragic plots, and his analytic concepts serve as a suggestive starting point for identifying the distinctive attributes of various non-Aristotelian modes of tragic construction.

Aristotle defined tragedy as "the imitation of an action that is serious and also, as having magnitude, complete in itself," in the medium of poetic language and in the manner of dramatic rather than of narrative presentation, involving "incidents arousing pity and fear, wherewith to accomplish the catharsis of such emotions." (See *imitation*; and for an enlightening discussion of the emotions, "pity and fear," refer to Martha C. Nussbaum, "Tragedy and Self-Sufficiency: Plato and Aristotle on Fear and Pity," *Oxford Studies in Ancient Philosophy*, Vol. 10, 1992, 107–59.) Precisely how to interpret Aristotle's **catharsis**—which in Greek signifies "purgation," or "purification," or both—is much disputed. On two matters, however, many commentators agree. Aristotle in the first place sets out to account for the undeniable, though remarkable, fact that many tragic representations of suffering and defeat leave an audience feeling not depressed, but relieved, or even exalted. In the second place, Aristotle uses this distinctive effect on the reader, which he calls "the pleasure of pity and fear," as the basic way to distinguish the tragic from comic or other forms, and he regards the dramatist's aim to produce this effect in the highest degree as the principle that determines the choice and moral qualities of the tragic protagonist and the organization of the tragic plot.

Accordingly, Aristotle says that the **tragic hero** will most effectively evoke both our pity and terror if he is neither thoroughly good nor thoroughly bad but a mixture of both; and also that this tragic effect will be stronger if the hero is "better than we are," in the sense that he is of higher than ordinary moral worth. Such a man is exhibited as suffering a change in fortune from happiness to misery because of his mistaken choice of an action, to which he is led by his **hamartia**—his "error" or "mistake of judgment" or, as it is often, although misleadingly and less literally translated, his **tragic flaw**. (One common form of hamartia in Greek tragedies was **hubris**, that "pride" or overweening self-confidence which leads a protagonist to disregard a divine

traditional ballad：传统民谣　23。

Tragedy：悲剧

　　这个术语泛指用文学的形式，尤其是用戏剧的形式，来表现造成主人公（主要人物）灾难性结局的严肃行动。对这种悲剧形式更为准确详细的讨论，恰如其分地说是始于——但不应终止于——亚里士多德在《诗学》（公元前4世纪）中所作的经典分析。亚里士多德的理论基于他对自己所能获取的范例的归纳之上，如希腊剧作家埃斯库罗斯、索福克勒斯和欧里庇德斯等人的悲剧。随后两千多年间，剧作家们发展了许多新颖的以灾难收场的严肃情节类型——这些类型是亚里士多德所无法预见的。牵强地把亚里士多德的分析方法运用于后世悲剧形式的许多尝试，只会混淆亚里士多德对戏剧的批评分类，模糊各种不同戏剧类型之间的重要区别；这些戏剧类型都被证明具有显著的戏剧效果。不过，如果能灵活运用亚里士多德的分析方法，那么亚里士多德的论述在一些方面仍然适用于许多悲剧情节，他的分析概念可以作为一个具有启发性的出发点，有助于辨认各种非亚里士多德悲剧结构模式的种种差异。

　　亚里士多德将悲剧定义为"对一个严肃行动的模仿，由于这一行动具有一定的长度，所以自身是完整的"，其媒介是诗的语言，表现方式是戏剧性的，而非叙事性的，涉及"引起怜悯与恐惧的事件，并以此达到情感上的陶冶。"（参见：**摹仿**；玛莎·C.努斯鲍姆所写的文章"悲剧与自足性：亚里士多德和柏拉图论怜悯与恐惧"，对"怜悯与恐惧"这一情感进行了富有启发意义的讨论，文章载于《牛津古典哲学研究》1992年第10卷第107—159页。）对如何准确解释亚里士多德提出的**情感陶冶**——希腊语中表示"净化""纯化"，或两种意思兼有——存在很大争议。不过，许多评论家都对下面两个问题有相同看法。首先，亚里士多德力图说明一个不可否认但值得注意的事实：许多表现苦难和失败的悲剧表演给观众留下的并不是情绪上的压抑，而是情感的宣泄乃至情感的升华。其次，亚里士多德把他所谓的"怜悯与恐惧的愉悦"这一作用于观众的独特效果，作为区分悲剧与喜剧或其他形式的基本方式，并把剧作家旨在最大限度地创造这种效果的努力，视为决定悲剧主人公的选择和道德品质、决定悲剧情节组织结构的原则。

　　因此，亚里士多德提出，如果**悲剧性英雄**既非完美无缺，又非邪恶至极，而是二者兼有，那他就能最有效地激发起我们的怜悯和恐惧；如果悲剧主人公"比我们好些"，即他比一般道德价值更高尚些，悲剧效果就会更加强烈。这样的人物由于错误地选择了某一行动而遭受从幸福到悲惨的命运转变，这种错误的选择是由于他的"**判断错误**"——他的"错误"或"误判"，或称为**悲剧性缺陷**（该词经常不是严格的字面对译）所造成的。[古希腊悲剧中常见的一种判断错误是**傲睨神明**，即导致主人公无视圣谕或违反某一重要道德法则的"骄傲"或过于自信。]

warning or to violate an important moral law.) The tragic hero, like Oedipus in Sophocles' *Oedipus the King*, moves us to pity because, since he is not an evil man, his misfortune is greater than he deserves; but he moves us also to fear, because we recognize similar possibilities of error in our own lesser and fallible selves. Aristotle grounds his analysis of "the very structure and incidents of the play" on the same principle; the plot, he says, which will most effectively evoke "tragic pity and fear" is one in which the events develop through complication to a *catastrophe* in which there occurs (often by an *anagnorisis*, or discovery of facts hitherto unknown to the hero) a sudden *peripeteia*, or reversal in his fortune from happiness to disaster. (See *plot*.)

Authors in the Middle Ages lacked direct knowledge either of classical tragedies or of Aristotle's *Poetics*. **Medieval tragedies** are simply the story of a person of high status who, whether deservedly or not, is brought from prosperity to wretchedness by an unpredictable turn of the wheel of fortune. The short narratives in "The Monk's Tale" of *The Canterbury Tales* (late fourteenth century) are all, in Chaucer's own term, "tragedies" of this kind. With the Elizabethan era came both the beginning and the acme of dramatic tragedy in England. The tragedies of this period owed much to the native religious drama, the *miracle* and *morality plays*, which had developed independently of classical influence, but with a crucial contribution from the Roman writer Seneca (first century), whose dramas got to be widely known earlier than those of the Greek tragedians.

Senecan tragedy was written to be recited rather than acted; but to English playwrights, who thought that these tragedies had been intended for the stage, they provided the model for an organized five-act play with a complex plot and an elaborately formal style of dialogue. Senecan drama, in the Elizabethan Age, had two main lines of development. One of these consisted of academic tragedies written in close imitation of the Senecan model, including the use of a *chorus*, and usually constructed according to the rules of the *three unities*, which had been elaborated by Italian critics of the sixteenth century; the earliest English example was Thomas Sackville and Thomas Norton's *Gorboduc* (1562). The other and much more important development was written for the popular stage, and is called the **revenge tragedy**, or (in its most sensational form) the **tragedy of blood**. This type of play derived from Seneca's favorite materials of murder, revenge, ghosts, mutilation, and carnage, but while Seneca had relegated such matters to long reports of offstage actions by messengers, Elizabethan dramatists usually represented them on stage to satisfy the appetite of the contemporary audience for violence and horror. Thomas Kyd's *The Spanish Tragedy* (1586) established this popular form; its subject is a murder and the quest for vengeance, and it includes a ghost, insanity, suicide, a play-within-a-play, sensational incidents, and a gruesomely bloody ending. Christopher Marlowe's *The Jew of Malta* (c. 1592) and Shakespeare's early play *Titus Andronicus* (c. 1590) are in this mode; and from this lively but unlikely prototype came one of the greatest of tragedies, *Hamlet*, as well as John Webster's fine horror plays of 1612–13, *The Duchess of Malfi* and *The White Devil*.

悲剧性英雄，如索福克勒斯《俄狄浦斯王》中的俄狄浦斯，引起我们的怜悯，这是因为他不是一个坏人，他本不该遭受那样大的不幸。但他又使我们感到恐惧，因为我们从我们自己更加无足轻重、易犯错误的身上看到犯类似错误的可能性。亚里士多德对"戏剧结构和事件"的分析也建立在同样的原则基础上。他指出，当情节中的事件经过错综复杂的纠葛发展到*结局*时（经常是通过*发现*，或通过发现主人公前所未知的事实）主人公的命运突然发生*突变*，或是他的命运从幸福到灾难的逆转，这种情节最能有效地唤起"悲剧性怜悯和恐惧"。（参见：*情节*。）

中世纪作家缺乏对古典悲剧的直接了解，也缺少对亚里士多德《诗学》的直接了解。**中世纪悲剧**只是简单地描述某位地位显赫的人物，命运之轮中无法预见的改变使他遭受从兴旺到不幸的厄运，不论他是否罪有应得。用乔叟自己的话来说，在《坎特伯雷故事集》（14世纪末）中"僧侣讲的故事"里，所有简短的故事都是这种"悲剧"。伊丽莎白时代是英国戏剧性悲剧兴起并达到全盛的时期。这一时期的悲剧大都源自英国本土的宗教戏剧：*奇迹剧*、*道德剧*；宗教戏剧不受古典戏剧的影响独立发展起来，但对英国悲剧的发展贡献最大的是古罗马作家塞内加（1世纪），他的戏剧早在古希腊悲剧之前便已广为人知。

塞内加式悲剧用于朗诵而非表演。然而，英国的剧作家却认为这些悲剧就是为了舞台表演而创作的。他们设计了五幕的戏剧结构，情节复杂，对话风格精巧正式。伊丽莎白时期的塞内加式戏剧有两条发展主线。其一由学院式悲剧组成，严格模仿塞内加的悲剧模式，包括采用合唱队，通常根据16世纪意大利批评家详尽阐述过的三一律规则构建而成。托马斯·萨克维尔与托马斯·诺顿共同创作的《戈尔伯德克悲剧》（1562）是英国最早的学院式悲剧。另一条主线的发展更为重要，是为大众剧场而创作的，被称为**复仇悲剧**或（以其最令人惊骇的形式）被称为**流血悲剧**。这类戏剧选取塞内加钟爱的谋杀、复仇、鬼怪、分尸和屠杀等题材；但塞内加把这类题材交由信使用长篇大论加以陈述，处理为观众看不到的舞台外行动；而伊丽莎白时期的剧作家则常在舞台上把它们表演出来，以满足当时观众对暴力和恐怖的兴趣。托马斯·基德的《西班牙的悲剧》（1586）开创了这种大众化戏剧形式；该剧以谋杀和复仇的欲望为主题，剧情包含鬼魂、疯狂、自杀、戏中戏、耸人听闻的事件和恐怖的血腥结局。克里斯托弗·马洛的《马耳他的犹太人》（约1592）和莎士比亚的《泰特斯·安特洛尼克斯》（约1590）也属于这种模式。这种生机勃勃但不大可靠的戏剧原型，也孕育了最伟大的悲剧之一：《哈姆雷特》，以及约翰·韦伯斯特在1612—1613年间创作的杰出恐怖剧《马尔菲公爵夫人》和《白魔》。

Many major tragedies in the flowering time between 1585 and 1625, by Marlowe, Shakespeare, George Chapman, Webster, Sir Francis Beaumont and John Fletcher, and Philip Massinger, deviate radically from the Aristotelian norm. Shakespeare's *Othello* is one of the few plays which accords closely with Aristotle's basic concepts of the tragic hero and plot. The hero of *Macbeth*, however, is not a good man who commits a tragic error, but an ambitious man who knowingly turns great gifts to evil purposes and therefore, although he retains something of our sympathy by his courage and self-insight, deserves his destruction at the hands of his morally superior antagonists. Shakespeare's *Richard III* presents first the success, then the ruin, of a protagonist who is thoroughly malign, yet arouses in us a reluctant admiration by his intelligence and imaginative power and by the shameless candor with which he glories in his ambition and malice. Most Shakespearean tragedies, like Elizabethan tragedies generally, also depart radically from Aristotle's paradigm by introducing humorous characters, incidents, or scenes, called *comic relief*, which were in various ways and degrees made relevant to the tragic plot and conducive to enriching the tragic effect. There developed also in this age the mixed mode called *tragicomedy*, a popular non-Aristotelian form which produced a number of artistic successes. And later in the seventeenth century the Restoration Period produced the curious genre, a cross between epic and tragedy, called *heroic tragedy*.

Until the close of the seventeenth century almost all tragedies were written in verse and had as protagonists men of high rank whose fate affected the fortunes of a state. A few minor Elizabethan tragedies, such as *A Yorkshire Tragedy* (of uncertain authorship), had as the chief character a man of the lower class, but it remained for eighteenth-century writers to popularize the **bourgeois** or **domestic tragedy**, which was written in prose and presented a protagonist from the middle or lower social ranks who suffers a commonplace or domestic disaster. George Lillo's *The London Merchant: or, The History of George Barnwell* (1731), about a merchant's apprentice who succumbs to a heartless courtesan and comes to a bad end by robbing his employer and murdering his uncle, is still read, at least in college courses.

Since that time most of the successful tragedies have been in prose and represent middle-class, or occasionally even working-class, heroes and heroines. The great and highly influential Norwegian playwright, Henrik Ibsen, wrote in the latter part of the nineteenth century tragedies in prose, many of which (such as *A Doll's House, Ghosts, An Enemy of the People*) revolve around an issue of general social or political significance. (See *problem play*.) One of the more notable modern tragedies, Arthur Miller's *Death of a Salesman* (1949), relies for its tragic seriousness on the degree to which Willy Loman, in his bewildered defeat by life, is representative of the ordinary man whose aspirations reflect the false values of a commercial society; the effect on the audience is one of compassionate understanding rather than of tragic pity and terror. The protagonists of some recent tragedies are not heroic but antiheroic, in that they manifest a character that is at an extreme from the dignity and courage of the protagonists in traditional dramas (see *antihero*); while in

在1585—1625年间这一短暂的戏剧繁荣时期，马洛、莎士比亚、乔治·查普曼、韦伯斯特、弗朗西斯·博蒙特爵士与约翰·弗莱彻，以及菲利普·马辛杰创作的许多重要悲剧与亚里士多德提出的准则大相径庭。严格遵循亚里士多德提出的悲剧性英雄与悲剧情节基本观念的戏剧为数极少，莎士比亚的《奥赛罗》便是其中一部。但是，《麦克白》中的英雄并不是一位犯了悲剧性过失的好人，而是一个野心勃勃的人。他有意利用自己的伟大天赋去达到邪恶的目的；所以，尽管他的勇敢无畏和自知之明获取了我们的某种同情，但他还是罪有应得地毁灭于在道义上优越于他的对手手中。莎士比亚的《理查三世》首先展现了主人公获得的成功，然后再表现他的毁灭；尽管主人公心狠手辣，但他的睿智，他的想象力，他对自己引以为豪的野心与狠毒的无耻直言都唤起我们极不情愿的钦佩。与伊丽莎白时期大多数悲剧一样，莎士比亚的大部分悲剧也引入了幽默诙谐的人物、事件或情景，即所谓的*喜剧性调剂*，也背离了亚里士多德的悲剧范式；这些喜剧性调剂或多或少都与悲剧情节有关，为的是增强悲剧效果。这一时期还产生了一种混合的模式：*悲喜剧*。这种非亚里士多德式的流行戏剧形式，产生了许多艺术上相当成功的作品。随后，在17世纪的王政复辟时期，兴起了一种奇特的体裁，它介于史诗与悲剧之间，被称为*英雄悲剧*。

在17世纪末之前，几乎所有的悲剧都是用诗体形式创作的，都以出身高贵的人物作为剧中的主人公，他们的命运影响了整个国家的命运。伊丽莎白时期少数次要的悲剧，如《约克郡的悲剧》（作者不详），以下层阶级的人物作为剧中的主要人物，但它使18世纪的剧作家普及了**市民悲剧**或**家庭悲剧**。这种悲剧用散文体写成，剧中主人公来自社会中下层且遭受了平凡的或家庭的灾难。乔治·李洛的《伦敦商人，或乔治·邦威尔传》（1731）就描述了一位商人的学徒怎样落入一个无情的交际花的圈套，最终陷入盗窃雇主、杀害叔父的悲惨结局。时至今日，人们至少在大学课程里还会阅读这出悲剧。

自那时起，最成功的悲剧都是以散文形式创作的，表现了中产阶级，有时甚至是劳动阶级的男女主人公。19世纪后半叶，影响深远的伟大挪威剧作家亨里克·易卜生用散文体创作的许多悲剧（如《玩偶之家》《群魔》《人民公敌》等），都围绕着具有普遍社会或政治意义的事件展开。（参见：*问题剧*。）现代更为著名的悲剧之一是阿瑟·米勒创作的《推销员之死》（1949）；这部戏剧的悲剧严肃性就在于，威利·洛曼在生活中遭受了匪夷所思的失败而成为普通人代表的深刻程度。这种普通人的抱负反映了商业社会虚伪的价值观，对观众造成的效果是一种深表同情的理解，而不是悲剧性的怜悯与恐惧。近代一些悲剧的主人公不是英雄式的，而是反英雄的，因为他们展现的性格特征与传统戏剧中主人公的尊严高尚、勇敢无畏截然不同（参见：*反英雄*）；但在近代的一些作品中，

some recent works, tragic effects involve elements that were once specific to the genre of farce (see literature of the *absurd* and *black comedy*).

Tragedy since World War I has also been innovative in other ways, including experimentation with new versions of ancient tragic forms. Eugene O'Neill's *Mourning Becomes Electra* (1931), for example, is an adaptation of Aeschylus' *Oresteia*, with the locale shifted from Greece to New England, the poetry altered to what is for the most part rather flat prose, and the tragedy of fate converted into a tragedy of the psychological compulsions of a family trapped in a tangle of Freudian complexes (see *psychoanalysis*). T. S. Eliot's *Murder in the Cathedral* (1935) is a tragic drama which, like Greek tragedy, is written in verse and has a chorus, but also incorporates elements of two early Christian forms, the medieval *miracle play* (dealing with the martyrdom of a saint) and the medieval *morality play*. A recent tendency, especially in some critics associated with *new historicism*, has been to interpret traditional tragedies primarily in political terms, as incorporating in the problems and catastrophe of the tragic individual an indirect representation of contemporary social or ideological dilemmas and crises. See Froma I. Zeitlin and John J. Winkler, eds., *Nothing to Do with Dionysos? Athenian Drama in Its Social Context* (1990) and Linda Kintz, *The Subject's Tragedy: Political Poetics, Feminist Theory, and Drama* (1992).

See *genre*, and refer to A. C. Bradley, *Shakespearean Tragedy* (1904); H. D. F. Kitto, *Greek Tragedy* (rev. 1954); Elder Olson, *Tragedy and the Theory of Drama* (1961); George Steiner, *The Death of Tragedy* (1961); R. B. Sewall, ed., *Tragedy: Modern Essays in Criticism* (1963); Adrian Poole, *Tragedy: A Very Short Introduction* (2005). For other theoretical treatments of tragedy, see Linda Bamber, *Comic Women, Tragic Men: A Study of Gender and Genre in Shakespeare* (1982); and Catherine Belsey, *The Subject of Tragedy: Identity and Difference in Renaissance Drama* (1985). Richard H. Palmer, *Tragedy and Tragic Theory: An Analytical Guide* (1992), is a useful survey of contested issues in the theory and criticism of tragedy, with many quotations by theorists from the ancient Greeks to the present. For references to *tragedy* in other entries, see pages *335, 411*. See also *heroic drama; tragic irony; tragicomedy*.

tragedy of blood: 409.

tragic flaw: 408; *300*.

tragic hero: 408.

tragic irony: 186.

tragicomedy: A type of *Elizabethan* and *Jacobean* drama which intermingled the standard characters and subject matter and the typical plot forms of *tragedy* and *comedy*. Thus, the important agents in tragicomedy included both people of high degree and people of low degree, even though, according to the reigning critical theory of that time, only upper-class characters were appropriate to

悲剧效果却包含了闹剧样式所特有的因素（参见：*荒诞派文学*、*黑色喜剧*）。

自从第一次世界大战以来，悲剧在其他方面也有创新，包括对古代各种悲剧类型的实验。如尤金·奥尼尔的《哀悼》(1931)就改编自埃斯库罗斯的《俄瑞斯忒亚》；戏剧的场景从希腊转移到了新英格兰，诗文形式改成了相当直白的散文体；命运的悲剧转换成陷入弗洛伊德情结（参见：*精神分析*）的一家人由于心理压抑而酿成的悲剧。T. S. 艾略特的《大教堂凶杀案》(1935)这出悲剧与希腊悲剧类似，不仅采用了诗体和合唱队，还融合了两种早期的基督教戏剧形式的元素：中世纪的*奇迹剧*（表现圣人的殉教事迹）和*道德剧*。近来的文学批评，尤其是与*新历史主义*有关的批评家，倾向于主要用政治术语来阐释传统悲剧，因为在悲剧性个人的困扰与灾难中，融入了对当代社会或意识形态的困境与危机的间接表现。参阅：弗罗马·I. 蔡特林与约翰·J. 温克勒合编的《与狄奥尼索斯无关？——社会背景中的雅典戏剧》(1990)，琳达·金茨所著的《主体的悲剧：政治诗学、女性主义理论和戏剧》(1992)。

参见：*文学类型*；参阅：A. C. 布拉德利所著的《莎士比亚悲剧》(1904)；H. D. F. 基托所著的《希腊悲剧》(1954年修订版)；埃尔德·奥尔森所著的《悲剧与戏剧理论》(1961)；乔治·斯坦纳所著的《悲剧之死》(1961)；R. B. 休厄尔主编的《悲剧：现代批评文集》(1963)；阿德里安·普尔所著的《悲剧简介》(2005)。近来有关悲剧的理论论述，参阅：琳达·巴姆伯所著的《喜剧女性，悲剧男性：性别研究和莎士比亚作品中的文学类型》(1982)；凯瑟琳·贝尔西所著的《悲剧的主体：文艺复兴戏剧中的身份与差异》(1985)。理查德·H. 帕默所著的《悲剧与悲剧理论：分析指南》(1992)，有效地概述了悲剧理论与批评中尚有争议的问题，并引用了古希腊至今许多理论家的观点。其他条目中提及"悲剧"的地方，参见第335、411页。另外也可参见：*英雄剧*、*悲剧性反讽*、*悲喜剧*。

tragedy of blood：流血悲剧　　409。

tragic flaw：悲剧性缺陷　　408；*300*。

tragic hero：悲剧性英雄　　408。

tragic irony：悲剧性反讽　　186。

Tragicomedy：悲喜剧

悲喜剧是*伊丽莎白时期和詹姆斯一世时期*的一种戏剧类型，它融合了*悲剧*与*喜剧*中标准的人物、题材与情节模式。因此，悲喜剧中的重要角色既包括出身高贵的人物又有出身低微的平民，虽然依据当时占统治地位的批评理论，只有上层

tragedy, while members of the middle and lower classes were the proper subject solely of comedy; see *decorum*. Also, tragicomedy represented a serious action which threatened a tragic disaster to the protagonist, yet, by an abrupt reversal of circumstance, turned out happily. As John Fletcher wrote in his preface to *The Faithful Shepherdess* (c. 1610), tragicomedy "wants [that is, lacks] deaths, which is enough to make it no tragedy, yet brings some near it, which is enough to make it no comedy, which must be a representation of familiar people.... A god is as lawful in [tragicomedy] as in a tragedy, and mean [that is, middle-class] people as in a comedy." (See *comedy* and *tragedy*.)

Shakespeare's *Merchant of Venice* is by these criteria a tragicomedy, because it mingles people of the aristocracy with lower-class characters (such as the Jewish merchant Shylock and the clown Launcelot Gobbo), and also because the developing threat of death to Antonio is suddenly reversed at the end by Portia's ingenious casuistry in the trial scene. Francis Beaumont and John Fletcher in *Philaster*, and numerous other plays on which they collaborated from about 1606 to 1613, inaugurated a mode of tragicomedy that employs a romantic and fast-moving plot of love, jealousy, treachery, intrigue, and disguises, and ends in a melodramatic reversal of fortune for the protagonists, who had hitherto seemed headed for a tragic *catastrophe*. Shakespeare wrote his late plays *Cymbeline* and *The Winter's Tale*, between 1609 and 1611, in this very popular mode of the tragicomic *romance*. The name "tragicomedy" is sometimes also applied more loosely to plays with double plots, one serious and the other comic; see *double plots*, under *plot*.

Refer to E. M. Waith, *The Pattern of Tragicomedy in Beaumont and Fletcher* (1952); M. T. Herrick, *Tragicomedy* (1955). Gordon McMullan and Jonathan Hope have edited a collection of essays on *The Politics of Tragicomedy: Shakespeare and After* (1992).

Transcendental Club: 412.

transcendental signified: 78.

Transcendentalism in America: A philosophical and literary movement, centered in Concord and Boston, which was prominent in the intellectual and cultural life of New England from 1836 until just before the Civil War. It was inaugurated in 1836 by a Unitarian discussion group that came to be called the **Transcendental Club**. In the seven years or so that the group met at various houses, it included at one time or another Ralph Waldo Emerson, Bronson Alcott, Frederick Henry Hedge, W. E. Channing and W. H. Channing, Theodore Parker, Margaret Fuller, Elizabeth Peabody, George Ripley, Nathaniel Hawthorne, Henry Thoreau, and Jones Very. A quarterly periodical *The Dial* (1840–44) printed many of the early essays, poems, and reviews by the Transcendentalists.

Transcendentalism was neither a systematic nor a sharply definable philosophy, but rather an intellectual mode and emotional mood that was expressed by diverse, and in some instances rather eccentric, voices. Modern historians

阶级的人物才适合于悲剧的主题，而中下层阶级成员只适合于喜剧主题；参见：*仪轨*。此外，悲喜剧中展示的严肃行动，往往预示着主人公的悲剧性灾难。但因环境突然逆转，主人公却有一个幸福的结局。就像约翰·弗莱彻在剧作《忠实的牧羊女》（约1610）的序言中所写的那样，悲喜剧"需要（即缺少）死亡，这就足以使之不能成为悲剧，但又让剧中的人物濒临死亡，这也足以使之不能成为喜剧，而这必定表现了我们所熟悉的人……[悲喜剧里]神的存在和悲剧里神的存在一样合情合理；悲喜剧里普通人物的存在也和喜剧中普通（即，中产阶级）人物的存在一样合乎情理。"（参见：*喜剧*、*悲剧*。）

按照这些标准，莎士比亚的《威尼斯商人》就是一出悲喜剧，因为它把出身高贵的人物和出身卑微的人物（如犹太商人夏洛克、小丑隆斯洛特·戈博）混合在一出戏内，也因为在结局审判的这场戏中，安东尼奥日益面临的死亡威胁由于鲍西娅的机智决疑而突然逆转。弗朗西斯·博蒙特与约翰·弗莱彻在《菲拉斯特》以及两人在1603—1613年间合力创作的许多戏剧中创立了一种悲喜剧模式。这种模式采用爱情、嫉妒、背叛、阴谋和伪装等迅速发展的传奇性情节。虽然剧中主人公似乎从一开始就面临着悲剧性的*结局*，但整出戏却以主人公命运的传奇性逆转而告终。莎士比亚在1609—1611年间创作的后期剧作《辛白林》和《冬天的故事》，都采用了这种非常流行的悲喜*传奇*剧模式。"悲喜剧"这一名称有时也用来表示具有双重情节的戏剧，即一种是严肃情节，而另一种是滑稽情节。参见：*情节*中的*双重情节*。

参阅：E. M. 韦思所著的《博蒙特与弗莱彻的悲喜剧模式》(1952)；M. T. 赫里克所著的《悲喜剧》(1955)。戈登·马克穆伦与乔纳森·霍普合编的近代论文选集：《莎士比亚以来的悲喜剧策略》(1992)。

Transcendental Club：超验主义俱乐部　　412。
transcendental signified：超验所指　　78。
Transcendentalism in America：美国的超验主义

美国的超验主义是一场以康科德和波士顿两地为中心的哲学与文学运动。从1836年到南北战争即将爆发之前，这场运动一直在新英格兰的知识文化生活中占据显著地位。这场运动是由一个后来被称为**超验主义俱乐部**的神体一位派讨论小组在1836年发起的。在七年左右的时间里，这个小组在不同的家庭中聚会，成员曾经包括拉尔夫·沃尔多·爱默生、布朗森·阿尔科特、弗雷德里克·亨利·赫奇、W. E. 钱宁与W. H. 钱宁、西奥多·帕克、玛格丽特·富勒、伊丽莎白·皮博迪、乔治·里普利、纳撒尼尔·霍桑、亨利·梭罗和琼斯·维里。季刊《日晷》(1840—1844)上发表了许多超验主义者早期的随笔、诗歌与评论。

超验主义既不是一门系统哲学，也不是一门能严格定义的哲学，而是通过形形色色、有时则是相当怪异的声音表达的一种思想模式和情绪。研究这场运动的

of the movement tend to take as its central exponents Emerson (especially in *Nature*, "The American Scholar," the Divinity School Address, "The Over-Soul," and "Self Reliance") and Thoreau (especially in *Walden* and his journals). The term "transcendental," as Emerson pointed out in his lecture "The Transcendentalist" (1841), was taken from the writings of the German philosopher Immanuel Kant (1724–1804). Kant had confined the expression "transcendental knowledge" to the cognizance of those forms and categories—such as space, time, quantity, causality—which, in his view, are imposed on whatever we perceive by the constitution of the human mind. Emerson and others, however, extended the concept of transcendental knowledge, in a way whose validity Kant had specifically denied, to include an intuitive cognizance of moral and other truths that transcend the limits of sense experience. The intellectual antecedents of American Transcendentalism, in addition to Kant, were many and diverse, and included post-Kantian German Idealists, the English thinkers Samuel Taylor Coleridge and Thomas Carlyle (themselves exponents of forms of German Idealism), Plato and Neoplatonists, the occult Swedish theologian Emanuel Swedenborg, and some varieties of Asian philosophy.

What the various Transcendentalists had in common was less what they proposed than what they were reacting against. By and large, they were opposed to rigid rationalism; to eighteenth-century empirical philosophy of the school of John Locke, which derived all knowledge from sense impressions; to highly formalized religion, especially the Calvinist orthodoxy of New England; and to the social conformity, materialism, and commercialism that they found increasingly dominant in American life. Among the counterviews that were affirmed by Transcendentalists, especially Emerson, were confidence in the validity of a mode of knowledge that is grounded in feeling and intuition, and a consequent tendency to accept what, to logical reasoning, might seem contradictions; an ethics of individualism that stressed self-trust, self-reliance, and self-sufficiency; a turn away from modern society, with its getting and spending, to the scenes and objects of the natural world, which were regarded both as physical entities and as correspondences to aspects of the human spirit (see *correspondences*); and, in place of a formal or doctrinal religion, a faith in a divine "Principle," or "Spirit," or "Soul" (Emerson's "Over-Soul") in which both humanity and the cosmos participate. This omnipresent Spirit, Emerson said, constitutes the "Unity within which every man's particular being is contained and made one with all other"; it manifests itself to human consciousness as influxes of inspired insights; and it is the source of the profoundest truths and the necessary condition of all moral and spiritual development.

Walden (1854) records how Thoreau tested his distinctive and radically individualist version of Transcendental values by withdrawing from societal complexities and distractions to a life of solitude and self-reliance in a natural setting at Walden Pond. He simplified his material wants to those he could satisfy by the bounty of the woods and lake or could provide by his own labor, attended minutely to natural objects both for their inherent interest and as correlatives to the mind of the observer, and devoted his leisure to

现代历史学家常将爱默生（尤其是《论自然》中的文章"美国学者""神学院献辞""论超灵""论自助"）和梭罗（尤其是《瓦尔登湖》与他的日志）视为这场运动的主要倡导者。爱默生在"超验主义者"（1841）这篇讲稿中指出，"超验的"一词源自德国哲学家伊曼纽尔·康德（1724—1804）。康德曾将"超验知识"局限于某些形式与范畴的认知，如空间、时间、量、因果关系等，在他看来，这些形式与范畴被强加于我们通过人类智力结构所感知的任何事物之上。但爱默生等人则扩展了超验知识的概念，认为它还包括超越人类感知经验局限对道德和其他真理的直觉认识；康德曾明确否认这种观点的正确性。除了康德，影响美国超验主义的思想先行者人数众多，形形色色，包括后康德主义的德国唯心主义者，英国思想家塞缪尔·泰勒·柯勒律治与托马斯·卡莱尔（他们自己也是德国唯心主义形式的倡导者），柏拉图与新柏拉图主义者，神秘的瑞典神学家伊曼纽尔·斯维登堡，以及一些形形色色的亚洲哲学。

不同超验主义者的共同之处更多体现在他们反对的事物上，而非他们提出的观点上。总体来说，超验主义者反对严格的理性主义；反对18世纪约翰·洛克学派的经验主义哲学，该学派从感知印象中提取所有的知识；反对高度形式化的宗教，尤其是新英格兰的加尔文主义的正统观念；反对他们发现在美国生活中日益占据主导地位的社会一致性、物质主义与商业主义。超验主义者，尤其是爱默生，申明的反对观点包括：相信建立在感觉与直觉基础上的知识模式的正确性，其结果便是接受对逻辑推理而言似乎是矛盾的事物；强调自我信任、自助、自足的个人主义道德规范；远离攫取和挥霍的现代社会，回归自然世界的情景与物体中，这些情景与物体被视为物质事实，与人类的精神方面相对应（参见：*对应*）；以及信仰人类与宇宙万物共同参与的天赐"原理"，或"精神"，或"灵魂"（爱默生的"超灵"），而不信仰形式化或教条化的宗教。爱默生提出，这种无所不在的精神，构成了一种"将每个人的特殊存在包含其中并使之与所有其他存在相互联系的统一体"；它在人类意识中表现为在灵感支配下的悟性的涌动；它是最深邃的真理的来源，是所有道德与精神发展的必要条件。

《瓦尔登湖》（1854）记录了梭罗如何检验自己独特的、极端个人主义的超验主义价值观；他远离社会的复杂与纷扰，回归瓦尔登湖畔的自然背景中，过着离群索居的自助生活。他简化了物质需要，利用森林湖泊富饶的物产或自身的劳动来满足物质需求，时常关注自然物体内在的趣味及其与观察者心灵之间的关联；

reading, meditation, and writing. In his nonconformity to any social and legal requirements that violated his moral sense, he chose a day in jail rather than pay his poll tax to a government that supported the Mexican War and slavery. Brook Farm, on the other hand, was a short-lived experiment (1841–47) by more community-oriented Transcendentalists who established a commune on the professed principle of the equal sharing of work, pay, and cultural benefits. Hawthorne, who lived there for a while, later wrote about Brook Farm, with considerable skepticism about both its goals and practices, in *The Blithedale Romance* (1852).

The Transcendental movement, with its optimism about the indwelling divinity, self-sufficiency, and high potentialities of human nature, did not survive the crisis of the Civil War and its aftermath; and Herman Melville, like Nathaniel Hawthorne, satirized aspects of Transcendentalism in his fiction. Some of its basic concepts and values, however, were assimilated by Walt Whitman, were later echoed in writings by Henry James and other major American authors, and continue to re-emerge, in both liberal and radical modes, in latter-day America. The voice of Thoreau, for example, however distorted, can be recognized still in some doctrines of the *counterculture* of the 1960s and later.

See *periods of American literature*, and refer to F. O. Matthiessen, *American Renaissance* (1941); the anthology edited, together with commentary, by Perry Miller, *The Transcendentalists* (1950); Joel Porte, *Emerson and Thoreau: Transcendentalists in Conflict* (1966); Lawrence Buell, *Literary Transcendentalism: Style and Vision in the American Renaissance* (1973). For a collection of writings on transcendentalism, see Perry Miller, ed., *Transcendentalists: An Anthology* (1971), and Joel Myerson, ed., *Transcendentalism: A Reader* (2000). See also *Encyclopedia of Transcendentalism*, ed. Wesley T. Mott (1996).

transformational linguistics: 198.

transformational-generative grammar: 198.

travesty: 39.

trickster: 9.

trimeter (trĭm′ ĕter): **219.**

triple rhyme: 349.

triplet: 375.

trochaic (trōkā′ ĭk): **218.**

trope (figurative) (trōp): **130.**

梭罗利用空闲时光进行阅读、沉思与写作。他不愿遵从违背自己道德观的社会要求和法律规定，宁愿坐一天牢也不愿向政府交纳支持墨西哥战争和奴隶制的人头税；另一方面，布卢克农场（1841—1847）则是那些对群居更感兴趣的超验主义者进行的一次为期短暂的试验；这些超验主义者建立公社的公开宗旨是同工同酬和平等分享文化利益。霍桑曾在布卢克农场居住过一段时间，随后创作了关于布卢克农场的《福谷传奇》（1852），书中表现出作者对布卢克农场的目标与实践深感怀疑。

超验主义运动及其对人类本性内在的神圣、自足、巨大潜能所持的乐观态度，并没有在南北战争及战后的危机中幸存下来。与霍桑一样，梅尔维尔也在自己的小说中讽刺了超验主义的某些方面。但是，沃尔特·惠特曼则吸收了超验主义的一些基本观念与价值观；后来，亨利·詹姆斯和其他一些美国主要作家也在作品中体现了这些基本观念与价值观。在当今美国，超验主义的一些基本观念与价值观，继续以自由或激进的模式重新出现。例如，我们仍然能在1960年代以来的反文化运动的某些学说中发现梭罗的观点，不论这些观点受到怎样的歪曲。

参见：*美国文学各时期的划分*；参阅：F. O. 马西森所著的《美国文艺复兴》（1941）；佩里·米勒带有评注的选集《超验主义者们》（1950）；乔尔·波特所著的《爱默生与梭罗：有分歧的超验主义者》（1966）；劳伦斯·布伊尔所著的《文学超验主义：美国文艺复兴的风格与想象力》（1973）；已编辑出版的文集及评论，参阅：佩里·米勒编选的《超验主义者选集》（1971）和乔尔·迈尔森编选的《超验主义读本》（2000）。另外也可参阅：韦斯利·T. 莫特主编的《超验主义百科全书》（1996）。

transformational linguistics：转换语言学　198。

transformational-generative grammar：转换生成语法　198。

travesty：效颦作品　39。

trickster：骗子　9。

trimeter：三音步诗行　219。

triple rhyme：三重韵　349。

triplet：三行联句　375。

trochaic：扬抑格　218。

trope (figurative)：(修辞中的) 比喻　130。

trope (liturgical): **224**.

troubadour: 66.

truth (in fiction): **128**.

type (in biblical interpretation): **181**.

type (in characters): **46**.

typological interpretation: 180; *17*.

trope (liturgical):(礼拜中的) 圣歌对白　224。

troubadour:行吟诗人　66。

truth (in fiction):(小说中的) 真实　128。

type (in biblical interpretation):(圣经释义中的) 原型　181。

type (in characters):(人物中的) 模式化人物　46。

typological interpretation:象征释义　180;*17*。

ubi sunt motif (oo' bē sŭnt mōtēf"): **229**.

understatement: **167**.

unintrusive (narrator): **302**.

unities, three: **405**.

unity of action: **295**.

unreliable narrator: **305**.

unstable irony: **185**.

utopias and dystopias: The term **utopia** designates the class of fictional writings that represent an ideal, nonexistent political and social way of life. It derives from *Utopia* (1515–16), a book written in Latin by the Renaissance humanist Sir Thomas More which describes a perfect commonwealth; More formed his title by conflating the Greek words "eutopia" (good place) and "outopia" (no place). The first and greatest instance of the literary type was Plato's *Republic* (later fourth century BC), which sets forth, in dialogue, the eternal Idea, or Form, of a perfect commonwealth that can at best be merely approximated by political organizations in the actual world. Most of the later utopias, like that of Sir Thomas More, represent their ideal state in the fiction of a distant country reached by a venturesome traveler. There have been many utopias written since More gave impetus to the genre, some as mere Arcadian dreams, others intended as blueprints for social and technological improvements in the actual world. They include Tommaso Campanella's *City of the Sun* (1623), Francis Bacon's *New Atlantis* (1627), Edward Bellamy's *Looking Backward* (1888), William Morris' *News from Nowhere* (1891), Charlotte Perkins Gilman's *Herland* (1915), and James Hilton's *Lost Horizon* (1934).

The utopia can be distinguished from literary representations of imaginary places which, because they are either inordinately superior to the present world or manifest exaggerated versions of some of its unsavory aspects, serve primarily as vehicles for *satire* on contemporary human life and society; notable examples are the fourth book of Swift's *Gulliver's Travels* (1726) and Samuel Butler's *Erewhon* (1872). Samuel Johnson's *Rasselas* (1759) presents the "Happy Valley," which functions as a gentle satire on humanity's stubborn but hopeless dream of a utopia. Not only does Rasselas discover that no mode of life available in this world guarantees happiness; he also realizes that the utopian satisfaction of all human wishes in the Happy Valley merely replaces the unhappiness of frustrated desires with the unhappiness of boredom;

ubi sunt motif：悲叹消失的岁月在哪里的题旨　229。

understatement：含蓄　167。

unintrusive (narrator)：非介入的（叙述者）　302。

unities, three：三一律　405。

unity of action：行动一致率　295。

unreliable narrator：不可信任的叙述者　305。

unstable irony：非指令反讽　185。

Utopias and Dystopias：乌托邦和反面乌托邦

　　乌托邦这一术语指的是表现了一种理想的但并不存在的政治及社会生活方式的那一类虚构作品。这一术语源自文艺复兴时期的人文主义者托马斯·莫尔爵士用拉丁文创作的一部作品《乌托邦》（1515—1516）。这部作品描述了一个完美的共和国，其书名由 eutopia（极乐地）和 outopia（乌有乡）这两个希腊词混合而成。这一文学类型第一个也是最伟大的范例是柏拉图的《理想国》（公元前4世纪下半叶）；该书用对话形式展现了一个完美的共和国永恒的理念与形式；这种共和国至多只能近似于真实社会中的政治组织。与托马斯·莫尔爵士的作品类似，后来的大多数乌托邦作品都虚构了一位具有冒险精神的旅行者到达某一遥远的国度，以此来表现作家的理想之国。自从莫尔推动了这一体裁的发展之后，许多乌托邦式作品纷纷问世；其中一些只不过是阿卡狄亚式的田园梦想，而另一些则意在作为真实世界中社会和科技改善的蓝图。这类乌托邦式作品包括托玛索·康帕内拉的《太阳城》（1623）、弗朗西斯·培根的《新大西洋》（1627）、爱德华·贝拉米的《回顾》（1888）、威廉·莫里斯的《乌有乡消息》（1891）、夏洛特·珀金斯·吉尔曼的《她乡》（1915）、詹姆斯·希尔顿的《消失的地平线》（1934）。

　　乌托邦与文学作品中所描绘的虚构之地不同，虚构之地远远优越于真实世界，而且夸张地展现了真实中的一些丑恶面，主要用来作为*讽刺*当代人类生活与社会的工具；著名例子包括斯威夫特的《格列佛游记》（1726）第四部和塞缪尔·勃特勒的《埃瑞洪》（1872）。塞缪尔·约翰逊通过《拉塞勒斯》（1759）中的"欢乐谷"，委婉地讽刺了人类对乌托邦固执而无望实现的梦想。拉塞勒斯不仅发现在这个世界上没有一种生活方式能够确保幸福，他还认识到欢乐谷中所有人类愿望得到乌托邦式的满足，只不过是用无聊引起的不悦来取代欲望受挫带来的不满而已；

see chapters 1–3. The term **dystopia** ("bad place") has recently come to be applied to works of fiction, including science fiction, that represent a very unpleasant imaginary world in which ominous tendencies of our present social, political, and technological order are projected into a disastrous future culmination. Examples are Aldous Huxley's *Brave New World* (1932), George Orwell's *Nineteen Eighty-Four* (1949), and Margaret Atwood's *The Handmaid's Tale* (1986). Cormac McCarthy's *The Road* (2006), set in a bleak, postnuclear landscape, represents a dystopian extreme. Ursula K. Le Guin's *The Dispossessed: An Ambiguous Utopia* (1974) contains both utopian and dystopian scenarios.

For utopias and dystopias based on future developments in science and technology, see *science fiction*. Refer to Karl Mannheim, *Ideology and Utopia* (1934); Chad Walsh, *From Utopia to Nightmare* (1962); Nell Eurich, *Science in Utopia* (1967); Frank E. Manuel and Fritzie P. Manuel, *Utopian Thought in the Western World* (1979). For collections of Utopian writings, see *Utopian Literature: A Selection*, ed. J. W. Johnson (1968), and *The Utopia Reader*, ed. Gregory Claeys and Lyman Tower Sargent (1999). Francis Bartkowski has analyzed *Feminist Utopias* (1989), from Charlotte Perkins Gilman's *Herland* (1915) to the present.

参阅:《拉塞勒斯》第 1—3 章。**反面乌托邦**(意为"不好的地方")这一术语近来用于指代某类虚构作品,包括科幻小说。这类作品表现了某一令人非常不愉快的想象世界;在这个世界中,当今社会、政治和技术秩序中某些令人担忧的趋势被投射到灾难性的未来终结里。反面乌托邦的例子包括:奥尔德斯·赫胥黎的《美丽新世界》(1932)、乔治·奥威尔的《1984》(1949)、玛格丽特·阿特伍德的《使女日记》(1986)。科马克·麦卡锡的《路》(2006)将故事背景设置在核子大战之后一派荒凉的景象中,代表了反面乌托邦的一种极致。厄休拉·K.列·吉恩的《一无所有:模糊的乌托邦》(1974),既包含了乌托邦式情节,也包含了反面乌托邦情节。

以未来科技发展为基础的乌托邦作品与反面乌托邦作品,参见:*科幻小说*。参阅:卡尔·曼海姆所著的《意识形态与乌托邦》(1934);查德·沃尔什所著的《从乌托邦到梦魇》(1962);内尔·尤里克所著的《乌托邦中的科学》(1967);弗兰克·E. 曼纽尔与弗里茨·P. 曼纽尔合著的《西方世界中的乌托邦思想》(1979)。关于乌托邦作品的合集,参阅:J. W. 约翰逊主编的《乌托邦文学选集》(1968),格雷戈里·克拉埃斯与莱曼·托尔·萨金特合编的《乌托邦读本》(1999)。弗朗西斯·巴特考斯基在其所著的《女性主义乌托邦》(1989)中,分析了从夏洛特·珀金斯·吉尔曼的《她乡》(1915)一直到当代的女性主义乌托邦。

variorum edition (văr ēōr′ ŭm): **33**.

Varronian satire (vărō′ nian): **354**.

vehicle (of a metaphor): **131**; *212*.

vellum: **32**.

verbal irony: **184**.

verbal meaning: **178**.

verisimilitude (vĕr′ ĭsĭmĭl″ ĭtood): **406**.

vers de société (vĕr′ dĕ sōsyātā″): **192**.

vers libre (vĕr lē′ br): **142**.

verse: **217**.

verse paragraph: **30**.

versification: **319**.

versions (of a text): **404**.

verso (vŭr′ sō): **34**.

Vice (the character): **224**.

Victorian and Victorianism: In its value-neutral use, "Victorian" simply identifies the historical era in England roughly coincident with the reign of Queen Victoria, 1837–1901. (See *Victorian period*, under *periods of English literature*.) It was a time of rapid and wrenching economic and social changes that had no parallel in earlier history—changes that made small-scale England, in the course of the nineteenth century, the leading industrial power, with an empire that occupied more than a quarter of the earth's surface. The pace and depth of such developments, while they fostered a mood of nationalist pride and optimism about future progress, also produced social stresses, class conflicts, and widespread anxiety about the ability of the nation and the individual to cope, socially, politically, and psychologically, with the cumulative problems of the age. England was the first nation to exploit the technological possibilities of steam power and steel, but its unregulated industrialization,

variorum edition：集注本　33。

Varronian satire：瓦罗式讽刺　354。

vehicle（**of a metaphor**）：（隐喻的）喻矢　131；*212*。

vellum：牛皮纸　32。

verbal irony：言语反讽　184。

verbal meaning：语言含义　178。

verisimilitude：逼真　406。

vers de société：上流社会轻佻诗　192。

vers libre：自由诗　142。

verse：韵文　217。

verse paragraph：诗段　30。

versification：韵律　319。

versions（**of a text**）：（文本的）版本　404。

verso：反页　34。

Vice（**the character**）：丑角（角色）　224。

Victorian and Victorianism：维多利亚时期与维多利亚时期的特点

如果保持价值中立，"维多利亚时期"仅仅指代英国的一段历史时期，时间大致与维多利亚女王的统治时期相一致：1837—1901。（参见：*英国文学各时期的划分中的维多利亚时期*。）这是一个经济和社会发生了前所未有的迅猛变化的时期——这些变化使面积很小的英国在 19 世纪中期变为占世界表面 1/4 以上面积的帝国并成为主要的工业国。这些发展的速度与深度激发了民族自豪感和对未来发展的乐观主义态度，但同时也造成了社会压力与阶级冲突；人们普遍对国家和个人处理时代积累的社会问题、政治问题与心理问题的能力感到焦虑。英国是第一个开发利用蒸汽动力及钢铁的技术可能性的国家，但未加控制的工业化既给日

while it produced great wealth for an expanding middle class, led also to the deterioration of rural England, a mushroom growth of often shoddy urbanization, and massive poverty concentrated in slum neighborhoods. Charles Darwin's theory of evolution (*On the Origin of Species* was published in 1859), together with the extension into all intellectual areas of **positivism** (the view that all valid knowledge must be based on the methods of empirical investigation established by the natural sciences), engendered sectarian controversy, doubts about the truth of religious beliefs, and in some instances, a reversion to strict biblical fundamentalism. Contributing to the social and political unrest was what was labeled "the woman question"; that is, the early *feminist* agitation for equal status and rights.

The Victorian age, for all its conflicts and anxieties, was one of immense, variegated, and often self-critical intellectual and literary activities. In our time, the term "Victorian," and still more **Victorianism**, is frequently used in a derogatory way, to connote narrow-mindedness, sexual priggishness, the determination to maintain feminine "innocence" (that is, sexual ignorance), and an emphasis on social respectability. Such views have a valid basis in attitudes and values expressed (and sometimes exemplified) by many members of the expanding middle class, with its roots in Puritanism and its insecurity about its newly won status. Later criticism of such Victorian attitudes, however, merely echo the vigorous attacks and devastating ridicule mounted against prevailing beliefs and attitudes by a number of thinkers and literary authors in the Victorian age itself.

Refer to G. M. Young, *Victorian England: Portrait of an Age* (republished 1977); David Thomson, *England in the Nineteenth Century* (1950); Jerome Buckley, *The Victorian Temper* (1951); W. E. Houghton, *The Victorian Frame of Mind* (1957). On Victorian attitudes to love and sexuality see Peter Gay, *The Bourgeois Experience, Victoria to Freud* (Vol. 1, *Education of the Senses*, 1984; Vol. 2, *The Tender Passion*, 1986); and on the undercover aspect of Victorian sexual life, Steven Marcus, *The Other Victorians* (republished 1974).

Victorian Period: 284; *189, 211*.

Victorianism: 419.

villain (in a plot): **294**.

villanelle (vĭl′ ănĕl″): **378**.

voice (in a literary work): **287**.

vraisemblable (vrā′ sŏmblä″ bl): **401**.

益扩大的中产阶级带来了巨大的财富，也造成了英国乡村地区的衰退、粗劣的城市化的迅猛发展和集中在贫民区的大规模贫困。查尔斯·达尔文的进化论（1859年出版的《物种起源》）和**实证主义**（认为所有正确的知识都必须以自然科学建立的实验调查方法为基础）对所有知识领域的影响引发了宗派论争，对宗教信仰正确性的质疑在某些情况下导致回归严格的圣经基要主义。给社会及政治造成动乱的还包括所谓的"女性问题"，即早期*女性主义者*鼓吹的平等地位与权利。

尽管有这样一些冲突和焦虑，维多利亚时期仍是一个轰轰烈烈、百家争鸣而且在知识与文学活动中经常自我反省的时代。"维多利亚时期"——更多的是**维多利亚时期的特点**——这一术语的使用在现代常带有贬义，意味着思想狭隘、对性的古板态度、维护女性"清白"（即性别愚昧）的决心、强调在社会上的体面。这些观念建立在日益扩大的中产阶级的许多成员所体现（有时则是身体力行）的态度与价值观这一确定基础之上，其根源是清教徒主义及其对新获得的地位没有安全感。许多维多利亚时期的思想家与文学家就曾对这些维多利亚时期流行的信念和态度进行过猛烈的抨击与辛辣的嘲讽，后来对此的批评只不过是重复了这些抨击与嘲讽而已。

参阅：G. M. 扬所著的《维多利亚时代的英格兰：一个时代的肖像》(1977)；戴维·汤姆逊所著的《19世纪的英格兰》(1950)；杰洛米·巴克利所著的《维多利亚时代的性情》(1951)；W. E. 霍顿所著的《维多利亚时期的思想状态》(1957)。有关维多利亚时期对待爱与性的态度，参阅：彼得·盖伊所著的《资产阶级的经验——从维多利亚到弗洛伊德》（卷一：理性的教育，1984；卷二：温柔的激情，1986）；关于维多利亚时期性生活的隐秘方面，参阅：斯蒂文·马尔库塞所著的《另类维多利亚人》(1974年再版)。

Victorian Period：维多利亚时期　284；*189, 211*。

Victorianism：维多利亚时期的特点　419。

villain (in a plot)：(情节中的) 反面人物　294。

Villanelle：维拉内拉诗　378。

voice (in a literary work)：(文学作品中的) 言念　287。

vraisemblable：貌似真实的　401。

wilderness romance: 99.

wit, humor, and the comic: At present both "wit" and "humor" designate species of the **comic**; that is, any element in a work of literature, whether a character, event, or utterance, which is designed to amuse or to excite mirth in the reader or audience. The words "wit" and "humor," however, had a variety of meanings in earlier literary criticism, and a brief comment on their history will help to clarify the differences between them in present usage.

The term "wit" once signified the human faculty of intelligence, inventiveness, and mental acuity, a sense it still retains in the term "half-wit." In the sixteenth and seventeenth centuries it came to be used also for ingenuity in literary invention, and especially for the ability to develop brilliant, surprising, and paradoxical figures of speech; hence "wit" was often applied to the figurative language in what we now call *metaphysical poetry*. And in the eighteenth century there were attempts to distinguish the **false wit** of Abraham Cowley and other metaphysical stylists, who were said to aim at a merely superficial dazzlement, and "true wit," regarded as the apt rephrasing of truths whose enduring validity is attested by the fact that they are universal commonplaces. Thus Alexander Pope defined "true wit" in his *Essay on Criticism* (1711) as "What oft was thought, but ne'er so well expressed." See *neoclassic*.

The most common present use of the term derives from its seventeenth-century application to a brilliant and paradoxical style. **Wit**, that is, now denotes a kind of verbal expression which is brief, deft, and intentionally contrived to produce a shock of comic surprise; a typical form is that of the *epigram*. The surprise is usually the result of a connection or distinction between words or concepts which frustrates the listener's expectation, only to satisfy it in an unexpected way. Philip Guedalla wittily said: "History repeats itself. Historians repeat each other." Thus the trite comment about history turns out to be unexpectedly appropriate, with an unlooked-for turn of meaning, to the writers of history as well. The film actress Mae West once remarked: "Too much of a good thing can be—*wonderful*." The resulting laughter, in a famous phrase of the German philosopher Immanuel Kant, arises "from the sudden transformation of a strained expectation into nothing"; it might be more precise to say, however, "from the sudden satisfaction of an expectation, but in a way we did not expect."

Mae West's remark is what the *psychoanalyst* Sigmund Freud called "harmless wit," which evokes a laugh or smile that is without malice. What Freud distinguished as "tendency wit," on the other hand, is aggressive: it is a derisive and derogatory turn of phrase, directing the laugh at a particular person or butt. "Mr. James Payn," in Oscar Wilde's barbed comment on a novelist of the 1890s, "hunts down the obvious with the enthusiasm of a short-sighted detective. As one turns over the pages, the suspense of the author becomes almost unbearable."

wilderness romance：荒野传奇　99

Wit, Humor, and the Comic：机智、幽默与滑稽

"机智"与"幽默"现在都是**滑稽**的种类，意即文学作品中任何一种旨在取悦读者或观众、令人发笑的因素，不论是人物、事件还是言语。不过，在早期的文学批评史上，"机智"和"幽默"曾有过多种含义。对这两个词的历史做一番简短的评论，将有助于阐明它们在当前用法上的不同。

"机智"这一术语曾被用来表示人类智力、创新精神与精神上的敏锐；"弱智"(half-wit)一词中仍然保留着这一含义。在16、17世纪，"机智"也用来表示文学创作方面的才智，特指发掘出色的、令人惊叹的、似是而非的修辞手法的能力。因此，"机智"一词常被用来形容我们现在称之为*玄学派诗歌*中的修辞性语言。18世纪曾有人多次试图区分亚伯拉罕·考利和其他玄学派文体学家的**假机智**与"**真机智**"。据说这些玄学派文体学家的目标仅仅是表面上的炫耀，而"真机智"则被视为用巧妙的措词对真理进行重新表述，这些真理的永久正确性可由其自身普遍是平凡的得以证实。所以，亚历山大·蒲柏在《批评论》(1711) 中将"真机智"定义为"所思虽常有，妙笔则空前"。参见：*新古典主义*。

"机智"这一术语在17世纪被用来指高超的、似是而非的文体风格，该术语现在最普遍的用法正源于此。**机智**现在指一种言简意赅的语言表达方法，作家旨在以此来造成一种滑稽的意外感；其典型形式就是*警句*。这种意外感通常由词语或概念之间的关联与区别造成；这种关联或区别使听者的期望落空，但却以出乎意料的方式满足了听者的期望。菲利普·奎达拉曾机智地说道："历史重演。历史学家彼此互相重复。"这番关于历史落入俗套的评论，以其意思上的意外转变，居然出乎意料地适用于撰写历史的作家。电影演员梅·韦斯特曾指出："太多的好东西真是妙极了。"这句话令人发笑，因为，借用德国哲学家伊曼纽尔·康德的一个著名短语，这种笑发自"从紧张的期待突然转化为虚无"。不过，更准确的说法应该是这种笑"发自对某一期待的突然满足，但这种满足的方式是我们所没有预料到的"。

梅·韦斯特的这句话是*精神分析学家西格蒙德·弗洛伊德*所谓的"无害机智"；这种机智会引起不带任何恶意的大笑或微笑。相反，弗洛伊德所谓的"意向机智"则带有挑衅性：这种机智以措辞上的嘲讽和贬义性转化，直接把某一特定人物或对象当做笑柄。1890年代，奥斯卡·王尔德在评论某位同时代的小说家时，语中带刺地说："詹姆斯·培恩先生以一位近视眼侦探的热情，对一目了然的事情穷追不舍。读者翻阅书本时，作者制造的悬念几乎让人难以忍受。"

Repartee is a term taken from fencing to signify a contest of wit, in which each person tries to cap the remark of the other, or to turn it to his or her own advantage. Attacking his opponent Disraeli in Parliament, Gladstone remarked that "the honorable gentleman will either end on the gallows or die of some loathsome disease." To which Disraeli rejoined: "That depends on whether I embrace the honorable gentleman's principles or his mistresses." *Restoration comedies* often included episodes of sustained repartee; a classic example is the give-and-take in the discussion of their coming marriage by the witty lovers Mirabel and Millamant in William Congreve's *The Way of the World* (1700), Act IV.

"Humor" is a term that goes back to the ancient theory that the particular mixture of the *four humours* determines each type of personality, and from the derivative application of the term "humorous" to one of the comically eccentric characters in the Elizabethan *comedy of humours*. As we now use the word, **humor** may be ascribed either to a comic utterance or to a comic appearance or mode of behavior. In a useful distinction between the two terms, a humorous utterance may be said to differ from a witty utterance in one or both of two ways: (1) wit, as we saw, is always intended by the speaker to be comic, but many utterances that we find comically humorous are intended by the speakers themselves to be serious; and (2) a humorous saying is not cast in the neatly epigrammatic form of a witty saying. For example, the chatter of the old Nurse in Shakespeare's *Romeo and Juliet* is verbose, and humorous to the audience, but not to the speaker; similarly, the discussion of the mode of life of the goldfish in Central Park by the inarticulate and irascible taxi driver in J. D. Salinger's *The Catcher in the Rye* (1951) is unintentionally but richly humorous, and is not cast in the form of a witty turn of phrase.

More important still is the difference that wit refers only to the spoken or written word, while humor has a much broader range of reference. We find humor, for example, in the way Charlie Chaplin looks, dresses, and acts, and also in the sometimes wordless cartoons in *The New Yorker*. In a thoroughly humorous situation, the sources of the fun may be complex. In Act III, Scene iv of Shakespeare's *Twelfth Night*, Malvolio's appearance and actions, and his utterances as well, are humorous, but all despite his own very solemn intentions; and our comic enjoyment is increased by our knowledge of the suppressed hilarity of the plotters who are hidden auditors onstage. The greatness of a comic creation like Shakespeare's Falstaff is that he exploits the full gamut of comic possibilities. Falstaff is humorous in the way he looks and in what he does; what he says is sometimes witty, and at most other times humorous; while his actions and speech are sometimes unintentionally humorous, sometimes intentionally humorous, and not infrequently—as in his whimsical account to his skeptical auditors of how heroically he bore himself in the highway robbery, in the second act of *1 Henry IV*—they are humorous even beyond his intention.

One other point should be made about humor and the comic. In normal use, the term "humor" refers to what is purely comic: it evokes, as it is sometimes said, sympathetic laughter, or else laughter which is an end in itself. If

机智应答是从击剑运动的词汇中借用的术语,表示一场斗智竞赛;在比赛中,每个人都企图胜过他人的言辞,或利用他人的言辞达到对自己有利的目的。格拉德斯顿在英国议会攻击他的对手迪斯雷利时说:"这位尊敬的绅士要么死于断头台,要么死于令人作呕的疾病。"迪斯雷利对此回应道:"那要看我是否信奉这位尊敬的绅士的原则,或者是否拥抱过他的情妇们。"*王政复辟时期的喜剧*通常都有持续的机智应答的片段。其经典例子是威廉·康格里夫《如此世道》(1700)第四幕中,米拉贝尔和米勒曼特这两位机智的恋人讨论他们即将到来的婚姻时进行的应答。

"幽默"这一术语可以追溯到古代的人体四液理论;这一理论认为,*人体四液*的特定融合决定了各种性格类型;到了伊丽莎白时期,该词的意义引申用于指*性格喜剧*中某个滑稽、乖戾的角色。现如今,**幽默**这个词可以表示某种滑稽的言谈、某种滑稽的外表或行为举止模式。对幽默言语与机智言语的实用区别,可以发现二者在以下一个或两个方面的差异:(1)正如我们之前所述,说话人总是故意使机智带有滑稽的成分,但许多我们认为滑稽性的幽默言语,其说话人的本意却是严肃的;(2)幽默的话语并不具有机智话语那种简雅的警句形式。如莎士比亚《罗密欧与朱丽叶》中老奶妈的唠叨在观众看来是幽默的,但对说话人本身而言就并非如此。类似地,在 J. D. 塞林格的《麦田里的守望者》(1951)中,说话含糊不清、脾气暴躁的出租车司机对中心公园里金鱼的生活方式发表的一番议论,虽是无意的但却是绝妙的幽默。这番议论也没有用机智的措辞转化形式来表达。

机智与幽默更重要的区别在于:机智只是指言辞或书面文字,幽默所指的范围则要广泛得多。例如,我们在查理·卓别林的模样、衣着和表演里发现了幽默;我们有时也会在《纽约人》杂志上无字的漫画里找到幽默。在彻头彻尾的幽默情景中,逗乐的来源可能是错综复杂的。在莎士比亚《第十二夜》第三幕第四场里,尽管马伏里奥的本意是严肃的,但他的外貌、行为和谈吐都十分幽默,而且由于我们知道密谋者(即台上隐匿的听者)压抑住的欢笑,所以我们从中获得了更多的喜剧乐趣。莎士比亚笔下的福斯塔夫式滑稽人物之所以出众,是因为他淋漓尽致地发掘了滑稽的所有可能性。福斯塔夫的幽默在于他的模样和举止;他的言谈虽然有时机智,但大多数还是幽默的。他的幽默言行有时出于无心,有时却也是有意地幽默;这些幽默的言行往往超出了他的本意——如在《亨利四世》上部第二幕中他突发奇想对心存怀疑的听众讲述起自己如何在公路抢劫中英勇地表现自己的那番话。

关于幽默和滑稽还需要指出的一点是,"幽默"这个术语一般用来指纯粹滑稽的事物:有时幽默会引起所谓同情的笑声,或者就是以引人发笑为其自身目的。

we extend Freud's distinction between harmless and tendency wit, we can say that humor is a "harmless" form of the comic. There is, however, another mode of the comic that might be called "tendency comedy," in which we are made to laugh at a person not merely because he is ridiculous but because he is being ridiculed—the laughter is derisive, with some element of contempt or malice, and serves as a weapon against its subject. Tendency comedy and tendency wit, rather than humor, are among the devices that a writer most exploits in *satire*, the literary art of derogating by deriding a subject.

On the alternative use of the term "comic" to define the formal features of a type of dramatic or narrative plot, see *comedy*; on the form of humor-in-horror in some present-day literature, see *black humor*. For diverse theories of wit, humor, and the comic, together with copious examples, refer to Sigmund Freud, *Wit and Its Relation to the Unconscious* (1916); Max Eastman, *Enjoyment of Laughter* (1936); D. H. Monro, *The Argument of Laughter* (1951); Louis Kronenberger, *The Thread of Laughter* (1952); Stuart M. Tave, *The Amiable Humorist* (1960); Jerry Palmer, *Taking Humor Seriously* (1994).

women's studies: 126.

wrenched accent: 218.

zeugma (zoog′ mă): **347**.

如果把弗洛伊德关于无害机智与意向机智之间的区分加以引申，我们可以说，幽默是一种"无害"的滑稽形式。不过滑稽还有另一种模式，可以称为"意向喜剧"；在这类喜剧中，我们取笑某人，不仅因为他可笑，而且也因为他受人愚弄——这种笑是讥笑，带有某种蔑视或恶意的成分，是对付其取笑对象的武器。意向喜剧和意向机智，而非幽默，是作家在讽刺中最常使用的手段。讽刺是一门靠讥讽来贬低某一对象的文学艺术。

关于"滑稽"一词用来指某种戏剧情节类型或叙事情节类型的形式特征，参见：*喜剧*；关于当今文学中采用恐惧中的幽默这一形式，参见：*黑色幽默*。有关机智、幽默与滑稽的各种理论及大量例子，参阅：西格蒙德·弗洛伊德所著的《机智及其与潜意识的关系》(1916)；马克斯·伊斯门所著的《笑的情趣》(1936)；D.H.门罗所著的《笑的理由》(1951)；路易斯·柯罗嫩伯格所著的《笑的思绪》(1952)；斯图尔特·M.塔夫所著的《可笑可爱的人》(1960)；杰里·帕尔默所著的《认真对待幽默》(1994)。

women's studies：女性研究　126。

wrenched accent：误加重音　218。

Zeugma：轭式搭配法　347。

Index of Authors

This index lists significant references to authors; it does not include passing references or the authors listed for supplementary reading. Following each name are the page numbers of general references and then, in alphabetic sequence, the page numbers of references to works written by the author.

Abrams, M. H., "Art-as-Such" 135; *The Mirror and the Lamp* 128, 138, 149, 320; *Natural Supernaturalism* 100; "Structure and Style in the Greater Romantic Lyric" 407; "What's the Use of Theorizing about the Arts?" 314.
Adams, James Eli, *Dandies and Desert Saints* 147.
Addison, Joseph, *Spectator* 114, 385.
Adorno, Theodor, 205–6.
Aesop, 9.
Albee, Edward, 2.
Alfred the Great, 279.
Alger, Horatio, 379.
Althusser, Louis, 206–7, 244.
Ammons, A. R., "Small Song" 144.
Apollinaire, Guillaume, 61.
Aquinas, St. Thomas, 181.
Aristophanes, 55.
Aristotle, 148, 212, 293, 295–97, 344, 409–10; *Poetics* 67, 86, 171–72, 342, 405–406, 408; *Rhetoric* 286, 342.
Arnold, Matthew, 162, 247; "Dover Beach" 115; "The Study of Poetry" 407.
Ashberry, John, *Three Poems* 319.

Auden, W. H., 355; "O where are you going?" 11.
Auerbach, Erich, *Mimesis* 83, 388.
Augustine, St., of Hippo (354–430), 181; *Confessions* 27, 56.
Austen, Jane, 74, 351; *Emma* 301; *Northanger Abbey* 38, 151; *Pride and Prejudice* 47, 184, 379; *Sense and Sensibility* 362.
Austin, John, 81; *How to Do Things with Words* 372–73.

Babbitt, Irving, 162.
Bacon, Francis, 341; *Essays* 114.
Bakhtin, Mikhail, 85–87, 245, 287–88, 312; "Discourse in the Novel" 86; *Problems of Dostoevsky's Poetics* 86; *Rabelais and His World* 86, 156.
Balzac, Honoré de, 334.
Bamber, Linda, *Comic Women, Tragic Men* 54.
Baraka, Amiri (LeRoi Jones), 29.
Barth, John, 2.
Barthes, Roland, 309, 312, 331; "The Death of the Author" 19–20, 311, 383; *Mythologies* 72, 359; *The Pleasure of the Text* 383; *S/Z* 401.

作者索引

本索引列出了重点提到的作者，不包括粗略述及的参考书目或补充阅读中所列的作者。每个名字之后是大致提到该作者时的页数，然后是提到该作者所创作作品（按字母顺序）时的页数。

艾布拉姆斯，M. H.，"像这样的艺术"，135；《镜与灯》，128，138，149，320；《自然的超自然主义》，100；"优秀浪漫主义抒情诗中的结构和风格"，407；"艺术的理论化有何用处？"314

亚当斯，詹姆斯·伊莱，《花花公子和沙漠圣徒》147

艾迪生，约瑟夫，《旁观者》，114，385

阿多诺，西奥多，205—6

伊索，9

阿尔比，爱德华，2

阿尔弗烈德大王，279

阿尔杰，霍拉旭，379

阿尔都塞，路易斯，206—7，244

阿蒙斯，A. R.，《小曲》，144

阿波利奈尔，纪尧姆，61

阿奎那，圣·托马斯，181

阿里斯托芬，55

亚里士多德，148，212，293，295—97，344，409—10；《诗学》，67，86，171—72，342，405—406，408；《修辞学》，286，342

阿诺德，马修，162，247；《多弗滩》，115；《诗歌研究》，407

亚斯比利，约翰，《三首诗》，319

奥登，W. H.，355；《何往？》，11

奥尔巴赫，埃利希，《摹仿论》，83，388

奥古斯丁，圣，希波的（354—430），181；《忏悔录》，27，56

奥斯丁，简，74，351；《爱玛》，301；《诺桑觉寺》，38，151；《傲慢与偏见》，47，184，379；《理智与情感》，362

奥斯汀，约翰，81；《如何以言行事》，372—73

白璧德，欧文，162

培根，弗朗西斯，341；《随笔》，114

巴赫金，米哈伊尔，85—87，245，287—88，312；"小说的话语"，86；《陀思妥耶夫斯基诗学问题》，86；《拉伯雷和他的世界》，86，156

巴尔扎克，奥诺雷·德，334

班伯，琳达，《喜剧女性，悲剧男性》，54

巴拉卡，阿米里（勒罗伊·琼斯），29

巴思，约翰，2

巴尔特，罗兰，309，312，331；"作者的死亡"，19—20，311，383；《神话学》，72，359；《文本的乐趣》，383；《S/Z》，401

Bate, Jonathan, *Romantic Ecology* 100.
Bate, Walter Jackson, *The Burden of the Past and the English Poet* 174.
Baudelaire, Charles, 5, 75, 398; *Fleurs du mal* 168, 397; *Little Poems in Prose* 318–19.
Baumgarten, Alexander, *Aesthetica* 4.
Baym, Nina, *Feminism and American Literary History* 99; *Woman's Fiction* 124.
Beardsley, Aubrey, 76.
Beardsley, Monroe C., 6, 175.
Beaumont, Francis, 412.
Beauvoir, Simone de, 122; *The Second Sex* 121.
Beckett, Samuel, 15, 185, 227; *Waiting for Godot* 2.
Beckford, William, *Vathek* 151.
Behn, Aphra, 282.
Belloc, Hilaire, 326.
Benjamin, Walter, 205; "The Work of Art in the Age of Mechanical Reproduction" 206.
Beowulf 132, 167.
Berry, Wendell, *The Unsettling of America* 98.
Bertram, William, *Travels* 96.
Betti, Emilio, 177.
Bialostosky, Don, *Dialogic Criticism* 87.
Black, Max, "Metaphor" 213.
Blake, William, 107–108, 153, 189, 231, 240, 397; *The Marriage of Heaven and Hell* 355; "The Sick Rose" 394.
Bleich, David, *Subjective Criticism* 331.
Bloom, Harold, 133, 173, 323, 332; *The Anxiety of Influence* 174; *The Western Canon* 141.
Bloomfield, Leonard, 194.
Blumenberg, Hans, *Work on Myth* 230.
Boccaccio, Giovanni, *Decameron* 252.
Bodkin, Maud, *Archetypal Patterns in Poetry* 17.
Boileau, Nicholas Despreaux, 39, 390.
Booth, Wayne, 138, 288; *The Rhetoric of Fiction* 92, 344; *A Rhetoric of Irony* 185.
Borges, Jorge Luis, 258.
Boswell, James, *Life of Samuel Johnson* 27, 385.
Bowdler, Thomas, *Family Shakespeare* 37.
Bowers, Fredson, 402.

Brecht, Bertolt, 7, 110, 205–6; *Threepenny Opera* 39.
Breton, André, *Manifesto on Surrealism* 392.
Brooks, Cleanth, 42, 170, 187, 241–42; *The Well-Wrought Urn* 68, 229, 267.
Brown, Norman O., *Life against Death* 317.
Brown, William Hill, 274.
Browning, Robert, "Meeting at Night" 264; "My Last Duchess" 94, 286; "Pied Piper" 116; "Soliloquy of the Spanish Cloister" 185.
Bryant, William Cullen, "Thanatopsis" 154.
Bullough, Edward, 92.
Bunyan, John, *Grace Abounding to the Chief of Sinners* 28; *The Pilgrim's Progress* 7, 8, 88, 95.
Bürger, G. A., "Lenore" 24.
Burke, Edmund, *Philosophical Enquiry into the Sublime and the Beautiful* 390.
Burns, Robert, 136, 394; "O my love's like a red, red rose" 130; "The Holy Fair" 355; "To a Mouse" 105.
Bush, Douglas, 119.
Butler, Judith, 126, 328; *Gender Trouble* 147, 328, 374.
Butler, Samuel (1613–80), *Hudibras* 39, 93.
Butler, Samuel (1835–1902), *Erewhon* 416.
Butor, Michel, *Second Thoughts* 304.
Byrom, John, 111.
Byron, George Gordon, Lord, *Childe Harold* 240, 326; *Don Juan* 26, 187, 293, 348–49, 377.

Calvin, John, 340.
Calvino, Italo, *If on a Winter's Night a Traveler* 304.
Camus, Albert, "The Myth of Sisyphus" 1.
Capellanus, Andreas, *The Art of Courtly Love* 66.
Capote, Truman, *In Cold Blood* 257.
Carew, Thomas, "A Song" 345.
Carlyle, Thomas, 189, 320.
Carroll, Joseph, *Evolution and Literary Theory* 74.
Carroll, Lewis, 192; *Alice in Wonderland* 95; *Through the Looking Glass* 13.
Carson, Rachel, *Silent Spring* 97.
Cary, Elizabeth, *The Tragedy of Mariam* 281.

贝特, 乔纳森,《浪漫主义生态学》, 100
巴特, 沃尔特·杰克逊,《过去的负担和英国诗人》, 174
波德莱尔, 查尔斯, 5, 75, 398;《恶之花》, 168, 397;《散文小诗》, 318—19
鲍姆加登, 亚历山大,《美学》, 4
贝姆, 尼娜,《女性主义与美国文学史》, 99;《女性小说》, 124
比尔兹利, 奥布里, 76
比尔兹利, 门罗·C., 6, 175
博蒙特, 弗朗西斯, 412
波伏娃, 西蒙娜·德, 122;《第二性》, 121
贝克特, 塞缪尔, 15, 185, 227;《等待戈多》, 2
贝克福德, 威廉,《瓦提克》, 151
贝恩, 阿弗拉, 282
贝洛克, 希拉里, 326
本雅明, 沃尔特, 205,"机械复制时代的艺术作品", 206;
《贝奥武甫》, 132, 167
贝瑞, 温德尔,《令人不安的美国》, 98
伯特伦, 威廉,《游记》, 96
贝蒂, 艾米利欧, 177
比亚洛斯托斯基, 唐,《对话批评》, 87
布莱克, 马克斯,《隐喻》, 213
布莱克, 威廉, 107—8, 153, 189, 231, 240, 397;《天堂与地狱的婚礼》, 355;《病玫瑰》394
布莱奇, 戴维,《主观性批评》, 331
布卢姆, 哈罗德, 133, 173, 323, 332;《影响的焦虑》, 174;《西方正典》, 141
布龙菲尔德, 伦纳德, 194
布鲁门贝格, 汉斯,《神话》, 230
薄伽丘, 乔瓦尼,《十日谈》, 252
博德金, 莫德,《诗歌中的原型》(又译《诗中的原型模式》), 17
布瓦洛, 尼古拉斯·德斯普鲁克斯, 39, 390
布思, 韦恩, 138, 288;《小说修辞学》, 92, 344;《反讽修辞学》, 185
博尔赫斯, 豪尔赫·路易斯, 258
鲍斯韦尔, 詹姆斯,《约翰逊传》, 27, 385
鲍德勒, 托马斯,《家用莎士比亚选集》, 37
鲍尔斯, 弗雷德森, 402

布莱希特, 贝尔托尔特, 7, 110, 205—6;《三分钱歌剧》, 39
布雷东, 安德烈,《超现实主义宣言》, 392
布鲁克斯, 克林斯, 42, 170, 187, 241—42;《精致的瓮》, 68, 229, 267
布朗, 诺曼·O.,《生与死》, 317
布朗, 威廉·希尔, 274
勃朗宁, 罗伯特,《夜半相会》, 264;《我那已故的公爵夫人》, 94, 286;《吹风笛的人》, 116;《西班牙修道院里的独白》, 185
布赖恩特, 威廉·卡伦,《死亡观》, 154
布洛, 爱德华, 92
班扬, 约翰,《罪魁蒙恩记》, 28;《天路历程》, 7, 8, 88, 95
伯格, G. A.,《勒诺》, 24
伯克, 埃德蒙,《崇高与美的理念之起源的哲学探索》, 390
彭斯, 罗伯特, 136, 394;《啊, 我的爱人像朵红红的玫瑰》, 130;《圣女》, 135;《致小鼠》, 105
布什, 道格拉斯, 119
巴特勒, 朱迪思, 126, 328;《性别麻烦》, 147, 328, 374
勃特勒, 塞缪尔 (1613—1680),《休迪布拉斯》, 39, 93
勃特勒, 塞缪尔 (1835—1902),《埃瑞洪》, 416
布托尔, 迈克尔,《三思之后》, 304
拜罗姆, 约翰, 111
拜伦, 乔治·戈登, 勋爵,《恰尔德·哈罗德游记》, 240, 326;《唐·璜》, 26, 187, 293, 348—49, 377

加尔文, 约翰, 340
卡尔维诺, 伊塔洛,《如果在冬夜, 一个旅人》, 304
加缪, 阿尔贝,《西西弗斯的神话》, 1
卡佩拉努斯, 安德烈亚斯,《优雅之爱的艺术》, 66
卡波特, 杜鲁门,《冷血》, 257
卡鲁, 托马斯,《不要再问我》, 345
卡莱尔, 托马斯, 189, 320
卡罗尔, 约瑟夫,《进化和文学理论》, 74
卡罗尔, 路易斯, 192;《艾丽丝漫游奇境记》, 95;《镜中世界》, 13
卡森, 蕾切尔,《寂静的春天》, 97
卡里, 伊丽莎白;《玛丽安的悲剧》, 281

INDEX OF AUTHORS

Castiglione, Baldassare, *The Courtier* 293, 339.
Caxton, William, 339.
Chandler, Raymond, 84.
Chaplin, Charlie, 355, 421.
Chartier, Roger, 36.
Chaucer, Geoffrey, 158, 222; *Canterbury Tales* 350, 366; *The Legend of Good Women* 266; "The Miller's Tale" 119; "The Monk's Tale" 409; "The Nun's Priest's Tale" 9–10; "The Pardoner's Tale" 10.
Chekhov, Anton, 365.
Chomsky, Noam, 194–95; *Reflections on Language* 164; *Syntactic Structures* 198.
Chopin, Kate, 275.
Chrétien de Troyes, 280.
Christie, Agatha, 84.
Cixous, Hélène, 125.
Cohn, Dorrit, *Transparent Minds* 380.
Coleridge, Hartley, 38.
Coleridge, Samuel Taylor, 129, 132, 137, 201, 230, 239, 396; *Biographia Literaria* 119–20, 139; "Christabel" 19, 222, 269–70; "Recollections of Love" 346; "The Rime of the Ancient Mariner" 24, 130, 348; *The Statesman's Manual* 395.
Collins, Wilkie, *The Moonstone* 85.
Collins, William, 390; "Ode on the Poetical Character" 8; "Ode to Evening" 11, 375.
Columbus, Christopher, 340.
Congreve, William, *Way of the World* 421.
Conley, Katharine, *Automatic Woman* 393.
Cooper, James Fenimore, *Leather-Stocking Tales* 317.
Copernicus, 340.
Cowley, Abraham, 263, 420.
Cowley, Malcolm, 276.
Cowper, William, *The Task* 51.
Crabbe, George, *The Village* 269.
Crane, R. S., 172; *Critics and Criticism* 149; *The Languages of Criticism and the Structure of Poetry* 138.
Crane, Stephen, 275, 335.
Crashaw, Richard, 25; "Saint Mary Magdalene" 59.
Culler, Jonathan, 402; *Literary Theory: A Very Short Introduction* 164, 314; *Structuralist Poetics* 297, 331, 382.

Cumberland, Richard, *The West Indian* 361.
cummings, e. e., 62; "Chanson Innocente" 142–43.

Dante (Dante Alighieri), 61, 293, 395; *Divine Comedy* 88, 95, 109, 182, 376, 395; *Inferno* 340; *Paradiso* 407.
Darnton, Robert, "What Is the History of Books?" 35.
Darwin, Charles, 74; *On the Origin of Species* 419.
Davidson, Donald, "What Metaphors Mean" 213.
Defoe, Daniel, *Moll Flanders* 15, 253, 334; *Robinson Crusoe* 253, 334.
DeMan, Paul, 3, 9, 80, 133, 311, 347; "The Rhetoric of Temporality" 396.
Denham, John, *Cooper's Hill* 158, 406.
Derrida, Jacques, 13, 77–80, 129, 133, 310; *Of Grammatology* 77; "Structure, Sign and Play" 309; *Writing and Difference* 79.
Descartes, René, 341.
Dickens, Charles, 156; *David Copperfield* 255–56; *The Old Curiosity Shop* 270, 362.
Dickinson, Emily, 275, 376.
Dilthey, Wilhelm, 162, 176–78.
Disraeli, Benjamin, 421.
Dollimore, Jonathan, 250.
Donne, John, 42, 101, 215–16; "The Canonization" 59, 94, 267; "Death, Be Not Proud" 267; "The First Anniversary" 341; "The Flea" 59, 94; *Holy Sonnets* 371; "Hymn to God the Father" 325; "A Valediction: Forbidding Mourning" 59.
Dowson, Ernest, 76.
Doyle, Arthur Conan, 63, 84.
Drayton, Michael, "Since there's no help" 371.
Dreiser, Theodore, 335.
Dryden, John, 27, 159, 215, 282, 300, 318; "Absalom and Achitophel" 7, 39, 355; *All for Love* 160; "Discourse Concerning Satire" 183; *MacFlecknoe* 353.
Dujardin, Edouard, 380.
Dunbar, Paul Laurence, 275.

卡斯底格朗, 巴尔达萨雷;《宫廷人物》, 293, 339
卡克斯顿, 威廉, 339
钱德勒, 雷蒙德, 84
卓别林, 查理, 355, 421
夏蒂埃, 罗杰, 36
乔叟, 杰弗里, 158, 222,《坎特伯雷故事集》, 350, 366,《好女人传说》, 266; "磨坊主讲的故事", 119; "僧侣讲的故事", 409; "尼姑教士讲的故事", 9—10; "卖赎罪券者讲的故事", 10
契诃夫, 安东, 365
乔姆斯基, 诺姆, 194—95,《语言反思录》, 164;《句法结构》, 198
肖邦, 凯特, 275
克里蒂安·德·特鲁瓦, 280
克里斯蒂, 阿加莎, 84
西苏, 埃莱娜, 125
科恩, 多里特,《透明的思想》, 380
柯勒律治, 哈特利, 38
柯勒律治, 塞缪尔·泰勒, 129, 132, 137, 201, 230, 239, 396;《文学传记》, 119—20, 139;《克利斯托贝尔》, 19, 222, 269—70,《爱的回忆》, 346;《古舟子咏》, 24, 130, 348;《政治家手册》, 293, 395
柯林斯, 威尔基,《月亮宝石》, 85
柯林斯, 威廉, 390;《诗人颂》, 8;《黄昏颂》, 11, 375
哥伦布, 克里斯托弗, 340
康格里夫, 威廉,《如此世道》, 421
康利, 凯瑟琳,《机械的女性》, 393
库珀, 詹姆斯·费尼莫尔,《皮袜子的故事》, 317
哥白尼, 340
考利, 亚伯拉罕, 263, 420
考利, 马尔科姆, 276
柯伯, 威廉,《任务》, 51
克雷布, 乔治,《乡村》, 269
克莱恩, R. S., 172;《批评家与批评》, 149;《批评的语言与诗歌的结构》, 138
克莱恩, 斯蒂芬, 275, 335
克拉肖, 理查德, 25;《圣女玛丽·马格德琳》, 59
卡勒, 乔纳森, 402;《文学理论简介》, 164, 314;《结构主义诗学》, 297, 331, 382

坎伯兰, 理查德,《西印度人》, 361
卡明斯, e. e., 62;《天真之歌》, 142—43

但丁 (但丁·阿里格杰瑞), 61, 293, 395;《神曲》, 88, 95, 109, 182, 376, 395;《地狱篇》, 340;《天堂篇》, 407
达恩顿, 罗伯特, "什么是书籍史?" 35
达尔文, 查尔斯, 74,《物种起源》, 419
戴维森, 唐纳德,《隐喻的意义》, 213
笛福, 丹尼尔,《摩尔·弗兰德斯》, 15, 253, 334;《鲁滨逊漂流记》, 253, 334
德·曼, 保罗, 3, 9, 80, 133, 311, 347; "短暂的修辞", 396
德纳姆, 约翰,《库珀山》, 158, 406
德里达, 雅克, 13, 77—80, 129, 133, 310;《论文字学》, 77; "结构、符号、人类科学话语中的游戏", 309;《书写与差异》, 79
笛卡尔, 勒内, 341
狄更斯, 查尔斯, 156;《大卫·科波菲尔》, 255—56;《老古玩店》, 270, 362
狄金森, 埃米莉, 275, 376
狄尔泰, 威廉, 162, 176—78
迪斯雷利, 本杰明, 421
多利莫尔, 乔纳森, 250
多恩, 约翰, 42, 101, 215—216;《圣徒追封》, 59, 94, 267;《死神, 别那么得意》, 267;《第一周年》, 341;《跳蚤》, 59, 94;《神圣十四行诗》, 371;《上帝天父颂》, 325;《莫为分离悲伤》, 59
道森, 欧内斯特, 76
道尔, 阿瑟·柯南, 63, 84
德雷顿, 迈克尔,《既然毫无指望, 就让我们吻别吧》, 371
德莱塞, 西奥多, 335
德莱顿, 约翰, 27, 159, 215, 282, 300, 318;《押沙龙与阿奇托菲尔》, 7, 39, 355;《一切为了爱》, 160;《讽刺对话》, 183;《迈克弗列诺》, 353
杜雅丹, 艾都瓦, 380
邓巴, 保罗·劳伦斯, 275

Eagleton, Terry, 207–8; *The Ideology of the Aesthetic* 4.
Eisner, Will, 153.
Eliot, George, 334.
Eliot, T. S., 42, 187, 241, 261, 360; "The Love Song of J. Alfred Prufrock" 60; "The Metaphysical Poets" 91; *Murder in the Cathedral* 411; *The Waste Land* 12, 226, 337, 355.
Ellis, Markman, *The Politics of Sensibility* 362.
Ellison, Ralph, *Invisible Man* 304.
Ellmann, Mary, *Thinking about Women* 121.
Emerson, Ralph Waldo, "The Transcendentalist" 413.
Empson, William, 14, 79; *Seven Types of Ambiguity* 13; *Some Versions of Pastoral* 269.
Engels, Friedrich, 203–4.
Erikson, Erik H., *Young Man Luther* 323.
Everyman 224.

Faulkner, William, 381.
Fetterley, Judith, *The Resisting Reader* 105, 123, 287.
Feydeau, Georges, 56.
Fielding, Henry, 160; *Joseph Andrews* 38, 297; *Tom Jones* 286–87, 295, 302; *Tom Thumb* 31.
Fish, Stanley, 312–13, 332–33, 388; *Surprised by Sin* 68.
Fitzgerald, F. Scott, *Tales of the Jazz Age* 276.
Flaubert, Gustave, 47; *Madame Bovary* 168, 302.
Fleming, Ian, 85.
Fletcher, John, 412.
Forster, E. M., 295; *Aspects of the Novel* 46.
Foucault, Michel, 90, 146, 163, 244–45, 249, 306, 309, 312, 359; *History of Sexuality* 328; "What Is an Author?" 19–20, 311; "What Is Enlightenment?" 107.
France, Anatole, 68.
Frazer, James G., *The Golden Bough* 16, 226.
Freud, Sigmund, 77, 320–24, 420; *Civilization and Its Discontents* 317.
Freytag, Gustav, *Technique of the Drama* 296.
Frost, Robert, 210.
Frye, Northrop, 231, 297; *Anatomy of Criticism* 17, 46, 54, 149, 184, 354, 378; *Fearful Symmetry* 397; *The Well-Tempered Critic* 385.

Gadamer, Hans-Georg, 90, 289, 336; *Truth and Method* 178–79.
Gallie, W. B., 234.
Gautier, Théophile, 4, 76.
Gay, John, *Beggar's Opera* 39; *Shepherd's Week* 269.
Geertz, Clifford, 90, 245.
Genet, Jean, 2.
Genette, Gérard, 234; *Narrative Discourse* 302.
Gibbons, Stella, *Cold Comfort Farm* 326.
Gide, André, *The Counterfeiters* 305.
Gilbert, Sandra, *The Madwoman in the Attic* 123; *No Man's Land* 124.
Ginsberg, Allen, 142; *Howl* 26.
Gladstone, William Ewart, 421.
Godwin, William, *Caleb Williams* 85.
Goethe, Johann Wolfgang von, 396; *Erlkönig* 24; *Maxims and Reflections* 395; *The Sorrows of Young Werther* 362.
Goldsmith, Oliver, 55; "Comparison between Sentimental and Laughing Comedy" 361.
Gomringer, Eugen, 61.
Gramsci, Antonio, 207.
Grass, Günter, 2.
Gray, Thomas, 298, 390; "Elegy Written in a Country Churchyard" 8, 154, 376; "Ode on the Death of a Favorite Cat" 26, 39; "Ode on a Distant Prospect of Eton College" 299; "Stanzas to Mr. Bentley" 283.
Greenblatt, Stephen, 22, 246–47; "Invisible Bullets" 249.
Greg, W. W., 402.
Grice, H. P., 179, 372; *Studies in the Way of Words* 90.
Gross, Milt, 153.
Gubar, Susan, *The Madwoman in the Attic* 123; *No Man's Land* 124.
Guedalla, Philip, 420.
Gutenberg, Johann, 32, 339.

Hall, Stuart, 72, 208.
Hamburger, Käte, *The Logic of Literature* 233.
Hammett, Dashiell, 84.

伊格尔顿, 特里, 207—8;《审美意识形态》, 4
艾斯纳, 威尔, 153
艾略特, 乔治, 334
艾略特, T. S., 42, 187, 241, 261, 360;《普鲁弗洛克的情歌》, 60;"玄学派诗人", 91;《大教堂凶杀案》, 411;《荒原》, 12, 226, 337, 355
埃利斯, 马克曼,《情感策略》, 362
埃里森, 拉尔夫,《隐身人》, 304
埃尔曼, 玛丽,《想想妇女们》, 121
爱默生, 拉尔夫·沃尔多, "超验主义者", 413
燕卜荪, 威廉, 14, 79;《晦涩的七种类型》, 13;《牧歌的一些形式》, 269
恩格斯, 弗里德里希, 203—4
埃里克森, 埃里克·H.,《年轻人路德》, 323
《每人》, 224

福克纳, 威廉, 381
菲特利, 朱迪思,《抗拒性读者》, 105, 123, 287
费多, 乔治, 56
菲尔丁, 亨利, 160;《约瑟夫·安德鲁斯》, 38, 297;《汤姆·琼斯》, 286—87, 295, 302;《大拇指汤姆的生与死》, 31
费什, 斯坦利, 312—13, 332—33, 388;《为罪恶所震惊》, 68
菲茨杰拉德, F. 司各特,《爵士时代的故事》, 276
福楼拜, 古斯塔夫, 47;《包法利夫人》, 168, 302
弗莱明, 伊恩, 85
弗莱彻, 约翰, 412
福斯特, E. M., 295;《小说面面观》, 46
福柯, 米歇尔, 90, 146, 163, 244—45, 249, 306, 309, 312, 359;《性史》, 328; "何为作者?" 19—20, 311; "什么是启蒙?" 107
法朗士, 阿纳托尔, 68
弗雷泽, 詹姆斯·G.,《金枝》, 16, 226
弗洛伊德, 西格蒙德, 77, 320—24, 420;《文明与它的不满》, 317
弗雷泰戈, 古斯塔夫,《戏剧的技巧》, 296
弗罗斯特, 罗伯特, 210
弗莱, 诺斯罗普, 231, 297;《批评的剖析》, 17, 46, 54, 149, 184, 354, 378;《可怖的对称》, 397;《好脾气的批评家》, 385

伽达默尔, 汉斯-乔治, 90, 289, 336;《真理与方法》, 178—79
加利, W. B., 234
戈蒂耶, 泰奥菲尔, 4, 76
盖伊, 约翰,《乞丐的歌剧》, 39;《牧人一周》, 269
格尔茨, 克利福德, 90, 245
热内, 让, 2
热奈特, 热拉尔, 234;《叙事话语》, 302
吉本斯, 斯特拉,《寒冷舒适的农庄》, 326
纪德, 安德烈,《伪币制造者》, 305
吉尔伯特, 桑德拉,《阁楼上的疯女人》, 123;《没有男性的领地》, 124
金斯堡, 艾伦, 142;《嚎叫》, 26
格拉德斯顿, 威廉·尤厄特, 421
戈德温, 威廉,《凯勒布·威廉斯》, 85
歌德, 约翰·沃尔夫冈·冯, 396;《魔王》, 24;《格言与感想集》, 395;《少年维特之烦恼》, 362
哥尔德斯密斯, 奥利弗, 55; "感伤喜剧与消遣喜剧的对比", 361
冈林格, 尤金, 61
葛兰西, 安东尼奥, 207
格拉斯, 君特, 2
格雷, 托马斯, 298, 390;《墓畔哀歌》, 8, 154, 376;《祭爱猫之死》, 26, 39;《伊顿公学远眺》, 299;《献给本特利先生的诗》, 283
格林布拉特, 斯蒂芬, 22, 246—47; "看不见的子弹", 249
格雷格, W. W., 402
格赖斯, H. P., 179, 372;《言语方式的研究》, 90
格罗斯, 米尔特, 153
格芭, 苏珊,《阁楼上的疯女人》, 123;《没有男性的领地》, 124
奎达拉, 菲利普, 420
谷登堡, 约翰, 32, 339

霍尔, 斯图尔特, 72, 208
汉伯格, 凯特,《文学的逻辑》, 233
哈米特, 达希尔, 84

Hardy, Thomas, 200; "In Tenebris I" 116; *Jude the Obscure* 335; *The Return of the Native* 19, 136; *Tess of the D'Urbervilles* 129, 186.
Harpham, Geoffrey Galt, *The Humanities and the Dream of America* 165; *On the Grotesque* 156.
Harris, Joel Chandler, 9.
Havel, Vaclav, 3.
Hawthorne, Nathaniel, 254; *The Blithedale Romance* 414.
Hazlitt, William, 68.
Heidegger, Martin, 289; *Being and Time* 178.
Heller, Joseph, 2.
Hemingway, Ernest, 276–77, 302, 378; "A Clean, Well-Lighted Place" 365; "Indian Camp" 386; "The Short Happy Life of Francis Macomber" 302, 365; *The Sun Also Rises* 385–86.
Henry VIII, 340.
Henry, O., 200, 295, 365.
Herbert, George, 61, 216; "Virtue" 63.
Herder, Johann Gottfried, 290.
Herrick, Robert, 281; "To the Virgins" 44.
Hertz, Neil, *The End of the Line* 392.
Hesiod, *Works and Days* 151.
Heywood, John, 225.
Hirsch, E. D., 178; *Stylistics and Synonymity* 388; *Validity in Interpretation* 177–79.
Hitchcock, Alfred, 85, 156.
Hobbes, Thomas, *Leviathan* 360.
Hogarth, William, 153.
Hoggart, Richard, *The Uses of Literacy* 72.
Holland, Norman, 322, 331.
Homer, 110, 113; *The Iliad* 108; *The Odyssey* 108.
Hopkins, Gerard Manley, 284; "Inversnaid" 98; "The Wreck of the Deutschland" 222.
Horace, 263, 354; *Ars Poetica* 21, 69, 82, 237, 326, 344; *Odes* 44.
Horkheimer, Max, 205.
Howells, William Dean, 334.
Hughes, Langston, "Mother to Son" 143.
Hulme, T. E., 170.
Hurston, Zora Neale, *Their Eyes Were Watching God* 157.
Husserl, Edmund, 289–90.
Huxley, Aldous, *Point Counter Point* 351, 355.

Huysmans, J. K., *À Rebours* 76.

Ibsen, Henrik, 410; *A Doll's House* 317.
Ingarden, Roman, 289, 330.
Ionesco, Eugène, 2.
Irigaray, Luce, 125.
Irving, John, 2.
Iser, Wolfgang, 330.

Jakobson, Roman, 132, 139–40, 197, 351, 387.
James, Henry, 47, 294, 303; *The Art of the Novel* 63, 257, 301; *Portrait of a Lady* 294, 380; "The Turn of the Screw" 305; *What Maisie Knew* 302.
James, William, 380.
Jameson, Fredric, 8, 207, 209; *The Political Unconscious* 208–9.
Jarry, Alfred, *Ubu Roi (Ubu the King)* 1.
Jauss, Hans Robert, "Literary History as a Challenge to Literary Theory" 336.
Jefferson, Thomas, 274.
Jensen, Wilhelm, *Gradiva* 322.
Johnson, Barbara, 81; *The Critical Difference* 81; *A World of Difference* 126.
Johnson, Mark, 53.
Johnson, Samuel, 83, 215, 238, 283, 354; "Life of Cowley" 59; "Life of John Denham" 406; "Life of Milton" 103, 162; *Lives of the English Poets* 27; "Preface to Shakespeare" 42, 406; *Rasselas* 15, 416.
Jones, Ernest, *Hamlet and Oedipus* 322.
Jones, Inigo, 210.
Jonson, Ben, 46, 55, 210, 262; "Drink to me only with thine eyes" 166; *Every Man in His Humour* 57; "To the Memory of My Beloved, The Author Mr. William Shakespeare" 22; *Volpone* 353.
Joyce, James, 45; *Finnegans Wake* 13, 95, 326; *Portrait of the Artist as a Young Man* 111–12, 148; *Stephen Hero* 403; *Ulysses* 109, 113, 363, 380.
Jung, Carl, 17, 323.
Juvenal, 354.

Kafka, Franz, 1, 8, 117, 156, 334.
Kant, Immanuel, 71, 168, 420; *Critique of Aesthetic Judgment* 4, 70, 92, 135, 391; "What Is Enlightenment?" 106.

哈代，托马斯，200；《在抑郁中》，116；《无名的裘德》，335；《还乡》，19, 136；《德伯家的苔丝》，129, 186

哈珀姆，杰弗里·高尔特，《人文学与美国梦》165；《论奇异艺术风格》，156

哈里斯，乔尔·钱德勒，9.

哈维尔，瓦茨拉夫，3

霍桑，纳撒尼尔，254；《福谷传奇》，414

黑兹利特，威廉，68

海德格尔，马丁，289；《存在与时间》，178

海勒，约瑟夫，2

海明威，欧内斯特，276—77, 302, 378；《一个干净明亮的地方》，365；《印第安人营地》，386；《弗朗西斯·麦康博的短暂幸福生活》，302, 365；《太阳照样升起》，385—86

亨利八世，340

亨利，O., 200, 295, 365

赫伯特，乔治，61, 216；《美德》，63

赫尔德，约翰·戈特弗里德，290

赫里克，罗伯特，281；《致处女》，44

赫兹，尼尔，《界线的末端》，392

赫西俄德，《工作与时日》，151

海伍德，约翰，225

赫兹，E. D.，178；"文体学与同义性"，388；《释义的合法性》，177—79

希区柯克，阿尔弗雷德，85, 156

霍布斯，托马斯，《利维坦》，360

霍加斯，威廉，153

霍格特，理查德，《文化的用途》，72

霍兰，诺曼，322, 331

荷马，110, 113；《伊利亚特》，108；《奥德赛》108

霍普金斯，杰勒德·曼利，284；《因弗斯内德》，98；《德意志号的沉没》，222

贺拉斯，263, 354；《诗艺》，21, 69, 82, 237, 326, 344；《歌集》，44

霍克海姆，马克斯，205

豪威尔斯，威廉·迪安，334

休斯，兰斯顿，《母亲对儿子说的一席话》，143

休姆，T. E.，170

赫斯顿，佐拉·尼尔，《他们眼望上苍》，157

胡塞尔，埃德蒙，289—90

赫胥黎，奥尔德斯，《针锋相对》，351, 355

于斯曼，J. K.，《逆流》，76

易卜生，亨里克，410；《玩偶之家》，317

英加登，罗曼，289, 330

尤内斯库，尤金，2

伊瑞格瑞，露丝，125

欧文，约翰，2

伊塞尔，沃尔夫冈，330

雅各布森，罗曼，132, 139—40, 197, 351, 387

詹姆斯，亨利，47, 294, 303；《小说的艺术》，63, 257, 301；《贵妇人的画像》，294, 380；《螺丝在拧紧》，305；《梅西知道的》，302

詹姆斯，威廉，380

詹姆逊，弗雷德里克，8, 207, 209；《政治无意识》，208—9

雅里，阿尔弗雷德，《于布王》，1

姚斯，汉斯·罗伯特，"作为向文学理论挑战的文学史"，336

杰斐逊，托马斯，274

詹森，威廉，《格拉迪沃》，322

约翰逊，芭芭拉，81；《批评的差异》，81；《差异的世界》，126

约翰逊，马克，53

约翰逊，塞缪尔，83, 215, 238, 283, 354；"考利传"，59；"约翰·德纳姆小传"，406；《弥尔顿生平》，103, 162；《诗人传》，27；《莎士比亚绪论》，42, 406；《拉塞勒斯》，15, 416

琼斯，欧内斯特，《哈姆雷特与俄狄浦斯》，322

琼斯，伊尼戈，210

琼森，本，46, 55, 210, 262；《用你的双眸给我祝酒吧》，166；《人各有癖》，57；《为了纪念我忠爱的朋友、作者威廉·莎士比亚先生》，22；《狐狸》，353

乔伊斯，詹姆斯，45；《芬尼根的觉醒》，13, 95, 326；《一个青年艺术家的画像》，111—12, 148；《英雄斯蒂芬》，403；《尤利西斯》，109, 113, 363, 380

荣格，卡尔，17, 323

尤维纳利斯，354

卡夫卡，弗朗兹，1, 8, 117, 156, 334

康德，伊曼纽尔，71, 168, 420；《判断力批判》，4, 70, 92, 135, 391；《论启蒙运动》，106

Kayser, Wolfgang, *The Grotesque in Art and Literature* 156.
Keats, John, 104, 221, 235, 239; "Endymion" 61, 104, 159, 220; "The Eve of St. Agnes" 113, 115; *The Fall of Hyperion* 95; "Ode on a Grecian Urn" 11, 16, 345–46; "Ode to a Nightingale" 60, 64; "Ode to Psyche" 60; "To Autumn" 8.
Keble, John, *On the Healing Power of Poetry* 320.
Kelly, Joan, 341.
Kermode, Frank, *The Genesis of Secrecy* 182.
Kerouac, Jack, *On the Road* 26.
King, Martin Luther, Jr., 345.
Kipling, Rudyard, 200.
Knapp, Steven, "Against Theory" 313.
Knight, G. Wilson, 170.
Kolodny, Annette, *The Lay of the Land* 98–99; *The Land before Her* 99.
Krieger, Murray, 243.
Kristeva, Julia, 401.
KRS-One, "Poetry" 272.
Kubrick, Stanley, *Dr. Strangelove* 2.
Kyd, Thomas, *The Spanish Tragedy* 409.

Lacan, Jacques, 125, 309, 324, 359.
Laclau, Ernesto, 208.
La Fontaine, Jean de, 9.
Lakoff, George, 53; *More Than Cool Reason* 214.
Landor, Walter Savage, 111.
Langland, William, *Piers Plowman* 11, 95, 222.
Lanier, Sidney, 275.
Lawrence, D. H., 316.
Lear, Edward, 192.
Leavis, F. R., 42, 242.
Leibniz, Gottfried, 154.
Lentricchia, Frank, 141.
Leonardo da Vinci, 339.
Leopold, Aldo, *A Sand County Almanac* 97.
Le Sage, Alain-René, *Gil Blas* 253.
Leverenz, David, *Manhood and the American Renaissance* 147.
Levin, Harry, 305.
Lévi-Strauss, Claude, 359, 381; *Structural Anthropology* 230.
Lewis, C. Day, *Poetic Image* 169.
Lewis, Matthew Gregory, *The Monk* 151.
Lillo, George, *The London Merchant* 410.
Lincoln, Abraham, "Gettysburg Address" 16, 343.
Locke, John, 413; *Essay Concerning Human Understanding* 213.
Lodge, Thomas, *Rosalynde* 54.
Longinus, *On the Sublime* 69, 389–90.
Lord, Albert, 265.
Lovejoy, A. O., 315.
Lowell, Amy, *Some Imagist Poets* 170.
Lowell, Robert, *Life Studies* 62.
Lubbock, Percy, *The Craft of Fiction* 301.
Lucretius, *De Rerum Natura* 88.
Lukács, Georg, 368; *Theory of the Novel* 109; *Writer and Critic and Other Essays* 205.
Luther, Martin, 165, 339.
Lyly, John, *Euphues: The Anatomy of Wit* 116.
Lyotard, François, 314.

Macherey, Pierre, *A Theory of Literary Production* 207.
MacKenzie, Henry, *The Man of Feeling* 362.
Maclean, Norman, 262.
Malory, Thomas, *Morte d'Arthur* 49, 280.
Mansfield, Katherine, "Bliss" 303.
Marie de France, 191; *Lais* 280.
Marlowe, Christopher, *Dr. Faustus* 31, 370; *Edward II* 50.
Márquez, Gabriel García, *One Hundred Years of Solitude* 258.
Marsh, Edward, 285.
Martial, 110.
Marvell, Andrew, 216; "The Garden" 131; "To His Coy Mistress" 44, 166.
Marx, Groucho, 131.
Marx, Karl, 203–4, 250, 368–69.
Mather, Increase, 189.
McGann, Jerome, *Critique of Modern Textual Criticism* 403; *The Textual Condition* 36.
McInerney, Jay, *Bright Lights, Big City* 304.
McKenzie, D. F., "The Book as an Expressive Form" 35; *Bibliography and the Sociology of Texts* 36.
Melville, Herman, *Moby-Dick* 395.
Meredith, George, *The Idea of Comedy* 56; *Modern Love* 371.

凯瑟,沃尔夫冈,《艺术和文学中的奇异艺术风格》,156
济慈,约翰,104,221,235,239;《恩底弥翁》,61,104,159,220;《圣阿格尼斯夜》,113,115;《海披里昂:梦》,95;《希腊古瓮颂》,11,16,345—46;《夜莺颂》,60,64;《心灵颂》,60;《秋颂》,8
基布尔,约翰,《论诗歌的治疗功能》,320
凯莉,琼,341
克莫德,弗兰克,《神秘的起源》,182
凯鲁亚克,杰克,《在路上》,26
金,小马丁·路德,345
吉卜林,拉迪亚德,200
纳普,斯蒂文,《反理论》,313
奈特,G.威尔逊,170
克罗德尼,安妮特,《地貌》,98—99;《在她之前的土地》,99
克里格,默里,243
克莉丝蒂娃,朱莉娅,401
KRS-One, "Poetry", 272
库布里克,斯坦利,《奇爱博士》,2
基德,托马斯,《西班牙的悲剧》,409

拉康,雅克,125,309,324,359
拉克劳,欧内斯托,208
拉封丹,让·德,9
雷柯夫,乔治,53;《并非只是冰冷的理论》,214
兰多,沃尔特·萨维奇,111
朗格兰,威廉,《农夫皮尔斯》,11,95,222
拉尼尔,西德尼,275
劳伦斯,D. H.,316
李尔,爱德华,192
利维斯,F. R.,42,242
莱布尼兹,戈特弗里德,154
兰特里夏,弗兰克,141
列奥纳多,达芬奇,339
利奥波德,奥尔多,《沙郡年鉴》,97
勒萨日,阿兰—勒内,《吉尔·布拉斯》,253
莱弗伦兹,戴维,《男子汉气概与美国文艺复兴》,147
莱文,哈里,305
列维-斯特劳斯,克劳德,359,381;《结构人类学》,230
刘易斯,C.戴,《诗学意象》,169

刘易斯,马修·格雷格里,《僧人》,151
李洛,乔治,《伦敦商人》,410
林肯,亚伯拉罕,《葛底斯堡演说》,16,343
洛克,约翰,413;《人类理解论》,213
洛奇,托马斯,《罗莎琳德》,54
朗吉努斯,《论崇高》,69,389—90
洛德,艾伯特,265
洛夫乔伊,A. O.,315
洛威尔,埃米,《一些意象主义诗人》,170
洛威尔,罗伯特,《人生写照》,62
卢伯克,珀西,《小说的技艺》,301
卢克莱修,《物性论》,88
卢卡奇,乔治,368;《小说理论》,109;《作家、批评家和其他论文》,205
路德,马丁,165,339
黎里,约翰,《尤弗伊斯:才智的剖析》,116
利奥塔,弗朗索瓦,314

马舍雷,彼埃尔,《文学生产理论》,207
麦肯齐,亨利,《情感男人》,362
迈克利恩,诺曼,262
马洛礼,托马斯,《亚瑟王之死》,49,280
曼斯菲德,凯瑟琳,《幸福》,303
玛丽·德·法兰西,191;《籁歌》,280
马洛,克里斯托弗,《浮士德博士》,31,370;《爱德华二世》,50
马尔克斯,加布里埃尔·加西亚,《百年孤独》,258
马什,爱德华,285
马提雅尔,110
马韦尔,安德鲁,216;《花园》,131;《致羞涩的情人》,44,166
马克思,格鲁乔,131
马克思,卡尔,203—4,250,368—69
马瑟,英克里斯,189
麦根,杰尔姆,《现代文本批评之评论》,403;《文本情境》,36
麦金纳尼,杰伊,《明亮的灯火,伟大的城市》,304
麦肯齐,D. F.,"作为一种表现形式的书籍",35;《书目学与文本社会学》,36
梅尔维尔,赫尔曼,《白鲸》,395
梅瑞狄斯,乔治,《喜剧的观念》,56;《摩登爱情》,371

Merleau-Ponty, Maurice, 289.
Michaels, Walter Benn, "Against Theory" 313.
Miles, Hamish, 362.
Miller, Arthur, *Death of a Salesman* 410.
Miller, Henry, 277.
Miller, J. Hillis, 290; *Charles Dickens* 291; *Theory Then and Now* 81.
Millett, Kate, *Sexual Politics* 121.
Milton, John, 162, 201, 338; "Comus" 210; *Il Penseroso* 8; *L'Allegro* 8; "Lycidas" 65, 102, 132; "Of Education" 83; "On the Morning of Christ's Nativity" 166; *Paradise Lost* 7, 30, 38, 89, 107–9, 110, 132, 155, 229, 267, 286, 300, 340–41, 346, 407.
Moi, Toril, 168.
Momaday, N. Scott, 99.
Monk, Samuel H., *The Sublime* 391.
Montagu, Lady Mary Wortley, 282; "The Lover: A Ballad" 45.
Montaigne, Michel de, *Essays* 27, 114.
Montrose, Louis, 245.
Moore, Marianne, "The Steeple-Jack" 169.
More, Paul Elmer, 162.
More, Sir Thomas, *Utopia* 416.
Mouffe, Chantal, 208.
Mukarovsky, Jan, 139.
Munch, Edvard, *The Cry* 117.

Nabokov, Vladimir, 277–78; *Pale Fire* 185, 258, 305.
Nash, Ogden, 349.
Nashe, Thomas, "Litany in Time of Plague" 12; *The Unfortunate Traveller* 253.
Neal, Larry, "The Black Arts Movement," 29.
Nietzsche, Friedrich, 49; *The Genealogy of Morals* 317.
Norton, Thomas, *Gorboduc* 409.
Nussbaum, Martha, 163, 360; *Women and Human Development* 164.

Odets, Clifford, *Waiting for Lefty* 89.
O'Neill, Eugene, *The Emperor Jones* 118; *Mourning Becomes Electra* 411; *Strange Interlude* 370.
Ong, Walter, 288, 344; *Orality and Literacy* 265.

Origen, 181.
Orwell, George, *Animal Farm* 9.
Overbury, Sir Thomas, 46.
Owen, Wilfred, 350.

Paine, Thomas, 274.
Parrish, Stephen, 403.
Parry, Milman, 265.
Passmore, John, *Man's Responsibility for Nature* 100.
Pater, Walter, 68–69; *The Renaissance* 5, 319, 326.
Patmore, Coventry, 123.
Peacock, Thomas Love, *Nightmare Abbey* 351; "The War Song of Dinas Vawr" 191.
Peirce, Charles Sanders, 357–58.
Pekar, Harvey, 153.
Percy, Thomas, *Reliques of Ancient English Poetry* 23.
Petrarch (Francesco Petrarca), 58, 293, 370.
Phillips, John, "The Splendid Shilling" 38.
Philo Judaeus, 181.
Pindar, 262–63.
Pinsky, Robert, 114.
Pinter, Harold, 2.
Plato, 148, 186, 230–31; *The Republic* 416; *Symposium* 292.
Plautus, 55.
Plotinus, 292.
Plutarch, *Parallel Lives* 27.
Poe, Edgar Allan, 84, 365, 397; "The Masque of the Red Death" 210; "The Poetic Principle" 5; *The Purloined Letter* 324; "The Raven" 337.
Pope, Alexander, 88, 158, 346, 348, 350, 353; "Epistle to Dr. Arbuthnot" 15, 286, 298, 354; "Essay on Criticism" 51–52, 114, 237, 264, 420; "Essay on Man" 155; *Imitations of Horace* 172; *Moral Essays* 354; "Of the Characters of Women" 159; "On Bathos" 25; *Pastorals* 268–69; "Rape of the Lock" 15, 38, 113, 184, 347; "The Universal Prayer" 83–84.
Porter, Cole, 60, 192.
Poulet, Georges, 290–91; "Phenomenology of Reading" 290.
Pound, Ezra, 170; "In a Station of the Metro" 157, 171.

梅洛-庞蒂，莫里斯，289
迈克尔斯，沃尔特·本，《反理论》，313
迈尔斯，哈米什，362
米勒，阿瑟，《推销员之死》，410
米勒，亨利，277
米勒，J. 希利斯，290；《查尔斯·狄更斯》，291；《此时与彼时的批评》，81
米利特，凯特，《性政治》，121
弥尔顿，约翰，162, 201, 338；《科玛斯》，210；《沉思的人》，8；《快乐的人》，8；《利西达斯》，65, 102, 132；《论教育》，83；《圣诞清晨歌》，166；《失乐园》，7, 30, 38, 89, 107—9, 110, 132, 155, 229, 267, 286, 300, 340—41, 346, 407
莫伊，陶丽，168
莫马迪，N. 斯科特，99
蒙克，塞缪尔·H.，《崇高》，391
蒙塔古，玛丽·沃特利夫人，282；《情人：情歌集》，45
蒙田，米歇尔·德，《随笔》，27, 114
蒙特罗斯，路易斯，245
穆尔，玛丽安，《尖顶》，169
莫尔，保罗·埃尔默，162
莫尔，托马斯爵士，《乌托邦》，416
墨菲，查特尔，208
穆卡诺夫斯基，詹，139
蒙克，爱德华，《呐喊》，117

纳博科夫，弗拉基米尔，277—78；《灰火》，185, 258, 305
纳什，奥格登，349
纳什，托马斯，《瘟疫年的祈祷》，12；《倒霉的旅行家》，253
尼尔，拉里，"黑人艺术运动"，29
尼采，弗里德里希，49；《道德的谱系》，317
诺顿，托马斯，《戈尔伯德克悲剧》，409
努斯鲍姆，玛莎，163, 360；《女性与人类发展》，164

奥德兹，克利福德，《等待老左》，89
奥尼尔，尤金，《琼斯皇》，118；《哀悼》，411；《奇妙的插曲》，370
翁格，沃尔特，288, 344；《口头和文字》，265

奥利金，181
奥威尔，乔治，《动物庄园》，9
奥弗伯里爵士，托马斯，46
欧文，威尔弗雷德，350

潘恩，托马斯，274
帕里什，斯蒂芬，403
帕里，米尔曼，265
帕斯莫尔，约翰，《人类对自然的责任》，100
佩特，沃尔特，68—69；《文艺复兴史研究》，5, 319, 326
帕特莫尔，考文垂，123
皮科克，托马斯·洛夫，《噩梦隐修院》，351；《黛纳斯·沃的战歌》，191
皮尔斯，查尔斯·桑德斯，357—58
贝克，哈维，153
珀西，托马斯，《英国古诗拾遗》，23
彼特拉克（弗朗西斯科·彼特拉克），58, 293, 370
菲利普斯，约翰，《耀眼的先令》，38
斐洛，尤迪厄斯，181
品达，262—263
平斯基，罗伯特，114
品特，哈罗德，2
柏拉图，148, 186, 230—31；《理想国》，416；《会饮篇》，292
普劳图斯，55
柏罗丁，292
普卢塔克，《希腊罗马名人比较列传》，27
坡，埃德加·爱伦，84, 365, 397；《红死病的假面舞会》，210；"诗歌原理"，5；《失窃的信》，324；《乌鸦》，337
蒲柏，亚历山大，88, 158, 346, 348, 350, 353；《致阿布斯纳特书》，15, 286, 298, 354；《批评论》，51—52, 114, 237, 264, 420；《人论》，155；《仿贺拉斯作》，172；《道德论》，354；《女人性格论》，159；"论诗歌中的突降技巧"，25；《牧歌集》，268—69；《卷发遇劫记》，15, 38, 113, 184, 347；《环球祷告》，83—84
波特，科尔，60, 192
普莱（又译布莱），乔治，290—91；《阅读的现象学》，290
庞德，埃兹拉，170；《地铁车站》，157, 171

Praed, Winthrop Mackworth, 394.
Propp, Vladimir, *The Morphology of the Folktale* 234.
Ptolemy, 340.
Pynchon, Thomas, 2.

Queen Latifah, "The Evil That Men Do" 272.
Quintilian, 343; *Institutes of Oratory* 130.

Radcliffe, Ann, *The Mysteries of Udolpho* 84, 151.
Radway, Janice, *A Feeling for Books* 36.
Ransom, John Crowe, 115, 241–42, 264; *The World's Body* 61.
Reinhardt, Max, 118.
Rice, Elmer, *The Adding Machine* 118.
Rich, Adrienne, 328.
Richards, I. A., *Philosophy of Rhetoric* 131, 212–13, 241; *Practical Criticism* 287, 379; *Principles of Literary Criticism* 6, 187; *Science and Poetry* 128.
Richardson, Dorothy, *Pilgrimage* 381.
Richardson, Samuel, *Pamela* 38, 254, 351, 361.
Ricoeur, Paul, 180, 313.
Riffaterre, Michael, 387–88.
Rimbaud, Arthur, 76, 398; *Illuminations* 319.
Robbe-Grillet, Alain, *Jealousy* 258.
Robertson, D. W., 182.
Rochester, John Wilmot, second earl of, "A Satyr against Mankind" 353.
Romance of the Rose, 95, 394.
Rorty, Richard, 314.
Rossetti, Christina, 315.
Rossetti, Dante Gabriel, "The Blessed Damozel" 315.
Rousseau, Jean-Jacques, 316; *Julie, or the New Héloise* 361.
Rubáiyát of Omar Khayyám, The, 45
Runyon, Damon, 200.
Ruskin, John, 261, 269–70; *The Stones of Venice* 156.
Rymer, Thomas, 83, 299.

Sackville, Thomas, *Gorboduc* 409.
Said, Edward, 207; *Orientalism* 306.
Sainte-Beuve, Charles-Augustin, 188.
Salinger, J. D., *The Catcher in the Rye* 301, 421.
Sapir, Edward, 194.
Sartre, Jean-Paul, 1.
Sayers, Dorothy, 84.
Saussure, Ferdinand de, 78, 193–96, 208, 309, 357–59, 381–82; *Course in General Linguistics* 193–94.
Schelling, F. W. J., 231.
Schiller, Friedrich, *Naive and Sentimental Poetry* 168.
Schlegel, Friedrich, 186, 231.
Schleiermacher, Friedrich, 176.
Scholes, Robert, 258.
Scott, Sir Walter, 191; *Ivanhoe* 256.
Scudéry, Madeline de, *Le Grand Cyrus* 351.
Searle, John R., 180, 372; *Expression and Meaning* 128, 214; *Speech Acts* 179.
Sedgwick, Eve, *Between Men* 146–47, 328.
Seneca, 409.
Shakespeare, William, 21–22, 27, 46, 50, 59, 131, 149, 156, 170, 318, 379, 421; *Antony and Cleopatra* 12–13; *As You Like It* 268; *Cymbeline* 326, 412; *Hamlet* 18, 266, 296, 322, 409; *1 Henry IV* 183, 300, 421; "It Was a Lover and His Lass" 337; *Julius Caesar* 300, 347; *King Lear* 105, 270; *Love's Labour's Lost* 116; *Macbeth* 363, 410; *Merchant of Venice* 412; *Othello* 166, 410; "The Rape of Lucrece" 376; *Richard II* 326; *Richard III* 410; *Romeo and Juliet* 296, 325, 421; *Sonnets* 11; *The Tempest* 105, 210, 249, 340; *Twelfth Night* 186, 353, 421; "Venus and Adonis" 104; *Winter's Tale* 50, 412.
Shaw, George Bernard, 318; *Mrs. Warren's Profession* 317.
Shelley, Mary, *Frankenstein* 356.
Shelley, Percy Bysshe, 42, 239, 397; *Defence of Poetry* 112, 347; "Epipsychidion" 293, 363; "Ode to the West Wind" 347, 376; *Prometheus Unbound* 210; "The Sensitive Plant" 398.
Sheridan, Richard Brinsley, 55; *The Rivals* 203.
Shklovsky, Victor, 139.
Showalter, Elaine, 121, 123; *A Literature of Their Own* 124.

普里德，温思罗普·麦克沃思，394
普洛普，弗拉基米尔，《民间故事形态学》，234
托勒密，340
品钦，托马斯，2

奎因，拉蒂法，"人之罪"，272
昆体良，343；《雄辩术原理》，130

拉德克利夫，安，《尤道弗之谜》，84, 151
雷德威，贾尼丝，《书的感觉》，36
兰塞姆，约翰·克罗，115, 241—42, 264；《世界的躯体》，61
莱因哈特，马克斯，118
赖斯，埃尔默，《加法机》，118
里奇，阿德瑞尼，328
理查兹，I. A.，《修辞哲学》，131, 212—13, 241；《实用批评》，287, 379；《文学批评原理》，6, 187；《科学与诗》，128
理查森，多萝西，《朝圣》，381
理查逊，塞缪尔，《帕美勒》，38, 254, 351, 361
利科，保罗，180, 313
里法泰尔，迈克尔，387—88
兰波，阿尔蒂尔，76, 398；《灵光篇》，319
罗布－格里耶，阿兰，《嫉妒》，258
罗伯逊，D. W.，182
罗彻斯特伯爵，约翰·威尔莫特，《对人类的讽刺》，353
《玫瑰传奇》，95, 394
罗蒂，理查德，314
罗塞蒂，克里斯蒂娜，315
罗塞蒂，但丁·加布里埃尔，《天女》，315
卢梭，让－雅克，316；《朱莉，或新爱洛绮斯》，361
《欧玛尔·海亚姆的鲁拜集》，4
鲁尼恩，达蒙，200
罗斯金，约翰，261, 269—70；《威尼斯的石头》，156
赖默，托马斯，83, 299

萨克维尔，托马斯，《戈尔伯德克悲剧》，409
赛义德，爱德华，207；《东方主义》，306
圣伯夫，查尔斯－奥古斯丁，188

塞林格，J. D.，《麦田里的守望者》，301, 421
萨丕尔，爱德华，194
萨特，让－保罗，1
塞耶斯，多萝西，84
索绪尔，费迪南·德，78, 193—96, 208, 309, 357—59, 381—82；《普通语言学教程》，193—94
谢林，F. W. J.，231
席勒，弗里德里希，《论素朴的诗和感伤的诗》，168
施莱格尔，弗里德里克，186, 231
施莱尔马赫，弗里德里克，176
斯科尔斯，罗伯特，258
司各特，沃尔特爵士，191；《艾凡赫》，256
斯古德瑞，玛德琳·德，《居鲁士大帝》，351
塞尔，约翰·R.，180, 372；《表达和意义》，128, 214；《言语行为》，179.
塞奇威克，伊芙，《男人之间》，146—47, 328
塞内加，409
莎士比亚，威廉，21—22, 27, 46, 50, 59, 131, 149, 156, 170, 318, 379, 421；《安东尼与克莉奥佩特拉》，12—13；《皆大欢喜》，268；《辛白林》，326, 412；《哈姆雷特》，18, 266, 296, 322, 409；《亨利四世》第一部，183, 300, 421；《那是一个情人和他的姑娘》，337；《尤利乌斯·恺撒》，300, 347；《李尔王》，105, 270；《爱的徒劳》，116；《麦克白》，363, 410；《威尼斯商人》，412；《奥赛罗》，166, 410；《鲁克丽丝受辱记》，376；《理查二世》，326；《理查三世》，410；《罗密欧与朱丽叶》，296, 325, 421；《十四行诗》，11；《暴风雨》，105, 210, 249, 340；《第十二夜》，186, 353, 421；《维纳斯与阿多尼》，104；《冬天的故事》，50, 412
萧，乔治·伯纳，318；《华伦夫人的职业》，317
雪莱，玛丽，《弗兰肯斯坦》，356
雪莱，珀西·比希，42, 239, 397；《诗辩》，112, 347；《厄皮塞乞迪翁》，293, 363；《西风颂》，347, 376；《解放了的普罗米修斯》，210；《敏感的植物》，398
谢立丹，理查德·布林斯利，55；《情敌》，203
什克洛夫斯基，维克托，139
肖瓦尔特，伊莱恩，121, 123；《她们自己的文学》，124

Sidney, Sir Philip, 112, 162, 339; *Apology for Poetry* 128; *Arcadia* 268; *Astrophel and Stella* 12; "Leave me, O love" 266.
Silko, Leslie Marmon, 99.
Sinclair, Upton, *The Jungle* 89.
Sinfield, Alan, 250.
Sir Gawain and the Green Knight 11, 49.
"Sir Patrick Spens" 23.
Skelton, John, *Colin Clout* 93.
Smith, Adam, *The Theory of Moral Sentiments* 360.
Smith, Barbara Hernnstein, *Margins of Discourse* 129.
Sondheim, Stephen, 211.
Sophocles, *Oedipus the King* 186, 322, 409.
Southey, Robert, 136.
Spender, Stephen, 130.
Spenser, Edmund, 162, 293, 370; "Epithalamion" 112, 337; *The Faerie Queene* 8, 16, 44, 88, 109, 295–96, 377; *Fowre Hymns* 166; *Shepherd's Calendar* 268.
Spiegelman, Art, *Maus* 153.
Spitzer, Leo, *Linguistics and Literary History* 388.
Spurgeon, Caroline, *Shakespeare's Imagery and What It Tells Us* 170.
Steele, Sir Richard, *The Conscious Lovers* 361.
Stein, Gertrude, 226, 276.
Sterne, Laurence, *Tristram Shandy* 187, 297, 361.
Stillinger, Jack, *Multiple Authorship and the Myth of Solitary Genius* 180, 404.
Stoppard, Tom, 2.
Storey, Robert F., *Mimesis and the Human Animal* 75.
Stowe, Harriet Beecher, *Uncle Tom's Cabin* 89, 270, 362.
Strout, Cushing, 273; *The Veracious Imagination* 257.
Suckling, Sir John, "A Ballad upon a Wedding" 113.
Surrey, Henry Howard, Earl of, 30, 370.
Swift, Jonathan, *Gulliver's Travels* 286, 353, 355–56, 416; "A Modest Proposal" 185, 355; *A Tale of a Tub* 167; "Verses on the Death of Dr. Swift" 353.
Swinburne, Algernon, 76, 348.

Taine, Hippolyte, 369.
Tanselle, G. Thomas, 404.
Tate, Allen, "Tension in Poetry" 400.
Tennyson, Alfred, Lord, 95; "Come Down, O Maid" 264; *In Memoriam* 169.
Terence, 55.
Theocritus, 96, 102, 268.
Theophrastus, *Characters* 45–46.
Thomas, Dylan, 60; *Altarwise by Owl-light* 371; "Do not go gentle into that good night" 378; "The Force That Through the Green Fuse Drives the Flower" 350.
Thomas, Francis-Noël, *Clear and Simple as the Truth* 386, 388.
Thomson, James, *The Seasons* 96, 149, 298–99; *The Tragedy of Sophonisba* 31.
Thoreau, Henry David, 98, 413–14; *Walden* 96, 413.
Thorpe, James, 404.
Thurber, James, *Fables for Our Time* 9.
Todorov, Tzvetan, *The Fantastic* 305.
Tolstoy, Leo, *War and Peace* 129, 302.
Tompkins, Jane, 362; *Sensational Designs* 36.
Toomer, Jean, *Cane* 157.
Turner, Mark, *Clear and Simple as the Truth* 386, 388; *The Literary Mind* 10; *More than Cool Reason* 214; *Reading Minds* 344.
Twain, Mark, *Huckleberry Finn* 317.
Tyler, Royall, *The Contrast* 274.

Verne, Jules, 356.
Virgil, 96, 102, 110; *The Aeneid* 108; *Eclogues* 268; *Georgics* 88.
Vivas, Eliseo, 243.
Voltaire, 155.
Vonnegut, Kurt, Jr., 2.

Waller, Edmund, "Go, Lovely Rose" 44.
Walpole, Horace, *The Castle of Otranto* 151.
Walton, Izaak, *Lives* 27.
Warren, Robert Penn, 187, 241.
Watt, Ian, 303.
Webster, John, 409; *The Duchess of Malfi* 266.
Weiskel, Thomas, *The Romantic Sublime* 392.

锡德尼爵士, 菲利普, 112, 162, 339;《诗辩》, 128;《阿卡迪亚》, 268;《爱星者和星星》, 12;《离开我吧, 那最轻易就能得到的爱轻如尘埃》, 266

席尔科, 莱斯利·马蒙, 99

辛克莱, 厄普顿,《屠场》, 89

辛菲尔德, 艾伦, 250

《高文爵士与绿衣骑士》, 11, 49

《帕特里克·斯彭斯爵士》, 23

斯克尔顿, 约翰,《科林·克劳特》, 93

斯密, 亚当,《道德情操论》, 360

史密斯, 巴巴拉·赫恩斯坦,《言语边界》, 129

桑德海姆, 斯蒂芬, 211

索福克勒斯,《俄狄浦斯王》, 186, 322, 409

骚塞, 罗伯特, 136

斯彭德, 斯蒂芬, 130

斯宾塞, 埃德蒙, 162, 293, 370;《婚曲》, 112, 337;《仙后》, 8, 16, 44, 88, 109, 295—96, 377;《赞美诗四首》, 166;《牧人月历》, 268

施皮格尔曼, 阿特,《莫斯》, 153

斯皮泽尔, 利奥,《语言学与文学史》, 388

斯珀金, 卡罗琳,《莎士比亚的比喻及其意义》, 170

斯梯尔, 理查德爵士,《自觉的情人》, 361

斯泰因, 格特鲁德, 226, 276

斯特恩, 劳伦斯,《项狄传》, 187, 297, 361

斯蒂林格, 杰克,《多重作者与孤独天才的神话》, 180, 404

斯托帕德, 汤姆, 2

斯托里, 罗伯特·F.,《模仿和人类动物》, 75

斯托, 哈丽特·比彻,《汤姆叔叔的小屋》, 89, 270, 362

斯特劳特, 库欣, 273;《真实的想象》, 257

萨克林, 约翰爵士,《婚礼歌谣》, 113

萨里, 亨利·霍华德, 伯爵, 30, 370

斯威夫特, 乔纳森,《格列佛游记》, 286, 353, 355—56, 416;《温和的建议》, 185, 355;《一个木桶的故事》, 167;《悼斯威夫特博士》, 353

斯温伯恩, 阿尔杰农, 76, 348

泰纳, 伊波莱特, 369

塔塞尔, G. 托马斯, 404

泰特, 艾伦,《诗歌的张力》, 400

丁尼生, 阿尔弗雷德, 95;《下来吧, 少女》, 264;《悼念》, 169

泰伦斯, 55

忒奥克里托斯, 96, 102, 268

泰奥弗拉斯托斯,《人物谱》(多译《品格论》), 45—46

托马斯, 迪伦, 60;《祭坛黄昏》, 371;《别轻柔地走进那美好的夜晚》, 378;《那通过绿色的茎催放花朵的力》, 350

托马斯, 弗朗西斯-诺埃尔,《像真理一样简单明了》, 386, 388

汤姆逊, 詹姆斯,《四季》, 96, 149, 298—99;《索弗尼斯巴之悲剧》, 31

梭罗, 亨利·戴维, 98, 413—14;《瓦尔登湖》, 96, 413

索普, 詹姆斯, 404

瑟伯, 詹姆斯,《当代寓言》, 9

托多罗夫, 兹维坦,《怪诞》, 305

托尔斯泰, 列夫,《战争与和平》, 129, 302

汤普金斯, 简, 362;《杰出的设计》, 36

图默, 琼,《甘蔗》, 157

特纳, 马克,《像真理一样简单明了》, 386, 388;《文学思想》, 10;《并非只是冰冷的理论》, 214;《阅读思维》, 344

吐温, 马克,《哈克贝利·芬历险记》, 317

泰勒, 罗耶尔,《对比》, 274

凡尔纳, 儒勒, 356

维吉尔, 96, 102, 110;《埃涅阿斯纪》, 108;《牧歌》, 268;《农事诗集》, 88

维瓦斯, 埃利西厄, 243

伏尔泰, 155

冯尼戈特, 小库特, 2

沃勒, 埃德蒙,《快, 可爱的玫瑰》, 44

沃波尔, 霍勒斯,《奥特朗托堡》, 151

沃尔顿, 艾萨克,《名人志》, 27

华伦, 罗伯特·佩恩, 187, 241

沃特, 伊恩, 303

韦伯斯特, 约翰, 409;《马尔菲公爵夫人》, 266

魏斯克尔, 托马斯,《浪漫的崇高》, 392

Wellek, René, 139, 389.
Wells, H. G., 356.
West, Mae, 420.
Wheatley, Phillis, *Poems on Various Subjects* 274.
White, Gilbert, *Natural History and Antiquities of Selborne* 96.
White, Hayden, 234.
Whitman, Walt, 275; *Leaves of Grass* 142.
Wiene, Robert, *The Cabinet of Dr. Caligari* 118.
Wilde, Oscar, 76, 420; *The Importance of Being Earnest* 56, 325.
Wilder, Thornton, *Our Town* 50, 294.
Williams, Raymond, 208, 250; *Culture and Society* 72.
Wilson, Edmund O., *Sociobiology: The New Synthesis* 74.
Wimsatt, W. K., 6, 351; *The Verbal Icon* 175.
Wittgenstein, Ludwig, 150.
Wittig, Monique, 328.

Wolfson, Susan J., *Formal Changes* 141.
Woolf, Virginia, 381; *A Room of One's Own* 121; *Orlando* 286; *To the Lighthouse* 302.
Wordsworth, Dorothy, *Journals* 27.
Wordsworth, William, 83, 239; *Lyrical Ballads* 238–39, 299; "Michael" 167, 269–70; "Nutting" 99; *The Prelude* 25, 28, 112, 239–40, 391; "She Dwelt among the Untrodden Ways" 169; "The Solitary Reaper" 233–34, 349; "Tintern Abbey" 30, 94, 286; "We Are Seven" 24.
Wyatt, Sir Thomas, 58, 370.

Yeats, William Butler, 45; "Among School Children" 347; "An Irish Airman Foresees His Death" 346; *A Vision* 231.
Yorkshire Tragedy, A 410.

Žižek, Slavoj, 392.
Zola, Émile, 335.

韦勒克,勒内,139, 389
威尔斯,H.G., 356
韦斯特,梅, 420
惠特利,菲利斯,《论各种主题的诗歌》, 274
怀特,吉尔伯特,《塞尔彭博物志》, 96
怀特,海登, 234
惠特曼,沃尔特, 275;《草叶集》, 142
韦恩,罗伯特,《卡利加里博士的密室》, 118
王尔德,奥斯卡, 76, 420;《认真的重要性》, 56, 325
怀尔德,桑顿,《小城风光》, 50, 294
威廉斯,雷蒙德, 208, 250;《文化与社会》, 72
威尔逊,埃德蒙,O.,《社会生物学:新的综合》, 74
维姆萨特,W.K., 6, 351;《语像》, 175
维特根斯坦,路德维希, 150
威蒂格,莫妮卡, 328

沃尔夫森,苏珊·J.,《形式印章》, 141
吴尔夫,弗吉尼亚(又译伍尔夫,弗吉尼亚), 381;《一间自己的房间》, 121;《奥兰多》, 286;《到灯塔去》, 302
沃兹沃斯,多萝西,《日志》, 27
华兹华斯,威廉, 83, 239;《抒情歌谣集》, 238—39, 299;《迈克尔》, 167, 269—70;《采坚果》, 99;《序曲》, 25, 28, 112, 239—40, 391;《她住在人迹罕至的地方》, 169;《孤独的收割者》, 233—34, 349;《丁登寺》, 30, 94, 286;《我们是七人》, 24
怀亚特爵士,托马斯, 58, 370

叶芝,威廉·巴特勒, 45;《在学童中间》, 347;《爱尔兰飞行员预见自己的死亡》, 346;《一种见解》, 231
《约克郡的悲剧》, 410

齐泽克,斯拉沃热, 392
左拉,埃米尔, 335